INVISIBLE WARS

THE COLLECTED DEAD SIX

To purchase any of these titles in e-book form, please go to www.baen.com.

INVISIBLE WARS

THE COLLECTED DEAD SIX

LARRY CORREIA
MIKE KUPARI

Acknowledgements

Far more people help in the creation of a novel than just the authors. The story that would become DEAD SIX began as an online serial at *www.thehighroad.org* titled *Welcome Back, Mr. Nightcrawler*. Thank you to the good folks of THR for letting us play in their yard. We would like to thank Chris Byrne and the Gun Counter for fixing the "computer situation." Their generosity is much appreciated. Special thanks go to Marcus Custer for his technical/tactical advice, he's like having your own personal Jack Bauer, only without all the yelling and whispering. John Shirley helped out big time on knives as did Ogre Rettinger on information security and Jeff More on the border. Once again, Reader Force Alpha rode to the rescue with their proofing, critiques, and vast stores of useful knowledge. Thank you all.

Contents

AUTHORS' NOTES

The story of how this series of books came to be dates back to 2003. I, a college student at the time, wrote a short story called "So There I Was" on an online discussion board called The Firing Line. It was inspired by things like *Cowboy Bebop, Kill Bill,* and *The Way of the Gun,* and while I had fun with it, it wasn't very good. It also wasn't very serious. It was told in the first person, starring a character who bore an unfortunate resemblance to myself, and was posted in a serialized format . . . by which I mean, I made it up as I went along.

Fast forward to 2006: I was living in a new state, I had spent a year and a half as a security contractor in the Middle East and post-Hurricane Katrina Mississippi, and my friends and I were hanging out on a new internet discussion board, this one called The High Road. (For the younger people reading this, please understand that this was before social media was ubiquitous. There was only MySpace, and that was relegated mostly to teenagers. People gathered on discussion boards relevant to whatever particular interest they held, and this is how I met a lot of my friends.) My time in the Middle East had given me a little bit of inspiration, and with that I decided to write a sort-of sequel to the original story. This one was entitled, "Welcome Back, Mr. Nightcrawler", as *Nightcrawler* was my handle at the time. (In case you're wondering, no, it wasn't inspired by the *X-Men* character.)

This story was more serious in tone, and was quite popular on the board at the time. Something else also happened then, something that would change my life forever. An accountant and gun store owner named Larry Correia (*Correia45*) approached me and asked if he could write scenes in my story, starring a different point of view character. This is the true origin of Lorenzo, my friendship with Larry, and indeed my writing career.

The readers loved the story as it continued. Two point of view characters facing off against one another, foiling each other, their stories separate but intertwined, doubled the fun to the audience. While it was fun for me, it was also a shrewd move for Larry, as in this way he began marketing himself. His first novel, *Monster Hunter International,* became very successful for a print-on-demand, self-published work. Eventually it was picked up by Baen, and now here we are.

By 2009, Larry's *Monster Hunter* series was becoming quite successful, and he insisted to me that we ought to turn our story into a novel. He'd already written something like seventy thousand words on a sequel we were planning, and he argued that people liked it and that it was better to get paid for all the effort we put into it.

I initially and repeatedly turned him down. I had no aspirations at being a novelist, and in any case I thought the story wasn't fit to print. I was a hobbyist, I said, and didn't have the talent to make it as a real writer.

Larry finally convinced me by reading a section of a novel from a best-selling thriller author, one who is widely known, famous, and doing quite well for himself. There were inaccuracies that a little bit of research would have prevented (Mormons aren't the least bit shy about discussing their beliefs and customs), a traditional tough-guy hero character (former Navy SEAL), some eye-rolling wordplay, and cringe-worthy dialogue.

Larry's argument moved me this time, and I agreed. I spent the next year and a half rewriting my entire portion of the novel, turning the character who became Constantine Michael Valentine from an unserious author avatar to a character with a life of his own. The book was published. Baen sent me my first copy while I was serving in Afghanistan as an explosive ordnance disposal technician in the US Air Force.

The moral of this story is perseverance. Larry never gave up, even when he had nothing to show for his efforts but a draft copy and a stack of rejection letters. Through practice, effort, and some luck, I went from being a hobbyist to having a writing career of my own.

Writing is a skill. Like any other skill, you get better at it only through practice. Innate talent is a factor, but it's a much smaller factor than planting your butt in the chair and typing the words. It can be hard work, tedious and frustrating, but this is the hill you must climb if you really want to write for a living.

I would like to thank Larry for everything he's done for me, including convincing me that I could do this. I would also like to thank Baen Books for giving a then-new author and his nobody coauthor a chance with an unconventional novel. Most of all I would like to thank *you,* the reader, from the bottom of my heart. Without you, none of this would be possible, and I sincerely appreciate your continued readership.

Mike Kupari
April 2019

�֍ �֍ ✖

When I first started reading Mike Kupari's online fiction serial, *Welcome Back, Mr. Nightcrawler,* he was only a few chapters in, but I was impressed. He was just posting new bits every few days, so it was rough, but it was a great story, and Mike was really good at dragging you in.

In fact, I got sucked in enough that after I read one scene in particular, I got the idea for the story of one of the side characters, and I really wanted to tell it. So I emailed Mike—who keep in mind, I only knew through talking about guns on the internet—and asked him if he would mind if I did a bit from that character's perspective and dropped it in there.

Mike said yes, and Lorenzo was born. I hurried, wrote a scene, and posted it. The readers went nuts. They thought we'd been planning this all along.

At that point, Mike and I figured what the heck, people are enjoying this, so I would keep writing scenes of Lorenzo reacting to the chaos caused by Valentine.

Keep in mind, we didn't really know what we were doing, and didn't have an outline. It was crazy. Every couple days Mike would post another scene. Then I would post a scene. Back and forth. Then as the inevitable clash of these two characters got closer, we actually had to hurriedly brainstorm a few things out, and then post it a couple of days later. Readers got to watch a real time rough draft taking form, and they participated by posting comments, feedback, and even soundtrack suggestions. After a few months, by some miracle, this slapdash story managed to have a coherent beginning, middle, and end.

And it was actually pretty good!

It wasn't until after writing a book with the guy that I actually met Mike in person. He's been like my brother ever since.

A few years later my writing career had taken off, and Mike has already told you the story about how I nagged him into turning *Welcome Back, Mr. Nightcrawler* into an actual novel. But honestly, it was good, and I knew he was good, way more talented than he gave himself credit for, and I wanted more people to read this cool thing we'd made.

Years later, we ended up writing this whole trilogy, and both of us having writing careers, all because a couple of guys decided to tell stories to their friends on the internet.

Larry Correia
April 2019

A NOTE FROM THE EDITOR

This work is the result of years of effort and is, to the very best of my knowledge, all true. Some of the names have been changed to protect the privacy of individuals involved, and the dates may not be exactly correct, but everything written here has been corroborated and verified to the maximum extent possible. Which, given the events, the secrecy, and the personalities of the individuals involved, is no small achievement.

It's hard to say for certain when the story truly began. The group that would become Majestic was founded more than a century ago, in the immediate aftermath of the Second World War. The Illuminati and the now-defunct Exodus organization both trace their lineage back to the Crusades, though how much of this is true, how much is propaganda, and how much has been lost to history is a matter of some debate.

The stories presented here are the stories I grew up with. They were told to me by my parents, as well as by Robert and Hector Lorenzo, Jill Del Toro, and Skyler Wheaton. I didn't learn many of the more grisly details until I was grown, and even then I was sworn to secrecy.

Compiling this work, corroborating the stories, interviewing the people involved, redacting what needed to be redacted, and actually getting it published took countless person-hours of work. It required a seemingly endless series of Freedom of Information Act requests, years of lobbying, several lawsuits, and a meeting with the President of the United States, and I could not have done it without the tireless efforts of my team. I would also like to personally and publicly thank Robert Lorenzo, whose honor, integrity, and dedication to upholding the Constitution made this possible. I would also like to thank the generous support of the Wheaton Foundation for Government and Corporate Accountability. Without the resources and financing of the WFGCA, this project likely never would have seen the light of day.

We don't learn from history by forgetting it, or by burying it in secrecy and lies. The machinations of governments, non-governmental organizations, and secret, powerful, unaccountable groups cost millions of innocent people their lives. Cities were razed, nations were plunged into chaos and violence, and in the case of China, the result was a bloody civil war that saw the first battlefield use of nuclear weapons since 1945.

Closer to home, a decades-long, invisible coup sought to wrest control of the United States from its flawed, but legitimate, government and place it in the hands of a cabal of shadowy individuals. It's no exaggeration to suggest that the entire world was threatened by the actions of a powerful few, moving in secret, protected by wealth and the bloated leviathan of government(s).

Had we stayed on this path, we might have seen the rise of a new technological dark age, and of an omnipresent, unaccountable, and perpetual surveillance state seemingly ripped from the nightmares of George Orwell and Ray Bradbury. The course of history was altered by actions of a few people, who through chance, luck, or providence, were in the right place, at the right time, and had the audacity to do what needed to be done.

Robert Heinlein once said that the price of freedom is the willingness to do sudden battle, anywhere, any time, and with utter recklessness. Driving this point home, the stories collected in this work aren't pleasant to read. The road the people involved walked was lonely and violent, and along the way they had to make many difficult decisions. I don't ask you to agree with the choices they made, only to understand how and why they made them. It is perhaps too easy to judge, from the comfort and safety of the present, and with the clarity of hindsight. It is important to remember that things we take for granted now were unclear or unknown at the time.

As we enter the latter half of the 21st century, it's critical that we understand the past. We very narrowly averted disaster, and will only avert it in future if we learn from history. The lessons are harsh, but we must face them with the determination to do better going forward. Future generations are counting on us.

—**Sarah Song-Valentine**

INVISIBLE WARS

WARS

THE COLLECTED DEAD SIX

DEAD SIX

by Larry Correia and Mike Kupari

"And by thy sword shalt thou live . . ."
Genesis 27:40

Prologue: Cold Open

VALENTINE
Sierra Vista Resort Hotel
Cancun, Quintana Roo
Southern Mexico
February 17

There was an angel standing over me when I opened my eyes. She was speaking but I could barely hear her. Every sound was muffled, as if I were underwater, except for the rapid pounding of my heart. *Am I dreaming? Am I dead?*

"On your feet, damn it!" the angel said as she grabbed my load-bearing vest and hauled me from my seat. My head was swimming, and every bone in my body ached. I wasn't sure where I was at first, but reality quickly came screaming back to me. We were still in the chopper. We'd crashed. The angel was pulling me toward the door. "Can you walk? Come on."

"Wait," I protested, steadying myself against the hull. "The others." I turned to where my teammates were sitting. Several of them were still strapped into their seats, but they weren't moving. Dim light poured through a gaping hole in the hull. Smoke and dust moved in the light, but behind that there was blood *everywhere*. My heart dropped into my stomach. I'd worked with these men for years.

"They're dead, bro," Tailor said, suddenly appearing in the door frame. At least one of my friends had made it. "She's right. We've got to get out of here before they start dropping mortars on us. This isn't a good place to be."

Still terribly disoriented, I shook my head, trying to clear it.

"You're in shock," the angel said, pushing me through the door of our wrecked NH-90 helicopter. "What's your name?" she asked as we stepped onto a large, tiled surface.

"V . . . Valentine," I stammered, squinting in the early morning sun. "Where are we?"

"In a pool," Tailor said, moving up a steep embankment ahead of me. "Ramirez is dead. Half the team's gone." He dropped the magazine out of his stubby, short-barreled OSW FAL and rocked in a fresh one. "Hostiles will be on us quick. You locked and loaded?"

My head was clearing. I looked down at the DSA FAL carbine in my hands and retracted the bolt slightly. A .308 round was in the chamber. My good-luck charm, a custom Smith & Wesson .44 Magnum, was still in its holster on my left thigh. I was still alive, so it hadn't let me down. "I'm ready," I said, following Tailor up the incline.

Our chopper had crashed in the deep end of a huge, pear-shaped swimming pool that had been mostly drained of water. It sat at an odd angle, still smoking, the camouflage hull absolutely riddled with bullet holes. The walls of the pool's deep end prevented the chopper from flipping over, but it was leaning to the side. There were deep gashes in the tile where the rotor had struck. The rotor had blown to pieces, and fragments were scattered everywhere.

"What happened?" I asked. The angel didn't answer at first. I remembered then; her name was Ling, the one who hired us. She followed me up the embankment, clutching a suppressed Sig 551 assault rifle.

"We crashed," she said after a moment, as if I didn't know that. We cleared the top of the incline. A handful of armed people waited for us in the shallow end of the empty pool. Aside from Tailor and me, only three were dressed in the green fatigues of my company, Vanguard Strategic Solutions. I closed my eyes and tried to catch my breath. Ten of us had left on this mission. Half hadn't made it. *Goddamn it . . .*

"You alright, Val?" Tailor asked. "I really need you with me, okay?"

"I'm fine," I said, kneeling down to check my gear. "Just a little rattled." We'd crash-landed in the middle of a deserted resort complex. The city had once been covered in places like this, but now they were all abandoned. In front of us stood a cluster of white towers that must have been a luxury hotel once. About a hundred yards behind us was the beach and ocean as far as the eye could see. The place had probably been evacuated back when the fighting started. It was dirty from disuse and littered with garbage and debris. Several plumes of smoke rose in the distance. Cancun had seen better days.

Ling brushed the dust from her black body armor. "Mr. Tailor. You're in charge now, correct? We must keep moving." I believed she was from China, but there was no accent to her speech.

With Ramirez gone, Tailor had just been promoted to team leader. He quickly looked around, taking in our surroundings. "And where in the hell do you want to go? This part of town is covered in hostiles." His East Tennessee twang were more pronounced with his anger.

"Somewhere that is not *here*. I have multiple wounded," Ling said, nodding toward the rest of her teammates, all members of the same mysterious *Exodus* organization. Like her, they were heavily armed and dressed in black. They were clustered in a tight circle near the edge of the pool, waiting for instructions. In the middle of them was a teenaged girl being tended to by their medic. "We have to get her out."

"Look, damn it," Tailor exclaimed. "We'll save your precious package. That was the deal." He jerked a thumb at the young girl as he spoke. "Let me try to get help again." Tailor squeezed the radio microphone on his vest and spoke into it. "Ocean-Four-One, this is Switchblade-Four-Alpha."

While Tailor tried to raise the base, our team sharpshooter, Skunky, ran over to see if I was okay. He was a skinny Asian guy and was in his mid-twenties, same age as me. "Dude, you're alive."

"I'm fine," I said, standing up. "What happened?"

"They hit us with some kind of big gun right after we took off. It punched that hole in the chopper. The pilots were hit with frag. We made it a few miles, but it was too much damage. They were trying to set us down when the pilot died. That's how we ended up in the pool."

Tailor looked over at us, flustered. "I can't raise the base. This is bad, really bad."

"*Switchblade-Four-Alpha, this is Stingray-Two-Zero,*" a new voice said, crackling over our radios.

That was the call-sign for our air support. One of Vanguard's Super Tucano turboprop attack planes roared overhead and began to circle our position. Vanguard was one of the best-funded private military companies in the business. We could provide our own air support if we needed to.

"Stingray-Two-Zero, this is Switchblade-Four-Alpha," Tailor said. "What's your status?"

"*We were going to ask you the same thing, Four-Alpha,*" the pilot replied. "*We've lost communication with the airfield. It looks bad down there.*"

"We've got multiple wounded and multiple KIA. We need an immediate medevac. Five of us, six Exodus personnel, and the package. Eight confirmed KIA, including the crew of the chopper." Switchblade-Four was down to just me, Tailor, Skunky, Tower, and Harper.

As Tailor talked to the pilot, trying to figure out what was going on, I looked over at Ling and her people and at the young girl that we'd gone through so much trouble to acquire. I didn't know who the girl was or why Exodus wanted her so badly. She had to be important, though, since Ling had offered us an ungodly sum of money to go into Cancun, guns blazing, to rescue her. The fact that we'd be violating the UN cease-fire hadn't seemed to bother her.

Tailor let go of his radio microphone. "Pilot says there's an armed convoy headed our way up Kukulkan Boulevard. Looks like Mendoza's militia. They saw us go down, I guess. Couple trucks full of guys and some technicals. He'll provide cover, but he's low on ammo."

"Just like us," Skunky interjected.

Ling put her gloved hand on Tailor's shoulder. "I need you to get your men moving," she said. "I'll contact my people to see if I can find out what's going on."

As Ling trotted off, Tailor turned back to us with a worried look on his face. "Val, Skunky, c'mon, we gotta go." Nodding, I followed him as he waved to the others. Standing away from the Exodus people, we huddled up. "Listen up, Switchblade-Four," Tailor said, addressing us as a team. "We're in some serious shit here. I don't know what's going on back at the base. I got a bad feeling." Tailor looked over his shoulder as an explosion detonated to the southeast. The Tucano had begun its attack run.

"This is the third time we've broken the cease-fire this month," Skunky said, anxiously grasping his scoped, accurized M14. "You don't think . . ."

"I know what *I* think," Tower, our machine gunner, said. Sweat beaded on his dark face. "I think they *left* us here."

That got everyone's attention. Being abandoned in-country was every mercenary's worst nightmare.

"It doesn't matter," Tailor said. "Everybody shut up and listen. I don't trust these Exodus assholes. When we start moving, y'all look out for each other. If we have to, we'll ditch these guys and head out on our own."

I flinched. "Tailor, they've got wounded and a kid. And where in the hell do you think we're gonna go?"

"Don't argue with me!" Tailor snapped. The pressure was getting to him. "We'll figure it out. Now get ready. We're moving out. Keep your spacing, use cover, and watch for snipers."

"*Get some!*" the rest of us shouted in response.

"Mr. Tailor, I've got some bad news," Ling said, approaching our group. She had a satellite phone in her hand. "I don't think anyone's coming for us."

"What?" Tailor asked, his face going a little pale.

"Something happened. According to my people, the UN shut down all of Vanguard's operations about an hour ago."

"The UN?" Tailor asked, exasperated. "But the Mexican government—"

"The Mexican Nationalist government dissolved last night, Mr. Tailor. I don't have all the details. I'm afraid we're on our own."

"All we have to do is get to the safe areas in the city, right?" Harper asked. Since the cease-fire, half of Cancun was controlled by UN peacekeepers.

Ling took off her tinted shooting glasses and wiped her brow on her sleeve. "I don't think that's wise," she said, putting the glasses back on. "All employees of Vanguard have been declared unlawful combatants by the UN.

I'm sorry, but we need to go, *now*." We all looked at each other, and several obscenities were uttered. We were now on our own in a country where we'd made a *lot* of enemies.

"They sold us out," Tower said. "I told you!"

Tailor spoke up. "It don't matter. Let's move." He took off after Ling. The rest of us followed, spacing ourselves out in a small column. Ling rallied the Exodus personnel, and they followed her as she climbed over the edge of the pool. Two of them were always within arm's reach of the strange young girl. We quickly moved across the courtyard of the resort complex, heading for the buildings. The grass was overgrown, and the palm trees were untended.

Tailor tried to contact the pilots for an update but got no response. It was obvious something was wrong. The small attack plane zoomed back over the resort in a steep right turn, ejecting flares as it went. An instant later, a missile shrieked across the sky, trailing smoke behind it. The Super Tucano exploded in mid-air, raining burning debris into the ocean below. A Rafale fighter jet with UN markings roared overhead, turning to the east.

Our entire group froze in disbelief. This day just kept getting better and better. Beyond the noise of the fighter's engines, the distinctive sound of a large helicopter approaching could be heard.

Tailor grabbed my shoulder and pulled me along. "Move, move, move!" he shouted, breaking into a run.

"Into the hotel, quickly!" Ling ordered. Behind us, a huge Super Cougar transport helicopter descended past our crash site and set down in the courtyard. Like the fighter jet, it bore UN markings. More than twenty soldiers, clad in urban camouflage and blue berets, spilled out of the chopper. They fanned out and immediately started shooting at us. Rounds snapped past my head as I ran across the hotel lobby. I jumped, slid across the reception desk, and crashed to the floor below. I landed on top of Tailor. Harper landed next to me.

"What do we do?" I asked, climbing off of Tailor. The water-damaged lobby was illuminated by hazy daylight streaming through the huge, shattered skylight. The wall in front of us was pockmarked with puffs of plaster dust as bullets struck. The reception desk was heavily constructed out of marble and concrete, so it provided decent cover. The hotel interior was ruined from disuse and stunk of rot.

"Why are they shooting at us?" Tailor screamed.

Ling was crouched down next to Tailor. She shouted in his ear. "I *told* you, they declared you unlawful combatants. We broke the cease-fire. They're just following orders!" She then reached up, leveled her assault rifle across the counter, and ripped off a long burst. "Protect the child!" The Exodus operatives under her command obeyed her order without hesitation. The two men guarding the young girl hustled her, crouched over, to the very back of the room. The rest started shooting, causing the UN troops outside to break their advance and dive for cover.

I glanced over at Tailor. "What do we do?"

Tailor looked around for a moment, the gears turning in his head. He swore to himself, then raised his voice so he could be heard over the noise. "Switchblade-Four! Open fire!"

My team was aggressive to the last. Tower opened up with his M60E4. The machine gun's rattling roar filled the lobby, making it difficult to hear anything. I saw a UN trooper drop to the ground as Skunky took the top of his head off with a single, well-placed shot from his M14. Harper's FAL carbine barked as he let off shot after shot.

I took a deep breath. My heart rate slowed down, and everything seemed to slow with it. I was *calm*. I found a target, a cluster of enemy soldiers advancing toward the lobby, and squeezed the trigger. The shortened alloy buttstock bucked into my left shoulder as I fired. One of the UN troops, much closer, tried to bolt across the foyer. Two quick shots and he went down. Another soldier crouched down to reload his G36 carbine. The palm tree he was hiding behind didn't conceal him well. The blue beret flew off in a spray of blood as I put two bullets through the tree.

I flinched. Something wet struck the right side of my face. Red droplets splashed my shooting glasses. Ducking back down, I reflexively wiped my glasses, smearing dark blood across them. Harper was lying on the floor, a gaping exit wound in the back of his head. Bits of gore and brain matter was splattered on the wall behind him.

I tugged on Tailor's pant leg. He dropped behind the counter. I pointed at Harper. My mouth opened, but I couldn't find anything to say. "He's dead?" Tailor asked, yelling to make himself heard as he rocked a fresh magazine into his weapon.

I nodded in affirmation. "We have to move! We're gonna get pinned down!"

"Got any grenades left?" Tailor asked. I nodded. He got Ling's attention. "Hey! We'll toss frags, then I'll pop smoke. They'll find a way to flank us if we stay here."

Ling shouted orders to the rest of her men. Tailor and I pulled fragmentation grenades from our vests and readied them.

"Frag out!" We lobbed them over the counter. The lobby was rocked by a double concussion as the explosives detonated nearly simultaneously. Dust filled the room, and the remaining glass in the skylight broke free and rained down on top of us. Tailor then threw his smoke grenade. It fired a few seconds later, and the lobby quickly filled with dense white smoke.

"That way!" Ling shouted, pointing to my right. At the far wall was a large doorway that led into the main part of the hotel. Her men filed past us at a run, stepping over Harper's body as they went.

One of Ling's men stopped. He was a hulking African man, probably six-foot-four and muscular, so broad that the rifle he carried seemed like a toy in his hands. "Commander, come on!" Behind him, a Chinese man fired short bursts through the smoke, keeping the UN troops busy as we fell back into the building. Then came the young girl, flanked by her two bodyguards.

The girl looked down at me as they hustled her by, and everything else dropped away. Her eyes were intensely blue, almost luminescent. Her hair was such a light shade of platinum blond that it looked white. It was like she was looking right through me. "I'm sorry about your friends," she whispered. At least, I could've sworn she did. I don't remember *seeing* her say anything, but I definitely *heard* her.

Tailor grabbed me by the arm. "Val, *go*, goddamn it!" It snapped me back to reality. He shoved me forward and we followed Ling's people into the building.

LORENZO
Disputed Zone
Thailand/Myanmar Border
September 6

Men with AK-47s waited for us at the gate, illuminated by the headlights of our stolen UN 6x6 truck. The guards approached the windows. One of them was wearing a necklace strung with dried human fingers.

"Decorative bunch," Carl stated.

The voice in my radio earpiece was not reassuring. "Lorenzo, I've got three at the gate. Two in the tower. FLIR shows *lots* of movement in the camp." Reaper was a quarter mile up the hill, one eye on the glowing blobs on his laptop screen and the other on the road to make sure the actual United Nations troops didn't show up.

I was signaled to roll down the window. Complying let in the humid night air and the scents of cook fires and diesel fuel. The lead guard shouted to be heard over the rumble of our engine. My Burmese was rusty, but he was gesturing with the muzzle of his rifle toward the only building with electricity, indicating our destination. I saluted. The guard returned it with a vague wave.

The heavy metal barricade was lifted and shuffled aside. Carl put the truck into gear and rolled us forward. "They bought it." The gate was shut behind us, effectively trapping us in a compound with a thousand Marxist assholes. My driver smiled as he steered us toward the command center. "That was the hard part."

"For you," I responded as I took my earpiece out and shoved it back inside my uniform shirt. Scanning across the compound showed that our aerial reconnaissance had been spot-on for once. The main generator was right where we thought it would be, ten meters from the loading dock. The machine was a thirty-year-old monstrosity of Soviet engineering, and our source had reported that it went out constantly. *Perfect.*

More soldiers, if you could use the term for a group this disorganized, were watching our big white truck with mild curiosity. Many of the local peacekeepers moonlighted smuggling munitions, so our presence was not out of the ordinary. I opened the door and hopped down. "Wait for my signal," I said before slamming the door.

Carl put the truck into reverse and backed toward the loading dock as a pair of soldiers shouted helpful but conflicting directions at him. The truck's bumper thumped into the concrete. The tarp covering the rear opened, and a giant of a man stepped from the truck and onto the dock. My associate, Train, spoke in rough tones to the thugs on the dock, pointing to the waiting crates of mortar rounds. They began to load the truck. The rebels paid him and Carl no mind. The various UN peacekeepers they had on the take changed constantly. Only the officers, like I was pretending to be, actually mattered.

The guard at the entrance held the door open for me as I walked up the steps. The building had once been part of a rubber plantation, and this had been a reception area for colonial-era visitors. It had been rather nice once but had slid into the typical third world shabbiness of faded paint, peeling wallpaper, and spreading stains. The air conditioner had died sometime during the Vietnam War, and giant malarial mosquitoes frolicked in the river of sweat running down my back. There was a man waiting for me, dressed nicer than the others, with something that casually resembled a uniform. The guard from the door followed me inside, carelessly cradling his AK as he stood behind me.

"Good evening," the warlord's lieutenant said in heavily accented English. "We were not expecting you so soon, Captain."

"I need to speak with your commander," I said curtly.

He looked me over suspiciously. I had practiced this disguise for weeks. The fake beard was perfection, my coloring changed slightly with makeup, my extra inches of height hidden with thin-soled boots and a slight slouch, and my gut augmented with padding to fill out the stolen camouflage uniform. I had watched the Pakistani captain, studying his mannerisms, his movements. I looked exactly like the fat, middle-aged, washed-up bureaucrat hack from an ineffective and corrupt organization.

Since the receptionist didn't pick the AK off his desk and empty a magazine into my chest, I could safely assume my disguise worked. I watched the guard over the tops of the Pakistani's spectacles. I had replaced the prescription lenses with plain glass after murdering the real captain this afternoon. Finally the lieutenant spoke. "Do you need more money?"

"Those border checkpoints won't bribe themselves open," I responded, my accent, tone, and inflection an almost perfect impersonation. I made a big show of looking at my watch. Carl and Train had better be loading that truck fast. "I must be back soon or my superiors will suspect something."

"General is busy man," he said, the sigh in his voice indicating what a bother I was being. He gestured toward his subordinate. "Search him."

I raised my arms as the soldier gave me a cursory pat down. I was, of course, unarmed. I couldn't risk the possibility that one of these amateurs might take their job seriously. Bringing a weapon into the same room as a rebel leader was a good way to get skinned alive. The search I received was so negligent that I could have smuggled in an RPG, but no use crying over spilt milk. I lowered my arms.

"Let's go." The lieutenant motioned for me to follow. The three of us went down a hallway that stank of cigarette smoke. The light was provided by naked bulbs that hummed and flickered with a weak yellow light. We passed other rooms flanked by soldiers. Quick glances through the windows showed village laborers, mostly old women and children, preparing narcotics for shipment. Revolutions need funding too. Finally we reached a set of double doors with a well-fed guard on each side. These boys were bigger, smartly dressed, wearing vests bristling with useful equipment, and kept their rifles casually pointed at me as we approached.

The general's personal bodyguards and the lieutenant exchanged some indecipherable dialog. I was patted down again, only this time it was brutally and invasively thorough, making me glad that my weapons were in the truck. The guard pulled my radio from my belt, yanking the cord out from under my shirt. He started to jabber at me.

"Regulations require me to have it at all times," I replied. The guard held it close to his chest, suspicious. "Fine, but I need it back when we're done here." The two led me into the inner sanctum while the lieutenant and the first guard returned to their post. That just left me with two heavily armed and trained thugs to deal with. The odds were now in my favor.

Now this room was more like it. Most warlords learned to like the finer things in life. While their army slept in mud huts and ate bugs, they lived plush and fat. Being the boss does have its perks. The furnishings were opulent, but random and mismatched, a shopping trip of looting across the country. It was twenty degrees cooler as a portable AC unit pumped air down on us.

The warlord was waiting for me, reclining in an overstuffed leather chair, smoking a giant cigar, with his feet resting on a golden Buddha. This man had spread terror over this region for a generation and grown obscenely rich in the process. He'd also become soft and complacent, which worked to my benefit. He was grizzled, scarred, and watching a 56 inch TV on the wall, tuned to some situation comedy that I couldn't understand. The volume was cranked way too high. "You want see me, Captain?" he grunted, puffing around the cigar. "What you want?"

He was ten feet away. I had a guard standing at attention on either side of me. "If I am to continue smuggling ordnance for you, I will need more money." I put on an air of meekness, of subservience, while in reality I was taking in every detail, calculating every angle. My pulse was quickening, but I gave no outward indication. I coughed politely against the cloud of Cuban smoke.

"Eh? I already pay you. Pay you good. Maybe too good . . ."

"They set up another checkpoint just north of the river. I'll need cash to pay off the garrison commander there."

The warlord sighed as he stood. "UN troops so greedy." He limped over to the wall and pulled back a tapestry, revealing a vault door, just where the informant had said it would be. "Old days, we just kill each other. Peacekeepers make it so complicated now. Peacekeepers . . ." He snorted. "No better than my men, but with pretty blue hats." No disagreement from me on that one. The UN was less than useless, though their ineptitude created plenty of business opportunities for men like me. "Maybe someday my country not have war. Then my men get pretty blue hats, and we can go to other countries and rape *their* women and take *their* money. Hah!"

I waited patiently for him to spin the dial. That vault was state of the art, rated TXTL-60, and would have required quite some time and a lot of noise for me to defeat on my own. Better to just have the man open it for you. I glanced over at one of the waiting guards. He had a Russian bayonet sheathed on the front of his armor. He smirked, taking my look to be one of nervousness. After all, what did he have to worry about from a middle-aged Pakistani who was just padding his paycheck? The guard turned his attention back to the TV.

"How much you need?" the warlord asked. The lock clicked. The vault hissed open.

The man at my right snickered along with the laugh track as my hand flew to his sheathed bayonet. "I'll be taking all of it." Steel flashed red, back and forth, and before either guard could even begin to react, they were dead. I jerked the knife out from under the second guard's ear and let the body flop.

"Huh?" The warlord turned and saw only me standing. His bleary eyes flicked down to see his men twitching on the ground, then back up at me, dripping bayonet in hand. Then he said something incomprehensible but obviously profane as understanding came. The general's pistol started out of his holster. I covered the distance in an instant and ran the knife up the inside of his arm before driving it between his ribs. I removed the gun from his nerveless fingers and left the old man tottering as I went back for my radio. The warlord went to his knees as I hit the transmit button.

"I'm in."

Carl came back before I even had the earpiece back in place. "Truck's loaded. Status?"

Stepping over the dying warlord, I glanced inside the vault. It was about the size of a walk-in closet. Rebellions ran on cold, hard cash. There were stacks of money inside. A quick check revealed that much of it was in euros and pounds, which was good, because many of the regional denominations weren't worth the effort to carry out.

"Status? Filthy rich. The intel was right on. Train, bring three of the big packs. You've got two guards in the entrance, three more in the hallway. Carl, you got a shot at that generator?"

"No problem."

"Execute," I ordered before noticing that the warlord was still breathing, gasping for air around a perforated lung, one useable hand clamped to his side, the spreading puddle of blood ruining the nice Persian rug beneath. I squatted next to him. "I must've hit you a little lower than expected. You should already be dead. Sorry about that."

"Who . . . who . . ." the old man gasped.

"You don't know me. It's nothing personal, just business." The lights flickered and died as Carl killed the generator. It was pitch black inside the old plantation. I rested next to the dying man and waited. The warlord finally breathed his last and embarked on his short journey to Hell. A moment later the door opened and a hulking shadow entered. Train pressed a tubular object into my hands and I quickly strapped the night-vision device over my head. The world was a sudden brilliant green. "You get them all?"

"Smoked 'em," he answered as he handed me my suppressed pistol. The can was warm to the touch. "Where's the cash?"

The two of us stuffed as many bills as would fit into the three big backpacks. I threw on one, and Train, being half pack animal, took the other two. I took point and led us out. One more guard blundered into the hallway from one of processing rooms. We didn't even slow as I put a pair of nearly silent 9mm rounds through his skull. Bodies were scattered around the entrance. It had started to rain. Carl started the truck as Train climbed into the back. I handed up my pack of cash.

I crawled into the cab and pulled off the NVGs. "Let's go." Carl nodded and put the 6x6 into gear. I kept my pistol in my lap, and I knew that Train was ready to fire a belt-fed machine gun through the fabric back of the truck, just in case the alarm was raised before we made it out.

The rain comes hard in Burma. The gate guards barely even paid us mind as the truck approached. I watched them through the windshield wipers as they sullenly left the security of their overhang to move the barricade. The man with the finger-necklace glanced back toward the command post and shrugged as he noticed that the lights were out again. We rolled through the gate uncontested, the muddy jungle road stretched out before us. We were home free. I activated my radio. "Reaper, we're out. Meet us at the bridge."

"On the way," was the distorted reply.

"We did it," I sighed. The spirit gum pulled at my cheeks as I yanked the fake beard off and tossed it on the floorboards. The glasses and idiotic blue beret followed. "There had to be close to a mil in the vault."

"That was too easy," Carl said, always the pessimist.

"No. We're just that *good.*"

There was a sudden clang of metal from the back, then a burst of automatic weapons fire. I glanced at Carl, and he was already giving the truck more gas. Somebody had raised the alarm. "Told you so."

"Lorenzo, taking fire," Train shouted into the radio. Then there was a terrible racket as he opened up with the SAW. Bullets quit hitting our truck, which was a relief, since it just happened to be filled to the brim with high explosives.

I checked the rear-view mirror. Through the raindrops I could see headlights igniting. They were coming after us, and they were going to be really pissed off. Train had just popped the men who would normally be moving the barricade, so that would buy us a minute, but our stolen truck would never outrun all of those jeeps on this kind of road.

It could never be simple. "Go to Plan B," I said into the radio.

We reached the bridge over the Salawin River nearly a minute ahead of our pursuers. A hundred yards long, it was the only crossing for miles and had been built by captives of the Japanese army in the waning of World War Two. The wood creaked ominously as our heavy truck rumbled over it. We stopped halfway across and bailed out. Headlights winked through the rain three times from the other end of the bridge, confirming that Reaper was waiting for us. Train tossed a bag of money to Carl and the detonator to me.

He shouldered the other two bags with one hand and carried the SAW like a suitcase.

The three of us walked to the waiting Land Rover. I could hear the approaching rebel vehicles. "Bummer about the ordnance," Train said. "That would've been worth some serious dough back in Thailand."

"Beats having our fingers end up on a necklace," Carl muttered.

We reached the waiting vehicle and piled in. Reaper scooted over as Carl got behind the driver's seat. Carl always drove. He spun us around through the mud so we could head toward the border. I glanced back at the bridge, noting the swarm of flashlights swinging around the UN truck. I waited until we were several hundred yards down the road before pressing the button.

The C4 that Train had stuck to the crates of munitions detonated. The truck was destroyed in a spreading concussion that blew the pursuing rebels into clouds of meat and turned the Say-Loo River bridge into splinters.

My crew gasped at the intensity of the display. "Impressive," I agreed before turning my attention to counting the money.

LORENZO
Bangkok, Thailand
September 7

My group had the private back room of the restaurant to ourselves. The food had arrived, the mood was happy, and the piped-in music was loud and had lots of cymbals in it. The crew was in high spirits. The job was a success. Some Burmese scumbags were a lot poorer, and we were a whole lot richer.

Reaper, our techie, was proceeding to get drunk. He was young, skinny, and it didn't take a whole lot of alcohol. Carl, our wheelman and my second-in-command, was slightly less sullen than usual, beady rat eyes darting back and forth while he chain-smoked cheap unfiltered cigarettes. Train, the muscle, was his usual good-natured self, laughing at every stupid comment. I was enjoying some nuclear-hot curry death mushroom dish and basking in the glow of another excellent score.

The beads leading into the private room parted, allowing a giant whale of a man in a three-piece suit to enter the room. He was taller than Train and probably weighed more than my entire team put together. He was freakishly large. My crew was instantly quiet. There was a slight motion to my right as Carl drew his CZ-75 and held it under the table.

"Lorenzo, I presume." The fat man pulled up a chair and sat. The chair creaked ominously under his mass. "Is that supposed to be your first name or your last?"

I finished chewing, savoring the eye-watering pain. "Neither. Who the hell are you?"

"My name is not important. I am the man that provided the information for your latest job. I take it that the warlord's vault was full, as promised."

I had never met the informant in person. The job had been arranged through intermediaries. That was normal in my line of work. The fewer people who knew me, the better, yet the fat man had found me, and I did not like being found. "We had an agreement. Your share will be left at the drop tomorrow."

Bald and sweaty, the giant shrugged. He was obese, but there was something about the way that he moved that suggested there was a lot of dense muscle under all that blubber. "Do not be alarmed. This is not a trap. Keep the money. Consider it a tip. You see, I work for Big Eddie." He trailed off as he spoke, smiling with that strange quality of the slightly schizophrenic. He must have noticed my unconscious flinch at the name. "Big Eddie has an assignment for you."

My crew exchanged nervous glances. *Oh hell no.* Everyone here knew what working for Eddie entailed. They all looked to me for confirmation. I slowly put my chopsticks down. "I retired from his organization. Me and your boss are square."

"I am afraid you are mistaken," the fat man stated. "Our employer does not believe in retirement, merely extended leaves of absence, and then only at his convenience. You have been away from the fold so long. He merely arranged this last assignment as a test to see if you had maintained your previous skill sets."

I had always known that some sort of reckoning would come. Standing to leave, I pulled some Thai baht from my wallet and threw them on the table. I had no interest in anything related to Big Eddie, one of the most brutal crime lords in history and an all-around bad dude. Prior jobs performed for the man had left me independently wealthy, but with a lot of scars and a trail of bodies from here to Moscow. "Come on, guys; let's go."

"Our employer insists that you are the only person who can complete this assignment. Your knowledge of languages, of disguises, your ability to blend in with any culture, to infiltrate any group, and your gift for violence are legendary. He spoke *very* highly of you, that there is no place safe from you, no item you cannot steal, no target you cannot eliminate. You, sir, are the best of the best, and he is prepared to compensate you generously for your valuable services."

It didn't matter how much money he was talking about, because it just wasn't worth it. "Tell him to find somebody else."

The fat man laughed, but it never reached his eyes. "Our employer said you would say that." He placed a manila folder on the table and shoved it toward me. He passed other folders to Carl, Train, and Reaper. "He said you should look at this before you make any rash decisions, Mr—" And then he called me by my real last name.

I froze. There was no way he could have known that. He opened the folder.

Pictures. Lots of pictures.

My crew began to flip through the pages of their files, eyes widening in shock, mouths falling open. Carl began swearing in Portuguese. Reaper, dumbfounded, stood and pulled his Glock from his waistband, letting it dangle, folder still open in his other hand. Finally, he raised the gun and pointed it at the fat man's head and snarled, "You're threatening my mom?"

"Of course." The fat man wiped his brow with a silk handkerchief as he began to read from my folder. "Mr. Lorenzo, your adoptive family consisted of six siblings, oh my, I do love large families. Robert, Jenny, Tom, George, Pat." He shoved a list of addresses toward me, paper clipped to a series of photos. "Big Eddie knows where each of them lives, where they work, what they do, and how to reach them at any time. Should you attempt to contact them, Big Eddie will find out, and he will be most displeased."

"They know about my daughter?" Train asked in disbelief, his big hands crunching the edges of the folder.

"You bastard." I knew he was not bluffing. Eddie was capable of *anything*. They must have been gathering this information on me for years.

"All five of your siblings are married. You have nine nieces and nephews, with one bundle of joy on the way," he told me as he passed me another stack of photos. School photos. I was across the table before he knew what was happening, my knife open and pressed hard between his second and third chin.

He didn't even flinch. "Your mother lives with your sister Jenny now, still in your hometown. On Tuesday evenings she goes to her book club. During the week she babysits while Jenny goes to work as the night manager of an International House of Pancakes."

I twisted the knife, and a small trickle of blood splattered on his white collar. His little pig eyes were hard and cold as he stared me down. "Your oldest brother, Robert, is, surprisingly enough, a federal agent. I take it he has no idea what you do for a living. He has a lovely home in the suburbs, a beautiful wife, a son, and two lovely daughters. You will take on this assignment or Big Eddie will take care of them first. You know how he feels about police officers."

"And if I just cut your throat and disappear?" I hissed, leashed anger bubbling to the surface.

"You won't. We've studied you. You will do what it takes to protect your family. Plans are in place so that if I do not return, or if you are not observed attempting to complete this assignment, then your family will pay the price. You may try to warn them, you may try to protect them, you may even attempt to locate our organization. If anyone is capable enough to try, it is you. But you cannot save all of them. You know how great our employer's reach is, and there is no place in this world where you can hide them all. At the first sign of a failure to fully cooperate, a terrible bloodbath will be on your head."

He wasn't bluffing. Eddie was more powerful than most governments, a shadowy figure involved in every criminal enterprise on the planet. I had never met him, and like many who had done his bidding, I suspected he wasn't a lone individual at all, rather a very ruthless organization. Either way, if Eddie wanted somebody dead, it was only a matter of time. I withdrew the Benchmade, wiped the blood on the fat man's shirt, folded the blade, and put it back in my pocket.

I lived under an assumed name. We all did. In this world, anything that was precious to you became a liability, potential leverage against you. How had Eddie found them? Where had I screwed up? I knew that if I tried to warn them, even if they believed me, there was no way I could protect them all. I slowly sat back down. My crew followed my example.

"That's better. Here is your mission packet. There are three phases. As you can see from the deadline, time is of the essence."

I opened the proffered folder, read a few lines, then laughed out loud. "You've got to be kidding. This is impossible."

"The clock is ticking, Mr. Lorenzo. Complete this mission or we will kill everyone you have ever loved." He gestured at the mushroom dish. "Are you going to finish that?"

"Shoulda just shot him," Carl muttered before downing the last of his beer. He crushed the can in his fist and tossed it out the fourth-floor window of our seedy Bangkok hotel room. Odds were that the can hit a tourist or a prostitute. "Suicide, this job, I tell you that. Better to run."

Train rubbed one callused hand across his face. Haggard, he looked like he'd aged ten years in the last hour. "And then what? Hide? Where are we gonna go?"

"*We* aren't the problem," I stated. Each of us was fully capable of going to ground and totally disappearing. The four of us exchanged knowing glances. If we thwarted Big Eddie, we were going to be knee-deep in dead babies. I hadn't even spoken to my family in years. They thought I was some sort of international businessman. I sent them a Christmas card once in a while, that kind of thing, but it wasn't like we were close. I'd checked out of the normal world. But I couldn't let my brothers and sisters pay for my sins. They weren't like me. They were *good* people. They were the only people who had ever shown me any kindness in my miserable youth.

We were quiet for a long time as my crew mulled over our predicament. Finally, I broke the silence. "Eddie's men will be randomly watching these people. As soon as any one of them is contacted, they'll kill all the others. We could maybe save some, but I don't want to take that chance. I'm in. If any of you want out, I understand. Take your share and go. If Eddie sees that I'm on my way to the Mideast, he'll know I'm working the job. It might buy you some time to get to your people."

Reaper immediately raised one bony hand. "I'm with you, boss." He was the youngest member of my crew. I had hired him in Singapore, where he'd been avoiding extradition to the US for a host of felony charges, and put him to work as our technical geek. I was the closest thing he had to a father figure, and that was just sad.

"This is going to be the toughest thing we've ever done," I warned. "There's no shame in backing out. We're probably going to get killed if we're lucky or thrown into the worst kind of prison you can imagine if we're not."

"I'm in," Reaper repeated with a lot more force than you would expect from looking at him. I had known that whatever I had voted for, Reaper would have my back.

I nodded. "Carl?"

My oldest friend grunted as he leaned forward in his chair. We had worked together for a very long time. When we had first met, Carl had been a Portuguese mercenary helping to overthrow an African government. Between the two of us we'd killed piles of people in dire need of killing, and quite a few who had just been in the wrong place at the wrong time. We'd robbed, conned, stolen, and murdered our way across four continents. The contents of Carl's folder were a mystery. He was like my brother, but I didn't know what he had left behind in the Azores all those years ago. He wasn't exactly the conversational sort.

Carl shrugged. "Whatever . . . I'm in."

The last member of my crew hesitated. I knew that Train's folder contained pictures of his estranged wife and little girl. Omaha, Nebraska wasn't out of Eddie's reach. Train's ex had divorced him while he had been serving time. She didn't like being married to a criminal, but she apparently had no moral problems cashing the checks he mailed to her after every single one of our jobs, either. Train loved his young daughter more than life itself, and I could see that fact roiling around behind his eyes as he made up his mind.

"I can't," he said simply. "Sorry, Lorenzo."

I nodded.

"Ah, Train, come on," Reaper whined. "We need you, big guy."

"I don't trust Eddie," Train spat. "And you'd be an idiot to trust him. He knows about my kid, man. I've got to go get her."

I extended my hand. He hesitated only briefly before crushing it in his big mitt. He was one of only a handful of people in this world that I actually trusted. I had worked with Train for nearly a decade and his decision didn't surprise me at all. For a man who could snap a neck with one hand, he had a remarkably soft heart. "Watch your back," I ordered.

He gave me a sad smile. We both knew that this was the end of a long run. "No problem, chief."

Train took his share of the money and slipped out that night. At the time, none of us had realized that our hotel room had been bugged even though we had swept the room.

The next morning I had awoken to a knock on our door. When I answered, gun in hand, the messenger was gone, but there had been a cardboard box left there addressed to me. The size and weight told me what it was even before I opened it. Train's severed head had been neatly wrapped in newspaper. The only other contents were a note.

I AM WATCHING YOU.

Chapter 1: Job Security

VALENTINE
ATC Research & Development Facility
North Las Vegas, Nevada, USA
January 18
0330

I made my way around Building 21, rattling door handles as I went. It was the second time I'd checked this building during my shift, and I didn't expect to find it unsecured. Still, the night-shift maintenance guys had a habit of leaving doors unlocked as they did their rounds, so I often had to relock them during *my* rounds.

Finding nothing out of place, I returned to the front of the building. Mounted on the wall next to the front door was a small metal button, resembling a watch battery. I retrieved from my pocket an electronic wand, and touched the tip of it to the metal button on the wall.

Nothing happened. "Goddamn it," I grumbled, wiping both the button and the end of the wand with my finger. The wand was my electronic leash. As I hit the buttons across the facility, the wand recorded the time that I was there, thus proving to my employers that I was actually doing my job. However, if there was any moisture at all on either the button or the wand, it wouldn't register.

I tried the button again. Still, nothing happened. Swearing some more, I pulled a small cloth out of my pocket and wiped down the button and the tip of the wand. Yet again, nothing happened. A pulse of anger shot through me, and I threw the wand against the steel door of Building 21. It bounced off, leaving not so much as a dent, and clattered to the concrete sidewalk below.

I took a deep breath and looked around. The sprawling ATC facility was dark, lit only by the amber lights around the buildings and along the roads. To the south, the omnipresent glow of the Strip lit up the sky. The night air was cool but had the familiar dusty stink of Las Vegas.

I looked down at the wand and frowned. Everywhere I'd been, everything I'd done, and *this* was what I was reduced to. I had seen combat on four

21

continents and had survived it all, only to be utterly defeated by badly designed electronics. I sighed loudly, though there was no one around to hear.

I picked up my wand and made one last attempt. Touching it to the button, the wand beeped loudly and registered the hit. Muttering to myself, I stuffed the wand back into my pocket and returned to my patrol truck. Building 21 was last on my scheduled rounds; I had nothing else to do but drive around for the remaining three and a half hours of my shift.

As I drove, I listened to a late-night radio program called *From Sea to Shining Sea*. It was basically four hours of people talking about conspiracy theories, aliens, ghosts, and stuff like that. Most of it was a bunch of hooey, in my opinion, but it was often entertaining. Listening to the conspiracy theories regarding Mexico, the United Nations, and Vanguard Strategic Services always gave me a chuckle. They had *no idea*. The host, Roger Geonoy, was talking about secret government black helicopters or something with a guest. The guest was a frequent visitor to the show and only called himself "Prometheus." He never gave his real name. Because, you know, *they* are listening. I barely paid attention as they went on about the supposed shadow government and its stealth helicopters. I did get another chuckle when Prometheus insisted that these choppers are sound-suppressed and can fly in what he called "whisper mode." I'd ridden in enough helicopters to know just how freaking loud they are.

As Roger Geonoy listened to Prometheus blather on about black helicopters and cattle mutilations, I remembered my last helicopter ride in detail. The noise of the engines, the roar of gunfire. The sickening sound of bullets hitting the hull. The shrieking of the alarm as we dropped into a drained swimming pool. The ragged, bloody hole in Ramirez' head. Doc's guts spilled out onto the floor of the chopper.

"Sierra-Eleven, Dispatch," my radio squawked, startling me. I realized that I'd been sitting at a stop sign for minutes on end. *From Sea to Shining Sea* had gone to commercial break. My heart was pounding.

Shaking it off, I answered my radio. "This is Sierra-Eleven."

"Electrical Maintenance needs you to let them into Building Fourteen," the Dispatcher said.

"Uh, ten-four," I replied. "Ten-seventeen." I took a deep breath and returned my attention to doing my stupid job.

Hours later, I pulled my patrol truck into a parking space behind the Security Office. Putting the truck in park, I finished the paperwork on my clipboard, recorded the mileage, and cut the engine. My breath steamed in the cool January air as I stepped out of the truck and made my way into the office.

"Mornin', Val," my supervisor, Mr. Norton, said as I passed his office en route to the ready room. "Anything happen last night?"

Pausing, I leaned into the doorway for a moment. "It was quiet, Boss." Leaning in farther, I handed him my paperwork. "Is McDonald here yet?"

"Yeah, he's on time today," Mr. Norton said. "Have a good weekend, Val."

"You, too, boss," I said, leaving the doorway and making my way down the hall. I pushed open the door to the ready room. My relief, McDonald, was standing by the gun lockers, seemingly half awake. He was *always* seemingly half awake and had a perpetual five o'clock shadow on top of it. I found him tiresome.

He had the muzzle of his pistol in the clearing barrel as he chambered a round. Stepping past him, I opened my own gun locker, drew the .357 Magnum revolver from the holster on my left hip, and placed it inside.

"Why do you still carry that thing? We've got the new nine-mils, you know," he said, holstering the pistol he'd just loaded.

"I shoot revolvers better," I answered, not looking at him. "Not much to pass on. It was quiet last night. Some contractors are working by the old warehouse on the south side, so make sure Gate Ten is closed and locked after they leave." I slung my gun belt over my shoulder and made my way out of the office and into the parking lot.

I found my Mustang and cranked it up. We weren't allowed to have personal phones at the facility, so I habitually left mine in the center console, turned off. The radio was playing the morning news, but I found it hard to pay attention. I'd lived outside of the United States for years; domestic news was something I was used to just ignoring. Frowning, I changed radio stations and listened to music for the rest of my commute home.

My apartment building was halfway across town. It didn't look like much, but it was cheap for Vegas and wasn't in a really bad neighborhood. It was an old motel that had been converted to apartments. The rooms were small, but there weren't a lot of gangbangers and hookers hanging around all the time, and the cops weren't there every night.

I made my way upstairs to the second floor. As I approached my door, I saw my next-door neighbor leaning against the railing. She smiled. "Hey," she said, sounding tired. She removed a pack of cigarettes from her jacket pocket.

"Mornin', Liz," I said, leaning against the railing next to her. She was wearing a blue uniform, like me, but she wasn't a security guard. Liz was a paramedic, and like me she also worked the night shift. She usually got home about the same time I did. Her curly red hair was pulled into a bun under her cap.

"Long night last night?" I asked as she dug for her lighter.

"Jesus Christ," she said. "Goddamn tweakers." Liz had been a medic for ten years and had seen just about everything.

"Here," I said, handing her my Zippo lighter. "You okay?"

"Thank you. I'm fine—my partner just had to fight with this one asshole." I'd never met Liz's partner, but apparently he was a big dude. That was probably for the best, as Liz herself stood barely five foot three. She paused while she lit her cigarette. She then snapped the lighter closed but didn't hand it back to me.

"That's an interesting logo on there," she said, holding my lighter up. It was matte black and engraved with a skull with a switchblade knife clutched in its teeth. I'd had the lighter a long time, and it was pretty scratched up. "Were you in the military?"

I didn't say anything. Looking over at Liz, I saw that she was studying me intently. "I was," I said at last. "Air Force. A long time ago."

"You're too young to have done anything a long time ago."

I chuckled. "I enlisted when I turned eighteen."

"I figured," she said, handing me the lighter. "You seem like the type. Was that your unit logo or something?"

"This? No. I was in the Security Forces. I did one stint in Afghanistan before I got out."

"What'd you do after that?" she asked.

"I went to work," I said awkwardly. I didn't know Liz all that well, and I wasn't used to talking about myself with people. "I was a security consultant for a few years."

"Consultant? What kind of work did you do?" she asked.

"Uh, the usual stuff," I said awkwardly. "Can't really tell you."

"Oh, whatever," she snorted, exhaling smoke.

"No, really," I said. "I signed a nondisclosure agreement." Leaving out the fact that my company no longer existed, I made a big show of yawning. "Hey, I think I need to hit the rack."

"You sure you don't want some breakfast? It's my weekend to have the kids. I'm making bacon and eggs in a little bit."

"Thanks, but I'm really tired," I said with a sheepish smile. I turned and unlocked my door.

"Hey, Val," Liz called after me just as I stepped inside. "I do PTSD counseling on the side. If you ever need to talk . . ."

I smiled at her again. "Thank you. I'm okay, really," I said, before closing the door. I locked it, dropped my backpack on the floor, and plopped down in front of my computer. I had one e-mail waiting for me.

Michael Valentine:

Have you considered my offer? You're an excellent soldier and you risked your life to save someone precious to us. Our organization could use people like you. I hope to hear back from you soon.

Song Ling

The e-mail was from a randomized address, so I had no idea where it was sent from. It included a footnote with a long phone number for me to call if I was interested, and it said that I could call that number from anywhere in the world.

Leaning back in my chair, I took a deep breath, and rubbed my eyes. I closed my e-mail browser and stood up. I wanted to take a shower and go to bed. I hoped that I wouldn't have nightmares this time, but I knew that I would. I always did.

VALENTINE
Las Vegas, Nevada, USA
January 18
1245

I awoke to the sound of my phone ringing. Noticing my clock, I realized I'd only been asleep for a few hours. I reached over to my nightstand, grabbed my phone, and looked at the display. I didn't recognize the number.

"Hello?" I asked, my voice sounding groggy.

"What're you doing, fucker?"

"Who *is* this?"

The voice laughed. "Has it been that long, bro?"

"Tailor?" I asked.

"What are you doing?"

"I'm sleeping. How did you get this number?"

"Well, get up! I'll be there in about half an hour."

"Be *where*?"

"At your apartment."

"What? How the hell do you know where I live? How did you get this number?" Tailor didn't answer. "Never mind. What do you want?"

"I'll tell you when I get there. Get dressed, I'm taking you to lunch. Don't dress like a slob, we're going someplace nice."

"But—"

"*Val.* Trust me."

I was quiet for a few seconds. "Fine. This better be good." I hung up on him, ran my fingers through my hair, and got up.

Twenty-five minutes later, there was a knock on my door. Now fully dressed and mostly awake, I crossed my small apartment and looked through the peephole. I saw Tailor's misshapen head, distorted through the tiny optic, his eyes hidden behind Oakley sunglasses. I opened the door.

"Tailor." His head was slightly less misshapen in person. Tailor grinned. He hadn't changed a bit. His dirty blond hair was buzzed down to almost nothing, as always. He was dressed casually but still looked uptight. He was wearing a nice leather jacket.

"Val." He stuck out his hand. I took it, and we shook firmly. "Long time no see, bro."

"C'mon in," I said, stepping aside.

Tailor looked around my apartment. "This is where you live? What'd you do, spend all your money?"

"I've got plenty of money in savings," I said testily. "I just wanted to keep a low profile. This place isn't bad." Tailor then noticed my blue uniforms hanging against the wall.

"You're a security guard?" he asked incredulously. "You've been in how many wars? And now you're a security guard?"

"Ain't much demand for my skill set, you know," I said, looking for my jacket. "Where are we going?"

"I found a steakhouse."

"You're buying me a steak? What? Okay, what the hell is going on?"

"Don't worry about it. I'll tell you about it over lunch." I looked at him hard for a moment. I was about to tell him to get the hell out of my apartment and go back to bed. Something told me to hear him out, though. I felt that I owed him that much; he'd saved my life more than once. I nodded, put on my sunglasses, and followed him out the door.

"It's good to see you again," I said from the passenger's seat of Tailor's Ford Expedition, looking out the window. Neither one of us had said anything since we'd left my apartment.

"You, too, bro," Tailor replied, his voice sounding unusually upbeat.

"So, where are we going?" I asked as he drove me across town. We were headed downtown, toward the Strip.

"Ruth's Chris," he said. "It's over on Paradise."

"Dude, that place is expensive."

"When did you become so *cheap*, Val?" Tailor asked. "Besides, I'm buying. Don't worry about it! You think I'd drag you out of bed and not buy lunch?"

"*Yes*," I said, folding my arms across my chest.

"Fair enough." A lopsided grin appeared on his face. "But I didn't this time."

A short while later, I found myself sitting at a booth in the steakhouse, waiting for my food. Tailor sat across from me. We both sipped glasses of Dr. Pepper and talked about nothing.

"Okay, Tailor, what's this all about? I haven't heard from you since Mexico. Now you show up on my doorstep and buy me an expensive steak. What's going on?"

Tailor set down his Dr. Pepper. "Have you thought about going back to work?"

"I *have* a job," I said, sounding a little huffy.

"What do you make, ten bucks an hour?" Tailor asked, sarcasm in his voice.

"I make *eighteen* bucks an hour," I said, sounding more than a little huffy this time. "And no one shoots at me. Also? I haven't been to a single funeral since I started."

"Okay, how's that working out for you? Are you happy?"

"What?"

"Are you happy doing this? Going to work every day like a regular guy? Is that what you want?

"Well, I . . ." I fell silent, and remained quiet for a long moment. I took a deep breath. "I *hate* this," I said quietly. "It's like . . . I try so hard to fit in, to understand people, to make this work. But I *can't.* I just . . ."

"You know what the problem is, Val?" Tailor asked, interrupting me. I raised my eyebrows at him. "You're a *killer.*"

"That's not it," I protested.

"The *fuck* it's not," he said. "How long have I known you? Four years, right?"

"Since Africa," I said, remembering my first deployment with Vanguard. It seemed like a lifetime had passed since then.

"Right. And you know what I've learned in all that time? You're a badass. You don't think you are, and you've got that baby face and stupid smile, and you act all quiet and shy. But when you strip all that away, you're a killer."

"So?" I asked. His analysis of my personality was making me uncomfortable. I looked around the restaurant, studying the other customers, watching the doors as people came in and out.

"See what you're doing right now? You're checking the exits, aren't you?" Tailor said.

"Fine. So I'm the problem. I'm some kind of badass that can't understand how to fit in the real world, just like in that old Kurt Russell movie. Is that it?"

"No. The problem isn't that *you* don't understand. It's that *they* don't understand," he said, moving his arm to indicate the other people in the restaurant. "*They* don't live in the real world. They haven't seen the things that you've seen or done the things that you've done. Most of these people have never killed a man or buried a friend. Hell, most probably have never even *fired a gun*. And there you sit, concealing a 44 Magnum, watching the exits, surrounded by people who just don't *get it*. You're a *killer*, Val, and no matter how long you work a bullshit nine-to-five job, you're not gonna change that."

I didn't respond for a few moments. "You're more perceptive than you look," I said at last, rubbing my eyes.

"The question is," Tailor went on, "what changed? It didn't used to bother you. I know you have nightmares, Val. Everybody has nightmares. Everybody has regrets. Well, except me. *I* don't. But most people do. It didn't used to eat you up. It's eating you up now. I can see it on your face. What happened?"

"*Mexico* happened, Tailor," I said flatly, looking him in the eye again.

Tailor took a deep breath and leaned back in his seat. "That was ugly, wasn't it?"

"Ugly? We got stranded in hostile territory, abandoned, left to *die*. We barely got out alive. So yeah, I guess you could say it was *ugly*."

"We got out, didn't we?"

"Only because of Ling and her people."

"It doesn't matter," Tailor said, taking another sip of his soda. "We lived."

"Tell that to Ramirez's family."

"Ramirez didn't *have* any family, Val," Tailor snapped, setting his glass down hard. "None of us did. It's why we were good at our jobs. It's why we got the good jobs, the good pay, and the good equipment. It's why we were on the Switchblade teams in the first place. We had nothing to come home to anyway. Ramirez is dead. Harper is dead. Tower is dead. *Everybody dies*, Val. You don't get to pick how or when. I worked with Ramirez longer than you. Don't you *dare* use his death as an excuse to mope around like a teenaged drama queen!"

I didn't say anything, and I didn't look at Tailor. We were briefly interrupted as the waitress brought us our food.

"Is that what's eating you, Val?" Tailor asked at last, chewing expensive steak with his mouth open. "Survivor's guilt?"

"You don't understand," I said quietly, cutting my steak.

"How the hell do *you* know what I understand?" Tailor said to me. "I've been doing this longer than you, Val. You think you've seen some shit? I've seen some shit, too. The difference is, I *deal with it* instead of letting it screw me up. Until you do that, nothing's going to change for you. Living in this dump, punishing yourself with a stupid job and a stupid life isn't going to make you feel any better."

I ate my steak in silence, not sure what to say. We were quiet for an awkwardly long time before either one of us spoke. I set my fork down and looked at my former partner. "What's this all about, Tailor? I know you didn't drive all the way to Vegas and buy me an expensive steak just to yell at me about my angst."

Tailor took a moment to finish chewing before he spoke. "I've got a job offer for you."

I raised my eyebrows. "I'm listening."

"You'd have to leave soon. Like in the next week or so."

"I'd have to break my lease."

"Will that be a problem?"

"No, I just won't get my deposit back. Who's it with?"

"I don't know," Tailor said, flatly.

"What do you mean, *you don't know*?"

Tailor leaned in, his voice hushed. "I think it's a front for the government. They're real hush-hush about everything. They just call it *The Project*. They're offering twenty-five K a month, plus expenses."

I almost choked on my Dr. Pepper. "Christ, that's like three hundred thousand dollars a year!" My annual salary with Vanguard had been about a hundred thousand dollars a year, plus operational bonuses. I only got paid that much because I was on one of the Switchblade teams.

"Tax-exempt," Tailor added.

"What? From a US company? No Medicare or Social Security?" By US law, if you were out of the United States for three hundred and thirty days of a year, you didn't have to pay income taxes. This capped out at eighty thousand dollars. Everything above that was taxable income.

"You get paid what you get paid. They told me they'd take care of the IRS aspects of it."

"And you're just trusting these people?"

"Val, they've already deposited a twenty thousand dollar signing bonus into my bank account. I trust *that*."

"Money talks, huh?"

"Money talks."

"Have you told anyone else about this?"

"I called Skunky," Tailor replied, sipping his soda.

"Really? How's he doing, anyway? Haven't heard from him."

"He lives in California now."

"Eew," I said, making a face.

"I know, right?"

"You know, you're not the first one to offer me a job," I said.

"Really? Have you been looking?"

"No. Every couple of months I get an e-mail from Ling. She wants me to sign up with her group."

"Val, that crazy Chinese bitch ain't gonna sleep with you."

"What? That's not—"

"Oh, the hell it's not," he interrupted, grinning. "Come on, Val, I know you. You've got a thing for Asians, and I watched you drool all over her from the moment she showed up. The puppy love was cute, Val, it really was."

"Hey, that *crazy bitch* saved our lives."

"Well, we wouldn't have been there if Exodus hadn't hired us in the first place. We were expendable. And we *paid* for it."

I sighed. "I know. It's why I haven't answered. Her group considers me some kind of hero, I think, because I saved that kid we rescued."

"Val, her group . . . how much do you know about them?"

"I've done some research. It's hard to find much. They're like global vigilantes. They kill slavers, drug runners . . ."

"That's just the beginning," Tailor said. "They're a very secretive, very well-funded transnational paramilitary organization. They're like a cult. They go around the world, shooting people and blowing shit up in the name of the greater good or something. The UN considers them a terrorist group."

"They didn't think too highly of Vanguard, either, Tailor."

"Look," Tailor continued, "I'm saying you might want to think twice before getting involved with some crazy terrorist group because you're bored and you're trying to get laid. I mean come on, this is *Nevada*. If you want to screw an Asian chick so bad, just go to a whorehouse."

My mouth fell open. "You . . ." I cracked a smile and began to laugh. "You're a *dick*, you know that?"

"Yeah, I know," he said matter-of-factly. "Even still, you shouldn't rush into something like that when you don't know anything about it."

"Says the guy who shows up on my doorstep and tries to get me to take a mysterious job with a mysterious company he doesn't know anything about," I said, a wry grin appearing on my face.

"Okay," Tailor admitted, "but we'll be there together. If there are any problems, well, we'll deal with it. We've been in bad situations before."

"The money's too good, Tailor. Something stinks."

"I know," he said again. "I think it's something to do with the Middle East."

"As in Afghanistan? I really don't want to go back to Afghanistan, Tailor."

"No, I think they're going to send us someplace that the US ain't supposed to be. I think that's why the pay is so good, and that's why there's so much secrecy."

"Huh," I said. "How'd you find out about this?"

"Friend of a friend got me in touch with this guy named Gordon Willis."

"Who's he?"

"I don't know. He's pretty cryptic about everything, but he's obviously got a lot of money behind him. All he'll say is that he represents the best interests of the United States."

"That sounds, um, *ominous.*"

"Right?" Tailor asked. "I know, Val, I know. Like I said, the money's real good. Everything I've seen from these people is on the ball. They pay in advance. And their cars have government plates."

"You're really going along with this?" I asked.

"I'm already signed up and everything. I ship next week. That's why I'm here, Val. I want you to go with me. Whaddaya say?"

I was quiet for a long moment, as our waitress brought us our check. "You know, last night at work I got bitched out by an employee at the facility. She showed up at the south gate at about zero-two-hundred and wanted a temporary badge. The south gate doesn't open until zero-six. So instead of going to the front gate, she sat there and bitched out the dispatcher on the phone until he sent me down there. Then she bitched *me* out until I issued her the temporary badge."

"That's bullshit," Tailor said. "You should've told her to go to the main gate or sit there all night."

"I can't. We're always getting nasty-grams in the e-mail from the Branch Office, reminding us that serving the client is the number one priority, that we're there to make things better for them, blah blah blah," I said, waving my arm theatrically. "Basically, if I enforce the rules I'm supposed to enforce, people complain and I get in trouble. If I *don't* enforce them, people complain and I get in trouble."

"Why don't you look for a new job?"

"Like I said, it's hard to get jobs with my skill-set. Normal jobs, anyway. I mean, what am I going to do, sell cars? Flip burgers? And I don't have anything else going on. I don't really have any friends here. I don't have a girlfriend. I mean, I guess I could go out to bars or whatever and try to pick women up, but what am I going to say? *Hey, baby, I know I'm emotionally damaged and unstable, and I spent the last five years shooting people for money, and now I'm a security guard and everything, but why don't you overlook all that and come have sex with me in my crappy little apartment?*"

Tailor let out a raucous laugh. "Then come back to work, Val. To hell with it."

"Yeah . . . yeah. I mean, why not? I can't possibly hate my life any more than I do now. Screw it, let's do this. It'll be good to work with you again."

"You sure, Val?"

"I'm sure. Hey, what did Skunky say when you called him?"

"He wasn't interested." Tailor shrugged. "Says he's got his own thing going on or something."

"I'm glad he's doing better than me. Come on, take me home. I've got some arrangements I need to make." Tailor grinned and stuck his fist across the table. I made a fist with my left hand and bumped it against his.

VALENTINE
Las Vegas, Nevada
January 19
1059

"Mr. Valentine! It's good to see you," the man said earnestly, giving me a firm handshake. "My name is Gordon Willis. This is my associate, Mr. Anders," he said, indicating a tall, muscular man with tan skin and cropped blond hair. Anders looked like an old Waffen SS recruiting poster. The *Übermensch* grunted. "Please, sit down," Gordon said then, indicating a chair on the opposite side of a cluttered desk.

Sitting down, I studied Gordon for a moment. He was in his late thirties or early forties, with a slick haircut and an expensive suit. He smiled with perfectly straight, perfectly white teeth, and observed me with piercing blue eyes. I immediately distrusted this man. He was slick, but my gut told me he was a snake. I tried to ignore it and listened to what he had to say.

"I trust Mr. Tailor has filled you in on the job opportunity I can offer you?" he asked, folding his hands on the desk in front of him.

"Uh, yes," I said, trying to quell my unease. "He didn't have a lot of details himself, but he told me about the pay. Twenty-five thousand dollars a month?"

"Yes!" he said, beaming. "Tax exempt, of course."

"How . . . how is that possible?" I asked. "The tax law says that—"

Gordon interrupted me with an obnoxious little chuckle. "Mr. Valentine, I'm sure you have a lot of questions. I'm afraid that there are a lot of things I simply can't tell you unless you sign. All I'm at liberty to say is that you won't have to worry about paying any taxes. We'll take care of the IRS documentation and filing for you. You'll keep every cent of what you earn."

"Who are you people?" I asked flatly, my eyes narrowing. "What's this all about? I can tell that this isn't your office," I said, moving my arm to indicate the small storefront we were sitting in. "You probably rented this place out a week ago."

Gordon sat back in his chair and studied me with a knowing grin on his face. "Mr. Tailor was right about you," he said. "You're very sharp." He then pulled a large manila envelope out of his desk drawer. He opened it and began to read to me. "Your real name is Constantine Michael Valentine, yet you somehow managed to get *Constantine* left off of your military ID." My mouth fell open, but I didn't say anything. I hadn't heard anyone say my real first name in years. "You served a four-year term of enlistment in the United States Air Force, including a six-month combat deployment to Afghanistan. You were involved in an incident there, and while you were discharged honorably you have a reenlistment code of RE-3. They asked you not to come back."

"Okay, so you were able to pull my DD214," I said. "Are you with the government?"

Gordon set the papers down before speaking. "Something like that. I'm afraid I really can't say much more at this time. Ever since Mr. Tailor indicated that you might be interested in the job I'm offering, we've been doing a very thorough background check on you. I know that you went from being a career contractor with Vanguard Strategic Solutions International to working as a night-shift security guard for a local defense contractor. Your annual income is about one quarter of what it was last year, and that doesn't include the generous operational bonuses or hazard pay that Vanguard was famous for."

"So?"

"So, Mr. Valentine, your friend Mr. Tailor told me that you're *better* than this. And you know what? I agree. I've studied your entire dossier, going back to when you were in high school. I know what happened to your mother, and I can only imagine the effect that had on you."

"Mr. Willis," I said coldly, "You have no *idea* the effect that had on me."

"Ah, I see," he said, his voice softening. "I apologize, Mr. Valentine. I didn't mean to bring up bad blood. All I was trying to say is that I think what I'm offering is perfect for you."

I sighed, pinching the bridge of my nose between two fingers as I did so. "Mr. Willis, what exactly *are* you offering me?"

"Straight to the point." He beamed. "I like that. You wouldn't believe how many guys we get through here that get intimidated when we pull out their file. I'm not going to lie to you," he said, leaning in closer. "This job is going to be dangerous. You'll have to be able to deploy right away."

"I see. That shouldn't be a problem. How dangerous are we talking here?"

"As I'm sure you've guessed," Gordon said, "absolute discretion is required. Look at the world situation right now, Mr. Valentine; war in Mexico, war in the Middle East, war in Southeast Asia and Africa, more in-fighting in Russia, and an uneasy cease-fire in China with a thousand-mile-long DMZ along the Yangtze River. The world is spiraling into chaos and our country's conventional military and intelligence assets just aren't enough to deal with it all."

"I've been shot at in half the places you just listed, Mr. Willis," I said. "I'm *well* aware of the geopolitical situation."

"I'm sure you are, Mr. Valentine. Since joining Vanguard you've been on—" he trailed off as he checked my file— "*five* major deployments overseas. Nearly five years of your life fighting other peoples' wars. I'm offering you a chance to serve *your* country again. There's a critical situation developing, and we need the best people available to manage it before it gets out of hand."

"Don't you have the CIA and Special Forces for that?" I asked. Something about this whole thing stank. The money was too good, and the facts were too few.

"As you can imagine, they're stretched thin as is," Gordon replied.

"I can't imagine you're having trouble recruiting people with the money you're offering."

"You wouldn't think so, but many of our candidates have the same professional paranoia as you, Mr. Valentine. Due to the nature of the situation, I'm simply unable to disclose much more than I've told you before you sign. Many otherwise promising candidates have balked at the lack of information."

I chewed on that for a moment. It was disquieting, to be sure, but I had a feeling there was more to it than that. "I see. Am I to assume that this will be a combat operation?"

"If all goes well," Gordon said, "the combat will be minimal. We're trying something new in our area of operations. You'll be trained in mission-specific skills above and beyond door-kicking and trigger-pulling. As I said, the utmost discretion is required. I'm also required to inform you that while you're away, you'll only have minimal contact with loved ones back home. We regret this, but security is necessary until the operation is completed."

"What kind of time frame are we looking at here?" I asked.

"Hopefully, we'll have everyone home by Christmas. Now, I'm sure you've heard that before, so I'm not going to mince words. The contract is for an undetermined period of time not to exceed three years. You're ours until the mission is over, basically. Obviously, at the pay rate we're offering, it's in our best interest to accomplish the mission as soon as possible." Gordon let out a convincing chuckle at his own joke.

"Tailor told me he got a signing bonus."

"Ah, yes!" Gordon said, retrieving another manila envelope from his desk.

He opened it and placed a piece of paper in front of me. It was a standard government direct-deposit form. "If you'll fill this out," he said, "we should have that in your bank account in three to five business days."

"And . . . you're sure there won't be any problems with the IRS? This is all going to my regular checking account with the Las Vegas Federal Credit Union and I'm not going to have the tax man breathing down my neck?"

"Don't worry, Mr. Valentine," Gordon said, grinning. "We're bigger than the tax man." That sounded more ominous than promising. I realized then that the big guy, Anders, was still standing in the corner behind Gordon and hadn't said a word the entire time. He observed me with a bored look on his face, but I didn't doubt that he'd made a plan to kill me the moment I walked in the door. These guys undoubtedly knew that I had a concealed-firearm permit, but they hadn't said anything about it.

"Who, exactly, is *we*?" I asked, looking over the contract Gordon had pushed in front of me. It was full of vague legalese and only referred to Gordon's organization as *the party of the first part.*

Gordon grinned. "I'm afraid you'll have to sign to get filled in on all of that, Mr. Valentine," he said and set an ornate pen down in front of me. "All I can say until then is that you'll be serving the best interests of the United States and will be protecting your country from enemies foreign and domestic."

I picked up the silver pen. It had XII, the Roman numeral for the number twelve, engraved on it. I wondered what it meant. I took a deep breath and signed the document. Gordon smiled.

"I guess I'll have to call my boss and tell him I'm not coming in Monday," I said.

"Don't worry about that," Gordon answered. "We'll take care of everything. You can take the direct-deposit form with you if you don't have your bank routing number available right now. Within forty-eight hours, you should receive a packet with everything you need to know. You'll be deploying within two weeks."

"Deploying where?" I asked, handing him back his pen.

"Everything will be in the packet," he said. "Until then, take some time to get your affairs in order. You'll likely be out of the United States for an extended period of time." Gordon stuck his hand out. I hesitated, then took it. He had an excessively firm handshake. "Welcome aboard," he said and stood up. I gathered my papers and stood up as well. "You did the right thing."

"I hope so," I said, taking my papers and turning to leave.

"Mr. Valentine?" Anders, the big guy, said as I opened the door. I turned and looked back at him. "If you fail to arrive at the deployment location at the appropriate time, we *will* come get you. It'll be best if you're punctual."

"I get it," I said and closed the door behind me. *What the hell did I just do?*

LORENZO
Confederated Gulf Emirate of Zubara
January 20

The marketplace was busy, the large Sunday crowds nervous. Change was coming, and the people could feel it. I made my way through the bustling place, gray and incognito as usual, dressed like the locals in a traditional white thobe and checkered headdress. In my line of work, you never stick out. It keeps you alive longer.

There were three sections of Zubara City (Ash Shamal, Umm Shamal, and Al Khor). Each was a narrow sliver of land extending into the Persian Gulf for a couple of miles. Half a million people were packed on those three little peninsulas, mostly Sunni, some Shiite, a mess of imported workers, and I was spending my day in the poor, dangerous one, Ash Shamal.

Nobody used the country's official name, or the abbreviation CGEZ. The Americans or Europeans who ended up here usually called it the Zoob. The rest of the world just referred to the tiny country as Zubara.

I got to the entrance of the club fifteen minutes early so I could survey the area. This neighborhood was one of the oldest in Ash Shamal, but there was much new construction underway. It was also one of the more traditional. It was interesting to note the fundamentalist graffiti that was popping up in many of the alleys, and even more interesting was that the local authorities hadn't bothered to cover it up. Either there was too much of it to keep up with, the official government types didn't bother to come into this neighborhood, or the cops actually agreed with the message. Either way, it was a grim omen.

Zubara was a relatively modern state, dragged kicking and screaming into the twenty-first century by the current monarch. Bordered by Qatar and Saudi Arabia, the tiny nation wasn't nearly as rich as its neighbors but was relatively clean, organized, and, by Arab standards, efficient. Zubara was one of the jewels of the Persian Gulf, but that appeared to be changing with the current power struggle, and my specialty was to capitalize on the inevitable chaos that would result.

I had spent my entire adult life in various third-world countries. I'd seen revolutions, famines, wars, and the utter collapse of societies. I made my living on the fringe of mankind. I didn't know what was going to happen here yet, but I knew *something* was coming.

Zubara would be just another job, just a little more difficult than normal, or so I tried to convince myself. It had been six months since I had been drafted for this job. Six months since Eddie had brutally murdered one of my crew just to let me know how serious he was. Half a year of preparation and groundwork to pull off an impossible mission. There was a bitter taste in my mouth as I prepared for this meeting.

I walked around the block to scope out the back entrance, just in case. There was some construction going on across the street, but the workers all looked like the normal Indonesians and Filipinos that did all the grunt labor in this country. I saw no indications of a trap. Making my way back to the front, I leaned against the corner of a building and watched the club. The man I was supposed to be meeting would probably be running late, like pretty much everything in this part of the world. I couldn't spot anyone else surveying the place, so it was either safe or they were really good.

Waiting gave me time to think, which was unfortunate, because right now thinking about what I was doing just made me angrier. This job sucked. It was suicide, and I had been forced into it against my will. It was going to take months to accomplish, but once this gig was completed, I was going to devote my life to finding the man who put me in this situation. I vowed that I was going to go on a killing spree that would become the stuff of legend.

My thoughts of murder were interrupted when a black Bentley parked in front of the club. The luxury car didn't seem out of place on the same street as a vendor selling live chickens, but that was the nature of the Middle East. The driver exited and held open the back door for his charge. The man that stepped out was in his forties, wearing a brown suit, white shirt, and no tie. This was pretty fashionable apparel in the region and was what all the cool terrorists were wearing.

He was early. *Amazing.* The driver stayed with the vehicle. I waited a few extra minutes, watching for anything out of the ordinary before I followed him into the club. The interior was dark and cooled by rows of ceiling fans. Inside, the social club was far nicer than its drab outside appearance suggested. It was relatively crowded by middle-aged men smoking hookahs, playing chess, and bitching about local politics.

The server acknowledged me as I entered, but I waved him off as I spotted the man I was looking for sitting at a table in the back. The server retreated deferentially.

The man saw me approaching and nodded once. I pulled up a chair and sat. "Lorenzo," he said before taking a sip of his pungent tea. "I didn't recognize you."

"That's the general idea," I responded. Say what you will about the man-dresses, they were actually pretty comfy and enabled me to conceal a few weapons. Even still, they do make you look like a big stupid marshmallow, and you can hardly run in one. I'd taken a few days to brush up my Arabic and perfect the local accent. I'd grown my beard out, and my natural features enabled me to pass for a native Zubaran rather easily. After all, I had a knack for blending in wherever I went. "Good to see you again, Jalal."

Jalal Hosani smiled. "No, it is not good, I am afraid. You are a wanted man in this country, if I recall correctly." His English was perfect. It should be, since he'd attended Oxford, paid for by his friends in the Qatari royal family.

"Actually, no. You're thinking of Syria, and the UAE . . . oh, and I think the Saudi courts want one of my hands. This is my first time in lovely Zubara. It's kind of nice, except that whole pending revolution thing. So, what brought you here?"

"Business grew difficult in Baghdad," he said with a casual wave of his hand, as if a couple hundred thousand American troops interrupting his illicit arms dealing was a minor inconvenience. Jalal pulled a silver cigarette case from his suit. He offered me one. I shook my head. "Still the health nut, I see."

I only smoked when the cover required it. "Cardiovascular fitness comes in handy in my line of work."

"About that." Jalal lit his cigarette and took a long drag. "What is your work this time?" He waited for me to respond, and when I didn't, he continued. "I see . . . Usually your work involves the involuntary transfer of wealth and countless murders. I can safely assume this will be the same?"

"But of course," I replied as I pulled a fat envelope from my man-dress and passed it over. "As usual, you don't want the details. I was never here."

Jalal raised his eyebrows as he flipped through the stack of money. He looked around the room as he shoved the money into his coat. "That is a considerable sum," he said. "A considerable sum indeed. You do realize, however, that there are men hiding in this country who are with organizations you have stolen from. In fact, I know that one *very* dangerous man happens to frequent this very club on occasion. I could just keep the money, say who you are, and—"

I cut him off. "I know who hangs out here." Everyone knew Zubara was a safe haven for various terrorist organizations. Diplomatically, the government was friendly to the US, and tolerated the Israelis, but the official government was growing weaker by the day. "Maybe you talk, and I end up on an Al Jazeera video getting my head sawed off?" I had robbed, conned, or defrauded every major criminal organization on earth at some point. It had made me both a lot of money and a lot of enemies. "We both know that won't happen, because you know I'd find a way to take you with me, and besides, I pay way better than those cheap bastards." I gestured toward the envelope.

"That's the first installment. I'll pay you double what I paid you in Dubai."

"It was only a hypothetical."

"And just so you know, I'm doing this job for Big Eddie. So if you *hypothetically* cross me, you *hypothetically* cross him, which means that he'll track you down to the ends of the earth and *hypothetically* feed your entire family into a wood chipper."

His eyes grew wide as he processed that information. Regardless of who you were in the criminal underworld, you were afraid of Eddie. He was evil incarnate. It was my ultimate trump card, because no one on Eddie's naughty list lived for long. Jalal's demeanor changed and he gave me a big smile, always the businessman. "Of course, my friend. How can I be of service?"

Jalal Hosani was a facilitator, not a man who got his hands dirty. He knew people. When you are operating in a new area, you had to have intelligence, and that meant knowing the right people. Jalal knew the right people. Of course, he would also sell me out as soon as it benefited him. So I had to make sure that the math stayed in my favor, because I actually kind of liked Jalal, snake that he was, and killing him would make me . . . sad. Sort of.

"Later on I'm going to need a source for equipment, weapons, vehicles. Usual stuff, but right now I need information. I need to know what's really going down in Zubara."

"The emir is having a battle against one of his generals for control of the government," Jalal said as if this were common knowledge. "The pro-Western factions are siding with the emir, the fundamentalists and Iranian puppets are siding with the general. It hasn't become violent yet, but it is only a matter of time."

I nodded. "I know that much. What I need to know is who all the players are, and then I'm going to have you do a few introductions for me. Which side are you on?"

"General Al Sabah is a very dangerous man, but the emir should not be underestimated." My old acquaintance appeared to give it some thought. "I suppose I will wait and see which side wins. That is always the side to be on."

"I killed a guy named Al Sabah once."

"It is a common name." Jalal shrugged. "Either way, most of the army is loyal to the general and his personal guard is growing with many foreign"— he paused, looking for the right word— "volunteers."

"You mean fundamentalist nut-jobs who got tired of getting their asses kicked up north decided to get a different job where they could still sock it to the Great Satan?"

"Something like that. Now let us get down to business." We spoke for another half an hour, during which he provided me with the low down on the various players in this unfolding drama. I was careful to give him no information about what I was actually doing here. I asked random questions about unrelated things, to cloud the issue just in case he was planning on betraying me. The meeting was beneficial, and I learned quite a bit more about the inner workings of Zubaran politics. Finally we were done, and Jalal, late for his next appointment, excused himself. We would be in touch.

I leaned back in my chair and watched him leave. The power struggle complicated things. Politics in this part of the world was like a high-speed chess game where the losers got put in front of a firing squad. Heightened tensions led to heightened security, which could prove to be a pain. If the situation deteriorated too quickly, it might spook our mark, and ruin Phase One. We would have to adjust accordingly.

A moment later the server approached me with a menu. The young man greeted me with a great deal of respect. "We did not know you were going to be visiting us today, Khalid." He addressed me by the fake identity I had been cultivating here over the last few months. "How can I be of service?"

Zubaran food was relatively bland for this part of the world, but it was tolerable, and scheming always made me hungry. "Kusbasi kebab, and make sure to spice it up this time. And fetch a chess board. I'll be meeting Al Falah for a match shortly."

He snapped his heels together and retreated toward the kitchen. The service here was excellent, as it should be, since I was their new landlord. I had bought the club outright as soon as I had arrived in Zubara. I checked my watch. My next appointment should be on the way.

At least for now, Phase One was proceeding according to plan.

Chapter 2: If You Die,
They Don't Have to Pay You

VALENTINE
Quagmire, Nevada, USA
January 30
1420

It was quiet in my Mustang, save for the noise of tires on gravel, as I made my way down the long, winding road to Hawk's home. I hadn't been down this road in months, not since I'd first settled in Las Vegas.

Hawk's real name was John Hawkins. I'd met him in Afghanistan years prior. He'd been the team leader of Switchblade 4, my team, before moving into the training section, then retiring. It had been Hawk who'd taught me how to shoot a revolver and instilled in me a love of Smith & Wesson .44 Magnums. Glancing in the rearview mirror, I saw that Tailor's Expedition was right behind me, shrouded in the cloud of dust my car was kicking up. Our two vehicles were laden with nearly all of my worldly possessions. It was surprisingly little, all things considered.

The dirt road passed through a barbed-wire fence, but the gate had been left open. Up ahead, I could see Hawk's ranch house and the barn beyond it. Several trees shaded the house from the afternoon sun. I could see a couple of horses absentmindedly chewing their feed, paying us no mind.

I came to a stop near Hawk's Dodge turbo-diesel pickup truck, and Tailor parked next to me. I stepped into the cool desert air, glad that I'd worn a jacket. Tailor joined me a second later.

"Place hasn't changed much," Tailor said, looking around.

"Look, he's got solar panels on the roof now."

"Hawk likes to live off the grid," Tailor said. "He's got his own water supply, his own food supply, and his own electricity. You could ride out the end of the world here."

I chuckled. "That's probably his plan." As we approached the house's large front porch, the door opened. Hawk stepped out into the afternoon air, squinting slightly in the light. He looked the same as ever, tall and fit, with rough features and hard eyes. His hair and goatee had more gray in them than they used to, but overall he was doing pretty well for a guy in his fifties. Hawk was wearing a tan button-down shirt, faded blue jeans, and cowboy boots. As usual, his Smith & Wesson Model 29 revolver was in its custom-made holster on his right hip.

Tailor and I both began to grin as we climbed the short steps. Hawk greeted us with a smile and roughly shook both of our hands. As always, his handshake nearly crushed mine.

"Goddamn, boys, it's good to see you," he said, his voice raspy and harsh. "How the hell are ya?"

"Doing just fine, sir," Tailor said.

"How 'bout you, kid?" Hawk asked me.

"Things are looking up."

"C'mon in, boys. Let's sit down before we start unloading your truck." Hawk opened the door and led us into his house. We followed him into the kitchen, where he had us sit down before opening the fridge. He still walked with a slight limp.

"You boys want a beer?"

"Uh, no thanks." I hate beer.

"We're driving," Tailor said. "Got any Dr. Pepper?"

Hawk turned around, closing the refrigerator door. He had in his left hand one large can of beer, and in his right hand two cans of Dr. Pepper. "I bought a case after Val called me," he answered, sitting down. "So, boys, why don't you tell me what's going on? Tailor, I haven't heard from you in a year. Val here hasn't e-mailed me in a couple of months. Then all of a sudden I get a call, asking me if I can store his stuff. So what's going on?"

"We're not supposed to talk about it," Tailor said. "It's a job. We're going to be gone for a long time, probably over a year."

"A job with who?" Hawk asked, sipping his beer.

"We're . . . not really sure," I said. Hawk set his beer down and raised his eyebrows. "I mean, I think it's the government. It's all very hush-hush."

"How's the pay?" Hawk asked.

"Insane," Tailor responded.

"We're not supposed to talk about it," I said, echoing Tailor's words.

"Don't give me that bullshit, boy," Hawk said. "You know I ain't gonna go calling the newspaper or anything."

"Does Quagmire even have a newspaper?" Tailor asked.

"Sure as hell does. The *Quagmire Sentinel.* Yesterday's front-page headline was about the truckload of chickens that overturned on the highway outside of town. There were chickens everywhere. Now, do you have any idea where they're sending you?"

"All they'd tell us was that it was someplace where the US doesn't have any ongoing operations," Tailor said. "So I'm guessing somewhere in the Middle East, probably."

"Or somewhere in Africa," I suggested.

"Christ, I hope not," Tailor said. "I don't want to go back to Africa."

"Me, either," I said. "But that's the thing, Hawk. They won't tell us anything. They just had us sign a three-year contract."

"Kid, are you telling me you signed a contract when you had no idea who you're working for or where you're going? Why would you do that?"

"Twenty-five *large* every month," I said. "They've already dropped a twenty-K signing bonus into my checking account."

"Damn," Hawk said. "That's good money. Hell, I haven't made that kind of money since Decker and I retook that diamond mine from the rebels. We got paid in cut stones. I still have some of 'em in the safe downstairs. Anyway . . . boys, are you sure about this?"

"No, I'm not," I said honestly. "But . . . Hawk, I tried living the regular life. I had a normal job and everything."

"You hated it, didn't you?" Hawk asked, studying me.

I hesitated briefly. "Yeah. I hated it. I don't know what's wrong with me. After Mexico . . . Christ, Hawk, most of my friends are dead now. How could I want to go back to that life? What's wrong with me?"

"Goddamn it, Val, we've been over this," Tailor said angrily.

Hawk interrupted him. "Hold on, Tailor. Val, we all go through this eventually. You get over it, and you go on to the next job. You miss that life because it's all you've done. You miss the money, the excitement, the shooting. It's normal. Anyway, you're good at it. I've never seen anyone run a six-gun like you. The first time I handed you a .357 you shot like you'd been born with it in your hand. Why do you think I talked Decker into hiring you? I saw what you did in Afghanistan. You cleaned out that Hajji nest like a pro, and practically by yourself."

"I got kicked out of the Air Force for that," I said.

"Forget 'em," Hawk responded. "The bureaucrats that run the military these days don't know talent when they see it."

"I know. Honestly? I don't feel bad about wanting to go back. I feel bad that I *don't* feel bad about wanting to go back."

"No point in trying to be something you're not, Val," Tailor said. "That's why I called you for this. I figured you wanted to go back as much as I did."

"Tailor's right," Hawk stated, a hard gleam in his eye. "You're a natural-born *killer*, boy, and you always will be. You're guaranteed to be miserable until you accept that."

"It's a good thing Tailor called," I said. "I was about to accept Ling's offer and join Exodus."

"I knew it!" Tailor exclaimed. "Hawk, will you talk some sense into him?"

"Kid, Exodus is bad news. Now, I know they helped you get out of there after things went to shit in Mexico, but that's probably only because you saved that Oriental girl's life. They're dangerous."

"So were *we*," I said.

"But we were professionals," Hawk replied. "They're true believers. That's a different kind of dangerous. Better to stay away from it."

"I don't have the best feeling about this gig, either," I said.

"You don't have to go."

"I already signed the contract."

"So? If you need to disappear, we can make that happen. It'll be a huge pain in my ass, but it's doable. I've done it before for other folks."

"No. I don't want to go on the run."

"The money's too good to walk away from," Tailor said.

"No kidding," I concurred, cracking a smile. "I'll be living large when I get back."

"Well, let's get to unloading your stuff, then," Hawk said, setting his empty beer can on the table.

As darkness fell, Tailor, Hawk, and I sat on the front porch, watching one of the most beautiful desert sunsets I'd ever seen. Hawk leaned back in his chair, sipping a beer. Tailor and I sat next to him, studying the shades of red and purple that filled the sky as the sun slowly sank beneath the mountains. Real moments of peace are hard to come by in life, and no one wanted to ruin it by talking.

The sun slowly disappeared, and the stars were increasingly visible overhead. It was cold out, and our breath smoldered in the chilly air. Hawk looked over at Tailor and me. "Now you listen, boys," he said, taking another sip of his beer. "A long time ago, I was on a job that paid too good to be true, too. More than twenty years ago now, I think. It was before we went legit and founded Vanguard. It was just Switchblade back then."

"What happened?" I asked.

"We were straight-up mercenaries. We worked for just about anyone that had the cash to pay us, and we didn't ask questions. We always got the job done, too. We spent most of our time in Africa. Business was good. Until this time we got in over our heads. We . . ." Hawk hesitated. "We basically overthrew the democratically elected government of Zembala."

"Where's that?" I asked.

"It doesn't exist anymore," Hawk replied. "It's called the Central African

People's Republic now. The government of Zembala was corrupt, teetering on collapse. They had tribal conflict, religious conflict, and the Cubans screwing around there, too."

"Fucking Cubans," Tailor and I said simultaneously.

"We had been paid to protect the president of Zembala. He was a real piece of work, let me tell ya. He was a lying, whoring drunk, and the validity of the election results were questionable. Anyway, he was hoarding the cash from the state-run diamond mines, trying to fund his army to keep the Commies from overthrowing him. We protected him. He didn't trust anyone from his own country. Too much tribal bullshit. We didn't have a dog in that race, so he trusted us. But we got a better offer." Hawk paused for a moment. "The Montalban Exchange, some big international firm, offered us a lot of money to kill the president."

"That didn't work out, did it?" Tailor asked.

"Christ Almighty, it was bad," Hawk said, finishing his beer and crushing the can in his hand. "Decker went for it. We killed the president. That was easy. It got complicated after that. We left the capital for Sweothi City, getting our asses kicked the whole way. There were only a few of us left. The Montalbans were supposed to have a plane there to extract us."

"There wasn't a plane, was there?" Tailor asked.

Hawk laughed bitterly. "Hell, no."

"How did you get out?" I asked. "Did the Montalban Exchange help you?"

"No, they didn't. They just left us to die. We hooked up with some Portuguese mercs and made a run for it. Decker sacrificed one of our guys, young fella named Ozzie, to distract the Cubans. He pulled it off, though. The rest of us managed to get on a plane to South Africa. Lost a lot of good men in that mess . . ." Hawk trailed off, looking toward the darkened mountains.

"Holy shit," Tailor said. "Ramirez never talked about that."

"And yet the story sounds strangely familiar," I said, giving Tailor a hard look.

Hawk opened another beer. "None of us talked about it. We made a mistake, and it got a lot of people killed. Well . . . even if we hadn't been there, the same thing probably would've happened. And Africa's *Africa*. Every time some politician sneezes over there a hundred thousand people get slaughtered."

"Africa sucks," I said, looking up at the stars. The time I'd spent there hadn't been so pleasant, either.

"It is what it is," Hawk said quietly. "You boys be careful over there, now. Always have a way out. Don't trust the people you work for. Remember, if you die, they don't have to pay you."

"Okay, Hawk," I said.

"I *mean it*, boy," he said harshly. "I've been to too many goddamned funerals already."

VALENTINE
Kelly Field Annex
Lackland Air Force Base, Texas
February 4
0545

Southern Texas was warm, even in February. It wasn't unpleasant, but it was a far cry from the harsh winters and lake-effect snow of Northern Michigan, where I'd grown up.

The last few days had been a whirlwind. Tailor and I had been flown from Las Vegas to San Antonio. From there we were hurried to a military installation that they tried to keep secret, but I knew it was Lackland Air Force Base. I'd gone to Air Force basic military training and Security Forces School here. They kept us cooped up in an old barracks for several days. Each day, more and more people would arrive. All told, there were forty-two of us living in the barracks, that we knew of.

Food, in the form of military MREs, was brought to us, and we weren't allowed to go outside. All cell phones had been confiscated, and those that had kept theirs hidden had found that they had no signal anyway, meaning our hosts were probably jamming them somehow. They also took all of our personal identification documents, like passports and driver's licenses. This caused all manner of outrage, but our employers insisted that these effects would be returned when the mission was complete.

People came and went from the barracks, but they weren't part of our group. No one knew who they were, so we all guessed that they were associates of Gordon Willis. I had to hand it to Gordon: he'd certainly managed to recruit an interesting bunch. As Tailor and I talked to, and got to know, the people that were presumably our new teammates, we learned quite a bit about them and how much we all had in common.

For starters, almost all of us had combat experience. Most were ex-military, like me, and of those, a few had been kicked out or had spent time in the Fort Leavenworth military prison. Others had an intelligence background, and most of us spoke foreign languages. Tailor and I spoke Spanish fluently. Very few of us had any close family. None of us were married.

There were a few women in the building, too, but they were confined to a different part of the barracks and weren't allowed near us. We didn't know how many there were. I guessed that they were afraid someone would end up pregnant or something. It seemed silly to me.

So there I was, standing on the ramp, looking at a plain white Boeing 767 jetliner that was waiting for us. The sun wouldn't be up for another hour. We stood there in a big cluster, smoking and joking, waiting for them to tell us to board the plane. A few of us, including Tailor and me, had formed into a little circle.

"Where are we going?" someone asked. "Anyone heard?" I turned around. The guy that had asked the question was named Carlos Hudson. He was a black guy from the south side of Detroit, originally. He was the only other Red Wings fan in the whole bunch, so he and I had hit it off.

"They haven't told us anything," I said. "They issued us a bunch of hot-weather gear, though. We're going to the Middle East."

"Oh, yeah, definitely," Tailor said, standing next to me.

"Why would they send us to there?" someone else asked. "What are forty-two guys going to do that half the US military can't?"

"Maybe we're going to Iran or somewhere, then," Hudson suggested. "You know, someplace the US ain't supposed to be?"

"Could be the Sudan," another guy chimed in.

"I do *not* want to go back to Africa," Tailor said for the umpteenth time, puffing a cigarette.

"Don't worry, boys, we're not going to Africa," a woman's dusky voice said. That's when I saw her. She was tall, probably five ten or so, and had auburn hair pulled back into a ponytail. She had curvy features hidden beneath khaki cargo pants and a sage green fleece jacket. A green duffel bag was hoisted over her shoulder, and it looked like it weighed as much as she did. She was flanked by three other women, but there was something about her . . .

"Who are you?" Tailor asked.

"McAllister," she said, sticking her hand out.

Tailor glanced at me, then shook her hand. "My name's Tailor," he said. "William Tailor. So, where *are* we going?"

"Zubara," she said.

"Where?" someone asked.

"The Confederated Gulf Emirate of Zubara," one of the other females, a tall black woman, said.

"It borders Qatar and Saudi Arabia," McAllister added. "The US has no real presence there."

"How . . . how do you know this?" I asked, stumbling on my words for some reason.

McAllister smiled at me. She had a mischievous . . . no, a *devious* smile, and beautiful green eyes. "I'm going to be in charge of our communications network when we get there. I've spent the last three weeks learning how their telecommunications setup works. Can't drop me in blind with equipment I've never seen and expect me to make it work." She maintained eye contact with me for what felt like a long time but in reality wasn't. "Anyway, that's all I know," she said then. "Well, we're getting some really good equipment, too."

Before I could think of anything else to say, the door of the plane opened, and the stairs were lowered down to the tarmac. A moment later, a black Suburban pulled up next to where we were all standing. Three men got out. Two looked like standard-issue contractor types, with their tactical cargo pants and tactical vests and whatnot. The third looked like something out of an old movie. He was probably sixty or so, with white hair and a black eye patch over his left eye. His face had hard lines in it. His remaining eye could bore a hole in you. He wore a bomber jacket that was undoubtedly older than I was.

"Alright, listen up!" he said. His voice was harsh and raspy. "I need you all to fall in and board that plane in an orderly fashion. This is your first assignment, and it's an easy one, so try not to *fuck it up*! I know you have a lot of questions. We have a long flight ahead of us. You'll be briefed in the air."

"But, um, sir, Gordon Willis told us that we'd have briefings and training before we deployed," some brave soul said.

"You were *lied to*, son. Now get on that plane so we can get going."

"Um, sir, who *are* you?" the same person, a red headed guy, asked. Some people just didn't know when to quit.

The old man, for his part, cracked an evil smile. "My name is Hunter, son. Colonel Curtis Hunter. I'm the *boss*. Now move out!"

We'd been in the air for a few hours, just wandering around the plane, killing time. The Boeing 767 jetliner was meant to hold hundreds of passengers in its standard form, but there were only about sixty seats in the front of the plane we were on. The rear was all for cargo. Tailor and I sat next to each other, talking, when Hunter's harsh voice came on over the intercom. "Listen up. Everyone wake up. I'm coming back to give you the first part of the briefing. McAllister, King, you two come up front."

I watched as McAllister and the tall black lady from the tarmac got out of their seats and made their way forward. After a few minutes, they returned, each carrying a bunch of manila envelopes. They walked down the aisle, handing them out to everyone.

"Thank you, stewardess," a smartass named Walker said. Walker was one of the guys that had been to Leavenworth. He'd been an Army Intelligence interrogator. Apparently he'd gotten in trouble for killing an insurgent prisoner in Iraq. He was short and suffered from obvious Little Man Syndrome. I had no idea how a dipshit like him scored high enough on the ASVAB to make it into Intelligence in the first place. "Could you bring me a Coke and some peanuts?"

"Shut your face, pencil-dick," McAllister said, dropping Walker's packet in his lap. Several guys started to laugh. Walker's face turned red, and he stood up. He grabbed McAllister by the arm, causing her to drop the rest of her packets. She was four inches taller than him.

"Listen, bitch," he started, looking up at her. She turned and punched him square in the face, just like that. He recoiled and let go of her. Blood came trickling from his nose. He came at her again, grabbing her with both hands. The next thing I knew, I was out of my seat, standing in the aisle.

"Val, what are you . . . ?" Tailor asked. I ignored him and moved toward Walker and McAllister. "Oh, goddamn it, Val," Tailor said, getting out of his seat and following me.

"What do *you* want, Valentine?" Walker didn't let go of McAllister. A couple more guys stood up. Walker was about to get his *ass beat.*

"What the hell is going on back here?" Colonel Hunter yelled, his rough voice clear over the drone of the engines. He had appeared from up front, flanked by two of the ambiguous security men. Both had their hands under their vests, probably ready to draw pistols.

"I'm fine, sir," McAllister said, pushing Walker off. She seemed embarrassed that people had come to her defense.

"I'm sure you are, Sarah," Hunter said, working his way through the crowd. "Mr. Walker, what is your problem?"

"Sir," Walker said, defiantly staring Hunter in the eye, "I just made a joke and this bitch—"

"That's *enough,* Mr. Walker." Hunter cut him off. He moved in closer. "Now you listen to *me,* boy. We aren't even in-country yet. If you're going to give me problems before we even get there, so help me God I will drop your ass into the ocean. I'm not joking. That's not some empty threat. You belong to me now. If you don't make it to Zubara alive, no one in my chain of command will give a shit. So I suggest you sit down and shut your mouth before you piss me off."

Walker looked around nervously. The rest of us had backed away, leaving him virtually alone with the scary senior citizen. After a long moment, he deflated. "Yes, sir." He sat back down.

"Better," Hunter said. "Sarah, Anita, please hand out the rest of the packets. Let's get this briefing started." McAllister and King both resumed handing out the materials. Tailor and I returned to our seats at the rear of the abbreviated passenger compartment and were the last to get the handouts. McAllister handed me mine without so much as making eye contact.

"Did I piss her off somehow?" I asked Tailor. He just shrugged and opened his packet. Inside was a bunch of documents, maps, and photographs.

"Gentlemen," Hunter said, using the aircraft's intercom so we could hear him, "as you're all probably aware, our destination is the Confederated Gulf Emirate of Zubara." There were screens all along the passenger section that displayed the briefing. The cabin lights darkened, and a large map of Zubara appeared. There wasn't much to it. It was a patch of desert with three little peninsulas sticking out into the Persian Gulf on the eastern side. Its borders touched Qatar in the north, Saudi Arabia in the west, and the United Arab Emirates in the southeast. The map then changed, from one of the entire country to one focusing on the three urbanized peninsulas.

"The capital city, and really the only city in Zubara, is Zubara City. It's made of three sections, Ash Shamal, Umm Shamal, and Al Khor. Over a million people are packed into these three pieces of land, including large numbers of immigrant workers from Pakistan and South Asia. For years, Zubara was a reclusive Middle Eastern emirate, founded on the supposed site of some ancient port city. It's rich in oil and natural gas but was very isolated. Without foreign investment, Zubara was unable to fully tap its natural resources, leaving the country much poorer than its neighbors.

"This made it a breeding ground for radical Islam. Over the years, Hezbollah, Hamas, and especially Al Qaeda were able to do a lot of recruiting here. Things started to change ten years ago. The old emir went on a vacation to Switzerland. His son, the current emir, had built a loyal following in the country's military and told his old man not to come back. Things have more or less been improving ever since." The map disappeared, and the picture of a middle-aged, mustachioed man, in an expensive-looking suit and traditional Middle Eastern keffiyeh headdress, appeared.

"This is the current emir," Hunter explained, "Salim ibn Meheid. He's tried very hard to force Zubara into the twenty-first century. He's attempted to crack down on terrorist recruiting and financing, has formally recognized Israel, though relations with the Israelis are strained, and has opened his nation's economy to foreign investment and development. As a result, billions of dollars are pouring into his country now, and oil and natural-gas output has doubled.

"There are problems, though. The biggest problem is this guy, General Mubarak Hassan Al Sabah." The picture changed again, this time to a man with a goatee in a gaudy tan military uniform, decorated with ribbons and medals.

"General Al Sabah has gained the loyalty of the army. Most of the army is made up of conscripts from poor families and volunteers from places like Iran, Iraq, Pakistan, and Yemen. General Al Sabah has created a cult of personality and has done everything short of openly defying the emir. The emir's economic policies have brought a lot of change to Zubara, and many Westerners. And while he's tried to crack down on the financing of terrorism, the general has proved an obstacle to that. General Al Sabah wants to be the Saddam Hussein of Zubara. He's built a network of contacts and allies, from the Iranians to Al Qaeda. All of his allies don't necessarily like each other now, but he apparently is able to keep them from killing each other long enough to focus on the Americans. Despite the emir's efforts, Zubara remains a safe haven for terrorists. This is where they do their banking. This is where their families live. This is where they recruit. This is where they go on vacation."

Hunter paused for a long time. "Gentlemen, I think you're beginning to understand why such tight security has been necessary in this operation. What we're doing here is radically unconventional. We're running a major operation with a skeleton crew. You make up the bulk of our forces. We have the support of the emir and a few people loyal to him, but we'll largely be on our own."

"What exactly is our mission, sir?" that same redhead asked.

"We're going to bring the war to their doorstep, son," Hunter replied. "We can't invade Zubara. It's not diplomatically or militarily viable. In any case, any attempt to bring in Americans would probably result in a coup attempt against the emir, which would surely bring the country into civil war. The mission would be over before it began. So we're doing things differently. It's called Project Heartbreaker. After you get off this plane, you're never to mention that name to anyone, *ever*. Anyway, through heavy use of human intelligence and years of planning, we've been able to track down a large number of bad people in Zubara. We know where these people live, where they work, and who they're dealing with. We're going to find them and kill them."

"Is that it, sir? Go to Zubara and kill a few terrorists?"

"You, ginger," Hunter said, pointing at the talkative redhead, "no more from you today. It's a lot bigger than that. We're bringing the war to their home front. The enemy will discover that there are no safe places, anywhere, for them to hide. Our small operational group is going to try something that's never been tried. Gentlemen, welcome to *Dead Six*."

Tailor and I looked at each other, grinning. Despite my trepidation about my new employers, I liked where this was going. I returned my attention to Colonel Hunter and his briefing.

✤ ✤ ✤

I had been in a deep sleep when someone pushed me on the shoulder. I sat up quickly, having been startled awake. I was in the window seat and had been leaning against the fuselage of the plane, using my jacket for a pillow. I looked to my right. Tailor was nowhere to be seen. The cabin was darkened, most of the window shades were pulled down, and it seemed that almost everyone was asleep. Sitting next to me was Sarah McAllister.

"What is it?" I said, rubbing my eyes.

"Hey." She sounded almost awkward. "I, uh, wanted to thank you, for, you know, standing up."

"It's okay," I said. "I mean—"

She cut me off. "But I can take care of myself. I don't need you to come galloping to the rescue."

"I saw that. You clocked him pretty good."

"I used to play hockey," she said. "When I was in high school."

"Seriously? Me, too."

"That's great," Sarah said flatly. "Listen. I know you and the others were trying to help, but you have to let me handle things or I won't get any respect around here. Does that make sense?"

It made a lot of sense, actually. "I wasn't trying to embarrass you. I just . . . it just happened, you know? I didn't really think about it."

"I know. I'm not trying to be a bitch or sound ungrateful, but there are four women here in the middle of all of you guys."

"You probably had wieners thrown at you from day one."

"Oh my God," Sarah said, rolling her eyes. "You have no idea."

"I didn't do that to get in your pants, if that's what you're thinking." I was being honest with her about that, too. Of course, I had no *objections* to getting in her pants, either.

Sarah smiled. "The funny thing is, I actually believe you. You know . . ." Sarah's voice trailed off and she leaned in close to me, squinting quizzically. I pulled back a little bit, not sure what she was doing. "Holy crap," she said, still too close to my face. "Your eyes are different colors."

This always makes me self-conscious. My left eye is blue. My right eye is brown. People usually react like that when they first notice. "Yes, they are."

"Are you wearing contacts or something?"

"No, I'm not." I gently pushed her back a little bit, out of my personal space. "I was born like that. It's called heterochromia."

"That's *so* weird," she said absentmindedly. "I'm sorry." Then she grinned. "I'll get out of your face now. I'll see you later, Valentine." Sarah touched me on the shoulder as she stood up and left the seat. I shook my head slightly and smiled.

LORENZO
February 5

Terrorist mastermind Ali bin Ahmed Al Falah sat across from me in the smoke-filled room. His guards watched me suspiciously. "Goat-fucker," he spat as my rook took his knight.

"Indeed," I replied as I pretended to study the board. For somebody who was supposed to be so damn nefarious, Falah sucked at chess. It was more challenging to put up a good match and then let him win than it was to actually play somebody good. And I didn't even like chess. "Your turn."

"Your mother was a whore, Khalid." Falah twirled the end of his bushy white beard. He looked vaguely like a Wahhabi Santa Claus as he contemplated his next move. I had left myself dangerously exposed and he could have checkmate in two, but apparently Falah was only strategic when it came to financing suicide bombings.

I had gotten to know Falah rather well over the last few months. As the new landlord of his social club, it had of course been necessary for me to meet my most prestigious customer. It had turned out that Khalid and Falah had a whole bunch in common and had become friends. Falah had taken a liking to my character and had taken Khalid under his jihadi wing.

Falah, wanted by both the Americans and the Mossad, was staying in Zubara, effectively out of their reach. Neither nation was willing to take official action in the tiny country right now, as perceived foreign involvement would only weaken the besieged pro-Western emir in the eyes of the populace. The old man talked a big game about sacrificing for the cause but had no desire to become a martyr himself.

There was a loud noise from downstairs in the social club, and one of the guards, an angry young man by the name of Yousef, went to check it. Falah always traveled with an entourage. Terrorists are kind of like rappers that way. Hell, his personal vehicle was a ridiculous yellow Hummer H2. It sounds ostentatious, but it wasn't really that odd in a country where this much oil money was flowing.

"Have you thought about what I suggested yesterday?" I asked.

He looked up, playing coy. "About the missiles?"

I nodded. "Yes. Remember, I am new to this, but I want to do anything in my power to help the cause. I do not mean to pry, but I believe our warriors could use the weapons."

"Ah, my young friend, I appreciate such enthusiasm," Falah laughed. "Of course, surface-to-air missiles would be incredibly valuable in the jihad against the American barbarians murdering our brothers."

I smiled. It was incredibly difficult to not ram my thumbs through the old man's eye sockets and wrench his miserable skull from his shoulders. It was even more difficult to pretend to be his buddy. The man I was playing a friendly game with was responsible for blowing up churches, businesses, and schools. I had no problem with killing, but I tried to keep my killing limited to scum like Al Falah. "Yes, of course."

Falah made his move. We had been playing chess together several times a week for months now. Occasionally he got one right. He leaned back and gestured proudly at what he had done. I barely noticed. "Ha. Get out of that."

"Hmm . . ." I made a big show of puzzling over his latest strategy. Inside I was praying that he was going to go for my offer of a meeting with the fictional arms dealers. The entire thing was totally fabricated. If he was stupid and greedy enough that he went for the deal, then it enabled me to end his pathetic life early and utilize his resources for Phase Two. I moved a pawn to enable him to beat me more easily. "Your turn."

"They will return soon, correct? I've thought about what you've told me about these businessmen you met, Khalid," he said, pausing for dramatic effect. "Tell them that I am willing to meet to discuss their offer. If it is as reasonable as you say, I will arrange the purchase."

"Most excellent, sir," I replied. *You'll be dead in a couple weeks, asshole.* "I will contact them immediately."

Falah gave me a devilish grin as he moved his queen. "Checkmate!"

"Indeed."

Chapter 3: The Zoob

VALENTINE
Fort Saradia National Historical Site
Confederated Gulf Emirate of Zubara
February 5

I didn't know what time it was locally when we arrived at our destination. I knew it was the middle of a moonless night. Our plane had landed at Zubara's only international airport but had taxied away from where the commercial airliners would offload passengers. Instead, our plane stopped at the far end of the airport, where the private and charter jets landed.

From there we were herded into a large, unmarked white bus. The bus's windows were so darkly tinted that you couldn't see out. The cargo from the plane was off-loaded onto the bus and a pair of trucks. The entire caravan was leaving the airport through a back gate within a half hour of the plane touching down. Compared to the seemingly endless flight from the United States, everything happened remarkably fast once we hit the ground.

I wasn't able to see anything of the city as we passed through it. The brief glimpse I got between the stairs of the jet and the door of the bus had told me little. It was cooler out than I thought it'd be, probably in the sixties. The air smelled of dust, burning natural gas, car exhaust, and an inadequate sewer system. It reminded me of Mexico.

The drive from the airport was long, but as near as I could tell, it was because we were winding our way around a cluttered city. I assumed the driver, who was one more of Colonel Hunter's security men, was taking a roundabout route to wherever it was we were going. It was the better part of an hour before the bus came to a stop. We all stood up in the aisle, clutching our backpacks, waiting for the line to begin moving, as Hunter's security guys tried to hustle us along. Tailor and I were two of the last ones off.

Stepping out into the cool night air, I took in my surroundings. We were in some kind of large compound surrounded by twenty-foot walls. The walls were made of stone, and looked old. Inside the walls were five large buildings, all of which looked new, plus a few old buildings off to one side.

"This some kind of fort?" Tailor asked.

"Looks like it," I replied. "Those buildings are new, though. So are those lights," I said, noting the new amber streetlights in the compound. "Looks like it's been improved over the years."

"This is Fort Saradia," Sarah said from behind me. I turned around quickly when she spoke, a little bit startled. Tailor looked at me funny and cracked a smile but didn't say anything.

"You know about this place, don't you?" Tailor asked.

"We got briefed before you guys. This place was a fort for the British in the nineteenth century. It was expanded over the years. The Zubarans used it as a small army depot for a long time. That's why half the wall looks new. They closed it down about twenty years ago. I guess they were going to turn it into a university or something, but that didn't pan out, either. Now it's a protected site."

"And that's why we're here, isn't it?" Tailor asked. "Because no one will come poking around, and those walls mean people can't see in."

"Pretty much," Sarah said.

"We can't spend all of our time here," I mused. "If we keep going in and out of the same place all the time we'll get spotted eventually."

"Nah, I bet this is just a staging area," Tailor suggested. "We probably won't spend much time here."

"You guys won't, but I will," Sarah said, grabbing her duffel bag as one of the security men tossed it onto the pavement. "All of my equipment is set up here."

"See? Like I said, it's a staging area," Tailor repeated. "A command center."

"There's my bag," I said. My large GI duffel bag had been dropped onto the pavement. I stepped forward and slung it. "So . . . where do we go now?" I asked. Tailor and Sarah just shrugged. Looking around, I could see that everyone else was just as puzzled as we were. A couple of the buildings looked like dormitories or barracks, but none of us knew what to do now.

The small cluster of security types standing around was no help. They'd hardly acknowledge us, much less tell us anything. Four of them were carrying carbines, too, so none of us got too pushy. All they would tell us was that Colonel Hunter would be along to brief us again. I wondered why they felt it necessary to have the briefing outside in the parking lot instead of in a building or something. I was tired, and so was everyone else. After a few minutes, I set my duffel bag down and sat next to it. Others did the same. A few minutes after that, the bus backed out of the large gate it had come in and departed, leaving us to sit on the ground.

Probably twenty minutes later, a white Toyota Land Cruiser came rolling up from the interior of the compound. It stopped a short distance from where we were all sitting. The doors opened. From the passenger's side, Colonel Hunter climbed out and strode toward us, flanked by yet another security guy. Most of us stood up as he approached.

"Gentlemen, welcome to the Zoob," he said, raising his voice so all of us could hear. "If you don't know already, we're currently at Fort Saradia, a few miles outside of the city. This will be our base of operations for the time being. Over there," he said, pointing to our right, "is the dormitory. Each of you has been assigned a room there. Your name is on the door of your room. The doors aren't locked. Grab your gear, find your room, and get some rack time. We'll be getting you up for more briefings in a few hours. Any questions?"

One guy spoke up. "Sir, what—"

Hunter cut him off. "Tough, I'm not answering any now. Move out!" Without so much as another word, Colonel Hunter and his entourage of security men piled into Land Cruisers and drove off, leaving us to carry our bags all the way to the dormitory. Tailor and I looked at each other, shrugged, and picked up our bags.

The dormitory had three levels. The stairs were on the outside of the building, with a set on either end. They led to an enclosed walkway that was flanked by rooms on either side. Tailor and I made our way down the first level, checking the doors on each side for our names. Each person's name was written on the door in magic marker.

I found my room eventually. It was on the north end of the third floor. "Valentine" had been written on the door. Someone had also drawn a rough picture of a heart with an arrow through it. Grumbling something unpleasant, I opened the door and stepped into the dark room.

A dusty smell filled my nose, and it took me a moment to find the light switch. As the old fluorescent light above my head flickered to life, it revealed a Spartan little room. It couldn't have been more than twelve foot by twelve. It looked like a college dorm room that had been abandoned years before. The walls were bare white cinder block, with no decorations. A simple bed with a thin mattress was shoved into one corner. A military-surplus wool blanket and a small pillow had been tossed onto it. Against one wall was a set of metal shelving. A small closet was situated on the other wall.

I set my bag down and began to explore my new room. On the far wall was a window and a door. The window was darkly tinted, and didn't open. The door opened outward to reveal a small balcony. From my balcony, in the cool, dry night air, I could see over the wall of the compound. The amber glow of Zubara City could be seen to the east. The wind was gusty and cold, so I went back into my room.

The other door in the room led to the bathroom. I crossed my room and pulled that door open. "Hey!" someone yelled, startling me enough that I stumbled back into my room. It had been a woman's voice. A second later, Sarah McAllister appeared in the doorway.

"Hey!" I said as she stepped around me, walking into my room like she owned the place. "What the hell?"

"Are you stalking me or something?" she asked.

I felt my face flush. "You're in *my* room!"

"I guess we share a bathroom," she said.

"I guess," I said. "Weird that they didn't separate males and females."

"This isn't summer camp," Sarah said, grinning.

"Do we have a shower, then?" I asked, poking my head back into the bathroom.

"Sort of," Sarah replied. To my right, at the very end of the room, was a square section that looked like the base of a shower. At about knee high, there was a spigot and two knobs. The spigot led to a hose, which in turn led to a shower head, clipped to the wall just above the spigot.

"Huh? So . . . what are you supposed to do, sit down in this thing?"

"I don't know," Sarah said. "You could use the spray-hose to wash yourself, I guess. There's nowhere on the wall above to clamp it, so we can't use it like a regular shower. Also, there's no curtain."

"And what the hell is that?" I asked, indicating another spray-hose. This one came out of the wall next to the toilet.

"It's for washing your feet," Sarah explained. "Most toilets over here have them. Local custom is you wash your feet after using the bathroom."

"What about your hands?" I asked.

"That's optional," she said, smiling.

"So this is it, huh? A shower, um, *thing* with no curtain, a toilet with a spray-hose on it, and a bare tile floor with a drain. Zubaran bathroom technology is a bit wanting."

"I'm going to take a shower," Sarah said. "Or I'm going to try. So get out of here. The door doesn't lock, so don't open it until I'm gone. *Stalker.*"

"I'm not stalking you!" I protested as Sarah shoved me out of the bathroom and slammed the door in my face. "Psycho," I muttered to myself as she turned the water on.

Exhausted, I kicked my boots off and climbed into bed. Pulling the rough wool blanket over me, I rolled over and was asleep in minutes.

I was abruptly woken a short while later. I sat up in bed, startled, not entirely sure where I was at first. Sarah stood over me, wearing nothing but a *short* pair of gym shorts and a T-shirt. Her hair was wet. She smelled nice; she *looked good.*

"Hey, Valentine," she said. "Do you have any toilet paper?"

"Huh? What're you doing in my room again?" I mumbled.

"*Toilet paper*. There isn't any. Did you bring some?"

"Actually, I did." I sat up. "I always bring toilet paper." I reached over and dug into my duffel bag. I handed her a roll that was wrapped in a plastic bag. "Anything else?"

"No, that's everything," she said, stepping back into the bathroom. "Nice try, though." She flashed me a smile before closing the door again.

"You're welcome!" I yelled at the door before laying back down. I had a smile on my face as I rolled over to go back to sleep.

VALENTINE
February 28

For the rest of the month of February, we remained cooped up in Fort Saradia. We had classes every day on topics ranging from fieldcraft to local history. Gordon Willis made several appearances to tell us what a great job we were doing and remind us of the importance of operational security. He seemed pretty useless, actually.

There was a lot of physical fitness training, too. It had been less than a year since I'd left Vanguard, but I'd gotten pretty out of shape. The first morning they had us running laps around the inside of the compound I thought my heart was going to explode. Tailor was even worse off than I was, since he was a smoker.

What we *weren't* getting was any firearms training, which bothered me, but I understood why. Fort Saradia didn't have a range of any kind, and was only a few miles outside of the city. There was no way to do a lot of shooting without drawing attention.

At least we did have weapons. I'd been inside the main building a few times and had caught a glimpse of the arms room. It was stocked with some of the most modern equipment I'd ever seen, and it was all brand new. Our armorer was a jovial guy named Frank Mann. He sported curly black hair and a bushy black mustache, and was eminently proud of his arms room. He'd been around the block a few times himself, so he, Tailor, and I became friends. In any case it's always a good idea to make friends with the armorer.

Tailor and I didn't tell him about the handguns we'd smuggled. Even though they'd prohibited cellular phones and some other items, they'd never bothered to search our belongings. I suspected Frank wouldn't care. He was as big a gun nut as Tailor and I, and I'd seen him packing what I assumed was a personally owned Glock .45 several times.

Toward the end of the month, things began to pick up. Every day it seemed that there were fewer and fewer of us. The word was that we were being divided up into small groups and sent off to safe houses to begin conducting operations. Sarah hinted that they'd been watching us to see whom we got along with, and who we'd work well with. Frank told me that he'd been issuing weapons to the people that were leaving. It seemed like things were finally going to begin. I was excited; sitting around in the compound had grown tiresome.

On the very last day of the month, I was told to report to the small briefing room in the admin building. It was mid-afternoon as I made my way across Fort Saradia. The sun was high in the sky; it was warm but not hot. A strong wind blew from the north. Every time it would gust, it'd kick up another huge cloud of dust. Other than the howling wind, the compound was quiet.

I was apparently the last one to arrive in the small briefing room. Colonel Hunter and Sarah were standing at the front of the room, talking quietly. A laptop was set up on a table, hooked up to a projector. A portable screen stood at the head of the darkened room.

"About time," Tailor said, sitting at one of the desks with a notebook.

"Are we taking a test or something?" I asked, sitting next to him. I briefly wondered if this was one of those crazy dreams where you're back in school and have to take an exam you haven't studied for.

"They're shipping us off," Hudson said from across the room. Sitting next to him was Wheeler, the guy who kept asking questions on the plane. He and Hudson had both been in the Rangers together. Wheeler was a slim, freckled redhead. Despite being from New York, he was a country boy. Wheeler had grown up hunting in the woods of upstate New York, or as he always pointed out, the "unpaved" part of the state.

"To where?" I asked.

"Downtown," Colonel Hunter explained, facing us at last. "You boys are ready. I'm shipping the four of you off to one of our safe houses in the city."

"Al Khor," Sarah said. "It's the upper class of the three peninsulas of Zubara City. It's where most of the government ministries are and where most of the Westerners live. It'll be easier for you to blend in there, but you will operate throughout the city."

"So, we're the last ones to leave, and we're getting an easy assignment," Tailor said. "Did we screw up somehow, sir?"

"You're the last team to leave, Mr. Tailor, but you'll probably get the first mission. I've actually been impressed with you boys, so I'm assigning you all to the same chalk."

"Just the four of us, sir?" Wheeler asked.

"You'll be fine," Hunter replied. "Mr. Tailor, you're in charge of this chalk."

"Yes, sir!" Tailor answered crisply. I groaned. Tailor kicked me in the shin under the desk.

"From your records, I know that Mr. Tailor has the most combat experience of you four," Hunter said. "Mr. Valentine, you're second-in-command."

"But, sir," Wheeler protested, "I mean, no offense to Valentine, but Hudson and I have been through a lot. We did two tours in Afghanistan together."

"I know that, Mr. Wheeler. However, Mr. Valentine has seen combat in Afghanistan, Africa, Bosnia, China, Central America, and Mexico. I didn't make the chain-of-command decision lightly. Do not question me, ginger."

Tailor snickered.

"Holy shit, Val," Wheeler said, looking over at me. I just shrugged.

"Moving along," Hunter said, "your first target is this man." Sarah pressed a few keys on the laptop. An image of a young Gulf Arab man, probably no older than me, appeared on the screen. He was wearing the traditional thobe and headdress. He had a baby face, with a thin mustache and a neatly trimmed beard on his chin. "His name is Abdul bin Muhammad Al Falah. He's a young up-and-comer in the Zubaran terrorist network. He's used his family's money and political connections to try to make a name for himself."

"He looks like a kid, Colonel," Tailor said.

"He's twenty-six," Hunter replied. "He's also, by all accounts, just a spoiled rich man's son. Our intelligence assets believe this is all a game for young Mr. Al Falah. And he's not been directly involved in any terrorist operations so far."

"So why is he important?" Hudson asked.

"He has connections. They're grooming him to be a player when he gets older. Your first assignment, gentlemen, is to locate and capture Mr. Al Falah."

"*Capture*, sir?" I asked.

"The junior Al Falah knows people," Sarah said, still sitting in front of her computer. "He'll be a very useful intelligence asset. He's relatively young and inexperienced, too, so it should be easier to extract information from him." Her voice was colder than usual as she spoke.

"Miss McAllister is right," Hunter said. "We need him alive, for the time being. You will interrogate him."

"Are we supposed to make him talk?" Wheeler sounded nervous with the idea. "Aren't there, like, *rules* about that now?"

Hunter scowled. "Rules? Does extracting information from this young man make you uncomfortable, Mr. Wheeler?" He didn't wait for a response. "You're not in the army anymore. This young man has been helping recruit the assholes who've been blowing up your old compatriots. I don't want rules, gentlemen, I want results."

"So, how are we supposed to find him?" Tailor asked.

"Our intelligence assets are working on that, Mr. Tailor," Hunter replied. "You'll be assigned to observe him yourself, and you'll be given a list of places he frequents. He's not a difficult man to track, and he has no reason to suspect he's in any danger here. Zubara has been a safe haven for terrorists for years. This should be an easy one."

"I'll be assisting during operations," Sarah said, taking over from Hunter, "as a sort of dispatcher. I'll be in radio contact with the other operational teams. I can update you on intelligence, give you instructions, and assist in translating if you need it. You've all been assigned radio call signs. Wheeler, yours is *Ginger*."

"Hey!" Wheeler protested. Tailor broke out in a laugh.

Sarah ignored our adolescent humor. "Hudson, you're *Shafter*."

"So the *black man* gets to be Shafter, huh?" Hudson growled. "Hell, why not *Dolemite*? Or how 'bout *Black Dynamite*?" The room immediately fell silent. Sarah looked at Colonel Hunter, not knowing what to say. Hudson could only maintain his indignant expression for so long before he started laughing. "Lord, girl, where did you come up with these?"

"They're randomly chosen by computer," Sarah insisted.

"Bullshit!" Wheeler snorted. Hudson slapped the desk and let out a raucous laugh.

"Gentlemen," Hunter warned, frowning. *Kill joy.*

Sarah continued. "Tailor, your call sign is *Xbox*."

"Xbox?" Tailor asked, sounding laughably butt-hurt. "Seriously?" Wheeler folded his arms across his chest and gave Tailor a look of smug satisfaction. I chuckled.

"And Valentine, your call sign is *Nightcrawler*."

"Nightcrawler?" I repeated. "How did you come up with *that*?"

Hunter finally cracked a smile. "You should've heard some of the ones she came up with for the other boys. Mr. Walker's call sign is *Lilac*."

"I thought you said they were randomly chosen by computer?"

Sarah tried as hard as she could to look innocent. "They are! Why would you think otherwise?" She flashed me a little smile and winked. Tailor, noticing, kicked me under the desk again.

VALENTINE
Ash Shamal District
March 11
1900

"This is Ginger. I've got eyes on the target," Wheeler said over the radio.

"Roger that," Tailor responded, his voice very hushed in my earpiece. *"I see him, too. He just passed my position."*

"*Ginger, Control,*" Sarah said over the radio, her voice very professional. "*Do you have a positive ID on the target?*" It was very important that we had the right guy, after all.

"*Uh . . . stand by.*" Wheeler and Hudson were both in our van, which was parked farther down the darkened alley to the south. To the north was the target building. It was a small building, only one story, constructed out of stucco and brick like most of the older buildings in the city. It looked out of place, though, surrounded by several huge, new, corrugated-steel warehouses. On the south side of the target building was a bright amber light. The rest of the alley was dark. Previously, our intelligence assets had made sure the other nearby street lights were out of commission, vandalized with a pellet gun.

"*Control, Shafter,*" Hudson said. "*I've got a positive ID on our target. He's got three others with him.*" The van had an impressive assortment of gadgets and equipment, including state-of-the-art night vision and thermal optics.

"*Copy that, Shafter,*" Sarah said, ice in her voice. "*You are cleared to engage. Capture the target. Kill the others. Control out*"

It was on. Shrouded in darkness, I peeked around the corner, looking north, up the narrow alley. Abdul bin Muhammad Al Falah and three compatriots slowly made their way toward me, talking loudly in the darkness. Al Falah and one skinny man were dressed in traditional Arab thobes, dark ones because it was cool out, and checkered headdresses. They were flanked by two serious-looking men in brown suits, probably bodyguards. Our target had what appeared to be a laptop bag slung over his shoulder. *Good.* It was likely we'd get at least some intelligence from his computer. Al Falah and his friend were having an animated conversation, their voices echoing loudly down the narrow alley. They acted like they didn't have a care in the world as they approached me.

The building at the end of the alley was some kind of terrorist hangout, used mainly for recruiting and propaganda. Al Falah frequented the place. Almost every night he would take a walk down the alley with another potential recruit. He'd go on and on about the jihad and other bullshit, wowing the recruits with his family connections and promising their families large monetary rewards if they would sign up to kill Americans. At first, I couldn't believe how brazen they were, walking down a public street discussing this stuff. After a few days, I realized that this was the reason we'd been sent to Zubara in the first place. *They'd never see it coming.*

"*This is Xbox,*" Tailor whispered, his voice hushed in my earpiece. "*They just passed my position. Four of 'em. The target, another individual, and two big fuckers, probably guards.*"

"Roger," I said, still peeking around the corner. Tailor was hiding behind a wall that separated the target building from a warehouse to its south. In the darkness, Al Falah and his escorts had walked right past Tailor's position without noticing him. His bodyguards were complacent, it seemed. *Good. Complacency kills.*

I looked down at my watch. The final call to prayer of the day would begin at any moment. There was a mosque only a block away. Once the call to prayer began, the traditional music would start blaring over a set of loudspeakers. This would last for a couple of minutes, and would give us a little cover if we had to make some noise.

I was wearing tan cargo pants, a black shirt, a black jacket, and a tan baseball cap. I looked unmistakably American, but I was dressed similarly to most of the Westerners running around Zubara, except for the holster on my left hip and the body-armor vest under my shirt. I reached under my jacket and drew the Sig 220 pistol I'd been issued. With my other hand, I reached into my jacket's inside pocket and pulled out a suppressor. I quickly screwed the two together, while taking one last look around. The sky was glowing from the lights of the city, so much so that I couldn't see any stars, even though it was clear out. All around us were typical city noises; we were only one block away from a busy main thoroughfare. The alley itself was peaceful, save for the prattling of Al Falah and his friend.

Suddenly, from the north, a recording of a man singing in Arabic began. It was 1907. The call to prayer had begun. I took a deep breath. "This is Nightcrawler," I said, whispering into my radio. "I'm moving." With that, I stepped around the corner, suppressed pistol held behind my back, and began walking purposefully toward my target. I kept my head down, so the brim of my ball cap hid my eyes. I hunched over, trying to hide how tall I was. My heart was pounding, but I wasn't really scared. I doubted Al Falah's half-assed bodyguards were much of a threat.

"*Xbox moving,*" Tailor whispered. To my north, past Al Falah and his compatriots, something moved in the shadows, another figure coming up behind them on the sidewalk. Tailor's shape was silhouetted against the amber light of the building at the end of the alley. The bodyguards hadn't once looked behind them yet.

I was getting close now. Looking up, I saw that the two bodyguards had noticed me. One stepped in front of the rest and began to approach. The other hung behind. Still, neither had looked behind them. Tailor continued his approach unnoticed.

The lead guard said something to me in Arabic, his voice raised to make himself heard over the blaring music. Al Falah and the other man stopped. I didn't understand the language, but I definitely got the gist from the tone of his voice. The thug was a tall man, with a bushy mustache. His right hand was beneath his brown jacket, resting on the butt of a gun. I made eye contact with him for the first time. He held his left hand up, signaling me to stop, still talking. He grew angry when he realized that I was a foreigner and took another step closer. He was only a few feet in front of me now. Young Mr. Al Falah had an obnoxious grin on his face; his friend seemed nervous.

My eyes darted to the left. Tailor was right behind the other bodyguard. His hands came up, extending his own pistol. He fired a shot; the muffled pop of the suppressed .45 round discharging was barely audible over the singing that echoed through the alley. Tailor's target dropped to the sidewalk.

The bodyguard in front of me turned around quickly, having heard the discharge. Before he knew what was happening, I had my own pistol up and put a .45 slug into his left ear. My gun was on Al Falah before the body hit the sidewalk. He and his friend both turned to face me, eyes wide, staring at my pistol. Tailor's .45 popped twice more, and Al Falah's friend fell to the ground, two gunshot wounds to his back.

Al Falah looked down at his companion, then turned around to see the muzzle of Tailor's suppressed pistol. He turned back to me, skin pale, eyes fixed on my pistol, and raised his hands slowly. A puddle formed on the sidewalk beneath him as his bladder let go.

An instant later, Tailor snapped open a collapsible baton and struck Al Falah on the neck. He cried out in pain and dropped to the sidewalk, falling into his own piss. I watched the street while Tailor zip tied our prisoner's hands. Al Falah looked up at me one last time before Tailor pulled a black bag over his head.

"Ginger, Nightcrawler," I said over the radio, "We got him. Get up here." I unscrewed the suppressor from my pistol and reholstered it. I then snapped open my automatic knife, cut the shoulder strap on Al Falah's bag, and pulled it off of him.

Without turning on its headlights, the van sped up the alley, coming to a stop right next to us. The sliding side door opened. Hudson jumped out, grabbed Al Falah, and effortlessly threw him into the van. He climbed back in, and I followed, laptop bag in hand.

Just as the call to prayer died away, Tailor noticed Al Falah's friend, lying facedown in his own blood with two bullets in his back. He was still alive. He groaned slightly and tried to move. Without blinking, Tailor stepped forward, shot him in the back of the head, then jumped into the van, pulling the door closed behind him.

We backed down the alley until we came to the cross street, turned on the headlights, and sped away into the night. Tailor called Control over the radio to inform them of our success. I slumped against the wall of the van and looked down at my watch again. *1909. Not bad.* Hunter had been right. It'd been remarkably easy.

Stepping forward, Tailor roughly pulled the black bag from Al Falah's head, knocking off his checkered headdress in the process. The young terrorist looked around, still groggy from the sedative and from being clocked by Tailor. His eyes grew wide as he became aware of the surroundings and his situation. He was handcuffed to a chair in the basement of our safe house. We had him shoved off into a corner. The only illumination was from a bright lamp we'd set up. I had to shake my head at the whole scene; it was like something from a bad spy movie.

Al Falah looked at Tailor, fear in his eyes. His mouth was slightly open, but he didn't, or maybe couldn't, speak. He then looked over to me; his eyes darted down to the pistol on my left hip. We'd removed our jackets in order to openly display our weapons.

To my left was Hudson. Al Falah seemed especially intimidated by him. Hudson, for his part, just folded his muscular arms across his chest and stared the skinny terrorist down, not saying a word.

"Do you speak English?" I asked. Our prisoner's eyes darted back to me. He didn't say anything.

"I know you can understand me," Tailor said, leaning in a little closer. He was probably right; almost all educated Gulf Arabs spoke English. "So we can do this the easy way, or we can do this the pushing-your-shit-in way. What's it gonna be, ace?"

Al Falah, for his part, seemed to have found a little bit of spine. He closed his mouth and sat up a little straighter in his chair, staring defiantly at the wall behind us. Tailor straightened up, then looked over at Hudson and me, grinning. It seemed that Al Falah didn't want to do this the easy way.

"Wheeler, go get Sarah," Tailor said then, talking over his shoulder. Wheeler, who was behind us, near the stairs, nodded and headed up to the main floor of the safe house. A few moments later, he clomped back down the stairs. Behind him, Sarah gracefully made her way down, clipboard in hand. She followed him across the darkened room.

The prisoner's eyes grew wide again when Sarah stepped into the light. He stared up at her shapely figure, and his mouth fell open again. She was taller than he was. She looked back down at him, not saying anything. Wheeler pulled up a second chair, and slid it next to her. She sat in it, crossing her legs and laying the clipboard in her lap. She clicked open a pen, leaned forward, and spoke to Al Falah in Arabic.

He looked back at us, then back at her, then back at us again, seemingly confused. Sarah repeated whatever it was that she'd said, her voice a little bit harsher. Al Falah seemingly balked at this and said something back.

"What'd he say?" Hudson asked.

"He just called me a cunt," Sarah said. "Said he doesn't have to answer to a woman."

"Really?" Tailor said. Without another word, he stepped forward and punched Al Falah across the face. The terrorist's head snapped to the side, and he cried out in pain. "Ask him now."

Sarah repeated whatever it is she said to Al Falah. His voice wavered, but the young terrorist apparently didn't tell Sarah whatever it was she wanted to hear. She looked up at us and just shook her head.

Tailor shrugged. "Okay, asshole," he said and punched Al Falah again. Hudson stepped around Sarah and violently struck our prisoner himself. Al Falah's head snapped back, and the young Arab cried out. Tailor and Hudson took turns hitting him a few more times. Hudson was strong as an ox and had to take it easy. A real shot from that man would have cracked Al Falah's skull.

"What are you asking him?" I said, looking down at Sarah.

"This kid is just a small fry. His uncle, Ali bin Ahmed Al Falah, is the real target. I'm asking about him."

I looked back up at our prisoner. Tailor and Hudson had stopped pummeling him for a moment. One eye was puffy and swelling shut, and blood was running from both his nose and lip. It was unpleasant, but this was war. If any of us were captured, we could expect worse. Sarah remained cool but seemed uncomfortable with what was happening. Nonetheless, she repeated her question, her voice sounding cold and harsh.

The young Al Falah spent a few moments staring at his lap, breathing heavily, blood dripping onto his clothes. He lifted his head back, still panting, and looked over at Sarah. He took a deep breath. Sarah lifted her clipboard just in time to block a blob of spit and blood. I had to give the kid credit; he'd certainly found his backbone. Not that it was going to do him any good.

"Oh, that's *it*," I said, speaking to Al Falah for the first time. I lifted my right foot and booted our prisoner in the chest. He gasped in pain, rocked back on his chair, and fell over backward, smashing his hands between the chair and the concrete floor. I moved forward, planting my right foot into his chest again, and drew my pistol. Holding the Sig .45 in both hands, I looked down at Al Falah, the sights aligned with the bridge of his nose.

"Valentine, no!" Sarah exclaimed, coming up out of her chair and putting her hand on my shoulder. "We need information from him."

"Tell him if he doesn't start talking I'm going to blow his head off," I said coldly. *The Calm* had overtaken me, as it often did right before I had to shoot someone. Sarah had sensed the change. She hesitated. "*Tell him*," I repeated, more firmly. Sarah stepped around me. Al Falah's eyes were focused on the muzzle of my pistol and nothing else. Sarah leaned down and spoke to him. Al Falah sputtered something back.

"What'd he say?" Hudson asked.

Sarah stood up and sighed. "He says he's prepared to die. I think he wants to. He's scared shitless. He thinks it'll make him a martyr."

"Fuck that," Tailor said, squatting down next to our prisoner. He reached into his pocket and drew his knife. With the push of a button, the blade snapped forward out of the handle. Tailor reached down and grabbed Al Falah's face with his left hand. "Tell him that if he doesn't start *talking*, I'm going to start *cutting parts* off him. Tell him we're *not* going to kill him. I'll just cut off his ears, his nose, his tongue, and put out his eyes, and knock out his teeth, and dump him on the side of the road somewhere. He can live the rest of his shitty life as a beggar, or he can kill himself and not get his virgins. I'm not gonna do him no favors."

"I . . ." Sarah said, hesitating.

"*Tell him!*" Tailor shouted, poking the very tip of his blade into Al Falah's face. There was no doubt that Tailor would do it.

Sarah steeled herself, leaned back down to our prisoner, and spoke to him again for a few moments. His eyes grew wider as he processed her words. He looked over to me, with the muzzle of my pistol still pointed between his eyes, then over to Tailor and the knife poking into his face. Apparently the short, scary Southerner with the disfiguring razor was the more frightening prospect of the two of us. Falah hesitated for what seemed like an eternity.

"I . . . I . . . okay," Al Falah then sputtered, speaking English for the first time. "I will tell you. I will tell you! Please . . ."

"That's more like it," Tailor said. He pushed the switch on his knife, and the blade disappeared back into the handle. I took my foot off of Al Falah's chest and holstered my pistol. Tailor and I then grabbed the back of his chair, hoisted him up, and set our prisoner upright again.

"Your uncle," Sarah said, sitting back down in her chair. "Ali bin Ahmed Al Falah. Tell me everything you know about him." The young Arab took one last look around the room, lowered his head slightly, and began to talk. He had a *lot* to say.

Stepping onto the roof, I saw Sarah silhouetted against the lights of the city. She was standing by the wall that ran around the roof of the house, smoking a cigarette. Hearing me open the door, she turned around briefly and nodded. I returned the nod, and stood beside her.

Below us was the small villa that we used for a safe house. The house itself was big, with no less than six bedrooms, two and a half bathrooms, and a big common area downstairs. In addition to that, it had a huge basement. Basements were rare in homes in the Middle East. The safe house also had a tall wall around it. Next to the house was a large carport that held four vehicles. In front of the house was a sort of garden with a grove of tall palm trees and a mess of ferns at their bases.

"Are you okay?" I asked, looking out over the city. "I didn't know you smoked."

"I don't," she said, exhaling a puff of smoke. "I mean, I quit years ago. I bummed one off Tailor. I just . . . sometimes when I get stressed I have one. That's all."

"Oh, I see. What's wrong?"

"I thought you were going to kill that guy."

"Sarah." I paused for a moment while I struggled to find the right words. "I *did* kill a man tonight. One of Al Falah's bodyguards."

"I know! I ordered you to. It's just . . . I don't know. I'm being stupid. I've never been part of an interrogation like that before."

"I was a little surprised to see you here," I said.

"I was surprised when they called me out. I guess the other Arabic speakers were busy. Walker was probably busy pulling somebody's fingernails out. I was told that normally I wouldn't leave the compound much. I'm not even supposed to know where all of the safe houses are!"

"You've never done an interrogation like that before, have you?" I asked.

"No. I suppose you've done a lot of them, right?"

"Not really," I said truthfully. "I was mostly a trigger-puller. We had intel specialists do that kind of thing."

"Tailor seemed like he was enjoying himself," she said hesitantly.

"Well . . . Tailor is *crazy*. He's always been like that."

"How long have you known him?"

"Years now. Since we were in Africa together."

"Do you really trust him?" Sarah asked, putting out her cigarette on the top of the wall and looking over at me.

"With my life," I replied. "I don't know if I'd trust him with anybody else's, though."

Sarah looked at me sideways, eyebrows raised. She then let out a sardonic chuckle. "You're funny, Mike," she said, calling me by my given name for the first time. We stood together, looking out over the lights of the city, for what seemed like a long time. Neither one of us said anything.

"You did fine, by the way," I said at last.

"What?"

"In the interrogation," I continued. "You really kept your cool in there. You really seemed like you knew your stuff."

"I've been trained," Sarah said, "by, um, our employers for Project Heartbreaker. I just didn't know how intense it was going to be."

"It gets easier. I mean, it sounds horrible, but you get used to it."

"I hope so," Sarah said. "We're just getting started."

"You hear something?" I asked.

"Oh, yeah." She looked back over at me. "We've got a list of targets a mile long. Terrorists, financiers, support people, recruiting people, you name it."

"You know all of the targets?" I asked incredulously.

"What? Oh, no. I just got a peek at it. It's not just names, either. It's places. Gatherings. *Events*. This is going to get *ugly*, Mike."

"That's what I figured," I said. "So, what happens to our boy downstairs?"

"Hunter's sending someone to come get him. I don't know what they're going to do with him now."

"They'll either make a deal with him in exchange for being a continuing source of information, or they'll put a bullet in his brainpan and dump him in the ocean. Either way, sucks to be him."

Sarah nodded. "His computer wasn't even password protected, either. There's a *lot* of information on there. Hunter was happy."

"Heh . . . I'm glad. So, do you know what's next?"

"His uncle. He's the next target for you guys."

"I figured. When?"

"Soon. Hunter said your chalk did so well that he's giving you that mission next. We've got some more intel to gather, but that's your next job. They'll be sending me information to brief you soon."

"Good."

"Mike . . . I saw something else. You know, when I was digging around. They're expecting heavy casualties for Dead Six. The operations they're planning are high risk and are planned with minimum possible manpower."

I sighed aloud, looking back out over the city. "Great."

"You just be careful out there, okay?" she said quietly. She was staring at me intently. We held eye contact for a long time.

"I will," I managed.

"What's *up*?" Tailor said, strolling through the door onto the roof, lighting a cigarette as he went. He was unusually upbeat and had a stupid grin on his face. He paused when he realized Sarah and I were alone together. "Am I, uh, interrupting something?" he asked, cigarette in mouth.

"No, no," Sarah said, stepping away from me. "I was just giving Valentine some info on what's happening next."

"We're going after his uncle, right?" Tailor asked, referring to the captive in our basement.

"Sure are," I answered.

The expression on Tailor's face changed almost imperceptibly. My friend might not have been *certifiably* nuts, but he sure did enjoy this kind of thing a little too much. "*Good.*" He grinned.

Chapter 4: Secondary Target

LORENZO
March 13

Falah had sounded nervous on the phone as he apologized for postponing our appointment due to family trouble. I played the concerned friend, even went so far as to offer my assistance, but he wouldn't elaborate about what was wrong. It wasn't until afterward that I got the word on the street that Falah's favorite nephew had disappeared. The bodyguards provided by his uncle had been found shot to death, along with one of their new recruits. I'd only met the kid once. He'd struck me as another obnoxious rich kid, wannabe-terrorist asshole.

Nobody had any idea who'd taken him. It wouldn't have surprised me if the senior Falah wasn't waiting by the phone for the ransom call right now. There was a subset of the criminal underworld that specialized in kidnapping the kinds of targets whose parents wouldn't involve the authorities. It was dangerous, but drug lords' kids were especially lucrative. But I knew of most of the crews who did that kind of thing professionally, and I didn't think any of them were operating around here.

Even the lowest of the low had families, easy targets that could be exploited for money, revenge, or leverage. Hell, I was a perfect example. Eddie had learned my real name, tracked down my family, and just like that, he owned me.

My family wouldn't even recognize me now. My older brother, Bob, the federal agent, always the righteous, morally grounded, overachieving tough guy would certainly slap the cuffs on me himself if he had even the slightest clue about the things I'd done, and he'd probably sleep well at night afterward. But he, and all the rest, were family, and I *owed* them. They wouldn't understand, but I was doing this for them.

In a way, I could understand Falah's worry. Even scumbags had loved ones. I just hoped he got that shit cleared up fast so I could hurry up and kill him.

VALENTINE
Al Khor District, Safe house 4
March 20
0745

Tailor and I made our way into the basement of the safe house, having been rousted out of bed by Sarah. We were surprised to find Colonel Hunter waiting for us, flanked as always by a pair of his nondescript security men. Several chairs had been set up. A laptop sat on a small table, hooked up to a portable screen. Wheeler and Hudson had been called away a few days prior and hadn't yet returned.

"Good morning, gentlemen," Hunter said. "I apologize for dragging you boys out of bed so early, but we've got work to do. We're ready to move."

"Are Hudson and Wheeler coming back, sir?" I asked as we sat down.

"I'm afraid not. I have them on another assignment right now. You two will be on your own. I have confidence in you."

Tailor and I just looked at each other. Sarah's face was a mask, but there was concern in her eyes.

Hunter turned on the big screen and began his briefing. "This is Ali bin Ahmed Al Falah. He's a Saudi national by birth but has lived in Zubara for over ten years. He's a wealthy, influential landowner and has connections to the Saudi royal family. He's also a *player.*" The man pictured was short and overweight. He was wearing a traditional checkered headdress and had a thick white beard.

The picture changed. It was now a much younger Al Falah, dressed in camouflage and holding an RPD machine gun.

"This is Al Falah in 1984," Hunter continued. "At the age of twenty-six, he dropped out of a Saudi religious university to join the jihad against the Soviets in Afghanistan. He fought with the mujahedin for two years before being wounded and returning to Saudi Arabia."

The picture changed again. This time Al Falah was shaking hands with an all-too-familiar man, and smiling.

"We believe this picture was taken in 1997 or so. Yes, that is Osama bin Laden. As I said, Al Falah is a player. He's very wealthy, both from his father and from his dealings in the oil and natural gas industry. He's respected, considered pious, and has an enormous family. Though polygamy is rare in Zubara, he's got three wives and probably nine children. He lives in a large walled compound outside of the city. Nice place—fountain, palm trees, you name it. He's got many servants and quite a few Indonesian slave girls as well."

Tailor and I were taking notes. Hunter told us it wasn't necessary. Sarah handed each of us a fat manila envelope.

"Everything you need is in here," Hunter said. "Al Falah never does anything himself. He's always the behind-the-scenes man, the one pulling the strings and providing the funding. We believe getting shot in the ass in the 'Stan probably led to this attitude. He raises enormous amounts of cash for various terrorist groups. He has several influential charities in Zubara, Kuwait, and the UAE that are all fronts for donating money to organizations like Hezbollah, Hamas, and Al Qaeda in the Arabian Peninsula."

"I'd do this one for free," Tailor muttered under his breath.

Hunter didn't seem to hear him. "Fortunately for us, this is one of the rare occasions where removing the man will remove the means. Al Falah does what he does through force of personality. He's well liked and respected. He goes to Friday services at mosque . . . well, *religiously*. He always fasts during Ramadan. People are happy to do business with him. Your mission, gentlemen, is to kill Ali bin Ahmed Al Falah. You can use any means you see fit. You are to keep collateral damage to an absolute minimum to keep the Zubarans from getting antsy. You can request any equipment you wish, but no other personnel are available at this time. Failure is not an option. Any questions?"

"This is . . . wow," I said, looking through the stack of documents.

"Welcome to Big Boy Town," Hunter said, cracking an evil grin. "You boys were picked for this assignment because I believe you can handle it. I didn't say it'd be easy. I'm giving you two a lot of leeway. Just get the job done. The best place to hit Al Falah is here," Hunter said, pointing to a picture that had appeared on the screen. "This is a social club that Al Falah frequents. It's a coffee house, or a tea house or something like that. Men go there to smoke hookahs, play chess, and shoot the shit. It's also one of very few public places he's regularly seen."

"How often does he go there, sir?" Tailor asked.

"Several nights a week, usually," Sarah said. "He likes to play chess with his friends."

"Where does this information come from, sir?" Tailor asked, looking at Colonel Hunter. "Is it reliable?" He seemed uncharacteristically concerned.

"Our intelligence assets are dependable enough, son," Hunter replied crossly. "We have our own people as well as contacts in the Zubaran intelligence services. This is an important job. This will be our first major hit."

"Anything else we need to know, sir?" I asked.

"As a matter of fact . . ." Another picture appeared on the screen. This one was of a pretty nondescript Gulf Arab man, in traditional dress, and was taken from far away. "Your secondary target is this man. He's the new proprietor of the social club. He appeared on the scene a few months ago. We don't know anything about him other than his name, *Khalid.*"

"Why's he important, sir?" I asked.

"He's hosting Al Falah," Sarah said. "He's a facilitator. We've picked up some unusual electronic chatter coming from the club. A lot of encrypted phone traffic, stuff like that. We have reason to suspect Khalid is part of the enemy's support network."

"Even if that's not the case," Hunter said, "everyone in Zubara knows who our target is and what he does. Part of our objective is to make the man on the street afraid to deal with the bad guys. So Khalid is your secondary target. Your tertiary targets are Al Falah's bodyguards and assistants. Eliminate as many of them as possible."

Tailor and I exchanged a knowing look. I felt a predatory grin split my face as I returned my attention to the briefing. This was the kind of job I'd signed up for.

VALENTINE
Ash Shamal District
March 25
1757

"Our boy's here," I said, looking through a pair of compact binoculars. Tailor was lying next to me, doing the same thing. One floor down and across the street from us, a bright yellow Hummer H2, followed by a white Toyota Land Cruiser, pulled to a stop in front of the social club. "Would you look at that?" I asked. "That's a pretty pimp ride he's got." Tailor chuckled.

The Land Cruiser's doors opened, and four men, presumably bodyguards, piled out. They were all dressed in cheap-looking suits without ties. As I watched, the driver got out of the Hummer, hurried to the other side of the vehicle, and opened the passenger's side door.

"There he is," Tailor said as a short, heavyset man in traditional Gulf Arab garb climbed out of the large yellow SUV. Tailor and I laid eyes on Ali Bin Ahmed Al Falah for the first time. We'd been coming to the same spot for days, watching the social club, waiting for him to make an appearance. Today we finally got lucky.

We were on the second floor of a half-completed building that stood directly across a divided street from the social club. It was going to be an office building of some kind, but construction had been halted. The second floor had large floor-to-ceiling windows on the sides. The glass wasn't installed yet. We lay on the floor, side by side, shrouded in the darkness the unfinished building provided, watching our target. The sun was low in the western sky behind us. People passing by on the narrow street had no idea we were there. Our vehicle was parked in the narrow alley behind the building, concealed from view.

Tailor reached into his backpack and pulled out a handheld device that looked like a satellite dish. He put on a set of headphones. "Let's see if we can hear what they have to say." Neither of us spoke Arabic, but we could connect the parabolic microphone to our radios and transmit the intelligence back to Control.

Al Falah made his way toward the glass front doors of the establishment, with his driver walking just behind. The other bodyguards fanned out and did a half-assed job of observing the area. As Al Falah approached, another man in similar Arab attire appeared from inside. The two men greeted each other warmly, grasping each other's right hands while putting their left hands on the other man's right shoulder. They then exchanged kisses on each cheek.

"That must be Khalid." I squeezed the transmit button on my tiny microphone. "Control, Nightcrawler. We have eyes on the primary, secondary, and tertiary targets. Intel was correct. This is the place."

"*Copy that, Nightcrawler,*" Control replied, all business. Anita King was on the radio instead of Sarah.

"Control, Xbox," Tailor said, "I'm transmitting now."

"*Copy that . . . receiving,*" Anita said. I could hear Al Falah and Khalid speaking in Arabic in the background. We observed Al Falah and Khalid for several minutes, until they disappeared into the club, followed by Al Falah's entourage.

"Did you get all that, Control?" Tailor asked.

"*Uh . . . roger that,*" Anita said. "*They were just greeting each other. Said something about a chess game, and that they were going to discuss a proposal.*"

"What kind of proposal?" Tailor asked.

"*They didn't say. Observe the area for as long as you can, then withdraw without being detected.*"

"Roger that, Control," I said. "Out."

Tailor looked over at me, then back through his binoculars. "I'm hungry."

"So, what do you think?" I asked. "How you wanna do this?"

"I say we get a scoped rifle and just pop him from here."

"Sounds easy enough. Do we have a scoped rifle?"

"There's an SR-25 in the safe house we can use. It's got a suppressor, too. From right here, we can lay down some fire, drop a bunch of these guys, and then bug out through the back."

"Did you get a good look at the bodyguards?" I asked. "I think they've got sub-guns."

"Probably little MP5s or something under their suit coats," Tailor agreed. "Probably can't shoot for shit. We should be okay." It was about sixty yards from our position to the front door of the club.

"Cripes, we should've brought the rifle with us. We could've popped him just now and had it over with," I said. We'd been ordered to observe the club and try to get a feel for Al Falah's routine. We knew where Al Falah lived, of course, but it had been deemed too risky to attempt to hit him there.

"Yeah," Tailor said, not really listening to me. "Can't see much in the windows. They're tinted. Al Falah won't sit by the windows out front anyway. He's a big shot, right? He'll have a private room in the back or something."

"Worse comes to worst we could enter the club," I suggested, even though I knew that wasn't a good idea. "Hell, no. Not with just the two of us. No, we'll have to hit him here. We'll only get one shot. If we fuck this up he'll go underground and we might lose him."

"You're right." I set my binoculars down. "You wanna take the shot, or you want me to?"

"You take the SR-25," Tailor said. "I'll grab a carbine and provide cover fire." Tailor wouldn't come out and admit it, but I was a more accurate shooter than he was. He was correct in his assertion that we'd only have one shot, too. There wouldn't be much room for error.

"I don't like it," I said. "Just the two of us versus five bodyguards—"

"That we *know* of," Tailor interjected.

"Right. Next time he could have more. One shot, maybe two, since the rifle's an autoloader, before his bodyguards can get him behind cover. A rifle I've never shot before, and who the hell knows who zeroed the scope or when." We didn't have access to any kind of a shooting range, and I doubted they'd let us risk taking the rifle out into the desert someplace to test-fire it.

"You're right," Tailor agreed, setting down his binoculars as well. "If they get Al Falah into that club, we'll have to go in after him. So you better drop him on the first shot. That's the best chance we got."

"Why are there only two of us? We could really use Hudson and Wheeler for this."

"I don't know," Tailor said. "I don't like it, either." I could only wonder what kind of operations the others were involved in if they could only spare two of us for a job they insisted was so important. As I continued to watch the social club, I couldn't help but worry that things were going to get ugly, fast.

LORENZO
March 26

The disassembled pieces of my pistol were strewn on the kitchen table of our rented apartment. I wiped the slide down with a rag while my crew slept. I found that I always woke up early on game day. Nervous excitement, I suppose.

It never hurts to recheck your equipment. I put a few drops of Slipstream lube on the frame rails of my STI 4.15 Tactical 9mm before fitting everything back together. The gun was a stubby work of lethal art. Phenomenally accurate and reliable, it was the pistol I used when performance was more important than deniability. I had a few Bulgarian Makarovs and old Browning P35s for that. I worked the slide back and forth quickly, feeling the familiar slickness of oiled metal on metal. I checked the chamber before aiming at Al Falah's picture that had been taped to the wall. The tritium sights lined up perfectly on the bridge of his nose as I pulled the trigger. The hammer fell with a snap.

Ali bin Ahmed Al Falah dies today.

The old terrorist bastard had dropped by the club yesterday. He was still distraught, but he wasn't going to let that get in the way of business. Our meeting was on.

An eighteen-round, flush-fit magazine went into the STI. I pulled back the slide and let it fly, feeding a Hornady hollow point into the chamber. If everything went according to plan, that same bullet would end up in one of Al Falah's bodyguards by the end of the night. He'd beefed up the number on his security detail since his nephew's murder. Sure, Al Falah was still calling it a kidnapping, but at this point I knew that was wishful thinking.

The call for prayer could be heard coming from the corner mosque as the sun rose. It was a mournful sound but I had spent so many years in places like this that I found it kind of comforting.

I showered, put on the obnoxious perfume that all of the men in this region wore, and dressed in my Zubaran thobe, vest, and head scarf. I'd tailored this one a bit with a few extra pockets, and I could hike up the idiotic skirt and run if I needed to. The reflection in the bathroom mirror was that of an Arab landlord who had become friends with a terrorist. Today would be the last day that this identity would ever exist.

If I were just here to assassinate this man, life would be simple. Murder is easy, no matter who the target. I needed him for so much more, hence the effort of fabricating Khalid. Al Falah needed to quietly disappear. A business meeting meant that he would probably have greater than normal security, but he would also need his computer to arrange the transfer of funds. I needed that computer for Phase Two and I needed Al Falah himself for Phase Three.

I splashed some water on my face and stared into the mirror. This was too damn complicated. If anything went wrong, there was going to be hell to pay. Shutting the faucet off, I dried my hands and prepared myself for what I had to do. My crew had woken up by the time I came out. The three of us ate breakfast in silence. There was a lot riding on today, and we all knew our jobs.

I holstered the pistol under my thobe, along with two more magazines and the Silencerco suppressor that would be attached to the end of the STI's threaded barrel. My radio went into another pocket.

"You ready?" Carl asked rhetorically, still chewing his Captain Crunch.

"I'm going down to the club," I answered in Arabic. "I'm expecting a busy day today."

VALENTINE
Al Khor District, Safe House 4
March 26
1955

I had the jitters. I always did before an operation. My nerves would smooth out as I got into the swing of things. Tailor and I were in the basement of the safe house, preparing our gear, getting ready for what was coming. Neither of us spoke. We'd go over the plan again later.

I'd gone through this routine many times before, and the jitters always passed, but it was different this time. It was just Tailor and me. No backup, no fire support, and our entire egress plan was to get in our car and drive away.

We'd gotten the word earlier in the day. Al Falah would be returning to the club tonight to broker some kind of arms deal with Khalid. Intelligence had given us the time of the meeting, but few other details. It was *on*.

But still my mind wandered. I had a lot of questions, many that I didn't dare to ask. I wondered about this intelligence. Where did it come from? Do they have someone inside Al Falah's network somewhere? Why not have *that guy* kill him? I wondered what happened to Wheeler and Hudson, too. Though they were supposedly assigned to our chalk, we hadn't heard from them in days.

I chided myself. So many questions, but now was not the time to worry about them. I returned my attention to my gear. Standing up, I slid on my body armor and adjusted the straps until it snugly conformed to my torso. It was a low-profile vest, black in color, with pockets front and back for hard protective plates. The plates, designed to stop rifle fire, were made of ceramic and were thinner and lighter than any I'd ever seen.

On my left hip was a high-ride concealment holster for my revolver. Tailor flashed me a smirk when I pulled the big wheelgun out of my bag, but I paid him no mind. It was my good-luck charm, and I had a feeling I was going to need some luck tonight.

I put on my jacket. It was loose-fitting, and like my body armor and T-shirt was black in color. In Zubara, it was still fairly cool out in March once the sun went down. I wouldn't look too out-of-place with a jacket on. The dark color of the jacket made it hard to tell I was wearing the armor vest underneath it.

Reaching down, I picked up my primary weapon and shouldered it. I pulled back the charging handle, observed that the rifle's chamber was empty, and let the bolt close. I then looked through the scope. The Knight's Armament SR-25 sniper rifle felt heavy in my hands. Its twenty-inch barrel was capped with a sound suppressor. A folding bipod was attached to its railed hand guards. I began to partially disassemble it so it'd fit in a discreet padded case.

While I did this, Tailor got his own equipment ready. His weapon was a 5.56mm FN MK 16 carbine, also with a suppressor. The carbine had the short, ten-inch barrel installed, making it very compact. Tailor removed the suppressor, then folded his carbine's stock. He was then able to fit it into his backpack.

As Tailor and I finished packing our gear, I realized Sarah had come down the stairs. Hunter had left her with us, as he'd been called away for something else. I wasn't sure why they left her at the safe house instead of bringing her back to the base where she belonged, but I was happy to have her around.

"Be careful," she said simply. The look on her face told me she wanted to say more.

"We'll be fine," I said, hefting my bag. I didn't mean to be dismissive of Sarah. It was just that I had my game face on and it was hard to be sociable. I looked her in the eye and touched her on the arm as I walked past. She didn't follow Tailor and me as we made our way up the stairs.

"Where *is* he?" Tailor whispered in frustration.

"Punctuality is not considered a virtue over here," I said absentmindedly, scanning the front of the club through the SR-25's scope. It was a lot more crowded than I would've preferred. By my count there were more than a dozen patrons, all of them Arab men, most of them in traditional garb, in the club now. I could see a few of them sitting by the windows, smoking, playing chess, and having animated conversations with a lot of hand gestures and laughter.

I looked up from the scope of my rifle and over at Tailor. His carbine was on the floor in front of him. He was propped up on his elbows, watching the front of the club through binoculars. I could tell he wanted a cigarette, but we couldn't risk the light signature. In order to have a clear shot, we had to get a lot closer to the window than I liked.

Another ten minutes slowly ticked by as the jitters got worse. Finally, a yellow Hummer H2 pulled up to the curb and parked, trailed by the same white Toyota Land Cruiser as last time. I quickly hunkered down behind the rifle as Tailor picked up his carbine and looked through the ACOG scope mounted on it. The jitters melted away. My heart rate slowed down. I felt my body relax as *the Calm* washed over me again.

A rough-looking man with a brown suit jacket and a bushy mustache got out. It was the same driver from the previous day. Through the rifle scope I could tell that he had a compact submachine gun hidden under his suit jacket. He hurried around to the passenger's side and opened the door.

Ali bin Ahmed Al Falah stepped out of his truck. He was on the opposite side of the Hummer, and I didn't have a clear shot, but there was no mistaking his squat stature and white beard.

"That's our boy," I whispered. "You confirm?"

"I confirm," Tailor said.

"Control, Nightcrawler," I whispered into my microphone. "We have eyes on target."

"*Roger that, Nightcrawler*," Anita said, her voice distant and professional. "*You are cleared to engage.*"

"Copy," I said, flipping the SR-25's selector switch from *safe* to *fire*. Al Falah, trailed by his driver, made his way toward the door of the social club. This time he had a large black briefcase in his hand. His four other bodyguards had piled out of the Land Cruiser and fanned out. To my dismay, they seemed more alert than they had the previous day.

"I'll hit his driver first, then switch to the other bodyguards," Tailor said. "You take out the primary target first, then the secondary target." The mission priorities were Al Falah, then Khalid, then the bodyguards. However, our *practical* priorities were to take care of the people who could shoot back as quickly as possible.

The front doors of the club opened. I recognized Khalid through the scope. As soon as the club's doors closed behind him, I swiveled the rifle on its bipod, placing the illuminated crosshairs between Al Falah's shoulder blades. I wasn't going to attempt a head shot, even at this close range, with a rifle I'd never fired before, not when it was this important. My finger moved to the trigger, and I exhaled.

Crack! The suppressed rifle's report sounded like a .22. The bullet smacked into my target in a puff of blood, a little higher than where I'd aimed, and tore right through him. Al Falah dropped to the ground like he'd been hit with a bat.

"He's down," I said calmly. Tailor fired off a double tap. Al Falah's driver went down as I swiveled the rifle toward Khalid. The other men standing around began to scurry like cockroaches. The patrons of the club seated next to the windows reacted in horror. Several got up. In a moment, the entire place would empty into the street. "I've lost Khalid!" I was getting tunnel vision through my scope. Somebody was shooting back at us.

"He's behind the Hummer!" Tailor said, firing off another double tap. There was someone crouched down behind the Hummer's engine block, concealed from my view. I didn't even see Khalid bolt for cover after I'd shot. *He's fast,* I thought. I then cussed at myself. *Damn it. I should've waited for them to shake hands. Probably could've gotten both of them with the same bullet.*

The two remaining bodyguards were hunkered down behind the Land Cruiser as Tailor began shooting at it. One of them was foolhardy enough to bolt for Al Falah; I caught him in my crosshairs and put a round through him as he ran. He stumbled as the bullet hit and face-planted onto the sidewalk.

I still didn't have a shot on Khalid. Swinging the SR-25 around on its bipod, I put two more rounds into Al Falah's body, just to make sure. The terrorist convulsed as the bullets hit him. Al Falah was *quite* dead.

Switching back, I rapidly fired into the boxy yellow truck, hoping a bullet would punch through and hit Khalid. Shot after shot, holes appeared in the hood and fender. Then my rifle *stopped.* I looked at the action; a fired case was sticking sideways out of the ejection port, mashed between the bolt and the breech face.

That same instant, Al Falah's surviving bodyguard raised his submachine gun over the ventilated hood of the Land Cruiser and ripped off an entire magazine at us. The bullets impacted all around us, kicking up clouds of plaster and dust as they hit. The noise panicked the patrons of the club, and they began to stream out onto the sidewalk, running in different directions. It was time to go.

Tailor roughly slapped me on the shoulder as he got up, changing magazines as he did so. I stood up, slung the SR-25's carrying case over my shoulder, and followed Tailor, trying to clear the jam as I moved.

We headed back into the building. A Range Rover came speeding around the corner and screeched to a halt next to the Hummer. Four more guys, armed with submachine guns and short-barreled Kalashnikovs, jumped out of the vehicle and fanned out. The bodyguard hiding behind the Land Cruiser leaned around the vehicle, pointed in our direction, and began shouting. As Tailor and I hit the stairs, our hiding place on the second floor of the half-completed building was hosed with automatic weapons fire.

LORENZO

Half a year of my life . . . wasted.

That was the first coherent thought that ran through my mind as Ali bin Ahmed Al Falah's chest puckered into a grapefruit sized exit hole right in front of me. Scarlet and white bits rose like a cloud as he went to his knees, heart torn in half and still pumping.

I had been on the receiving end of gunfire so many times that I instinctively bolted for cover behind the nearest vehicle. Flinching involuntarily as I wiped the fine mist of Al Falah off my face, I honed in on the shooter's position across the street. I wasn't the only one. "Achmed, up there!" the first bodyguard shouted as he lifted his MP5. Two rapid shots came from the building, and the guard went down hard, disappearing from view on the other side of the yellow Hummer. One of the other bodyguards returned fire.

My ear piece crackled. "*Who's shooting? What the hell's going on?*"

"I don't know! I didn't fire!" The sniper hammered two more rifle rounds into the fallen man's back, and now the closest bystanders realized what was happening and ran away screaming.

"*Who did, then?*"

"A sniper wasted Falah." I pushed myself tight against the wheel as the sniper fired a couple of rounds into the Hummer. The window shattered, and the nearest guard fell, missing half his face. A Range Rover screeched to a halt and the rest of Falah's men piled out.

"*Witnesses?*"

"Bunches," I replied.

Carl said, "*Roger that.*" Then there was a stream of profanity so vile that it made me cringe more than the incoming sniper fire. "*A public killing! This ruins everything!*"

The voice on the radio changed. It was Reaper. "*Lorenzo! We still need his computer.*"

"*Get it! Get the case!*" Carl bellowed across the channel. "*I'm on the way.*"

I risked a peek. The other guards were blasting the crap out of the building. Bystanders were running for their lives. Bodily fluids were draining all over the street, and there it was, a plain leather briefcase, still clutched in Falah's twitching hand. I had to move now, because some asshole had just blown my carefully laid plans. Starting toward it, I stuck one hand under my thobe and grabbed the butt of my STI. I had spent three months wearing a dress, and I was not leaving without that damned case.

The shooting had stopped. The new guards were shouting and pointing at the sniper's building. One young man jumped from the vehicle and sprinted toward me. He knelt next to his former boss, barely even registering that I was there, recognizing me from previous visits. The Range Rover tore away, probably in pursuit of the shooter. *Good.*

"Khalid! Call for doctors!" he shouted. It took a split second for me to realize that was supposed to be my name. Look one way, look the other. People moving, pointing, talking on cell phones, no other guards in sight, this could still work.

"At once!" I answered as I reached down and grabbed the case. Al Falah's hand wouldn't let go when I pulled. He had it clutched in a literal death grip. I tugged harder, hoping that the guard would keep trying to hold the contents of Al Falah's chest in rather than pay any attention to me.

The guard looked up in confusion. "What are you doing? Why—" I kicked him in the teeth, sending him reeling into the gutter. Jerking the case into my arms, I ran back into the club. I pushed past the startled onlookers, their attention mostly on the bodies in the street. Some of them were just realizing that I had booted a man with a submachine gun in the face and robbed the dead. I jerked up the thobe and ran like hell back into the club, through the kitchen, past the startled employees, out the back door, and into the alley. I heard the door slam closed behind me.

I rounded the corner. The stinking alley was empty except for overflowing dumpsters and graffiti-sprayed walls. Carl wasn't here yet. "Where are you?" I hissed. "I've got it. I'm at the back of the club."

His voice was slightly distorted in my ear. "Coming. I almost got hit by some crazies having a car chase or something."

I glanced back to the club. Nobody had followed yet, but it wouldn't be long. I jerked my head around at the noise of an engine. A vehicle pulled into the alley, only it wasn't Carl's van, but another car full of angry Muslims, and I immediately recognized the driver screaming into his cell phone as Yousef, one of Al Falah's men.

No cover, no place to hide. No time to run. Yousef's eyes widened when he saw me there, splattered in his boss' blood, stolen briefcase in hand. He was probably on the phone with the guard I had just booted. Ten yards to that vehicle, Yousef behind the wheel, one passenger, no other options, and the

9mm was in my hand before I even thought about it. Car doors flew open as my STI cleared leather.

Time slowed to a crawl. The passenger was quicker, coming up out of the vehicle, stupidly leaving cover, stubby black MP5 rising. Dropping the case, my hands came together, arms punching outward, the gun an extension of my will. The front sight entered my vision, focused so clearly that the bad guy was only a blur behind it. I stroked the perfect trigger to the rear.

The sound should have been deafening, but it seemed more of a muted thump in the narrow alley. The heavy 9mm had virtually no recoil, and I fired as fast as the sights came back into place. The man with the submachine gun fell, his weapon tumbling from his hands. My muzzle moved, seemingly on its own, over the driver's windshield where Yousef, face betraying his shock, was slower to react, cell phone falling from his open hand as he wrestled with his seat belt. The glass spiderwebbed as I opened fire, obscuring my target. Uncertain as to his fate, I continued firing, pumping round after round through the car. The slide locked back empty. The spent magazine struck the ground as I automatically speed-reloaded.

I had done this kind of thing a few times.

Carl's white van careened wildly into the alley, locked up the brakes and narrowly stopped inches from the car's bumper. "Down! Down!" he screamed out the window, creating a weird off-time effect as my radio earpiece repeated it a millisecond later. Without hesitation I flung myself into the garbage. The muzzle of a Galil SAR extended from the van's window as Carl fired over my head. The cracks of the .223 were ear-splitting compared to my 9mm.

Rolling over, I could see dust and debris spraying from the club's rear exit. The guard I had kicked a moment ago was sliding limply down the door frame, already on the way to his seventy-two-virgin welcoming committee.

"Let's get out of here!" Carl shouted. I scrambled to my feet, grabbed the case, and ran past the shot-up car, keeping my gun up, scanning for threats, and pulled myself into the already moving van. We sped off into the streets, Carl's beady eyes flickering rapidly back and forth, looking for cops. I reholstered my gun and watched as my hands began to shake.

"Did you get the computer?"

"Yeah, I'm fine. Didn't get hit. Thanks for asking," I replied.

He rolled his eyes. I opened the case, and inside was the unharmed laptop. So at least we hadn't screwed *everything*. Months of planning and preparation, Phase One almost done, Phase Two ready to go, and all screwed because some mystery person whacks *my* target in public. *Damn it. Damn it.* Could we still pull this off? We had to. We sure couldn't afford to fail.

I closed my hand into a fist as the trembling continued. I was going to figure out who screwed us, and I was going to make them pay.

Chapter 5: Grand Theft Auto

VALENTINE

"Nightcrawler, Xbox, this is Control, report! Give us a status update!" Anita sounded anxious over the radio.

"We're fucking busy right now!" Tailor snapped. We quickly moved down the two flights of stairs and out the back door of the building. We stopped at the fence. Tailor went through the hole we'd cut first, his carbine pointing to our left, up the alley. I followed, pointing the heavy SR-25 to our right. I was startled when four muffled shots rang out; one of the bodyguards had come around the corner, and Tailor had cut him down. The man crumpled to the ground, his MP5K clattering on the pavement.

Moving quickly, I opened the door of our truck, an extended-cab Toyota pickup, and tossed my gear onto the backseat. I then climbed into the driver's seat. Tailor jumped into the passenger's seat. I put the pickup into gear and stepped on the gas.

"Look out!" Tailor yelled. The bodyguards' Range Rover had pulled into the alley ahead, blocking our exit. They got out and started shooting. Worse, the alley wasn't wide enough to turn around in. Swearing aloud, I threw it into reverse and stomped on the gas.

We backed down the alley entirely too fast. Tailor fired through the windshield, his suppressed rifle hissing and snapping loudly in the passenger cabin. The enemy took cover behind their truck and returned fire. Several stray rounds peppered the front of our vehicle.

Scrunching down, hoping the engine block would provide me with protection, I tried to navigate the Toyota down the alley in reverse by using my side mirror. Rounds came whizzing through the windshield. I hit the walls five or six times, smashing through garbage cans and terrifying stray cats. Seconds later, Al Falah's bodyguards piled back into their truck and started down the alley after us.

We exploded onto the main road, still in reverse, and were nearly broadsided by a minibus. I cut the wheel to the right and stomped on the brakes. Cars swerved around us, horns screaming as they went. I put the pickup back into drive and hit the gas. We got moving just as Al Falah's men made it onto the street.

I sped along, having turned the wrong way to use our preplanned egress route. They were in close pursuit. At that time of the night, the roundabouts in Zubara were clogged with traffic. I didn't want to get in a gunfight in the middle of a traffic jam, too many bystanders, too many witnesses. I hung a quick right, turning down a narrow side street. Such streets in the city had one lane going each way, with a small roundabout at each intersection. In the middle was a raised concrete divider, almost like a sidewalk, making left turns difficult.

The street was mercifully free of traffic, but within seconds, Al Falah's men began firing at us again. Rounds entered through the back window and hit the tops of our seats. Tailor and I were hunkered down about as far as we could go.

"Will you please shoot *back*?" I screamed. He turned around, twisting to his left, and returned fire through what was left of the back window. Hot brass peppered me in the side of the head. I flinched and almost went off the road. "Be careful!"

As Tailor swore at me, we came to the first roundabout. My heart fell into my stomach as I realized a large truck full of sheep had broken down in the middle of it, blocking the road. Several cars were stopped around it. There was no way past. At the last instant, I cut the wheel to the right. The Toyota bucked as we jumped onto the sidewalk. I had to swerve again to avoid hitting a planted palm tree. It was hard to see clearly; the windshield was full of bullet holes and was covered in a spider's web of cracks.

I laid on the horn as terrified pedestrians jumped out of our way. Clear of the traffic jam, I swerved back to the left, ripping off the truck's passenger-side mirror on another palm tree as we landed back on the street. The pursuing Range Rover was right behind us now. Two men were leaning out of the windows, firing at us with pistols. I snarled in pain as a round clipped my right shoulder, causing me to almost lose control of the truck. The sudden swerving of the vehicle made Tailor drop his spare magazine as he was trying to reload.

To hell with this, I thought. "You buckled?"

"What? Why?" Tailor shouted back. I floored the brake pedal.

The Range Rover smashed into the back of our truck, crumpling the bed and tailgate. Our perforated rear window shattered completely. The big SUV considerably outweighed our little pickup. We fishtailed to the left; the Range Rover went on and crashed into a parked car.

Our ride was trashed, but we were stopped, and we were alive.

Dazed, I unbuckled myself, opened the door, and literally fell to the pavement. I somehow managed to get to my feet and looked over at our pursuers. The driver and the front passenger hadn't been wearing seat belts. They appeared injured or dead. The airbags had deployed.

I looked around. Cars drove by, slowing down to gawk at the wreck. We didn't have much time. With my left hand, I swept my jacket to the side and drew my revolver. I brought the gun up, pointing it at the Range Rover, but pain shot through my right shoulder as I attempted a two-handed hold. I remembered then that I was bleeding, and was suddenly aware of the pain. Holy *crap* did it hurt. I winced, but continued on, holding my .44 Magnum one-handed.

Approaching the SUV carefully, I looked for signs of movement. I stumbled as I walked, and couldn't hear very well. The driver begin to stir behind his airbag. He tried to open his door, but it crunched up against the smashed tailgate of our pickup.

He didn't see me. I fired. A fat .44 slug tore through his head, splashing the airbag with blood. I fired again, putting a bullet into the passenger. He looked dead, but I wanted to be sure.

There was a third man in the backseat. He sat up, obviously dazed. There was a cut on his forehead; blood was pouring down his face. He placed his hand on his head as he came to, not noticing me at first, but he froze when he saw the big .44 leveled at him. His eyes went wide. My hand was shaking. I could hear sirens in the distance. We had to go. We weren't supposed to leave witnesses. I pulled the trigger again. The terrorist disappeared behind the door in a small puff of blood.

My ears were ringing. My heart was pounding. I was injured. *The Calm* had worn off, and I was half in shock. I took a deep breath, reloaded, then holstered my revolver. I moved to the passenger's side door of our pickup. Tailor was starting to come around, but he was in a daze.

"C'mon, bro, we gotta split," I said. "Cops are coming."

"Yeah . . . yeah . . . okay . . . You get 'em?"

"I think so. C'mon, let's go!" I grabbed the SR-25 and its carrying case from the backseat. My shoulder screamed in protest as I hefted the rifle, but I didn't have time to worry about it. Tailor stumbled and nearly fell down but was able to retrieve his backpack, his carbine, and the spare magazine he'd dropped onto the floor of the truck. We then hurried away from the scene of the crash, heading up the street a short way before turning into a narrow alley.

Rounding the corner, we were immediately illuminated by headlights. *Oh, hell.* The vehicle, a small French Renault, came to a stop just under a streetlight. I could see the driver. He appeared to be a Westerner.

Not sure what to do, I leveled the SR-25 at the Renault. "Get out of the car!" The man hesitated, then raised his hands, seemingly in shock. I squeezed the trigger. The suppressed rifle cracked thinly in the night air, and the Renault's left-side mirror exploded as a 175-grain match bullet tore through it. "Now!" I ordered. The driver stepped out of the vehicle. I lowered my rifle and moved toward him. "I'm sorry," I said without looking at him. "We need your car."

"Bloody hell! Just take it! Don't shoot!" He was British.

Tailor stepped up to him. "Drop your cell phone," he said levelly, even though he still looked a little wobbly.

"Are you mad? You're taking my car, do you have to take my bloody mobile, too?"

I'm not going to repeat the swath of obscenities that Tailor let out at that point, but an instant later the unlucky British man dropped his phone onto the ground. Tailor stomped on it, smashing it.

"Get out of here!" he yelled. The terrified man ran off down the street.

"You drive," I said.

"Why?"

"I'm *bleeding,* that's why!" I said as I tossed my weapon into the little French car's backseat.

"Fine," he said. We got in, Tailor put the car in gear, did a three-point turn in a narrow driveway, and we took off down the alley, away from the crash scene, just as the police arrived.

LORENZO

We drove south toward our apartment. After a few minutes I was positive that nobody was after us. Our vehicle was as bland and common as could be had in this city, even though Carl had worked it over so that we had some speed on tap if necessary.

Carl's Portuguese accent was a lot more pronounced when he was enraged. "Everybody knows Falah's dead. We're screwed!" he bellowed as he slammed his fist into the steering wheel. His eyes flickered back to the mirror as the sound of a siren went behind us, but it was heading for the scene of the crime and not our way. He continued, slightly calmer. "What now?"

"Pull over." My mind was racing. The mission depended on making Al Falah disappear. "Nobody has to know he's dead."

"And how're we supposed to do that, genius?" Carl pulled us into the lot of the Happy Chicken on Bakhun Street and parked the van behind a brand new Audi A8.

I got on the radio. "Reaper. Come in."

"Gotcha, boss."

"You've got the police band. Figure out where they're taking Falah."

Carl's eyes studied me in the rear-view mirror. "You've got to be shittin' me . . . No. You're not," he sighed. "We're gonna die."

"Eventually."

Reaper was back in a matter of seconds. "Security forces are freaking out. How many people did you guys kill down there?" I looked at Carl and held up two fingers. He gave me one back, but he used his middle finger. "Never mind. Ambulance is en route to the hospital in Ash Shamal under police escort."

I glanced back the way we had come. The hospital was just off Bakhun, which was the major four-lane through this peninsula. The ambulance would have to pass us. We could still intercept them. "Reaper, I want you to flood their emergency system with calls. Give them a bunch of shooters randomly killing people at the *north* end of Ash Shamal," I ordered. Carl looked at me in confusion. "Let's see what we can do about that police escort." Zubara was a relatively quiet city by this part of the world's standards. If they just had a bunch of people get popped in the district, they would be quick to jump at another call.

"Too late." Carl glanced back. "I hear sirens. Here comes the ambulance."

Through the window, I saw a pudgy, well-dressed Zubaran approaching the Audi with a sack of fast food in hand. He raised his key fob, and the car's alarm beeped. "I've got an idea."

There was no time for subtlety. I slid open the van door and hopped out. I could hear the sirens now, too. They would be passing by any second. The driver of the Audi was just sitting down as I caught the closing door with my body. He looked up in surprise and started to say something. I grabbed the keys from his hand, slugged him hard in the mouth, and jerked him onto the pavement.

The Audi started right up with a purr. I slammed it into gear and roared out of the parking lot. A dozen cows had given their lives for this interior. "Nice car," I muttered as I shifted into second. Oncoming traffic had to stomp the brakes to avoid hitting me, then I was out on the road, northbound, the GPS told me in Arabic.

On the other side of the divider a police car zipped by, blue lights flashing, heading south. Right behind it was the ambulance. Zubaran emergency vehicles used that obnoxious European-style siren. I grabbed the radio. "Carl, I'll take the cop car. Run the ambulance off the road!" I shouted as I cranked the wheel and gunned it over the mound of dirt that served as the divider. German cars have great suspension but I still managed to almost bite my tongue off as I crashed onto the southbound lane. I hastily put my seat belt on. The GPS told me I had just done something very bad.

Drivers in this part of the world didn't pull off to the side for emergency vehicles. If you're dying in the Middle East, don't do it during rush hour. Traffic here was a constant battle of wits and honking horns. The ambulance was weaving between cars ahead of me. A Toyota tore off my passenger-side mirror, and the driver honked. Revving the powerful engine, I was doing sixty by the time I passed the ambulance. The police car, some little Euro sedan, was right ahead of me. The Audi pulled alongside effortlessly.

The cops glanced over in confusion. The look here for security forces was Saddam Hussein-style mustaches and big mirrored shades. I drifted right into them, slamming into their side, shoving them hard to the right. The cops started yelling, and the passenger was going for his gun. I drifted left a bit, then swerved back with more energy, smashing the hell out of their little car.

The driver overcorrected, turning too far to the side, and the car spun out of control in a haze of rubber smoke before crashing violently into the rear end of a parked SUV. I applied the brakes and came to a smooth stop.

The cop car was at an angle, sideways, half on top of the other vehicle. Those guys wouldn't be causing me any trouble for a bit. I could see the flashing lights of the ambulance as it slowed to a crawl behind me. Stepping on the clutch, I shifted into reverse. "Carl, where are you?"

"Right behind the ambulance," he replied.

"Hit the brakes," I said as I stomped on the gas. Even in reverse this car was pretty damn quick. I braced myself as the Audi's trunk collided with the front of the still-moving ambulance. My world came to a violent lurching halt. The rear window shattered and glass ricocheted around the cab as the air bag knocked the shit out of me.

It took me a blurry second to get the seat belt unbuckled and to collapse out the door into the street. Got to hand it to those Germans, they crash test their stuff really well. I staggered to my feet and pulled my gun. It wasn't necessary though. The ambulance crew were groggily moving, knocked silly by the impact. The siren was still wailing.

Carl was at the back of the ambulance, dragging Al Falah's corpse out. The cars around us had stopped, and there had to be at least a dozen eyes on us. I limped around the back to help. "Hurry up," Carl grunted as he pulled the limp body toward our van. I grabbed his legs and lifted. He weighed a ton. We got to the van and tossed him inside, I was in right behind.

The van's tires squealed as Carl got us out of there.

VALENTINE
Al Khor District, Safe House 4
March 26
2355

Tailor and I were surprised to find Gordon Willis waiting for us back at the safe house. As before, the big guy named Anders was with him, giving us a hard stare but not saying a word. Suffice to say, Gordon wasn't happy. The two of us sat on folding chairs in the middle of the big house's living room while Hal, one of our medics, worked to patch us up. I was sitting there, shirtless, as Hal worked on the wound on my shoulder. All while Gordon royally bitched us out.

It turned out Gordon's cool demeanor came unraveled when he was mad. It was a little amusing to see the smooth-talking slickster sputtering and raising his voice. Yelling didn't really suit him. He wasn't unhappy about Al Falah; we'd done quite well in that regard. As we described what happened, I could see the anger in his eyes. We failed to kill the secondary target Khalid. We lost our vehicle and had to exigently acquire a new one. Worst of all, we were *seen*.

I honestly don't know what the hell he expected. We were ordered to do the hit in public in the middle of the city; of *course* it was going to make noise. I thought that was the *point*.

Looking over at Tailor, I could tell he was kind of tuning Gordon out too. As Gordon blathered on about operational security and his expectations of us, Hunter stood quietly in the corner. Sarah leaned against the wall behind him, looking at me with an expression on her face that I couldn't read. I wondered what she was thinking. One of Hunter's security men stood by the door, giving Anders the stink eye.

After a few minutes of ass-chewing, Gordon visibly shifted gears, and the slickness returned. He plopped down on the couch across from Tailor and me and began to speak once more as I put my T-shirt back on.

"Well, what's done is done," Gordon said, straightening his tie. I wondered why in the hell he was wearing a suit. "Now we need to focus on the next mission. I need you two to be ready to move on this in a few days."

Tailor and I looked at each other. I *was* able to read the expression on his face. I had a bad feeling too. "What's the next mission, sir?" I asked.

"Ms. . . . uh . . . McAllister, right? Ms. McAllister, would you hand them the mission packets, please?" Sarah rolled her eyes and stepped forward, handing out manila envelopes to each of us.

"Your next mission will be pretty simple, boys. You're going to return to the social club you snatched the younger Al Falah from and clean it out. The other two men in your chalk . . . um . . ."

"Wheeler and Hudson," I interjected, my voice flat.

"Yes, Weiner and Hudson," Gordon replied, "will be rejoining you for this one. It'll be a straight-up enter-and-clear. Are you up to it?"

I sighed and looked over at Tailor. He nodded at me, ever so slightly. "What's the plan, sir?" I asked after a moment. Tailor and I listened as

Gordon went over the plan. He droned on for a long time. The man sure liked listening to himself talk. He asked us if we had any questions.

"When do we roll on this?" I asked.

"In the next few days," Gordon said. "Word will be sent down soon, so be ready to go on short notice. Anyway, gentlemen, I need to get going." Gordon stood up. Tailor and I followed suit. Gordon shook my hand vigorously, squeezing tightly, then did the same to Tailor. He then nodded at Anders, and the two of them strode out of the room.

"You heard the man, boys," Hunter said after Gordon was out of earshot. "Be ready. The order to move will come down without much warning. You're going to be operating at a high tempo for the time being. I need you boys to stay sharp. No alcohol, no sneaking off, nothing that will slow you down, until further notice. Tailor, I need you and Valentine to plan your routes to and from the target building, including contingency plans. I trust things will go smoother this time?"

"It would've went smoother if we'd had some backup," Tailor said.

Hunter shook his head. "Gordon had the rest of your chalk on a wild goose chase. We sent a dozen men to hit a building, and no one was even home. Complete waste of time, unlike your next job, where I can promise you'll have a target-rich environment."

"Roger that, Colonel," Tailor said.

"Outstanding." Hunter turned to the medic. "Hal, you're coming with me. Singer's chalk is coming back from a mission tonight, and they've got some injuries. The doctor could use your help."

Hal nodded and began to pack up his jump bag. "Valentine, make sure you change that bandage in the morning," he told me. "I'll check you out when you get back to the fort."

"Sarah, do you want to come back to the compound tonight, or do you want to come back tomorrow?" Hunter asked.

"I, uh, need to pack my stuff, Colonel," Sarah said, seemingly surprised by the question.

"That's fine," Hunter said. "You can ride back to the fort in the car that brings Hudson and Wheeler here. Let's go, Conrad," he said, addressing his security escort. It was the first time I'd heard him name one of his bodyguards.

After a few moments, Hal finished packing up his bag and shouldered it. With that, Hunter, his security, and the medic left, leaving the three of us alone in the big house. Sarah flopped down on the couch where Gordon had been sitting.

"This isn't looking as good now," I said after a long moment.

"At least we'll have full chalk this time," Tailor said. "What happened today was *bullshit*."

"What are you going to do?" Sarah asked.

"What can we do?" I said. "We're going to do the mission and hope we don't get killed."

"I don't know about y'all, but I'm going to *bed*," Tailor said, standing up. Without another word, he disappeared up the stairs, leaving Sarah and me alone in the dimly lit living room. I stood up and sat down next to her on the couch. The metal folding chair was making my butt hurt, and I was still sore from the crash.

"Where'd you get the tattoo?" she asked, breaking the awkward silence after a few moments. She'd seen it while I'd had my shirt off. "Were you in the military?"

"Air Force."

"Really? Me, too. What did you do?"

"Security Forces. You?"

"Radio Communications Systems. I cross-trained as a Cryptologic Linguist after four years. Did three years of that after a year at the DLA," Sarah said, referring to the Defense Language Academy in California.

"So that's how you speak Arabic," I said. Sarah nodded. "Hell, I was all proud of myself for learning *Spanish*. And I only did that after all the time I spent in Central America."

"In the Air Force?"

"Uh, no. I was in Afghanistan for six months, but I got out after that. I was hired by, um, a contractor, after that."

"You did construction?"

"No, not that kind of contractor. I worked for Vanguard."

Everyone had heard of Vanguard. We'd been in the news a lot last year. "You were a *mercenary?*" she asked incredulously.

"Basically," I said. "Tailor hooked me up here. How 'bout you?"

"I . . . This is embarrassing, but I ran into some financial problems. I had this boyfriend that . . . well, he was an asshole. Basically, he spent all of my money, ran up my credit cards, stuff like that. He got into drugs. I tried to help him. Before it was over, my credit was ruined. The cops arrested him, found his cocaine in my apartment. I lost my security clearance. My career was over. I got out last year. There's plenty of work out there for people with my background. Almost none for people who can't get a clearance, though."

"So how'd you end up here?"

"I was living in a crappy apartment, working a crappy job, when I was contacted with this offer. How could I refuse? A chance to go do something again, to use the skills I learned."

"And make a pile of money while you're at it," I suggested.

"Obviously," she said, smiling again. "I don't know why I'm telling you all this. You're easy to talk to. So, where'd you get the tattoo?"

"What? Oh. I got it in Nevada." I turned toward her and rolled up my left sleeve, showing her the tattoo on my shoulder. It was a skull clutching a switchblade knife in its teeth. It had the words "Abandon All Hope" written around it. "It was after we got back from Bosnia. This is the Switchblade logo."

"Switchblade?" Sarah asked. "Didn't you just say you worked for Vanguard?"

"Vanguard Strategic Solutions International," I said. "But the Switchblade teams were the best the company had. We were the lifers. Most guys worked short-term contracts, six months to two years. A few of us stayed full-time. We got better training, better benefits, better equipment, and much better pay."

"Sounds good," Sarah said, sounding unconvinced.

"It was dangerous as hell," I said honestly. "But my team was lucky. We did really well. Then Mexico happened."

"You were there?" Sarah asked. "During the fighting, I mean?"

"You could say that. Our last mission was an absolute clusterfuck. We lost . . ." I trailed off for a second. "Well, we lost damn near everybody. Our chopper was shot down in Cancun, and the UN came after us."

"Wait, what? Why?"

I paused for a moment. "It's . . . complicated."

It must have been obvious I didn't want to talk about it. "I'm sorry," Sarah said. "How are you feeling? You had a pretty rough night tonight." She lightly placed her hand on my leg.

"I'm . . . fine," I said, my heart rate suddenly increasing.

"I was worried about you." She didn't break eye contact.

"This isn't the first time I've been shot. I got lucky. This will heal up okay. It'll just be another scar," I answered, obviously full of shit.

"Whatever you say, Mr. Tough Guy," she said, that devilish grin appearing on her face again. A moment later, the smile faded. She stared into my eyes for what seemed like a long time, her mouth open slightly. "Hi," she said, leaning in a little bit closer. The tone in her voice was ever-so-slightly different now. Then she leaned forward and kissed me, *hard*.

"Sarah, I—"

"Just relax," she whispered, her mouth inches from mine. "It'll be fun. I promise." This had all come out of nowhere. I was so dense about stuff like this and was never much of a ladies' man. I wasn't sure what to do. But as Sarah pushed me back onto the couch and climbed on top of me, it became pretty clear what *she* wanted to do. I wasn't about to argue.

LORENZO
March 26

Reaper was clicking away madly, his Rob Zombie T-shirt stained with energy drink, head bobbing back and forth rhythmically to whatever was on his iPod as he glared at the gibberish on Falah's laptop screen.

"He looks kinda like a *galinha* when he does that," Carl said from the kitchen table. Then he moved his head back and forth, except Carl had no rhythm to speak of, and no neck, either, so it was more like he moved his face back and forth in a very poor imitation of the scarecrow-like Reaper.

"He does have that chicken vibe going on," I replied as I moved the ice pack to a different spot on my face. That airbag had really clocked me. As soon as the swelling went down enough, I was going to go shave. The police were already looking to question Khalid about today's events. Too bad he no longer existed.

"I can still hear you guys," Reaper said without looking up from his multiple screens. He had been engrossed in those since we had gotten back.

"How?" I asked incredulously. I could hear the metal coming out of his earpieces from across the room. That mystery was going to go unanswered as Reaper suddenly pumped his fist in the air.

"Cracked it!"

Thank goodness. This was big, but I had faith that Reaper could do it. "Well, that's a little anticlimactic," I said. Carl grunted in agreement and popped open another beer. It wasn't that you couldn't get alcohol in Muslim countries; you just had to know where to look. "Me crashing a hundred-thousand Euro car was way cooler."

Reaper yanked out the earpieces. "I'm in. I've got everything. His password protection was pathetic. I own you, punk-ass bitch! Ha!" he shouted like he had just won a multiplayer death match rather than broken into a terrorist financier's personal files.

I approached and stood over Reaper's shoulder. "Look for anything on Adar. We need his contact info. If it isn't under Adar, look for the Butcher. It's time for Al Falah to call his pet psycho home."

I called the Fat Man at the number provided in the folder from Thailand. I'd already had Reaper take a shot at figuring out where it originated, but it was even more secure than my personal communications, bounced off of who knew how many satellites and scrambled in every way imaginable.

The Fat Man knew who it was before I even spoke. "Hello, Mr. Lorenzo. How goes it?"

"Phase One is complete. We've implemented Phase Two," I said.

"I shall pass that on to our employer. We had heard that there had been a few complications." His voice was without inflection. He wouldn't even give me a clue if he had just woken up or if it was late at night. Nobody even knew what time zone Big Eddie was in. "Nothing you couldn't handle, I assume."

"Of course not."

"By the way, some of our men attended your niece's dance recital. Rachel, I believe her name was. Let's see, she belongs to your brother, Robert. They recorded the recital for Big Eddie. He commented that she is very graceful and talented for such a young girl."

"I told you. I'll *do* the job," I stated.

"Of course you will. Eddie just likes to keep track of his employees. It is what makes him such an effective leader. Keep up the good work." Then he hung up. I carefully put my phone away before smashing my fist into the wall.

Chapter 6: From Sea to Shining Sea

VALENTINE
Ash Shamal District
April 1
2005

"*Xbox, this is Shafter,*" Hudson said over the radio, breathing hard. "*We're in position.*"

Tailor looked over at me. I nodded, and he spoke into his radio. "Copy that. Stand by. Control, Xbox, we're standing by."

"*Xbox, Control,*" Sarah said, sounding as calm and distant as ever. "*Execute. Be careful,*" she added, her voice softening just a bit.

I smiled to myself. "This is going to be a turkey shoot," I said, observing our target building through binoculars one last time. "You think they'd have beefed up security after we snatched the Al Falah kid out here."

"They did," Tailor corrected. "Look. That guy right there, he's got a rifle."

"What is that, a G3?" I asked absentmindedly. "Look, another guy in the doorway. Looks like he's got a sub-gun."

"I think they're wearing vests," Tailor said. He patted the driver on the shoulder. "Let's go. Shafter, Ginger, stand by to execute. When you hear shooting, enter and clear. Watch for friendlies—we'll be coming in from the other side."

Hudson acknowledged. Our driver, a guy from another chalk that everyone called Animal, flipped on the headlights and stomped on the gas. Our up-armored van roared down the narrow street toward the social club.

The little side street had several cars parked on either side. Tonight was the most popular night, and it seemed that the disappearance of Al Falah hadn't deterred the enemy from using the place. The two armed clowns outside wouldn't pose a problem. Our plan was laughably simple: take out the two armed guards outside, then enter and kill every son of a bitch in the place. Tailor and I would enter from the front, while Hudson and Wheeler would enter from the rear. The rear door led down into a basement, where we believed there might be a weapons cache. Animal was going to stay with

98

the van. He was from Singer's chalk; he'd been hurt and couldn't run, but he could still drive.

The terrorist with the G3 rifle was meandering up the street, checking the parked cars when he was illuminated by our headlights. I saw him clearly; he was wearing black fatigues, a ski mask, a blue body armor vest, and a chest rig for spare magazines. He looked pretty squared away, and our van's windshield probably wouldn't stop direct hits from a 7.62x51mm weapon.

That didn't deter Animal. He swerved the van right at the terrorist. I braced myself. The man in the black fatigues dodged to the left. He wasn't fast enough. Our heavy, armored van came to a stop with a crunch of twisting metal and shattering glass. The little Toyota sedan we hit crumpled and was pushed up onto the curb. The man in black was pinned between our van and the Toyota, his legs and hips crushed.

"Move, move!" Tailor shouted, pulling the van's right-side door open. I shouldered the paratrooper SAW I was carrying and headed for the door. I heard two quick shots as Animal leaned out the window and blasted the pinned terrorist with his .45. I ignored it as I ripped off a short burst at the man guarding the door, my machine gun roaring loudly in the narrow alley. The 5.56 mm bullets punched through him, splattering blood on the wall behind. He was so surprised he hadn't even gotten his weapon ready.

I came up to the door. Tailor was right behind me. Stepping over the body, I reached forward and yanked the door open just as a long rattle of automatic fire could be heard from behind the building. I held the door open, and Tailor tossed in a pyrotechnic distraction device. We would've used grenades, but we didn't know where Hudson and Wheeler were. A couple seconds later the device detonated, blasting the room with a head-splitting concussion.

Tailor and I stormed inside, weapons at the ready. The doorway dog-legged around into a main room. We rounded the corner. The social club was in chaos. Men were running in every direction, shouting and screaming in Arabic. Billiards tables lined one wall, and couches lined the other. The air stank of smoke from cigarettes, hookahs, and our flash-bang. Terrorist propaganda and Islamic flags were plastered all over the walls.

Men ran toward us, trying to get out of the building. They were either too confused and didn't realize we were there, or thought we were their own armed guys. It didn't really matter. I leveled my machine gun and squeezed the trigger.

It was a massacre. Tailor and I moved laterally across the main room, firing at anything that moved. A door burst open and a pair of men came running in, armed with assault rifles, but we cut them down before they even realized what was happening. The crowd of terrorist recruits turned, trying to escape down the stairs, tripping over overturned chairs, bodies, and each other as they fled. It didn't do them any good.

"*We're in the basement,*" Wheeler said over the radio. The men trying to flee out the back entrance were gunned down as they came upon Wheeler and Hudson.

The whole thing was over in a matter of minutes. I stood amongst the carnage in the social club, pulling a fresh belt of ammunition onto my weapon's feed tray. The machine gun in my hands was hot to the touch; I'd gone through a hundred-round belt in less than two minutes. Probably two dozen bodies lay on the floor, ripped apart by gunfire. The air stank of powder, smoke, and death.

Tailor lit a cigarette, his carbine dangling from its sling. "April fool, motherfuckers," he said, snapping his Zippo lighter shut. My hands started to shake. *The Calm* was wearing off, and soon I'd be hit with a flood of emotions as adrenaline dump shocked my system.

The only people we'd let out of the building alive were three Indonesian girls Hudson and Wheeler found in the basement. They were drugged up and had been used as playthings by the terrorist recruits. We found a weapons cache also. AK-103 assault rifles and GP-30 grenade launchers from Russia. G3 rifles from Iran and Pakistan. Rocket-propelled grenades and launchers from China. Thousands and thousands of rounds of ammunition. So we dumped some gas, popped a thermite grenade, and burned it all.

As we hurried outside, we noticed that the air reeked of gasoline. In the few minutes we were inside, Animal had kept himself busy by dousing all of the cars parked on the street with gas. As we backed down the street, Hudson tossed a road flare out of the van, igniting the gas and setting the whole row of cars ablaze, just like the building.

The fire quickly spread to the neighboring warehouses. Before long, the entire block was engulfed in flames. It took the city firefighters all night to put the inferno out. In the morning, they found an Ace of Spades playing card stuck to a light pole at the end of the street. Our little calling card been Colonel Hunter's idea. I liked it.

LORENZO
April 10

I stood on the balcony of our apartment. It was part of a complex at the south end of the city, near the intersection of old world and new money, oil-rich and third world poor. The compound itself was relatively modern, but more importantly, it was landscaped in such a way that we had quite a bit of privacy. We had some university students sharing one wall, and an old couple below us, but they all kept to themselves. We entered only through the attached garage, and that was in a van with tinted windows. The ID I had used to set up the lease was a top-of-the-line forgery of a Zubaran Oil Ministry employee who worked weird hours, and our only paleface, Reaper, never went outside anyway. We might as well have been invisible.

The balcony was where I came to contemplate. Every wall inside our hideout had something mission related tacked up, as I had to memorize a lot of facts and faces, but that could get obnoxious after a while. I had brought the manila folder from Thailand with me and had been absently flipping through the photos. It had been a long time since I had seen most of those people, and I had never met any of the kids, and now they were all going to die if I didn't play my cards right.

Over the last few weeks there had been shootings, bombings, and all manner of craziness. Normally Zubara was a quiet place, but now there were blue uniformed SF troops on every corner, and random checkpoints set up by the secret police. There was a war going on, and it was making life difficult for us honest criminals.

I suppose I could call myself an honest criminal. I had tried being a regular criminal, but I found that I didn't have the stomach to lie to and steal from normal folks. Terrorists on the other hand had lots of money, were fun to lie to, and nobody seemed to mind when I occasionally killed them. And it was easier to sleep at night since I was able to convince myself that I used my sociopathic tendencies for good. *Mostly*.

The local news was full of stories about random murders and disappearances. Somebody was going down a checklist of the Zoob's terrorist underworld like a bad issue of *The Punisher*, and the worst part was that we had no idea who it was. The word on the street was that it was the emir's secret police killing men loyal to General Sabah, but from what I had seen, this was too professional for those thugs. My money was on the Israelis, but even that didn't make any sense. The hits were stirring up the fundies and talk of revolution was becoming more and more common. If the emir lost power, then the Izzies would have yet another oil-rich country hating them and funding Hezbollah and that struck me as a bad thing, but then again, I had never been the diplomat type.

So if it wasn't the emir, and it wasn't Mossad, who was raising so much hell in the area? It couldn't be the CIA, as they were way too obvious. I had no evidence, but I was sure that whoever had blown Falah's heart out was one of them. Having some sort of hit squad mowing down the people that I was supposed to be infiltrating was definitely screwing with my work. It didn't really matter, though. I just had to keep a low profile until I could get to Adar. *Piece of cake.*

The sliding door opened and Reaper appeared, gangly and squinting at the sudden brightness. The boy really needed to get more sun, but that would take him away from his precious computers and high-speed Internet.

Reaper was an interesting case. He'd been one of those super-genius kids, awkward and goofy as hell I was sure, and he'd been attending MIT when he was fourteen. When I'd met him six years ago he'd been on the run from the law. Ironically enough, he had the most serious criminal record of my crew. My rap sheet only showed a handful of juvenile offenses whereas Reaper, the child prodigy, had been an overachiever and been indicted for several hundred counts of felony fraud, hacking, and embezzlement before he was old enough to drive.

Time magazine had written a cover story about him. Reaper had used that as his resume when he'd asked to join my crew.

He shuddered. "Man, it's hot."

I chuckled. "Wait until summer. It's barely ninety. How's your machine thingy coming?"

He shrugged. He'd been working on the device for Phase Three for weeks now. His room was covered in bits and pieces of the complicated gizmo. "I thought about going with a low-inductance capacitor bank discharge, but I said hell with it, the explosive pumped flux compression generator will be so much *cooler.*"

"You know, I dropped out of high school specifically so I wouldn't have to know what any of those words meant."

"I thought you dropped out to commit a triple homicide."

"Quadruple," I corrected him. "All I need to know is will it work and will it be ready in time?"

I knew it would be. Reaper had an IQ that was off the charts. He could process data like I could languages. "Starfish will be good to go, but we'll need a couple of test runs out in the desert, just to make sure."

"You named it Starfish?" It didn't resemble a starfish, it looked like a big tube in an aluminum housing. "That's cheesy."

"Cheesy *awesome,*" he answered with pride. I'm sure the name had some sort of geeky historical reference. Reaper changed the subject and pointed at the folder in my hand. "You been thinking about your family?"

I shrugged. "A little, you know . . ." In actuality, I was terrified a bunch of my nieces and nephews were going to get shot in the head for something that they didn't even know about, but I couldn't let that show to the kid. He needed me to be sure, indomitable, fearless, all that leadership crap.

Reaper looked slightly embarrassed. "You worried about them?"

"Only if we fail." The rest went unsaid. We both knew what would happen then: Eddie would kill everyone that had ever mattered to us just out of principle. But he hadn't come out here to talk about that. "What've you got?"

"Adar bought the spoofed e-mails. He just wrote back. He's leaving Iraq today. He'll be back in a couple of days."

I nodded. As long as he had the box, everything would be fine, but from everything I had learned, he *always* had the box. It was his prized possession and life-insurance policy. "Good. We'll intercept him at his safe house outside of town."

"You think he's as scary as the rumors make him out to be?" Reaper asked. The word on Adar made him sound like some sort of jihadi Jack the Ripper. If Adar had been born into some other society, he probably would have been a serial killer. But luckily for the young murderer from Riyadh, Falah had recruited him and put his natural talents for cruelty to good use for their cause. "I mean, come on, we've dealt with some crazies, but this guy takes the cake. Dude, he like *eats people* and stuff."

"No big deal." I clapped my young associate on the back. "So he's bug-nuts crazy and I get to kill him. I told you this job has some perks."

"There's more," Reaper said. "I just heard on the news, they're evacuating the American embassy. There's a big mob protesting in front of it. The State Department said that all Americans need to leave Zubara right away." His grin exposed a bank of grossly crooked teeth. "I'm guessing that doesn't apply to us."

I hadn't been back in my home country in forever—too many laws, too much order. Life out on the fringe was much more to my liking. "It looks like the Zoob's heating up. Don't worry, we'll be out of here before the place totally melts down."

"I don't know, chief," Reaper said slowly, like he was the one with all the experience. "This shitty little country is important to a lot of powerful folks, shadowy, scary, secret government crazy shit. I wouldn't be surprised if there was a bunch of stuff going down."

Oh, not again. I rolled my eyes. "You've been listening to that conspiracy theory talk-radio show again, haven't you?"

"*From Sea to Shining Sea*?" Reaper shrugged. "You know, it isn't always just space aliens and Reptoids of the Hollow Earth. Their political analysis is awesome. Way better than the propaganda you get from the regular news. You really should listen. I've got it streaming right now if you want."

I snorted. "If I'm ever commissioned to rob Atlantis, I'll tune in. In the meantime, you worry too much."

"I'm just saying, I got a bad feeling about this is all."

VALENTINE
Fort Saradia National Historical Site
April 11
1230

"Cover me, goddamn it!" Tailor snarled as fire poured onto his position.

"Hang on, hang on," I said. I had a situation of my own to deal with. There were at least four bad guys coming up on my left.

"I need help now or I'm gonna die! Shit. I'm hit!"

I could see where Tailor went down. I started for him, but the distraction cost me. I didn't see the guy with the chainsaw until it was too late.

"Come and save me, damn it."

There was blood everywhere as I was cut in half. "Too late. I'm dead." I tossed the vibrating controller on the couch. Tailor swore at me first and then the Xbox.

The biggest open room on the first floor of the dorms had been turned into the rec room. We'd scrounged up a couple of games, a bunch of free weights, and a dart board. Our chalk was enjoying the break. Wheeler was spotting Hudson, as our big man bench-pressed enormous amounts of weight. Wheeler saw that we were toast and got excited. "About time. Our turn. Wrap it up, Hud."

Hudson grunted as he shoved up three hundred pounds for the ninth time. He was actually scary. "One. More."

"You suck, Val," Tailor whined as his character was curb-stomped to death. "You completely and utterly suck. You sucked so hard you choked on your suck. You suck at horde mode."

I raised an eyebrow. "It's this stupid controller. I hate playing shooters on a console. A keyboard and mouse is superior in every way."

Before Tailor could rebut and begin another nerd argument, Hudson racked the weights and stood up. "Get outta my chair, Tailor." He grinned. "Let me show you how it's done."

"How about me and you play, Hud?" Tailor asked him. "Let these uncoordinated monkeys go play Candy Land or something. Leave the horde to the real men."

"It's my turn," Wheeler insisted. "Just because it's your call sign doesn't mean you can hog it all day. Here, I'll pull all the weights off for you, and we'll see if you can do just the bar. Val, you better be ready to spot so he doesn't drop it on his concave chest and hurt himself."

Tailor flipped them both the bird as he passed over his controller. "Screw you, Wheeler, you soulless ginger. It ain't my fault I want to enjoy the finest recreation that Club Sara-Dia has to offer."

"Saradia," Hudson corrected as he flopped onto the couch. "Say it with me. Saw-radia."

"Sara-*Dia*!" Tailor exclaimed, needlessly accentuating his twang.

"Now you're just messing with me," Hudson muttered.

"What?" Tailor asked. "Sara-Dia."

"Hell, I can't tell if you're Southern or handicapped," Wheeler said. "But I repeat myself."

We were becoming a tight crew. One of the things I'd missed after leaving Vanguard was the camaraderie. It was good to have the R&R time together. Too bad it was temporary.

One of the colonel's security men appeared in the doorway. "Tailor, Valentine, Mr. Willis needs to speak to you right away." He didn't even wait for the response.

Tailor groaned. "Oh, what now?"

"Come on, man." I headed for the door. "This is why we're paid the medium bucks."

"I'm management. I should be getting bigger bucks." Tailor reluctantly followed. He stopped at the doorway to shout at Hudson and Wheeler. "Sara-*Dia*!" Then he ducked around the corner as Wheeler chucked an orange Fanta can at him.

The two of us headed across the courtyard. Tailor seemed to be in a better than normal mood, but shooting people in third-world nations was his element. "How's Sarah doing?"

"She's good," I replied, suspicious. "Why?"

"I bet," he said, smirking. I raised an eyebrow at him. "Val, I know you two are getting it on. She jumped your bones in the safe house, didn't she?"

I chuckled. "As a matter of fact—"

Tailor laughed. "I hope you at least turned the couch cushions over." I felt my face flush, and Tailor laughed at me again. "It's about time, anyway. That girl's been after you since the day you met."

"This whole thing is insane," I said. "I mean, it's intense. I feel like a teenager. I don't know how it's going to work out, but—"

"Goddamn it Val, there you go again!" Tailor said, interrupting me. "Quit overthinking it! You always spaz out and scare the girl off."

"When did I ever," I began.

Tailor interrupted me again. "Remember Teresa?"

"Oh . . . right," I said.

"I'm always right," Tailor insisted. I was dubious about that claim, but in this instance he was. Teresa had been a medical assistant with Vanguard, and she was the last woman I'd almost had a relationship with. I more or less pushed her away. I had to give myself credit, though. I was trying *really hard* to avoid doing the same thing to Sarah. "I'm serious. Stop being such a big spaz-girl. I can't have you worrying about some bullshit angst when we're out in the field."

"I'll be fine," I said. Tailor doused his cigarette as we entered the building. Gordon Willis and Colonel Hunter were waiting for us in the classroom.

Gordon greeted us enthusiastically. As always, he was wearing a suit. Anders was there also, leaning against the back wall, looking bored. "Mr. Tailor! Mr. Valentine!" Gordon said, vigorously shaking our hands. "Great to see you boys again. Damn fine work you're doing out there. Your hit on the terrorist recruitment house went off without a hitch. Now, our Zubaran counterparts were pissed that you caused so much collateral damage." Gordon leaned in closer and theatrically lowered his voice. "Off the record, boys, I don't give a shit about that. I'm glad to see you mopping the floor with hajji."

"Wait a minute," Tailor said. "You sure as hell gave a shit *last* time."

"I see where you're coming from, Mr. Tailor. Last time there was some concern that making too big of a splash too soon would cause some of our known targets to go to ground. We were able to keep things under control, and that didn't happen. The plan now is to kick it in high gear, keep hammering the enemy, so they don't have any safe places to hide."

Tailor and I looked at each other. I could tell Tailor wanted to get in Gordon's face, but I shook my head ever so slightly. He just frowned and sat down.

"Have you had a chance to look over your mission packets?" Gordon asked as I took my seat. We hadn't. "Well, I guess that's why we're having this briefing, isn't it?" Gordon said, laughing at his own joke. Tailor and I ignored him and opened our packets. "As you can see, gentlemen," Gordon continued, "we don't have a lot of information on the next target. His name is Adar. We believe that he is originally from Saudi Arabia. We don't know if Adar is his real name. We also suspect that he has ties to the Saudi government, but we're not sure what those ties are."

I looked through my packet as Gordon talked. This guy had spent years running all over Southwest Asia killing American and British soldiers. There was only one photograph, and it was taken from far away. He was a pretty nondescript looking guy, with short hair and a trimmed mustache. He was braced against the cinder block wall, looking out a window, carrying a Russian SVU bullpup sniper rifle affixed with a sound suppressor.

"I've heard of this guy," Tailor said. "Read about him on the Net. They say he's killed over a hundred Americans. The army thinks he's a myth, nothing but terrorist propaganda."

"If only that were the case," Gordon said, doing a very good job of feigning sincerity. "Adar is quite real, and that number is probably accurate. We don't know who he really is, who he works for, or who trained him, but he's a definite threat. Eliminating him will help me prove to my superiors that Project Heartbreaker is a worthwhile cause."

"So we've been able to track him down, then?" I asked.

"Exactly!" Gordon said, sounding upbeat. "He keeps a home in Zubara, in the village of Umm Bab, near the Saudi border."

"So, the US has been trying to find this guy for years, but all of a sudden we find out where he lives? How do we know this information is good?" I asked.

Gordon didn't bat an eye. "Twenty-four hours ago, we intercepted an e-mail from Adar. He's returning to Zubara and will be staying at his house here. However, if it turns out Adar isn't there, we'll just cancel the operation and go back to square one. If the information proves to be accurate, you two are going to go in and kill Adar."

"What? Just the two of us again? What about Hudson and Wheeler? They were assigned to *me*." Tailor was visibly agitated now.

"The operational plan calls for two shooters, Mr. Tailor," Gordon said dismissively. "I wasn't able to get clearance for any more than that."

"Shouldn't this get the priority?" I asked. "I mean, we need to get this guy, right?"

"I'm going to level with you boys," Gordon said, leaning in closer. "My superiors don't consider Adar a priority target. Eliminating him is a way of garnering more support for Project Heartbreaker, especially from people in the Pentagon. I was able to get approval for this operation, but you two are the only ones I was able to commandeer, if you will, to do the job. People in my chain of command have security concerns. It's not that I don't trust you, but . . . well, let's just say that this operation will be a little unorthodox."

I wasn't sure what to think. Gordon sounded sincere, but he *always* sounded sincere. Adar certainly was a worthy enough target; I'd heard of him too. I sure as hell didn't like the sound of *unorthodox* though. "It's not that killing Adar isn't worthwhile, sir," I said cautiously. "It's just . . . look, we almost got killed on our first mission because we were outnumbered. If we'd had Hudson and Wheeler with us, the complications would've been avoided entirely. Because there were just the two of us, we had to improvise."

"And you lost one of my trucks," Hunter growled, speaking for the first time.

"Exactly," I said. "With more eyes on the target, more shooters, we could've wiped out all of Al Falah's bodyguards in a less than a minute. As it was . . . well, things went to shit."

"I understand where you're coming from, Mr. Valentine," Gordon said, looking me in the eye. "I don't like having to take risks like this. But it needs to be done. This Adar has killed over a hundred American soldiers. Let's *get* this guy. Can I count on you boys?"

Tailor and I looked at each other again. "We'll get the job done, sir," Tailor said.

"Great!" Gordon said, slapping me on the shoulder. I winced as pain shot through my arm; he managed to hit me right where the bandage was. "You boys go ahead and look over those mission packets. There's a lot of information in there. I'll be contacting you as soon as we have confirmation that our target is on the ground." Gordon's cell phone began to ring. "Excuse me," he said, answering it. He left the room with his phone in his ear and Anders in tow.

We waited until we heard the outside door close. "Colonel, you didn't buy any of that horseshit, did you?" Tailor asked. "Isn't there some way we can get more guys for this?"

Hunter's face was a mask. "I'm afraid not, son," he said, turning to leave. "It's not my decision. Wheeler and Hudson will be staying here. You boys relax now, but stay sharp. And don't discuss this with anyone, not even your teammates. You won't get much notice for this one. Don't leave the compound." With that, Hunter left the room, leaving Tailor and me alone.

Chapter 7: Black Helicopters

VALENTINE
Fort Saradia National Historical Site
April 15
1700

Colonel Hunter and Sarah were waiting for us in the classroom. One of Hunter's security men had come looking for us in the chow hall and ordered us to go in for a briefing.

"Gentlemen, I'm glad you made it," Hunter said, sounding slightly agitated. "I know this is short notice, but you two are rolling out tonight. We believe our target has returned to his compound." Sarah handed each of us a fat new mission packet, full of maps and photographs.

Tailor and I sat down in the classroom, opening our packets as we did so. "Has this Adar guy come back, then, Colonel?" I asked.

"We believe so," Hunter said. He clicked his laptop and a video appeared on the big screen at the front of the room. It was footage from a thermal camera, taken from an aircraft. A pair of SUVs could be seen rolling into a compound. Eight people got out after they stopped.

"This is Adar's place in the village of Umm Bab. It's about fifty kilometers southwest of here. This video was taken fourteen hours ago."

"Wait, what's that?" Tailor said, pointing at the screen. Hunter replayed the segment of the video. It appeared that one of the people was being dragged into the house, struggling.

"We don't know," Hunter said bluntly. "Our boy has an ugly reputation. That individual could likely be his next victim. That's not our problem."

"Where did we get this video?" I asked. "Do we have a drone out there?"

"Yes," Sarah said from the back of the room. "Our, um, support network was able to acquire several UAVs for us."

"We've had UAVs watching Adar's compound since Gordon came and talked to you boys," Hunter said. "Nothing's come up until today. No one has left the compound since this was filmed. You'll be rolling out shortly. Gordon wanted to move sooner, but I told him I wasn't going to try this in broad daylight. You'll have the cover of darkness at least."

"Wait, how do we know that Adar's there, then?" I asked. "Did someone on the ground ID him? Are we just going by this footage?"

Hunter and Sarah exchanged a glance. Hunter then came around the table and leaned against it. He looked tired. "Yes," he said flatly. "Look, boys, I'm not any happier about this than you are. Frankly, I think this whole mission is bullshit. I told Gordon I don't want my men risking their lives on his pet projects when we're running with a skeleton crew to begin with. I was overruled on this one."

"Is there any way we can get more guys, Colonel?" Tailor asked.

"No, Mr. Tailor, there isn't," Hunter replied.

"So how are we going to get there?"

"A truck will be waiting for you by the gate," Hunter said. "First you'll need to go to supply. Get your gear and draw your weapons before you get on that truck."

"Wait, we're going to just *drive* there?" Tailor asked incredulously.

"Don't worry about it, Mr. Tailor," Hunter said dismissively. "Your transportation needs will be taken care of. The organization that has oversight of our little mission has a few assets. Everything else you need to know is in your packets, including aerial photos of the target compound. You'll need to plan your operation while en route."

"What? Colonel," I began.

Hunter cut me off. "This is *not* a democracy, Mr. Valentine!" he barked. "Now get your ass to supply and get kitted up! Move out!" Tailor and I looked at each other, and stood up. Sarah gave me a worried glance as we left the classroom.

VALENTINE
Confederated Gulf Emirate of Zubara
April 15
2045

"Control, Nightcrawler, radio check," I said, squeezing the transmit button on my headset.

"*Read you loud and clear, Nightcrawler,*" Sarah replied, all business.

"Alright, let's go over this one more time," Tailor said, concentrating on one of the aerial pictures of Adar's compound. We were in the back of a large, windowless van driven by Hunter's man, Conrad. He ignored us as we talked. The interior of the van was lit by a red light. "We'll use the assault ladder to hop the wall here," he said, pointing a gloved finger at a spot on the picture.

"Right," I said. "We'll come down behind the shed, here, and stash the ladder there."

"We then move across the compound to the back door, here," Tailor continued.

"Then we enter and clear. As if it's going to be that simple."

"It is that simple. Doing that without getting killed is the hard part."

I leaned in close to Tailor so that Conrad couldn't hear me. "This whole thing is screwed up, dude. We're going to clear a house that we *know* has eight people in it, with just the two of us. We don't know the interior layout. We don't know their security measures. All we know is that one or two guys patrol the yard every half hour or so."

"What I want to know is how we're supposed to get close to the place by just driving up to it," Tailor said. He had a point. The compound was in the middle of the village of Umm Bab. "Too much risk of being seen. Small town like that won't have much traffic at night."

"Well, why don't we ask him, then?" I suggested, nodding my head toward our driver.

"What the hell, why not?" Tailor agreed. "Hey, buddy?" he said, moving to the front of the van and tapping the driver on the shoulder.

"What is it?" Conrad said, seemingly irritated that we were talking to him.

"How the fuck do you intend to get us to that compound without getting our asses shot off?"

"Yeah," I said, chiming in, "what are we going to do, just drive up to the front gate and hop over it with this gay little ladder they gave us?"

Conrad was visibly annoyed now. "I'm not driving you to the target," he answered curtly. "I don't even know where it is. I don't know what your objective is. I had no idea it was a 'compound' until you two idiots told me. I'm just dropping you off at a predetermined location. Someone else is taking it from there."

"Wait, what?" I asked. "Where are we going from there?"

Conrad sighed. "Again, guys, I *don't know*. I don't *need to know*. I'm just the driver, okay?" He spoke to us like an elementary school teacher lecturing his class. "Maybe you two should just concentrate on whatever it is you're doing back there and let me drive."

"Listen, asshole," Tailor said, his eyes narrowing. Before he could say anything else I put my hand on his shoulder and shook my head. He plopped back down to his seat, flipping Conrad the bird as he did so. "Pissed me off," Tailor muttered as he picked up his packet again.

I leaned back against the wall, rubbing my eyes. We'd been driving for over an hour, and I had no idea where we were. They hadn't issued us much in the way of equipment, either. We were each given a set of fatigues, in the blotchy A-TACS pattern, and body-armor vests. We wore night-vision goggles up on our heads. The goggles themselves were state of the art and were lighter than any kind I'd used before.

Another piece of equipment I'd never used before was the strange weapon in my hands. "What the hell *is* this thing?" Tailor asked, as if he'd read my mind. We'd each been issued a weird, boxy little .45-caliber submachine gun with a folding stock and a fat suppressor on the end.

"It's a KRISS Vector," I said after a moment. "I read about these in a gun rag. They came out a few years ago." Each of our weapons was painted to match our fatigues and was topped with a holographic sight.

We carried the rest of our gear in pouches on our vests. Tailor had been issued some kind of tactical PDA with a GPS locator built into it. It had the coordinates preprogrammed, as well as a bunch of mission-specific information. I wondered why in the hell they didn't just give us that in the first place instead of bothering to print out the mission packets. My .44 was on my left thigh. I had a feeling I was going to need some luck tonight.

After a seemingly endless drive, the van rolled to a stop. "We're here," Conrad said, looking at us in his rearview mirror. "This is where you two get off. Leave your mission packets in the van." Tailor opened the back doors and climbed out.

"Where are we?" I asked, stepping out after him, slinging the folded assault ladder over my shoulder. The van had pulled off to the side of a long dirt road that cut through the desert. Far off in the distance, I could see the amber glow of Zubara City. The moon wasn't out yet, and the stars were bright overhead.

Conrad shut the van's engine off and killed the headlights. Suddenly it was dead quiet; nothing could be heard except the faint sound of the wind and the rustling of our equipment.

"We're in the middle of nowhere," Tailor said, his face illuminated by the small screen on his GPS. "What the hell? We're even farther from the target than we were at the fort!"

"Hey man, are we in the right place?" I asked, approaching the driver's side door of the van. Conrad had gotten out and was leaning against the van. He reached underneath his 5.11 vest and retrieved a pack of cigarettes.

"We're in the right spot," he said nonchalantly, lighting up. "Your ride will be here shortly. Smoke 'em if you got 'em." Tailor just shrugged, leaned against the van himself, and lit up a cigarette.

Minutes ticked by. None of us spoke. I gazed up into the night sky; it was the first time I'd been able to see the stars since I'd arrived in Zubara. I don't think any of us wanted to ruin the rare quiet moment we were having.

The quiet was suddenly interrupted by a low beeping sound. Conrad pulled out a device that looked like a pager and read the little display. "Your ride is here," he said, putting the gadget back into his pocket. Tailor and I looked around. No lights could be seen on the road. Not a single car had driven by in the few minutes we'd been standing there.

"Where?" I asked. Conrad just shook his head like I was stupid. A moment later, I heard a dull *thwup-thwup-thwup* noise. It sounded like a helicopter off in the distance.

"Is that a chopper?" Tailor asked.

"Something like that," Conrad said. I wondered what in the hell he was being so coy about. I quickly found out. The *thwupping* noise grew louder, but the helicopter still sounded far off in the distance, and it was difficult to tell which direction it was coming from. Then I saw a black shape slowly moving across the sky; the helicopter was a lot closer than it sounded.

"Now, what the hell is *that*?" Tailor asked as the helicopter approached.

"I have no idea," I said. Seeing new and strange things had become the theme of the evening, it seemed. I'm something of an aviation buff. As a matter of fact, I have a private pilot's license. But I'd never seen anything like the machine that was setting down in the desert in front of us.

It wasn't very big, maybe the size of an old Huey. Its hull was painted black and was made up of oddly curved and faceted surfaces. The chopper looked like a bastard love-child of a Huey and the RAH-66 Comanche. It kicked up a cloud of white dust as it touched down onto the bleached, rocky Zubaran desert, but it still was ridiculously quiet. The muted whine of turbine engines could be heard over the dull *thwupping* of the rotor. The rotor blades themselves appeared to be very wide and were oddly shaped.

"It's a stealth helicopter," I said, somewhat in disbelief. There I was, working for a secret government organization, engaged in an honest-to-goodness black operation, and I was about to climb onto a genuine *black helicopter*. I shook my head. Tailor laughed to himself.

The chopper settled onto the desert floor, and an off-kilter-looking door slid open on the side of the fuselage. The interior cabin was lit with a red light.

"Let's go!" Tailor said, slapping me on the shoulder. He took off toward the chopper at a jog, and I followed. We both crouched down as we approached the aircraft. The unbelievably quiet rotor was still turning. We climbed into the small cabin. A bench was in the middle, with five seats facing outward on each side. As we sat down and strapped ourselves in, the sliding door closed itself.

"Here," the copilot said, reaching back toward me. He was wearing a black flight suit and a helmet with night-vision goggles mounted on it. He handed me a bulky little flash drive. "Updated mission information." I took it from him and handed it to Tailor. Tailor pulled the PDA out of its pouch on his vest and plugged the drive into it. We both studied the screen as the helicopter lifted off, carrying us into the night sky.

I closed my eyes briefly, trying not to think about my *last* ride in a helicopter.

"Thirty seconds!" the copilot said. "We won't touch down." Tailor and I nodded. The stealth helicopter was running dark, flying low over the desert floor toward the village of Umm Bab. We were slowing down now. I unbuckled my seat belt and readied myself.

"We're at the LZ!" the pilot said. The door on the chopper slid open. Cool, dusty desert air rushed in. "Now!" Without replying, Tailor stood up, made his way to the door, and jumped out into the darkness. Following suit, I stepped up to the door, bent down, and jumped out.

We were a little higher up than I thought. I landed hard, swearing aloud as I flopped onto the rocky desert floor, rolling onto my side. We were so obscured by fine dust that I could hardly see anything. Tailor grabbed me and pulled me upright as the muted sounds of the stealth helicopter faded away. The dust cloud began to settle, leaving us alone in the desert.

"Where are we?" I asked as I quietly chambered a round on my weapon.

"That's Umm Bab over there." He pointed toward the amber lights in the distance. "Control, Xbox," Tailor whispered into his headset. "We're on the ground."

"*Copy that, Xbox,*" Sarah replied. "*Proceed to the target.*" There was some static interference as she spoke. We were a long way from the fort.

"Roger," Tailor replied. "Let's move, Val." Flipping down his night-vision goggles, he took off toward Umm Bab at a fast walk, submachine gun held at the low-ready. I pulled my own NVGs down over my eyes and turned them on. The dark desert was now bright green. The stars overhead were incredibly bright, and the lights of Umm Bab were almost blinding.

I stood up and followed Tailor. I unfolded the stock on my weapon and turned on the holographic sight, setting it for night-vision mode. Carrying the assault ladder on my back, I moved through the darkness in silence. It took us a long time to reach the outskirts of the village. The moon was set to rise at 0122, and we wanted to be out of the open desert before that happened.

Tailor broke into a run and took cover behind a high wall that surrounded a large house. Once he was in place, he signaled for me to follow while he kept a lookout. I quickly ran to him, crouching down next to him against the wall. "Over there," he said. "The target house is just down this street. Follow me to the alley. Watch out for dogs." In Zubara, like many

Middle Eastern countries, one could occasionally find packs of feral dogs roaming the streets.

Tailor nodded, stood up, and quietly moved toward the alley. I followed, constantly watching our backs while Tailor led the way. We came to the end of the wall. Tailor leaned around it. He used hand signals to tell me it was clear, then disappeared.

Checking our six one last time, I peeked around the corner. Tailor was a few meters up the alley, crouched behind a large trash bin, waiting for me. I could see no other movement in the alley, and mercifully no lights. The alley itself was narrow, barely wide enough for a truck to drive down. The back walls of compounds lined either side. There was no movement, except for a single black cat trotting along the wall. I signaled for Tailor to advance again. He moved forward, another twenty meters or so, before crouching down in front of a parked pickup truck. The cat took off running and disappeared. Tailor leaned around the vehicle and signaled for me to move forward. In this fashion we leapfrogged toward our target as quietly as possible.

Just after midnight, we arrived behind Adar's compound, in the exact spot we'd picked out from the aerial photos. I began to unfold the ladder, locking it into its extended position. I leaned it up against the ten-foot wall. Tailor and I froze when we heard someone loudly talking in Arabic on the other side of the wall. Tailor mouthed the word *shit*. I whispered that I'd go check it out and began to climb the ladder as quietly as I could.

Reaching the top of the wall, I laid eyes on Adar's compound for the first time. The house was large, square, and made of white stone. A lush garden of palm trees and ferns sat in the middle. There was also a fountain, loudly splashing water into an artificial pond. I was grateful for this as the noise of the water could cover our footsteps.

Below me was the shed, and *directly* below me, leaning against the wall I'd just climbed, was an Arab man wearing a suit. He was smoking a cigarette and talking to somebody on his cell phone. *Shit.*

I turned around and looked down at Tailor. I held up one finger, telling him that there was one guy. I pointed down, indicating his location. I held my hand to my head, mimicking a phone, to tell Tailor what he was doing. Tailor nodded and dragged his finger across his throat. I nodded back.

Turning around again, I shuffled forward onto the top of the wall, as slowly as I could, so as not to make noise. The man was oblivious to my presence. His lit cigarette was as bright as a flashlight through my goggles, and it illuminated him clearly.

I brought my weapon around, being very careful not to let it touch the top of the concrete wall. I waited. I didn't want to interrupt the call, just in case he was talking to somebody who might tip these guys off.

After a moment, he snapped the phone closed. I was ready. Leaning a little bit farther forward, I aimed for the top-rear portion of my target's head, just as he began to walk back to the house. The suppressed submachine gun clicked and hissed as I fired a two-round burst, and the man collapsed to the ground, blood pouring out of the back of his perforated skull. The strange submachine gun had surprisingly little recoil.

I gave Tailor the thumbs-up and took one last look around the compound. There were bright lights on the front of the house but none on the rear. Seeing no movement, I climbed over the wall and dropped ten feet to the ground below. I landed hard in the dirt between the shed and the wall, and my ankle stung a little. I ignored it, ran forward, and grabbed the dead man's feet. As Tailor cleared the top of the wall, I dragged my victim into the darkness behind the shed.

Above me, Tailor carefully maintained his balance while he pulled the ladder up over the wall. He handed it down to me. I held it as he quickly climbed down. Once he was on the ground, he covered the courtyard with his weapon as I laid the ladder down in the dirt behind the shed.

"Control, Nightcrawler, we're inside the compound. Proceeding to the house."

"*Roger that, Nightcrawler,*" Sarah replied, her voice still shrouded in static. "*Is that you behind the shed?*"

"Uh, affirmative," I said.

"*Understood. I see three heat signatures.*"

"One of the tangos," Tailor said. "He's down."

"*Copy that,*" Sarah replied. "*We just got the UAV in place. We'll be providing overwatch.*"

"Roger that. Out." I was happy for the cover of the aerial drone, of course, but I wondered why in the hell they didn't have it there from the get-go.

"Nice work," Tailor said, indicating the dead man. "You see the back door?"

"Yes," I said, peering around the shed. The house was only about fifty feet from our position, but we'd have to bolt across the courtyard and hope we weren't seen.

"I'll cover you."

"Roger," I said, as Tailor positioned himself to cover the courtyard with his weapon. He gave me the high sign when he was ready. "Moving!" I said, and ran toward the house as quickly and as quietly as I could. I was across the courtyard a moment later. I took a knee, and leaned around the corner of the building, covering the courtyard for Tailor. He then ran from the shed to my position, and crouched down next to me.

Together we moved to the back door of Adar's safe house. It was locked.

"Can you pick it?" I asked.

"Probably," Tailor replied, lifting his night-vision goggles up onto his head. I covered him as he pulled out some bump keys and began to work on the door. It wasn't the best lock ever designed, and thankfully the door wasn't dead-bolted. It was open in a few seconds.

I turned off my NVGs and lifted them off my face. Giving my eyes a moment to adjust to the darkness, I nodded to Tailor. We readied our weapons, and Tailor quietly opened the door. It led into a large kitchen, but no one could be seen, and the lights were off. Tailor and I crept inside, silently closing the door behind us.

Music could be heard from the next room. It sounded like a radio or a television, and we could hear men talking in Arabic. We moved through the kitchen, and I risked a peek around the corner into the other room.

It was a living room. Against the far wall was a huge television. Four more men sat around it watching a porno flick. Cheesy music, grunting, and moaning resonated though the house. I looked back at Tailor and told him what was happening through hand signals. Three men were sitting on a couch, facing the television. Their backs were toward us. The fourth sat in a chair off to the side. He'd be able to see us if he looked away from the TV.

Through hand signals, Tailor told me what he wanted to do. Tailor crawled up right next to me, very slowly so as not to make noise, and stood up. We simultaneously leaned around the corner, bringing our weapons to bear. A short burst from Tailor's Vector tore into the head of the man sitting in the chair. Tailor's target slumped forward, his blood pouring down his neck.

At the same time, I put the reticule of my holographic sight on the back of the couch and held down the trigger. The .45 rounds ripped through the couch in puffs of fabric and stuffing. I swept from right to left, stitching bullets across them. The men gasped as bullets tore into them, but they were quickly silenced. Tailor switched targets and emptied the rest of his magazine into the three men as well.

It was over in seconds. They never knew what hit them. We both quickly changed magazines and moved into the living room, doing our best to cover all angles. The men on the couch had been thoroughly ventilated. A few stray rounds had gone into the far wall, but the television was still blaring pornography at an unpleasantly high volume. A cloud of smoke hung in the room, and the air smelled like burnt powder.

This is too easy, I thought, but I wasn't about to get complacent. Complacency is what had gotten these assholes killed. We still hadn't found Adar, and we knew from the surveillance that three more individuals were in the house.

"Control, Xbox," Tailor whispered. "Main floor clear. Four more tangos down. Sweeping the building now." I could barely hear Sarah's voice. She was drowned in static. Tailor tried again, but he got the same result. Something in the area was interfering with our transmissions.

Tailor pointed up. He proceeded to an ornate staircase, weapon shouldered and at the ready. I followed, constantly swiveling my head around to make sure no one was coming up behind. The top of the stairs revealed a wide hallway, with a few doors on either side. Strange music resonated through the upper level, and it included people chanting in some language that wasn't Arabic. At the end of the hall was a closed door that probably led to the master bedroom.

Tailor started down the hallway, and I followed. Most of the doors on either side were open, and we carefully checked each one before proceeding past. One was locked, so we kept going.

A toilet flushed. Tailor and I froze and swung our weapons toward the bathroom door just as it opened. The man inside was buttoning his shirt back up when he saw us. He had a pistol in a shoulder holster. His eyes grew wide, and he reached for it, but he wasn't nearly fast enough. His white shirt splashed red as we both hit him with a two-round burst. He fell over backward, hitting the hardwood floor with a thud.

Tailor immediately swung his weapon toward the door at the end of the hall. I swung mine back toward the stairs. Back to back, we waited for a long moment. Nothing happened. The strange music was the only sound that could be heard. The upstairs of the house must have been sound-dampened or something. Sweat trickled down Tailor's blackened face. He nodded at the door at the end of the hall and started toward it. All of the rooms in the upstairs hallway were now empty. If Adar was in the house, he was through that door.

The bizarre chanting music grew louder as we drew closer, but it was muffled enough that I still couldn't tell what language it was. As we approached the end of the hall, I felt strange. Apprehension grew in me. My heart rate sped up. *The Calm* was wavering. Something was wrong.

I put a hand on Tailor's shoulder. He stopped and looked a question back at me. My mouth opened, but I couldn't think of anything to say. Looking irritated, Tailor just jerked his head at the door and reached for the handle. He signaled me to go right while he'd go straight. It's hard to properly cover the angles in a room when there're only two of you. We'd have to be quick. He hesitated for a long second, hand hovering over the handle, then grabbed it and slammed the door open. Together, we rushed into the room.

The bedroom was huge. Directly opposite the door was a large four-poster bed, with some kind of big painting hung above it. Against the far wall was a mirrored dresser, a desk, and what looked like a vanity.

Adar stood in the middle of the room. He was taller than I thought he'd be. He was also completely naked and splattered with blood. He clutched some kind of curved dagger in his hand.

In front of him, hanging from the ceiling, was a woman. Her hands were bound over her head. Her hair, matted and wet, hung down in her face. Blood dripped from her ravaged body onto plastic sheets spread across the floor. She'd been utterly mutilated. Adar had split her open like he was cleaning a game animal. Bloody lumps that appeared to be internal organs had been neatly arranged on the dresser. Behind them was an iPod and a set of speakers, the source of the strange music.

My stomach lurched. My mouth fell open. It felt like my balls were trying to crawl up into my stomach. It took me a moment to process what I was actually seeing. I could hear a strange buzzing in my ears over the bizarre rhythms of Adar's music.

"Jesus Christ," Tailor said, turning toward Adar. I don't know why neither of us fired. The whole thing was surreal.

Adar, as if noticing our presence for the first time, turned toward us. His face was a mask. If he was surprised or afraid, he didn't show it. My heart was racing now. My knees were weak, and I thought I was going to fall. I wanted to turn and run out of the room. Adar spoke to us then. He said something in Arabic that I didn't understand. Blood trickled from the corner of his mouth as he talked. I looked over at the dead girl again, then back at Adar. I felt numb. Adar smiled. I closed my eyes . . .

"*Val!*" Tailor yelled, startling me.

I blinked, realizing then that my revolver was in my hands. Confused, I slowly reholstered it.

"*Nightcrawler, Nightcrawler, Control, what's your status?*" Sarah asked, the concern in her voice obvious. I tried to speak but couldn't.

That's when I saw Adar. He was lying on the floor, on his stomach, in a huge pool of blood. Some of it was his, some of it was the girl's. A gory wound protruded from the center of his lower back. There was another exit wound on the back of his neck; he'd been nearly decapitated.

"Get it together, goddamn it!" Tailor yelled, grabbing my body armor and shaking me.

"I'm . . . what happened?" I asked. "I think I blacked out."

"You fucked him *up* is what happened!" Tailor said, letting me go. He walked across the room, stepping over Adar's corpse, and smashed the iPod. The horrid music silenced, Tailor keyed his microphone. "Control, Xbox, radio check."

"*Loud and clear, Xbox,*" Sarah replied, relief obvious in her voice. "*What's your status?*"

"The target's dead," Tailor said. "We're fine. Stand by." He looked up at me. "Why didn't you just shoot him with your submachine gun?"

"I don't know." I didn't remember shooting Adar. "Why didn't *you* just shoot him?"

Tailor hesitated. "I don't know, either," he said. "Fuck it, it's *done*. Let's check for intel and get the hell out of here. This place is freaking me out."

Nodding, I looked around Adar's room. The mirror behind him had shattered, presumably from my bullets passing through him. The painting above the bed depicted a horrific monster, a mass of tentacles and teeth, devouring a girl. I looked back over at Adar's victim. I felt dizzy, turned, and threw up on the floor.

"You alright, Val?" Tailor asked, calmer now.

"No," I replied. "We can't leave her like that!"

"What? Val, we gotta go, man, we don't have time to —"

"*We can't leave her like that!*" I shouted, standing back up.

"Listen, goddamn it!" Tailor said. "She's dead! You can't—"

"Tailor, *please*," I said, much more quietly this time.

He mouthed another curse word. "Fine. Let's hurry this up. We have to get out of here." I closed my eyes as I held the girl's feet. Tailor stood up on a chair and snapped out his automatic knife. He used it to cut the ropes that she'd been hung with and grabbed her shoulders. He helped me gently lower her body.

"Oh, *God*," Tailor said, making himself look up at the ceiling. The girl's head had flopped back as we carried her; her eyes were gone. Empty red sockets stared up at my partner. "This is fucked up. This is *fucked up*," he said. Doing our best to ignore it, we carried her to Adar's bed and wrapped her in the sheets. Tailor quickly looked away, sweat trickling down his face.

"Hey look," I said, noticing for the first time a small safe. It was mounted in the wall next to the bed, and was open.

"Let's . . . let's check it out," Tailor said, regaining his composure.

Inside was a stack of American hundred-dollar bills. "Wow."

"There has to be fifty thousand dollars here," Tailor said. He began stuffing the money into his assault pack.

"I don't suppose you're going to report that," I said as I rummaged through the safe, stuffing documents into my pockets. At the very back of the safe, my hand touched something solid.

"What's that?" Tailor asked as I pulled it out.

"I don't know," I said. It was a small wooden box wrapped in a plastic bag.

"Take it. Grab everything else you can find. We've gotta bounce, man. We been here too long." We took one last look around the room but didn't find anything else. As we turned to leave, I pulled an Ace of Spades out of my pocket and dropped it onto Adar's back.

He hadn't stopped smiling, even in death.

Chapter 8: The Intern

LORENZO
April 16

The house was too quiet.

I should have known something was wrong as soon as I saw the compound's front gate left open. After doing a quick pass by, we had modified the plan. Carl had parked a klick down the road, and I had snuck up on the isolated compound, consisting of a single large house surrounded by a ten-foot brick wall, on foot. It had been purchased by Al Falah as a safe house for his associates.

Approaching as quietly as possible, I had paused and scanned the gate repeatedly. The plan had been for both of us to sneak in, kill Adar and anybody else there as quickly as possible, grab the box, and get the hell out, but now that situation looked fishy. So I'd snuck in to take a quick peek. I was wearing body armor, covered with ammo and explosives, and had a short AR-15 carbine, and even weighed down that much I was far stealthier than most. Not trying to brag, but I would have made a damn good ninja.

The compound had appeared utterly dead, so I had sprinted right up to the door. Lights were on but nobody was home. Sweeping inside, I paused as I saw the first perforated corpse. "Somebody beat us to it," I said into the radio as I surveyed the destruction in the living room. Brass casings rolled underfoot and the room stank of the recently dead.

"*What do you mean?*" Carl's voice said in my ear.

"I mean that the guards are dead and the place is shot to hell. Somebody's been here already."

"*Did they get the box? If those no-good thieves got the box, I swear I'm gonna—*"

"Dude, we are no-good thieves. Chill." I moved quickly through the room, careful not to step in any of the spreading puddles. Empty extended Glock magazines were on the carpet. Could this be the work of the same hitters that had screwed up Phase One?

I kept my rifle up as I moved through the house. It was dead silent, but there could still be somebody here.

"I bet it was those guys that almost botched the Falah job." There was a single body half in the bathroom with a cloverleaf of bullet holes in his chest. I approached the bedroom door quietly, my suppressed 5.56 carbine at the ready, the red dot of the Aimpoint sight floating just under my vision, though I had a sneaky feeling that Adar wasn't going to be a problem. The bedroom door slowly swung open. Adar was obviously dead. There was a second form under a blood-drenched sheet. I lifted it slowly.

I must have made some sort of strange noise into the radio.

"Lorenzo? What is it? Are you okay?"

"Better than the residents. It's a bloodbath in here." I hadn't seen anything like this since Chechnya. That girl had been mutilated, dissected. Somebody had shot the hell out of Adar, too. I did a quick once over of the room, discovering that the stories about the Butcher of Zubara hadn't been exaggerated. "Carl, Adar cut this girl . . . like . . . I don't know what."

"No time for that. Find that box. Hurry before somebody else shows up."

Blood was *everywhere*. Adar hadn't just been dropped, he'd been methodically taken apart. There was a blood-stained Ace of Spades playing card left on the perforated corpse. *What the hell?* Then I noticed a discarded revolver speed loader, five spent cases, and a single live .44 magnum cartridge. I picked up the round and examined it.

"Clint Eastwood was here."

"Huh?" Carl responded. *"Quit screwing around."*

Shoving the cartridge into my pocket, I kept searching. The safe had been cleaned out, Adar's belongings had been rifled through, and I felt a sinking feeling in my gut that what we had come for was already gone.

The shooters had missed something.

"One second." Having years of experience looking for bugs and planting them, I knew that most people would have missed Adar's hidden camera. Apparently he liked to record his torture sessions. I followed the wire back behind the bed and found the recorder. It was still running. Maybe this would tell me who our mystery shooters were. I took the DVD out of the machine and hurried back down the stairs.

"I can't find the damn box."

Carl swore over the radio again. *"Someone took it already, you think?"*

"I think so. I'm leaving the duplicate anyway. Odds are whoever took it doesn't know what it's for, but the prince's people have to think it's been destroyed." I took a small box from a pouch in my armor. It had been carved to very exacting specifications from some very specific pieces of wood. Pressure on some hidden indentations caused the intricate box to slide open, revealing the delicate key inside. I pulled the duplicate out and held it up to the light. This part had been trickier, since there were no recorded measurements for the actual device, but I was about to melt it into slag anyway, so it didn't really matter. I twisted the base of the key, and dozens of tiny pins moved freely down the sides of the shaft. I placed it in the safe and started setting the bomb.

The incendiary device would immolate the entire room, burning a hole through the floor in seconds. This whole house would be nothing but ash and bones in a matter of minutes, and it was all so Adar's extended family would think his box was toast. I set the timer for five minutes. Plenty of time to be down the road.

"Hurry up," Carl said. "*I'm getting nervous.*"

"I know," I answered, already heading for the exit, knowing with dread certainty that the box had probably been taken from the upstairs safe by the shooters. I made sure the DVD was still in place. Those shooters had my box, and I had to get it back, no matter what.

"*Lorenzo, you better hurry.*"

"What?"

"*Two cars full of bad guys pulling into the compound. Run!*"

I ran downstairs and crouched near the rear exit. The door was open, and the arriving headlights illuminated the back wall of the compound. The cars pulled to a stop and doors opened. Someone began to sing, drunken and off key. Adar must have been planning a homecoming party, and more guests had just arrived.

Not wanting to find out what kind of people a terrorist invited to a torture party, I tried to think of a way out, *something, anything*. If I made it to the back wall, I would surely be spotted before I could scale it. I could try to Rambo my way out, but from the noises coming from the yard, there were several bad guys.

"Carl, how many we got?"

"*Couldn't tell. It was too dark when they pulled in. Want me to come in shooting?*"

"Hold on that. I've got an idea." I moved quickly back into the home. The doorbell rang, long and raspy, and someone on the other side laughed. I had seen the fuse box in my search. The bell continued, the user obviously becoming frustrated. I pulled my pack off, removed my night-vision monocular, and strapped it onto my head. In another pouch was a small Semtex charge, and I squished it against the circuit breakers.

The ringing quit, and loud knocking started. The laughter was gone, and now voices called out with some concern. The radio initiator blinked green in my hand, we had contact. The charge would only kill the lights in the house, but hopefully this would be enough of an edge. I moved back toward the side entrance.

Now they were pounding on the front door. I pulled a frag from one of the MOLLE pouches on my armor and, staying low so as to not blot out the light coming through the peep hole, slid up to the door. I pulled the pin but carefully kept the spoon down until it was wedged tightly against the door's base plate. The grenade had a five-second fuse, and it would be one heck of a surprise for our party guests. It's those little touches that show you care.

Back toward the side door now. The pounding turned to kicking. I kept moving, wanting to get some space between me and that frag. The side door was in view, the rear wall of the compound visible through the portal, still illuminated in the headlights. A shadow moved on the back porch: a man with a gun. They were coming. I flipped down the monocular, and the view for one eye turned a pixilated green.

"Adar!" one of the men on the back porch shouted. The front door cracked and splintered on its hinges.

"Hide-and-seek time." I took a deep breath and mashed the initiator.

There was a *bang* as the house plunged into darkness. My world was now a super illuminated green. I raised the AR to my shoulder, realized that I had not turned down the Aimpoint for night vision use as the dot appeared blindingly fuzzy, cursed under my breath, turned the knob to dial it down, and moved my hand back to the grip. Behind me the front door crashed open.

Five.

A man in a suit and headdress moved through the rear entrance into my sight, blinking stupidly, pistol held before him like a talisman to ward off evil.

Four.

I flipped the selector to semi and pulled the trigger twice, the dot of the Aimpoint barely moving as it bounced across his torso. The suppressor was deadly silent, but each bullet still made a very audible *chuff* noise as it violated the speed of sound.

Three.

I moved forward, sidestepping, gun still at the ready, slicing the pie, more of the back porch swinging into view. The first man was falling, a second man was behind him, looking surprised in my pixilated world, lifting his Tokarev sideways, gangster style. The dot sight covered his face. *Chuff.*

Two.

There was movement behind me, the rest of Adar's guests piling into the entryway, surprised by the darkness. A few random gunshots rang out as they attacked the shadows.

One.

The concussion of the grenade was sharp inside the structure. Even with a few walls between us I could feel the impact in my eyeballs. Gliding over the bodies of the men that I had just shot, I took the corner slowly, watching for movement. Somebody started screaming.

There were two figures standing in front of the fancy fountain, easy targets. The carbine met my shoulder, but I stopped. Only one of the targets was a man, the other was female. The man had a subgun in one hand, and a rope leading to the bound wrists of the young woman. Her head was hung down, hair covering her face. He was staring, slack jawed, at the smoking front door of Adar's home and his dying and injured companions.

Having seen that poor girl upstairs, I just reacted. I flipped the selector to full auto. The man never knew what hit him as I stitched him from groin to neck in one burst. The bullets were tiny, but they were *fast*, and at this range they fragmented violently, ripping through flesh and leaving softball-sized exit wounds. He stumbled back, falling into the fountain with a crimson splash, jerking the rope and sending the girl sprawling. I dropped the mag and reloaded as I scanned for threats, trying to break the tunnel vision. *Clear.*

Instead of heading for the back wall, I sprinted toward the captive. She appeared to be in a state of shock, probably a young Filipina worker. I'm a killer, and a thief, and a con man, and a hired gun, but I was not a monster, and in Zubara, girls like this were treated like slaves or worse.

"Come with me," I said in Arabic, helping the girl to her feet, then quickly switching to Tagalog. "Come with me now or these men will kill you." She looked at me, stunned or bewildered, probably drugged and incoherent.

"*Lorenzo, what's happening?*" Carl's voice was tense.

"Pick me up at the front gate," I replied tersely. "We need to go, lady." I gestured with my gun in the direction to move. "Now!"

"You're an American!" she shouted in English. "Oh, thank God!"

"Uh . . ." *That was unexpected.* "Yes! I'm here to rescue you . . . or something. Let's go."

The van barely slowed as I shoved the still-bound girl into the back and climbed in after her. The incendiary bomb detonated with a brilliant flash that crackled from every window. I slammed the door as Adar's burning compound shrank in the distance.

VALENTINE
Fort Saradia National Historical Site
April 16
0400

Alone in my room, I sat on the floor, my back to the wall. I was still wearing my cammies. My body armor was lying on the floor next to me. The door to the balcony was open; a cool breeze drifted into the room.

On the floor next to me was Adar's strange little box. I'd given it a half-hearted examination; it was some kind of puzzle box, made of wood, ornately carved. It looked very old. I tried for a minute to open it but quickly gave up.

I don't know how long I'd been sitting there when I heard someone knocking on my door. I didn't answer it. I didn't want to talk to anyone. After a few moments, the knocking stopped, leaving me alone with my thoughts. Our trip back from Adar's compound had been long, but I barely remembered it. We'd been debriefed by Gordon as soon as we'd returned to the compound. He, of course, had been overjoyed, especially at the intelligence we'd gathered. Tailor neglected to mention the fifty thousand dollars he'd stuffed into his backpack. I'd forgotten to turn over the puzzle box.

I couldn't sleep. Every time I closed my eyes, I could see that dead girl hanging from Adar's ceiling. I wondered what her name had been, where she'd come from, how she'd ended up there. It reminded me so much of what happened to my mom, it *hurt*. My stomach was still twisted into knots, hours later.

I took another swig from the large plastic bottle in my hand. I'd managed to bum some booze from one of the other guys. I didn't know what in the hell it was. It tasted terrible, but it was alcohol, and it was potent. It'd *do*. As I took another drink, my bathroom door suddenly opened. Sarah walked into my room.

"Hey," I said, not looking up at her.

"Mike? Are you okay?" she asked, standing over me.

I raised my eyes up to hers. "Not really," I said. I took another sip.

"What happened?" she asked, sitting on the floor next to me. She saw the bottle in my hand. "Are you drinking?"

"Yes, I am!" I said, loudly slurring my speech and saluting her with the bottle. Sarah grabbed it out of my hand. "Hey!" I protested, but she ignored me. She lifted it to her nose and made a face when she sniffed it.

"What is this stuff?"

"I was drinking that," I said testily.

"I think you've had enough, Mike," she said firmly.

"Just leave me alone, okay?" I snatched the bottle back from her.

"Mike, please, just tell me what happened. I'm here for you. *Talk* to me."

"No, goddamn it, I don't want to *talk* about it!" I snapped. "I just want some peace and quiet! You think all because you screwed me it gives you the right to march in here whenever the hell you want?"

Sarah huffed loudly and quickly stood up. "Look, I read the report, okay? I know what you found in there."

I let out an obnoxious drunken snort. "Oh, do you? So you know that he cut her open, cut out her organs, and put them on his shelf like bowling trophies?"

"Oh my God," Sarah said. We'd kind of left that part out of our report.

"So don't barge in here and tell me I can't have a goddamned drink!"

"I'm just trying to *help* you."

"I don't need your help!" I shouted, slamming the plastic bottle down on the concrete floor. "You're not my damned mother! She's been dead since I was a kid. You know what? I get by just fine."

Sarah's expression softened a little. "How did she die?"

"She was murdered. I came home one day and found her cut to pieces, just like that girl. My dad's dead too. So are half my friends. You know what? I don't *care*. I *kill people* for money. Shooting people is my *job*. I can handle it. I always handle it. I don't need your help. I don't need your pity. And I don't need *you*. So just march your little ass the hell out of here and leave me alone!"

Sarah's eyes flashed with anger. "I don't need this. Go ahead, drink it all! Drink yourself to death if you want. I hope you choke on it!" She turned on a heel and stormed out of my room, slamming the bathroom door behind her.

A pulse of anger surged through me. I picked up the ancient puzzle box and threw it against the door as hard as I could. It crunched loudly as it hit, and fell to the floor, broken. I stared at the bathroom door, breathing heavily. I just wanted to be left alone. I just wanted Sarah to come back. I wanted another drink. I didn't want to drink anymore.

A sickening pit formed in my stomach as I realized what I'd done. *Good job, Ace,* I thought. *You managed to drive her away, too.*

"Shut up," I said aloud. *It's not my fault. I had a bad night.* There was comfort in self-pity. I lifted the plastic bottle to my lips and began to gulp down the rest of the pungent mystery alcohol. It burned on the way down, and I thought I was going to throw up. I let the empty bottle clatter to the floor.

I slumped back against the wall and closed my eyes. The room was spinning, and it wouldn't stop. My thoughts became even more sluggish than they were before, and it was difficult to concentrate on anything. I had a hard time remembering what I was so upset about. I drifted off to sleep.

LORENZO

The van slalomed around the corner as we headed back toward town. I bounced painfully against the wall. The girl I had rescued was sitting next to me, head flopped back on the seat, totally out. Apparently she'd been drugged by the bad guys.

"Easy, Carl, don't get us killed."

"Don't you tell me easy! Plan, Lorenzo, we had a plan. Who the hell is this broad?" He swung us around a truck full of sheep, and when I say full of sheep, I mean that literally, like it was piled full with legs sticking out the top. "She was not part of the plan. I would have remembered that."

"They were going to torture her. I couldn't just leave her. She sounded like an American before she passed out. We can just drop her at the embassy gates and take off."

"Is that what you think now?" He gestured out the window at the Zubaran police vehicles streaking in the direction we had come from. "Cops crawling everywhere. And you forgot, because of the mobs of angry assholes, they evacuated the embassy."

To accentuate his point, I saw a man on the sidewalk getting the hell kicked out of him by some of the Zubaran secret police. "Okay, our place is closer. Get us off the streets." The whole city had gone nuts.

"I'm not taking her to our place. With what we're working on, nobody can see that."

"Do it, Carl." I ordered. My crew was loyal, and I seldom had to pull rank, but this was *my* crew, and it wasn't a democracy. The driver swore, his beady eyes glaring at me in the rearview mirror. We reached the compound in minutes. We entered through the attached garage so no one would see us carry the girl in.

Reaper met us at the door. He had a Glock shoved in the front of his pants. "What happened out there? Police bands are screaming about some massacre. Did you get the box? Hey . . . who's the babe?"

"Lorenzo decided he's Batman, sneaking around at night and rescuing people," Carl spat. I ignored him and carried the girl up the stairs and into the apartment. I laid her gently on the couch. She was still out.

"Where's the box?" Reaper asked.

"Somebody beat us to it and whacked Adar." I put the DVD in his hand. "The shooters are hopefully on this, and we need to figure out who they are. We need that damn box."

"On it, chief." He ran for his computer.

I flopped onto the couch next to the girl. My hands were starting to do the post-action shake. No matter how many times I did something like this, that part never changed. Carl sighed, folded the stock of his stubby Galil, and set it on the coffee table.

"Pretty bad in there, I guess?" he asked slowly, sitting down. We had been working together for over fifteen years now. We'd met in Africa, where he had been working as a mercenary, and we had both gotten screwed over by our respective employers. Working with me had proven more lucrative, and we'd been together ever since, through all sorts of craziness, and it still took me a moment to realize that Carl was *trying* to be comforting. He just wasn't very good at it.

"I shot three of them. Took out some more with a grenade." I shrugged. "The guys before me made a real mess."

Carl regarded me suspiciously, wheels turning, probably wondering if I was going soft on him. "Couldn't happen to a nicer bunch." He gestured at the girl. "And what do we do with her now?"

I studied her for the first time. She was young. Probably in her twenties. I had thought that she was from the Philippines when I had first seen her, as most of the servant girls in Zubara were imported from there or Indonesia. They were literally a slave class. Now I wasn't so sure. She would have been unusually tall for a Filipina and didn't look quite like most of the servant girls I had seen here. She was snoring peacefully in a drug-addled haze. One eye was badly bruised, and it made me glad that I had shot those men.

"I couldn't leave her. You should have seen the girl upstairs," I said. Carl didn't respond. Acts of mercy were few and far between in his life. I patted her down: no documents, no passport. Something caught my eye. "Check this out." I held up her wrist. She had a gold ring on one finger.

"What's that say?" he asked, squinting his beady eyes.

"California Polytechnic University, San Luis Obispo."

"Think she stole it off a tourist, I hope?"

"I'm thinking that we're going to need to come up with a pretty good cover story for when she wakes up." I gestured around the room. Hundreds of pictures were tacked on the walls. Posters of Al Falah, Adar, building schematics, road maps, and miscellaneous paper littered every corner of the room. A scale model of the Phase Three target was on the coffee table, and there were at least ten visible guns, and that wasn't counting the RPG in the corner.

Carl took his time responding. He would have just left her there. Hell, I don't know why I hadn't just left her behind. We were thieves, not heroes. "You're the one with the imagination. I just drive good and shoot people."

"Guys, come check this out," Reaper called excitedly from the other room. "I've got your shooters."

We entered the makeshift computer room and hovered over Reaper's shoulder. He was playing some Finnish goth-metal over the speakers. "I'm skipping past the torture porn. This Adar guy was one screwed up son of a bitch . . . and *here* is where your shooters come in."

"Why isn't there any sound?"

"Audio's all screwed up, chief. It's all static. The DVR probably didn't burn the disk properly."

"Slow it down." There were two men, dressed in camo, faces smeared with black greasepaint. They were armed with blocky submachine guns. One was just over six feet, kind of stocky, and left handed. The other was thin, a lot shorter, probably about my size. Both were Caucasians. "They're Americans."

"How can you tell already?" Reaper asked.

"That's A-TACS camo. Not that common. They're either Americans or Canadian airsofters. Look how they move, too. Pretty typical Western CQB doctrine."

The two had entered the room at the same time, weapons shouldered. The shorter one covered the room to his front, while the taller one peeled off to the right. *They've done this before.*

Their professionalism seemed to fall apart a second later as the bigger one froze when he saw the girl hanging from the ceiling. Adar turned toward the shooter with a strange look, almost a smile, on his face.

The shorter of the two shooters kept his weapon pointed at Adar. The other one just flipped out. First he said something to Adar, but the Butcher didn't seem to respond. He just stood there, smiling. It was creepy. The shooter then dropped his subgun, leaving it to hang on a single-point sling, reached down to his left thigh, and drew his handgun.

"What the hell is *that*?" Reaper asked.

"That's a .44 magnum," I said as the shooter put a round into Adar's left knee. The kneecap exploded into blood and pulp, and the Butcher of Zubara dropped to the floor. The other infiltrator flinched and covered his ears as the powerful weapon discharged.

From there, the shooter proceeded to take Adar apart piece by piece, systematically. Adar tried to say something, holding up his right hand, only to get it blown off. The next round went into Adar's left bicep, mangling his arm in a spray of blood.

The shooter's accuracy was impressive. The fourth slug went into Adar's gut. The fifth went into his neck, nearly taking his head off. The shooter then reloaded automatically, mechanically, without thought. *Damn, he's fast.* He had the gun reloaded and the cylinder closed before the emptied speed loader hit the floor. I absentmindedly pulled the .44 shell out of my pocket. I flipped it end over end between my fingers as I watched.

After the execution, the two shooters seemed to argue for a moment, then cut the mutilated girl down.

The pair then quickly ransacked the bedroom. Before they left, the tall one dropped the Ace of Spades onto Adar's bleeding corpse. A grotesque grin remained on the Butcher of Zubara's face.

"Who are these *fodas*?" Carl asked.

"Who the hell carries a *revolver* anymore?" Reaper asked.

Somebody who's really good with one and knows it, I thought. "Like I said, Dirty Harry."

"Look at these guys!" Carl was pissed. "What's with the camouflage? Kids these days all want to wear camouflage and gear and play dress up! How are they going to explain that if they got picked up by the cops?"

"They'd just shoot the cops." A professional should never be this brazen when there were more subtle ways available to pop somebody. "Play back when they're arguing." The taller shooter was young. He didn't have a killer's face, but there was no hesitation when he'd stitched those massive slugs through Adar. "He's definitely American. Looks pretty corn-fed. He's a pasty northern Midwesterner, probably has a cheese-wedge hat at home."

"How can you tell when you can't hear what he's saying?" Carl asked suspiciously.

"It's in the way he moves. I do this for a living, remember? His mannerisms, his gear, his clothing, all point to the USA. He might as well be wearing an Uncle Sam hat."

"I guess. Well, when you play an Arab, I don't recognize you, down to the dress and the perfume. You say he's American, I believe you," Reaper said.

"Go back a bit." Carl frowned. "These guys have to stick out. How many Americans are in Zubara?"

"Officially? A couple thousand," Reaper replied automatically. "And thousands more assorted Europeans. Mostly in Al Khor. If these guys have been operating in the poor side of town, they'd totally stick out."

"Reaper, grab my notepad from the living room. We've got contacts in every district. I'm going to give a few of them a call."

Reaper nodded, adjusted his Glock, and left the room.

"Kid's gonna shoot his balls off, carrying his gun like that." Carl said. Reaper flipped him the bird on his way out.

"We don't have very good health insurance in this business, either," I muttered, studying the faces of my new adversaries. These men were standing in the way of me completing Phase Three. Until I had that box, all of our work was worthless. Without that box, our families belonged to Big Eddie. I did not know who these mystery shooters were, but my new mission in life was to find them and kill them if I had to. I blew up the picture until it became grainy, zooming in on the tall one. These men knew their business. This was going to be a challenge.

There was a sudden crash and a surprised yelp from the living room. Carl and I both drew our guns and moved apart. I disengaged the safety on my

STI and pointed it at the doorway. Carl took up position behind the desk, CZ extended in front of him.

"Reaper?" I shouted. "You okay?"

Our guest had awoken. Reaper stumbled into the doorway, his arms raised in a surrender position. The girl stood behind him with his Glock 19 pressed into the base of his neck. I didn't have a shot.

"Sorry, chief," he said slowly.

The girl glared over Reaper's shoulder. The drugs must have worn off enough for her to come to, and she was obviously angry and confused. Her eyes darted about between us. "Nobody move! I'll shoot this guy right in the head," she ordered. I had been right. She was an American, and she apparently knew how to use that Glock. "Who are you people? What am I doing here?"

"That's kind of complicated."

She tightened her grip on the Glock. I could imagine a 9mm exploding through Reaper's head. "Give me the short version, asshole!"

"Okay. So there I was, minding my own business . . . and I ran into some very bad men who had you tied up and were taking you into a house where you were going to be tortured to death on video. I, uh, rescued you." The girl looked kind of out of it, disoriented and scared. She was still under the influence of whatever drug they had given her. And her finger was resting on the trigger that decided whether one of my crew lived or died. "We're friends."

"You expect me to believe that?" she shouted, blinking rapidly. Reaper cringed as she banged the Glock into the base of his skull.

"Look, we're not your enemies. See?" I slowly placed my 9mm on the table and stepped away. "Carl, put your gun down."

"But—"

"Do it!" I ordered. Even worse than her killing Reaper would be the noise. Our complex was crowded with rental villas, and I had no doubt that Zubaran fuzz would be crawling all over a gunshot call within minutes. Carl grudgingly responded and placed his CZ on the floor. "My name is Lorenzo. I saw that you were in danger, and I helped. I brought you back here, because the streets are covered in cops, and all hell has broken loose out there. Let me help you." Why had I brought her to our hideout? Damn needless complications.

"Okay, I don't think you're with those men that grabbed me, but who are you, really?" She was scared, but she was hard, and her grip on the gun didn't loosen. "You're an American, at least."

"You first," I suggested soothingly. Plus it gave me a moment to try to think of some sort of plausible cover story.

"I'm with the US government," she snapped.

You have got to be fucking kidding me. "Good," I said as calmly as possible. If I had brought a fed or a spy back to our hideout, it was either screw the mission or kill her. Neither one sounded like a good option. I caught Carl casting me a look, letting me know how stupid he thought I was. "We're on the same side. We're on a top-secret mission. And if you blow Special Agent Wheaton's brains all over the walls, you're going to have some explaining to do to your superiors, and I probably won't be able to get the security deposit back on this apartment."

When you have to lie, you might as well reach for the stars.

"Are you Dead Six?" she asked unsteadily. Her eyes had narrowed to dangerous slits, and her teeth were a hard white line on her darkly tanned face. I paused, not sure how to answer. "Are *you* with Dead Six?" she repeated.

Fifty-fifty chance on this one. "Yes."

"I knew it!" she shouted as she stepped back from Reaper. The muzzle of the Glock was swinging toward me. The 9mm hole looked unnaturally large as the contents of my stomach turned to ice. I threw myself to the side, but I already knew it wouldn't be fast enough.

Click.

Reaper disdained holsters, and since he tended to just shove the gun in his pants, he usually carried chamber-empty. Carl and I called him a sissy for doing that, but as I hit the floor, I was mighty glad Reaper was a sissy.

The girl apparently knew guns, and she instinctively reached up with her left hand and began to rack the slide. The world seemed to dial down into slow motion as Reaper spun and charged her, his stringy black hair rising like a halo. He hit her hard, and they both disappeared into the living room.

I was up in a flash, moving toward the scuffle. In the corner of my vision, I saw Carl scooping up his gun. Reaper and the girl were wrestling for the Glock, the muzzle pointed upward between their faces. He was much taller, but she was stronger than she looked.

Beginning to lose the struggle, she let go of the gun and threw her elbow into Reaper's temple. His head snapped back like his neck was a spring. Our techie went to the ground in a heap, but at least he took the Glock with him.

Carl had drawn down on her. "Don't shoot!" I shouted as I leapt over Reaper. "Too loud!" The girl had gone into a crouch, hands open in front of her face. Carl turned and disappeared from the room. *Thanks for the help there, buddy.* The girl circled, waiting for me. Apparently this chick knew how to fight, and I didn't like hitting girls.

"Just calm dow—" She cut me off with a snap kick at my groin. I swept one hand down to block, but it had just been a feint. She hit me with a back fist on my cheek hard enough to rattle my teeth. That hurt. I stepped back, eyes watering, and cracked my knuckles one-handed. "Oh, it's gonna be like that, huh?"

"I'm not going to let you kill me, too," she spat. She charged with a scream, throwing wild punches. She was desperate, but I was a professional. I dodged and swept them aside, waiting for a clean shot. She fought surprisingly well for a girl, and if it wasn't for the fact that I was going to have to knock her the hell out, I could almost admire the ferocity.

Suddenly Reaper's terrible music began to blare, painfully loud. The speakers on the computer probably near overload. *What the hell?* Carl came storming back into the room. He had my pistol and was screwing my sound suppressor onto the end of the threaded muzzle. It was difficult to hear him over the noise. "I'm too old for this hand-to-hand crap." He raised the 9mm and fired. The Zubara phone book sitting on the couch exploded into confetti. The *thump* of the silenced gun was barely discernible over the wailing guitars. He turned the gun on the girl. "Cool down, missy, or your head gets the next one."

Eyes wide, she slowly raised her hands in surrender. I slugged her hard in the stomach, knocking the wind out her and sending her to the floor. Violence against women doesn't count when they start it, and I wasn't going to trust her as far as I could throw her. Somebody banged on the other side of the living-room wall. Our neighbors were probably cursing us.

"You got her, chief?" Carl asked with a grin. "I'm gonna turn this garbage down. Kids today, Reaper, how can you listen to such noise?" Our techie moaned on the floor in response.

"Reaper, you okay?" I asked. The girl had gotten to her hands and knees, gasping. Flicking open my Benchmade, I placed the knife against her neck. She felt the steel there and froze, knowing that this fight was over. Reaper grunted, indicating that he would live. "Good. Grab some rope."

The three of us and our captive were in the living room. The music was turned off, and everyone was a whole lot calmer. The girl was sitting on the loveseat, hands tied behind her back and, just to be safe, ankles tied together, too. I had my suppressed pistol in my hand, Carl had a beer, and Reaper was holding an ice pack against his head. "No wonder they drugged her," he muttered.

"Okay, let's try this again, without all the hitting and shooting and stuff. Who are you, and why were you being held by Adar's men?"

"What's an Adar?" she asked.

"Evil, crazy guy, planned on doing really bad things to you and then selling the video to demented freaks to masturbate to, but sadly he's on an express train to hell right now. That's an Adar," I said patiently. "And your name?"

She answered sullenly, realizing that she might as well cooperate. "My name's Jill . . . Jill Del Toro. I used to work at the American embassy."

"Used to? Who were you with? State Department? CIA? NSA?"

"Um . . . the Department of Agriculture."

I raised one eyebrow. "Okay, then. Please tell me that was some sort of cover, and you're some sort of super spy or something?" I didn't want to think that somebody from the Department of Cows and Plows had almost been the death of my team of professional killers.

"No, that's Rob Clancy stuff. I was temporarily on loan to the State Department, but I was basically a receptionist . . . well . . . I was an intern."

"Tom Clancy," Reaper corrected. "Wait . . . intern? What the hell?"

"You got beat up by an intern," Carl laughed. "Oh, man. That's good."

"I'm working on my master's degree, political science, and was doing a tour of US aid programs around the Middle East. Did you know they actually have dairy farms in Saudi Arabia?"

"Fascinating. Stick to the subject," I ordered, gesturing with my 9mm for emphasis.

"I found out about something that I wasn't supposed to. I saw them kill the assistant-ambassador. The Dead Six guys tried to shoot me, but I ran. I got lost in town, and that's when those crazy guys grabbed me and stuck a needle in my arm. I woke up here." She sighed. "I swear, I don't know much about Dead Six, but I know you plan to kill me, so let's get this over with. I'm not going to beg."

"Tell me what you do know about Dead Six first."

"I know you're some sort of secret death squad. The ambassador was told not to talk about it by your boss, that Gordon guy. You guys killed Jim Fiore for asking too many questions, and I was just in the wrong place. I don't know anything!" The girl looked like she could cry, but was too mad. "Screw it. So let's do this, you *pinche pendejo* cowards."

"Did she just call us what I think she called us?" Reaper asked.

"I think so." Carl chuckled approvingly.

The girl was tough, and pretty, too. Even tired, dirty, with one blackened eye, and being generally disheveled, I could tell that she was probably normally very attractive in an athletic kind of way. Her hair was long and extremely dark. On the other hand, I was probably old enough to be her dad, or at least her dad's younger brother. "Calm down. We're not Black Flag, or Dead Six, or Ninja Force Alpha, or whatever, and we're not going to kill you," I said.

"Really? Who are you then?" There was a sudden hope in her voice. She studied the pictures and maps on the walls, the piles of weapons and equipment, and the model building on the table. "Wait a second . . . What the hell are you?"

"Well, we aren't the good guys," Carl grunted, "if that's what you're hoping for."

"We're criminals," I stated. "You got a problem with that?"

"But . . . you're not going to kill me?"

"Only if you give me a pressing reason," I responded, deep in thought. This Dead Six, whatever the hell that meant, was who had Adar's box, and, if this Jill was telling the truth, which my gut told me she was, then I now held something that *they* wanted.

I had a witness to their black op. I wasn't adverse to the idea of arranging a trade. Worst case scenario, I could use her as bait. Sucked for her, but that wasn't my problem. I jerked my head at Reaper. "Check her out." He looked at me in confusion. I sighed. He really didn't get to spend much time around women that weren't being paid to pole dance. "On the *computer*."

"Oh, gotcha," Reaper replied as he left the room, returning a moment later with his laptop. He started doing his thing while Jill glanced between us suspiciously. It only took him a few seconds. "You're dead," he said without looking up. "Officially at least."

"That was quick." I said.

"It wasn't like I had to look hard." He flipped the screen around so I could see it.

It was on the *Drudge Report*. The headline said Four US Embassy Staff Killed in Zubara. It took me a second to scan the article. Apparently during the evacuation, an embassy car had been struck by gunfire then firebombed. It was a terrible tragedy, killing the assistant to the ambassador, two US Marines, and an intern. This was sure to cause even more strain in the already tense relations, blah blah blah. I turned the screen so Jill could see it. "That's a nice picture they got of you," I said.

"Oh my God." Jill turned almost as white as Reaper. "I can't believe this."

"I hate to break it to you, but some very powerful people have decided that you being alive is inconvenient," I replied, wheels turning. Dead Six had marked her for death. I could use her. *Which meant that she needed to trust me.* "Believe it. You've got nowhere to run." I pulled out my knife and flicked it open. "If you promise to quit hitting us and taking my people hostage, I'll let you loose. But if you try to run off, I'm going to have to shoot you, okay?"

"I promise."

"What are you doing?" Reaper asked, suddenly wary at the idea of turning this particular firecracker loose. "You sure this is . . . ?" He trailed off as I glared at him. "Never mind."

"Jill, is it?" She nodded. I proceeded to cut the rope around her wrists. "The way I see it, you have a problem. You've been declared dead by some sort of black operations guys. Official channels will only hurt you, not help you. This country has gone crazy. There's a war going on, and you're now in the middle of it. If the government finds you, then you're dead. If the secret police find you, then you're dead. And if you get picked up by the kind of people I saved you from tonight, you're worse than dead. You will need the assistance of, shall we say, a criminal element to get out of this country alive. Preferably honest, and dare I say, charming criminals, versus the standard underachievers who gravitate toward that career field."

She rubbed her wrists. "And you know where I can find some people like this, I assume?"

"Perhaps. We have a very difficult job to do, and I think that you might be helpful. You don't have any moral qualms about helping us out, in exchange for us getting you out of the country, do you? Considering that the kind of people I rob are the kind of people who want you dead."

"Okay," Jill answered after a long pause. "This . . . this is a lot to process. Can you really help me?"

"I can, but you have to help us first."

"You can't be serious, chief," Reaper stated. The side of his head was turning a nasty shade of purple.

Jill nervously looked around the room, obviously unsure of what to do. "Well, you saved my life. What is it you need from me? How can I possibly help you guys?"

"We'll worry about that later," I said, sounding as reassuring as I could. I'm really good at sounding reassuring when I need to. "For now, welcome aboard."

Carl began to laugh, a deep, rumbling belly laugh. The mercenary did not laugh much.

"What's so funny?" I asked.

"We got us an intern. Haw!"

While Carl was busy changing the license plates on the van and Reaper was tending to his bruised face and ego, I showed the video of the two shooters to Jill. I made sure to back it up far enough for her to see what I had saved her from. She visibly cringed and had to look away when she saw the mutilated girl.

"That would have been you," I said patiently. "Now I need you to keep watching." If anything should make her thankful for me coming along, that had to be it. Watching Adar get blasted seemed to cheer her up. Unfortunately she didn't recognize either of the Dead Six operatives.

"The only ones I ever saw was a really normal-looking white guy, probably forty-five or so, named Gordon. The other two I didn't get as good a look at, well . . . because they were trying to kill me. One had real short hair, looked like a former soldier, the other I didn't see hardly at all, but he was this really big, muscled blond guy. All of them wore suits. Gordon did all the talking," she explained. "Sorry. I don't even know if Gordon was his first name or last."

"Won't be his real name anyway," I responded. "Start from the beginning."

She sighed as she pulled up a seat. I could tell that she was exhausted and emotionally fried. "Originally I was working out of the embassy in Doha, Qatar. It's a lot bigger. But they were short clerical staff here, so I got volunteered. At the time everybody told me how *boring* Zubara was supposed to be. I had never even heard of the place before. It wasn't supposed to be anything big, just catching up on basic paperwork so the ambassador could go around shaking hands. This was supposed to have been my last week, then I was going home."

"Bummer," I said, shoving her a bottle of water and a couple of pills. She looked at the pills suspiciously. "Ibuprofen," I explained. "Sorry about punching you, but you brought it on yourself. Then what happened?"

"Well, there really aren't that many Americans here, and those that do live here are pretty self-contained, oil or natural-gas guys, with their own compounds, so it wasn't like they ever needed us. There really wasn't much for us to do. It isn't like this is an important assignment. The ambassador's this old guy, used to be the mayor of some town in Kentucky, got the job because he worked on the president's political campaign. He just drank and slept all day." She actually smiled at the thought. "That's your tax dollars at work."

I just nodded. I hadn't paid taxes in, well, *ever*.

"Then it started getting crazy."

"I was here for that part." I didn't add that I had probably contributed to that state of affairs.

"Some men had been killed while trying to murder some of the locals. They appeared to be Americans. The Zubaran security forces freaked out at us, but the ambassador assured them that it wasn't us. Then more and more bad things started happening, and we got the word to pack. It was the assistant to the ambassador, a guy named Jim Fiore, real nice guy, who took care of all the day-to-day stuff. He kept calling people in Washington, trying to figure out what was going on."

"Like who?" I asked. If I could narrow down what kind of operation Dead Six was, it might help me track them down.

She shrugged. "It wasn't like I got to hear the calls. That's way over my piddly clearance. I just know that he was in his office on the phone non-stop for two days. He used to talk to this old army buddy of his all the time, I think he's an FBI agent now, but other than that, I don't know. There were three of us left to help Jim at that point. We were mostly just shredding papers, and it wasn't like there was anything important in there, it was just standard procedure. There was a mob outside the gates, protesting, burning flags, and it was pretty scary, but they hadn't turned violent yet other than throwing some rocks at the gate."

"When did this Gordon show up?"

"It was the last day of the evacuation. Everybody else had left except for us and some of the Marines, but they were all manning the gate. I had been assigned to be Mr. Fiore's secretary. His regular one had been diagnosed with pancreatic cancer last month and had to fly home . . . uh, never mind, doesn't matter. So I was working for Jim, and he was still making phone calls. I was in back shredding papers when Gordon came barging in." Jill's voice grew quieter. "He started yelling, telling Jim that he needed to shut up, and quit asking questions, that none of this was his business. Jim got all angry and said that Dead Six was destroying the country. That was the first time I had heard the name."

"So they shot him?"

"Oh, no, not then. The Marines would have torn them apart, I don't care who they were. No, when Jim said Dead Six, Gordon got all quiet, like he was surprised at the name, and said that they were done here. Then he left. It wasn't until later . . ." Jill paused to wipe under her eyes. It almost made me feel bad for using her. "About twenty minutes later we left for the airport with an escort, two Marines, both really cool guys that I knew. We were almost there when the Marines got a call that that there was another riot on the route that we were on, and we were supposed to take a different way. We pulled off onto this quiet street and there was another government car there waiting to meet us."

I nodded. That's probably how I would have done it.

"Two guys, the Marines acted like they recognized them, they walked right up to the windows like they were friendly as could be and just started . . . started shooting . . ." Jill paused for a really long time. "I'm sorry . . ."

Brutal. "How'd you get out?"

"They shot the guards in the front seat first, probably because they were more scared of them. They just shot *forever*. Mr. Fiore was hit, blood was going everywhere, but he opened the door and managed to get out while they were reloading."

"Typical mistake. Bullets act weird when you're shooting through window glass. You get a lot of deflection with handguns," I explained. She looked at me with bloodshot eyes. She had been crying. It made me uncomfortable. "Sorry."

"Mr. Fiore, Jim, was a tough dude. He grabbed the big blond one and I just ran. I ran while they shot him over and over and over. I didn't look back, but I could hear him screaming. I *felt* the bullets go by me. I just ran between the houses until I couldn't anymore."

Jill had started weeping. This wasn't exactly my cup of tea. What was I supposed to say? *Sorry your life is ruined and your government wants you dead, but shit happens.* I awkwardly reached over and patted her on the knee. It seemed like the human thing to do.

She continued. "I hid in an alley for hours. I didn't speak the language. I was scared to death. When I finally saw a police officer, I ran over to him. He talked to me long enough to find out I was an American. He called someone on his radio. Then he had me sit in the back of his car while we drove across town. I thought he was taking me to the police station, but instead he took me to those assholes who drugged me." She wiped her nose and sniffed, regaining her composure. "And after seeing that video, thanks for taking care of them."

I smiled. She was actually kind of cute. A little while ago she had been trying to kill me, and now she needed a *moment*. "It was no problem." I wasn't the best at comforting people, but I was pretty good at killing people.

"Look, I'm about to pass out. I've had a hell of a day. Do you have a place I can sleep?"

I nodded. "Yeah, we've got a spare bedroom. Just . . . you know."

"Don't try to escape or you'll shoot me," she replied. "Where would I go? Who would I call? I've got no family. I can't call my employers. I'm assuming that everybody I know has their phone tapped already. Don't worry. I won't do anything stupid."

I showed her to the spare room. There was no window, no phone, and the way I slept, she would have to be a ghost to sneak out, but I would rig the door with a motion detector after she fell asleep. The apartment had an alarm, and I'd arm the perimeter, too, just in case. "You've got a bed, pillow, and a minimal number of roaches. Sorry I don't have any spare girl clothes, but I can come up with something tomorrow. The bathroom's that door there, complete with actual toilet or squatty hole and spray hose. Personal preference, I guess."

Jill paused in the doorway. "I just realized. You saved my life, and I don't even know your name."

I gave her a weak smile. "I'm Lorenzo. The skinny one you beat up is Reaper. The hairy one is Carl. And if you're wondering, yes, those are all made up and won't do you a bit of good."

"Good night, Lorenzo. And thanks." She closed the door.

Carl was waiting for me around the corner. "You're an idiot," he whispered.

I nodded. "So what's new?"

The short Portagee folded his burly arms and glared at me. "You're jeopardizing the whole job to take in some broad. You forget the part where Big Eddie kills everybody if we screw up? How does this help us?"

"I take it you heard her story?"

"I listened in. She doesn't know squat about these Dead Six *fodas*. She's useless."

"Helping her was the right thing to do," I said.

Carl snorted. "And since when did you start caring about what's *right*? I've known you a long time, Lorenzo. You don't care about right and wrong. When you meet people, they go in one of two groups: Are they a threat, or can you use them somehow? I was surprised you cared so much about this family of yours, that I've never heard you talk about, to risk your neck."

That was because the people in that folder were the only people who had ever been decent to me, but that went unsaid. "I like a few people."

"I shouldn't count," Carl replied.

"Of course not. You're unlikable," I said. Carl nodded as if this was the wisest thing he'd heard. "Look, I've got other things in mind for the girl. Dead Six will be looking for her. She's an in against them. And if they want her bad enough, they'll trade us that damned box."

Carl rubbed his stubbly face as he thought about that. "That's cold, even for you. I don't know. I'm gonna have to sleep on that. Whatever you do, don't tell Reaper. The kid will never go for it." He turned and walked away, shaking his head.

Sometimes it's hard being the bad guy.

The Fat Man picked up on the first ring. "Hello, Mr. Lorenzo."

Did he ever sleep? "We've completed Phase Two, but there's been a complication."

"Our employer does not like *complications*."

"Adar is dead, but his box is missing."

"My goodness. That certainly is bad news. I do hope that this will not unduly hinder you."

"I need information. I need to know about an American operation being conducted in Zubara called Dead Six. At least, the operatives I saw were American. I believe they have the box. If any of Eddie's people hear anything, I need to know."

"But of course," the Fat Man said. "Is that all?"

"That's all. Is this the part where you randomly threaten children to keep me in line?"

"Good-bye, Mr. Lorenzo." And he was gone.

Chapter 9: The To-Do List

VALENTINE
Fort Saradia National Historical Site
April 16
0900

I opened my eyes to the sound of someone pounding on my door. My head throbbed with each blow. Using the wall to prop myself up, I struggled to my feet and answered the knock.

It was Conrad, Hunter's security man. Next to him was another guy I'd seen before but whose name I didn't recall. They were dressed like twins in 5.11 vests and Oakley sunglasses. "Valentine, come with us," Conrad said bluntly.

I looked at my watch. "What's happening?"

"Just come with us." Conrad put a hand on my shoulder and pulled me out of the room.

"Hey!" I protested, groggily. My left hand reflexively reached for my S&W .44; it was still in its holster.

"Hold it right there!" Conrad's partner shouted, immediately producing a pistol from under his vest. He held the Sig 220 in a tight two-handed grip, pointed at my right ear.

"Whoa whoa whoa!" I said, raising my hands, head pounding with each word. "Everybody calm down! What the hell's going on here?"

"Put your hands behind your head!" Conrad's partner demanded.

"Do it," Conrad said. He yanked my .44 out of its holster and stuffed it into his waistband. I had little choice; I slowly laced my fingers behind my head. Conrad then shoved my face into the concrete wall. Pain shot through my skull at the impact. They kept me pinned as my hands were pulled behind my back and roughly zip-tied together. Conrad spun me around, and his partner punched me in the stomach, *hard.*

I doubled over, gasping for air. Conrad was holding my zip-tied hands and wouldn't let me fall. "Hunter is waiting for you," he said. The two men shoved me toward the stairs and marched me across the compound. Conrad had his hand on my shoulder while his partner stayed a few paces away, ready to shoot me if I ran.

It had been a long time since I'd been that hung over, and I wasn't handling it well. The morning heat was oppressive. Once we cleared the shade of the covered hallway, it felt like the sun would burn my hair off. I squinted in the light, and my head ached with each step.

Other Dead Six personnel watched quietly as I was paraded across Fort Saradia. I was furious. Beyond that, a small pit was forming in my stomach. As we grew nearer and nearer to the admin building, I began to wonder if Hunter was going to have me shot.

"Wait, wait, we gotta stop." I leaned forward and threw up.

"Heh, looks like our boy doesn't feel so good," one of the security men said. Conrad and his partner had a good laugh at my expense before dragging me along again.

As we approached the administrative building, Sarah stepped out into the morning sun, putting on sunglasses as she cleared the door. She froze when she saw me being pushed along by Hunter's men, blood trickling down the side of my head, hands tied behind my back. Her mouth opened, but she didn't say anything. I just looked at the ground.

A few minutes later, I was sitting outside of Hunter's office, being watched by one security guy while Conrad was inside talking to the colonel. After a short time I was marched in and pushed into a chair in front of Hunter's desk.

Looking around, I realized I'd never actually been in the office before. It had once belonged to Fort Saradia's commanding officer. It was under new management now. Several screens were mounted in various places, and bundles of wires were strung along the floor and ceiling. Maps of the city, of the CGEZ, and of the entire Middle East were hung on the walls. The air stank of cigar smoke. The two security men loomed over me as I sat there.

Hunter regarded me quietly. His gaze was hard and unsettling. He had only one eye, but it could look at you twice as hard.

"Colonel?" I began, choosing my words carefully. "What did I do?" I struggled to think clearly; my head felt like it was full of peanut butter.

"Gentlemen, take a walk," Hunter said, dismissing his two men. As they left the room, he turned his attention to me. "Miss McAllister informed me that you were drunk off your ass last night and seemed unstable. And now Conrad tells me you went for your weapon when they woke you."

Hunter paused for effect. "Mr. Valentine, we're having this little chat to determine if you're still fit to go on missions. So tell me, son, what the hell is your problem?"

"It was . . . bad . . . last night, sir. I did things I regret. I was under a lot of stress. I took it out on Sarah, and I shouldn't have. But I don't understand why I got dragged in here at gunpoint."

Hunter studied me for a moment before speaking. "I know all about you and McAllister, by the way. I know you've been diddling each other like a couple of high-school kids. I don't give a damn about that. I'm only telling you so you're not under the impression that anything happens around here without my knowledge. What I do give a damn about is one of my best men trying to drink himself stupid after a mission, especially given the operational tempo we're dealing with. I seem to recall telling you no alcohol until further notice. As a matter of fact, you're supposed to go out again tonight."

"But sir!" I protested. "I'm—"

"Hung over?" Hunter interjected. "I can see that. You look like hell, Mr. Valentine. You reek of alcohol. What the hell were you drinking, Av-Gas?"

"I . . . don't really know, sir. I don't remember much."

"I bet," Hunter said. "I'm asking you again, now, what's your problem?"

"There were some things we left out of our report, sir," I said quietly. "About what we found in Umm Bab."

"Oh?" Hunter asked, raising the eyebrow above his eye patch. I spent the next few minutes recapping the grisly scene we discovered in Adar's bedroom. My voice broke a few times as I talked about the mutilated girl.

Hunter quietly let me finish. "Well, that makes sense now," he said at last. He thought about it for a long, uncomfortable moment. "I guess you're lucky."

"Sir?"

"You heard me. My first inclination was to throw you in the brig for a couple weeks. Unfortunately, we don't have time for that, and we're too short on personnel. You will not jeopardize this mission. Another episode and I'll send you home."

I couldn't believe what I'd just heard. "Send me *home*?"

"Well, I'll send you back to Gordon Willis. He'll probably make you disappear. I doubt you'll end up back wherever it is you came from. I've only sent one person back so far, and I don't know what happened to him. If you follow orders until the project is over, you won't have to find out. Am I making myself clear, Mr. Valentine?"

"Perfectly, sir," I replied.

"Outstanding," Hunter said.

"Sir, can you untie me now?"

"In a minute. Listen up. Your next mission is very important. So far, the project has been going well. Very well. We have the enemy running scared, and the rumors are flying. Many suspect Americans, but we're too aggressive. Most think it's the Israelis, or the emir's secret police. The nice thing about shaking the bushes like that is that once in a while something good comes running out."

"I'm not sure I follow you, sir."

"We've been approached by a contact that wants to make a deal. She's willing to exchange information for protection. We're working on setting up the meeting now. The name she gave us is Asra Elnadi. We believe she's a former partner of one of the local arms dealers, Jalal Hosani."

"I've heard that name before."

"Mr. Hosani is on our to-do list. He's been running guns to anyone in the region with the cash to buy them. As a matter of fact, we think he provided most of the weapons you torched in Ash Shamal. But he's not the issue right now. Our contact says she left Hosani to go work with one of his competitors, a Russian syndicate run by one Anatoly Federov. He's on the list, too, and he's higher up on it than Hosani. He's not only running guns but is providing explosives and advisers. The training he offers is a lot better than the Iranians."

"So what's the deal?"

"It's simple, really. She wants to meet with our people. She'll divulge everything she knows about both Federov and Hosani if we get her out of the country."

"Do you think she's worth the trouble?"

"I do. So here's what's going to happen." Colonel Hunter spent the next few minutes giving me a brief rundown of his mission plan. I listened intently, despite being in pain and having my hands tied behind my back.

It was simple enough. One of our people would meet Asra at a predetermined location. We'd screen her, make sure she checked out, and would then bring her to one of our safe houses. If she was legit, we'd get her out of the country. Hunter seemed reasonably confident that things would go smoothly, but operational experience had dulled my optimism somewhat.

Half an hour later, I left Hunter's office and headed down the hall to the security office, rubbing the raw spots on my wrists where the zip ties had been. My head still ached, and all I wanted to do was crawl back into bed.

Conrad was sitting at a desk, clicking away at a laptop when I walked in. I spotted my .44 sitting on a shelf behind his desk. "I'm here for my gun," I said simply. I really didn't feel like having another conversation with this asshole.

Conrad didn't look up from his screen. "Well, if it isn't Doc Holliday looking for his big shootin' iron."

My head still throbbed, and I felt a surge of anger shoot through me. "Just give me my gun so I can go," I said, stepping closer to Conrad's desk.

"The colonel thinks you're hot shit. That's the only reason you didn't end up in the Gulf," Conrad said, grabbing my revolver from his shelf. "You know what I think?"

"I don't really care," I stated. "Just give me my gun."

"I think you're just a dumb kid who's in way over his head," Conrad said, pretending to examine my revolver. He then set it down on his desk with a clunk.

The muzzle was facing toward me as I grabbed the .44. As I stood up, I flipped the gun around in my hand and extended my arm. I aligned the sights on the bridge of Conrad's nose. I'd had enough of these people.

I pulled the trigger.

Click! Conrad raised an eyebrow as the revolver's hammer fell on an empty chamber. I pulled the gun in close to my chest and hit the cylinder release. The security man had unloaded it before giving it back to me. I could tell the moment I picked it up. Smart move on his part.

He put his hand on the butt of his gun. "You trying to scare me or something? I'm with the *organization*," he sputtered, like I knew what he was talking about. "You're a fucking *temp*. You're *nothing*."

"I'll see you later, asshole," I said. I holstered my gun, turned on a heel, and left the office.

I made my way downstairs and out the front door, almost crashing into Sarah as I stepped back into the heat. "Michael!" she said, seemingly unsure of what to say. "What happened to you?"

I almost laughed. "What *happened?* Hunter was ready to shoot me, that's what happened!"

"Michael, I didn't mean for—"

I cut her off. "No. Just stop. I learned a long time ago not to fish out of the company pond, and this is why. As soon as I piss you off, you run to the boss, and I get the *shit* kicked out of me. So just stay away from me, alright? I got a mission to plan." I stepped around her and walked away, not looking back.

It took me a few minutes to get back up to my room. Sweat was trickling down my face by the time I made it to the third floor of the dorms, and I thought I was going to pass out. I locked the door behind me, cranked the air conditioner up, and sat down on my bed.

I noticed something shiny on the floor by the bathroom door. It had fallen out of the old Arabian puzzle box. The object was silver in color and had a silver chain attached to one end. I grabbed the chain and picked the trinket up.

It was roughly cylindrical, a few inches long and maybe as big around as a ballpoint pen. Surprisingly heavy, the object was intricately carved and looked as it if had many moving parts. It also looked very old. The top of the object, where the chain was attached, appeared to be a knob. I gently tried to rotate it to see if anything would happen.

To my surprise, the thing audibly clicked and more than a dozen tiny metal pins of varying lengths popped out of the shaft. Rotating the knob the other way caused the pins to disappear again.

I sat back down on my bed, playing with the trinket, wondering what it was. It seemed like a key of some kind, but that was only a guess on my part. Whatever the object was, it was still in my hand when I fell asleep.

I told myself it was a coincidence, but I had the most macabre, horrifying nightmares of my entire life.

LORENZO
April 16

I was wandering the local market when my cell phone buzzed. It was secure, encrypted, and not very many people had my number. *Caller unknown.* Glancing around, there was nobody close enough to eavesdrop, and there was enough background hum from the various vendors and customers that listening in would be difficult. Half the Arab world was on a cell phone at any given time anyway.

"I heard you were looking for me," Jalal Hosani said, cutting right to the point. I had been trying to reach him all week. If anybody knew what was really going on, it would be the local neighborhood arms smuggler.

"I need some information."

"As do I." There was a long pause on the other end of the line. "Are you involved in what has been happening?"

"Not my style. You know that." I had the professional reputation of being a man of subtlety. "I was actually going to ask you the same question."

Jalal actually laughed. "Are you serious? I've been afraid to stick my head out in public for fear of losing it to these men leaving the playing cards."

I paused in front of one of the carts. They actually had good-looking chili peppers, and I was a bit of a connoisseur. Even the smell was *hot*. I gestured for them to fill a bag. "So, how's business treating you?" I asked as I passed over a few riyals to the eager vendor and put the peppers with the rest of the supplies I'd purchased.

"Well, half my customer base is dead or hiding, but the other half has been stocking up on guns in response, so overall it has been good. At this rate we'll be in full-fledged revolution in a matter of months." Jalal said that like it was a good thing, simply a business opportunity. "Why are you curious? I thought a *patriot* such as yourself would be glad to see such enemies of your homeland eliminated."

I wasn't going to lie. If it wasn't for Dead Six having my box, they could burn the entire city down and I wouldn't give a damn. "They took something that belongs to me. I need to find them."

"Not that I know where they are, but if I were to find such a thing, that information would be incredibly valuable to many people. I'm sure General Al Sabah, for instance, would be willing to pay a fortune."

"So would Big Eddie," I responded as I stopped in front of another booth featuring camel, the other, other white meat. *Yum.* "He's got deeper pockets than the general, but you know how he feels about being exclusive," I bluffed. I didn't have access to Eddie's resources, but I would cross that bridge when I came to it. "Does the name Dead Six mean anything to you?"

"Perhaps," Jalal responded after a moment of thought. "I will be in touch." The call ended.

I shook my head. Hopefully Jalal would come up with something. That man had his finger on the pulse of the city's criminal heart. Now I was just going to have to work my sources until I found something about Dead Six that I could use. *Well, why the hell not?* I ordered a pound of camel. You only live once.

The short walk back to the apartment compound gave me a chance to think. I had one weapon I could use against Dead Six to get them in the open, young Jill Del Toro, but I was hesitant to utilize her. The idea made me uncomfortable. Carl had been right. I used people. That's what I did. It didn't mean I had to like it.

Carl had said that he was surprised that I was sticking my neck out for my family. They weren't even my blood relations, but they had taken me in. They were the only people who'd ever been good to me. I had grown up on the streets, son of a drug-addled whore and a homicidal beast of a man. I'd been put to work stealing as soon as I was old enough not to get caught, and I had been an overachiever in that respect. By the time I was ten, there wasn't a lock I couldn't pick, no pocket I couldn't get into undetected. I had been a tiny shrimp of a kid, and though that had been handy for fitting through various unsecured windows, it had made me look like an easy target for the other predators. I had solved that by developing a reputation for savage violence. Pipe, knife, chain, brick, it didn't matter. I never fought *fair*. Cross me and I kill you.

I had kept that attitude into adulthood, and it had served me well. There had only been one point in my life where I hadn't had to fight to survive. It had been brief, but I had appreciated it. The people in that manila folder were responsible for that, and I would be damned if I was going to let Big Eddie hurt them for it.

If that meant I had to hurt some other seemingly decent person . . . so be it. In the end it was all just an equation. Whatever I had to do to reach my goals was what was going to happen.

So why did I feel like such an asshole? I sighed as I ascended the steps to our apartment, bags in hand. This was why I stuck to robbing criminals, terrorists, and scumbags. The unfortunate downside of my time with a real family was that I had developed a finely tuned sense of guilt, damn Gideon and all his morals. I had managed to utterly squash my conscience for years, but it was bugging me now.

The apartment smelled . . . *really* good. "Okay, we're in a Muslim country, where did you guys find *bacon*?"

Carl poked his head around the corner from the kitchen. "Same place I find beer. Whenever you buy groceries, everything is too hot or weird with tentacles and eyeballs and shit."

"You do realize that the greatest thing your explorer ancestors ever accomplished was introducing the chili pepper to Thailand? That was awesome. That whole slave-trade thing . . . not so good." I tossed my headdress on the couch and followed the smell of pig. Carl was cooking and Reaper was sitting at the table, listening to his conspiracy-theory radio.

Carl looked at my bags as I started unpacking. "You bought camel? Fucking *camel*? See? What did I just say?"

I realized the shower was running. "Where's the girl?" I asked suspiciously.

"Jill's in the bathroom," Reaper replied dismissively.

I thought about it a second. "How long?" I snapped.

Reaper looked up, stringy hair in his face, disheveled as usual. He tended to keep weird nocturnal hours, fueled by sugar and energy drinks. "Uh . . . ten minutes?"

"There's a window in there." If she ran, it could ruin everything. I was across the apartment in an instant and jerked open the bathroom door. The room was fogged with steam. Jill was just stepping out of the shower, naked, absolutely gorgeous, and reaching for a towel. I froze.

"Hey!" she shouted as she quickly covered herself. "You mind?"

I backed out and closed the door.

Carl was waiting for me as I returned. "Thought of that. Window's too small, and it's a twenty-foot drop onto asphalt." He shoved me a plate. "Jackass."

Reaper was looking at me in awe. "So . . ."

I nodded. I was guessing that Jill worked out. *A lot.* "Smoking hot."

"I knew it," he sputtered, then grinned. "You know, we haven't had a girl on the team since Kat—"

"She's not on the *team*," I snapped. "Don't get too attached. Got it?"

Reaper looked down. "I just meant . . . never mind." He stuck his earpieces back in. Carl studied me for a moment. I gave him a look just daring him to respond. He went back to his bacon.

Jill joined us for breakfast a minute later. Apparently Reaper had decided to help out and had loaned her a Rammstein T-shirt. She accepted the offered plate and sat down across from me, looking a bit indignant. "Next time you should knock."

I took my time and finished chewing. "Next time you shouldn't get kidnapped by terrorists."

"Touché," she replied. "Fair enough. But just so you know, I'm not going to try and escape, I promise. Who am I going to run to? The cops? That worked *real* good last time. So . . . mind if I ask a few questions?" When I didn't respond, she must have taken that as a yes. "What kind of criminals are you?"

The other two looked to me and waited, as if saying, *this should be interesting.* "The strong silent type that doesn't talk about their work in polite company," I replied slowly. "As in, it's none of your business."

"Okay, fine. How about, what do we do now?"

Pausing, I wiped my mouth with a napkin. It wasn't like I could just tell her I was waiting for some sort of contact so I could trade her for the box. I took a moment to compose my response. "*You're* going to lay low. *We're* going to find Dead Six."

"Well, I know why I don't like them, but what's in it for you?" She was suspicious of my motives, which meant she wasn't stupid.

"Let's just say that they have something I want and leave it at that."

"When you find them, are you going to . . . *kill* them?" she asked.

"That's a definite possibility. Does that offend you?"

"No. I just wanted to see if you needed any help." Jill actually smiled. "It's still kind of sinking in, but these people ruined my life. As long as they're out there, I can't go home."

I don't think she realized yet that she could never go home. Once you've witnessed a rogue government operation murder US citizens and they'd already reported you as KIA, it was time to just walk away and get a new name. She was now on the official to-do-list. "This isn't amateur hour. We're highly trained professionals. What exactly are you bringing to the table?"

"I can take care of myself," Jill responded.

"No kidding," Reaper said. His face was still swollen. "Where'd you learn to fight like that? Not that I couldn't have, you know . . . taken you out, but you surprised me is all." Carl and I both openly scoffed at him. Reaper couldn't fight his way out of a cardboard box. "Whatever."

"My dad owned a martial-arts studio. He taught us how to defend ourselves. I grew up in kind of a rough neighborhood, so it came in handy a couple times. Dad was a good teacher, used to fight professionally even."

Carl scowled. His favorite thing in the world, other than chain-smoking and complaining, was to watch people beat each other bloody senseless on TV. There wasn't a lot of televised bullfighting, I suppose. "Del Toro . . . Tony 'the Demon' Del Toro?" he asked. Jill nodded in the affirmative. That must have been impressive or something from the approving look Carl gave her. "Like ten years ago, I watched him on pay-per-view almost tear this guy's arm off. I hate those Brazilian jujitsu guys. Guy needed his arm tore off, cocky *fodas*, so I remember the Demon."

"Being able to punch out Reaper is great and all, but we're talking about a team of assassins who've been ripping through fundamentalist murderers like it's nothing," I said coldly. "Do you even know how to shoot?"

"Dad taught me how to use a gun," Jill said defensively. That alone meant nothing. There were lots of people that *thought* they knew how to shoot. Usually if they could hit anything, they were too slow, or if they were fast, then they couldn't get reliable hits under stress. The kind of shooting I was good at was all about putting a bunch of bullets into my opponent before they could do it to me, and that was not how most recreational types did it.

"Uh-huh. Do you speak Arabic? Can you pass for a local?" In fairness, I already knew the answer to those. And with a little bit of coaching, I could easily get her to pass for one of the local imported Filipina workers: she had the features. Worst-case scenario, the women in the old part of town all wore hoods, and in the most traditional didn't even let their eyes show. "Can you *not* stick out like a tourist?"

"Well . . . no."

"Ever killed anybody?"

She shook her head.

"Thought so. You're going to stay here, keep your head down, and do exactly what I tell you to. When we come up against Dead Six, they won't hesitate. You run into that guy with the .44 magnum from the video and he'll *eat* you."

"Phrasing!" Reaper injected. Jill scowled at him.

"So to speak," I corrected.

"Your old man retired now?" Carl asked, trying to return the conversation to something more interesting to him. "Haven't seen him fight in forever."

"Passed away," she said. "I lost both my parents in a car accident. My brother was a Marine, just like dad had been, but he was killed in the war a couple years ago. I've got no close family left. So there won't be anybody demanding to see my supposedly dead body, either."

"They burned the embassy car anyway. If these guys are as professional as they seem, they probably found another girl to stick in the car before they lit it up. Nobody is going to recognize that body anyway," I said. "Hell, that's probably why they burned the car. They wouldn't have bothered if they'd nailed all of you." I didn't add that that was how I would have done it.

"And if I was missing, presumed taken by the terrorists, then that would have forced a big response from the government," Jill added. She caught on quick. Dead Six was running quiet. I'm guessing having the American populace watching the news and demanding a rescue mission was not on their itinerary.

Reaper chimed in. "There won't be an official investigation anyway. These black ops always squash that. There won't ever be an autopsy to show it isn't really you, either. Dental records won't matter. I bet you ten bucks they already cremated them all!"

Reaper was talking out of his ass. "When did *you* become such an expert on secret government operations?"

"I tell you, man, you really need to listen more. The truth is out *there*." He was getting defensive. "Roger Geonoy had an expert on *Sea to Shining Sea* last night. See, there's an Illuminati plot to control the world's oil supply, but that's just the beginning."

"Oh, not again," Carl muttered.

"Seriously," Reaper said, wide-eyed. "A cabal of powerful European bankers and stuff, it all makes *sense*. Did you know that the US government couldn't account for billions of dollars last year? Where do you think it all goes, man? It's for the secret war against the Illuminati."

"And they're going to release Loch Ness Monsters into the Gulf to disrupt the tankers," I added. "How nefarious."

"Only if the aliens from Roswell he's always talking about say so," Carl said. "Shut up already, Reaper."

"What is it that he does for you . . . exactly?" Jill asked.

"He's the brains of the operation."

But the kid wasn't going to be deterred. "Okay, so you don't believe in *my* conspiracy theories, but we're conspiring to break into a thousand-year-old secret vault for a mythical crime lord, so we're trying to track down a secret government death squad that kills witnesses, and there's apparently a conspiracy to overthrow the emir, but the second I say Illuminati, I'm the crazy one."

"Yes," I answered without hesitation.

Jill looked around the table. "Maybe I was better off with the terrorists."

Chapter 10: Hurt

Ash Shamal was the poorest of Zubara's three urban districts, and the most dangerous. Parts of this district were hotbeds of Islamic fundamentalism, and the streets weren't safe for Westerners, especially at night. Much of that was our fault. Since Project Heartbreaker had begun, it had stirred up a hornet's nest on the poor side of town. The locals were outraged over Dead Six's dirty work. Most of them seemed to think it was the Israelis. Certain people used this misconception to their own personal advantage.

By *certain people* I mean General Mubarak Al Sabah. The emir considered the popular general to be a threat, but for whatever reason couldn't just have him shot. Word on the street was General Al Sabah's faction of the army was making deals with local terrorist cells. Now, most of these so-called *cells* were just groups of angry, ignorant locals that claimed to stand against "Zionism" and "American Imperialism" and all that bullshit. In reality, they had no training, no equipment, no organization, and most of them weren't eager to go off and die for the jihad.

That was, of course, until General Al Sabah started using his connections to equip and train the locals. He was slowly building a small army in Ash Shamal. They were, at best, poorly trained rabble, little more than cannon fodder. But we believed Al Sabah was going to make a move on the emir soon, and he'd need all of the help he could get.

Facilitating these jihadi militias was one Anatoly Federov, the Russian arms dealer Hunter had briefed me about. He supplied them with brand-new hardware from Russia and advisers on how to use the equipment. Al Sabah, in turn, promised to be a very powerful friend to Federov when he managed to overthrow the emir.

Dead Six had no intention of letting that happen. From what I'd heard, we had plans to kill both Federov and General Al Sabah himself. One thing at a

153

time, though. In order to kill someone, you have to find them, and find a way to get to them. Powerful people surrounded by many heavily armed friends are notoriously difficult to get to, for obvious reasons.

That is, unless the powerful person's disgruntled business partner decides to cut a deal with the people gunning for him in order to save her own ass.

Enter one Asra Elnadi. According to our information, Ms. Elnadi was an Egyptian-born businesswoman who had been educated in Paris. We didn't know a lot about her history beyond that. We did know that for a few years she had been the business partner and lover of Jalal Hosani. Yet something went wrong, and Asra left Hosani in order to team up with Federov, taking a bunch of his business contacts with her. Federov became a major player in the Gulf; Hosani's business stagnated, and he went from being a rising-star arms broker to a second-rate gunrunner.

Hell hath no fury like a woman scorned, or so goes the ancient cliché. Project Heartbreaker had brought a different kind of hell to Zubara, and people like Asra were scattering like cockroaches. Normally you step on the roaches as they run, but occasionally you make a deal with one to get to another, more powerful cockroach.

Okay, that analogy kind of fell apart, but you know what I meant. Through some unknown—to me, at least—back channel, Ms. Elnadi had managed to contact Dead Six and offered to squeal. She was afraid of us, sure, but she was more afraid of her current boyfriend. There was only one problem: despite her expensive European education and status as an international businesswoman of ill repute, Ms. Elnadi didn't speak English. Furthermore, she had an intense distrust of men and apparently insisted on meeting face-to-face with a woman, one who spoke either Arabic or French.

The result of all this skullduggery and intrigue was that I found myself driving across town in a nondescript Toyota Land Cruiser, sitting next to Sarah McAllister in awkward silence.

We were taking two vehicles. Sarah and I were riding in the Land Cruiser, and would be the ones to actually make contact with Asra Elnadi. Tailor, Hudson, and Wheeler were following us in a van. The plan was for them to hang back until we arrived at the meeting, then fan out and provide overwatch as best they could. Asra wouldn't be expecting Sarah to arrive alone, but we feared that too much of a show of force would spook her. If we lost her, we'd probably never find Hosani or Federov. If all went well, the only people she'd actually see would be Sarah and me.

"Shafter, Nightcrawler, radio check," I said, squeezing the transmit button as I talked.

"Loud and clear," Hudson replied.

"We're almost there," I said to Sarah, keeping my eyes on the road. I was

tense, and not just because I was uncomfortable being around Sarah. Keeping
a low profile for the mission meant that I'd be alone, at least for a short time,
if things went south. It also meant that instead of wearing full battle rattle and
carrying a rifle, I was in street clothes and a wearing a low-profile vest with
thinner plates and less coverage. In a big backpack in the backseat was my FN
MK 17 7.62x51mm carbine. With the short thirteen-inch barrel fitted and the
stock folded, it could be concealed in a pack with a couple of spare
magazines.

Sarah had barely said anything to me the entire trip. She wasn't enjoying
the ride any more than I was, but we had a mission to complete. We were
both trying really hard to be professional.

"Are you armed?" I asked as I maneuvered the Land Cruiser through a
roundabout.

Sarah seemed surprised by the question. "They gave me a forty-five."
Sarah, like me, was wearing an untucked, short-sleeved shirt over her T-shirt
and body armor to conceal her weapon.

"Okay," I said. "If the shit hits the fan, fall back to the truck and let me
cover you. If I get hit, get in the truck and leave without me."

She was quiet for a moment. "Mike, you don't have to."

"Yes, I do. You're a mission-essential asset. It's my job to get you in and out
of there alive. If it gets bad, you grab our target and get her out. If you can't
do that, leave her with me and get yourself out. This is how it works. Okay?"
She briefly looked like she was going to argue with me, but simply nodded.

Asra Elnadi insisted that we meet in a freight yard near the Ash Shamal
docks. She told us that she'd be coming alone. This simplified things for us a
little, as we'd only have one person to exfiltrate. Nothing complicates a simple
extraction mission more than the would-be extractee showing up with an
entourage of friends and family.

Using a GPS unit in the truck, I navigated my way through a labyrinthine
maze of old warehouses and stacked shipping containers. The Ash Shamal
docks were one of the busiest ports in the Persian Gulf, and the surrounding
facilities were huge. They were also uncontrolled. There were no fences, no
cameras, no access control points, and as near as I could tell, no security. The
harbor police occasionally did patrols through the docks at night, but those
patrols had fallen off as violence had risen in the district. The police in the
Zoob were probably either sympathetic to General Al Sabah's fermenting
revolution or didn't want to get killed in it.

It was just after midnight when we finally arrived at the predetermined
meeting point. It was a large, open area surrounded by walls of shipping
containers stacked four and five high. There were a couple of small buildings
and a long, metal sunshade, under which dozens of forklifts and utility

vehicles were parked. Along the rear of this concrete pad was a massive warehouse. The area was dark, save for lights on the front of each of the buildings.

I killed the headlights as we slowly rolled into the open, noticing an Audi sedan parked between two forklifts. "Xbox, Nightcrawler, I think I have eyes on the package. Where are you?"

"*We're almost in position,*" Tailor replied. "*Okay,*" he said after a few moments. "*I can see you.*"

"Where are you?"

"*I'm on top of a stack of conex boxes to the south of you. Gotcha covered, nice and quiet.*" This meant that Tailor was providing overwatch with a suppressed rifle. It was too dark for me to see where he was, but from on top of any of the stacks of containers he'd have a commanding view of the area, especially using the thermal scope Frank had pulled out of the armory.

"*Nightcrawler, Shafter,*" Hudson said. "*We're just around the corner. We can be on top of you in a couple seconds.*"

"Roger that," I said as I got out of the truck.

I looked over at Sarah. "You ready?" She nodded again, not looking at me. I reached into my pocket and took out a flashlight. I flashed it at the Audi three times, paused for a few seconds, then flashed it a fourth time. The Audi's headlights flashed back at me five times. The dome light came on briefly as the driver's door opened. A slender female figure climbed out of the car and closed the door behind her.

Sarah and I approached slowly. I stayed a few paces behind Sarah and scanned the area. Even though I had Tailor watching me and some backup, something was bothering me. I felt vulnerable.

"Stay here," Sarah said. "I'm going to go talk to her." She then keyed her own radio microphone. "Xbox, I'm making contact with the package now."

I waited for him to acknowledge Sarah before speaking. "If this takes too long, I'm going to grab her and throw her in the truck. If she tries to get back in her car, draw down on her."

Sarah looked a question at me. "Hunter's orders," I said. "She's coming with us whether she likes it or not. I was told to shoot her if she tries to run. So you need to make sure she understands that the only way she's getting out of this alive is if she does what you tell her. If she gets cold feet, I'll put a slug through her. If I don't, Tailor will. Clear?"

"Yeah, clear," Sarah replied, walking away from me. I didn't know what the hell she was being so touchy about. The fact that Asra Elnadi was a woman didn't make her a good person. She was a black-market arms dealer who sold weapons to terrorists. If she hadn't come to us first, she'd have probably ended up dead when we went after Federov. Maybe it was a chick thing.

I was standing about fifty feet away from Sarah when she addressed the target in Arabic. I constantly scanned the surroundings. I was gripped by a sense of unease that I just couldn't shake. Was it because of the previous night, or was it something real?

"*I've got the package in tow,*" Sarah said over the radio, sounding relieved. "*So far so good.*"

I activated my microphone again. "Xbox, Nightcrawler, you see anything?"

"*Negative,*" Tailor replied. "*It's quiet. Why? Something up?*"

"Just a bad feeling."

"*Hang on,*" Tailor said. "*I just had a door open. . . . There's a couple guys walking up some exterior stairs.*"

It might not be anything, I thought, just somebody working late, but it didn't make me feel any better. I couldn't see anything moving in the darkness. "Xbox, where?"

"*Two hundred meters due north of you. They're on a catwalk on that three-story warehouse. Shit, they just walked behind something. I lost them.*" I could see the building in question but couldn't make out any details from here. There was a long pause as Tailor searched through his scope. "*They were carrying boxes or something, but it's hard to see details through this thing.*"

Sarah seemed to have our contact under control and was gently leading her my way. I wished she'd hurry the hell up. Asra was babbling away, nervous. The arms dealer had a high-pitched voice. Something she said seemed to spook Sarah, and they started moving quicker. She sounded nervous over the radio. "*The package thinks she might have been followed.*"

My attention focused back to the warehouse. I'd just caught a tiny flicker of movement at the top.

"*Okay, I got visual on one of them again. He's setting down his box.*" Tailor sounded uncertain. "*Wait. Shit. It's a weapon, I say again, he's got a weapon. Get out of there, Nightcrawler! Engaging!*"

Sniper. "Understood, moving!" I said, breaking into a run. There was no cover where we were. We had to get out of there. "Sarah!" I yelled, digging the Land Cruiser's keys out of my pocket. "Get her in the truck!"

"*I heard him!*" Sarah said, grabbing the package by the arm and pulling her along. Asra balked at this and began chattering at Sarah. She seemed like she wanted to know what was going on. There wasn't time for that. I caught up with the two women, took Asra by the other arm, and hauled her roughly back to our Toyota.

She struggled and bitched at me. I looked over at Sarah as my left hand went to the butt of my gun. "Tell her that Federov is coming for her, and if she doesn't get into that truck right now I'm going to fucking *shoot* her." Sarah conveyed my warning to Asra. The arms dealer's eyes went wide, and she complied with my command. I hurried for the front seat. Muffled cracks echoed across the storage yard; Tailor had started shooting.

"Xbox, do you have—" But a deafening *bang* cut me off. Bits of metal flew from the hood of our truck. I lurched to the side and threw myself to the pavement behind the car. The next bullet exploded through the engine block, destroying it. Asra started screaming. "Out! Out!" I shouted, crawling toward the women. Windows shattered as huge bullets lanced through our ride.

Sarah reacted quickly, getting as low as possible. I reached up, got a handful of Asra's suit jacket, and yanked her to the ground. We were pinned. The sniper had something huge, and by the rate of fire, semiautomatic. Our Toyota wasn't cover, it was just concealment.

"*Got one. Shit! Can't spot the other guy. Shot's blocked. Moving!*" Tailor shouted.

A hole as big around as my fist punched through the Toyota's side panel. The bullet dug a divot into the ground, launching stinging asphalt bits. If we ran for the nearest conex, not all of us would make it, but if we sat here, we were as good as dead.

Asra stood, panicking, trying to flee. Sarah knocked her down before I could. A bullet whined through the space she had just filled. Sarah threw her body on top of our package to hold the struggling woman down.

This day just kept getting better and better. The sniper had disabled our vehicle first so we couldn't run. The only reason we hadn't been hit yet was luck.

"*This is Shafter. We've got multiple vehicles inbound from the east at a high rate of speed. We got more company!*"

"Copy!" I said. Another heavy slug plowed through our truck, showering me with shattered safety glass. "Hurry!"

"*Got you, fucker,*" Tailor gasped as he opened fire. The gun was suppressed, but the supersonic bullets cracked by over our heads. "*He's down! I got him!*"

I rolled over. Sarah was still on top of the flailing woman. "Are you hit?" She shook her head. Asra was in shock, covering her ears with her hands and babbling like an idiot. "Shut her up!" Fluids were pouring from our perforated truck. More bad guys were inbound. It was time to go. "Shafter, we need extraction, *now!*"

I scanned nervously out the window as we raced away from the scene of the shootout. This was exactly why we always tried to use multiple vehicles. The colonel was going to be pissed that we'd lost another one. Wheeler was driving, Hudson was riding shotgun. Tailor was in the back of the van, scanning out the rear window with his rifle in his lap. Sarah and I were in the back, too, as was our guest. Asra Elnadi was still prattling on about something.

"What's she saying?" Hudson snapped.

"She says she's very sorry. Federov must have had her tailed, and . . ." Sarah scowled. "Mike, she says you'll regret roughing her up, and that she'll complain to our superiors and have you punished."

I looked over at her incredulously. The arms dealer was an attractive woman of about forty. Her mascara was running badly. She glared back at me with an indignant look that said *don't you know who I am*?

I made a face at her and turned toward Tailor. "What took you so long back there?"

"There was a crane in the way. I couldn't get a shot. I had to run a ways."

"If you didn't smoke so damn much, you'd have gotten there faster."

He turned around and grinned at me. "You ain't worth that!"

Conex containers were flying past as we sped out of the port, pulling onto a main road. Wheeler had been trying to keep our speed reasonable, so as to not draw attention to us, but he floored it now that we were in the open.

"Damn it. A bunch of sedans just pulled out behind us," Tailor snapped. "They're on us."

"They weren't in visual range," Wheeler said tersely. "How're they following us now?"

"She's been bugged," Hudson said. Asra shrieked at me as I ripped her purse away, but sure enough, I found the little tracking device a second later. I passed it forward, and Hudson tossed it out his window. Too bad they had a visual on us now, which meant we either had to lose them the old-fashioned way, or shoot it out. "Pat her down, Sarah." Sarah didn't complain, but Asra Elnadi certainly did. "Tell her that she can either let you do it, or I will." Once that was translated, it finally shut her up.

We raced south, toward the main part of town. There was more traffic here, which we could use to our advantage. "I'm going to get on the parkway," Wheeler said as he took the turnoff. It made sense. It was way too easy to get lost on the backstreets. Hudson was on the radio with Control, trying to get us some help. Several sets of headlights were gaining rapidly on us. They'd followed us onto the parkway.

"Shit! Shit! Shit!" Wheeler suddenly applied the brakes. Traffic had slowed to a stop.

"Oh, God, what *now*?" I asked in frustration. Then I saw the flashing lights. Zubaran security forces had set up a checkpoint. Two police cars were parked there, along with an army APC, and the road had been funneled down to a single lane in the center. Camouflaged soldiers and blue-suited police officers were stopping each car, checking the occupants. One car had been pulled off to the side to be searched.

This was new. Our antics had been causing the Zubarans some serious problems, but this was the first time we'd run into a random checkpoint.

"It's the damned curfew!" Wheeler said, looking around anxiously. There was nowhere to turn off. They'd placed the roadblock such that anyone pulling onto the parkway would be committed, and flipping around would bring us right back to the pursuing mobsters.

"They've stopped," Tailor reported from the back. "They see the cops too." At least Federov's men weren't stupid enough to start a gunfight with the police right there, but we were trapped. "We've got to go through. Hide your guns."

They were still searching that one car, and it appeared they only left room enough to search one at a time. We might get through this. Other cars were being waved through with just cursory examinations. But then again, we were a carload of obvious Westerners. Dead Six had provided us all with forged documents for just this contingency, but if the car got searched and they found our weapons, we'd have a serious problem.

"Let me do the talking," Sarah suggested. She was the only one of us that spoke the language.

Hudson thought about it for a second and then struggled to maneuver his bulk between the seats so Sarah could get up front. It was rather difficult for him, but finally we got Sarah into the passenger's seat before we were close enough for the troops at the checkpoint to see us.

It took forever for the line of cars to move forward. The soldiers ahead seemed to be as unmotivated as third-world armies normally were on this kind of duty. We had a good chance of breezing right through this. As an added bonus, we'd be long gone before Federov's men could make it through. There were over a dozen soldiers and cops manning the checkpoint, but only a few of them seemed to be engaged in doing any actual work. The rest stood around shiftlessly, smoking or talking to each other.

Tailor stashed his rifle under a blanket. "Everybody stay calm, but if this goes south, lay down as much fire as you can. Wheeler, drive right between those cop cars and get us the hell out of here. Sarah, your job is to make sure we don't have to do that? Got it?"

Sarah just nodded. Hudson was sitting on the other side of Asra now, looking really uneasy. He and Wheeler had spent a lot of time manning checkpoints in Iraq, and I figured he'd much rather be on the other side of the roadblock right now. "Wheeler, be cool, man. Just be cool."

A few minutes later it was our turn. Wheeler rolled his window down as a soldier walked up to the van. The soldier was young, but he seemed like he was on the ball. He kept one hand on the pistol on his belt as he scowled at the carload of Westerners. The back of the van was dark, and had no windows. He didn't seem to have a flashlight.

The soldier said something. Wheeler just smiled and passed over his papers. Sarah responded in Arabic, but the soldier snapped back at her harshly. He either didn't like being addressed by someone he wasn't talking to, or he didn't like being addressed by a woman. He studied Wheeler's papers intently, looking for any discrepancies. It was just our luck that we'd found one of the only people in the Middle East who gave a shit about doing a good job. Even better, he spoke English.

"Americans?"

"Yes, sir," Wheeler responded, cheerful as he could be. "We're working on the natural-gas pipeline for Zubara National Energy."

The soldier nodded but seemed suspicious. "What is your business in Ash Shamal? This is a dangerous place for Americans at night."

Wheeler had already thought of the cover story. "We had to pick up some diagrams at the Ash Shamal branch office. It took longer than expected, and I got lost in the dark."

The other soldiers were all sitting on their asses, but many of them had rifles close at hand. The cupola on top of the armored car was manned and equipped with a machine gun. The car ahead of us pulled away, giving us a clear shot to freedom. Wheeler's eyes flicked nervously forward. The young soldier was nodding as he thought about Wheeler's story.

"Foreign criminals are murdering people in this part of the city. There was a shooting down at the harbor. Do you know anything about that?"

"No, sir," Wheeler replied cautiously.

"No?" the soldier asked sarcastically, and leaned farther in. Sarah tried to speak to him again, but he ignored her. *Damn it, why wouldn't he just let us go?* His gaze lingered on Asra and her smeared makeup. Then he studied me and Hudson for a moment. My carbine was in the backpack between my legs. I moved one hand to the sliding-door latch. The soldier removed his head from the window and addressed Wheeler loudly. "Step out of the car. All of you, step out of the car."

"Officer, can't we—" Wheeler began to speak but stopped as the soldier suddenly yanked out his pistol and stuck it in our driver's face. "Whoa! Hey, man! Relax!"

"Out of the car!" the soldier shouted. The other soldiers and police officers looked up in confusion. The APC gunner swung the machine gun around so it was pointed at our van.

I didn't have my own window. I could only see the soldier's extended gun hand now. More troops appeared behind us, curious at the commotion. They tried to look in through the tinted back windows. Tailor reached under the blanket. Sarah was shouting something in Arabic. The soldier was shouting back at her. Somebody banged something hard against the opposite side of the van. Asra flinched so violently that it made me jump.

Then there was a gunshot. *The Calm* slowed everything down. I looked just in time to see the soldier's gun move down out of recoil. Wheeler said something unintelligible. A small amount of blood splattered against the interior of our windshield.

"Drive!" Tailor shouted. The rear glass shattered as he opened fire through it, killing a soldier. Another gunshot roared through the van. Sarah had pulled her .45 and fired out the driver's side window, right past Wheeler's face. I slid the side door open and brought my carbine up even though the stock was still folded. The soldier that had been questioning us was hitting the pavement, a hole between his eyes. I pointed the carbine up at the gunner in the cupola and fired five or six times. The first shots missed but at least one went home, dropping the gunner down into his hatch in a puff of blood. I shifted to the next target, a police officer who was clumsily trying to draw his pistol. Two rounds went through his chest. The soldier next to him was trying to bring his rifle to bear, which had been slung across his back. We began to move as I popped off three more shots. I watched the soldier collapse to the ground as we sped by.

Tailor kept firing at the checkpoint through the back window, forcing the troops to keep their heads down as we made our getaway. He flipped around as I slid my door closed, noticing the blood on the inside of the windshield. "Who's hit? Wheeler? Sarah?"

"I'm fine!" Sarah shouted.

"I'm okay," Wheeler hissed, concentrating on the road. "Asshole shot me in the arm."

Tailor turned back around. "Get us out of here." He went back to shooting.

Asra had been screaming. I hadn't heard her over the gunshots. "Shut up!" Hudson bellowed at her as he moved up between the front seats. "Let me drive," he said. "Let Val look at that, man."

"I'm okay!" Wheeler snapped. "I'm fine! Let me drive!"

Tailor dropped the empty magazine out of his carbine and looked over his shoulder. "Val, we—" He was cut off as the van swerved violently to the right. Tires squealed, and we were thrown around the cabin.

When I looked back to the front of the van, Sarah was reaching over, holding the steering wheel. Wheeler was slumped forward and wasn't moving. Just like that, he was gone.

It took us over an hour to get to the safe house, even though it wasn't all that far from the port. The Zoob had already been in a heightened state of alert because of our exploits and the subsequent spike in terrorist attacks. A shootout at the docks and another at a police checkpoint had put the city on lockdown. We had to go very far out of our way to avoid more checkpoints.

Two vehicles were waiting for us at the safe house. One of them was driven by two of Colonel Hunter's security men. They grabbed Asra Elnadi and drove off with her before we even got in the door. The other, a van, was driven by Hal and one of the other medics.

Other than some cuts and bruises, I was unscathed. The same went for Tailor, Hudson, and Sarah. Wheeler was dead. The bullet had struck him in the bicep, traveled through his arm, and entered his chest through the armpit opening of his armor vest. He hadn't even known that he was dying. There was nothing we could have done for him. My shirt was sticky with his drying blood.

After the four of us had been seen by the medics, we assembled outside by the garage. Hal backed his van up to the open garage door and gave us a body bag. Together, and in silence, Hudson, Tailor, and I stripped Wheeler of his equipment. When that was done, Tailor and I stood back while Hudson quietly said a few words to his old friend. We then carried Wheeler's body to the medics' van. It was the closest thing the affable former army paratrooper would ever get to a proper funeral.

"Tailor?" Hal said, approaching us after a while. "Hunter wants you to come back for debrief."

"What?" Tailor said, sounding agitated. "We had kind of a bad night."

"I know, but he wants you to come back. Valentine, McAllister, he said there'd be a car for you two sometime tomorrow."

Sarah seemed suddenly uncomfortable. "Wait a minute. Don't they need me to debrief Asra?"

"You're not the only one that can speak Arabic, you know. Besides, you're exhausted. You're in no shape to do any work tonight. Tailor just has to give a report. Then he can go to bed."

"Why not just bring us all back?" Hudson asked. He hadn't spoken in a while. "They need someone to stay here and watch the house or something?"

"Well, there's only one extra seat in the front of the van," Hal said. "And . . ." he hesitated. "I didn't figure anyone would want to ride in the back with Wheeler."

"I will," Hudson said. "It's no problem."

"You sure, man?" Tailor asked.

"Yep," Hudson said. "Wheeler and me, we zipped six of our soldiers into body bags last time we were deployed. We carried them away. Stayed with them for as long as we could. I'll ride with him one last time. I owe him that much. He never would've come over here if it wasn't for me."

"Okay," Hal said quietly. "We need to get going now."

"There any food in this place?" I asked. Hal just shrugged. "Yeah, I'll be fine. I just need to get some sleep."

"Take it easy, bro," Tailor said as he climbed into the van. It disappeared through the gate, leaving Sarah and me standing alone under the stars. We had the big house all to ourselves. *Awkward . . .*

"Mike, I'm sorry about Wheeler," she said as we went inside. "Are you okay?"

"I just need to take a shower."

"Me, too," she said. Fortunately, the big house had two bathrooms, so it wasn't an issue. The medics had brought fresh clothes for us to the safe house, so we wouldn't have to run around in blood-stained khakis for the rest of the night.

After my shower, all I wanted was to get some sleep, but sleep just wouldn't come. The longer I lay there, the madder I got that I couldn't sleep. I rolled over, then rolled over again. I was too hot, so I cranked up the air conditioner. Then I was too cold. Then my foot itched. Then I had to go to the bathroom. Then . . .

"Fuck!" I snarled, throwing my pillow across the room. "Goddamn it!" I stood up and began to pace around in the darkness. The clock on the nightstand said 4:45 and I was still awake. I stormed across the room, picked up the clock, yanked the cord out of the socket, and threw it against the wall. It smashed into pieces of broken plastic.

I stood there, breathing heavily, ridiculously mad but unsure of what I was mad at. I just wanted to go to sleep and forget things for a while.

Wheeler was dead. Yesterday he was there, today he was gone, just like that. I had no one to talk to, nothing to distract me, and no alcohol to numb me. All I could do was sit there, awake when I should be sleeping, thinking about how I'd watched my friend die and what I could have done differently. It was *killing* me.

There was a quiet knock on my door. It was Sarah. "Mike, are you okay?" she asked. Her voice was slightly raspy, like she'd been crying.

"Yeah, I'm . . . yeah . . ." I said, even though I was anything but okay. Sarah opened the door a little bit and peeked in at me.

"Can I come in?"

I sighed. "Sure," I said and sat down on the bed. I turned on the stupid-looking lamp that sat on the nightstand. Sarah was wearing the same short shorts and T-shirt she'd been wearing the first time she came into my room, our first night in-country. It was strange, but she looked a little older now.

"You broke your clock," she noted. "And you look like hell." I became suddenly self-conscious and looked around for my T-shirt.

"It's been a bad night."

"I know," Sarah said. She crossed the room and sat down next to me. "I've been in my room crying for an hour."

"Are *you* okay?" I asked, looking over at her.

"I don't know why I was crying," she said. "I don't feel anything. I didn't feel anything when Wheeler died. I didn't feel anything when I killed that solder. I didn't feel . . ." Tears welled up in Sarah's eyes, and her hands started to shake. "I didn't feel anything at all."

"That's normal," I said. "It's adrenaline. You're going through adrenaline dump right now. Makes you crazy."

"How do you *do* this?" she asked, wiping her eyes. "I saw you. You shot those three guys dead like it was nothing. It took like four seconds. I mean, oh my God, how do you do it?"

I shrugged. "It's what I do. It's all that I do, I guess. I try not to think about it."

"I just want to go home," Sarah said, sounding like she couldn't cry anymore. "I hate this country."

Me, too. "But, hey, we're alive. Right now that counts for a lot."

"Thank you," she said. Sarah then yawned widely.

"You should get some rest," I suggested. "You're exhausted. I am too."

"I know," she said, rubbing her eyes. "I just don't want to be alone right now. This big house is too quiet." Sarah looked down at her lap for a moment, then back up at me. "Is it alright if I sleep in here?"

"What?" I said, surprised. "I mean . . . sure. If you want."

"Don't get the wrong idea," she said more sternly. "I just don't want to be by myself. Okay?"

"It's fine."

"Are you sure?" she asked.

"I'm sure," I said, trying to sound reassuring. "Lay down." Sarah thanked me again, gave me a small kiss on the cheek, and slid under the covers on the right side of the bed. I turned the lamp back off and laid my head on the pillow. This time sleep quickly overtook me.

It was daylight out when I awoke. My clock was still smashed on the floor, so I wasn't sure what time it was. I took a deep breath and closed my eyes as the events of the night before came back to me. I relived, in my mind, watching Wheeler die, and I quietly swore to myself.

There are always doubts when a teammate dies. You question yourself, and your confidence is shattered. *Did I do everything I could? Was there any way it could have been avoided? Did something I do cause him to get killed?* The hardest thing to do after losing one of your own is to go back into combat again, burdened with the knowledge that your surviving teammates are all counting on you. I've known guys that could never get over that hurdle, and I've seen it end careers.

In my case, that wasn't really an option. There was nothing I'd have liked more than to simply quit and go home, but it seemed like the only way to go home early was in a body bag.

It was then that I noticed something warm and soft pressed against me. Sarah, still asleep, had wrapped her arm and one leg around me. She quietly slept, her face a few inches from my right ear, her auburn hair splashed across the pillow.

God, she's beautiful. Sarah opened her eyes then, as if my thinking about her woke her up.

"Hey," I said, looking into her eyes.

"Hey, you," she replied. "You make a good pillow."

"I'm glad you think so. I can't feel my right arm."

"I'm sorry," Sarah said with a little smile. "You want me to move?"

"Not really," I confessed. "This is . . . nice. A nice way to wake up."

Sarah agreed. "Yeah," she said, squeezing me a bit tighter. "So tell me. Why is it every time you almost get your ass shot off you end up in bed with me?"

I had no idea how to answer that. I just looked at her, mouth slightly open, and she giggled. "Um . . ."

"Yes?" she asked.

"Because you're the Queen of Crazy Town?" I suggested tentatively.

Sarah gently pushed my face away and laughed. "I can see where I gave you that impression. What time is it, anyway?"

I shrugged. "My clock is still broken."

"Well . . . they'll call before they send a car," Sarah said. "We could be here all day. They're trying to limit traffic outside the compound during daylight hours or when the roads are busy. You know, because of the checkpoints." Sarah trailed off and exhaled heavily.

"Listen," I said. "You did good out there. You weren't trained for that kind of job, but you held it together. You did what you had to do. No hesitation, nothing. I'm impressed." I really was.

"You don't have to say that to make me feel better."

"I'm not," I said sternly. "Your quick thinking is probably the reason more of us didn't get killed. I'm proud of you."

"Thank you," she said softly. She kissed me sweetly.

Smiling, I turned toward her a little and gently brushed a stray strand of hair out of her face. She closed her eyes as I caressed her cheek. Her right hand slid up to my shoulder, pulling me closer to her. I scootched over a bit and kissed her, deeply. She made a very soft, pleasurable sigh and ran her fingers through my buzzed hair.

I rolled onto my back, pulling Sarah with me. Straddling me, she only stopped kissing me for a moment and pulled her shirt off over her head. She leaned forward again, kissing me passionately, her hair tickling my face and my neck.

Sarah and I made love for a long time, and, for a while, I was able to stop thinking about all the things that were bothering me. Like how horrible it was that we were fooling around like a couple of high-school kids on prom night just hours after we watched one of my guys bleed to death. Or how I treated her the night I got drunk. Or what was going to happen between us after this. However it played out, it was going to be *complicated*.

At that moment, though, with her in my arms, I didn't worry about any of that. I was *alive*, goddamn it, and so was she. For the time being, that was all that mattered.

VALENTINE
Fort Saradia National Historical Site
April 18
1230

I stepped into my room and closed the door behind me, looking down at the sheet of paper in my hand. Hunter had given it to me after Sarah and I returned from Safe House 5.

It was a BOLO, or "be on the lookout" alert, passed down from Gordon Willis. The photocopy was about a young woman named Jillian Del Toro. She had been an intern at the US Embassy in Zubara, on loan to the State Department from the Department of Agriculture. She was a low-level employee but apparently had access to one James Fiore, the assistant ambassador. Fiore had been killed by the enemy after the US Embassy was evacuated. According to the dossier I'd been given, Jill Del Toro was apparently selling embassy secrets to General Al Sabah's intelligence people and had gotten Fiore killed.

Del Toro was still at large. She wasn't considered dangerous, but she was a traitor, and Gordon wanted her brought in, dead or alive.

I studied the picture of the young woman. Miss Del Toro was twenty-five years old, fresh out of college. She was beautiful, with dark hair, bright eyes, and a very pretty face. Maybe it was just me, but she didn't look like a traitor.

I was probably being naïve, I thought, but something about this whole thing didn't sit right.

Of course, very little of what was passed down from Gordon Willis sat right with me. I tossed the BOLO on my bed and sat. As I did so, I noticed the strange key that I'd found in Adar's safe, still sitting where I'd left it.

I reached over and picked up the ancient-looking trinket and examined it again. Turning the knob on the base caused dozens of tiny pins to pop out of nearly invisible recesses in the object's shaft. I twisted the knob the other way, and the tiny pins smoothly disappeared.

Sarah and I hadn't really gotten any sleep, and I was tired. I was off for the rest of the day and decided then that I was going to take a nap. Before I could lie down, there was a soft knock on my door. The door opened and Sarah stepped into my room, quietly closing the door behind her.

"Hey, you," she said, smiling widely when she saw me. I felt a smile appear on my own face as I stood. She met me in the middle of my room, stepping into my arms and kissing me.

In some subtle way, Sarah was a different person to me now. At first, she was just some chick I thought was hot. Then we talked a bit, and then we slept together. But now we'd been in combat together, bled together, buried a friend together. We were more than friends and lovers now. We were *comrades.*

"Hey yourself," I said, not letting go of her. "What's going on?"

"What's that in your hand?" she asked, indicating the strange trinket I was holding.

I held it up. "I don't really know, but watch this." I twisted the knob again, causing the pins and teeth to reappear. Another twist of the knob retracted them.

"Wow," Sarah said, taking it from my hand to examine it. "Where'd you get this? It's pretty."

Suddenly, I felt uncomfortable. "I found it the other night," I said, sitting back down on my bed. "It was in a safe in Adar's house."

Sarah looked down at the trinket, apparently not bothered by where I'd gotten it. "Why didn't you report it?"

I shrugged. "Hunter didn't ask about it, so I figured they weren't looking for it anyway. It's just some doodad I found. I've collected a bunch of crap since I've been here, you know. Besides, I forgot about it. That was kind of a bad night."

The expression on Sarah's face changed subtly. "Yeah, it was," she said. All at once I felt butterflies in my stomach. Something was bothering her. "We need to talk about that," she said.

I sighed, lowering my eyes. "Okay." I patted the bed next to me so Sarah would sit down. "So let's talk."

"You hurt me," she said, crossing her legs as she sat down. "I came in here trying to help you. You screamed at me, swore at me, and told me to get out." Sarah's voice was perfectly calm as she spoke. I felt like curling up into a ball.

"I was drunk," I said after a moment. Sarah's eyes flashed. I raised my hands in surrender before she got too upset. "I'm not using that as an excuse," I said quickly. "I'm really not. It's just a fact. I had a bad night. Seeing that girl . . . it just . . . I was still in shock. I couldn't handle it. It doesn't matter, though. I shouldn't have taken it out on you. Like you said, you were trying to help me, and I pushed you away. I'm sorry. I'm not just saying I'm sorry, either, I really mean it. I . . . I didn't mean to hurt you."

"Well, you did," she said coldly, fidgeting with the key in her hands. I started to say something, but she interrupted me. "But you know what? It's okay. I mean, it's not okay, but it's okay."

I gave her a sidelong glance, not really sure what to say. Sarah laughed, lightening the mood in the room just a little bit. "Have I mentioned I'm crazy?" she asked.

"I gathered," I said, allowing myself a half smile.

"I'm also confused." Sarah exhaled heavily and continued fiddling with the key, trying to think of what to say. "After the other night, I think I got it," she said. "I mean . . . Jesus Christ, I killed a guy, and I cried my eyes out. You go out and do that every day, and they just expect you to keep on doing it and not break down. You broke down, didn't you?"

I looked down at the floor, lowering my head just a little. "When I saw that girl, I . . ."

"I know," Sarah said quietly. "I know. It really bothers you when men hurt women, doesn't it?"

I was surprised by the question. "I guess. I mean . . ."

"I can tell," she said. "Even when you were dragging Asra Elnadi along, you were very careful with her. You probably didn't even bruise her arm."

"I would've shot her if she ran," I said levelly. "Just like I was ordered to."

"I know," Sarah said. "It would've bothered you for a long time, though, wouldn't it?" I nodded my head slightly. "I read your file. I know about your mom. That had to have been awful."

I had just been a teenager when she'd been robbed and murdered by some random meth-heads. "It was, but it's been a really long time."

"I didn't get you at first, you know," she said. "I mean, you're cute and everything, but I didn't think you'd be good for much more than a roll in the hay."

"You think I'm cute?" I interjected, trying to deadpan.

"Shut up," Sarah said, grinning and giving me a little shove. "I'm serious. I didn't think we'd . . . you know . . ."

"Yeah," I said. "This is kind of intense, isn't it?"

Sarah nodded. "But I get it now. I know you guys are under a lot of pressure out there. I mean, oh my God, look at how many people we've lost already!"

"Sarah—"

"I'm not finished. That doesn't change what happened. I came here to help you. You yelled at me and made me feel like a piece of shit." Sarah's cool words hurt me like I was being stabbed. "And I need to know where we stand, right now. Because if this is how you are . . . I'm sorry, I mean, I know what you're going through now, but if this is how you are, I'm not going to be a part of it. I spent three years in a bad relationship, and I'm not going through it again."

I was quiet for a few moments as I tried to figure out what to say. The thought of driving her away terrified me. The thought of trying to build a relationship with her, in the middle of war, also terrified me. I wasn't sure which scared me more. Sarah gave me a hard look, swallowed, and spoke again. "Mike, if you want me in your life . . ."

"I want you in my life," I said awkwardly. "You're just . . . you're amazing. I can't even tell you. I—"

Sarah gently placed a finger over my lips, silencing me. "It's okay. I just needed to hear you say that. Thank you."

We sat together, quietly looking into each other's eyes for a long time. Butterflies danced around in my stomach, and I couldn't think of anything else to say. Right then I knew that I was falling in love with her. It was an amazing feeling, and it scared the hell out of me. I didn't even know if either of us was going to make it out of Zubara alive.

As I looked into her eyes, I asked myself, is it worth the risk? I realized that I'd already made my decision, even before I asked the question. This woman had seen me at my best and at my worst, and she still wanted to be with me. What kind of fool passes that up?

I took the silvery trinket from Sarah's hand, opened the chain, and gently hung it around her neck. She'd said it was pretty.

"Are you giving me this thing? Too cheap to buy me a real present?" She laughed.

"I found this thing that night," I said awkwardly. "So . . . I'm giving it to you, as a promise of a fresh start."

Sarah crinkled her brow at me. "That is so cheesy, but really sweet too. So yes, I accept your token of apology." She laughed again. "Oh, I almost forgot. You're off for the next three days at least."

"The next three days? Are you serious?"

"I talked to Hunter for you. I convinced him you and your chalk need a break. So you don't have anything to do for the next three days but lounge around the fort and relax."

"What about you?"

"I have a briefing I have to be at in . . ." Sarah glanced at her watch. She wore it upside down, so that the face was on the underside of her right wrist. "Four hours. I don't have anything to do until then."

"I can think of something," I said coyly, knowing I sounded more dorky than suave.

"Oh really?" Sarah said, sounding coy herself, as she moved in to kiss me again. "Sounds interesting . . ."

Some time later, Sarah and I lay together in my bed. She was asleep in my arms. Her hair smelled like strawberries. She was a quiet sleeper.

I don't know how long I lay there, holding her in my arms, thinking about things, before I feel asleep. What chance did Sarah and I have in this place? What else could I do? Could we get out somehow? Even if I could find a way to escape Zubara, would I be able to convince Sarah to go with me and leave everyone else behind?

Chapter 11: For the Good of the People

LORENZO
April 20

I punished the bag until my knuckles bled.

It was an eighty-pound leather punching bag that I'd found used in a local market. Some duct tape, and it was good as new. I'd hung it up in the corner of the garage and was using it for some stress release. I worked out religiously every morning, but this was different. I'd already been striking the bag furiously for half an hour, and stinging sweat was leaking into my eyes.

I imagined that the bag was Big Eddie. If I could get my hands on whoever he was, I was going to absolutely destroy him. The nerve, the *audacity*, to threaten me, to force me into this . . . I was going to make him pay. I'd worked for him for years, doing his bidding, stealing things, killing people, robbery, extortion, you name it. I had been his lapdog, and I didn't even know if he was real. Disgusted with what I'd become, I had eventually walked away, naively thinking that I could be safe from his machinations. But somehow he'd figured out who I really was, and that had given him leverage. With a shout, I stepped back and side kicked the bag so hard that a jolt of electricity traveled up the bones of my leg.

I switched my mental picture, and now the bag was the Dead Six operatives. My life was growing complicated, and I didn't like that one bit. My elbows left skin on the bag as I nearly bent it in half with the impacts. Nobody knew a thing. Reaper's electronic digging couldn't find them. Hosani hadn't called me back. None of the urchins, scumbags, villains, and criminals I'd contacted had a clue who they were. They were ghosts.

They'd slip up eventually. Everyone did, and then I would take them. But what if I couldn't find them before Eddie's deadline? Or even worse, what if their operation finished, and they just went home? And the worst possible scenario: Adar's box had already been shipped back to the US and was sitting in some CIA warehouse where they had no clue what they even had.

If that was the case, then I would just have to proceed without it. And that meant my odds of success went from slim to near zero. If the pace of the killings tapered off, then I was going to have to assume the worst, and then I would have to do my worst. I'd have to stick Jill out in the open and see what happened.

Here I was, perfectly willing to take an innocent woman and basically sentence her to death. What kind of monster was I?

You're soft. Weak. I slammed the bag again and again, breath coming in ragged gasps. Even a couple of years ago, I would have handed her off in a heartbeat. The problem was that she wasn't just a number in an equation now. She'd been living here for a couple of days. She was a decent, kind, trusting person. She was the sort of person that I had avoided all of these years, because they were exactly the type that I didn't want to hurt. I hung out with evil for a reason. She was just a scared girl who only wanted to go home.

With that bleak thought, the last of my energy evaporated, as even I have my limits, and I just hugged the bag close to stop the swaying. Every muscle in my body was on fire, and sweat drizzled down my face and onto the bag, but the leather was cool under my skin.

"Anybody ever tell you that you're kind of intense?"

I hadn't heard her enter over the rhythmic pounding in my ears. Jill was standing at the base of the stairs into the apartment, watching me. I pushed away from the bag. "Yeah, I get that once in a while. . . . What're you doing up so early?"

"Couldn't sleep," she said with a shrug. The bruised discoloration around her eye had subsided and she was looking better. "I've got a lot on my mind. You know."

I walked around the front of the van. "Understandable. But if you've come to talk about it, you've really got the wrong guy," I said as I picked up my shirt. My torso and limbs were crisscrossed with scars from bullets, knives, burns, and shrapnel, and most of them had not been stitched up by actual medical professionals, either. It always made me a little self-conscious.

"If I wanted somebody in touch with their emotional side, I'd talk to Carl," she replied sarcastically. "Wow. You know, you're pretty ripped for an old guy. . . ."

"I'm not *that* old." Well, I had been in junior high the year Jill had been born.

"Easy there. I was just trying to make a joke. Seriously, though, you're going out looking for Dead Six again today, aren't you?"

"That's the plan," I answered as I pulled the shirt over my head. It was instantly drenched with sweat. My muscles ached. "I'm going to check out Al Khor today." It was the safest, and therefore most boring, part of town. It was also the most modernized section and was where the Americans and

Europeans tended to live. There was a possibility that someone over there had seen our shooters.

She was regarding me strangely. "Take me with you."

I stopped. "Why?"

"I've been cooped up in here for days. I'm bored."

As a professional liar, I'm a master of knowing when I was being lied to. I just waited. She rolled her eyes. "Fine. It's just something I have to do. I have to feel like I'm doing *something*. This might just be business for you, but this is personal to me. These people killed my friends, and they tried to kill me. Then they burned them. They were good men, and they deserved better. I have to do this."

Sighing, I studied her. I could understand that feeling. I could even kind of respect it.

"Please?"

I didn't say anything as I pushed past her and climbed the stairs. My silence must have hit a nerve, as she immediately blew up. "Damn it, Lorenzo! I'm not some useless child. I don't care what your stupid secret mission is! I—" She was cut off as the bundle of clothing hit her in the face.

"Get dressed," I said from the top of the stairs.

"Is this a burka?"

"Sort of. If you're going to be here, you might as well learn how not to be totally useless. I said get dressed. You coming or what?"

It is surprising how foggy it can get along the Persian Gulf in the mornings. A fat gray cloud hung over the city, and only the lights at the tops of the buildings in the Khor district were visible as we crossed the bridge.

"Is this really necessary?" Jill asked through the bag that was covering her head. "Can I take this off yet?"

"Think she's lost enough?" I asked Carl. He shrugged. "It's for your own good, Jill. If you're captured, this way you can't be tortured into telling them where our hideout is."

"You mean if I run away, I can't sell you out," she snapped. "Well, duh. I was lost in the first couple of minutes, but that was a while ago, and now we're on the Gamal bridge going over the ocean. I can tell. The embassy is only a couple miles from here. It's the only big bridge in town, and it sounds like we're on a big bridge, so unless we drove all the way to Dubai while I wasn't paying attention, can I please take this stupid bag off now?"

Carl leaned over from the driver's seat. "She's got a point."

"Next time, it'll be a blindfold *and* a gag," I muttered. "Okay. Take it off."

Jill complied. "See? Told you."

"Goodie for you. Now listen carefully. I'll be talking to a lot of people.

You're going to do exactly what I tell you, when I tell you, and you are not going to talk. At all. You sound like an American and walk like an American. Hell, you've been eating American food, and you even smell like an American. Keep your head down, shoulders slumped, because you're too damn tall, and stay behind me."

"I've been around this part of town before," Jill replied.

"Not like this you haven't. There's a lot of women around, and in Khor, most of them are dressed pretty normal. You're not one of them. You're invisible. You're going to play my obedient little wifey-poo, which means you carry the shopping bags and mostly just watch. I'm going to teach you how to blend in. We'll be in radio contact with Reaper back at base if we need him."

"What's Reaper do?"

"Besides play video games and watch porn?" Carl responded. "I'm not sure."

"Reaper's tapped into *everything*. Hacking, information piracy, anything complicated. In a way, he's as good at what he does as I am at what I do. Hell, he could screw with the traffic lights here from our apartment if we need him to." In truth, behind Reaper's pathetic tough-guy facade lurked the soul of an über-nerd who should have been working for NASA.

"What's your job, Lorenzo?"

I smiled. "I'm management." In actuality I wore a few hats, none of which Jill needed to know the specifics of. I was the master of disguise, the acrobatic second-story man, the con, the swindler, the lady's man, certified locksmith and safecracker, a ruthless fighter with hand or blade, and wasn't too shabby as a gunslinger. "These guys do all the work. I take the credit."

"What's Carl do?"

"Drive and shoot stuff," he explained. "People are stupid, so talking to them, that's Lorenzo's job."

"Carl's always my backup when we work. He's the getaway driver and heavy artillery."

"How many guns do you have in here?"

"A few . . ." And an RPG and a mess of Semtex, but she didn't need to know that.

"Can I have one?"

"No," Carl and I responded simultaneously.

This part of town was sleek, modern, damn-near swanky. Most of the buildings looked new, all glass and concrete. It had been less than a decade since the current emir had deposed his father. The old emir had been a pretty typical dictator, and he'd stuffed his Swiss bank accounts fat while most of his people lived in poverty. The current emir was a decent enough sort by all accounts. Sure, he was still ruthless and brutal, but he'd decided that the days of his country being a cultural backwater were done. He'd made friends with the West, told the Fundies to chill out, brought in big-time infrastructure investments, and even went so far as to say crazy, controversial stuff like Israel shouldn't be burned into nuclear oblivion. Like I said, pretty decent by this part of the world's standards.

And Al Khor was the shining example to the rest of the world that Zubara didn't suck anymore. I don't know if the emir was jealous of the nearby UAE or Qatar, but he was doing his best to keep up with the Joneses. Fueled by oil money, Zubara now had three hospitals, a university, luxury hotels, a big museum, a fancy new zoo, and, very impressively for a city of under a million residents, *two* Bentley dealerships.

Too bad the emir had stepped on so many toes in the process, because the line of people mean enough to take him down was getting longer and longer.

"*Sabah! Sabah! Sabah! Sabah!*" the crowd at the end of the street chanted, led by some professional agitator in a black hood with a bullhorn. They were a hundred yards away, and there were probably fifty of them, all relatively young and nicely dressed, probably students, and they were stacked in front of one of the tall municipal buildings. They were waving signs with pictures of a bearded man wearing a purple beret. Since there weren't any rocks or Molotov cocktails being thrown, it was relatively boring.

I stopped to watch. Jill halted obediently behind me. In true chauvinistic style, I had loaded her with a bunch of bags full of items purchased from the local shops. If you were going to be questioning merchants, it helped to spread a little love in the process. Jill had followed me for hours now, not understanding a word that passed between me and the various people I'd spoken with. I wondered if she was sick of it yet.

Glancing back, I saw that she was waiting patiently, burdened down by fifty pounds of miscellaneous crap that was probably just going to get thrown away after Reaper picked through it for souvenirs. Interviewing merchants looking for Dead Six had been an utter waste of time. Only Jill's dark eyes were visible under the blue silk scarf. Those eyes drifted over to the protestors, then back to me, wondering what was up.

The sidewalks were relatively crowded with the late lunch crowd, and we were right in front of a café filled with government employees, who were trying to eat and watch the protestors at the same time. Nobody was close enough to hear me speak English, so I leaned in.

"General Sabah's supporters are getting braver. See, with all of the killings lately, his followers are getting fired up that the emir isn't doing enough to stop it. If the emir loses enough support from the right people, then I bet you money the general is ready to have a coup to restore order, for the good of the people, of course."

Jill looked around nervously. I signaled that she could speak. "They talked about the general at the embassy. That's one of the reasons we got the order to get out. He hates Americans."

There was a concrete bench nearby, and these sandals were hurting my feet. I gestured for her to take a seat. A bunch of pigeons immediately surrounded us. They were probably escapees from the rooftop cages that littered the city. Pigeons here were a delicacy, and these once-fat things were reduced to scavenging for crumbs. I shooed one away.

"Men like him hate whoever is convenient to put them into power, and then they'll hate whoever's convenient to keep them in power. Sabah's side is supported by the Iranians. The emir screwed up. The Zubaran army hardly has any natives in it. Once the people started getting rich, they farmed out all the low-paying jobs to imported labor, and they included the army in that." I gestured around the street. "Notice that all of the waiters, taxi drivers, janitors, they're all Indians, Filipinos, Malays, or Sri Lankans? Sabah did the same thing with the military, but he filled it with Iranians and Syrians."

"So why doesn't the emir just fire the general?"

I pointed at the mob. "Because of useful idiots like them. The emir wouldn't just fire Al Sabah, he'd execute him if he could get away with it. But then half the city would get burned down, and that's assuming the emir's got the manpower to take him anyway. I'm guessing probably a quarter of the security forces would go with the emir, if that. Either way, an overt move by either one to topple the other would blow this place right up. I've seen it before."

"Where?" Jill asked, obnoxiously curious.

"Sixteen years ago I helped overthrow the democratically elected government of an African country," I explained. "It wasn't pretty. When a country collapses, the scumbags run free, raping and murdering. It's like nothing you can imagine. Think slaughter on an industrial scale. You take any city, take away their electricity, food, and water for a week, and it'll turn into *Mad Max*, guaranteed. And there's always some asshole ready to take those things away for his own benefit. I've seen it up close in Africa twice, Mexico, Chechnya, Haiti, Burma, Afghanistan, you name it, anyplace that has fallen apart, I've been there, and I see it coming soon to Zubara. I can *smell* it."

Jill studied the mob. "You've seen a lot of suffering."

I snorted. "I've *caused* a lot of suffering. Naw, that's just what I do. I seek out chaos. I make my living off the men that cause chaos. Assholes like Sabah are my meal ticket. Regular thieves steal from normal people. I steal from assholes."

"So, you're trying to say you're Robin Hood?" Jill scoffed.

"No, of course not. Assholes just have more money, and it isn't like they can cry to the cops when they get taken. It's worked out well for me."

"So, you justify being bad by only victimizing bad people."

"It's like karma, or something . . ." I trailed off as I noticed a black limo roll past us. It parked before the protestors at the front of the building. Apparently the mob was blocking the garage. A group of blue-uniformed security forces came down the government building's steps and surrounded the limo, rifles shouldered. The mob pulled back instinctively in the face of the guns. A young man in a designer suit stepped from the back of the limo.

"I think that's the Interior Minister," Jill said. "He's like the emir's nephew or something. He came to an embassy function once."

I surveyed the crowd. The students were full of noise but weren't so tough facing half a dozen men with rifles. In fact, they were quieter now. The chanting had stopped. The black-hooded agitator with the bullhorn was suspiciously missing.

"Jill, get up. Let's go." I stood. She started collecting the bags. I grabbed her arm. "Leave them."

The emir's nephew was met by an older man in a suit. They greeted each other warmly, surrounded by their loyal security forces. The young man adjusted his tie and smiled. My eyes narrowed as I picked out one person moving against the tide of the mob. Jill sensed the urgency in my grasp and sped up. We walked quickly back the direction we'd come. "Don't run. Don't look suspicious. Don't look back. When I push you down, cover your ears and keep your head *down*."

I glanced back. We were too far away to understand whatever it was the suicide bomber screamed. Probably just a teenager, he opened his vest, exposing stacks of gray wrapping his torso, and raised his arms wide. There was a long moment in time as the security forces and the nephew froze and the crowd right around the bomber instinctively recoiled. The pigeons leapt skyward in a cloud. I threw my arm around Jill's shoulders and took us both to the pavement.

The blast rippled across the ground and through my lungs. The concussion was massive. A wave of sound and energy rolled over us. Windows half a block away shattered.

Lying there, eyes clenched shut, hands pressed flat over my ears, I kept my weight on Jill, but no secondary explosions came. I uncovered my ears. First I could only hear a high-pitched whine, and that eventually settled into car alarms. Then I could finally hear the screaming of the wounded. As I rolled over, a wall of smoke and dust hung around the front of the government building.

People were wandering, dazed, bloody. Mangled bodies were splayed everywhere. The limo was twisted back into itself, jagged metal protruding. Severed limbs and bits of tissue littered the street. The shattered steps that had held the Interior Minister were coated in a red slurry of ribs and organs. The mob was *gone*.

Children were crying. A dog was barking. Where the hell had a dog come from? Already people were pulling out their cell phones. Some idiot's first inclination was to use his camera phone to take a picture of the carnage.

I got shakily to my feet. The café we'd been standing next to was a mess. Tables overturned, awning broken and hanging at a bizarre angle. One of the waiters was down, a giant chunk of hurled glass embedded in his throat, gurgling and thrashing on the sidewalk. Jill grabbed my thobe and hauled herself to her feet. Her facial scarf was dangling down her chest as she looked about in bewilderment, a stream of blood trickling from her nose.

"Got to keep going," I ordered. I put my hand on her shoulder and propelled her in the correct direction.

"Okay. Okay." Snapping back to reality, Jill realized her face was exposed and pulled the scarf back into place. We walked briskly down the street, part of a herd of humanity trying to get away from the terror. I guided her into an alley. Already I could hear the first sirens.

The alley was dark and cool. I got us behind a loading dock. "Hold your arms out," I ordered. Jill was confused but did exactly as I ordered. I ran my hands down the insides of her arms, then through her voluminous robes, patting her down, looking for blood. I'd seen people bleed out from shrapnel wounds to arteries without even knowing they'd been hit. Torso clear, legs clear. *No blood except the superficial amount on her face.* "Are you all right?"

"I'm . . . I'm fine. All those people . . ."

"Dead," I responded as I took my radio earpiece out of my shirt. "Nothing you can do about it. Hang on! Carl, come in, Carl!"

"What was that?" he bellowed in my ear.

"Suicide bomber. We're moving back toward Ensun and the Gamal Parkway on foot. Once we're clear of the responders, I'll call for pickup."

"Stay low and watch your back," Carl ordered.

"You, too." I pulled the earpiece out. "We've got to keep moving. This place is going to be swarming with security forces fast, and we don't want to get picked up for questioning." Jill nodded quickly. Her head was still in the game. *Good.* I took a handkerchief out of my vest and roughly wiped the blood from under her nose. "Keep your head down and keep up with me."

We went out the other side of the alley and started walking. The streets were full of workers now as people flooded out of their respective buildings to see what was going on. A pillar of black smoke rose into the air behind us.

The war had just arrived in Al Khor.

We were back in the apartment within an hour of the bombing.

My crew sat around our kitchen table. There was a white leaflet in the center. These things had been posted all over Ash Shamal within minutes of the explosion. I'd had Carl pull over and pick one up from one of the little kids that were passing them out on every single corner in the neighborhood.

The leaflet told all about how over twenty innocent students, most of them from this very district, were peacefully protesting in front of the interior ministry and had been massacred by the emir's personal guard. Apparently there had been another attack by the Zionist murderers, this one against the emir's own family, and he was still too emasculated to root them out; rather, he reacted in a heavy-handed and inept way against the innocent students of Ash Shamal's madrassa. Zubara needed the strong leadership of General Mubarak Al Sabah to get us through these tough times, not the Jew-loving emir . . . so on and so forth.

"That's such bullshit," Jill spat as Reaper finished translating it for her. "That's not what happened at all."

"Reality never matters," I muttered. "Just feelings. Get the masses riled up enough and you can do anything. Propaganda doesn't have to be true—it just has to *feel* true to enough stupid people. Make them feel picked on, then fill them full of hope about how you'll change stuff. Works every time."

"I so hate this place." Jill put her head down on the table. "Have you got any more of that ibuprofen? My head's killing me," she muttered through her arm. Shockwaves tend to have that effect on people. Reaper got her the bottle.

Carl glanced at me. "The bomb, how big?"

"At least twenty pounds. I was too far away to get a good look, but I'm guessing it was packed in nails or something from the mess it made."

"Good thing you weren't close enough to get a good look or we wouldn't be talking right now. These guys ain't fucking around," Carl responded. He'd been at the receiving end of a bombing during a job involving the Tamil Tigers several years back. That one had been wrapped in industrial staples. My friend still had one embedded in his back. It occasionally set off metal detectors. Carl didn't like bombs, unless he was the one setting them.

I sighed. This was it. If the country was moving into a full-blown revolution, then Dead Six was sure to bail. It was now or never. I glanced over at Jill. It was time to put her out there and see who tried to kill her. She still had her head down. She'd had a really tough day. *Shit.*

"How're you doing, Jill?" Reaper asked, a real note of concern in his voice.

"I'm fine," she lied. She slowly raised her head and moved her long hair out of her eyes, neatly tucking the stray strands behind her ear. She was remarkably composed, all things considered. "I've just never seen anything like that before. It was terrible, absolutely terrible."

"It's probably going to get worse," I added, "before we can get you out of here safely." *Lies.*

"So what do we do now, chief?" Reaper asked hesitantly.

I didn't know what to do. My one option sucked. Even the hardened killer, Carl, didn't like it, and Reaper would probably openly revolt. *I have to figure out how to play*—then my phone buzzed. It was from another unknown number. I flipped it open.

"Hello, my friend," Jalal Hosani greeted me. "I do not have much time."

I covered the speaker and mouthed *Hosani* to the others. Jill looked round, still confused. She was still in the dark about everything related to this job, and I intended to keep it that way. "What've you got?"

"I have some information about those friends you've been seeking to reunite with. I'm happy to say that they're still in town. I will need you to meet me the day after tomorrow. I will call you that morning with the location."

"Thank you, my friend." I said. "And how *appreciative* will I need to be for you doing this favor for me?"

"Do you remember how appreciative you were of the favor I did for you in Dubai? I believe that five times that should suffice."

I had paid him a hundred thousand American dollars for what he'd done for me that time, and that had been outrageous. So now Jalal was asking for *half a million.* "You've got to be kidding . . ." Reaper and Carl looked with mild curiosity. I took a pen and wrote *$500 K* on the bottom of the leaflet.

"Holy shit," Reaper said.

"Be cheaper just to beat it out of him," Carl suggested.

"Believe it or not, there are other people who would be even more appreciative of this information. But we are such old friends that I thought you should have the first opportunity. And also, I do believe that I will be going on a vacation shortly after, as the climate around here has gotten a little *warm* for my tastes, so I would like physical appreciation, rather than digital."

He wanted half a million in *cash.* "Physical?" I responded slowly, looking to Reaper, who thought about it for a second, then nodded in the affirmative. "Okay. But two days is short notice—are you cool if it is European appreciation?" Reaper hurried from the room.

"English, Euro, or other?"

"You picky bastard. Well, mostly British, God save the Queen, and some Continental, because I do love all those pretty colors, you know how it goes. And for this much love, it had better be damn worth it."

"Such a sense of humor! You are a good friend. I will be in touch." He sounded happy, and he should be.

I put the phone away. "Greedy, conniving son of a bitch."

"What just happened?" Jill asked.

"For information on Dead Six, Lorenzo just agreed to fork over half a million bucks," Carl explained. "Lorenzo has always sucked at negotiation."

Jill seemed absolutely stunned. "Where in the world are you going to come up with that kind of money? That's insane!"

Reaper came back into the room with a backpack and a big silly grin on his face. He dropped it in the middle of the table with a theatrical grunt. Carl, temporarily inconvenienced, was forced to move his beer out of the way. "I'll have to pull some out and recount it," Reaper said as he unzipped it. This particular bag was mostly U.K. pounds, neatly stacked 100 pound notes, fifty per stack, rubber-banded together. There were at least fifty stacks in this particular bag that we had smuggled into the country. Reaper pulled one out and flipped through it. "I'll have to check today's exchange rate first."

Zubara had been a British protectorate, and they still had a lot of influence here. So we'd smuggled in mostly pounds. We also had a mess of euros, dollars, and a giant pile of local riyals.

Jill made a whistling noise as she opened the bag wider. "The movies always make it look so much bigger. . . . How'd you get all this?"

I'd been stealing professionally for years from everybody from Al Qaeda to FARC, from the Yakuza to the Russian Mob, and I was about the best in the world. My exploits were the stuff of legend. I was worth a lot more than Jill could easily comprehend. I wasn't even really sure how much I had stashed in various encrypted accounts around the world dating back to my days working for Big Eddie. Personally, I was easily worth millions. I could have given up this lifestyle years ago, but then again it had never been about the cash. It had been about the *challenge*.

"I told you assholes always have more money," I answered with a smirk.

Chapter 12: Broken Arrow

VALENTINE
Location unknown
April 21
0700

Nine of us sat in the back of a V-22 Osprey, wondering where in the hell we were going. Well, eight of us were wondering. The ninth, Anders, seemed like he knew what was going on, but he wouldn't tell us anything. We'd been suddenly roused from bed and rushed to the desert, where we'd been picked up by the Osprey.

Anders wasn't really part of Dead Six. He answered only to Gordon and seemingly came and went as he pleased. I'd heard that he'd helped on a few missions, and he had a ruthless reputation. He never spoke to anyone else, and his background was a complete mystery. Holbrook was former Navy and said that he'd spotted a SEAL trident tattoo on Anders' forearm. Other than that, we knew nothing about the guy.

Tailor and Hudson were with me, as was Singer's entire chalk. Also with us was a new guy, a heavy-set dude with a buzzcut. His name was Byrne, and he was Wheeler's replacement. Like me, he was former Air Force. We'd heard that new guys were showing up here and there to augment our losses. Obviously, those rumors were true.

Singer *had* been around since day one, and he was a solid team leader. Tall, lanky, and possessed of a sick sense of humor, Singer had probably the best track record of any of the chalk leaders, a fact which drove Tailor insane. With him were Holbrook, Cromwell, and Mitchell, all good guys.

We were roused out of bed in the middle of the night and were driven out into the desert again. Instead of the stealth helicopter they'd flown us around in before, I was surprised to be picked up by the awkward-looking tiltrotor aircraft.

We'd been in the air for over an hour. No one talked; it was too loud in the back of the aircraft. We were all wearing earplugs, and most of my teammates had fallen asleep. The tiltrotor's cramped cabin was illuminated by red overhead lights. Anders sat toward the rear, away from the rest of us, and was carefully studying something on a PDA.

We were all fully kitted up in battle rattle, too. My MK 17 rifle was slung across my chest, with the muzzle hanging between my knees. My vest was covered with magazines, grenades, and other ridiculously heavy crap. We'd even been given fancy new A-TACS camouflage fatigues to wear.

Pulling my hat down over my eyes, I tilted my head back and tried to fall asleep. I figured the Osprey would either have to land or refuel sooner or later, and maybe then Anders would tell us what was going on. Until then, I was going to rack out for a while.

I don't know how long I'd been asleep when Anders kicked me, but it couldn't have been very long. Startled, I sat up, pulling my hat off my head. Anders had strolled, hunched over, down the cabin and roused all of us. He turned around at the front of the cabin, sat in one of the chairs, and addressed us as a group.

"Listen up!" he said, raising his voice over the dull roar of the engines. "This mission is the highest priority operation we've received. You men make up the best teams Dead Six has, and that's why you were selected for this operation. You need to understand that everything you're about to hear is need-to-know only. Do not discuss this operation with anyone. Not your friends, not the other chalks, not the admin pogues, no one! Am I making myself clear enough? If there's an OPSEC breach on this, I'm going to fuck your world up. Understood?"

We all nodded haltingly. None of us liked being threatened by this douche bag.

Anders continued unfazed, holding up the PDA so we could see the screen. We leaned in to try to make out the small picture he was showing us. "Your objective is this. This is the warhead to a Russian RT-2PM Topol ICBM. It has a yield of five-hundred and fifty kilotons."

Anders pushed a button on his PDA, then held it up again, showing us a new picture. "This is what the physics package of the warhead looks like if it is removed from the reentry vehicle. This part is where the nuclear reaction takes place and is all that is required to produce a yield. As you can see, this part is small enough to fit in the trunk of a small car." The eight of us looked at each other. "I think you can see where this is going," Anders said dispassionately. "This particular warhead, so far as we know, was removed from its missile and was to be destroyed in accordance with the START treaty. It disappeared years ago and has never been accounted for. At this moment, the warhead is on a truck, headed for a remote airfield in Yemen. From there, we expect it to be flown covertly to Zubara and delivered to General Al Sabah. For obvious reasons, we're not going to allow this to happen. We're flying nap-of-the-Earth right now. We'll arrive at the target site just before dawn and intercept the warhead before that plane takes off. Our mission is to secure the warhead and eliminate anyone involved in the delivery. We will take *no* prisoners. Any questions?"

We had none. "Good," Anders said. "Each chalk will operate as a fire-team. The plane will be waiting on the ground when we get there. Tailor, take your chalk and secure the aircraft. Singer, take your chalk and secure the truck. It's probably escorted, and there could be heavy resistance. Be aware that the situation can change at any time. If we get there and it's obvious the plane hasn't been loaded yet, I want both teams to hit the truck. No matter what, we have to secure that warhead."

"What will you be doing during all this?" Singer asked.

"Whatever I feel like. I have the RADIAC equipment," Anders said curtly. "I'm also a trained medic. I'll be on the ground with you and will direct you over the radio as the situation develops. Do your job."

I sat back against my seat and looked at the floor. The tension in the air was making me uncomfortable. Nobody liked being around Anders. Why would they only send eight guys, plus Anders, for such an important mission? You'd think they could at least spare a third chalk to stop General Al Sabah from obtaining a nuclear weapon! *What the hell is going on?*

VALENTINE
Somewhere in Yemen

Tailor had his arm over my shoulder as I helped him along. Blood trickled from a wound on his right calf, and he was limping pretty badly. The wound didn't look that bad, but even "minor" gunshot wounds hurt.

We hobbled down the ramp of a damaged An-74 transport plane, back out into the early morning sun. The notional airstrip we were at didn't look like it had been used in decades. There was nothing left but a short, cracked runway, a ramp half covered in desert sand, and one road leading off into the hills. The terrain around us was rugged and mountainous. A cold wind blew steadily across the flat spot the airfield had been built on.

We'd arrived right in the middle of the transfer of the nuclear warhead. It had already been loaded on the plane, but the convoy that transported it hadn't yet left when we came upon the airfield. We took them by surprise, landing right in the middle of their deal.

It was a bloodbath. More than twenty-five bodies littered the area around the transport plane. A convoy of trucks sat shot-up and burning behind the damaged aircraft. Once we had confirmed that the weapon was on the plane and not in the trucks, the modified Osprey had done a strafing run with a chin-mounted gun turret. Both chalks had struck with the element of surprise and liberal use of 40mm grenades. The Yemenis had been quickly overwhelmed.

Which isn't to say that things went well for us. Singer was on the ground in front of us, gurgling and gasping for air. Blood poured from a sucking chest wound near his armpit. The bullet that hit him had missed his ceramic plate and plunged deep into his chest, probably tearing through his lungs.

Cromwell had ripped off Singer's vest and was hastily applying a pressure dressing. It just wasn't enough. "Christ, I can't stop the bleeding!" he cried. "Hang in there, boss! Where's Anders? Anders! I need a medic!"

Anders strode up from behind the wreckage of a 6x6 truck, satellite phone in hand. "What's the matter?" he asked casually, stuffing the phone into a pouch on his vest.

"I can't stop the bleeding!" Cromwell repeated. "I need your help!"

Anders, not moving with any particular urgency while Singer suffered, squatted down, smacked Cromwell's hand aside, and began to inspect the wound. He stuck his face in close.

"There's nothing I can do," Anders said emotionlessly. "Tension pneumothorax. He sucked in too much air from the entrance wound. His lungs have collapsed." He stood up and wiped the blood off on his pant legs. Singer had stopped moving. "He's dead." The tall operative then turned on his heel and headed for the ramp of the An-74.

"Hey!" I said, unable to hide the anger in my voice. "Tailor's hurt, too!" Tailor winced as he put weight on his hurt leg and babbled a short stream of obscenities.

"He'll be fine. You've got combat lifesaver training, right?" Anders said, not looking at me as he walked up the ramp into the aircraft.

"Fuck you, Anders!" Tailor said. Anders ignored him and disappeared into the plane. "Shit . . . Val, I gotta sit down. Help me out here." I supported Tailor's weight as he lowered himself onto the edge of the plane's cargo ramp. He extended his wounded leg. "Take a look at that, will you?"

Slinging my rifle behind my back, I snapped out my automatic knife and cut his pant leg away. He had a nasty gash in his left calf. I pulled out a bandage and applied pressure to the wound. Tailor grunted and swore as I did so.

"Cromwell," Tailor said, forcing himself to talk through the pain. "You okay, buddy?"

Cromwell and Holbrook were kneeling next to Singer. Holbrook gently pushed Singer's eyelids down.

"He's gone," Cromwell said. Furious, he stood up and stomped away. Holbrook fell onto his butt and sat there, staring at his dead friend.

"Holbrook?" I asked.

"Singer's dead, man. Singer's fucking dead." He put his bloody hands over his face.

Their chalk's fourth man, Mitchell, had caught a round in the throat on the way out of the Osprey and was dead on the spot. Hudson and our new guy, Byrne, stood back cautiously, scanning the horizon for reinforcements. The Osprey we'd arrived on had landed and was waiting for us.

Anders came out of the plane, stowing the radiation detector. He was talking on the radio. "Tarantula, this is Drago. Package is secure . . . Roger that." He strode down the ramp and started giving orders. "Valentine, Holbrook, bring that nuke out here. I've got a strike team coming to secure it."

"Strike team?" Tailor snarled. "Where were they while we were getting shot at?"

Anders glared at him, nostrils flaring. "We needed to get here before this thing moved." Anders saw Holbrook sitting there, with his head in his hands, and came over and kicked him in the side. "Get off your ass. I gave you an order."

Suddenly, Holbrook stood, bloody hands clenched into fists. "You let Singer die!"

Anders shrugged. "Shit happens."

Holbrook lost it. He swung for Anders's face, but the big man moved shockingly fast. He easily ducked aside, but followed up with an elbow that got Holbrook square in the face. Then Anders hurled him headfirst into the ramp. Tailor and I barely got out of the way. Anders's heavy boot slammed down on Holbrook's back. Holbrook cried out in pain.

Singer's chalk was tight, and Cromwell saw his buddy go down. He came running. Anders saw him coming and calmly readied himself. Cromwell threw a punch that Anders easily blocked. Anders then slugged Cromwell in the teeth. Cromwell swung wildly, but Anders let it sail past before surging forward and grabbing Cromwell by the armor and then wrapping his big left arm around his throat. Somehow Anders had pulled his combat knife and it was pressed against Cromwell's jugular.

Instinctively, I jumped up, pulling my rifle around from where it had been slung behind my back, but Anders was too quick. A pistol appeared in his other hand, and, faster than I could blink, I was staring down the barrel of a .45. I froze. Anders's pistol was a big H&K MK 23. He spoke very slowly. "Got a problem, Valentine?"

I was *Calm*. I didn't say anything, but Tailor did. "Fuck you, Anders!" Of course, *he* wasn't the one with a gun stuck in his face. Now Tailor had his .45 out and leveled at Anders. "Let Cromwell go!"

"Safety that sidearm and place it on the deck, Tailor, or I shoot your girlfriend in the face."

"Easy, Tailor," I suggested. Holbrook was moaning, trying to rise. Cromwell was turning red; his eyes were focused on the blade pressed against his neck. Hudson had come running and was now covering Anders with his SAW.

The hulking operative took it all in calmly. He showed no fear at all. "Shoot me and you walk home." There was nothing but barren rocky desert as far as the eye could see. We'd have better odds of surviving a walk across Mars. Anders glanced around. "I hear Yemen is nice this time of year."

Tailor slowly lowered his weapon. "Stand down, Hudson," he ordered. Anders waited, keeping his gun on me for longer than he needed to, just because he was a douche. Finally he put his arm to his side, but he didn't holster. Anders let go of Cromwell, and he fell, gasping, to the ground.

"That's better. Now quit your crying and secure that package before I get angry." Anders turned and walked away. He casually stepped over Cromwell. "Get this piece of shit onto the bird."

We watched as the second Osprey dusted off. Anders's mysterious strike force had arrived a few minutes before and secured the package, all while keeping a suspicious eye on us. Thankfully, Anders went with them. Holbrook and Cromwell were both still dazed. Hudson and Byrne were helping them onto the aircraft ahead of us. I was supporting the still-limping Tailor. In the distance we could see dust from approaching Yemeni reinforcements. They were still a ways off.

"Hey, Val. Remember back in Vegas when I said you were a killer?"

"What about it?" I grunted as I helped him along.

"Well, you ain't in the same league as Anders. That fucker *scares* me."

"Tailor, can you see where this thing is going?"

"Yeah, I can," he replied. He pulled out a cigarette and lit it. Tailor's hands were shaking.

"The money isn't looking so good anymore."

He had talked me into this, and he knew it, but it wasn't in Tailor's nature to admit making a mistake. "Not really."

"We need to make a Plan B, bro."

"You think so?"

"I think so. I think we might need to disappear in a hurry. They obviously think we're expendable. Have you checked your bank account?"

"No, why?"

"I can't access mine from the computers at the fort."

"You think they're not paying us?"

"I've heard the others talking. Nobody can check their accounts. Hunter said he'd ask Gordon about it. Remember what Hawk said?"

"If we're dead they don't have to pay us. Son of a bitch," Tailor said tiredly. "I think you're right. I think we might need to ditch these guys. This is Mexico all over again."

"Got any ideas?" I asked as I helped him up the ramp.

"Not really."

"I might."

VALENTINE
Al Khor District
April 22
2100

It was a typically warm and dry night as Tailor and I made our way down the sidewalk, trying not to draw attention to ourselves. Al Khor had the most Westerners of any of the Zoob's three urban districts. A few weeks prior, it wouldn't have been unusual to see quite a few Brits and Europeans out and about.

Things had gone downhill since then, and now Westerners were abandoning the city. A string of car bombings and other attacks kept most Westerners indoors at night. The streets of the city were still jam-packed with traffic, and the sidewalks were only a little less crowded, but you could feel the tension in the air as the tiny little nation held its breath.

Project Heartbreaker was at the same time wildly successful and a miserable failure. We did indeed have the terrorists on the run here. Several of our chalks were sitting at safe houses, idle, because there wasn't much to do. We were literally running out of targets. To that end we'd begun casting the net wider, expanding operations into neighboring Qatar and the United Arab Emirates.

According to our intelligence contacts, including those ostensibly working for the Emir, the terrorists were scared shitless. Horror stories about the men who leave the Ace of Spades had spread as far as Afghanistan and Indonesia. The local press had picked up on it here and there, too, but the Zubaran government had, for the most part, quashed that before it became an issue. Dead Six had become the Bogeyman that terrorists looked under their filthy beds for.

At the same time, the Confederated Gulf Emirate of Zubara was slowly tearing itself apart. The fear and chaos we'd caused was intended to be inflicted only upon the terrorists, but it had quickly spread to the wider community. General Al Sabah was now positioning himself to be the new Iron Man of the Arabian Gulf, and had half the Zubaran Army on his side. The emir was on shakier ground than ever. It seemed very likely that the emir's regime would fall, not to Islamic Fundamentalist fanatics as originally feared but to a militant opportunist who wanted to become a world power broker overnight.

The entire situation was a confusing mess that threatened to send the region spiraling into chaos. On top of it, we'd paid a steep price for our questionable success. Almost one-third of our personnel had been killed in action at this point.

I was terrified of what would happen to Sarah if we stayed in the Zoob. So Tailor and I had talked it over for a long time. I then talked to Sarah, while Tailor talked to Hudson, and that was as far as the talking went. There were others I liked, others I'd have liked to bring in, but I couldn't trust anyone else. We were getting out.

That was easier said than done, of course. I could, I suppose, have just gone to the airport, whipped out my passport, and tried to buy a plane ticket, but that would've created questions. In any case, I was sure Gordon's people had mechanisms in place to catch us if we tried to run. So we'd have to be clever.

I'm not really that clever. I'm not the guy that comes up with cool tricks or brilliant plans. Neither is Tailor, regardless of what he might tell you. But you don't have to be clever if you have clever friends.

Tailor stood watch while I entered a phone booth outside an Internet café. Zubara still had pay phones aplenty, unlike the United States. Foreign workers fresh from South Asia didn't have cell phones that worked in the country, so they often made use of the pay phones until they got situated. I had a cell phone myself, of course, but it was issued by Dead Six, and I wasn't about to use it for this.

I pulled from my pocket a wrinkled piece of paper. Scrawled on the paper, in my own handwriting, was a long telephone number. Using a prepaid international calling card that I'd bought with cash, I dialed and waited. It took several seconds to connect, then began to ring.

Ling answered the phone on the second ring, sounding a little sleepy. I had no idea what time it was where she was. For that matter, I had no idea where she was.

"Um, hello?" I said awkwardly, hoping like hell she wasn't pissed that I'd ignored her e-mails.

"Who is this?" Ling asked firmly.

"It's Valentine. Remember Mexico?"

Ling was quiet for a second. "Michael Valentine? This is a surprise."

"I'm sorry," I said. "I hope I didn't wake you."

"It's three o' clock in the bloody morning here," Ling said, not actually sounding irritated. "Of course you woke me. Are you calling to take me up on my offer?"

"Actually . . . I need your help."

"Is that so? What sort of help?"

"I'm in kind of a bad spot here, and I need to get out of it."

"Where are you?"

"The Middle East."

"It would help if you were more specific, Mr. Valentine."

"I'm in the Confederated Gulf Emirate of Zubara."

Ling paused for a moment. "Oh. Oh, I see. Yes, I can see where you might be in some trouble then. How did you come to be there?"

"That's a long story."

"Can I safely assume that you've been getting into trouble there, or perhaps causing trouble yourself?"

"That'd be a safe assumption," I said, nervously looking around. Tailor gave me a thumbs up through the glass.

"Very well," Ling said. "What sort of help do you need, then?"

"I need to get out of here," I said flatly. "As soon as possible. Normal methods of transportation aren't workable. I need to just disappear."

"Just you?" Ling asked.

"No, me plus three others. People I trust. I don't care how we go, and right now I don't even care where we go, we just need to go."

"What's going on?"

"Look, I can't stay on the line too long. If we're gone too long they'll notice, and then there'll be questions, and that will cause problems."

Ling chewed on that for a moment. "I see. I see. So tell me, honestly. Why should I help you? How can I even trust that you're not now working for someone trying to set a trap for my organization?"

"Because a bunch of my friends died trying to help get that girl off that boat before she disappeared. Because I, personally, risked my life to keep her safe, even though you never even told me why she was important. I have money. I'll pay if I have to. I just need your help."

"As luck would have it," Ling said after another long pause, "I'll be in that part of the world shortly. Do you have a way for me to contact you?"

"Not securely, no," I admitted. "I have a phone, but it's probably monitored. I'm on a pay phone right now."

"I see. Okay, I'll need you to call me on May fourth. We'll set up the meeting then.

"Meeting?"

"Yes. I want to meet with you face-to-face. If all goes well, we'll have no problem getting you and your friends out quickly after that."

"Can't we all just go the first time? Things are circling the drain here."

"We can do it my way, or I can go back to bed, Mr. Valentine," Ling said, ice in her voice. "It's up to you."

I exhaled. "Okay, okay, we'll make it work. I'll call you on May fourth and we'll go from there."

"Good," Ling said. Her voice softened just a bit. "Please be careful."

"Thank—" Ling hung up on me before I could finish thanking her.

Chapter 13: Hasa Market

LORENZO
May 3

I was in the kitchen when my phone buzzed, indicating a new text message.

Hasa Market. 4:00 at the fountain.
Wait for further instructions. Come alone.

I scowled. *Come alone?* Why did he need to specify that? Did he somehow think that this was all some sort of scheme to get him into the open? Was he afraid Dead Six was coming for him, too? Or maybe he thought that I just wanted to get the info out of him and then cheat him out of the money. . . .

Or it was a trap for me. There were plenty of people in this country who would pay Hosani good money for my head. "Carl, check this out," I called.

My partner joined me a second later. He only glanced at the phone for a second. "Trap, it sounds like, maybe."

"Could be. But we need the info. It's worth the risk."

"You going alone?" Carl asked suspiciously.

"Of course not. Hasa is a busy place. It's that fish *souk* right off the docks at the end of Umm Shamal. Plenty of places for you guys to stay incognito."

Carl shook his head. "No vehicles in there. I can blend in. Reaper, not so much." That was true. Our techie was about the palest white boy we were going to find in five hundred miles. I had given Jill crap about walking like an American, but she was a master of disguise compared to Reaper. "I miss Train."

I missed Train, too. The big guy had been a virtual killing machine and had been great backup for situations like this. "We'll stick Reaper in the van back a ways. He's our ride out if we need him. We'll stay in radio contact." I tried to keep Reaper away from the hands-on part of the work. It wasn't exactly his area of expertise. But he was street-smart enough to keep his eyes open for anything suspicious.

"One problem," Carl said slowly. "What about the girl?"

"Aw, hell." He had a point. We couldn't just leave Jill here alone. I suppose we could have tied her up, but that didn't really go along with trying to get her to trust us. If this meeting didn't go well, she was still my ace in the hole. The other times I had gone out since she'd been here, there had always been at least one member of my crew here to make sure she didn't try anything stupid. She had behaved, so far. *Drugs were an option.*

Then Carl surprised me. "We take her." He caught my look of confusion. "Extra eyes we could use. I saw her after that bomb went off. She was tough. Most folks don't do that good first time they see a bunch of guts blown all over the street. We used to have a girl on the team."

He knew how much I hated when he brought up that bit of our past. "Her and Kat don't have very much in common," I said.

Carl shrugged. "Personality? No. But both pretty girls, skinny but still with big tits and a nice ass. The good parts are in common." As usual, Carl was a subtle poet of a man. "Pretty girls come in handy in this business, go places we can't, talk to people we can't. But that's not what I meant. This girl, she's a good girl."

"Carl, oh man, I can't believe this," I laughed. "You're getting soft in your old age. She's grown on you, hasn't she?" I didn't think Carl was capable of actually *liking* anyone.

That got him. He raised a meaty hand threateningly and waved one stubby finger in my face. "We'll stick her in the van. Make her feel helpful. This don't change nothing. It sure don't change the plan. So don't you give me no shit about getting soft. I've burned fucking *villages*. Got it?"

"Got it."

"Good." He folded his arms. "That said, I don't like your backup plan no more."

"Me either," I said slowly, but it wasn't like he had a better idea. For us, it was either find Dead Six or die. Nothing else would stop Big Eddie's rampage. "Hosani had better come through."

The four of us were gathered around the kitchen table. I had just outlined what was going down this afternoon. Reaper pulled up a Google Earth view of the Hasa neighborhood on one of his laptops.

"That's a pretty open area, Chief," Reaper said. "I can't see them trying to take you out in the middle of all that." The market was right off the docks. There were warehouses to the north, and a school and a mosque to the southwest. There were three roads in. At any given time of day, the place was packed with witnesses.

"If it is a trap, they'll send another text, telling me to walk somewhere

else quieter. That gives them a chance to see if I've got anybody tailing me."
I nodded at Carl. "You'll need to be discreet."

"What do you want me to do?" Jill asked quickly. It was almost like she was eager to prove that she was worth something.

I glanced at Carl. He shrugged. I already knew his opinion.

More than likely, nothing was going to happen. Hosani would give me an address or something, and I would slide him the backpack of cash. That was it. Odds were that this was going to be relatively boring. But then again, I had thought the same thing about Al Khor, and that had ended up with blood raining from the sky.

I placed the Bulgarian Makarov in the center of the table with a metallic clunk. "You said you know how to use this?"

She looked at me suspiciously for a second, then back to the gun, then back at me. "Who am I supposed to shoot?"

"Nobody in particular. You're going to be a lookout if Hosani tries to bring in help or if Dead Six shows up. Early warning, that's it. This is just for self-defense."

"Got anything bigger?"

"No. You get the *chick* gun." I rolled my eyes. "That's one of the most common guns in this part of the world for a reason. It works. It's concealable. And that's really important because like most shitty countries, Zubara's got strict gun-control laws. So unless you want to go to prison forever, don't get spotted with this. If you need to ditch it, I'm not worried about it, just drop it in a garbage can and keep walking."

Without further hesitation, she picked up the gun. I noted that she was careful to keep it in a safe direction and her finger was indexed outside the trigger guard. Maybe she had been taught well. "It's . . . double action. The safety works backwards from Dad's Beretta . . ." It took her a second to find the magazine-release. The Makarov had its magazine release button in the heel of the grip, unlike most American guns. She dropped the magazine on the table, then pulled the slide back, looking inside the empty chamber. She grinned maliciously. "Do I get bullets, too?"

I had to admit that she had a pretty smile. "We'll work up to that."

VALENTINE
Fort Saradia National Historical Site
May 3
1030

Tailor, Hudson, Byrne, and I were already sitting in the classroom when

Hunter came striding in, Sarah in tow. "I'll be brief, gentlemen," he said, opening his laptop and hooking it up to the display screen. "You're moving out shortly."

"We were told that we've got a lock on our next target, sir," Tailor said.

"That's right," Hunter replied, bringing up a picture on the screen. "This is your target, Jalal Hosani." Hosani was an average-looking Middle Eastern man, with styled hair and a scruffy, stubbly goatee. He was dressed in a brown suit and a white shirt with no tie, as was the fashion. "He's going to attempt to flee Zubara today. He's not going to get out of the country alive."

"How do we know this, Colonel?" I asked.

"Asra Elnadi," Hunter replied. "During her interrogation, she told us that one of Hosani's bodyguards was an ex-lover of hers, and they kept it on the sly. She was able to contact him and get him to sell out his boss."

"No employee loyalty," Byrne suggested.

"Not in this business, son," Hunter said. "With his boss skipping town, this guy's probably out of a job anyway. So he tipped off our contact without knowing who she's working for."

"How do we know this information is credible?" I asked.

"I made it clear to Ms. Elnadi that there would be severe consequences if the information she gave us proved to be false," Sarah said coolly. "She's afraid of us. I don't think she'd try anything stupid, especially since we've kept her alive so far."

Hunter switched the screen to a map of the city. "The target will be attempting his escape from a small warehouse that he owns in the Hasa Market, in Umm Shamal. This warehouse is right on the pier. According to the information Ms. Elnadi gave us, Hosani owns a boat. His escape plan is to load up his boat, hoist anchor, and sail away. Asra's ex-boyfriend told her that he's meeting someone in the warehouse around sixteen hundred hours, and that he'll be leaving immediately after.

"There are several places he could go, so if we lose him he's probably gone for good. Your mission is to intercept Jalal Hosani at the docks and kill him. There are no secondary targets. Tertiary targets are any of his employees and bodyguards that you encounter."

"We're going to kill him in the middle of Hasa Market in broad daylight?" I asked. "Sir, that's one of the busiest markets in the city. It'll be packed by mid-afternoon."

"I'm aware of that, Mr. Valentine, but it is this or nothing. Any questions?"

We had plenty of questions. We spent the next two hours in the classroom, formulating the plan.

LORENZO
May 3

I had been dropped off several blocks from the Hasa Market and had walked in. Umm Shamal was the middle peninsula and was relatively middle-class, so I wore jeans, a soccer jersey, and a good pair of running shoes instead of sandals. I carried the money in a small backpack.

I liked baggy jerseys. They were handy for hiding stuff, including the relatively soft Level IIIA armor vest. My STI 4.15 Tactical was on my hip, concealed beneath my shirt. Between it and the two spare longer twenty-two-round magazines on my off-side, I had sixty-three rounds ready to go. Also concealed on me was my Greco Whisper CT knife. It had a five-and-a-quarter-inch blade and was perfectly balanced. If Hosani tried anything, I was going to stick to my promise to take him with me.

There was one benefit if I bought it today. Once Big Eddie found out, that would probably get Carl and Reaper off the hook, temporarily. But he had leverage on them too, so even though they couldn't do this job, he would find some way to use them again. Believe me, I'd thought about faking my own death rather than finishing this job. But if Eddie ever got any inkling that I'd cheated him, he'd kill every single person in that folder.

The market was bustling with humanity. It was a miniature city, with buildings made from portable stands and wandering streets of weathered stones. This was where all the small-time fishermen sold their catch, so it was the best place in the city to get fresh fish. The violence in poor Ash Shamal and rich Al Khor hadn't really hit here yet. This was the part of town where the actual work got done. This was the home of the regular people, and they just wanted to live their lives in peace, earn their money, and raise their kids. Too bad for them they were stuck between a bunch of fanatics.

There was a line of speakers placed over the central row of booths. They were playing traditional music, which was actually kind of pretty in a haunting way. Every now and then the music would cut out and a fast-talking announcer would tell the customers about some special at one of the booths.

The fountain dated back to the British and was styled to be vaguely ancient Greek. It was out of place between all the tan brick buildings. I took a seat on the edge of the fountain, waited, and watched bus drivers and school teachers buy sea bass. My Bluetooth earpiece wasn't very out of place in this group.

"I don't see anything yet," Carl said. I knew he had stationed himself at the opposite end of the market near the corner of the school. He had dressed in full-on man pajamas and baggy vest. Carl was too stocky and muscular to pass for a Zubaran, but there were a lot of foreigners in this country, actually more foreigners than natives since the boom began, and he had grown a bushy beard that would make any mullah jealous. "I'm at the bootleg DVD table."

"Anything interesting?"

"They've got a Robert DeNiro five-pack. I'm watching the windows on the mosque. If I was gonna snipe you, that's where I'd be."

That was comforting.

"Lots of traffic, but nothing suspicious," Reaper said. He and Jill were parked about a block away to the south.

I noted a man standing near one of the fish stands. Skinny guy, wearing Ray-Bans, he was making good use of the crowd to cover himself but was obviously watching the people clustered around the fountain, waiting for something. He had the look of a local, so that was probably one of Hosani's men.

My phone buzzed. The text was short.

Walk north. Go to the first warehouse.

So the exchange wasn't going to be in public. The thin man saw me looking at my phone, right on schedule, so now he knew who I was. I bent down, as if to tie my shoe, but primarily so he couldn't see me speak. "Got the message. Moving north to the first warehouse. I've got at least one guy watching me. Stay low." I adjusted the backpack and started pushing through the crowd in the direction of the docks.

VALENTINE
Umm Shamal District
May 3
1555

Hasa Market was a sprawling, confusing maze of tiny shops, stands, and carts that emanated out from an old fountain in the square. To the north were a trio of warehouses on the pier. Tailor parked our Land Cruiser between a mosque and a small schoolhouse on the west side of the square.

Hudson and Byrne were supposed to park their vehicle on the opposite side of the square. As much as we could, we always took two vehicles on a mission. It gave us a backup option should we not be able to make it to our own vehicle. Also, we figured that with all of the chaos we were about to cause in Hasa Market, we'd have less chance of getting snagged by the cops if we split up.

The situation still sucked. Four of us were going into an unknown building against an unknown number of opponents. Because we had to go through a crowded marketplace in the middle of the afternoon to get to that building, we could only bring weapons that we could conceal, i.e., handguns. Going into a gunfight with nothing but a handgun is stupid and should be avoided if at all possible.

Unfortunately, it wasn't possible. Hunter had suggested that we use compact assault rifles, concealed in backpacks, that we could drop if we needed to disappear into the crowd. Gordon Willis had overruled him on that one, apparently. He said it caused an unacceptable risk of getting made.

It seemed the risk of us getting our asses shot off trying to go into a gunfight with nothing but pistols didn't bother him. By that point I'd had more than my fill of Gordon Willis. But there was nothing we could do except carry on with the mission and try not to get killed.

Tailor and I made our way through the cluttered mess of Hasa Market, doing our best not to be noticed. We were both wearing khaki cargo pants, dark T-shirts to conceal body armor underneath, sunglasses, and untucked shirts to hide our sidearms. We looked undeniably American, but even with the recent chaos, no one seemed to pay us any mind.

The market stunk of fresh fish, and squawking seagulls filled the air. The rows of booths, carts, and shacks weren't laid out in any discernible order. They were gaudily decorated with what looked like Christmas lights, loudspeakers playing music, and signs in six languages. Most of the shoppers at Hasa Market weren't Zubaran citizens, or even Arabs. Most were imported labor from India, South Asia, and the Philippines.

The market sold more than just fish. Goods of every variety could be bought, from bootleg DVDs to clothes to medicine of dubious medical value imported from Asia. As Tailor and I made our way past various stands, the vendors would blurt sales offers out at us in broken English, telling us they had a great deal that was perfect for our needs.

"Lo siento, no hablo Inglés," is all we'd say in return. Tailor and I both spoke Spanish fairly well and had decided that with this many witnesses around, we'd avoid speaking to each other in English if at all possible. Half the world spoke English, including people in the Middle East. You'd be a lot harder pressed to find a Middle Easterner that spoke Spanish.

I did have to speak English into my radio, so I squeezed the transmit button and spoke softly. "Control, Nightcrawler, target building in sight." Tailor and I studied the warehouse though the crowd, trying to discern the best way in.

"*Control copies,*" Sarah replied. Hearing her voice in my ear comforted me in a strange way. "*You are cleared to engage. Be careful.*"

LORENZO

The noise of the market was muted here by the thick walls of the surrounding buildings. The skinny guy was still following discreetly. I had to cross a narrow street, and, glancing both ways, I saw no vehicles other than parked delivery trucks. It was late enough in the afternoon that all the day's deliveries had been made. It smelled like fish.

There was a man, wearing a nice suit, waiting for me at the side door of the first warehouse. "Mr. Lorenzo," he said in rough English. "I need search you before come in."

"Tell Hosani to kiss my ass. If he's got a problem, me and my big bag of money will just go home."

The guard nodded. "He said you say something like that. I just want make sure you right man." He opened the door into darkness.

The interior of the warehouse was dark and cool. Crates were stacked up in neat rows. The roll-up door at the rear of the building was open, and a few small fishing boats were tied there, as well as one nice fifty-footer.

I spotted Hosani in the shadows under the catwalk by the glowing ash of his cigarette. There were a couple other men standing toward the back of the warehouse, and, from the sound, at least one pacing the metal catwalk above. If he wanted to take me out, I was well and truly screwed.

"Hey, Jalal. You didn't need to bring your whole gang," I said with forced joviality, mostly so Carl would hear and know that there were a lot of men with guns here.

"Don't flatter yourself," Jalal said. "This is how everyone in my line of work has to travel now, in groups, and in secret. I'm only doing this as a favor, and then I'm getting on that boat"—he waved his cigarette toward the back of the warehouse—"and going someplace safe."

"I thought this was good for business."

He adjusted his coat as he put his lighter away, exposing the butt of a compact pistol. Hosani sold guns, but I'd never seen him actually use one. He really was nervous. Earlier I had thought Dead Six was unprofessional because of their lack of subtlety, but now I could see the logic behind it. Their targets were *terrified* of them.

"These Americans who leave the playing cards, they're only part of the reason I'm leaving. This Dead Six, as you called it, is part of something bigger. I do not think they even realize who they are really working for." He trailed off with a wry smile. "But as they say, why buy the cow when you can get the milk for free? My appreciation?"

"Of course." I tossed him the backpack. He unzipped it and glanced inside, rifling quickly through the stacks of British currency. "You can count it. I won't be offended."

"I don't feel like sticking around any longer than I have to," he responded as he zipped the bag back up and put it over his shoulder. "I've got to warn you, Lorenzo. I don't know what Big Eddie's commissioned you to do, but it isn't worth going after these people."

"That's not an option."

VALENTINE

We paused for a moment, allowing our eyes to adjust to the darkness. We were in the warehouse. I slid my sunglasses up onto my head and pressed onward. The small side door we'd come through led into the main room of the warehouse, but it was stacked from floor to ceiling with racks and shelves full of boxes. Voices could be heard echoing through the building, but we couldn't see anyone.

We crouched down and quietly weaved our way through the maze of racks and crates. The roll-up door at the north end of the warehouse was open to the docks, flooding the center of the floor in brilliant daylight. Above that door was a metal catwalk. There was someone up there. We'd have to take him out before Hudson and Byrne came in, otherwise he'd be above and behind them as they entered from the other side of the building.

I came to a spot where I could see the main floor through a narrow gap between two crates on the shelf in front of me. Tailor had his 1911 Operator drawn and watched my back as I tried to ID my target.

There were at least four more men in the building aside from the man on the catwalk. Two of them were standing off to the side, in the shadows, probably more bodyguards. The other two men were more interesting.

One of them was a fit-looking man wearing a soccer jersey and jeans. He had on sunglasses and had a scruffy, unshaven face, so I couldn't get a good look at him. A backpack was slung over his shoulder.

The other man was facing away from me. He wore a dark suit and had a lit cigarette in his hand. I couldn't quite make out what he was saying over the noises of the city and the harbor, but he was discussing something with the man in the soccer jersey. He paced as he talked, and turned around so I could see his face. There was no doubt about it. It was Jalal Hosani. I looked over at Tailor and nodded. Through hand signals, I told Tailor I was going to shoot

Hosani from our current position. Hosani was only about fifty feet away, I could make the shot easily. Tailor told me he'd cover the catwalk.

I aimed my revolver through the gap in the crates, placing the tritium front sight on Jalal Hosani's chest. I wasn't going to attempt a head shot at this range. If he was wearing a vest, the impact of a fat .44 hollow point would still probably break some ribs. Hudson and Byrne would be in the building before he could get away.

Hosani turned away to face the man in the soccer jersey. I adjusted my sight picture and aimed in between his shoulder blades as Jersey Guy tossed him a backpack. Hosani opened the bag and rifled through it. My finger moved to the trigger. I exhaled.

LORENZO

Jalal took a long drag off of his cigarette and shook his head as he exhaled. "Very well, my friend. It's your funeral, as they say. For my part, I—" Jalal's white shirt exploded in a spray of red, and a sledgehammer weight collided with my chest.

Jalal's blood was on my face, in my eyes, and I could taste it in my mouth. He collapsed into me, clawing at my shirt, but he was already dead and didn't even know it yet. I stumbled and fell, taking us both to the concrete. The bullet that had torn through his torso was stuck in my vest, and waves of pain radiated out from the bruised tissue underneath.

There was more shooting. Muzzle flashes back and forth across the warehouse as Hosani's guards went down, one after the other. There was a scream from above, and the man on the catwalk flipped over the edge and landed a few yards away, bones audibly cracking on impact.

It was the shooter from Adar's video, the tall one with the .44. He was moving smoothly down the aisle of crates. He had this calm look on his face, just kind of concentrating, like he was reading an interesting book or something. I shoved the twitching corpse off and jerked my pistol out. I didn't have a shot. He caught the movement and ducked down as I started cranking off rounds. My bullets flung splinters from the surrounding boxes as I scrambled to my feet. I kept firing, forcing him to keep his head down as I moved.

I flinched as a bullet impacted a support beam right next to me. There were multiple shooters. Jerking my head in the direction of the shot, I saw the shorter man from the Adar video vaulting over a railing. He disappeared between the crates. Now I had at least two of them hunting me.

I slid to my knees behind a crate. "Carl! Dead Six is here!" I instantly dropped the mag, stuffed the partially expended one in my pocket, and slammed a new one home. Pain radiated through my chest with every breath, and that was even after the bullet had zipped through Hosani. That wasn't a pistol, that was a cannon.

There was movement in the sunlight at the open dock door as someone else swept inside. *I have to get out of here.* There was a door to the side, offices or something. I leapt to my feet and sprinted through the doorway. It was a hallway, several doors branching off in each direction. *Shit.* Speeding right to the last door, I discovered it was locked. I took a step back and kicked it open, flinging it open with a bang. It was just a janitor's closet. No windows. No exit. The shooters were moving up behind me. I was trapped.

VALENTINE

Wooden crates splintered and fragmented above me as I ducked behind a crate and hoped that its contents were substantial enough to stop handgun fire. The man in the soccer jersey had spotted me.

I reloaded, punching my revolver's ejector rod and twisting a new speed loader into the cylinder. I then squeezed my radio's transmit button. "Xbox, I'm pinned down! Get this guy off me!"

"*I'm on it!*" Tailor replied. Seconds later more gunshots echoed through the warehouse as Tailor opened up with his .45. "*You can move!*"

"Roger! Moving!" I replied, coming to my feet again. I snaked through the maze of crates and shelves, revolver held out in front of me in both hands as I moved.

"*Xbox, Shafter, we're entering now!*" Hudson said over the radio. Tailor acknowledged him, and I wondered what in the hell had taken Hudson so long. I realized then that it had only been a minute since I'd fired the first shot.

"I've lost that shooter!" Tailor snarled, frustration obvious in his voice. In less than a minute we'd wiped out all of Hosani's guards except one. It kind of pissed me off, too.

I cleared the maze of crates and found myself in the open area in the middle of the warehouse. Jalal Hosani's corpse lay splayed out on the floor in a large pool of blood, a ragged hole between his shoulder blades.

"Careful," Tailor warned as Hudson and Byrne approached. "We still got one shooter out there, the guy in the jersey."

"Which way did he go?" I asked, kicking Hosani's corpse to make sure he was dead. He was. I dropped an Ace of Spades onto his back.

"You two," Tailor said, pointing at Hudson, "cover us. Val, follow me, I think he went through this door." The four of us split into pairs again.

Hudson and Byrne exited the way they'd come in, through the open dock door. Tailor extended his 1911 and led me behind another shelf of crates, through a door that was hidden behind it.

It led to a short hallway. Our two teammates stayed behind, covering the doorway while Tailor and I made our way down, weapons at the ready. There were two doors on one side and one door on the other, but all three were closed. At the end of the hallway, there was a partially open door. A small sign above the door read Custodian in English and Arabic. It was a janitor's closet. A backpack with a broken strap lay on the floor, a few feet from the door.

My eyes caught a flash of movement in the darkened closet. Tailor and I spread out to either side of the hallway and continued to inch forward. We were wide open, and doorways were fatal funnels.

Shit, I thought bitterly. *I wish we had grenades.*

"Hey! Why don't you come out and die like a man?" I shouted. I looked over at Tailor and shrugged. When all else fails, *negotiate.*

LORENZO

Please, don't let them have any grenades.

"Hey! Why don't you come out and die like a man?" one of them yelled. Despite his raised voice, he sounded very calm, almost conversational.

"Why don't you come down here and get me then?" I shouted around the corner. The closet was decent cover, the walls were solid, and if they wanted me, they had to come down that fatal funnel of a hallway. The first one to stick his head down here was going to die, and they knew it.

"Who the fuck are you?" one of them yelled, clearly agitated. Apparently they weren't used to somebody speaking English. He was obviously a Southerner.

"Nobody worth dying over," I responded. "You better hurry. Somebody had to hear all that shooting. You don't have much time."

"We'll make time," stated the calm one.

Carl came over the earpiece. He was out of breath. "*Some skinny guy saw me coming in the market and tried to stab me, so I broke his head.*" So Jalal's man had tried to stop my friend. That was a fatal mistake.

"There are at least three shooters. They've got me pinned down."

"*I'll circle around,*" he said. I could hear the Dead Six men talking back and forth in hushed tones down the hallway. The nearest two were speaking in Spanish, but they shouted at someone else in English that they would take care of me.

"*We're on the way,*" Reaper said. "*But I'm stuck behind some trucks.*"

"*I'm coming to help.*" The female voice over the radio took me a second to process. I could hear the van door open.

Idiot. "Jill, stay put!"

BOOM BOOM BOOM BOOM

I jerked away from the doorway as the walls shattered. The giant .44 Magnum slugs tore through the building materials with unbelievable fury. The smell of solvents filled the air from leaking containers. I stuck my gun around the corner and fired several wild rounds in response.

"Val! Holy shit, look at all this money!" They'd found the backpack.

"That's mine!" I shouted. "Assholes!"

"Not anymore, motherfucker!" shouted the obnoxious one. "*Ha!*"

VALENTINE

"This is taking too long," I said, dumping a fresh speed loader into my .44. "C'mon, man, we gotta go!" Tailor nodded, slung the backpack full of money, and led the way. I backed down the hallway, keeping my gun trained on the closet at the end of the hall. We'd already told Hudson and Byrne to head back to their vehicle, and the cops would be all over Hasa Market before too long.

"Control, Xbox," Tailor said, speaking into his radio. "Target neutralized. Egressing now. Will update as I can." Sarah acknowledged him on the radio as we reached the door at the other end of the hallway.

"It's your lucky day, asshole," I said to the man in the closet, even though I doubted he could hear me. Tailor and I then turned and bolted back through the warehouse.

LORENZO

It was quiet. I risked a peek. I couldn't see anything, but that didn't mean they weren't just waiting quietly to blow my head off.

"*Lorenzo, there are four of them. Two came in the back. They're heading west toward the street.*" Carl said. "*Those two fodas from the video just walked out the front. They're heading south through the market, trying to play it cool.*"

The ones with the box were the ones that mattered. "Tail them. I'm on my way," I responded, already heading for the exit. I shoved the STI back in its holster as I hopped over the bodies of Jalal and his men. There was no way I was going to let them get away.

The market was continuing as normal. The walls of the old warehouse and the music must have muffled the gunshots enough not to spook the crowd. I walked quickly, as running would have drawn too much attention. A woman gasped and pointed at me. Glancing down, I realized that I was still splattered with Jalal's blood. "Shit," I muttered.

"*They're moving south,*" Carl reported. "*I'm on them.*"

"Where?" I hissed. The woman was pointing at me and pulling on her husband's sleeve. I ducked my head and turned, moving deeper into the throng.

"*By the fountain.*"

"Reaper, move up on the entrance. Be ready to roll. Carl, we need one of them alive."

Carl came back. "*I've been made.*"

Then there was a gunshot.

VALENTINE

Guns holstered, Tailor and I pushed our way back through Hasa Market, south, where our vehicle was waiting for us. We nervously eyed the crowd as we walked, checking over our shoulders for the guy in the soccer jersey. I didn't know who he was, but I knew he wasn't just another militant asshole.

There wasn't time to worry about it. We'd been lucky, so far, in that no one had heard the shots or called the police, but I didn't want to find out how long that luck would hold. All we had to do was make it back to our truck and we were home free.

Not necessarily, I thought bitterly, remembering the night Wheeler died. We cleared the tangled mess of the marketplace and came upon the open area that surrounded the old fountain at the center. Like the rest of the market, it was choked with people, but it wasn't nearly as claustrophobic as the maze of shops and carts.

Gun. I noticed it so instinctively that I almost didn't realize it. Everything slowed down as *the Calm* kicked in again. On the other side of the fountain there was a man with a gun. He was short and squat, with a dark face and a scraggly beard. He was staring at me intently, and through the bustle of the crowd I could see him trying to bring a pistol to bear. He was dressed in local garb, but, like the man in the soccer jersey, I didn't believe he was some random Zubaran citizen.

Before I'd finished processing that, I realized my gun was clear of its holster and that the front sight was aligned on the man with the gun as he brought his own pistol up. His eyes grew wide as a gap appeared in the crowd; I had a shot. I fired.

I *missed*. My bullet struck the edge of the fountain, blowing off a small chunk and ricocheting off into the distance. My revolver's roar echoed through Hasa Market, and all at once everyone froze, heads turning to see what was happening. People around us stared at us wide-eyed, mouths agape.

"Oh, shit," Tailor said, his .45 already drawn. More shots rang out as the man with the gun fired at us, using the edge of the heavily constructed fountain as cover. Tailor and I shot back, moving laterally as we fired, trying to hit the gunman without killing anyone in the crowd.

All at once the marketplace was in chaos. People screamed and began to stampede in every direction. Tailor and I were nearly crushed by a throng of people trying to get away from the shooting. We couldn't even see the shooter through the morass of panicked shoppers, much less get a bead on him.

"We're compromised!" Tailor shouted, straining to be heard even though I was only a few feet from him. "Let's get the hell out of here!" He struggled to reload his .45 while he talked.

Following his lead, I lowered my now-empty revolver and began to push my way through the crowd. We headed west, toward the mosque. Our Land Cruiser was parked in an alley between the mosque and a school next door. After a few seconds, the crowd thinned a little, and I had room to breathe. I emptied my gun's cylinder and reached for my belt again.

Someone crashed into me as I drew the speed loader from my belt, causing me to drop it. My speed loader bounced off the concrete and rolled away. Swearing, I shoved the hapless person aside and crouched down, grabbing my loader.

I stood up, pausing to twist the cartridges into the cylinder, when someone shouted at me to stop in heavily accented English. I froze and looked up. About ten feet to my left was a Zubaran police officer. His pistol was pointed between my eyes. He held a radio in his other hand.

Two puffs of blood and uniform material erupted from the Zubaran police officer's side as Tailor double-tapped him. The cop staggered, and Tailor put a third round into his head. He dropped to the concrete like a sack of potatoes, his pistol clattering as it hit. I made eye contact with Tailor, nodded at him, and we took off at a run toward the mosque.

Looking back through the crowd, I couldn't see the stocky man who had shot as us by the fountain. But as we crossed in front of the school, I noticed a woman in a black burka running determinedly in our direction across the lawn of the mosque. She produced a small pistol from somewhere just as I rounded the corner into the alley.

LORENZO

I spotted the two Dead Six operatives fifty yards ahead, moving fast, straight for the mosque. That had to be where they'd left their car. I raised my gun, but there were too many terrified people stampeding between us, then they were around the corner of some booths and out of sight. "Damn it! Carl, flank around the mosque and hit them from the other side. Reaper, get your ass up here now."

I took off after them, darting between people. Some lady saw my gun and bloodsoaked countenance and screamed. That caused a bunch of other people to shriek and point, and a lot of them were already on their cell phones. This was so not good. "*Reaper*! We need immediate evac!"

"*Almost there!*" he responded.

There was a winding alley between the one-story school and the much taller mosque. The east end dumped into the market, and the west onto a quiet street. That's where I would have parked. I caught a glimpse of a khaki-clad figure duck into the alley. *Got you.* I moved up along the school wall, gun at my side. I was going to drop whichever one I saw first, then try to shoot the legs out from under the other.

Most of the people from the market were moving away from the two Caucasians and the men chasing them, and maybe that's why the woman with the veil stuck out so quickly. Jill Del Toro was coming across the lawn of the mosque, directly toward me, only she was going to reach the alley a few seconds before I was. She reached into her clothing and out came the little Makarov.

I ran faster, forcing myself forward. Jill brought the gun up in both hands, but she made the classic mistake of letting her gun lead around the corner, telegraphing her presence. And *he* had been waiting for it. One hand clamped around her wrist, jerking her forward. Jill disappeared.

Chapter 14: Anger Management

VALENTINE

I grabbed the woman's arm with my right hand, crushing her thin wrist as roughly as I could. I used her momentum, vaulting her around the corner. She cried out in surprise as I wheeled her around a full two-hundred and seventy degrees, and gasped for air when I smashed her against the wall of the mosque, my forearm on her neck. In the same instant I brought my own gun up, leveling it between her eyes, and I froze.

The veiled woman was now staring down the barrel of my .44 Magnum, dark eyes wide with fear. Her right hand went slack, and the little Makarov pistol clattered to the pavement. She stopped struggling, and I asked myself why I hadn't already fired. I couldn't find an answer. Tailor asked what was going on. I didn't answer him either.

I reached forward with my gun hand and ripped the woman's veil off of her head. The black veil covered a very pretty face. She was young, with tanned olive skin and night-black hair. She was Hispanic, or maybe of Philippine ancestry, and she looked . . . *damned familiar.*

Holy shit, I thought, suddenly remembering where I'd seen that face. "Jillian Del Toro?" I asked cautiously. Her eyes suddenly went even wider, and the color flushed out of her face. I couldn't believe it. It was the woman Gordon had put out the BOLO on.

I noticed something out of the corner of my eye: movement. Everything moved in slow motion as I watched, my consciousness still enveloped by *the Calm.* The man with the soccer jersey was approaching from my right, weapon drawn. He was running straight at me, hoping I wouldn't notice him in the mass of panicked, fleeing shoppers.

I yanked Jill Del Toro's arm forward as hard as I could, twisting to the right as I did so. She gasped in pain again. I let go of her hand and clamped my right arm around her neck. I pulled her against me and tightened my arm as I brought my revolver over her left shoulder and leveled it at the son of a bitch in the soccer jersey.

"Lorenzo, look out!" Jill Del Toro screamed. I tracked him with my gun

209

and fired. Jill winced as the gun discharged a foot from her face. He dove aside. The .44 slug smacked the corner of the school, smashing a small piece of brick into a cloud of dust.

I tightened my grip on Jill and hunched down behind her. The man in the jersey, Lorenzo, hovered just around the corner, where I couldn't get a shot at him. He didn't seem willing to risk a shot at me under the circumstances, either. Tailor was coming up behind me, pistol drawn.

"Just let the girl go," he said from around the corner. He spoke flawless, generic, unaccented English. "We can all just walk away."

"Listen, asshole," I growled, slowly backing down the alley. "I've had just about enough of you today. Why don't you come out so we can finish this?"

"Yeah," Tailor said, "we got your girl and your money bag. Having a bad day?"

We could hear police sirens in the distance. "What's it gonna be, ace?" I asked calmly, continuing to back down the alley, pulling the young woman with me as I went. "Cops are coming."

"Lorenzo!" the woman cried out, fear now obvious in her voice. I caught a flash of movement at the edge of the school. My revolver barked as I popped off another shot, taking another chunk off the corner of the building. Jill cried out again.

A couple of long seconds ticked by, and there was no response. Tailor and I made eye contact. I dropped the muzzle of my gun as he crossed in front of me, weapon held at the ready. He checked around the perforated corner of the school as I covered the opposite corner.

"He's gone," Tailor said, stepping back around the corner. He looked at Jill. "Guess your boyfriend got cold feet, bitch."

I couldn't help but smile at the absurdity of the situation. I yanked Jill Del Toro around and began to force her back toward our car.

LORENZO

I left her.

"Fall back, Carl. Fall back!" I ordered. The sirens were wailing. The security forces would be here any second. Everything was ruined. Jill had gotten herself captured. Dead Six had won. She was as good as dead. The mission was screwed. The only option left was self-preservation. I would have to figure out what to do about Eddie later. "Hurry."

"*I'm almost there!*" Carl responded.

"Leave them!"

The van tore around the edge of the school. I waved both hands overhead so he'd see me. Reaper stomped on the brakes, and the van screeched to a halt. I yanked open the side door. "Back up, grab Carl, and let's go."

"Where's Jill?" Reaper shouted.

"Go!" I bellowed.

But he hesitated. "She's one of *us*."

I froze, half in, half out of the van. My first inclination was to reach forward and smack Reaper on the side of his stupid head. In a minute we'd be fighting half the cops in Zubara. I was a thief. You run. That's what thieves do.

But he was right.

Something *snapped* just then.

I couldn't leave her.

Things had changed. She wasn't just bait. Jill wasn't just somebody I could use and throw away anymore. Reaper was right. She was one of us. "Son of a bitch!" I grimaced. Reaper must have seen it. Instead of putting the van into reverse like I had ordered, he stomped on the gas, narrowly avoiding running down a bunch of innocent bystanders, and headed straight for the alley.

"Carl, turn around and take them out!"

He was out of breath from running. "*Make up your mind!*"

The alley was probably forty yards long, five yards wide, and their car had to be parked either in it or on the exiting street. Trying to walk down that alley would get me killed, and shooting it out down the alley would only get Jill killed, and either way the cops were going to kill all of us in a second anyway. I needed to get on top of them, *fast*. The school wasn't very tall at all. I had an idea. "Reaper, pull right up to the front door of the school."

"What?"

"Just do it! Then back up and block that alley."

He did as I said, actually crashing our bumper into the front steps. But I didn't feel it as I was already out the side of the moving vehicle before impact. I stepped onto the bumper, the hood, the windshield, and finally onto the van's roof. I ran, jumped, and caught the edge of the roof with my hands. Pulling myself up, I scrambled onto the roof of the school.

I ran up the angled tile of the roof, parallel with the alley. This was idiotic. Half of Zubara was probably watching this moronic stunt, and I was sure that I'd be nicely silhouetted for the police snipers. The STI materialized in my hand as I approached the edge. Glancing downward, there were the assassins. The tall one was struggling against Jill, trying to force her into the backseat of a car, while she was fighting like crazy, but he outweighed her by eighty pounds. The Southerner was watching back down the alley, wearing *my* backpack, 1911 extended, waiting for me to appear at the end.

"What are you doing?" he shouted. "Cops are coming. Just shoot her already!"

The tall one grunted a response that I couldn't understand. He was hugging Jill's arms tight, but she just kept swinging her legs and jerking her head back into his face. I had no idea why he hadn't already shot her. Dead Six must have decided they wanted Jill alive for some reason. There was no time to think. The second Reaper appeared at the end of that alley, that psychopath was going to light him up. I punched my gun out, sights lining up on the Southerner's head.

There was a door into the alley from the mosque. It swung open directly behind the man, and he instantly spun toward it. There was a kid, probably all of six years old, standing there, and the kid was right behind my target. I was putting two and a half pounds of pressure on a three-pound trigger when I froze, thinking of the bullet that had passed through Jalal that was still throbbing, stuck in my vest.

I couldn't kill a kid. I'd never killed a kid.

The child looked at the Southerner, at his gun, and then over his shoulder, right at me. The Dead Six operative instinctively turned, following the kid's gaze. He saw me, eyes narrowed, and his gun flew up. Chunks of tile erupted skyward as I moved back from the ledge. Bullets just kept tearing through the mosque, searching for me, as he ran for the car.

At the end of the alley, our white van appeared, blocking their exit. They would cut Reaper to ribbons. I had to take them out *now*.

I took a few steps back, trying to remember the exact position of their car, hoped I was right, then ran forward and jumped off the edge.

VALENTINE

Jill Del Toro struggled mightily as Tailor snapped off several rounds at the man she'd called Lorenzo. I turned back to our Land Cruiser and, despite the girl's thrashing, pulled the passenger's door open. We had zip-ties in the glove box, and I was going to restrain the girl in my arms before I gave in to the temptation to *shoot her*. The terrified young child had disappeared back inside. We were out of time and had to get the hell out of there.

"Just shoot her and let's go, Val!"

CRUNCH! I looked up in surprise as Lorenzo fell off the roof of the school. He put a dent in the roof of our Land Cruiser as he landed. He tried to do a shoulder roll to dissipate his impact but ended up rolling down the windshield and falling off the hood of the truck. He disappeared over the truck as he hit the pavement on the other side.

He reappeared a split-second later, pistol leveled at me across the hood of the truck. He was listing slightly to one side, and blood started to trickle down his face, but he had a killing look in his eyes.

"Lorenzo!" Jill screamed again. Before Lorenzo could turn around, Tailor was behind him, pushing his pistol into the back of his skull.

"Drop it, motherfucker!" Tailor growled. Lorenzo let his gun fall. Then there was more movement as someone ran up the alley from my left. I'd been so fixated on Lorenzo that I hadn't noticed. Neither had Tailor, who, with a metallic *CLANG*, crumpled to the pavement as he was smacked in the head with a goddamned shovel.

LORENZO

CLANG!

Carl hit the Southerner unbelievably hard, collapsing the man in a heap. *I told him to take one of them alive.*

The tall one shoved Jill down as his hand flew to his gun. Carl was already diving behind the trunk as the Magnum spit flame. I hit the ground as he reflexively turned on me next. Brick dust rained down on me when he fired, pulverizing the wall where I had just been. The shooter with the hand cannon was circling the back of the car, wearing that look on his face again, like everything else in the world had just stopped, and that all that mattered was taking out the garbage.

Carl was going for his pistol but was struggling to get it out, snagged on the unfamiliar clothing. The left-handed shooter came smoothly around the back of the car, doing the math, deciding to take me out first, like he had all the time in the world, mammoth handgun leveled right at my face. Time dilated until I could see the cylinder rotate another giant hollow-point into position behind the barrel. Guns are scarier when you can actually see the bullets.

He twitched at the last possible instant, .44 slug digging a divot into the pavement next to my face, fragments raking bloody chunks from my upraised hands. The shooter jerked as another round struck him in the chest. I looked through the open door to see Jill shooting him with my pistol, then back in time to see him go down.

The police sirens were right on top of us. Reaper was honking the horn.

"Come on!" Carl shouted. He had leapt to his feet, tossed the shovel, and was trying to pick up the man he'd knocked out, pulling him by one limp arm. I moved to help but saw the man crawling around the back of the car, his buddy's 1911 in hand. Carl grimaced as the bullet struck him in the back. "Aaarg! I'm hit!"

"Run!" I shouted. The shooter ducked back down as Jill started punching holes in the trunk. I grabbed Carl by the vest and tugged him along. "Back to the van!" Jill kept shooting. "Jill, move!" She finally complied and ran after us. We reached the van a second later, and I shoved Carl in first. Jill leapt in after him. A new .45 caliber hole magically appeared in the sheet metal next to my hand. My opponent stood up and reflexively dropped the empty magazine from the .45 in his hands. He cursed as he realized he didn't have a reload. I made eye contact with my nemesis.

This isn't over.

There were flashing police lights coming up behind him. He tossed the empty gun into the car and went back for his friend, who was still wearing my backpack. I dove into the van and jerked the door closed. "Drive, Reaper, drive!"

Reaper did his best to get us out of there and managed to scrape all the paint off our passenger side on an approaching police car. The screech of metal on metal filled the compartment. Carl grimaced.

"How bad?" I asked.

"You know how hard it is to get a clean, untraceable, vehicle? How much work I put into this engine? I'm gonna have to burn it now. I didn't want to have to use the spare yet. It ain't as nice—"

"I meant the bullet."

"Vest stopped it, bet I piss blood tonight, but I better drive before *galinha-boy* kills us all." Carl crawled forward and started yelling at Reaper to get into the passenger seat. There was a brief lull as Reaper got out of the way; then the van really started to roar. Even kidney-punched with a .45, Carl was the best getaway driver in the business. We still had a chance.

I was lying on the floor of the open cargo area, breathing hard and sliding about as Carl took us around corners on two wheels, sirens screaming right outside our back window, when I saw Jill looking at me strangely. "You okay? Are you injured?"

She didn't answer for a long enough time that I started to worry she'd taken a blow to the head. Then she finally spoke. "You came back for me. You weren't going to. You were going to save yourself, you could have, but then you came back."

"Yeah." That made me uncomfortable. Of course I had been ready to ditch her. I don't know why I'd changed my mind, but she had ended up saving my life, not the other way around. "Can I have my gun back?" She realized that it was still in her hands, then passed it over. "Go take a seat and buckle in."

"Thank you," she said softly as she moved forward.

Every cop in Zubara was going to be looking for our van. "Reaper, get on your computer and get rid of this pursuit. I want zero security forces communication. Screw with them however you want."

"All of them?" he asked, opening his machine. He sounded eager. I didn't normally just turn him loose like that. It was kind of scary.

"Use your imagination." There were two police cars directly behind us on the narrow street. "Carl, you want a hand losing these guys?" I shouted.

"If you don't mind me doing *all* the work!"

That sounded like a yes. I pulled up the rug in the back and opened a secret compartment, took out the stashed carbine, turned on the Aimpoint, and pulled back the charging handle. One thing I liked about this particular type of Toyota van was that you could open the back window. The muzzle cleared the window as I took a sight picture. It was difficult with the swaying of the shocks, but this wasn't rocket science.

Unlike Western police agencies that relied on communication, tire spikes, and road blocks, Zubaran cops hung their guns out the windows and randomly started shooting, which was a whole lot more dangerous to the neighborhood than it was to the people they were pursuing. I was doing the populace a favor. I pumped half a dozen rounds through the radiator of the first car before the cop panicked and jerked the wheel to the side, spinning out of control. The second car T-boned them.

I rolled the window up and sank to the floor. Reaper was clicking away like mad, destroying thousands of man-hours' worth of Zubara's communications programming, Carl was driving like a Formula One champion, and Jill was just watching me with this indecipherable look on her face, probably thinking about how, for the first time in her life, she'd just shot somebody, and it had saved a life. My life.

It had been a long afternoon. And it had all been for nothing.

"*Control, this is Nightcrawler, we've got a situation.*" I recognized that voice, even distorted over an unfamiliar radio. He sounded like he was in pain.

"*Go ahead, Nightcrawler,*" said an unfamiliar woman's voice. "*Are you alright?*" I could sense a note of *personal* concern slipping through the professionalism.

"Where's that coming from?" I asked quickly.

Carl took one hand off the wheel long enough to hold up a small radio. "It fell off the one I knocked out." He risked a look back at me. "Told you I do all the work around here."

"*I'm okay. Xbox is hurt. I've lost the cops and I'm heading to the safe house.*"

"*Nightcrawler, what's Xbox's status?*" the girl asked.

"*I don't know.*" He sounded worried. They weren't just teammates. They were friends. *Nightcrawler* . . . so that was the name of the guy I had to kill. What a stupid call sign. "*Xbox took a bad hit to the head. Some asshole hit him with a shovel!*"

"Where'd you find a shovel anyway?" I shouted.

Carl shrugged. "I passed some construction guys digging up pipes. You know, knock one cold, to interrogate. Seemed like a smart idea at the time." Good thing that the shovel was the official martial arts weapon of the Portuguese. It came from all of that dairy farming and hitting cows they had in their genes or something.

We were now listening in to Dead Six's encrypted communications. This was huge. "Carl, have I told you yet today that I love you?"

The next voice that came on was older, gruff. He had the air of command. "*This is Big Boss. Nightcrawler, was the target neutralized?*"

"*Yes, sir.*"

"*Are you sure, son?*"

"*He was dead before he hit the floor, sir. The guy he was meeting with got away. I don't know who the hell he was. He looked like a local, but he didn't fight like a local. He was good. Really good, sir. That girl that Bureaucrat put the BOLO on was there, too. I almost had her, but she escaped. She's working with the shooter. Called him Lorenzo.*"

There was a pause. "*Understood, Nightcrawler. Did you notice anything else about this man? Any way to identify him?*"

"*He was average looking, could've been Arab, could've been Mexican. I couldn't really tell. He did carry some kind of high-cap 1911. Xbox tried to take him prisoner, but that kind of backfired on him. Are the others okay?*"

"*Shafter and Anarchangel are on their way to the safe house. Zubaran communications are going wild. People saw you. You screwed up out there, son. I want a full briefing as soon as you get back. Bureaucrat will be mad as hell.*"

"Reaper, can you track this?" I asked hopefully.

"I can try. Give me a second, though," he responded. He was right. Eluding pursuit was more important. "I'm routing every cop in the city back to the Hasa Market where we're holed up in a hostage standoff." The boy was creative when you gave him some leeway. "We've got a room full of school kids and a sack of anthrax!"

"Don't overdo it," I warned.

The radio crackled one last time. "*Nightcrawler out.*"

You just wait.

The stolen radio sat in the middle of the computer table, volume cranked all the way up. Reaper had removed the back plate and attached a few mysterious wires to various things and was tapping away on his computer, looking at waves, graphs full of quickly scrolling numbers, and other things far beyond my meager comprehension. He'd already made sure that the radio didn't have any sort of tracking device that could lead back to us. He was in the zone. I had pulled up a chair and was sitting there, pad of paper and pen in hand, scribbling furious notes each time someone from Dead Six spoke.

It had taken forever to get home. After being routed in the wrong direction, the police had actually caught on that they were being screwed with. Then Reaper had introduced a ferocious virus into their system, crashing the entire Zubaran security forces' communication network. We had parked the van in a ditch a few miles away and then walked home.

Jill, apparently not sure what else to do, was sitting across from me, nervously fiddling. The one called Nightcrawler—or Val, as Jill had said the Southerner had called him—had roughed her up pretty good, but she seemed okay to me. I'd been too engrossed with the radio on the walk home to talk to her. Carl had checked Jill's minor injures, then had grabbed a beer, flopped onto the couch, and was watching TV. The selections in this part of the world were out of date and he was watching the end of a poorly dubbed episode of *Three's Company*. He ripped the Velcro on his vest and tossed it on the floor, absently rubbing the bruise on his back.

Dead Six's communications were thoroughly connected. Within ten minutes of Reaper's virus attack, they had informed all of their operators that the security force's comms were disrupted and to take advantage of that if they needed to. It pissed me off that some of our work might somehow benefit these jerk-offs.

"Any luck?" I asked.

"I can't get a fix on the transmissions. This encryption is intense," Reaper muttered. "Whoever set this network up is good, really good."

"You're better," I stated. "Find them."

"It doesn't work like that," he said. "It's all about the math. If we hadn't found this unit already open, I wouldn't ever have cracked it. Even then, I can't access any of the other channels. I can't triangulate location because they're bouncing these things off everything. Their crypto guy's got mad skills."

I scowled. Reaper was usually unbearably cocky about this kind of stuff. I didn't like him sounding humble. That couldn't be good. Shaking my head, I went back to the chatter. This was the operational channel of the day, and Dead Six was apparently a busy bunch. I had noted every call sign used or referred to, and they had mentioned eight different individuals so far. I had no idea if that was all of them or just a fraction.

I got the impression that this channel was for the operators in Zubara, but from the dialog I could tell that this was bigger, and there were other active channels, and probably command channels beyond that. Big Boss was the operational commander. He answered to somebody called Bureaucrat, who apparently had a sidekick called Drago, but neither one of those had spoken yet.

There were two other operations being conducted today in the Zoob. Unfortunately they all spoke in vague generalities about their locations, like "we're on the street," or "by the mosque," or "we're waiting in the parking garage." No names, just random call signs. Nothing I could use to track them. The people they were either murdering or spying on were simply referred to as the targets, never by name.

"*Nightcrawler, this is Control.*" It was the girl from earlier. Her voice was young, American. Her tone told me that she was close to this Nightcrawler. "*Big Boss wants an update on Xbox's status.*"

The voice that came back sounded tired. "*He's got a concussion. I think he'll be okay. He's pretty screwed up, though, kind of . . . like punch-drunk stupid or something.*" His accent was from the northern Midwest, Michigan, or maybe Wisconsin. It wasn't thick, though. He'd probably traveled. There was another voice in the background. I recognized the accent. "*Yes, I am talking about you, asshole. . . . No sign of traumatic brain injury. Um, I think. It's hard to tell with him. He's awake, anyway.*"

It sounded like the Southerner laughed and then said "*Tell Sarah Ah said hi,*" or something like that. He sounded like he was from East Tennessee, and not from the rich side of town. I quickly scribbled "Sarah?" after the note for Control.

"*How are you doing?*" she asked. That was real concern. I was right. There was some emotion there.

"*I'm fine. Had a close one today, but I'm fine,*" Nightcrawler answered slowly. The kid didn't just sound physically tired, but weary, burned out. *Good.* From what I'd heard in the last little while, their operational tempo was brutal. They were being driven hard, and hopefully that meant they would slip up soon.

"*What happened?*" Control asked.

"*It was that girl. The one Bureaucrat wanted so bad. I don't know. I just . . . she caught me off guard.*" I glanced over at Jill and gave her a big thumbs-up. It would have been better if she had shot him in the face, but she was new at this and wouldn't have thought of a vest. Jill shrugged. Nightcrawler continued. "*Then there was that other guy, the one with the tricked-out 1911. The girl called him Lorenzo. He's good. He, I don't know, fell off the roof of this mosque, landed on our truck, and started shooting.*"

"*He fell off the roof? He kept shooting after that?*"

"*It wasn't that high. I mean, I fell off the roof of the barn once when I was a kid. I ended up in the emergency room, though.*"

"I didn't *fall*," I said to the others. "I meant to do that."

"*Don't worry,*" Control said. "*We'll find him. I need you to be careful out there.*"

"*Don't worry. I'll be fine.*"

Damn right you're fine. You didn't report my sack of money, either, you piece of shit. "They're sloppy on the radio," I said.

"You're just annoyed," Jill said.

Control came back. "*They want to debrief you right away. Big Boss is sending a car to pick you up. I'll . . . I'll see you soon.*" She was trying to be professional, but was . . . she was in *love* with him. *Holy crap, this gets better and better.*

Nightcrawler came right back. "*I'll—wait a second. What?*" There was some commotion in the background. "*I don't have your radio. . . . What do you . . . Son of a bitch! Control, Xbox's radio is missing. Repeat, his radio is gone.*"

"Are you sure?"

Brief pause. "*Yes. It's missing.*"

"No!" I shouted as I leapt from my chair. "Damn it, no!"

"*Hang on.*" Sarah, or whatever her name was, went right into full-blown damage control. "*Attention on the net. ComSec breach. I say again, ComSec breach. Emergency protocol in force, Zulu One. I repeat, Zulu One.*"

Then the radio went to static.

They'd changed to a different encrypted channel. "Reaper!"

"They're gone," he replied.

"Not good enough! Find them," I bellowed.

"I'm trying, but this stuff is hard."

Gone!

A bubble of rage uncorked from my soul, rumbled to the top, and erupted like a festering boil. All this work, all the killing, all the effort, all for nothing.

I just lost it.

With an incoherent roar, I picked up my chair and hurled it into the kitchen, shattering it against the far wall. "This Nightcrawler asshole has screwed me *three* times now! *Three times!*" I slammed my fist through the nearby Sheetrock, scattering tacked-up photos of the Zubaran underworld like confetti. "Falah, Adar, and now Hosani! And I even kind of liked Hosani! Worthless asshole cock-sucking son of a bitch!"

Jill and Reaper recoiled as I stomped past. "Every step of the way, every part of this suicide mission, complicated because of that piece of shit. *Damn it!* Not only does he have *my* box—he's got *my* money! And I've got—" I kicked a hole through the kitchen door. "*Nothing!* It isn't enough for him to ruin my life, but *no*, I get to make him rich, too. I swear I'm going to gut him like a fish. I'm going to pull his eyes out and skull-fuck him to death! I'll tear his throat out with my *teeth*!"

Carl, having seen a few of my outbursts over the years, calmly turned up the TV volume and sipped his beer.

The neighbors started banging on the wall, demanding quiet. My first inclination was to pull my gun and shoot them through the wall. If they wanted loud, I'd show them loud. But I just stood there, breathing hard, chest heaving, veins popping out in my neck, left eye spasmodically twitching, fists clenched so hard that I was shaking. Big Eddie was going to murder *everyone*, and all because I couldn't catch Dead Six.

So what the hell do I do now?

"Are you done throwing your sissy tantrum?" Carl asked over the sounds of *Walker, Texas Ranger* speaking in Arabic. "Or should I go get more furniture for you to break?"

Deflated, back to the wall, I sank slowly to the floor. "I'm out of ideas."

Reaper had instinctively moved his body to protect his precious computer equipment from my fury. He'd rather me toss him across the room than one of those hard drives. "I can keep trying," he assured me. The kid wasn't used to me not having all the answers. "There's got to be a way. You always figure out something."

I shook my head. "We need to start thinking about how we can protect our families. How can we get all of them out of Big Eddie's reach?" But I knew that was futile before the words even left my mouth. He had us by the short hairs, and there was nothing we could do. "Jill, you did your part. I'll get you out of the country. I've got resources, friends. You—"

"Lorenzo!" Jill snapped. "You're not out of options yet."

I laughed, and it wasn't a happy noise. If only she knew. Up until a few hours ago, *she* had been my final option. But somehow things had changed. I stood up. "You don't have a *clue* what you're talking about," I said.

Jill's eyes narrowed dangerously. "Yes, I do." Her voice was barely a whisper, but somehow that got everyone's attention more than my ranting. "We all heard what they said. This Bureaucrat wants me dead, and I'll bet you money that's Gordon. You can still use *me* to get to *them*. I know you've already thought of that."

That perked Carl's interest, and he turned down the TV to listen to my response.

"I wouldn't do that."

"Yes, you would. I'm not stupid, Lorenzo. That's why you've kept me around. I figured that out in the last few days. I could see it in your eyes. You didn't like it, but I was insurance."

"I wouldn't do that *now*." That time I said it with more force.

And she knew I was telling the truth. "What changed?"

I didn't have an answer. "Nothing."

But she wasn't going to be deterred. "There's no such thing as *nothing*."

Reaper shook his head. "No way, man. Bullshit. Lorenzo wouldn't sell you out. That's . . ." He turned to me, scowling. "No way."

I looked Reaper square in the eyes. "I was going to do what I had to do. This isn't about me. This is about your mom, and Carl's family, and a bunch of little kids I've never even met, and for Train. I know what Eddie can do. I've seen it. What would you do if you were in my place?"

He looked around hesitantly. "I don't know."

I turned back to Jill. "But I'm not selling anybody to Dead Six."

Jill smiled. "So, you *do* have a heart."

It was really *tense* in that apartment right then. "Look, sorry about . . ." I waved my throbbing hand at the new holes in the wall. "Whatever. Just leave me alone. I'll . . . we'll think of something in the morning." I went to my room and closed the door, utterly defeated.

She didn't bother to knock.

I was sitting on the edge of the bed, staring at the folder of family photos in the dim light, absently spinning that blood-stained .44 Magnum cartridge between my fingers, and I looked up to see Jill's silhouette in the doorway, hands on her hips. "Carl wanted me to tell you that he and Reaper went to pick up the spare car." Closing the folder, I set it aside. "What's that?" she asked.

Sighing, I responded. "This? This is a forty-four Magnum round. It came from the man that shot me today. And these," I said, gesturing at the photos, "are a bunch of innocent people who are going to be hurt because of what I am."

She waited. "Well . . . what are you?"

I shrugged. "I don't know anymore."

"I do," Jill said. She came inside and softly closed the door behind her. There was a sudden energy in the room. "I know *exactly* what you are."

I recognized the look that she was giving me. I'd seduced more women than I could count, but it wasn't like they *knew* me. I couldn't do this. Not with her. This wasn't right. I stood. "Listen, I—"

"You're a thief, and a liar, and an all-around jerk," she said with this mischievous little smile. "You're this just *horrendous* asshole that takes advantage of everybody around him, and uses people whenever it's convenient. And you're so *short*. I don't know what the hell I'm thinking."

That was unexpected. "Me, either."

"But . . ." Jill was closer now. She stopped, so close that I could just barely feel the soft curves of her body against me. It was electric. It had been a *long* time. "You're also the man that saved my life."

Her fingers were soft on my cheek. Then I was pulling her tight. Against all reason, I kissed her. She responded, quickly, aggressively. She felt so very good. "You don't have to do this," I said, and I meant it.

She whispered in my ear. "I know."

Wide awake, I stared at the dark ceiling, listening to the night sounds of Zubara coming from the open window and Jill's rhythmic breathing next to me. Her head was resting on my shoulder, and she had fallen asleep with one hand caressing the mottled scars on my chest.

Man, I needed that.

I moved the hair from her face, and she shifted slightly tighter against me in response.

What the hell was I doing? Men like me weren't allowed to have relationships. It wasn't that I wasn't attracted to her. . . . *Are you kidding?* She was beautiful and had an unbelievable body. No problem there. I'm only human. There was nothing I'd rather do, but I actually . . . hell. *I don't know.* It wasn't like I was used to *feelings.*

Jill was different than the others.

But I couldn't afford affection. Affection was weakness. I'd only ever had one serious relationship, and that had ended really badly. In the terrible world I inhabited, sex was business and love was for suckers. Loyalty was just something that could be used against you by anybody more ambitious than you were, my current predicament being a perfect example.

On the one hand, I felt like the biggest jerk in the world, like I was somehow taking advantage of this poor scared girl who had looked to me for protection, though it wasn't exactly like I had initiated this. On the other hand, I was thinking about how stupid I was. The cold, calculating part of my brain was warning me that Jill was probably just doing this to cement her chances of me not selling her out, that somehow she was better at emotional manipulation than I was. Maybe the con was getting conned.

Then again, I was at least a decade older than her, probably more. Since I spent my days murdering scumbags, it seemed odd that I would have some sort of moral hang up about that, but I did feel like a dirty old man. On a strictly practical note, it made me really glad that at forty I had the physical conditioning of an Olympic athlete. *Holy crap, the girl is energetic. Or maybe I'm just getting old.*

So I lay there, beating myself up, yet somehow feeling strangely happy. It was kind of weird.

Jill stirred. "You awake?" she asked softly.

"Just thinking is all."

I could see the whiteness of her smile in the dark. "Don't worry. We *will* find them." That hadn't been what I was thinking about at all. In fact, this was the first time in weeks that every one of my thoughts hadn't been driven by revenge. And for some reason, I liked how she said *we* would find them.

"You know, Jill, you're really pretty when you're homicidal."

She giggled. "You think too much. Wanna go again!"

Maybe life doesn't have to totally suck.

Chapter 15: Pancakes

LORENZO
May 4

For some reason, despite massive setbacks, Dead Six boning me at every turn, being half a million dollars poorer, getting shot the day before, and still unable to get Adar's box, I felt better today than I had in quite a while. I had gone out onto the balcony and was staring at the sun just beginning to light the morning fog. Carl joined me a few minutes later, leaned on the balcony, and regarded me suspiciously. As usual, we were the first up. "You kids get that out of the way finally? Been sniffing around each other like horny teenagers since she got here."

The call to prayer began to resonate across the city. "Why, Carl, my good man. I have no idea what you're talking about."

He grunted. "Sure. So, what now, genius?"

I had been thinking about that. "You've seen the e-mails to Al Falah. The big meeting is on for June eighteenth. So we've got just over a month to get ready for the Phase Three."

"So we go in, but without Adar's box, we just die? Good plan."

"I might be able to pick it."

Carl nodded. "It's like a thousand years old and has something like *two hundred* tumblers, and if Reaper's numbers are right, you've got ten minutes maybe to get through before a couple hundred pissed off Saudis start shooting at you."

We had been through all this before, but it never hurt to go over the options again. "Explosives."

Carl knew his bombs better than I did. "That much reinforced material." He held up a stubby finger. "First, too loud. Pissed Saudis, remember?" Then another. "Second, you won't be able to smuggle enough in to make a shaped charge that can punch through."

"What if I were to find explosives inside the palace?"

"Ten minutes," Carl said. "Good luck. It's true what they say." He took a swig of his beer, breakfast of champions. "Getting laid makes you dumb."

224

"There are four other keys in existence. Adar only had one. We've got a month. We could steal one of the others," I suggested. Carl started to count on his fingers again. "I know, I know. One's been missing since the Third Crusade. The others are well guarded, and any attempt to take them would cause the vault's security to triple and probably get the meeting canceled." Adar, the exiled heir, had been our only hope.

"Maybe we try something different," Carl said.

"Find Big Eddie and kill him before he kills us? I'd love to. Since nobody knows who he really is, if he's really even one man at all, and he works through layer after of layer of anonymous intermediaries, how do you suggest we do that?" I had been Big Eddie's single most effective thief for years, and I had never met the man. The intermediaries I had worked for had never met the man, either, and the second I started looking, he'd somehow know. "It'd be like catching the devil."

"I was just sayin'. I suppose I could just lay around in my underwear, get drunk, and watch TV until we run out of time."

"That's always an option. I'll keep working the streets. Dead Six will screw up. They're only human," I said. My phone buzzed. "Unknown number," I said suspiciously as I opened it. "Yeah?"

"Hello, Mr. Lorenzo." It was the Fat Man, sounding as ominously vacant as usual. "Our employer was wondering if you had made any progress in retrieving his box."

Oh, now it was *his* box. "Not yet. Dead Six is slippery."

"I understand. Disappointing, but I do understand. Big Eddie believes in fully supporting his employees with all of our organization's resources. His eyes are everywhere. Be ready on the eleventh. I will be in contact at exactly seven-fifteen in the morning, Zubaran time. I will give you the exact location of Dead Six. You will need to act quickly. There will be no second chance."

I was so shocked that I almost said thank-you.

"And as your immediate supervisor, I need to warn you. Big Eddie is concerned that you are not showing proper motivation. Motivation is very important, Mr. Lorenzo." His voice was urgent. "Fear and pain, these are good motivators, but loss . . . loss is the finest of them all. Please don't make me have to motivate you further. If I do not get a favorable report from you on the eleventh, I will be forced to use extreme motivation. Do you understand me, Mr. Lorenzo?"

"I hear you." *Psycho.* "Just get me the location and I'll handle the rest."

"I like pancakes." Then he hung up.

What the hell? Carl was looking at me strangely. My face must have betrayed my confusion. "The Fat Man's going to give us Dead Six next week."

My burly companion was actually shocked. "That's like a miracle."

"And he said he likes *pancakes*."

"Huh?"

My phone buzzed again a moment later. I had received a video message. There was no sound. It was the Fat Man, the bloated monstrosity, wearing a giant white suit, almost filling my phone's screen. His bulk was squeezed impossibly into a restaurant booth, plate after empty plate stacked before him. He was shoveling pancakes into his mouth like some sort of industrial harvesting machine, barely pausing to breathe. He made a show of seeing the camera, stopped mid-mouthful, and made a big fake smile. His dark, empty eyes didn't smile with his mouth. His face was stained with whipped cream and syrup. The lettering on the window behind him was backward, but read IHOP.

The camera angle changed, moving over his shoulder, and sitting at the table directly behind him were my mother and my younger sister, Jenny, still in her uniform, probably taking a break from work, having an animated conversation, oblivious to the sociopath stuffing himself a few feet away. The camera panned back to the Fat Man, and he waved at me.

The son of a bitch was in Texas, personally keeping tabs on my mom.

Is it still considered a miracle if it comes from the devil?

VALENTINE
Fort Saradia National Historical Site
May 4
1205

Sarah was anxiously waiting for me in her room when I returned. My trip outside the compound had taken longer than I'd expected. The real trick had been convincing the guys at the motor pool to not log that Tailor and I took one of the vehicles for two hours. That hadn't been a problem, either. Things were getting bad enough that few of us that were still alive gave a crap about the rules anymore.

Sarah opened the door quickly when I knocked, and kissed me as I stepped inside. "I was worried," she said. The situation in the Zoob had been steadily deteriorating, and our shootout with that Lorenzo guy at the Hasa Market hadn't helped. It was getting difficult for us to move around the city quickly, as we had to spend a lot of time going around checkpoints.

"Sorry it took so long," I said. "Traffic. We had to go way the hell out of our way to avoid being stopped."

"I know," Sarah replied. "I'm just glad you're back. How did it go?"

"We're on," I said. I retrieved a piece of paper from my pocket. "She'll be here soon. She wants us to meet her in person. If she's satisfied that we're legit, she'll arrange to pick us up shortly after that."

"Wow," Sarah said. "Wait, she wants to meet all four of us? In person?"

"I'm afraid so. We're going to have to find a way to get you, me, Hudson, and Tailor out in town, together, without raising any suspicions."

"Shit," Sarah said. "I could talk to the other controllers. They could cover for us."

"Can you trust them?"

Sarah's expression sank. "I don't know. I can't believe we're just going to leave them. I mean, Anita is my friend."

I put my arms on Sarah's shoulders and looked down into her eyes. "Listen to me. I know this is hard. I don't like the idea of leaving Byrne, Frank, Cromwell, or Holbrook behind, either. I've been through a lot of shit with those guys. But it took a lot of doing just to get the four of us out. The more people I try to bring in, the greater the risk of compromise."

"I know, I know," Sarah said, sounding exasperated. "I get it. We need to be secretive about this, otherwise your friends will get pissed and leave us."

"I'm not worried about that," I said. "Sarah, if Ling thinks I'm screwing with her she'll have us all *killed*. These are dangerous people."

"I don't like it."

"I don't like it, either," I said honestly. "But it's the best I could do. Look . . . if you're having second thoughts, we don't have to go. Tailor and Hudson can go by themselves."

"Mike, you don't have—"

I interrupted her. "Yes I *do*, damn it. If you stay I'm staying. I'm not leaving without you."

Sarah's eyes widened slightly as what I'd just said sunk in. She shook her head slightly and gently put a hand on my cheek. "You're so stupid," she said. She then leaned in and kissed me, deeply and for a long time.

"What do you mean, 'stupid'?" I asked. We leaned in close together, so that my forehead was touching hers. I looked down into her eyes.

Sarah smiled. "I mean you say ridiculously sweet things like that and you're not being ironic. You're completely sincere, and you have no clue how rare that is. You're like a character in a bad romance novel."

"Well, it's your own fault, you know. You jumped me, remember?"

"I know," Sarah said. "Crazytown, remember? I warned you."

"You did. But listen," I said, seriousness edging back into my voice, "I'm asking you. Please, leave with me. This whole thing is going to hell in a ham sandwich. We have to get out while the getting's good. So let's go! Run away together."

"Go where?" Sarah asked. "I mean, really, Mike, where can we go?"

"Anywhere we want," I said, trying to sound more confident than I really was. "We can travel the world for a while until this whole thing blows over. I don't think Project Heartbreaker is going to be around much longer. This country is falling apart. After things calm down, we can go home."

"Can I at least leave a note for my friends, warning them to get out?"

"Why not? They'll assume we bugged out on them anyway. It's not like I was planning to fake our deaths or anything. Tailor will be pissed, though."

"Fuck him," Sarah said dismissively. "He's the one that got you into this mess, isn't he? If he gives you any shit, I'll break his stupid face." She smiled again, and a surge of triumphant relief washed over me. I knew she was hesitant to just disappear and leave the others behind. I'd been terrified that she'd want to stay behind.

"I have something for you," Sarah said. She handed me a brown envelope. It contained all of my personal identification documents, including my passport, that had been taken from me before we left the States.

"How did you get these?" I asked.

"I have access to the safe," she said, eyes twinkling mischievously. "It's not like anyone goes in and checks to make sure your papers are still there."

I shook my head slightly. "You're amazing, you know that?"

"So tell me," Sarah said after a moment. "Who is this Ling woman? You haven't exactly been forthcoming about your history with her. Is she like an ex-girlfriend or something? You need to tell me the whole story."

Sarah was right. I owed her that much. I had avoided talking about Mexico the entire time I'd been in Zubara. As time went on, the parallels between our doomed mission in Mexico and Project Heartbreaker had made me increasingly uncomfortable.

"No, nothing like that," I said honestly. "I met Ling in Mexico last year when the situation had already gone to shit for Vanguard. We'd been contracted by the Mexican Nationalist Government to help secure some trouble areas in the southern part of the country. Some drug lords turned warlords had cut out little empires, so the government hired Vanguard to do a lot of high-risk operations."

"High-risk operations?" Sarah asked suspiciously.

"VIP protection, search-and-destroy missions, things like that. It was our biggest contract ever. Decker, my old boss, hired a ton of extra guys and brought in every team in the company."

"Including yours," Sarah said.

"Switchblade Four. We got the most critical assignments, raids on the bad guys, ambushing militia convoys, stuff like that. We were making progress until the UN moved in. Thirty thousand peacekeepers came in and unilaterally cut a cease-fire with the warlord in Cancun."

"Where does Ling come in?"

"We'd been sitting on our asses for days when she approached Decker with a business proposal. She said that there was a Cuban-flagged freighter docked in Cancun that was full of weapons going to the warlords, but she doesn't give a crap about the weapons. She says there's something else on the freighter, something her group, real secretive bunch, really wants. A girl."

"A girl?"

"Fourteen years old. A prisoner. Ling told Decker, that her organization was willing to pay a crazy sum of money if we'd provide airlift and help get this girl back."

"Why did they bring you guys in?"

"I'm not sure. I never really asked her, and she didn't volunteer a lot of information. Anyway, Decker asks for volunteers, says there'll be a huge operational bonus to the team that goes. We volunteered."

"What happened?"

"Well, we got the girl," I said, my voice softening just a bit. "Stirred up a hornet's nest. Our chopper got hit on the way out. We went down at this abandoned resort hotel, landed right in an empty pool. Then the UN showed up and started shooting at us. Once the government collapsed, Vanguard was declared war criminals."

Sarah was suspicious. "This group that Ling works for, who are they?"

"Exodus." The look on Sarah's face told me she'd heard of them.

"Are you sure?" Sarah asked.

"That's what she told me."

"I thought they were a myth. Wow."

"I know, right? The whole thing was crazy. But it was *so* much money."

"Mike, tell me what happened," Sarah said, looking into my eyes.

I took a deep breath, glanced away for a second, then met Sarah's gaze again. I hadn't told anyone aside from Hawk the full story of what happened in Mexico. "Exodus thinks I'm some kind of hero."

VALENTINE
Umm Shamal District
May 5
0200

It took us over two hours to get to Ling's designated meeting spot. As was the usual case now, we had to go way out of our way to avoid downtown areas, major intersections, and other places where there were likely to be military or police checkpoints. The tiny Emirate of Zubara was holding its breath, waiting for the civil war to start.

It had taken some doing, but Tailor had managed to talk the motorpool into letting him sign out a Land Cruiser without it going in the books. I don't know who he begged, threatened, or bribed, but whatever he did, it worked. He, Sarah, Hudson, and I rolled out of the gate at Fort Zubara without so much as a second look from the guys standing watch.

The location Ling had given me was a construction site. The project, a shopping complex funded by a European firm, had been suspended indefinitely due to "security concerns," so we'd probably have the place to ourselves.

Hudson was driving as we pulled off of the street and into the site. The whole project was just a big hole in the ground surrounded by stacks of supplies and materials, much of which appeared to have been vandalized and looted. The gate at the front truck entrance had been left open, just as Ling said it would be.

No one said anything as we followed the road deep into the hole that was to be the foundation of the shopping center's underground parking lot. I was nervous. The last time I'd worked with Exodus it had cost several of my teammates their lives. They were a bunch of trigger-happy fanatics. If anything went wrong, the four of us would probably end up dead.

We stopped about fifty feet from an abandoned crane in the very center of the site. At least we wouldn't be visible from the road. It was about as secluded as you could get in the middle of a city. As per Ling's instructions, Hudson blinked the headlights three times, then turned them off.

Several floodlights snapped on. Startled, I squinted into the blinding light. I looked over at Hudson, nodded, and opened my door.

"Be careful," Sarah said from the backseat.

I tried to give her a reassuring smile. "I'll be fine."

Stepping onto the ground, I closed the door behind me and moved slowly to the front of the Land Cruiser. I took off my overshirt, revealing both my holstered revolver and my body armor. Holding my right hand up in the air, I slowly drew my gun with my left hand and laid it on the hood of the truck. I then stepped forward, both hands in the air over my head.

For a few tense moments, I walked toward the crane, almost holding my breath. I was following Ling's very specific instructions to the letter, and they hadn't shot me yet, but I couldn't shake the sense of unease. I was vulnerable, helpless, and hated it. A bead of sweat trickled down my head, and it wasn't just from the warm night air.

Ling appeared from behind the crane, alone. She confidently strode toward me, closing the distance in a matter of seconds.

"You can put your hands down now, Mr. Valentine. It's fine," she said, not quite smiling.

Feeling silly, I slowly lowered my hands. "You're alone?" I asked, looking around.

"Of course not," she said. "My men are observing you and your friends. Just a precaution. Please do not take offense."

"None taken," I said, looking down into her dark eyes. "Thank you for coming. I need your help."

"So you insist." She looked past me at the Land Cruiser. "You can tell your friends to come out. I won't have them shot." The corner of her mouth turned up in half a wry smile.

I nodded and squeezed my throat mic. "It's clear. C'mon up." I looked back at Ling. "You want them to leave their weapons?"

"No, it's fine," she said dismissively. "I'm not worried."

"You don't have to drop your weapons," I said into my microphone. "Bring my gun up." I heard doors slamming behind me as my friends climbed out of the truck.

"So, Mr. Valentine, to business," Ling said, not wasting any time. "I apologize for dragging you out here like this, but I always prefer to deal face to face."

"I remember," I said flatly.

She didn't bat an eye. "And frankly, I'm curious to just who it is you wish me to help smuggle out of this country." Tailor tapped me on the shoulder and handed me my gun. I quickly holstered it. "Ah, Mr. Tailor," Ling said, "it's good to see you again."

Tailor nodded but didn't say anything. I then introduced Ling to Hudson and Sarah. Sarah seemed to pique Ling's interest a bit.

"I think I understand now, Mr. Valentine," Ling said, excessively polite as always. "Is this your girlfriend?"

"Uh . . ." I mumbled, surprised by the question.

"Yes," Sarah said levelly. "I'm his girlfriend." She gave Ling the evil eye, but the Exodus operative either didn't notice or didn't care.

"This makes more sense now," Ling said thoughtfully, looking at Sarah. She smiled. "Yes. Well, this is very unorthodox, but I see no reason I can't help you while I'm here. Like you said, Mr. Valentine, my organization owes you a great deal, and we've never had a proper chance to repay you."

"You'll help us get out of Zubara?" I asked.

"Yes," Ling replied. "Unfortunately, it won't be right away. We have business in the region and aren't ready to leave yet."

"How long will it be?" I asked. "I'm not trying to look a gift horse in the mouth, but time is a factor. Things are rapidly going south here."

"I'm aware," Ling said. "However, I still have a job to do myself. Your transportation out of Zubara is a freighter that my organization owns and operates, and it's still at sea."

"You flew here, right?" Tailor asked. "Can't we fly out on that plane?"

"No, you can't," Ling replied, almond eyes narrowing slightly. "I, too, have orders I must follow. The freighter is the only method of transport I'm to make available to you four. It will arrive when it arrives and leave when we've finished here. You can choose to be on it or not. It was the best I could do."

"It'll be fine," I said.

"Mike, I don't know about this," Sarah said quietly.

"Yeah, man," Hudson said. "Are you sure about this?"

"Guys, please," I said. "This is our only shot. Remember what happened to Singer? I trust *these* guys more than I trust Gordon Willis and his cronies."

"You're right." Hudson nodded.

"I trust *you*," Sarah said, looking up into my eyes. I smiled at her, then looked over at Tailor.

His brow was furled unhappily. He didn't say anything for a moment, then nodded. "Fuck it, we don't have a choice."

"Okay," I said, looking back at Ling. "We're in. How do you want to do this?"

Ling smiled as if oblivious to the near-argument we'd just had right in front of her. "Here," she said, handing me something from her pocket. It was a cell phone. "This is secure. A number I can be reached at is programmed into it. Use it sparingly and keep it with you. I'll contact you when we're ready to leave. I'm afraid it might be short notice."

"It's fine," I said. "We'll make it work. Do you have an approximate time frame?"

"Possibly a week. I know that's a long time, given your circumstances, but as I said, it was the best I can do." She looked down at her watch. "I need to be going now. We've been here too long, and I have a lot of work to do myself. It was good to see you again, Mr. Valentine." Ling smiled at me. "Please be careful. I'll be in touch."

VALENTINE
Fort Saradia National Historical Site
May 8
0800

It had been several days since our meeting with Ling, and there'd been no word from her since. This wasn't unexpected, but it was nerve-wracking. The goal now was to stay alive long enough for Ling to get us out of the country. It would suck to get killed so close to being home free.

There was another problem, too. The longer we waited, the greater the chance one of us would get second thoughts. I knew Tailor wouldn't change his mind. Once he made a decision, he always went through with it, even if it wasn't really a good idea. I wasn't so sure about the rest of us.

Especially Sarah. The idea of just leaving her friends and running away from Project Heartbreaker bothered her, a lot. Hell, it bothered me. Aside from Tailor and Hudson, there were a quite a few guys that I was friends with, and I hated to think what would happen to them after we disappeared. But I didn't know them that well. I wasn't sure if I could trust them. If I told them we had a way out, what would they do? Would they report it to Hunter or Gordon Willis? Would they want to come along? If so, would Ling and her people agree to that, or would they call the whole thing off since we tried to change the deal?

My greatest fear was that Sarah would decide she didn't want to go. There was no way I was leaving without her, either, so that meant I had to stay as well. That thought terrified me. Not because I was worried about myself; I was worried about what would happen to Sarah. I didn't think I could bear it if anything happened to her.

Project Heartbreaker was falling apart around us. I didn't know how Gordon and his people would handle doing damage control and cleanup. There was the possibility that it might involve Mr. Anders just murdering us. One way or the other, I really didn't want to wait around to find out.

Despite all this, the missions didn't stop coming, and they seemed to get more and more ridiculous as time went on. Our casualties had been severe. We were losing guys left and right, and yet they kept asking more and more of us.

We had just gotten briefed by Gordon on our next operation. Our chalk, plus Cromwell, Holbrook, Animal, and another new replacement named Fillmore, were all present. Our assignment was, to be blunt, *fucking ridiculous.*

Seems there was this Spanish billionaire-aristocrat-industrialist named Rafael Miguel Felipe Montalban who was the head of the Montalban Exchange, one of the largest and wealthiest corporations in the world. According to Gordon, this guy was using his money to fund General Al Sabah in Zubara and had his hands in other things as well. Conveniently, he was sailing up the Persian Gulf on his insanely luxurious yacht, the *Santa Maria.*

No problem, right? We'll just blow up the yacht, take this guy out, and be home before beer-thirty. But no, Gordon says, that won't work. Instead we were to be inserted onto the yacht via helicopter, storm the ship, and capture Rafael Montalban alive. We were then to retrieve him and his personal laptop computer and bring them back to base.

Basically, Gordon was asking us to risk our lives to capture a guy when it was completely unnecessary. They were tracking Montalban's yacht by satellite. They had an armed UAV ready to drop a pair of guided bombs onto it at a moment's notice. If they wanted this guy out of the picture, all they had to do was say the word and he'd be on the bottom of the Gulf.

Except Gordon wanted him *alive*. He wouldn't even explain why. Eight of us were going to board two of Gordon's stealth helicopters, fly out over the ocean, and board Montalban's yacht in force. Just like last time, he was only sending in eight guys when dozens would be preferable. He assured us that Montalban's security detail, though highly trained, would be caught completely off guard and that we'd have the initiative the entire time.

I thought Tailor was going to blow a gasket. Holbrook and Cromwell didn't really get vocal until Gordon explained that Anders was coming along to provide support. Gordon probably very nearly avoided getting *decked*.

I explained that I'd never been trained on rappelling from a helicopter, much less onto the back of a moving ship at night. Gordon said rappelling wouldn't be necessary. The yacht was big enough that it had not one but two helipads, one on top and one on the stern.

We'd been given a lot of information on the *Santa Maria*. Photos taken from the UAV stalking it. Plans from the builder, reports on Montalban's security people. The plan was simple enough. Chalk 1 would touch down on the helipad at the top of the ship's superstructure. They would then proceed in and take control of the bridge. Chalk 2 would land at the stern, enter the ship, disable the engines, then begin hunting for Rafael Montalban. Once we captured him, the choppers would pick us up. We'd fly off, and the UAV would prang the *Santa Maria*, sending it to the bottom and killing everyone still alive on board.

The two helicopters would orbit the area for as long as fuel permitted. One would have a machine gun to provide fire support. Anders would be riding in the other, armed with a sniper rifle, to pick off targets of opportunity on the deck. Anders was going to be riding in Holbrook and Cromwell's chopper. I imagined what a fun ride *that* was going to be.

Chapter 16: Surface Tension

VALENTINE
Somewhere over the Persian Gulf
May 9
0155

Dark water flashed below us as the strange black helicopter skimmed the deck at speed. Inside, we were bathed in red light as we made final checks on our equipment and communications.

Tailor, Byrne, Hudson, and I huddled together, going over the plan one last time. Just inside the starboard-side door sat a crewman manning a machine gun. The stealth helicopter flew with its doors closed to maintain its small radar cross-section. When the door opened, the entire gun mount swung out, allowing the chopper to lay down suppressive fire.

"We have the target on FLIR," the copilot said. "Stand by. Touchdown in three minutes."

"Going dark," the pilot said, and the internal red lights switched off. My active hearing protection minimized the noise of the chopper, but I could hear the pounding of my heart. It was that last-minute adrenaline spike that you get right before showtime. With the onset of that adrenaline, my pulse slowed and my thoughts coalesced as *the Calm* washed over me. Tailor reached over and slapped me on the shoulder.

"Thirty seconds!" My grip on the cut-down Benelli M4 shotgun tightened. The side doors quietly slid open, and the chopper was filled with the roar of rushing air. The door gunner slid his weapon mount into position. Below us, I could clearly see the *Santa Maria,* well-lit and steadily cruising though calm seas.

My stomach felt the sudden drop as our helicopter rapidly descended upon the *Santa Maria*'s aft helipad. The yacht rushed up toward us, and with a heavy *thud* we were on the deck.

Tailor was out the door first, his carbine up and ready. I was right behind him. Following me was Hudson with the SAW, and then Byrne with another carbine. As soon as we were clear, the chopper dusted off. The door gunner opened up as the chopper ascended, raking the foredeck with a stream of tracer fire. We moved together in a tight line, rushing for the superstructure, trying to cover as many angles as possible. Shouting could be heard. An alarm sounded.

The aft superstructure served as a hangar for a small helicopter. We kicked in a personnel door and entered as our second chopper landed above us. The ship's interior lights were on. A door at the opposite end of the hangar opened as we passed by the *Santa Maria*'s helicopter. Two men in suits, armed with MP7 submachine guns, burst into the room. They hesitated for a brief moment when they saw us. We'd caught them completely off guard. Tailor cut down one while I put a magnum buckshot load through the other. Both men were dead before they hit the floor.

"Clear!" Tailor said.

"Clear! Reloading!" I repeated, thumbing another shell into my shotgun.

"Clear!" Hudson and Byrne repeated.

"Alpha Team, this is Bravo Team," Tailor said. "We're in the hangar. What's your status?"

"*Bravo Team, Alpha,*" Holbrook replied. "*We're crossing the sundeck, heading for the bridge. We—shit!*" A long burst of automatic weapons fire rattled over the radio. "*Encountering stiff resistance.*"

"Roger that." Tailor looked back at us. "Engine room. Let's go!" We followed Tailor into the bowels of the *Santa Maria,* encountering terrified crewmembers as we went. The engine room was on the lowest deck, in the aft of the yacht.

We cleared a tight, spiraling staircase and immediately came under fire from down the passageway. Tailor jumped back in the stairwell, stumbling backwards and crashing into me.

"Shit," he snarled. "That was close."

"What?" I asked.

"I think they've got guys at both ends of the passageway. The hatch to the engine room is sealed."

"Frag?" I asked, mind racing.

"Frag," Tailor concurred. We each pulled a hand grenade from our vests. Squeezing side by side, we moved as close to the doorway at the bottom of the stairwell as we could and pulled the pins. At the same time, we reached around the doorway and threw our grenades. Mine went aft, Tailor's went forward. They went bouncing down the passageway. We withdrew into the stairwell and crouched down. Men were shouting in the corridor. The *Santa Maria* was rocked by two deafening blasts a second later as the grenades detonated.

"Move, move, move!" Tailor shouted. We spilled into the passageway as rapidly as we could, weapons leading us around the corners. Tailor angled to the left, while I angled to the right. The two men that had been guarding the hatch to the engine room were dead.

I dove to the deck as a burst of automatic weapons fire roared behind me. Bullets zipped over my head and pocked the hatch to the engine room. Tailor fired off several short bursts in response. I rolled over onto my back, leveling my shotgun down the passageway just in time to see Hudson crouch in front of me, SAW shouldered. He ripped off a long burst while Tailor reloaded.

"Byrne!" Tailor shouted. "We'll hold 'em off. Get that fucking hatch open!"

"Moving!" Byrne replied. He was carrying on his back a compact Broco cutting torch. The three of us provided him with covering fire as he set his equipment up. Without hesitating, he pulled welder's goggles down over his eyes and ignited the torch.

Byrne first cut a small hole in the hatch and punched out the circular piece of hot metal in the center. I warned my teammates and tossed in another grenade. The blast slammed the narrow corridor. Byrne fired the torch up again and resumed cutting.

Minutes ticked by at an agonizingly slow pace as our teammate cut his way through the watertight hatch. We were vulnerable in the narrow passageway, and the ship's security complement knew right where we were.

"I'm through!" Byrne shouted as he extinguished the torch. Tailor and Hudson covered forward while Byrne and I went aft to clear the engine room. A couple of full-force kicks and the cut-through hatch slammed to the deck in a deafening clatter. The engine room was dark and filled with smoke from my grenade. We switched on our weapon lights, sending bright columns of light piercing into the hazy darkness.

A crewmember was lying on the floor by the hatch with blood leaking out of his ears. He wasn't moving. I couldn't tell if he was unconscious or dead.

"Damn," Byrne said, looking down. "Do you—" *BRRRRRRRP!* One of Rafael Montalban's security men appeared from behind a fixture. His MP7 was extended in one hand, like a pistol, while he covered his bleeding ear with the other.

Snapping the shotgun up, I fired. Two loads of buckshot tore into the bodyguard in a splash of blood. As he hit the deck, I caught movement out of the corner of my eye. I swung my weapon around, firing twice again, dropping another crewmember that was running toward me. I quickly scanned the engine room for any more threats. Then I noticed Byrne lying on the floor, staring up at the ceiling, his right eye wide open. What was left of his left eye was hidden under a puddle of blood. A bullet had punched right through his safety glasses and into his head.

Enveloped in *the Calm,* I didn't feel anything as I looked down at his lifeless body. No, that would come later.

"Clear!" I shouted. "Man down!" Tailor and Hudson came in a second later. I was crouched by Byrne's body, thumbing more shells into my shotgun.

"Goddamn it!" Hudson cursed, punching the wall so hard I thought he'd break his hand. He looked down at me. "What are you doing?"

"I'm taking the torch," I said. "We might need it again."

Tailor quietly swore to himself. He then squeezed his throat mic. "Alpha Team, this is Bravo, engine room secured, what's your status?"

"*This is Alpha!*" Holbrook replied, sounding shaken up. "*We've got the bridge secured. Commo equipment is trashed. They're trying to retake it, but we'll hold 'em off. Animal is down, KIA.*"

"Roger that," Tailor said flatly. "We're down one, too. Disabling the engine now. We're then going after the target."

"Good luck," Holbrook said, and the radio went silent.

Our first objective was complete. The *Santa Maria* was dead in the water. The engine was disabled, the radio was smashed, and the bridge was controlled by Holbrook's chalk. It was now up to the three of us to find Rafael Montalban and capture him.

The two choppers circling were watching for lifeboats or swimmers. No one had left the yacht. Rafael Montalban was on board somewhere. Tailor figured that he'd be holed up in the security office. It was at the end of a passageway on one of the lower decks, and was defensible. If we didn't find him there, we were going to head to his stateroom next. If he wasn't there either it was going to be a room-by-room, deck-by-deck search until we found the son of a bitch.

We encountered almost no resistance as we crossed the yacht. Sporadic gunfire could be heard coming from above us. Holbrook reported that Montalban's security force made their attempt to retake the bridge, and failed. We expected the remainder of the security contingent to be protecting the man himself.

We were right. We came under fire as soon as we set foot in the passageway that led to the security office. Instead of a few disorganized guys in suits with machine pistols, we were now encountering guards in body armor, armed with G36C carbines and Benelli shotguns. To make matters worse, we were outnumbered.

But *they* were outgunned. The *Santa Maria* shuddered with another concussion after Tailor sent a grenade rolling down the passageway. As soon as it detonated, Hudson leaned around the corner and laid down suppressive fire. Tailor and I quickly advanced up the corridor. There were several compartments on either side of the passageway, with a few of Montalban's remaining bodyguards using the doorways as cover. We were sitting ducks as we moved down the hall. We had to use overwhelming firepower to keep their heads down.

My shotgun wouldn't penetrate their vests, but a shotgun with a holographic sight on top of it makes for comparatively easy head shots. We brutally cut down the rest of Montalban's security force in that passageway. When the shooting stopped, six men lay dead on the deck in a mix of spent brass and spilled blood. The air stunk of smoke and burnt powder. Only the three of us remained standing.

I used the brief lull to pull more shells from the bandolier across my chest and thumb them into my shotgun. The weapon was hot to the touch. My cheek was sore from the pounding the stock gave it. Even an autoloader could be rough with three-inch Magnum buckshot.

As expected, the hatch to the security office was sealed from the inside like the engine room had been. According to the ship's schematics, these were security features in the event the *Santa Maria* was overrun by pirates. The security office was designed as a sort of panic room where Rafael Montalban and his personal guards could hold out until assistance arrived.

No assistance was coming. Our choppers had impressive electronic warfare suites and were effectively jamming all transmissions that weren't on select frequencies, like our radios. And your typical pirate didn't have access to a Broco torch.

My teammates covered me as I fired up the torch and began to cut through the hatch. This one was less substantial than the engine room hatch had been, and the cutting went faster.

It was done. Tailor was ready, MK 16 carbine shouldered. I dropped the torch, doffed the welder's goggles, and clicked off the safety on my shotgun. Hudson had just finished loading a fresh hundred-round nutsack into his saw and nodded at us.

Tailor kicked in the hatch. The last three bodyguards were waiting inside, sporting compact assault rifles and body armor. My team swept into the security office all at once. We didn't use grenades this time. We needed Montalban alive.

The first guard was ducked behind an overturned metal desk. He fired off a burst as we came into the room. Hudson replied with the SAW, tearing through the desk and ventilating the man trying to hide behind it. At the same time, another guard leaned around a corner, G36C shouldered. Tailor and I hit him at the same time. The guard was ripped apart by the barrage of buckshot and 5.56mm rounds and collapsed to the deck.

We didn't stop. Moving through the office, we turned a corner. A hammer weight slammed into my chest as a loud handgun discharged in front of me. I yelled that I'd been hit and stumbled backward, falling to my butt. The shot was answered with a hail of gunfire that was over in a second.

"Val! You alright?" Tailor asked, crouching beside me.

"I'm fine! I'm fine!" I gasped, looking down at my chest. The bullet had blown open two of the shotgun shells on my bandolier and lodged in my front armor plate. I was okay.

Tailor extended a hand and helped me to my feet. I shook my head and stepped around the corner. Two men had been holed up at the back of the office. One was a big guy in a dark suit, with an ear bud. He was dead on the floor with about a dozen exit wounds in his back. His pistol lay on the deck in a pool of his blood.

The other man was still alive. He was an older gentleman, with graying hair and a neatly trimmed goatee. He had an aristocratic air to him and was wearing what looked to be a very expensive suit. He stood against the wall, eyes wide, with his hands on top of his head. Hudson had the barrel of his SAW practically shoved up the man's nose.

My eyes narrowed. "Rafael Montalban?"

"Yes," the man replied. "What is the meaning of this?" I had to give the guy credit. He hadn't pissed himself or anything. He had some semblance of backbone at least.

"Don't worry about it," Tailor said harshly. "You have a computer?"

"I have many," Montalban replied with an aloof sniff.

"We're only concerned with the one," Tailor said. "You know the one I'm talking about." Tailor was bullshitting the guy. All we'd been told was to get his laptop. We had no idea which laptop or what they were looking for.

Rafael Montalban frowned. "You've been well informed. It seems I have a leak in my organization. I'd speak to my head of security about it, but I'm afraid you just killed him." He nodded to the dead man on the floor.

"Just show us where the laptop is, playboy," Hudson growled. "I ain't in the mood for any bullshit."

"It would seem not," Montalban said, his English only had a hint of a Spanish accent. "Very well. It's in a safe in this office. This way." Hudson led Rafael Montalban around the corner. Tailor and I looked at each other and shrugged. *I can't believe that worked.*

Tailor bent over and picked something up. "Here," he said, handing it to me. "He shot you with this."

I looked down at the gun in my hand. It was a Korth .357 Magnum revolver, beautifully engraved, with a brightly polished blue finish. The grips were genuine ivory and had what I guessed was the Montalban family crest inlaid in them in gold and silver. I'd just been shot with a ten thousand dollar gun.

After Rafael Montalban opened the safe and retrieved the laptop, Tailor made him boot it up and enter the password. He then shoved the laptop into his backpack and keyed his microphone. "Control, this is Xbox. Bravo Team has secured the package and the target, repeat, we have the package and the target, both intact. Requesting immediate extraction."

Gordon Willis himself came on over the radio. "*Excellent work, boys!*" he said enthusiastically. "*Your ride will be there shortly. Over and out!*" Tailor rolled his eyes.

"*Xbox, this is Control,*" Sarah said then. "*What's your status?*"

"One KIA on our team," Tailor said. "It was Anarchangel."

"*Control, this is Joker,*" Holbrook said, sounding very tired. "*We've got two KIA, Animal and Linus. I'm wounded but still mobile. Copy?*" Sarah acknowledged while the three of us swore aloud. Linus was Cromwell's call sign.

I didn't really listen to the rest of the radio chatter. We were ordered to gather up and stand by for extraction at the aft heliport. We still had to use caution. Most of the *Santa Maria*'s crew was still alive. Even though we'd wiped out Rafael Montalban's security detail, there was no telling who'd be waiting around the corner, ready to be a hero.

"Gentlemen," Rafael Montalban said, sounding detached and aloof. "Surely we can come to some sort of understanding? I assure you I can triple whatever it is you're being paid. People died tonight, yes. Your people and my people. But we can all walk away from this." Montalban then winced as Hudson roughly pulled his arms behind his back and secured them with a zip-tie.

"There's no going back for us," Tailor said, lighting a cigarette.

"I see," Montalban said, discomfort apparent in his voice. "I'm going to ask you again. Let's talk about this like civilized people. Believe me, gentlemen, I'm a man of means. And I'm *not* a man to be trifled with. I have powerful friends."

"I think you better shut your mouth, playboy," Hudson said roughly. "Your friends ain't here."

Tailor gestured at our prisoner. "Bag this motherfucker." Rafael Montalban was forced to his knees. Hudson pulled a heavy black sack over his head and slapped him upside the head to shut him up. Tailor led the way down the corridor as we marched the Spanish billionaire topside.

I looked at the ornate revolver in my hand again. Feeling a slight twinge beneath layers of *Calm*, I ejected the one spent case and five unfired rounds and stuffed the gun into a pouch on my vest. Rafael Montalban wasn't going to need it anymore.

✛ ✛ ✛

The extraction from the *Santa Maria* went smoothly enough. The other chopper landed first, depositing Anders onto the deck. He collected the laptop from us as soon as we made it topside. Holbrook and Fillmore boarded that chopper with Anders. It lifted off and hovered nearby while the other one set down.

As Hudson, Tailor, and I shoved Rafael Montalban onto our stealthy helicopter, we noticed the survivors of the Santa Maria's crew quietly watching us from a distance. Some looked angry, others looked terrified, but most appeared in shock. None had offered any further resistance after we'd wiped out the security detail.

I looked at them one last time as we lifted off. They were all dead, and they didn't even know it. It felt wrong. A lot of people had died, and I found myself wondering why. The helicopter's door slid shut as we ascended into the night sky. I quickly grew tired as the chopper droned on. *The Calm* was wearing off, and I began to get the shakes. I was experiencing adrenaline dump. Closing my eyes, I tried to concentrate on something else.

I couldn't wait to see Sarah when I got back. I'd probably go straight to bed and fall right to sleep. Holding her in my arms helped me forget things for a little while. In the morning, we'd probably hold a memorial service for the three men we'd lost. I'd been to several such services already. There were no bodies this time. Our friends' remains had been unceremoniously dumped into the ocean.

The events of that night strengthened my resolve to escape Project Heartbreaker. We'd gone from meticulously hunting terrorists to recklessly killing the employees of a European billionaire, with no regard whatsoever for our safety. I'd had *enough*. I was done doing Gordon Willis's dirty work. He could find another damned errand boy.

My thoughts were interrupted when the chopper's copilot called my name. I left my seat and went forward.

"You have a call," the copilot said, handing me a headset.

"Who is it?" I asked, my voice raised so I could be heard over the noise of the chopper's engines.

"Gordon Willis," the copilot replied. I pinched the bridge of my nose, took a deep breath, and put on the headset.

"This is Nightcrawler."

"*Nightcrawler,*" Gordon said. "*Listen up. Damn fine job you did tonight. I'm proud of you. But something's come up. We have a slight change in our game plan. Can you handle that?*"

"What kind of change?" I asked, my voice flat.

"*I just got confirmation from Drago,*" Gordon said, referring to Anders by his call sign. *"Everything we need is on that laptop. Excellent work securing it with the password already entered."*

"So, what's the change?" I repeated.

"We no longer need Rafael Montalban alive. Liquidate him immediately."

"What?" I snarled, furious. "Three guys *died* trying to get that asshole, and now you tell us you don't need him? What the fuck are you doing, Gordon? Who in the hell is making these decisions?"

"Nightcrawler, I know you've had a bad night, but—"

"I haven't had a bad night, goddamn it!" I snapped, shouting into the microphone. "A bad night is when you get a flat tire or you break your cell phone. Tonight I killed a bunch of people and three of my teammates died, and now you're telling me it was for *nothing*?"

"Mr. Valentine!" Gordon barked, ignoring radio protocols. *"We'll discuss this when you return. Believe me when I say that tonight's operation was* not *for nothing. You have your orders. Carry them out."* The radio fell silent. I ripped the headset off and threw it to the deck. I closed my eyes tightly for a moment, swearing to myself. Taking another deep breath, I regained my composure and warned the pilots about what was going to happen.

"What was that all about?" Tailor asked. I didn't say anything in response. I just pointed at Rafael Montalban and dragged a finger across my throat. Tailor's eyes flashed with anger.

"Jesus Christ, you gotta be shittin' me," Hudson said, shaking his head.

I steeled myself; I had my orders. I turned to face Rafael Montalban and pulled the bag off of his head. He squinted in the red light, obviously confused.

"What's happening now?" he asked, still sounding defiant. "Have you come to your senses, young man?"

"This is where you get off," I said levelly.

"I . . . don't understand," Montalban replied hesitantly.

"You will." I pushed a button on the hull. The chopper was filled with a windy roar as the door behind our prisoner slid open. His eyes grew wide at the sudden realization of what was happening. He looked out at the blackness behind him, then back at me.

My .44 was already in my hand. I fired from the hip, putting the bullet through his chest. He didn't even scream. Before he could crumple to the floor, I kicked the dying man in the chest. Rafael Montalban, aristocrat, billionaire, industrialist, and head of an international conglomerate, tumbled out the door and disappeared into the darkness. Holstering my revolver, I closed the door and sat back down. I held my head in my hands.

The subsequent trip back to Fort Saradia was long and uneventful. I slept through most of it. The choppers had landed somewhere in the desert again. The five of us piled into a large van for the long drive back to the city. I didn't wake up again until we crossed into the fort.

Upon arrival we were immediately herded into the briefing room. Colonel Hunter and Sarah were both waiting for us. We shuffled into the room, still in our body armor, weapons slung, and tried to sit at the desks with all of our gear on.

When I stepped into the room, I made eye contact with Sarah, who was standing back by Hunter. I knew I looked like hell. I wanted nothing more than to stride across the room and take her in my arms. I didn't think the colonel would approve. I managed a smile for her to let her know I was okay, even though I wasn't really. I just didn't want her to worry, even though she undoubtedly would anyway.

The debriefing went by quickly. Hunter just wanted to get through it while the mission was fresh in our minds and let us get some sleep. It had been a tough run. Holbrook had a bandage on his arm. I had a .357 slug stuck in my vest. Three of our teammates were on the bottom of the Persian Gulf. Bad op.

We all chimed in during the debriefing. Sarah recorded and Hunter listened intently as we retold the events of the mission, from beginning to end. Fighting fatigue, I explained the entry into the engine room and how Byrne died. The image of him lying on the floor, left eye socket filled with blood, flashed in my mind and I stumbled on my words. Tailor interjected and continued the narrative.

Hunter leaned against a desk, arms folded across his chest, and listened quietly as I explained the events of the return flight. His one eye studied me as I recalled Gordon's order to kill Rafael Montalban. Sarah put a hand over her mouth when I described dropping him into the ocean.

"So tell me," Colonel Hunter said, "where is this laptop? You retrieved the target's laptop computer, correct?"

"Yes, sir," Tailor replied.

"So where is it?" Hunter repeated.

"We gave it to Anders," Tailor said, sounding confused.

"What?" Hunter said, anger rising in his voice.

"Anders was waiting for us on the deck of the ship," Hudson said. "He took the laptop from us. Did we do something wrong, Colonel?"

Hunter didn't say anything for a moment. "No, boys, you did fine. Where is Mr. Anders now?"

"He stayed on the chopper after it dropped us off, sir," Holbrook said. "He's wherever those stealth birds go, I guess."

"I see," Hunter said, rubbing his chin. It was obvious that something was very wrong, but he didn't want to discuss it with us. At that point I was so tired I didn't really care. I just wanted to go to bed and forget this day had happened. "That's all I have for you, gentlemen. Go get some rack time. You won't have anything else scheduled for as long as I can manage it. You've all been busting ass for a long time. You deserve a break. Tonight, after sundown, we'll have a memorial service for Cromwell, Byrne, and Blutarsky. Dismissed."

We all got up to leave. Sarah crossed the room and threw her arms around me. She squeezed me tightly, then stepped away.

"I was worried," she said simply.

"I'm okay," I said, smiling a little. "It was a bad night. But I'm okay."

"Ms. McAllister, you can smother Mr. Valentine with affection later," Colonel Hunter said. "I need to speak with him. You, too, Tailor." Sarah's face turned red, and I felt myself flush a little.

"Oh, for God's sake, Val, everyone knows," Tailor said. "It's not a secret."

"Did you guys think you were keeping it a secret?" Holbrook asked, standing by the door. "Wow, that's funny," he said humorlessly, then stepped out of the classroom. Hudson and Fillmore followed.

"I'll see you later," Sarah said, squeezing my hand. She left the room, leaving Tailor and me alone with Colonel Hunter.

"Is something wrong, Colonel?" Tailor asked.

"You're goddamned right something's wrong," Hunter growled. "I'm not yelling at you, son, don't worry. You boys took a bad situation and made it work, like you always do. Matter of fact, I'm damned proud of you all."

"With all due respect, sir," I said, "this is *bullshit*. You told us we'd be fighting terrorists. You told us we were taking the war to their backyard. You said we were accomplishing something here. So what did we accomplish by kidnapping some rich guy off of his yacht? What did we accomplish when I murdered him and dropped him in the ocean? What the fuck are we *doing* here, sir?" I realized then that I'd almost been yelling at Colonel Hunter. He didn't seem fazed.

"I don't know," Hunter said.

"Um . . . what?" Tailor asked.

"I don't know what you accomplished, boys. I'm going to level with you here. I saw Gordon's intelligence on Rafael Montalban. His organization definitely was funneling money to General Al Sabah and other radical elements throughout the region. We've known about that for years."

"Then why haven't we done anything until now, sir?" I asked, more than a little confused.

"It's . . . *complicated*, son," Hunter said. "This stuff is way above my pay grade. We're talking about national foreign policy stuff here. International business, transnational interests, and supranational organizations. Rafael Montalban was connected. He had ties to the leadership of the European Union. He had ties to the UN Security Council. He had . . ." Hunter paused. "Well, let's just say the man had a lot of powerful friends."

"And we took this guy out," Tailor said. "Is that good?"

"I don't know," Hunter said. "He was a power player, but he was just one man. There are many others to take his place. Rafael Montalban has a younger brother, Eduard, who will probably take over for him. Killing one man won't break the Montalban Exchange. It won't stop the flow of money to the enemy. Christ, if that was all it took, we'd have killed all those sons of bitches years ago."

"What sons of bitches?" I asked.

"Never mind. Doesn't matter. Anyway, boys, I want to thank you for the work you've done. You two, in particular, have been the sharp end of the stick for Dead Six since your first operation. And it hasn't gone unnoticed."

Tailor and I looked at each other. "What do you mean?"

"For my part," Hunter said, "I'm going to tell Gordon that I'm taking you two off the mission roster. Hudson also. Hell, Holbrook, too. Fillmore, he spent the last two months sitting in a safe house. He's raring to go, still. But you boys need a break."

"I appreciate that," Tailor said.

"Gordon Willis wants to see you both," Hunter said. "He'll be here in a few minutes."

"What the hell does he want now?" I asked ruefully.

"I think he wants to offer you two a job," Hunter replied.

"What?"

"Project Heartbreaker is a temporary assignment, as you two are aware. I'm sure you've guessed that we have a much larger organization that's supporting our mission here. Well, we also have an active paramilitary branch that's always recruiting. I think Gordon wants to offer you a position there."

"Wait," Tailor said. "Who the hell does Gordon work for, exactly? The CIA?"

Hunter didn't blink. "Just like when you signed up for Project Heartbreaker, there are a lot of things you don't get to know until you sign the paper. Even then, there are a lot of things you don't get to know. I know you're angry. Just . . . think real hard before you make any rash decisions, boys. We could use you. It would probably be . . . better if you signed on. It's not always like this. I've been doing this for a long time. There are a lot of things going on right now that I don't like. Back in the old days a cocksucker like Gordon never would've . . ." He trailed off. "Never mind. Excuse me, gentlemen. I'm tired, too. Stand by. Gordon will be here in a few minutes. Remember what I told you." Colonel Hunter left the room without another word.

"He didn't *tell* us anything," Tailor grumbled. "I'm sick of all this innuendo and double-talk. People need to quit dropping hints and shit. They either just need to tell us straight up or shut their mouths."

"Skullduggery gives me a headache," I said, rubbing my temple. My shoulders sagged from the weight of my body armor and gear. I still had a shotgun slung across my back. I just wanted to take a shower and go to bed. I was in no mood for any of Gordon's bullshit.

But even when Gordon wasn't around, he could still piss you off. Another twenty minutes ticked by before Gordon strolled into the classroom. He had his suit jacket hanging over the crook of his arm. He tie was loosened and his shirt collar was unbuttoned. It was as casual as I'd ever seen him. He was wearing a leather shoulder holster with a Glock tucked under his left arm. He looked like a TV cop.

"Mr. Valentine!" he said jovially, vigorously shaking my hand. Gordon was one of those people who seemed like he was trying to crush your fingers during a handshake. "Mr. Tailor! Good to see you both. How was your flight?"

"I shot a man and kicked him out of the helicopter, Gordon," I said.

"I know. Nicely done, Mr. Valentine. Excellent work rolling with a changing situation. I know things were tense, and I know you gentlemen have been under a lot of pressure. Please believe me when I say your efforts are paying off."

"Is that so?" Tailor asked.

"It certainly is!" Gordon said. "We've been watching you two very closely. I'm prepared to offer you, both of you, full-time positions with my organization."

"What organization is that, exactly?" I asked.

Gordon smiled. "You know the drill, Mr. Valentine. Need-to-know. And unless I can count on you to make a commitment, you don't need to know."

Tailor lit a cigarette, not bothering to ask if it was okay to smoke in the classroom. "What exactly are you offering us?"

"A full-time job," Gordon replied. "You two would start right away. We'd have you on the next flight out of Zubara. You'll head back to our training center stateside for indoc and processing. After a couple weeks of R&R, of course. Paid R&R. You two have more than earned it."

I was speechless. Tailor kept asking questions. "So we'd just leave?"

"I'm going to level with you," Gordon said, leaning in conspiratorially. "And this goes no further than you two. Project Heartbreaker is winding down. Your mission tonight was probably the last major operation we're going to take on."

"What? What happened?"

"I had to fight to make Project Heartbreaker happen," Gordon said. "My superiors never really believed in it. It was a constant struggle to get funding and resources. That's why you were always so short on manpower and equipment. That's also why we ran you so hard. We had no choice. I never wanted to send you two out on missions, alone, with no back up. A lot of decisions made over my head forced my hand, I'm afraid."

"Like risking our lives to capture some guy then changing your mind later and ordering me to kill him?" I asked bitterly.

"Yes, like that," Gordon said. "I hated to do that, Mr. Valentine. I still think Rafael Montalban would've been an excellent asset. But the situation changed, and so did my orders. I asked you to carry them out, and you did. That sort of dedication and ability to adapt to a dynamic situation is why we're having this conversation right now. It's no accident your chalk was sent after Rafael Montalban. My organization needs people of your caliber."

"Okay, okay," Tailor said, interjecting before I could say anything else. "What would this position involve?" I couldn't believe it. *Is he seriously interested in Gordon's offer?*

"You'll work for me. Things are changing quickly. I need people I can count on so we can stay on top of things. I need people who can carry out tough jobs despite limited resources and information. The pay is *far* better than you're making now. You won't have to deal with any bureaucratic bullshit. You two will answer only to me."

I found it darkly humorous that Gordon didn't consider himself a bureaucrat. "You mean like Anders?"

"Yes!" Gordon beamed. "As a matter of fact, Anders is my right-hand man. You'll be working with him a lot. He's spoken highly of you both."

"I'll bet," I said. "Did he tell you he let Singer bleed to death without even trying to help him?"

"I was fully briefed on that operation, Mr. Valentine. I know that was tough, but the import—"

I cut him off. "Tough? *Tough?* Is that what you'd call that? We've had thirty percent casualties, and you call that tough?"

"You need to control your temper," Gordon snapped. "I'm trying to offer you a job!"

"Don't fuck with me, Gordon. I've seen full well what your jobs involve! And I'm sick of this shit!"

Tailor stepped between me and Gordon, trying to calm me down. I don't know if it was fatigue, stress, or a combination of the two, but I was on the verge of blowing up completely. My heart was pounding in my chest. I was so mad I was almost shaking.

"Fine!" Gordon said, gesturing sharply with his hands. "I'm trying to do you a favor. If this is how you want it, forget it. Mr. Anders warned me about this. He told me that when things start to get tough and you lose a couple guys, you fall apart. I didn't believe it. I've seen your record. But you know what? He's right. You can't handle it, Valentine. You're not cut out for this. This was a mistake. I need solid, dependable men. I don't need guys that turn to mush when we take a few casualties. Shit happens. People die. That's the way it is."

Something clicked just then. I stepped back and straightened myself out. My eyes narrowed. My face went blank. Tailor saw the expression on my face. His eyes went wide, and he turned to Gordon.

"Listen, you wanna leave now," he said. "Val had a bad night. Bad timing, you know?"

"It doesn't matter," Gordon said. "Forget the whole thing. You two want to go down with this ship, you're more than welcome. We can always get more. You know how many people there are like you out there? Half burned-out shooters, desperate for their glory days and the old run-and-gun, who jump at any offer we give them? They're all so eager, and they don't ask a lot of questions. You, for example."

"Gordon, I'm warning you," Tailor said.

"I'm not afraid of you, Valentine," Gordon said, looking at me over Tailor's shoulder. He gestured to the pistol under his arm. "I'm not some paper-pushing desk jockey, you know."

"Gordon, there's no way you're going to get that gun out before Val blows a hole in your chest. Everybody just calm down now!"

"I'm perfectly *calm*," I stated. "I'm not angry at you because my friends died. We knew the risks when we signed up. I'm angry because my friends died as a direct result of your incompetence and blatant disregard for our lives. So I'm going to have to decline your offer." I turned around and walked away, but paused at the door. "Gordon, if I ever see you again, I'll kill you." I turned and left the room.

Chapter 17: The Coup

LORENZO
May 10

The news was grim. There had been an explosion at the palace. The emir was dead. Until further notice, a curfew was in effect at eight o'clock every evening. The radio's volume had been turned up, and the crowd of foreign workers, mostly Pakistani and Sri Lankan, gathered at the café were all listening carefully, many of them surely wondering just how bad it was going to get, but too poor to leave their relatively good-paying jobs to fly home. The news report ended on the high note that the heroic General Sabah had personally assured the destruction of the Zionist backed criminals, and all the workers went back to their cheap food.

"Tomorrow's the big day. Are you nervous?" Jill asked.

"Of course not," I lied. "I eat commando death squads for breakfast."

The two of us were not that far from our apartment. Tired of waiting for the Fat Man, and feeling the need to keep busy, we had continued our search for Dead Six. It had been just as fruitless as before. Zubara was a big city, and nobody we talked to recognized the Americans of Dead Six. I don't know where they bought their food, or who did their laundry, and apparently none of them had ever taken a taxi, and it was really pissing me off.

Jill Del Toro's education was coming along. She'd been my shadow for the last few days. She no longer walked like an American in public, and I was pretty sure I'd gotten her to the point that she was street-smart enough to not just get randomly murdered on her own. Today she was playing a relatively convincing imported Filipina. I'd helped her with her makeup so she'd look more forgettable. She looked like a cleaning lady and I looked like I should be unclogging drains.

It turned out that both of us were fluent in Spanish. Jill's paternal grandparents had been Mexican immigrants, and her dad had met and married her mom while stationed in Subic Bay. So we could converse freely here, as hardly anybody except for the occasional Filipino or European spoke Spanish in the Zoob and it didn't stick out in public like English did.

She'd come along pretty well. If she had the inclination, I thought she could actually have a future as a criminal. She was certainly a good liar. "I'm not worried, either," Jill said with confidence.

The last few days had been kind of awkward. Neither one of us talked about what had happened between us, which was good, *I think*, because that would have just needlessly complicated things. I had to keep my mind on business. "There's something important I need to talk to you about."

"Yes?" Jill responded quickly.

"It's about tomorrow's job," I said.

"Oh." She went back to her food, stabbing an olive with her fork.

"I don't know what's going to happen. This could be something simple and I can just walk right in and grab the box, or it could be crazy. I just don't know. We're going to have to come up with a plan on the fly. So I might need your help, I might not."

"I'm ready. Dead Six ruined my life, Lorenzo. I'll do whatever I have to do. I already showed you I'm willing to shoot them. What more do you need me to prove?"

I smiled. *She was aggressive.* "That's not what I meant. Tomorrow, we either succeed or fail. After that, it's on to Phase Three, and that's my problem, not yours."

"When will you tell me what that even is?"

"You really don't want to know. Let's just say that it's stupid and dangerous. But that's not what I'm talking about. What I'm trying to say is that after tomorrow, you're done."

She looked up from her lunch. "What do you mean?"

"I told you that if you helped me, I'd help you. I've had Reaper working on fake papers for you. I've got contacts I can refer you through. Basically, after tomorrow, you can go back to the US if you want." I would need to walk her through all the details of setting up a new life, but she didn't belong here, in this disintegrating shit hole, not anymore.

"Home?" Jill seemed shocked. Not upset, just surprised. "I . . . I don't know what to say."

"We'll worry about tomorrow first." I noticed some blue uniforms coming down the street. The security forces were randomly rousting people off the streets for questioning. It would be best to avoid that. I pulled out my wallet and threw down some riyals. "We'll talk about it later."

VALENTINE
Fort Saradia National Historical Site
May 10
1400

Following Sarah, I stepped out into the harsh desert heat. We made our way down the stairs of the dorm, followed by everyone else who'd been inside. Sarah and Anita had gone around banging on doors, telling everyone to follow them to the chow hall. She'd come to my room last.

Everyone kept asking her what was going on. She would only tell them she didn't know why, but Colonel Hunter had ordered an all-hands meeting. Something big had gone down. We hadn't had a meeting like this since our first night in-country.

For my part, I could guess what was happening. Gordon had told me that Project Heartbreaker was winding down. I wondered if, hell, *hoped* that the Project had been canceled and that we'd all be going home.

We all filed into the chow hall, and people began to sit down. Several of Hunter's security people were standing around, looking just as confused as the rest of us. My old buddy Conrad was there, too, looking as dickish as usual.

Aside from the support staff, only fifteen members of Dead Six were present. I knew another ten or so were still out at safe houses throughout the city. Even still, a lot of faces were missing, and almost a third of the guys present had been wounded.

Even our support staff hadn't been untouched. Sarah, Anita King, and another controller whose name I couldn't recall were there. But the fourth controller, a woman named Evelyn Majors, had been killed in action. She'd been sent in to a captured enemy safe house to help gather intelligence. The whole place had been wired. It blew up, killing her and all of Hansen's chalk. A couple of the logistics guys had been killed by a suicide bomber downtown.

We sat around talking for a few minutes. The dull roar of conversation quickly dropped away when Colonel Hunter came purposefully striding into the room. He stopped at the front of the chow hall, near the carts where the food was served.

"Listen up, everyone," he said, his raspy voice echoing through the now-quiet cafeteria. "Two hours ago there was an explosion at the Royal Palace. The emir is dead. It's been confirmed. General Al Sabah has declared martial law and has effected a nationwide curfew. He's deploying half the Zubaran Army throughout the city in order to lock everything down.

"Not all of the Army is on his side. According to our information, one of the emir's sons is still alive and is trying to rally support. General Al Sabah claims that the emir's son assassinated his father in a coup attempt. We have every reason to believe that General Al Sabah was the one behind the bombing. Either way, a civil war is about to break out in this country, and our support network is gone."

"What does this mean, sir?" someone asked.

Hunter looked thoughtful for a second. "Without Zubaran support, we can't function. We can't get supplies in and out of the country, and half of our best intelligence came from the emir's secret police. This is a crippling blow to our operations. Project Heartbreaker has failed." Hunter let that sink in for a moment before continuing. "I've been in contact with higher authority. I spoke with Gordon Willis half an hour ago. Project Heartbreaker has been terminated. Dead Six is being disbanded. We're all going home."

The chow hall erupted in clapping and cheers before Hunter could even finish saying it. Sarah leaned over and hugged me tightly in my seat. I could scarcely believe it, even though I'd sort of known this was going to happen. I was going to have to call Ling and tell her we wouldn't be needing her assistance after all. A big smile formed across my face.

"Okay, okay, listen up!" Hunter shouted. "Getting home is going to be a long and painful process, folks. There's going to be out-processing, nondisclosure agreements, and more paperwork than you can imagine. We're still working on getting all your pay problems straightened out, too. Worse, you're not leaving Zubara on a plane."

"How are we leaving then, Colonel?"

"The situation in the Zoob has deteriorated enough that they're not willing to risk our jet. Tomorrow night, around midnight, a boat will be coming for us. It'll moor at the dock on the north side of the fort. You're all going to board that vessel, and you'll be on your way. Before ten people ask, I have no idea where that boat is going. I won't be on it."

I barely listened to the rest of Hunter's briefing. He went on about how we needed to pack our stuff and start breaking down everything in the fort as quickly as possible. Instead my attention was focused on Sarah. She was beaming at me, a bright smile on her face. We were going to have to have a long talk about the future, about *us*. I knew it wasn't going to be easy, either. But after everything we'd been through already, I knew we could make it.

As it would turn out, I didn't know *anything*.

LORENZO
May 11

My phone sat in the middle of kitchen table, and I just watched it . . . waiting. The others had joined me, and the four of us were in a circle, kind of quietly looking at that phone like it was a magic oracle that was going to spit out the answers in a rhyming riddle or something. We had spent the last week preparing for today. Our equipment had been checked and rechecked. My crew was ready for anything. I didn't know what the Fat Man's message would bring, but I knew with dead certainty that he would call. Big Eddie's people were extremely reliable.

And punctual. The phone buzzed. I pushed the button for speaker phone.

The Fat Man spoke. "Dead Six is supposed to leave Zubara tonight. They will be told to gather in the old Fort Saradia compound to await evacuation. A boat is supposed to pick them up at midnight."

Reaper was already pulling up a map of the area and getting details on the old British fort. "How many men?" I asked.

"Approximately twenty-five remaining combat personnel and a dozen or more support staff. They will have all their equipment, and they will be alert. The last of them have been recalled already. Fort Saradia was their base of operations. All of their personnel will be on-site before sundown. They will need to be inside before the curfew to avoid suspicion."

Reaper turned his laptop so I could see the fort. It was a big square of tall mud-brick walls on the coast just west of the Ash Shamal peninsula. A single road led to it, weaving through encroaching housing and terminating right at the front gate. The fort itself was big enough to fit a football field inside and had several interior buildings. That was a lot of area to cover. "Do you know where the box is being kept?"

"I do not have that information."

Of course. "Anything else you can give me?"

"I would strongly suggest that you accomplish your mission before midnight. You do not want to be there after midnight."

"What happens then?"

"I cannot tell you, but Dead Six will be dead by dawn. Do you understand me, Mr. Lorenzo?"

I hope you choke on a pancake and die. "Tell your boss I'll get the box." I hung up. The group was quiet as I studied the satellite photo of the fort. Something was going down, something huge.

Tonight I would bring the fight to Dead Six.

VALENTINE
Fort Saradia National Historical Site
May 11
1500

I found myself alone in my room, packing my belongings. Almost all of my clothes were stuffed into my duffel bag. In the short time I'd been in the Zoob, I'd somehow managed to acquire a second duffel bag's worth of crap, and I was busy sorting through it all.

All of the gear I'd been issued was on my bed, laid out for sorting. We were told to just throw away the various fatigues and other clothing we'd used. Colonel Hunter told us to keep our body armor and weapons with us until we were on the boat and out of Zubaran waters. The situation downtown had rapidly deteriorated, and there'd been sporadic fighting throughout the tiny country. Rumors were flying about the emir's son planning a last-ditch attempt to retake the Royal Palace. We all figured Zubara would be a war zone before the night was out, and we wanted to be ready in case anything spilled over onto our doorstep.

So the MK 17 SCAR-H carbine I'd claimed back in February was lying on my bed, complete with grenade launcher, weapon light, and ACOG scope. I hadn't yet reassembled it after giving it a thorough cleaning. That rifle and I had been through a lot together, and it hadn't let me down. I wished I could keep it.

My body armor and load-bearing vest were on the bed as well. The armor still had Rafael Montalban's .357 slug buried in it. My vest was stocked with ammunition and even a couple of grenades. The colonel had been adamant about us being ready to fight in case something bad happened, and none of us argued with him. There was no sense getting killed on your last night in-country.

I'd lined my various souvenirs up on the metal shelf that sat against the wall of my room until I figured out where I was going to pack them. The strange wooden puzzle box that I'd found in Adar's safe was there, and I'd managed to sort of put it back together. Next to it was Rafael Montalban's elaborate Korth revolver. I'd found my harmonica, too, which I was happy about. I hadn't played it once since I'd been in the Zoob and had actually forgotten I'd brought it.

On the floor next to the shelf was a backpack full of money. It was my share of the loot we'd stolen from the man named Lorenzo. We'd split it four ways between Tailor, Hudson, Wheeler, and myself. Hudson was taking

Wheeler's share. He said he'd make sure Wheeler's parents got the money. I had no doubt in my mind that he'd honor that promise.

I'd planned to use that money to pay Exodus for safe passage out of Zubara. Happily, I wasn't going to need their services now, which meant I could keep the money. My share amounted to about a hundred and twenty-five thousand dollars' worth of British pounds. I also had, stashed somewhere else, a smaller pouch with my half of the money from Adar's safe. *The spoils of war . . .*

I called Ling on the phone she'd given me and told her the good news. She congratulated me but said that if the situation changed I could still call her. We'd made a deal and she'd honor it, she said. She told me that her people would be in Zubara for a few more days, though they were still leaving earlier than planned because of the looming civil war.

There were two quick knocks on my bathroom door, and Sarah came into my room. I smiled as soon as I saw her, and her eyes lit up. We embraced and kissed.

"Hey, you," she said, looking up into my eyes. "Getting all packed up?"

"You know it," I said. "I can't believe how much crap I've accumulated since I've been here. I hope they don't charge us for luggage." I laughed.

"I wonder how long it'll take us to get home?" Sarah said. "I mean, this boat could be going anywhere."

"It could be weeks," I suggested. "Or longer. Who knows? Hell, who *cares?* The important thing is we're getting out of here."

"I can't believe it," Sarah said, looking down. "After everything we've been through, all the people we've lost, we're just leaving. It was all for nothing."

I sighed. She was right. A lot of people had died, and we had nothing to show for it. "I know," I said. "The important thing is we're still alive. We have each other. We're going home. All things considered, I'll settle for that."

Sarah gave me a sad smile. "Me, too. So, uh, where are you going when you get home?"

"I don't really have a home," I said. "The closest thing I have to family is a cranky old bastard named Hawk. He lives in a little town called Quagmire, Nevada. I'll probably go there, since I don't have anywhere else to stay. What about you?"

"I managed to get an e-mail off to my mom, telling her I'm coming home," Sarah said excitedly. "She doesn't even know where I've been. Not really, anyway. I gave her a story, told her I was working as a translator for an oil company. I'll probably go back to Modesto, where she lives. I don't have anyplace else to stay either."

I chewed in my lip for a moment. "Modesto is a long way from Quagmire," I said.

"You know, I hate living in California anyway," Sarah said, smiling again. "I could, I suppose, be talked into leaving. You know, with the right incentive package."

I raised an eyebrow theatrically. "Baby, I've got an incentive package right here," I said, gesturing to myself while grinning stupidly.

Sarah laughed out loud. "You're cute when you're being a retard, you know that? Are you asking me to move in with you?"

"Eh, you might want to let me find a place to live first," I said.

"Oh no, it's not going to be that easy," Sarah said, eyes twinkling. "You're going to have to meet my mother first."

"Oh boy," I said without enthusiasm.

"Stop it, my mom is a sweet lady."

"Wow," I said after a moment. "This is all surreal. We're really doing this, aren't we? Holy shit. We're going home!"

"I know, right?" Sarah said, squeezing me again. "Thank God."

I closed my eyes, holding Sarah tightly. "Thank God."

LORENZO

Carl and I sat in the van. It had turned out to be the hottest day so far this year, so of course, the air conditioner in our secondary van had died. We had one other vehicle stashed in a storage unit but it would stick out way too much in this neighborhood. The heat was like a stifling blanket, burning the air in my lungs. Sweat dripped down my back and pooled in my armpits. I finished the bottle of water and tossed it. Tonight was the night.

"You ready?" Carl asked from behind the wheel.

"Yep." I cracked the vertebrae of my neck after securing the transmitter around my throat. This was it. "Radio check."

"I can hear you fine. I've got a clear view of the gate, and the guards don't seem to be checking anything," Jill said. *"I think it's too hot for them to care."*

She was out of sight, a couple hundred yards up the road, closer to the fort. Alone, unarmed, and ready to step out into traffic on a moment's notice. She sounded excited.

"I've got you, chief," Reaper's voice echoed in my ear. I knew that he would be sitting in the darkened apartment, half a dozen screens open in front of him, joystick in hand, four radio channels going at once, processing absurd amounts of information, and totally in his element. Even though he was ten miles away, Reaper was going to be my eyes. "Little Bird can see the van just perfect, nice and bright on thermal, too."

Circling high overhead was Reaper's favorite toy and the single most expensive thing that I had ever purchased, and that included sports cars, yachts, and houses. Little Bird was basically the world's fanciest remote-controlled plane. Well, at least that a regular person could actually purchase. No matter how bad Reaper wanted one, we couldn't afford a Predator drone.

L.B. had a wingspan of only ten feet. When you took it apart, the whole thing fit into two big suitcases. It wasn't fast, it didn't have any guns, but what it did have was the ability to stay in the air for damn-near forever running off what was basically a glorified leaf-blower engine, all while snooping with every type of camera you could think of. It was like having my own portable spy satellite.

Old Fort Saradia was visible at the end of the road. Those twenty-foot walls had been built over a hundred years ago by the British Empire. There were only two entrances, one off the road, and a smaller one on the opposite side overlooking the rudimentary dock, and thermal showed that both of them were being guarded.

Inside the walls were several other buildings. Some old battered historical things, then a couple of large steel buildings that dated back to the forties, and finally a dorm that had been built more recently when Fort Saradia had been used briefly as the oceanographic institute for the emir's new university. The whole thing was supposed to be unoccupied now except for a couple of caretakers.

"You gonna stick with the plan this time, Lorenzo?" Carl asked.

"Sneak into a den of professional killers, find the box, walk back out. Right?" I was nervous, but I tried not to let it show. The shakes would come later, now I needed to be cold and professional.

"Walk in the park," Carl muttered. I knew he didn't like this at all. He wanted to go with me, but Carl was a warrior, he wasn't built for stealth. And no matter how satisfying it would be, kicking in the door, guns blazing, was just going to get us all killed.

Rather, I was going to do what I did best. And that meant being one sneaky son of a bitch. I needed to be fully in touch with my inner ninja. I checked my gear again. I was moving light. Speed and silence mattered more than firepower. Forty of them, one of me, it didn't matter what I was armed with. If I got caught, I was going to die. I had my STI, several extra mags of 9mm ammo, the excellent Silencerco suppressor, a pair of knives, one fixed blade and one folder, radio, lock picks, night-vision monocular, and finally a length of piano wire tied between two small wooden dowels. I'm an old-fashioned kind of guy.

My clothing was neutral, all gray and tan, cargo pants, plain long-sleeve T-shirt, soft desert boots, one of those cargo vests with ten million pockets, and even a khaki ball cap. The Dead Six types that we had seen tended to be dressed in that contractor-chic style, so I hoped that if somebody spotted me, their first inclination would be that I was just one of them, and by the time they recognized that I wasn't, they'd be quietly dispatched.

After some internal debate, I had worn my lightweight, concealable armor vest, because even though it made me a little less mobile, this was a very trigger-happy bunch that we were dealing with. It would stop pistol rounds, but rifle bullets would still zip through like it was made of butter.

Now we were waiting. From the Fat Man, we knew that all of Dead Six was coming here, and with the curfew in effect, they couldn't risk being randomly pulled over anymore than we could. Once Carl dropped me off and picked up Jill, he was going to park out of sight.

We were hoping for a vehicle that I could either carjack or ride unnoticed. Preferably the latter, as the former introduced some real bad complications into the mix. It was too early in the evening to start popping people. Reaper had already notified us of a couple of potentials, but they had been traveling too closely together. Luckily, the fort was the only thing at the end of this road other than shabby ramshackle housing, so if it was any sort of decent vehicle, it was obvious where it was going.

I didn't like this plan. There were way too many things to go wrong. But if this didn't work, then I was going to be reduced to trying to climb over walls that were probably under video surveillance. "I hate winging it," I muttered. Carl grunted in affirmation.

"I've got a truck on camera. He's at the base of the road, ETA, one minute," Reaper said. *"No thermal hits from the back."* Carl started the engine. The plan was to come up behind potential vehicles and tail them to the last roundabout. If it was a good one, we'd go for it. If it wasn't, then we'd take the turn and come back here to wait for the next target.

It was a Mitsubishi truck, with a ragged tarp covering the back. It passed us slowly. The driver was a blond Caucasian and the passenger was a black guy, so they probably didn't live here. It didn't have a tailgate, so that was one less thing to worry about. "This one looks good," I whispered. Carl nodded and rolled out behind him. "Jill, the white truck. Get ready to intercept." I pulled the hat low onto my head and placed my hand on the door handle. The metal was scorching hot to the touch.

"Have visual. Truck's coming toward the roundabout. Distraction time," Jill reported matter-of-factly.

"Good luck, everybody," I said. The van rolled up behind the Mitsubishi. "Now, Jill. Go! Go!"

I opened the passenger-side door. We had disabled the interior lights. The truck was slowing on the roundabout. We had one shot. Jill was dressed as a local, weighed down with bags of groceries. She blundered right into the path of the truck, playing oblivious to the hilt. The driver of the Mitsubishi hit the brakes. Red lights illuminated my world. I was out of the van in a heartbeat, Carl pulling the door closed behind me. I could see the passenger's profile in his mirror, his attention on Jill.

The tarp was dusty with talcum-powder sand. Trying not to make a sudden impact against the shocks, I slid under and right onto the burning heat of the truck's diamond-plate bed. The horn sounded, making me flinch involuntarily. I heard Jill shout back at the driver and could imagine her shaking her fist.

"I'm in," I whispered.

Jill heard and continued on her way across the road. Carl pulled through the roundabout and headed in a different direction. I lay on the metal that was hot enough to fry bacon and tried not to cry. The truck rolled forward. I slowly shifted myself around on the greasy, hot surface until I was squished in the shadow of the cab as much as possible. After another minute we left the paved road and the tires began to make a different noise on the gravel. We were getting close. The brakes whined as we stopped.

"*You're coming through the gate,*" Reaper informed me.

I could barely hear the passenger. "Hey, Studley, what's up, dawg?" I couldn't make out the guard's response. "We've got the last of the stuff from Safe House Five. . . . I know, right?" There was laughter.

"*Interior guard is waving them past. You're inside.*" Then music started playing in my earpiece. It was some techno-remix of the *Mission: Impossible* theme.

"Turn that shit off," I hissed.

It stopped. "*Sorry, just trying to set the mood.*"

The brakes whined as we rolled to a stop. The smell of diesel was strong in the air. The engine died with a gurgle, and the doors slammed. I heard voices speaking in English, somebody laughed, and then it was quiet.

"*They're walking away from the truck. You're parked just south of Building One.*" I had memorized the overhead layout of the place, and we had numbered every structure inside. "*You've got somebody on the wall directly above you. Hold on a second—I'll warn you when you're clear.*"

I scurried around until I could see out the back. The interior of the fort was getting darker by the minute. There were only a handful of exterior lights scattered about, and luckily most of them were low wattage. Once it was fully dark, this place was going to be my playground.

I'm coming for you, Valentine.

Chapter 18: Civil War

VALENTINE
1955

As darkness fell on the tiny Gulf emirate, the Zubaran Civil War began in earnest. Fighting had broken out all across the city as forces loyal to the Royal Family clashed with the numerically superior forces of General Al Sabah. According to news reports, there was heavy fighting near the palace. As expected, the Royalists attempted to retake Zubara's seat of government.

By now, most everything we were taking with us was packed onto pallets, ready to be loaded onto the boat when it arrived. Everything else was being systematically destroyed. We were leaving nothing behind for the Zubarans to capture.

A lot of us didn't have anything to do. Everything had been broken down and packed away, so we didn't even have a television to watch. We ended up gathering on the roof of the dormitory, where we had a pretty good view of the city, to watch the fighting.

It was like a grim fireworks show. The occasional stream of tracer fire arced into the darkened sky. We could see flashes and hear distant rumbling as both sides shelled each other with artillery. Jets roared overhead, and ancient air-raid sirens screamed throughout the city. Several large fires had broken out. Volleys of rockets were exchanged. We watched in awe as a Zubaran jet, engulfed in flames, plunged into the bay.

I sat on an old metal bucket and played my harmonica. I was rusty, but I'd been pretty good back in the day. I played a sad, lilting tune. I didn't know what it was called, but no one seemed to mind me setting things to music as we watched Zubara burn.

"We caused this," Anita King said. She stood near me, arms folded across her chest, looking off into the distance. "We destroyed this country."

"We were trying to prevent this," Holbrook said, looking through a pair of large military binoculars.

Tailor's face was briefly illuminated as he lit a cigarette. "This was bound to happen sooner or later," he said, snapping the lighter shut. "There was no way a handful of guys was going to come in and change the course of this country."

"Then why did you sign up?" Holbrook asked.

Tailor shrugged. "It was something to do. I was bored." He cracked a smile, and Holbrook shook his head.

Frank Mann, the armorer, was with us. "It's been nice working with you guys," he said. "You didn't abuse my weapons. I appreciated that." We all chuckled.

"You know what really pisses me off?" Holbrook asked. "You know they'll try this again."

"Who?"

"Whoever the hell we work for. These black-ops guys. Project Heartbreaker failed. But you know they're going to try this again somewhere else. Might be a year from now, might be twenty years. But they *will* try again. And a handful of guys will die trying to accomplish a mission an entire army would have trouble with."

He was right. If Gordon Willis was representative of whatever shadowy organization he worked for, I knew they'd try something like this again. Our employers had no regard for human life, neither ours nor those of civilians caught in the crossfire. They would do anything, no matter the cost, to accomplish their ambiguous and convoluted goals. We were the ones that paid the price.

Whoever they were, they were powerful, well-funded, and connected. And they were arrogant. I had no doubt in my mind that they'd try again someday. A strong wind gusted from the ocean. A storm was coming, unseasonably late in the year.

LORENZO

I hung from the underside of the stairs of the big forties- era structure we had christened Building Two, sweat rolling down my face and stinging my eyes. My grip was tight on the hot metal bars, and I prayed that the Dead Six personnel standing ten feet away would hurry up and find a better place to be.

"*Aqua Teens* is way better than *Venture Brothers*," the first argued. There were some clicking sounds, and then a lighter flame appeared, briefly highlighting the two men. I could hear him take a long drag. The nearest light was burned out, and it was dark enough that I could only see the glowing red embers.

Using the thermal camera on Little Bird, Reaper had warned me right before the Dead Six men had turned the corner. My awkward perch was the best that I could come up with on short notice.

"Dude, you're stupid," the second replied. "*Venture Brothers* has Brock Samson. *Brock Samson*, man. All you got is a milkshake. Quit hogging that."

Who argues about cartoons in the middle of the night? Ignoring the growing pain in my arms, I contemplated shooting them and getting it over with, but it was too damn hot to have to drag their bodies to a hiding place. Luckily, after a few minutes the two super geniuses decided they needed some munchies and went back inside. The smell from Building Two's open door told me that it was the chow hall.

I slowly lowered myself to the floor, careful to settle my weight without making a sound. Checking my watch, I cursed the delay. I didn't know what was going down at midnight, but I didn't want to be here to find out. I'd crept around the first few buildings now and I still hadn't seen Nightcrawler. My best bet was to isolate him and find out where the box was. If he had any clue how incredibly valuable it was, he had more than likely kept it for himself. If not, I could certainly carve the box's location out of him.

Building Three looked liked like the living quarters, so that's where I'd start. I could stick to the shadows under the wall of the old steel building all the way there. It took nearly twenty minutes, since I had to low-crawl through a few narrow patches between rays of naked light, but this was my element, I was a ghost, I was a predator. Move . . . stop, wait, listen . . . move. Every time I heard Reaper's voice I would freeze and wait until the danger passed. There was one final wide space to cross, but it was relatively dark and scattered with miscellaneous barrels and bits of cover, and then I was in place.

Building Three had a covered stairwell on both ends. Reaper's thermal camera couldn't help me once I was under a roof. I heard the footsteps coming and unconsciously calculated where they would be looking as they descended. I pulled into the darkest corner, hand coming to rest on my Greco Whisper CT. The 5-inch blade came out slowly, not making any noise, and I held it in against my body. A bearded man came down the stairs, whistling. *If his eyes so much as flick in this direction . . .*

Knives aren't for fighting. Knives are for *killing*. I was already visualizing his death, when luckily for both of us, he just kept going, opened the door, and walked out. I started breathing again and sheathed the blade back under my vest.

The second floor. *Hall clear.* I couldn't believe it. Their names were actually *written* on the doors. The first door said McAllister. The next door read Valentine and had a stupid heart with an arrow through it. Jill had thought that she'd heard Nightcrawler called Val back at the Hasa Market.

The door was locked, but I picked it in under five seconds. I drew my 9mm, screwed the suppressor on, and entered the room without hesitation. Thankfully the hinges did not squeak.

The nearest exterior lights of the compound provided enough illumination to see by through the open balcony door. The balcony was empty. The bed was unoccupied. I checked the bathroom. The shower was damp, and there was still condensation on the mirror. He had not been gone long. Music came from the other bedroom attached to this bathroom. I had to hurry. I closed the door. If anyone returned, it would at least give me a brief warning.

Some weapons were thrown on the bed. There was a disassembled 7.62mm SCAR sitting on top of some armor. The armor itself was stained with dried blood and had a bullet impact on the trauma plate. I could not help but notice the oddball sidearm still holstered on the green web gear, a weird, customized S&W .44 Magnum. That was probably the same gun that had blasted a hole clear through Hosani and into me. I'd found the right room.

I began to ransack the room, going through the footlocker and checking the contents, trying not to disturb the scene. If the box wasn't here, I was going to hit the main building next, and the last thing I wanted to do was raise an alarm in this ant's nest. Clock was ticking. The shooter was bound to be back any minute. Nothing of interest so far. Closet next. Random gear and clothing had just been dumped in here. He must have known that this was temporary.

On the floor was a plain duffel bag. Unzipping it revealed a whole bunch of money. I was positive that some of the rubber-banded stacks had come from me. *Bastard*. But on top of the money was a small wooden box. *Could it be?* I picked it up. It felt exactly like the replica I had left to be mangled in Adar's house fire.

YES! YES! YES!

"I've found it," I whispered into the radio. The others, even Carl, actually cheered. Leaving the money, I stuffed the box into my vest. All that cash . . . It would just slow me down, though. The oldest, scariest part of me was really tempted to stay there until Nightcrawler came back, just so I could murder him on general principle, but it was time to go. "Prepare to extract. Reaper, how's it look out there?"

"*Compound looks clear right around you, but I can't see under the overhangs.*"

"*Military vehicles? Lorenzo,*" Carl's voice sounded urgent. "*There's something weird going on down here.*"

"What've you got?" Something moved in the corner of my vision. "Wait—"

Lights flashed inside my skull, and the world exploded in pain.

VALENTINE

My hand hurt. I hadn't busted anybody in the head like that in a long time. The stranger in my room flopped to the floor like a sandbag. My mind raced as I tried to figure out what was happening. *Who is this guy? Are the Zubarans coming after us?*

I'd crossed over from Sarah's room by hopping the balcony. I'd left my balcony door open, so the guy hadn't noticed when I came in. He'd been huddled over by my closet, holding something in his hand. I was on top of the guy immediately. I didn't give him time to breathe. I slammed my knee into his spine, putting all of my weight on it, while I checked him for weapons. I found some kind of fancy 1911 pistol, a boxy custom job with a wide-body frame, tucked in a holster on his right side. I had a hard time pulling the pistol out, since there was a long suppressor screwed on the end. My own gun was still in its holster, sitting on my bed across the room. I swore at myself for leaving the room unarmed. It was a stupid thing to do, given the circumstances.

I swiped off the safety of the stranger's gun as I stood up, and kept it pointed at him. My eyes darted to the gun in my hand, and something clicked in my brain. I stepped around the splayed-out intruder and hit the light switch.

"You!" I snarled. "It's you!" I couldn't believe it. It was the guy from Hasa Market. Lorenzo, the girl had called him. "What the fuck are you doing here?" I said and kicked him in the ribs as hard as I could. He gasped in pain, and I kicked him again. He flopped over onto his back. "What did you think was gonna happen here, asshole?" I asked. "Huh? You got some balls, man, I'll give you that." I tried to kick him a third time. He was ready for it. He spun around on his back, feet moving so fast I couldn't keep up. He kicked the pistol out of my hands. It flew across the room and slid under my bed.

Lorenzo tried to scramble to his feet, but I was on top of him. I grabbed his tan vest, hoisted him up, and slammed him against the cinder-block wall. He was still disoriented. I reached behind him and clamped onto his vest again. I was a lot taller than Lorenzo. I pulled his vest up from behind and down over his face. I leaned into him then, punching him in the head over and over again, hockey-brawl style.

I thought I heard Lorenzo say something, but I couldn't understand him. Then the building was rocked by an explosion outside.

LORENZO

My brain must have really bounced off the inside of my skull, because I couldn't remember how I'd ended up on the floor with a mouth full of blood. My earpiece was lying next to my head, and I could barely hear Carl screaming about something.

Someone was talking, angrily asking me questions. The kick that landed in my ribs was unbelievably hard. The second was even worse. It was that son of a bitch, Nightcrawler. There was a gun in his hand. My gun, *damn it*! He tried to kick me a third time, but I reacted and kicked my gun across the room. Strong hands grabbed me, jerking me to my feet and hurling me into the far wall. He pulled my vest over my head and was on me in a second, knuckles slamming into my face repeatedly.

I slid down, shaking my head, trying to focus, which is difficult when you're getting punched. I couldn't hear Carl, but he could still hear me through my throat mike. I needed a distraction. "Carl, hit it."

A concussion shook the room as Carl radio-detonated the Semtex plastic explosive I had left in the Mitsubishi. Nightcrawler spun, surprised by the noise. I shoved myself upright as he turned back to me. I kicked him in the chest. Dust flew from my boot as he crashed back into the wall next to the bed. I moved in while he was off balance and threw a knee to his side. He grimaced but stayed up. I followed with an elbow to his face, but he blocked it with his forearm and then used his size advantage to shove me back with one big meat hook against my sternum.

The kid was bigger and stronger, but I was faster. He was using a form of Krav Maga, but he was rusty. He didn't practice much, I could tell. I locked up on his arm, spun inside of it, and slugged him in the kidney, then put my foot on the inside of his knee and forced him down. I jerked up on his arm, trying to snap it at the elbow. He crashed into the shelf, snapping boards and sending things flying. He shouted incoherently as his other arm came around with something shiny and metallic and caught me on the side of the head. *Thunk!*

I must have gone out for a second. I was down, blood spewing from my mouth. The room spun as I refocused, again on the floor, and at the blood-stained Korth revolver that he'd just hit me with.

I rolled out of the way as his foot kicked through empty air. I was back up in a split second, trying to make distance until I could see straight. I was dizzy, but my blade appeared in my hand, like I had willed the Greco there with anger alone. His hand came out of his pocket, and a switchblade opened with an audible *snik*. Time slowed down as we focused on each other.

"Oh, it's on now," he said as he pointed the knife at me, chest heaving, gasping for breath.

I spat out a bunch of blood. "On like Donkey Kong, motherfucker."

We charged.

VALENTINE

I had to finish this. The warning klaxon was screaming, and I could hear people shouting outside. Lorenzo had a hard gleam in his eye, and I knew he meant to kill me.

He lunged. I dodged to the right and tried to slash at him with the Infidel automatic knife in my left hand. His hand arced around and put a gash up my left cheek, barely missing my eye. It wasn't deep, but Christ it was close. I slashed at his abdomen as he pulled away and managed to clip him.

Lorenzo only took a moment to recompose and came at me again. I could tell he was a better fighter than me. He fought like a wounded animal and was extremely fast. This guy was dangerous. But he was injured. I still had the advantage.

He slashed at my face. I leaned back and dodged it, but just barely. I tried to stab him in the abdomen. He moved to the right, avoiding the thrust. His right hand came back down, trying to cut open my left arm. I twisted to the left at the last second. He sliced upward, nicking my arm.

He didn't let up. As I recoiled in pain, he brought his left elbow up and smashed it into my face. Lights flashed in front of my eyes. I dropped my knife. Lorenzo then snap-kicked me in the chest, sending me crashing to the floor.

He was on top of me in an instant. I kicked out, nailing him in the groin. Lorenzo grunted and gasped for air, face turning red. I turned around, fumbling for any kind of weapon. My hand found the rock I used to prop the balcony door open. Grasping it, I sat up and threw it at Lorenzo as hard as I could. His hands flew up to cover his face. The white, softball-sized Zubaran rock hit him in the forearms. He reeled back.

I only had a second. I sat up and dove toward my bed. I desperately grasped for my holstered revolver sitting on my armor. Lorenzo reached me before I could reach my .44, trying to plunge his blade into my back.

LORENZO

It should have been over by now. I should have been able to take him, but those initial hits had left me disoriented, sluggish. Before I could drive my knife into his spine, his enormous boot hit me in the stomach. My abs absorbed the hit, but I staggered back, gasping for air. The kid was pulling that big .44 now, the muzzle swinging toward me.

I stepped into him, knife humming through the air. He raised his right hand to hold me off and I opened his forearm, splashing the walls with red droplets. The kid screamed as the blade struck. But I was too late, he swiveled the big revolver into me from a low retention position.

The concussion was deafening in the little room. The mammoth slug hit me square in the chest. My armor stopped it, but I couldn't breathe. It was like being hit with a bat. Fire washed down every nerve. It took everything I had to stay on my feet. We locked up, me trying to keep that gun away and his blood-slick hand wrapped around my wrist to keep my knife at bay.

I got my fingers around the cylinder of the Smith and wouldn't let it turn as he squeezed the trigger. I could feel his other hand slipping off my knife, and as soon as he let go I was going to plunge it into his neck. We spun around, shoving and grunting, stumbling over the junk on the floor. He was shouting in my ear.

All coherent thought had ceased. It was kill or be killed. No time for fear, no time for pain. I kept throwing knees, trying to tear him down. He head-butted me in the face, smashing my nose, but he stumbled back as well. My eyes filled with involuntary tears, and my hand began to slip from the cylinder.

Desperate, I dropped my knife, reached across his torso, and got my thumb under the hammer of the Smith just as it fell, blocking the shot. His wounded hand now free, the kid swung for my face. I ducked, pushed the gun away from me, and hit him repeatedly, forearms, fists, elbows, knees, every time that gun came back around, I hit him again. He went to his knees, still trying to shoot me. I stepped back and snap-kicked him in the face.

He landed flat on his back with a huge crash.

That had to do it. I bore down on him, ready to beat his head in. He jerked the gun up.

BOOM!

There was a flash of light as he fired, so close that fire engulfed my vision. He missed, but pain like nothing I had ever felt before pierced the right side of my skull. The bullet skimmed past my head and blew a chunk from the ceiling, but I was already falling, clamping one hand over my bleeding ear.

My balance was just gone. I could barely think. I wanted to vomit. All I could hear was this terrible grinding noise as my eardrum died. He was rising, wobbly, seeing two of me. Then I saw tiny green lights under the bed, the night sights from my 9mm. I snatched it into my hand, rolled over and stood, gun punching out, finger already on the trigger.

I was staring down the barrel of his .44. The suppressor of my gun was inches from my opponent's face, centered on the bridge of his nose. Our fingers were on the triggers, both of us just ounces of pressure away from oblivion.

We glared at each other. Each of us battered, cut, bleeding, and pulped. I was blowing frothy blood bubbles every time I exhaled. He moved his mouth. He was talking. *Holy shit, I'm deaf!* I could barely understand him. "What the hell are you doing here?"

Careful not to let my gun move, I reached into my vest, grimacing as my hand brushed the area that was now one massive spreading bruise, and pulled out Adar's box. "I've got what I came for."

Nightcrawler was confused. "That? I don't even know what that is!"

"I'll be going now," I said.

He was shaking badly, and blood was dripping from his forearm, but it wasn't pumping like I'd severed the artery. *Too bad.* "I don't think so."

I didn't hear the door open behind me, but I did feel the terrible impact as they smashed a rifle butt over my head. I ended up on the floor. The last thing I remember was looking at the ceiling, surrounded by angry shadows pointing guns at me. I couldn't understand a word they were saying over that damn *ringing,* and then everything faded to blessed black.

Chapter 19: Best Laid Plans

VALENTINE

It was like an old John Woo movie. Lorenzo and I stood in my little room, not six feet from each other, guns drawn. Neither of us fired. I don't know why. My arm was bleeding badly and burned with pain. I was dizzy and felt sick. It hurt to breathe. Only *the Calm* kept me focused enough to stay in the fight. I barely noticed the pain, and even though I was terrified, I felt no fear.

He was so focused on me that he didn't notice the door opening behind him. Tailor, Hudson, and two of Hunter's security guys came rushing in, weapons at the ready. I lowered my gun just as Hudson bashed Lorenzo in the head with the buttstock of a carbine. The intruder's gun clattered to the floor as he collapsed. He lay there for a second, staring bleary-eyed at the ceiling before losing consciousness.

I stepped back, setting my revolver down on the bed, and clutched my bleeding arm. *The Calm* was wearing off, and I was beginning to notice the pain. And holy crap did it hurt.

"Michael!" Sarah said, pushing her way through the men in my room, holstering her Sig .45. She threw her arms around me and hugged me tightly. "What happened?" she asked. "Your face! You have a cut on your face! I was walking back to the dorm when I heard the shots. Oh my God! Your arm!" She turned to yell at Hunter's men as they picked Lorenzo up off the floor. "Get a medic up here right now! He's injured!" Shouts went out for the doc.

"Val, what the fuck happened up here?" Tailor asked. He lowered his carbine as Hunter's two security guys dragged Lorenzo away.

"That's the guy from Hasa Market," I said, wincing with the pain.

Nervously, Tailor looked around for anyone who wasn't in the know. "Did he come back for his money?"

"He was in here looking for that puzzle box I found in Adar's safe. I jumped him. Son of a bitch is a hell of a fighter. If I hadn't got the drop on him he'd have sliced me open." I said, straining. "Where the hell is Hal? Christ, I'm bleeding like crazy here." I wiped the blood from my cheek, smearing it across my face.

270

"Stop being a pussy," Tailor said. "Focus. You sure he wasn't after the money?"

"He only seemed to care about the box."

Tailor looked thoughtful. "Shit. We need to tell Hunter."

"You're going to tell him about the money?" Hudson asked, concern in his voice.

"No. Especially not this dude's cash," Tailor said. "We found that box and a bunch of money in Adar's safe. We'll just tell Hunter about the box and shut up about the rest."

"Damn." Hudson whistled. "You guys find a lot of money laying around, don't you?"

A moment later, Hal, the medic, came rushing into the room, carrying his jump bag. Tailor gave everyone the eye so there would be no more talk about the money. "Everybody get back," Hal said. "Let me see him. Sit down on the bed, Valentine. Goddamn, you got yourself all cut to shit, didn't you?" He looked me over, illuminating my wounds with a small flashlight. "Yeah, that one on the cheek is going to leave a nasty scar. Not too deep, though. Let me see your arm. Wow, yeah, you're going to need stitches on this." I winced as he poked and prodded the bleeding gash. "Quit being a little girl," Hal chided. "Holy shit, you're lucky. Any deeper and this would've severed your radial artery."

"Just patch me up, Doc. Was anybody hurt in that explosion?"

"I don't think so," Hudson said. "I was outside when the truck blew. Nobody was nearby. Did that guy have something to do with that?"

"I think so. Hal, please hurry. I need to talk to Hunter right away."

"Just hold still," Hal said. "This is going to hurt."

He wasn't kidding. Hal expertly stitched up the long gash on my arm without bothering with anesthetic. He then bandaged my face and stuck cotton balls in my nose to stop the trickle of blood. Lorenzo had elbowed me pretty hard, but my nose wasn't broken.

I turned to Sarah as Hal applied the last of my bandages. "Go get your body armor on and tell Hunter I'll be there in a minute. Tell him that the guy we caught is the same shooter from Hasa Market. They call him Lorenzo. Bring the puzzle box to him, too. We have a major security breach here. Somehow this guy was able to track us back to the fort. If he found us, Al Sabah's forces might have, too."

"Okay," Sarah said. She picked up Adar's puzzle box and turned to leave the room. She paused by the door and looked back at me.

"I'll be right there," I said. "Don't worry." Sarah flashed me a worried smile and was out the door.

It wasn't until after she'd left that I remembered that the key Sarah was wearing on her necklace had been inside that box.

LORENZO

I woke up in terrible pain. "What time is it?" I asked.

"Time for you to start talking," a voice said. The screeching banshee death wail in my right ear had calmed down enough that I could hear, but I had the worst headache ever. Waves of throbbing suffering cascaded through my skull with each heartbeat. Every bit of me hurt.

There was a blinding light aimed at my face. The light moved away, and I blinked in confusion. It had been a flashlight. "All yours, sir," a young man said. "He'll live as long as you want him to."

"Thank you. That will be all, Hal," said the man with an eye patch. He was probably sixty but looked tough for his age. The medic picked up his bag and left us. We were in an old room. It smelled of mildew and decay. The walls were made of rough, crumbling brick, and down the center of the room was a line of rusty iron bars cemented into the floor and ceiling. *A jail?* On the other side of those bars were two other men, both armed and watching. I was sitting on the floor, back to the damp wall. When I tried to move, a chain clanked. My left arm had been handcuffed to a bar.

The old man was sitting on a folding chair, just out of reach. "This was the original brig for Fort Saradia. Appropriate right now, don't you think?" He took his time lighting a fat cigar, finally blowing a pungent cloud of smoke in my direction.

I took stock of the situation. I couldn't have been out long. My vest was gone. My shirt had been torn open, and there was a spreading black and purple blotch over most of my chest and stomach. Something was packed into my ear, and the blood that coated my neck and chest was still slick. I tugged on the cuff. The bar was rusty, but solid.

He got tired of waiting for me to answer. "Why is this important?" he asked, cigar in one hand, Adar's box in the other. "It's an Arabian puzzle. Very old from the looks of it."

"I'm into antiques." It hurt to talk. My face was too swollen. I bet I looked like a mess.

The old man smiled, only there was nothing friendly about it at all. This dude was dangerous. "I don't think you realize the world of shit you've gotten yourself into, boy, or maybe you do. Maybe you know exactly who you're messing with."

I recognized the voice now. I'd heard him on the radio. "So, Big Boss . . . How's Nightcrawler?" I chuckled. "Did I manage to take his arm off? You Dead Six guys get good medical, right?"

Big Boss scowled. That had gotten his attention. "Mr. Valentine will be just fine. You, I'm not so sure about." He didn't seem concerned to drop actual names, which meant he wanted me to know I was dead, no matter what. The only question was how much it was going to hurt first. "I'll ask you, just one time, who you are and who you work for. You will answer me truthfully, or I'm going to make you suffer in ways you can't even imagine."

That's where he was wrong. I had one hell of an imagination. And I just had to keep these people occupied until whatever apocalyptic thing the Fat Man had been talking about happened at midnight. "I'm not telling you shit. I'll only talk to Gordon. I don't have time for his flunkies."

Big Boss nodded. "I see. Either you know what you're talking about, or you're full of shit and I know where that missing radio wound up. Speaking of radios, who were you talking to on yours?" Big Boss pulled my radio out of his shirt pocket. "I tried to be polite, but someone just started calling me names in what I believe was Portuguese. They're not answering now, for some reason."

"They're picky like that."

Big Boss paused to address the two men who had been watching. "Conrad, Walker, come here for a minute. And remove your sidearms. I'm afraid this one's tricky." The two men drew their pistols and placed them on a table, then came through the bars. The gate had probably been missing for years.

One was a taller dude, and he accidentally bumped his head on the only light bulb, sending it swinging wildly back and forth, casting crazy shadows in the old brig. The other was about my size, with sunglasses perched on his head, who looked like he knew his way around the intricacies of hurting people. They grabbed on and smashed me into the wall.

"To warm up, I want you to take our friend here and break every one of his fingers." Big Boss paused as the door opened.

A woman entered. Young, auburn hair tied back, and rather cute, she was totally out of place in this dismal setting. She seemed a little ruffled when she saw the two goons holding me. It was pretty obvious what was about to happen. "Colonel, we've sighted the boat. It'll be at the dock in a few minutes."

Big Boss glanced at his watch. "They're early. Spread the word and start loading. I'm on my way down."

The two thugs were dragging me to my feet. I didn't resist and the handcuff scratched its way up the bar until I was standing. The girl's voice sounded familiar too. It was worth a shot. "Hey, Sarah." She twitched in surprise. *Yep, that was her.* "Sorry about cutting up your boyfriend."

"You bastard," she spat. "I'll—" Then her eyes flashed as she changed her mind. She crossed quickly into the cell, apparently surprising the men holding me. She cupped her hand and smacked me upside the head, right across my bandaged ear.

The pain was nauseating. I grunted, but forced it into a laugh. "What kind of limp-dick carries a gun like that anyway? He's compensating for something." I forced myself to laugh so hard I started wheezing. It actually hurt. And that's when I saw the briefest flash of a metallic trinket hanging inside her shirt. The necklace looked familiar. *No. That's impossible.* But then she was backing away, hands balled into fists, and it was out of sight.

She was *really* pissed off now. She was about to come at me again when the old man spoke up. "That'll be *all*, McAllister," he said gruffly. Sarah gave me one last defiant look before leaving.

Big Boss then turned his attention back to me. "Don't worry, friend. This won't take too long. I'll have you singing like a bird by the time my men get packed. I was interrogating communists when your mommy gave your daddy the clap for the first time." Big Boss strode out, pausing just long enough to drop the box and my radio on a table by the exit.

"Don't hurry on my account," I called after him.

He paused and smiled. "Oh, don't worry. You don't have to wait up for me. Walker, start with the pinky."

Oh hell.

"Yes, sir," said the shorter one cheerfully, obviously excited. The other dude slammed his weight into me, pinning me into the wall. I thrashed, but with my wrist handcuffed, it wasn't like I had a lot of maneuverability with that hand. The one called Conrad punched me in the stomach, which got my attention just long enough for Walker to latch onto my fist. While I struggled, he pried my pinky loose and yanked it back. I screamed as it broke with a sick crack.

VALENTINE

Goddamn it, I thought to myself bitterly. *I knew it was too good to be true.* I cursed myself for staying with Dead Six. We should've used the confusion of Project Heartbreaker being terminated to sneak out and link up with Ling's people. We could've slipped away, and with everything being packed up and shipped out, they'd have had no time to try to find us. It would've been perfect.

Instead, here I was, decked out in full battle rattle with a rifle slung across my chest and a bandage on my arm. The fort was on full lockdown. Everyone healthy enough to hold a weapon was kitted up and told to be on the alert.

Despite Hal's painkillers, I hurt, and my face was bruised and swollen. Worse, the sky had clouded over. Thunder rumbled overhead; it was threatening to rain.

Most of us were standing by on the docks at the north side of the fort. They sat just beyond a huge stone arch in the old wall of Fort Saradia. Colonel Hunter had ordered patrols of the compound as well. Every person that could be spared hurriedly loaded equipment onto the dock. Word was Hunter was going to try to get the boat to come sooner. My own personal gear, including a backpack full of money, was still in my room. I *really* hoped I'd have time to get it before we had to board the boat.

We were prepared for the worst. We'd emptied the armory and broken out all of our heavy weapons. We quickly set up defensive fighting positions covering both the gate and the docks, backed up with machine guns, RPGs, Javelin missile launchers, and everything else we had lying around. If the Zubarans came looking for a fight, they were in for a big surprise.

We couldn't take everything with us. I was shocked at how much weaponry they'd stockpiled in our armory. Most of it had been locally acquired, either captured or given to us by the Zubarans. There was a lot of Chinese and Russian hardware. We'd rigged the supply building, where the armory was, with explosives. As soon as we cleared out, we'd blow the rest of it in place so General Al Sabah's troops couldn't make use of it.

Sarah was with me. Her hair was pulled back into a ponytail. She'd put on her body armor like I asked. It was soft armor, useless against rifle fire. We couldn't find any regular armor that would fit her. She carried a MK 16 5.56mm carbine in her hands and had her Sig .45 on her hip. Sarah had a serious look on her face as she kept watch over the harbor.

God, she's beautiful.

"I've got a boat in sight!" someone shouted. He was looking out over the bay with a pair of night-vision binoculars. "It's a ways out, approaching slowly."

"Is that our ride?" someone else asked. "Did the colonel talk them into showing up early?"

"Sarah, go tell Colonel Hunter we have a boat in sight," I said. Most of our radios were packed away, and our network had been dismantled. We had to communicate the old-fashioned way.

"Okay. I'll be right back." Sarah trotted off, disappearing from sight.

The group was smoking and joking, eager to head for home. Holbrook, the only surviving member of Singer's chalk, was telling everybody that the beers were on him as soon as we got to a non-shitty country. Now I could see the lights of the boat. They were growing quickly.

"Gimme those." Tailor stole the binocs from the guy using them. He scowled. "Val, that boat looks too small. . . ."

There were several quick flashes from the boat. I could see them clearly without night vision. The sound came an instant later. "Get down!" I screamed, pulling Tailor to the ground. The tracers were high, hitting the fort wall behind us, showering us in dust and debris. But then the gunner adjusted fire and walked the bullets into the dock. Chunks of concrete and wood went flying as heavy rounds punched through walls, equipment, and men. Two streams of tracers zipped from the boat as it hosed our position with twin fifty-caliber machine guns.

"Return fire!" Tailor yelled, trying to make himself heard over the chaos. A fire erupted behind us as the boat's armor-piercing/incendiary rounds ignited something flammable. "Take that boat out! Somebody grab a Javelin!" Fillmore and Chetwood ran for the missile launcher.

The boat was still hundreds of yards out. It gunned its engines and sped up, continuously firing on our position. Several men were able to bring their weapons to bear and return fire, but to no effect.

Through the three-and-a-half power magnification of my ACOG scope our attacker looked like a patrol boat of the Zubaran Coast Guard. Leaning around the barricade of sandbags I was using for cover, I squeezed the trigger, popping off shot after shot at the incoming boat. It strafed the dock again, twin tongues of flame tearing into our position with lethal results.

"Where is that goddamned Javelin?" Tailor screamed again, firing his weapon as he did so. I looked around, trying to figure out what happened to our missile crew. They were on the other side of the entrance to the dock, about twenty-five meters from my position. Fillmore and Chetwood were lying behind a pile of sandbags, blood everywhere. Chetwood had been decapitated. Fillmore was missing an arm and screaming his head off. *Christ . . .*

"I got it!" Holbrook shouted. He slung his weapon behind his back and ran into the open just as the incoming patrol boat opened fire again. I watched in horror as a heavy .50-caliber round smacked into him, punching through his body armor like it wasn't there. The bullet exploded out his side in a spray of blood, guts, and bits of shattered ceramic. Holbrook didn't make a noise as he went down.

If we didn't get that missile, we were all dead. "Tailor, I'm going," I said, feeling no fear as *the Calm* pushed all emotions aside. Without hesitation, I sprinted for the other position and jumped over Holbrook's body. I made it across. I dropped to the deck and slid to a stop on my knees. I roughly pushed aside Fillmore and picked up the Javelin launcher. Shouldering the heavy beast, I looked through the sophisticated sight and pointed the weapon toward the Zubaran patrol boat.

The Javelin achieved missile lock. I pressed the firing stud. The missile's expelling charge caused it to belch out of the launcher. A fraction of a second later the rocket motors ignited, sending the missile roaring up into the night sky on a column of smoke. It took the missile a few seconds to arc through the sky. It came screaming down, slamming into the boat from above and detonating. The hull was ripped in half in a flash of light.

My comrades on the dock stood up and cheered, holding their weapons in the air while the sinking boat burned. For my part, I simply dropped the Javelin launcher and exhaled heavily, taking stock. Fillmore was already gone. My pant legs were coated in the blood of my dead teammates. The patrol boat's strafing run had killed several of us, and the screaming told me others were wounded. Thunder rumbled overhead again, and the rain began. Within moments it was pouring.

Seconds later something shrieked overhead and detonated inside the compound. Then there was another, then another. The ground rumbled as mortars struck the armory and the admin building. My heart dropped into my stomach. *Sarah!*

"Val, where are you going?" Tailor shouted as I took off at a run.

"I have to find Sarah!" I said, not looking back.

LORENZO

The big lump of meat, Conrad, let go of me, and I sank to the ground, retching. Walker didn't just snap my finger bones, he broke them slowly, grinding away, joint on joint, until he was sure he'd hit every nerve bundle. He was a fucking *artist*.

"Two down, three to go," Walker said. "And I'm just getting warmed up on this one. This is going to be a long night. You really shouldn't have come here. You're my bitch now."

"No shit," I gasped. I had no weapons. They'd searched me, disarmed me, and I was already hurt and handcuffed to a wall. Options were limited. There was no room for error. I had to kill both of these men. I felt around the wall behind me. *This place is old and crumbling. There has to be something I can use. There.*

"Ready for the next one, Stan?" Walker asked.

Conrad shrugged and started in. "Sure, but I don't get off on this like you do." He grabbed me around the back of the neck and dragged me up the wall, loose brick scraping my back. He slugged me in the stomach again, hammering the tissue that had already been pulverized by a stopped bullet. It hurt so *bad* that I just wanted to curl up into a ball and die, but that's why I did all of those damned sit-ups. I took it. I had to let them think I was helpless, but I still had one hand free, and I clutched the chunk of brick tight.

There was a burst of noise from outside. Walker and Conrad glanced at each other. "Gunfire? Who's shooting?" Walker queried. My hearing was still all buggered up. I had no idea. "Check it out," he snapped. Conrad let go of me. This was my chance. I slid to floor, limp, gagging, as if that last punch had leveled me.

"Okay," Conrad said, jogged toward the exit. I waited until the door closed.

But Walker wasn't stupid. He'd stepped out of arms' reach to wait for his backup. *Chicken shit.*

I crawled to my knees. I had to make this count. "Wait? You hear that?" I gasped, looking toward the door.

Unconsciously, he turned. "Wha—" But was cut off as I hurled the brick as hard as I could. His glasses flew off and he stumbled back, hands clutched to his face, screeching in pain, one eye obliterated. I scrambled for him, but the cuff chain snapped tight, just short, just out of arm's reach. *Shit!*

"Help!" Walker, blinded, was tripping, stumbling, but getting farther away. "Conrad! Help!" he cried.

His aviator shades were at my feet. I snatched them up, ripping them apart, knocking the remaining lens out. I bent the wire spine straight and went to work on the cuffs. Men like me have an instinctive fear of being in handcuffs, so I had practiced this a few hundred times. I could pick a handcuff with a toothpick. "Maybe Big Boss will lend you an eye patch, asshole!"

The door flew open and Conrad ran back in, shouting, "We're under attack! It's the army." Then he collided with his bleeding friend. "What the hell?"

"My *eye*!" Walker screamed. "He put out my eye!"

The cuff clicked loose and I ripped my damaged hand out, leaving a lot of skin behind. I crossed the cell, reaching up and swatting the lone light bulb, shattering it and plunging us all into darkness. They never saw me coming.

I kicked Conrad's ankle out from under him. The bone splintered and he toppled down to my level, where I ridge-handed him brutally in the throat. Conrad choked, gagging, still confused as to how I got all the way over here. I grabbed him by the hair and slammed his face into my knee, knocking half his teeth out. He was down.

Walker was groping about, searching for his gun. They'd left them on the table by the door. He found the table just as I found him. My arm slid around his throat, injured left hand putting pressure on the side of his head as I cranked back, taking us both to the ground. He thrashed, kicked, elbowed me in the side, but once I'd cut the flow of oxygen off to his brain, he was out in ten seconds. The elbow hits got weaker and weaker, then finally stopped. When I was convinced the struggle was over, I rolled his unconscious form off.

Gasping, I struggled to my feet. There were flashes of light coming through the narrow windows. A high-pitched whistle terminated in a explosion against one of the walls. The compound was under attack. I had to get the hell out of here. I ran my good hand over the dark table until I found what I'd come here for. The box went into one pants pocket, radio into the other. I kept Walker's gun.

The two men were groaning, stirring. I could have just put a bullet into both of them, but I might need the ammo. I booted Conrad in the head once more to be safe, then rolled Walker over, stripping him of two spare magazines. Blood flow restored, the man was starting to come to.

Being an asshole, I just couldn't help myself. Squatting down, I grabbed all the fingers on Walker's right hand. "Wake up." Then I cranked them back so brutally hard that they touched his wrist, breaking every one of them so fiercely that the skin of his palm split open. He sat up, screaming, so I smashed him in the face with his own gun.

It was time to go.

VALENTINE

Fort Saradia was in utter chaos as mortars rained down on us. I left the relative safety of the stone archway that led to the docks and ran into the open, desperate to find Sarah. She was probably either in the admin building or the old brig, where they'd taken Lorenzo.

The admin building was easier to get to, and it was where Hunter's office was, so I started there. Hearing the screams of more incoming shells, I huddled by the wall of the closest building and covered my head. Two big military trucks, wearing Zubaran Army markings, were parked by the north wall of the supply building. Those trucks had been sitting in the compound since day one, but we hadn't used them. I hoped they'd protect me from fragmentation.

Five more mortars exploded in the compound. The first one didn't hit anything. The second struck the admin building. The third hit the dormitory building and destroyed several rooms on the top floor. The fourth hit the big gas tank directly west of my position. Hot wind blew across my back as the fuel tank erupted in a huge fireball and burned. I didn't see where the last mortar hit, but it was close. The barrage ended. An assault was coming, and we were undoubtedly outnumbered. Through the torrential downpour, I saw the survivors from the docks running back into the compound, toward my position, as they prepared to make a stand.

I had my own mission, though. Clenching my MK 17, I took off at a run again, rounding the east corner of the supply warehouse. One of the shells had struck the ground right next to the building, making a small crater and collapsing part of the wall. I didn't stop to see if anyone was hurt inside. I jumped over the crater and continued running.

A loud crash echoed across the compound. I stopped and took cover. A French-built Leclerc tank smashed through the front gate, busting the heavy metal doors open. The turret had been turned around to keep from damaging the barrel. As it cleared the gate, it began to swing its gun around, looking for a target.

A few seconds later, a Javelin missile shrieked down onto the tank and slammed into the top of the turret. The missile hit with a loud metallic *BANG*, sounding like someone hitting a metal plate with a sledgehammer. The tank rumbled to a stop just inside the gate, burning. Brilliant flames shot out from under the turret as the ammunition inside cooked off and burned.

The destroyed tank effectively blocked other vehicles from entering the gate, but that didn't stop the onslaught. Armed troops began pouring into the compound, coming around the tank on both sides. They were a mix of Zubaran Army regulars, with their desert-camouflage uniforms and helmets, and irregular militia, who wore black fatigues and masks over their faces.

Holy shit. There's a lot of 'em. I backed up and dove into the mortar crater and used it for cover. I acquired a target through my ACOG scope, a militiaman with an RPG, and popped off a shot. He dropped to the muddy ground. I shifted my carbine to the right and fired three shots at another cluster of soldiers, Zubaran regulars. One went down, but the others took cover behind the tank.

They just kept *coming.* To my left, my teammates had gotten a couple of machine guns set up. They tore into the soldiers as they filed in past the tank, but the enemy was relentless. I fired continuously, pausing only to change magazines. I don't know how many I hit. More than a dozen Dead Six operatives were all firing into the same enemy position, mowing down the Zubaran soldiers, but there were too many of them. Rounds began to strike the dirt around my little crater, and the wall behind me. I suddenly felt very vulnerable. Taking a chance, I came to my feet and ran for the admin building, bullets snapping past me as I went. I hugged the wall, hoping the hostiles wouldn't see me through the rain.

Thunder clapped overhead, barely audible over the roar of the battle as I reached the admin building. My heart sank when I saw the damage. A mortar had struck the roof, partially caving in the second floor. Hunter's office was on the second floor. *Oh God, no . . .*

My *Calm* began to fail. I was nearly in a panic. I busted the ground-level door open and entered the building, heading for the stairs.

"Sarah!" I shouted, hoping she would hear me. It was dark inside. The impact had knocked out the main lights. The emergency lights had kicked on, but they didn't provide much illumination. I switched on my weapon light as I vaulted up the stairs two at a time. "Sarah!"

I made it to the second floor and shined my light down the hallway. The roof had caved in at the far end of the hall where Conrad's office was. A small fire burned within, and the hall was quickly filling with smoke. Hunter's office was closer. The door had been knocked off the hinges, and the ceiling was cracked all the way down the hall, but the roof hadn't caved in yet. The old building's solid construction was the only reason it had been able to withstand two direct mortar hits.

"Sarah!" I shouted, growing desperate.

"Here!" Sarah replied, her voice resonating through the low-pitched roar of the battle outside.

"Sarah, where are you?" I shouted, running into the hall.

"I'm—" She coughed. "I'm in here!"

I followed the sound of her voice to the first room in the hall. The door was open. A smear of blood was on the floor, leading into the dimly lit room. I found Sarah sitting on the floor. She was holding Anita King in her arms. Anita was dead.

"Oh God, are you alright?" I cried, dropping to my knees and throwing my arms around Sarah. She had a few cuts and bruises. Blood trickled from a scrape on her arm.

"She's dead," Sarah said. "She . . . she was in the hall when the shell hit. She got hit by shrapnel or something. She wasn't wearing her vest. I . . . I just stepped in here. I was knocked down. Anita died."

"Sarah!" I shouted, shaking her. "Hey! We can't stay here. I need you to focus, okay? Are you hurt?" She was shell-shocked.

"I don't think so," she responded, still sounding distant. "I just fell down when the shell hit. I think I hit my head on the floor."

"C'mon, we gotta go," I said.

"I can't leave Anita."

"We have to. She's dead. There's nothing you can do for her now. Come on now, *please!*"

Sarah took a deep breath and jerkily nodded her head. She gently lowered

Anita's body to the floor, and I extended my arm. Sarah grabbed it, and I pulled her to her feet.

"Come on, we have to get out of here," I urged. "Are you sure you're okay?"

"I'm fine," she answered, sounding more collected. She brought her slung carbine around and grasped it in her hands. "I'll be okay. Let's go." I nodded and led the way back into the hall, heading for the stairs.

"Wait!" Sarah cried. "The Colonel! He was in his office!" She turned and ran down the hall to Hunter's office without waiting for me. I swore aloud and followed.

Hunter's office door was lying on the floor in the hall. Sarah stepped on it as she crossed into the room. I coughed in the smoky air as I followed. The office was smashed. Part of the ceiling had collapsed and fallen right on Hunter's desk.

"Mike!" Sarah was kneeling on the floor next to the pile of rubble that had come from the ceiling. Colonel Hunter was trapped under the debris. It had all come down right in his lap, smashing his chair to the floor and crushing him.

"Colonel!" I crouched down next to Sarah. "Jesus," I said, surveying the damage. It was bad. Hunter was broken and bleeding. A massive pile of blocks and rebar had landed on his abdomen. Only one of his legs was visible under the rubble.

"Valentine?" Hunter asked weakly, blood tricking from his mouth.

"I'm here, sir," I said, leaning in so I could hear him over the noise of the fighting outside. "We're gonna get you out of here. Hang on."

"Bullshit," Hunter wheezed. "I ain't goin' nowhere. You . . . you get her out of here, you hear me, boy?"

"Yes, sir," I replied solemnly.

Hunter coughed up a small amount of blood. "You know I was supposed to leave last night? All of us were. Not you guys, but the support staff. I said no. I told Gordon I wasn't leaving until all my guys got out. I think maybe that wasn't such a good idea," he said, somehow managing a raspy laugh.

"What happened, Colonel? That boat was a Zubaran gunboat. It strafed the docks, killed a bunch of us." Sarah gasped as I told them that. "What the hell is going on?"

"Gordon Willis sold us out," Hunter said quietly. "He . . . he told the hajjis where we are. Made a deal with somebody. Same thing with that raid on Montalban's yacht. That was his own idea, not a sanctioned hit. Gordon's playing both sides. Son of a bitch sold us out."

My eyes narrowed, and my hands clenched into fists. I was so angry I was shaking. I closed my eyes for a second and tried to remain focused.

"Take this," Hunter said. He pushed a small object into my hand. It was a thumb drive. "Everything on Project Heartbreaker is on here. I've been doing some homework. Everything I found out about Gordon's double-dealing is on here, too."

"What do I do with this, sir?" I asked. The thumb drive had Colonel Hunter's bloody thumbprint on it.

"Give it to the right people," the colonel replied. "Find someone you can trust. Be careful. This is a lot bigger . . ." Hunter's voice trailed off. He coughed up more blood.

"Colonel! Stay with us!" Sarah cried.

"This is bigger than you know," Hunter whispered, his one eye staring at me intently. "There's something else, too, not on the drive. Another project. Like Red, only bigger this time." Hunter trailed off again. His breathing was ragged now. Blood bubbled out of his nose. "Project Blue's ready. You've got to . . ." His words tapered off, too faint to hear.

Hunter was almost gone. "I can't hear you. What?" I asked urgently.

Suddenly he grabbed my armor and pulled me close with surprising intensity. "*Evangeline!*" he hissed. Then his grip relaxed. His eye unfocused. "Find—" He coughed, painful and wet, gasping for air as his body shut down.

Colonel Curtis Hunter died before he could finish that sentence. I quietly swore to myself before gently closing his eye. I pocketed the thumb drive and stood up.

"What was he trying to say?" Sarah asked.

I shook my head. "I hope it's on this drive. I hope it's not for nothing." I stepped across the room and looked out the window. My remaining teammates had fallen back to the supply building behind my position. They were being pushed back to the docks. Enemy troops continued to pour in around the disabled tank, spreading out through the motorpool as they entered the compound. There was literally a heap of dead Zubaran militiamen all around the tank, but more kept coming, stepping over their dead comrades. General Al Sabah was using the local radical militants as cannon fodder.

Sarah huddled close to me. "What are we going to do?" There was fear in her voice.

"I still have the phone Ling gave me." I was scared too. "If we get out of the compound, we can contact her. She said the deal was still on if we needed her help. We can—"

Before I could finish that thought, the entire compound was rocked by a huge explosion. The concussion hit my face through the shattered windows. A section of wall just down from the gate was blasted high into the air. I turned and shoved Sarah to the floor, covering her with my body as pieces of the wall rained on the compound.

I risked another look out the window. Through the new hole in the wall, dozens more soldiers streamed into the compound, a lot more Zubaran regulars, supported by some kind of wheeled armored car. They had to be hitting us with a company-sized element, if not bigger.

Sarah shook her head. She grabbed my hand and held it tightly. "We're . . . we're going to die here, aren't we?"

I stood there helplessly watching as the Zubarans pushed my remaining friends back even farther. The compound was being overrun, and they weren't taking prisoners. I looked down at the floor, then over at Sarah. I nodded slowly as my last hope died.

Sarah closed her eyes for a second while she took a deep breath. "Promise me you'll stay with me until the end," she said, looking into my eyes.

"I promise," I replied. "I won't leave you. No matter what." Tears welled up in Sarah's eyes as she leaned forward and kissed me. I stepped back and steeled myself. "Are you locked and loaded?"

Sarah pulled back the charging handle on her carbine slightly, checking the chamber. "I'm ready."

"Stay behind me. Stay low. Move when I move, stop when I stop. We're going to circle around the backside of the building and link up with our guys on the other side. Let's go," I said, leading the way out of Hunter's office. Zubaran soldiers were running past the admin building, one floor down from where I was. I didn't have much time before they entered the building. It's a strange feeling, knowing you're running off to your own death.

I didn't make it three steps before my phone rang.

Chapter 20: Rain

LORENZO

It had begun to rain, giant, stinging drops falling like some sort of biblical vengeance.

I was pulling myself around the back corner of the brig when a Zubaran armored car came through a breach in the wall. Soldiers in desert camouflage scurried through behind it, firing wildly at anything that moved. Muzzle flashes were coming from everywhere as Dead Six returned fire.

Really. Not. Cool.

Deaf in one ear, every inch of me hurting, and with two broken fingers, I crouched in the shadows and called for help. "Reaper! Come in Reaper! This is Lorenzo. Come in, damn it!" I shouted into the radio.

"Lorenzo! You're alive! Get out of there. The army is attacking!"

No shit. "Status?

Carl responded. *"The road's blocked. I can see five armored cars. There's a company-sized element hitting the compound now, mix of regulars and militia. You've got an unknown number of troops sitting in reserve about a click off the gate."*

"What about the dock?" If I could get out the back way, I could swim for it.

Reaper came back. *"There's a couple patrol boats out there now."*

Something whistled off to the side and exploded against Building One. The army was launching RPGs. I ran a few feet to the side and took cover behind a low wall. Hunkering down, I watched the battle between Dead Six and the army unfold. The Americans were putting up a fight, taking defensive positions around the buildings, but there seemed to be an unending stream of fanatical fighters pouring in. Bullets were flying in every direction, some leaving visible trails, the rain was so thick. A few Dead Six ran past, carrying heavy weapons, but they were too preoccupied to notice me hiding in the mud.

"What's your status?" Carl demanded.

I had broken at least one rib, if not more, and one lung felt like it was full

285

of burning hydrogen instead of air. "Oh, I'm doing just *swell*. But the exit's blocked." Just as I said that, the armored car exploded, lifting and flipping its turret on a pillar of fire and throwing fragments fifty feet into the air. "Damn! Really blocked. I'll think of something."

"*Lorenzo, be careful.*" It was Jill. She sounded terrified.

"Get off the line!" I snapped. There was no time for sentimentality. Off to my right, several grenades exploded around the parked cars, shredding some of the Dead Six personnel. One of the Americans, badly injured, stumbled, confused, in the direction of the enemy, raising his empty hands in surrender and was shot dead on the spot. They weren't taking any prisoners. "Reaper, can you keep L.B. in the air in this weather?"

"*Yeah, chief. It's all-weather capable.*"

"I need you to be my eyes. I'm at the east wall, by the old brig, uh, Building Six."

"*Lots of heat blooms from the explosions. Wait. I see you.*"

I had to get out of here. The army was bottlenecked with that APC blocking the hole in the wall and a tank burning in the main gate. As long as they kept trickling through, Dead Six could hold them, but I didn't want to be out here in the open when either side started getting desperate. Dead Six personnel had moved out of the dorm to hold the gates, so they should be empty. "I'm going to take cover back inside the apartments. Let me know when I've got company." Both sides of this battle would kill me, so it was time to do what I do best in situations like this. *Hide.*

Slipping through the rapidly growing puddles, I had just reached the dorm when I was forced to dodge into a doorway to hide. Some more Dead Six men ran past, guns held high, faces grim. Once they were gone, I ran up the stairs, sprinted down the hall, and ducked back into the Valentine's room. At least it was familiar, and I really didn't want to participate in the war unfolding outside.

"Reaper, status?"

"*Dead Six is fighting like crazy, but more Zubarans are inside. You better think of something fast, boss, because they're coming in force now.*"

Plan. I needed a plan. The rain drumming the roof was louder than the gunfire. My eye landed on the bug-out bag filled with *my* money.

VALENTINE

I looked at my cell phone like I'd never seen one before as it beeped and buzzed in my hand. Tailor was calling.

"Hello?" I said awkwardly, pressing the talk button.

"Where the *fuck* are you?" Tailor screamed in my ear.

"I'm in the admin building," I hissed, trying not to make too much noise. "I found Sarah. Hunter, too. Hunter's dead."

Tailor swore. "You have to get back here, right now!"

"Get back *where?*" I asked, exasperated.

"The north side of the supply building. We've . . . shit, choppers inbound! I'll call you back!" The line went dead.

"What is it?" Sarah asked. As if to answer her question, a Zubaran Army Mi-17 helicopter came in low over the compound. It slowed and came to a hover between the admin building and the dormitory. It was so close I could see up into the open back door. I pushed Sarah to the floor and lay on top of her, hoping the troops in the back of the helicopter couldn't see down into the window.

"Stay down," I told Sarah over the roar of the chopper's rotor. I poked the top of my head over the bottom of the shattered window frame so I could see. The door gunner on the left side was constantly firing. The chopper's hull was pinged and dinged by bullets as my teammates returned fire.

Ropes dropped from the chopper's open back door. Zubaran Special Forces soldiers, clad in their distinctive blue camouflage fatigues, began to fast-rope to the ground. They were inserting them right in the middle of the compound.

Four soldiers had reached the ground when an RPG rocket punched into the chopper's front-left quarter, right behind the cockpit, and exploded. The chopper spun wildly once, flinging a soldier out the back door, before going nose down and slamming into the dirt. Pieces of the chopper's rotor shot across the compound as it landed right on top of the troops it had just inserted.

My phone buzzed again, and I ducked back down. "Tailor!" I said, pushing it to my ear.

"Listen," Tailor said. "You have to get to the north side of the supply building. We wired up the west wall with explosives. As soon as it blows, we're going to make a break for it. We've got those two trucks, the Army ones. We can't wait. Another APC just came in through the hole they breached. The chopper wreck will hold up the armor for a minute, but they'll get around it." The Zubaran vehicles had to go up the narrow corridor between the admin and supply buildings and the dormitory. The west side of the compound was blocked by the remains of an old stone wall that was part of the original British fort.

"Okay, we're moving," I said.

"Val, we can't wait," Tailor repeated. "If you're not here in a couple minutes . . ."

"Leave without me. If I'm not there in a minute, it means I'm dead. Good luck, bro."

"Good luck."

Stashing the phone, I quickly outlined the plan to Sarah.

"That's crazy!"

I agreed. "But it's the only chance we've got. Come on, we have to go. It's not far." We had one shot, and we were going to take it. I checked out the window. The Zubarans were still advancing. It was too risky to go back the way I'd come in. Cautiously, I led the way as we entered the stairwell, hoping we could make it to the first floor unnoticed. The admin building only had one set of stairs, and they landed on the first floor right by the east-side door.

We were on the landing between the first and second floors. I held my hand up, signaling Sarah to stop, and peered around the corner. The ground-floor landing appeared to be clear but was illuminated from the outside. Problem was, a squad of Zubaran soldiers had hunkered down by that door to shoot at my comrades.

The door was still open to the outside. There was no way we'd get by unnoticed. *Shit.*

"Hang on," I whispered to Sarah. "Cover your ears." I pulled a grenade from my vest and grasped it tightly in my hand. I peeked around the corner again and, sure enough, saw movement and shadows. The enemy troops were still there. I pulled the pin, leaned around the corner, and tossed the grenade down the stairs.

BOOM! The concussion was deafening as the grenade detonated. We had no time to waste. I slapped Sarah on the shoulder and quickly made my way down the stairs.

On the ground-floor landing was a dead solider. As I came down the stairs, another man entered the building, G3 rifle held at the hip. I snapped off a shot at point-blank range, aiming high so my shot would clear his body armor. The bullet tore through the soldier's throat. Before he hit the floor, I was on the landing. Just outside the door was another wounded soldier. Two of his comrades were leaning over him, tending to his wounds. One was looking up at me as I appeared in the doorway. I shot him in the face, shifted over, and shot the other before he could react. I left the unconscious Zubaran alone and rounded the corner, heading deeper into the admin building.

We entered the operations center. It had been gutted, with all of the valuable equipment removed or destroyed. Crossing the ops center, we cleared its back door and entered the short hallway that lead to the north door. Sarah watched our backs. With the noise of the battle going on outside, I couldn't hear very well. For all I knew another squad of Zubarans was parked just outside. I decided to crack the door as quietly as I could and take a peek.

The door was stuck. I swore aloud.

"Mike, they're coming!" Sarah said. She had the door to the ops center cracked and was watching the way we'd come in. Before I could say anything she stuck the muzzle of her carbine through the door and fired off a long burst. "I got one!" she shouted.

"Get down!" I screamed as bullets punched through the metal doors and zipped down the hall. Sarah ducked to the floor, stuck her carbine through the door again, and fired off the rest of her magazine on full auto.

She looked over at me. "What are you waiting for?"

"Reload, reload!" I shouted. "The door is stuck! I can't get it open!"

"Kick it or something!" Sarah yelled, fumbling as she tried to insert another magazine into her weapon. "I'll hold 'em off!"

"Short, controlled bursts!" I shouted, then turned back to the door. I kicked it as hard as I could. It budged a little. More shots punched through the door and came down the hallway. One buzzed right past my ear. "Fuck this," I said to no one in particular. I backed up, stuck my right shoulder out, and charged at the door, yelling like a madman as I went barreling down the hallway. I hit the door, and it popped wide open. I flew out into the rain, tripped, and landed face-first in the mud, right on top of my weapon.

I grunted and pushed myself up. A Zubaran militiaman stood behind me, to my left. He was standing against the wall of the admin building, rain drizzling off of the mask he wore. He was pounding on his M16 in a vain attempt to clear a jam. He looked up at me, eyes wide. It was too late for him. I rolled to my right and yanked my revolver out of its holster. Extending my arm, I snapped off a shot. The .44 roared in the narrow alley. Blood splattered on the wall behind the militiaman and he crumpled to the mud in a wet heap.

I reholstered my gun and pushed myself off the ground as Sarah came running out the door. "Mike, they're coming!" she warned, pressing herself up against the wall. "Are you okay?"

"Good to go!" Swinging my rifle around, I leaned around the door frame and popped off four or five shots down the hallway, scattering the Zubaran troops advancing through the ops center. The door at the end of the hall was open. My middle finger moved to the trigger of my under-slung grenade launcher and squeezed. The weapon bucked under my arm, launching a 40mm high-explosive round with a loud *POOT!* Before I could finish ducking out of the way, the round exploded in the ops center, right in the middle of the cluster of enemy soldiers.

"Watch the door, watch the door!" She shouldered her weapon and covered the hallway as she crossed. It was clear. "Let's go!" I grabbed her by the arm and pulled her close to me. Sarah covered to the east while I risked a look round the west corner.

"Shit!" I said, pulling back just in time. Several rounds snapped past me. Maybe a dozen Zubaran regulars were creeping up the side of the admin building. "We can't go this way."

"Over here!" Sarah said, pointing to the chopper wreck with her carbine. I removed my last hand grenade from my vest and lobbed it around the corner, up the west side of the building. Sarah and I bolted for the chopper. The grenade detonated behind us a few seconds later.

We dashed into the open, running past dazed, wounded, and surprised Zubaran troops around the wreck of the Mi-17. We turned north and ran alongside the supply building. It wasn't that far. I could feel my heart pounding in my ears as I sprinted with sixty pounds of gear on. Thunder crashed again. The rain was pouring harder than ever. Tracers flashed by, but we kept running. There were bullets buzzing from every direction. Rounds splattered into the muddy ground ahead, barely missing Sarah's legs. *Smack!* My leg came out from under me. I stumbled and fell into the mud. It burned. Blood leaked from a gash in my calf. I grunted in pain.

"Mike!" Sarah cried, looking back. She stopped running and turned around.

"No, Sarah, don't stop!" I screamed. "Keep going!"

But she didn't listen. She started toward me. A hole was torn in her vest as a bullet punched right through it. A second bullet hit her a little lower, in the stomach. A third went into her side. Sarah's face went blank. She collapsed to the muddy ground.

"*Sarah!*" I screamed. My voice sounded like it was coming from far away. I couldn't feel my wounded leg anymore. I pushed myself up off the ground. Bullets zipped past me as I limped to her. My left leg buckled. Every time I put weight on it, I began to fall. The wind was knocked out of me as a bullet struck me in the back, cratering on the ceramic plate in my vest. It felt like I'd been hit with a sledgehammer. I fell again.

I crawled through the mud, bleeding, dragging my weapon on its sling. On my hands and knees, I reached Sarah and lifted her head up. She was completely limp, nothing but dead weight. Her pupils were dilated. Her beautiful face was smeared with mud. I held her body close to me as blood poured from her vest. I couldn't breathe. I couldn't move. The rain poured down relentlessly. Sounds began to fade out. Everything sounded muffled, like I was underwater, except for my own ragged breathing and the pounding of my heart.

I was being shot at. I ignored it. The strange key I'd given Sarah was hanging around her neck, drenched in blood. I grasped it in my hand. There was a concussion. Then everything went black.

My eyes opened. I don't know how long I was out. I was lying on my back, staring up into the rain. Sarah's key was still in my hand. My ears were ringing, and I could barely feel anything. I couldn't see out of my right eye. Warm blood, my blood, was pouring down my face.

I saw Sarah out of the corner of my eye. She was just a few feet away, but out of my reach. I couldn't sit up. I was bleeding badly. I was about to die. Holding my last breath, I stretched my hand out and reached for her.

Then she was out of reach altogether. My last conscious thought was the realization that I was being dragged away.

LORENZO

"Squad of soldiers is heading right for your building. Eight of them."

Carl's voice now. He had a laptop in the van and could watch the videos, too. "The dorm's a good position for them to take. Gives them cover and elevation against Dead Six. They'll use the windows on the west-facing rooms." Carl knew, because that's exactly what he would have done in this situation, and he had a lot of experience leading infantry in combat. Unfortunately, that was the building I'd picked to hide in.

I grabbed the bag of money. I'd slip out the north stairs. I'd just reached them when a sudden rhythmic beating rocked across the compound. "What's that?" I shouted.

"*Helicopter incoming!*" Reaper answered. "*Where'd that come from?*"

The stairs were exposed to the open air. Suddenly a chopper appeared through the rain, slowing to a hover thirty feet off the ground, rotating as the door gunners blasted the living hell out of Building One with belt-fed machine guns. Ropes spilled from the open doors, and blue-camouflaged Zubaran Special Forces started fast-roping down. These guys were everywhere.

Then there was a terrible bang, like a clap of thunder. The side of the helicopter seemed to collapse into itself, belching smoke and launching one of the soldiers out the open rear door. The chopper fell from the sky. The rotors hit, hammering the mud into a circular plume before fragmenting into thousands of lethal bits. Fire, blood, oil, and flesh sprayed in every direction. I ducked as a chunk of the broken rotor screamed past and hit the stairwell just over my head.

Looks like I'm not going that way. I ran back inside the dorms. I needed a way out. The weight of the money gave me an idea.

"*Soldiers are in your building,*" Carl insisted. "*Whatever you're gonna do, do it quick!*"

"Roger that." I picked a west-facing room, whose door was unlocked, and hurried inside. It was a mirror image of Valentine's room. I dumped all the cash on the bed and spread it around, trying to make the money look as tempting as possible. That was one expensive distraction. Walker's gun was still in hand, a .45 Sig 220. I pulled the slide back slightly. There was already a round chambered.

There was a crash as another dorm door was kicked in, followed by automatic weapons fire and a scream. I entered the small bathroom, shoved the pistol in the back of my waistband, and stood on the toilet. I placed my hands on the opposite wall and slowly levered myself into position, "walking" with my hands until I was above the door frame. Every bit of pressure against my left hand caused unbelievable agony. Palms pushing out and boots pushing back against the opposite wall, holding myself there by muscle tension alone, I was now out of view of anybody looking through the bathroom door.

I knew how third-world armies cleared rooms and you did not want to be at ground level.

Drops of blood fell from my lacerated face and hit the floor. My arms began to vibrate from the strain of holding myself there. My swollen, broken fingers throbbed. More gunfire ripped through the dorm. They were spraying down each room as they kicked in the doors. *Hurry up.*

There were shouts in the hall, someone barking orders, and then they were here. The soldiers fired, bullets shredding through furniture. Dust erupted below as projectiles shot through the bathroom walls. I held my breath as a rifle barrel appeared through the doorway under me and shot the shower square into porcelain shards. The muzzle blast pounded upward. Flinching, I slipped a bit, biting my lip and praying for gravity to fail. I held on. The rifle disappeared.

Persian. "Look at all this money!"

"Praise be! It's a fortune, Mohammed."

Arabic. "What's all this? You two, keep moving."

"But, sir!"

"Move, dog. That is an order. And close the door."

The stomping of boots. *Wait for it.* Gunfire in the next room. Give him a second. I drew the Sig in my blood-soaked right hand and cocked the hammer, only one handed on the wall now, injured and too weak to hold me, slipping. The others were still shooting.

Go.

I dropped, landing feet first in a crouch. One soldier, an officer in the desert camo of a Zubaran regular, was standing at the bed. He looked up, both hands filled with rubber-banded stacks of currency, surprise registering on his face just as the front sight covered it. Masked by the cracks of rifles in the next room, I fired.

The bullet hit him in the sinus. He went down with a spray of blood and snot painting the wall. I de-cocked the Sig and shoved it back in my waistband as I moved. This was my ticket out. I pulled off the ragged remains of my shirt as the gunfire continued and more explosions ripped through the compound.

The officer was dead, eyeball dangling on a bloody cord from the shattered orbital socket. That's what he got for being greedy. He had a captain's insignia on his collar. I unbuttoned the bloody uniform jacket, tore it from the twitching corpse and put it on. He was much shorter than me, and my wrists dangled naked from the sleeves. There was more stomping of combat boots outside the door now. This building was clear. I didn't have much time. I tugged on the officer's blue beret.

One problem, he didn't look anything like me at all. *Shit.* It was dark, but I couldn't bank on that. I needed a distraction. They couldn't see my face.

"Sir?" someone shouted through the door in Arabic. "The colonel says we need to fire from these windows at the Americans." They started banging.

I saw the dangling eyeball and had an idea.

Falling into the hallway, I pressed the blood-soaked pillowcase against my face. "Aaaiiiii!" I screamed, my voice unnaturally high pitched, as I had no idea what this officer sounded like. "Booby trap! Booby trap!"

"Captain!" one of the soldiers shouted. "Are you all right?"

"My eye! My eye!" I held out my hand with the officer's eyeball in it and showed it to him. "Aaaaiiii!"

"Merciful Allah!" the soldier screamed, recoiling. "Get him out of here! Medic!"

Hands grabbed me by the arm and pulled me along, I kept my head down and weaved, crying and sobbing. Then we were outside, the rain pelting us mercilessly. The black night was lit by hellish fires, and smoke obscured everything. Good for me, as I was only partially in the enemy's uniform. The Zubarans were in the middle of a coup, most of these guys were Sabah's irregulars, so hopefully there were a lot of new faces. We were heading for the breach in the wall.

I looked back over my shoulder as I was pushed past the burning APC and into the rift. A couple Dead Six were leapfrogging their way toward the gate, firing at this position, their only hope for escape. Desperate and stupid, they were cut down one by one. The soldiers passed me off to other waiting hands outside the wall and returned to the fight. I discreetly tossed the eyeball in a puddle.

"Hang on, Captain. I've got you," someone shouted. I couldn't see him, as I was still covering my face with the pillow. Strong hands shoved me down. There was a lot of screaming and crying around me. The army had taken an absurd number of casualties. "I'll be right back," the medic said. All he saw on me was a head injury and it wasn't squirting. He had more important things to worry about right now. Lifting the bloody rag, I saw the medic kneeling next to me, up to his wrists in another soldier's pelvis, trying to clamp off a severed femoral artery. He was shouting for assistance.

Through the jagged breach in the old wall, I could see Dead Six, still fighting. There were fewer of them, and they were taking fire from multiple directions now. Most of the buildings were on fire, the rain pummeling giant clouds of steam into the air. Some Dead Six were fighting their way past the helicopter crash, using whatever cover was available. There was the kid, Valentine, and he was making a mad dash away from a bunch of pursuing soldiers. The girl, Sarah, was right behind him, as they headed for the back wall.

Seeing Sarah reminded me of what I'd noticed briefly in the brig, but that was impossible. That couldn't have been the key. I'd gone through hell for this thing. I pulled Adar's box out of my pocket and tried to work the puzzle, but it had been *broken*. The pieces had just been stuck back together. The box slid open, revealing . . . *absolutely nothing*.

Well, fuck me. I jerked my head up. Sarah was forty yards away, running for her life. Valentine's leg was shot out from under him. Sarah turned, screaming, and went back for him. Then several bullets struck, and Sarah fell in a fog of blood.

I stood. I had to get that key. The medic was screaming at me to get down.

There was the kid. He got up, fell, got up again, got shot in the back, went down, but starting crawling to his girlfriend. He reached her, shell-shocked, looking for something that wasn't there, oblivious to the inevitability of his death and the carnage around him. Several grenades exploded between us, temporarily hiding him from view. The gunpowder cloud was gradually crushed by the rain, revealing Valentine on his back.

"*Cover me!*" I bellowed in Arabic. Back through the breach, I sprinted through the rain, bullets screaming past in both directions as the last of Dead Six retreated, water geysering up as the newly formed puddles were struck. I slid in the mud, sprawling down next to Sarah.

Sarah was dead, eyes open, crimson stream trickling from her mouth, white shirt soaked by rain and blood. She was wearing a few necklaces, and right in the middle, riding on a fragile chain was the *key*. Grabbing the chains and ripping them off, I held it up to the light of the fires, other trinkets dangling below. Unlike its last holder, the key was undamaged.

I glanced at Valentine. He was badly injured, blood pouring from his head, staring, incoherent, smoking shrapnel embedded all over his armor. He'd be gone soon. I shoved Sarah's jewelry into my pocket. The main fight was heading past me. There was a roar as Dead Six breached the west wall. Soldiers were swarming after them. I turned to leave.

Valentine stirred. He was dying, but he only seemed to care about the dead girl. He reached one blood soaked hand plaintively for her. It was the arm that I had slashed, red stain soaking through the bandage.

He was reaching for Sarah, but it felt like he was asking for *my* help. It was crazy. He was too out of it to know I was there.

Compassion. Criminals aren't supposed to have any.

Screw him. But still, I hesitated. *He deserves to die. But not today. Not like this.* "Damn it." I didn't know why, but I grabbed the drag handle on the back of his web gear and jerked. Agony tore through my injured torso. I pulled him through the mud, back toward the hole.

It took the last of my strength to drag his unconscious weight through the breach. The Army had seen me run out, and not realizing who I was, welcomed me back. Dozens of Zubaran Army regulars were leaping from the backs of trucks, running into the compound to mop up the slaughter. I was so covered in blood, filth, and mud that I was utterly unrecognizable at that point.

Somebody saw the insignia on my collar. "Captain!" a soldier shouted. "What are you doing?"

"We need this one alive. Get him in the truck," I ordered.

The American kid was unconscious on the seat beside me. A medic had done a competent job stopping his bleeding before we had departed, supposedly for the hospital. I had waited until we were out of sight of the compound and past several other APCs set up as a roadblock before I clubbed the driver and tossed him onto the road. I was kind of making this up as I went along.

"Reaper, I'm back."

"*Where are you?*"

"I'm driving a Zubaran Army pickup south on the main road. What's left of Dead Six?"

"*Okay, I'm pulling back for a better view.*" Reaper's voice was intense in my good ear. "*The last of them blew a hole in the west wall of the compound and moved south through the shanty town past the roadblocks. Looks like they're in two army trucks. No sign of pursuit.*"

They had to be going to a safe house. "Track them," I ordered.

"*They're heading south on Balad.*" He continued to give me directions as I drove like a madman, keeping the hammer down and blowing through roundabouts like they weren't there. The windshield wipers couldn't match the intensity of the deluge, and I could barely see. Headlights flashed behind me. Carl and Jill had caught up.

Valentine moaned. He didn't look good, pale and shaking from blood loss, and I wondered if my act of kindness/stupidity would have been for nothing. Reaper informed me as the Dead Six trucks pulled into the back of a slaughterhouse a mile south of here.

"*Lorenzo, what are you doing?*" Carl asked. "*Do they have the key or something?*"

This was idiotic. *I am an idiot. Why am I doing this?*

I didn't know, but it was too late now.

"No, Carl. I've got it. Just hang on." I looked down at Valentine. "You owe me," I whispered, even though he couldn't hear. "You owe me big."

I arrived a moment later. The garage door of the slaughterhouse was still closing, light leaking out from beneath. I laid on the horn, and after a moment the door stopped and then reversed its motion. Leaving the kid behind, I bailed out of the cab, and hobbled toward the headlights of Carl's van. Armed Americans came out of the slaughterhouse and approached the still-running Army truck.

I slid into the passenger seat of the van, and it was moving before the door closed.

No amount of rain could wash Zubara clean tonight.

Chapter 21: Nefarious Master Plan

LORENZO
May 12, 2008

The light streaming through the window was blindingly bright. Cringing as the bandages around my chest tightened, I raised one hand to block the sun from stabbing through my eye sockets.

"So, you're awake." Jill Del Toro smiled as she opened the curtains. "How do you feel?"

That was a stupid question. "Ever take a contact shot to the chest with a .44 Mag?" I asked rhetorically. My voice sounded funny. Sadly, I already knew that as bad as my ear was ringing, I had done some serious damage. When that ring went away, I'd have lost a range of hearing forever.

"Uh . . . nope. Can't say that I have."

"What time is it? How long have I been out?" After getting patched and stitched from the Dead Six gig, I had gone right into a fuzzy, painkiller-induced sleep.

"It's five in the afternoon. Don't feel bad. You looked like hell."

I studied my left hand. Carl had taped all the fingers together. He was a decent doctor. He had certainly gotten enough practice on me over the years. "Well, I got pistol whipped with a ten-thousand-dollar Korth. Funny, it felt the same as getting pistol whipped with a Ruger. Who would have thought?" I looked under the sheets. I wasn't wearing any pants. "Please tell me Carl's got the key? Really intricate antique thing?" Jill nodded. "Oh, thank you."

I'd done it. After all that, we'd gotten the key.

The gloating almost made up for the physical suffering. Good thing painkillers tipped the scale in gloating's favor. "Has there been any backlash from our little escapade?"

"It's all over the news. The police are saying it was a terrorist group and that they've been eliminated. The emir was murdered last night. General Al Sabah is getting all the credit for tracking the assassins back to Fort Saradia and eliminating them."

I nodded. So, just like that, the bad guys had won.

She slowly sat on the edge of the bed, her manner serious, her voice somber. "I watched the video from Little Bird. I saw them die. I saw them all die."

"Those kinds of things happen in this world."

"Dead Six ruined my life. They murdered my friends. I didn't think I would mind seeing them all killed, but that . . . I just don't know." She trailed off. "That just seemed so *wrong*."

I could tell she was really upset, just trying not to let it show. "Well, it wasn't really the trigger pullers' fault. They were probably kept in the dark and just given orders. It was that one guy from the embassy that wanted you dead."

"Gordon," she sighed.

"I don't think he was there," I said. "Sorry."

"Now him, when he gets his, I want a front-row seat. That last girl, though, when she got shot, and he tried to protect her? That was the girl from the radio, wasn't it?"

I nodded. "His name is Valentine. Her name is . . . was . . . Sarah."

Jill bit her lip. "That was the saddest thing I think I've ever seen. But I have to know. Why did you go back for him?"

I'd gone back for the key, but I'd taken him with me, and I didn't even know why. The bedroom door opened. "Because Lorenzo's an idiot," Carl said as he entered the room with a sandwich on a plate.

"Hey, you brought me some dinner. Thanks."

"Get your own," he responded as he took a bite. "Why the hell did you save him anyway? That just complicated everything. Lucky you didn't get shot. You just can't stick to a plan, can you? Why do you keep screwing up simple things?"

Jill gave him a look that would have killed most men with a soul. "I thought it was brave, and if it wasn't for Lorenzo *screwing up* I'd be dead."

Carl ignored her and chewed his sandwich. "Last time I checked, we're not the good guys."

I shrugged, not really knowing the answer myself. "Must have been the blood loss. I was kind of out of it. I wasn't thinking clearly." That seemed to placate Carl, though Jill's expression indicated she knew I was lying. "Well, at least we got the key, which means Phase Three is a go." That reminded me, I had better call the Fat Man before he got jittery and started eating my family members.

"Can I know what that is now?" Jill asked. We both looked at her, but neither responded. "This *Phase Three*. I think I've proven my worth around here. You got your stupid box, so what's the deal? I can't believe what you went through to get it, either. Not that it hasn't been fun, but I would like to get back to someplace without terrorists and mercenaries and crazy people."

I had been giving this some thought, and now was as good a time as any.

"Okay, but do me a favor first. There's a big freezer in the garage. Could you get me an ice pack out of there first? My face really hurts."

"Okay, sure," Jill said as she left.

Carl raised a single bushy eyebrow as I rolled out of bed and winced as my feet hit the floor. "Are you crazy?" he asked.

"Well, I'm thinking about offering her a real job. We need to see if she's up for it," I explained as I walked gingerly to the mirror. My equilibrium was off, and it hurt to inhale. "I think she's tough enough. Dude, just trust me."

"Okay. Whatever. But I'm getting worried. Lately you've not been yourself. This job's affecting your brain. We're not in the helping business. Survival first. Everything else, second. You can do good deeds on your own time. I'm here to keep Big Eddie from skinning me alive. Other than that, I don't give a shit."

I examined my battered face in the mirror. I had really taken a beating. Nobody would ever accuse me of being pretty, but once the swelling went down, I would probably be back to my forgettable average self, just how I liked it. "Have I ever been wrong, Carl?"

"Constantly," he replied. There was a frightened scream from the garage. "See."

So Jill had found the freezer. "All part of my nefarious master plan. Come on."

I ran into her on her way out of the garage. Jill nearly took me down as we collided, causing me to wince in pain. "Somebody want to tell me why there's a dead guy in the fridge?" she shrieked.

She was actually taking it pretty well.

"Why is there a dead body in the freezer?" Jill shouted. "That scared me!"

Taking it well . . . relatively speaking.

"Hey, it worked for Walt Disney." I opened the freezer door wider. Carl and Reaper were leaning on the van, enjoying the show. "Jill, allow me to introduce you to Ali bin Ahmed Al Falah, terrorist financier, evil genius, slave trader, gun runner, and huge Streisand fan. Seriously. I can't make this stuff up." Falah's body had been crammed into the freezer. Skin gray, beard flecked with ice, his frozen eyeballs were staring at us.

"His pictures are all over the living room," she asked suspiciously. "What kind of sick game is this?"

"Mr. Falah here was a *very* bad man. I've got pictures of him hanging with Osama. Phase One of this job consisted of me following him, watching him, learning his habits, how he talked, how he sounded. I took on the persona of a man named Khalid. I actually bought Falah's social club so I could get into his circle of friends."

"Why?"

"Because I need to be able to impersonate him so well that people who've known him for years wouldn't be able to tell. Freeze pop has a standing appointment for a party that I need to crash. Plus, we needed his cash. This James Bond crap is expensive."

"I do like my toys," Reaper explained. "It is hard to hack half of the Zubaran government with sucky equipment."

"Did you really need those big speakers, though?" Carl asked him.

"Helps me get in the mood."

"Anyway, I arranged a meeting between Falah and some imaginary Russian arms dealers to take place at my club. The plan was to get him inside, make him disappear, and I replace him. Nice and simple."

The idea didn't seem to shock her. "And that got screwed up when Dead Six assassinated him?"

"Exactly. When they put a bullet in his heart, we had to improvise. Luckily, all of his guards got killed, too, so though there were witnesses to the shooting, none of them were real chummy with Al Falah." I gestured at the dead fat body wrapped in plastic. "I had planned on making him go away, nice and quiet. The ground work was already laid—now it was just messier. I made some calls as if I was him, telling his associates that I had faked my own death to go into hiding." I left off the fact that I had even sent hand-forged letters to his children and wives. That seemed a bit grim. "Reaper had already taken command of all of his e-mail addresses—"

"I'm like the grand pimp mack daddy of identity theft," Reaper said proudly.

"So as far as the terrorist world knows, Al Falah is alive and well and living incognito, hiding from the Americans. Since he was in such mortal danger, he asked for his dear old friend, Adar Al-Saud, to come and assist him. Adar's a psychopath, but he's one very special psychopath."

On cue, Carl reached into his shirt and pulled out the key. It was still riding on Sarah's chain. It spun, reflecting the light. "Adar's daddy was an important man. Not many folks get access to the place we're going. They sure don't make them like this anymore."

Reaper took the key from him. He twisted the base slightly, causing dozens of perfectly carved, delicate pins to extend in various directions. It was remarkably complex. "They *never* made them like this. I'm telling you guys, man didn't have the mechanical ability to design something like this a thousand years ago. This would be tough to do with modern CNC machining." Carl quickly took the key back before Reaper could suggest something about space aliens.

"So, you need to pretend to be Al Falah for Phase Three? Do you really need to keep him in the freezer, though?" She looked ill. "That's just gross."

I nodded. "All part of the plan. Mr. Falah here still has one last job to do." I patted him fondly on his frozen shoulder. "He's going to throw the hounds off the scent long enough for us to get away."

"Okay, I get it. I get it . . . That's a lot of effort to steal . . . what?" Jill asked. "What could possibly be so important? Zillions of dollars? Somebody's Fabergé egg collection? The Holy Grail?"

My crew traded glances. This part was hard to explain. "We don't actually know *what* it is, just *where* it is," I said slowly.

"Look, if you feel the need to keep me in the dark still, that's fine, but don't treat me like I'm stupid."

"No, really." I raised my hands in surrender. "They said that it would be the only thing there, it's portable, and that we couldn't miss it. They drew a rough sketch of it, but I don't have any idea what it's supposed to be." I held my open hands about two inches apart. "All I know is that Eddie wants it very badly."

"I can't even find it on the *Internet*," Reaper exclaimed, because, you know, that's the source of all knowledge in the universe.

Jill was incredulous. "All this . . . and you don't even know what you're stealing? You guys are nuts."

"No, Eddie's nuts. We're just too good at what we do."

"Man, close the fridge. That's freaking me out," Carl said.

After briefing Jill on the highlights of the utterly insane and possibly suicidal plan, we took a little drive in the van the next morning. I did not tell her where we were going and once again made her wear the blindfold so that she would not be able to lead anyone back to our hideout. She was quiet as we drove through the streets of Zubara, probably thinking about what I had told her. I didn't speak either, mostly because my face still really hurt. Carl was a decent medic, but having a mercenary smash your nose back into place and pull a broken tooth with a pair of pliers didn't exactly qualify as quality medical care.

The streets were relatively quiet. Supporters of the emir had seen which way the wind was blowing. The ones that had enough money to cause trouble were on their way to Europe or Saudi Arabia. General Al Sabah owned Zubara now, and he was an astute enough man to not rock the boat more than he needed to.

Once I was sure that we had taken enough turns, I told Jill she could take her blindfold off. She rubbed her eyes as she adjusted to the light. The ocean was a brilliant blue out her window.

"So, where are we going?"

I didn't answer. "Now that you know about the job, and you know how dangerous it's going to be, I'm giving you an option." She waited, watching seagulls spiral over the passing beach. "This next part is going to get complicated and I don't normally recruit interns from the Department of Agriculture. This is a job for professionals, and I'm going to need a professional, not an amateur."

"I never claimed to be anything I'm not."

"True." I parked the van at the end of a long wooden pier. There was a fifty-foot boat moored at the end. "Look, I promised that if you helped us, I would get you out of the country safely. And you've held up your part of the bargain. It was like you were part of the crew over the last few weeks. So now it's time for me to hold up mine."

She looked at the boat and then back at me. "I see . . . I thought you were going to ask me to keep help you with Phase Three."

"Yes, I am. But if you want out, now's your chance. That boat is headed for Bahrain. I know the captain. He's a decent man, and he'll take you to another friend of mine. From there, you'll board a plane and take a circuitous route back to the US. Tickets and instructions are in the bag."

"I can't go back to the States. Gordon's people will kill me."

I patted a leather bag on the seat beside me. "There are some new papers in here. Forged passports, driver's licenses, social security numbers, birth certificates, everything you need, all clean, courtesy of Reaper, on the house. His work is as good as you'll ever find."

"He's really sweet," Jill said simply. "Squirrelly, but sweet."

"I've left contact information for an old acquaintance of mine. I've already spoken to him. He's agreed to help you get a new life set up. He's done this kind of thing before, and he owes me a favor." He hadn't been the first person I'd thought of, but as I'd gone down my list of other contacts in the States, most of them were either dead, in prison, or way too untrustworthy to send Jill to. Even though our last parting hadn't been friendly, at least the old guy was honorable, so Jill would be in good hands.

"You will never be able to go back to where you're from. You can never let your picture show up in the newspaper. Don't end up on TV. And never get in trouble with the law. You get fingerprinted, and Gordon's people will find you and kill you. You will never able to let anyone know that you're alive. You can never contact any family or friends."

Jill sighed. "I told you, Lorenzo. My family is all dead. . . . Maybe that's for the best. Look at the mess it's gotten you guys into."

That was a bleak way to look at it, but probably true. "You'll have to start over. I can tell you right now that it'll be extremely hard." Pushing the bag over, I continued. "If you choose to go home, you can't be Jill Del Toro ever again."

She opened the bag and pulled out some passports. "Peaches LaRue? Delilah B. Sweet?" she said incredulously.

"Reaper has a thing for strippers. Take it as a compliment." I shrugged. "There's a couple thousand dollars in cash in there and a bank card to a Chase Manhattan account with a hundred and fifty thousand in it. That's from me. Use it to get your new life started, but spend it gradually so it doesn't attract a lot of attention. Consider it a going-away present." I nodded at the boat. "All you need to do is get on there, and never look back."

She glanced at the boat, at the bag, and then back at me. "You said you were giving me an option. What's behind door number two?"

"I won't lie. Carl thinks I'm insane to offer you a job, but I've got a good feeling about you. I think you're sharp and tough. Plus, a pretty girl does come in handy."

"So, you think I'm pretty?" Now she was just being coy.

"Well . . . duh. I think you'd work out well. You help us complete Phase Three, and I'll make you a full partner. The money is good. You get to live a crazy life, bouncing around the Third World, robbing and conning assorted warlords, terrorists, scumbags, and lunatics, until eventually one of them catches and tortures us to death, or we're nabbed by some government, that'll just throw us in jail forever."

"Gee whiz, what's the downside?"

"You don't want to be around Carl on casual Friday."

She studied the contents of the bag. I did not envy her choice. Both options required her to give up her entire life. Jill bit her lip as she studied one of the driver's licenses. "How long do I have to decide?"

"The boat leaves in ten minutes." I glanced at my watch. "Make that seven. I talk too much."

"I've got a few questions. . . ." She paused, then gave me a dangerous look. "And don't you dare bullshit me. I want the truth. Why do you do this, Lorenzo?"

"This job? It's for my family, and I'm working on a way to make sure Big Eddie won't ever threaten them again."

"No, I know about them. Why do you do *this*?"

I studied the wheeling birds and the sparkling water. Why did I do it? It had all started as some sort of game, a challenge, a competition against the world. I had been the juvenile delinquent, the black sheep, the rebel. The first to fight, the first to cheat, the one that had to win, even though it didn't matter what I was winning, or what I was losing in the process. One day I had just walked away, fell off the grid, disappeared into the stinking underbelly of the world. I had become a predator of the predators, the ultimate rush, the perfect challenge.

Now I was just tired. And I didn't want my family, who were just normal, decent people, to pay for my sins. But even once this job was done, and even with Big Eddie either satisfied or dispatched, I couldn't imagine myself doing anything else.

"Hell if I know. It's what I do." She nodded as if that made perfect sense. "Boat's about to leave," I pointed out.

"Do you do a lot of bad things?" she asked.

"Depends on your perspective."

"I know I can do it if I have to, but I don't like to hurt people," she stated.

"I don't, either. But most of the things I deal with don't rank as people."

Jill turned her head, like she didn't want to look at me. "Is that the only reason you want me to stay? Because I might come in handy?" She was fishing for something.

God, she was beautiful. She was good and decent and strong. She deserved better than this, better than me. "What do you want me to say, Jill? I don't think I'm the man you think I am."

"And . . . I know you're wrong. I can see it. I just wish you could too." Jill turned back. Her eyes were full of moisture. She kissed me gently on my battered lips. She slung the bag over her shoulder, opened the door, and stepped onto the sand. She had a beautiful smile full of perfect white teeth. "Thank you for saving my life, Lorenzo."

"You're welcome."

"I just don't think I could do the kind of things that you do. It's nothing personal, but I just don't know if I could live in your world."

So that was it.

I held out a slip of paper. "That's a number I check periodically. If you ever change your mind, or if you ever need me for anything, leave a message. don't use any names. I'll know who it is."

She took the paper from my outstretched hand. "Thanks. You know . . . if things were a little different . . ."

"Things will never be different." I smiled. "If you change your mind and decide to come with me, you don't have to wear the blindfold back to base."

"Goodbye, Lorenzo," she said softly. "Good luck. Thank you for everything." Jill closed the door and walked down the pier.

I watched her climb onto the boat. She never looked back.

Chapter 22: Casualties

VALENTINE
Location Unknown
Date/Time Unknown

Someone was singing. It was a woman's voice, soft and warm. It seemed to fade in and out. I couldn't tell where it was coming from. I couldn't see anything or feel anything. That voice was the only thing I had to focus on as I tried to collect my thoughts. It was like a dream.

I don't know how long it took, but eventually I was able to open my eyes to find an unfamiliar gray ceiling. The singing continued, but now I could hear it clearly. I wasn't alone, wherever I was. The room I was in was small. The walls appeared to be metal. Against the far wall was a small desk. A woman sat at the desk, facing away from me, hunched over a laptop. She had long black hair.

My mouth was so dry I couldn't speak. My throat was sore. All I could manage was a hoarse, raspy cough. The woman in the chair perked up and turned around, pulling small white earbuds out of her ears as she did so. *Ling?*

Ling stood up and quickly crossed the room. "Mr. Valentine!" she said. "My God. You're awake." I struggled to sit up. Ling helped me. I pulled an oxygen line from my nose. I had all manner of tubes, hoses, and IVs stuck in me. A cardiograph rhythmically beeped with the beating of my heart. "You should leave those in," Ling said.

"Where am I?" I croaked. "What happened? How . . ." I trailed off, coughing again. It hurt to talk.

"Hold on," Ling said, hurrying to the door. "I'll get the doctor!" She was gone, and I was alone again.

A minute later, several people rushed back into the room, including a man who strongly resembled Albert Einstein. He had a bushy mustache and a wild shock of white hair. He was wearing a lab coat. He put a hand on my shoulder and asked me to look at him. I slowly turned my head, only to have a flashlight shined in my eyes. I flinched; it was so bright it hurt.

305

"I'm sorry about that, Mr. Valentine," the doctor said. He had a German accent. "You've been in a coma for more than a week. Oh. Forgive me. I am Dr. Heinrich Bundt."

I took several deep breaths. "Where am I?" I asked again.

"You're on the *Walden*," Ling explained. "It's an Exodus ship. You're safe here."

"How did I get here? Why . . . ?" I trailed off again. My head hurt.

"You were very badly injured," Ling said. "We almost lost you."

Dr. Bundt straightened his glasses. "Mr. Valentine, I'm afraid you sustained a coup-contrecoup injury. That is to say, a traumatic brain injury affecting both your frontal and occipital lobes."

"Brain injury?" I muttered, suddenly very worried about my aching head.

"That's correct. You had a subdural hematoma to both the front and back of your brain. We were forced to place you in an induced coma after neurosurgery. Given the—"

"Wait, wait, wait," I said, interrupting. "What the hell did you do? Drill a hole in my head?"

"That's correct," the doctor said, sounding very reassuring, all things considered. "It was necessary to drain the hematomas to reduce the pressure on your brain. You should consider yourself very lucky that you suffered no permanent brain damage, given the time that elapsed between when you were injured and when we were able to treat you."

"So . . . am I going to be okay?"

"Time will tell, but I believe so."

I rubbed the sides of my head. "Where's Sarah?" The room suddenly got very quiet. Ling, the doctor, and a couple of orderlies just looked at each other stupidly.

"Where is Sarah?" I demanded, sitting up.

"Mr. Valentine, *please!*" Dr. Bundt said.

"Let me talk to him," a familiar Tennessee twang said. "Give us a minute." The doctor, Ling, and the orderlies left the room, leaving me alone with Tailor. "Hey, brother," he said quietly.

"Tailor, where the hell is Sarah? What happened?" I was getting scared.

"Christ . . . You don't remember, do you?"

"Remember *what*, Tailor?" I asked, a pit forming in my stomach.

"Sarah didn't make it, bro."

I looked at Tailor for a few seconds, then closed my eyes. My stomach twisted into a knot. I rubbed my head again, struggling to remember. Images flashed in my mind. I fell into the mud. I was hit. Sarah turned around. She came back for me. I was screaming at her to keep going, but she didn't listen. She was hit. She went down. She died.

"Oh God," I said, burying my face in my hands. "Oh my God." The knot in my stomach began to hurt. My chest tightened. It was hard to breathe.

"Yeah," Tailor managed. "Bad op, man."

"Bad op," I repeated, my voice wavering. "What the hell happened? How did I get here?"

"You were hit," Tailor said. "So was Sarah. A grenade went off near you. Hudson saw you go down, then lost you in the smoke. There was a lot of shooting. Then the charges on the wall went off. We had to go."

"Why did you come back for me?"

"We didn't. I told Hudson to get in the truck. We took off. I thought you were dead."

"Wait," I said, rubbing my eyes. "How did I end up here, then?"

"We managed to get out of the city, just by pure luck," Tailor explained. "We went to that contingency safe house south of the Al Khor district. You know, the one Hunter told us to never use unless it was a dire emergency. We made it. Somebody else knew about it, though, because after we got there a truck rolled up, dumped you, and took off."

"What?"

"I'm serious," Tailor said. "Someone pulled you out of the fort, tailed us to the safe house, left you, and disappeared. I have no idea who."

That didn't make any sense. "Was it the Exodus guys?"

"They say they don't know anything about it. That's what I'm telling you. I have no idea how you made it out of there alive. Anyway, I used that phone Ling gave you, got a hold of her. Took some doing, but I was able to talk her into getting us out. Told her you were wounded. That seemed to work. I think she likes you."

"Who's left?" I asked.

"You and me," Tailor replied. "Hudson. Frank Mann. That Nikki chick that translated the documents. One of Hunter's security guys. Baker's entire chalk. Hal the medic. Couple other guys. Eleven total. Would've been twelve, but Cox bled to death in the truck."

"Eleven," I lamented. "Jesus Christ."

"Hey, man," Tailor said, trying his best to sound consoling. "At least that many got out. Could've been a lot worse. We're still alive."

"Still alive." I looked up into my friend's eyes. "Tailor, I . . . Sarah's dead. She . . . I promised her I wouldn't leave her. I don't know what I'm going to do now."

Tailor's brow crinkled with concern. "You're going to get some rest, bro," he said. "I'm going to get the doc. Don't worry about anything. We'll talk later. Okay?"

I didn't respond. I just closed my eyes again.

VALENTINE
Exodus Ship *Walden*
Port of Mumbai, India
May 16
0700

I was alone in my little metal room, picking at my food, when Tailor came in. "How you doing, Val?" he asked.

I shrugged. "I walked all the way to the galley and got this food," I said. "I'm mobile again, anyway." The wound to my left calf had gone deep, but it hadn't shattered the bone or cut anything vital. It was slowly healing.

"That's good," Tailor said. "I need you mobile. We're pulling into port right now. The crew says we should be at the pier in less than an hour."

"So?"

"So, we're leaving," Tailor said. "I collected your stuff for you. It's in a bag ready to go. Hudson's trying to find you some fresh clothes. You're hard to fit, you big son of a bitch." I was five inches taller than Tailor, and that always seemed to piss him off just a little.

"Where in the hell do you think you're going to go?" I asked. Tailor's plan sounded ill-thought-out to me.

"Val, listen. Between me and Hudson we've got three hundred and seventy-five grand, okay? We have plenty of money. It's enough for all of us to find room and board for a while, get some supplies, and lay low."

"Lay low?"

"Right, until things calm down. Then we can start thinking about going home, if it's safe. Now come on. You gonna be ready to go? You feel okay?"

I gave Tailor a hard look for a long moment. "Tailor, I'm not going anywhere," I said flatly.

"What are you talking about? We know for a fact that this ship is going to dock in Mumbai. We're getting off here. We don't know where in the hell they're going after this. We need to go while the going's good."

"Tailor, I'm not running away to India. I'm not going to go hide in a dirty safe house somewhere. I'm staying right here."

"Goddamn it, Val," Tailor said, anger rising in his voice. "Don't argue with me. You're not thinking clearly right now. Trust me. Get your shit and get ready to go."

"*Trust* you?" I said. "Trust you? Tailor, trusting you is how I ended up in Zubara in the first place!"

"Well, shit happens!" Tailor said, louder still. "I didn't force you. You wanted to go just as bad as I did, and you damn well know it. Now we need to get off this boat before these Exodus nut-jobs drag us off someplace and we disappear!"

"No, goddamn it! I'm sick of your shit! These 'nut-jobs' have saved our lives *twice* now. Maybe you didn't notice that they didn't charge you for getting out of Zubara? They helped us even though they're not getting anything out of it!"

"That we know of," Tailor interjected. "You don't know what they're planning. You can't trust these people. You don't know them. You need to listen to me. We both know I'm right."

"Listen to you? *You* were ready to take Gordon up on his offer!"

"What? Val, I—"

I cut Tailor off. "Shut up! If I hadn't been ready to shoot him, you would've probably signed up and left the rest of us behind! I know you, man. I *know* you. You just can't pass up an opportunity like that, can you? You know what the difference between you and me is? I don't know why the hell I do it. You, you do it because you're addicted to it. You're a goddamned war junkie!"

"You're about to piss me off, Val," Tailor warned, pointing a crooked finger at me.

"I don't give a shit!" I shouted. "Go ahead, get mad! What the fuck are you going to do? *Huh?* I have *nothing left*, Tailor! So hit me! Shoot me! I don't care! You'd be doing me a favor!"

Tailor's harsh expression softened just a little. "Val . . . ," he started.

I interrupted him again, much more quietly this time. "Tailor . . . I'm just tired. I can't do it anymore. Hell, it's all I can do to get out of bed. I've spent the last three days trying to think of reasons to bother, and I keep coming up short. I'm not going."

"I've already talked to the others, Val. We're going."

"I know. I understand. It's okay. If you guys want to go, then go. I know how it is, man. Don't worry about me. I can take care of myself."

"I've gotta go get ready," Tailor said. He turned to leave, but paused by the door. "I'll see you around, man," he said, and was gone.

VALENTINE
Exodus Base
Somewhere in Southeast Asia
May 20

Strange music echoed in my ears as I pushed open a heavy wooden door. I crossed the threshold and entered the room beyond, despite the suffocating sense of apprehension that squeezed my heart. Directly across from the door was an ornate four-poster bed. A painting hung on the wall above it, but I couldn't make it out.

Slowly I turned, looking across the room I was in. It was familiar; I'd been here before. At the far end of the room a woman hung from the ceiling, her hands bound above her head. I approached her, unsure of what was compelling me onward. The apprehension was turning into dread. My skin began to crawl.

I looked up at the girl as she hung from the ceiling, motionless. Her body had been cut open, her organs removed. Black hair hung down over her eyes, and her face was shrouded in darkness. I tried as hard as I could to focus on her, but I just couldn't make out her face.

I couldn't stand it anymore. I was overwhelmed by fear and confusion. I knew where I was, but I couldn't remember where that place was or why it was important. I didn't know how I got there. I turned to leave.

Something clamped down on my arm as I turned around, and squeezed. The girl was now standing behind me, grasping my arm with her hand. She lifted her head, the dark hair moving aside. It was Sarah. Her eyes were gone.

"You said you'd stay with me."

My eyes snapped open as I was wrenched back to consciousness. I sat up in bed, looking around the room, trying to remember where I was. It was dark. I nearly knocked my lamp off the table trying to turn the light on. The little fluorescent bulb flickered to life, and the room was illuminated with pale light.

My heart was pounding so hard I could feel it in my ears. I sat in bed for a few minutes, breathing through my nose, trying to calm down. I'd had that nightmare before. I had a nightmare every time I went to sleep.

I sighed and rubbed my face with my hands. The clock on the wall told me it was just after three in the morning. There would be no getting back to sleep tonight. Resigned to that, I swung my legs off the bed and stood up.

Exodus had housed me in a small metal Quonset hut that, despite its utilitarian appearance, was actually pretty comfortable. It lacked a kitchen but had its own bathroom. (In any case, I'm a terrible cook; I was more than happy to get my meals from the nearby cafeteria.) I headed into said bathroom to take the first leak of the day.

My heart was finally slowing down as I washed my hands. I missed Sarah so much it hurt. I knew her death wasn't my fault, but that didn't make it any better. She died because she came back for *me*. Worse still, *she* died and *I* lived. That was so unfair it made me sick.

Sarah was one of the kindest people I'd ever known. I, on the other hand, had spent most of my adult life shooting people for money. I had blood on my hands, and I knew it. If anyone deserved to die, it was *me*. Worst of all, I'd broken my promise to her. I told her I'd stay with her until the end.

Looking down at my hands again, I realized I'd been washing them for several minutes straight. I got lost in thought like that once in a while, especially since I'd woken up on the *Walden*. I wondered if it was a side effect of them drilling holes in my head.

I turned off the water and looked at myself in the mirror. I barely recognized the man that looked back at me. My hair was buzzed short, military style. There was a horizontal cut across my forehead, just above the hairline over my right eye. This had been from a Zubaran grenade, I think. Another gash went from my left cheek up my face, splitting my eyebrow in two. Lorenzo, whoever the hell he really was, had given me that one. Missed my eye by a fraction of an inch. My right arm had been similarly carved up.

There were more still-healing scars from where Exodus doctors had treated my injuries. There was the mark on my shoulder from where a bullet grazed me after we assassinated Al Falah. Yet another one cut across my left calf, where a Zubaran bullet had winged me and caused me to fall on my face. Small frag marks peppered my arms and legs. I frowned at my reflection in the mirror before turning off the bathroom light.

Later in the morning, I found myself sitting on the bed, digging through the backpack that served as my bug-out bag. Inside were all the things I thought I'd need for a quick escape, or if I had to be on the go for a while. I'd had it with me when I'd been hit at Fort Saradia.

I laid several stacks of bills on the bed, my half of the money we'd taken from Adar's safe. It was a shame I'd lost my share of Lorenzo's money. I found a zippered pouch. Inside were my driver's license, passport, concealed firearms permit, and other personal identification documents that had been confiscated from me. I wondered if it was safe to use any of these documents. Were they looking for me? Did they think I was dead? Would I get flagged at the airport or something?

Hidden beneath a box of .44 Magnum ammunition was an envelope. I'd tried several times before to open it, but hadn't been able to bring myself to do it. But this time I succeeded. I carefully opened the envelope and removed the pictures inside.

These were the only pictures I had of Sarah. She'd gotten her hands on one of the cameras we had and used the equipment in the lab to print out photographs before clearing the camera's memory.

The first was one of me. It was an awful picture. I wasn't even looking at the camera. I was standing by a building, sunglasses up on my head, mouth open. I'd been halfway through a sentence when Sarah jumped me with the camera. It was a completely natural picture. The next one was of the two of us together. I had my arm awkwardly around Sarah's waist as she pulled me close to her. She had a bright smile on her face.

My God, she was so beautiful. I stared at the pictures for a long time. My hands started to shake. I set the pictures down and buried my face in my hands as my chest tightened. There, alone in my room, I sat on my bed and wept for the first time that I could remember.

Some time later, I noticed something else in the bag as I put the pictures away. It was Colonel Hunter's flash drive, with his bloody thumb print still on it. I had forgotten completely about it. I held it in my hand and struggled to remember, there was something important about what was on here. Information he wanted me to see. I had to take a look.

I made my way across the Exodus base in the early morning darkness. The base was a walled compound that seemed to have sprouted out of the jungle, big enough to house a couple hundred people. The low, utilitarian buildings were interspersed between huge trees and thick vegetation, permanently shrouded in shadow by triple-canopy tree cover overhead. Misty shafts of light would poke through the trees during the day, giving the base a very ethereal look, but right now it was dark.

The compound sat on a flat spot between thickly forested hills and a rocky beach. The dense tree cover probably made the place difficult to study from the air or by satellite. I could faintly hear the low rumble of waves over the constant din of nocturnal animals and insects, generators, and a few vehicles.

Across the rocky beach was a dock big enough to service a ship the size of the *Walden,* though that ship was long gone. On the other side of the compound, in a narrow clearing, was a short airstrip, and planes would occasionally come and go. Only one road led out of the compound. Out the gate, the gravel path wound its way through the hills until it disappeared.

Many areas of the small base were off-limits, at least to me. An armed patrol roved the facility, and guards were posted at the entrances to a couple buildings. These areas were fenced off from the rest of the compound, even. Vehicle traffic was sparse, but there was a motorpool.

I'd been here for a couple of weeks, but hadn't ventured out much without Ling. While everyone I met was exceedingly polite, I was regarded as an outsider. No one spoke to me unless I engaged them in conversation first, except for Ling and Dr. Bundt. But I'd been around enough to know where to find a computer.

There was an Internet cafe in the compound, apparently for use by transient Exodus personnel who needed to check their e-mail or something. I'd been past it several times before, but had never gone in. What did I need to get on the Internet for? I was scared to even check my e-mail, lest the people behind Project Heartbreaker realize I was still alive. I suppose I could've at least checked the news or something, but honestly, at that point I didn't give a good goddamn what was happening to the rest of the world.

Entering the café, I noted that it was all but deserted at this early hour. Out of fifteen computers, only two were occupied. A squat Asian man sat behind a desk near the door, reading a newspaper in a language I didn't recognize.

I approached his desk. "Uh, good morning," I said awkwardly. "I need to use a computer."

"You come right place," he said with a thick accent, not lowering his paper. "This Internet place. Many computers. Here." He began to slide a laminated card across the desk to me, but stopped. "Wait. You guest. You can't get on Internet. Information security rules, okay? Sorry!"

"Listen, I really need to use a computer."

"No Internet, okay? Sorry!" he said, sounding testy.

"Listen. I don't need the Internet. I just need to use a computer. Please."

The clerk folded his newspaper in a huff and thought for a moment. "Okay. Use computer ten. Internet not work. Okay?"

"Uh, okay," I said. "Um, thank you." I turned on my heel and headed for computer number ten.

The computer, like most Internet cafe machines, was a few years old and was pretty beat-up. But it would do for my purposes. I fished Colonel Hunter's thumb drive out of my pocket and plugged it into a USB port. It took a few seconds for the computer to read the drive, then a window popped up displaying all of the available files. It wasn't even password protected; Hunter had put this together in a hurry.

There was more information on the drive than I could've imagined, hundreds of files. One was an initial proposal, more than five years old, describing the theory behind Project Heartbreaker. It was written by someone named Walter Barrington and was vague, at best.

> The use of a DEAD unit would accomplish overall regional goal, but with limited chance of blowback to core elements. See success of D2 and D3 in completion of Project Red in China. The failures of D4 in Chechnya and the eradication of D5 in Mexico were unforeseen setbacks, but in no way undermine the viability of the DEAD program as some program administrators have alleged. I am certain Zubaran security could be achieved with a limited expenditure of resources.

They had done this before.

There were personnel files for every member of Dead Six, including our field leaders. I found mine. It proved to be a fascinating if vaguely surreal read. It was almost frightening how much they knew. My Air Force service, details of my time with Vanguard, bank statements, phone records, everything about me up until my recruitment. After that were newer entries about my performance in Zubara, evaluations, even notes regarding my relationship with Sarah. Apparently, I had gained Hunter's admiration, though he'd suspected I was a flight risk.

There were bios for every one of us, nearly clinical assessments of our suitability. There was one common thread in the pre-recruitment section. Nobody of importance would notice if we were gone.

The meat, the part that Hunter had entrusted me with, came from his personal logs. There were two sections, official daily entries reporting back to some unknown overseer about our operations, successes, goals, and losses. *April 1—Successfully neutralized terror cell in city. 20+ kills. No losses.* It was all very professional. In addition to the official entries, though, were his notes, almost like personal journal entries. Apparently these had not been sent in with his reports. *April 1—Tailor's chalk hit a club. Murdered a bunch of them. Burned it down. Sent a real message. Good op. Not getting support from above. Logistics are a nightmare. I've got a bad feeling about this one.*

I began to skim.

April 15—Tailor and Valentine eliminated Adar. Gordon screwed them, sent just the two of them. Said he wasn't authorized more, but I think it was a test. I think he's eyeing them for Direct Action jobs. They got the job done, though. Chalks are running without enough support. Intel is shit. They're lucky to be alive. Two chalks have taken casualties now because of Gordon's bullshit. I don't know what he thinks he's doing, but nobody will answer my questions.

It seemed that Colonel Hunter had grown increasingly disaffected with the project as time went on. He distrusted his superiors, especially Gordon Willis.

April 18—I got confirmation today. The hit on the assistant ambassador was Gordon's call. Anders pulled the trigger. That was unnecessary. They were being evacuated anyway. They were no threat to OpSec. This was not part of the plan. This is not what I signed up with the organization for. Things have changed over the last twenty years, and not for the good.

Frustratingly, there was almost nothing *about* his organization on the drive other than a few scattered opinions. It was, however, pretty clear that whatever the late colonel's organization was, it was powerful, it operated strictly behind the scenes, and it had been around for a long time.

April 21—Singer is dead. Two chalks took heavy casualties. Gordon didn't give two shits, and now I know why. Gordon secured another asset for Project Blue. Blue is so much bigger, but still. As much as I dislike Gordon, I can't believe he'd compromise this entire operation just to boost his career.

That was one of the few mentions of Project Blue, but there was a lot more about Gordon. I learned a great deal about the man. Hunter had despised him and didn't trust him in the least.

May 5—We're done. I've not got the order yet, but I can read the writing on the wall. Project Heartbreaker is Gordon's baby, his ticket to upper-management. He lobbied for a DEAD op in Zubara. But by last month our superiors knew we were done. Zubara has spiraled out of control and I simply don't have the manpower to do anything about it. Too much reliance was placed on indigenous assets. The Emir is too weak. The best I can hope for is that we can kill a few more of these assholes before we pack it in. Gordon's withdrawn. He knows his career is shot.

By May 7, Gordon Willis had received orders to wrap up Project Heartbreaker as quickly and quietly as possible and prepare to withdraw all assets from Zubara. The hit on Rafael Montalban had taken Hunter by surprise. Even his official report had plainly stated that Gordon had ordered the op over Hunter's objection.

May 10—Gordon is up to something. Orders were hands off on anyone from the Rivals. Montalban was not on our list. Moving on someone as high up on their hierarchy as Rafael Montalban is an act of war. Gordon had to have cut a deal with somebody. This puts us all in danger. Our organization isn't ready for that kind of fight. The bastard. He'll hang for this.

The lack of details about Montalban's rival group was also frustrating. It was as if Hunter had expected whoever read this to already know about them. I sat back from my computer and pinched the bridge of my nose, closing my eyes tightly for a moment. I realized I'd been reading for two hours and had scarcely learned a thing. What did he expect me to do with the information on this drive? Who could I give it to that would make a difference? Who would even believe me? I'd have a hard time proving that I'd been in Zubara at all, much less that there had been some kind of international conspiracy afoot there. Still, I wasn't ready to give up just yet. I rubbed my eyes and continued to read. There was only one entry left, dated the morning of Dead Six's betrayal.

> *May 11—Preparations for the evacuation have been made. I pushed for one last mission targeting General Al Sabah, hoping that maybe we could leave this country a little better off, but was denied. Gordon Willis left ahead of the rest of us. Probably hoping for a head start so he can try to explain this all away before I can file my official report. I think I know what he's up to. Turns out Rafael Montalban's second-in-command was his younger brother, Eduard. I've gathered some evidence that Eduard has been in contact with Gordon. I think the Montalbans just had a coup, only our organization will get the blame. I don't know why Gordon did it. He either got paid off by Eduard, or worse, he's more ambitious that I thought. Worst case scenario, he's trying to force us into a war so we can initiate his precious Project Blue. Even Gordon can't be that crazy.*

I could figure out the rest. Instead of waiting for Hunter to burn Gordon to their mysterious organization, Gordon had turned the tables and sold us out to General Al Sabah.

> *Recording any of this is a direct violation of OpSec, but I have a bad feeling about tonight. This file is my insurance policy. The first DEAD unit was stood up thirty years ago. Detachment One, protecting the world from communism. I was on D1. We accomplished a lot of good, killed a lot of bad guys, saved a lot of lives, but things changed. We've changed. The organization has gone bad, turned rotten. I don't recognize it anymore. Men like Gordon Willis run it now. I used to be proud of what I did, but not anymore.*
>
> *The plan is to evacuate by ship. A handful of D6 have been approached and accepted permanent positions with the organization.*

Gordon had tried to hire me and Tailor, and I had nearly shot him. The personnel files were still open in another window. It looked like some of us on the chalks had been approached, and it appeared several had agreed.

Sarah hadn't been approached, though; neither had Anita King. In fact, there was a note on all the support staff files that they were *unsuitable for recruitment*. Curious, I continued with Hunter's final entry.

> *The recruits and I will rendezvous with a chopper in the gulf for transport home. As for the rest, once out to sea, the evacuation ship will be destroyed, terminating the remainder of D6 deemed to be security risks.*

Shocked, I stopped reading. I must have made a noise, since the man running the café gave me a disapproving look before going back to his paper.

> *It pains me. These boys fought and died thinking they did it for their country. I was the same way once. But most of these boys were dead before they left the States. They didn't even know it. It was Gordon's suggestion to our superiors when this mission started to go off the rails. Anyone who might talk about our operation was to be eliminated. The control staff especially knew too much. Gordon decreed that they were to be on that boat, no matter what. I disagreed, but he outranked me. Too dangerous, he said. Deniable and expendable, he said. Then, when command agreed with Gordon's plan, I knew for sure that this outfit had gone straight to hell.*
>
> *I'm amazed that command went along with this. I'm fighting to get the order rescinded. I volunteered to stay, to try to force their hand. Majestic used to mean something. I can't let this stand.*

Majestic? Was *that* who I'd been working for? I'd heard the name before, but only on *From Sea to Shining Sea*. I thought they were just some ridiculous conspiracy theory. It seemed less ridiculous now that I'd ridden in a few stealthy black helicopters.

But there it was, in black and white, right in front of me. I had worked for Majestic. And not only had Gordon Willis betrayed us, but he'd apparently betrayed them as well. More importantly, he had personally and deliberately orchestrated Sarah's death. If the Zubarans hadn't killed her, then Majestic would have.

I sat there staring at the screen. My heart began to pound so hard I could feel it in my chest. My hands were shaking. A pit formed in my stomach. I felt something well up inside of me that I hadn't felt since the morning my mother was murdered. My eyes narrowed slightly, and I scrolled back through the documents to confirm something I'd seen. Yes, there it was. Gordon Willis's home address.

I stood up from the computer and shoved the thumb drive back into my pocket. I left to find Ling; I needed to talk to her. It was time for me to go home.

Ling was teaching children to fight.

I found her near the docks, working in a large structure with corrugated steel walls and a dirt floor. It had been a storage building once, but it had been turned into a training dojo. Ling was standing in front of twenty kids, boys and girls, the oldest maybe sixteen, the youngest approximately twelve, while she yelled at them in Chinese. Though I hadn't made any noise, she turned when I entered, giving me a small nod, as if to say *give me a moment*.

Turning back to her class, she continued shouting. There was nothing gentle about her commands. I only knew a handful of words in Chinese, but I gathered that she was not pleased with their efforts. The children were all barefoot, wearing shorts and T-shirts, and every last one of them was drenched in sweat. At Ling's command the kids broke into pairs and immediately set about trying to murder each other. It wasn't the sort of sparring you'd expect from children being taught martial arts. They fought each other viciously. The soft dirt floor had seemed odd at first, but as I saw a teenager go bouncing across it on her head, I could understand the logic.

"Shen?" Ling asked. "Would you continue the lesson?"

There was movement in the doorway I'd just come through. A short Asian man wearing green fatigues passed by. I had not heard him at all. He dipped his head, giving me just the briefest acknowledgment as I jumped in surprise. He took Ling's place in front of the class as she approached.

"How long has he been following me?"

"Since your arrival," Ling explained. "Shen is very good at what he does." Shen caught one of the teenage boys by the wrist, mid-punch, and began to berate him for something in Chinese. He proceeded to demonstrate by putting the kid in an arm bar and then tossing him on his face until the kid desperately tapped the dirt for mercy. "We meant no offense, but you are a stranger here. Some were nervous about your presence. Your status has allowed some leeway, but I needed to placate others. My apologies. You are looking well," she said, sounding slightly less serious. "Are you feeling better?"

"Much." My health was improving, but my mood wasn't. Shen kicked a girl's legs out from under her. "He was in Mexico with you, wasn't he?"

"Yes. He is alive because of you. All of us from that day are."

I shrugged. The attention made me self-conscious. "I just did what anyone would have done. It was nothing."

Ling shook her head. "No. It is the reason you are here. Your actions in Mexico earned our gratitude. You alone risked your life against impossible odds to ensure our survival. Exodus does not take its debts lightly. You are a bit of a legend in some circles."

That explained some of the odd looks I'd gotten while I'd been here. These Exodus people were a strange bunch. "Hey, how is . . . you know, *the girl?* The one we rescued? Is she here?"

Ling smiled at me. "She will be disappointed to learn that she's missed your visit, assuming that she doesn't already know. I'm afraid she's not here. She is well."

I had about a thousand more questions about the mysterious girl we rescued in Mexico, but the look on Ling's face and the tone of her voice told me she wouldn't answer any of them. My thoughts were interrupted when one of the kids screamed when a punch landed way too hard. "That's pretty rough," I suggested. "Aren't they a little young for this?"

Ling thought about it for a moment. "And how much older were you when you killed the men who murdered your mother?"

How the hell had she known that? I was sick of everyone knowing more about me than I did about them. It was none of her damn business. When I didn't respond, Ling continued. "It takes dedication to become a member of Exodus."

"You're teaching little kids to kill."

"I'm teaching them how to *survive.* They are all volunteers. These *children* have seen horrors that even you cannot imagine. Yes, we teach them to fight, to kill, and when they're older, someone like me will lead them into battle. Several of these children have already seen war. Others, like that young man there, were forced to watch as their family was murdered by the agents of a genocidal tyrant. That girl was abducted from her home and sold into slavery. They were all forgotten by the world and survived their ordeals only by the grace of God. We teach them the skills they need to not only survive, but *prevail.* They will go from being helpless to being able to help others."

This was very personal for her; I could hear it in her voice. "You went through something similar yourself once, didn't you?"

The look she gave me was cold. "I'm assuming you did not come here to judge my organization or my beliefs. So, what is it that I can do for you, Mr. Valentine?"

"I need transport back to the States."

Ling studied me with her dark eyes as she thought about my request. "There is nothing for you there now."

I answered without hesitation. "There's one thing."

"Of course." Ling thought about it for a moment. "Walk with me, Michael."

There was a rocky path down the shore. Ling led the way. Walking was still difficult, and after a few minutes of exercise, I'd developed a terrible headache. Ling sat on a big chunk of volcanic rock and gestured at a spot for me to sit. "I apologize. I just wanted someplace private to talk. It is easy to forget you recently underwent surgery."

"I'm fine," I insisted, carefully making my way across the rocks before sitting down. The sun was climbing into a brilliantly blue sky over the jungle behind us as incoming waves gently rolled in. It was quite a view.

Ling was quiet for a few moments. She brushed a loose strand of her long, black hair out of her face as she looked out over the ocean. I couldn't guess what she was thinking; I'm pretty perceptive, I think, but this woman was impossible to read. Before I could say anything, though, she asked me a question. "What changed?"

"What do you mean?" I asked.

"You've been with us for quite a while now, and seemed content enough with our hospitality. Until this morning, that is, when you suddenly decided you need to return to the United States. I don't need to tell you how risky that could be for you. Your former employers are not people to be trifled with. Right now they most likely think you're dead. Is it not better to go on letting them think that, rather than to risk being tracked down?"

Ling knew more about Project Heartbreaker than she let on. Once again, the Exodus operative seemed to know a lot more about what was going on than I did, and I was getting sick of it. I'd had enough of being the last one to know everything.

"Look," I said, trying to be firm without being rude. "I don't really want to get into it. Nothing personal. I just thought about it last night, and I think it's time for me to go home. I mean, I can't stay here forever."

She raised an eyebrow at me. "I see." She sounded dubious. "I take it you learned something new while using the computer this morning?"

I took a deep breath before I said anything. I hated being spied on, but there was nothing to be gained by getting angry with Ling. I needed her help. "Yes, I did, but I don't want to talk about it. I'm sorry to impose on you again. And please don't think I'm not grateful for everything you've done for me. You saved my life, and the lives of my friends. But I really can't stay here."

"When I was thirteen," Ling began casually, looking out over the ocean again, "my parents were arrested by State Security. They were Christians and tried to flee with me to the South when the war started. I was sent to a Communist Party School to be reeducated. I never saw them again."

"That's . . . awful," I said hesitantly. "I didn't know."

"Four years later I was conscripted into the Women's Auxiliary of the People's Liberation Army. I was wounded in the Third Battle of Shanghai later that year. Our forces were in complete disarray after Shanghai was destroyed by a nuclear weapon. A corrupt officer sold me and a dozen other women to a band of human traffickers from South China in exchange for the equivalent of five thousand dollars. I spent the next two years in hell before I was rescued by Exodus. Like the children you met this morning, I immediately volunteered. I've been here ever since."

"Why are you telling me all this?"

"I realized that I know everything about you, Michael," she said, casting me a sidelong glance, "and you know nothing about me. I can tell that bothers you. I will arrange for you to return to America if you wish. But will you please tell me why?"

My expression hardened as I carefully chose my words. "They told me I was doing a great thing, that I was serving my country. We went over there for that reason. For many of us, it was a second chance, an offer of redemption. They sent us on missions that were so dangerous it was a joke. Many of my friends died in the process. We never quit. Not a single one of my teammates asked to go home."

"Until you contacted me," Ling injected.

"It wasn't about me anymore. It was about Sarah. And I saw the writing on the wall. I didn't trust the people I worked for. I was worried they'd leave us hanging if things went south." I shook my head bitterly. "I hate it when I'm right."

Ling gave me a faint smile. "Michael, I could tell that the night you and your friends met me in Zubara. I knew right away it was about her."

"We went over there trying to do the right thing. No matter what they asked of us, we did it. We accomplished the impossible. I did terrible things, killed so many people, because they told me it was necessary. They told me I was protecting my country. And what did we get for it? They turned us over to the people we'd been fighting and left us all to die. Their brilliant plan didn't work the way they thought it would, so they made a deal with the enemy because suddenly we were inconvenient."

"And who is 'they'?" Ling asked.

"They're called Majestic, but it's just a name. I don't know if it really means anything. I was given a lot of information by my boss before he died, and even with all that, I don't really understand everything that was going on. There are too many layers to know who's really pulling the strings, you know? But I do have one name. Gordon Willis. He was the guy that recruited me. He's the one that sold us out. He's the reason Sarah's dead."

Ling gave me a hard look for a few seconds. "I see," she said at last. "It is as I thought. I could see it in your eyes when you found me this morning."

"See what?"

"The hatred, the anger, the desire for revenge. I know these things very well. These are the things that motivated me to join Exodus in the beginning. I volunteered with the idea that I would eventually track down the PLA officer that sold me and my comrades to the slavers. I fantasized about that often when I began my training. And when I was done with that corrupt officer, I was going to go after the Communist Party running dogs that took me away from my parents." Ling actually chuckled, as if telling a silly story about her petulant youth.

"I take it that didn't work out?"

"Of course it didn't. I don't know the name of the officer that was responsible for what happened to me, even if he survived the war. Exodus doesn't have the capability to overthrow the communist government of North China. And operations aren't planned around the angry wishes of eighteen-year-old new recruits. People who join Exodus only to seek revenge don't last very long."

"Ling, I see where you're going with this, but I don't—"

"*Do* you now?" Ling said sharply, interrupting me. "I told you all this because I want you to know that I understand how you feel. I know too well the bitter taste of betrayal, the frustration of being powerless to change a vile injustice. I understand the desire to avenge your dead comrades and bring justice to those responsible, probably better than you do. I'm not trying to talk you out of doing what you think you need to do."

I said nothing. Now I was just confused.

Ling smiled. "Surprised? Exodus's reason for being is to fight for those who can't fight for themselves, to avenge those that the world has forgotten, and speak for those who have been silenced. Look around you. The world teeters on the brink of the abyss; civilization dangles by a thread. On every corner of the earth there is oppression, injustice, slavery, and tyranny. In far too many places freedom is being stamped out under a jackboot. In other places, people are slaughtered wholesale for being the wrong race or religion. Meanwhile the so-called *civilized world* blithely ignores these horrors so long as they don't interrupt the latest reality-television program."

I was taken aback. Ling was one of the most reserved people I'd ever met.

"For six hundred years," she continued, "Exodus has stood alone against the darkness. For six hundred years, we've fought for the dignity and the freedom of the individual. For generations we've fought, and died, for the idea that every human life has value, and that the individual is as important as the kingdom or the state. We fight for the idea that every person is accountable for his actions, no matter how powerful or exalted he may be."

My God, I thought. *The woman is a fanatic.*

Ling straightened her hair and blushed slightly. "I apologize, Michael. I get carried away on occasion. I am very passionate about this, I'm afraid."

"I can, uh, see that," I managed. *Crazy,* I didn't add.

"I do have a point," Ling said, obviously a little embarrassed. "As I said, I'm not trying to talk you out of doing what you think you must do. My whole life is dedicated to bringing vengeance to the corrupt and the wicked. I am in no position to lecture you about doing the very same thing in your own way."

"I don't understand," I said. "Why did you bring me out here?"

"Really, Michael, I just wanted to talk to you. You obviously had something on your mind."

"So . . . you'll help me go home, then?"

"Yes, of course," she said. "It might take a little time, but we will find you a safe way to return to the United States, if that's what you really want. We'll be sorry to lose you, but I'm not going to stand in your way." Ling's expression hardened. "I do have some advice for you. There's a very fine line between avenging those who have been wronged and seeking revenge for your own gratification. It's easy to stray from one side to the other. Once you start down that path, it becomes harder and harder to turn around. There's no telling where it will lead you, and you may not like where you end up. You may find yourself digging your own grave in addition to your enemy's. Are you prepared to deal with the consequences?"

"I don't know," I said honestly, looking out over the ocean. "But I don't have anything to lose. They took everything from me. My life, my friends . . . Sarah. What else can I do?"

"Would Sarah have wanted you to make this choice?"

Ling stared at me for a few seconds. I really didn't have an answer to that. The question made me uncomfortable. After a moment, Ling's expression softened. I could almost see the gears turning behind her dark eyes, but as usual she gave no indication of what she was thinking. I was taken by complete surprise when she grabbed my hand and squeezed it tightly.

"Walk with God, Michael," she said. "And please be careful." She let go of my hand, stood up, and turned away. She paused after a few steps and looked over her shoulder. "It will take me a few days, maybe a bit longer, to make the preparations. I'll come get you when it's time."

Ling then walked away without looking back.

Chapter 23: The Heist

LORENZO
June 15

Countdown to D-Day.

The radio was on in the background. Just as I had expected, General Al Sabah's true colors were showing. All of Zubara's major industries had been nationalized, and if you didn't like it, too bad, please line up against that wall and wait your turn. The brain drain of the upper-class fleeing was already starting to affect the running of the country. People who had cheered the general's rise to power a few short months ago were cursing now as their property was confiscated. The university had been closed down, the remains turned over to the craziest mullah he could find. The Zoob was toast.

People never learn. It made me kind of melancholy. I had liked this city. But it didn't matter, we'd be leaving for our meeting in Saudi Arabia shortly, and I didn't plan on ever coming back. I'd had some good times here. Shaking my head, I went back to work comparing three different shades of brown contact lenses so that I could match Falah perfectly. *Good times?* I was just being stupid. Carl shouted for me from the garage.

"What do you think?" he asked proudly when I came down the stairs. He was gesturing at the massive black car that filled the entire space. "No more of that pussy van. This is *class*." It was a Mercedes-Benz 600 luxury car, built in 1968. When I had explained the plan to Carl, he had been very specific about what kind of vehicle we would need. "Six point three liter V8, single overhead cam, Bosch *mechanical* fuel injection, hydraulic suspension, sweet mother of God, it has hydraulic windows and trunk lid."

"You're starting to sound like Reaper," I said.

Carl shook his head at my apparent lack of appreciation for automotive excellence. "No soft electronics, genius. I've worked this baby over. She's cherry. I don't know where Hosani found her, but damn." He whistled.

"Maybe he bought it off Fidel Castro?"

Reaper was in the backseat, bolting Starfish down. Our testing yesterday out in the boondocks had shown it was ready to go. He chimed in. "Pol Pot,

Kim Jong Il, and Ceaucescu drove one of these, too. Idi Amin, Ferdinand Marcos, all the real bad asses. This is the ultimate dictator dope-ride."

"Don't forget Elvis Presley," I added. "And the Popemobile."

"See," Carl insisted. "Those guys *know* class." He turned back to the car sadly. "Too bad we've got to trash her."

"Every mission has casualties. We're sacrificing her for the greater good." I put my arm over his shoulder. "Dude, we live through this and I'll buy you *two*."

Carl patted the hood fondly. "I'm gonna hold you to that, Lorenzo."

LORENZO
East of Riyadh, Kingdom of Saudi Arabia
June 18

Phase Three begins.

The palace compound rose out of the bleak desert like some ancient monument. It was the only human habitation for miles, with nothing but sand stretching in every direction as far as the eye could see. It had once been an oasis and was now a self-contained miniature city. Isolation was the complex's first layer of defense. There was no way to sneak in. If you wanted to get through those walls, you needed an invitation.

Behind the walls lived a staff numbering in the hundreds, and only a select few of them were ever allowed to leave. Every inch of the interior was constantly monitored. The security here was so unbelievably tight that only once a year were outsiders allowed into the inner sanctum.

The temperature outside was so bad that the window glass of the limousine was scorching hot to the touch, but the overburdened air conditioner kept me semi-comfortable in my traditional robes and additional fake fat padding. Starfish was sitting on the floor next to my legs, black and ominous. "Reaper, is this thing going to give me cancer?"

"Probably not. Now back to quizzing. Third wife's name and birthday?" Reaper spoke from the front seat. He looked much different with his hair in a neat ponytail and wearing a suit. Both he and Carl were sporting the black-sunglasses bodyguard look.

"Sufi. August twentieth, 1985," I answered, switching back to Arabic. I tugged on the fake beard that had been weaved into the real one I'd grown out over the last two months and dyed gray. "She is a shrill little harpy, who will give a man no rest."

"What do you think about football?" Carl asked.

I checked the glued on latex attachment on my nose. It itched horribly but looked perfect. "It is a pathetic distraction that takes our young men away from more important pursuits, such as jihad or reading the scriptures," I replied, knowing that my tone and inflection was a perfect match to the hours of recorded tapes of Falah's conversations. Then in my own voice in English, "But I think Al-Nasiffia will take the regional championships."

"Quit screwing around, you need to be in character." The palace was growing larger through the window. We were close now. The walls were forty feet tall and thick enough to withstand anything short of 105mm direct fire. FLIR cameras swiveled downward to examine us. The massive front gate hydraulically opened as we neared.

I cleared my mind. For the next few minutes, I needed to think and act as if I were Ali bin Ahmed Al Falah, terrorist scumbag. We passed through the tunnel in the wall and entered the Garden of freaking Eden. A paradise waited inside the walls. It had trees, orchards, a lake with spiraling fountains, and behind that was the palace itself. The small model in our hideout had not done the thing justice. It was *huge*.

But I wasn't here for the palace. I was after what was *under* it.

My trained eye picked up the multitude of cameras and guard posts watching us. We stopped at the base of the palace, and I prepared myself as my "bodyguards" exited and opened my door. Carl extended a hand and helped me out. The heat was like a blast furnace.

I was in character now.

A hulking brute of a man approached, with four rifle-armed guards trailing behind him. He looked awkward in a suit. "Ali bin Ahmed Al Falah, my name is Hassan, and I am the director of security for Prince Abdul."

"What happened to Adar?" I asked suspiciously. "He was in charge of security the last time I was here."

"He left for other opportunities," Hassan replied without hesitation. In reality he had left for Iraq, where there were more opportunities to hurt people, until Falah had called him to Zubara.

"Of course. I had not heard from my old friend recently. I've been worried about him."

"Please come with me, sir. The other guests have already arrived."

I followed Hassan up the stairs, Carl and Reaper behind me, and the four guards behind them. I spotted at least one sniper on the roof. There were two helicopters parked on a nearby pad. Several other limos and expensive super-cars were parked just forward of mine. Through the steel-reinforced twelve-foot front doors, cold air washed over us as we came into the entryway that was bigger than the largest house I'd ever lived in. A solid gold chandelier was overhead, and the best word to describe the interior of the palace was opulent. Paintings and statues that would have been centerpiece attractions at the finest museums in the world lined the walls, mere trinkets here. The prince had some cash.

Hassan gestured toward a metal detector manned by two more guards. Adar's box was safely concealed inside my padding. Whatever metal the key was made out of didn't trigger metal detectors, we'd already checked. I stepped through, clean, followed by my crew.

Nobody brought weapons anywhere near the prince.

It beeped as Carl stepped through. The four guards lifted their guns slightly. Carl raised his hands. "I got a piece of metal stuck in my back," he stated. Two other men appeared and immediately led Carl aside for a more invasive search. As a VIP, I knew that I would be spared such indignities.

Hassan held up one gigantic hand to stop me. "I apologize for the inconvenience, but surely you must understand, with all the questionable activity concerning your disappearance and the resulting confusion, I need to be sure of your identity before I allow you into the presence of Prince Abdul." He held a small box with a scanner window in his other hand. It had two lights on it. One red. One green.

"But of course," I replied. Without hesitation, I put my right thumb on the window.

Reaper had spent hours testing the prosthetic attachment. It was a relatively new technology, and the single, tiny piece of etched, synthetic flesh glued to my hand had cost a ton, and just to be on the safe side, I was wearing one on each finger. Micro engraved with preprogrammed whirls and ridges, it was the most practical way to fool a fingerprint machine. The machine would only read Falah's fingerprints.

The red light lit up.

Not cool. A single bead of sweat rolled down my back. The guards shifted, spreading out around me.

Hassan shook his head. "Technology, it never works right. Please try again, sir."

I put my thumb on the glass. Hassan nodded at the guard behind me. If this didn't work, we were going to die. Horribly. Turn green, you little bastard.

Green light.

"Ah, excellent. I apologize for the inconvenience." Hassan smiled. His teeth looked slightly pointed. "There is just one more thing. I have someone who wishes to speak with you, an old friend who was most shocked by your sudden disappearance." He clapped his hands.

"Please hurry," I said with some exasperation. This was not good. We had not planned on anyone close to Falah being at the palace. He was known to these people, but only because of an annual meeting. Conning a close associate was a thousand times more difficult than mere business acquaintances. "I do not wish to be late."

A young man in a gray guard's uniform came around the corner. "Al Falah!" he exclaimed, his face lighting up. "Oh, I was so sure you had been murdered."

Flash back to the apartment, hours spent going over the cards, each card a picture of one of Falah's people, with a name and a description on the back. Carl had quizzed me mercilessly, hammering these strangers into my brain. "Rashid!" I exclaimed. "What are you doing here?" *Really, what was he doing here?* Rashid was one of the bodyguards that had supposedly been killed during the hit. He had been in the chase car that had taken off after the sniper. This was way too close.

I'd been practicing for weeks, talking like Falah, moving like him, watching videos, listening to phone calls, and then finally watching him in person in the club, conversing with the man, playing games of chess against him, all coming down to this.

"I saw you get shot, and then we chased the assassins. They crashed into our car. I was the only one who lived. I woke up, and there was this tall American standing over me. He pointed this huge revolver at my face. I prayed for my life. He fired, but the bullet only grazed my head." He eagerly indicated a long scar going down the side of his head. "I thought I was dead, but Merciful Allah spared me!"

Valentine, you cock-fag sack of shit monkey-humping pus ball!

I smiled broadly. "How fortuitous."

"But how did *you* live?" He studied me carefully, obviously suspicious. Apparently he'd shared his concerns with Hassan also, because the tall man had that look in his eye that suggested he was ready to break me in half at a moment's notice.

"I hired Khalid, from the club, to stand in my place. I had heard rumors of Americans operating in the city, and it worried me. Allah smiled upon me, as I had been wise to do so. Rashid, I'm so very glad to see that you are alive." I spoke as he spoke. I moved as he moved. I was Ali bin Ahmed Al Falah.

"As am I to see you." He grinned, buying the act, then nodded at Hassan. "I am working for the prince now, but I would be honored to serve you again, should you ever need me."

"Of course. Thank you, my son."

Hassan gestured toward the epic marble staircase. "Right this way, sir. The meeting is about to start. Your men will stay here, and we will provide them refreshment." I nodded at Carl and Reaper. They knew what to do.

There was an elevator shaft in the center of the staircase. Hassan and I traveled up several floors. The motors were utterly silent, and it was the smoothest elevator I'd ever ridden. The control panel was encrypted, and the basement levels couldn't be accessed without authorization from central control. Even the carpet inside the elevator was so thick that I left footprints.

"The prince respects you a great deal," Hassan said, attempting small talk. "He was worried that you might have been hurt in the recent unpleasantness."

"I am only sorry that so many of our brave brothers gave their lives to the cowardly Americans," I answered. "And I'm greatly troubled that I would have caused a man as noble as Prince Abdul any distress. I do hope that he will accept my humble apologies."

The door whisked open at the top floor. We exited into a long hallway, and Hassan led the way into a meeting room the size of an aircraft hangar.

It was only because of Big Eddie that I knew anything about this meeting which was conducted annually in extreme secrecy. By special invitation only, it was a gathering of the region's movers and shakers, and a handful of special guests from the rest of the world. Businessmen, politicians, scions of powerful families, royalty, and propaganda masters, some of the most important string-pullers on Earth were gathered here. Unspeakable things were planned in this room, agendas set, and massive checks written. This was where the real behind-the-scenes action took place.

Reaper's conspiracy-theory radio would have a heart attack.

The guests were milling around, eating endangered species off a buffet table that could feed Ecuador for a year, mingling and waiting for their host to arrive. I recognized many of them from the flashcards, others from the news. I stayed in character, passing through the room, looking for familiar faces, watching for anyone who might know the terrorist financier that I was pretending to be. In this crowd, Falah was a low-level player. He barely ranked an invite only due to his many contacts. If a bombing was going down within 1,500 miles, Falah probably knew about it beforehand.

The prince had not arrived yet. In a country with 4,000 members of the royal family, he was not even close to being the heir, but through malicious use of his fortune, Prince Abdul had carved a place for himself as the ultimate arbiter of power in the Middle East, and since the world's economy had stupidly become dependent upon this region's resources, the decisions he made affected every person on the planet. He had his fingers in everything, oil, war, politics, even entertainment. Nothing happened here unless the prince had knowledge of it. OPEC was his bitch.

The annual meeting was held for two reasons. First, so the prince could set his agenda for the next year, and coerce or bribe the various VIPs to work together to accomplish his goals. Second, it was to stroke his massive ego. He liked being so important that presidents and dictators jumped at his command. Factions that absolutely hated each other came together for this meeting, all evil but each hoping to be the side that curried the prince's favor this year. This must be what Satan's throne room was like.

Of the hundred or so guests, there were maybe a dozen Europeans, a few Asians, and a handful of Africans. I recognized one American, a former senator who was surely here lobbying on behalf of something nefarious.

There was one man standing to the side that I knew immediately, not from the flashcards but from the protestor's signs. General Al Sabah had come himself to pay respects to the ultimate Godfather. He looked a little uncomfortable. Maybe his ascension hadn't had the prince's blessing, but he'd earned his way in through ruthlessness. I'm sure he'd fit right in.

Flash back to the model. Remember the layout. Focus on the mission.

A hand fell on my shoulder. I slowly turned. It was one of the Europeans. "Ah, Mr. Al Falah. What a pleasure to meet you," the man said. He didn't look like much.

Falah's English was rough, halting, and so was mine. "The pleasure is mine . . ." I did not recognize him from the flashcards. "Mister?"

"Montalban. Eduard Montalban." He smiled, but his eyes were pools of nothing. I had looked into serpent's eyes that held more soul. He leaned in close and hissed in my ear, "But for you, Lorenzo, my friends call me Big Eddie."

I couldn't speak. Big Eddie was *real*.

His accent was British, and his manner was effeminate. His nails were manicured, and each finger had some form of expensive jewelry on it. Probably only in his thirties, with Flock of Seagulls hair and dark circles under his eyes, he looked skinny and weak. He even spoke with a bit of a lisp.

All this time, I had been picturing Lex Luthor, and instead I got Carson from Queer Eye. It was a bit of a shock. As Carl would say, Big Eddie was a *poofter*. This really wasn't what I had expected.

But I would be a fool to underestimate him. I knew for a fact that he was directly responsible for hundreds, if not thousands, of murders. He was a pure killer. This man had more blood on his hands than anyone could ever imagine.

"Nice to meet you, Mr. Montalban. I do not believe that I've seen you at this meeting before." It was difficult to stay in Al Falah mode and not just snap his neck. The room was lined with guards, and I wouldn't make it ten feet. I could live, well, die with that, but it would seal my crew's fate as well.

"No. You would be correct. This is my first year. Normally my half-brother represents the family interests." Eddie did not blink as he appraised me. My initial take had been correct. There was no soul in there. He was empty.

"It is unfortunate that he could not make it."

"Yes. His boat exploded. Bloody sad bit of business, that." He glanced over his shoulder at the American delegation. "That Senator Kenton is a batty shit, isn't she? Hag just won't shut up. Her people are a constant pain in my arse."

"Indeed. Filthy Americans," I responded. *What was he doing here?* I struggled to be polite while the wheels in my brain were turning. "So, what is it that you do, Mr. Montalban?"

"The family business." He waved his hand dismissively. "Shipping, mostly. All the oil in the world won't do any good if they can't move it, you know. I don't trouble myself with the details." Then Eddie leaned back in and whispered into my good ear. "Just a slight change of plan, chap. You just keep up the good work. Pretend I'm not here." His closeness made me cringe.

"This wasn't part of the deal," I whispered.

"I make the deal. You do what I say." He must have caught the murderous glimmer in my eye. "That would be a mistake, my friend. Even if you succeeded in taking me out, your family would still die."

"What do you want?"

His breath stank of menthol lozenges. "Why, you're a legend. The family wouldn't be where it was today if it hadn't been for you. I just wanted to meet you in person." He reached up and tugged on the end of my beard. "I'd say face-to-face, but this is close enough. You're probably the best employee I've ever had. When you quit, I was simply *heartbroken.*"

I had been warned back then. Nobody left Big Eddie's service. *Nobody.* "Yeah, me, too."

"Do your job. Now get back to work." Eddie adjusted his silk tie as he walked away, waving foppishly at someone else, returning to the party.

Focus on the plan. Deal with Eddie later. It took me a moment to compose myself. Why had he bothered? It didn't make any sense. *Shit.* He'd told me his name. He was going to kill me.

Servants in tuxedos began to usher the guests away from the buffet and toward a rectangular table the size of a basketball court. Bummer, since the harp seal looked delicious. The meeting was about to begin. I could only hope that Reaper and Carl were ready. I checked Falah's Rolex, the meeting was exactly on schedule. It was time.

Hanging back, I waited for the group to begin to sit in their assigned places around the giant table. The room gradually darkened; projectors came out of the ceiling and displayed images and maps on the walls. The prince entered the room, and the power brokers politely clapped. Prince Abdul was one of the richest people in the world. If he woke up with a tummy ache, gas prices would go up fifty cents a gallon by lunchtime, so you damn well better believe they clapped.

While the main attention was elsewhere, I grimaced, stumbled, and caught myself on the edge of the buffet table. There was a servant by my side almost instantly.

"Are you all right, sir?"

"My arm hurts. Oh, my chest." I gasped and wheezed, doing my best to contort my face. The servant was on a radio, and I had a guard on each arm helping me toward the exit within seconds. In the background, the prince was giving his opening comments. Most of the power brokers did not notice my exit. Big Eddie winked.

We had memorized the layout of the palace. Every room and corridor was known to me. I knew exactly where I was as the guards pushed my wheelchair down the marble hall. The infirmary was the tenth room on this wing. The guards chattered into their radios, asking for one the prince's physicians to meet them.

"Oh, the pain." I was really milking it. "It is my heart again. Summon my men; they have my special medication."

"Do as he says!" one of the guards ordered as he rolled me into the white-walled room filled with state-of-the-art medical equipment. They gently lifted my padded bulk onto a padded table. There were two guards in the room now.

This was right where I needed to be. The building plans indicated that the infirmary backed up to the secondary security-control station. They shared the same wiring conduit behind the walls. The plans said that the access panel was ten feet from the northwest corner. Reaper figured that it would look like a half-size metal door with electrical warning stickers on it. *There*.

"Dr. Karzi, it is Al Falah, one of the guests. He has fallen ill. He says it is his heart," one of the guards exclaimed as an older man entered the room, pulling a white smock over his starched shirt and tie. He rudely pushed the guard aside and pressed his fingers against my neck. He scowled.

"That is odd," he muttered. "Describe your pain."

"It hurts." I held up my arm and risked a glance at my watch. I had been playing sick now for three minutes, which meant Carl had probably tripped Starfish's timer by now. "I need my men . . . my medicine . . ." On cue, Reaper appeared, being led by a third guard. He gave me an imperceptible nod.

The doctor began to open the front of my traditional dress. "Your heart rate is only forty beats per minute. Something is abnormal." There were some downsides to having ice water running through your veins.

"I have his medication," Reaper said, holding up the briefcase he had been allowed to obtain from our car. Sadly, there were no guns in it, because we had been certain that even in this scenario, they would probably still give it a cursory check. He opened the case.

The doctor was going to figure out something was wrong any second now. The guards looked more concerned for my health than for any trickery. Well, they should be concerned; Al Falah was buddies with every badass terrorist in the business. I was the equivalent of a rock star to these guys.

Several stories below, Starfish was counting down to firing. I was technically illiterate, but Reaper had done his best to educate me. Starfish was a NNEMPD, a Non-Nuclear Electromagnetic Pulse Device. When Starfish's timer hit zero, it was going to use a small amount of explosives to cause a compressed magnetic flux. It would nail every electronic device within a couple hundred yards with the equivalent of getting struck by lightning ten times in a quarter of a second.

Reaper came out with a syringe full of amber liquid. He tapped it and squirted a bit out to remove the air bubbles. The doctor glanced at him. "This isn't a coronary. What is his condition?"

The lights went out, plunging the room into pure black.

"Just plain mean," Reaper answered.

I nailed the doctor with an elbow to the face and then sprung off the table, moving in the direction of the three guards. I couldn't see, but I had been expecting this. They were caught by surprise. A shape moved in front of me. I kicked straight out, low and fast, and caught someone in the knee. There was a scream. A hand grabbed my thobe and pulled. I grabbed the wrist, twisted it, and levered it down, snapping bones. I palm-struck that guard in the throat and put him down.

The emergency power kicked on a second later. The place was certainly efficient. The third guard was down, Reaper's syringe in his neck. The man with the broken knee fumbled with the strap over his pistol. I snap-kicked him in the face, and he was done.

Reaper retrieved the briefcase and sprinted to the access panel. He opened it, revealing a twisted pillar of wires and fiber-optic cables. He immediately went to work. Starfish wasn't powerful enough to destroy everything, just the unshielded electronics that were close to it. It was at ground level and wouldn't travel very far. Inside the palace, it would have fried a lot of stuff, but the main security system would be shielded. But that was okay. We didn't want to take it out; we only needed to give them a surge hard enough to force them to restart.

I pulled the syringe out of the guard, moved to the next one, and poked him in the side, careful to only give him a few CCs of the powerful horse tranquilizer. The doctor moaned and crawled toward one of the guard's squawking radios. "Nighty night, Doc." I stuck him in the arm and gave him the last of the drug. He sluggishly rolled over, smiled stupidly at me, giggled, and was out.

"*System report. What caused the power surge?*" It was Hassan's voice on the radio. I picked it off of the guard's belt. Apparently it hadn't been hot enough to fry these.

"*Unknown, sir,*" someone else responded. "*The system has gone down. We'll have it back up shortly.*"

"*Find out, or I'll have you fed to the tigers,*" Hassan snapped. "*Taha, report.*"

The line was quiet.

"*Taha. What's the status of our guest?*" Hassan sounded angry. He did not seem like the kind of person I wanted to deal with when he was angry. I had to assume that one of these men was Taha.

I made my voice as neutral as possible. "Dr. Karzi says that it was just gas. Al Falah is resting." I began to remove weapons from the guard's duty belts. FN FNP 9mms, good guns.

"*Fine. Get him back here as soon as you can. Hassan out.*"

I checked my watch. "Forty seconds," I said to Reaper.

"Working on it." He was flipping through wires like a man on a mission. "Get my computer." I pulled the laptop out of the briefcase, opened it, and waited for his next command. It was already running and on the correct screens. We had practiced this a few times. This was his gig now.

From Big Eddie's intel we knew that the palace compound was a closed system. There was no way to hack into the security from the outside world. If you wanted to take over, you needed to be in the belly of the beast. The design parameters told us that we had one minute from a power outage for the system to reset, and then we'd be locked out. It was a narrow window, but it was all we had.

Reaper picked a fat yellow cable and did his magic to it, clamping some sort of ring around it. He plugged a USB cable into his machine and then pushed me rather rudely out of the way.

"Thirty seconds."

"I know. I know," he muttered. Screens flashed by as he paged through them. "Come on, baby, come on."

I stuffed two of the FNs inside the thobe and left the third on the countertop by Reaper. I stuck four extra magazines into my pockets. Might as well be ready, because if he couldn't get us into their system, we were going to have a whole lot of explaining to do. And when I said explaining, I meant shooting. I also took one of the radios.

"Twenty seconds."

Numbers were scrolling through a box on the screen. Another box was gradually filling up with asterisks below it. This was hard to watch, and my stomach felt sick at the tension. The computer beeped.

"Ten. Why did it beep?"

"Shut up, Lorenzo!"

"Five."

The screen changed color, and Reaper clapped his hands together above his head. "I so rock! We're in. I think I should be the new sysadmin." Reaper began to tab through windows. Alarm systems, cameras, laser arrays, surface-to-air missiles; you name it, we had it. He immediately found the camera for the infirmary. It was a black-and-white image of the two of us standing over the computer, with a bunch of people lying on the floor. He fiddled with the track ball, and the camera rotated until it was looking at the far wall. Now it was an empty room.

"I'm going," I said. I reset the timer on my watch. "Mark, ten minutes. Then we blow this sucker." From our best estimates, that was how long we figured we had before system command figured out that they were compromised and the whole place locked down on red alert.

"I know the drill," he replied, not taking his eyes from the screen. Of course he did. We had practiced this a hundred times. He was already screwing around with the palace's communications. In a few seconds, the only people who were going to be using the radio net in this place were the ones Reaper was going to allow to do so. He didn't need to do anything to the outside equipment; Starfish had destroyed most of that. So now he was randomly closing down interior systems. Hopefully they'd think that it was some sort of equipment malfunction and not that they were being violated by people like us.

At ten minutes, I exited, took a quick glance down the hallways, and then walked purposefully toward the main elevator. Some servants noticed me, but I smiled at them like I belonged there, and they let me pass. I entered the elevator and waited for the doors to close.

Nine minutes left. The elevator was secure and plated in gold and polished mirrors. You needed a card key to access anything other than the main floors. Only a handful of the staff here had the card necessary to do so. I didn't even press any buttons, and the car began to move smoothly down. A digital display counted rapidly into the negative numbers as we headed deep into the bowels of the palace.

My radio beeped. I pulled it out. "Go."

"I'm in control now. I've locked out everyone else. They're confused, blaming it on the surge. You've got two guards standing at the base of the elevator shaft, and you're going to walk right into them."

"Put me through to them," I said, then cleared my throat. I had only spoken with him for a moment, but I needed to do a real convincing Hassan, real quick.

"*You're on,*" Reaper said, and the radio clicked.

"All guards on basement six report to the level command post." I could only hope that those were the correct terms, as that was what they had been labeled on Big Eddie's stolen plans. "I want you there immediately."

"*But, sir, you said not to leave our—*"

"Tigers! I will feed you to the tigers! Hassan out." I shouted.

"*They're moving, Lorenzo,*" Reaper said.

At seven minutes the elevator slid to a halt at negative six and the doors whooshed open. This was the lowest floor, chiseled out of the solid rock and containing one very secure vault. The hallway was empty. The concrete floors echoed as I walked down them. The level command post was just around the corner. I needed to get past it to get to the vault room.

I slid along the cold wall. Even the desert heat couldn't reach this deep into the Earth. I carefully took stock of the command room. I could see at least a half a dozen men through the glass doors, most of them standing, looking around nervously, waiting for Hassan to arrive.

I checked my watch. Six minutes. There was no way I was going to get past there without getting spotted. I pulled out the radio. "Need a distraction at the guard room."

"*I'm looking through the menus. Hang on.*"

The clock was ticking. I was going to give him thirty more seconds, and then I would try to sneak past on my own. Knowing that I was probably going to get spotted, I pulled one of the pistols and checked the chamber. No time for thought, once you pick a course of action, you were committed, and you'd damn well better see it through.

"*Got it.*"

The guards shouted in confusion as the fire sprinklers came on. I was immediately drenched in the downpour. I moved quickly while they were either looking up or covering their heads. I ran, splashing down the hallway, and pushed my way through the heavy double doors at the end. Once again, I didn't even have to swipe a card.

"*Oh shit. I screwed up, chief.*"

"What?" I stared at the mighty vault door. It was enormous, a circular stainless-steel ultra-modern monolith to security engineering. To a thief like me, it was the most intimidating thing I had ever seen. Multiple combination locks ringed the device, over a dozen giant bolts were compressed into the tempered steel at different angles. The fact that the sprinklers in here were dumping water everywhere made the scene slightly surreal. On the other side of that vault were the greatest treasures in the world, wealth beyond all comprehension.

But that wasn't what I'd come for.

"That command turned on all the fire sprinklers in the palace. I'm watching the cameras. Everybody is freaking out!"

I continued down the hall. The carved stone became rougher and rougher and the passage started to trend sharply downward. I was now in the ancient tunnels that predated the construction of the palace. There were no sprinklers here, but their water flooded in a fast trail past my feet to disappear ahead of me.

"The IT guys know something is up," Reaper exclaimed. *"Hurry."*

They were ahead of schedule. Why was it that nothing ever went according to plan?

The tunnel opened into a larger room. A string of lights had been bolted into the ceiling. The room was perfectly square, every surface covered in carved writing. I didn't recognize any of the words; everything was too archaic. There was a circular indentation on the floor. The room felt *ancient*.

And it should. This space had been carved over a thousand years ago by unknown hands. Discovered by Saladin's armies, it had been used to house his most valuable possessions. Or so the Fat Man's report had said. All I knew was that the thing I sought was under my feet.

There were only a handful of these keys still in existence, passed down from fathers to whoever was the best warrior among their sons for hundreds of years. Over time they had gained something of almost religious significance. It was prestigious to be the bearer of the key, even though the reasons had long since been lost to the sands of time. Eddie's file had said the prince didn't understand what he was sitting on, except that it was prestigious and therefore had to be hoarded.

I found the keyhole in the center of the floor, a bizarrely geometric shape, going straight down. Standing in the indentation, I took the key out. I had to turn the base slowly until the protruding spines lined up with the hole. I inserted it until it clicked into the lock. As I twisted the base back, there was a cold hiss of air around me and the stone under my feet began to shudder. Steps appeared one by one as the floor sank. I leapt back in surprise. I had expected a simple door or something, not an elaborate construction that seemed to work like oiled silk even though it was a millennium old.

Holy shit, that's cool.

Within thirty seconds a narrow staircase had materialized, shooting straight down into the darkness. The steps were tiny, brutally steep, and made for feet far smaller than mine. I went down, and after a few steps I made out a faint glow. The stairs terminated in a stone wall carved with a three-foot skull. The skull had curving ram's horns. The light was coming from inside the skull's open mouth.

There it is. Whatever it is. It was sitting in the alcove formed by the mouth. It was vaguely Egyptian looking, almost like one of those beetle things they carved on the pyramids. A scarab, I believe they were called. It was only two inches of intricately carved black metal wrapped around a gold blob. At first I thought the center was glass, but it was different somehow, almost like crystal. With a shock I realized that the center was actually where the light was coming from.

I was scared to touch it. Maybe it was *radioactive.* "Shit," I muttered. I didn't have time for this. I reached inside the alcove and scooped up the thing. It was surprisingly heavy. I froze as I felt it shift in my palm, for an uneasy second thinking that it was alive, but it was the golden interior. It was some sort of dense liquid shifting about sluggishly. I felt incredibly nervous, like I was a child screwing around with something that I really shouldn't be. There was an unbelievable temptation to just put it the hell back.

This thing wasn't natural. It was somehow *wrong.*

Reaper pulled me back. *"Time's up, Chief."* I looked at my watch, I had only been down here for ten seconds, but it had felt like forever in the dark. *"I gotta go. I've set the system for our getaway and crashed everything else. I locked the sprinkler controls. I've opened every gate except for the one that leads to the water main. I'm going to pump half the Gulf in here before they get that door breached, punk-ass newbs tried to mess with me. Elevator is running freely now. The guests are trying to get out. All hell's breaking loose. Shit. Some guards are coming this way, gotta run."*

"Go, I'll meet you at the car," I said, stuffing the scarab inside my clothing. I didn't have time for metaphysical bullshit. I had a job to finish. I ran back up the stairs, reached the top, twisted the key free, and sure enough the stairs began to rise, one by one. I knew that within seconds it would be like I had never been here.

There was no way that stealth was going to work now. I drew one of the FN pistols and kept it low at my side as I hurried up the tunnel. The sprinklers were still pumping. One of the guards stepped into the raining hallway from the control room, shouting into his blocked-off radio. He heard my footfalls and turned just in time to catch a face full of steel slide. The shock reverberated down my arm, and the guard rebounded off the wall. I was past him, in a full-on sprint now. Voices shouted behind me. I extended the 9mm as I ran, not even looking as I fired wildly down the corridor, just trying to keep their heads down.

Bullets whizzed past. I spun to the side as I slid into the elevator. Projectiles impacted the wall, shattering the polished glass. Mashing the up arrow repeatedly, I leaned the gun around the corner and cranked off wild shots until the slide locked back empty. The door slid closed, bullets clanging off the exterior.

I dropped the spent mag on the soggy carpet and reloaded. The elevator car vibrated slightly as pulleys lifted me toward safety. I pushed the button to stop at the lobby floor. The doors opened onto pure pandemonium. Water was pouring down the walls, collecting in chandeliers, and ruining antique furniture. Billionaires were pushing to get out the entryway, and the prince's men were trying to stop them. A fight had erupted between one of the bigwig's security detail and some of the gray-uniformed guards.

I collided with a fat, bloated slug of a man. He glared stupidly at me with little pig eyes and tried to push his way into the relatively dry elevator. "Hey, you're bleeding," he said nasally in American English as he pointed at my robes. "What happened in here?" Not seeing any guards looking in my direction, I grabbed him by the throat, yanked him into the car, broke his nose with a head butt, kneed him hard in the crotch, and then slammed his face repeatedly into the wall. He collapsed in a whimpering heap in the shell casings and broken glass.

Nonchalantly as possible, I stepped into the indoor rain and pushed through the chaos. Carl magically appeared at my side. "Wow, you really kicked Michael Moore's ass," he whispered. I turned back briefly. It had kind of looked like him . . . *Naw.*

There was Reaper, also heading toward the door. Hassan was blocking the door with his bulk, shouting for order and begging the VIPs to calm down. I saw Eduard Montalban at the foot of the stairs, a grinning caricature of a human being. In sharp contrast, the Fat Man stood behind him, holding an umbrella open over his employer. Big Eddie golf-clapped for me.

Hassan finally relented, surely not willing to risk the prince's wrath, and let the sodden guests through the door. We shoved along with the rest of the sheiks, royalty, CEOs, and scumbags into the scorching desert air. Hassan was too busy screaming into his nonresponsive radio to notice me exit. Steam immediately rose from my man-dress as we headed for the car.

The crowd was spreading when the first explosion went off. It was at the opposite end of the compound, but it sent the group into an even bigger frenzy. Reaper had set the mines along the opposite perimeter to detonate randomly. He was grinning from ear to ear, enjoying the up-close view of his handiwork.

The radio under my thobe began to speak. It was my voice in panicked Arabic, the audio file recorded back at our hideout and set to play on the radio net as a final distraction. It was going to repeat every thirty seconds, and it was the only thing that was going to broadcast over their intercoms and radios. "*We're under attack. Forces are breaching the north wall. All guards to the north wall. Evacuate the guests. The prince does not want them found here. Let everyone out the gates!*" I opened the door and slid into the backseat of our Mercedes. Carl and Reaper jumped in the front.

Around us, other drivers were attempting to start their expensive cars to no avail, their modern electronics all hopelessly fried by Starfish. "Go!" I shouted. We were spinning tires and leaving rubber on the pavement in an instant, zipping through the gardens, through the tunnel under the wall, and then we were out into the blinding desert. The acceleration sucked, but within a few minutes our land-yacht was doing a hundred.

We had done it. We had pulled it off. The palace was shrinking in the distance. All three of us began to whoop and cheer wildly. Carl screamed out happy profanities. Reaper punched the ceiling. We had done the impossible. Phase Three was done. This suicide mission was done. *Screw you, Eddie. We got your stupid treasure.*

Then the adrenaline began to subside, and my hands began to shake. That is when I noticed the blood and felt a burning sensation in my back. I stuck one quivering hand under my thobe and probed around. It came back slick and red.

Nothing ever goes according to plan.

"Ow! Carl, careful!" I snapped. "That hurts."

"Quit your crying. Here you go." He waved a bloody Leatherman multitool in front of my head with something held in the pliers. I opened my hand and he dropped a bullet fragment onto my palm. Carl poured something stinging on my back then started to tape down a bandage. "That's it. Must have bounced off the elevator wall and got you. I thought the way you were whining you might actually have gotten hurt or something."

The limo was still cruising across the bleak desert. Reaper was driving now, so Carl could play medic, and had taken us off the main road and deeper into the dunes. The car kicked up a massive sand plume behind us. "We're almost there," he shouted into the back compartment.

"Good," I answered as I threw the waterlogged and bloodstained mandress on the floor. Carl handed me a T-shirt. "As soon as we stop, you guys grab Al Falah out of the trunk, shove him back here, and we'll light this sucker. I'll get the van ready."

"What, you get one little hole in you and you think you don't have to lift the fat guy?" Carl asked with a grin. Even a bitter and angry fellow like Carl had to be in a jovial mood after pulling off a heist like this. He started to undo his tie. "At least he'll be thawed. When he wouldn't bend, it was a hell of a time getting him in the trunk."

They'd identify the burned corpse as Al Falah, probably assumed murdered by his co-conspirators, which would totally point the investigation in the wrong direction at first. Eventually an autopsy would show that he'd been dead for a long time, but by then we'd be well out of the country.

I tried to turn serious for a minute. "Guys, I've just got to say. You were amazing back there. The EMP was awesome. You took down security in record time, everything. That was damn near perfect . . . except for the sprinklers."

"Yeah, what the fuck was that?" Carl shouted before he called Reaper something unpronounceable in Portuguese and threw his tie at the driver.

"Hey, I had to improvise," our techie answered defensively. "Next time, you do the computer stuff and I'll do the kung-fu ninja stuff. How hard could it be?"

"Well, either way, we're done." I pulled the scarab from my pocket. It still made me uncomfortable. "We got his damn . . . whatever."

"Rub it and see if it grants three wishes," Reaper suggested.

"Whatever, Aladdin, Big Eddie will be in contact and we can arrange a handoff. And I didn't get the chance to tell you—I met Eddie. He was there at the meeting."

"No way," Carl said. "Was he there because of us?"

I shrugged. "I don't know. But he felt the need to talk to me in person, which can't be good."

"Do you think our families are off the hook?" Reaper asked quietly.

"I think I've got an idea to guarantee Eddie sticks to his word. I'll fill you guys in on the way to the border."

An ancient oil rig appeared ahead of us. It had long since fallen into disuse and was slowly decaying back into the desert. There was a wooden shack behind it where we had stashed our van. A few minutes to destroy the evidence, and we'd be on our way toward the border. We parked near the dilapidated shed. Old canvas tarps whipped in the wind.

I stepped into the searing heat, savoring the *freedom* of it, and went to unlock the padlock we had left on the shed. Carl pulled out a pair of binoculars and scanned the desert we'd just traveled. "Lorenzo, we've got dust behind us. We're being followed."

I shouted back as I unlocked the door. "How far?"

"We've got maybe five minutes," he responded. "How'd they find us?"

I'd hoped that Starfish would have bought us more time. "Eddie probably had a bug stuck on our car during the meeting," I shouted. Well, it was either Eddie's goons or the prince's men. Eddie must have decided he couldn't trust us to hand off the goods, that double-crossing bastard, and heaven help us if it was Hassan. I shoved the door open. The white van was a welcome sight. "Hurry up and move that body! We've got to roll."

I was getting into the van, looking for the ignition key, as Carl was unlocking the limousine's trunk. Reaper was getting out of the driver's seat.

"They won't be able to catch us, Lorenzo. Nobody can catch me," Carl said as the trunk lid opened.

CRACK!

I jerked my head in surprise, jolted by the unexpected noise, dropping the keys to the van's floorboards.

Carl's beady eyes narrowed in momentary confusion, bushy brows scrunching together as he looked into the trunk. The first bullet had struck him square in the chest, leaving a red hole on his white dress shirt. The second concussion came a split second later. Blood spurted from Carl's neck, his hands flying reflexively to his throat as he fell sprawling into the sand.

Time jerked to a screeching halt.

"*Carl!*" Reaper screamed. Someone was crawling out of the trunk.

I was moving, the FNP coming out of my waistband.

The man twisted to the side, one foot hitting the ground, the other still bent in the trunk. He extended a small B&T machine pistol in one hand, seeking Reaper.

"Down! "Down!" I pushed around the van door, punching the FN out, the front sight moving into my field of vision, finger already pulling the trigger back.

Too late.

The submachine gun bucked, brass flashing in the sunlight. Reaper jerked violently to the side, spinning, crashing into the limousine's hood as the window beside him shattered. I fired, the 9mm in my hand recoiling, the front sight coming back on target, firing again.

The man dove from the trunk, rolling in the sand on the other side of the limo. I moved laterally, gun up, tracking, searching, looking for another shot. He opened up from under the car. Bullets stitched across the shack behind me, flinging splinters into the air. Metal screeched as something struck the van. I was running now, not even thinking about it, trying to flank around the side of the car.

He rose, looking for me, glaring over the top of the limo, stubby black muzzle swinging wide. He was a tiny, dark-skinned man, drenched in sweat. Still moving, I saw him first, centered the front sight and fired. His head snapped back violently, visible matter flying as I shot him in the face. I hammered him twice more before he disappeared.

I lowered the gun. Multiple dust plumes were closing in the distance. Reaper was dragging himself up the car hood. He screamed as the pain hit him. I grabbed him as he started to fall again. "Can you move?" I shouted.

He grimaced, biting his lip, tears running down his cheeks. "Yes."

"Get in the van. Hurry!" Reaper lurched away. I ran for Carl.

My friend was gasping, shaking, blood streaming between his fingers as he kept pressure on his neck. He focused on me as I knelt beside him. "Get him?" he wheezed. There was a massive quantity of blood already spilled on the sand.

"Yeah, I got him. Hang on, man, I'm gonna get you out of here."

Carl closed his eyes. He grabbed my hand and squeezed.

Then he was gone.

"Carl?"

The cars were closer now. I knelt by the body of my friend, pistol dangling from my numb fingertips. I wanted nothing more than to stay here and wait for them to arrive.

Then all of this would have been for nothing.

I stood, dragged Carl's body to the limo, gently set him in the driver's seat, then went to the trunk. Falah's body was still cold. It was probably the only thing that had kept the assassin alive in the heat, lying on that ice block, waiting for his chance. He must have gotten in while we were at the palace. I retrieved the white phosphorus grenade from under Falah, pulled the pin, and tossed it into the Mercedes. It ignited behind me in a billowing wall of chemical flame.

Carl would have liked the Viking funeral.

Reaper was sobbing when I got into the van. "Dude, the fuckers killed him." He was cringing from the pain, holding his hands tightly to his wounded side. "Eddie did this. Bastard's gonna pay."

I found the keys on the floorboard. The goons were inbound. It was going to be a race to the border now.

Chapter 24: Welcome Back, Mr. Nightcrawler

LORENZO
June 18

I was certain we had lost them after we had crossed the border. A gentle breeze had calmed the raging temperature. The sun was setting over the desert, and if it hadn't been such a terrible day, I would have thought it was beautiful. I cradled the rifle in my arms and scanned the horizon.

Part of me was secretly praying for cars to appear on the road. Carl had been my best friend.

The village was small, consisting of a few small compounds and some outlying buildings. The van was well hidden. I sat in the shade beneath an awning, gun in hand, black and gold scarab in a pouch I'd tied around my neck. In the distance dogs barked and children laughed.

It had been my fault. I should have seen it coming. I should have done *something*.

There was movement in the doorway behind me. "Your friend will live. He was struck twice, but the wounds were superficial. Given time to heal, he should have no permanent disability."

"Thank you, doctor," I replied, never taking my eyes off the horizon.

"I'm afraid I'm no Doctor," the Qatari answered. "I failed from an American veterinary school."

"Good enough." I lifted the rubber-banded stack of money above my head. He took it. This particular establishment had a reputation within the criminal element of the region. "When can I move him?"

"I would not move him until morning. You may sleep in the guest room. I shall have my servants prepare it." He turned to leave.

"We were never here," I stated.

"But of course."

Carl's duffel bag was open on the bed. I found the manila folder with the mission details and dialed the Fat Man's number on my untraceable cell phone.

I had checked on Reaper before retiring to the guest room. He had been asleep, and had looked terrible, even paler than normal, with bandages all over his skinny chest, and buried beneath IV bags. A heart monitor kept a steady pace. He would be fine, but the sight of what was left of my crew filled me with rage.

"Yes," the Fat Man answered on the other end of the line.

"I want to talk to Eddie."

There was a pause. "Mr. Lorenzo, Big Eddie does not speak with the help. I am his intermediary and—"

"Put him on or I toss the scarab in the ocean," I stated calmly.

"Think of your family before you make any rash decisions."

Part of my family had been shot in the throat this afternoon. I was not in the mood to play games. "Do it."

There was a moment's hesitation. "Please hold."

I rummaged through Carl's bag while I waited. We had worked together for so long that it still hadn't sunk in that he was really gone, corpse burned to ashes on a Saudi dune. Death was always a possibility in this business, but you never really got used to it. I found another folder in the bag. It had *Carlo Gomes* written on it in black marker. It was the information about his family that the Fat Man had originally given us in Thailand.

I opened Carl's folder. The man had never talked about his people. There were a handful of photographs. They were marked Island of Terceira. The pictures were all very old. Beneath each person's photo had been handwritten the word *deceased*.

Carl had no family left. Eddie had never held leverage on him . . .

Carl had done it for us.

"Ah, Mr. Lorenzo. Good to hear from you." The oily sound of Eddie's voice uncorked a clot of rage in my soul.

"Why did you do it, Eddie? Why'd you try to kill us?" I hissed.

"Just business. I'm sorry about that. I saw the opportunity at the meeting. I realized what you had done. Brilliant move, I must say, but with the cameras around the cars disabled, I sent one of my men to accompany you. I thought I would tie up some loose ends."

I was a *loose end*. He did not even sound defensive. That was just what our lives were worth to him.

"I was going to give it to you."

"It was a calculated risk."

"I should just destroy this thing and walk away," I said, trying to keep my voice as neutral as possible.

"Do so and you will have a much shorter Christmas card list. The original deal is still in place." He laughed. This was amusing him. "See, Lorenzo, you're a pawn."

"I guess that makes you the queen."

"Fair enough. But you will bring me that phylactery, or I give the order and your loved ones get fed to the sharks. Listen to me carefully, chap. You do not have any idea what you have. The contents of that thing are more important than you can even imagine. I've strangled children for far less, and I sleep very well at night. You will give it to me or you will have—"

I cut him off. "Now you listen to me. You harm any of my relatives and I'll give this thing back to the prince and tell him who hired me to steal it."

Eddie let out a long breath. "You bloody fool."

"No, you're the fool. You screwed up. I know who you are now," I snapped. "Mr. Montalban."

"I suppose that was a mistake. You know what they say about hubris," Eddie said slowly. Whatever stupid bit of arrogance had caused Eddie to reveal himself to me at the meeting was going to be his downfall. "Let's be reasonable, Lorenzo."

"Reason went out the window when your boy crawled out the trunk. You'd better pray that none of my nieces falls down and scrapes a knee, because I'll assume you were behind it." I seized the moment. I was tired of being pushed around, and now it was time to push back. "We trade. You get your bug right after you transfer twenty million dollars into my Swiss accounts. Then you walk the fuck away. You ever contact me again, I call the prince. If I die of anything other than old age, I'll have somebody else contact the prince. You ever look at my family cross-eyed again, I call the prince. If one of my brothers gets prostate cancer, I'm going to hold you responsible."

"And call the prince, yes, yes, I get it. . . . You know, Lorenzo, I never took you for a tattletale. But that's why you were always my favorite. You'll do anything to get the job done. Very well, I can deal. Fair enough." I could tell that he didn't think it was fair at all. Fair was not a concept a man like Big Eddie understood. Someway, somehow, he would find a way to kill me. There was no turning back from this point. For this to end, one of us had to die. "When can I have it?"

"I'll be in touch." I hung up.

I awoke with a start. It was dark, and I lay there for a second, heart pounding. The house was quiet, but I snatched up my rifle and went to the window anyway. There was no movement outside. No dogs barking. *All clear.*

But I stayed there, watching, waiting, too wired to return to bed. I was letting this get to me, letting it affect my judgment. There was a cough from next door. *Reaper.* That's what had startled me awake. I put down my rifle and went to check on him. Surprisingly enough, he was awake too. Sitting up in bed and looking out the window, white bandages reflecting the moonlight.

"How you feeling?" I asked.

"Carl's gone, man," Reaper said as he wiped one hand under his nose. "Holy shit, I didn't think Carl could die. He was too *angry* to die. It's dumb, but like if he got shot, he'd just get more pissed off . . . Shit . . . That sounds stupid. He wasn't the Hulk."

I pulled up a seat. "I know how you feel."

He got really quiet for a while. This was hitting him worse than me. "Man, it's been so long. . . . Carl was always there for me. I don't know if I ever told you, but when I met you guys . . . I was really scared." He said that as if it were some kind of revelation, and maybe to him it was. "I was all alone. I didn't know where to go, and you gave me a job, gave me a *mission*. You know, I never fit in back home."

I nodded, as if that were a surprise. "Me, either."

"Okay, this might come as a shock, but I wasn't as tough when I was a kid. I was kind of a nerd," he said, like he was admitting something shocking. "I got picked on a lot. I was always the smartest kid, but I was so much younger than everybody else, so I was like a weirdo."

"You were like Doogie Howser."

"Except straight. Totally straight," he corrected me. "Then my mom got remarried, and my stepdad was like this super tough-guy fucking lumberjack or something, and my step-brother was Johnny Football Hero, and he got all the chicks, and there I was, this little scared dork *weakling*. . . . I could never live up to their standards. I *hated* them."

I wondered if this was how some of the genius super-villains from the comic books started out. I just kept nodding.

"So I showed them. I'd be way more bad-ass than they could ever be. It was time to Fear the Reaper, you know what I'm saying? I had *skills*, man."

"Two hundred felony counts is pretty damn impressive for a teenager."

"Well, I wasn't as clever as I thought I was back then." Reaper smiled sadly. "I scared the shit out of the government, though! I crashed a bank and turned off all the lights in Boston, just because I *could*. They wanted to make an example out of kids like me. Mom was heartbroken, and you know what the weirdest thing was? My stepdad, the *asshole*, he's the one that helped me the most. He gave me a plane ticket to a place with no extradition and told me it was 'time to be a man' . . . that was the nicest thing anybody had ever done for me."

Shit. If Reaper started crying, I wouldn't know what to do.

He started crying. "You guys took me in after that. You were my family. *Family* . . . But now? First Train, now Carl. They were my *brothers*. We're all that's left, and look at me. They almost got me. I've never been shot before." He blinked the tears away. "This shit just got *real*. Eddie's going down. Eddie and that fat fucker in the white suit, both. I'm gonna kill them, Lorenzo, I swear to God, I'm gonna kill that fat bastard if it's the last thing I do. I'm gonna wipe that smile off his fucking face."

I patted him on the arm. I had a hard time with emotions, but revenge, that I could understand. "That's the spirit."

"They're gonna *fear* the Reaper," he vowed.

VALENTINE
Quagmire, Nevada
June 21
1500

The Nevada sun blazed overhead as I hiked up the road from the Greyhound bus station. Quagmire's bus station wasn't really a bus station. It was a tobacco shop and party store that the Greyhound bus occasionally stopped at. Hawk knew I was coming, but he didn't know what time I was getting in. No one was waiting for me.

I thought about calling him. I had a prepaid phone that I'd purchased after I landed in the States. I decided I'd just walk. I was probably being paranoid, but I was very leery about using a cell phone still. It was a good hike to Hawk's ranch, but I knew the way. I shouldered my duffel bag and started down the road.

I was walking up Main Street in Quagmire when a big Ford pickup, adorned with an NRA and a US Marine Corps window sticker, slowed to a stop next to me. The driver, a crusty old guy wearing a NASCAR hat, rolled down his passenger-side window and got my attention. I immediately tensed up. I was unarmed, save a pocket knife I'd bought at a Wal-Mart. My left hand slid down to my pants pocket, where the knife was tucked away.

"You need a lift, son?" he asked. I had a big green military duffel bag, and my hair was still buzzed short. He probably thought I was a vet coming home. *Close enough.*

I relaxed some and moved my hand away from my pocket. "If it's no trouble," I said, stepping closer to the pickup.

"Where ya headed?"

"You know the Hawkins place? It's on the north end of town."

"Oh hell," the man said, grinning. "I know Hawk. C'mon, get in. Toss your bag in the back. I'll give you a lift. It's no trouble." I thanked the man, threw my heavy bag into the back of his truck, and jumped in.

We rolled past the limits of the town, following a well-worn dirt road. About half a mile down it, we passed through a gate that had been left open, ignoring the NO TRESPASSING signs that were fading in the desert sun. The truck left a cloud of fine dust in its wake as we neared the house at the end of the road.

It was a modest-looking two-story ranch house, very unassuming and unremarkable in appearance, just like its owner. There was more than immediately met the eye. The old man stopped his truck by a well-used, dusty Dodge turbo diesel pickup. I thanked him and got out. As soon as I grabbed my bag, the old man turned around and headed up the road again, leaving me standing in his dusty wake.

The sun was intense overhead. I squinted even through my sunglasses. I slowly walked toward the house, bag in hand. On the porch, in the shade, Hawk sat in a rocking chair, reading a newspaper and sipping ice water. "Hawk," I said, stepping onto the porch. He didn't get up, but I knew he recognized me. If he hadn't, I'd have been staring down the barrel of a .44 Magnum before I even got close.

Hawk folded his newspaper and set it aside. "Good to see you, kid," he said simply. "I was glad to hear from you. I kind of figured you were dead."

"You were almost right," I said levelly.

"Where's Tailor?"

"I don't know," I replied truthfully. "He was alive last time I saw him. It's a long story."

Hawk nodded and stood up. "C'mon in." He led the way into his house. It was air-conditioned and mercifully cool inside. I was immediately greeted by a pair of big mutt dogs that wanted to be petted. Their tails wagged back and forth as they sniffed me. I smiled and set my duffel bag down.

Hawk shooed the dogs away and led me to his kitchen. He motioned for me to sit down and went to the refrigerator.

"Want a beer?" he asked.

"No thanks," I said quietly.

"Ah," he said thoughtfully. "Didn't think you would. Here." Hawk turned around and placed a ice-cold can of Dr. Pepper in front of me. The man knew me well. He then pulled out another chair and sat down, popping open a can of beer. "So, where ya been?"

I didn't answer at first. I took off my baseball cap and sunglasses. Hawk got a good look at the scars on my face for the first time. He just nodded.

"Start talking, kid."

I sat in Hawk's kitchen and told my story for more than half an hour. Where I'd only told Ling a little bit about what had happened, I poured my guts out to Hawk. I knew I could trust this man. I told him everything. Gordon Willis. Project Heartbreaker. Zubara. The fighting, the killing, the loss, all of it.

My voice wavered a little as I recounted the night Sarah died. He sat back in his chair, rubbing his chin when I told him about the man called Lorenzo that had showed up in my room. He raised an eyebrow when I told him about how I'd first encountered him, and nearly captured a woman named Jillian Del Toro, but he didn't say anything.

Hawk's eyes narrowed a little when I described Sarah's death and explained that I didn't know who pulled me to safety. He would just nod and sip his beer, not saying anything, until I finished.

Hawk looked thoughtful for a moment. "Bad way, kid," he said simply. "So you haven't heard from Tailor?"

"No. He has no way to contact me."

"He hasn't called here," Hawk said. "Eh. No worries. Tailor can take care of himself."

"Did you get the package I sent?"

"I got it," Hawk said. Ling had helped me ship my revolver and my knife to Hawk. They were both disassembled and placed in a box full of random machine parts I found. They apparently made it through customs. "Your .44 is all cleaned up and put back together. They're up in the room I made up for you. I put your other guns up there, too. Figured you'd wanna go shooting while you were here."

"Thank you," I said, looking down at the table. I didn't know what else to say.

"No sweat, kid," Hawk said after a moment. "You know you always got a place here. Now listen. I need to go water the horses. You can come help if you want, but you're probably tired."

"If it's okay, I'd like to go upstairs and lie down. It's been a long day."

"No problem," Hawk said, standing up. "Your room is first one on the right upstairs." I thanked Hawk again and made my way up to the room he'd prepared for me. I opened my duffel bag, found some comfortable clothes to sleep in, and crawled into bed. I was asleep in minutes.

It was dark when I awoke. I sat up in bed, sweat beading on my face. My heart was racing. I fumbled with the lamp next to the bed until I got it turned on. My eyes darted around the room. I was breathing hard. There was nothing there. I was safe in bed. Exhaling slowly, I rubbed my face with my hands. The clock said it was just after midnight. My mouth was so dry it felt like my tongue had swollen up. I climbed out of bed and headed down to the kitchen.

It was cool in Hawk's house as I padded down the stairs. I was only wearing a pair of shorts. It was quiet. Hawk was undoubtedly in bed already. I made my way into the kitchen but didn't turn on the light. I grabbed a cup and opened the fridge, pouring myself some water from the filtration pitcher.

I stood upright as a key hit the lock on the front door. I could hear the door swing open, then close again. It was then locked. I relaxed a bit. Hawk must've gone out late or something. No one breaking in for nefarious purposes would have a key and not even try to be quiet. I stepped away from the refrigerator, cup of water in hand, and stepped toward the door to the front room.

"Hawk?" I asked, squinting into the darkness. A moment later, someone appeared in the kitchen doorway and switched on the light. A woman stood not five feet from me with a blank look on her pretty face. She wore a short pink jumper, like a waitress uniform, and tennis shoes. She carried a purse under her arm.

Her eyes went wide when she saw me standing there in my shorts. It hit me then. I recognized her. It was Jillian Del Toro. *Jesus Christ. It can't be.*

I think she recognized me, too. Dropping her purse, her hand flew behind her back. Before I could say anything, she'd produced a Smith & Wesson M&P compact pistol and leveled it at my face. Her nametag said Peaches.

She sure as hell didn't *look* like a Peaches. She had an intense gaze; it was a mix of obvious fear and anger. I looked back down at the pistol in her hands. It was shaking slightly, but it was close enough that I could see the rifling in the barrel. It was a 9mm.

I dropped my water cup on the floor and slowly raised my hands. "Please," I said. I was very calm. "Put the gun down. I'm just as confused as you are. I'm not going to hurt you."

"You shut up!" she said fiercely. "I know why you're here!" Her grip on the pistol tightened.

"I'm getting a cup of water," I said, nodding to the puddle on the floor. "I'm standing here in my *shorts* for Christ sakes." *The Calm* was wavering as I became agitated.

"Shut up!" Jill shouted. "You're Dead Six! You're here to kill me!" I visibly halted when she said the words "Dead Six."

"Dead Six is done now. I barely got out alive."

"I know that! But what are you doing here?"

"I was *getting* a God damned cup of *water!*" I said, almost shouting now. "What do you think, I came to Nevada and infiltrated Hawk's house in my fucking underwear so I could kill you?"

"Just shut up!" Jill snarled. She shifted her weight forward slightly. Her pistol was in arm's reach. *Close enough.*

Moving quickly and following through, just like I'd been trained, my hand shot up and grabbed the pistol. I forced it upward, yanking both of her arms up with it. I was taller than Jill, and stronger. I twisted the pistol in her hands and slammed my other arm into her sternum. There was a chance she'd pull the trigger, but it wouldn't hit anything but the ceiling. The blow knocked her off balance. She stumbled backward and lost her grip on her gun.

I have to give her credit. She didn't stay down. She immediately got back up and came at me. In one smooth motion I shifted the pistol to my right hand, grasped the slide with my left, and racked it as I extended my arm. An unfired cartridge ejected and bounced off the floor. Jill froze as I pointed the S&W at the bridge of her nose. Her eyes were wide with terror, but she didn't blink and didn't cringe. *Ballsy.*

"Now that's *enough,*" I said firmly but calmly. I sidestepped to the left, shifting the pistol to my left hand then gripping it with both hands. "Just calm down, okay?"

"What the *hell* are you doing, boy?" Hawk's gravelly voice boomed. I froze, and my head snapped around. Hawk was standing in the other doorway to the kitchen with a Remington 870 shotgun in his hands.

"Hawk!" Jill cried. "He's from Dead Six! They found me!"

"Hawk," I said. "This is the girl I told you about! She was over in the Zoob! She shot me in the back!"

"You pointed a gun at my face and took me hostage!" Jill snapped back.

I was pissed off now. "Well, what the hell—"

"Both of you shut up!" Hawk said, lowering the shotgun. "Damn it, Val, you give that girl her gun back. Jill, you holster that gun and calm down." Giving Jill a dirty look, I dropped the magazine out of her gun, locked the slide back, and handed it to her. She snatched it out of my hand. I gave her the magazine a second later. She didn't reload it.

Hawk sighed. "Both of you relax. This is my fault. I guess I should've told you about each other. Val, I was gonna say something to you when you got up. You're both guests in my house, though. I expect you to behave yourselves. Now you damn kids go to bed. We'll straighten this all out in the morning." Hawk turned and left the kitchen, leaving Jill Del Toro and me alone. She folded her arms across her chest and looked at the floor. I shuffled my feet. Neither of us spoke until we heard the door to Hawk's room close.

Jill glared at me. "It's *your* fault."

Hawk roused me out of bed at six in the morning and told me to go feed the horses, reminding me that he wasn't running a bed-and-breakfast. Half an hour later I was in the barn, carrying big bales of hay from the loft out into the field. The horses were already happily munching on their grain in their stalls. I was going to spread the hay around outside to keep them busy while I got to cleaning. See, I had to shovel the horse shit after I fed the horses. Living on a ranch is a lot of fun, let me tell you.

I hauled another hay bale through the barn, this one for Hawk's ill-tempered stallion. I was wearing leather gloves. My .44 was holstered on my left hip, out of habit more than anything else. After everything that happened, I really didn't like going around unarmed.

Jill Del Toro was standing in the barn, dressed in jeans, a T-shirt, and work gloves when I came back in. She carried a pitchfork and a shovel in her hands.

"Hey," she said, sounding much more amicable than the night before.

"Mornin'," I said, nodding at her. "Hawk drag you out of bed too?"

"What? No, I worked swing shift last night. He lets me sleep in on my days off."

"Must be nice," I grumbled.

"Look," Jill said awkwardly, "I'm sorry about last night. You know, for trying to shoot you."

"Well . . . I'm sorry I hit you," I said.

"It's just that I saw you, and I remembered from before, when you grabbed me, you know, and I kind of freaked, and—"

I held up my hand. "Hey, it's cool. I know what it's like to be twitchy." We both fell silent for a few uncomfortable seconds.

Jill looked me in the eye. "Can I ask you something? How . . . *whoa*. Your *eyes* are different colors!"

I rolled my mismatched eyes and sighed.

"I'm sorry!" Jill insisted, embarrassed. "I've just never seen anyone like that before. I can't believe I didn't notice last night."

"What were you going to ask me?"

"Oh, right. How did you end up here? Where do you know Hawk from?"

"I was going to ask you the same thing," I said. "I know Hawk from way back. I used to work for him. Hell, my stuff is stored here. My Mustang is still in his garage. Unless he sold it. The question is, what the hell are *you* doing here?"

"We were in Zubara after that night. You know, when the fighting started. Lorenzo got hurt pretty bad dragging you out of there. He—"

I interrupted her. "Whoa, whoa, whoa. Stop. Hang on. Back up the truck. What the hell do you mean, *Lorenzo dragged me out of there*?"

"Oh . . . you don't know?"

"No, I don't know! The motherfucker showed up in my room, pulled a knife on me, gave me *this*," I snapped, pointing to the scar on my face, "and *this*," I added, indicating the scar on my arm, "and I still don't know what he was after. Now you're telling me he *rescued* me?"

"Hey!" Jill said. "Your friends broke his fingers. They were torturing him!"

"What the hell was he doing in our compound in the first place?"

Jill deflated a little. "That's, uh, that's a long story," she said.

"We've got a lot of shit to shovel," I suggested.

"Fair enough," Jill replied. We spent the next two hours doing various farm chores as Jill told me her story. She'd been an intern at the US Embassy when she had a run-in with Gordon Willis. Gordon had some embassy staff murdered. She went on the run, was kidnapped, and was eventually rescued by Lorenzo, in the very house where I'd blown Adar's head off. The whole thing made my head spin.

I told her parts of my own tale as well. She laughed nervously when I explained that Gordon had described her as a dangerous traitor.

"I'm sorry about Sarah," Jill said eventually.

"How did you know?"

"We had one of your radios for a while. and I was watching on camera when she . . .when it happened. Lorenzo has this little drone airplane."

I exhaled. "Thank you. I'm doing okay, all things considered. So . . . where is Lorenzo now?"

"Honestly?" Jill said. "I have no idea. I haven't tried to contact him. He could be anywhere."

Chapter 25: Undocumented

LORENZO
June 22

This part of the Red Sea was really more of a dirty blue.

The boat rocked in the mild waves, Saudi Arabia behind us and North Africa somewhere over the horizon. The air smelled of fish and diesel fuel. I leaned against the railing, contemplating our next move.

Reaper was sleeping in one of the passenger cabins. It had only been a couple of days since he'd been shot, and he was still looking haggard. My back still ached from the ricochet that I had picked up in the elevator, and the last member of my crew was dead. Right now I wanted to get as far away from this damnable place as possible. Our next stop would be Egypt. There was a safe house in Cairo that we could hole up in while we formulated a plan to deal with Big Eddie.

Eduard Santiago Montalban. Half brother to the billionaire businessman murdered recently in the Gulf. Raised in Hong Kong, educated at Eaton, and as far as the world knew a useless fop that lived off the family wealth. He was all over the high-society pages, philanthropist, humanitarian, playboy, all that bullshit.

In actuality, he was the one that took care of the dirty side of the Montalban family business: murder, extortion, bribery, money laundering, slave trading, you name it, Big Eddie was involved. All the years that I had worked for him, I would never have guessed who he was. At times, I'd thought that he was imaginary, a name put onto some cartel of powerful individuals. Surely, one man wouldn't be capable of that much evil.

Allowing me to find out his true identity would be the biggest, and last, mistake that Eddie would ever make.

We would arrange a handoff for the scarab to string him along, but I planned on getting to him first. He was so fixated on getting it that a preemptive strike would be the last thing that he'd expect.

And what was in there that made it so valuable? The metal was something hard and black that I couldn't recognize. The glowing amber liquid was a mystery. Nervous that I'd had it next to my skin for so long, I'd had Reaper check it with a Geiger counter. It wasn't radioactive, and he couldn't recognize it, so Reaper had hypothesized that perhaps the glow was some sort of bioluminescence. In other words, it might be alive.

Maybe it was some sort of bio-weapon? But its setting didn't make any sense for that. Reaper, being absurdly inquisitive, had wanted to crack it open so he could get a sample to test. I'd shot that down, because I was afraid that opening it would kill us all. I just wanted to get rid of it as fast as I could. Maybe I was psyching myself out, but it made me uncomfortable just looking at it. All that we knew for sure was that it was more valuable than all of the other treasures in the prince's vault and that Eddie was willing to kill crowds of people to get it.

My cell phone began to vibrate in my pocket, interrupting my thoughts of revenge. Glancing around, I made sure that there were no other passengers along the railing, just a couple of filthy seagulls. It was a forwarded voice mail from another one of my numbers. Suspicious, I punched in the security code. I did not give that phone number to very many people.

"You said not to use any names, so I hope you recognize my voice." It was Jill Del Toro. "I hope you guys are doing okay with that thing you were working on. The date's passed. I'm settled in pretty good here, thanks to you." I was embarrassed to find myself grinning stupidly, not the way a cold-blooded criminal was supposed to act, but it was good to hear the recording of her voice. "You said to contact you if I needed help. There is something going on, something related to what happened before, from when you found me. I don't know who else to turn to. Lo—" She caught herself then continued. "Please call me."

She rattled off a phone number and the message ended. I dialed the number; it had an American area code, but I didn't know which state it was for. An answering machine picked up.

"Hi, you've reached Peaches. Leave a message." It was Jill's voice; damn Reaper and his stupid stripper-name fake IDs.

"Got your message. I, uh . . ." What was I supposed to say? It wasn't like I didn't have more important things going on. Eddie needed to be dealt with. I had a mystery bug full of something glowing and apparently alive, and a crown prince who would have me fed to his tigers if he found out I'd been the one to steal it. My family was still in danger, and the only surviving member of my crew was healing from multiple gunshot wounds.

She had never even been a real member of my team. Like Carl said, she was just some stray that I had saved from Adar's goons. She had even turned her back and walked away, so as not to sully herself in my gritty illegal world. I was a hardened, professional criminal. I didn't have time for helping people out of sentimentality.

"I'm coming. Call me when you get this and let me know where to meet you." I folded the phone and stuck it back in my pocket. "Fuck!" I shouted. The seagulls scattered, squawking at my vehemence.

Screw it. I was running out of friends. I could arrange a meeting with Big Eddie in the States just as easy as I could meet him in Egypt.

Change of plans. I was going home.

LORENZO
Santa Vasquez, Mexico
June 24

The chubby man wiped his brow as he entered the little office. Massive sweat rings had pooled in his armpits. He'd been working outside on the tiny airport's asphalt runway, and it was over a hundred degrees. He dropped the bag containing his lunch on the desk and immediately turned on the oscillating fan, sticking his face directly in front of it. He never heard me rise from behind the filing cabinets.

I wrapped my arm around his throat, other hand clamping over his mouth, locking him right down. "Make a noise and I'll snap your neck," I whispered. He nodded slowly. "Good. Don't reach for the gun in your desk. I've already taken it. Go for the knife in your pocket and I kill you. Comprende?" He nodded again. I removed my hand slowly but kept up the pressure so he could barely breathe.

"What do you want?" he whispered, terrified.

I slowly reached down and lifted his lunch bag from the table, bringing it up to our faces, and smelled it. Ham, eggs, bacon, guacamole, jalapeños, on fresh baked bread, *oh yeah* . . . I hadn't eaten since the flight. I was starving. "I want your lunch. Dude, *Lomitos Argentinos*? This stuff is going to kill you. I see Juanita's still trying to fatten you up. It's working." I patted his gut.

He hesitated. It had been years. "*Lorenzo?*"

I let go of his throat. "What's up, Guillermo?"

He spun around, eyes widening in shock. "*Pendejo!* You scared the piss out of me!"

I put my finger in front of my lips, signaling the need for quiet. "I snuck in. I didn't want anybody else in your outfit to know I was here. What's up, man?" I grinned.

He crushed me in a hug. "You always were a scary bastard," he said as we clapped each other on the back. Guillermo let go and studied me. "But what're you doing here? I thought you guys were in Thailand? Where's Death Train? Where's Carl? The asshole still owes me money."

Guillermo Reyes and I went way back. I shook my head. "Big Eddie killed them."

"Oh, shit. Sorry, man," he said. "That sucks. They were good men, honorable men. I hadn't heard . . ." Realization dawned. "Hey, man, I don't do *nothing* with Big Eddie anymore. He's too crazy. The money's not worth it. That man gives me nightmares."

"I know," I said quickly. "I don't want you to get involved."

It was obvious that was a relief. "Well, thanks for sneaking in. Last thing I want is being seen with somebody Big Eddie's looking for. I like not getting my house burned down with me in it, know what I mean?"

"I need a favor."

Guillermo scowled. He knew exactly what kind of favor somebody like me probably needed. "I'm a legitimate businessman now."

"Legitimate my ass. That's why this dinky airstrip has fifty flights a day taking off? Sightseeing?"

He smiled; once a crook, always a crook. "Smuggling is a legitimate business. All right, I still owe you a favor."

Once upon a time—well, about eight years ago— Guillermo had pissed off a certain group of drug dealers. They'd decided that for his disrespect the lovely young Reyes family needed to die. But before that could happen, Carl, Train, and I had made all those bad men go quietly away forever. We'd staged our own little *Dia De Los Muertos*, only with real dead people, *and* kept their money. Good times.

"*A* favor? You owe me like five." He had three kids, so he knew exactly what I was talking about. "But I'm not picky. I just need intel. It's been a really long time, and I need to cross the border tonight." It would have been nice to fly directly into the states, but since I had no idea what the mystery item in my possession was, I had not wanted to try to bluff my way through US Customs. Those guys were actually really good at their jobs. The officials at the Mexico City airport were a lot easier to work with once you passed over the *mordida*. Reaper was still in Cairo recuperating. Once I had a clue where I was going, he would just fly directly there to meet me. Travel was much simpler when you weren't smuggling glowing beetle vials.

"Whoa. Lorenzo is going back to the States? Are you loco? You need a place to hide, I can help you. I've got a little place back in the mountains. Beautiful. You stay there as long as you want."

"No. I've got to do this. I just need to know where it's safe to cross." The last time I'd been here, Mexico still had a semi-functioning government. I didn't know what the border was like anymore. For all I knew, the Americans had actually secured it since then. "I only need to get into Arizona."

Guillermo plopped into his seat and opened his lunch. He pulled a giant knife from his pocket, flicked it open, and sliced his messy sandwich in two. He passed me the smaller side. "So, you were thinking that with a full-on revolution south of the border, your countrymen would actually be paying attention?" He laughed. "Man, you worry too much. Paying attention would cost money and be *racist*. Some movie stars said so. The military is for rent in this State. You got some extra money and I'll send you across with an army tank if you want."

So, just as lax as usual. *Figures.* "No tanks."

"Seriously, man. It's so open that it's getting bad for business. I'm a professional, I run a *clean* outfit, but now I've got to compete with every coked-out asshole who's just itching to shoot up innocent bystanders. And those UN *pinche* faggots—gotta bribe them more often than I did the old *Federales*. And you won't believe this. I've got rag-heads sneaking across the border to blow shit up. Hell, about once a week now I get some dude named Achmed, pretending to be Mexican, crossing the border with bombs or poison gas or some scary shit. You know me, I kill those *putas* on sight."

"That's mighty nice of you, Guillermo."

He snorted. "They start blowing up schools in Happytown, USA, and it turns out they crossed here, and then the US overreacts once the shit's already blown up, and it'll kill business for us regular guys. It'll go from one Border Patrol per hundred square miles to a thousand Navy SEALs. I know how you Americans do it. You love to lock the barn after all the horses are gone. It's getting bad lately. The world's getting crazier, I tell you."

It was kind of sad when smugglers were our first line of border security. The food was amazing. Juanita was still a great cook. "Got a map?"

Santa Vasquez *stank*.

The smell was a combination of chemicals, garbage, open sewer, and crowded humanity. I had been all over the Third World, and this town had to be in the middle of the list of olfactory offenders. It was worse than Afghanistan, where the stink of dried human waste was embedded into the dust, but it was far better than the shallow-grave smell of Bosnia back when everything fell apart there.

The town was on the other side of the sagebrush-covered hillside, but the prevailing winds still carried the funk toward the Arizona border. It was night and dark enough that I could barely make out the rest of the group stumbling northward. During the day illegals tended to walk in bunches, but at night they unconsciously strung out into a single-file line. I could hear the sloshing of the milk jugs of water that everyone else was carrying. The ground was rough, uneven, and strewn with trash.

I was dressed like the other border jumpers. Rough jeans, a button-down work shirt, and a ratty ball cap. I was unshaven and had not bathed since my flight had landed in Mexico City yesterday morning. I was traveling light, just a small pack and some water. The drug mules were the ones with the burlap forty-five-pound backpacks, and their tracks tended to leave deeper heel prints. Those were the ones that the Border Patrol paid extra attention to, and those boys knew how to track. Once I split off from the herd, I didn't want my footprints to stand out.

It was late June and hot, but my body was acclimatized to the Middle East. This was pleasant by comparison. We were 5,000 feet farther above sea level than I was used to, so I was a bit out of breath. The border was a hundred yards away, and Guillermo said that the terrain was rough enough and covered in ocotillo that it was a rare occurrence to have Border Patrol vehicles in the area. Since I wanted to be discreet, Guillermo had pointed me to this section. The path was through a rough, hilly area. If any of my fellow travelers got picked up by the USBP, they would be detained, given a Capri Sun drink and a picante-flavored cup of noodles, fingerprinted, and bussed back across the border. For me, I was armed, smuggling something priceless, and had no idea what kind of flags my fingerprints might raise in America, so better safe than sorry.

Jill had not called me back yet, and it was beginning to worry me. I had left a message with the Fat Man to tell Eddie that I would arrange a drop-off within the week. The last thing I wanted was for him to get jumpy. When Eddie gets jumpy, people get burned.

There was movement in the sagebrush ahead. Instinctively, I took a knee and crouched low. The other illegals—technically I suppose I was an illegal, too, even if I was an American citizen—kept walking. They were talking, laughing; a few had ear pieces in and were listening to radios or iPods. I had the impression that most of them had done this before. Pulling the night-vision monocular from a pocket, I pressed it to my eye and scanned the horizon.

Vehicles at the border. *Damn it, Guillermo.* Staying low, I moved off to the side. Thousands of people walk across this border every day, and I have to blunder into a section that was actually covered by *La Migra*. We were in a natural gully with rocky hills surrounding us. It looked like it would be one heck of a climb. I sighed. Apparently I would be taking the high road.

Twenty minutes of hard scrambling later, I was on the top of the rocky hillside. The terrain up here was horrible, but I was certain that I wouldn't run into any more inconveniences. Only a crazy person or somebody who really wanted to avoid getting spotted was going to take this path into Arizona.

Somebody was coming.

Give me a break. I settled myself into a depression in the rock beneath some prickly pear and scanned through my monocular. Three men were on the steep hillside above, moving through the shadows. They were dressed similar to me, each carrying a heavy pack, and were having a tough time moving through the thick brush and cacti. Probably drug runners. I stayed hidden. Most mules were unarmed, just regular Josés roped into carrying the packages in exchange for passage, but in every group there was usually one actual bad dude with a gun.

I watched them pass. Two of them had long tubes strapped to their packs. They paused just past me at the lip of the hill and examined the trucks parked below. One of them pointed and spoke. It wasn't in Spanish. My ears perked up. I recognized the language. *No way.* I crawled forward slightly, careful to not shift any of the rocks. Scorpions crawled under my body. The man said something else before turning toward the border and continuing on.

What the hell were Chechens doing crossing the American border?

Guillermo hadn't been kidding. It was getting crazy around here. I refocused the monocular and took a closer look. Those tubes looked suspicious.

Oh, wow.

I pulled my STI 9mm from my holster, the Silencerco suppressor from my pocket, and began screwing them together. *Not in my country, assholes.*

A few hours later, I stood inside a gas-station phone booth in a town north of Nogales, Arizona. It was close to three in the morning and the little desert town was utterly silent. A stray dog watched me from under the gas station's neon sign. Loud insects buzzed around the glass.

"Sheriff's Department."

"Listen to me very carefully," I said, adding a Mexican accent to my voice. "There are three dead men on the American side of the border, just north of Santa Vasquez."

"Okay, and who is this?" The deputy sounded almost bored. Apparently multiple dead bodies were not that strange of an occurrence on the border.

"I'm the man that killed them."

"Wait, what?" *That* got his attention.

"The men were crossing the border. They were Chechen terrorists." I was careful not to touch anything in the booth in a way that would leave fingerprints. My rough clothes were splattered with dried blood.

"Chechens, like from Chechnya?"

"Yes. Write this down." I rattled off the GPS coordinates. "That's where you'll find the bodies. There's a missile hidden under some rocks ten meters east of the bodies."

"A missile?"

"Look, I'm just a coyote," I lied, "but I don't want guys like that shooting down airliners, you know what I mean. I'm calling because one of them talked before he died. There will be a second group crossing the border in the same area just before dawn."

"Sir, I need—" I hung up the phone and quickly walked to the still running Ford Explorer. The last Chechen had talked all right, encouraged by some expedient use of my Greco knife. There had been a vehicle waiting for them, but I didn't feel the need to tell the deputy about where I had left the driver's body. Besides, I had needed a ride.

I had dealt with people like them before, bloodthirsty fanatics who just plain liked to kill innocent people. The average American had no idea what was waiting for them out in the world, and there was some serious badness crawling across the country's soft white underbelly. At first I had assumed that it was just random chance that had allowed me to bump into those men, but I had a sneaky suspicion that Guillermo might have put me on that particular path for a reason, and probably saved him some work, the sneaky bastard.

Warning the cops about the second group of Chechens would count as my good deed for the day. Never hurts to put a check in the positive-karma box. I wiped some of the dried gore from my hands with a rag as I drove north. That third terrorist had been pretty tough, but everybody talks eventually. In the back seat was the second portable Russian surface-to-air missile launcher. I figured it might come in handy.

Flagstaff was my next stop. If my attempt on Eddie failed, then I knew he would kill my family purely out of spite. They deserved a warning. And there was only one person I could think of who might be clever enough to reach them all without Eddie's goons finding out.

Too bad he was an FBI agent. I bet you thought *your* family reunions were awkward.

LORENZO
Flagstaff, Arizona
June 25, 2008

My brother's house was in the suburbs. It had been easy enough to find with the address written in Eddie's folder. The sun had been coming up by the time I found the place, so I had just done a quick drive-by. I had no way of knowing if or how Eddie was monitoring them, so I didn't want to risk a visit during the daytime. Plus, I looked like I was here to pick fruit, smelled horrible, and was still splattered with at least a pint of Chechen.

I checked into a cheap motel, cleaned up, shaved, and slept until sundown. My dreams were strange and featured those dancing hippos from the old Disney movie until they were violently torn apart by an alligator with an effeminate English accent. I woke in a foul mood. Jill still hadn't called back, and frankly that was really beginning to gnaw at me. I called in an update to Reaper before leaving for Bob's place. At least he was sounding healthier, eager for revenge, and was ready to fly out as soon as I needed him.

There was another Ford Explorer in the motel parking lot. Using my Leatherman, I swapped license plates then headed back to the suburbs.

Bob had a great security system. It took me almost three whole minutes to figure out how to circumvent it after I'd climbed over the back fence. Luckily he didn't have a dog. He was allergic to them.

It didn't seem right to break into my own brother's house, and it certainly wasn't the best way to make an impression, especially considering that I hadn't seen him for years and he had no idea what I actually did for a living. But I couldn't risk just knocking on the door in case Eddie was watching the place. The last thing I wanted to do was contact him at work while he was surrounded by other Feds. I've got an aversion to cops. Nothing personal, mind you, just that our philosophies on life tended to diverge rather abruptly.

It was nearing midnight as I crept through the house. There were kids' toys scattered across the carpet and dozens of pictures on the wall. The kitchen was empty, and there were crayon drawings held onto the fridge with magnets. It was a really nice house. Clean, organized, but with that little bit of chaos that healthy kids always managed to bring. It reminded me a bit of Gideon's house, and that thought brought back memories. Gideon Lorenzo had been a good man to take me in. Compared to how I'd grown up, their house had seemed so warm, and I never had to worry about being hit with randomly thrown beer bottles.

Suddenly the room was bathed in scalding light, blinding me. It had to be one of those eyeball-melting police flashlights. "Don't move!" a deep voice bellowed. It was a command voice that was used to being obeyed. I slowly raised my hands to the surrender position.

"It's me, Bob." Hands open, I turned toward the giant in the doorway. "Shoot me, and Mom will be pissed."

The brilliant light moved to the side, leaving white ghosts floating in my eyeballs. "Hector?"

It had been a long time since anybody had called me that.

Robert Lorenzo was big man, six and a half feet tall, broad and barrel-chested. He looked nothing like me at all, which wasn't a surprise, considering that I was a foster kid.

The Lorenzos were good people. I'd never really felt like I had fit in, no matter how hard I'd tried, but they had loved me as if I were one of them regardless. They were hard-working, honestly religious, salt-of-the-Earth decent folks. My real father had been a petty criminal, crackhead, piece of filth, and Gideon Lorenzo was the judge who had finally sent him away for murder.

Gideon had never confided in me the logic behind taking me in. I just remember him staring down at me from that tall judge's seat while I had been giving my eyewitness testimony against my real father. His kind eyes had filled with involuntary tears as I'd talked about how I'd watched my mother get her head kicked in, even after I had tried to defend her by stabbing my father with a fork. I had been twelve.

Four years. For four years I had lived with the Lorenzo family. Then something terrible had happened, popping the happy bubble where I'd briefly gotten to live like a normal person. I had violated Gideon's deathbed final wish, but my services had been needed to make things right, and I did what I had to do.

While in their care, I had never officially taken their last name. After I dropped off the grid, I'd lived under many different names, changing identities like clothing. Eventually I'd started going by Lorenzo. It had seemed like the thing to do at the time. It had seemed *right*. If only I had realized that it would eventually come back to haunt me.

"So, you want to tell me how you broke into my house?" Bob asked as he settled onto his couch. He put his bare feet up on the coffee table. His Remington 870 was leaning against the arm of the couch.

"Always right to the point with you, wasn't it?" I dodged. "Where's the wife and kids? How's Gwen?"

"Visiting her mom. You'll like her. She's nice. Now back to the B and E." Bob looked like Dad before he had died. The resemblance was almost eerie. The last few years had rendered him totally bald, but that wasn't a surprise, as he'd starting losing his hair at sixteen. "You could have knocked. I almost plugged you back there. I'm a light sleeper."

Real light, apparently. I had been in full ninja mode. "The door was open," I lied.

"No, it wasn't," Bob said with finality. "It was locked, and the alarm was armed. It's been forever since I've seen you, and you sneak into my house in the middle of the night. Why?"

I had to be careful here. He was my older brother, and he was damn smart. I had known him very well once, but we were almost strangers now. "I need your help."

"What's going on, man?" Just like his father, there was no way I was going to be able to lie to this man and get away with it. I just hoped that he wouldn't try to arrest me. That could get messy.

"I had to sneak in because there are people watching your house. You're in danger, the whole family is in danger, because of me, and I'm here to warn you."

Bob laughed. "You always were a hoot. No, serious, what's going on?" After a moment of studying my grim expression, he realized I was for real, and then there was a hint of anger in his voice. "What have you gotten into?"

The Lorenzos had always been a real law-and-order bunch, except for me, obviously. I leaned back on the comfortable couch and groaned. This wasn't going to be easy. "Do you know what I do for a living?"

"You work for some international-relations firm. That was what the last Christmas card said, which, by the way, is the only reason any of us even realized you were still alive. You've only visited Mom, what, once since you ran off and joined the Peace Corps." He said that with just a hint of disdain. Bob had joined the Army.

"About that . . ." We had been close once. He was only a couple of years older than me, and after Dad had died Bob had become the family rock, while I had run off. This was a lot more difficult than I had thought it would be. "I'm not a businessman. I was never in the Peace Corps. I think they're a bunch of hippies. Look . . . I'm . . . I'm a crook."

"Crook? Like a criminal?" The last little bit of a smile faded. His normally jovial face grew hard, and now he really reminded me of Dad. "What kind of crook?"

"A very good one. Ever hear of the Cape Town diamond-exchange robbery?" I asked. He slowly nodded. I was sure the FBI had passed around a memo about that one. It had been rather impressive. "That was me. Bangkok National. *Me*. Bahrain Museum of Antiquity. *Me*. Vladivostok gold-train heist, all me." Bob's eyes grew wide. Of course he had heard of those. They were some of the more infamous robberies of our generation. "After that, I decided I didn't like robbing normal people and I started to rob from other bad guys. Those jobs you probably haven't heard about, but I'm pretty good at this stuff."

"You can't be serious," he stated.

"I worked for a man called Big Eddie for a long time, the crime lord who has a piece of everything in Asia. I'm assuming the FBI's heard of him?"

"Of course. The organized-crime guys have a task force dedicated to just that group. Personally, I thought he was a fairy tale."

"Oh, he's real." I tossed the manila folder from Thailand on the coffee table between us. Bob picked it up and started to leaf through the family pictures. "He had one last job for me, and he gave me this to assure that I'd do it. I know he'll hurt every single person in there, and I need you to get to them first, as quiet as you can."

My brother crumpled the edges of the folder as he read. I could see the realization that I was telling the truth dawning on his face. "I can't believe this. This . . . this is nuts. Sure, you were always pushing the boundaries, petty theft, joyriding cars, stupid crap, but this?"

"Bob, I know this is a shock, but listen to me. You can't be obvious. Big Eddie will find out. You can't bring in the FBI. Eddie has men on the inside. He will find out. This man sits on Satan's right hand. You have no idea what he's capable of. I need you to help me stop him."

"I can't believe you're some sort of international super thief, I mean, come on man, you were such a . . ."

"Dork?" I offered. It was true. Bob had been the tough one.

"No offense, but heck, when we were kids, when I played football, you did *gymnastics*."

"It comes in handy. I'm a good second-story man."

"You were in the *drama* club. You were really good at it too, before you dropped out."

I shrugged. "Playing pretend comes in handy," I answered, my voice a nearly perfect impression of his own. I'd always had a gift for being someone else. Compared to some of the cons I had pulled off, sophomore-year *Hamlet* was a piece of cake. "Do you believe me?"

He rubbed his face in his hands. After a long pause, he looked me in the eye. "Yes. I can see it. You always were the crazy one." I could tell that this was breaking his heart. He had always looked out for me, like a good big brother. "Hector, you've got to come in with me. The FBI can protect you. *I* can protect you. You can testify against this Big Eddie. I can get you into the witness-protection program."

"Bob. This is bigger than that. Way bigger." I stood. "Please, just get everybody to safety. You don't have much time. And you've got to keep it low profile. Nothing official, because he *will* know. You're the only one that can do this. Eddie tried to kill me. He shot one of my friends and murdered the others. He cut one's *head* off. I've stalled him for now, but the man is a snake, and he'll bite soon. It's his nature."

My brother stood, too. He towered over me, and his face was dark, clouded with anger. The shotgun was still leaning against the couch.

"You gonna try to arrest me?" I asked. Bob was a good and honorable man, and I did not know what I would do if he tried. "If you do, then you're signing our family's death warrant. As soon as Eddie finds out I've made contact with you, they're all dead."

"What do you plan on doing?" Bob was seething.

"I'm going to kill Eddie first."

"You're a murderer, too?"

No point in beating around the bush. "Bob, I shot three Chechens and tortured a fourth one to death before I ate breakfast this morning. What do you think?" I answered, hard and low.

He was taken a back. "That was you? I saw the bulletin about the SAM and the bodies. ICE nailed some more coming over at dawn with missiles because of an anonymous tip. The report said that one of them had been cut to ribbons, bullets in the other one's heads, execution style. . . . I can't imagine my little brother doing that." Bob slowly sat back down. "What have you become?"

"I'm a monster," I answered truthfully. "But I'm still your brother. Protect them, Bob. It's up to you." I turned and walked for the back door. I'm sure this was a lot to take in.

"Hector."

I stopped, hand on the doorknob. He sounded broken. It tore my heart open. "Yeah, Bob?"

"Be careful, little bro."

"You, too," I answered as I slipped out the door and into the night. I had to pause to wipe my eyes before scaling the back fence.

Chapter 26: Quagmire

VALENTINE
Quagmire, Nevada
June 28
0500

The sun wouldn't be up for a while, but the little diner where Jill worked opened at five. The place opened at oh-dark-thirty so the local ranchers could get their breakfast and coffee. She was on early shift today and was probably getting ready for the early birds. At this hour, she'd be the only one there, doing both the cooking and the serving. The regular cooks and waitresses came in later in the morning.

I hadn't planned on being up that early, but I still had terrible nightmares sometimes. Once I woke up from one of those, I was up for the day. Hell, I didn't want to go back to sleep anyway. I was hungry, too, so off I went to the only place in town where I could get breakfast at that hour without cooking it myself.

A few days earlier, Hawk and I had pulled my Mustang out of his shed and dusted it off. He'd taken very good care of it. The oil had been changed, the tank was full, and the registration fee had been paid for me. I'd missed my car, and it was nice to have it back.

The diner Jill worked at was called Shifty's, which I thought was hilarious. The place had been a staple of Quagmire life for forty years. The food was good, too. I'd eaten here every time I'd returned to Quagmire over the past few years. It was a decent place for Jill to work while she tried to figure out how to start her life all over again.

Really, I was in the same situation. After being gone for months, I was back in the United States, home sweet home. Nothing had changed. The fall of Zubara had been pretty big news while it was happening, but the press had no idea there was direct American involvement. The only ones that even suspected that were conspiracy nuts like Roger Geonoy and the kooky guests on *From Sea to Shining Sea*. I began to wonder if any of their other stuff about aliens, ghosts, and demons was true, too.

Anyway, I was in an interesting situation. It was as if the last six of months of my life had never happened. Save for the scars on my body and the ache in my heart, it would've been easy to pretend that all was well and that everything was normal.

And let me tell you, it was tempting. Back at the Exodus base I had been so filled with rage that I was ready to track Gordon Willis down and murder him. That had been my primary motivation for returning home, after all. But now that I was here . . . well, let's just say that reality had sunk in a little bit.

Having a quiet life and working on Hawk's ranch had done me a lot of good. My mom used to say that taking care of animals, especially horses, was good for the soul. She was onto something, I think. Hawk wouldn't come out and say it, but I think he really enjoyed having Jill and me around. He was old enough to be our father, and had lived alone since his wife, Elaine, died.

Seeing Jill every day had been nice, too. The girl was an absolute sweetheart, and she was beautiful too. After losing Sarah, I was completely disinterested in any kind of romantic pursuits, but . . . well, Jill was easy on the eyes, especially in the little cutoffs and tank top she wore when working in the garden. If things had been different . . . But they weren't.

In any case, I wasn't ready for anything like that, and Jill was still going on and on about how dreamy Lorenzo was. I felt bad for the girl. She was young and, despite everything she'd been through, naïve. Lorenzo wasn't coming back for her, period, end of story. I don't care if he did save my life; it was plain to see what was going on. I just didn't have the heart to tell her. She'd figure it out eventually. Probably better that she came to the realization on her own.

The question remained, though: What in the hell was *I* supposed to do? Aside from Hawk and Jill, I didn't really have any friends. I had nowhere else to go. And what was I going to do, go find a job? I didn't have a fake ID or alternate passport or anything. For all I knew, the moment I popped up on the radar, Gordon Willis's organization would come swooping down in their stealthy helicopters and make me disappear into the night. I was scared to drive my own car anywhere beyond the bounds of Quagmire.

I had thousands of dollars stashed away, so I wasn't hurting for money at the moment. I wasn't about to try to access my old Las Vegas Federal Credit Union account, and I doubted I'd ever been paid a dime for my service in Zubara. But I still had access to my old offshore account with the Bank of Grand Cayman. As far as I knew, my former employers had never found out about it. They probably didn't look real hard, considering they were planning on killing me anyway.

But I couldn't stay in Quagmire forever. It was a small town in the middle of nowhere, which seems like a good place to hide, but it's really not. People noticed a new face in Quagmire, especially one as scarred up as mine. Sooner or later somebody would notice me, and being noticed could get me killed. Not just me, either, but Hawk and Jill also.

Besides, I wasn't about to just stay in Hawk's spare bedroom, mooching off his hospitality until my savings ran out. I was determined not to be a burden on him or put him at risk. I had to leave Quagmire, and soon. But where would I go? My original plan of hunting down Gordon Willis seemed, as Ling suggested it would, silly now. The injustice of what that man had done still burned a pit in my stomach, and I hated him all the more for being powerless to change it, but what could I do? Even if I could get to him without getting picked up, would killing him change anything?

Sighing, I shook my head. Five o'clock in the morning was no time to be making big life decisions, especially not on an empty stomach. I pulled into the empty parking lot of Shifty's and parked my Mustang. Jill liked to walk to work. It appeared I'd be her first customer.

The place was dark. *Weird*, I thought. *Where is she?* Jill should've been there for at least half an hour already, but the diner was still locked up. No one had been in.

Suddenly worried, I looked around the parking lot. Jill had left Hawk's house an hour ago. It didn't take that long to walk to the diner. I hadn't seen her anywhere along the way. It's hard to miss the hottest girl in town in a pink miniskirt jumper and white sneakers, after all.

I couldn't see anything out of the ordinary. I was so upset I was on the verge of panic. If somebody had just driven up and grabbed her on the way to work, how would we ever know? *Oh, God. Oh, God, no . . .*

Something caught my eye then. A faint glow in the darkness, coming from the weeds across the parking lot. It was only there for a moment, then disappeared. I broke out into a run, pulling a small flashlight out of my pocket as I did so. It had come from near the entrance to the parking lot. There were some scrubby little weeds near the edge of the sidewalk.

There. On the ground was Jill's cell phone. The screen had illuminated for a moment and I was lucky to have seen it. Nearby was her purse, its contents spilled out onto the ground. A little bit farther away from the sidewalk I found Jill's gun.

Picking up the little S&W compact, I checked the chamber and magazine. It hadn't been fired. She'd either drawn it and been disarmed or it had been found and tossed. Jill had been taken. There was no doubt about it. They'd snatched her off the side of the road. I lifted her phone, intending to call the sheriff. Jill had been kidnapped, and there wasn't any time to worry about that.

It hit me then. What if they were looking for me? What if they took her because they thought she could lead them to me? A knot formed in my stomach. It didn't make any sense, but what else could it be? Why would anyone kidnap a waitress in Quagmire freaking Nevada? It couldn't be a coincidence. I couldn't call the sheriff. They'd be waiting for me. But if I didn't call, how would I ever find Jill? I had to do something. They were going to hurt her, or kill her. *Damn it! What do I do?*

I noticed the screen on her phone then. It was open to her address book. There were only two entries, and one of them was Hawk. The other . . . *well, holy shit.*

The phone rang six times before it was answered. On the other end of the phone was a voice I'd not heard in a long time.

"Jill?" he said.

"Guess again, Lorenzo."

LORENZO
Somewhere in Arizona
June 28

I had just hung up on the Fat Man. The meeting had been arranged for a few days from now.

Reaper's snooping had shown that Eddie, like all good international playboys, had a penthouse in Vegas. I had arranged the handoff for some innocuous shopping center with plenty of eyewitnesses, just like they would have expected. My gut told me that though Eddie wouldn't dare show his face at the handoff, he wouldn't be able to wait to see his treasure. So it seemed logical that he would be staying at his local residence.

And the night before the handoff, I was going to break in and take care of business. The place wasn't in his name, rather owned by one of the Montalban family's shell corporations. Reaper, more dedicated than I had ever seen him, had been doing a lot of digging and had compiled quite the list of properties, from private islands to penthouse suites spanning the globe; Big Eddie certainly got around.

The Fat Man had sounded suspicious. They'd probably thought I would have still been somewhere in the eastern hemisphere. Screw them. Las Vegas seemed like as reasonable a place for a drop as any. I could have picked a hundred other cities in twenty countries and Eddie probably had a place there, too.

He wouldn't be expecting me to take the fight right to him. Reaper was en route, and the plan seemed to be coming together. Plotting revenge gave me a feeling of smug satisfaction.

I would be in Vegas before lunch, leaving me with plenty of time to scout the place, take care of some business, catch up on some sleep, and get some Thai food. There was this one little hole-in-the-wall place off the strip . . . My phone rang. I was expecting Reaper, but the caller ID was a surprise. I stared at it for a moment. I had arranged for the drop to be in Nevada once I had figured out that was the prefix from Jill's phone, but now with the handoff arranged . . . *She sure has lousy timing.*

I flipped the phone open. "Jill?" I asked.

"Guess again, Lorenzo."

It definitely wasn't Jill. The voice was familiar . . . from Zubara. *It can't be.* "Valentine?"

"Yeah."

It took me a long moment to wrap my brain around this. How had Dead Six found her? Valentine, the killer with the .44 Magnum, and he was only alive because of my stupidity. I should have killed him when I had the chance. "If you hurt her, I swear I'll—"

He cut me off. "Shut up. Listen to me."

"No, *you* listen to *me!* I'll cut your eyes out if you don't put her on," I shouted into the phone.

"Goddamn it, if you want that girl to live, *listen to me.*"

"What did you do with her?" I asked before he could say anything else.

"For Christ sakes, I didn't do anything with her. Somebody else did. They took her."

"*Who* did? Where?"

"I don't know. Who else have you pissed off?"

Answering that accurately would require a lot of time and thought. "Where was she taken?"

"Quagmire. It's in Nevada."

"I've never been there, but I know where it's at. I'm a few hours away," I said, stomping on the gas. The terrorists' Ford wasn't built for speed, but I would make it work. "What happened?"

"They grabbed her on the way to work. I was going to stop in and say hi, get some breakfast, but she never made it. I found her stuff on the ground in the parking lot."

"Wait, what are you talking about? What's Jill doing hanging around with *you*?" My hand tightened on the phone so hard I thought it was going to break.

"She was in Quagmire when I got there."

"Then what are *you* doing in Quagmire?"

"None of your goddamn business," Valentine said. "Try to keep up. I was in Quagmire. I met the girl there, your little sidekick that shot me in the back in the Zoob. Something happened. She was taken. I don't know who did it. I found her phone. I called you. Still with me?"

"Yes," I said, trying not to let my frustration bubble over into anger. "Could it have been Gordon? Jill told me about a run-in at the embassy with somebody named Gordon Willis." There was no response. "Valentine?" I wondered for a moment if the line had gone dead.

"Yeah, you're right. I thought they were looking for me. But I think they were looking for *her*. They're good at cleaning up the loose ends."

"You know this Gordon Willis?"

"Long story. Look, if they have her, they're going to make her disappear. We don't have any time."

"That's not going to happen. I'll be there in a few hours," I repeated.

"Can I ask you something?" Valentine said after a long pause.

"What? Go ahead."

"Is it true that you pulled me out after I went down? In the fort, I mean."

"Yeah, I did."

"Why did you do that?" he asked.

"I . . . I don't know. You don't sound very grateful."

"I'm *not*," he said harshly. "Call me when you get here."

The line went dead.

LORENZO
Quagmire, Nevada

Quagmire was a typical, pissant desert town. The only things that looked new were the McDonald's and the slot machines. Nothing interesting ever happened in towns like this. It wasn't the kind of place that attracted rogue government operators, that was for sure. This should have been a great place to disappear.

You would think.

Valentine had given me directions to a small ranch on the outskirts of town. Even in the middle of the day, the roads were mostly deserted. If this was a setup, I was walking right into it.

The house was far enough out of town and away from any neighbors that there could be a ton of gunfire and nobody would notice. It was rather isolated on its own gravel road, surrounded by barbed wire and trees. Some horses studied me stupidly. I hate horses.

The weight of the STI on my belt was comforting, but if this was a professional trap, it wouldn't do me a bit of good. Somebody would snipe me from the trees or a SWAT team would toss flash-bangs and then swarm around every corner. I walked up the porch, knocked, and waited. If I was the hitter in this situation, this is when I would just shoot them through the door.

There was a noise as the door was unlocked. Then it creaked open.

Valentine.

This was the first time I'd seen him in person without immediate violence. He was just over six foot. Dark hair, a face that made him look too young, muscular, but he really didn't look like much. Yet I had already gotten my ass kicked once by this guy, so I knew that looks could be deceiving. His face was still healing from where I had cut him, and that wasn't the only scar visible. Valentine looked older now than when I had met him before, tired and run down. Zubara had taken a lot from him. His eyes were different colors. I'd never noticed that before. It was weird. It made it a little unsettling to look him in the eye. It kind of pissed me off.

"Hey."

"Hey." He leaned his head out of the doorway and looked around the gravel driveway. I don't know what he was expecting to see. It wasn't like I would need to bring friends if I was going to waste him. Valentine regarded me warily, like most people would look at an unfamiliar dog. Finally he turned into the entry, nodding his head for me to follow.

The living room was vaguely rustic, with antlers mounted on the walls and a few pictures over the fireplace. It didn't feel like his place. It was an awkward moment. Neither one of us offered to shake hands. I stepped inside and he gestured toward a chair.

"No thanks. I'll stand." It was slower to draw from a hip holster while seated and I didn't trust him as far as I could throw him.

"Suit yourself." He closed the door.

"Anything new on Jill?"

"Nothing. There's not much to Quagmire, so she's probably not here. I don't know where they've taken her. We didn't get the authorities involved. Hawk called her boss at the diner and said she had to leave for a family emergency, so no one in town is suspicious."

"The cops can't do anything I can't," I said. The FBI handles all kidnapping cases, and I really didn't want *them* involved in this. Especially not my brother.

"Like I said, they must've grabbed her on the way to work. I found her purse, her phone, and her gun lying on the ground. She didn't get a shot off or anything. I have no idea who would've taken her."

"Maybe they were looking for *you*," I snapped. "What the hell are you doing here anyway?" It infuriated me that Jill might've gotten caught up in Valentine's mess. I swear this kid destroys and ruins everything he comes into contact with. He was the bane of my existence, and it was all I could do to not punch him in his stupid face then shoot him between his stupid mismatched eyes.

"Maybe they were looking for *you*," he retorted. "Or did it never occur to you that hanging out with a guy like you could be bad for your friends' health?"

My muscles tightened. My fists clenched. A vein bulged in my forehead. Valentine didn't know about Carl or Train, but that was about the worst possible thing he could've said to me. I was very close to pulling out my STI and putting a bullet in this asshole.

He must've read my body language. The expression on his face subtly changed. "Go ahead," he said, staring me down. "*Pull* it. You better be quick, motherfucker."

"You don't know when to quit, do you?" I growled, tensing up.

"Because you know what will really help you find Jill? Shooting *me*. Assuming you're faster than me, which you're not. And then if you do get her back alive, you can explain to her how you murdered me in a tantrum because I said something that made you mad. After she's spent days telling me what a great guy you are, I'm sure she'll understand."

I grudgingly had to admit to myself that he had a point. This pissing contest was getting us nowhere. Jill's life was in our hands. I exhaled heavily and tried to force myself to relax. Valentine did the same. "Sorry . . . I've been driving all day." I relented and sat in down in a chair. "Why did you call me, Valentine?"

"Jill's a nice girl. She told me her story, you know. She was doing fine until she got caught up in the crap that we got caught up in. You and I, and the people we associate with, came into that girl's life and screwed it up royally. And now, either because she knows me or because she knows you, her life is in danger. *Again*. She deserves better than that. I don't want to see anything happen to her. And I didn't know who else to call. What are the cops gonna do? The people that might be after us are more than the sheriff can handle. Also . . ." Valentine trailed off for a moment. "Jill told me you saved my life. There've been times when I wish you'd have just left me there, too. But debts have to be repaid all the same. We owe her a debt, too. We brought this on her. So you and I, we need to make this right." He was quiet for a moment. What he'd just told me had obviously been hard for him to say. "You know, I honestly don't know what she sees in you."

"Hell, me either," I said, but really I was just trying to be agreeable. I happen to think I'm a pretty amazing guy.

In all of my life, no matter how bad things got, I never once wished I was dead. My survival instinct is too strong. I know I'm not going to live forever, but damn if I'm not going to try. I don't give up. I don't quit. And I'd kind of assumed Valentine was much the same. I'd seen him in action, after all. He was a hardened killer, the man that had thwarted me at every turn, my *nemesis,* but all I saw was a broken young man who'd watched his girlfriend get shot to death right before his eyes. He couldn't have been much more than twenty-five, and he acted as if his life was over. They'd taken everything from him. That's when it hit me, slapped me right in the face. I finally understood why I had dragged him out of Fort Saradia.

I'd felt *sorry* for him.

I hadn't known that I was capable of pity. I shook my head, and then it was gone. Men like us didn't need pity, just a balancing of the scales. As far as I could see, what Valentine needed was a cleansing vengeance, but there wasn't time to ponder on his questionable mental state. We had work to do. "Do you know how they found her?"

"I don't know. She's been here longer than me. She works at a little diner in town called Shifty's, but lives under an assumed name, Peaches."

"Right."

"It seems we have a mutual friend here. Everyone in town thinks . . . well, thinks Jill is Hawk's illegitimate daughter that he was reunited with. Hawk didn't try to dispel the rumors. Thinking she was Hawk's daughter kept horny ranch hands from sniffing around, and it was better than the town thinking he'd shacked up with a woman young enough to be his daughter, I guess. Hawk's been letting me crash here, too."

Hawk? I looked around the living room. Suddenly everything seemed to fit. I knew this wasn't Valentine's house. It was *Hawk*'s. I knew that Hawk would take care of her when I sent her to him. I never imagined she'd end up living in his house.

"How do you know Hawk?" I asked. "And what are you doing living over his garage like the Fonz?"

"You making a scrapbook?" Valentine retorted. "That's none of your business. And no, he wouldn't tell me anything about you, either."

Of course. Hawk was a professional. "Let's keep it that way. Where is he?"

"He's out in town talking to some people, trying to find out if anyone saw anything. He'll be back soon. But money says she's long gone by now. I wish I had more to tell you."

"I've called in some help. My associates will be here soon." It sounded more important to say *associates* rather than lone techno-geek. "They're good at shaking the trees and seeing what falls out. Right now your buddy Gordon Willis is the only lead we've got. He's a federal employee of some kind, right? It's a start." There was the outside chance that Bob might know of him, too, but I didn't say that.

My phone rang. "Hang on." I was hoping that it would be Bob with good news about how he'd arranged to get the family to safety, but I didn't recognize the number.

"Mr. Lorenzo." The voice was electronically distorted, drastically deep.

"Yes?" My frown must have indicated to Valentine that something was up. He stood, looking nervous, and peeked through the blinds.

"We have your friend, Jill Del Toro. If you ever want to see her alive again, you will do exactly what I say."

"I'm listening," I replied calmly. Inside I was raging, wanting to kill, to murder, to drive my knife through someone's trachea and shower in the arterial spray. "What do you want?"

"You have two videos of Americans in Zubara. One video of two Americans executing a man. A second aerial video of a gun battle between Americans and the Zubaran army. You will deliver those to us. You will do so in person. If you do not, Miss Del Toro will die."

Videos? I hadn't even thought of those since getting the key back. As far as I was aware, Reaper had them on his laptop. Jill must have told Gordon's men about them while being interrogated. "Let me speak to Jill so I can know she's okay."

The line was silent for a few seconds. Then Jill's voice, desperate, "Lorenzo! It's a tra—" Then she was gone.

Of course it was a trap. Why else would they want me in person? I could easily have made copies. The videos were just an excuse. They wanted the witnesses dead. Back to the distorted voice; the speaker sounded vaguely demonic. "Where are you now?"

"Maine." My cell phone was untraceable.

"You have twenty-four hours to get to Nevada. We will contact you then."

"I want to see her in person or you don't get the videos."

"Of course." The line went dead. I resisted the urge to chuck the phone across the room.

Valentine scowled at me. "They'll be waiting for you. You know it's a trap, right?"

I nodded. "They won't expect *you*, though. Feel like making some trouble?"

Valentine actually grinned. It was an unpleasant, predatory expression, like a wolf eyeballing a rabbit. "I need to break in my rifle anyway."

"We need to make a plan."

"How about we drive there and shoot everybody?"

"Except for Jill," I corrected. "But that'll do." We were going to need a little more finesse than that, probably, but that was pretty much what it amounted to. Valentine held out one hand. I didn't trust him. I didn't like him. But I knew he could fight, and he was the best option Jill or I had right now.

We shook on it.

Chapter 27: Last of the Gunslingers

VALENTINE

Once again I was in the middle of somebody else's fight. The story of my life, right? Well, not so much this time. I had reason to believe that Gordon's group was behind the abduction. It wasn't really through any desire to repay Lorenzo for saving my life, because *fuck him*. But I liked Jill. And like I told Lorenzo, she didn't deserve to die because of her association with *us*.

As for Lorenzo . . . he was a strange one. He was constantly on edge, with a sort of angry nervous energy. I didn't trust him, though I really didn't think he'd try anything while Jill's life was on the line. Frankly I couldn't see how somebody with a heart of gold like her could fall for such a prick.

Lorenzo was hard to describe. He was short, six inches shorter than me at least. I couldn't tell what ethnicity he was. His skin was a pretty indistinct shade of brown that could've originated from dozens of countries. His black hair was cropped short, and he had some kind of permanent stubble thing happening on his chin. His eyes were like knives, and I swear he was always watching you.

He had gone into the other room to make a phone call, muttering about "gathering intel" or something. I listened to his half of the conversation through the door all the same. Some guy named Bob had been pissed about something but had known right away who Gordon was. The conversation had ended abruptly after that.

A couple hours later, Lorenzo's so-called associates arrived. His associates consisted of exactly one skinny Goth kid dressed all in black, carrying a laptop. He had a big hockey bag slung over his shoulder.

The kid was a trip. Black fatigue pants, combat boots, black Rob Zombie T-shirt, black trench coat, and his hair hanging in front of his eyes. He had piercings in his nose and ear. He had tattoos on what small amount of his pasty white skin could be seen.

He looked surprised when he noticed me sitting against the far wall.

"Who the hell are you?" he asked.

"Who the hell are *you*?" I retorted.

"Wait . . . it's you! You're that guy!"

Raising my eyebrows, I looked over at Lorenzo. *Seriously?* Lorenzo just shrugged.

"What are you doing here?" the kid asked.

"I'm going to help you get Jill back so I can get on with my life," I said, going back to my cleaning. On a table in front of me was my disassembled DSA FAL carbine. It had a short, sixteen-inch barrel, a folding stock, and rail hand guards. It was equipped with an ACOG scope and a weapon light. It was nearly identical to the carbine I'd carried while on Switchblade 4. Also on the table was my beloved .44, a S&W Performance Center Model 629 Classic. It had a five-inch heavy barrel, a smooth, stainless-steel cylinder, and a black Melonite finish on the rest of the gun. Lorenzo had given me a dirty look when I pulled it out. I just smiled at him in return.

Lorenzo addressed his associate. "Reaper, this is—"

"I know who he is," the kid interrupted. "Is he for real?"

"He's for real," Lorenzo replied.

Reaper, I guess his name was, stared at me. "Dude, what's wrong with your eyes? They're like totally different colors. That's fucked up."

Lorenzo ignored him. "Let's get started. How are we gonna do this?"

"I'm still on board with the 'go in and kill everybody' plan," I said. "Or did you get enough information to make a better plan than that?"

"No." Lorenzo frowned. "We need to find Jill first. We still need more information. Their *meet* will be a turkey shoot. I called somebody earlier who might know. He's working on it now." Reaper raised an eyebrow, but Lorenzo didn't elaborate about his mysterious phone call.

"I don't think we have a lot of time," I said. "We don't know what we don't know. We'll just have to go in and play it by ear."

"Not really my style," Lorenzo said.

"Mine, either," I confessed. "But nobody ever tells me what the hell is going on, so I just roll with it. You guys got weapons?" If they didn't, Hawk sure had a basement full of them.

"Hells *yeah*, we got weapons!" Reaper said. He picked up the hockey bag and dumped it out onto a table. Lorenzo rolled his eyes as weapons, magazines, radios, body armor, and night-vision equipment came clattering out of the bag, landing in a heap on the table.

So *this* was the crack team that had managed to track down Dead Six and infiltrate our compound. I shook my head and went back to my cleaning.

Reaper handed a carbine to Lorenzo, who proceeded to check it. Some kind of short, select-fire AR-15, with a twelve-inch barrel and a suppressor. Reaper pulled from the bag a Glock 17. He inserted a magazine, chambered a round, then stuck the pistol in a shoulder holster under his trench coat. On his belt he had more magazines. He then picked up what I assumed was his primary weapon.

"Benelli M1," Reaper said proudly as he started stuffing 12-gauge shells into every available pocket. "Semi-auto, short barrel, badass all the way."

"That's actually a Benelli *M2*," I corrected. Reaper frowned. I wondered how well Reaper could use his shotgun, though. He looked like an extra from *The Matrix*. Reassembling my rifle, I watched the two of them get suited up. I could tell they'd been working together since . . . well, probably since that kid graduated from high school, which couldn't have been all that long ago. Still, for old friends, they didn't talk much. It might've been because of my presence, but then, professional thieves probably have some weird interpersonal dynamics going on.

Like I've got any room to talk, right?

Hawk came home while we were still playing dress up. He scowled first at the strangeness that was Reaper, then at me, then finally gave Lorenzo a silent nod. "Been a long time."

"Hawk," Lorenzo responded uncomfortably.

The two stayed, exchanging a look that I couldn't decipher. There was a lot of history there, and I couldn't tell if they were friends or enemies or maybe somehow both. Finally, Hawk spoke. "No sign of the girl. No one in town knows anything."

"I guess we keep waiting," I said.

Lorenzo reached into his pocket as his phone vibrated. "Yeah?" He listened for at least a minute straight. "Okay, I got it. Thanks. I'll be in touch."

Hanging up the phone, he looked at me.

"What's the word?" I asked, fiddling with my thigh holster like a woman adjusting a stocking.

"Our next stop is a closed rest stop down the highway. Out past it is an abandoned prison work camp. That's where they're holding her."

"You're sure of this? Can your friend be trusted?"

"Oh, I'm sure. He's like a brother to me."

LORENZO

The four of us were still in Hawk's house, readying equipment. We would be leaving in a few minutes. At one point I caught Hawk studying me. He motioned for me to step aside to speak. I stopped loading magazines long enough to follow. He had aged a lot since I had seen him last. I knew Hawk was at least a decade older than I was, and there had apparently been some hard years in there. His hair was grayer, his face lined and creased by the sun and wind of several continents, and he'd picked up a limp at some point.

When we were out of earshot, Hawk began to speak. "You know, I thought you were dead. Everybody from the old crew thought for sure those Cubans had got you in Sweothi City."

"It was better that way," I answered. "Some of us didn't part on the best of terms. I figured it would be easier for everybody if Decker assumed I was dead."

Hawk nodded sagely. "That was probably smart. Adrian wasn't the kind of man that I'd want holding a grudge against me, so I suppose it was for the best. Well, I was glad to hear from you. I always hated losing men. I just wished you would have called sooner, because that's one less thing I would have had gnawing at me, Ozzie."

It had been a long time since I had gone by that name, just one of many in a long line of aliases. "I go by Lorenzo now."

"That's what Jill told me. That girl wouldn't shut up about you. She's got quite the fondness for you. She talked a lot, but I'll admit, it was nice having a young lady around. You've changed more than your name, *Lorenzo*. You're a different man than you were back in Africa."

"What makes you say that?" I asked slowly.

"The man I knew back then was a stone-cold killer who only thought about himself and back-stabbed anybody who got in his way, unless you just happened to somehow become one of his friends, and he didn't have hardly any of those. A man so twisted up inside and scary driven that it even got to worrying somebody like Decker. Why do I think you changed? Because for a woman that good to take a liking to you, you're either a better man than I remember, or you're a whole lot better con." The old mercenary gave me the smallest bit of a grin. "And Val might not think so yet, but you did the right thing helping him. That boy's like a son to me. Don't you tell him I said that."

"You don't have to come with us, Hawk."

He was solemn. "True. I don't. I'm retired. I've got a nice place, just how I like it. Comfortable, I suppose. But you know, I think I took a liking to that girl too. Hell, Val and that little lady damn near killed each other in my kitchen when he first got here. Had to separate 'em like a couple of squawkin' kids." Hawk let out a raspy laugh. "He's sure got a soft spot for the females. And they're about the same age. They got along after a while. Gave her someone else to blab about you to. I was getting tired of it."

I laughed along with him. We'd overthrown a country together once. Hawk was the last of the gunslingers, and there was nobody alive I'd rather have at our side.

Valentine appeared in the doorway. "It's time." He was dropping rounds into his revolver and snapped the cylinder closed. Well, maybe Hawk wasn't the *last* of the gunslingers.

VALENTINE

It was a long drive out of Quagmire to the rest stop, following a lonely two-lane highway with sparse traffic. We were far away from the nearest interstate, and there wasn't much going on out here. The rest stop itself was closed, but you could still pull off into the parking lot. Sitting in that parking lot was a nondescript black Suburban. I watched Lorenzo get out of his car, and I could tell he was surprised.

Anxious, I got out myself, my hand hovering over my pistol. All four of us had on body armor and other assorted battle rattle. I hoped like hell it wasn't a cop. At best, he'd think we were a bunch of militia nuts or mall ninjas. Or maybe we could pass ourselves off as airsofters. Anyway, I doubted most militia nuts were nearly as armed and dangerous as we were.

From out of the Suburban stepped a big guy, tall, barrel-chested, and muscular. He and Lorenzo were exchanging words as I approached, and the bald man seemed none too concerned that Lorenzo was dressed in full tac gear. I could tell they knew each other. Was this the "Bob" guy Lorenzo had been talking to on the phone? Why would he be here?

That's when I noticed the government plates on the Suburban. "Well, fuck me," I said to myself. There were Feds here. Lorenzo had called a Federal Agent. Was this a setup? Had this entire thing been some overcomplicated scheme to turn me over to the government? It didn't make any sense. My mind raced. Adrenaline surged.

"Lorenzo, you need to tell me what the hell is going on here," I said calmly. My right hand had reflexively found its way to my chest, resting on my plate carrier. My left hand was on the butt of my .44. "Why is there a Fed here?"

"No! It's cool! It's cool!" he said excitedly. "This is my brother, Bob. He's—"

I unsnapped the retention device on my thigh holster.

"Listen to me!" Lorenzo insisted. "It's not like that. He's my *brother*. He wasn't supposed to *be* here. He's supposed to be getting his *family* to *safety*!" Lorenzo glared at the other man.

"So," I said, *Calm* wavering as I grew angry, "you called a *Fed*. Your brother the *Fed*. You idiot! Why in the hell didn't you just have me call the cops if you wanted the Feds involved? Jesus, why don't we just the ATF and the Secret fucking Service while you're we're it! Hell, we can get the DEA and the Coast Guard in on it, too, and have a giant fucking federal law-enforcement jamboree!"

"Look, kid," the big man said, "I don't know who you are and I don't care. I'm here to help my brother get his girlfriend back."

"She's not my girlfriend!" Lorenzo sputtered. The big man grinned. I relaxed slightly. Though they didn't look anything alike, they sure acted like brothers.

"This is Bob," Lorenzo sighed "Bob, this is—"

"Don't you *dare* tell him my name!" I yelled, wheeling around.

Lorenzo laughed. "I'm just kidding, relax."

It was going to be a long night.

LORENZO

Valentine stomped away, muttering and swearing. I turned back to Bob and whispered, "What're you doing here?"

"I've got a contact in Vegas I was going to see. Let's just say he's *outside* my chain of command, but he's really good at hiding people. Don't worry. I've got things moving to protect everyone from your boss." My giant of a brother nodded after Valentine. "Your friend seems a little tense."

"He's wound kind of tight. But back to the question, what are you doing here? What about the family?"

"The family will be fine. I've put some things into motion. You should have come to me sooner." Bob shaded his eyes and scanned the horizon. "Look, Hector, this Gordon Willis you asked me about, he's not just a low-level chump. He's more important than that. I don't think you realize just who he works for, but it's bigger than you can imagine. If he has your friend, she's in big trouble."

"You can't do this, you're the law. You're a *cop!*"

"I won't be for long if anybody ever finds out about this," he answered. "Maybe we can share a cell."

"But these are *your* people."

He raised his voice. "These are not *my* people. My people take an oath to defend the Constitution, and I'm sick of watching men like Willis shred it. People like him work in a different kind of government than the one I signed on to. Black, secret, unaccountable. We're not even supposed to ask questions about his operation. He's had suspects taken in, no evidence, no investigation, no trial, and they just disappear into thin air, forever. These aren't even bad guys they're rolling up. They're regular folks who've asked too many questions about the wrong powerful people."

This was kind of a scary paradigm shift. Bob had always been the good one and I had been the bad one. *Simple.* "But you've always been so . . . law-abiding."

"There's a higher law, and it's time that these men had to answer to it." Bob was truly angry, red-faced and nostrils flaring, like the very idea of Gordon's outfit offended him to his core. "I'll take the risk."

"You're familiar with them?"

"You have no idea," Bob stated coldly. "Let's just say that you don't know as much about me as you think you do and leave it at that. I can't let you go in there with just these guys." He gestured at the other three. "Who are they, anyway?"

"You can call the big kid *Nightcrawler* since he's so worried about me telling you his name. The old guy is Hawk. The other kid goes by Reaper."

"Okay, then I'm Colossus and you can be Wolverine. Doesn't anybody have a normal name in your business?"

"Actually, I go by Lorenzo," I responded, slightly embarrassed.

Bob just stared at me. "Seriously? Wow, man, that's *devious*. And what part came as a surprise when Big Eddie found his way past your masterful secret identity? You were only *raised* by Lorenzos."

Reaper walked up. "If we've all got superhero names, then Jill should be Aquaman since she's been kidnapped twice." I just looked at him like he was stupid. "What? Didn't you ever watch *Super Friends*? Aquaman . . . you know, always got captured? Never mind." Reaper wandered off.

"*Super Friends* was off the air before that kid was born," Bob said.

"I know, but he spends a lot of time on the Internet."

"You guys done screwing around?" Valentine growled as he approached. "Let's get going. We're kind of conspicuous hanging around in all of this crap," he said, indicating the pouch-laden plate carrier and battle belt he wore.

He was right. We needed to get going. "We're not here to arrest them," I warned Bob.

My brother shook his head sadly. "Willis's men aren't the type you can arrest. They're a bunch of professional killers. Castoffs who've gotten kicked out of every reputable organization there is because they're too violent, too crazy, or too corrupt. Operations like his attract them like flies."

"How do you know all this?" Hawk asked suspiciously. Switchblade hadn't always been a respectable mercenary company, so Hawk had developed an appropriate paranoia about the law.

Bob shrugged. "A man has to have a hobby. Mine is collecting trivia about scumbags." My brother was being evasive. Somehow he knew exactly who Gordon Willis was, knew something about his organization, and apparently hated them with a passion. "The old work-camp is over that rise. We used to use it to hole up Mafioso witnesses out of Vegas. Word is that Willis's men are using it for something now,"

"Let's get these cars hidden, then sneak up on the camp and see if we can spot Jill," I suggested, hefting my AR-15. "If we're lucky, maybe we can get her out with minimal shooting."

"I wouldn't bet on that." Bob turned, opened the back of his Suburban, and pulled out a long black Remington 700 sniper rifle, with a suppressor, bipod, and US Optics scope. He worked the bolt and chambered a round. He put the heavy barreled rifle over one shoulder. Bob almost seemed to be looking forward to this. Maybe I *didn't* know him as well as I thought I did. "When the shooting starts, take them hard and fast."

"That's what *she* said!" Reaper quipped.

"You. Stop talking," Valentine ordered.

Reaper grinned, gesturing with his stubby shotgun. "Then let's go." The bravado was forced. The kid was tough, but he wasn't a warrior like the rest of us, but God bless his techno-geek soul, he was ready. "Let's smoke these fags."

Hawk adjusted his old South African army vest. "Yep." Then he spat on the ground.

Valentine raised an eyebrow. "Smoke these fags?" he asked, looking at me incredulously. "What have you been *teaching* this kid?" I held up my hands in surrender. A general has to fight with the army he's got.

The five of us climbed the sagebrush-and-scrub-tree hill. The sun was rapidly setting. I suggested we track farther to one side so that we could attack out of the sun. Valentine didn't seem to care one way or the other, Bob and Hawk thought it was a good idea, and Reaper was used to following my orders.

We picked our frequencies and checked the radios on the walk in, and they worked fine. We had no plan and no intel. Our group had never worked together before, and there wasn't a lot of trust.

"So why do you guys use those old Belgian rifles?" Reaper asked Hawk and Valentine at one point, displaying his ignorance. "Those are the same kind as those rusty poacher guns from all over Africa, right? Why don't you get something *new*?"

Hawk grunted. "They're all over Africa because they still work, kid. Besides, you can dress 'em up if you want. Look at his," he said, indicating Valentine's railed-up FAL. "You can bolt ten pounds of crap on it if you want." Valentine's rifle was fitted with a Tijicon scope and had a flashlight bolted to the hand guards. It looked heavy, but he didn't seem to mind. "And it's at least a manly thirty caliber, unlike Lorenzo's pussy twenty-two."

I paid Hawk's opinions on terminal ballistics no mind. I'd lost track of how many people I'd killed with a short-barreled 5.56 over the years. I preferred lots of little bullets to a few big ones, but then again, anybody worth shooting once was worth shooting five to seven times.

"M-16s are poodle shooters," Hawk said. "That's all they're good for."

"I'm pretty good with a FAL," Valentine answered Reaper, not looking up from the trail through the sagebrush.

"How good is pretty good?" Reaper asked. The kid just didn't know when to quit.

"Look," Valentine said levelly, pointing the knife-edge of his hand at Reaper. "This isn't a *game*, okay? You need to focus, or you're going to get yourself *killed*. Now either lock it up or go wait in the car!"

Reaper seemed taken aback by Valentine's harsh words. "Okay, okay! Sorry. I miss a lot. That's why Lorenzo makes me use the shotgun."

"Super," Valentine muttered. "You know, we really ought to be quiet."

"Kid's right. Quiet down. They might have sentries posted at the top of the hill," Hawk suggested.

"They won't," Bob replied. "They've been operating above the law so long, they think they're untouchable. The idea of us coming to them will never even enter their minds."

"I hope you're right," Hawk muttered.

After half an hour of walking, we hunkered down in the rocks overlooking the old prison work camp. It looked like a ghost town out of an old western movie. There were several wooden buildings, in two horizontal rows heading away from us, paint long since peeled, signs long since faded. One larger building was directly below us, newer, built out of cinder blocks; it looked like it had been a truck stop or some sort of garage back in the days before the freeway bypassed this little settlement. Fence posts stuck out of the ground like random teeth in a broken jaw, the barbed wire mostly rusted away.

There were several vehicles parked on the broken asphalt around the garage, new vehicles, black sedans, a Chevy passenger van, and another G-ride Suburban. There were a couple of men standing around the cars, smoking, talking, long guns visible slung from their backs.

"Damn, there's a lot of them," I said.

Bob extended the bipod legs on his sniper rifle and hunkered down, scanning through his scope. "I've got three in the parking lot. At least one moving inside the garage." After a moment he stopped, then cranked up the magnification. "Hector, take a look at the window on the left."

"Hector?" Reaper laughed. "Your real name is Hector?"

"Shut it . . . *Skyler*," I answered. Reaper was immediately silent. Valentine snorted as he tried to suppress a laugh.

"Yeah? Well, what the fuck kind of name is *Nightcrawler*?" Reaper asked defensively.

"It's French," he replied, looking through the scope on his rifle. He then turned to my teammate. "You know that's not actually my name, right? Just like you, Reaper isn't your real name. *Skyler* is your real name, and I think it's pretty." Valentine cracked a smile again.

I shushed Reaper before he could retort. Bob moved aside and I got behind the Remington. It took a moment to find the right window on 14X magnification. The glass was gray with filth and hard to see through. "That's her." Jill was slumped in a chair, long black hair obscuring her face. Seeing her there filled me with fresh anger.

The terrain leading up to that window was rough enough that it gave me an idea. I didn't want to endanger the lives of these men any more than I had to. I moved into a crouch and examined each of them in the fading light. "Okay. Here's the plan. I'll sneak up on that building, break in, and secure Jill. If everything works out, I can get her out of there before they ever even know we were here."

"That's just stupid," Bob said. "There's no way you could sneak in there under their noses."

Reaper just looked at him and grinned. "Dude, you have *no* idea. Your brother could steal cookies from the Keebler elves."

Hawk reached over and tapped Valentine on the arm, gesturing down the hillside. "Check out that ravine," he said. He'd always had a good eye for terrain.

Valentine nodded. "While you're crawling through the weeds, we'll take Marilyn Manson here and head down that way. It'll put us closer so we can back you up if this all goes to shit." He looked to Bob. "You good enough with that rifle to give us some cover?"

My brother nodded. Before I had dropped off the grid, Bob had already been a champion rifle competitor. When we were teenagers, I had spent my free time boosting cars, while he had shot coyotes for the local farmers. Bob was better than me at most things, and shooting was probably toward the top of that list, and that was before he had joined the Army and become some sort of Green Beret or something.

"He'll do fine. We all will." This was it. This wasn't a heist, it wasn't a job. These men were here to help me. This was a rescue mission. I'd led many crews, but usually for money. I didn't know how to motivate people with pure intentions. Awkwardly, I put my hand out, palm down. "Thanks, guys."

Reaper enthusiastically put his on top of mine. "Anytime, chief!"

It took a moment before Bob followed suit. "No problem, bro."

Valentine looked at us incredulously. "Are you guys for real?"

"I'm not really good at saying thank you, okay?"

Valentine glanced over at Hawk, who just shrugged, then back at us. "You guys are so *gay.*"

Reaper yanked his hand back, embarrassed. Okay, so maybe it was corny. I took one last look at my friends—and Valentine—nodded, and disappeared into the weeds.

Chapter 28: The Calm

VALENTINE

Lorenzo's little buddy tagged along as Hawk and I made our way down the ravine, practically crawling along as we went. There were several cars parked outside of the building that Jill was being held in, and there were armed men standing watch outside. They didn't seem particularly alert, but it wasn't quite dark yet and I didn't want to blow our cover.

I was most worried about them spotting Reaper. Where Hawk and I were dressed in earth tones and flat colors, Reaper was dressed entirely in black. Black sticks out pretty clearly against a dusty brown hillside in the Nevada desert. Worse, the kid just didn't know how to move. We had to crawl along more slowly than we would have otherwise, making sure Reaper utilized available cover and concealment.

Lorenzo, on the other hand, moved like a ghost. I tried to track him as he crept down the hill parallel to us, but quickly lost sight of him in the sage. Grudgingly impressed, I had little doubt Lorenzo would make it all the way down without being spotted.

LORENZO

There was probably only a few minutes of weak daylight left coming over the hills by the time I crept up on the cinder-block wall. My load-bearing equipment was coated in dirt, twigs, and dead sage. I hadn't been seen.

"Looking good," Bob's voice said in my ear. *"Guards are leaning on the cars out front. I don't see any movement in the back room. There are a few men inside the next room."*

Crouching below the window, I cradled my nose-heavy AR in my strong hand and reached up and tested the window. It was the multi-paned, hinged type. It moved slightly. It was unlocked. Just then my phone began to vibrate. I pulled it out of my pocket, glanced both ways, still clear, and flipped it open. "Hello?" I whispered.

"*Mr. Lorenzo.*" It was the digitally altered voice. I could hear the real voice through another broken window fifteen feet away. "*Where are you?*"

"I'm going through Las Vegas now," I whispered. "Bad reception here."

"*You will proceed to Quagmire, Nevada, and wait for further instructions.*" The normal human voice came through the window a split second before the distorted voice.

"Sorry, you're breaking up." I closed the phone and put it back in my pocket.

"Lost him. He says he's in Vegas," the voice said. "Send the strike team to Quagmire."

"Should we take the girl, sir? He said he wanted to see her alive."

"They all say that. Keep her alive long enough to talk on the phone if we need her. Then put a bullet in her. Remember, we want this Lorenzo alive. Eddie won't give us anything for him dead."

Eddie? How could Gordon the government guy be involved with Big Eddie? This didn't make any sense. Valentine must have picked that up from my microphone. "*I recognize that voice. Gordon's here. You don't touch him. He's mine.*"

"Let me get Jill first. Then you can go on a killing spree," I whispered.

"*A bunch of men in SWAT gear are loading into the passenger van,*" Bob noted calmly. There was the sound of a door sliding shut, and then a large engine revving. They were going to set up an ambush for nobody. I crouched lower as the headlights briefly swung past the cinder-block wall.

This was as good as it was going to get. "I'm going in." I sprung up and took a quick look through the dirty window. Jill was still slumped in a chair. There was nobody else in the room. The room was filled with old trash, rusted metal, and broken bits of wood. Thick spiderwebs clouded the corners. I pushed the heavy panes open slowly, rust binding in the hinge, begging to let out a screech. I gritted my teeth, pushing, praying for silence. Finally it was open wide enough to scramble through.

The door to the back room opened. I slid back down the outside wall. A man was coming into the room. He was wearing a suit, and a cigarette dangled from his lips. He was small, weasel-like, and had an MP5 slung over one shoulder. "Hey, baby. The boss man says we don't need you much longer."

Jill raised her head for the first time. There was duct-tape over her mouth. Having held her against her will once myself, I could understand the need for the tape. She struggled against the chair. The fierce anger in her eyes was very familiar. The man closed the door behind him. "See, the way I figure it, I'm your only hope right now. You do me a little favor, and maybe I do you a little favor, know what I mean?" If he was any more of a slimeball he'd be leaving a trail.

The man leaned the MP5 against the wall. He took his suit coat off, threw it on top of the gun, and began to loosen his tie. "You know you want it anyway, baby. Make this good for me, and I can talk the boss into letting you go." Jill just glared at him.

I found the small dowels in my pocket, palmed them in one hand, then slowly put my hands on the windowsill and began to lever myself through as silently as possible. If I could take this guy out quietly, we still had a chance.

The man had his back to me, distracted as he ran one hand through Jill's hair. She jerked her head away. "Fine, you wanna be a bitch, whatever. I like it when they fight." He laughed.

What happened next was a surprise. Jill's hands came around in a blur, bloody tape still tied around her wrists. She must have been working those against the back of the chair for hours. She slugged him right in the throat. He made a terrible *gahhwk* noise and stumbled. Then Jill stuck one thumb into his eye and locked the other hand around his larynx. The man started to scream, but she cranked down on his throat and choked it off. Her knee found his crotch, so violently hard that I cringed.

He punched her in the side, she cranked down harder, crushing his windpipe, forcing him to his knees. I pushed myself through the window, landing on my hands and rolling. The would-be rapist was on his back now, with Jill bearing down on his throat with both hands. He grabbed her by her hair and jerked her down, but she kept cranking on his neck.

The door opened. I stepped behind it without thinking, a dowel in each hand. "Davis, what the hell are you doing in here?" the second man asked. He stepped into the dark, his imagination filling in the blanks about the struggle before him, drawing all the wrong conclusions. "Can't you just keep it in your—" I kicked the door closed after he stepped through, the length of piano wire stretched between the two dowels coming down over his head. I crossed my arms and tugged with all of my strength.

He never knew what hit him. The second man struggled, leaning forward I followed, all my weight dragging the wire inexorably through his flesh. The wire grated against vertebra in a matter of seconds, and we both fell to the ground in a spreading puddle of red. His head was barely attached.

I rolled off the twitching body and moved to assist Jill, but she didn't need any help. She leaned back, shaking. The man's eyes stared blankly at the ceiling, his tongue almost bit off between his teeth. Jill stood, angrily ripped the tape from her face, and kicked the body once.

"Jill? Are you okay?" I whispered, the sound of conversation barely audible on the other side of the door. The rest of Gordon's men hadn't heard. She fell into my arms and sobbed. "It's okay. I've got you."

"You came for me." She was trembling. "I thought I was dead. . . . I've never killed anyone before."

"It's okay; he deserved it. Let's get out of here."

We weren't out of the woods yet. The radio crackled. "*Lorenzo, did you get her?*" It was Hawk.

"Yeah, we're coming out. Two down."

"*Hold on. There's more vehicles coming in,*" Bob said. "*I've got an SUV and a couple of sedans.*" Headlights came through the window. Our escape route was illuminated.

"*Are they holding a convention?*" Hawk asked.

"*Lots of men moving now. These new ones seem to be paying attention. Don't move,*" Bob insisted. "*These aren't government.*"

"What's wrong?" Jill asked desperately. She was wearing some sort of pink waitress outfit, but it was filthy and blood splattered. She looked exhausted. "Is that Carl on the radio?"

She didn't know. It just strengthened my resolve. I had to get her out of here. "We can't sneak out. We're stuck. We might have to fight our way out."

"*Lorenzo, we're in position. Just say when,*" Valentine said. His demeanor had changed. He wasn't the sarcastic, nervous asshole he'd been before. Now he sounded utterly *calm*. I'd seen him in that state before. I could only imagine what kind of childhood he must've had to have gotten so messed up.

Jill knelt by the nearly decapitated man and removed a Glock from his belt. She checked the chamber then stuck it into her waistband. "There's a subgun under that coat." She followed my pointing finger and nodded. I leaned against the door and listened. There were more voices on the other side now.

"So what do you want, Gordon?" Oily, British accent, effeminate. "I've got important business to conduct. I don't have time to drive out to middle of the bloody desert. I had to fly into a pathetic little airport in the middle of this dreadful desert just to get here. And it was *closed*. There was nothing there but an empty hangar! I had to land at a closed airport like . . . like some kind of *vagrant!*"

Eddie?

"I would think by now you would trust me." The voices were muffled through the ancient wooden door, but that had to be Gordon. "Why the entourage?"

"Associates of mine from Las Vegas. I had them pick me up. But I didn't bring them just because I don't trust you. I also have some personal business to conduct in the area." In other words, these were the men that he was planning on using to kill me at the scarab drop.

"Well, Mr. Montalban, as for your personal business, it turns out that there might be another favor I can do for you."

"Removing my brother from the equation did improve my affairs rather immensely. But all part of fulfilling Project Blue, to the benefit of your employers, of course. And in addition I paid you rather handsomely, so I would hardly call it a favor."

"As was part of the agreement. My partner is at the Alpha Point for Blue now."

"I always keep my promises, Mr. Willis. So tell me why you dragged me out here to this filthy, dreadful little place."

After all of this, Eduard Montalban was in the next room. He'd killed my friends, tried to kill me, and had threatened my loved ones. All thoughts of escaping quietly were dismissed. There was no way he was getting out of here alive. I looked to Jill, eyes wide, stubby machine gun shaking in her hands, and she understood. I pulled a frag grenade from my vest and put one hand on the door knob. "Get ready," I whispered into the radio.

"This thief, Lorenzo, that you asked me to keep an eye out for—"

Eddie cut him off. "Lorenzo is why I came to America in the first place."

"How much would he be worth if I was able to deliver him into your hands?" Gordon asked.

Eddie didn't hesitate. "Though a challenging diversion, he's worth nothing; But he has something in his possession, an antique piece of *jewelry*. For that, I'd give you ten million."

"What if I told you that a person of interest we were looking for was picked up by facial-recognition software while passing through Las Vegas? Once flagged, SIGINT eventually pinpointed her in Quagmire. Surprisingly enough, under interrogation it turns out she's friends with this Lorenzo of yours. My men will be picking him up shortly, right down the road. And for you, a special deal. I've *neglected* to mention any of this to my superiors."

"Of course. But if your men screw this up and I don't get my property back, I'll hold you responsible." A small dog began to bark in the next room. Who the hell brings a dog to a meeting like this?

"It's already in motion," the government man said. Somewhere, an armed squad was lying in ambush for us. They hadn't the faintest idea where we actually were.

"I hope you realize who you're dealing with, Gordon. Underestimating a man like Lorenzo can be fatal."

Damn straight.

I opened the door.

VALENTINE

My blood had run cold when I'd heard Gordon's voice. Then *the Calm* had washed over me, and suddenly I felt very detached. I couldn't believe it. I had all but resolved myself to disappearing quietly. I had convinced myself that getting to Gordon was impossible, that it was just an angry fantasy. Now Gordon had been dropped right into my lap. He'd injected himself back into my life and screwed it up all over again. Beneath *the Calm,* at the outermost limit of my perception, I was seething with anger. He wasn't going to get away this time. He wasn't going to do this to me *twice.*

Reaper and I were in a shallow ravine that was about two-thirds of the way down the steep hill we'd come from. Hawk had crawled another twenty feet to a better position of cover. At the top of the hill was Bob with his rifle. At the bottom of the hill was the cinder-block building where they were holding Jill.

"Reaper, keep your head down," I said. The nearest visible bad guy was far out of range of his stubby shotgun. "I'll tell you when to move. Stay alert."

There were two parties of men hanging around outside. One was presumably from Gordon's group, since they had been driving the government Suburbans. Only three of them remained outside, doing a very poor job of keeping watch. The rest, more heavily armed in SWAT gear, had piled into a van and left. I figured that was the group that was supposed to be ambushing us at the arranged meeting point.

But several other cars that had just arrived, and these new guys were anxious. A handful of men got out and entered the building, including one of the biggest, fattest men I'd ever seen. This giant whale of a man was probably close to seven feet tall and had to weigh four hundred pounds.

"Who's the fat guy?" I whispered into my radio.

"*Unknown,*" Bob tersely replied.

"Fat guy?" Reaper asked, suddenly sounding even more anxious. Before I could stop him, he poked his head over the ravine to see. A shocked look appeared on his face, and he immediately dropped back down.

"What is it?" I asked. But Reaper wouldn't tell me anything. He just whispered into his radio that "the fat man" was here. Lorenzo clicked his microphone in reply.

Bob had said over the radio that these new arrivals were more alert, and that was definitely true. Compared to the government suits, the new guys looked like they belonged in a European fashion magazine, and they were all openly carrying weapons. Some had MP7 submachine guns, some had G36C assault rifles, and all were alert.

I was startled by the sound of a muffled explosion. The windows of the cinder-block building blew out, and the prison camp suddenly came alive.

The men outside were all startled by the blast. I put my aiming reticle on the upper chest of one of the new guys. He was hanging back by a sedan, his carbine shouldered, obviously providing rear security. I swiped my selector switch to the fire position and squeezed the trigger. I hit the man in the sternum, and blood from the giant exit wound on his back splashed onto the car door. He crumpled to the ground, landing in a small cloud of dust.

One of the others running full tilt toward the building caught a round in the chest and almost did a cartwheel into the dirt. With my hearing protection in I couldn't hear the distant crack of Bob's suppressed rifle, but I knew it was him. Another shooter, one of Gordon's men, had drawn his pistol and was about to open the door to the cinder-block building. Before I could drop the hammer on him his head exploded into a red cloud, and down he went. Bob again. *Damn. Dude knows how to shoot!*

The others had turned around and were running back toward their vehicles. I fired at one of them and missed, leading him too much. But he froze when he saw the bullet impact the dirt, like a deer in the headlights. I squeezed the trigger again, and down he went. Scanning through my scope for targets, I lined up one of the new guys just in time to see a muzzle flash. Sand and tiny pebbles hit my face as his bullet impacted the dirt a few feet from me. I ducked back down into the ravine and was out of his line of sight, but more and more bullets snapped overhead and hit the rocks around us. Off to the side, Hawk slid into the gulley, calmly rocking a new magazine into his rifle.

Reaper was to my left, trying to become one with the earth. His already pale skin had gone white, and he had a death grip on his little shotgun. I could tell that this really wasn't his cup of tea. Honestly? I wasn't exactly having the time of my life, either, but there are worse ways to spend your time.

I got on my radio. "Bob, they got me pinned down. Help me out here."

"*Roger,*" was all Bob said in response. A moment later, he spoke up again. "*Hey, Nightcrawler . . . I got another one, but the rest are hunkered down pretty good. If you follow that ravine, it works its way down the hill and it'll get you closer.*" I signaled Hawk and used my hands to indicate for him to cover us. "*It looks shallow as you get to the bottom, but there are some big rocks down there that'll give you cover. You'll come out pretty close to the corner of the building. Just make sure you watch both sides. Guys could come around the building either way. You up for it? I can't get Lorenzo on the radio.*"

"Roger. Moving." I looked over at Reaper. "You ready?" He looked back at me, eyes wide but full of surprising determination. He nodded. "Alright, then. Follow me."

Hawk popped back up, firing, trying to keep the bad guy's heads down as Reaper and I moved. We snaked our way down the ravine, trying to stay out of sight. I could barely hear the occasional snap of a rifle bullet coming from Bob's position, always followed by sporadic, sometimes automatic, weapons fire in response. They didn't know where he was, and he was picking them off one by one.

We made it to the rocks at the bottom of the hill. We had to crawl from the end of the ravine, little more than a shallow gulley at this point, to the rocks. Reaper followed close, breathing hard and sweating heavily in his black trench coat. I crawled to the far left edge of the rocks, still in the prone. I was very close to the cinder-block building, and there was only one door on the side that was facing me. I also now had a clear view of the men taking cover behind the SUV, busily shooting at Hawk's position.

I snapped off a shot, and one of the men fell. The other surprised me by how quickly he reacted and returned fire. I pushed myself back behind the rocks while he popped shot after shot off at us. He suddenly shifted his fire back toward Bob's position after a near-miss from my sniper overwatch. I rolled out from the side of the boulder and fired twice. "He's down," I said into my radio.

I was about to make a dash for the door when one of Gordon's men came around the corner of the building to my left. He fired a burst at me. The bullets impacted the rocks, sending dust and debris flying. I let myself fall to the ground and scrambled behind cover. A second burst narrowly missed me, and a third one peppered the rocks I was now hiding behind.

I moved to my right and came up firing. My rounds hit the ground and the wall near the government guy just as he disappeared back around the corner. I held my fire but kept my sights on where he was. He'd either come back out or circle back around the building. Hawk was covering my right flank, so I wasn't worried about that. Sure enough, he did a quick peek, broadcasting to me where he was. As soon as he stepped around the corner, I opened up on him. At least three of my rounds tore through him.

I ducked back behind the boulder. "How are you doing?" I asked Reaper as I removed the nearly spent magazine from my rifle. He just nodded at me as I pulled another one from my vest and locked it into position. "Okay," I said, "head for the door."

I dashed from behind the rocks with Reaper right behind me, running so fast that we smacked into the wall. I pointed down the wall of the building, indicating to Reaper that he needed to watch that corner. Reaching down, I tried the handle. The old door wasn't locked, but it was stuck.

Subtlety was never my strong point. I nodded at Reaper and kicked the door in.

LORENZO

I threw open the door, taking in the scene in an instant. There was Eduard Montalban standing in the filthy abandoned garage. Next to him was the hulking Fat Man, who looked like Moby Dick in his white suit. Eddie was wearing a silk shirt, Flock of Seagulls hair combed high, little yippy white poodle-dog under one arm, the smirk on his face turning to disbelief as he saw me. Gordon and one of his men had their backs to me and were just beginning to turn as they saw Eddie's shock. Both sides had several goons arrayed across the room, but none of them would be fast enough to stop me.

The grenade left my hand, spoon popping off in mid-flight. "Hey, Eddie," I stated as the grenade struck the concrete floor, bounced, and spun between Gordon's legs.

"Bloody hell!" Eddie shrieked. The poodle started barking.

Chaos. The Fat Man was far faster than he looked. He spun about, one massive arm sweeping Eddie up, lifting his employer and shielding him as they dove away. Gordon acted in pure instinctive self-preservation, one hand coming up, grabbing the government man next to him by the necktie, and yanking hard. The man, taken by surprise, toppled over on top of the grenade as Gordon hurled himself into the old oil pit.

I ducked back around the corner.

THUMP.

I felt the pressure in my teeth. Gordon's guard absorbed most of the blast and saved the others. The walls were sprayed like a red Jackson Pollock. Decades of dust and cobwebs were dislodged from the ceiling, obscuring everything.

Jill pulled her fingers out of her ears and actually smiled at me. I motioned for her to stay put before taking a quick peek through the doorway. The windows had all been shattered. Dust whirled. One of the goons was screaming. There was gunfire coming from outside.

Something moved in a pile of dust. *The Fat Man.* The back of his white suit coat was shredded and burned. Small spatters and trickles of blood covered his back. He pushed himself up with one arm, Eddie still held protectively beneath him. I raised my AR, taking the safety off, finger moving onto the trigger, red dot settling on the Fat Man's back.

The wall next to me exploded in a shower of cinder fragments, and I jerked the trigger as I cringed, missing my target entirely. Something sliced hot across my cheek and I fell into the back room, bullets screaming through the doorway overhead. I scrambled to the side as the floor erupted into dust.

"Lorenzo!" Jill shouted as I rolled toward her. She raised the MP5 and fired out the doorway. A man cried out in pain.

Still prone, I leaned around the doorway and spotted a government man moving through the dust, firing his M4 at us. Jill shot again, and the man stumbled. "They've got vests on!" I shouted as I put the Aimpoint on him and cranked off several quick shots. Soft armor would stop her 9mm, but not my 5.56. He fell to his knees and Jill's third shot hit him in the bridge of the nose. I scrambled farther out, searching for Eddie.

The spot where the Fat Man had fallen was empty.

"Shit!" I shouted. More shapes were appearing in the dust. I fired at anything that moved. That damn poodle was still barking. Bullets impacted our wall, digging fierce pits into the cinder-blocks, or skipped across the concrete and smashed our room into debris.

Flipping the selector to auto, I emptied the rest of my magazine into the confusion, then rolled inside, fumbling at my vest for a reload. There were a lot more bad guys than I had expected, but they were being hit from multiple directions. Jill was crouched behind me. I made eye contact and gestured violently toward the window. We had to get out of here. "I'll cover you," I said as I slammed the magazine home and slapped the bolt release.

"Quit shooting! Stop it!" Eddie was screeching. The random gunfire tapered off and died. "I need him *alive!*"

"Go!" I shouted to Jill, leaned out, and fired in the direction of Eddie's voice. There was a rusted truck parked near the main door, and it sounded like he had come from behind it. I stitched a line of impacts across the truck body, the clang of hot lead on metal louder than my suppressor. Jill sprang up and pushed her way through the window. Within seconds, multiple rifles opened up on my position. I fired until she disappeared, going clear through my second magazine.

"Damn it!" Eddie shrieked. "I said quit *shooting*! Next one of you wankers shoots at him and I'll slit your throat myself! Lorenzo!" I pulled back, reloading again. I could feel the heat rising from my rifle. "Listen to me carefully. I just want what's mine. I don't care about you."

Red laser dots flashed on the far wall. Bright flashlights illuminated the doorway. If I tried to move, I was dead. Rather than fire and maneuver, I'd allowed myself to get pinned down. At least Jill had gotten out. "Bob, the hostage just went out the window. Cover her. I'm stuck," I whispered. There was no response. I grasped my radio. The box had been smashed by a round. *Damn.*

"I'm listening, Eddie," I shouted back. The gunfire outside continued. It sounded like the others were busy. "What're you offering?"

"Give me the scarab, you and all your people walk, and I pay you *double.*"

"Sounds tempting," I lied. We were dog food the second he had it. I didn't dare stick my head around the corner, and I couldn't try to move across the doorway. There was a large piece of broken mirrored glass on the floor. Grabbing it, I held it up and used it to peer around the corner.

"Yes, it is tempting. We both know you're stuck, and it won't take too many bullets to carve through that wall. My associate is setting up a belt-fed as we speak. . . ." There was a sudden burst of much louder gunfire, and the wall above me exploded into shrapnel. The sound was horrendous. The gun fired so fast it was like a buzzsaw. I covered my head and tried to make myself as small as possible as I was pelted with jagged bits. The poodle yelped. "Hush now, Precious, the bad man won't scare you anymore," Eddie soothed. "You've got ten seconds, Lorenzo."

Moving the broken shard of glass, I scanned the garage. Multiple bright weapon-mounted lights shined back at me, and there was the Fat Man, a terrifying German MG3 machine gun on a bipod resting on the old truck hood, pointed right at me. I coughed as more dust settled onto my face. Hopefully Jill and the others would make it out of here, because I didn't think that I would.

But at least I could take Eddie with me. "I've got to know. What is it? Why is it so important?" If I could keep him talking, maybe I could figure out where he hiding.

"Is Willis around?" Eddie asked. "Or any of his men?"

"No, sir. He took off running into those old buildings," a voice behind one of the bobbing weapon lights answered.

"Well, chap, you might as well know. Gordon and I may be from rival organizations, but I'm helping him accomplish something for his employers, and in turn he's helping me get the position I so rightfully deserve among my peers. And you are going to help keep me there. The thing you stole? It isn't even for me. There's a certain individual, who even I am scared of, and he'd do *anything* to get that scarab. Now quit stalling. Time's up, Lorenzo. Where . . . is . . . *my* . . . *property*?"

The scarab was sitting in a Velcro pouch on my armor. I held the AR tight and did one last pass with my makeshift mirror: three lighted weapons trained on my position, and a belt-fed machine gun. It was Butch and Sundance time.

Then there was another reflection shifting in the glass, the flash of a pink waitress dress creeping up behind the Fat Man.

Oh, please no.

No time to think. I sprang up, muzzle rising as I heard the *brraaappp* noise of the little MP5 in Jill's hands on full-auto. The Fat Man jerked as her bullets stitched up his side. The MG3 fired wildly past me, tearing a gash of dust and pulverized cinder block up the wall. My Aimpoint settled on the first weapon mounted light and I fired twice, shifting immediately to the next light and firing again.

I was blinded by the scalding beams, burning bullets zipping around me, through my clothing, feeling them parting my hair, buzzing past like angry bees. There was the third light, dancing with muzzle flashes, and I pulled the trigger twice more. Jill was shouting as she fired.

One of the lights was weaving, a shadow appearing behind it. My gun moved back toward him, but I tripped on some debris, sprawling forward, jerking the trigger as I went, supersonic lead filling the empty air where I'd just been. The other light swung upward, briefly illuminating the bloody ceiling as the man holding it went down. The Fat Man grunted under the impacts as Jill shot him again, and finally he and the heavy machine gun disappeared behind the truck.

There was only one weapon light shining now, swinging wildly toward Jill. We fired at the same time. The bulb shattered.

The room went dark.

I gasped for breath as the filthy dust stirred. My good ear was ringing from the gunfire, but above that I could hear a man crying and the sounds of someone breathing froth through a torn-open chest.

This time the flashlight piercing the darkness was mounted to *my* gun. "Jill!" I shouted. I only activated the light for a split second to find my way, then it was back out to avoid being a target and I was moving to the truck and the last place I'd seen her.

"Lorenzo!" she hissed at me. "Over here."

I found her in the dark, kneeling behind some rusted junk. The empty MP5 had been tossed, and she had a pistol in her hands. She flinched as my hand touched her shoulder, but at least she didn't shoot me.

"Are you okay?" I whispered, crouching beside her. I didn't know who was still alive in the garage.

"I'm okay." She gestured at the Fat Man, his massive, sprawled, white-clad form standing out in the dark. "But he's not. Shot him like ten times."

I didn't know why, but I hugged her then, held her tight, my face pressed into her soft neck, her dark, blood matted hair pressed against my cheek. That lasted for a few seconds as there was more high-powered rifle fire nearby, several back and forth volleys. The others were still fighting.

Back to business . . .

"Did you see which way Eddie went?"

"The one that looked like he came from an episode of *I Love the Eighties*, with the poodle?" I nodded, somehow in the dark she could tell. She pointed out the large front door. "He headed for those old buildings."

I couldn't let him get away. I stood, dropped my partially expended magazine, and drew a new one from my vest. "Head for the hills to the west. I have a friend out there. He'll get you out of here."

"I'm coming with you," she answered defiantly.

"This isn't a democracy. You're—" Something stirred behind me, gliding into the garage, a shape with a weapon. I turned, pulling the rifle to my shoulder. The man was in my sights, but I knew I was too late.

We both froze. Guns raised, death only a tiny bit of pressure on a trigger away.

"Valentine," I acknowledged, relieved, and lowered my carbine.

Valentine's FAL hovered on me for just a fraction of a second. *That son of a bitch,* I thought. *He's actually thinking it over.* I glared at him for an instant, daring him to pull the trigger. His expression changed almost imperceptibly and he lowered his weapon. "Is Jill okay?"

Before I could answer, Reaper swept into the room, trench coat billowing like something out of a bad vampire movie. Man, I hated that stupid coat. He grinned when he saw us. "I'm glad to see you guys. I've been trying to get you on the radio. Bob says that that van full of SWAT dudes has turned around and is on its way back. We've got to go." Reaper shone his light around the room, seeing the multiple bodies and blood still dripping from the ceiling. "I love what you've done with the place."

Valentine was all business. He quickly scanned the dead. No quips. No jokes. Only: "Where's Gordon?"

"He went that way." I nodded toward the ghost town.

"Then let's go."

VALENTINE

I turned to leave, but paused. I looked back at my . . . companions? I don't suppose we were friends. Standing close to Lorenzo was Jill, a gun in hand, her hair a mess, blood-stains on her pink jumper.

"You alright, darlin'?" I asked of Jill. She nodded at me but said nothing. She was hovering close to Lorenzo. I managed half a smile for her, then put my game face back on. Gordon was out there somewhere, and he wasn't getting away.

"*Val, what's your status?*" Hawk asked over the radio.

"Cover the entrance. I'm coming out."

"What's the plan?" Reaper asked.

What is it with these people and their stupid plans? A plan is just a list of things that don't happen after the first shot is fired, and the situation had already gone straight to hell. "Gordon's back there somewhere," I said, gesturing to the door. "I'm going to find him and kill him." My blood was running cold.

"That's it?" Jill asked, speaking up at last. "You don't know how many of them there are! You're going to get yourself killed!"

"The van full of SWAT guys is coming back," Reaper said again.

"This is gonna get interesting." I moved forward and opened the door. It was mostly dark outside now, and only the last bit of sun crept over the hill to illuminate the interior of the long-abandoned prison camp. There was a row of buildings along each side of a gravel road. Barracks, mostly, but utility buildings, a mess hall, things like that. The tall fence that had once surrounded the place was falling down, and several of the structures had been vandalized.

I moved out the door. Lorenzo stepped out behind me, with Reaper behind him. He made Jill stay inside. *Good*, I thought. I didn't want her to get hurt, especially after all this.

I moved to my right, edging towards the corner of the building. It was shadowed here, and I was thankful for that. The next building over didn't have any windows facing my position, but others did, and I was exposed.

Hawk came over the radio. "*Val, I'm moving up on you. Cover me.*"

I leaned around the corner. The road that led into the camp was lit up by the headlights of the van. It was rapidly approaching our position, leaving a long dust cloud behind it.

"You see the van?" Lorenzo asked. He was now right behind me.

"Got it," I said.

"We should move over there," he said, pointing to the next building. "Find some cover and light 'em up as they come out. We—"

His voice was cut off by the loud bark of my carbine. He hissed an obscenity, but then opened fire as well. Hawk joined him an instant later. I couldn't see anything but the dark mass of the van beyond the blinding headlights, but that was enough. The glowing red reticle of my scope was centered on it, and I let go. I fired as rapidly as I could, my rounds tearing into the van, my face illuminated briefly by each muzzle flash. The van skidded to its right and crashed into the far corner of a building. My bolt locked back, and my rifle was empty. I looked back at Lorenzo as he dropped the magazine out of his carbine.

"Let's go. I couldn't have gotten them all."

LORENZO

Valentine ejected the empty magazine from his rifle, flinging it away from him as he rocked it out, and locked a new one in place. The bolt flew forward with a clang.

"Let's get them," Jill said. I turned. She was right behind me, one of Eddie's goon's G36 carbines in her hands. Before I could even tell her to go back, she snapped, "Shut up, Lorenzo, I'm coming." Her tone suggested that there wouldn't be any arguing.

Valentine grinned at me. *Asshole*. I shook my head while walking quickly toward the smoking wreck. "Stay low. Hawk, cover us. Valentine and Reaper, flank right. Jill, stay behind me. That little pad on the front grip activates your flashlight. Leave it off until—"

"I'm not retarded. I can use a stupid light. Come on already," she hissed. "Gordon's going to get away."

Fair enough.

There was no discernible movement around the van. Steam was rising from the smashed-open radiator. I sprinted the last few feet and stuck my muzzle through the driver's side window just as Valentine threw open the rear doors. The driver was dead, his face mashed against the wheel, blood leaking from his ear. The passenger's brains were sliding down the dash. The back was empty, but there was some blood. The others must have bailed out.

There was a raised wooden walkway on both sides of the rectangular barracks. Reaper's boots echoed hollowly on the wooden planks as he walked toward the open doorway. Suddenly, he and Valentine both crouched down. I stood there stupidly for an instant before realizing that they were still in communication with Bob. I grabbed Jill by the wrist and pulled her down beside the van.

A supersonic crack whistled overhead, and someone screamed inside the darkened barracks. Reaper threw himself flat as the SWAT team inside fired wildly through the plank walls in response. Valentine disappeared in a flash, moving to the building's corner. Jill and I were in the shadows, and the SWAT guys were firing at nothing.

"Reaper, stay down!" I had one frag grenade left. I pulled it from its pouch, yanked the pin, and chucked it through the barracks window. A few seconds later, the barracks shook and bits of jagged metal hummed through the air, seeking flesh.

"Now!" I shouted. Reaper popped up, turned on his Surefire light, and leaned across the barrack's window. The stubby 12 gauge belched fire three quick times. You didn't need to be a good shot at conversational distance. Off to the side came the thunderous crack of Valentine's .308.

"Clear!" he shouted.

"Scratch two more assholes," Reaper responded.

But how many did that leave? I sprinted toward the barracks, vaulted over the railing, and landed beside Reaper. Hawk was running up behind us. The railing next to my head made a hollow *thunk* noise as a bullet smashed into it. I pressed tighter against the wall. Jill was still prone by the van. "Everybody down! That came from the water tower!"

"Bob, sniper on the water tower. Take him out," Valentine ordered as he walked calmly into the barracks. "Hey, Lorenzo. We've got to keep moving."

I scanned the town. There were only intermittent patches of amber lighting, and most of the ramshackle buildings were deadly ambushes waiting to happen. I pulled out my night-vision monocular, pressed it to my eye, and scanned around the corner.

Through the NVD I could see a man with a rifle standing at the top of the water tower's ladder. There was another crack, and the man toppled from his perch, fell two stories, and landed lifelessly in a cloud of dust. My brother was a damn fine shot.

Hawk clambered up the steps and took cover next to me. "Val, if that G-man's running from you, he's probably holed up in that last big building." It made sense, it was the easternmost position they could fall back to. To get back to their vehicles they would have to either fight past us through the southern row of buildings, or they'd have to try to cross back between the buildings on the north side. Each time they left cover, we could engage them, and to reach a car they'd be visible to Bob. Holing up to wait for reinforcements would be the smart thing to do.

"The mess hall? I'm on it. Come on." He disappeared into the shadows of the barracks, heading for the back door.

"Doesn't he ever plan anything?" I grunted. There couldn't be many of Eddie's goons or Gordon's men left, but the element of surprise was gone, and they would be waiting for us somewhere in that twisted labyrinth of junk and jagged wood. The four of us stood and followed Valentine into the darkness.

Chapter 29: Dropped Call

VALENTINE

Gordon. I was so close now I could taste it. I could sense his presence. I can't remember ever being more focused, more intense, yet so detached. *The Calm* had never been this overwhelming before. My survival instinct had been turned off. This was *it*. I only had to live long enough to kill Gordon. After that it didn't matter.

I entered the darkened barracks, stepping over the bodies of Gordon's men. It was a mess in there; Lorenzo's grenade had done the trick. The rest of the building was virtually empty, with little more than old frames for bunk beds. At the far end was another door. That's where I was going. Gordon was hiding in this camp, somewhere, and I was going to find him.

I slowed to a fast walk as I approached the far door, my rifle up and at the ready. There were no windows on the ends of the buildings, just narrow ones along the walls. Moving to the right side of the door frame, I pulled the door open and peeked out. It was about twenty feet to the next barracks building, and its door was closed. There could be shooters on the buildings across the road, so I'd have to be careful. I looked back at Lorenzo, and with hand signals told him to cover that direction. He shifted his carbine to his left shoulder and stacked behind the doorway.

I dashed across the gap between the barracks. On the other side, I pressed myself against the wall and crouched down. At the same time, Lorenzo was leaning out of the door, his weapon covering across the road.

Flipping around, I pointed the muzzle of my rifle at the door and reached for the handle. It was locked and made of metal. It looked too solid to kick down.

"Reaper!" I hissed, trying not to make too much noise. "Get up here with that room broom! I need you to bust a lock!" The kid came running out of the barracks in a crouched jog, weapon in hand. He didn't even stop to look at the buildings across the way. He obviously had complete confidence that Lorenzo would cover him. The kid pressed himself against the wall on the left side of the door frame, opposite me.

"Use that shotgun to blow the lock on this door so we can keep moving!" Reaper pointed the stubby muzzle of his weapon at the door's handle and flinched as he pulled the trigger. The shotgun roared, and the door handle exploded.

There was no time to pause. Reaper turned away, and I booted the door in. A man was crouched about halfway through the building. I snapped off two shots at him, then ducked back out of the doorway, crouching down in case he fired through the wall. He fired two more shots through the doorway, then it was quiet. I leaned in and saw him, slightly magnified through my rifle's scope. One of my rounds had gone through his abdomen, and he was now slowly crawling toward the far door, leaving a thick trail of blood in his wake.

I walked up quickly and stomped down on his back. He shrieked in agony. "Where's Gordon?"

"I don't know who that is!" he cried, blood pouring out of the exit wound beneath my boot. I shot him in the back of the head, shattering his skull like a watermelon with a blasting cap in it.

"Clear!" I shouted. The room was suddenly quiet. The air stank of burnt powder and dust. We crossed the room and opened the door at the far end. The doorway to the next barracks was closed, and again we had to contend with the gap between the buildings.

I peeked outside and nearly lost my head. The shots were coming from the barracks building across the way. I fell back inside the doorway just in time to avoid being hit. The shooter then began to pepper the wall with rifle fire. Bullets tore through and snapped angrily overhead.

"Everybody down!" Hawk shouted. Lorenzo furiously started low-crawling toward the back of the building. I crawled forward and got as close to the door as I could.

The shooter was still firing through the wall, about one shot every second. He was focusing on our end of the building, though. Looking back, I saw Lorenzo pop up and fire off a long burst from his carbine. The suppressed weapon sounded like a rapid series of hissing pops as it fired.

Still in the prone, leaning out of the doorway, I began to fire at the building across the road. Lorenzo's bursts of fire had shattered the windows and stitched the wall, but the shooter was nowhere to be seen. We both paused for a moment and waited. A second later, he popped up again in the exact same spot. Both Lorenzo and I lit him up. I don't know how many rounds the shooter took, but he fell from sight and didn't appear again.

"Keep moving," I ordered, scrambling to my feet and heading for the next building. I took up position on one side of the door, and Lorenzo was on the other a second later. Hawk wasn't looking so good.

"You okay?" I asked.

"I'm too old for this shit," he answered.

"Do you have any more frags?" I asked. Lorenzo shook his head. *Damn it*. We were going to have to do this the hard way. I reached down and opened the door. We were answered with weapons fire, only this time there were multiple shooters. Lorenzo and I both leaned in and returned fire. Lorenzo mashed himself up against the fence that connected the buildings as one of the shooters inside returned fire through the wall. There was no way we were getting through that door without getting killed.

I decided to take a chance and flank them. I took off at a run up the right side of the building. Gunfire echoed through the camp as I made my way along the wall. I stopped about three-quarters of the way down and began to fire through the wall into the barracks. This way, my companions wouldn't be in the line of fire and there was a chance I'd actually hit one of the bad guys. If nothing else, it'd distract them long enough for the others to make a move. I burned off the rest of my magazine as fast as I could pull the trigger.

My rifle's bolt locked open. I began to jog back to the rear of the building, reloading as I went. A tiny bit of movement in the periphery of my vision alerted me. I spun around, seeing a man in a dirty suit, limping badly, blood pouring from wounds on his arms and legs. He raised a handgun. I turned toward him, reaching down for the revolver on my thigh. I felt a thump as a round smacked me in the chest plate. I lost my balance and fell.

The shooter aimed unsteadily, pistol wobbling in one bloody hand, just as my .44 cleared its holster. I took a bead on him and fired between my knees. His head snapped around in a pink cloud. Rolling back to my hands and knees, I scrambled ahead, heading back to the others.

The others were behind cover in the entrance of the final barracks. Lorenzo was nowhere to be seen. Rifle still slung across my chest, revolver held at the ready, I jogged down the length of the barracks, passing Reaper and Jill and stepping over dead bodies. It looked like I had managed to plug somebody through the wall after all.

"Everybody okay?" I got a chorus of nods in response.

I looked out a window just in time to see Lorenzo enter the mess hall building.

"Where's *he* going?"

"I don't know," Reaper said. "He just took off."

"Let's go!" Jill said, a fire in her eyes.

Holstering my Smith & Wesson, I pulled a fresh twenty-round magazine from my vest and locked it into my FAL's magazine well. I looked back at my companions and was out the door.

LORENZO

Valentine was a killing machine.

The last of Gordon's SWAT team were gone, shot to death through the barracks walls. Bodies twisted into unnatural positions, hands curled into claws, staring blankly at the beams overhead. I stepped quickly through the mess, shell casings spinning away underfoot. Hawk had been firing from the window, hammering his Para FAL at someone in the northern buildings. Reaper and Jill were back toward the entrance.

I crouched near the rear door and scanned the last building. There was no visible movement, but there had been earlier, and none of the men that we had killed were Eddie or Gordon. Process of elimination left that one.

Elimination. Sometimes I make myself smile.

There was a noise, high pitched and repetitive over the ringing in my ears. It was coming from the cafeteria. The noise seemed out of place in the ghost town.

Barking. It was Eddie's poodle.

I'm by nature a cautious man. You do not live long in my business by charging into situations, but caution went out the window when I heard that sound. Eddie's presence here tonight was like a gift from heaven, and I wasn't going to leave without sending him to hell.

"I'm going in," I said into my radio, took a quick look, didn't see any obvious threats, then sprinted for the cafeteria, realizing halfway across that I didn't have a working radio. Too late to turn back. I covered the last bit of distance and slid to a stop in the gravel next to the open doorway.

The old mess hall was a huge building. I rounded the corner and activated my flashlight. The interior was a mass of old tables, most of them broken and sticking up at odd angles. The light created horrific shadows dancing on the walls. Nothing moved, but you could have hid an elephant in here and I wouldn't have seen it.

That annoying barking came again, a high-pitched yipping, louder now, off to the side. My light illuminated another door, probably to the kitchen. I moved through, using what cover was available, ready to shoot at any second. The kitchen was empty also, just some dust-coated countertops, old bottles, and a rusting industrial-sized stove. There was another door, and the barking was coming from inside.

I kicked the door open, the old bolt tearing right through the age-softened wood. Rickety stairs descended into the darkness.

Man. What I'd give for another grenade.

The yippy dog was really freaking out now. I cracked the vertebra in my neck. This was it.

I swept around the corner, light stabbing into the darkness. Below was a small pantry, filled with empty shelves, probably sunk into the ground to keep the food from the desert heat. Eddie's poodle was in the center of the room, its leash tied around a beam.

The dog was snarling at me. I moved the light around, but there was nobody else in the room. There was a dusty tarp hanging in one corner, big enough to conceal a man.

I started down the steps, gun up, finger on the trigger, Aimpoint dot floating on that tarp. My heart was pounding. Was that Eddie behind there? I took aim and stitched a line of shots up it. The AR moved slightly under recoil as something shattered and fell behind the tarp. The poodle yelped in surprise and whimpered.

If Eddie was hiding in there, he wasn't happy.

The first gunshot struck me low in the back. I stumbled forward, accidentally discharging my weapon as another round tore down my arm. I tried to turn back toward the kitchen, but as my boot landed on the next step, the ancient stairs broke and gave way under my weight. Windmilling, off balance, another shot sparked off my AR's receiver and I crashed halfway through the stairs, legs dangling over the pantry, jagged wood stabbing into my arms. The door to the giant stove was open now and a hand with a pistol extended out of it. I saw the muzzle flash, and something tore along the side of my scalp, snapping my head back. Another shot thudded into my armor as the rest of the staircase collapsed around me.

The air exploded from my lungs as I landed hard in a pile of dust and wood. I lay there for a split second, lights exploding behind my eyes. I had walked right into it, focused on the noise, and waltzed right past Eddie's ambush.

Choking, gasping, I pushed myself deeper into the corner under the broken stairs as I drew my pistol. My body was on fire with pain, and blood was running out of my hair and into my eyes. My protesting lungs wouldn't fill with air at first, but I forced back the rising tide of panic. The bag containing the prince's treasure had somehow spilled free and was resting on the floor a few feet away, just out of reach.

"Lorenzo, I thought you were supposed to be good at this," Eddie said from above. He peered over the edge at me, smiling, H&K P7 in one hand, his silk shirt filthy with old rust, puffy hair matted with cobwebs. He moved back over the threshold as I raised my gun and fired. The bullet smashed into the ceiling.

I kept the shaking front sight aimed at that doorway and tried to breathe.

The basement was dark. My AR was smashed on the ground beside me. I had no cover. At least that dog had shut up. I glanced over at the Precious's last position. It looked like I'd accidently shot the poodle before the stairs had fallen on it. *Ouch.*

"You know you're not the first one to come after me. Did you really think it would be that easy? You probably did. I try to cultivate a certain manner. It tends to cause men like you to underestimate me." Eddie's effeminate voice was safely out of sight above. "Where's the scarab, Lorenzo?"

"Sorry about your dog." I coughed and used my sleeve to wipe the blood out of my eyes. If Eddie was going to finish me, he needed to stick his gun over the edge. So I only had one shot. The STI slowly quit shaking. Blood trickled down my lacerated arm and pooled inside my armor.

"I'll buy a new dog. The scarab is irreplaceable."

Come on, Eddie. Just a peek. "It must be worth a fortune."

"It's not the money. It's the *sentimental* value. The man that wants that thing is far more dangerous than me. He'd crush the prince like a bug. But if I have it, he'll do anything I ask. You have no idea how important that bloody thing is. This is your last chance, Lorenzo. Where is it?"

It was sitting right there in the dust, but I wouldn't give him the satisfaction. "Someplace you'll never find it," I answered, and it wasn't a stretch of my acting ability to sound injured. "So let's get this over with."

Eddie was quiet for a moment. "You realize, of course, that I'm still going to kill your family. It's a matter of principle now."

"Of course," I answered as I blocked out the pain, the throbbing in my head, the ringing in my ears, the blood in my eyes, and focused on that glowing front sight. *One shot. Just one shot.*

Then there was a gunshot, not from a handgun, but the thunder of a .308 round, followed by several other deep booms from Reaper's Benelli. They were close.

"Sounds like your mates are here. I'm afraid our time together has come to an end."

"Yeah, that's too bad." *Front sight. Front sight. Come on.*

"Farewell, Lorenzo."

I was waiting for it. *Please, God, just one shot.* But Eddie didn't appear at the edge. Rather, there was a scratchy clicking noise. *A lighter?* Then a glass bottle with a flaming rag stuck in the top flew through the doorway. I watched in horror as the Molotov cocktail sailed across the room and shattered against the far wall. The liquid inside spread across the walls and wooden shelves, ignited, and bathed the tiny room in heat and flames.

I pushed myself to my feet, scrambling, searching for handholds to get out of the deathtrap. The fire was spreading, eating up the dry wood, leaping up the walls, licking at me, singeing my clothes. The heat sucked the moisture from my eyes, and the poison smoke billowed into my lungs.

Eduard Montalban chortled like a deranged schoolgirl as he fled the kitchen. I screamed as the flames tore at me.

VALENTINE

The smell of smoke hit my nostrils as I reached the mess hall. The door was already open. I crouched and studied the darkened interior. Hawk crouched across from me and shined his flashlight into the room. Smoke was drifting up through the floorboards, obscuring everything.

Hawk killed the light and glanced at me. "What do you want to do?"

Jill and Reaper were still shadowed in the safety of the barracks. I keyed my radio. "I don't see Lorenzo, I—" I froze. Something moved quickly at the far end of the room, headed for the door. I flashed my weapon light, and there he was.

Gordon.

My former employer flinched in the blinding light, his normally expensive suit covered in dirt and rust. He had a handkerchief pressed to his mouth because of the rising smoke and had just reached the back door. He looked back at us for an instant, then dove through the doorway. I opened fire, rattling off half a magazine at where Gordon had been, then firing through the wall at where he might be. Before Hawk could stop me, I took off in pursuit and disappeared into the smoke.

LORENZO

The world was engulfed in flames. Fire moved like a living creature, consuming everything around me. I reached for the scarab, but the fire drove me back. There was no time to retrieve it, and I stumbled away. The heat was unbearable, my exposed skin was burning. My mind swam through incoherent thoughts as my lungs pumped poison gases into my brain.

Not like this. I can't go down like this.

The fingernails of one hand tore off trying to pull myself up the wall to reach the doorway. It was only about a dozen feet, but it seemed a million miles away.

Calm down. Hold your breath and fucking climb.

I unsheathed my Greco knife and stabbed it into the planks high above my head. Driven with the strength of desperation, the blade stuck deep. I only had one chance. With my clothing burning, driven by adrenaline, I pulled on the knife while I jumped, boots scrambling for purchase, bloody fingers tearing at the boards above. The remaining cartridges in my AR began to cook off, sounding like firecrackers inside the conflagration.

Somehow I found purchase, dangling by my fingertips. I was halfway there. *Shit, it hurts.* I jerked the knife out, raised it overhead as I began to slip, and slammed it home again. The next few seconds were a blur of pain, tearing muscles, and fire, always the fire. Finding fingerholds when there were none, I reached the jagged broken top step, got one hand onto it, and pulled myself upward. By a miracle, it held.

I crawled onto the kitchen floor. Black smoke billowed through the doorway over me, filling the room. Face on the ground, I opened my mouth and inhaled. I immediately began to cough, violent spasms that were like vomiting pain.

"Lorenzo!" someone shouted. Hands grabbed me by the straps on my armor and pulled me across the kitchen. Black combat boots stomped ahead of me. Reaper. "Holy shit! You're on fire!" He whipped off his giant coat and covered me with it, beating at my back and legs.

Finally I rolled over and gasped, precious air filling my lungs. He was pulling me outside the burning mess hall. It took a moment for my head to quit spinning. Jill was staring down at me, her hands on the side of my face. She was saying something.

"I'm okay," I rasped, trying to sit up. Pain like electric current moved through my limbs.

"You know fuck-all about okay." She pushed me back down. "Hold still. You're hurt."

Pain was replaced with anger. Anger was replaced with rage. I grabbed her arm. "Where's Eddie?" I snapped.

"I don't know," she cried. "You're hurting me."

I immediately let go. "Sorry." I left a soot-black, bloodstained handprint on her arm. "Help me up," I ordered. Jill and Reaper both took an elbow and helped me stand. Reaper pushed me a small bottle of water, and I sucked at it greedily. It burned going down my parched throat. After a few seconds, I had to stop and puke the water and a bunch of soot up, then I went back to drinking. They both wore looks of shock as they studied me. I had to look pretty bad.

"Screw it. I'll live," I wheezed as I tossed the bottle, sounding like a ten-pack-a-day smoker. "Status?"

"Bob's pinned down. Somebody got back on that machine gun. Valentine saw Gordon. He and Hawk went that way." Reaper pointed toward the garage. "We haven't seen Eddie."

The scarab was still down there, lost in the flames, probably melted. Whoever wanted that thing so badly was probably going to be pissed. I patted my side. At least I had stuck with my training and reholstered my pistol even while standing inside a fireball. I pulled the gun now and let it dangle at my side.

"Quit staring. Let's go help my brother."

VALENTINE

Gordon was not going to get away. *The Calm* was failing, replaced with rage. I was hunting him like an animal, and I'd never felt more alive. I think I actually had a smile on my face.

"Val! Wait!" Hawk shouted, struggling to keep up.

It was dark. The air was filled with smoke. My eyes welled with tears, and my lungs ached. My focus was on the back doorway and the pitch-black space that Gordon had escaped into.

Bob was saying something over the radio, sounding scared, but I couldn't understand him over the beating pulse in my head. Gordon had to die first; then I could care about everyone else's business. I reached the doorway. I pulled up against the frame and flashed my weapon light before stepping through. *Clear.*

I stepped forward and was immediately cracked across the chest with a 2x4. I lurched back, disoriented, and fell to the ground. The man was on top of me in an instant. I raised my hands to protect my head as began to bludgeon me with the board.

My attacker swung again. The board struck my arm, and shocking pain flooded all the way to my shoulder. My arm went numb. I struggled for my pistol, but he slammed the board down on me again. The man raised the 2x4 over his head, meaning to swing it down on me like a sledgehammer. He left an opening. I planted a size-twelve boot right in his nutsack.

He stumbled back, giving me a moment of respite. Before he could recover, someone jumped over me and dove into my attacker. I was dazed. My head was swimming, and it felt like my skull had been split open. I was too dizzy to rise.

I could barely see what was going on. Two men fought viciously in front of me, moving so fast in the dark I couldn't tell who was who. I then heard Hawk grunt in pain as the two shapes moved apart. There was sudden flash of steel as a knife darted between them. I raised my gun as one of the shapes tottered forward, went to his knees, and fell face-first to the floor.

"Hawk?" I asked. "You okay?"

It took him a second to respond. "Fine," he grunted as he emerged from the shadows, holding his old Randall knife in one hand. His other hand was clamped against his side. "He stabbed me. Not too bad, though." Despite his injury, Hawk helped me to my feet. I wobbled but was able to stand.

Is it Gordon? My deceased attacker was wearing a suit and was about the right size. I swung my rifle around and thumbed on my flashlight. I don't know who the man was, but it wasn't Gordon Willis. Probably one of his flunkies. The side of his neck had been split open from his collarbone to his ear. *Damn.* Hawk spat.

Gunfire echoed from the direction of the garage. Beyond that I could hear the noise of an engine turning over.

Gordon was getting away.

LORENZO

Reaper was in front now as we hurried back toward the garage, trying to stay in the shadows as much as possible. We could see a stream of tracers flying from the side of the garage up into the hillside where we had left Bob. I stumbled along, one arm over Jill's shoulder as she kept me upright. The mess hall was burning bright, and the flames had spread to the surrounding buildings. The camp was coming down.

I avoided taking a mental inventory of my injuries. Nothing seemed to be bleeding very fast.

We all instinctively ducked as we were suddenly illuminated by car headlights. Somebody had made it back to the vehicles. There was a sudden roar from a powerful engine, and one of the Suburbans sprayed gravel as it turned around and tore away from us.

That's when I saw Valentine emerge from one of the buildings on the other side of the horseshoe. "*Gordon!*" he screamed, running right into the middle of the road, oblivious to danger. He snapped his FAL to his shoulder and fired at the Suburban. Several holes were punched in the back of the SUV before Valentine's bolt locked back. He rapidly reloaded, once again flinging the empty magazine away and rocking in a new one, but it was too late. By the time he dropped the bolt on a live round, the Suburban had dipped into a gully and disappeared from view.

Valentine slowly lowered his rifle. He stood there quietly, seething, staring at the horizon as if he could will the Suburban to come back. Hawk appeared behind him, limping badly. His rifle was slung, his .44 dangled from one hand, and his other hand was pressed against a wound on his side.

Hawk caught my look. "Keep moving! I'm fine." Another burst of machine gun fire tore into the hillside. All of us flinched in that direction. *Bob.* I was running now, the others right behind me. Valentine saw us and followed. My 9mm was at the ready as I moved around the corner of the garage.

The MG3 was braced over the hood of a sedan. A giant white shape was manning the gun, firing short bursts onto a patch of darkened mountain where my brother had gotten pinned down. It was the Fat Man. The back of his white suit was shredded from my grenade. Blood ran from dozens of injuries. Maybe he had on some kind of body armor, or maybe he was just that tough, but somehow the son of a bitch was still alive. I could feel the others behind me, five of us in a row now. I settled my front sight on him and fired, still walking forward.

He grunted, raising the machine gun off the hood of the sedan. I fired again. Valentine's rifle bucked off to the side. The Fat Man began to turn, surprisingly enough, a strange smile on his face even as our bullets struck home. Jill was shooting her pistol now, cranking off shots as fast as she could pull the trigger. I kept shooting, but impossibly the Fat Man stayed on his feet as bullets puckered into his bloated frame, tearing him apart. Reaper's buckshot rocked him slightly, sending the MG3's muzzle into the dirt. I kept firing, front sight tracking back down; now I was shooting for his head. One of Hawk's .44 slugs erupted through his cheek, and he spit teeth but stayed upright. Still closing, Reaper hit him again, the buckshot in a tighter pattern now, taking the Fat Man's kneecap off.

His ponderous weight hit the hood, sliding inevitably toward the earth, leaving a trail behind him. He was reaching into his coat, somehow finding the strength to go for his gun. Jill fired her last shots into his neck. He was still smiling a toothless death's head grin, one eye missing now, as he hit the ground.

"Fucking die already!" Reaper shouted, stepping on the Fat Man's arm, pinning the gun, extending the stubby 12 gauge toward that nebulous smile. *BOOM BOOM!* Point-blank range. It wasn't pretty. Reaper stepped back and wiped his arm across his blood-splattered face. "You ain't coming back now!"

I shoved a fresh magazine into my STI. "Get Bob on the radio."

"He says he's okay," Reaper answered. "And—"

"Down!" Valentine shouted. He was closest to Jill and shoved her aside. I hit the deck as another sedan tore past us, muzzle flashes strobing out the open window, bullets whizzing past. Eddie's maniacally grinning face was illuminated for a brief instant. He must have gotten into the car while we were distracted by the Fat Man. Hawk fired his .44 one-handed at the speeding car as it bounced down the road. The concussions were deafening, but then the car was around the hillside and out of sight.

"Everybody okay?"

"I think so," Jill answered from the ground.

"Reaper?" *No answer.* I scrambled over to my friend. He was on his back next to the headless body of the Fat Man. "Reaper? Reaper!"

A bullet had smashed his chest plate. He was bleeding badly from the side of his head. I shook him. He opened his eyes, looked around in confusion, then grimaced. "Ow, shit, that hurts." He rolled over and put his hands on his skull. "He shot me, and I hit my head on the car. So quit yelling at me! Oh, man, he shot me in the arm too." Sure enough, there was a wound on his bicep. Jill knelt by his side and put pressure on it. "I hate getting shot!"

"You'll live," Jill said.

I could be relieved later. I pulled Reaper's radio off his vest. "Bob. Can you hear me?"

"*Yeah, bro. I'm good. That was close.*"

Somehow we had all survived. "If you see another car moving down the road, kill the driver."

"He's already around the hill. I can't acquire."

I swore as I keyed the radio again. "Get down to the road as fast as you can. We'll pick you up in a minute."

"*I'm on my way,*" he answered.

I stuffed the radio in my pocket. Valentine had picked up the big MG3 and taken up a defensive position. I started for the closest sedan. The door was unlocked. No keys of course. I whipped out my multitool and cracked open the cover beneath the steering wheel. It took all of thirty seconds to get the car hot-wired, and that was between bouts of violent coughing and blood trickling down my arms and making my hands slippery. The engine turned over as I struck the wires together.

The others were already cramming into the sedan. Valentine had to maneuver the German machine gun to make it fit. The entire prison camp was burning bright now, and we needed to get out of here before the authorities showed up. I slammed the car into gear and floored it as soon as everyone was inside.

The car was dying. Something must have been hit as we were unloading on the Fat Man. All the warning lights were on. The engine was coughing almost as badly as I was. Jill was squished against me, with Bob and his body armor taking up most of the front seat. All of us were filthy, sweating, and half of us were bleeding. Bob's shocked reaction to seeing me under the car's interior lights when we had picked him up told me about how horrible I looked.

"We're almost where we left the vehicles," Bob stated calmly. He was covered in desert dust. His rifle was between his knees. The fire from the work camp was just a visible glow over the hill behind us.

"Status back there?" I asked. "Hawk? Reaper?"

"It's a shallow cut." Hawk had his shirt open and had shoved a pressure bandage on his side. "Nothing bad."

"The kid's going to be okay. Bullet grazed his bicep, missed the brachial artery. I've got the bleeding under control," Valentine said from the backseat.

"I suck at this stuff," Reaper whined. "I keep getting shot."

"You'll be fine," Valentine said flatly.

"Bob, I need you to get these guys out of here before the cops show up. They need medical attention. Think you can handle it?"

"No problem," my brother answered. I knew that he'd been some sort of medic in the National Guard, an 18 Delta he'd called it. "But I think you need a hospital."

"It's better than it looks," I lied. There were deep lacerations on my face, scalp, and down my arms. My hands were a blood soaked mess. I had first degree burns on much of my body, and from the throbbing nerves down my back and legs I knew that there were some spots that were much worse. I couldn't stop coughing.

But there was no way in hell Eddie was going to get away.

"*Holy shit!*" Reaper suddenly freaked out. "Look at this! Look at this!"

"Crap. What?"

"I think it's Eddie's tablet!" he exclaimed.

"So?"

"He's *logged* in!" Reaper cackled in glee. I was too out of it to see the significance. Gunshot wound forgotten, Reaper madly started fiddling with the little gizmo. "Oh, now this, I am good at!"

The car died as we rolled into the rest stop. I jumped out and started toward the stolen Explorer. "Where do you think you're going?" Jill asked.

"After Eddie." I opened the door. "He told Gordon that he'd flown into a nearby airport."

Valentine spoke up. "There's only one around here. It's not far."

"You're injured! You need medical attention!" Jill insisted. She was right, of course. I was running on nothing but adrenaline and anger now.

"I'll be fine," I said. "I'll hook up with you later." I didn't want them with me. Gordon had probably notified the authorities, and surely word would reach the cops in Quagmire about the massacre at the old work camp. I grabbed the wheel. My vision was blurred and my head was swimming. Bob was helping Reaper into the back of the G-ride Suburban.

Valentine tossed the keys to his Mustang to Jill. "Follow Bob," he told her. "And take good care of my car."

"Lorenzo . . ." Jill trailed off. She was filthy, stupid pink outfit splattered with blood, her hair tangled with dirt, hanging like a dark shadow over half her face, a stolen handgun dangling from one hand.

She was beautiful.

"I know," I rasped.

Valentine opened the passenger-side door and slid in, maneuvering the big German machine gun to fit between us.

"What the hell are you doing?"

"Just *drive*." He slammed the door.

I pushed the Ford up to a hundred and five. It wouldn't go any faster. The highway was virtually deserted, and I had the gas pedal floored. I wasn't worried about being pulled over. God help the stray Highway Patrolman that got between me and Eddie.

Valentine held onto the *oh, shit!* handle as we barreled down the road. I passed a slow-moving semi truck like it was standing still, pulling back into the right-hand lane just in time to avoid hitting another car head on. The Explorer was vibrating like hell.

"We're almost there," Valentine said. "This airport has been closed for years. Your guy must've had his boys come pick him up. There's nothing there but a few run-down buildings."

In the back of my mind, I wondered why Valentine came with me. I doubted he'd tell me if I asked. Just then, my cell phone vibrated, disrupting my thoughts. I pulled it out of my pocket and hit the talk button.

It was Eddie, sounding as shrill and oily as ever. "Ah, Lorenzo. Just checking. I thought that was you I saw standing on the side of the road back there. Did I kill any more of your friends with my little drive-by? It was so invigorating! Like one of your American rap-music videos!" The psychopath giggled.

"No, Eddie, you're a lousy fucking shot." The sound of his voice made me push the gas pedal that much harder.

"You certainly are hard to kill."

"You won't be," I promised. "What do you want?"

He laughed, somehow managing to sound girly and sadistic at the same time. "To taunt you, of course. My plane is taking off as we speak. I imagine that you're trying to catch up with me, but you will be too late. As soon as I hang up, I'm going to ring one of my associates, and then the fun will begin. I'm not just going to have your loved ones killed, I'm going to have them tortured first. I'm going to take your little nieces and nephews, and I'm going to have them raped in front of their parents. I'm going to make them *watch*. I will—"

I ignored Eddie's ranting. "Where do we turn?"

"Right here, right here!" Valentine said, pointing.

"Hang on!" I'd nearly missed the turnoff. Hitting the brake, I cranked the Explorer to the right, nearly putting it up on two wheels.

"Ow! Damn it!" Valentine snarled as the heavy machine gun slid over and struck him. We sped down a narrow. deserted road. The airport wasn't far. After a minute or two we shot through an open gate on a rusted chain-link fence and careened onto a wide-open paved area. I smashed the brake, making a tight turn as we crossed a parking area, passed the dilapidated remains of a hanger, and sped onto the tarmac. The airport obviously hadn't been used in years. The runway and taxiways were cracked and faded, with weeds springing through splits in the pavement. Eddie's car, now empty, was parked off to the side.

"There!" Valentine shouted, pointing down the runway. At the far end was a speeding Gulfstream jet. Its engines screamed as it built up speed.

Eddie was still going on, screeching like a lunatic. "—you hear me? Nobody crosses Big Eddie! *Nobody*! I've got to make an example out of you, Lorenzo. Everyone needs to know the consequences of my displeasure!"

The Explorer skidded to a stop, leaving a trail of rubber. Valentine leapt out, pulling the machine gun with him as the jet jumped into the air. He set the barrel over the junction of the door and frame, crouched down, and squeezed the trigger.

The MG3 roared, sending a stream of tracers down the runway after the climbing jet. He hosed the rest of the belt, at least fifty rounds, at the target. Bullets streamed into the air, but fell short. The jet was just too far away. The MG3's bolt flew forward on an empty chamber. That was it.

"That's the best you've got, Lorenzo?" Eddie cackled. "Not a scratch on me!" I stuck the phone in the front of my armor.

"Shit!" Valentine shouted. "I'm out! He's gonna get away!"

"No," I stated calmly. While he was shooting, I had limped around to the back door. I opened it, ripped the concealing blanket aside, and pulled out the portable surface to air missile that I had stolen from the Chechen border jumpers. "He's not."

"What the . . ." Valentine said, observing my weapon in awe.

I set the heavy tube on my shoulder, took one step around the Explorer and looked through the scope. I had read the instructions earlier, and it seemed relatively straightforward. I found the red and green flashing lights of Eddie's jet, centered them in the circle, and hit the lock button. It took a few seconds for the sensor to read. It made a noise like a microwave oven saying that the hotdogs were done.

I pulled the heavy trigger.

FOOOOOM!

The concussion was horrendous. The initial charge threw the missile straight out. A split second later the rocket engine ignited in a massive gout of flame and soared after the jet with a shrieking noise like some obscene bird of prey. The impact staggered me. I pulled the phone out of my armor with my shaking left hand.

"—should have just given me the scarab. I'll—"

I cut him off. "Hey, Eddie . . ."

"What is it, Lorenzo?"

"See you in *hell*."

"What are you . . . evade! Evade!" I could hear him screaming at the pilot while an alarm went off in the background. Eddie was rich enough to afford a missile detection system for his private jet.

Not that it did him any good. A fireball blossomed in the night sky. The entire jet was illuminated for a brief moment as one of the rear engines was engulfed, sparks drifting toward the ground like a demented fireworks display. A wing broke off just as the sound of the first impact reached us. The plane rolled over, trailing smoke, and crumpled into the desert floor in a ball of fire.

I looked down at the phone.

Call Disconnected

Elapsed Time: 4:33

The wreckage continued to burn. It was over. Big Eddie was dead.

My body began to shake, to tremble. All of the pain that I had forced aside came rushing back, staggering me, sending me to my knees. A year of doing the impossible, my loved ones held hostage, my friends in danger, some hurt, some killed, all had come down to this.

It was over.

"We better get out of here before the cops show up," Valentine said. "I don't want to try to explain to them where you got a Stinger missile from."

I was leaning against the SUV, shaking. I couldn't believe it. I was in shock.

"How about I drive?" Valentine suggested, "Since you're having, um, a moment?"

I jerkily nodded and climbed into the passenger seat. I closed my eyes. The pillar of fire that had been Eddie's plane burned onto the inside of my eyelids. "It's over," I said.

Valentine put the Explorer in gear. "Sure, whatever." He thought for a moment. "So. Who was that on the plane?"

I let the pain carry me into the dark.

. . . over . . .

Chapter 30: What Happens in Vegas . . .

VALENTINE
Las Vegas, Nevada
June 29
0300

Somehow I ended up back in Las Vegas. It was like I couldn't escape that place. It had been Bob's idea. Vegas was the nearest big city, and we needed a place to go. We found a crappy motel in a crappy part of town, the kind of place where call girls hang out in the lobby and they don't bother asking for ID, and checked in.

Hawk had gone home. As far as I knew, neither Gordon Willis nor any of his surviving men had identified any of us. At least I hoped not. We made a pretty big mess and shot down a private jet. There was bound to be a shit-storm over it, and we decided it was best if we scattered before anyone figured out what happened. If they traced it back to Hawk, or any of us for that matter . . . I didn't know what would happen, but I knew it would be bad.

Bob insisted that Gordon Willis and his people weren't part of the legitimate government. As much as they'd use every resource to figure out what happened, they'd try just as hard to keep things quiet. That made sense to me. I knew things about Gordon that Bob didn't know. I knew what Gordon did. He was a traitor, not only to his country, but to Majestic, the shadowy organization he served. He was probably running just as far and just as fast as we were.

We all had injuries, but with some rudimentary supplies we were able to sort ourselves out. Bob was a medic, and a good one at that. Between the two of us we had gotten the others patched up. Lorenzo had been put down with a significant amount of painkillers. He probably should have been taken to a burn unit for a few spots on his back and legs, but that would've attracted attention, so he was going to have to make do.

Reaper was so preoccupied with the tablet PC he'd found that he barely noticed as we closed the hole in his arm. Jill only had nicks and bruises, but mostly she had just needed to crash. She'd had a hell of a day. All things considered, the girl was doing okay. She was tougher than she looked.

I'd been so close to killing Gordon I could taste it, yet he got away. I needed to get some air, and on top of it I was starving. I left our motel room to get some food. Bob Lorenzo insisted on going with me, which was both annoying and suspicious. It was annoying because I was contemplating just ditching those guys and taking off on my own. That was going to be a challenge riding with the hulking FBI agent in his G-ride SUV.

The ride was awkward, for me at least. I didn't know Bob, and even though we'd just gone through some shit together, I sure as hell didn't trust him. It was obvious he wanted to talk to me about something, and I wasn't comfortable with it.

Bob was quiet for a long time as we fought our way through Vegas traffic. "So, who are you really, Mr. Nightcrawler?" he finally asked. He didn't look at me.

"Are you asking me as a cop, or are you asking me as a guy who just helped me kill a bunch of people?"

Bob didn't respond for a long time. "Don't judge what you don't understand."

A sardonic grin split my face. "My name is Michael Valentine, and I understand things a lot better than you think."

"I believe you," the big man said slowly. "You used to work for Gordon Willis, right?"

I was quiet for a few moments before I answered, trying to choose my words carefully. My gut told me I could trust Bob. Recent experience taught me that I couldn't trust anyone. "Yes. Until a month ago, anyway."

"You seem to have some kind of grudge. Were you in Majestic?"

That's who Colonel Hunter had said he answered to. "You could say that. To answer both your questions, I mean. I wasn't really aware of who I was working for until recently. I'm not sure what Majestic is. All I can find on it is a bunch of Internet conspiracy-theory crap."

"It's just a name. It's every secret, every abuse of power, every bad thing you can imagine. They used to exist to protect us, but now they just exist to consolidate their power. I'm guessing you were Dead Six, then."

I raised an eyebrow.

"You fit the profile," Bob said. "Young, probably former military, and you're not wearing a wedding ring so I'm guessing you're single. No family, either, right? Don't get excited. I've been looking into this stuff for a long time. I was waiting for someone involved in that to pop up. It's my lucky day, I guess."

He knew too much. He looked over at me and squinted. Was he doing the math? Trying to decide if he could get to his sidearm before I could get to mine? Bob was a Fed; was he in on this?

My face went blank. "You've got a forty-cal Sig in a strong-side, thumb-break cop holster that's stuck behind your seat-belt buckle. You won't get it out fast enough."

Bob chuckled before turning back to the road, shaking his head slightly. "Well, I'll be. You're quiet. You're used to people underestimating you, aren't you? But you turn it on like a light switch when you feel threatened. That's something else. But listen, I'm no friend of Gordon Willis. Trust me on this one. Let's just say that keeping up on current events is a hobby of mine. You could go so far as to say that I'm a bit of a conspiracy theorist, or at least my bosses seem to think so. Dead Six was one tiny operation out of many, all of them secret, most of them illegal, and half of them pure evil, all run by men like Willis, and if you get in the way of their power, you die."

"What do you know about Project Heartbreaker?"

"Officially? Nothing. Unofficially, an old friend of mine was the assistant ambassador in Zubara. We were on the same ODA. He knew that I was . . . *obsessed*, I think, was the word he used, about things like this. When things started to go bad there, he called me up, wondering if I could do some checking for him. I did, and found the stink of Willis and his people all over it. I've been doing research into him and the others like him for years. So I did some poking, through sources you wouldn't understand and I wouldn't tell you about anyway, and I learned about Dead Six. I told my friend, Jim Fiore, about what I'd found, and he was dead within forty-eight hours. I warned him not to talk, but he wouldn't listen."

"Why are you telling me this?" I asked.

"Because I want your help," Bob answered. "Because I *need* your help. You know things. Come with me. There are plenty of us in the government, the *real* government, who would love to see these people stopped. We can protect you. You can help us put a stake through their heart once and for all. There are still ways to work through the system. If we shine the light of day on these cockroaches, they'll scatter. If you come help me, we can . . ." Bob trailed off as I chuckled at him. "What is it?"

"You think I haven't heard this line of bullshit before? Come sign up with us, serve your country, fight the bad guys, blah blah *blah*. It's the same crap every time. Well, you know what? I'm *done*. I'm done signing up. I'm done joining the cause. I'm tired of being somebody else's damned *pawn*."

"It's not like that."

"Oh, the *hell* it's not," I said bitterly. "It's always the same. I'm just an asset to you. I used to work for a PMC. I know all about being a commodity. At least Vanguard was honest about it and had a good benefits package. What are you offering me besides a bunch of rhetoric and empty promises?"

Bob frowned. "I don't think you understand the gravity of the situation. These people are *destroying* this country. What you've seen is just the tip of the iceberg. If we—"

I cut him off. "No, *you* don't understand," I said harshly. "I *don't care.*"

We were stopped at an intersection, waiting for a light to turn green, which seemed to take an eternity. Bob gave me a hard stare. I could almost see the gears turning behind his eyes. His expression softened a bit. "What the hell happened to you, kid?"

I looked down at my lap and exhaled. "That's a long story."

"More importantly," Bob continued, returning his attention to the road as we started moving again, "what are you going to do now? You can't hide at your friend's place forever. If certain people find out you're alive, they'll kill you and everyone you know. How long do you think you can stay on the run?"

"Who said anything about running?"

Bob shook his head. "The best defense is a good offense, huh?" he asked sardonically. "I've known a lot of guys like you. Most of them were Special Forces."

"I was in the Air Force."

Bob laughed, somewhat defusing the tension in the car. "You know it won't work, right? I mean, you know that, don't you? Majestic is too big to just take out. You can't kill the beast by running in and shooting everybody. You have to be smart about it."

"I'm not interested in killing the beast," I said. "And there's only one person I need to shoot."

"You intend to kill Gordon Willis, don't you?" Bob asked levelly. I didn't answer. That in and of itself was answer enough, I suppose. Bob shook his head again. "It's a suicide mission. Majestic won't let you touch him, and even if you succeed, you're a dead man."

"See, there's where you're wrong," I suggested. "You don't know everything I know. I don't think Majestic's got Gordon's back anymore."

"What are you talking about?"

"Gordon's gone off the reservation. Project Heartbreaker failed because of his dirty dealings."

Bob seemed surprised by this. "What? How do you know this?" I didn't answer him. He looked frustrated at my intransigence. "It doesn't change anything. Killing him won't change anything. Right now you think it'll settle the score, right whatever wrong happened to you. Trust me, even if you succeed, it won't change. You won't get the satisfaction you want. They'll kill you, and it'll have all been for nothing."

In my mind I saw Sarah falling to the mud like a puppet with the strings cut. *Not for nothing,* I thought.

We went through the drive-through of some all-night burger place. Bob ordered. I was distracted. What *would* happen if I killed Gordon? Would I even succeed? I knew where he lived. I knew everything about him. It was all on Hunter's flash drive. But would I be able to find him? What if he went into hiding?

If those thoughts weren't troubling enough, something else crossed my mind. Ling warned me about trying to exact revenge. She asked me if I thought that was what Sarah would have wanted me to do. I still didn't have an answer that I liked.

"I'm asking you one last time. Don't do it, kid. I don't know what happened, what you lost out there, but I can see that pain inside of you. Don't let the pain steer you." Bob set the bags on the seat and started driving. "Don't throw your life away for nothing." I glanced over at him. He seemed sincere enough. Was it possible he was actually being straight with me?

I wasn't used to that. "I'll think on it," I lied.

Bob started to speak again but had to stop to answer his phone. He listened for a minute, speaking occasionally, before hanging up. "Looks like there's been a terrorist *incident* in my area of responsibility. They want me out there ASAP."

I shook my head at the surrealism of it all as we pulled back into the motel parking lot.

Bob put the Suburban in park. "Will you at least think about what I said? Look. You're right. I don't know you. I'm not trying to help you out of pure altruism. But you helped save my brother's life. Are you sure you want to go it alone?"

"No," I replied honestly. "But it's all I can do. Listen, there is something I can do to help you," I said as I reached into my pocket. I retrieved Colonel Hunter's blood-stained flash drive and handed it to Bob.

"What is this?" he asked. The white piece of plastic looked tiny in his huge hands.

"It's everything," I said. "Everything on Project Heartbreaker from start to finish. The planning, the logistics, the personnel and assets involved. Almost everything, anyway. We picked up a nuke in Yemen, too. No idea where that ended up."

Bob's eyes went wide. He looked at the diminutive piece of electronics as if it were a holy relic. "What? Where did you get this?"

"It was compiled by Colonel Curtis Hunter, the field commander of Dead Six. The last thing he did before dying was give this to me. I've gone over it. Hunter suspected Gordon's activities for a long time and dug up as much as he could. There are still big pieces of the story missing. The stuff highlighted in green is my own notes. I filled in the gaps where I could, but there's a lot I don't know and a lot Hunter couldn't find out. But the hit on your friend at the embassy is detailed on there, though I don't think you'll be able to pin it on anyone. A lot of the info has been sanitized."

Bob couldn't take his eyes off the flash drive. "Why are you giving this to me?"

"You can use it more than I can," I said honestly. "It will help you. It has the complete files of all of the people recruited for Dead Six, from the time they were approached to the time they were killed or went missing. All are listed as KIA or MIA. I've edited my own file, changed it to a confirmed KIA."

"Why did you do that?"

"I was thinking about releasing this whole thing to the news. But I don't know if that would do any good. So I'm giving it to you instead. If you do go public with this, make sure they think I'm dead. Okay?"

"I will," Bob answered solemnly.

"We were serving our country," I said quietly. "A lot of my friends died taking the fight to the enemy's doorstep. And they sold us out and left us to die. Somebody needs to tell the world what happened. Most of us didn't have any family at all. But some did. Their families deserve to know how they died."

Bob gave me a look that told me he respected what I said. He'd been a soldier. He understood. I got out of the car, pulling most of the food with me.

"Valentine, wait," Bob said, quickly shoving the thumb drive in his shirt pocket. "What if they don't kill you? What if you're captured? They'll find out everything. Everyone that's helped you, including me, will be put in danger."

I looked at the ground for a moment. I really didn't have a rebuttal to that. Bob didn't want to let me go, but I'd made it clear that he couldn't stop me. Had I really thought this through? Where would I end up if I went down this road?

My expression hardened as I buried my self-doubt. I didn't have a choice. Bob was right. I couldn't run forever. I wasn't going to run off with him, either. He struck me as a sincere man, but also a lone nut who was short on friends. At least if I went my own way, I had a say over where I ended up.

That's what I told myself, anyway. Bob wished me luck. I nodded and turned away, not looking back as he drove off.

LORENZO

Somebody was singing.

I awoke in a strange hotel room. There were bandages on my head, arms, and the back of my legs. My lungs ached and I could still feel the smoke in my sinuses. An IV bag was hanging from the wall light above me. I tracked the tube down and it disappeared under the gauze on my forearm. I hurt everywhere and my eyes grated in my sockets as I scanned the room. Reaper was asleep on the other bed, his arm wrapped in white and strapped across his torso. The kid was snoring.

I could hear the shower running. The singing was Jill. She was off-key and loud, but she sounded happy. It was a good sound.

The scarab. There was a momentary flash of panic. It was gone. I'd sacrificed so much to get it. . . . The last I'd seen, it had been in the basement of a building collapsing in flames. Then I relaxed. It didn't matter now. Eddie was dead. I was free. I'd never even known what it was, except that it cost too many of my friends' lives. Hopefully the fire had destroyed it, and if it hadn't, then it could stay buried in the desert forever.

I had never even known who it was for. Whoever the important man was that Eddie had been getting the scarab for more than likely didn't know anything about me . . . *Probably.*

The hotel door clicked as somebody used a card key to open it. Instinctively I looked around for my gun. It was nowhere to be seen. I relaxed as I realized it was Valentine. He entered the room with a fast-food bag in one hand and one of those cardboard drink trays full of sodas in the other. "Yo."

"Hey," I responded. "Where are we?"

"Vegas. Wanna hit up a strip club?"

"Only if we can't get Siegfried and Roy tickets."

"What? Siegfried and . . . No, man, one of 'em got eaten by the tiger. Long time ago."

"No kidding? Leave the country for a while and everything goes nuts."

"Tell me about it. Everybody is okay. Hawk's back at his place keeping a low profile. We figured that Quagmire might be a little hot, so we came here. There's no place to disappear like Vegas. Since they grabbed Jill they never saw Hawk with either of us, so he should be in the clear as long as I don't contact him." Valentine set the food on the table and pulled up a chair. "Your little buddy's been busy, going hog-wild over that computer he found. He passed out about an hour ago. He takes his Internet very seriously, doesn't he?"

"That's a bit of an understatement. How's Jill?"

Valentine nodded in the direction of the bathroom. "She'll be fine."

I had to smile. "I think she'll be okay. So what's our situation?"

"Jill insisted that I bring you here, and she's hard to say no to. Your brother's a decent medic, and he got you patched up before he had to go.

Apparently some terrorist shot down an airplane in Quagmire with a surface-to-air missile. The terror alert is at red level right now."

"What's the world coming to?"

He looked exhausted. "Jill filled me in on Big Eddie. So your boy is dead. That's two Montalbans I've either killed or helped kill. How weird is that?"

"What are you going to do now?" I asked, already knowing the answer.

"I don't know," he stated flatly.

He might not know, but I knew where his road would lead. I had seen this kind of attitude before, depressed, violent, hovering on the fine line between homicidal and suicidal. Valentine had a weight on his shoulders, and I didn't know if removing it would free him or destroy him.

It wasn't in my nature to offer, but I did anyway. I'd been surprising myself a lot lately. "You want help?"

"What? No."

I nodded. "I understand."

"You won't see me again," he said, "but there is one thing. Listen to me. Your two friends here, Jill and Skyler? You get them out of this life. Look at me. Whatever it is you see? That's their future unless you stop now. You know as well as I do that once you get in, you don't get out."

I glanced over at the bathroom door, then back at Valentine. I cringed at the thought of Jill becoming . . . like *him*.

"I gotta go. Your gun is in the drawer. I got you guys some food. I hope you like burgers."

"Only communists and hippies don't like burgers. Thanks."

"No problem."

"No, I meant . . ." I shrugged. I couldn't have done it without his help. "You know."

He gave me a small nod in acknowledgment. "Just remember what I said."

We were no longer enemies, but we certainly weren't friends. "You want to stick around and say good-bye to Jill?"

"I need to go. Besides, all she does it talk about you. I'm kind of sick of it. I honestly don't know what she sees in you."

"Well, I did take a guy's head off with piano wire for her."

Valentine shrugged. "Girls like romantic gestures like that. Look, I gotta split. Take it easy."

"Watch your back," I told him.

"Watch the news." He didn't look back.

Epilogue: Requiem

VALENTINE
Arlington, Virginia
July 4
2245

Sweat beaded on my face as I cleared the top of a tall fence and quietly landed in the grass. I crouched down for a moment, shrouded in darkness, and studied my surroundings. Directly in front of me was a full-sized swimming pool. Beyond that was a palatial home, situated in the more expensive half of a gated community of "rich-bitch" estates. The air smelled like gunpowder from the fireworks being set off in the streets.

I was dressed in dark clothes and had black grease paint smeared onto my face. My S&W .44 Magnum revolver was concealed under my shirt. I double-checked my coordinates on the GPS one last time; I had to make sure I had the right house. Satisfied, I stood up and moved silently across the darkened backyard toward the house. Gordon Willis didn't know it, but he had *company* tonight.

The back patio door was glass. I risked a peek inside and saw no movement. The house was mostly darkened but had enough lights left on that navigation wouldn't be difficult. I'd have to be quick. There was probably some kind of an alarm system; as soon as I busted through the door, I'd have only moments to do what I'd come to do.

Taking one last look around, I reached for the door and tried the handle. It was unlocked. Grinning to myself, I silently entered Gordon's house, shocked that a man like him would be so lackadaisical in his home security. I drew my revolver as the door closed behind me. The tritium front sight glowed green in the dim light.

The house was lavishly furnished with tacky postmodern décor. Half the stuff in the large downstairs recroom looked like it came from Ikea. An expensive-looking pool table sat in the middle of the room. I searched the downstairs area in silence. The lower level was deserted, but I could hear sounds of movement coming from somewhere in the house. My grip on

429

my weapon tightened slightly as I made my way up the stairs to the second floor.

I walked down the second-floor hall. The first door on my left led to a bedroom. The bed was covered with pillows and stuffed animals, and posters of several teen pop idols decorated the walls. A pit formed in my stomach, and I felt *the Calm* begin to waiver. It had never occurred to me that Gordon might've had a daughter. *Shit.* I noticed that the drawers on the girl's dresser had been pulled open and emptied. Had Gordon and his family fled? If so, who was in the house?

I steeled myself and quietly returned to the hallway, padding along on the carpet. At the end of the hall was a door to what looked like a master bedroom. The door was open, but I couldn't see any movement inside. There was a room kitty-corner to it, also with the door open. I froze when I heard someone cough loudly from that room.

My eyes narrowed as I brought my weapon up in both hands. I took one last deep breath and swiftly entered the room. I was surprised by what I saw.

Gordon Willis sat at a desk, facing the doorway, with his face buried in his hands. A large bottle of vodka sat open on his desk, and I could smell booze in the air. Next to the bottle was a Glock pistol. The room was some kind of study.

Gordon looked up when I entered the room, eyes wide. He swore aloud and reached for the pistol. My revolver roared in the confines of the study. The slug shattered the vodka bottle, blasted through Gordon's hand, and smacked into his desk. Gordon screamed in pain, clutching his pulped right hand with his left. The Glock was sent clattering to the floor.

He stared at the blood pouring down his arm for a moment, then looked up at me. "What took you so long?" he asked heavily, convulsing with pain. "What are you waiting for?"

"It was a long drive from Nevada," I said coldly.

Gordon froze and stared at my face intently for a moment. "V . . . Valentine? They sent *you*?" He paused for a moment, grunting in pain. "Jesus, I should've known. Well, just . . . just get it over with." He looked down at his desk.

"Gordon," I said slowly, keeping my weapon trained on him, "who is it that you think sent me?"

"What? You mean you're not . . ." Gordon trailed off for a moment. He then let out a pained laugh. "You picked a hell of a day to show up."

"What are you talking about?" My patience was running out.

Gordon nodded his head at his computer screen. *The Drudge Report* had a lead article about Project Heartbreaker and the abandonment of American personnel in Zubara. Bob Lorenzo had come through. He'd leaked Hunter's flash drive, or at least part of it, to the public. "They told me there was no reason for my family to suffer," Gordon said slowly, grasping his bleeding hand even tighter. "They let me send my wife away with my little girl. They . . . they told me to wait here. They said they'd come for me."

"Who?" I asked. "Majestic?"

Gordon managed a sardonic, half-in-shock smile, all while tears of pain were leaking involuntarily from his eyes. "You think you got it all figured out because you found out a name?" He scoffed, wincing in pain as he did so. "You have no idea the forces that are at work here, kid. This is *bigger* than us. They know everything now. They know about the deal I made with Eduard Montalban. They even found out I was proceeding on Blue!"

"I'm not working for anybody. You don't know why I'm here, do you?" Gordon looked at me in silence, inebriated from both shock and alcohol. My face hardened. "Her name was *Sarah*."

"What? Oh . . . right . . . McAllister. I was sent a report about you two."

"I know. I read it. She's dead because of you, you son of a bitch!"

"I know," Gordon groaned, squirming from the pain. "What do you want me to say? I was cleaning up loose ends. It was part of the deal. But that's all ruined now. They found out."

I smiled coldly. "Hunter gave me a lot of information before he died. I made sure it got into the right hands."

"*You?* You did this? Do you have any idea the damage you've done? Well you'll find out soon enough. Or not. I don't know. They'll probably just kill you. You should've taken me up on my offer."

"And you should've listened when I told you not to fuck with me." Then I shot him through the heart. The bullet punched through the back of his chair in a splash of blood, and Gordon tumbled to the floor.

I stood there for what seemed like a long time, not moving. I slowly lowered my gun. It was done; Gordon was dead. I'd avenged Sarah.

Yet I felt no satisfaction. Nothing had changed, except I'd ended one more life. Ling had warned me that if I went down this road, I might not like what I found when I reached the end. She was right. I'd reached the end, and I felt *nothing*.

Turning to leave the room, I nearly ran into the barrels of several suppressed weapons. A full squad of men dressed in tac gear was standing in the hall.

"Drop your weapon!" one of the men commanded.

Very slowly, I laid my revolver down on the carpet. I stepped back and placed my hands behind my head. The men in the hall rushed me then. I was turned around and slammed against the wall. My hands were roughly pulled behind my back and cuffed together.

Searing pain shot through me as one of the men shoved a high-powered taser into my back. I gasped for air, my knees buckled, and I fell to the floor. A black bag was pulled over my head, and I was hit with the taser again.

I found myself wondering if they'd come for me, or if they'd come for Gordon. I doubted I'd live long enough to find out.

LORENZO
Somewhere in the Caribbean
August 28

"It has been a month since billionaire philanthropist Eduard Montalban was killed in a tragic plane crash. The FAA has concluded their investigation and have determined that his Gulfstream jet was brought down by a mechanical failure as the pilot attempted an emergency landing at an airport in rural Nevada. According to the National Transportation Safety Board, there is no evidence that the plane was brought down by a surface-to-air missile, as was originally rumored," the anchorwoman said. Like most cable news people, she was easy on the eyes yet hard on the brain.

The screen switched over to a prerecorded press conference. The caption on the bottom of the shot said Special Agent Robert T. Lorenzo, FBI. Bob looked awkward on camera, enormous behind the podium, and the press spotlights caused a reflection from the top of his bald head. "I can assure you that there is no need to panic. There's absolutely no evidence that there are any anti-aircraft missiles in the United States. Air travel is perfectly safe." My brother lied well. It must run in the family. "The reports of a wild west-style gunfight in the Nevada desert beforehand are nothing more than unfounded rumors passed on by conspiracy theorists. Mr. Montalban's death was a tragic accident. He was a great humanitarian and will be missed by all."

They showed a file photo of Big Eddie waving to the crowd at some bigwig charity function, supermodel on one arm, poodle in the other.

Good riddance. *Freak.*

How could such a pathetic shell of a man cause so much suffering? I didn't think I would ever understand what made him tick, what motivated him to threaten me. The wicked trinket that had cost Train and Carl their lives was buried in a pit of ashes in Nevada. It had gone from one hole in the desert to another. It could rot in those ruins forever for all I cared. It seemed fitting.

The picture changed back to the vacuous reporter. "But with the recently revealed secret files concerning Project Heartbreaker, new questions have been raised. According to the files anonymously placed on the Internet,

Eduard Montalban's older brother, Rafael, was one of their targets in the Middle East and was assassinated by members of the rogue operation codenamed Dead Six. Now members of Congress are questioning the NTSB's ruling and demanding that the investigation be reopened."

The picture changed to footage of several men in suits leaving a courthouse. A mob of reporters screamed questions at the men while mirrored-sunglass-wearing security rushed them into large black cars.

"In related news, the Project Heartbreaker hearings have continued. The president has vowed that the perpetrators will be found and that no secrets will be kept from the American public. The House Minority Leader has insisted on the appointment of an independent commission to—"

Jill picked up the remote and killed the TV. "That stuff will rot your brain."

She was wearing a simple white dress and had flowers in her hair. Through the window behind her, I could see the pristine beach stretching into the distance, bright green trees rising behind. Brilliant blue waves were washing onto the sand.

"I was hoping to hear something about what happened to Valentine," I explained. "After he got arrested, he just disappeared into the system. Even Reaper can't find any information about where they sent him."

"You don't even know it was him. They did rule Gordon's death a suicide."

"Suicide?" I snorted. "Five bucks says the kid killed him."

"Maybe." She grabbed my hand and pulled me up. "Come on. We're on a tropical island in the middle of nowhere, and you want to watch the news? That's just wrong." She dragged me up the stairs and onto the deck. Our yacht rocked gently against the wooden pier. I wasn't wearing a shirt, and the sun beat down on the mass of scars that was my back.

It had been one of Big Eddie's boats, but it was mine now. In the confusion immediately following his death, we had gone to work embezzling as much of his fortune as was possible. Eddie's computer had been packed with valuable information. He wasn't worried about password security, because only a fool would steal from Big Eddie. But he was dead now, and you'd never find a bigger pair of fools than me and Reaper. With the contacts I had made in all of my years of doing Eddie's dirty work, and with Reaper's mad skills, we had been able to make an absurd amount of his wealth disappear into a maze of foreign banks before news of his demise spread and his accounts had been locked down.

Basically, we were now obscenely wealthy. In fact, this little island had been Eddie's also. Most of it, anyway. It did have a little town on it. The rest was mine now. Apparently the Montalbans hadn't even used the place in years. Reaper had found it in his frenzied searching of Montalban shell-corporation properties. Jill and I had been holed up here together for the last few weeks. With such a huge burden lifted from my shoulders, they had been some of the happiest days of my life.

And what we did together during that time was none of your business.

My family was safe, and as far as all of them except Bob knew, I was still just the flaky world traveler. Reaper had taken his share of the loot and gone his own way. He'd kept in touch and kept asking if I wanted to go back to work. I always turned him down. Valentine's final words still haunted me.

"Want to head into town?" Jill gestured inland. Her arm was darkly tanned. "We haven't gone dancing for a while."

"I need to talk to you about something," I said. "Something serious."

She stopped smiling, folded her arms, and leaned on the railing. "I'm listening."

"With all of the information about Dead Six public, and with Gordon dead, you aren't in danger anymore."

"I know," she said slowly.

"You don't need to stay hidden. You can be yourself again."

Jill turned away, scanning across the beach as the wind whipped her dark hair around her shoulders. We'd spent a lot of time together recently. Being in hiding tends to do that to people. I was older than her, wearied and scarred by the world. She was a beautiful young woman with her whole life ahead of her. I was a criminal, wanted by the law in a dozen countries and wanted dead by hundreds of evil men. We both knew that though my life was calm and happy now, there was no guarantee that my past wouldn't catch up with us eventually. And for men like me, sometimes the past comes back to haunt you, while other times it comes back to cut your head off.

She'd be better off without me. She'd be safe, no longer a target. "Jill, what I'm saying is, you can go home."

Jill continued to watch the surf and the wheeling seagulls. It wasn't like she needed to stick around for the money. She'd helped us loot Eddie's fortune and had gotten an equal share. The only reason she had to stay now was me.

"You know what, Lorenzo? I think I am home." In one smooth move, she pulled her dress over her head, tossed it on the deck, and dove into the perfect blue water.

I grinned stupidly and followed.

My first official act as the island's new owner had been to change the name from Montalban Island to St. Carl.

It had a nice ring to it.

Home.

Sweothi City

by Larry Correia

Sweothi City, Central African Republic
December 15th, 1993
1:25 PM

The hotel had been evacuated since the government had collapsed and revolution had spilled over the countryside, but the lobby still stank of stale cigarette smoke and sweat. Random cries, crowd noise, and honking horns resonated through the windows as the seemingly endless mob of refugees surged through the streets.

The refugees did not know they were doomed. With the *Mouvement pour la Libération du Centrafricain* (MLC) rebels tearing up the Ubangi river basin, there was no escape. And from what I had seen in the last forty-eight hours, they didn't take prisoners. The CAR Army was in shambles from the coup, with half of them joining the rebels, and the other half fleeing for the Congolese border.

The lobby had become our improvised command center. Furniture, debris, and even some of the planking from the walls had been stacked against the doors to deter adventurous looters. Ramirez was on the roof, armed with an ancient DP machinegun and a radio. So far the MLC hadn't made a move against the city, but they were massing, and every escape route was blocked.

There were twenty men in the lobby, two separate groups forced together, uneasy allies with only one chance for survival. You could feel the anxiety in the air, a physical buzz, almost louder than the refugee train outside. All of them were filthy, armed to the teeth, exhausted, and aware that death was coming, and it was coming hard and fast.

SWITCHBLADE was headed by Decker, the dispassionate mercenary leader. Someone had scrounged up a chalkboard, probably stolen from the missionary school next door and he was busy drawing a rudimentary map of the city and the route that the rebel army was most likely going to use to assault it. O's were the bad guys. X's and arrows showed his plan. Each X was one of us. Each arrow was an order given in a cold, emotionless, voice.

There weren't very many X's on that map. There were a whole lot of O's.

Hawk, the weathered gunslinger, was second in command. The man always made me think of those gun magazines I had read as a kid, with the stories about blazing sixguns on the border. He was seemingly unfazed, even in our current situation. Cuzak sat on a barstool, head wrapped in a blood stained rag, still in shock from the landmine that had splattered Irwin all over the rest of us. Areyh, the former Israeli commando, was squatting next to the board, memorizing the plans while he ran a bore brush frantically through a filthy Galil. Doc was our medic, and he was off to one side attending to one of the wounded Portuguese mercs. I had a feeling that Doc was going to have a long day.

And me.

And that was all that was left of the illustrious mercenary company called SWITCHBLADE.

F***ing Decker. F*** Decker and his f***ing mission. He should have listened to me. If he hadn't been so damn sure of himself, so damn proud, Irwin, Slick, and Sam would still be alive.

I hid my emotions behind a mask of mud and dried blood, and went back to dispassionately cleaning the Yugoslavian RPK that I had stolen, listening to Decker's defensive plans, but already making plans of my own.

The other half of our ragtag group of survivors was all that remained of the Portuguese mercenary company out of Angola. They had been hit worse than we were. Nobody had expected the rebels to be this well organized and equipped, but apparently the Montalban Diamond Exchange had brought in a large group of Cubans to train up the disorganized MLC. The Ports had lost most of their leadership in the last skirmish, and the only thing holding them together was a short, angry, hairball of a man named Sergeant Gomes.

"If we put up enough of a fight along these streets, then the rebels will commit their reserves. Currently that reserve is blocking here, and here. And as far as we can tell, those are the shock troops. The groups moving into the city now are the irregulars. With them out of the way, we can then retreat down Kahiba Road toward Manova-Gounda. Then it's a straight shot, fifteen clicks, to the airfield," Decker explained calmly. "The plane is fueled, and ready to go, but they will not wait for us if the rebels approach the airfield. We do not have much time."

He was calm now. The Belgian was always calm. He was calm when he got us into this suicide mission. Calm when we overthrew a government and brought hell down on these people to placate a diamond company, and he would probably be calm when I put my knife in his throat. I snapped a fresh drum into the Yugo and worked the charging handle.

"It'll be tight, but we can fit in the truck, all of us," the leader of the Portuguese said, referring to the deuce and a half they had stashed in the hotel garage. His English sounded strange, and had probably been taught to him by an Afrikaner. "Who's gonna cause enough problems to get a division of rebels to concentrate enough to let us slip out though?"

"We'll need a diversion. Someone will need to cause enough resistance to stall the irregulars, here," he gestured at the board, "long enough for them to call in the Cubans and the trained MLC. We'll need someone who can fight, and then slip away once we escape, someone who can disappear, go to ground. Stealth will be their only chance to evade capture." He looked right at me as he said it.

So he knew.

I should have kept my mouth shut after this operation went to hell. But I didn't. I violated my own rule of always being the grey man, the one that didn't draw attention, the thief in the background. I had let my emotions get the better of me. And Decker must have sensed my anger.

And over the last year, he had seen what happened to people who made me angry.

So this was how it was going to be.

"Ozzie," he nodded toward me. "I think you would be the only person who would have a chance." Decker was good, very good. He didn't display any indication that he was disposing of me. Rather, he was just the good leader, picking the best man for the job. "We're counting on you. Force them to pull their reserves, if not, we'll have to try a frontal assault, and since they have those APCs, it would be suicide in the open."

The only surviving radio in the room suddenly crackled with static. Every head in the room swiveled towards it. "This is Ramirez. Militia forces are moving into the south end of the city. Looks like they're going to burn it all."

The room was silent, then broken by a fit of coughing from one of the wounded mercs who'd caught shrapnel in the lung.

"Do you mind if we have a word about this, in private?" I asked, perfectly calm.

Decker made a show of looking at his watch. "Certainly." He gave an imperceptible nod toward Hawk. They had been around, and knew what was happening. "But we'd best hurry."

"No s***," Sergeant Gomes said, as a mortar shell exploded somewhere in the city.

"It didn't have to be like this," Decker said, as he strolled into the side room. He had his back to me. The spot between his shoulder blades and the ALICE suspenders was an inviting target, and I could feel the heavy weight of the combat knife on my hip. But Hawk was trailing behind me, and as fast as I was, I knew that Hawk was that much faster with that big magnum revolver.

"It is what it is," I replied, too damn tired to try to put on any sort of act. "We killed the president. We caused this. The diamond exchange used us, and you let them."

"How long have you been with SWITCHBLADE?" he asked, already knowing the answer. "A year, yes, a year. And honestly . . ." he finally turned to face me, his eyes sad, his spirit injured by the events of the last two days. "I saw great things in your future. You were nothing but a common thief when you joined us . . ."

"I was an *exceptional* thief."

He ignored that. "But I saw a leader, a man that could make a difference. I could see you taking over, and running this organization." Decker was sincere, at least. That I could tell, but sincerity doesn't make a rattlesnake any less venomous.

"If you haven't noticed, half your organization's dead, because you screwed up."

"I know . . ." Decker said, his voice cracking, the pain obvious. "This is the end of SWITCHBLADE. Even if we make it out, the diamond exchange will have us hunted down like dogs. I'm sorry about the men. They . . . they were like family to me." I could hear the creak of gun leather as Hawk shifted behind me.

Also true, but it didn't make me hate him any less right then.

"And I know that's why you're going to do your best to slow down these rebels. Because I know that Ramirez, and Doc, and Cuzak are like brothers to you, and you won't let them down," Decker said simply.

"True," I answered.

"You had better hurry." Decker put his hand on my shoulder. "I'm sorry," he said. And I believed him.

And that was the only reason I decided not to kill him.

The refugees were panicking now, turning from individuals, into a deadly entity, discarding and crushing bits of itself underfoot. Screams filled the air. In the distance could be heard the boom of mortars and sporadic automatic weapons fire. The boards that had been blocking the front door flew into the street in a spray of dust as I booted them hard and pushed my way into the street.

It was hot. Muggy, sticky hot, and sweat rolled down my back and soaked my camouflage. The air stank of oil and smoke and fear.

The group had been low on ammo after two days of furious combat and retreat, but I had still commandeered every piece of hardware that I could carry. I had the RPK in hand, our last RPG slung over one shoulder, Cuzak's Ithaca 37 over the other shoulder (he was in no shape to fight anyway), a Browning Hi-Power on my belt, and every spare round of ammo and frag grenade that I could scrape up. Any more munitions and I wouldn't be able to move. Tsetse flies kept landing on my face to probe the dried blood patches.

Doc had tried to stop me. He understood what was happening, that I was a threat to Decker, and therefore expendable. I had just shook my head, and made him promise to get the wounded to safety. Cuzak hadn't said a word, but he shook my hand solemnly, knowing what I was about to do. If I had one weakness, it was that when I occasionally made a friend, I was too damn loyal.

And it was about to kill me.

Decker gave me a brief nod. Hawk tipped his hat in my direction. Areyh spit on the floor.

So this was the end of SWITCHBLADE.

The others exited, fanning out, forming a perimeter around the hotel, where they would hold until Ramirez, acting as our spotter, could see that the road was clear. If I failed, their only choice was to attack straight into the Cubans and try to break through to the airfield. They would never make it. I walked away, the deadly mob of women, children, and old men parting before me like water, leaving the last year of my life behind, and knowing that I was probably going to perish in the next few minutes. The terrified Africans moved out of my way, my anger like an invisible plow.

The CAR was a blighted land. Torn by war for generations, poor beyond all comprehension, and I knew that probably half of these refugees would be dead in the next ten years from AIDS even if they managed to somehow survive the machetes of the approaching rebels. And we had come here, paid in blood money, to topple their corrupt government, and install another corrupt government that the diamond exchange liked better. And even then, the exchange had sold us out.

What a waste.

Then there was someone pushing forward with me. Sergeant Gomes, the Portuguese mercenary, appeared at my side, his burly form cradling the Port's PKM machine gun. A stubby Steyr Aug was tied around him with a discarded web belt serving as a sling. His oddball camouflage was ripped, blood stained, and every exposed patch of skin was covered in caked on mud. He looked hideous.

But happy. "Let's kill us a bunch of these rebel sons of bitches," he grinned, his beady eyes narrowing dangerously.

"What're you doing?" I shouted over the chaos.

"My men? They're in no shape to fight. So I figure, nothing I can do for them," he shrugged. "You could use the help. Might as well go fight."

I couldn't argue with that.

He stuck out his hand. It was calloused and strong. "Call me Carl."

I had been going by Ozzie for the last year, but I knew that I couldn't go back. Even if I lived through this battle, it would be best if I disappeared. I knew that the diamond exchange could not afford to allow any of SWITCHBLADE to survive, knowing the things that we knew. And if they didn't get me, then Decker might very well try, just to tie up loose ends. It was time to start over, to disappear, to become grey again.

I said the first name that popped into my head.

"Lorenzo . . . My name is Lorenzo."

Sweothi City, Central African Republic
December 15th, 1993
2:15 PM

The crowd thinned out enough for the two of us to break into a run, counter intuitively, toward the sound of gunfire. Normally I was the type that liked to plan, but there was no time for that.

This part of Sweothi City was rougher than the rest. Half the buildings were the stacked mud brick type, but compressed between them was a maze of shanties built out of things like chicken wire, packing crates, and old tires. Some of them were already burning.

Carl grabbed me by the arm and pointed down the street into the emptying marketplace. Black smoke was rising from the neighborhood behind it. "The irregulars will come through here."

"How do you know?"

"I've been fighting in Africa since my people lost Mozambique. They'll come through here because they're stupid rabble and it's obvious. They'll want to loot the shops, rape the stragglers." He swept his hand to the right, and pointed down the other intersection. "When the Cubans come, they'll move up this street, and then try to flank us through the shanties on the north. That's how those commie bastards will do it."

I nodded quickly, trying to burn the layout into my mind.

"Stick and move. Don't let them pin you down. Most of these s*** birds can't shoot, but they shoot a lot." Carl hefted the massive PK. "Always attack. Make them react. Got it?"

"Got it."

My pulse was pounding in my head as I turned and headed into the market and toward the rising smoke plumes of black tire-fueled smoke. The 75 round drum in the RPK was heavy and pendulous at the balance point as I let the muzzle lead the way. I moved in a crouch, Carl slightly behind me, gun shifting toward every sudden flash of movement. Several scrawny dogs ran past, tails between their legs.

Then I saw the first of the rebels. I raised my fist, signaling contact. We both crouched low and moved into the shadows beneath a meat stand. A thick black cloud of flies covered the hanging goats and chickens. A can of generic bug spray was under foot, surely used to spray the meat down to keep the flies off.

The first of the MLC were making their way through the bazaar, kicking over stands, and picking up anything left that looked shiny. They really were rabble. Nothing like the disciplined troops we had fought earlier. Most of them were scrawny, malnourished, conscripts wide-eyed with fear, or barely coherent on khat. I hunkered down, waiting for more of them to come into view before I opened fire.

Then there was a scream to the side. A woman. Carl and I both jerked toward the noise, just in time to see two of the rebels dragging a young girl by the hair from one of the brick houses into the street. She was hysterical, with tears running down her dark cheeks.

Carl's machinegun shifted toward the two men, but I grabbed his arm and shook my head. The rebels hadn't seen us yet. I jerked my thumb toward myself, made a slashing motion across my throat, and then pointed at the two would be rapists. Carl nodded, and trained his weapon back at the rebels collecting in the market. We only had one belt for the machine gun, and needed to make the most use of it.

I put the RPG, RPK, and Ithaca on the ground, as quietly as possible, and drew the Vietnam-era Air Force knife from my belt. I slid under the booth, and crawled through the dirt, brushing between hanging meat and half gutted chickens, using every shadow and piece of cover. Luckily my Rhodesian camouflage was so crusted with filth that I was the same color as the earth. I covered the thirty feet to the first rebel in a matter of seconds. This was my element. No one could move quieter or faster than I could.

The men were distracted. The first had shoved the girl down and was trying to rip her clothes off as she thrashed and screamed. He was obviously inexperienced at this whole pillaging thing, and the girl was wailing on him.

The second man got tired of waiting, lowered his machete, and pushed the younger man aside. "*Ashti sangha m'baka*, dummy."

I moved in a blur, my knife humming through the air. I hit the first man in the base of the neck. The knife jabbed in under his ear, and out in a flash of red. The second man had time to turn, shock registering on his face, just as I kicked his knee cap backward. He went down on top of the girl. I grabbed him by the hair, jerked his head back, and slashed him across the jugular.

Neither man was making noise now, but both were thrashing, spraying arterial fluids everywhere. They would be dead in seconds. The girl looked up at me in shock as I grabbed the rags that served as her assailant's shirt and hauled him off of her.

"Run."

She heeded my suggestion, leapt to her feet, and bolted, trying to hold her torn clothing closed. I heard motion coming from the open door of her house, and quickly moved against the hot brick wall. Dripping knife held in a reverse grip, close to my chin.

Another rebel walked out of the house, AK in one hand, dangling useless, the other hand was holding some gaudy, cheap, necklace up to the sunlight. He was grinning from ear to ear, pleased with his plunder.

Enjoy it, mother-f***er.

He paused, realizing that his two friends were the source of all that blood, just as I grabbed him by the top of the head, jerked it back, and rammed the combat knife straight down, just above the junction of his neck and sternum. I used the knife against his ribs like a lever to force him to his knees as I sawed through his aorta. I yanked the blade out and let him thud lifeless to the ground. I wiped the knife on his pants, sheathed it, and grabbed his AK. The whole thing had taken less than twenty seconds.

Carl was staring at me in slack-jawed wonderment as I slithered back through the hanging meats.

"Filho da Puta . . ."

"Yeah. I get that a lot," I muttered as I slung the RPG tube and the shotgun. I now had a Kalashnikov in each hand. This was getting kind of extreme.

"Contact right," Carl hissed.

Sure enough, there was the main body of the irregulars. Now they were clustered in the marketplace, fighting like dogs over the scraps of a ruined civilization. There were at least thirty of them, armed with everything from meat cleavers to grenade launchers, and they were not in the least bit worried about resistance.

"On three," his voice was a whisper as he slowly extended the PKM's bipod. "One mag, then run like hell back to the intersection."

"One." I proned out behind the AK, using the magazine as a monopod, and centered it on a knot of men. They were less than one hundred meters away.

"Two," Carl hissed as he took up slack on the trigger.

"Three," I moved the selector to full.

BBBBRRAAAAAAPPPPP . . . BBBBRRAAAAAAPPPPP . . .

The PKM was horrendously loud as it cut a swath through flesh and bone. Whole knots of the rebels disintegrated in clouds of red as the 7.62x54R tore into them in great piercing blows. As Carl was swinging the reaper's scythe, I tried to pick out anything he was missing. I centered the front sight on a running rebel, and cranked off a burst.

The wall three feet to his side exploded under the impact.

"Damn it!"

The sights on this thing were so far off that aiming was useless. I held the trigger down and swept the muzzle across the market, emptying the magazine in one burst. I let go of the AK and let it flop to its side. I was to Carl's left, and the steel cases from the PK hit me with brutal impacts. I scooped up the RPK and prepared to cover his withdrawal.

Carl was saying something repetitive in Portuguese with every burst. In seconds, our hundred-round belt was gone. "Moving!" Carl shouted as he jumped up from behind the smoking beast.

"Move!" I answered as I scanned for threats. Carl ran for the intersection while pulling the Aug from its makeshift sling. The market was a mess, with the dead and dying spread everywhere. The rebels were in disarray, but that wouldn't last long. Already there was movement as more came in from the south. I sighted in on one charging man, and stroked the trigger. The Yugo barked, and the man pitched forward into the street. At least *this* one was sighted in.

"Go!" Carl shouted as he took up position behind a brick wall.

I sprang to my feet, and leapfrogged past him, sliding into a position behind a bank of broken cinderblocks. The RPG on my back made it hard to maneuver, and damn near impossible to get low.

Several of the very brave, or very stupid, moved out into the open. In African warfare, you could often get away with this, as the fundamentals of marksmanship were not really known or taught by very many people here. For Carl and me, however, marksmanship was apparently not a problem. The rebels went down in a quick hail of gunfire.

The street was silent.

We had bloodied them, but I didn't know what it was going to take to get those Cuban's attention and get them off that damn road.

"Give them a minute, to get puffed up, get over the shock, and then they're gonna charge. Then it won't stop until we're dead, or they're dead. So let the dumb ones get popped in the open, and then we'll fall back into the houses and alleys," he jerked with his head in one direction, "and counterattack. When we hear the commie's vehicles, move so we can hit the intersection."

And then it was *on*. Rebels poured through the marketplace. Some ran straight at us, firing from the hip, others hung their guns around corners and blazed away. It was chaos. None of them could shoot worth a damn, but they made up for it in volume. Bullets tried to fill all the empty spaces. The cinderblocks around me exploded into powder and clouds of dust, and I swear some of those guys must have been shooting black powder from all the smoke. I fired at everything that moved and put rounds through anything that looked suspicious.

"Reloading!" Carl shouted as I hammered a line of impacts through some shanties. "Move to the buildings! Go! Go!"

The whole world had gone insane. I was up and moving as fast as I could, hot lead all around me, sounding like angry bees. The RPK sparked hard and spun from my hands, torn nearly in half. The hot muzzle smashed me in the face and my feet flew out from under me. I crashed into the gravel as gouts of flame tore all around.

"Technical!" Carl shouted as he lumbered past me, grabbing me by the straps of my LBV and pulling me up. This particular technical was a red Toyota pickup with a massive 12.7 DhSK machine gun mounted on the back. I hadn't heard it roll up behind us in the intersection.

The huge gun tracked over us, spitting bullets past, and into the soldiers on their own side. Carl shoved me through an open doorway and into the cool darkness.

I lay on the floor, breath coming in ragged gasps. It was actually quiet. Or I think it was quiet. It was hard to tell over the ringing in my ears.

"Are you hit?" Carl shouted as he quickly poked his head through the door.

"I don't think so," I answered.

"Good." Carl pulled back, just as the doorway exploded into mud fragments. The DhSK was seeking us again, probing for us with bullets bigger than my pinky finger. "*Fodas!*"

Now it was brighter as sunshine streamed through the fresh new holes in the wall. This home was a simple, one-room dwelling. There was a backdoor. I crawled toward it, rolled over, yanked Cuzak's 12 gauge, and kicked the simple plywood door open. Leaning out, I could see that the door led into an alley. I scanned the other direction and—

CRACK

"Damn it!" I screamed as the bullet flew through the plywood and past my face. I fell into the dirt alley, right at the feet of a rebel. He looked down at me in surprise as he tried to work the bolt on his Mosin Nagant. I smashed the Ithaca's steel buttplate into his groin. He stumbled back as I rose and smashed his skull with another butt stroke. I brought it down twice more in rapid succession, each impact a meaty thud. He slid slowly down the wall.

Someone else appeared around the corner, and I raised the shotgun without thinking, front bead centering on his head. I froze, as the unarmed old man raised his open hands and begged for his life. My trembling finger had almost pulled the trigger.

"Get down!" I shouted at the old man as the DhSK raked through the house again, with the bullets passing through multiple walls and into the alley. The old man vanished back around the corner.

I had to take out that machine gun. Now. I sprinted down the alley in the direction of the noise. I could hear Carl breathing hard as he tore after me. The alley was long, and twisty, with each mud house having a backdoor. "Watch our back!" I shouted as I thought about all those openings behind us.

The Aug barked twice. "On it!" Carl answered.

There was movement ahead, one of the plywood doors flew open, and the muzzle of an SKS snaked through. The rebel stepped through the doorway and I blasted him in the face with a round of double aught, pumped it, and swung around the door. The little house was packed with soldiers. Packed.

They looked at me. I looked at them. That one second stretched into eternity.

Then everybody moved.

Cuzak's gun was the old style with no disconnector, so you just held down the trigger and pumped and it kept shooting, it also had an extended magazine, but I didn't stop to think about those facts at the time.

BOOM BOOM BOOM BOOM BOOM BOOM click

"*Meu Deus*," Carl gasped as he viewed over my shoulder.

I reached one shaking hand into my pocket, pulled out some more buckshot, and started feeding them into the loading port.

"We've got to keep moving."

2:22 PM

Sweothi City, Central African Republic
December 15th, 1993
2:35 PM

"We need to kill that technical!" Carl shouted into my ear as the walls exploded around us from heavy machinegun fire. Whoever was manning that DhSK was just working it back and forth across the houses. They didn't know which house we were hiding in, or we would already be dead.

"Ya think?" I screamed back.

This was the third home we had leapfrogged into after the shotgun massacre. The area was covered in rebels now, shooting at anybody who didn't look like they were from around these parts. Carl and I sure didn't look like locals.

"You gonna use that thing—" he gestured at the end of the RPG launcher sticking above my shoulder like a psychotic blunderbuss. "Or just carry it around all day?"

I flipped him the bird, and pulled the heavy tube around in front of me. "Head for the alley so the back blast don't kill you."

He nodded once, rolled over, and low crawled for the back door. I knew once I opened that front door, I would have a clean shot at the intersection, but every scumbag in a three block radius was going to zero right in on us. I wouldn't have much time.

I made sure the rocket was fully seated, the hammer cocked on the launcher, and push button safety deactivated. This was it. I stood, risked a quick peek through one of the approximately fifty-caliber holes through the wall, and spotted that damn little Toyota, parked in the middle of the road about ninety meters away. The tube settled heavy on my shoulder.

The plywood door flew open with a bang, powered by my boot and a whole lot of adrenalin. I centered the front sight through the lowest aperture, focused on it, with the Toyota a blur behind.

But then something caught my attention. I don't know if it was the rumble of the heavy engines, or the crunching of debris under its tires. The RPG dipped slightly as I turned toward the lumbering thing coming from the direction, that sure enough, Carl had predicted the Cubans would use.

"BTR!" I screamed, as I pivoted toward the massive Soviet armored personnel carrier. It was all angles and armor, ugly, and swarming with Cubans. I aimed the RPG at the new, deadlier threat, and yanked the trigger. The tube boomed against my face and years of dust billowed from every surface inside the tiny African home. The rocket streaked to its target. It was deafening and awe inspiring.

The front of the BTR seemed to shiver for a brief instant before the grey steel tub belched flames in every direction. Several quick, massive blasts shuddered through the hulk, and I could see figures tossed, wind-milling, and spinning through the air.

I had not seen the second BTR enter the intersection. But it had seen me. Its cannon swiveled toward me. I turned and dove back into the house.

Suddenly the world was white. Brilliant flashing white. Up was down, and the ground was somehow now far below. It came up to meet me, very quickly.

Then nothing.

2:37 PM

Bob looked grim when he walked out of the hospital room and into the hallway. His eyes were red, puffy from crying, and at that moment he looked aged far beyond his seventeen years. My heart broke when I saw him, because Bob was our rock.

"Mom's on her way," I said quickly. She had been hysterical on the phone.

My older brother put one massive hand on my shoulder, using me to steady himself on wobbly legs. He towered over me, intimidating in his size and mass, though he never meant to be. "Dad wants to talk to you," he croaked. Bob then let go of me, and seemed to melt, as he slid down into one of the waiting-room chairs. "You better hurry." He put his head down and started to sob.

Several members of the hospital staff were clustered nearby, watching us. It was a small town, and everybody knew my foster father. They were all stunned by the senseless act of violence that had ripped our little community. I gathered up my courage, and headed for the door.

There was only one bed in the room. A bank of archaic instruments were beeping and clicking behind it. Doctor Smith nodded at me, placed his clipboard down on a small table, and silently left the room. The doctors had done everything they could, but the thugs that had attacked my father had been thorough. If Gideon Lorenzo lived it would be a miracle. Tubes and mysterious bags descended from the ceiling. Through the tangle, I could make out my father.

"Dad?"

"Hector . . ." he wheezed. His bandaged head tilted slightly in acknowledgement.

I moved to his side. He looked bad, with great dark circles around eyes so laced with blood that I couldn't help but blink in sympathy. Always an amazingly strong man, it was shocking to see him in this state. I felt like someone had punched me in the throat. He was a good man, an honorable man. The idea of him being mortal had never entered my mind.

"I've got to tell you something . . ."

I waited, hot tears streaming down my face. This was the man that had taken me off the streets. This was the judge that sent the miserable wretch that had been my real father to prison. The Lorenzos had taken me in, welcomed me into their happy home, let me know what real family and loyalty was like. And now he was dying.

"What, Dad?"

"I'm worried about you . . ." His voice was barely a whisper. "I see things . . . in your future. Bad things." I wiped my running nose on the back of my hand, and leaned in close. His red eyes were open wide, staring right through me. "You have a streak in you. You're good, but you have . . . an evil inside. Don't let it out. Please, whatever you do, don't let it out."

"I won't."

I flinched involuntarily as his hand clamped onto my arm, suddenly strong.

"Don't avenge me. Leave it to the law, boy," he hissed. "*Don't let the evil out . . .*"

Then he was gone.

I stumbled back, crashing hard into the wall, instruments scattering across the floor, the strength gone from my legs. The machines began to scream and nurses rushed into the room. The wall was hard against my back, and the floor was cold beneath my legs. Bob was a hulking shadow in the doorway. A doctor began to pump his hands up and down on my father's chest. I heard a wailing as Mom arrived, her hands pressed to her mouth, but the noise still coming through. I wanted to move to help her, but my body wouldn't respond. Her scream was the word no, over and over.

My ears were ringing.

2:38 PM

My ears were ringing.
   Where am I?
   "Lorenzo! Come on!" Someone slapped me in the face. Hard. "Move, damn it!"
   I woke up, and everything hurt. I was on my back, at an awkward angle, the Ithaca under me, stabbing me in the kidneys. It was hard to breath and the air was choked with dust and smoke. I raised my shaking hands in front of my face and saw that they were covered in blood and I had no idea if it was mine.
   "What the hell was that?" I blurted, sitting up, and feeling something grate unnaturally in my chest.
   "The Cubans are dropping mortar rounds right ahead of their advance."
   "They can do that?" I quavered as Carl pulled me up.
   "Apparently. Good thing they missed. Can you move?"
   "I think so." Pain was shooting through me, but everything seemed to be connected. The house that I had been hiding in was . . . gone. "That was a *miss*?"
   The area was now overlaid in swirling dust and smoke from the burning BTR. That mortar round had raised a mess. I could see flashes of movement through the fog, but I was lucky to see ten feet. This was our chance. We had accomplished our mission and gotten the Cubans to abandon their post. "Carl, head for where the technical was. Let's hitch a ride."
   "Good idea," he coughed as he inhaled a lungful of particulate. He pulled a black bandana out of his pocket and quickly tied it around his face like some bandito. *Nice.* I started toward where I thought the intersection was. Carl grabbed me by the shoulder, turned me 180 degrees, and shoved. I had really gotten turned around.
   It hurt to move. It hurt more to breath. I was confused and disoriented, but I would be damned if I was going to die in this forsaken hell-hole. I hefted the

shotgun and ran through the rubble and over the occasional body. This dust screen was going to settle fast.

It was like something out of a nightmare. Shapes appeared only to fade away through the haze. I slashed my leg open on a protruding piece of jagged rebar, scattering red droplets that disappeared into the ground like it was covered in sawdust, but I couldn't even think of slowing down. A rebel materialized in front of me, and I instantly shot him through the heart with the 12 gauge. More men were moving to the side, and I fired at them as I sprinted past until the firing pin landed on an empty chamber.

Then we were out of the cloud, but we were in the open, running down the middle of a dirt street. My eyes gritted in their sockets, locking onto the technical, now only twenty meters away. A rebel was charging straight at me, a machete held high overhead, spittle flying from his lips. He was screaming something.

I tossed him the Ithaca. He caught it, looked at it in surprise, and then I crashed into him with my shoulder, bowling both of us to the ground. My combat knife was already coming out of the sheath as we hit. He screamed as I drove it between his ribs, but he still struggled to bring the machete into play.

Carl stepped past me, Aug shouldered, and opened fire on the Toyota. There were two men in the back, and both of them shook as the angry Portagee put bullets into them. The driver's window shattered as Carl shifted targets.

The rebel and I rolled across the ground, locked in a dance to the death. I blocked the machete with my forearm. It cut deep, but he didn't have the room to swing it. I pulled the knife out, and slammed it in again, and again, and again. Finally, he quit moving.

"Lorenzo, quit screwing around!" Carl shouted, as he scanned the wall of dust and flames. "We've got to go."

I rose, panting, and sheathed the still bloody knife. Angry bullets whined past my head as more rebels saw us. "I'll drive."

"No, I drive. Nobody can catch me." Carl answered as he opened the Toyota's door, grabbed the dead driver, and hurled him out. "Get on that gun!"

I vaulted over the side of the pickup bed, landing on a pile of hot 12.7 brass. Carl revved the engine. Then the smoke wall opened and a great screaming beast roared through, muzzle flashes erupting from its machinegun.

"BTR!" I screamed as the APC rolled over a knot of rebels. But Carl was fast. He slammed the Toyota into gear and put pedal to metal. I slipped on the brass, and bounced off the truck bed walls as Carl cranked the wheel and took us through the rubble. I looked up in time to see an unlucky rebel bounce off the front fender and fly through a scrap-wood shanty.

Bullets puckered through our technical as we tore down the street and right through the militia. The remaining windows shattered. Carl bellowed in rage and pain as something struck him. I crawled up to the DhSK, but it was empty, with the feed tray cover locked open. I yanked the Browning 9mm from my holster and fired at the rebels one handed, the other holding onto the rollbar to keep from being tossed out.

We seemed to be going unbelievably fast.

The BTR was right behind us. For being so big, damn that thing was quick.

"Get on that gun or we're gonna die!" Carl yelled, as he cranked the wheel and we took a corner far too fast.

THOOM

The 37mm cannon round flew past and most of the marketplace disappeared. The shockwave rocked the little technical onto two wheels, and then back. I spotted a big, green ammo-can and opened it. There were the huge 12.7 rounds, linked in a rusty, metal belt. I hoisted it out, put the belt in place, slammed the cover down, and yanked back on the charging handle.

I swiveled the DhSK around, but the BTR hadn't followed us around the corner.

But there were plenty of other targets.

I opened fire on random MLC rebels as we drove by. The muzzle blast from the big Russian was like a mushroom cloud. The recoil shook the Toyota down to its suspension. Carl took another corner, trying to head south, out of the city, but the streets were a maze.

Suddenly the brakes locked up, and we slid to a halt. I had the gun trained to the rear, and craned my neck around to see what the problem was.

The road was on fire.

For a good thirty feet, the road was nothing but a blazing oil slick, with flames taller than I was. This had been the source of the great pillar of smoke that we had homed in on to get to the marketplace. It must have been some sort of gas station before the rebels had blown it up. There was no other way past.

I turned back. The way we came from was swarming with rebels, looking like ants. A bullet sparked off the Toyota's tailgate. Ants with AK-47s.

The tail lights lit up, signaling that we were in reverse. Another bullet smashed one of the lights. We started back toward the pile of rebels.

"Carl? What are you doing?" The only remaining taillight shattered. Another round cut a chunk from my ear.

"We need a running start."

"You've got to be kidding me . . ." I laid on the DhSK like it was the hammer of Thor, sweeping it across the street. It ain't pretty what one of these things does to a human being. I held the trigger down, the concussion so deep that I could feel it vibrating the jelly in my eyes.

Carl stopped, ground the transmission, and floored it.

I dropped down, threw my arms over my head, and tried to think happy thoughts.

Fire. Everywhere. Holy s***.

It was hard to explain. I opened me eyes, and could see it, like it was a living thing, coming up over the edge of the truck, leering down at me, hungry and angry. The heat hit like a sledgehammer, evaporating all of the moisture from my skin. I held my breath, but could feel the poison crowding up my nostrils. It wanted to eat me.

Then we were through.

I jumped back up. The DhSK's wooden spade grips were on fire. I smothered them with my shirt. The Toyota's paint was burning, the wind quickly beat it out.

Carl turned back around and looked at me through the shattered rear window, beady eyes gleaming through a layer of soot over his bandito mask, and said, "Hey, Lorenzo, your hair's on fire."

Well f*** me. I rubbed it out.

This road seemed to lead to the edge of town. I could see down it, a straight shot, and in the distance was open country and room to run or hide. Carl shifted gears and we continued to accelerate.

Then I saw it.

The BTR was running parallel to us. It was one street over to the right, separated from us by a single row of mud houses and shacks. The grey hulk was going to intercept us. The Cubans inside opened up through their firing ports. Most of the rounds smashed into the buildings, but at each gap, some passed through. Tracers stabbed a dotted line across the road.

Two could play that game. I grabbed the smoking handles and swiveled the DhSK.

"Hey!"

"Yeah!"

"BTR on our right. Will 12.7 pierce their armor?"

"Hell yeah! They're light plate."

I wasn't going to try to time it between the houses. We were almost out of town, and I didn't want to square off with this thing in the open. I mashed the butterfly trigger down.

The DhSK roared. Homes disintegrated as we played tag to the death with the Cubans at fifty miles an hour. The mighty 12.7 rounds crashed into the monstrosity, zipping right through the armor and through the crew inside.

The BTR swerved hard toward us, smashed through a house, actually got some air, and careened onto our street. I kept the DhSK on it the whole time, stitching it from end to end, opening it like a teenager shooting a pop can with a .22. The BTR continued on at an angle and smashed through another house and disappeared onto another street.

"I think I got him!"

"No." Carl pointed out the window. The BTR was now traveling down the street to our left. The 37mm cannon was rotating toward us. I cranked the DhSK back around and opened fire, bouncing wildly as the Toyota careened down the rutted road. Carl stomped on the brakes. I flew forward and smashed into the cab as the cannon bloomed flame. The round narrowly missed us and a pile of shanties exploded into flames and shrapnel.

I spit a mouthful of blood onto the roof and shoved myself back onto the machinegun. The BTR was slightly ahead of us on the next street over. Carl suddenly accelerated. Somehow I knew exactly what he was doing. I cranked the DhSK around toward the front.

Carl swerved, crashing us through a fence made of sticks and cardboard. A pile of chickens fell victim to the Toyota, and suddenly birds and feathers were flying everywhere. We seemed to be airborne for a brief second, then the tires struck earth, and we were behind the speeding BTR.

I mashed the spade grips, the sight lined up on the rear end of the BTR. The muzzle brake reverberated painfully off the Toyota's roof. Carl stuck his fingers into his ears, and steered with his knees. Round after round ripped through the armored vehicle from end to end, and it careened wildly to the side and crashed into a ditch, flames suddenly licking out of its ports.

Carl pulled his fingers out of his ears, put one on the wheel, and one on the gear shift, and hammered the little Toyota forward. We zipped past the now burning BTR and toward freedom. A hot wind struck my back as it exploded behind us. Another black, oily, cloud was rising above Sweothi City as we sped onto the highway and past the sign pointing toward the Congolese border.

2:52 PM

The man looked up at me in fear, as he thrashed against the duct tape that held his wrists to the heavy chair. The old warehouse was deserted and I knew that nobody would hear him scream. "Please, come on, man, don't do it!"

I held the syringe up to the flickering fluorescent light. "You know what this is?"

"No please, come on, I'm begging you."

Did my father beg? No, of course not.

"It's heroin. Mostly. The rest is drain cleaner. The heroin is to make this plausible. You're just another scumbag junkie, got some bad stuff, had an overdose. There won't even be an investigation. The drain cleaner is so this will hurt. A lot."

"You can't do this. T-Bone will kill you. He'll kill you, man!" the thug screamed.

Did my father threaten violence? No. I'm sure he hadn't. He was a man of peace and justice.

"T-Bone's dead. I got him already. He fell out his apartment window. Landed on one of those pointy fences. Real nasty." I gave a fake shudder. "The others are dead too. Ice got shot in a drive by shooting this morning. Little Mike is floating in the river. He fell in, couldn't swim. Especially with those cinderblocks I tied to his legs."

His eyes were wide. I could smell the fear. "Who are you!"

"A year ago, you were passing through a little place outside Georgetown. You beat a man to death. He was a good man. Why? Why did you do it?"

"I don't know man! I don't remember . . . He had a nice watch, or something. Come on, man, he was just some dude! We didn't mean to kill him. Just mess him up, take his s***."

I stabbed the needle into his arm and smashed the plunger down. I tossed the now empty syringe aside. He began to convulse as I cut the tape and stuffed the evidence into my pocket. He fell to the floor as I walked away. I shut the lights off on the way out and left him in the dark to twitch and foam. I started walking, and didn't look back. I was sixteen years old.

The thing is, when you let the evil out, it's hard to put it back.

Sorry, Dad.

10 Kilometers east of Banti-Guonda, Congo
December 16th, 1993

Dreams of home. So very long ago.

I woke up sore when I heard the sound of the airplane. The stitches on my arm, back, and legs were tight and itchy. Carl did good work. He was already awake, cleaning his Aug while leaning in the shade beneath a crumpled tree. He had a bandage wrapped around his torso, over the carpet of black hair that was his body. The ruined Toyota was hidden in the bushes.

He squinted at me with beady eyes. "Bush plane's coming in. You think we can trust this guy?"

I yawned. "Yeah. He's good people . . . Phil specializes in helping people move valuable things. He owes me a favor. So, Carl, you think about what you're going to do now?"

"I don't know." He shrugged. "My company's gone. Most of us died in the coup. I don't even know if my men made it out."

"They're with Decker. They made it." I answered truthfully. As much as I hated the man, he was extremely good at what he did. "You know, I'm now out of work myself." I pulled a black bag out of my pocket and tossed it to Carl.

He caught it absently, opened the drawstring, and shook some of its contents into the palm of his hand. He whistled.

"SWITCHBLADE had a few simple rules. The leader always got a double share, and he was the only one that has access to the Swiss bank account. Since the diamond exchange crossed us, I'm pretty sure nobody got paid. So we looted some of the treasury while we were in the palace. The six still gets a double share."

Carl's hand was filled with diamonds.

"I took the liberty of lifting Decker's shares. And to think he called me a *common* thief. I'm pretty sure he'll be massively pissed when he finds out. Good thing he thinks I'm dead." I knew that was for the best. I would gain nothing by tracking Decker down. It was time for the evil to be put away once and for all.

"Not a bad haul," Carl said, as he poured the diamonds back into the bag. He started to hand it back.

"No, that's your share. I've got mine."

"Serious?"

"Yeah, I've been thinking . . ." I said as the bush plane approached the runway, landing gear extended. "I'm going to go on my own, form my own team. Be my own boss. But I'm going to need help. Have you ever thought of stealing stuff for a living?"

"Can't say I have," he answered. "Unless you count twenty years of plundering Africa, but I'm sick of this place."

"Well, I'm thinking about only robbing bad people. They've got all the money anyway, and screwing with them is a lot more fun."

The little plane touched down with a squeak of tires. Carl chewed his lip for a moment, then extended his hand.

I shook it. "Carl, I think this could be the beginning of a beautiful friendship."

SWORDS OF EXODUS

by Larry Correia and Mike Kupari

*"The price of freedom is
the willingness to do sudden battle anywhere,
any time and with utter recklessness."*
—Robert A. Heinlein

Prologue: Set in Stone

SrA VALENTINE, M.
521st Expeditionary Security Forces Squadron
U.S. Air Force
Zargabad District, Western Afghanistan
Seven Years Ago

My shoulders ached. Dust filled my nose as the column came to a halt. I let my M4 hang on its sling as I pulled off my eye-pro and wiped my face with my shemagh.

Word came down the line that we were going to be here for a while. The cavalry soldiers we were embedded with fanned out and took up good defensive positions. Being a team of enablers, we were just expected to stay put unless they needed us. That was okay with me. My rucksack wasn't sitting right on top of my body armor and needed to be adjusted. After a quick check of my area, to make sure I wasn't near any pressure plates, I set my pack down and plopped down next to it.

"That's a good idea," said my partner. Senior Airman Arlene Chambers was a dog handler. Her military working dog, Muttley, was tired from the oppressive heat and sat next to her, panting.

At least there was shade. The village of Murghab was so far from the nearest US FOB that our only support came via helicopter, and was uncomfortably close to the Iranian border, but it was picturesque in its own way. Our patrol had come down a narrow dirt path that ran alongside a small, babbling creek. On the other side of the trail was a six-foot mud wall. Behind the wall was a row of tall poplar trees that sighed in the hot breeze and kept us out of the sun.

A Cavalry NCO stopped to check on us as he made his way up the line. "How you doing, Air Force?" Sergeant Hanover wasn't really checking on *us* so much as he was checking on Chambers. She wasn't the only female out with us in Murghab. We had a two-woman Female Engagement Team up in front, interfacing with the Afghan women as part of our ongoing counterinsurgency efforts, but Chambers was easily the *best looking* female out with us, and she knew it.

My partner smiled at him. "Oh, I'm a little tired but good to go." She cracked open a bottle of water and tilted it forward. Muttley lapped at it eagerly, wagging his tail as he drank.

"How's the dog doing?" Hanover asked, kneeling down so he could pet Muttley.

"He's hot, but I'm watching him. He'll be good for the rest of the op I think. We're still flying out after sundown, aren't we?" There had been talk of extending our mission another day. It'd already been two days since a pair of Chinooks had dropped us off outside of the village.

"I'm okay too," I said with a sarcastic grin. "Thanks for asking."

Hanover laughed at me. "Patrol's been extended."

"What's going on?" Chambers asked. "Why are we stopping now?"

"We ran into some contractors up there. PMC guys in armored trucks. The ANA commander is flipping out because I guess nobody told him they were operating in 'his' AO. Our 'terp is trying to convince him that nobody told us, either, but he's pretty pissed." We'd only been operating with this Afghan National Army unit for a couple of days, but it had already become apparent that its commander enjoyed theatrical temper tantrums if it helped him get his way. I guess he thought it showed his men that he was willing to stand up to the Americans. All it really did was make Captain Drake, the Cavalry troop commander, want to punch him in the face. Hanover's radio squawked. "Alright," he said. "I gotta get up there. We'll call you if we need the dog to check anything." Muttley was pretty good at sniffing out explosives and drugs, both of which could easily be found in Afghanistan.

"Have fun!" I said encouragingly as Sergeant Hanover jogged forward. I then stood up to stretch. So far, the mission to Murghab had been a bust. No contact with insurgents, no weapons caches, and thankfully no IEDs. It had been three days of just walking around, talking to the locals. It was still better than sitting back at the Expeditionary Air Base, stuck in a guard tower for twelve hours at a time. At least we got to get out into the war.

I scanned the village for threats, doing my best not to get complacent, as the leadership dickered with the ANA, the locals, and the PMC guys. Across the creek were more buildings made of mud, then a two-story mosque that was a lot nicer than anything else in the village. It wasn't made of mud, which was pretty remarkable for a village this remote, and was topped with a blue minaret. The generator behind it indicated that it even had electricity. *Fancy.*

Up the trail, I could see the PMC vehicles Hanover told us about. They were MATVs, like the ones US forces used, but painted white instead of tan. The dirt road they were parked on was one of few in the village wide enough for a big vehicle to use. The contractors were clad in Desert Tiger Stripe fatigues and mismatched head gear, and a couple of them were walking down the line with Captain Drake.

The ANA took the halt to mean that it was chow time. They were easy to spot in their mint chocolate chip digital camouflage fatigues, and were already stripping off their armor, laying down their weapons, and breaking out the rations. ANA units varied widely, from *pretty decent* to *dangerously incompetent*. This particular unit gravitated more toward the incompetent end. When we bedded down in strongpoints for the night, they busted out the hashish and started getting high. It was ridiculous.

"Great," I said to Chambers. "The ANA's hungry. We're going to be here for a while."

Chambers stood up, keeping one hand on her M4 and another on Muttley's leash. "They already had breakfast a few hours ago!" It was only about ten thirty in the morning, but we'd been on the move since first light.

"Second breakfast, I guess. Like hobbits."

Chambers laughed at me. "Nerd."

"I'm just saying. Afghanistan would be way nicer if hobbits lived here instead of Afghans." I paused for a second and looked around. "Hey . . . where'd the little dusties go?"

"Yeah, you're right," my partner agreed, looking around. A troop of Afghan children, aged five to probably thirteen, had been following us around all morning, begging us for treats and candy. "I haven't seen them in a while."

The air was suddenly filled with music as the nearby mosque began its call to prayer. Islamic music blared tinnily over a loudspeaker, making it difficult to be heard.

"That's weird too," I said, raising my voice. "Don't they usually do it after noon?"

A wry smile appeared on Chambers' face. "Do you think they have an atomic clock in there or something? This is Afghanistan. It's whatever time they say it is."

"You don't know that. Maybe they have a sundial or some—"

Chambers suddenly fell to the ground, landing in a puff of moon dust. She had a very surprised look on her face. I was about to ask her if she was okay when I saw the blood. I'd heard the shot. It just happened so fast it didn't register. My heart dropped into my stomach as I processed what was happening. "Medic!" I screamed. "Contact right!"

The ambush began in earnest. I fell to my knees and tried to apply pressure to Chamber's wound as gunfire erupted from every direction. I tried to ignore that and focused on keeping my partner alive. Bullets buzzed and snapped overhead like so many angry hornets, pock-marking the mud wall we'd been leaning on. I screamed for the medic again as blood poured out from under my hands. Chambers' eyes were wide as she writhed in agony. Muttley whined and licked her hand.

Oh God, oh God, oh God! I let go of the wound long enough to fumble for my medical pouch. I had some hemostatic gauze in there that might stop the bleeding. The bullet missed the plate on her vest, blasting right through the soft armor of her vest and deep into her side.

"I got this!" A Cavalry medic materialized at my side. "Give me that." He took the gauze package out of my hand and went to work. I didn't move. "Hey!" he said, looking up from Chambers to stare me down. "I got this! Cover me!"

I nodded my head, turned, and tried to process the chaos around me. The ANA had been caught completely off guard. They scrambled for the weapons they'd laid down, and most of them didn't have time to get their armor back on. A low *BUUUUUURRRP* sound echoed through the village as the PMCs opened fire with the minigun mounted on their MATV.

The mosque. The shot had come from the mosque. Above the cacophony of battle a very loud rifle report resonated from the direction of the mosque. An ANA soldier's chest exploded, sending him tumbling to the ground in a cloud of dust.

"Shooters in the mosque! Shooters in the mosque! They have a fifty-cal up there!" No one seemed to hear me. Orders were shouted over the radio. Complex ambush. Many insurgent personnel. Multiple wounded. KIA. Assault through. MEDEVAC delayed until attack helicopters could be spun up to escort.

Boom! Someone found an IED. *Christ.* All the while, the medic struggled to stabilize Chambers. She was either unconscious or dead. I couldn't tell.

Something strange happened to me then. There was a coldness deep in my belly. It slowly made its way up, enveloping my heart and spine. My heart rate slowed, and my breathing slowed with it. The sounds of gunfire faded just a little, and everything seemed to slow down enough that I could process what was going on.

I was *Calm.* I hadn't felt like that since the day my mother died. My fear faded into the background. A plan rapidly formulated in my mind. The Cav guys were getting ready to counterattack, but this village was prepped for an ambush. There would be IEDs. The soldiers would have to move carefully, sweeping everywhere they went. They wouldn't get to the mosque before the shooters got away.

That wasn't going to happen. Before I realized it, I was moving. I left my partner with the medic and slid down into the ditch, splashed through the creek, and scrambled up the other side. Sprinting forward, I slid to a halt behind a mud wall, next to the two contractors who had been talking to Captain Drake. One had his head wrapped in a brown bandanna and carried an AA-12 automatic shotgun. The other was a grizzled-looking SOB with a trimmed, graying goatee, a body armor vest loaded with ammunition, and a brown South African-style bush hat. Around his waist was a leather gunbelt. A big revolver hung from one side, and a big knife hung from the other.

The old guy snapped off several shots from his stubby FAL carbine before covering back down behind the wall. The heavy rifle had a deep bark to it, being more powerful than the M4 I was carrying. "There are shooters in the mosque over yonder, son," he said to me, coolly. "You boys might want to do something about it."

A hole exploded in the mud wall we were using for cover as the enemy sniper put a round from his fifty through it. "They have a fifty-cal rifle up there," I said. "We need to take it out before the MEDEVAC chopper arrives. I can't do it by myself!"

"What about the rest of your troops?"

"I'm in the Air Force. My partner will die if that chopper is delayed. Will you guys help me or what?"

The old man with the FAL nodded. "Alright then, let's get it done. Lay down some fire, I'll move first." As he bounded off to the right, seeking the cover of another building, I started rapidly firing shots into the second level of the mosque. Civilians were running around in terror in front of it, and I hoped my rounds were going over their heads. The other contractor, the one with the shotgun, removed the drum from his weapon and replaced it with a box magazine that I guessed was loaded with slugs. He looked through the holographic sight bolted to the top of his boxy weapon and tore into the mosque.

These contractors didn't seem to be concerned with the rules of engagement. Neither was I. You couldn't tell who was who. The snipers in the mosque weren't the only enemy personnel shooting at us. The ones we could see were dressed the same as the Afghan villagers. Some of them may have *been* Afghan villagers. I didn't give a damn.

A man dressed in dirty white linens stepped around the corner of a mud hut. *Weapon!* He had an AK-47-type rifle with the stock folded. I put my red dot on his chest and cranked off probably half a dozen shots. He fell to the ground and I shifted my fire back to the mosque. The Cav soldiers behind me opened up on it as well. Several M4s and a SAW streamed rounds into the building.

"Now! Move!" the old contractor shouted. He leaned around the corner and fired. His friend with the AA-12 and I bounded over the wall and sprinted forward and to the left. The big rifle in the mosque roared again, kicking up a huge divot on the trail behind me. We took refuge behind a small building before the sniper could fire again.

From behind me, I could hear one of the Cav NCOs shouting at me. "Airman Valentine! Where the fuck are you going?" I ignored him. More shooters appeared in the doorway of the mosque, firing on us even as civilians ran into the building past them. We shot back. People fell to the ground. There wasn't any going back now.

Coughing from the smoke and dust, I removed the partial magazine from my M4 and replaced it with a full one. I stood above the bodies of two dead men. Unlike the Taliban insurgents we normally encountered, these two looked like they'd been pretty squared away. They both wore desert camouflage uniforms, and each had been wearing body armor. On the floor in front of them was a Steyr HS50 rifle, a monstrous bolt-action chambered for .50 BMG.

"Holy shit, son." It was the leader of the contractors. The old man shook his head. "I think these boys are Iranians, judging from the equipment."

"Huh," I said absentmindedly. I was going through adrenaline dump and was coming down off of *the Calm*. My hands were shaking. I could barely stand.

"You okay, kid?" he asked.

"Yeah . . . yeah. I just need a minute."

"That was some damn fine work . . . C'mon, let's get back downstairs. Your friends are here." We were on the second level of the mosque. The two contractors and I had cleared the place before the Cav had arrived. "What's your name, kid?"

"Valentine. Mike Valentine."

"John Hawkins," he said. "People just call me Hawk. I'm with Vanguard Strategic Solutions International." He handed me a business card. "When you get out of the Air Force, you give me a call. I'll put you to work making four times what they pay you for this."

I nodded jerkily and put his card in my pocket as we arrived on the lower level of the mosque. My heart dropped into my stomach when I took in the carnage.

The air was dirty and stunk of burnt powder. Several dead bodies were scattered on the floor in pools of blood. Several more Afghans were wounded. Only a couple of the Afghans had been armed, but they'd used the civilians seeking shelter in the mosque as human shields. I didn't know whose rounds had struck who, but it didn't make any difference to those that had been hit.

"Holy fucking shit." One of the Cavalry soldiers appeared in the doorway. He turned and yelled for a medic. The same medic that had been treating Chambers pushed past him and ran to a wounded Afghan man. I left Hawk where he stood and approached the medic, stepping over bodies as I went.

"What happened to Chambers?"

He took a deep breath and shook his head. "I'm sorry, man. She didn't make it."

I nodded at him as my chest tightened, but I couldn't choke out any words. I knew he'd done the best he could. I wasn't angry at him. I just needed air. The mosque felt as if it was suffocating me. The air stank of death. The wounded survivors stared at me with wide eyes. The dead seemed to be staring at me too.

Stepping back out into the sunlight, I leaned against the wall of the mosque and slid down to the ground. I unsnapped my helmet and set it on the ground next to me. I took off my safety glasses and buried my face in my hands. People came and went past me, but I paid them no mind.

After a few minutes, I was tapped on the shoulder. It was Captain Drake. I immediately came to my feet. "Relax, Valentine," he said calmly. "What the hell happened?"

He listened quietly as I explained, his face a mask.

When I was finished, he simply nodded. "We got a problem. You ran off with some civilian contractors without orders from any of my NCOs. There are a bunch of dead civilians in there. You've been briefed on the ROE. You know how this is going to play out, don't you?"

I felt like I was going to throw up. My partner was dead and I was probably going to be court-martialed. This day couldn't have gone any worse. At that moment, if I could've gone back in time and taken that bullet for Chambers, knowing full well that I was going to die, I would have done so.

But there is no going back, is there?

The Cavalry officer put his hand on my shoulder. "I'm sorry about Airman Chambers. And between you and me, that was some impressive shit you pulled off there. I can't believe some Air Force puke can shoot like that. I'll vouch for you when the time comes. I'll tell them the truth, but I'll vouch for you."

"Thank you, sir."

He left me alone.

In the distance could be heard the sound of a helicopter.

The room rattled slightly as an outbound C-130 took off. I stood at the position of attention in the office of Colonel Christopher Blair, the commander of the 521st Air Expeditionary Wing. I had on a clean uniform and was freshly shaved. I was in enough trouble without going in front of the Wing King looking like a bag of ass. The colonel told me to stand at ease after he sat down. I relaxed a little and moved my hands behind my back.

"Senior Airman Valentine," he began, folding his hands on his desk, "I'm afraid I'm in kind of a bad position here. On one hand, your actions in the village of Murghab were commendable. You advanced under fire and without support onto an enemy position, and cleared that position with almost no help. Senior Airman Chambers was killed by an enemy sniper team, and your actions resulted in that sniper team being neutralized. On the other hand," he gestured at the computer on his desk, "your actions, while not technically insubordination, did involve you disregarding your chain of command, standing general orders, and the rules of engagement. Furthermore, you were aided by employees of a PMC, which is to say, civilians. As a result, six Afghan noncombatants were killed and four more were wounded."

"Sir, the enemy personnel in the mosque were using those people as human shields. They were also firing indiscriminately through the crowd."

"So the report says. That works in your favor. Not working in your favor is the fact that you and these two civilians entered and cleared a mosque without any Afghan personnel with you, which is a violation of the current ROE."

"Sir, we were under direct, immediate, and lethal fire from that position. Half our ANA had either been killed or run away. The ones that stayed were shooting up the entire village in a panic. They were useless."

"Also noted, Airman. Now listen to me. You stirred up a shit storm. An epic shit storm. The Afghan government is calling for you and the contractors from Vanguard to be put on trial by an Afghan court. There is no way that is going to happen, but they're incensed, to say the least. Worse, the Army wants to crucify you. A lot of people who weren't on the ground with you say that you're an undertrained Air Force kid with no business being in their battle space. They say you blatantly disregarded the ROE, killed a bunch of civilians, and they want you court-martialed. You committed the mortal sin of creating headaches for staff officers somewhere."

"Sir—"

"Now, before you get too upset, the Cavalry unit you were with spoke very highly of you and Airman Chambers. They said you two had been a valuable asset to them on other missions and that you made the best decision you could while under fire."

"What does the Air Force say, sir?"

"I'm going to be honest with you. Some people above my level are telling me to throw you under the bus, recommend you for a court martial, and wash my hands of you. If word of this gets out, they say, it'll reflect badly on the Air Force, and the last thing we need is more bad PR."

I took a deep breath and lowered my head slightly. I was going to Fort Leavenworth. I could already see it.

Colonel Blair ignored my moping and continued. "It's more complicated than that, however. You also uncovered the first concrete evidence we've had that Iranian special operations forces are in Afghanistan. The Afghan government has been denying this for years, even though we've suspected all along they've been dealing with the Iranians on the side. That causes nothing but headaches for the brass and their bosses on the civilian side. So as much as they want you crucified, they want this thing quashed so they can deal with it on the down-low. It hasn't gone public yet, but it will if you're put on trial. And believe it or not, there are a few people on the Air Force side who are willing to go to bat for you."

"So what's going to happen to me, sir?"

"Right now? Nothing. Your leadership put you in for the Combat Action Medal, which I intend to sign off on. You've earned that much. But you're not going out on any more missions with the Cav, or anyone else. You're not even going to stand watch. I told your squadron commander to put you in the armory or some other place out of sight. You're going to stay there, keep your head down, and finish out your deployment without any more incidents. You lost your partner out there. Take some time for yourself. Believe me when I say I don't want to see your name come across my desk again. Your term of enlistment is up in, what, a year?"

"About that long, sir."

"Right. You're going to just get out. As a matter of fact, you're not going to be allowed to reenlist, but in exchange for you quietly getting out of the Air Force and keeping your mouth shut about this whole thing, you're not going to be court-martialed. Your punishment will be handled administratively, and this verbal counseling session will suffice, as far as I'm concerned."

"Thank you, sir."

"Look," the colonel said, his demeanor softening. "I'm sorry about Airman Chambers. The official notifications have all been made, but I'm still working on the letter to her parents. We lost one of our own out there, and you were in a bad situation. I don't think what's happening to you is right. I think you should be getting the Bronze Star instead of punished. But there's not much else I can do for you. The best thing you can do is go along, get along, and just leave the military behind."

"I understand, sir," I said quietly. "Thank you."

Hours later, as the Sun sank slowly over the horizon, I found myself wandering the base alone, reflective belt around my waist.

I found a good spot where there wasn't too much background noise, and pulled one of my unit's satellite phones out of my pocket. I unfolded the antenna and, in the failing light, strained to read the card in my hand.

John Hawkins, Director of Special Tactics Training, Vanguard Strategic Solutions International.

I wasn't getting out for almost a year. I wondered, is it too soon to call? *What the hell,* I thought. *It's worth a shot.* That phone call changed my life.

LORENZO
Kuala Lumpur, Malaysia
Seven Years Ago

Hari Merdeka is Malaysian Independence day, and this particular one was one hell of a party. The place was packed with the rich, famous, and powerful, all struggling to hear each other over the extremely loud band. The crowd was Malay, Indonesian, Thai, Indian, Chinese, with a smattering of Westerners, all of them wealthy, many of them distracted by the huge fireworks over the city, and the remainder were schmoozing or cutting deals. For a supposedly Muslim country, there was a surprising amount of very expensive alcohol being consumed, and most of the beautiful women gyrating on the dance floor were thousand-dollar-an-hour prostitutes.

The restaurant was forty stories above the street, suspended at the intersection of two ultramodern buildings. It was a five-star luxury establishment, most of which was currently open to the night air, a veritable hanging garden over the busy street below. The massive Petronas Towers were visible through the rooftop tropical forest. Occasionally, a really bright firework would illuminate the catwalks above us, and you could just make out the shadows of the guard force stalking about, watching the crowd.

Security was tight, but fragmented. There were private guards for some of the more important people, and the perimeter staff made up of hotel employees. I had passed through two sets of metal detectors to get to this point. The food in the dinner cart I was pushing had been tasted by three separate people to check for poison. The guards had forced the chef, his assistant, and the waiter who would be delivering it, played by yours truly, to try some. The foie gras had been delicious.

I passed swiftly between the kitchen and the private dining area, with two black-suited men flanking me. They had patted me down before I had picked up the food, just to be certain, and they kept an eye on me the entire time. They were big for Malays, thick with muscle, shoulder holsters poking out from their unbuttoned coats. This particular private dinner party was a little on the paranoid side.

You would be too if you had stolen from Big Eddie.

Another guard was waiting, and he held open the heavy wooden double door for me and my goon escort. Away from the teeming crowd, the screeching pop band, and the Japanese businessmen eating sushi off of naked chicks, the private dining area was silent, almost peaceful. The roof on this section had not been retracted, and the restaurant had been decorated in the manner of a Zen garden, with lots of those funny little trees and sand with designs drawn in it.

It was a large room, normally capable of holding fifty diners, but tonight there was only one group allowed inside. The proprietors knew that these people needed privacy to discuss their business.

This latest guard held up his hand. I had been through this a few times tonight, to take their orders, to bring their drinks, I knew the drill. I left the cart, and raised my arms for yet another very thorough pat-down. The first two guards did one last check of the large dining cart, lifting up covers and steaming trays, looking under the fabric, probably checking to make sure no guest had managed to stick a bomb onto it in the minute it had taken to walk here from the kitchen.

Grimacing as the guard checked what would be a very uncomfortable place to carry a weapon anyway, I thought about the plan and tried to look as unthreatening as possible, which is actually pretty easy when you're as forgettable as I am. Tonight I was wearing a tuxedo like the other staff, but with the red sash of the chief waiter. My ID said that my name was Pard and I was a resident of the Salpeng Valley and its Tamil minority and I had worked here for five boring years. Being just another nobody was my specialty.

"Smells great," grunted one of the guards as he finished checking the food.

"Well, you're eating noodles when you're off shift, so don't dwell on it," said the other as he straightened my sash and patted me on the shoulder. "You're good. Make this quick and get out of here. The boss is talking business."

"Of course, sir." I rolled the cart toward the diners. Only one guard stayed at my side, the other two took up positions back outside to dissuade partygoers in search of privacy. The heavy door closed behind them.

The dinner party consisted of two men and a woman. The males were

Indonesians in very expensive suits. The woman was a stunning blonde in a slinky black dress. They were seated on thick cushions around a short table. Another guard stood at attention a few feet behind his principle, the Browning Hi-Power in his shoulder holster plainly visible under his open coat. Only the guard noticed my approach. I slowed, but he nodded for me to continue. Ever subservient, I dipped my head, rolled the cart into position, and began removing steaming lids.

The woman was speaking. "Big Eddie will not tolerate you operating in the Strait of Malacca without his permission. That last freighter you hijacked belonged to him, and he is not pleased." Her voice had a slight European accent. "This is not a fight you want to pick." She really was a looker. Her hair had been pulled back into a tight bun, revealing a very perfect neck. She had movie-star looks, a body better than any of the professional girls at the party, and the eyes of a serial killer. I knew her *very* well.

The man laughed. "Katarina, please, I've had far too pleasant an evening to entertain idle threats. My people have controlled the Strait from Selenor to the sea for ten generations." His name was Datuk Keng and he was a pirate. He didn't look like a pirate in the traditional sense, lacking parrot, eye patch, or wooden leg, but believe me, he was the real deal. Keng had approximately three hundred men under his direct command, and they specialized in taking down merchant cargos, selling the boats, and holding the crews for ransom. "You can tell Big Eddie that if his ships are to pass through the Strait, then he must pay for protection like everyone else."

"Our records indicate that Big Eddie owes us twenty-five million in passage taxes." The other man at the table was Keng's assistant. Even pirates need accountants nowadays. "Ten thousand per shipment, plus interest and penalties for sixteen months of noncompliance."

"You really think you can extort money from someone like Eddie?"

"Ahh . . . dinner has arrived," Keng said merrily. "Ms. Katarina, I'm the king of this world. I can do whatever I want. Take that back to your employer, and tell him that twenty-five million is my final offer."

I placed the first dish of five-star goodness in front of Datuk Keng and made eye contact with Katarina.

"Smells wonderful," she said. Translation: Negotiations failed. Time for violence.

Two guards behind me, two more outside, but they were bored. This was just another meeting. They were pirates, tough guys, brutes. This standing around stuff dulled the senses, and I was just the submissive little waiter, whom they had dealt with all night long. *Complacency kills.*

"I must implore you one final time, don't force this issue with Big Eddie, or he will kill you."

Datuk Keng scowled, all pretenses of cordiality gone. Now I could see the man who plundered ships and murdered sailors. His face creased with rage. "You dare threaten me? I'll make this quick—"

I moved with lightning speed, reaching into the nearest guard's coat. The problem with shoulder holsters? The guy standing in front of you can draw your gun faster than you can. I popped the snap, yanked the Browning, and tossed it to Katarina.

She caught the Browning by the grip and leveled it at Keng.

"I'll make it quicker." *BLAM.*

Datuk Keng's head snapped back in a spray of red. The guard tried to hit me, but I blocked it with my elbow, grabbed him by the tie, and fell, choking off his air and taking us both to the ground. That's why I won't wear a tie.

Katarina brought her hands together smoothly and pointed the gun at the second guard. He froze, hand on gun. She smiled. There was no question how that was going to play out. He raised his trembling hands slowly, aware that the only reason he wasn't dead was because we didn't want to make any more noise.

I rolled, sprang to my feet, grabbed a serving platter, and smashed the second guard in the head. He went right down. Then I kicked them both repeatedly in the face—tuxedo shoes are not the best for beating people senseless—until I was sure neither would be causing any trouble. One quick glance at the exit wound on the back of Keng's skull told me *mission accomplished*, now to get out of here in one piece.

I removed the other Browning from the second guard's belt and two spare magazines from his offside, stuffed those in my pocket, grabbed his radio, and headed toward the door. We had no idea if the room was insulated enough to dampen the sound of a gunshot.

Katarina placed the 9mm muzzle against the accountant's head. He began to whimper and plead for his life in Indonesian. "Listen to me very carefully." Her voice was utterly cold and distant. "Big Eddie wants his money. You will repay him triple the value of his stolen cargo. You will also pay him ten percent of all future takes. You will clear every attack with us from now on. Or we'll burn your little pirate kingdom to the ground. We can find you anywhere. We can reach you anywhere. You work for Big Eddie now. These negotiations are closed. Do you understand?"

He started to respond, she smashed him in the head with the butt of the gun. "In English!" This was the part of negotiation that Katarina excelled at.

"Yes, yes! Whatever you say, please don't kill me!"

Kat called over to me. "Status?"

I had taken up position behind a wooden column and had the gun trained on the door. There was no traffic on the radio. I was really glad that the party was so blaringly loud. "They probably thought it was fireworks."

"Good." Katarina turned her attention back toward Keng's assistant. "We'll be in touch." She hit him in the head with the pistol again, hard enough the sound of the blow made me cringe. The assistant flopped onto the floor unconscious.

"Let's go," I said as I changed the radio to a predetermined channel and hit *transmit*. "We're on the way down. Prepare for pickup."

"*On the way,*" Carl, my partner in crime, responded over the airwaves. I knew that the car was already in motion and he would be waiting at the service entrance in exactly two minutes. Carl was reliable. I stuffed the Browning into my waistband and made sure my tuxedo covered it. The radio went into a pocket.

"Damn it!" Katarina hissed as she lifted the cloth of the cart. "The soup spilled. I can't ride in there. You know what this dress cost me?"

"Just go," I grunted. She had just murdered a pirate, but she was worried about her outfit. My girlfriend was psychotic. "You got a better way to walk out of here past twenty security guards?"

"You are handsome when you're stern, Lorenzo," she replied as she ducked under the cloth, slipped out of her high heels, and folded herself into an almost impossible position. "And you look like a Bollywood James Bond in that outfit. Very handsome."

"Shut up," I grumbled as I flipped the cloth down to conceal her, then pushed the cart to the door. It was heavier now. Katarina was taller than I was and extremely athletic, so she added a lot of weight to the cart. Not that I would ever guess her weight out loud, since she made her living killing people for an organized crime syndicate.

And I was what? Her *helper*?

It was a pretty shitty job when you thought about it that way.

We walked right out. I kept my head down, eyes averted. The guards at the door grunted at me as I passed. From observing them, I knew that they had approximately two to three minutes before another radio check, plenty of time to get out of here.

The crowd was thicker now, more people accumulating around the railing. The fireworks show was reaching its climax and the city was beautiful in the smoky light. Weaving the cart between socialites, I kept my head down and kept moving, not paying any attention to the sparkles or explosions. I risked one last glance back toward the private area as I reached the kitchen. One of the guards was pulling out his radio, checking in prematurely.

As soon as I was into the kitchen I was moving fast, the doors swinging wildly behind me. I nearly ran over one of the chefs, and collided with another waiter. The kitchen smelled of exotic meats and curry, lots of curry. Flames were leaping from a grill under a row of neatly carved chickens. We had to get out of here, now.

"Pard? What's going on? Is Mr. Keng not happy with his food?" the chef asked nervously.

"He's really not happy," I responded as I threw back the cover. "We've got to move."

"Which way?" Katarina asked, sliding out of the cart. I took off running. She carried her five-inch heels in her hand so she could keep up with me as she followed.

"Pard? What's going on?" the chef shouted after us, totally unaware that the man he thought he was speaking to was on a boat to India with a ten-thousand-dollar bribe in his pocket. I shoved past more kitchen staff, leaving them confused with what an Anglo woman in a party dress was doing running through their work space. I went right to the freight elevator and mashed the button furiously.

"What about the security check on the first level?" Katarina asked as the elevator started down.

I pulled out the stolen radio. "Carl, put the kid on."

"This is Reaper."

"Reaper . . ." Katarina hissed, rolling her eyes. "Such a terrible nickname."

"I need you to jam Keng's channel. Then I need to know what's going on at the first floor checkpoint. And tell Carl and Train we've been spotted. This might get hot."

"Okay," Reaper responded, sounding slightly distorted as the radio waves passed through layers of concrete and steel. *"Their channel is now filled with crap."*

"You know, if he's over sixteen I would be stunned." She bent over and put her shoes back on.

"He told me he's twenty-one, and he's a technical wizard. And since our last tech guy got blown up in Singapore . . ."

Reaper came back. *"I don't think they were able to contact security, but they may try the courtesy phones. I'll kill those."*

"Do it."

"On it," he responded enthusiastically. *"Reaper out."*

"What kind of name is that supposed to be?" Katarina snorted.

"I told him he couldn't go by his real name. Too dangerous." The floor numbers changed rapidly, but I didn't know if we would be fast enough.

"Yes, real names are dangerous in this business . . ." She put her hands on my shoulders and pushed me slowly back against the elevator wall. "Hector."

"Business, Katarina. Stick to business," I grunted as I pushed her away. She was the first person I had told my real name to in years. It was stupid, and weak, but infatuation does that to a man. She did that fake pout that I had found cute at first, though now it was just annoying.

"Whatever you say, Lorenzo, darling." She was beautiful, lethal, and I had been lonely. I had let her suck me into working for Big Eddie, and what a mistake that had been. Bad guy. Villain. Robber. Thief. Look up the definition and there was my picture. It was what I was good at. I was probably one of the best in the world. It was all that I knew, and all that I could do. And honestly, I loved it. I was a predator, through and through. But since everything had fallen apart back in back in Africa, I had tried to only prey on other bad guys. They had more to take, and I could always console myself that when I had to off one of them, I left the world a better place. According to my twisted moral code, they were fair game. Normal people were off limits, but working for Big Eddie, those lines often blurred. I had seen how real evil operated, and I was employee of the month.

I hate what I've become.

Concentrate on escaping. Be bitter later. I yanked the waiter's sash, opened my coat, undid my tie, and tried to look casual, sloppy. Just a guy wrapping up a night on the town and taking home a professional girl. I grabbed Katarina around the waist—her abdominal muscles were hard as rock—and held her close. "Look like we're guests leaving the party." She held out the other 9mm.

"Take this."

"Why?"

"Where am I supposed to conceal a full-size pistol in this thing?" she growled, gesturing at her dress.

True enough. She couldn't hide most of herself in it. I took the gun and shoved it into the front of my pants and made sure the cummerbund hid it. I didn't like carrying a cocked and locked handgun over my manhood, but didn't have time to think of a better spot.

First floor. The elevator clanked to a stop and the doors hissed open. Katarina giggled loudly and snuggled up; she was a superb actress. I did the half-drunk wobble out onto the linoleum. This was the service entrance, and guests shouldn't be coming down this way, but it was a heck of a party upstairs, and what happens in Kuala Lumpur, stays in Kuala Lumpur.

A few workers noticed us, but the place was swamped tonight. What was another drunk and his harlot? An older woman behind some sort of registration desk was wearing a traditional headscarf, and she shook her head sadly at the sight. She was old enough to have watched her traditional backwater country super-modernize, and all of the ancillary moral decay that came with it.

"Excuse me, sir. You should not be in this area," she said politely.

I waved my hand in her general direction. "We're leaving," I said dismissively, playing the lost rich guy. Katarina giggled again. The woman frowned, apparently deciding that she needed to notify somebody of lost guests, and lifted her phone. She jiggled the receiver a few times when she didn't get a dial tone. *Way to go, Reaper.* We continued down the hall.

The area terminated in some doors and a loading dock. Several workers were moving in cartons of food and booze from a truck. Carl would pick us up on the other side.

Katarina's nails sank into my arm. I froze. Several men were entering, squeezing around the delivery truck. They had the look of toughs, not dressed for a quality event. The guy in the lead was still wearing his sunglasses at close to midnight, was plainly hurried, and was talking into a cell phone. *Can't jam everything, damn it.*

He saw me as I saw him, across twenty feet of concrete and harsh fluorescent light, and he knew that these were the people who had just shot his boss in the face. His hand moved in a blur as he shouted to the other pirates.

Katarina had her arm around me, and her hand was only inches from the Hi-Power in the back of my waistband. I felt it leave as she dove to the side. I drew the second gun as I went the other way.

It was *on*.

The gun in my hand was a worn old military model. I punched the gun straight out, shifting focus from the pirate to the rudimentary front sight. I fired twice as I moved against the wall. Now I was crouching, moving forward into the loading area. I had to get out of that fatal funnel. Had to attack.

Katarina had the same idea. There were multiple gunshots from her side. The lead pirate stumbled, dropped his cell phone, started to turn toward her, black gun coming up in his hand. I nailed him again, and then he was down. The workers were screaming, scattering, hitting the floor, or running.

The other pirates were in a bad position, squeezing past the truck with no place to maneuver. It was like shooting fish in a barrel. I took the left. Katarina took the right. The wall behind me exploded into concrete fragments. The noise was deafening in the echoing space. A worker trapped in the crossfire spun, vegetables flying out of the cardboard box in his hands. A fine particulate mist seemed to hang in the space that he had filled. I fired down the narrow passage, dropping another pirate.

"Magazine! Magazine!" Katarina shouted. I reached into my pocket and tossed one to her. She was at slide lock, gun empty, and barely looked up to catch the mag. She slammed it home, dropped the slide, and kept shooting.

I dove behind a stack of boxes. Bullets zipped right through. Glass bottles shattered, splashing me with wine older than I was. There was only one more pirate on my side of the truck, and he was firing wildly, trying to retreat, to get away from us. He disappeared around the rear of the truck . . . only to reappear a moment later, falling head-first onto the pavement. The crack of a .223 echoed through the alley.

The radio crackled. It was Carl. *"Got him! Now hurry up. There's more coming. It's like a fucking pirate convention out here."*

"Clear right!" Katarina shouted. I pulled the last mag and reloaded without thinking.

"Clear left. Let's go." The worker who had been shot was still moving, but he wouldn't be for long. Blood was welling from his chest in great violent gouts. He was lying on his back, hands twisted into claws, blood flowing from his mouth as he coughed. His dark eyes were open, staring at the buzzing fluorescents, seeing Allah, or Buddha, or Vishnu, or who knew what in this country.

Standing over him, gun dangling loose in my hand, I froze. I had seen this hundreds of times, and didn't know why this hit me. He looked right at me, and extended a hand, probably wondering why I wouldn't help him, wondering why he hurt so bad, why his heart was pumping blood out of his chest instead of to his brain . . .

"Lorenzo! Let's go!" Katarina shouted.

The old lady with the headscarf pushed past, oblivious to danger, oblivious to the stranger with the gun. She fell at the young man's side, cradled his head in her hands, and began to scream. He was already dead.

"Murderer!" she shrieked in Malay.

"But I didn't kill him," I said in English, but she wasn't paying attention. She was trying to stop the bleeding that had already stopped forever.

"Lorenzo!" Katarina shrieked. I snapped out of it and ran for the exit.

The next hour was a blur. There were more of Keng's men in the alley. And I killed them as I had killed so many before. The cops arrived, and Carl eluded them by driving like a madman through the streets of KL. Nobody could catch Carl, nobody.

All I could think of was that old woman with the headscarf. *Murderer . . .*

Dawn found us at a safe house in the Malaysian countryside. We pushed the van with bullet holes into the lake. Datuk Keng was dead. Big Eddie's work was done.

The new guy, Reaper, may have been young, but he'd done well. Carl had cracked open a beer and was sitting on the couch, surly as usual. Train was his usual jovial, goofball self. A nerdy computer kid, my best friend the angry mercenary, and a mountain of muscle with a teddy bear's heart. This was my crew, this was my family. They did this for me. They were watching the news coverage about what the local authorities were calling the Independence Day Massacre.

I left the room, wanting to be by myself. Carl studied me as I walked away. He knew me better than anybody, and I had no doubt he knew what I was about to do. I watched Katarina through the window as she paced back and forth on the lawn. She was on her cell phone, giving details to Big Eddie's representatives. She was dressed down now, just wearing normal clothing, not made up at all, and even then I had to admit that she was probably the most beautiful woman I had ever known, and fun, and amazingly smart, talented, pretty much everything I could ever want.

Too bad she was evil.

I overheard Reaper whisper to Train. "A massacre? Man, that was crazy. I've never seen anything like that before . . . How many people have you guys killed?"

"That's a stupid question, kid." Carl muttered. "Really stupid."

"Sorry."

"I can understand you asking," Train said. "Me, I've had to do it a few times. Carl here, if you had to get all of the people he's killed together, you would probably fill a bus. A big Greyhound bus. He and Lorenzo were mercenaries in Africa for a few years."

"Dude . . ."

"Shut it, Train," Carl growled.

"What about Lorenzo?" Reaper asked with a reverent tone.

"Lorenzo, well . . ." Train hesitated.

Carl responded. "If I need a bus, then Lorenzo needs a football stadium. Now both of you shut up."

I sighed, and banged my head against the window.

I intercepted Katarina on the lawn as she hung up her phone. She got right to business. "Big Eddie is not happy." Her accent was Swiss. She was half Spanish, half Swiss, and sometimes when she wasn't playing at being something else, her accent was very obvious. It sounded like "*Big Eddie eez not happy.*"

"And why's that?"

"Too much attention. Too much collateral damage. He says that next time—"

I cut her off. "There is no next time. You tell him I'm *done.*"

"Lorenzo . . ." she spoke calmly. "Think this through. Nobody is ever *done* with Eddie."

"I am. Sorry, Kat, it's over."

"Are you talking about our employer, or are you talking about us too?" She looked sad, and even bit her lower lip, but I knew that was an act. A year ago I would have believed she was capable of sadness but now I knew that it was fake. Any normal human emotions Katarina had, had long since been expunged.

"Both."

"I thought you loved me . . ." she said, voice cracking, and this time, I almost could believe her. *Almost.* I turned my back on her and walked away.

Chapter 1: Paradise Lost

LORENZO
St. Carl Island
The Bahamas
February 6th

Seven years ago. Why was I dreaming about seven years ago? The clock by the bed told me that it was three in the morning. I was having a hard time sleeping again, just too restless.

Jill grunted in her sleep. Trying not to wake her, I got up carefully and went to the bathroom. The nondescript face in the mirror stared at me. *What's your problem, Lorenzo?* It was weird to think about Kuala Lumpur again. It had been a turning point for me. Of course, Eddie had come back to haunt me, dragging me into the mess in Zubara, but he was dead now and I was still alive. So what had I become? I was a free man. I was my *own* man. I was a retired thief. I was wealthy. I was in a relationship with a wonderful woman, even though I didn't deserve her.

But at what cost? *A football stadium.* The face in the mirror scowled. That's what Carl had described. So what was I now? For some reason, the words of my foster father were on my mind that morning. I could hear his deep voice, fading on his death bed. Warning me about good and evil . . .

I wouldn't be getting back to sleep tonight.

"Welcome to St. Carl!" the waitress said with extra cheer. Those simple words got my attention. St. Carl was a small enough island that anyone who wasn't a regular got that greeting, especially during the off season when tourists were few and the staff was hungry for tips. The room was kept dark, in sharp contrast to the bright Caribbean sunshine trying to force its way through the now-open entrance. The lunch patrons were sitting in a few tight clusters, mostly workers from the nearby docks, and a handful of others, all of whom I recognized, but I didn't know the three newcomers standing in the doorway.

The lead was a striking woman of Chinese descent, dressed casually, but

477

not casually enough to pass for a St. Carl resident. Her black eyes were scanning across the room, looking for something, or someone. She was flanked by two men, one short Asian guy built like a cage fighter, and the other, a black man so tall he almost had to duck to get through the door, with a shaved head and more muscle than a side of beef.

Tourists, my ass. The door closed behind the three, plunging the room back into a nice, muted grey. I like grey. People like me just kind of fade away. I went back to my lunch, enjoying the spices and the ache in my muscles. Unable to go back to sleep this morning, I had got in a workout. I wasn't close to my peak, but I'd still done thirty pull-ups, a hundred push-ups, and thirty minutes straight on an eighty-pound punching bag. Not bad for a *gentleman of leisure* on the wrong side of forty.

The woman said something, quietly enough that I couldn't hear, and the waitress waved them toward the bar. I noted that the woman kept scanning, always looking, dividing the room into quadrants, and giving every occupant a once-over. She made eye contact with me, but I just kept chewing my food like any other slack-jawed yokel, just an everyman, not worthy of any attention. I had developed this ability with a lifetime of practice. I was good at appearing unremarkable.

I was also a master of reading people. It was a gift. Two seconds of eye contact told me everything that I needed to know about her. This woman was a killer, and she was hard, but I didn't get the vibe that she was here to kill anyone in particular. She was here on business.

The woman broke away and headed for the bar. She stopped while the tall man pulled a wicker stool out and waited for her to sit. She crossed her legs gracefully, smiled at the bartender like a lion would smile at a gazelle, and placed several folded pieces of currency onto the bar. Beckoning him closer, conspiratorially, she started asking questions. The bartender, always a sucker for a pretty girl, took the money, scratched his head, looked around the room, shrugged, and pointed right at me.

And here we go. I sighed and took another bite.

The woman stood, delicately adjusted her blouse, and walked toward me. Her men took up positions at the bar, still close enough to shoot me if necessary. I waited for her to approach. The weight of the compact pistol on my belt, concealed under an untucked cotton shirt, was reassuring.

She stopped, hovering next to my table, while I nonchalantly finished my larb. Why Thai food for breakfast in a hole-in-the-wall restaurant on a flyspeck island in the middle of nowhere? Because I *said so*.

Of course the bartender knew me. I own most of this damned island.

"Are you Lorenzo?" she asked politely in perfectly nuanced English. Such a mundane statement seemed vaguely threatening when she said it.

I made her wait while I took a long drink of water. Most everything I ate was seasoned to be lethally hot. "At times," I replied, pushing my dish away and wiping my mouth on a napkin. "Have a seat." She did. It had been a while since anyone other than my Jill had called me that name on St. Carl.

"My name is Song Ling." She got right down to business. "I have need of your services."

I raised an eyebrow. "You must not have gotten the memo, lady. I'm retired."

Nonplussed, she reached into a pocket and pulled out a business-size envelope. "You will want to see this." She held it out to me, her blood-red fingernails bright over the white paper. The nails were kept short, like those of most women more concerned about trigger control than fashion.

I was forced into my last job, too. It too had started with a messenger giving me an envelope, though Ling was far more attractive than the psychotic Fat Man who had served Big Eddie Montalban. That particular envelope had been filled with information on my extended family and threats against their lives. I had pulled off one of the most daring heists of my career, but the costs had been far too high. Too many people, friends and enemies both, had died because of the contents of that last envelope.

I didn't take it.

"Ling, was it? Look, I'm sorry that you came all this way for nothing, but I'm not interested." I pushed back my chair and stood. I could see both of Ling's goons tense up. "I hope you enjoy your stay on St. Carl. The rock shrimp really is good this time of year. You should try some. My treat. And then have a nice trip home."

"Your brother said you would react like this." She didn't even look at me. She placed the envelope on the table and spun it. "I didn't pick you out of the crowd. You look nothing at all like him. I was expecting a man of greater . . . stature."

I paused. That would explain how she found me. *Son of a bitch.*

"I was a foster kid," I said as I sat back down. The envelope sat between us. Ling didn't speak. I had been correct in my earlier assessment, she was a hard one. "How do you know Bob?" I asked, because of course, of all my brothers, it had to have been him. For some reason she didn't strike me as the type of person that ran in the same social circles as my straitlaced, honorable, FBI Agent older brother.

She opened the envelope and pulled out a torn paper napkin. It had been scribbled on with black ink. She shoved it toward me. "He gave this to me, right before he was chased down, beaten unconscious, and taken away. That was . . . " she theatrically looked at her watch. ". . . seventy-two hours ago. I do not know if he is alive or dead."

"What?" I snatched the napkin from her. I recognized Bob's blocky handwriting.

HECTOR—NEED HELP. REMEMBER Q?
THEY KNOW.
DON'T WORRY ABOUT ME.
HE IS IN NORTH GAP.
HE IS THE KEY.
YOU MUST SAVE HIM.

The bottom half of the napkin was missing, torn off.

Q? Quagmire. Quagmire, Nevada. They know? Eddie's dead. His organization is destroyed. Gordon . . . The shadow government types. They must have found out about Bob helping us in Quagmire.

The Quagmire Incident had made national headlines the year before. Everybody knew about how a civilian jet, owned by billionaire philanthropist Eduard Montalban, had allegedly been shot down by a surface-to-air missile. That part was actually true. I knew because I was the one who had fired the missile. The rest of the story had never made it to the news, nothing about the gun battle with a bunch of secret government agents in an abandoned prison work camp ever made it beyond the usual conspiracy-theory sites. Except all of that was true as well. Bob had been there for every bit of it.

"Who's in North Gap? What does that mean?"

"North Gap is a decommissioned US Air Force radar station in the State of Montana. It is now used by a covert organization within the United States government. It serves as a secret prison and interrogation center for high-value, high-risk subjects. I'm here to offer you a trade, Mr. Lorenzo. You help me rescue someone from this facility, and I'll give you all of the information I can to help you find your brother. We will lend you our full assistance and allow you to use our intelligence network for this end."

"What happened to my brother? Where was he when he was taken? Why was he with you?"

Ling folded her hands neatly on the table. "Do we have a deal or not, Mr. Lorenzo? I do not have much time."

I could feel the anger bubbling to the surface, the same killing anger that I had used as a tool for so long, the same evil that I had thrown into the deepest, darkest well of my mind to be locked up safely for the last six months. "How about you tell me where my brother is right now or I cut your eyes out?" Her men sensed the change, and started to rise from the bar, hands moving under their shirts.

Ling didn't flinch. She casually raised her hand, and her goons grudgingly lowered themselves. The rest of the patrons kept eating, unaware that for a split second the room had teetered on the edge of a gunfight.

"Read your brother's words. That isn't what he wants. This is bigger than your brother. Greater than you, than me, than all of us." She spoke with the sincerity of a true believer, and those were the most dangerous kind. Ling produced a smartphone, tapped the screen a couple of times, then laid it on the table so I could see it.

"Do you know this man, Mr. Lorenzo?"

I looked at the picture on the screen. My eyes narrowed. "Yeah . . . I know him."

Ling leaned forward. "One life for another. Your brother is an honorable man, Mr. Lorenzo. I want no harm to come to him. Right now, my people are doing everything they can to locate him. But your brother insisted that finding this man was more important than his own safety. Please. We need your help."

I glanced down at the image again. A young man, with a young face, but hard eyes. His hair had been shaved off, and his face was crisscrossed with scars. As a matter of fact, I'd given him one of those scars.

Valentine.

VALENTINE
Location Unknown
Date/Time Unknown

You're a natural-born killer, boy.

Hawk had said that. I found myself thinking about his words and that day I first met him in Afghanistan. It had been a bad day but it changed me, set me on the path that I'd walked ever since . . . a long, winding, bloody path that ended with me in a small, windowless cell.

Sitting against the wall, I stared blankly into space. Footsteps would occasionally echo from the hallway outside my door. Every so often an ancient industrial heater would come on, filling the hall with a dull roar while it ran and kicking up small clouds of dust from the vents. Fluorescent lights buzzed unendingly; they never turned them off. I didn't know if it was night or day. I could sometimes hear voices from outside, but I was never directly spoken to while I was in this room. I wasn't allowed to speak. If I made noise, they came in and sedated me, or worse. So I sat quietly, back to the wall, and lost myself in thought.

I didn't know where I was, exactly. It was cold, and there were thick pine forests in every direction. I had been outside a few times. It may have been on a mountaintop somewhere, or up in Alaska. I had no real way of keeping track of time. This had to be intentional. I didn't know how many days, or weeks or months, I'd been in this place, but I grew increasingly certain that I would never leave. I knew that there was more snow on the ground the last time I'd been outside than there was the first time they'd let me out, so it was probably winter.

Of course, they hadn't let me out in a while, as part of my punishment for stabbing one of the guards in the knee with a pen.

Despite ending up in prison, I didn't regret knowing Hawk. The man was like a father to me, and I hadn't even known I'd been lost before I met him. I joined the military because I just didn't know what else to do with myself, volunteered for Afghanistan for the same reason.

My time with Vanguard Strategic Services International was something of a blur now, even though my career had lasted nearly five years. The deployments were all different, but they were all the same, too. We fought for the people who could afford to pay us in wars the rest of the world generally didn't care about. Others fought for duty, honor, and country. We fought because it was our job.

I was good at it. It's what I'm best at. A natural-born killer. Deep down, I'd always known. I killed my first man as a teenager. I grew up that day. I changed. And I knew I was different. I began to look at the people around me the way a wolf looks at a herd of deer.

Somehow I held on. My teammates kept me sane. We went through a lot of bad days and a lot of good ones. We fought together, partied together, and mourned our dead together. I traveled all over the world, and was paid a lot of money for what I did.

It all came crashing down in Mexico. Only three of us survived that mission, and our employer was forced out of business. My entire life was gone in the span of a couple of days.

I tried. I tried to return home, to the US, and get a regular job. I tried to live my life as a respectable citizen. I did that for almost a year, and I was completely miserable. Restless, disconnected from the people around me. When my former teammate Tailor showed up on my doorstep with a job offer, the deal was sealed.

Project Heartbreaker, they called it. We did good work, at first. I met the first woman I ever really loved. Her name was Sarah, and she made me a better man.

She died in a little country called Zubara. Most of us did, betrayed by the same shadowy organization that had brought us there. They were just cleaning up loose ends. Some of us managed to escape with our lives, and those who did went into hiding.

Not me. I was done running. I tracked down Gordon Willis, the man behind the entire operation, and shot him through the heart.

Then they caught me. So there I was, some time later, in a windowless cell, wondering when they were going to get around to killing me. I wondered if anyone had any idea what happened to me. *Did anyone even care?*

My eyes snapped into focus as the tromp of combat boots echoed down the hall. Three people, it sounded like. It didn't seem like it was mealtime, and they never sent three men just to slide my tray of slop through the door. I took a deep breath, and tried to steady myself as I stood up. I knew what was coming next.

A key hit the lock. The door swung inward. Three men in black uniforms strode in. I recognized all of them. I'd seen them all before. Reilly, Smoot, and Davis. They didn't speak as they shoved me against the wall and cuffed my hands together and shackled my feet. They jabbed me in the side to get me going, hard enough to leave a throbbing pain. I shuffled up the hallway, chains clinking like an inmate at the county jail.

There was a time when I'd tried to resist, tried to make myself a pain in the ass, hoping for rescue or escape. In my confinement, I'd worked out, doing push-ups and sit-ups in my cell to stay somewhat fit. As time went on, that hope faded. I gave up exercising. What as the point? I was going to die in this place. I was too much of a liability for them to ever let me go.

I hung my head slightly, but said nothing, as I clattered along in chains.

LORENZO

I studied the image for a time. "I don't know what happened to him. Once he popped that guy in Virginia, he just dropped off the grid. I figured the secret government types murdered him." I slid the phone back to Ling.

"From what your brother has told me, you owe him a great deal." Ling's dark eyes almost bored holes into me. Of course she was right. Jill would be dead if it hadn't been for Valentine, but that wasn't the sort of thing Bob should be sharing. How much had my brother told this woman?

"No disagreement there, but the way I see it, the way *he* saw it, we're even. No offense, lady, and in normal circumstances, I'd love to go take on the entire US government to rescue somebody who shot me with a .44 magnum, but it sounds like my brother's in trouble. Family comes first."

"How noble of you," Ling said flatly. "My organization is searching for your brother as we speak, and as soon as we have information on his whereabouts, we will act. I understand your frustration. But until we are able to locate Bob, there is little that can be done."

"You might be surprised," I muttered.

"Perhaps not. I know exactly what you can do. You are one of most accomplished thieves in modern history. The Vladivostok gold train robbery, the Bahrain Museum of Antiquity heist, the South African Diamond Exchange, and rumors of many others. You are a master of disguise, stealth, and various intrigues." She smiled as she saw my reaction. Yep, the old poker face was out of practice. Island living makes a man soft.

"You missed a few of my greatest hits, but apparently you know me. So who the hell are you supposed to be?"

"I am a strike team commander for the organization called Exodus. I assume you are familiar with our work?"

I nodded slowly. Of course I knew about them. Anyone who worked in the circles I did had heard of Exodus. "You kill people. Slave traders mostly. Criminals, terrorists, drug lords . . ." Mostly I knew about them from their reputation, and it was a grisly one. They were a bunch of pseudo-holy-warrior kooks who never took prisoners and rarely left witnesses. "You pop anybody you decide is evil enough."

"There's a lot more to it than that, but you are fundamentally correct. This does not bother you, I trust."

I smiled. "I'm morally ambivalent."

"So your brother implied. Given your reputation, I'm surprised you haven't crossed paths with our organization before."

"I try not to take sides. And, no offense, I'm too good at what I do to be snared by a bunch of vigilante fanatics with automatic weapons. Please continue, Miss Ling."

Ignoring the slight, Ling glanced around the restaurant to make sure no one was listening before continuing. "My organization was working on a matter of some significance. We were planning a mission against a very high-profile target. Have you heard of Sala Jihan?"

"The Pale Man?" I snorted. Every professional criminal who had ever worked in the Eastern hemisphere had heard of him, but it was all legend and nonsense from the superstitious or crazy. He was central Asia's cross between the boogieman and Jack the Ripper. Villagers had been telling scary stories around campfires about him for hundreds of years. "I don't have time for fairy tales."

"He is *quite* real, I assure you." Her flash of anger was very convincing. "Or at least some slave-trading warlord wants people to think he is real, and that he has returned. Someone calling himself Sala Jihan appeared a few years ago, and during that time, he's amassed an army and now controls the trade of slaves, illicit arms, and drugs across south and central Eurasia."

"That part of the world was Big Eddie's territory," I stated.

"Eduard Montalban was not in the same league as Sala Jihan."

"Then you didn't know much about Big Eddie."

"He was a bored rich man's son. A sociopath, of course, and dangerous, but in the end all of his power came from his family. His older brother is dead now, of course, and so is he. Thanks to you. That was well done, Mr. Lorenzo."

I happened to agree, but I was growing impatient. "What does any of this have to do with Bob?"

"Your brother was looking for someone with some extremely vital information. This individual he was searching for was also being pursued by a certain US government agency which I believe you have some experience with. The person Bob was after had fled to Sala Jihan's territory. It is easy to disappear there."

I had always thought of my brother as the law-abiding, rational one. That was why it had been kind of shocking to see him shoot some of his fellow federal agents, without hesitation, back in Quagmire. I could see Bob putting what he thought was *right* and *good* ahead of what was *practical*. I was the practical one of the family. "So where is he now, and how many people do I have to kill to get him back?"

"We're working on that. But first we need you to help us rescue Valentine. Read your brother's words. It's what he wants."

"And why the hell is Valentine so important?"

She didn't get a chance to answer. One of her bodyguards, the tall black man, approached quickly and tapped her on the shoulder. "Ma'am, I received. We need to leave."

Ling brushed her hair back and stood. "We need your help, Mr. Lorenzo. Our plane will be leaving the airfield in ninety minutes. Gather your equipment and meet us there. If we do not see you, then we will attempt this rescue without you. The choice is yours."

I stayed seated and stewed for a moment. Technically, I owned the airfield on St. Carl, and this woman had landed on my runway without my permission. Of course, I leased it to the island, and tourist planes weren't uncommon, but I was already angry and that just made it worse. I repeated my question. "And why is he so important?"

She looked at me like I was stupid.

"We never leave a man behind, Mr. Lorenzo. Your brother understood that much."

"Reaper." The phone picked up as I charged up the stairs to my home. The beach stretched for a mile in each direction below me, and my boat was rocking softly at my nearby dock. Seagulls squawked overhead. Ling and her men were on their way back to the airstrip. I was supposed to grab my stuff and meet them there.

"Hey, Chief! What's up? Haven't heard from you in forever."

"Where are you at?"

"I'm kicking ass and taking names. Can I call you back?" I could hear clanking and something roaring in the background. Reaper played a lot of video games. "You like that, *bitch*? Huh? Witness my perfection! Go cry to momma, *noob*!"

"No. This is serious."

"Oh shit." Reaper was suddenly all business. "This line is secure. What do you need?"

"I've got some work for you to do." I looked at my watch. "Find out everything you can about a decommissioned air force base in Montana called North Gap. Then I want you to get my brother's file from the FBI database and forward it to me. I want to know where he was, and what he was working on."

"Wow. Jumping right back into the deep end." Reaper whistled. "That's gonna be a tough one. I'll get on it." For most people, a request to break into a secure government database would seem a bit odd. For Reaper, it was the kind of thing he did for kicks. "It might get really expensive."

"I'll cover it. And get me everything you can find on Valentine."

Reaper was quiet for a moment. "Like from Zubara? That Valentine?"

"Yes, that Valentine. Find me everything you can on him. Everything. I want to know where he came from, where he's been, and what happened to him after Quagmire."

"I'm on it!" Reaper paused for a second. "Are we back, Chief?"

He'd been bugging me about once a month for the last half a year about resuming our life of crime. Even though he was the only surviving member of my last team, and he was now independently wealthy from our looting of Big Eddie's treasury, he just couldn't leave it alone. I suppose some of us just aren't good at walking away.

"We're back."

"Sweet! I'm on this!"

I pocketed my phone as I stepped into the entryway. "Jill! I'm home. We've got to talk." My voice echoed through the vast space of vaulted ceilings, but no answer came. My home was huge. The average slum apartment I had lived in as a kid could fit in the living room. This had been the Montalban family vacation home on this island. The walls were white, the floor made of bright local wood, and an ocean breeze caused the curtains to flow softly over the very expensive furnishings. For a place that Big Eddie had hardly ever visited, he had spared no expense. "Jill!"

"I'm up here." Jill's voice came from upstairs. I ran, my sandals slapping on the marble stairs, then softly as I hit the thick carpet of the second floor landing. She was waiting in the bedroom, a large cardboard box open on the bed, packing peanuts strewn everywhere. She was wearing the little orange sundress that I loved on her, and didn't look up as I entered. "Those antique candelabras I won on eBay got here, and look! They're so pretty! I'm going to put these up in the dining room. So how was lunch, honey?"

I didn't respond. I stepped past her, opened the door to the closet, and examined the three black duffel bags sitting on the floor. The first bag was set up with US currency and clothing that would fit in most places in America. I grabbed it and dragged it out. I reached up a shelf and grabbed another black case, this one carrying my disguise kit and other tools of my former trade. I hadn't asked, but I assumed that Ling's plane would have spots to smuggle weapons past customs. It was kind of a given in these kinds of social circles. The last duffle was my go-bag, with weapons, ammunition, and gear kept ready.

After a moment, I turned around and faced Jill. She stood there, looking confused, with a silver thing in her hands. It was designed to hold candles, but had a lot of points and edges. Knowing her temper, I was concerned that I was going to have to dig it out of my forehead when I told her that I was about to jeopardize my retirement and take off with a bunch of nut jobs to attack a secret government base to rescue a mercenary.

"What's going on?" Jill asked. Her dark eyes narrowed dangerously. Her hair was pitch black, and tied casually in a ponytail. Her skin was bronzed. Island living had been good to her. She was just as beautiful as the day that I had rescued her from a band of Zubaran terrorists. Considering that the first time we had ever actually spoken, she'd attempted to shoot me, our relationship had come a long way. "That's your bug-out bag." She looked back up at me, an edge in her voice. "Lorenzo, what did you *do*?"

I grabbed Jill gently by the arms, partially to comfort her, and partially to prevent her from getting a good swing with the candle holder. The running joke was that Jill was half Filipina, so when she got angry, people got stabbed. I didn't know how she was going to take this. "Listen to me. Bob's in danger. He's been kidnapped," I said as calmly as I could manage. Jill gasped. She loved my brother. He'd helped save her from Gordon Willis, after all. "It's a long story. I'm going to get him back, but first I need to spring Valentine out of jail."

Jill looked confused for a moment. She hadn't heard that name in a while. "Valentine? Michael Valentine? He's still alive?" She'd known him a lot better than I had, since they'd spent some time together at Hawk's ranch. "I thought he was dead."

"I'll call you and explain everything. I don't have time now. There's a plane at the airfield leaving soon. I need to be on it."

She tossed the candlestick holder on the bed. "I understand. I'll grab my bug-out bag." Jill didn't have my background. She wasn't really a criminal, but she was tough. She adapted and overcame adversity no matter what, a trait which I really admired. Sometimes I worried that she had adapted to life with me a little too well. She hadn't even flinched at what I'd said. We were still technically newlyweds, but we had been through a lot together, so I knew how she was going to react to what I was going to say next.

"Jill . . . no."

She blinked rapidly, the way she always did when I said something stupid. "What do you mean, *no*? Bob's in trouble. We have work to do!"

"No, just me. It's too dangerous. These people I'm going with, I don't trust them. They're bad people." *Here comes the stabbing part.* "I need you to stay here."

"*What*?"

"I can't risk you, and I've got work for you to do, and I'll call and tell you, but I just don't have time now. I have to go."

"Lorenzo, you don't have a team anymore. Carl's dead. You never work alone."

"I called Reaper," I said defensively.

"Reaper hasn't done anything for the last six months but play video games and waste money on lap dances. He's not exactly in practice. If you don't know these people, then you need me to watch your back."

"Jill," I looked into her eyes, "do you trust me?"

She looked away. We'd been living an idyllic existence, my violent past left far behind. The evil that had plagued all my days had been locked away, seemingly forgotten, never to be brought out again. The horrible things that had befallen Jill were buried with them, and we'd begun a new life together.

That time ended now, and it was a lot to take in. Finally she turned back to me. "Yes."

I kissed her and held her tight. "I love you," I said softly, then let her go, her hands lingering on mine as I drew away. I slung the rifle case over my back, and grabbed my other bags. "I gotta go."

She followed me down the stairs and across the lawn. I stopped at my climate-controlled tool shed, unlocked the heavy padlock, and went straight to one of the wooden crates. This was the stuff I wasn't comfortable storing in the house. Jill fidgeted as she watched my preparations. She knew full well what I was doing.

"Be careful."

"Always."

Chapter 2: Head Games

VALENTINE
Location Unknown

My shackles clinked as I was led down to the last room on the right side of the corridor. A pit began to form in my stomach. This was the *information extraction* room. I had been in there several times before, but couldn't recall exactly how many times. Nor, for that matter, could I remember how long it had been. I just knew that this was where they took me when they wanted me to tell them something.

The room was a little bit colder than the corridor. Machines and equipment that I couldn't identify lined the walls. At the back of the room was a large tubular tank that resembled an MRI machine or something.

Near the center of the room was a chair like you'd find in a dentist's office, except this one had built-in restraints. My three escorts sat me down in the chair. Davis held me in place while Smoot stood watch, taser at the ready. Reilly then fastened both of my wrists and both of my ankles to the chair before doing up the waist and head straps. Once I was restrained, they raised the chair so that I was almost in a standing position. Several suction cups with wires leading to them were connected to my head. A band was put around my arm to monitor my heart rate and breathing. An oxygen tube was jammed up my nose. Machines in the room blinked to life as they were brought out of standby mode.

In front of the insane dentist's chair was a regular chair. That was where *she* always sat when we did this. The door to the room opened again. High heels clicked on a cold concrete floor as a pale, fortyish woman strode across the room. She sat stiffly in the chair in front of me, crossed her legs, and tapped on her iPad for a few moments.

"Good morning, Mr. Valentine." She didn't bother to look up.

My eyes narrowed. "To what do I owe the pleasure this time, Doc?"

Her name was Dr. Silvers. Olivia Silvers. She didn't look like much. Pale skin, thin build, flat hair, but she was in charge here, and she was an ice-cold bitch. I hated her with the utmost intensity, but in my present position, the

489

most I could do would be to verbally abuse her. Her retaliations for that kind of behavior had convinced me that it wasn't worth the trouble.

It's not that they necessarily tortured me. They hadn't pulled out my fingernails, smashed my kneecaps, or anything like that. Hell, they didn't even waterboard me. Nothing that base. These people had other ways, sophisticated, monstrous ways of getting inside your head.

First would be the needles and then would be the questions. Sometimes the questions didn't make sense. Other times I didn't know the answers, but she'd keep asking. Sometimes they'd put something in the oxygen tube in my nose. Other times they'd put things in my food and I'd wake up in the chair. Or I'd have a nightmare about being in the chair and wake up back in my room. Sometimes I'd remember things that didn't actually happen. It was hard to tell what was real.

Whenever I resisted or fought back they'd just beat the shit out of me and throw me back in my room. Sometimes they'd withhold food or leave me strapped down for days on end. One time, they left me out in the snow for a few hours. They let a big guard dog attack me once for the time I'd stabbed Smoot with the pen.

Dr. Silvers looked up at me over her spectacles. She must have practiced that disinterested, condescending expression in the mirror, since she was very good at it. "The last time we talked, you told me about the death of your mother."

"I did?"

"You were quite talkative. You described the events of your mother's death in great detail to me, and I told you I'd look into the matter for you."

I'd been too drugged to remember. I sure as hell wouldn't have talked to Dr. Silvers about it. But deep down, I knew that I had told her everything.

"The men that murdered your mother were William and Jesse Skinner. The Skinner Brothers were, at the time, the subject of a multi-state manhunt. They'd been terrorizing small communities in the Upper Midwest for a year when you encountered them. The older of the two, Jessie, was suspected of multiple counts of armed robbery, rape, and murder. William was a high-functioning psychotic with extremely violent tendencies."

"I know all that. They killed my mom, for chrissakes. I went to court and was interviewed by the cops over and over. Why are you telling me this?"

"Oh," Dr. Silvers said, unperturbed. "Last time we spoke, you were having trouble remembering, so I looked into the matter for you. In any case this is what I want to talk about today."

"You want to talk about my mother?"

"Not specifically. I want to talk about what happened to you when you found her dead, when you realized that you were in danger. What did you call it!"

I looked down at the floor. "*Calm*. I was calm."

"Yes," she said, eyebrow raised. "I want to talk about this sense of calm with you."

Why is she asking me about that? It was hard to remember what we'd talked about before. I knew I'd been grilled about Gordon Willis a great deal. There had been a sense of desperation in the way she'd asked. He was one of theirs, but he'd gone off the reservation. He'd been working with Eduard Montalban, and I told them that too. I don't remember telling them about my involvement in Eduard Montalban's death, but for all I knew, I'd already betrayed Hawk, Bob Lorenzo, and . . . the other Lorenzo, too.

But why was she asking me about *the Calm*? Why was she asking me about my mom? I couldn't figure out what she wanted, and that scared me.

Dr. Silvers stood up, and stepped closer to me. "Michael," she said softly, her lips inches from my ear. "You are a unique individual. What we're doing now is figuring out the best course for you going forward. Do you understand?"

"No," I managed. I felt strange. Groggy, but my heart was racing. They were doing something to me again. I could feel it.

"That's alright," she said, not quite smiling. "I'll be with you on this journey, every step of the way."

I don't remember much after that.

LORENZO
Somewhere over the Caribbean
February 6th

The ocean flashed by below us. I leaned my forehead against the Plexiglas window as the plane, a loud, rattling, turboprop Cessna Grand Caravan, banked toward the west, giving me one final look at the white sand and green tropical forest that was St. Carl. I sighed, mentally shifted gears, and returned to business.

The plane had an unusual interior layout, with limited seating. A curtain hung between the pilots' seats and the rest of the cabin. The back half of the cabin had a gurney and some medical supplies, presumably for Valentine. The hulking black man sat directly across from me, a bemused expression on his face. He looked me in the eyes, but didn't say anything. It was pissing me off.

"So who are you supposed to be?"

"My name is Antoine," he replied over the noise and vibration of the engine. The accent suggested West African. A folding table was between us, and it concealed his hands. He either had them folded in his lap or was pointing a gun at me. He smiled, his gleaming white teeth contrasting with his dark skin. The plane vibrated as we gained altitude. My Gearslinger bag was in my lap, one compartment unzipped. I thought about my next move. I didn't trust these people, and they didn't trust me. They were *right* not to trust me.

"Thank you for coming with us, Mr. Lorenzo. Your help is greatly appreciated," Ling said calmly. She sat kitty-corner across from me. "Exodus is very—"

I cut her off. It was time for business. "I don't give a shit about you or Exodus, or how much you appreciate anything. I'm here for my brother. You're very lucky that I believed you when you said you don't know where he is. If I didn't, you'd be spilling your guts to me right now, literally, if necessary."

"You could attempt that," Ling said diplomatically. Antoine grunted, obviously protective of her. Shen sat across the narrow aisle from me. He looked relaxed, but I could tell it was a facade. He was ready to pounce if I made a wrong move.

"But that would take too long, and I'm sure you've got some sort of arrangement with your handlers. I know how this game is played, and I'm too old for it."

"Indeed."

"So that's why we're going to play a different game, I call it defining the working relationship." My hands moved with lightning speed. I reached into the unzipped compartment and found a round, metal object. Before Ling or either of her companions knew what was happening, I slammed the hand grenade down onto the plastic table. I raised my left hand, with the grenade's pin looped around my finger. The only thing preventing it from initiating was the death grip I had on the spoon.

Shen drew a pistol in a flash, and had it pointed at my left ear. Antoine's left hand had never come out from under the table, but my suspicion that he had a pistol in it was confirmed by the way he moved. Ling smiled slightly.

I stared her down. "If I let go, it goes off, with a lethal radius bigger than your airplane. Try anything, we all die. Am I making myself perfectly clear?"

Ling nodded slightly at Shen, so he refrained from blowing my brains out.

"I've found it's harder for people to lie when they're about to get blown up."

"I'm telling you the truth. I don't know where your brother is."

"Cut the bullshit. You think you can just come to my island, land this piece of junk on my airfield, and blackmail me into going along with this? Do you know who you're screwing with? You come into *my* house and threaten me? Really?"

Antoine's pistol came out from under the table. He raised the big FNP-45 up and pointed it between my eyes.

"Look at me, Lorenzo," Ling ordered. "I'm telling you the truth. My people are doing everything they can to find your brother."

I glared at her. She glared right back. She wasn't cracking.

Antoine was starting to look nervous, and I could see his finger tightening up on the trigger. The hammer started to creep imperceptibly back. He was going to shoot me, and try to grab my hand before I let the grenade go. I shifted my glare to him, daring him to try.

Reaching across the aisle, Ling placed her tiny hand on his massive arm. "No need, Antoine. He knows I'm telling the truth. What of your lady, Mr. Lorenzo? All she will know is that you got onto a plane with another woman and were never seen again."

I showed no emotion. I wasn't going to give them anything. I wasn't going to let up. I had to know the truth. "Ever see what happens to bodies in the ocean? Half of you will wash up on a St. Carl beach, bloated, green, crabs living inside. It's pretty gross . . . Where is my brother?"

She didn't blink. "My soul is prepared, Mr. Lorenzo. Is yours?"

A cold bead of sweat rolled down into my eye. I blinked it away. This woman was either as cold as ice or was giving me a performance worthy of an Oscar. *Damned true believers.* They were calling my bluff. *Shit.*

Ling folded her hands across her chest and stared at me, daring me to do it. I actually cracked a smile. Shaking my head, I very carefully slid the pin back into its hole, and folded it down on the other side. "I gotta hand it to you, lady. You've got some brass balls."

Antoine was up in a split second, moving amazingly fast for a big man. He grabbed the grenade and snatched it away from me. I let go without a fight. "The grenade has been safed," Antoine confirmed.

"Thank you," Ling said. She was calm, but seemed visibly relieved. "Shen?"

Shen skull-punched me so hard it was like getting cracked with a bat. Lights flashed before my eyes, and my face hit the table. *So she has a temper after all . . .*

Gideon Lorenzo, my foster father, was a big man. Physically intimidating, with one of those bald heads that managed to gleam in the sun. I always felt kind of dwarfed in his presence. "You want to look at the target, but the front sight is the important part. Focus on the front sight. The target is going to be blurry behind it." He was standing slightly behind me and his deep voice boomed even through my ear plugs.

The old Colt Series 70 bucked in my hands, and this time the can flew off the fence. I did what he had taught me, and focused, and pulled the trigger straight back to the rear. Seven shots, and I got five that time. I was getting the hang of this.

"Much better," he said.

"Way to go, bro," Bob said. My brother was sixteen, and nearly as big as Dad. I was fourteen, and a shrimp in comparison, but I didn't have any of those Lorenzo family monster genes. According to the wall lines in my real father's mug shot—the only picture I had of him—he was only five foot five. "You should stick with the 1911, you stink with the revolver."

"Bob . . . " Dad said sternly.

"I'm just saying. Hector can't shoot a round gun to save his life."

I was careful to keep the muzzle downrange like Dad had shown me as I reached over and slugged Bob in the arm. Realistically the muscles on his arm were so thick that he wouldn't have felt it anyway, but he made a great show of being injured.

"No horseplay," Dad ordered. "Bob, go pick up those targets. Hector will help me pick up brass. Remember, always leave the range cleaner than you found it. Your mother will have dinner ready soon."

I put the .45 back in its case, ditched my ear plugs, and started picking up brass. Dad grimaced as he sat down next to me. He had ruined one of his knees in Vietnam, and I knew it was bothering him lately. He watched Bob go downrange, and waited until he was out of earshot. I could tell he wanted to say something.

"Hector, I just wanted to let you know. Your real father's parole hearing was today."

I kept looking for brass. "I'm assuming they're keeping him in."

"Yes."

"Good. Hope he rots in there forever."

Dad cleared his throat. "You know, someday he may be fit to return to society. A man can be redeemed."

"Redemption?" I snorted. I was fourteen and knew everything. "How can somebody like him make up for what he's done?"

One giant hand clamped onto my forearm. I looked up from the brass pile. "Hector, listen to me. You might not believe me now, but no matter what somebody has done in their past, they can be forgiven. They can make up for what they've done. There still needs to be justice, and that person has to pay for what they've done first, but anyone can be redeemed. Just remember that."

I went back to picking up brass. "That's insane."

"He's insane."

"Obviously." Ling's voice. "Unfortunately we need him. We don't have the numbers for a frontal assault."

"They might kill Valentine as soon as we attacked anyway. No, you're right, Ma'am. If we're going to free him, then we need this man, even if he is unpredictable," Antoine responded. "Did you think he was bluffing?"

"A Godless, self-absorbed narcissist like him would never willingly sacrifice his life for the sake of others, much less in a childish attempt to prove a *point*. Frankly, I'm rather surprised that the fact his brother is in danger was enough to compel him to do this," Ling responded with some contempt. "However, he's very good at what he does. His reputation indicates that."

"Everything we have heard about this Lorenzo says that he's a ghost. He can go anywhere. The fact that we happened to encounter his brother, just when we needed a man like him, is I think, providence. Please let me speak to him."

I didn't recognize the latest voice, and it was close. I groaned as I cracked open my eyes. The side of my head throbbed and the light streaming through the plane's windows stabbed through my eyeballs and into my brain. The speaker was sitting across from me, a concerned look on his face. I was still in my chair.

Albert Einstein? I thought groggily. He was an older man, with wispy strands of white hair poking out from around his ears, and a mustache like a boot-brush. He studied me from behind his thick glasses. He was actually wearing a bow tie.

"Good afternoon," he said with a thick German accent. "I am Dr. Bundt." He was holding my STI 9mm casually in his bony fist, pointed toward my chest. "I'm afraid Shen hit you a little hard. I apologize for getting off on the wrong foot, but you were threatening to blow us up." His smile seemed genuine.

"Who're you?" The lump on my head hurt like a son of a bitch. Ling and Antoine were seated around me. Shen must have gone up front, behind the curtain. Brilliant Caribbean clouds scrolled past the windows.

"As I say, I am Dr. Bundt. I oversee the treatment and well-being of those unfortunate souls that we rescue. As you may expect, I have gained some experience in helping people."

"Ironic," I said, nodding toward my gun.

"Oh, this?" He turned it around and held it out to me. I glanced toward Ling and Antoine, waiting to see which one was going to shoot me first, but neither moved. "Go on, take it." He shook it slightly. I took the gun slowly, the textured grip was familiar and comforting. I didn't do anything stupid, figuring that they had probably unloaded it while I was out. I reholstered without looking. "No more of the threats, yes? We have a common goal. Both of us want to see your brother rescued. He is very well respected in our organization now. He was most insistent that rescuing Mr. Valentine should be our first priority."

"My brother, the *Fed*, is friends with a bunch of terrorists?" I snorted.

"I see there is much about your brother you do not know," he said. "I think you will be very surprised when you see him next. In any case, if I were you, I'd be careful about using the word *terrorist*, Mr. Lorenzo. Is it not true that you were the right hand of Eduard Montalban?"

I rubbed the knot on my head, not wanting to argue. Hopefully Shen at least broke a finger or something. "Will you *please* tell me what is so important about that kid?"

"Mr. Valentine is one of us, though only in an honorary sense."

"One of you? When did that happen?"

"Mexico," Ling injected harshly. "A few years ago. He saved many lives, including mine."

Touched a nerve there. Ling had a personal stake in Valentine, and always looking for an angle, I filed that potentially useful information away for later.

Dr. Bundt continued. "In any case, that fact was irrelevant to your brother. For him, young Mr. Valentine was far more important than that. Bob believes Valentine was the key to something very important, something which could have grave repercussions for all mankind."

"And what would that be?"

"This I do not know. All he was able to convey to us was that there are powerful forces moving right now, and that something inside Mr. Valentine's head may be the crux of it all." Dr. Bundt shrugged his bony shoulders. "I do not know any more than that, I'm afraid. Once we rescue your brother you can ask him yourself. He was most adamant, though, that we need to get Mr. Valentine back alive."

"I wouldn't get too worked up either way." That stupid kid getting himself captured in Virginia could have compromised everyone that he'd been involved with, including me and Jill. If I found him alive I was going to choke the shit out of him.

"So what do you say, Mr. Lorenzo? We cannot complete this mission if we are at each other's throats."

"Fine. But understand this, Doc. You people fuck with me and I'll kill you all."

Ling smiled as if she'd just thought of something funny, then stood up.

"This is going well," she said, and went forward.

VALENTINE

I'm having the strangest dream.

The images were confusing at first, but soon they formed a thread, a narrative, a story. *My* story. On some level I knew the thoughts were my own, but they felt unfamiliar and half-remembered. A memory of a memory.

I stood in a palatial bedroom, not sure of when I was there. An ornate, four-poster bed sits against one wall. Above it hangs a hideous painting of some tentacled monstrosity devouring a girl.

I'm not focused on the painting, though. A girl hangs from the ceiling by her bound hands. Her night-black hair is wet with blood. Her body has been ruined, mutilated, split open and dissected. She stares at me, judging me, damning me from empty sockets. The holes where her eyes should have been are black pits, so deep and dark that I fall right into them. I want to look away, but the darkness calls to me, invites me to give myself up to it.

I answer its call, and down I go, into the abyss.

You're a natural-born killer, boy. The words sound different this time, almost mocking me. Who had said that to me? What does it mean? I couldn't remember. I was lost in the darkness and couldn't find my way.

I found myself on a dusty trail in Afghanistan, next to a wall made of mud. The village around me is desolate and empty. I am utterly alone. My only companion is a dead body, laying in the dirt next to me, wrapped in a poncho.

I can't see her face, but I know it's Arlene Chambers.. We're waiting for a helicopter that wasn't coming. I look down at her unmoving form and place a hand on it. It's like touching a piece of driftwood, cold and dead.

It should have been me.

Why am I still alive?

Am I?

I cover my face with my hands, and the ancient, immutable dust and rocks of Afghanistan, witness to thousands of years of bloodshed, fade away. I am back in the abyss, and again, I welcome it.

Before I realize what's happening, I'm in a small village somewhere. I've been here before, but I can't remember when. This time I'm not alone. It's dark, but there are fires, enough of them that I can see. People are running for their lives. Men, women, children alike, fleeing in terror.

There's noise, gunfire. A large armored truck, an MRAP, slowly rolls through the village. A faceless machine gunner in the turret mows down anything that moves in front of him. Men in uniforms, carrying rifles, walk alongside it, shooting.

Why are they killing all these people?

I see a few more men, coming up behind the vehicle. These men are bulkier, stronger, and wear armor. One carries a FAL rifle in his hands, and shoots a terrified old man as he runs down the street.

Stop it! Why are they doing this? Who are these people?

The shooter with the FAL rifle is undeterred, unaware of my pleas. He reloads his rifle, quickly and smoothly, and fires again. A car pulls out into the street, desperately trying to get away, but it's no use. The machine gunner and the man with the FAL rifle tear into it. It rolls to a stop, crunching against a wall, its passengers' lives having been snuffed out.

I move closer to the man with the FAL, furious now. I don't know what's going on, but I desperately want to make him hear me. I'm like a ghost, silent, invisible. I have no mouth, and I must scream.

STOP IT!

The man with the rifle is aware of me now, somehow. He turns to face me, a cruel smile on his face. "Stop what?" he asks. His voice is familiar. It's mine. He's *me.*

No! I didn't do that!

"Didn't you?" he asks, still smiling. His voice sounds distant, like an echo. I look down, and now the rifle is in my hands. It's still hot to the touch. I can feel the heat of the fires, smell the exhaust of the truck, and hear the screams and gunfire clearly.

No! I protest. *It wasn't me! I didn't kill all those people!*

The ghastly mirror image grins at me malevolently. "You did kill a lot of people. You're a natural-born killer, remember? This is your natural environment."

The burning village is gone, and suddenly I'm in a helicopter. Dim red lights provide all the illumination I have. My .44 Magnum revolver is in my hand. Rafael Montalban is in front of me, on his knees, with a surprised look on his face. I fire, the gun bucking in my hand. Before he can scream, I kick him out of the aircraft. He falls away into the darkness and disappears.

The other one is next to me again, whispering in my ear. "It's what you do. It's *all* you do."

No . . . please stop. God, please, make it stop.

He laughs darkly. "God can't find you here. It's just you and me."

Leave me alone! I scream, in silence. The other is gone then, and I'm alone, floating in a void.

Is this hell?

I don't know how long I wondered that, but I wasn't afraid. After a while, I felt nothing at all. I drifted alone in darkness for ages, wondering about my state, but only barely. I was detached, wholly separate from myself, and I didn't have it in me to care. No one else did, why should I?

Suddenly I was aware of my body again. I'd returned to my corporeal form. My arms and legs began to feel heavy. My back was against warm metal. I was lying on something. Muffled sounds pierced the blackness. Metallic sounds, then voices. Then there was light, blinding white light. With the light, my skin felt cold, and I began to shake.

I didn't know what was happening. I still couldn't see anything. But one clear voice pierced the confusion, a cold, dispassionate woman's voice.

"Log that as eighteen hours, thirty-six minutes in the tank," Dr. Silvers said.

"That's amazing," a nasally man's voice replied. "I wasn't sure we'd be able to keep the program going for that long."

"Neither was I," Dr. Silvers said. "Mr. Valentine keeps exceeding our expectations."

The last image that crosses my mind, before mercifully losing unconsciousness, is of the sky, on fire.

LORENZO
Somewhere over Texas
February 8th

I looked up from the file in my hand, rubbed my eyes, and glanced out the window. Brown fields stretched for miles below. Somewhere down there was where I had been born. Somewhere to the east was where I had been taken in and raised by the Lorenzo family. Ling was sitting across from me, the folding plastic table in between us.

"So, what do you think?" she asked.

"Tough, but doable. This is pretty detailed information about the security at North Gap." We had floor plans, an incomplete list of personnel files, and even some intercepted e-mail traffic from somebody named Dr. Silvers. "How'd you get this?"

"Your brother gave it to me," she said simply. "Once he found out that we wanted to rescue Valentine, he provided everything. He has been looking into this secret organization, which he referred to as Majestic, for quite some time."

"And how exactly did you come into contact with Bob?" Ling was silent. She could tell I was fishing. "Fine. Be like that. What other resources do we have?"

"You're looking at them." She gestured at the others on the plane. "My sword is the only one which can be spared at this time."

"Sword?"

"An Exodus strike team. Most of our people are occupied with other operations." She didn't seem inclined to elaborate further.

"Flight plan?"

"We will be landing at a small airfield in Montana, approximately two hundred miles from the target. Dr. Bundt and Elvis will stay with the plane." Elvis was the pilot. I'd only seen him briefly, and he didn't seem to be the talkative sort. "We will need to secure secondary transportation from there."

"I've boosted a few cars in my day, won't be a problem."

"I imagine."

"Have you thought about our getaway? How you're going to get Valentine out of the country? These Majestic assholes may be illegitimate, but they have full access to all of the investigatory powers of one really big-ass government machine. If Valentine's important enough to get locked in a secret prison, they're going to be pissed off when they find out he's gone."

She shook her head. "This has all been rather . . . *hasty.* I'm still not sure how we're going to get Valentine out without them killing him."

"Don't worry. I'll come up with something. I always do."

Chapter 3: The Princess of Montana

LORENZO
Bozeman, Montana
February 10th

"You're serious. *This* is your plan?" Ling was incredulous.

I held up the spaghetti-strapped tank top and the denim miniskirt. "Come on. You need to look the part."

Ling glanced around the Walmart, embarrassed. She caught the skimpy top when I tossed it to her. "This is . . ." she looked at the tag, "a size too small."

"Changing room is right over there." I nodded my head.

"But . . ."

"Look. I know you don't trust me but you need to work with me here. We're going to an oil roughneck town in the middle-of-nowhere Montana, not the French Riviera. So unless you want to put Antoine in drag, this is the best I can come up with."

Antoine grunted.

Ling gave me a dirty look and went into the changing room.

"I hope your boss can lighten up for this," I told Antoine, "or at least fake it. She's a little intense."

Antoine folded his massive arms and glared at me. Over the last few days I had discovered that he was very protective of Ling. She was clearly his superior, but he seemed almost like a father figure. Shen, on the other hand, was a cipher. He hardly ever spoke. He stood a short way away from us, and seemed to be uncomfortable shopping at Walmart at two o' clock in the morning. Every freak, junkie, and crazy in Bozeman was wandering around the huge store, making a nuisance of themselves as the hapless employees tried to buff the floors and restock the shelves.

"You are from here?" Antoine asked me out of the blue.

"Not here, specifically. Born and raised in the US. Only been back briefly a handful of times over the last few years . . . And every time it seems a little bit worse, a little rougher."

501

"Indeed." Antoine looked around the gigantic store filled with more food and goods in one night than whatever West African village he hailed from had probably seen in its history. He chuckled, surely thinking *whatever you say, fat American. First world problems.* "Times are hard."

I may have detached myself from the world, didn't mean I didn't pay attention to current events, especially those that could present job opportunities. I was retired, not dead. "The economy is shit, but this country has bigger problems."

"I do not understand." Antoine looked to his partner. Shen as usual had nothing to say. "Compared to most of the world, this place is a paradise."

"Listen . . ." It was hard to explain. "I've lived in every shit hole on Earth, and they're all the same. It pisses me off to see the same thing creeping in here. There are always assholes who want to hurt the regular people, and then along come the control freaks who want to capitalize on fear of the scary assholes to control the regular people. The scary assholes just don't care, so repeat, repeat, repeat. Government's like a ratchet, and it just keeps on cranking down. This isn't the country I grew up in anymore. People got too scared of the assholes so now the ratchet's getting real tight. People think they're trading chaos for order, but they're just trading normal human evil for the really dangerous organized kind of evil, the kind that simply does not give a shit. Only bureaucrats can give you true evil."

"Exodus stands against any entity which would deprive man of his freedom."

I laughed. "Good luck with that. My brother and Valentine exposed a rogue federal agency killing folks and breaking every law you can think of. It was a big deal. They called it Zubaragate. It was all over the news for a couple of weeks, but what changed since?"

"Nothing," Antoine admitted.

"Nothing. Valentine's in prison and Bob's missing, and not a damn thing changed, because a majority of the people are stupid, willfully ignorant, naïve fools, who expect bureaucrats to save them and wipe their asses for them, and the ratchet just keeps on getting tighter."

"I am surprised this offends you."

I glanced over at him. Antoine was smarter than he looked. I had said too much. These people weren't my friends. They didn't deserve a look inside my head. "Yeah . . . Too much control. Too many people watching. I don't like people watching me." My phone vibrated in my pocket, interrupting my thoughts. It was Reaper. *Good.* This conversation was starting to piss me off. I tapped the Bluetooth headset in my ear.

"Go," I said.

"Go where?"

I sighed. "What do you want, Reaper?"

"I got Bob's file, and some other stuff. I'm sending it to you now." My phone buzzed in my hand as it downloaded the data packet. At least the cell service was better than it used to be.

"How much did you get?"

"Not as much as I wanted, Chief. I went in sideways, compromised another agency's system, gave myself the title of personnel manager, then requested some files. Tried to stay away from anything that would be classified, good thing too, 'cause once I did the whole system came crashing down. They were on me hard. I was lucky to get what I did. Bob's file was flagged."

"Of course it was. Did they track you?"

"Please. I'm The Reaper." He was always *The* Reaper when he was bragging. "Get this," he continued. "Bob was fired from the FBI. He went off the reservation, disobeyed a direct order, was working on a forbidden investigation, stuff like that."

This just kept getting better and better. "What the hell did Bob get himself into? Did they find out about his involvement with our incident last year?"

"I don't know. The reprimands and personal notes weren't classified. He was looking into something they told him not to look into. He tried to gain access to compartmentalized data. He pissed somebody off, that's for sure. It's no wonder he left the country. These people are scary."

Reaper was just telling me like it was, but it wasn't what I wanted to hear. So I changed the subject. "How's Jill doing?"

"She's a little freaked out. Worried about you, but she's okay. By the way, did I ever tell you there are some *seriously* hot girls on your island? Dude! I'm gonna have to get a vacation place out here. You want me to go wake up Jill?"

"No. I'll call her later."

"Hey, one more thing. Check this out." My phone vibrated again as Reaper sent me another file.

"What is it?"

"You wanted me to find everything I could on Valentine, right? Just look. You're going to love this."

What now? I retrieved my phone from my pocket and tapped the screen. I pulled up the image Reaper sent me. It was a picture of the cover of an issue of *Soldier of Fortune* magazine from several years ago. The screen was too small to read all of the print. The cover photo was a group of men in Tiger Stripe camouflage fatigues, carrying FAL rifles.

"What is this?"

"Just what it looks like. That's our buddy Valentine on the cover of *Soldier of Fortune*."

The cover headline read, "Switchblade Teams: Elite Special Purpose Units from Vanguard in Action!"

So that's why he'd been tight with Hawk . . . That tight-lipped old bastard had once been his boss. We'd worked for the same bunch, only I'd been there back before they'd gone all corporate and legitimate. "Unbelievable. Have you found anything else out?"

"Oh, tons. He's never been careful about information management. Between that and the Dead Six files that got dumped during Zubaragate, I found everything on him, easy. It's all there."

"Thanks. I'll go through it when I have time. I'll check in later." I dropped the phone back in my pocket as Ling came out of the dressing room. I cracked a mean grin and whistled. The outfit was just as sleazy as I hoped. And Ling certainly had the body for it.

"I look like a Bangkok whore," she said, awkwardly trying to pull the too-short skirt down a little farther. The revealing top she was wearing had *Princess* written across it in pink bubble letters.

"Yes, *Princess*, yes you do. It's perfect. Now if you could just try not to be so scary all the time, we might be able to pull this off."

Shen and Antoine were stonefaced. They looked at each other, at their superior, at me, and then back at each other. Ling glared at them.

"Not a word!" she snapped, spun around, and stomped back into the changing room. "So help me *God*, Mr. Lorenzo."

VALENTINE
North Gap, Montana

Seated in my usual spot on the floor, I stared into space and tried not to think. My head hurt. My mind was sluggish. I felt like I had just woken from a dream. Or maybe I was still dreaming. I couldn't always tell.

They had put me in the machine they called *the tank* multiple times now. I had only the dimmest recollection of it. It seemed to me that they drugged me before putting me inside it, but they had been drugging me so much the drugs didn't always work anymore. I remembered a mask being put over my entire face, covering my eyes, ears, nose, and mouth. Something else was wrapped around my waist. Other things were plugged into my body, and they'd put me in.

I wasn't sure what the machine did but I knew that somehow Dr. Silvers was drilling into my mind. I'd have vivid dreams, frighteningly real dreams, that seemed to come from someone else. I knew things that I hadn't known, and had forgotten other things altogether. I lowered my head and rubbed my temples. Trying to make sense of anything just made my head hurt worse. I didn't know why they just didn't kill me and be done with it.

Footsteps echoed down the corridor. It wasn't just combat boots on the cold concrete floor, though. I heard the click of pumps and the shuffling of sneakers. I didn't move as they unlocked my door. I didn't stand up. I merely looked up dispassionately, and wondered what they wanted with me now.

Smoot entered first, followed by Davis. They were dressed in black fatigues and black combat boots. Smoot drew a taser from a brown plastic thigh holster and leveled it at me. A red laser dot appeared on my chest. He fanned out to the side, keeping the laser on me, as Davis went the other way, armed with a baton. There was another guard waiting in the hall as backup.

Dr. Silvers entered the room next, rolling her eyes and shaking her head slightly at the overt display of force. It was plain to see that she held her security force in some contempt. As usual, she was dressed in slacks, a turtleneck sweater, and low pumps. A wrinkled white lab coat completed her look, as if she were beating us all over the head with the fact that she was a doctor of some sort.

Behind her was Neville, her assistant and toady. A thin, wiry man with unkempt hair, Neville had a nasal voice and seemed extremely awkward in all of his interactions with other people, especially the guards. When she didn't have him doing other things, he followed Dr. Silvers around like a beaten dog, espousing platitudes about her brilliance. I couldn't tell if she enjoyed his sycophancy or merely tolerated it.

She stood over me for a moment without saying anything. This whole thing was very unusual. I couldn't remember the last time I'd talked to her when I wasn't doped up or restrained.

"I'm not going to get up, if that's what you're waiting for."

She didn't respond. She just exchanged a glance with Neville, then crouched down so she could be face to face with me. "How are you feeling today, Michael?"

I blinked rapidly. "How am I feeling?"

"It's a simple question."

"I feel like I went on a bender, ate a bunch of mushrooms, then got roofied. What the hell have you been doing to me?"

Dr. Silvers did something unusual then. She kicked her shoes off, then sat cross-legged on the floor, facing me, like she was addressing a frightened child. The two guards looked at each other with stupid expressions on their faces.

"When you first arrived," Dr. Silvers began, "my organization was in a state of panic. My superiors didn't know what to do with you. Project Heartbreaker had utterly failed. Then the worst breach of information security in our organization's history occurred. It quickly became apparent that your Dead Six superior, Curtis Hunter, was the man who compiled all of that damaging information. From that information, though, we learned that Gordon Willis had betrayed us and was secretly in league with Eduard Montalban. The team sent to bring in Willis found him dead by your hand. Tell me, Michael, what were we to think?"

I didn't say anything.

Dr. Silvers didn't let my lack of participation in the conversation faze her. "As I said, they were in a state of panic. Gordon Willis had proceeded on Project Blue without any authorization from our superiors."

"I don't know what Project Blue is," I managed weakly. I'd told them that a hundred times.

"I know you don't, Michael. Unfortunately, you killed Gordon Willis, the last man we could locate that knew anything about Project Blue. My superiors were convinced you were in on his plot with the Montalbans."

"I'm not *in* on anything," I said. "I killed Gordon because he fucking deserved it."

Dr. Silvers put an icy hand on my forearm in an attempt to be comforting. I almost flinched at her touch. "I know that now. We've learned everything you know and it isn't anything more than we already know. The only other people alive who might know, like your friend Bob Lorenzo, have gone to ground."

My heart dropped into my stomach. I didn't remember ever telling her about Bob. I had been sure that despite everything they'd done to me, I hadn't given him up. I was wrong. I'd betrayed him. Who else had I given up? Hawk? Ling? Lorenzo? Well, screw Lorenzo, but Jill? I felt sick, and lowered my eyes. Dr. Silvers regarded me silently for a few moments, until I was able to speak.

"I don't understand," I managed. "Why am I still here? I told you I didn't know what you wanted to know. What do you want from me?"

"To be honest, we established that you'd been telling us the truth some time ago. We so desperately hoped you could tell us who Colonel Hunter's Evangeline was. Once it became apparent that you were of no value in that regard, my superiors wanted you liquidated. Just one more loose end tied up."

"Then why haven't you killed me yet?"

Dr. Silvers leaned in closer. She stared me in the eyes. "Because you have such potential, Michael. You are an exceptional individual, and you've already done great things for our organization. Your record from Project

Heartbreaker is phenomenal. The fact that you survived Gordon Willis' attempt to sanitize the operation speaks volumes about your abilities, to say nothing of the fact that you managed to track him down and kill him all on your own. All of that natural talent, that drive, needn't go to waste."

My eyes grew wide. I was afraid. The clouded memories, the strange impulses, the vivid dreams and lucid nightmares. "What . . . what the hell are you doing to me?"

Dr. Silvers smiled at me for the first time. "Nothing you didn't agree to when you signed your contract, Michael. I'm just protecting our investment."

"I hate you."

"I know. That will pass in time. You'll see."

Anger pulsed through me. Every muscle in my body tightened. "Someday, I'm going to kill you."

She gently placed a cold hand on my cheek, like a mother comforting an upset child. "I very much doubt that."

I drifted in darkness, not sure if I was asleep or awake, or even if I was alive or dead. Images passed through my mind, fragments of memories, out of order, disconnected, adrift. They were but moments in time, seemingly unrelated to one another, but somehow I knew they were all mine.

I saw my father when I was young. He was giving me a tour of his airplane, the massive B-52 he flew for the Air Force. I was sitting in his seat, the navigator's seat, marveling at all of the dials and buttons and screens, an anachronistic mix of three decades of technological development. Then I was standing in a cemetery, looking down on my father's grave. It was raining, and the little American flag placed on it had fallen over. I was repairing a fence line with my mother, on the back twenty acres of our farm. A tree had fallen over and broken one of our fence posts, tearing down the electric fence with it. I was a teenager, and I carried off pieces of the tree as she cut them with a chainsaw. She put the saw down, wiped her brow, and smiled. There was something wrong with her face. There was blood. Her eyes were locked open, wide, her face a mask in death. I tried to close my eyes and look away, but the moment was lost and the sadness faded with it.

I was lost in the darkness for a long time. Moments of my life came and went, each time growing blurrier, more distant, until it felt like I was watching someone else's life.

I was sitting on a couch next to Sarah. She was playing video games against Tailor in Zubara. She was better at them than I was, and Tailor was getting increasingly, comically irritated, and kept insisting that girls weren't supposed to be good at video games. Hudson and Wheeler were there, laughing, making fun of Tailor just to get him riled up. I looked over at her as she concentrated on the screen, and my heart moved. She was gorgeous, and she didn't know it. She thought her nose was too big and was self-conscious about it. She worried about her appearance, but she was beautiful, and I loved her.

From the back of the van, I watched helplessly as Sarah shot a Zubaran soldier through the window. The soldier fired too. Wheeler was hit. The Zubaran solider died. Wheeler died too. He was slumped over the steering wheel, unmoving. Sarah looked at me, as if asking me to do something, to fix it, but there was nothing to be done.

She was in my arms, warm and soft, I held her tightly, and I was afraid. I was afraid we'd never leave Zubara alive. I was afraid that I'd be the death of her, like I seemed to be for everyone else in my life. I wanted to push her away, tried to push her away, but my heart couldn't bear it.

She stayed with me. She stayed with me and it cost her life. It was raining. We were running. Gunfire was coming from every direction. I was hit in the leg and I fell. Sarah stopped and turned, coming back for me. I screamed at her to keep going, but she didn't listen. She was hit. I crawled to her, but she was already dead. There was blood. I wanted to die with her. I was ready to die. It was my time. In that moment I felt relief, as if a great weight had been lifted from my soul. It was over.

Somehow I could see myself, from above, like I was flying above my own body. My clothing was muddy and torn. Sarah's body was next to mine. My arm reached out for her, but she was too far away. There was someone else then, a dark figure moving quickly, pulling me away from Sarah.

Lorenzo. I met him again, but I couldn't remember when or where. We fought together later, I dimly recalled. We shared something, a bond that kept our fates lashed together. Death followed us everywhere we went. It took everyone around us, but kept passing us over. If anyone deserved to die more than me, it was Lorenzo. But somehow, we both managed to survive. It wasn't fair. It wasn't right. But even though I was ready to die, even though I promised Sarah I'd stay with her until the end, Lorenzo saved my life. I hated him for it.

My body moved slightly, and I became aware of it once again. I was still immersed in the darkness, but I retained my corporeal form. I felt warmth on my back as I slowly gained awareness. I realized I was laying on my back. It was like that fleeting, lucid moment between sleeping and awake, when you can still see your dreams but know they're not real.

A woman was singing quietly. I couldn't make out the words, but the voice was familiar. It was Ling. Ling was singing, not for me so much as for herself, but I remember clinging to the sound once. She was pulling me up by my vest, helping me out of a wrecked helicopter. She was standing in pale light in an empty construction site, her dark eyes impossible to read. She was standing over me when I awoke on a ship. The wind was in her hair as she sat on a rock, with the ocean crashing ashore behind her. *I wonder where she is?* The singing faded quickly. The images grew blurry. Her voice was gone, replaced with the hum of the machine and the sound of water going down a drain. A noise resonated somewhere in the distance, and suddenly I felt cold. I began to shiver.

The light was blinding. It appeared suddenly, white light so bright it hurt my eyes. My face and ears burned as the mask was pulled off my head. My eyes wouldn't focus, and I could barely move, but I could hear again.

"Dr. Silvers! D . . . Dr. Silvers!" Neville whined. I hated the sound of his voice. "Look at these numbers!"

"I can see them from here," Dr. Silvers sounded tired. "Wait . . . is he conscious?"

Neville sounded pensive. "He shouldn't be. I don't see . . . oh my. Yes, he's definitely awake."

I tried to sit up. Neville gasped. Dr. Silvers called for the guards, and I was pushed back into the tank. Exhausted, confused, blind, and in pain, I let myself slip from consciousness. I had nothing left in me.

A fleeting thought passed through my mind, a surge of anger so intense it startled me: *I'm going to kill you all.*

You're a natural born killer, boy.

Chapter 4: Golden Manatee Nights

LORENZO
Tickville, Montana
February 13th

The shadow government had a nickname: *Majestic.* They even used it for themselves like some sort of in-joke. I saw that name over and over as I pored through the information Reaper had sent me. Much of it came from the information Valentine had given to Bob the year before and it was borderline crazy town. If I hadn't been reading leaked classified documents, I'd have assumed it was all a bunch of bullshit.

Reaper was giddy with excitement. He still religiously listened to that late-night conspiracy theory radio show, *From Sea to Shining Sea,* and having me be forced to seriously entertain such things was simply awesome for him. I had to hang up on him so I could concentrate.

Picture the government, by the people, for the people, all that crap. Picture it as a body, made up of cells that were bureaucrats and elected officials. Each cell had a job. Sometimes the cells were replaced, but the body stayed about the same, except this one just kept getting bigger and fatter. Now picture Majestic as a cancer invading the body, slowly but steadily spreading. A black shadow on an X-ray, a secret conspiracy of very powerful people, steering that body to accomplish secret goals. Ever since the Zubaran coup there had been hearings, trials, special prosecutors. Thanks to Bob's data dump, people had been fired, and a few had even been sent to prison— and mostly pardoned—but the cancer was still there. Who were they really? Who did they work for? What were their goals?

Beats the hell out of me. Ling, with all of the intelligence assets of the Exodus organization at her disposal, didn't know any more than I did. I guess it didn't really matter. I had a job to do one way or another.

Lucky for us, my brother had managed to gather a lot of info about where Valentine was being held. It was obvious to me that Bob had help. You don't have that long a career in Army Special Forces and then the FBI without making some contacts. He'd managed to get us the location, a list of assigned personnel, almost everything except a prisoner list. I suspected there was no prisoner list. Even bureaucrats didn't like to make lists of people who weren't supposed to exist.

This particular corner of Majestic's invisible kingdom was a secret prison and interrogation center. North Gap was a desolate little radar base dating back to the early Cold War. Now it was staffed by about two dozen people, with a cover story about it being a weather research facility for the National Oceanic and Atmospheric Administration. Bob's FBI file indicated that he had been reprimanded for demanding to speak to some of the people held here. Apparently they didn't like when people rocked their boat.

Back in Quagmire, Bob had warned me about the guys that made up this organization. Gordon Willis' men had been the dregs of law enforcement and military service. Men too violent, unstable, amoral, or crazy to work in a normal system, but still capable and having valuable skills. The staff at the North Gap facility seemed to be cut from the same cloth. Most of them were former employees of the Bureau of Prisons or different police agencies, kicked out for various reasons. Our target tonight was no different. Roger Smoot had been a prison guard, with allegations of multiple assaults, rapes, and possibly even murders of female inmates. Yet before the official inquires had concluded, Smoot had been whisked off the radar by Majestic and given a new job.

We had picked Smoot for two reasons. He was approximately my size and build, and in an afternoon of poking around Tickville, Montana, we had found out that he usually spent his evenings at a local dive of a bar called the Golden Manatee. What would possess anyone to name an establishment that, I can't say. There was a yellow neon blob above the entrance that I think was supposed to be a manatee.

Tickville was a pimple of a town which served one purpose. It gave the local oil roughnecks a place to get drunk, blow their money, and find some action. That was pretty much the basis of the economy and the Golden Manatee was the highlight of Tickville culture.

It was snowing as we pulled into the parking lot of the Golden Manatee. Our stolen ten-year-old Ford Taurus station wagon fit in reasonably well with the beat-up pickup trucks and other crappy cars in the parking lot. Even with the heater on full blast, I was still painfully chilled to the bone. I had gotten used to a constant temperate weather for the last year, and Tickville in February isn't close to St. Carl at any time of the year.

We made our way inside. Ling drew the attention of every man in the place from the moment she walked in. I could tell she didn't like being the center of attention, and was already in a foul mood when we sat at the bar.

I tried to listen to the nearest conversations, trying to get a feel for the place. Some Department of the Interior administrator, who had probably never lived anyplace that wasn't completely paved, had recently put five thousand men out of work in this area with the stroke of a pen, killing drilling on federal lands in order to protect *pristine wilderness*, and you could feel the resulting surliness in the air. As somebody who lived his life off the grid and avoided authority, I wasn't exactly an expert on domestic policy, but anybody who thought it was a better idea to buy their oil and give tons of money to monsters like Adar, General-turned-President Al Sabah, and the Prince instead of the folks in Tickville was a fucking imbecile.

For the first hour we sat there, Ling kept her long coat on, and tried not to draw attention to herself. Even so, she'd been hit on or offered drinks by one knucklehead after another. Her patience was wearing thin, and I found it hilarious.

"He'll be here soon," I said calmly as I swirled the straw in my five-dollar, watered-down bar Coke.

"And if he doesn't come tonight?" she asked. I had to struggle to hear her over the distorted country music blasting from the jukebox. In one corner of the bar was a game where drunks could sock a punching bag to test their strength. It made a ridiculous amount of racket, even louder than the music.

"Then we come back *tomorrow.*" I didn't like Ling's attitude. She thought *she* was in a hurry? It was my brother who needed help. If Valentine rotted in a secret jail forever, it really wouldn't hurt my tender feelings. "Hey, look on the bright side," I said, trying to lighten the mood. "They've got punch cards. Ten dinners here, and you get a free basket of mozzarella sticks."

"As if you could make it ten times without contracting botulism . . . Look, Mr. Lorenzo, I can tell you don't like this any more than I do." She was trying to sound more diplomatic.

"True. I normally prefer more time to plan. A job like this? I would probably watch the target for weeks, get to know his mannerisms, the way he talks, the way he sounds. This is going to be a challenge."

There was a loud crash near the jukebox. Two men had gotten into a fight over the music. The guy voting for Lynyrd Skynyrd won by knocking the other guy over, toppling a small table and some stools in the process. The bar patrons cheered and laughed. Since nobody was squirting blood, the lady running the place didn't seem to care.

A few minutes later, a big man shuffled up and sat at the bar next to Ling. He wore a flannel shirt with the sleeves cut off. His face was covered in a short beard, but his head was shaved. His arms were covered in intricate tattoos, including a big one of Captain Morgan striking his famous, trademarked pose. *Classy.*

"Hey, pretty lady," the Captain said. "Buy you a beer?"

It was all I could do to not laugh at the look of revulsion on Ling's face, but she quickly hid it. She shook her head at him, sort of giggling, putting on the *shy Asian schoolgirl* bit. "No, thank you." *Giggle.*

Captain Morgan was undaunted, and it was plain to see he considered himself a smooth operator. "C'mon, baby. We don't get too many oriental women here. Where you from?"

"I am from China," she said, her accent suddenly thick. "Preeze, I have drink with my friend." She looked up at me while lacing her arm around mine, wearing a big fake grin.

"Fine, snooty bitch," El Capitan said, shooting me an evil look. "I'll see *you* later, cocksucker." He spat, pointing a crooked finger at me.

I rubbed my hands across my face. "Thanks a lot," I said to her, not looking up.

"I apologize for that. It would complicate things if I had that *zhu tou* pawing over me when the target walked in," Ling said over the sounds of "Sweet Home Alabama." She grabbed the glass in front of her and pounded it down in one gulp. "I'm really not such a prude, Mr. Lorenzo. It's just . . . I am often in a bad mood before a mission, because I worry about my team and have much on my mind. Now I'm worried about Valentine as well." She signaled the bartender, who came by and poured her another shot.

I watched the door. More people were piling in, but still no Smoot. Shen and Antoine were parked outside. For some reason I figured a 6'6" West African and Jet-freakin'-Li would stick out a bit. I was dressed like the other patrons, lots of flannel and denim, and could easily blend in with the crowd.

"Yeah, I've been meaning to ask you something."

Ling waited, staring at her reflection in the dirty bar mirror. She was wearing too much purple eyeliner and tacky lipstick. I had helped her with her makeup—don't laugh, I'm a professional.—It's not that she couldn't do it herself, it was just that when she did it, it was *tasteful.* "Yes?" she asked, looking not at me, but over my shoulder, studying the crowd.

"Level with me here. What's the story with you and the kid? This is personal for you, isn't it?"

Her gaze shifted so that she was looking me in the eyes. I could tell that my question had surprised her. "I . . . I owe him my life. I've helped him before. I helped him escape Zubara. He was very badly injured and nearly died. I was there when he woke up and remembered that the woman he loved had died."

Her name was Sarah and I'd watched her die. Around her neck had been an ancient key that I'd needed, and I'd risked my life to grab it. Instead of leaving Valentine to die there with her, I'd dragged him to safety. I didn't know if Ling knew that, but now wasn't the time for storytelling. Besides, there was more to her story than that. My gut told me Ling had feelings for the kid. There wasn't any point in asking about that. It didn't matter, for one thing, and she probably wouldn't admit it, for another.

"He's here," Ling said, looking at the door, eyes narrowing. Standing in the doorway was our target, one Roger Smoot.

Smoot had a shock of red hair. His face was also red from the cold, and he had the huge capillary-strewn nose of a man who drank too much. His beady eyes surveyed the crowd, looking for fun or trouble, or maybe both. A couple of regulars shouted at him from one of the pool tables, daring him to throw down some money on a game. Smoot waved back and headed their way.

"He's armed." Smoot had something bulky under his jacket. "Strong side hip. Give him a minute to settle in. Don't make this too sudden, or he'll get suspicious. Don't make it too easy for him." Ling pulled off her coat and handed it to me. She ran her fingers through her hair and adjusted her top, so she looked more . . . *perky*. Ling really was hot, and she apparently knew how to work what she had. "Err . . . never mind. You ready?"

"Of course. Honestly, Mr. Lorenzo, do you think this is the first time I've executed a honeypot? It doesn't mean I have to like it." Ling flashed me a warm, sultry smile that almost fooled me. She slammed down her third shot in one gulp, then slid off the bar stool with catlike grace. She stalked toward the pool tables to the sound of Steppenwolf's "Magic Carpet Ride"—I was really glad the classic rock guy had won that fight. Ling's transformation was amazing, and every set of eyes in the room locked onto her.

So much for blending in. I'm afraid Ling was a little too much for poor little Tickville. The only way we were going to pull this off was if Smoot was, in fact, as stupid as his file suggested he was. I watched as Ling threw down a twenty and joined the game of pool.

Ling was good. Within fifteen minutes she was acting like she had had too much to drink, was bending over the pool table with a little too much enthusiasm, and was now Smoot's best friend. Smoot seemed to be enjoying himself, and I caught him giving one of his buddies a high five behind Ling's back. I had to admire her professionalism.

Smoot's file listed ten different accusations of extremely violent behavior against incarcerated women. I felt no guilt in unleashing Ling on him. After *impressing* Ling with his charm and mad pool skills, she returned to the bar and retrieved her coat. She was smiling, laughing, waving back at him.

"He is revolting. We're going to the motel," she muttered under her breath before going back to her new special friend.

Ling and Smoot left. A blast of winter air snaked across the bar before the door closed behind them. I waited a moment, then followed. Shen and Antoine would pick me up in front and then we'd tail Smoot back to Ling's place, which, in this case, was a cheap motel we had picked because it was mostly empty and had a poorly lit parking lot. I had no doubt Ling could handle herself, but her men didn't like the idea of leaving their commander alone with a rapist any longer than they had to.

The jukebox changed to Black Sabbath. *Good stuff.* I hadn't gone by the name of Ozzie during the time I worked with Switchblade for nothing.

Evil minds that plot destruction

Sorcerers of death's construction

I hummed along as I gently moved through the crowd. We had lots of work to do tonight so I was a little preoccupied. I froze when a hand landed on my shoulder.

"Where you think you're goin', shitface?" It was Captain Morgan, and he was drunker and braver than when Ling had insulted his manhood by refusing his offer of a beer. "You're friends with that oriental bitch."

"Hey, man, she blew me off too. Let me buy you a beer," I turned around, all smiles. The Captain's hand curled around the collar of my flannel shirt. "Man, I love this song. Don't you love this song?"

Now in darkness, world stops turning

As the war machine keeps burning

"You think I'm stupid? I saw you talking. Thinking she's all too good for me? Then she leaves with that fuck head? Like he's better than me?" He was shouting now. A couple of other guys stood behind him, obviously his friends, grinning stupidly. "And you, you little prick. I never seen you 'round here before. Where the fuck do you get off comin' in here and stealin' all the pussy?"

And here we go. Years of experience told me how this was going to turn out.

"Didn't Patrick Swayze beat you up in *Road House*?"

The Captain's brow scrunched in drunk confusion. "Huh?" Then in drunk anger. "Oh, you wanna dance, boy? You think you're tough?"

It doesn't matter what country you're in. There are places like the Golden Manatee everywhere and the inhabitants are always the same. The adrenaline began to flow as Ozzie got to my favorite part of "War Pigs."

Day of judgment, God is calling

On their knees, the war pigs crawling

Begging mercy for their sins

Satan laughing spreads his wings

"All right now," I said, as I grabbed the hand on my shirt, dropped my elbow, and bowed my head. The Captain screamed as the pressure hit his wrist. He went right to his knees. "I don't want any trouble," I said calmly. He reached into his pocket with his other hand and pulled out a knife. *Idiot.*

I levered his arm and snapped his wrist before stepping back and kicking him in the face. I was wearing heavy work boots to fit in with the crowd, and the steel toe removed his front teeth.

"He hit Chet!" someone shouted. *This asshole looks like a Chet.* One of Captain Chet's friends charged me. I ducked the clumsy blow, and brought my knee into his stomach. The moose kept going, and went head first into the pool table.

"The Mexican broke my arm!" Chet screamed from the floor. I suppose all brown people look the same to guys like Chet. "Help me, Timbo!"

A giant of a man stood up from a nearby table, dumping the two girls sitting on his lap to the floor. "Who hit my little brother?" He bellowed. That had to be Timbo, and he was bigger than my old buddy Train, bigger than Bob, bigger than Antoine, like *holy shit, that's one big motherfucker* big.

"The Mexican!" the Captain cried, pointing his good arm at me. *So much for low profile.*

"Come on, boys, let's get him!" Timbo said. Half a dozen other brutes stood up from their tables. The number-one sport in Tickville was whooping ass, and it looked like I was playing for the visiting team.

The sound of a shotgun getting a shell pumped into the chamber was loud enough to hear over the jukebox. All eyes fixated on the owner, a heavyset, surly-looking, middle-aged woman named Betty. "Take it outside, Timbo!" she ordered. "You wreck my place one more time and I swear to Christ I'll have the sheriff lock you up for a month!"

I'm a tough guy, but I'm a lot smarter than I am tough. While everyone was distracted by Betty's shotgun, I sprinted for the door, ducked an eight ball that somebody chucked at me from the pool table, knocked down a waitress, "Sorry!" and was out the door. A bottle shattered on the door frame next to me. *So long, suckers.*

Then I collided with two more big guys coming in from the snow. "Watch it, asshole." One grimy hand latched onto my left coat sleeve.

"Sorry," I replied, as I tried to shove past them.

"Grab him, Frank!" Timbo yelled from inside the Golden Manatee. "He beat up Chet!"

"He didn't beat me up!" the Captain protested, cradling his damaged arm. "He suckered me with some kung fu shit! Hold that son of a bitch!"

"You got it, bro," said Frank as he squeezed my arm.

How many brothers does this asshole have? I clamped onto Frank's hand with my right, levered my left elbow up and over, and broke his forearm.

His head dipped down and intercepted with my knee at a remarkable velocity. I pulled away, dodged a wild swing from the other guy, started to run, and slipped in the snow. I hit the ground hard, scrambling to get away.

The crew from the Golden Manatee was piling out now, chanting, "Fight! Fight! *Fight!*" Except for Frank, who started screaming when he realized the floppy lump inside his forearm was a bone.

I felt a hand the size of a canned ham clamp onto my collar, lift me effortlessly, and toss me onto the hood of a nearby pickup. Timbo was strong.

"He broke two of our guys' arms! Who's gonna run the pumps on Monday?"

"Two arms? *This guy's* got two arms. Eye for a tooth, asshole!" Timbo shouted. He was a biblical scholar too. I rolled to the side as he clubbed a dent into the hood of the truck. I landed on my hands and knees, kicked out, and connected my boot with his shin. "*Aaarrgh!*"

"He kicked Timbo!" There was a collective gasp from the crowd. They had fanned out, and now I was completely surrounded. Apparently, nobody was allowed to hit Timbo, because the circle was closing on me rapidly.

"There a problem here, gentlemen?" Antoine's voice boomed over the crowd, muted slightly in the drifting snow. Shen stood slightly to his side, arms loose and ready. Their breath formed steam halos around their heads.

"Me and Master Blaster here just had a little disagreement is all," I said.

"Why don't you all step away from my friend?" Antoine's tone made it clear that this wasn't a polite suggestion. He didn't look like a man to trifle with. He cracked his knuckles loudly.

Timbo was squatting, rubbing his ankle furiously. "Well, looks like we're about to have us a good old-fashioned rumble. We got a wetback, a nigger, and a . . . a . . . "

"Chink?" Shen supplied helpfully.

"Yeah. A *chink*! Get 'em, boys!" Timbo ordered.

A pair of burly-looking black men, more oil workers by the look of them, appeared behind Timbo. "What the fuck did you just say, cracker?" One of them socked one of Timbo's friends in the side of the head and pandemonium ensued.

"Don't kill any of them!" I shouted at Antoine. I had serious doubts that we were sticking with the low-profile plan at this point. I think Timbo thought I was pleading for my friend's lives. He couldn't have been more wrong. He grinned at me evilly, and charged.

Then it was on like a bad episode of *The A-Team*. There were eight of the locals against the three of us. Behind them, a dozen other locals brawled with each other, with more and more roughnecks running to join the fight, crew on crew, hitting people without even knowing what was going on. The parking lot of the Golden Manatee had turned into a rumble.

Shen got a running start, and slid through the snow, right into the leading pair of roughnecks. His hands were moving so fast it was hard to track. One of the men doubled over gagging and the next stumbled back, holding his nose, blood streaming between his fingers. Antoine was right behind. He caught one fist sailing toward Shen, spun the man off the ground, and tossed him a good ten feet into the tailgate of a truck. It rocked on impact.

I was on Timbo like white on rice. He was powerful, but he was sloppy and untrained. I moved between his arms and started hitting him. I hit him in the eyes, the nose, he kept moving back, trying to make room to swing. I kept on him, all knees and elbows, not wanting to break my hands. It was nonstop punishment. Timbo was a giant punching bag.

A worker took a swing at Antoine and hit him right in the face. Antoine swayed back slightly, and smiled, actually smiled, before he punched the man once. The blow made a sound like a bat hitting a watermelon and the man collapsed into the snow. Shen went after the next man, spin-kicked him in the sternum, and followed up with a flurry of blows to the face before he even had a chance to fall down. These guys were brawlers. Shen and Antoine killed slavers and warlords for a living. The last fighters took a look at the two of them beating the shit out their friends, then turned and ran. Apparently they were the smart ones.

Timbo was swooning now, blood rushing out of his nose, his mouth, and one ear. "Fall down already!" He finally got enough distance to launch one of those haymakers, but I was faster and kicked him on his inner thigh. He toppled over as his leg went numb, femoral artery temporarily stopped, making a noise like a felled tree.

The locals cheered and continued to brawl with each other. There were now probably twenty-five men beating the hell out of each other in the parking lot and it had spilled out into the street. I looked down at Timbo, backed up a step, and punt-kicked him in the ribs. He bellowed and flopped over, looking like some sort of injured walrus, or, well, I suppose *manatee* would be more appropriate. The others that attacked us were lying in the snow, moaning, whimpering, one man was vomiting from where Shen had punched him in the stomach, and another was actually, literally, crying for his mother.

All three of us grinned at each other. Nothing like a fist-fight for a team-building exercise. These Exodus guys were actually kind of fun to hang out with.

"Better go before the cops get here." I was surprised to discover that I was totally out of breath. It had been awhile since I had gotten my violence on.

"Are you okay?" Shen asked.

"It must be the altitude," I answered.

"Americans," Antoine lamented, shaking his head. "We must hurry!"

Antoine pulled our beat-up station wagon into a dark spot in the motel parking lot. We had rented three rooms on the far edge of the building. Ling's was the one on the end, and the other two were a buffer zone, just in case we needed to make a little noise. Smoot's car was parked in front of the last room and the lights were on inside. Luckily there were only a few other cars in the lot. The government plates told me which one was Smoot's ride.

"I'll go first."

"I'll come with you," Shen spoke from the backseat.

"Okay, Antoine, stay here."

"Very well," he said curtly. What could I say? I'd just watched this guy toss a full-grown man like a shot put. I assumed that being sneaky wasn't his specialty. I had disabled the interior lights, so it stayed dark when I opened the door. Shen nodded at his partner as we got out of the car and made our way toward the motel.

We had broken the bulbs in the overhang earlier that day so this end of the building was cloaked in darkness. We made no noise as we crept up to the window. I had to admit, Shen was pretty good. Not as quiet as me, but pretty damn sneaky. I risked a peek. Ling and our target were both sitting on the bed. Smoot stood up and walked into the bathroom. I signaled Shen to wait at the entrance. He squatted in the shadows.

I pulled my key card and unlocked the door. The door creaked slightly as I slipped through, carefully testing the carpeted floor before I let my boot touch down. We had planned for inadvertent noise, and Ling had turned up the radio. She was sitting on the bed, glancing at her watch. I could hear Smoot talking in the attached bathroom.

"Yeah, I can't really talk about what I do. You know how it is with government work."

"That is *so* exciting," Ling answered, playing up her accent, sounding again like the stereotypical naïve, passive, easily-impressed Asian schoolgirl. She saw me in the doorway. I gave her a thumbs up and started slowly into the bedroom. Ling mouthed the words *about time*. I heard the faucet shut off. *Damn it, he's coming back.* The closet door was slightly open, so I ducked inside, trying not to rattle the hangers.

The closet door was the slatted kind, and I could peer through it. Smoot came back into the room, now not wearing a shirt, and placed his gun on the night stand. Ling made a show of staring at the Glock 23 all wide-eyed.

"Don't let that thing intimidate you, baby. I take care of bad guys with that. See, that's the kind of thing I do. 'Sides, I got an even *bigger* gun to show you." He laughed and sat on the bed beside Ling, facing away from me. "So whaddaya say, baby?"

He put his bulbous nose against her neck. Ling looked right at the closet door, and mouthed the word *now*. I had to admit that I didn't attack because I was enjoying her discomfort. It was payback for getting me into that bar fight. I'm a bad man.

"The fact I'm a highly-trained badass scares people, but don't worry, we're safe here. Just relax." Ling looked like she was about to vomit. She mouthed the word *now* again. Smoot sloppily kissed her neck, and pulled one of the spaghetti straps down over her shoulder. She narrowed her eyes, and said "Now," out loud.

"Okay, baby, don't worry," Smoot said happily. "You want it now, we can do that." Ling's dark eyes flashed, and she pushed him away. "*Rowr,*" he said. "So you like it rough? You are a dirty little . . . *HURRK!*" Smoot's voice was cut off in a gurgle as Ling smashed him in the throat with the knife ridge of her hand. He rose, hands clutching his throat, gagging, as Ling spun, her tiny denim skirt riding high, and kicked him in the side of the head.

"Oh shit!" I exclaimed from inside the closet at the spectacular impact of her heel to Smoot's skull. Smoot hit the bed, eyes rolled back, totally out. Shen leapt into the room, having heard the noise, and ready to take down the target. Ling pushed the spaghetti-strap back over her shoulder.

"*Now* would be a good time, Mr. Lorenzo!" she snapped, glaring at me through the slats on the closet door.

I fell out of the closet laughing. Ling cursed in Chinese, turned on her heel, and stormed into the bathroom, slamming the door behind her. Shen looked at me, obviously confused, and he seemed unable to find anything to say.

Chapter 5: My Funny Valentine

LORENZO
North Gap, Montana
February 14th
0400 Hours

I was exhausted. Preparations had taken all night, another downside of this sort of rush job. Normally I would have taken weeks to prepare my disguise, to converse with the target, learning their speech patterns, their mannerisms, the quirks that make them who they are. Usually by the time I'm ready to impersonate someone, I've become that person. Give me enough time and I could fool their own mother. Today, I'd be lucky to not get shot at the first checkpoint.

Smoot's uniform was just a touch too big, but there was no time to tailor it so that it would fit me exactly like it had fit him. The black BDUs had been in a duffle bag in the back seat of the government Chevy Tahoe.

The heater was running full blast, but I was still freezing. The road to the radar station was winding, and there was a sheer drop off one side of the mountain if you happened to hit a patch of unexpected ice. The wipers beat a steady cadence to keep off the steadily falling snow.

"Don't let that thing intimidate you. Don't let *that thing* intimidate you," I coughed, that didn't sound right. "Don't let that thing intimidate you." His accent had been Irish, Boston, but not thick. He hadn't lived there for a long time. *Don't lay it on. Clip the words faster.* "Don't let *that thing intimidate you.*"

I checked my face in the rearview mirror. I wasn't happy. The molds had barely had time to cool for the latex nose and chin, the hair color wasn't quite the right shade of red, and even with makeup, my skin tone was a little too dark to match his pasty complexion. It takes experimentation to get things like that perfect, and I didn't have time to experiment.

This is never going to work.

I had spent half the night interrogating Smoot. He thought it was to gather intelligence about the security at the North Gap facility. That was only partly true. Mostly I was listening to how he talked, how he acted, to get a sense of him as a person. Of course, it was always better to observe a subject in their natural environment. Unfortunately, zip-tied to a chair with Shen occasionally hitting you is not a natural environment.

To say that Roger Smoot was a dirtbag was an insult to honest, decent bags of dirt. Getting inside his head had made me want to take a shower. His laptop had been in his car, filled with every weird, deviant, sicko thing you could think of. Unfortunately, there weren't very many job opportunities for me to pretend to be a decent human being.

The headlights cut a swath through the darkness. An old sign indicted that I was only three miles from the radar station.

This is it.

My phone buzzed. "Go."

"Hey, it's me."

"Jill?" I was surprised. I had been expecting Ling to check in to tell me they would be pulling off to await my signal. It was good to hear her voice, but right now I needed to get into character. "What's going on?"

"You didn't call me back last night. I just wanted to make sure you were okay." Her voice cut out as she spoke. I barely had any signal.

"Sorry. I'm fine. I had a lot of stuff to take care of last night." Like kidnapping, torture, etc. "I don't have much time. I've got to go. I'm about to go get the kid. I'll call you when I can."

"Okay, be careful. Please." She was tough, but I could hear the nervousness in her voice.

"I love you, Jill. I'll be fine."

"Okay, you better be, and happy Valentine's Day."

"Oh, I forgot. I'll do something nice for you when I get home."

"I love you, Lorenzo." The line went dead.

Valentine's Day. Hi-fucking-larious.

There was a guard shack at the end of the road. A hydraulic gate blocked the entrance. There was a chain link fence running around the entire property, but the real security was the host of motion detectors and thermal cameras. If Exodus had launched an attack, they would have been spotted miles away, and that probably would have ended with Valentine getting a preemptive bullet to the brain.

I stopped the Tahoe in front of the gate. The lights were on inside the shack, and a man dressed in black fatigues looked up from the flashing glare of a TV screen.

Plan A was to pass for Roger Smoot. Plan B was to pull my suppressed pistol from under the seat and shoot this man in the face. I was really rooting for Plan A. I rolled down the window. A jet of freezing air flooded the car as the intercom buzzed.

"Hey, man. How was leave?" He sounded bored. I didn't recognize the guard from any of the personnel files, but we had no idea how up to date those were.

"Dude . . ." I could tell Smoot was a braggart, a jerk, and in his mind, a ladies' man. "I totally scored with this hot chick. You should have seen her. Young, Asian, stacked like you wouldn't believe."

"In Tickville? Fuck you, you did not." He shook his head. The gate started to rise. I waved, and put the SUV back into drive. Suddenly, the gate stopped. The intercom buzzed again. "Hey, wait a second . . . " I placed my hand on the grip of my STI 9mm and mentally shifted to Plan B.

"Yeah?"

"You still owe me fifty bucks from poker night, asshole."

I let go of my gun, raised my hand, and flipped him the bird. "I'll pay you when I pay you! Now open the goddamn gate. I'm gonna be late." He laughed, and the gate rose. I stepped on it.

My headlights illuminated a few old dilapidated houses. Cookie-cutter, cheap base housing. A deer leapt across the road, and I had to admit that my nerves were wound tight enough, that it startled me.

I pulled my phone. "Ling. I'm in."

"Copy. We're at the bottom of the hill."

"There's one man in the guard shack. I couldn't see what kind of weapons. The glass wasn't thick enough to be bulletproof."

"Godspeed, Lorenzo." Ling's voice cut out.

Interrogating Smoot had showed me that there was no way I was going to get any weapons or electronic devices into the building. The Glock that Smoot had been carrying was personally-owned. I was going to leave it in the truck because everybody, even the guards, got checked at the entrance. Their duty weapons were stored in a locker inside.

The main building dated back to the early '50s. It was a three-story building, ugly and imposing, with very few windows. There were a couple of large radar dishes on the roof, and one giant revolving ball radar that had been rusted solid for decades. There was a second chain link fence around the building, only this fence was topped with razor wire. I parked next to the other cars took a deep breath, and stepped out into the cold.

Whatever is in Valentine's head better be worth it, Bob, because I'm freezing my ass off out here.

There was a single gate in the fence. There was another intercom, a keypad, and a camera that was looking right down at me. I pushed the intercom button.

"Identify," the bored voice said. The camera made a mechanical noise as it tracked on me.

"Roger Smoot."

"Enter your password." I typed in the four-digit number that Smoot had indicated. Since I had been rather persuasive, I was relatively sure that he had finally given me the right number. The light blinked green. *Good serial rapist.*

"Stand by for thumbprint scan."

Smoot had said that sometimes the electronics weren't very reliable when it was below freezing. "Hurry up, man. It's cold out here." I dramatically shoved my hands into the pockets of my black fatigues, and found the cold lump waiting for me. The box lit up, I pulled the thing out of my pocket and smashed it against the pad. The pad blinked twice as it scanned the print, and the gate unlocked.

I pushed the gate open and shuffled toward the main entrance. Somebody had shoveled and thrown down salt, causing a layer of cold slush to form. A heavy-set, jowly man in a black uniform and a coyote-brown gun belt opened the security door for me.

"You're late."

"I'm hung over too." I followed him in and nonchalantly tossed Smoot's severed thumb in the snow behind me. He wouldn't be missing it.

VALENTINE

There was a dull throb in the back of my head as the ceiling slowly came into focus. I didn't move. My muscles were cramped and I ached all over. I was dizzy and nauseated on top of it. My heart was racing, as if I'd woken from a bad dream. It's a hell of a thing, waking up and realizing you're still in the nightmare.

But I was still in my cell, so that's how it was. I had long since given up hope that this particular nightmare would ever end. I didn't move, didn't attempt to get up because I had no reason to. Why bother? What did I have to gain from getting up?

Whatever else Dr. Silvers' machines, methods, and drugs were doing to me, having to relive the nightmares of my past were the worst. So much death. So many dead faces, blankly staring at me, silently accusing me.

The ache wasn't as bad as it had been last time. I didn't know. I didn't care. A sense of ambivalence had overtaken me. It was more than ambivalence, it was apathy. I just didn't give a damn anymore. Whatever Dr. Silvers was doing to me, it was working. I couldn't even muster the will to sit up. My grasp was slipping. The painful memories were still painful, but more distant now. It was like being *Calm,* but all the time. As I lay there in the dark, I idly wondered what would happen to me if I let go entirely.

Just lay here and die, I thought. *No one would blame you. No one will ever know. You've already been forgotten.* I grew angry at the thought. So angry my body felt hot, like I was burning with a fever. My hands balled into fists, my jaw clenched. A singular, overwhelming impulse filled my consciousness: *kill them all.*

The fog in my mind cleared as I seethed, and I became more aware of my surroundings. *Wait a minute. The lights are off.* The surge of anger subsided somewhat, and my muscles relaxed. I didn't realize it before, but the lights were off in my cell. They never turned the lights off. The maddening buzz of the fluorescent tubes had ceased. The only light came from under the door to the hall. Had the tubes finally burned out? They'd been on, constantly, from the first moment I'd been tossed into that cell. The darkness was strange, but comforting. My cell felt different. It was like hiding under the blankets when you're a little kid. I'd given myself up to the abyss, and I felt at home in it.

I blinked hard as the room spun. I'd never done drugs in my life. Never so much as puffed a joint. Now? I could only imagine the chemical concoctions that they were pumping through my body. If I thought I had any future, I'd have been deeply concerned about the long-term side effects. I actually made myself laugh out loud at that thought. *Holy hell, I'm going insane.*

"And to think we always said *I* was the Queen of Crazy Town."

The voice had come from the darkness, only a few feet away. Someone was sitting on the edge of my bed. I stayed perfectly still, breathing loudly though my nose, jaw clenched, as I tried to stave off panic. My earlier sense of detachment was replaced entirely with fear.

"It's okay," she said. The voice was familiar. Friendly. It came from nearby, but was at the same time distant. Like an echo, or a memory. I clenched my eyes shut as I realized the room was now very cold, like they'd left a window open or something. "Please," she insisted. "You can open your eyes. It's okay."

If I'm insane I might as well embrace it. I willed myself to sit up. The room spun so badly that I thought I was going to fall out of bed. It settled down after a moment.

In the dim light, I couldn't see much of her. An outline, a shadow, more of a presence. But there was no doubt about it. It was her.

It was Sarah.

I looked down at the bed. I couldn't face her. I couldn't bear it. I just shook my head and tried to focus. "I . . . I missed you," I managed. The words came out as little more than a throaty whisper.

"I know," Sarah said. There was a sadness in her voice that hadn't been there before.

"I'm sorry I left you."

"You didn't. You stayed until the end, just like you said you would."

"I . . . what . . . what are you doing here?"

"A better question is, what are *you* doing here, Michael?"

I looked up at her. It was easier to see now. Her face was as I remembered it. Auburn hair cascaded over her shoulders. Her eyes were a luminescent green. I blinked hard to make sure I wasn't imagining it. She was still there when I opened my eyes. "Even for a ghost, you're being awfully cryptic."

Sarah smiled as she leaned closer. "Let go. Please, just let it all go. Let me go. You'll need to if you want to survive," she whispered into my ear. Then she pulled away. It was like she was fading into the darkness. "You don't have much time left."

"Sarah, wait!" The words were hollow in my empty cell. I was alone. I was sweating, breathing heavily. I was dizzy, shaking.

Oh, God. I buried my face in my hands. *Oh God, oh God. What are they doing to me? Is any of this even real?*

"Mr. Valentine, can I be honest with you for a moment? I'm a little disappointed in you right now." The new voice came from my right, from the far side of the room. I could just barely see someone standing there, nothing more than a shape, out of the corner of my eye.

Gordon?

The dark figure hung there, but I couldn't bring myself to look directly at him. A bead of sweat rolled down the side of my head. The room was too cold. The air was heavy and stale, oppressive, even.

"You had a great deal of potential," Gordon Willis said. "You still do. My former colleagues here certainly seem to have picked up on it. A lot of people would kill for some of the opportunities you're being presented with. Heh, no irony intended, of course."

"This isn't happening," I said aloud. "This isn't real. This isn't real." I clenched my eyes shut and brought my hands up over them again. "Oh God. It's not real. It's the drugs. It's just the drugs."

"You didn't mind your dead girlfriend visiting," Gordon sounded disappointed. "Maybe it's the drugs, maybe not . . . Maybe in that messed-up head of yours I represent Majestic and all it stands for, so I'm just here to gloat . . . I must admit, this isn't what I was expecting. Of course, I wasn't expecting you to murder me in my own home, either, so I guess you're just full of surprises." He laughed.

"Go away!" I screamed. "You're not real!"

"I don't know what to tell you about that. I'm trying to be straight with you here."

Even in death he was full of shit. "What do you want from me?" I asked, finally looking over at him. Gordon was leaning against the wall. His shirt collar was unbuttoned, and a designer tie hung loosely around his neck. Behind it was the dark and bloody wound where I'd shot him.

"You're a survivor, Val. You mind if I call you Val? Anyway, you're definitely a survivor. More than you can say for me, right?" He laughed at his own joke again. "So putting yourself in my shoes, you can probably understand my surprise at finding you like this. Not at all what I was expecting. You never struck me as a quitter."

Gordon got closer to me. I looked away and shut my eyes again. "This isn't happening," I repeated to myself. "It's the drugs. This isn't real. This isn't real." I held myself in my arms, rocking back and forth. "God, please, make it stop. It's not real. It's not real."

"There are things in motion now that can't be stopped. You can be a part of it or not. But you're better than this. You have a unique opportunity here. Don't let it pass you by."

"Leave me alone!" I jerked upright in bed. My eyes were wide, and I was covered in sweat. My heart was beating so hard that I could almost hear it. Slowly, very slowly, I looked around my room. I was alone. The lights were still off. I hadn't dreamt that part at least.

Even as Dr. Silvers' techniques and contrivances had torn me down, even as I wanted to just give up and die, a part of me still resisted. The more times they fed me to the machine, breaking down my will, the angrier I became. Two halves of my mind were at odds with each other. Even as I contemplated trying to kill myself, I darkly desired to kill Dr. Silvers, to kill Neville, to kill Reilly and Smoot and Davis and the rest. *To kill them all.* Each time they worked their horrors on me, I came out more broken, more disconnected, but at the same time stronger, angrier. Hatred and apathy battled for control of my will.

My head suddenly hurt, as if merely thinking about it was giving me a headache. What was happening to me? Was I going crazy? I could've sworn I actually heard an audible click as my brain shifted gears. The misery, the anger, the rage, the fear, the regret, it all coalesced, condensed into a tight little ball of determination. A familiar cold wave washed over my body then. The jumbled thoughts rapidly fluttering through my mind slowed and focused.

For the first time in a long time, I was *Calm.*

I'm getting out of this hole.

LORENZO

The first floor of the building had an entry control point, a break room, and lockers. The second floor was offices, though Smoot said they weren't used much. The top floor was the control center, which was where I needed to go to disable communications and shut down the security cameras. The basement was where the prisoners were held, and where the uglier side of what they did here went on. Smoot had told me all about the mind games.

"You look terrible," the guard said as he ran the metal detecting wand over me. He looked like an out-of-shape bull. There hadn't been a file on this one.

"I was up all night, if you know what I mean."

"Yeah, whatever, Roger. Grab your gear and head up to the control room."

Luckily he gestured in the direction of the locker room while he was talking. I walked away, trying to look casual. The interior was old and run down, a relic from the Cold War. The modern computers and equipment inside looked entirely out of place. I made my way to the security lockers Smoot had told me about. I found his locker and, using his key, opened it and took stock of his equipment.

Inside were several sets of the black fatigues. Body armor, holsters, a helmet, and other gear were all in coyote tan, which must've looked really stupid with black uniforms. I put on Smoot's duty belt, only to find it was a little too big for me. I had to quickly cinch it down so it wouldn't look off. I buckled it around my waist and grabbed his issue weapon, another Glock 23. There was a knife too, a CRKT folder. I tested the edge, found it relatively sharp, then stuck it in my pocket.

Smoot told us quite a bit about the operations at North Gap. He had considered it a shit detail. Apparently Majestic had several out-of-the-way places like this. Prisoners came and went, but Smoot insisted that there weren't that many currently being held here. All of them had been picked up domestically, and he never knew the why. He knew who Valentine was, since the Zubaran info dump had made him something of a celebrity, though he had no idea why he was still being held, nor did he care, hated the guy though. Valentine had once stabbed him in the knee with a pen. Smoot didn't like it when I'd laughed in his face about that. I have room to talk. Valentine had done worse to me. I still can't hear right in one ear, the bastard.

Lucky for me, not all of the staff would be on duty at any given time. They worked in shifts like anyone else, and most of them would be in their residences in the refurbished base housing, asleep. If things got loud, that would probably change in a hurry. Smoot said that there were always at least two guards in the basement level at all times. As a rule, no guns were allowed down there except under extreme circumstances. Only a moron would let somebody like Valentine anywhere near a firearm. A couple more men would be in the control room on the third floor. I found the elevator and made my way up.

The radar station was tapered, so that the top floor was not nearly as large as the bottom. There were windows at this level, but it was dark outside. There were several desks with computer monitors, and three bored-looking men in black fatigues. Bundles of cables were strung across the room. Screens for controlling and monitoring the security systems were mounted on one wall.

One of the guards was using the Mr. Coffee. The second was screwing around on Facebook, and the last one was actually doing his job and watching the camera feeds. Thankfully, none of them bothered to do more than glance in my direction.

"Smoot, what's up, dawg?" the one at the coffee machine asked. He was tall, skinny, and dark. I remembered his picture from the files. Local law enforcement background, until he'd lost it and beaten a prisoner to death. Perfect Majestic material. He had a complicated Slavic last name. I'd just think of him as Mr. Coffee.

"Hey." When you're trying to impersonate somebody, it's best not to talk much. You don't want to give them much to work with. "'Sup?"

"You hear what happened to Randy?" the one reading Facebook asked. I drew a blank on him. "Guess what happened while you were on leave?"

"Uh . . ." I was scanning back and forth. I needed to kill their alarms. I didn't know what kind of response would happen when a secret prison that wasn't supposed to exist was attacked, and I didn't care to find out. There wouldn't be much time before one of these assholes realized I wasn't who I was supposed to be, and I didn't want to start shooting until I could disable the comms.

"Randy got temped to Arizona, where it's warm. They're actually giving him something interesting to do. Lucky son of a bitch."

"Oh?" There was a fuse box on the wall, an ancient metal monstrosity with heavy cables running into it. I could just kill the power to the entire building. That could work. In the far corner was a big locker. That had to be where the long guns were stored.

"Uh-huh. Apparently higher authority asked Silvers if she could spare somebody for an op down there, and she picked Randy. Some FBI puke was poking around in organization business, and then he disappeared."

Bob? "Okay."

"Nobody knows where this FBI dude went. He just dropped off the map. They've been watching his house, but he hasn't come home. His wife and kids are there, so they're gonna raid the place, have a few words with the family. I bet the organization's going to try to apply some *leverage*, if you follow me."

Everything just changed.

"Man, wish I could've gone," Mr. Coffee said, taking a sip. "Anything to get out of this shithole."

The guard at the monitors finally spoke. "Screw that noise. This job is a cake walk. Steady pay, free housing, and we don't actually do any work. I don't know what you vaginas are whining about."

I casually made my way over to the bank of screens, to see what he could see. The facility didn't have a huge number of cameras, but it had enough that Ling and her people wouldn't make it to the building undetected unless I did something.

Facebook Guy disagreed. "Dude, this place blows! It snows half the year, there's nothing to do in town, and we don't get any action!"

"Action? To hell with that," the monitor-watcher rebutted. "I was in the operations division for a while, until I got shot . . ." I recognized him from the files. *Frost.* Former Army, drummed out for criminal misconduct, then recruited by Majestic.

I studied the screens. Several of them showed prisoners in their cells. Most of them were sitting on their beds or on the floor, not doing anything interesting. The fourth cell was different. Unlike the others, it was dark, and the camera was on IR mode. The prisoner was sitting up in bed. It looked like he was talking to someone that wasn't there.

"What're you doing?" Frost asked.

"Valentine?" I nodded toward the bank.

Frost looked at the monitor I suspected, confirming I had the right man. "Yep. Your buddy. How's the knee, by the way?" he laughed.

I smiled like that was hilarious. "What's he doing?"

"Talking to himself," Frost suggested. "I don't know. Silvers made your boy down there her pet project. I don't know what she's doing to him, but he's fucked *up.*"

"Who cares?" Mr. Coffee whined. "I'm sick of sitting up here, freezing my dick off, watching Silvers play head games with the prisoners. I want to get out there and get some action. Maybe get laid once in a while." I casually made my way over to him, as if I was going to get a cup of coffee.

"You say that like it's fun and all until command screws up and you get your asses shot off," Frost said.

Mr. Coffee rebutted. "Frosty, nobody wants to hear your war stories again." Frost gave him a dirty look and went back to watching the screens. Mr. Coffee then popped me in the shoulder. "Now this guy, he's got a way with the ladies." He laughed. "They should have sent you to Arizona, dawg. You'd probably get that FBI guy's old lady to talk." He guffawed at his own humor.

My pulse was racing. I struggled to stay in character. "Booyah! You know it, dawg!" Smoot habitually said 'booyah.' In general, he talked like a douchebag, and anybody who said *booyah* and *dawg*, I had no problem sawing their thumbs off. "When are they doing it?"

"What?" Facebook guy finally looked up from his monitor. "Geezus, Smoot, you look like shit. You got gonorrhea again?"

"When are they raiding the house in Arizona?"

"Randy said tomorrow night. Why, you wanna beg Silvers and try and get in on it?" He took another sip from his mug. "You really itching to get out of here that bad?"

I started to laugh, laugh like Mr. Coffee had said the funniest goddamn thing in the world. Then I hit him, palm-struck him in the face. I smashed his coffee mug into his teeth and up his nose. His head snapped back in a splash of coffee, blood, spittle, and broken porcelain. Before he could react, I grabbed the back of his head and smashed his face into the desk.

"What the fuck!" Frost shouted, jumping up from his row of monitors, stunned that one of his friends had just brutalized the other.

Facebook Guy was staring at me, wide-eyed, from his chair. He was in shock, stammering for words. I didn't give him a chance to speak. I grabbed the pot of hot coffee and lobbed it at him as hard as I could. The pot shattered on his face, sending scalding hot coffee and broken glass into his eyes. He let out a blood-curdling, high-pitched scream, fell out of his chair, and clawed at his eyes.

Frost fumbled for his gun.

I was faster.

BLAM

The .40 round entered just below Frost's left eye and took the back of his head off.

Mr. Coffee was still dazed, trying to get off the desk. No need to make extra noise, Smoot's knife came out in a flash. I plunged it into his throat and slashed my arm outward. Mr. Coffee's eyes were wide with shock as he gurgled and choked on his own blood. He slid down the desk in a red smear as his life poured out, but I'd already turned my attention to Facebook Guy. He couldn't see and had panicked, ineffectually slapping at my hands until I stabbed him in the throat. His screams turned into a sickening gurgle. Warm blood spilled out of the wound, and he went limp. I stepped back, trying not to get too much of it on me.

I stood up, surveying the carnage in the control room. These motherfuckers were going after Bob's family. *My* family. A radio on Frost's desk beeped. "Control room! Report in! We heard a gunshot! Report!"

I snatched it up. "This is Smoot. Frost had a negligent discharge."

"Frost did? You guys okay?"

I looked around at the bodies on the floor. "Uh, yeah. Scared the shit out of us. He was trying to teach us how to quick draw a pistol and he put a round into the floor." I paused for effect and moved the radio away from my mouth. "Yeah, Frost, I'm telling on you. You almost shot me."

"Put him on."

"Uh, he's kind of shaken up right now. He won't take the radio."

"For Christ's sake. I'll be there in a minute. Take his gun away."

I reholstered the Glock. The security camera feed showed a man on the first floor running for the stairs. I only had a moment. I flipped the radio to the channel I knew Ling would be listening to.

"I have control of video and comms. Execute, execute!"

VALENTINE

A gunshot echoed through the quiet building. It was muffled, as if it had come from above, but there was no mistaking that sound. Something was happening. I didn't know what, but this might be the only chance I was going to get. With the onset of *the Calm*, my thoughts were clear and rational. The dark, bubbling anger from before was pushed to the background. *They might be distracted. I'm not going to get a better chance than this.* I swung my feet over the edge of the bed and stood up.

I nearly fell. My legs were weak and quivering. It took me a moment to steady myself. At last my head stopped spinning and I felt . . . not *good*, exactly, but better than I could recall. *The Calm*, with its clarity and sense of purpose, steadied me. I smiled in the darkness. I'd missed this feeling.

I was getting out, and I was going to kill as many of my captors as I could in the attempt. They might kill me, but the fear was pushed aside by the single-minded, determined focus *the Calm* brought with it.

I went for the door. *Locked.* No surprise there. There was also a camera. It was up in the corner, bolted to the ceiling so it could see the entire room. A red light glowed by the lens, as if to let me know I was being watched. I didn't know if the camera had a night vision mode, but I assumed it did.

There was a cable leading from the camera, across the ceiling, through a small hole drilled in the wall, and out into the hallway. The rooms of this building were made of cinder blocks and concrete. They'd made no effort to hide the camera's power and feed cable, just bolted it onto the textured ceiling. I could barely make out the black line in the darkness, but it was there, just too high for me to reach.

Stepping back across the room, I pulled my bed into place beneath the camera. This was easy, because my bed was basically a gurney with wheels. Shakily, unsteadily, I climbed up and carefully stood. I smiled for the camera as I grabbed onto the coaxial cable and tugged.

Nothing happened. *Shit.* I tugged harder. Still nothing. It was on there really solidly. They could see me on camera. I didn't have time for this. I grabbed the cable with both hands and put my body weight into it. The cable ripped out of the camera. The fasteners holding it to the ceiling gave way. My bed rolled out from underneath me and toppled over with a crash. I landed hard on the floor.

Well. That probably got their attention. I didn't have a lot of time. They'd be coming for me. I needed a weapon. I looked down at the cable in my hands, and smiled. A pair of boots stomped down the hall. Gathering up the cable in my hands, I pressed myself against the wall behind where the door swung when it opened, and waited. The heater kicked on, filling the entire hallway with an obnoxious rumbling sound.

Keys jingled, then hit the lock. I could hear voices on his radio. The volume was up too high and the tinny noise echoed in the hallway, intermixed with static.

The door swung open.

It was now or never. Stepping around the door, I looped the heavy-gauge coaxial cable around the guard's neck and yanked it as hard as I could. I let myself fall. The thrashing guard went down with me. He was panicking, kicking, twisting, desperate for air. His hands clawed as his throat, but I held on for dear life. He tried to reach me, but I was underneath him. There was nothing he could do. His gurgles and gasps grew more desperate, his thrashing wilder. He kicked the door and the wall, tried to bash my face with the back of his head, but I didn't let go.

Then he went limp.

I held on for a few moments longer, making sure he was done, before pushing the heavy man off and sitting up. I was panting. My arms felt like lead and my hands were raw where the coaxial cable had dug into them. Luckily my grip had lasted longer than his air.

There had only been one of them. They usually sent two or more. Something was happening, maybe related to that gunshot. I didn't have time to sort it out. I had to move.

In the light coming from the hallway, I could see the dead man's face. It was Reilly. His eyes were grotesquely rolled up into his head and his crushed throat was purple. I smiled viciously at the corpse and began to strip the equipment off of his duty belt.

No gun. Of course Dr. Silvers didn't let them carry guns down here anymore. But he had other goodies for me: an aluminum side-handle baton, keys, handcuffs, and a radio. There was too much of it for me to carry in my hands. Unbuckling his duty belt, I rolled Reilly over and took it off of him. He was a fat man, and I'd lost quite a bit of weight during my stay. His belt was way too big for me. I looped it over my shoulder like a bandolier and stood up.

It was time to go.

LORENZO

Ling acknowledged she was on her way. I lunged across the control room for the weapons locker. It had an electronic lock with a keypad. I had no idea what the combination was. This was why I hated rush jobs. Given time to think I would have remembered to beat that combo out of Smoot too. I swore and futilely slammed a fist into the metal door. More guards would be here in seconds and it would be nice to have something bigger than a pistol. At least I could take everyone else's ammo.

There was movement on one of the screens as I looted Frost's corpse. Valentine was standing on his bed, smiling at the camera. It was almost as if he was looking right at me. His face was green and white, his eyes shining creepily in the camera's night vision mode. He messed with the camera, and then the feed was cut.

What the hell was he doing? But I didn't have time to worry about it. The door opened and another man in black fatigues appeared in the stairwell. It was the guard that had checked me at the door. He strode in purposefully, loudly cursing as he moved. "Jesus tap-dancing Christ, Frost, I'll have your ass for this. Silvers is going to blow a gasket when she . . . when she . . ." He trailed off when he saw the puddle of blood and coffee coagulating around the desks.

I came from his periphery, so fast he couldn't react, and brutally smashed Frost's baton onto his shoulder. He bellowed in pain and stumbled back against the wall. Spinning the baton so that the short end was forward, I punched it into his sternum. He made a noise like a cat trying to cough up a hairball, and for a moment I was afraid he was going to puke on me. I whipped the baton around and cracked him in forehead. He fell to the floor after that, blood pouring down his face. I removed his pistol and shoved it into the back of my waistband, then I stood over him, with the baton pushed against his top lip. He was too dazed to do anything.

"S . . . Smoot!" he stammered. "What are you doing?"

"Smoot's dead." It had to be strange to hear an alien voice coming out of a coworker's face.

"Who are you? What's going on?"

I cracked him in the shoulder with the baton. He cried out.

"What's your name?"

"What?"

"Did I fucking stutter? Your name! What. Is. Your. Name." I jabbed the nightstick into his side.

"Greg!" he blurted out, wincing with pain. "Greg Spanner!"

Spanner . . . I seemed to remember bribery, stealing from evidence rooms, and witness intimidation, so no wonder he was a supervisor here. "Okay, Greg. Listen to me very carefully. How do you check in with your command?" The longer that Majestic didn't know that we had been here, the greater our chances of getting away.

"I can't tell you that." It looked like Greg was trying to find his backbone.

"That's what those assholes said." I gestured to the corpses. "See how that turned out? I'm not going to ask you again, Greg. You're either an asset or a liability."

"It's Silvers . . . Silvers!" I jabbed him again, just to keep him talking. It wasn't surprising that he was less than eager to lay down his life for a super-loyal organization like Majestic. "She sends in a status report every day!"

"How?"

"E-mail." He cringed as I raised the stick, tears streaming down his cheeks. "No, really, she sends an e-mail! Every morning, really early! She works all night most of the time, and sends the SITREP in before she goes home!"

"That's it?"

"Yeah!" He nodded rapidly. "It's on the secure network, though!"

"Lackadaisical motherfuckers!" I spat.

VALENTINE

The hallway was dimly lit.

I crept past the other locked doors, my footsteps covered by the constant rumbling of the industrial heater. White light filled a spot on the floor further down the hall.

I wasn't sure what to do. I wasn't sure what was driving me. I didn't have a plan. There was only the powerful impulse to get out and to kill anyone who got in my way. My thoughts were a whirlwind, too jumbled for me to even follow, but occasionally they'd slow down into a moment of pure clarity. I really wanted to see the sky again. The soles on my laceless shoes were soft and didn't make much noise.

The next section of hallway went right past Dr. Silvers' office. Her office had a window in it, to give her a nice view of the scenic hallway I guess. Venetian blinds were hung over the window, but they were open enough that I could see through. I darted across the hall so that I was next to the window. Through the slatted blinds, I could see Dr. Silvers at her desk, idly typing away on the computer on her desk.

Ducking under the window, I crept down the hallway toward the open door. I had to move very slowly. I was far enough away from the heater that it would no longer cover any inadvertent sounds I made. Reilly's belt was still slung over my shoulder, and I had to be careful not to let any of his equipment scrape against the concrete floor. Past the window I stood up, back to the wall, and moved on as silently as I could to her office door. It was open.

A nasal voice came from inside. "Reilly's been gone for an awfully long time. We haven't heard anything else about the incident upstairs, either. Do you think everything is okay?"

Dr. Silvers let out a long sigh before responding. "I'm sure they're doing paperwork, Neville. One of those cretins almost shot his foot off. I swear I'm going to ban guns in this facility completely, take all of their toys away. I'm surrounded by idiots."

"But what about Reilly, Doctor? It shouldn't take that long to just check on a noise. And shouldn't Smoot be on shift by now?" *A noise? Didn't they see me disable the camera? Wasn't anyone monitoring the cameras?*

"Smoot is probably upstairs too, gawking with the other idiots. Now quit gibbering. Go check on him yourself if you want. I'm trying to work."

Very carefully, I peeked around the corner. The front part of her office had a countertop with a coffee machine on it. Neville was there, making a fresh pot. Seemingly unaware that Dr. Silvers didn't want to talk to him, kept flapping his mouth at her. "Have you sent in the daily SITREP and report to higher, Doctor?"

Dr. Silvers muttered something to herself. "Yes, Neville, I have. Perhaps you'd also like to follow me to the restroom and remind me to wipe my ass?"

Neville laughed nervously again, even though it was pretty obvious Silvers wasn't joking around with him. It made me happy that she found him just as insufferable as I did, but he persisted. The fool never did know when to shut his pie-hole. "Doctor, perhaps if you just called Reilly on the radio . . ." He trailed off as Dr. Silvers let out another long sigh.

"I'm sure he's just dawdling, Neville, but if it will make you feel better. Soothing your paranoia is apparently the only way I'm going to be able to get any work done this morning."

My eyes went wide as I remembered that Reilly's radio was still in its pouch, on his belt, over my shoulder. Dr. Silvers hit the transmit button before I could turn his radio off. The radio squawked.

Oh shit.

I heard her stand up. "Reilly?" she asked, calling out into the hallway.

"I can't see anything, Doctor," Neville whined.

"Go look," Silvers ordered.

I moved while Neville hesitated. Drawing Reilly's baton from the belt, I lunged around the corner. Neville was so shocked he didn't even have time to react. I held the baton by the side handle, with the short end pointing forward. I was on top of Neville before he could even step back. My hand on his shoulder, I slammed the blunt aluminum baton into his gut, over and over again. I shoved him back, flipped the baton around, and whacked him upside the head. Neville's head snapped to the side and he flopped to the floor. I didn't let up. I raised the baton over my head, clutching it in both hands, and savagely beat the little bastard's skull in.

Spittle flew out of my clenched teeth as I clubbed him. I was on an adrenaline high like I'd never experienced. I didn't know what was happening to me, but killing Neville was the greatest feeling I'd ever known.

The Calm was gone. There was only rage.

Panting, sweat pouring down my face, I rose over Neville's lifeless form. Across the room, behind her desk, Dr. Silvers was pressed up against the wall. Her eyes were wide, a look of horror covered her face. I'd never seen her afraid before, and it made me so happy I laughed out loud. She'd mashed the alarm button and a loud warbling noise began to sound. It probably alerted the entire facility. I laughed at that, too. My hope of escape was extinguished, but I wasn't done just yet.

LORENZO

Greg Spanner, clad in black and covered in blood, blubbered on the floor of the control room after I'd beaten the hell out of him and threatened his life. Not too surprisingly, he felt talkative.

"Next question, Greg," I said. "That weapons locker over there. What's the combination?"

"One, twenty-five, thirteen!" he gasped, struggling to fight back tears. I had broken this guy, and he couldn't maintain his dignity. He was scared, he was confused, and all he knew was that he didn't want to die.

I'm good at this sort of thing. Once you push someone over the threshold, where they become more worried about living than anyone's opinion of them, they can be very useful. It doesn't work so well on the strong-willed, the true believers, fanatics, or people who've undergone intense training, but for low-level, wannabe jack-booted thugs like Spanner this technique was perfect.

"Now look at me, Greg. I'm going to go over there and see what's in that locker. You stay right there. If you get up, I'll shoot you. If you try to crawl away, I'll shoot you. Are we clear?"

"Who are you?"

That was the wrong answer. I kicked Greg in the stomach. He folded onto himself like wet origami. "Am I making myself clear?" I pulled his Glock.

"Yes!" Greg cried. "I swear!"

"Good. Stay put." I made my way across the control room and punched the numbers into the gun locker. Inside were several M4 carbines, a couple of shotguns, and ammunition for both. I took one of the carbines, turned on its EOTech sight, slammed a magazine into it, and worked the charging handle.

That's when the alarm went off. It was an obnoxiously loud klaxon, something originally intended to alert the residents of North Gap that Soviet missiles were inbound. My first thought was that the gun safe was alarmed somehow, but I didn't think Spanner was brave enough to try and trick me. "What's going on?"

"I don't know!"

Stepping over Frost's body, I checked the bank of monitors. The screen for Valentine's cell was still dead. There was movement on another screen. *Holy shit.* Valentine was out of his cell, viciously beating someone with a nightstick. Even in the gritty black and white I could tell he was painting the walls down there.

The son of a bitch picked a hell of a day to escape.

"Come in Ling," I said, keying the radio.

"I hear a siren. We just cleared the checkpoint," Ling replied. "Status?"

"We've got a problem. Our boy is out of his room."

"Say again?"

"He's out of his cell! He's escaping! He just beat the shit out of some skinny guy and somebody tripped the alarm." There was motion on many of the monitors now. They were coming out of the nearby housing and running through the snow and there was movement on the level below me. "Every guard in this place is on the move."

"You have to slow them. You have to get to Valentine before they do."

"Then you better go loud. Greg!" I snapped as I dropped the mic. "How do I kill the power in—" He was gone. *Son of a bitch.* The door to the stairwell was swinging closed. He'd run for it.

Chapter 6: Pushed Too Far

VALENTINE
North Gap, Montana

Dr. Silvers stared at me, wide-eyed, as the alarm sounded. Guards would be here in seconds and this time they'd probably kill me. I didn't have much time, but I didn't *need* much time.

I lunged toward her. She gasped and made for her desk, yanking open a drawer. A gun was in her hand. I was on top of her before she could bring it to bear. I brought the baton down, smashing her wrist. The pistol clattered to the floor as the doctor shrieked in pain. I scrambled over the desk, powered by desperation and a euphoric surge of adrenaline, and came down on the other side. My free hand clamped around Dr. Silvers' throat, and I shoved her back against the wall. I dropped the baton, wrapped my other hand around her neck, and squeezed.

The normally ice-cold scientist writhed and squirmed as color flushed her pale face. She tried to scratch at me with her uninjured hand, but it did her no good. A puddle formed at her feet as her bladder let go. Her eyes began to roll back in her head. Darkness clouded my vision. A vicious grin split my face as I throttled this woman, a dark joy that I'd never felt. I was excited to watch her die.

I hesitated. My grip relaxed a little. Something was holding me back. I thought of Sarah, the last woman I'd seen die. Was that it? I tried to focus, to finish Silvers, but I just couldn't. The adrenaline rush receded. My hands hurt from choking her. The alarm was still screaming, but no one had come yet.

I let go of Dr. Silvers. Gasping and coughing, she slumped to the floor. I stepped back. My hands were shaking. My knees were weak. I felt dizzy and sick. I sat on her desk to avoid falling over.

Then the lights went out, shrouding us in complete darkness. Thankfully that silenced that annoying alarm. Dr. Silvers was too busy coughing to speak. The emergency lights kicked on a moment later, dimly illuminating the room with an eerie glow.

"M . . . Michael," the doctor managed. She always used my first name when she was trying to get into my head. It wasn't going to work this time. "Listen to me. You're not yourself. It's the drugs." She coughed again.

I cast a dark shadow across her face as I stood back up. "What did you do to me?"

"What did I do?" she wheezed. "My God, look at you! You escaped! You killed Neville without even blinking! I assume you killed Reilly as well?"

Why is she so excited about this? "I did."

She grasped her broken arm, obviously in pain, but she'd regained some composure. "Listen to me. You've been subjected to several experimental drugs as part of the procedure. They're still in your system. The rage, the aggression, the anger . . . you're having a reaction. You have to let me sedate you. I can help you, Michael. If you don't let me help you you'll die."

Shouts echoed throughout the building. Somebody started laughing. It took me a moment to realize it was me. They were coming and I didn't know why they hadn't gotten here already. Something else was going on. I had to make a decision before I ran out of time and squandered the only chance I was going to get.

Without taking my eyes off of Dr. Silvers, I reached down and found her pistol, a compact Glock. I racked the slide. No unfired cartridge was ejected, meaning she hadn't had a round chambered. If she'd gotten the gun on me before I broke her arm it wouldn't have done her any good. It figured, she didn't allow the guards to have guns down here but she had no problem violating her own rules. The little pistol had luminescent night sights, three green dots glowed above the slide. The dots made me think of fireflies, which told me I was still very high.

"Get up," I told her.

"Michael, please," she pleaded. "You can't—"

I cut her off. "Get up or I'll kill you where you sit." *The Calm* was returning. The rage subsided as my heart rate steadied. I was in control again.

Dr. Silvers still hesitated. I didn't. Reaching downward, I grabbed her by the collar of her white lab coat. She cried out as I yanked her to her feet. I pushed her ahead of me and wrapped my right arm around her neck. I leveled the Glock over her left shoulder and pushed her forward.

"Shut your mouth and *walk*."

LORENZO

The main fuse-box killed the power and that annoying siren, but then dim emergency lights had kicked in. I didn't have time to figure out how to shut those off so it would have to do. Most of the exterior lights were on another circuit and stayed on, but the relative darkness inside the building would help me. Last I'd seen on the monitors, several guards had come from the barracks and were standing outside the main building, pounding on the door. I had to get downstairs before Spanner or somebody else let them in.

Just then, the courtyard was illuminated with headlights as a beat-up station wagon came tearing up to the chain link fence. It did a tight one-eighty turn, skidding in the snow, and slid to a stop. Ling, Shen, and Antoine rolled out of the vehicle and immediately opened fire on the Majestic guards stuck outside. *Perfect timing.*

I made my way down the stairs, carbine shouldered, carefully checking the corners. *Nothing.* The stairwell was dark, illuminated only by one weak red light. I could hear shouts below me. I knew from the cameras there were more guards in the building. Carefully I leaned around the edge, trying to cover every possible angle, by myself. Stairwells are dangerous as hell to clear. A shadow moved below and I lunged back.

BLAM BLAM BLAM BLAM

I struck the wall hard, bullets whizzing through the space I'd been standing in. Puffs of dust and fragments kicked up as they struck the wall. I couldn't let him pin me down so I stuck the M4 over the side and fired several wild rounds at where the flashes had come from. The noise of the short-barreled carbine was brutal in the enclosed concrete space. *Great. More hearing damage.*

Then there was light below as someone opened the door to the second floor. I fired again as his shadow moved through and was rewarded with a startled cry. The door slammed shut behind, plunging me again into darkness.

I took the stairs two at a time, flying blind, and only hesitated a split second before jerking open the door to the second floor. Light flooded past, and there was blood splatter on the door. I ducked back as the holes appeared in the metal door, .40 caliber bullets flying through. He kept shooting, and I could hear the bullets impacting the wall behind my back. More beams of light shot into the darkness as they poked more holes in the door.

Then it was quiet, save for the muffled echoes of gunfire outside. It sounded like Ling was in a full-on gun battle with the rest of North Gap's personnel.

Doorways are fatal funnels. You don't ever want to get stuck in a doorway. There wasn't enough light in the stairwell for him to see my shadow, so I risked a peek through the crack, and caught a glimpse of a man running down the hall. I jerked the door open, and went through fast, crouched low, moving as swiftly as I could, but he was gone.

I was on the office level, lit only by emergency lights. *Where are they?* There was a trail of blood across the floor, leading into an open doorway. I approached silently. I could hear them speaking over the ringing in my ears and the blood thundering in my head.

"Oh man, oh man, oh man." He sounded like he was in a lot of pain, and it wasn't Spanner. "He shot me. What's going on?"

"I don't know! I don't know!" That *was* Spanner. "No one is answering on the radio. Who's shooting outside? We're under attack!"

WHUMP!

A concussion rang out from outside. Ling was using hand grenades. The lady wasn't messing around.

"Holy shit!" the injured guard said. "We're gonna die! Oh my God, we're gonna die!"

"Shut up and watch the door, you idiot!"

No hesitation. I came around the corner and put two rounds into the wounded guard's back, shifted my sight picture, and put two rounds into Greg's chest. They went right down. I turned back into the darkness. "Ling, what's your status?"

Back in the stairwell, the radio crackled to life. It was Ling. "There are a lot of them out here. We had to retreat to cover. They got the door open. At least five more personnel entered the building, all armed, and they have a dog. The rest are coming after us. We may not be able to assist you right away."

"On it," I acknowledged. My plan would've been working *perfectly* had that asshole not decided to escape.

VALENTINE

One floor above us was the ground level. I forced Dr. Silvers up both flights of stairs, using her as a human shield. There was a landing here, a small room with two doors. One led to the rear courtyard. The other led to the main level, where everything else was. On a row of hooks on the wall hung several bulky winter coats. Next to the door was a well-used metal snow shovel. Gunfire had been echoing throughout the building and from outside. I was pretty sure I'd heard a detonation, too, like a grenade or something. I didn't know what the hell was going on and I didn't want to find out.

I peered out the small, square window into the courtyard. It was surrounded by a fence topped with razor wire. It was lit by overhead lights. A small whirlwind of powdery snow blew across the open area.

"You'll never make it, you know," Dr. Silvers said. Her voice was raspy. "Where the hell do you think you're going to go?"

I let go of her, stepped back, and leveled the Glock 27 at her face. She didn't flinch. She just clutched her broken arm and stared me down.

"I ought to kill you." My grip tightened on the little pistol. My finger made contact with the trigger.

"Then do it," she said calmly. "I'm in no position to stop you."

I really and truly did want to kill Dr. Silvers. I hated her. I didn't know what had stopped me from strangling her to death before, and I didn't know what was stopping me from shooting her in the face now. Whatever it was, I just didn't have it in me.

There was another loud noise nearby, like a door being kicked in. Now was not the time for a moral quandary. Stepping forward, I raised the gun and cracked Dr. Silvers upside the head with it. She cried out in pain. Before she could fall I shoved her backward. She tumbled down the stairs and landed in a heap on the landing below.

Without pausing, I threw on one of the heavy coats, opened the door to the courtyard, and dashed into the cold night air. Being out of shape and exhausted, my dash was really more of a slow jog. The fence seemed farther away than I'd thought.

I didn't even come close to making it. Before I knew what was happening I was on the ground in the snow. Someone had tackled me from behind, slamming me down and knocking the wind out of me. I nearly lost my grip on the pistol.

Furious, I kicked and struggled. The man that had tackled me swore aloud and his grip loosened enough for me to roll over. He had a baton in his hand but couldn't bring it to bear. I twisted onto my side as he tried to reestablish his grip on me. It was Davis. His eyes went wide as he realized I had a gun. He blocked it and my first shot went into the air. He was right on top of me. The next shot was close and hot and loud, right above my face, but it hit him in the chest, which gave me time to lever the pistol up beneath his chin. I was splattered with blood and brains the instant I pulled the trigger. I kicked Davis' limp body off of me and staggered to my feet.

The door I had just come through popped open. There were black-clad men inside.

Sticking the pistol outward, I popped off several shots. The guards trying to funnel through the doorway were forced back. The slide locked back empty, so I dropped the Glock in the snow, scooped up Davis' baton, and turned and ran for the fence again.

It was a strange feeling, like when you're still dreaming, but you're almost awake. It didn't seem real. I ran and ran, but the gate didn't get any closer.

Darkness crept into my peripheral vision. My breathing was labored, and I could still feel my heart pounding in my ears. Then I smacked into the fence, shaking the thin layer of snow off of the top and causing it to fall on me. Confused, I dropped the baton and began to climb.

A terrible electric pain shot through me, and I lost my grip on the fence. I fell to the ground, and the pain stopped almost immediately. Looking behind me, I saw another man in black fatigues holding an air taser in his hand. One of the wires had fallen out of my back, probably because of the puffy coat I wore. I started climbing again.

Something clamped onto my right leg, and I screamed out loud as teeth broke the skin. A dog, *that fucking German Shepherd*, latched onto my calf. My grip gave out and I fell to the ground once again.

I found the baton. Twisting around, I struck the dog hard, smashing into the side of its neck. It yelped and let go. Everything slowed down once again, except my heart, which was beating so fast it felt like it was going to explode. Dr. Silvers had been right. The drugs were doing weird things to me. I felt my lips curl back in a snarl and my fingers grasped the baton so hard it hurt. Sweat was pouring down my face, stinging my eyes. My leg was bleeding, but the pain seemed distant somehow. A red haze clouded my vision as I focused on the snarling German Shepherd. *That dog. That goddamn fucking dog.*

It was named Gonzo.

I don't remember anything after that.

LORENZO

I ran for the stairs, leapt down most of them, and entered a darkened room on the first floor. Men in various states of dress, all armed, were moving through the building.

"Smoot! What's going on?"

Not knowing if my disguise had been damaged, I tried to keep my head down. "Valentine's escaping."

"We're under attack!"

No shit.

They ran through the break room, a small entry room, and out a back door and I followed. Gunshots echoed from outside. From the rear of the group, I couldn't see what was happening.

"I want him alive!" a woman shrieked. She had platinum blonde hair, a bloody lab coat, and was limping her way up a flight of stairs that led down into the basement. Blood was trickling down her face and she held her right arm as if she was injured. *Dr. Silvers, I presume?*

Before anyone else could make it outside, more shots rang out. Bullets zipped into the doorway. That had been close. One of the men in front of me, dressed in civilian clothes and carrying a pistol, snarled in pain as a round struck him in the wrist. Now Valentine had almost shot me too. Dude was on a roll.

The gunfire let up and the guards rushed forward. A man lay dead on the ground, skull emptied. The guards and Silvers rushed forward. I hung back so I could keep everyone in sight. "Get him. Hurry." The doctor saw me. "Smoot, where the hell have you been? Valentine is escaping!" More gunfire resonated from the other side of the building. Exodus was still in the fight.

"He dropped his gun. Sic the dog on him!"

Valentine had reached the perimeter, but the guards had converged on him. Valentine hit the fence climbing like mad, only to be pulled down by a huge dog. It dragged him through the snow by the leg. It yelped and let go as he smacked it with a stick, but it circled around for another attack. The North Gap guards clustered around the scene, apparently confident Valentine was out of ammunition, and happy to give the dog a minute to work.

Valentine rose, screaming like a berserker. His face was covered in blood. His clothing was ripped, a baton in one fist, and every vein and muscle bulged on his face. The dog, snarling, leapt at him.

Valentine clenched the baton in both hands, holding it horizontally. The dog's slobbering jaws clamped onto the stick, and Valentine wrenched it brutally to the side. The German Shepherd's spine snapped audibly. Its limp form slammed into Valentine, pushing him back against the fence.

He tossed the dog aside and screamed for more. I had never seen a man so angry.

"Now!" One of the guards ordered. Pairs of taser barbs latched into Valentine's body. He twitched as electricity crackled through his muscles. They hit him long and hard, multiple guns sparking.

"Take him," Dr. Silvers said raggedly, walking through the snow with a limp. "Do not kill him! I'm not going to tell you idiots again!" The remaining guards swarmed forward, clubbing Valentine with their batons, sticks rising and falling rhythmically. Four men all tackled him at once, and even then they could barely contain his rage beneath their weight.

Enough of this shit. There were five of them left alive. They all had their backs to me. I was the only one armed with a rifle. I raised the stubby carbine and pulled the trigger. The gun roared in the cold air. I put a round into each of them, and 5.56 makes a horrible mess of people at such close range. I wheeled around and double-tapped the man who had been hit in the wrist. Then I went back and plugged each of the guards again, just to be sure.

It was suddenly very quiet. I stood there, hot carbine in my hands, bolt locked to the rear. Dr. Silvers was the only other person standing. She didn't move, she just stood there, staring at me, wide-eyed. She began to shiver, realizing that I was not who she thought I was. The shock of it hit her like a train.

A shape moved in the carnage. Valentine slowly rose, pushing limbs off of him. Now he stood, coated in a pink mush that was half snow and half blood. He saw me, surely not understanding why one of his tormentors had murdered the others, but it didn't seem to matter to him. He looked at Dr. Silvers intently, his bloodied form heaving as he gasped for air. Valentine got up, made it a few halting steps toward her, but then he began to shake, fell to his knees, and face-planted in the snow, like a puppet with its strings cut.

Chapter 7: The Sum of Our Parts

LORENZO
North Gap, Montana

The gray sky was slowly brightened as the Sun climbed over the horizon. It was still overcast and lightly snowing, but the darkness was receding to the west.

Near as I could tell, we had killed every last one of the North Gap facility's personnel, except for Dr. Silvers. There was a chance that there were some in hiding and they'd called for help. So we needed to get the hell out of Dodge.

But first, I found Dr. Silvers' office and ransacked it, taking everything I could get my hands on. Shen and I searched for intelligence on the Majestic organization while Ling and Antoine got Valentine secured for transport. I wasn't ever going to get a better opportunity to learn about the organization that was after my brother, and after everything I'd risked and everyone I'd killed, I wasn't about to let that opportunity go to waste.

Reaper would love this. The chance to explore an actual shadow-government secret interrogation facility? The kid would probably pee himself with conspiratorial glee. Looking around the basement, I began to wonder if maybe there wasn't a lot more to Reaper's conspiracy theories than I thought. The place was full of strange machines that I couldn't identify, like some kind of science-fiction torture dungeon. One of the computers in that room had a red sticker on it that said *Secret*. Which meant it could probably access the secure network Greg Spanner had told me about. I snagged every electronic storage device that wasn't nailed down.

Shen had broken open a metal container with a crowbar. He called me over to see something.

"What is it?" I looked into the storage bin he'd busted the lock off of. Inside were what looked like Valentine's personal belongings from when they'd nabbed him in Virginia. Clothing, wallet, watch, keys, that sort of thing, but right on top was a large, stainless steel .44 magnum revolver. I picked the Smith & Wesson up, opened the cylinder, and inspected it. "I hate this gun." For good reason. Valentine had basically shot me three times with the goddamn thing in Zubara, once right through an arms dealer. My tinnitus was a permanent reminder of how much I hated that gun, but Shen didn't know all that, and he looked puzzled. "Never mind. Grab it all."

Ling was waiting for us on the first floor. All three of the Exodus people were dressed in Mossy Oak camouflage we'd picked up in town. Dr. Silvers was with her, zip-tied to a chair. The good doctor was bitching at Ling about something when we came to the top of the stairs. Ling stared her down and said nothing until we entered the room.

"Did you find everything you were looking for?" she asked me.

"Yeah. We should go." We'd only been in here for a few minutes, but already that felt far too long.

Dr. Silvers saw her iPad in my hands, and her eyes went wide. She began to say something, but Ling jabbed her with the suppressor of her MP-9 subgun and told her to be quiet.

"It says I need a passcode to unlock this." I held up the iPad. "What is it?"

"Go to hell."

"Kneecap her," I said.

"Wait . . ." She hadn't even given the Exodus folks a chance to be threatening. "Seven, three, one, nine."

I tried the code and it worked. "Awesome."

"What of the other captives?" Antoine asked.

"Not our problem," I said. They might have been pure as the driven snow, but on the other hand, they might deserve to be in a place like this.

"Unlock their doors," Ling ordered. "We do not have time to sort out who they are. They are on their own."

I shrugged.

Dr. Silvers finally piped up. "You people have a lot of nerve, coming in here. Do you have any idea the hornet's nest you've just kicked? Do you have any idea at all what you're bringing down on yourselves?"

"Not entirely, but I'm sure we'll figure it out. Thanks for the hard drives."

The Majestic scientist shook her head in bewilderment. "You. You're not Roger Smoot. Who are you? What the hell is going on? Why did you take Valentine?"

I smiled at her but offered no answers.

She grew frustrated. "It doesn't matter. You will never get away with this. We're too powerful. We're everywhere."

"You mean Majestic?"

She sneered at me. "They'll catch you, and then they'll bring you to someone like me. They'll drill out every last piece of information you know. There's nowhere you can run to, noplace you can hide, where they won't find you. Sooner or later, you'll end up in a place like this, and someone like me will be there to make you regret this decision. I promise you that . . ."

Ling stepped in front of Silvers. Her dark eyes were like daggers. Silvers trailed off as the Chinese Exodus operative stared her down. "You never imagined this day would come, did you?" Ling asked quietly. "I know your kind. You sit here in your little kingdom, removed from the world, committing your little atrocities because it's your job. You say you do these things because powerful men tell you to, but really, you do these things because you enjoy them. You never imagined that you'd have to account for your actions, did you?"

Dr. Silvers said nothing. Fear was on her face.

"Of course you didn't," Ling continued. "You never dreamed such a thing could happen, that one day it would all come crashing down, that your insulated world would fall apart. That day has come."

The doctor stumbled on her words as she tried to speak. "If . . . if you want information . . ." she trailed off as Ling seemed unimpressed with her attempt to negotiate. "What is this?"

"I would like nothing more than to shoot you and be done with it, however . . ." Ling's eyes narrowed. "My order has an old saying, when a criminal has been caught and justice must be satisfied, the wisest judges are his victims . . . Carry her downstairs. Leave her bound. Unlock the doors. We will let her prisoners decide her fate."

"No! No!" Silvers began to scream as Shen and Antoine picked up her chair and carried her away.

"Harsh." Then I thought of the weird machines. "But fair."

"I am confident she will receive as much mercy as she has given . . . Come, Mr. Lorenzo, we've been here too long already."

I followed her outside. Valentine was wrapped in a blanket, passed out in the back of our car. He looked like shit. "Son of a bitch better live." I muttered. "I didn't just audition for public enemy number one for nothing."

Ling glared at me. "How can you—"

"Be so heartless?" She was obviously distressed by Valentine's condition, and she had to suppress anger at my callousness to his fate. I'd grown to like the Exodus operatives over the last few days, but that didn't make me their errand boy. "I just killed a whole mess of people to get your boyfriend back. I fulfilled my part of the bargain. So where the fuck is my brother?"

Ling sighed. "Altay Krai, in the Golden Mountains."

"The Crossroads?"

Ling nodded.

I couldn't believe it. I knew that area well. "Shit . . . Bob, you stupid idiot . . . And the rest of the note?" I demanded. Ling reached into a pocket on her black fatigue shirt and pulled out half a paper napkin and handed it over. It was the bottom half of the note that Bob had left me. "You had it the whole time?" I shouted. I was used to being lied to, but it didn't mean I had to like it.

"Yes. It wasn't my wish to be untruthful."

"Well, you did a bang-up job."

"It was your brother's idea."

Son of a bitch. I unfolded the torn napkin. "It's blank."

"Bob said you wouldn't trust us. He said you would not help unless you had an incentive."

I didn't answer. I was too mad. But Bob had been right. I stood there in the gently falling snow and the grey light of the Montana sunrise and cursed him to hell.

"Bob said you were the only man who would be able to free Valentine, and even at the last moment, when your brother knew he was going to be captured or killed, the very last thing he did was write that note and make us swear to free Valentine, no matter what . . ." Ling paused, uncomfortable. "He said you would react exactly as you did, and that you only had one weakness we could exploit."

"Loyalty," I spat the word.

"Yes, your brother knew that you would do anything to help those few people you've claimed as your family. But Bob said that Valentine was more important, or rather, something he knows, is so important that . . ." She trailed off.

"What?" I did not like where this was going, and the combination of fatigue and anger boiling through my system was threatening to blow.

"That if you tried to hinder us, or betray us, or anything that would stop us from retrieving Valentine, we were to kill you," Ling stated calmly. "If necessary," she added, almost as an afterthought.

It was like being hit in the stomach with a hammer. I could taste sour bile in the back of my throat, and the idea of being betrayed by my own brother physically hurt. The napkin was still in my hand. I crumpled it into a tight ball and squeezed until my fingers ached.

What did Valentine know? What was so important that Bob would jeopardize his own life, ruin his career, endanger his family, and be willing to sacrifice his own brother? "Damn it, Bob . . ." That didn't matter now because tonight Majestic was going after Bob's wife and kids. His family. *My family.* I didn't know if I could do anything, but I wasn't about to do *nothing*.

"Ling, change in plans. We need to go to Arizona."

We drove down a lonely two-lane highway, heading into the sunrise, as we made our way back to the airport. The sooner we were in the air and the farther from North Gap we got, the better off we'd be. The longer it took them to discover our attack, the greater our chances of getting away. Every minute we traveled increased the diameter of the search they would have to undertake, and since we were talking about an outfit that probably had access to spy satellites and massive databases, I hoped to turn minutes into hours.

Valentine was in the back, on a litter, still unconscious. Shen had hooked him up to an IV. Our wagon had a poorly-done tint job on the windows that kept our patient out of the sight of prying eyes. That would be important when we stopped for gas. Antoine drove just below the speed limit. We wanted to avoid attention and law enforcement at all costs.

Ling and I went through Dr. Silvers' iPad. I was definitely curious about what they were doing to the kid, but I wasn't nearly as interested as Ling was. I was mostly looking for anything that would help me figure out what happened to my brother.

Some of the hard drives we grabbed were sure to be encrypted. I didn't know much about that kind of stuff. That's why I had Reaper. Silvers had used her iPad to keep notes on her work, and she'd been lousy with information security. I'm sure Majestic, being secret black-ops types, had rules against this sort of thing, but over the years I'd found that the know-it-all academic types considered themselves too smart to listen to mere operators. Silvers had been interrogating him about something called Project Blue, and specifically, something called the Alpha Point. Ling didn't know what that meant either.

"Big Eddie mentioned this back in Quagmire," I muttered. Ling looked at me curiously. "That's why Gordon Willis turned traitor. Those two were in on it together. It's something huge."

"Your brother was concerned about it as well, but he was unclear on what it entailed. It was this search that brought him to The Crossroads."

"Do you know who this Evangeline person is?"

Ling shrugged.

They'd sure worked him over good trying to find out. Whoever she was, Valentine had no clue one way or another. Dr. Silvers had become convinced of that early on.

So why did they keep him alive?

VALENTINE

The morning Sun was still below the horizon as I turned onto the long gravel driveway that led to our house. I'd been driving a long time and was happy to be home. Three of my friends and I had gone on a road trip to Detroit, and we'd driven all night on the way back. I'd dropped them off at their houses before heading home myself.

As I pulled to a stop in front of the house, I was making plans to sleep through the day. It was my last day of Spring Break, and I'd have to be back in school the next morning. I doubted that I'd get much sleep. Knowing my mom, in a few hours she'd drag me out of bed to help shovel the horses' stalls.

I parked next to my mom's pickup. There was a truck, one I didn't recognize, parked in the drive. I quietly made my way to the front door, wondering who could be over so early.

Holy crap, *I thought.* I wonder if Mom had some guy over while I was gone? *I was uncomfortable with that thought. Being honest, I couldn't blame her. It'd been eight years since my dad had died. My mom had been alone for a long time.* Maybe she has a boyfriend?

Those thoughts faded away as I walked into the house. I expected to find my mom sitting at the table, eating some toast and smoking a cigarette like she always did.

Whatever I may have expected, it wasn't what I found. The kitchen was trashed. There was broken glass everywhere. The chairs around the table were dumped over. The refrigerator was wide open, and food was out on the counter.

My mom was on her back in a chair that was lying on the floor. She stared up at the ceiling and didn't say anything.

"Mom?" I asked, stepping closer. There were extension cords wrapped around her, like she was tied to the chair. Her shirt was stained with little red blotches; around her was a pool of dark red liquid.

"Mom?" I repeated. Why is she lying on the floor wrapped up in extension cords? Is this a joke or something? *It clicked a second later.* My mom is dead. *She'd been tied to a chair and stabbed over and over again.*

My breathing sped up. My heart began pounding so hard it felt like it was going to burst out of my chest. I became dizzy. My knees went weak. My stomach twisted, and pain shot through my groin. My mouth was dry. There was a loud buzzing in my ears. I stepped back, stumbled, and fell to the floor. My mouth was open. I was trying to scream, but no sound came out.

After a few seconds, I was able to tear my eyes away from my mother's brutalized body. A black and white lump lay in the next room. It was my dog, Buckwheat. He'd been killed too.

Something strange happened to me then. The dizziness stopped, my heart rate slowed, and the buzzing in my ears faded away. My head cleared. The shock and pain drifted into the background as the Calm overtook me for the very first time.

Focus, I thought to myself. Somebody did this. They might still be here. You have to get out of here and call the Sheriff. *I gritted my teeth and managed to get to my feet.*

It was in that moment that a man walked in from the next room. His image was forever burned into my mind: he had on cowboy boots and dirty, stained jeans. He wore a dirty white t-shirt and an old acid-washed jean jacket. His hair was long and uncombed, and his face was covered in stubble. His eyes were wide and his pupils were dilated. Hanging from his belt was a large hunting knife in a leather scabbard. Behind him was another man, taller and skinnier, with pale skin and no hair.

"Jesse, look!" the skinny guy said, pointing at me. "There's someone else here, Jesse!"

"It's just a fucking kid," Jesse said, wiping his nose with his hand. "How you doing, kid? Where's your mom keep the cash?"

"Let's cut him up, Jesse!" the skinny guy said excitedly, wringing his shirt in his hands. "Let's fucking cut him up!"

Jesse turned to his friend and shoved him. "Goddamn it, Billy, calm the fuck down! We been here too long already."

"But, Jesse, please!" Billy said, his voice getting even more high-pitched. "It'll just take a minute! Look how surprised he is! He came home and found his mommy all cut up! Surprise!"

Jesse slapped Billy, causing him to let out a squealing cry. "Get a hold of yourself, Billy! We don't—"

Billy interrupted Jesse. "He's getting away!" Jesse turned around to see me running up the stairs. The skinny one, Billy, took off after me, but I made it upstairs before he did. I rounded the corner, ran down the hall, and burst into my mom's bedroom. I slammed and locked the door behind me, just as Billy crashed into it.

"Come out, kid!" Billy said, almost giggling with excitement. "Come on out!"

My heart was pounding in my chest, but my head was clear. The shotgun! My mom had a pump shotgun in her closet. I hoped to God it was loaded, because I didn't know where she kept the box of shells.

Vaulting across the room, I pulled open the closet door and pushed my mom's clothes aside. In the back corner was a little-used Remington 870. I heard a crash as Billy began slamming his body against the flimsy door. I grabbed the shotgun and stepped out of the closet, opening the action as I did so. It was loaded. I slammed the pump forward, pushing the shell into the chamber, just as Billy cracked the door open. His arm reached in and began fumbling for the lock.

I was completely calm as I brought the stock of the shotgun to my left shoulder, pointed it at the door, and squeezed the trigger. The shotgun barked loudly in my mom's bedroom, and blew a hole through the door. Billy shrieked in pain and his arm disappeared back through the door.

Pumping another round into the chamber, I pulled the bedroom door open. Billy was lying on the floor trying to hug himself. Just below his left armpit was a gory wound. Blood was pouring onto the floor.

"Jesse, help me!" Billy cried, his screeching voice gurgling as blood filled his lungs.

I was on autopilot. It was like playing one of my first-person-shooter video games. I wasn't afraid or upset. I felt nothing. I stepped over Billy and pointed the shotgun at his face. "Surprise," I said, and squeezed the trigger again. Billy's head exploded in a mass of brains and blood.

I looked up, pumping the shotgun again, just as Jesse appeared at the end of the hall.

"Billy!" he said excitedly, seeing me standing over the remains of his partner. "You killed my little brother!" I pointed the shotgun at him and fired again. I missed. The mirror at the end of the hall exploded in a shower of broken glass as Jesse disappeared back into the stairwell.

I ran down the hall after him, chambering another round in the shotgun. I rounded the corner and looked down the stairs. Jesse was pulling a pistol from his waistband. He looked up and saw me point the shotgun at him. He turned to run, stumbled, and fell down the last few steps. His gun clattered across the floor and out of sight. I fired again, but missed again, blowing a hole in the wall of the stairwell. The intruder rounded the corner at the base of the stairs as he bolted for the door.

I went after him, running down the stairs as fast as I could. I went through the kitchen just as Jesse burst through the front door. I fired yet again. The buckshot ripped through the screen door and shattered one of the potted plants hanging on the porch, but I missed my target again.

Jesse jumped off the porch and ran for his truck. I stumbled on the steps and fell to the ground, skinning the heel of my hand in the gravel and dropping the shotgun. I didn't even feel it. I pushed myself up, grabbed the 12-gauge, and pumped the last round into the chamber. On my feet again, I took off in a run.

I caught up with Jesse just as he pulled open the door of his truck. He hurriedly tried to climb in, but I was right behind him. I aimed for the back of his head and fired. Jesse's head exploded, spattering the interior of his pickup with the contents of his skull. His lifeless body slumped forward onto the seat, slid off, and crumpled to the ground by the running boards. It left a stream of blood as it went.

I stood there, frozen, pointing the now-empty shotgun into Jesse's blood-spattered truck for what seemed like a long time. I heard a faint ringing in my *ears, and my hands began to shake.* The Calm *was wearing off, and I was rapidly going into shock. I slowly lowered the shotgun and turned away.*

In a daze, I made my way back to the house, stopping only to throw up once. I sat on the porch, resting the shotgun next to me, and stared off into the distance. I didn't feel anything inside. I'd always imagined that when you killed someone for the first time, it'd be dramatic, or emotional, like in the movies. Now that I'd done it, I didn't see what the big deal was. I just sat there, not feeling a damned thing, as the Sun climbed into the sky.

LORENZO
Connley Field, Montana
February 15th

The tiny airport was uncontrolled. There was no tower, and only the most rudimentary of hangar facilities. Our Cessna was almost ready to roll, and Antoine and Shen were gently loading Valentine in. It had taken us hours to get here, stopping only for gas. We could have used a closer airport, but the nearer we were to the target, the more attention we would be sure to draw. This one had a great combination of obscurity and lack of witnesses.

"I understand what you feel you must do, Lorenzo," Ling said as she handed my bag to me from the back of the station wagon. "But I see one possible problem. If you encounter any Majestic agents—"

"And this plane was nearby both times? They'll focus on us like a laser beam. It won't matter where we go, they'll track us down. I know." We both knew how our foes would react, and the radar coverage over North America was just too good for them not to pick out the pattern. The government, when properly motivated, could process a whole lot of data very quickly.

But I had to go. I couldn't just call Bob's wife, Gwen, and tell her to run, because surely the phone would be tapped. I had nobody in that area who I could rely on, and we were short on time, with the clock ticking toward the scheduled raid. "I can't just leave them. If these were normal government types, I wouldn't worry. But these people . . ."

"Yes, I know." Ling had just got done reading a whole lot of disturbing notes and emails about Silvers' interrogation techniques.

I barely knew my sister-in-law. In fact, I had only met her twice, but I wasn't about to let her be taken away by the kind of people who thought it was fun to give Valentine enough drugs to pickle an elephant and employed people like Smoot. "Then you know I've got to do this."

"It endangers my men and jeopardizes our mission."

"My mission is to get my brother back, and I'll be damned if I bring him home and his wife and kids are rotting in some secret prison shit hole . . . Look, you drop me off in Flagstaff, then take right back off. Even as powerful as Majestic is, it'll still take them time to put it together. There's an airfield in Santa Vasquez, Mexico. I know a guy there, and you can get a new plane, nice and clean. I'll cross the border and meet you there, and if I'm . . . held up, you just bail without me."

Ling folded her arms and studied me. "Bob was right about one thing."

"What?" The Cessna engine turned over with a cough and a belch of oil smoke.

"You love very few people, but to those, you are extremely loyal."

It was a stupid weakness. "Don't rub it in."

"I meant it as a compliment," she said sincerely. Ling folded her arms and studied me. "You helped us. We will take this risk."

"Thanks." Then I noticed something about the airfield. I stopped, tilted my head, and thought about it for a moment. It was stupid, but it could work. "Maybe we don't need to land. That way if I screw up and attract any attention, you guys are still in the clear." I pointed at a large green sign on a nearby hangar. "I've got an idea."

The hangar had a padlocked chain on the door, and was clearly closed for the winter. Ling followed my finger and read the sign.

SKYDIVING LESSONS AND RENTALS

"You can't be serious."

"Ms. Ling, serious is my middle name," I said with a smile.

I woke up looking at Albert Einstein again.

"Good evening, Mr. Lorenzo," Dr. Bundt said over the noise of the Cessna. The good doctor had come to the rear of the plane and sat next to me. "We'll be passing over Flagstaff in thirty minutes."

"Groovy." I yawned and stretched. At least I had managed to get a couple of hours of sleep. The view out the window showed that it was nearly dark. Perfect. "I'll get ready. We'll need to pick a good spot. We've got to avoid witnesses, but someplace close enough that I can catch a ride into town."

"Understandable. You have done this before, I assume?"

"Jumped out of an airplane? Yeah, a few times." When Big Eddie had commissioned me to rob the Cape Town Diamond Exchange, my team had inserted with a HALO jump. We had practiced a multitude of times, jumping five or six times a day in the week leading up to the actual heist. Of course, one of Eddie's men had landed on a wrought-iron fence and disemboweled himself, so I couldn't exactly say that it had been *flawlessly* executed. I changed the subject. "How's your patient?"

Ling was forward of us, sitting on the floor, leaning on the fuselage, next to the unconscious form of Valentine. The table had been removed, and Valentine was stretched out. He still looked like shit.

Dr. Bundt shook his head. "At this point, I do not know. He'll live, but I do not know what shape he will be in. The boy has seen some serious trauma, and has been heavily medicated for quite some time. He still hasn't woken up."

"Well, when he wakes up, the kid and I need to talk." It was not a request.

"It may not be that simple, I'm afraid. Not everyone comes back fully from that kind of trauma."

"He's tough," I said simply.

"If only that were all there was to it. You see, when someone faces something so horrible, when something breaks inside their—"

I cut him off. "Whatever, Doc. I know how horrible works. Some people wimp out, let the hurt, the evil, *own* them. Others lock it up and hide it, and some people are really smart, and they keep it, and learn to use it as a weapon."

He paused, studying me. "And I assume that you are the latter?"

I had already said too much. "Don't bother to psychoanalyze me, Doc. You're wasting your time."

"It is what I do," he said simply. "But if I were to make an educated guess, in a professional capacity, I would say that you had a very horrible childhood, violent, poor, probably a criminal background, most likely abusive. I can tell that by your reputation and behavior. You trust no one. Your natural instinct is to dislike everyone you meet. Your first reaction is to view them either as a threat or something you can use to your own advantage. Basically, you are what I believe you Americans would refer to as an *asshole*."

"I'm the nicest asshole you'll ever meet. You know I'm not paying for this session, right?" I moved over to check my stolen parachute.

He followed me. "But that's not all you are. I can only assume that you had some respite, some brief time where you actually learned to love. Where you actually learned about family and loyalty, and that not everyone in the world existed just to prey upon one another. I can tell this by the way you speak about those that you consider your own. For them, you are very protective. Perhaps those good times were somehow taken from you, rendering you bitter and full of hate for so long—"

"I'm not one of your freed slaves in need of fixing. Now if you'll excuse me . . ." I hoisted the parachute and headed forward.

His bony hand clamped down on my wrist. "Mr. Lorenzo, if I can ever be of assistance . . ."

I sighed, crouched uncomfortably in the cramped compartment. He meant well. "Dr. Bundt, just so you know. When I was a kid, I watched my old man beat my mother to death. I stabbed one of his eyes out with a fork when he came for me next. The judge that put my dad in prison took me in and gave me a home. He was a good man. A few years later, some scumbags killed him for his watch. So I hunted them down and murdered every last one of them. I've spent the time since hurting people and taking their stuff. So there really isn't much you can tell me that's going to fill me with warm fuzzies, if you know what I mean."

"See? I was actually pretty close," he said happily.

I gently removed his hand from my arm. "Score one for psychiatry." I moved toward the cockpit. Ling was asleep, still holding Valentine's hand. I'd suspected there were some feelings there, at least on her side of the equation. Antoine and Shen watched me carefully step over them as I made my way to the cockpit.

"We're getting close," the pilot said without turning around. "This area's actually really forested. Where do you want to get out?"

"That's the highway below us. I just need to be close enough to run to it. Pick me a good, open field where I won't break my neck, and I'll try for that. I'll get ready, you just give me the signal."

The pilot nodded. As I turned back around, Shen spoke.

"Was Doctor Bundt trying to analyze you?"

It took me a moment to respond. I could count the number of times that Shen had initiated conversation in the last week on one hand. "Yeah, apparently my psychological profile says I'm an asshole."

"I could have told you that," he said, and actually grinned. Shen extended his hand. I shook it. He had a grip that could bend rebar. "It was a pleasure working with you."

"Yes, I thought I was going to have to kill you at first, but I would work with you anytime," Antoine said simply. "It was an honor."

Well, I'll be damned.

"Thanks, guys, but this is only a detour. I'm not dead yet." I passed forward a note that I had written some instructions on. "When you get to Santa Vasquez, the man you need to speak with at the airport is Guillermo Reyes. He runs all of the smuggling through that area. Tell him I sent you, and he'll arrange for new tail numbers and transponder. Don't let him give you any shit. Shen, would you help me at the door?"

Shen moved to assist as I struggled into the chute. I had checked it on the ground in Montana, and it had appeared to be relatively new, in good condition and packed correctly, rigging seemed nice and tight, and if it wasn't, at least I wouldn't have to worry about it for very long. My Suunto watch had an illuminated altimeter, and had always been very accurate in the past. The light was fading, and I was planning to open low enough that hopefully I would minimize any witnesses.

I was dressed in jeans, a baggy grey long-sleeve shirt, and the same boots I had been wearing in Tickville. The holster for my STI 9mm was a standard concealment rig, nothing really jump capable, so I fixed that by zip-tying the STI's grip to my belt. I had a pouch for the suppressor, and I hoped that it would hold, same with my two spare magazines. You may think something is securely attached to your person, but hitting the ground after a jump has a tendency to separate a lot of gear from their owners.

"There's a good pasture ahead. Looks fairly flat. The highway is one mile to the west," the pilot shouted. "Get ready."

I noticed Ling watching me. We had woken her. Her black eyes were difficult to read.

"If you don't hear from me in six hours, assume I'm dead," I said as I pulled the stolen goggles over my eyes. "I'm sorry about what I said earlier."

"No, you're not. But thank you for saying so. Good luck, Lorenzo," she said, smiling, still holding Valentine's hand. "See you in Mexico."

Shen opened the door behind me. The roar of the passing airstream was deafening. The pilot pumped his fist in the air. It was time to go. I gave the Exodus operatives a wave, and stepped backward into the hundred mile-an-hour sky.

It had been awhile. The feeling was terrifying and exhilarating at the same time. The wind tore at my clothing, battered my face, and sucked the moisture right off my grinning teeth. I could only vaguely see the color and texture of the ground. The Sun was setting, and I knew that the odds of someone seeing the grey, terminal-velocity blur that was my silhouette was slim. I held my arms at my sides, clenched tight, legs extended, head down as I tore through the air at absurd speed.

There was the highway. The headlights were beacons. I could see the field that the pilot had picked out, a giant strip a slightly different shade of brown than the rest of the countryside. The numbers on my altimeter were changing rapidly. I'd changed the ground level on it before jumping, which was good because Arizona was a lot closer to the sky than Saint Carl.

Jill would really love this. She's never jumped before. I can only imagine how fun she would think this is.

Strange, the thoughts that wander through your head when you're streaking toward the ground at a speed sufficient to turn you into a red paste. Here I was, taking a stupid risk with a very high potential for death, and I was thinking about Jill. Well, that was understandable, since she was the best thing that had ever happened to me. Someone like me certainly didn't deserve someone like her. Hell, someone like me didn't deserve to be alive at all, let alone happy. It was probably best not to think such bad karmic thoughts while whistling through the air, flipping gravity the bird.

Pay attention. The ground was closer now, and every fiber of my being told me to deploy the chute. I'd disabled the automatic deployment preset. I checked my altitude again. Still a little too high on the horizon. A single police report that might show up in a government database would defeat the purpose of this idiotic stunt. I waited.

I flared my arms and legs out, feeling the current change over my body, turning myself into a giant air brake. The ground was close, screaming toward me. *Ground! Ground!* I told the panicky part of my brain to shut up. *NOW!*

I pulled the hacky-sack-looking ball from the base of my pack. The pilot chute shot out, but the big ram chute seemed to take forever to unfurl. The slider kept it from opening so fast that the straps would smash into me. That was always the sucky part. The parachute cracked and snapped above me. I glanced up. Nice and open, and I was shedding velocity.

It was only open for a few seconds, then there was the earth, scrolling beneath me at too high of a speed. This part was always really difficult in low light. Flare too soon, stall and free fall the last little bit, flare too late and you hit the ground too hard. I was out of practice, but landing felt pretty clean. My boots hit the ground running. I made it about ten huge steps before I stepped into a soft depression and pitched sideways, twisting my ankle before landing on my hand, elbow, shoulder, and then I was rolling in a mass of dirt clods, parachute fabric, and cord.

Yep. It's been awhile.

I lay in the dust, spitting dirt and catching my breath under a pile of blue fabric. My right ankle throbbed. Not my best landing by any means, but it would do. I untangled myself and stood. The field was dark and quiet in every direction. All clear. I checked my gear. One spare magazine was somewhere in the dirt, but I didn't have time to look for it.

Unbuckling the chute, I crumpled it into a ball in my arms and began to limp in the direction of the highway. That had been fun, but now it was time to catch a ride.

I had thrown the chute in a drainage ditch. I had no doubt it would be found shortly. Everything I knew about agriculture could be written on a 3x5 card, with plenty of space left over, so I had no idea how often people checked those kinds of things, but all I needed was a day or two.

My ankle was good and swollen by the time I reached the highway. I stepped out in front of the first set of headlights, waving my arms above my head. It was a pickup truck. The driver hit the brakes, and I had to step back onto the shoulder to keep from getting run over. The Dodge stopped twenty meters past me. I trotted up to the window as the driver rolled it down.

"What the hell's the emergency?" He was an older man, with a puffy trucker hat and a scruffy grey beard. Both the driver and the passenger, a younger clone of the driver, eyed me suspiciously. "You look like hell," he drawled.

"I've had a rough night. I need a ride into town."

"Where's your car?" he asked. The old man kept his right hand down at his side, probably on his gun. This was Arizona, after all. "I don't pick up hitchhikers." Smart people in Arizona.

"Long story." I knew that I looked suspicious. Especially since I still had Smoot-colored hair, was dusty, and I was walking along a highway in the middle of nowhere. "It's embarrassing, okay?"

He put the truck back in drive and started to roll.

"Okay! Okay!" I said. The old man braked. "I had a fight with my girlfriend. I called her fat, 'cause she's totally let herself go. We pulled over so I could take a leak. She was mad, and drove off without me. My cell phone's in the car. I fell in a ditch running after her. Just give me a lift to the next place with a phone, and I'll call one of my friends in Flagstaff to pick me up. Come on, man, please?" I'm a very convincing liar. Might as well cut to the chase. I held up one hand with several twenties. "I can pay you for gas!"

He looked at me disdainfully and spit a mighty stream of chew out the window. "Get in back," he said with a jerk of his head.

Chapter 8: Shadows

LORENZO
Flagstaff, Arizona
February 15th

It was a school night, so hopefully Bob's kids would all be home and not out screwing around. All I needed to do was break in without being seen by the government agents who were surely staked out around the place, convince my sister-in-law—whom I barely knew—to trust me, and get them out of there without being spotted. Then somehow I needed to get them across the border, and to someplace safe. *This sucks.*

I made one pass through Bob's nice suburban neighborhood in the Jeep Cherokee that I had boosted from the truckstop on the outskirts of town. I knew where Bob lived because I'd broken in the last time I'd been here. *He really should just give me a key.* I spotted the watchers on the end of the street in an unmarked surveillance van. There was no one in the cab, heavily tinted windows all around, the standard stuff, it was really obvious. I tried to look nonchalant as I cruised past them, by the front of Bob's house, and around the corner.

I parked on the cul-de-sac that backed up to the Lorenzo family's backyard and checked my watch. It was pretty late and there was no one outside. It was drastically warmer than Montana, and happy insects swarmed the street lights. Some neighborhood dog started barking in the distance. It took me a few moments to pick the yard to cut through, no sign of pets, no motion-detecting lights, and it didn't look like anyone was home. It was a straight shot through the yard and over the back fence.

Two minutes later I was using my bump keys to break into Bob's back door. He still had the same high-tech alarm system. This time it took me almost a minute and a half to bypass it. All that soft island living had made me sloppy.

The lights were on inside the Lorenzo house. The TV was playing in the family room, something obnoxious with a laugh track. A radio was on upstairs. I crept through the kitchen, trying to formulate a plan. This woman had married my brother, so I had no doubt that I was a split-second from getting a load of double-aught buckshot to the face if I startled her.

There were children's toys scattered across the living-room floor. The wall was covered in family pictures. They were all happy and smiling. I listened to the sounds of the house. Something was wrong. There were supposed to be several people home, but it didn't feel right. I had broken into a lot of homes, and I knew how an occupied house felt. Nobody was here.

The bedroom closets were open. Clothes were spread on the beds. It felt like they had bailed out of here in a hurry. There was a pink Post-It note stuck to the mirror just inside the front entryway. The message had been written in neat, cursive handwriting. The pen was still lying on the hardwood floor directly below the mirror.

> Dear Government Assholes,
>
> I've been married to an FBI agent for fifteen years. Did you honestly think I would be stupid enough not to notice your van full of idiots watching my house and following me around?
>
> I don't know what you've done with my husband, but we have made contingency plans. You will not find us. You will never find us. But my husband will find you. You picked the wrong family to fuck with. Bob is ten times the cop you pussies are.
>
> > Hugs and kisses
> > Gwen Lorenzo
>
> p.s. Kiss my ass and die, you filthy,
> crooked sons of bitches.

It shouldn't have surprised me that the Lorenzos had a bugout plan. I was rapidly discovering that there was a lot I didn't know about my relatives. It looked like my mission had already been accomplished. I was willing to bet that Gwen and the kids had gone out the same way that I had come in, probably had somebody waiting to pick them up in the cul-de-sac. Hell, I might have passed them on the way into the neighborhood.

It appeared that Bob had married up.

"Well, since I'm here . . ." I muttered to myself. I might as well see if he'd left any clues as to what he had been working on that was so damned important.

His office was the only locked room in the basement. It took me ten seconds to pick. Judging from the looks of the place, he took after Dad. The desk was a mess of papers, a type of organized chaos that the Lorenzo men seemed to cultivate. Every wall had pictures, newspaper clippings, maps, timelines, and hundreds of Post-It notes stuck up. Under the notes were awards, commendations, citations for bravery, framed and then forgotten, things that most people would have thought to be very important, but Bob was too personally humble to worry about things like that. There were five guns hung on the wall behind the desk, muzzles pointed down in a half circle, the main rifles of WW2, an M1 Garand, a Russian Mosin Nagant, a British Enfield, a German Mauser, and a Japanese Arisaka, and that was the only space without notes taped to it. That's because those had belonged to our father.

I scanned the notes. Names, dates, some circled, some with question marks after them. A lot of it was from the data that Valentine had dumped on the internet before he wasted Gordon Willis. There were a few familiar words that popped up a lot, like *Blue* and *Alpha Point*. The most common word was *Majestic*. It appeared over and over again. It was everywhere, oftentimes with an exclamation point behind it, like an angry afterthought.

Majestic is the shadow government. Majestic is the cancer.

There was a handwritten note on the top of the desk.

> *To whom it may concern,*
>
> *If you're reading this, I can only assume that I am dead. I hope you're not one of them. If you are, congratulations, you bastards win again. I've made arrangements for my family. If I disappear they know to go someplace where you'll never find them. They know nothing, so leave them out of it. I've kept them in the dark to protect them.*
>
> *If somebody else finds this, I hope this information proves of more use to you than it has to me. I have spent the last few years of my life learning about a secret government organization usually known as Majestic.*
>
> *They are the end result of secrets and decades of lies. At one time they existed for a good reason, to defend our country, to do the dirty jobs that others could not do, but they've become corrupt, perverted. They exist only to grow in power. They are in every facet of the government. The Bureau is infested with them. They're watching my every move.*
>
> *I first found out about them as a young agent, after they arranged the murder of several witnesses to their crimes. These were innocent people. Since then I've been watching them, learning, and what I've found out is terrifying. They're always in the shadows, pulling the strings. They are above the law.*
>
> *They are not evil. Just like a disease isn't evil. It just is. Majestic is a disease. May the truth be the cure.*
>
> *Robert T. Lorenzo*

I began flipping through Bob's ramblings. If I hadn't had first-hand experience with this sort of thing I would've thought it was the rantings of a crazy man. He'd been working on this for a *long* time, way before he'd gotten Valentine's information from Zubara.

Just like Silvers, Bob had been preoccupied with this Project Blue. There was a printout with a few photos on it. *Four Majestic operatives were involved with the creation and implementation of Project Blue.*

I didn't recognize the first man, he looked like a politician type. Under his name had been written *Former Senator Barrington, head of operations, killed under mysterious circumstances.* The second man I had seen briefly in Quagmire, Nevada last year. He was a popular guy in my house, since he'd tried to have Jill murdered. *Gordon Willis, murdered/possible suicide in Virginia. Head of Majestic black ops.* The third picture was somebody else I'd met in less than perfect circumstances, mostly because his men had just captured me and he had my fingers broken during an interrogation. *Colonel Curtis Hunter, Dead Six field commander. Killed in Zubara.*

The last spot was blank except for where Bob had drawn a giant question mark. Apparently he didn't know who the fourth man was.

Blue was the doomsday option against Ill.

I paused. I hadn't seen a note that explained who or what "Ill" stood for. I doubted Majestic needed a doomsday option against Illinois.

Four operatives knew about Blue. Barrington came up with the plan. He enlisted the other three to implement it. Willis took command when Barrington was killed. Hunter and unknown subject set the Alpha Point. Hunter got cold feet. He must have realized that Majestic was up to no good. Gave up Majestic to Valentine when Willis betrayed Dead Six in Zubara. Two down. Before Willis can bring more operatives into the plan for Blue, he dies.

Four men knew about Blue. Three are dead. Majestic scraps Blue. But the final operative has gone rogue. Why? Maybe he thinks Majestic killed his compatriots?

Majestic is panicking. I've watched these bastards for years, and I've never seen this before. Majestic doesn't know what Blue entails and they're scared of it. Zubaragate hurt them. If information on Blue leaks, it will kill them.

My phone rang. "Damn it." I didn't have time for this. I had to know what was going on. "What?" I snapped.

"It's me," Reaper said quickly. "I've intercepted some traffic. They're keeping the details hushed up, but there's been an alert out of Montana. Dude, they know."

I can't get Valentine out of North Gap. The only other person alive who knows about Blue is the final operative. Majestic was looking for him in a place called The Crossroads, he's tied to some sort of mythical figure known as

Sala Jihan, the Pale Man. I've got to find the final operative. It is the only way to destroy Majestic once and for all.

"Boss, are you listening? The government knows!" Reaper insisted.

"Okay. I've got to go." I put my phone away. I had to get this stuff out of here, fast. The goons outside would probably move as soon as they got the word. I looked for something to shove paper into, and spotted a small garbage can. It would have to do. I dumped the can's contents on the floor. At the very top was a crumpled letter from the FBI telling Bob that he was fired from the bureau for gross misconduct.

CRASH! I cringed at the sound of the front door splintering open.

Discretion is the better part of valor. I comforted myself with that platitude as I ran away like a coward. I've done my fair share of fighting, but I always try to fight on my terms. I always have a plan. I always ambush. And when I don't have the element of surprise, I retreat. I'm a thief first and foremost, and thieves who pick fights tend to die young.

The Majestic goons got the call and moved right in. At least two hit the front door, and the third circled through the backyard. I hid behind the fridge, my 9mm in one hand, garbage can full of paper in the other, and waited for the Majestic goon to kick in the back door, stomp through the kitchen, and run right past me.

They were expecting a woman and some frightened kids, an easy target, probably lots of screaming and crying, real obvious stuff. I waited for the man in the suit to leave the kitchen, and he headed down the stairs to the basement. I slipped across the floor without a sound, paused briefly at the back door to scan in both directions, figuring correctly that they'd rushed in rather than form a perimeter, and then took off in a full sprint for the fence. It was wood, five feet tall, and I vaulted it without slowing.

I landed with a grunt on the neighbor's lawn, having forgotten about my swollen ankle. The yard was dark, a couple of big bushes, a swing set moved slightly in the breeze, but it appeared to be clear. I hadn't been spotted. Seventy feet and I would be back to my stolen Jeep and out of here.

"Move and I'll shoot you down where you stand," a man said from behind me, utterly calm. I hesitated, my pistol at my side. I could spin and dive, factor in his reaction time. *Ca-click.* The sound of a hammer being cocked was piercingly loud. "You're fittin' to get tumped. Drop your piece."

The voice had a slow drawl to it. My trained ear told me probably Arkansas, and somebody who meant business. The gunman was ten feet behind me, and was just another shadow in the bushes. He had me dead to rights. I tossed my STI on the grass. "I'm guessing you aren't the guy that owns this house."

"Nope. Turn around real slow-like." I did as I was told.

The man moved forward, the glint of a revolver coming out of the darkness. He was keeping his voice down. "Well, if it ain't Bob's kin, his brother, the thief."

"I know you?"

"Nope. And you never will. I asked around about your rep after Bob met you last, so I don't think we'd make good friends. I only recognize you because of the old family pictures on his wall. Bob's a sentimental type . . . I watched you go in his house, all sneaky. Real smooth."

I had been pretty sure that nobody had been watching. This guy was good. "And I'm assuming that you're not with them," I said calmly, nodding back toward the house. "Who're you?"

"Let's say I'm a friend of the family." He moved closer. He was probably in his early fifties, tall and lean, his face weatherbeaten and creased, long hair tied back in a ponytail, and eyes that scanned me like a wolf. His revolver was classic blued steel and polished walnut, and the front sight never wavered from my heart. "I owe Bob a favor. Me and him share some mentors, if you know what I mean . . ."

"You're an agent? Some sort of operator?"

He snorted. "I'm no G man."

"You're the one that helped Gwen and the kids get away?" Our voices were barely whispers. On the other side of the fence I could hear the angry shouting of the Majestic men as they found the note left for them.

"That's what I do. Where you take things, I hide them. Where you hunt things, I protect them. The family's safe. I aim to keep them that way. That's all you need to know, brother."

"Tell Gwen I'll bring him back," I stated.

"I reckon you will." He lowered the hammer, tucked the gun back under his nondescript denim shirt, and faded back into the shadows. "My gut tells me Bob underestimates you about as much as you underestimate him. Nice to meet you, *Uncle Hector*. You won't see me again." He was gone as suddenly as he came.

I retrieved my gun and files, made it to the Jeep in record time, and drove out of the neighborhood as fast as I could without drawing undue attention to myself. Even then, I almost managed to run over a fat guy out power walking. A yellow Mustang left the cul-de-sac a moment after I did, headed in the opposite direction.

The man in the shadows . . . I had only spoken to him for a moment, but from what he said, and the steel in his eyes, I knew exactly what he was. I had dealt with his kind before. They were my antithesis.

A black Suburban with red and blue wig-wag lights flashing inside its windshield passed me as I left the subdivision. I turned onto the main road and headed for the highway. I left no trace that I had been in my brother's home, so the road south should be clear. I had only slept a couple of hours in the last two days, and I was a long way from Mexico.

My thoughts returned to the man in the dark. I'd spent most of my career in countries that didn't have much in the way of professional law enforcement, and men like that always appeared eventually. They were the ones who took care of problems society couldn't, protecting innocents and their valuables from men like me, and usually disregarding the laws to do it. They weren't organized, but the sorts that drifted into that line of work inevitably knew each other, and shared information about my kind. That fellow with no name had probably dealt with a lot of people like me, and more than likely left them in shallow graves.

Majestic would never find that family. Bob had chosen well.

LORENZO
Santa Vasquez, Mexico
February 16th

The Sun was approaching its high point as I rolled into the Santa Vasquez airport. At this point I was running on nothing but energy drinks, and my brain was twitchy from fatigue and caffeine. The trip across the border had been uneventful, and the only people that had seen me take a cow trail across were a couple dozen illegals. The last time I had been through those hills, I had ended up running into some Chechens. Heading south was a lot easier than heading north.

Airport was a generous term for an asphalt strip surrounded by corrugated tin shacks. It didn't look like much, but I knew there were probably a good thirty to fifty flights landing here every day, and I was willing to bet that almost all of them were somehow drug related. Mexico had calmed down a bit since the revolution, but it had been business as usual here the whole time.

My nose was assaulted with the burning chemical stench of Santa Vasquez as soon as I stepped out of the Jeep. It was winter, so it was only in the nineties. Good old Mexico.

I spotted the Exodus Cessna parked in one of the sheds, and started toward it, still holding the garbage can under one arm. I saw the hulking form of Antoine first. A broad smile split his face when he saw me.

"Glad to see you, my friend," he shouted.

"Let's go home," I said simply.

Chapter 9: House Guests

VALENTINE
Location Unknown
Date/Time Unknown

When my eyes opened next, I was staring at an unfamiliar ceiling. I was lying in a clean, soft four-poster bed. A ceiling fan lazily rotated above me. It was a much more pleasant setting than the last place I'd woken up in. My head began to spin as soon as I sat up. As I waited for the dizzy spell to pass, the sounds of water running, or rain, resonated in the background.

The last thing I remembered was being in the snow. I'd been in pain. I remembered fear, then rage, then violence. I'd been trying to escape from . . . where had I been? I rubbed my face and tried to think. My head throbbed. My body ached. I had gaps in my memory and thinking hurt. It was like the worst hangover ever.

Had I really escaped? Gone were the cold cinder block walls and concrete floors. There was no hint of chill in the air. Instead I found myself in a cozy wooden bungalow with nice furniture. The windows were open, but covered by screens, and shaded from the sun by low hanging eaves. There was a screen door at one end of the room. Beyond it was a wooden deck and a cluster of tree trunks.

Where the hell am I? Is this another one of Dr. Silvers' tricks? Pain shot through my leg as I stood up. It had been bandaged, and my clothes had been changed. Instead of my blue sweats, white T-shirt, and shoes with no laces, I was wearing only a t-shirt and a pair of gaudy swim trunks. I had no idea where my shoes were. My body protested with each movement as I hobbled toward the door. The pain in my right leg calmed to a dull throb after the initial shock, nothing I couldn't deal with. Barefoot and confused, I quietly pulled the door open and stepped onto the deck. What lay beyond took my breath away.

White sand stretched out in front of me until it met clear blue water. The sound of gently rolling waves filled the air, and I could hear the cries of seagulls. I stepped off the deck and onto the sand; where the deck had been rough and cool, the sand was warm and soft. I kept limping forward, out from under the shade of a clump of palm trees, toward the water.

I felt the sun on my neck for the first time that I could recall. I looked up into the deep blue sky, squinting in the light as puffy white clouds drifted overhead. I looked back at the bungalow, and then again toward the water.

This isn't real, my mind protested. Scattered memories came back to me; I'd been deceived before, by Dr. Silvers' machines, her mind games, her tricks. But the sand was warm between my toes and the wind was gentle on my face. I could smell the salt in the air. It certainly *seemed* real.

I wandered across the beach, not at all sure where I was going. No one else was around. I hadn't gotten very far before exhaustion caught up with me. I had no idea how long I'd been in that bed, and it was obvious that I was in bad shape. I focused on a clump of palm trees ahead of me and made my way toward them. My head still ached and I wanted to get out of the sun.

In the shade, the sand was much cooler. I sat down, facing the water, and just stared into the distance. I'm not sure just how long I stayed there, listening to the waves, trying to clear my head.

"Michael!" someone cried. The woman had a clear soprano voice. I rolled my head and saw a woman standing on the beach, holding something in her hand. I couldn't tell who she was, but she turned in my direction and began to run toward me. "Michael!" she repeated as she got closer. I rubbed my eyes. When I looked up again, the woman was kneeling next to me.

"Ling?" I croaked. It couldn't be real. I refused to accept it. Yet I was looking into the dark almond eyes of someone I never imagined I'd see again. She threw her arms around me and pulled me against her. The last time I'd seen her, we were on a different beach, and she certainly hadn't given me a hug. "Is it really you?" My voice was a hoarse whisper. Her neck was smooth and soft against my cheek; her hair was wet and smelled nice. She squeezed me tighter and rubbed her hand up and down on my back.

"It's really me," she said. "I'm sorry I wasn't there when you woke up. I was in the shower."

"Can I have some water? I'm . . . I'm really thirsty."

"Here, drink," she said, handing me a plastic bottle. I lifted it to my lips and reveled in its icy coldness. I downed the whole thing, coughing when it was empty.

"Jesus," I said, my voice clearer now. "That's good. What happened? How . . . where are we?"

"Someplace safe. Our host would prefer I not tell you the name of this place."

"You helped me escape from . . . from . . ."

"North Gap. The place you were held is called North Gap. It's in

America, in Montana. We got you out." The concern was apparent on her face. Ling gently placed a hand on the left side of my face. I recoiled slightly as she touched me, but fought the urge to pull away. "Are you all right?"

I tried to speak, tried to answer her, but I didn't have the words. "Thank you," I said. It was all I could manage. I was suddenly too emotional to say much more.

"You are safe now. It is a long story, and you need to rest."

Ling and I sat there, looking out over the water, for a long time. The waves rolled in and out. A sailboat slowly moved across the horizon. Part of me was still expecting to wake up any time, to find myself attached to one of Dr. Silvers' infernal machines. I'd been so far gone that I'd been talking to the dead. The rational part of my mind never expected to actually escape. I was just trying to give them a reason to kill me, to end it all.

A seagull landed nearby and studied us greedily with its beady little eyes. I was free. I was alive. Ling, like a guardian angel, had come to my rescue. The gull was soon joined by one of his friends, then another, then another.

"Are you ready to go?" Ling asked.

I was free. Tears welled up in my eyes.

"No."

LORENZO
St. Carl Island
February 17th

"Looks like sleeping beauty's awake." I put my bare feet up on the banister and leaned back in the wicker chair. The ocean breeze was cool, and the palm trees around the front of my house swayed gently.

"Really? Oh good," Jill said as she came out of the house, drying her hands on a towel. "He's even walking? Good for him."

I gestured with my drink toward the beach. "Yeah, I think he's lost, but Ling found him." Valentine and Ling were sitting under one of the trees, facing away from us, and looking out over the gentle waves. The ocean was a brilliant blue beyond them, and they appeared to be deep in conversation. Some seagulls had surrounded them, preparing to attack. St. Carl had some aggressive seagulls.

"Oh, they make a cute couple. I like Ling, she seems really nice. A little intense, but nice." Jill said as she sat down next to me. She had pulled her hair up into a bun while she had been cleaning and organizing gear. I couldn't help but smile when I saw the grease smudge on her cheek.

"He's a schizo mercenary, riddled with PTSD, and she's a terrorist with ice water for blood. *Cute* isn't the first word that comes to mind. I'm sure they'll have a bunch of beautiful little sociopathic killing machines someday."

"Like you have any room to talk," Jill said curtly. "How many countries are you wanted in again?"

"Fifteen. Well, sixteen, but I don't think Somalia is technically a country right now." She had me there. Jill was the most normal person currently residing at Casa De Lorenzo, but that wasn't saying a whole lot. She'd been dragged into my world against her will, just a witness who'd been in the wrong place at the wrong time. Jill was a survivor, and she'd taken to it well enough. Though it pained me to admit it, if it hadn't been for that kid lying down there on my beach right now, Jill would certainly be in a shallow grave in Quagmire, Nevada.

"You know, you don't need to be so pissy about this. I really like Val. You did a good thing getting him out of that horrible place."

"I didn't do it for him," I said sullenly. "He better be worth it."

Jill laughed at me. Her dark eyes twinkled when she laughed. "You know, you can actually admit to doing a good deed once in a while. It won't ruin your image."

I didn't respond to that. Jill was an honest-to-goodness decent person. She saw the best in everyone, even me. Of course, she was wrong about me. I wasn't a good person. I certainly wasn't worthy of her, but she seemed to disagree. I made a show of finishing my drink, sat the glass down, and stood. "Well, I'm going to have a few words with Mr. Valentine."

Jill's hand clamped down on my wrist. She was not a very big person, but she had the iron grip of someone who had grown up in a martial arts studio. When most little girls were playing with dolls, Jill's dad had her punching speed bags. "No," her voice was firm.

"Jill. I just killed like a dozen people. He owes me, and the son of a bitch is gonna talk."

She didn't let go. "Sit . . ."

"Honey . . ."

". . . *down*."

She wasn't going to budge on this one. I could tell. I flopped back into the chair with a pensive grunt. "Let's not fight in front of the terrorists."

Jill didn't take the bait. "First off, if those men in Montana were anything like the ones that had me in Nevada, they don't count as people. Second, you're going to leave him alone. Val's been through a lot of trauma. They need some time, and the last thing they need is you going in there and being your usual pushy self. You're not exactly in touch with your emotions."

"I've got plenty of emotions." I started to count on my fingers. "Anger, hate, revenge—"

"Revenge is not an emotion."

"You've been watching those relationship shows on cable again, haven't you?" From the look on her face, my attempt at evasion was going down in flames.

"I'm serious, Lorenzo. Leave them alone. You can harass him later, and when you do, you'd better be nice."

I sighed. "I'm not good at *nice*."

"You're nice to me. Besides, we have a few days before Reaper completes our covers anyway."

I bit my lip and watched a seagull land on the porch railing. It looked at me with its evil little rat eyes, contemplating where to poop. "On our covers . . . The Crossroads is one of the most dangerous places in the world."

"We've been over this," Jill said sharply. Meaning that we'd already had a fight once. "I'm going with you. You need somebody you can trust. And besides, I do okay at this stuff, remember?" She stood, kissed me gently on the forehead, and headed back into the house. "End of discussion."

This domestication thing certainly had its ups and downs. With few exceptions, I had spent most of my life only looking after myself. It was hard to deal with having to protect somebody else who was just as bullheaded as I was. Half of me was proud of her, wanting to help save my brother, to watch my back, and though she wouldn't admit it, I knew she wanted revenge on Majestic for shattering her life. The other half of me was kind of pissed that she wouldn't just agree to stay home where it was safe.

In the distance, Ling snuggled closer against Valentine. I wanted nothing more than to go down there and get an answer as to just what in the hell made him so damned special. The seagull cocked its head at me.

"Little fucker," I said as I pulled my STI with my right hand and my Silencerco Osprey suppressor with my left. I started to screw them together while the seagull stared stupidly at its coming demise.

"No killing gulls on the porch!" Jill shouted from inside.

Shit. "Yes, dear," I answered as I stuck my gun back in its holster. "It's your lucky day, punk." The gull emptied its bowels all over my porch, squawked at me, and flew off. It's a sad day when a man gets no respect in his own house.

VALENTINE
St. Carl Island
February 18th

It was all a lot to take in. The thing that really boggled my mind was the fact that it was February. Between not having any way to keep track of time and Dr. Silvers' mind games, I had no idea I'd been in North Gap for so long. And now I was on Lorenzo's island. According to Ling, he owned most of it. That was just weird.

The first time I'd actually *met* Lorenzo was in Zubara. I put a bullet through an arms dealer named Jalal Hosani, and that same slug hit Lorenzo . . . who unfortunately had been wearing a vest. The night that Fort Saradia fell to the Zubarans, Lorenzo had broken into my room, trying to steal an old Arabian puzzle box that I'd taken on one of my operations with Dead Six. I closed my eyes as that memory came back to me. That was the night Sarah died. I would've died with her if he hadn't dragged me out. We'd met one last time, this time as reluctant allies to get Jill back from Gordon. We parted ways when I'd gone after Gordon. I'd never known much about him, hadn't wanted to, and figured I'd never see him again.

The snarky thief had done quite well for himself. Somehow he now basically owned an island and lived a life of leisure and luxury. Meanwhile I was getting mind-fucked by a mad scientist working for a shadow government organization. It hardly seemed fair, all things considered.

Returning my attention to what I was doing, I clicked through the files on Ling's laptop. I was alone in the bungalow, but before Ling left she showed me all of the information that they'd recovered from North Gap. Much of it was about me. It was unsettling, to say the least. Dr. Olivia Silvers had taken me on as a pet project. Originally, they were interested in me because of Project Blue. Once they realized I'd told them everything I knew, Silvers opted to keep me there for her own purposes, stringing her superiors along that I might still be useful. I suspected that her doing so was the only reason they hadn't just taken me out back and shot me. I basically owed her my life.

I wasn't going to send her a thank-you card.

I had barely been able to sleep the night before. I'd been drugged, sedated, restrained, exhausted, and unconscious for so long that I just didn't want to lie in bed anymore. Then there were the dreams. They weren't *nightmares,* exactly. These dreams were different. There were numbers that didn't mean anything to me, places I wasn't familiar with, and people I mostly didn't recognize, voices, overlapping and contradictory, some familiar, some not. They had to be subconscious leftovers from my time in Silvers' tank.

One person I did recognize from the bizarre dreams was Lorenzo's brother, the *other* Lorenzo, Bob. Probably because I had given him up. He was the one I'd given Colonel Hunter's flash drive to, and he'd dumped that information onto the internet. From what I'd heard from Ling, Project

Heartbreaker was now a well-known government scandal. From what I'd heard today, it turned out that Bob had been trying to expose them for years. I regretted not trusting him more when we'd last spoken. I wanted to find him. We needed to compare notes.

Ling's rescue had retrieved a box with all the things that had been in my possession when I had been captured. My custom Smith & Wesson 629 Performance Center Classic .44 Magnum revolver was returned to me, complete with holster, the couple boxes of ammo I had in the car when they took me, and speed loaders. I'd meticulously cleaned and function-checked the heavy stainless-steel firearm. It felt good in my hand. My arm felt more whole when I held it. Having it on my hip again was a welcome comfort. It wasn't just my gun, though. My clothes were in there, loose-fitting now, since I'd lost weight in captivity, as well as my shoes. I found my Benchmade *Infidel* automatic knife, too, which I was happy to have back. More important than that was my father's harmonica. I'd been carrying it everywhere since Afghanistan and was happy I didn't lose it.

Staying focused was difficult. I looked at the screen again. I had just watched a security-camera video of one of my interrogation sessions. It was a surreal experience. You'd think it'd be hard to watch, but I found myself oddly detached from it all. My concentration was interrupted by a knock on the door. "It's open."

Lorenzo stepped into the little beach house. "Hey," he said awkwardly.

"Yo," I said. Lorenzo was an unassuming-looking man. He might be Mexican, sort of, maybe Middle Eastern, or even Indian. He had tanned skin, dark hair, and no really remarkable features. His face was accented only by unshaven stubble, like a permanent five o'clock shadow. He was shorter than me, but muscular. His eyes always seemed to be watching you and he moved like he was wound pretty tight. It was really hard to tell how old he was, probably somewhere between thirty and forty-five. It was probably closer to the higher end just because of his apparent level of experience.

"You were in Switchblade, huh?" he asked.

I looked up at him. "Yeah . . . yeah I was. Switchblade Four, to be specific, for a few years. How'd you know?"

"Reaper did some digging on you. You guys made the cover of *Soldier of Fortune*."

I smiled. "Yeah, I remember that. We all had to pay up, a case of beer each."

"Who was your team leader?"

"Huh? Ramirez. Jesus Ramirez," I said, pronouncing his name "*hey-sous.*" "But we all called him . . ."

"You all called him Jesus," Lorenzo interrupted, pronouncing it like Jesus from the Bible. "And everyone would make bad puns about when Jesus is coming back, or Jesus is watching you, or Jesus saves."

I looked around nervously, not sure what to say. "Uh . . . Yeah, we did. Did you know him?" Lorenzo knew Hawk somehow, but neither man ever told me what their history was.

"A long time ago, back when he was the FNG. So Ramirez was a lifer?"

"I guess so. He was older than most of the team leaders. He'd been in that spot for a while, but was getting ready to move over to training, with Hawk, or maybe Corporate, when . . ."

"How'd he go out?"

"Helicopter crash. Mexico."

Lorenzo's face was a mask. If he was bothered by Ramirez' death he didn't show it. "Was Decker still in command?" he asked, the tone of his voice changing slightly. It sounded like there was some bad blood there.

"Not really. Decker was the CEO and head of Operations for all of Vanguard, but I only met him a few times. I heard he still did training and stuff, but I never saw him on any of our ops unless he was showcasing us for potential clients. He was the corporate front of Vanguard. He wore a suit instead of fatigues and surrounded himself with lawyers and accountants."

An unfriendly smile appeared on his face. "That's Decker for you."

"How do you know Decker? Or Ramirez? Or Hawk, for that matter."

"That's none of your business, kid," he said levelly. He was quiet for a moment, took a deep breath, then looked me in the eye like he was trying to bore a hole through my face. "I worked with Decker, and Hawk, and Ramirez a long time ago. Before there was a Vanguard corporation, before Decker became Mister *Legitimate Businessman*. It was just Switchblade back then. It was a different world. It was before PMCs got big, went mainstream. We did the dirty work."

"So did we," I suggested. "We just had PR firms to put a pretty face on it all. So what happened between you?"

"Things got complicated," Lorenzo said. He pulled out a chair, flipped it around, and sat across from me, leaning on the chair-back. Between us was a small wicker table with Ling's laptop on it. "I need to ask you some questions."

My eye twitched involuntarily. "What is it?"

"I'm not going to pretend that I busted you out of there because I like you. No offense."

"None taken."

"My brother came into contact with your girlfriend in Asia."

"He did?"

"Did she tell you?"

"Obviously not."

"My brother told Ling that there was something in your head important enough to die for. Now, I risked my life getting you out of there, I brought you into my home, and I want to know what it is."

I shook my head and chuckled to myself.

"What the hell are you laughing at?" Lorenzo growled. He was agitated.

"I don't know," I said simply.

"You don't know what?"

"Whatever it is your brother thinks I know, I don't know."

"*What?* He talked on and on about Project Blue. What the hell is Project Blue?"

My eyes narrowed. "I don't *know.*"

Lorenzo came up out of his chair. I stood up too, trying to back away. He grabbed me and pushed me against the wall, spilling my chair over as he did so. I was still shaky enough that I couldn't put up much resistance.

"What the fuck do you mean *you don't know?* My brother was willing to get me *killed* over this! He's probably dead now because of it, and you're telling me you don't know? You're fucking *lying*! Tell me what—" Lorenzo abruptly fell silent as I pushed the muzzle of my revolver into his chin.

"I don't know," I said quietly. "They asked me the same thing. I told them I didn't know. They kept me in solitary confinement, I told them I didn't know. They moved me to some secret prison, and I told them I didn't know. They used drugs on me, and I told them I didn't know. They shocked me with tasers, attacked me with a dog, beat me with sticks, left me out in the snow, fucked with my mind, and I kept telling them I don't know. I don't fucking know what . . ." I began to cough. I'd been screaming in Lorenzo's face. His eyes were wide, but hard. "I don't know," I repeated, trying to catch my breath.

"I saved your life, *twice*," he spat, still not moving. "I risked my life to go get you, because my brother thought you were worth it. And you mean to tell me that it was all a *mistake*?" His voice was cold and level, and he was so mad he was nearly shaking. "Then you come into *my house* and stick a gun in my face?"

I met his glare. I was *Calm*. Lorenzo's life was in danger, even if he was too stubborn to realize it. "Get your goddamn hands off me before Jill has to come down here and clean your brains off the ceiling fan." Lorenzo stared me down defiantly, but his grip on my shirt loosened. I pushed him away and backed up until I was leaning against the wall. I kept the gun trained on him. The thief was livid. He stood there, glaring at me, looking like he wanted nothing more than to break my neck. My gun didn't waver. He was pretty fast with a pistol but I wasn't going to give him a chance.

"I'm sorry, Lorenzo. I'm sorry you all went through this for me. You think it's what I wanted? You think I wanted Ling to risk her life for my sorry ass? All I wanted was to die, this time and the last time. Twice in a row you got involved, didn't let me die when I was supposed to, and both times you got pissed at *me* because of it. I'm sorry, okay? I don't know what Project Blue is, and I don't know why it's so important to Bob or Majestic. The last thing Colonel Hunter told me before he died was 'Evangeline,' and he didn't say who that is or why she's important. He didn't say anything about Project Blue. I'm sorry, but I just don't know."

Lorenzo didn't say anything else. He just turned and walked out of the beach house. After he left, I set the revolver down and buried my face in my shaking hands. I hoped that Ling would get back soon.

LORENZO

"What's wrong, chief?" Reaper asked, looking up from the multiple computer screens that now filled one of my spare bedrooms. His stringy black hair was draped over half of his pale face. Even a few days of glorious St. Carl sun couldn't darken Reaper. The boy had no pigment. "You look pissed."

"Son of bitch pointed a gun at me, in my own fucking house. My own house!" I punched the door frame hard enough to hurt my hand. "I should have taken that .44 and shoved it up his ass. And this is after I saved his miserable life, the lousy, screwed-in-the-head, ingrate mother—"

"Say what?" Reaper cut me off as he pulled his iPod earbuds out. I could hear the blaring death metal from ten feet away.

I bit my lip. Yelling at Reaper, however tempting, wouldn't help anything. "Nothing. Never mind. How are you doing on the cover identities?"

Contrary to what you see in movies, you can't just create a whole new identity on a whim. It takes preparation and resources. Some countries were easier than others. In the third world, it was a piece of cake, wave around some money and tell people whatever you wanted. In nations that had computerized recordkeeping, professional police that actually investigated things, photo ID, taxes, and other horrible things like that, it took a lot more work. The key was always some sort of number. A number let you create history. In the US, it was a social security number, and most of the developed world had some sort of equivalent. There were people who made huge sums of money farming these things. For cheap, you end up with an ID that is being shared by hundreds of illegal aliens. For guys like me, you end up with a social security number that belongs to somebody who actually existed, but never developed any of their own history. Invalids, for example.

In the modern world, people don't just pop into existence anymore. Those golden days were long gone. Now when you created an identity, you had to groom it. I had a dozen names ready to go from six different countries. Each of those imaginary people had jobs working for corporations that were wholly owned by other international corporations, and so forth, in a maze of shells actually owned by me. These imaginary people got paid a salary, which of course flowed back into other accounts that I controlled, which then went back to the corporations, to pay them again later. They all traveled for a living, with addresses consisting of PO boxes. And once a year, they even automatically filed taxes in their respective nations, just like my shell corporations did. I kept quite a few clueless accountants very happy. Keeping these things up cost me a lot of money, but they were oh so worth it.

Reaper spun his chair back around and pointed at the screen. "Me and you, no problem, I've got like twenty to choose from. For the others, I'm using some of the IDs I created back when we were in Malaysia. They were the escape set I developed that we never ended up using . . . I was thinking, the Exodus guys have their own, but if they needed one for Valentine, I could use one of Carl's old ones and shop the picture. Carl was too short, but we could always say he had a growth spurt."

I didn't know what Exodus' next move was. Shen, Antoine, and Dr. Bundt had been hanging around a lot before, but I hadn't seen any of them in the last couple of days. They had gotten rooms at the little tourist hotel in town, probably to give Ling time alone with the kid. Dr. Bundt had been mildly annoying, but I had actually enjoyed working with Shen and Antoine. Neither one talked a lot, and both liked to hit people. You can't ask for much more than that. Ling could sit around and mope with her boyfriend for all I cared, as long as they did it someplace far away from my people.

"You'll have to ask them. Valentine might not live that long, but whatever gets him off my island faster, awesome. . . . " Having the most wanted man in the world staying in my guest house didn't really fit with that whole *low profile* vibe. "And when we find Bob?" We would need ID for my brother to get out. Of course, that was assuming this was still a rescue mission, and not just to identify his remains.

Reaper handed me a Russian passport. I opened it, and there was the picture that Reaper had lifted from Bob's FBI file. "You said your brother spoke Russian."

"FBI started him in organized crime, Russian mafia stuff in New York, or at least that's what Mom said on a Christmas card one year." She had always been so proud of him. I had no idea what the cards she had sent to the other kids had said about me. Probably some variant of "Crazy Hector is still screwing around, wasting his life." "I'm assuming this ID was groomed for Train?"

"Yep, they're both fuckin' monsters, so the stats work. And the peace day resistance . . ."

"Piéce de résistance," I corrected.

"Whatever, the best part," he grinned when he handed me the next ID. I knew he had millions of dollars in the bank, but he had never found the time to get his crooked front teeth fixed. "Jill will have to pretend she's ten years older, but she does speak Spanish fluently. She's a businesswoman with a mining company based in Madrid."

"That was fast."

"Well, I originally developed this one for Ilsa, She-Bitch of the SS."

"Katarina wasn't *that* bad."

"To *you*," he snorted. "She hated me. Dumping that psycho was the best thing you ever did."

"What do you have left?"

"I'm fleshing out our Spanish mining corporation. We've even got a bitchin' webpage. Jihan's slave mines are turning out a lot of metal. It will take a couple of days for the money to transfer over. Jill's going to be the negotiator. You're the interpreter. I'm a technician. I've contacted Uri in Volgostadorsk—"

"Little Federov? The gun runner?"

"Obviously. Our mining company is going to bribe him not to molest our *survey gear* on the rail line to The Crossroads. You know how those greedy Russian bastards are, and I don't want my good shit stolen."

"How much?"

"A hundred grand."

"Our gear damn well better be left alone. You do remember I stabbed Uri's brother in the kidney, right?"

"No, a mysterious super-thief who worked for Big Eddie stabbed his brother. You're just a lowly interpreter. And it was in the spleen, not the kidney. You're thinking of the other guy. Train shot Federov's cousin in the kidney."

"Oh yeah, that was awesome." I chuckled. "Good times . . . Speaking of which, I'm a little rusty. I'm going to go shooting."

"Actual targets, or seagulls? 'Cause I don't think Jill likes it when you shoot the seagulls."

"A seagull *is* an actual target. I think of them as my own interactive pop-up range." I needed the practice, and besides, it helped me blow off steam.

My performance in Montana hadn't been good enough. I'd been slow. I'd let some wounded jackass escape. I'd missed a few shots and my reactions weren't what they used to be. That was simply unacceptable. The paper targets had been shredded, replaced, and shredded again. I'd lost count of how many hundred rounds I'd fired today, but there was a pile of spent brass in the sand underfoot, and my thumbs hurt from loading magazines.

The island wasn't that big, but I was using suppressed weapons, and the Montalbans had fenced off this secluded area. There wasn't a damn thing else I could do until Reaper was done with his prep work. It gave me time to train and time to think.

Bob had been taken in The Crossroads. He'd been poking around in a warlord's business, so that wasn't a surprise. My one supposed lead was a basket case who apparently knew jack and shit about what this was all about. The timer beeped. I shouldered my new Remington ACR and put a controlled pair into each of the target's center of mass. I checked the timer's recording of the last shot. *Not good enough.* I reset the timer and went again.

I didn't know if I could trust Exodus, but what choice did I have? They were up to something in The Crossroads, but wouldn't divulge what it was. That meant that the only resources I could really rely on were me, Reaper, and Jill, who I wasn't comfortable with taking at all. Not that she hadn't proven herself capable at this sort of work, but taking her to The Crossroads filled me with dread.

I heard the four-wheeler coming a long way off. It made a lot more noise than a 5.56 with a can on it. I emptied the carbine's magazine into the last target's head, put it on the table to cool, and waited for Jill to arrive.

She parked behind me and killed the Honda's engine. "What're you doing?"

I shrugged. "Practicing."

"You're sweating."

That's because I'd been doing a set of push-ups or sprints between the strings of fire. Shooting was more challenging when your arms burned and you were short of breath. "It's a warm day."

Jill got off the four-wheeler and came over. "What's wrong, Lorenzo?"

"Valentine pulled a gun on me."

"Shocking. I warned you not to be pushy . . . And you didn't kill him."

"Thought about it," I muttered.

"I'm impressed. What else is bugging you?"

She knew me too well. I'd thought long and hard about this. "The idea of you going to The Crossroads. I really don't think you realize what that place is like or what the kind of people who work there are like."

"I understand the risks." She folded her arms. "I know what I'm doing. We play it low key. We're just investigating. We're not looking for a fight.

Come on, you've taught me all sorts of stuff. You admitted yourself that I'm talented at your sort of business."

"You're a talented *beginner*."

"I can take care of myself." Jill went to the table, picked up my STI 9mm, lifted it and quickly shot the furthest target twice in the chest, and after the briefest instant, square in the face. She'd become an excellent shot.

"The men that took Bob aren't made out of cardboard."

"Neither was the Fat Man or the other jerks I shot that night."

That was true. She'd never choked under pressure yet. "I don't want you to get hurt . . ."

"Well, duh. And?"

I sighed. "I need help, but I don't have to like it, and I sure as hell don't like putting you in danger."

"You're cool putting Reaper in danger. I'm tougher than Reaper."

"Sure, but I'm not . . ." I hesitated. "I'm not in love with Reaper."

"Wow." Jill looked at me for a long time, but luckily she didn't get all weird on me. "That's remarkably sentimental by your standards. And good about Reaper, because *ewww* . . . that would be awkward for everybody." Jill grinned.

"Here's the thing. The Crossroads is a city of bad guys. You're not a bad guy, Jill."

"Nope. I'm not. You know I've got no interest in the things you've done in the past, and if this was just some heist then I'd tell you to go to hell, you're on your own. Because I'm not a bad guy, but this time, *neither are you*. You rescued Val from evil men. You're going to The Crossroads on a *rescue mission*. For once, relatively speaking, you're not the bad guy here."

"I . . . Well . . ." *Holy shit. She was right.*

"Listen, I know you're scared." She held up a hand before I could protest. "Yeah, yeah, you're not afraid of anything, whatever. Spare me. I have to do this. Bob didn't hesitate to help when I was the one in danger. He's off on a mission to bring down the bunch of corrupt assholes that ruined my life. So what kind of hypocrite would I be if I stayed here safe in my island mansion while you go off on a dangerous rescue mission and get killed because I wasn't there to help?"

We'd already had this fight, and I'd already had to admit she was right. I needed help, but I certainly didn't have to like it. "Fine." I tossed her another mag of 9mm. She caught it. "Get to work then."

VALENTINE

The deep rhythm of the rolling waves helped clear my head.

It had been an emotionally overwhelming few days. Dr. Bundt had sat me down in the beach house to look me over. It was strange to see this man again. The last time we'd met, I'd just woken up in another unfamiliar place, on board an Exodus ship, after having a traumatic brain injury where he'd had to drill a hole in my skull to drain a subdural hematoma.

Sitting there, getting quizzed, while he'd shined lights into my eyes, had just been too much. I'd been poked and prodded and questioned enough. I found myself having an anxiety attack, almost a panic attack. I stood up so fast I startled the old man, and took off out the door. I had gone back to my shady palm tree, sat down on the sand, and stared out over the water, trying to regain my composure.

Hours passed with nobody showing up, leaving me alone with my thoughts. The sky was on fire as the Sun slowly sank below the horizon. The clouds burst with shades of red and purple, and the sky itself was almost golden. A few days before, my only goal in life, as I dimly recalled it, had been to live long enough to see the sky again. Now I was in paradise, watching the most beautiful sunset I'd ever seen. For the last couple of days I hadn't known hunger, fear, nor cold. I'd had plenty of rest, good food, all the sunshine I wanted.

It was too much. It was just too much. Completely overwhelmed, I sat under that palm tree and stared helplessly into the sunset until the sky darkened. The stars began to shine overhead when the Sun finally sank below the sea. There are few things more routine and constant than the rising and setting of the Sun, but at that moment, you would have thought I'd never seen it before.

Ling came to me as the horizon darkened. I was so lost in thought I didn't notice her approach. "Hello," she said, pulling me back to reality. "Dr. Bundt told me what happened. He said it was best to give you some time to adjust. I hope I'm not disturbing you."

"It's fine," I said simply.

Ling seemed unconvinced. She sat next to me in the sand. "I know what it's like, you know." I looked a question at her. She brushed a few errant strands of hair out of her face before explaining, "When Exodus rescued me, I was still very young. Yet in those years I'd lost my family, fought in a war, been injured, and barely avoided being killed in the destruction of Shanghai. Yet after surviving all of that, I was made a slave. They kept me chained to a bed in a shack, letting me outside only to relieve myself. I wanted to die. I gave up hope completely.

"When Exodus saved me, it took a long time for me to accept it. I didn't speak for almost a month. I was afraid to. I was afraid it wasn't real, as if . . . well, it seems silly now, but I had this idea in my head that if I spoke, it would break the spell, end the dream, and I'd wake up under my tattered blanket, still chained to that wretched bed."

I said nothing, but I was consumed with a feeling of guilt. Well, not guilt exactly, but rather shame. I looked over at Ling and wondered. This woman was about the same age as me, maybe a couple years older. She had easily seen as much, if not more, horror in her life than I had. From what little I knew of her captivity, it had been far worse than mine. I feared many things during my short time in North Gap, but I'd never once been concerned that I was going to be gang-raped. Feeling pathetic, and not sure what to say, I wrapped my arms around my legs and stared at the sand.

Ling startled me by placing her hand on my shoulder. "I'm not telling you this to make you feel bad, Michael. I'm not trying to . . . how would you say, *one-up* you with my own story. It's important that you understand you're not alone. I know what you've been through. Many of us do. People like you make up the heart and soul of Exodus."

Her face was illuminated by the same milky moonlight that shimmered off of the calm Caribbean Sea. "Are you trying to recruit me?" I asked flatly.

She smiled at me and squeezed my shoulder. "No. Though I think you'd make a fine addition to our order. I tried to recruit you for some time after seeing what you were capable of in Mexico. But after all you've been through, after all that's happened, and knowing you as well as I do now . . . no. You're not ready, Michael. Exodus isn't a job. It's a lifelong commitment. It's an oath. You don't just join, you become part of it, and it becomes part of you. Much devotion is required. You . . . your heart belongs elsewhere, I think. Your loyalties lie elsewhere. You just do not know where that is now that you have been betrayed by your country. Am I incorrect?"

I had to think about that for a moment. Normally I didn't like it when people analyzed me, especially after months at the mercy of a mad scientist drilling into my subconscious with drugs and machines, but coming from Ling, it didn't feel invasive. I wasn't being prodded or interrogated. Her simple honesty put me at ease.

"No. Maybe. But it wasn't my country that betrayed me. The *government* did. There's a big difference. Our system was never perfect, but I think it's falling apart now. I mean, that's no surprise, things had been getting worse for a long time. I lived out of the country for almost five years straight when I worked for Vanguard. Every time I came home things seemed a little bit worse somehow. Even the government isn't just some big faceless entity. It's people. People did this to me. They chose to do this to me. They made their decisions, and I made mine. They're probably used to there not being any consequences for those decisions, but I made sure at least one of them paid a price."

Ling smiled. "Now you sound like an Exodus operative. Powerful men deserve their day of reckoning as much as anyone else. They too are answerable for their actions, even if they don't think they are. It makes no difference if they're warlords, criminals, or excuse their actions with the supposed legitimacy of government. They're just men, as you say, and men must be held to account."

"You're going somewhere with this, aren't you?"

"I am." She hesitated for a moment, looking out over the shimmering ocean. "It took a lot of doing to arrange for your retrieval. Many in our organization did not want to risk it. We're already considered a terrorist group by the United Nations. We almost never operate inside the United States in any capacity. The last thing Exodus wishes is to risk the attention of the US government. I had to pull many strings. It was made clear to me that under no circumstances was I, or anyone on my team, to be captured alive."

"So why did you do it?" I'd been wanting to ask her that since I woke up. "What on earth compelled you to risk so much on my account?"

"Because Robert Lorenzo said you might know something about this Project Blue, and that that knowledge could be used as a weapon against this shadow government organization, Majestic." She hushed me before I could once again protest that I knew nothing about Project Blue. "They are an example of everything we stand against. Agent Lorenzo was wrong about Project Blue, but he was not completely wrong. You still have knowledge that can hurt them. You know things, have seen things, even done things on their behalf. That kind of information is power."

"Bob already used everything I knew. It caused a huge scandal that was almost completely forgotten, what, six months later? It just got passed over and the media went onto the next story. God forbid they risk making some politician they like look bad."

"It is as you say." Ling nodded. "The corruption runs deep. But you did hurt them, whether you realize it or not. You have the power to hurt them again, should you choose to. As does Agent Lorenzo, if we can find him."

If only I had the answers everyone thought I did. Majestic was terrified of Project Blue. They were so compartmentalized, so secretive, that even they didn't even seem to know exactly what it was Gordon had unleashed. Colonel Hunter's notes had mentioned Dead Two and Dead Three being involved in a *Project Red* in China. The Second Chinese Civil War had broken out when I was in grade school, and continued off and on again for the better part of a decade before the final cease-fire. Nukes had been used and millions died.

Millions died. A pit formed in my stomach. My own Dead Six had been involved in an intervention in a foreign country. Had D2 and D3 been doing the same thing? Had Project Red started the Chinese civil war?

Ling didn't seem to notice my racing thoughts. "I met Bob Lorenzo by chance," she explained. "He told me there were four men who knew about Project Blue. Three of them are dead. One was a United States Senator, the other two were your former superiors, Curtis Hunter and Gordon Willis."

I clamped my eyes shut. "Jesus."

"I think you can see why Agent Lorenzo was so interested in you."

"So who was the fourth guy?"

"I do not know. Neither did Bob. He didn't know the man's identity, but his investigation indicated that he had fled to The Crossroads." Ling said that last part like she expected it to mean something to me.

"Don't know it."

"It's a lawless region, the intersection of North China, Russia, Kazakhstan, and Mongolia, kept lawless by the inability of those nations to control the remote parts of their territories."

"Okay. This is where you met Bob? What were you doing there?"

The Exodus operative looked at me for a moment, but said nothing. She was hesitant again. "We are planning a very large operation there. The Crossroads is controlled by a powerful warlord known as Sala Jihan. The profits come from his mines, mines that hundreds, maybe thousands, of slave workers die in every year. It's not a secret, simply another blight on the world that Western media ignores."

"You didn't answer my question."

Ling's expression hardened. "Exodus intends to eradicate Sala Jihan and remove his vile stain from the earth." Ling was a very well-spoken, calm, almost dispassionate woman. Half the time she seemed very cold. Seeing that fire in her, the true believer, still surprised me, even though I already knew it was there. *But holy crap, there was the crazy.* Ling continued, "In Agent Lorenzo . . . Bob, we found a kindred spirit. Before he was captured he asked me to find you. He said you would be able to help."

"What the hell do all these people expect me to know?"

"Michael . . . I have no right to ask this of you. You've been through enough, but in order to secure my organization's blessing on the rescue attempt, I told them that you would be an asset to us."

And there it is. "I thought you said I wasn't cut out for Exodus?"

"That's not what I said. It's not like we're above taking in outside help, as you're well aware." She waved her hand, indicating Lorenzo's island. "Lorenzo is going to The Crossroads to search for his brother. I promised him that we would do everything we could to help him in this endeavor if he helped us save you, and Exodus always fulfills its covenants. But for you,

Michael, there is no obligation. You do not have to come with us, but I'm asking for your help."

I blinked hard. This was insane. "What is it do you think I'm going to be able to do?"

"I *know* what you can do. You're a warrior," Ling said. "I also know what you've been through. I do not wish to place such a burden on you. Let me ask you this: if not with me, where will you go? Majestic will not stop hunting you. They may have the entire intelligence apparatus of the United States at their disposal. Anyone you associate with, anyone who shelters you, will be in danger. Exodus is uniquely prepared to deal with people in your position. Let me help you one more time, Michael. I'm not forcing you to join. I'm not forcing you to fight our battles. I swear to you, you can walk away if you wish."

"I'm not sure what to do, Ling."

Standing up unexpectedly, she brushed the sand off of her pants. "All I ask is that you weigh your options carefully. Whatever you decide, a plane will be here tomorrow, and I will be leaving on it. Sleep well, Michael." Ling walked away without looking back.

LORENZO
St. Carl Island
February 18th

We'd had one final meeting with Ling to discuss travel arrangements and contacts in The Crossroads. I was far more comfortable seeing to my own than tagging along with Exodus. She'd told me that their little turboprop Cessna would be leaving and a larger, longer-range jet had just landed to take them to Europe in the morning. Of course, it had also landed on my airfield without my permission. At this point I think Ling was doing that just to piss me off.

Antoine passed on several contacts and specific intros to use with Exodus operatives in the region. Shen updated Reaper on some of the radio frequencies and code phrases we could use to communicate, though I was positive he didn't give us any of the important ones. Ling hit it off with Jill by complimenting her decorating of the living room. It was a real chick bonding moment. Everything was now set for our meet in The Crossroads.

That left only one thing in question.

"What the hell do you mean, *you're not sure if Valentine is going with you?*"

"Easy, Lorenzo," Jill put her hand on my arm.

"I always mean exactly what I say," Ling stated. "Michael is not my prisoner. He is free to do as he pleases. If he does not wish to accompany us on this mission, then that is his choice."

"Holy shit, Ling. After all we went through to get him . . . And you want to just leave him . . . And on my island? Oh fuck that. Get him *off* my island."

"What would you have me do?"

"Have Shen choke his ass out or Antoine can throw a bag over his head and carry him, I don't care!" Considering how wanted Valentine was, he'd been here too damned long already. "I don't give a shit what you do, as long as he's on your fucking airplane in the morning, because otherwise I'll—"

"He's no trouble," Jill interjected. "We've got space."

"Oh, hell no!" I shouted.

"I know you don't like him, but we're not going to be here anyway! He's been through a lot of trauma, Lorenzo!"

"Trauma is when Majestic finds out he's here and then *kills us*, Jill." Shen, Antoine, and Ling exchanged glances and then politely backed away from the table like they totally weren't paying attention to the erupting argument. "Stop right there. You Exodus bastards aren't sneaking out of this one. Get Valentine out of here or I will."

"And what do you intend to do with him?" Jill demanded.

"He can learn to *swim*. Or hell, I'll be generous. I'll give him an inflatable raft. Haiti's that-a-way."

"Mike helped save my life, Lorenzo," Jill shouted. "Maybe you should go inflate that raft for yourself."

"Oh, snap," Reaper said. "Somebody's sleeping on the couch tonight!" I glared at him. "Never mind."

Ling shifted. I looked to see what had gotten her attention. Valentine was standing in the doorway, looking pale and tired.

"Oh good, our house guest has arrived. Feel like apologizing to me?"

Valentine didn't say anything in response.

"Apologizing for what?" Ling asked.

"Sticking a gun in my face under my own roof."

"Sorry," he said, totally not meaning it. Valentine nodded at Jill. "Good to see you, Peaches." She smiled at the use of her alias from Quagmire, because of course this asshole would be charming to my girlfriend. Then Valentine looked at Reaper. "Good to see you too, Skyler."

Reaper frowned at the use of his hated real name. "I'm with Lorenzo. This fucker's got to go."

"Yeah, about that, we were just discussing your leaving on a jet plane tomorrow."

"Or we were discussing about how you were welcome to stay here until you felt better," Jill added.

I turned back to her. "No. We weren't."

"He's been through a lot, Lorenzo. He's a *good* man." Jill was starting to get her *stabbing face*. "If it wasn't for him, I'd be dead."

"You still might get the chance if he gets spotted and they track his escape back to us! Do you feel like becoming a fugitive again? Because that's what we'll have to do if they connect us."

"Mike can stay here as long as he needs to. That's what Hawk did for me!"

Of course, she'd bring somebody doing a good deed into it. I smashed my hand into the table. "Damn it! He's—"

"Gone," Ling pointed out.

I looked back at the doorway. Sure enough, Valentine had left.

Apparently he'd made his decision.

LORENZO
St. Carl Island
February 19th

I'd gone to the airport to see them off. Ling hadn't seen Valentine, and she seemed a little sad about that. I was sad too, because now I was contemplating how to get rid of him, up to and including murder, without my girlfriend finding out of course.

However, it turned out that Valentine had decided to leave after all. He showed up as Exodus' Gulfstream jet was being loaded, with all of his earthly possessions shoved into one of my laundry bags.

"Hey," he said when he saw me hanging out by the hangar. "Jill gave me a lift. She's back by the gate."

"She's nice like that. So, what are you going to do?"

Valentine stopped and looked over the St. Carl airfield, at the brilliant green trees surrounding it, and then across the vast ocean. "I don't know. All I want is to be left alone. I don't want anybody else dying because of me."

"I know that feeling well." I didn't *hate* Valentine exactly, but he had a way of screwing up my orderly existence that was borderline supernatural. "Maybe I'll see you in The Crossroads, but if not, good luck."

The plane was warming up behind us. "If I think of anything else, anything that can help you find your brother, I'll call." What remained unspoken was how unlikely that really was.

There was still one thing that was bugging me, though. Mostly because it had come up during my argument with Jill, and I actually didn't know the answer. "The news said that Gordon Willis offed himself. I bet Jill five bucks that was a crock and you murdered him."

"Yeah, I killed him. Shot him in cold blood, right in the heart, right in his own house . . . Do you think that'll make Jill think less of me?"

I shrugged. "Hard to tell. It wasn't like she was his biggest fan."

"I heard her stick up for me last night. She called me a good man. I don't even know why that matters to me. Do me a favor . . . Don't tell her the truth. Make something up."

I could respect that. "You know Majestic will never rest." The assumption was that I would probably never see Valentine again, so I might as well say it. "They'll find you eventually. Me springing you will just make them think you're even more valuable than they thought before. They'll hunt you to the ends of the earth until they find out what they want to know about this Project Blue."

"I'm beginning to get curious myself," he replied with a wry smirk. "When you find your brother, tell him I'm sorry that I didn't know what he thought I knew. I . . ." Valentine trailed off, looked away for a second, and sighed. Finally he held out his hand. "Thanks for getting me out of there."

I hesitated, then took his hand and shook it firmly. He gave me one last nod, and then left to face his destiny, a man living on borrowed time. I watched the plane leave St. Carl, and bank sluggishly toward the west.

Jill was waiting for me at the airfield's gate. "So was I right?"

"You were right. Gordon committed suicide."

"Told you so. I win."

I handed her a $5 bill.

Chapter 10: Blue Eyed Girl

VALENTINE
Location Unknown
February 21st

The flight from the Caribbean was long, punctuated by a refueling stop, but I spent much of it sleeping. Dr. Bundt told me that I needed rest, and offered me a sedative. I refused. I'd spent more than enough time pumped full of drugs. I wanted my mind to be clear, even if clarity hurt.

I was still in shock. My entire world changed in an instant when I woke up on Lorenzo's island, and already it was changing again.

We touched down at a bustling airport in a picturesque coastal city. I didn't know where we were, and didn't bother to ask. The Exodus jet taxied to a private hangar, where three large BMWs with tinted windows were waiting for us. I was hurried into the back of one of the cars and we sped across the city, eventually leaving the urban landscape and the sea behind.

We drove for over an hour, far into arid, mountainous countryside. Our destination was a sprawling estate surrounded by rugged, rocky terrain. At its center was an ancient, partially-crumbling castle tower. It was accompanied by many newer-looking buildings, including a mansion that overlooked a cliff.

A short while later I was left standing alone in a large, ornately-decorated office. The far wall was one large bay window that stretched from floor to ceiling. Through it rugged mountains, brown under a clear blue sky, stretched out as far as the eye could see. I moved closer to the window and looked down. The mansion was built on the precipice of a cliff. Beyond the glass was a vertical drop that had to be several hundred feet.

"Impressive, isn't it?" someone asked, in an Oxford English accent. "Forgive me, Mr. Valentine, I didn't mean to startle you." An older, well-groomed gentleman in an expensive-looking grey suit walked confidently across the room and stuck out his hand. At his side was a much younger, prim-looking woman in a pencil skirt and high heels. Her hair was done

591

up in a tight bun and thick-rimmed glasses adorned her face. She held a tablet computer in her hands. The man looked me in the eye as I shook his hand.

"Who are you?" I asked.

"Mr. Valentine," the woman said, in a Mary Poppins English accent, "allow me to introduce Sir Matthew Cartwright, High Councilor of Exodus."

"Thank you, Penelope," he said, sounding just a bit embarrassed. "Of course, with your current popularity, that is an alias. I do not intend offense."

"Understandable, *Sir* Matthew."

He smiled. "The Sir part is correct, but the Crown hands out titles like candy these days, so pay it no mind."

"High Councilor? So you're the Exodus commander?"

"One of thirteen, actually. It's mostly a formality. Exodus is an organization which takes pride in its traditions. In any case, welcome to Azerbaijan."

Azerbaijan. A little country on the Caspian Sea, I recalled, used to be part of the Soviet Union. "So, does this *Council of Thirteen* run Exodus then?"

"Run it?" He seemed taken aback by the question. "It would seem that Ling hasn't told you much about our organization, has she?"

"She's told me practically nothing."

"Yes. Quite the stickler for operational security, that one. Well, it's all for the best. But since you're here, I think it's only fair that we pull back the veil just a bit, as it were, wouldn't you agree?"

"Uh, sure," I said. He seemed excited to tell me all about Exodus. Despite everything I had to admit I was curious. For all that I'd done with Exodus, the Mexico op, fleeing Zubara, staying at their secret base in Southeast Asia, and being rescued by Ling, I still knew very little about the organization. They were well-funded, with a global reach, and had access to state-of-the-art equipment. I also knew that if Ling was typical of their membership, they pursued their goals with a passionate tenacity bordering on fanaticism. That tenacity had saved my life multiple times, however, so I could hardly complain.

"Our lineage can be traced back a very long time, to the Crusades, in fact. Our founders were wise men, knights, scholars, men of the cloth, originally brought together on a quest to free the Holy Land. They were no strangers to war, but the corruption they found disgusted them, craven acts of barbarism from both sides, fueled by greed and lust, burdensome truths, even by the harsh standards of the day. The needless suffering they witnessed had disgusted them. *Verily I say unto you, inasmuch as ye have done it unto the least of these my brethren, ye have done it unto me.* A secret meeting was held in Constantinople, and a pact was made."

"I see." I hadn't been expecting an in-depth history and philosophy lesson.

"These men decided to pursue a higher calling, of protecting the common man, the poor and the downtrodden from the injustices of the mighty. It was a noble goal, quixotic even, and like many such things, it failed for a very long time. Sadly, it still does, occasionally."

"Ling told me Exodus goes back six hundred years."

"Correct. Our organization, as it exists today was based upon that earlier pact, but was founded in the fifteenth century, during the waning days of the Byzantine Empire. This time we had a few more persuasive leaders, and Exodus was born. In a world filled with evil, we would be a sword of righteousness."

"They call you people terrorists." I didn't have to specify who *they* were. The United Nations, INTERPOL, and numerous national governments were all on the list.

Sir Matthew chuckled. "Indeed they do. Supposedly, our world is made up of orderly nation-states and codified international law. You and I both know that there is an entire world that exists in the cracks between those borders, beneath that thin veneer of societal order, Mr. Valentine. Civilization only ever dangles by a thread. We bring justice to the truly evil. Many of our warriors are former victims themselves, willing to save others from the depravities they themselves have experienced. Exodus does not bow to diplomatic or economic pressure. We are not beholden to the weak wills of politicians. We don't negotiate with evil. We do not care what is popular, we simply care that things are *right*."

I raised an eyebrow. "Who picks what is right?"

"A fine question," Sir Matthew agreed. "A question which would surely be debated by our membership, which is why Exodus does not waste time delving into the grey areas. Why muddle things when there is so much pure, unquestionable evil to go around? I speak of real evil, Mr. Valentine: the massacres, the brutality, and the slavery that goes on, ignored by the civilized world, every single day. I've read your dossier, about your career as a mercenary. You've seen these things for yourself, have you not?"

Before I could answer that, the heavy wooden double doors that led to the office flew open. In rushed a slender young woman with hair that was such a light shade of platinum blonde that it almost looked white. I hadn't seen her in a couple of years, and she'd definitely grown, but there was no mistaking this girl.

"Michael!" she said, hurrying across the room and throwing her arms around me. I felt myself blush a little as she hugged me enthusiastically. "I'm so happy to see you!"

I composed myself and stepped back a bit. "You've grown," I managed. In the time since I'd last seen her, the gangly teenager had matured into a lovely young woman with striking features. She was still short, the top of her head not quite making it to my shoulder, but her hair was longer, almost reaching to her waist.

"Yes. I understand that the two of you have already met," Sir Matthew said. He seemed uneasy for some reason. I didn't think it'd be possible, but Penelope looked even more uptight. *Did I just commit some kind of faux pas?*

"Michael saved my life," the girl said.

"Mexico," I agreed. "It's been a long time, kiddo. And I don't even know your name."

"I'm sorry about that." Her intense blue eyes looked deeply into mine. It was almost unsettling. She had the most unnatural eyes I'd ever seen, and that's coming from somebody with heterochromia. It felt like she could see through you. "My name is Ariel."

"Like in *The Little Mermaid*?"

"I loved that movie when I was little. That's where I picked my name from."

"Wait, what? You picked your name?"

She ignored my question. "Come with me! Let's go for a walk. I want to show you around. You've been through a lot."

Sir Matthew protested. "Ah, My Lady, Mr. Valentine and I have much to discuss . . ."

"Later!" she said, interrupting him. "There'll be plenty of time to talk about the work later. He needs to relax! You have no idea what he's been through!" She tugged on my arm and began to lead me out of the room. I looked an apology to my host.

He shrugged. "As you wish, My Lady. Mr. Valentine, we'll talk later."

Ariel was visibly fighting off tears as we casually strolled down a long hallway. Brilliant sunlight spilled into the corridor from a row of floor-to-ceiling windows on one wall. Paintings and tapestries lined the other wall. It was a really nice place, even with a teenage girl trying not to cry.

"I'm sorry, Michael," she said, rubbing her eyes. "I get overwhelmed sometimes. Seeing all the scars on you was just too much."

Most of my scars were covered by my clothing, so I wasn't entirely sure what she was talking about. The girl was strange, there was no doubt about it. I can't say I've spent a lot of time around teenaged girls, but this one was a lot more emotional than I was prepared for. "It's okay."

"No, it's not!" she insisted. "Every time the work comes into your life, you suffer. You lost so many friends to save me. And Sarah . . . Michael, I never knew her, but I'm so sorry."

"How do you know about Sarah?"

She hesitated for the briefest instant. "Ling told me."

I closed my eyes for a moment and took a deep breath, remembering the vivid dream about Sarah I had when I was still in captivity. It seemed so real that it still shook me to my core. "It's okay," I repeated. "It is what it is. I made choices, and I have to live with the consequences of those choices." I didn't want to talk about it anymore. That didn't seem like the sort of thing you should dump on a teenage girl.

"Things will get better for you." Ariel sounded remarkably confident in her statement. "They will. I know it's been a hard road for you, and I don't think it's over yet, but someday things will be better for you. You'll see. You are supposed to be here."

"Why? Why did Exodus get me out of that hole? Why risk so much on my account? Ling saved us in Zubara. As far as I'm concerned, any debt owed to me from Mexico was squared."

"Ling proposed the operation." Ariel's demeanor visibly changed. She sounded less the emotional teenager and more like a veteran commander. The transition was almost unreal. "The organization wasn't very receptive to it. The operation at The Crossroads is our priority. There aren't a lot of people to be spared, much less aircraft and intelligence and everything else that would be needed. Sir Matthew didn't think it was worth the risk to save you. We're always hesitant to do anything in the US. He lobbied the Council against Ling's proposal. But you are too important."

"I don't know anything about Project Blue, if that's what you mean."

"I know. I don't know anything about it either, and that troubles me. But you're still important."

"Okay, hang on a sec. What is it you do for Exodus anyway?"

"Things . . . I don't know."

"Things?"

"I'm like an advisor."

"Kiddo, please don't be offended by this, because you're obviously a very smart girl, but how are you at all qualified to advise an international, clandestine, completely-illegal paramilitary organization?"

Ariel covered her mouth with one hand and giggled like I'd just said something funny. "I have a . . . unique way of seeing things. Patterns, connections, causalities that other people don't see. That's how I help with the work, and that's how I know you're important, Michael. I just know it. I wanted to find you ever since you disappeared. I just didn't know where you were, until Ling met Agent Lorenzo."

"That was a crazy coincidence."

"I don't believe in coincidence," Ariel said firmly. "Fates intertwine. It's all connected, even if we can't see the end yet."

I said nothing. I didn't believe in fate, and I certainly didn't want to get into some kind of philosophical argument with the strange girl, but when she put it that way, with such determined conviction, I began to wonder.

Ariel continued after taking a deep breath. "After Ling found out where you were, I knew we had to get you back. When I was being held by those men in Mexico, I gave up. I know what it's like to be left in a dark place without hope, and so does Ling. We were the ones that lobbied the Council. But we couldn't spare a lot of people."

"So Lorenzo was brought in."

"Yes. I hated to do it. He was trying so hard, living on the edge of peace, and we pushed him back over. I hate myself for it but it needed to be done. His own brother knew it needed to be done." Ariel sniffled a little. "Do you know how hard it is for someone like that to change his destiny? It scares me to think what we might have unleashed."

"Don't get all metaphysical on me, Ariel. Lorenzo's a dangerous, angry little man, but he's just a man. If he hadn't been smart enough to wear a vest one day in Zubara, I would've shot him dead, and that would've been the end of him."

My young companion looked thoughtful for a moment. "And then you, yourself, would have died in Zubara too, am I wrong? Fates intertwine, Michael. Remember that. We needed him because it wasn't your time, so it must have been the right thing to do," She sounded more upbeat and very confident. I didn't bother asking her how she knew about Lorenzo saving my life. Exodus knew a lot more about me than I was comfortable with.

"I thought I was a dead man," I said. "But then there was Ling, waiting for me when I woke up. Just like before. My guardian angel."

Ariel smiled at that. "She loves you, you know."

Huh? "Whoa, whoa, whoa. Love is a pretty strong word, don't you think?"

"I don't think, I *know*," Ariel insisted. "She loves you. Duh. You can't be that surprised."

I thought about it for a moment. "We've hardly spent any time together. She never, you know, flirted with me or anything. She was always all about business."

"You don't know anything about girls, do you? Do you remember, back in Mexico, when we found our way back to the group? You appeared unexpectedly, carrying me in your arms? You were a mighty white knight, dressed in green, but you know. That's when she fell for you, in that moment."

Just like a Disney movie, except for all the guns. "Heh . . . I guess it was pretty dramatic." I didn't think of it that way at the time, but I had been busy trying to stay alive.

"I saw it on her face in that moment, even though she couldn't admit it to herself. It really came together for her while she was taking care of you after you got hurt. The first time, I mean."

I'd been unconscious on that Exodus ship for a long time with Ling watching over me. "Florence Nightingale syndrome?"

"Something like that. I don't think she's admitted it to herself. She's been hurt before. She's not ready yet."

"What should I do?" *Why am I asking this girl for advice?*

"I don't think you're ready either, Michael," said Ariel, looking up into me with that eerie gaze of hers.

I hadn't had nightmares about Sarah's death for a week. That was progress, I suppose.

Still unsure of what to say, and more than a little uncomfortable at how insightful she was, I changed the subject. "Listen, about this thing in Central Asia, I don't know much—"

"Exodus buries the work in layers of deceit. I hate it. I hate all the secrets and lies. But it's necessary. Sala Jihan has ways of finding things out."

"Sala Jihan. The warlord?"

Ariel looked up at me like I'd said something strange. "Yes," she agreed. "He must be stopped. Besides, you're a wanted man. Majestic is almost everywhere, but they're not allowed in The Crossroads. Jihan's shadow may be the safest place for you. There are some places that even Majestic can't go."

"So where do I come in? I'm not in any kind of shape to do much right now."

"Every little bit helps, Michael," Ariel said with a smile. "The right man in the wrong place can make all the difference in the world. You're supposed to go, because remember, fates intertwine."

"I have a confession to make, Michael," Ling said, breaking the silence as we boarded an ornate elevator. She pushed the 'basement' button.

After some of the weird things I'd heard from Ariel, this should be good. "Okay."

"The reason I've brought you here is in the hope that you would be persuaded to help Exodus in The Crossroads."

That was her confession? After what Ariel had said part of me had been wondering if Ling would come out and say she had feelings for me, but right now she was all business. "Ariel seems to think I should go." Ling had insisted that my going with her off of Lorenzo's island in no way obligated me to go to war with her. This was the first time she'd brought it up since we got on the plane.

"The young lady is full of surprises . . . and is surprisingly perceptive. So?"

"I . . . I don't know."

"I have an ulterior motive for asking you to come on this operation with us. It's not just that we need every possible body. I told the Council you'd be an asset to us. Exodus doesn't like bringing in outsiders, but we're going to have to rely on them a great deal in this case." The elevator came to a stop. The mirrored doors opened, revealing a very spartan underground level. "Saving Ariel in Mexico made you a hero in the eyes of many. Having you on board would be excellent for morale."

I exhaled heavily, suddenly feeling very silly. "Really?"

Ling always had one hell of a poker face. There was nothing to be gained from trying to read this woman when she was being professional. She left the elevator and started down along concrete hallway. "Really," she confirmed. "It's a rare thing for someone who is not a member of the order to risk so much, and sacrifice so much on our behalf."

Following along, I wondered if my reputation had been somewhat inflated. The thing in Mexico was more luck than anything else, and I'd hardly done it singlehandedly. We passed strangers in the hall. All of them were watching me. "I hope I live up to everyone's expectations," I managed.

Ling flashed me a brief smile. "I reported events precisely how they occurred, but I must warn you. People who weren't there may have heard, and then embellished it in the retelling. I have heard some interesting versions of what happened in Cancun. The fact you singlehandedly held off a battalion of UN peacekeepers and the cartel is remarkable."

"Great." I sighed.

Ling paused, and turned to face me. The expression on her face softened. "I'm . . . I'm sorry," she said, looking down briefly. "I'm putting you under a great deal of pressure, aren't I? Please forgive my presumptuousness."

"There's nothing to forgive. I owe you my life. Asking me to help out after all you went through to get me isn't unreasonable. I just . . ." I trailed off. I was having a hard time putting it into words. "I don't know what it is you think I can do. I don't want to let you down."

"I *know* what you can do," she insisted. "I've seen it with my own eyes."

"Mexico was a long time ago."

"Not that long. And you have only grown in experience since then, am I wrong?" She didn't wait for me to answer. "Michael, I . . . like you. Even so, I would not ask you to come with me if I did not think you would truly be an asset to the operation. I believe in you, even if you do not, and I believe we need your help. Many of our members are inexperienced in combat. For quite a few of them, this will be their first time going into battle. They're well-trained and enthusiastic, but inexperienced and outnumbered. Having a seasoned veteran with us, even if only in an advisory role, will be beneficial."

I chewed on that for a second. Somehow, I had gotten the idea that Ling was asking me to come along out of pity or something. I know it sounds dumb, but after everything I'd been through I wasn't necessarily thinking straight. Her little pep talk was good to hear, and it wasn't like I didn't have experience in training other forces. In my time at Vanguard, I helped train multiple armed forces, from Africa to South China. Corporate called it "partnership."

That sounded right. *Partnership.* With Exodus. Just an advisory role. *I can handle that.* I looked back up at Ling. "By the way, why are we in this basement? Where are we going?"

"We need to outfit you with equipment for the operation. You'll need weapons, body armor, clothes to wear, cold-weather gear, and so forth."

"I haven't said I'm going yet."

"You haven't said you are not. Come on, we have everything you may need."

"What are my needs, exactly?"

"If you decide to join us you'll be with me. What I'm going to be doing remains to be seen, I'm afraid."

"It's not like you to not have a plan."

Ling smiled again. "No, it's not. My mission was to rescue you. There was no guarantee that operation would succeed or that I would return alive. They planned the operation at The Crossroads with the assumption that I would be unavailable."

"Assume the worst-case scenario until proven otherwise." That attitude had kept me alive, even if it brings frequent accusations of pessimism and cynicism.

"You and I will be among the last to arrive at The Crossroads," she said. "Shen and Antoine are already on their way there."

We reached a large supply room, where paramilitary clothing and gear of all sorts was stored on racks and in bins. The room smelled like a surplus store. Two attendants spoke briefly to Ling in French. One of them pulled out a measuring tape.

"Hold on," I protested.

Ling tilted her head to the side. "Humor me, Michael. You need new clothes one way or the other." It was true; I'd been wearing the same set of clothes I'd had on when I was captured the year before.

They took my measurements, then went to work supplying me with new clothes. I was skinnier than the last time I'd done something like this. "So Shen and Antoine are already gone? They're breaking up your team?"

"My team has been broken up for quite some time. Shen and Antoine are all who remain. They'll be put to better use elsewhere." There was sadness behind Ling's professional mask. "But I still need soldiers I can count on."

Sometime, when we were alone, I resolved to ask her about what happened to her team. Right now I felt like I was being swept along by a very strong current. "So, if I was to say yes, how would we get there?"

"There are only two practical ways into The Crossroads," Ling replied. "Rail and road. There is an unpaved airfield, but in the winter it is snowed over and requires a short-field-capable aircraft fitted with skis. Arriving there by air would likely attract more scrutiny than we want. We'll be flying into Kazakhstan and traveling the rest of the way by road."

"You just drive there? Even in the winter?"

"The Kazakh government expends a lot of effort to keep the mountain roads accessible year round, to help the mountain villagers, of course. Obviously this has nothing to do with the wealth generated by the illicit flow of drugs, arms, and slaves."

The quartermaster brought me several sets of green fatigues and a set of winter overwhites. "Like I haven't had enough snow lately." One attendant fitted me for body armor while the other attempted to find a pair of boots that would fit me. He said something to Ling in French. "What did he say?"

"He said that Americans have very big feet."

I was given a backpack, hats, gloves, goggles, a face mask, knives, a radio, rope, even an ice axe. It was a ridiculous amount of gear, so much that I had to borrow a hand cart to transport it down the hall with. "Jesus," I said, looking at my cart full of swag. "You guys don't screw around with gear issue, do you?"

"It wouldn't do for a person of your reputation to show up poorly prepared. We will go by communications and get the encryption loaded into your radio before we depart. Communications are going to be difficult, at best, during this operation."

"I can imagine." The more dudes you have running around with encrypted radios the less likely it is that anybody will be able to hear anybody else.

"And here we are," Ling said. "The armory." A set of heavy vault doors had been opened, but a locked gate was installed behind them. Two men were present in the vault. One was armed with a pistol on his hip. The other had some kind of large revolver in a shoulder holster. *A man after my own heart!*

I pushed my little cart off to the side of the hallway as Ling spoke to one of the armorers. She showed him some kind of identification badge. He studied it closely before letting us in. Exodus ran a very tight ship.

My mouth fell open. I have been through a lot of combat in my life. War has been my profession for years. But behind that paper-thin veil of stoic professionalism, I'm a gun nut at heart, and the racks of weapons left me salivating. "Which one do I get?"

"Whichever one you want, Michael," Ling replied. The pistol-packing armorer didn't say anything but gave me the stink eye. *Fair enough. I wouldn't want some jackass poking around in my gun safe either.* The one with the big wheelgun, a short, dark-skinned man of ambiguous ethnicity, grinned widely at me with extremely white teeth. He could recognize a fellow enthusiast.

I returned my attention to the racks, only giving a cursory glance at the heavier weapons. I wasn't interested in carrying an M240 through the mountains in waist-deep snow. No, I was looking for a rifle. Something that suited me. There were plenty to choose from. One rack had nothing but SIG 551 carbines fitted with all of the latest accoutrements. Another contained similarly-updated Steyr AUG bullpups. Against one wall was a rack of M4-style rifles; against another were HK G36s.

"Maintaining this many different systems has to be a strain on your resources."

Near each rack were bins full of magazines and boxes of tools and parts. In a way, it made sense, though. Exodus is a clandestine organization that operates outside of the law. I wasn't sure how they acquired weapons, but I was certain it wasn't the legal way. It's probably easier to keep your weapons purchases on the down low if you buy small lots from a variety of sources, rather than trying to standardize across the board.

"Exodus purchases what we can, where we can, with few questions asked."

In addition to the racks of rifles, there were more specialized weapons, like bolt-action sniper rifles and shotguns, but that wasn't my thing. I was getting discouraged. I could see nothing but rows of 5.56mm assault rifles.

As if reading the disappointment on my face, the revolver-toting armorer approached me, still smiling. "You no find what you like?" he asked in heavily-accented English.

"These are all five-five-six. Got anything bigger?"

The armorer's beady eyes lit up. He crossed the room, rummaged around for a few seconds before returning with a rifle in his hands. "HK G3," he said eagerly, handing me the rifle. I grasped the folding charging handle and retracted the bolt slightly, checking the chamber, before shouldering it. "Seven-point-six-two. Gun for *real* man."

The rifle's stock had been replaced with a Spuhr adjustable one from Sweden. The iron sights had been cut off, as the stock rendered them unusable. The weapon was fitted with an extended optics rail, and had an ELCAN 1x/4x scope mounted on it. *This will do.* I felt the corner of my mouth curl up in a grin. "Okay. I only need one more thing. Do you have any forty-four magnum ammunition?"

The armorer's eyes lit up. "Forty-four!" He stepped back and reached for the big revolver slung under his left arm. I tensed up as he drew it, but relaxed once I realized he just wanted to show it off. It was a stainless steel Taurus .44 Magnum with a six-inch barrel. "Like Dirty Harry!" he insisted. He reholstered his gun and disappeared into the back again. The other armorer silently sat in his chair and glared at me. The six-gunner returned with half a dozen boxes of Czech and Serbian .44 Magnum ammunition, all jacketed hollow points.

"Will that suffice?" Ling asked, eyebrows raised.

I set the rifle in the padded case I was given, and zipped it up. "Oh yes. I think I'm all set here."

Ling looked me over. "So I assume this means you're *in,* as they say?"

The rifle felt good in my hands. I had nothing else to live for. I was the most wanted man in the world. A knight had just given me a talk about fighting evil and a strange girl had gone off about fate.

"Looks like it."

"We're going into harm's way, Michael," Ling said. "You don't have to go with us."

"So you keep insisting."

I'd spent most of my life fighting other people's battles. My body was weak and my mind traumatized. I wasn't in any shape to fight, and I wasn't really sure what I was fighting for. But what was I supposed to do? Turn back now, after all Ling had done for me, and let Exodus down? They thought me a hero. Would they think me a coward if I walked away? Why did I care?

Ling awaited my answer.

"Would I have to give the rifle back?"

"I'm afraid so," Ling replied.

"I get to keep it when we're done, though."

Assuming I'm still alive . . .

✢ ✢ ✢

The Exodus mansion had an impressive library.

After a couple of long meetings with Sir Matthew and some of his functionaries, where we discussed the terms of my agreement with Exodus, including modest compensation, I was allowed to roam much of the mansion at will. We would be departing for Kazakhstan soon, and things were going to kind of suck after that, so I was enjoying the luxury while it lasted. I had a huge, soft bed to sleep in, hot baths whenever I wanted, and all the food I could eat. It was amazing.

The other residents of the mansion, or the staff, or whoever they were, generally kept their distance. Everyone was exceedingly polite, but I was still an outsider and they were generally leery of me. The only ones that ever really talked to me were Ling and Ariel.

Sir Matthew was proud of the mansion's library, and I could see why. There were thousands of books there, ranging from ancient volumes to an entire shelf of paperback pulp novels. A bookish person could keep himself busy in there for a long time. There were many comfy places to sit, with cozy reading lights, and a cheery fireplace crackled and popped in the corner.

I wasn't there to read, though. The library had a computer, and for the first time in a long time I was able to get onto the Internet. I had been out of the loop since my capture the previous summer. I had no idea what all was going on in the world. I had heard bits and pieces about the fallout of Bob Lorenzo dumping, to the press, Colonel Hunter's flash drive, but I wanted to see for myself.

I spent several hours in front of that computer, clicking away at news sites, and catching up on blogs I used to follow. I downloaded a .PDF of *The Project Heartbreaker Commission Report*, which resulted from the Congressional Committee appointed to investigate. It was a long read, hundreds of pages, so I mostly skimmed.

I was startled when the quiet room was suddenly filled with the clicking of high heels. Penelope, Sir Matthew's assistant, quickly walked into the room, carrying a couple of books. There was surprise on her face when she noticed me sitting in front of the computer.

"Ah, Mr. Valentine," she said. "I didn't know you were given free run of the premises. I trust you've been making yourself comfortable?"

She said disdainfully. Cripes. "Yeah, everyone's been super nice. I appreciate that."

"Well, feel free to use our facilities. I might remind you that while you're using the computer, please don't access any social media or personal e-mail. I'm sure an individual of your experience is familiar with operational security, so I shan't lecture you."

That sounded like a lecture to me. "See, I'm glad you said something.

Hell, I was going to whip out my cell phone, hold it up over my head, make duck lips at it and snap a pic of myself, slap it up on Facebook, and tag myself in it so all my friends would see."

Penelope's brow furled into an unattractive glower.

"Actually, turns out I can't do that," I continued. "I don't have a cell phone. Or Facebook. Or . . . " I paused, thinking about it for a second. ". . . *friends,* for that matter. So no worries, hey?"

The uptight Englishwoman composed herself. "Please forgive me, Mr. Valentine, I did not mean to offend you. Please excuse me." She hurried out of the room, heels clicking as she went. She took the books she'd brought in back out with her.

I had no idea why Penelope disliked me so much. I simply shook my head and returned my attention to the screen, scrolling through the file.

"She is *such* a bitch sometimes," Ariel said.

"Gah!" I jumped up in my chair.

The strange platinum-haired girl was standing right in front of the desk, looking through me with her eerie gaze. Her eyes reflected the flickering light of the fire and shimmered. She grinned at me. "Did I scare you?"

I laughed. "Holy hell, kiddo, you're like a damn ninja. I didn't hear you come in."

"I learned to be sneaky when I want to be," she said mischievously, leaning on the desk. Dressed in blue jeans and a T-shirt, she looked like a perfectly normal American teenager, except for her weird eyes. "And you do so have friends. *I'm* your friend, stupid. Whatcha doin'?"

"Just reading up on everything I missed, while I was . . . you know, *in captivity.* What is that woman's problem with me?"

"Penelope? Oh, she's nice most of the time. She just doesn't like you."

"Yeah, I can see that. What the hell did I do?"

"Don't worry, you didn't do anything. She's mistrustful of outsiders, like a lot of people in the organization are. I think you also remind her of her ex-husband. He was handsome, like you, a tough military guy."

When I looked at myself in the mirror, I saw an emaciated shell of the very average-looking person I used to be. I felt neither handsome nor particularly tough, but I found myself blushing at the compliment all the same.

Ariel giggled, and leaned over to see the screen. "So what are you reading . . . oh." Her demeanor darkened, and some of the light left her eyes.

"It's the *Project Heartbreaker Commission Report,*" I said quietly. On the screen was picture of a man with a hard face and an eye patch. *Hunter, Curtis Alan. Lieutenant Colonel (Ret.), US Army. KIA in Zubara.* "I knew these people," I said absentmindedly, as I scrolled through the faces of the dead.

"Worked with them, fought with them, mourned our dead with them. We destroyed a nation together. We . . . " I trailed off.

McAllister, Sarah Marie. Fmr. US Air Force. KIA in Zubara. Sarah looked a bit younger in the picture than she had the day she died. It probably came from her old military ID.

Ariel gently placed a hand on my shoulder. Tears were trickling down her cheeks. "She was beautiful," she sniffled, sitting down next to me.

I took a deep breath. "Yeah, she was. She didn't know how beautiful she was, either."

"I'm so sorry." She squeezed my shoulder more tightly.

"For a long time, I felt like I was supposed to have died there. I told her I'd stay with her until the end. I promised her. I couldn't keep her safe, I couldn't protect her, but I promised her that much. I was supposed to die in the mud at Fort Saradia, next to her."

There was a fierce light in my young companion's eyes, reflected firelight. "No, you *weren't!* I already told you. It wasn't your time. You need to listen better, damn it!" She punched me in the shoulder.

"Ow! Okay, okay, I'm sorry. I was just saying. For a long time that's how I felt. I resented Lorenzo for saving me. I resented him because I owed him a favor and he's a giant asshole, and I resented him because I felt like I broke my promise to Sarah."

"But you didn't, did you?"

"No . . . no, I guess I didn't." I thought back, again, to the frighteningly real dream I had. In that dream, Sarah's eyes shined like Ariel's sometimes seemed to. It was so vivid, so intense, that I wanted it to be real, even though I knew it was just a drug-induced hallucination. I shook my head. "It's still hard. I miss her every day."

"Things will get better for you," Ariel said quietly. "I just *know* it. Please be strong, Michael. Please don't give up. You saved me. You're my knight too." She hugged me tightly, tears in her eyes. I awkwardly patted her on the shoulder, worried that someone was going to walk in and get the wrong idea.

I grabbed the mouse and kept scrolling. "Don't worry, kiddo," I said, trying to sound comforting. "I'm stubborn. I'll be okay."

"I wish you didn't have to go to The Crossroads," Ariel whispered. "I'm scared. I have a bad feeling."

I smiled. "I thought you said things were going to get better for me?"

"I've been wrong before," she said ominously.

I stopped scrolling when a very familiar face appeared on the screen. It, too, was an old picture. From my last DOD ID card, if I remembered right. *Valentine, Constantine Michael. Fmr. US Air Force. KIA in Zubara.*

Before handing over Colonel Hunter's flash drive to Bob Lorenzo, I changed my own status from "MIA" to "confirmed KIA." I figured if they thought I was already dead, it'd give me a better chance of staying off the radar. A good theory, and one that might've worked if I hadn't gotten my stupid ass captured.

I nodded at the picture. "Ever feel like someone just walked over your grave?"

Ariel sat up and wiped her eyes, but didn't say anything. I closed out the report and asked her if she was okay.

"I actually came down here to tell you something, Michael," she said. The tone of her voice was subtlety different. "Majestic doesn't know where you are right now, and they're panicking. You're dangerous to them, because of what you know, because of the scars they left on you, and because you escaped. You're safe for now, I think, but they will never stop hunting you. You have to find Mr. Lorenzo's brother. The two of you might be able to end this. Maybe."

"Don't you worry. If Bob Lorenzo's at The Crossroads, I'll find him and we'll find a way clear of all this." *Another good theory.*

"There is one more thing. Promise me you'll watch over Ling."

"Ling can take care of herself, I think."

"Promise me! She's the closest thing to family I have. Please."

"Okay, honey. I'll do everything I can to bring her home safe. I'll stick with her through the whole thing."

"You promise?"

"I promise."

Ariel seemed content with that answer, and smiled.

Chapter 11: Tourists

LORENZO
Altay Mountains, Russia
March 10th

The train wheels beat rhythmically on the steel tracks. Our private passenger compartment was old-school comfortable, with thick couches, real wood paneling, and an actual bearskin rug on the floor. The bar was stocked with expensive vodka and caviar. As wealthy western businessmen, we rode first class. I had scouted the other passenger cars, and they were typical Russian, the middle cars were run-down utilitarian things housing ethnic Russians and some replacement soldiers for their outpost, and the cars at the end of the train were pure third world, unheated splintery wood, almost cattle cars that were packed with Kyrgyz and Uzbek workers.

The massive diesel engine labored to get us through the mountain pass. Jill tugged on the bottom of the black window curtain. It rolled up with a snap, revealing a glorious view. We were 6,000 feet above sea level and climbing. The peaks of the Golden Mountains towered far higher around us, and my lungs ached from the lack of air. North Gap, Montana had been pleasant in comparison. I knew I had better get used to it though. The Crossroads itself was at 8,000 feet.

"It's so pretty," Jill said. "All that snow . . ."

I looked past her. Huge white drifts covered miles of black rock. Giant angled sheets of ice reflected the sunlight so clean and white and brilliant that it made my eyes hurt. Behind those black rock walls were mile after mile of glaciers, one of the greatest reserves of fresh water on Earth. Miles of pristine evergreens were interspaced with sluggish glacial springs.

"Looks cold." I was feeling disagreeable. We were behind schedule. A late snowstorm had held us up in Volgostadorsk. We were supposed to have flown in, but reports said that it was going to take some time to clear the runways with that typical Russian enthusiasm and efficiency. In other words, the one plow was broken down, and the guy that could fix it had to sober up first. The delay had put me in a foul mood. Well, fouler than normal.

"I think it's the most beautiful place I've ever seen," Jill said. Reaper looked up from his laptop, squinted at the bright light, grunted, and returned to his files. Reaper didn't appreciate any beauty that wasn't pixilated. Well, unless you count strippers. Jill shook her head sadly. "You guys have no appreciation for nature."

"Nature's an evil whore who'll kill you in a heartbeat," I replied. Even though I didn't like people, I liked being surrounded by them. The wilderness made me uncomfortable. In a crowd, I can fade away. In the woods, I was pretty much clueless.

"It's supposed to be spring, but when the Sun goes down tonight, it'll be ten degrees below zero. A blizzard here can kill you in a manner of minutes. There are packs of wolves in that forest where the males weigh a hundred and fifty fucking pounds and eat their body weight in meat every few days," Reaper said. He looked up from his computer. I raised an eyebrow. "Wikipedia," he explained.

This territory held the intersection of Russia, China, Kazakhstan, and Mongolia. Only Russia and China officially touched, with the Kazakhs and Mongols being separated by about twenty miles. Historically this area had been a crossroads of the ancient world, and the birthplace of the Turkic people. For most of the last couple centuries it had been a kind of no man's land, populated by small villages and ethnic minorities. Over the last fifty years there had been a few border skirmishes, and one really unlucky Russian military disaster, but mostly this area had been ignored. It was steep, cold, hard to get to, and generally considered the ass end of the universe by everyone involved.

That had all changed about twenty years ago, beginning with a natural gas pipeline from southern Siberia into North China, and that had led to the construction of the rail line through the mountains. Then an oil pipeline had crossed it from Kazakhstan through Mongolia which had brought its own railroad. These lines had intersected in a mountain valley that at the time had held nothing but an abandoned Soviet military base and the ancient ruins of some people that had long since been forgotten, and a small town had sprung up at this new intersection.

Then an enterprising businessman known as Big Eddie had decided that this little crossroads was a superb hub for trafficking in all sorts of illicit goods. Afghan and Kazakh opium heading east, north, and south, the Russian Army selling off everything that wasn't nailed down, and Chinese military hardware heading every which way. The Crossroads became a kind of international super-flea market of illicit goods. Soon every criminal, terrorist, and wannabe warlord converged on it, looking to buy and sell. People like that needed neutral places to meet and conduct business, and

Big Eddie kept the peace. That mountain village had turned into a boomtown of the criminal underworld, and the boom had brought the deals and the money. Every faction on Earth wanted a piece of the action.

But The Crossroads wasn't all fun and profit. Criminal factions tend to solve their problems with violence, and old grudges die hard. The factions needed muscle, and this attracted the mercenaries, Muslims run out of Chechnya, Mongols hungry for work, Uyghur, Kazakhs, Kyrgyz, Han, and every other group you could think of. If a rough man needed work, there was no better place to find it than The Crossroads.

Once it was found that the surrounding mountains held huge stores of gold, silver, copper, and zinc, all in a place where there was no government interference or regulations on how to get at that wealth, legitimate business had flocked to The Crossroads, and the area exploded. After a few years the town had swelled to almost twenty thousand people. And it was a *tough* town. All four of the legitimate governments that bordered The Crossroads were happy to look away from the bad things that happened there, as long as they got paid.

It had been the crown jewel in Big Eddie's empire. Of course, none of the residents and visitors to The Crossroads knew who he really was, only that he ran the show with an iron fist, and he always got a cut of the action. Apparently that had changed rather drastically when I had shot that poodle-petting freak out of the sky, but nature abhors a vacuum, so now there was someone new at the top of the food-chain.

That's where we came in.

"We'll be in The Crossroads in a matter of hours. From here on out, we're in character. Get used to it. I don't want any—" There was a knock at the cabin door. "Hang on. I got it."

A waiter was in the hall, pushing a steam cart. The terrain flashed by behind him through the opposite bank of windows. We were entering a valley. He was a young ethnic Uzbek, and spoke in poorly accented Russian. "Good afternoon, sir. Lunch is served," he lifted the cover and displayed his wares. "Today, fresh salmon from Katun River, with potatoes in lamb bone marrow pudding." It actually looked really good, but I had eclectic tastes.

First class so totally rocks. "Wonderful," I reached into my pocket for a tip. The train lurched as the brakes were forcefully applied. I stumbled and caught myself on the doorframe. The screech of metal on metal echoed up through the carpeted floor. The waiter braced himself and kept his cart from spilling. "What's going on?"

"I not know," he answered, looking bewildered. "No stop here."

"Giant wolf on the track," Reaper suggested from behind me.

"No." I saw the pillars of black smoke out the window. There was, or had been, a small village here. The homes had been tiny wooden things with thatch roofs, and there had only been five or six of them at the most. All of them were burning now. There were bodies strewn around in the bloody snow, none of them were moving. The train finally came to a full stop, with our car looking right at the remains.

"What the hell?" Reaper said as he looked over my shoulder. "Whoa." Jill pushed past me and into the hall and stared out the window. Other first-class passengers left their cabins and joined us, staring at the scene. There was muttering and gasping.

A blast of freezing cold and the smell of smoke flowed through the hall when the rear door opened. "Make way! Move aside!" The soldiers from the next car were pushing their way forward, in their greatcoats with AK74s in their hands.

"What is this?" asked a large man with a Ukrainian accent, gesturing at the carnage. "What happened?"

"Sala Jihan happened," muttered a wizened old Uyghur man who was now standing next to Jill. She was frozen in shock. I don't think she had seen anything like this before. I had warned her about this part of the world. It was no place for the good. "The Pale Man sends a message to these people."

The lead soldier grabbed the waiter by the shoulders and shook him. "Go forward and tell the engineer to get this thing moving. He should not have stopped. Go! *Now!*" The waiter ran from the car in the direction of the engine.

"Aren't you going to help those people?" the Ukrainian businessman asked.

The old Russian soldier had a master sergeant's insignia on his great coat, and he looked like he had been around this rodeo a few times. "They are beyond help, Comrade . . ." *Yep, he was old guard . . .* "This is not our affair. There's no use in getting involved."

"But we are still in Altay! This is your jurisdiction!" The Ukrainian demanded. The train lurched forward with a *chug chug* noise as we restarted our journey.

"We may still be in Russia, according to the map," the soldier said with some resignation. "But it is not our *jurisdiction* anymore." The Ukrainian began to bluster. Some of the other passengers began to shout. The younger soldiers looked jumpy with their Kalashnikovs as the train car rolled forward. I grabbed Jill by the arm and tugged her back toward me. She was still transfixed on the village.

Then it was suddenly silent. Every one of us was looking out the window, without the words, as our train slowly moved past the things only a few feet outside the window. Some villagers had been left as an example. They had been impaled on stakes along the tracks. Even after all of the horrible things that I had seen in Chechnya, Bosnia, and Africa, I couldn't accurately describe what had been done to these people, flayed, burned, tortured, exposed muscle and dangling skin, white teeth and open eye sockets, and things I couldn't really understand.

I pulled Jill closer, and forced her eyes down. I shouldn't have let her come. The crowd tracked on the examples, heads moving as one as if in slow motion, as the train built up momentum and left them behind. Finally, the Ukrainian spoke, his voice quivering and higher pitched, like a child that had just woken up from a nightmare. "What manner of man could do something like that?"

The old Uyghur spoke again. "Is not man." He spat on the floor. "Is demon."

We all went back into our cabins and closed the doors, lunch forgotten.

LORENZO
Crossroads City
March 10th

"Welcome to the wild-wild-middle," Reaper said as he stepped from the raised platform of the train station and into the slush-and mud-covered street. The air smelled like cooking smoke, diesel fumes, and unwashed people. It was remarkably cold, but the street was crowded with busy people from every culture you could think of. The music of twenty languages bombarded my ears.

The surrounding mountains around us had been stripped of all their trees, and the amount of growth that had occurred here since my last visit was positively shocking. I grunted as I lifted my bags, marveling at the sprawling development that had seemingly sprung up overnight. The Crossroads had exploded.

The three of us were dressed in Mountain Yuppiflage, brightly colored, Gore-Tex parkas and snow pants. We looked like typical Europeans or Americans at a ski resort. I hated wearing anything colorful, but we had a cover to keep up. My coat was puffy, green with big black stripes. I was wearing a black neoprene skull cap and Bolle sunglasses. I hadn't shaved for the last few weeks and had a pretty decent beard going. Then again, I was one of those guys with a Homer Simpson face who could grow a goatee in forty-eight hours. The last time I'd been in The Crossroads I had been clean shaven with long hair, and that had been seven years ago, so hopefully I wouldn't run into anyone who would recognize me.

Jill's coat was yellow and Reaper's was red. With his hair pulled back in a ponytail and the facial piercings gone, Reaper actually could be pretty convincing as a professional techie type. He carried a briefcase filled with information about our make-believe mining concern. Jill was going to play the part of our young go-getter junior executive in search of cheap ore.

"Which way to our hotel?" Jill asked in Spanish. Her breath formed a steam halo around her face. We would be in character from here on out. "You, find out where the hotel is, and then get my luggage."

"Yes, ma'am," I answered humbly. For somebody with no criminal past, Jill had no problem playing pretend, either that or she just really liked ordering me around. I examined the crowd, looking for a potential guide that wouldn't just rip us off or lead us down some alley to get robbed and murdered. The throng of people was pushing and shoving, unloading cargo from the train, yelling in a dozen different language, and just taking care of random bits of business. They were dressed in everything from expensive Western clothing, like us, to Russian-style long coats and fur hats, to traditional robes and fur coats. Almost everyone appeared to be armed. The people who weren't, were either too poor to afford a gun or too rich to bother, and those guys were obviously flanked by armed henchmen.

I picked out a kid, probably eight years old, who was begging by the entrance to the first-class car. He held out his hands as I approached. I wasn't quite sure what he was, so I started with Russian. "Do you know where the Glorious Cloud is?" He cocked his head, so I asked him the same thing in Chinese. My Chinese wasn't as good as my Russian, but apparently he understood and replied with some rapid-fire chatter in a dialect that I barely understood. I held up some cash. We had a guide.

The boy led us through the streets of Crossroad City. The main road from the train station was asphalt and I think the side streets were gravel. There was so much snow and mud slush that it was hard to tell. I saw a few motor vehicles, usually bigger trucks, Russian 4x4s, a few horses and yaks, and surprisingly enough, bicycles. I wasn't sure how the riders managed to stay upright riding through ice, but they did. There were a few waiting rickshaw drivers who shouted for our business, but Ling had told me the Exodus meetingplace was near the train station. Being on foot gives you a better feel for a place anyway.

The buildings were of every sort imaginable, from concrete bunkers, to mud-walled compounds, to wood-frame buildings that would look normal in suburban America. The streets didn't even vaguely resemble straight lines. There was no rhyme or reason to how Crossroads City was laid out. There was no zoning here. Hell, there was no law whatsoever. People built whatever they felt like.

I watched the people. Business was being conducted on every corner. There was no central marketplace because the entire town was the marketplace. You could go to any street here, buy three machine guns, a sack of opium, and a chicken, and have change left over. One man handed over a small stack of currency to a street vendor, and the vendor passed back an RPG rocket.

"Gift wrap that for you, sir?" Jill giggled.

"Quiet." I could feel eyes on us. Everyone was watched here. Every worker, every peasant, and every hired tough was a potential spy.

The nicer buildings had sign posts in front of them. There usually wasn't anything actually written, just carved symbols, but I recognized a lot of them, Red Dragon Triad, Luminous Path, Chechen Brotherhood, Russian mob, Al Qaeda, Yakuza, heck, even the Sicilians had a rather nice brick rambler. Since I had left, The Crossroads had grown into a super criminal United Nations. If a mob boss six thousand miles away might need to get some particular bit of rare merchandise, or place an order for a huge amount of product, or even just have his emissaries sit down across the table from their rivals, this was the place.

Each faction had some toughs hanging out by their front entrance. Normally I would expect all sorts of posturing between the groups, but they seemed to ignore each other. All of them glared at us *legitimate* businessmen. As we passed in front of the sprawling Russian compound, one of the drunker Russians shouted something profane at my girlfriend while simulating something really nasty with his AK. *Classy bunch.*

We had to step aside to keep from being run over by a giant septic-pumper truck. "Well, at least they don't just throw it in the street, like most of the places we've worked," Reaper muttered. "Though they're probably gonna go dump it in the water supply."

This was Reaper's first time here. He'd probably be surprised that even criminal scumbags didn't want nasty water. "You had your shots."

"Stop, thief!" one of the street vendors shouted in Chinese. Ironically, three quarters of the people on the street looked up to see if they were the one being talked about. A young man in a fur robe crashed past me, pushing his way through the crowd and past the Russian compound, a bag of grain thrown over one shoulder. The various factions' toughs laughed and pointed.

The thief didn't make it far. A black shape materialized from around the corner ahead of the runner, and moved to intercept at an astonishing rate of speed. There was a sound like a watermelon hitting a bat, and the thief's head snapped back. He did most of a flip before landing in the snow.

The crowd froze. The noise in the immediate area died down to muted whispers. The man in black stood over the twitching thief. The new arrival was short and broad, cloaked from head to toe in some thick, shapeless furs with a large hood. Under the hood was a black mask and round, tinted goggles. The goggles surveyed the crowd, and I swear that even the Yakuza and the Chechens shrank back under that gaze. Canvas bandoleers of rifle ammo crossed his chest in an X, on top of that was a leather necklace strung with wolf teeth. He had an ancient M44 Mosin-Nagant bolt-action rifle in his hands, and a single drop of blood fell from the stock from where he had brutally clubbed the runner.

"One of the Brothers!" a nearby street vendor hissed. The black-clad man's head snapped in the direction of the voice, and the vendor fearfully averted his gaze.

The thief moaned, spat out a mouthful of blood, and started to rise, sack of grain spilled open beside him. He rolled over, realized who had taken him down, and immediately began to cry. I didn't know what language it was, but begging for mercy sounds pretty much the same everywhere. Without a word, the man in black flipped out the M44's bayonet and stabbed forward once. The scream turned into gurgling as the spike was twisted. Then the street was quiet again. The man jerked the spike out in a red splash. The tinted goggles surveyed the street once more before he wiped the blood off his bayonet on the thief's pants. He turned and walked away, never having said a word.

A moment later the street came back to life, as if nothing had ever happened.

The crowd was ignoring the dead body, except for a couple of street urchins who were already stealing his shoes and coat. Our guide looked wistful at the missed opportunity. "Who was that?" I asked the kid, putting my forefingers and thumbs in a circle over my eyes like I was wearing goggles. The boy said something I couldn't understand.

"The Brothers are the Pale Man's personal bodyguard. They keep the peace in town," said one of the more sober Russian mafia who had sauntered up behind us. He took a drag on his cigarette and blew it out in a cloud. "They don't ever talk, and they never show their faces. Nobody smart fucks with them."

"I don't think they're so tough," said the drunker Russian that had been offering his sensitive undying love to Jill just a moment before.

"Like I said, nobody smart fucks with them," said the first. "Shut the fuck up, Gregor. War between houses and stealing in general is bad for business. The Brothers kill anybody that messes with that, unless they take a liking to you—then they drag you off to the slave mines." I was supposed to be the interpreter, so I quickly translated all this into Spanish for Jill, and the lead

Russian took that as an indicator as to who was supposedly the boss. "Welcome to The Crossroads, lady. Should you businessfolk need any assistance, some of my men are always looking for freelance *security* work. And most of them are smarter than Gregor here. We're much more reliable than those slant-eyed homosexuals." He nodded down the street toward the other factions' houses.

"We'll keep that in mind, thank you," Jill responded politely, glancing nervously toward the dead thief, who was now missing most of his clothing. Even the grain was gone. "Are they just going to leave him there?"

The Russian shrugged. "It serves as a warning. If he's got family, they'll collect him eventually. Or not. The wolves creep into town at night when nobody's around, take care of it." He laughed, but I didn't think he was making a joke. "Enjoy your stay here."

I said goodbye to the Russian killers and we continued on.

A minute later our guide pointed at a wooden, three-story building, with a giant porch that circled the entire thing. Surprisingly, it looked rather nice. Nobody ever said anarchy had to be uncomfortable. There was a sign over the double door written in a few languages. I was able to read the third one down: *Glorious Cloud Hotel.* A roughly-carved wooden dragon was wrapped around the sign pole, breathing wooden fire. I gave the boy about $20 worth of rubles, and the way his face lit up, I could tell that was a big deal, easily worth passing up on looting the dead guy's shoes.

The interior of the Glorious Cloud was immaculately clean, and once the door was closed to the chaos of the street, the hotel lobby was peaceful and smelled like incense. The lady behind the desk was elderly Han, and extremely polite. She took our money, handed us a key, explained the meal schedule, and pointed us up the stairs to our rooms.

I handed her one final coin. "A tip." She took the coin, and rubbed her thumb around the outside edge without thinking. She looked at me curiously when she found that one edge of the coin had been smashed flat.

"Will you be staying until the thaw?" she asked.

"I'm told the forest is beautiful in spring." I completed the Exodus code phrase.

"Thank you, kind sir. Please enjoy your stay at The Crossroads."

The view out our window was spectacular. We were on the top floor, and the town stretched out below us in a confused mass before sprawling out into the edges of the mountains. The Crossroads were situated in an X-shaped valley. Each leg was about nine miles long, with the bottom two descending into China. Lake Tansai and the big dam built by the Russians was barely visible in the distance. Against the mountains a few miles away was the abandoned military base which had been taken over by Sala Jihan and turned into a fortress. If my brother was still alive he would be in there. The entire mountain around the base was torn open by a gash that could probably be seen from space. Those were Jihan's mines.

The Glorious Cloud's rooms were small, but clean. Reaper was off taking care of our *survey* gear that porters had delivered to the hotel.

I felt Jill's arms encircle me from behind. She squeezed me tight and tucked her face against the back of my neck. I could feel her warm breath. "You okay, honey?" I asked quietly. I had to remember, this was my world. Not hers.

"Yeah, I'm fine. I've just never seen anything like that before."

I didn't know if she meant the thief getting executed in the street, or the villagers' bodies left up as warning signs. Either way, it wasn't a pleasant welcome. "I know. I warned you about this place. I shouldn't have let you come."

"I didn't give you a choice. Don't worry about me. I'll be fine. I'm not going mushy on you. I have to do this. Bob's my family now too, and not only that, I owe those Majestic assholes."

"They did ruin your life."

"I can't say they ruined it anymore now, can I?" She squeezed me tight, as if afraid to let go. "But they did change it pretty drastically. I have to help you do this, you know that."

I gently disentangled myself, turned to face her, and took her into my arms. I well and truly loved this woman. "You really did beat me down over you coming on this job."

"Yeah, that was like our first real couple fight." She grinned. "Unless you count when we first met and you punched me in the stomach."

"Well, you tried to shoot me first."

"Fair enough." She snuggled in closer. "You know what else? We've been laying low on St. Carl for so long, we've never actually taken a trip before. This is our first vacation together."

"Hmm . . . Hadn't really thought about that," I said. "We should make the best of it." Then she bit the bottom of my ear. I checked my watch. Exodus could wait.

"Thank you for meeting with me, Mr. Lorenzo."

"Nice place you've got here. Wasn't this in *Raiders of the Lost Ark*?"

"I haven't seen that film." Ibrahim was an Iraqi Kurd. He was about my age, and appeared to be in extremely good shape. His greying hair was kept short, and his dark eyes studied me carefully as I sat across from him. The Exodus operative and I were sitting at a table in the rear of a bar near the hotel. The room was dark, smoky, loud, filled with boisterous drunken Mongolians, and reminded me of a third-world version of the Golden Manatee. "So, you're the man that freed Michael Valentine?"

"Yeah. That was loads of fun."

"His reputation is great amongst the men, and having a hero figure along for this sort of operation is good for morale."

"So Valentine's a hero figure now."

"You are not familiar with his exploits on our behalf in Mexico?"

"No, and it would be impossible for me to care less."

"Nonetheless, you have our sincere thanks." Ibrahim chuckled. "Shen told me that you were not friends with Valentine; however, Shen spoke very highly of your bravery and skills."

"Shen's here?" I glanced around the bar. I had no doubt there were some other Exodus types hidden among the patrons, but I hadn't seen him, but he was one of the only people I'd ever met who might be as unnoticeable as I was.

"He and Antoine are in The Crossroads. They will be assigned to one of the swords in anticipation of our assault, an assault which will have better odds of success now, thanks to your actions."

"Save the flattery, Ibrahim. I know the deal. So, has Ling kissed and made up with your superiors?" I asked with a smirk. "Invading Montana had to piss them off."

"How did you know that?" Ibrahim was suspicious.

"Ling was motivated. Even if your bosses had told her no, she would've still gone for it. Antoine and Shen would follow her no matter what . . . Chill out. You don't have a leak. I'm good at reading people. It's what I do. Whatever permission Ling had to pull off that stunt wasn't given *too* freely. Exodus is a low-profile bunch, and that certainly wasn't low profile. You might be happy to have your motivational poster on heroism, but that's a happy bonus is all."

"You are perceptive," Ibrahim was nodding. "Shen also warned me about that."

"Good. So we won't waste any time blowing smoke up each other's asses. Has there been any sign of my brother?" Behind me there was a crash as two Mongolians got into a fight. The topless dancing girl was knocked off her table.

Ibrahim shook his head. "Sadly, no. I can show you where he was attacked after speaking with Ling, the market overlooking the arena, but there has been no sign since. My people have been listening, but no one has spoken. Ling was the last person he was with, before he was captured near the fighting pits. I'm sorry." He must have seen my face darken, and attempted to change the subject. "After what Shen told me about you, I am glad that you and your people are here to join us."

"Listen, I think you and your folks are doing a good thing. Killing slavers is like killing cockroaches, but just so we're on the same page, I'm here for my brother. Nothing personal, I'm not the joining type. I'm going to meet with this Jihan asshole, see what we can find out, and go from there. If my brother's dead, I'm going home, but I'll pass on any intelligence I can gather just on the general principle that I don't like asshole warlords."

"I understand. The path that God has chosen for me is not for every man, but nonetheless, I appreciate your offer. And if your brother is still alive and being held in the fortress or in the mines . . ."

"Then, I'll gladly help you stack the bodies so deep they'll call it Great Wall of China, the Sequel."

Ibrahim laughed and struck the table. "Excellent, my brother!" He raised his cup of tea, I raised my drink. "To killing assholes!" It was good to see that not every team commander in Exodus was as intense as Ling.

"So what can you tell me about the situation? A lot of things have changed since I was here last."

"When Big Eddie died, there was a battle for control of The Crossroads. Whoever controls this place runs Central Asia. The Russian Mafia and the Triads lost a lot of men, as did the other factions that joined in. It was chaos. A situation which Exodus loved. While The Crossroads was unavailable, the evil which feeds upon this place was stymied. It was a glorious, but for all too short time. By the way, thank you for killing such a terrible man."

"Yeah, I'm all about making the world a better place."

Ibrahim swirled his tea and studied it. "Then after a few months of fighting, a new group arrived here. A man had taken the name of Sala Jihan, the Pale Man. Are you familiar with the old tales?"

"A little. Mostly campfire stories to scare little kids. Eat your vegetables or the Pale Man will come and get you, that kind of crap."

"Yes, the Pale Man supposedly terrorized this land a thousand years ago. Born of human mother and sired by the devil, he reigned with blood and fire. His slave armies crushed everything in their path." Ibrahim paused to take a drink. "He was a force of incredible evil. Finally, he was defeated by a great Mongol prince and imprisoned deep beneath the earth, but the local tribes maintain a tradition. There is a prophecy that someday he will return and reclaim his throne of blood."

I laughed. "Don't tell me you think this is the same guy?"

Ibrahim smirked. "No, of course not, but I think we are dealing with a very talented and evil man, who took the name of someone the locals are already terrified of and used that to his own advantage. In the many years

I've been in the Order, I've never seen a man such as this. His people came into this valley, and within three days he had utterly defeated the Mafia and the Triads. He impaled many of them on stakes in front of their houses, declared peace, and moved into the old base on the mountain. He's gotten the money flowing again, so the other factions are happy . . . for now."

"Think we could use that for our advantage?"

Ibrahim shrugged. "With as many spies as there are in this place, I'm hesitant to approach anyone. Certainly one faction would love to take Jihan's place, but as they say, it is the nail that sticks up that gets hammered down. Big Eddie's old faction, now called the Montalban Exchange after his real identity became known, seems like the most likely candidate to attempt a coup. It is led by one of Eddie's former lieutenants. They have a reputation for ruthlessness. Frankly, I don't care who takes over afterward, but Jihan must die. In the last year, he has systematically enslaved tens of thousands."

"You're exaggerating."

"Some things I do not joke about, my friend." Ibrahim reached into his shirt and pulled out a folded sheet of paper. It was a map of Asia. There were hundreds of red dots scattered around the map. "Each of those dots is, or was, a village. Jihan contacts the local governments, finds out who the troublemakers are, and then makes them go away. The Chinese hate the northern Uyghur minority, for example, so should one of their villages be raided, they do not care."

"That's a lot of dots."

"The youngest men are taken into his army and brainwashed as child soldiers. You will see them around town. Their faces are disfigured with a branding iron. He keeps a garrison at his base and uses them as guards over the mines. Do not let the fact they are slaves cause you to underestimate them."

"I've dealt with child soldiers in Africa. I know the deal."

"Not like this, you do not. His indoctrination techniques are very effective. The young women are sold internationally, through the various factions, for uses which I'm sure you understand. Everyone else works in the mines."

"I saw the mines from my hotel window," I said patiently. "You can't tell me there's ten thousand people housed there."

"Obviously not. There's a fifty percent fatality rate in the first month. The bodies are thrown into a very large hole . . ." He must have seen the look of disgust cross my face. "He works them to death, weeds out the *unsuitable*, and replaces them with more. Are you certain you still want to go home if your brother is dead?"

"I'm not a good guy, Ibrahim. That's a job for guys like you and

Valentine. My concern is me and mine. That's it. People like me don't adopt causes."

"Not the most honorable philosophy."

"It's kept me alive." I shrugged. "And your assets?"

"I have a few swords here. The others are staged in Mongolia, waiting for me to summon them." He smiled, knowing that I knew he was being purposefully vague as to their strength. I didn't even know how many men made up a sword.

"So what are you waiting for?"

"There are others available. They're wrapping up their tasks and then coming here. In the meantime, we're trying to gather as much intelligence as possible. We will need every man possible. We believe there are several hundred slave soldiers guarding Jihan's fortress."

"ETA?"

Ibrahim smiled again. "And I tell you this, and you find in your meeting with Jihan, that perhaps he would be willing to trade your brother for information about a gang of assassins plotting against him? Please, Mr. Lorenzo. The only way you will know our plans is if you volunteer to accompany us. No offense."

"None taken." This was business after all. "One other question. Who are the Brothers?"

"You saw one?" he asked. I nodded. "They are the Pale Man's elite personal guards. Since they never show their faces, never speak in public, and always dress the same, we don't know how many there are, but they enforce his rule in town. Everyone is scared of them. They are brutal."

"How many would you estimate there really are?"

"There are at least three."

I snorted. "Three goofy little bastards have managed to terrorize a town full of psychos, murderers, and hired thugs?"

He smiled at me. "You saw one, so I'm assuming you saw him murder someone."

"How'd you know that?"

"Because that's the only time you see them. If they reveal themselves, then somebody is about to die. Trust me, Mr. Lorenzo, the Brothers are very good at what they do. They and a small garrison of perhaps twenty slave soldiers have kept the factions from warring more effectively than hundreds of Big Eddie's mercenaries ever did. You must understand, this is a superstitious place, and Jihan has used that as a weapon. Do not underestimate his forces. These are not the back-country thugs you might be expecting. So, what is your plan?"

"We have a business meeting scheduled for tomorrow at the fortress. I'm going to—" There was a sudden loud crash at the front of the bar, followed by a lot of shouting in Mongolian. Two people seated near the entrance stood and headed directly back toward us. I placed my hand on my pistol, but Ibrahim signaled for me to wait.

"They're friends. What is it?"

The first spoke. "Montalban Exchange is starting some trouble out front. They're looking for somebody and want to come in." He was a handsome young man, and surprisingly enough had a bland American accent. "They're led by that big Viking-looking dude."

The second was a female, with the hood of her coat up, and a scarf covering the lower half of her face. She had really pretty blue eyes. "The Mongols disagree." She sounded Russian. "I think they're going to fight." She discreetly took a Makarov from inside her coat and placed it in an outside pocket, so it would be easier to shoot some unsuspecting sap.

"We'd best be going then." Ibrahim stood. "Mr. Lorenzo, this is Svetlana and Roland, two of my sword. You can reach us through the Glorious Cloud should you have any further information you wish to share. We'll be in touch. May Allah grant you good fortune on your mission."

Chapter 12: The Greatest Trick the Devil Ever Pulled

LORENZO
Sala Jihan's Fortress
March 13th

A weather-beaten statue of Stalin looked out over the valley. The concrete features had been mostly obliterated by wind and rain, but even then the blank eyes of the Man of Steel seemed to follow us as we drove past.

A Land Cruiser had picked us up in front of the Glorious Cloud, exactly on time. The driver was a young man with a large brand scar on each cheek. He had not said a single word the entire thirty-minute trip. None of us spoke either. Jill was nervous. I wanted to reach over and squeeze her hand, but that would have been out of character for a translator and his boss, so I refrained.

The road skirted the edge of the river and passed through the old dry lake bed before climbing into the mountains. The terrain at this altitude consisted of rock and scrub brush. There was no way to approach without being seen. The maps showed a possible path through the mountains to the back of the fortress, but it was impassable for vehicles and would be a difficult trek on foot.

The walls were tall, thick concrete. Guards paced atop, watching our approach through binoculars. The walls were too smooth to scale, and too tall to hit with ladders. Our driver steered the Land Cruiser between concrete barricades designed to keep a truck bomb from getting a good run at the entrance. The steel gate was already open, waiting for us. I noted the thickness of the gates as we passed through. Short of a tank or a whole lot of explosives, I didn't see Exodus getting through that quickly either.

Through the tinted glass of the Land Cruiser, I could see that the inside of the fortress was made up featureless concrete bunkers, each with its own heavy steel doors and narrow, metal-shuttered windows that served as firing ports. There was a raised concrete landing pad, sufficient for a few helicopters, though nothing was parked there now. The snow suggested that nothing had landed there all winter.

Reaper was gawking at something out his window. Behind the landing pad was a small hill with a tank parked on top of it. *Shit. That's no tank.* Instead of a single large barrel poking out of the turret, it had four smaller barrels and a rotating radar dish on top. It was a ZSU-23, a nasty antiaircraft machine, and unlike most of the military equipment rotting in this part of the world, it appeared well maintained. Four 23mm autocannons would rip the hell out of anything Exodus tried to land here.

The Land Cruiser stopped, and our doors were immediately opened for us by waiting staff. None of them would make eye contact. Behind them were more emotionless child soldiers. The oldest was maybe sixteen. They were of various ethnicities, but all were dressed in snow camouflage, wearing some sort of load-bearing vest, and carrying an AK or SKS. Each one had savage burn scars on their cheeks or forehead.

"Greetings and welcome." A muscular man in a business suit approached. His face was unscarred. He was here voluntarily. "I am Talak Aziz. I will be your escort during your visit here. After so many e-mails it is a pleasure to meet you in person, Ms. Garcia and Mr. Cook." He nodded at Jill and Reaper. I smoothly translated everything that he said into Spanish. Jill smiled and nodded as Talak gestured us toward the entrance of the largest bunker. "You will need to go through our security check, for your own protection, of course."

"Of course," Jill responded.

The soldiers gave us a thorough pat-down and even had a metal detecting wand. A woman checked Jill. We had left everything dangerous, sharp, pointy, or flammable at the hotel. This meeting was just to gather intelligence on our foe, nothing more.

Satisfied that we weren't assassins, Aziz took us inside. The entryway for this bunker had been decorated with expensive Persian rugs and Japanese landscape paintings. It was surprisingly nice compared to the stark exterior. A slave girl took our coats and disappeared. We were led through the bunker to a meeting room set up in much the same manner as the entrance, and we were seated on cushions. Talak remained standing as he introduced us to the men in European business suits who were already waiting. I struggled to keep up and to correctly pronounce everyone's name. They were all older, professional, and had that stink of dirty money on them.

I was disappointed. These were Jihan's functionaries, the guys that actually handled the business end of things, the money changers, the accountants. They were here to discuss the exchange of slave-mined ore for cash, and the shipment thereof to our subsidiaries for processing. They were talking dollars a ton and how much different countries' customs officials cost to bribe. I wanted to meet *The Man*.

Jill did a superb job. Reaper had coached her well. She played the part of a junior executive whiz-kid rather well. Her nervousness was actually perfect, because to Jihan's functionaries it read as her being scared about brokering a big-money deal. She was the only woman in the room. They probably thought she was the negotiator because she was pretty. Jill knew nothing about the technical end of things, wire transfers, transportation, amounts required, and the methods of exchange, which was obvious to the functionaries, but she wasn't supposed to. That's where Reaper came in. He didn't look like much, but if he hadn't damaged it with all the death metal and Red Bull he'd probably have an IQ up around Stephen Hawking's. He'd memorized every mineral-business-related factoid known to man in the last few weeks.

Meanwhile I looked unimportant, translated, and soaked up everything I possibly could about these people and their operation. Aziz was doing the same thing as me. You could hang a fancy suit on a killer gorilla, but it was always going to be a killer gorilla at heart.

Jill and Reaper wasted an hour butting heads with the hirelings, but it was a waste of time. I had only gotten a look at the security arrangements for a few seconds. This was not helping our mission at all. We hadn't fabricated an entire corporation, wired millions of my own money into it, and come all this way to look at spreadsheets.

Jill must have been feeling the same way. "My superiors were hoping that I could meet this Sala Jihan." As I translated that last bit, the hirelings stiffened up. Talak shifted nervously. "He's a very mysterious figure."

"Ms. Garcia, I'm afraid that will not be possible," stammered one of the functionaries. "Sala Jihan does not participate in these sorts of activities. He is a very busy man, and has engaged us to represent him."

"Yes, it wouldn't be proper," said an older Chinese man with a bad hairpiece. "We can assure you that we are fully vested with authority—"

Jill held up her hand. "And I can assure you, gentlemen, I am here to arrange the purchase of millions of dollars of precious metals a year from your operation. My superiors insisted that I not agree to anything until I have met the head of your organization in person."

"As you are aware, Sala Jihan's methods are different than what you are used to in the west." I tried not to chuckle as I translated that. *No shit.*

"Meaning that he uses slave labor?" Jill replied. The men shifted awkwardly. "We're fully aware of that, but we're expecting an emerging demand for copper that is unprecedented from the Indian market this year, and my company intends to fill that need. We don't care about the slaves. We care about building a long-term relationship so we can make a lot of money before one of our competitors grows the balls to come here themselves. You are sitting on billions, but you're limited to what you can sell through greedy mobsters. My company is offering a legitimate distribution channel. We feel the profit opportunity outweighs the possible negative press, but my superiors don't even know that Sala Jihan is *real*. I meet him, or there will be no deal."

The hirelings looked at each other, fearful of losing this deal, but more scared of contacting their boss. Talak actually choked when I translated *cojones*. He spoke up. "I will inquire if the Master is available. In the meantime, please continue with your negotiations." The big man left the room.

The meeting continued, only now that they knew Jill was playing hardball, it was a lot more heated. Ironically, since our entire operation was imaginary, Jill was having quite a bit of fun sticking it to them and playing up the heartless corporation angle. Twenty minutes later the door slid open and Talak entered, looking rather grim.

"The Master will see you now."

The trip across the compound alone was worth it. I was able to see more of the security, where the interior choke points were, where the vehicles were parked, and and where the guards slept. All of that would be good stuff to pass on to Ibrahim. Most importantly, I was able to spot which building had been the Russian brig. A handful of prisoners watched us from the other side of the bars with eyes pleading for mercy. It was very possible that—if he was still alive—Bob was inside that prison building. I scanned every window, but unfortunately didn't see a single giant, bald Caucasian.

Talak took us to a concrete slab with an elevator shed on top of it. Behind the shed was a giant circular depression in the snow. A Brother stood to the side of the door, studying us with goggled eyes, arms folded, and weapons slung over his back.

"He seriously lives in a missile silo?" Reaper asked. Talak didn't bother to respond, he only nodded at the guard, who continued to watch us soundlessly. The faceless black mask was strangely intimidating, but he stepped out of our path.

The elevator car was basically a steel frame with a mesh wire floor to stand on and handrails to hold on to, and a giant exposed pulley above us. It swayed dangerously as we stepped into it. Talak picked up a wired control box and punched the down button. With a lurch, the car began to descend. It was dark and strangely humid inside the shaft.

"I cannot promise a long visit," Talak explained, only his eyes and teeth really showed up in the dark. There wasn't a single light installed on the car. "He is a very busy man and agrees to speak with very few. You are rather fortunate."

"That will be quite all right," Jill responded after I translated, obviously agitated. I had forgotten that she was a little bit claustrophobic.

Talak turned to me, and the look he gave me indicted that this message was for me alone. "Listen, translator, if your employer says anything insulting, I would caution you not to relay it, or you will not make it out of this hole, because he *will* kill the messenger. Understand?"

I nodded slowly.

"Excellent."

After what seemed like forever, the car clanked to a halt, and Talak opened a scissor gate. We stepped into some sort of control room. The ancient computers were covered in cobwebs and dust. Punch cards were slowly eroding into the floor. He pointed at the far door. "Through there is the Master's living quarters. I will wait here for your return. Are you certain you wish to do this?"

If they wanted to kill us, they would have just done it on the surface and saved themselves the work. This was just more of that superstitious weirdo crap that Jihan was using to control The Crossroads. I glanced at Reaper. He looked even whiter than usual. Jill was sweating, surely thinking about the tons of rock crushing down above us. This Jihan really was a master of the mind fuck. "Ma'am," I gestured forward.

Jill swallowed hard. "Of course." She screwed up her courage and went through the far door. There was a long hallway, interspersed with submarine-style blast doors. They were currently open, but I made note that if Ibrahim needed to get down here, he was going to need to need explosives, cutting torches, and time.

We emerged into the flickering light at the bottom of the silo. It was a big area, the giant missile long since removed or launched. The open space spiraled up toward the surface, finally disappearing into shadow. I had been expecting some sort of palatial thing, with gold and diamonds, and the gaudy things that warlords liked to adorn themselves with to impress the fearful, greedy, and stupid. This was nothing like that.

The space was mostly open. The outer ring was just a walkway that circled the entire room. A catwalk extended to the center, where there was a circular concrete pad about twenty meters across. The base of the concrete disappeared into a pool of dark water that had settled in the bottom of the silo. The center pad had no decoration, just some nice, but very basic furniture; a bed, and some wardrobes, mirrors, and cabinets. On the far side of the pad was what appeared to be an altar, illuminated by candles and two large, metallic pans that were burning wood and incense. The crackling fire was the only source of light, and the smoke drifted toward the top of the silo.

"Weird," I muttered.

"I am Sala Jihan," a voice boomed from the island. "Come closer."

Jill started down the catwalk, with me right behind her. Reaper lagged a little bit behind. The metal echoed under our boots, and through the steel mesh, you could see down into the water. I couldn't see the bottom.

Sala Jihan was waiting for us, reclined on a plush red couch, facing the catwalk. He was wearing what looked like a red silk bathrobe tied with a black sash, was barefoot, and his hair was wet, like he had just gotten done swimming. The legendary Sala Jihan lived up to his title, the Pale Man. His skin was white, not like Reaper, but like a cave fish, almost translucent. I thought he was an albino until I saw his pitch black eyes.

Two more Brothers flanked Jihan. Even here in the near-dark they were still wearing their goggles. I didn't see any weapons, but I had no doubt the squat little men were fully ready to destroy us.

"Hello, I am Maria Consuela Garcia, and these are my associates—"

Jihan silenced her with a wave of his hand. "I know who you are," he answered in perfect Spanish. "Your translator will not be necessary," then he switched to accentless English. "Or would you prefer this?"

"Either will do," Jill responded slowly.

Jihan stroked his face thoughtfully. He had a thin mustache, pointy goatee, and long black hair. He was kind of like me, difficult to guess an age, but he appeared relatively young and fit. "I do not normally agree to meet outsiders. What would you ask of me?"

"My company just wanted to know what manner of man we were dealing with."

Jihan smiled. Perhaps it was a trick of the light, but his teeth looked like they had been sharpened, then his lips closed and I could no longer tell. He gestured at his surroundings. "I am but a humble man who likes to dig in the Earth. I find precious things as I dig, and sell them to people like you. It funds my . . . hobbies."

He exuded evil. It was hard to explain. A man like me needed to be an expert judge of character. I had known truly evil men before, but not like this. They say the eyes are the window to the soul, and in some of those men, I had seen broken souls, or in the case of Eddie Montalban, an emptiness. But in these black orbs, I saw something . . . *else*.

"Thank you," Jill said, her voice quavering slightly. She felt it as well. "I, uh . . . well . . ."

I noted the altar behind him. I had just assumed that Jihan would have been another Muslim warlord, but that altar was from something different, something *older*. "And what is it that you're digging for?" I asked, not knowing why I spoke, but regretting it immediately.

The warlord turned his head slightly, as if noticing me for the first time. The two Brothers visibly tensed beneath their robes. Jihan paused for what seemed like an eternity, studying me. It was as if somebody had turned on a million candle power spotlight, and I wanted nothing but to slink away and hide.

Finally he broke the awkward silence. "You are no mere translator, little man." He let that hang. I didn't respond, rather I tried to look as pathetic and bewildered as possible, but his black eyes were on me like a CAT scan. He continued to stroke his goatee. "You are a killer of men . . . a son of murder. So tell me, Maria, why did you bring an assassin into my home?"

My stomach rolled over in an acidic lurch. Nobody ever saw anything in me that I didn't want them to see. I was grey, unreadable. *What kind of man is this?*

"He's also my bodyguard," Jill spoke quickly. "The Crossroads have a reputation for being dangerous, and my company felt that security wo—"

He raised his hand to silence her. I felt the adrenaline begin to flow, fully expecting him to give the order to have the Brothers gun us down. Jihan smiled again, those strange eyes never breaking away from my own. "Yes, this country is quite dangerous." Something large splashed in the water under the catwalk. Reaper jumped. "It is wise to have one such as this to do your bidding." He gestured at me. His fingernails ended in points. "You may return to your organization and tell them that you have spoken with Sala Jihan, and that I am real. The precious things I take from the earth are yours to purchase. You may go now."

"But I was hoping to—" Jill began.

"That will be all." Jihan said in a manner that left no doubt that we would be feeding whatever the hell was in the pool if we didn't go away right now. The Brothers stepped forward and escorted us to the edge of the catwalk. I couldn't wait to get out of there. We walked—entirely too fast—across the catwalk back to the outer concrete ring. The Brothers stopped at the edge and folded their arms, a definite barrier to reentry.

"One last thing, oh, son of murder." Jihan's voice boomed behind us. I froze, a feeling of dread tingling up the base of my spine. Then I pushed Jill after Reaper out the blast-door exit before turning around.

"Yes?"

Jihan rose, the flames and smoke dancing behind him. "Where you have gone, death has followed like a loyal servant, but do not think to return to this place . . . For here, death answers only to me."

I nodded once, turned, and left the room.

We'll see about that.

✤ ✤ ✤

"Shit! What the fuck was that?" Jill shouted once we were back in the relative safety of the Glorious Cloud and away from spying ears. "Weird-ass bizarro shit! Did you feel that?"

Of course I had. Sala Jihan gave off a vibe similar to a bag of serial killers and electric eels, but I played the stoic. "Feel what?" I muttered.

"It was like all of the good in the universe got squished at the door to that place. Just, kind of . . . hell, I don't know . . . wrong." Jill threw up her hands in frustration, lacking the words to explain it.

"He's a slave-trading warlord. I warned you before we ever came. You wanted to play this game? Well, that's the opposing team. What did you expect? A nice house in the suburbs with a white picket fence, maybe some garden gnomes?"

"Not that, that's for sure," she answered. "There's something wrong with that man."

"He's messing with your head. It's his MO. That's how he runs this place so well. Yeah, he's one evil son of a bitch, but he's only human."

"I don't know, Chief." Reaper spoke for the first time. He was even paler than usual.

"Oh, not you too!" I said in exasperation. "Reaper, we've been through so much craziness, and you're gonna let this guy scare you?"

He bit his lip and looked down, embarrassed. "Well, yeah."

"Damn it! Don't be such a pussy," I spat. It wasn't fair. Jihan's act had shaken me as well, but I couldn't let it show. I had a mission to accomplish, and if my brother was alive, he was probably in that fortress. "Can I count on you or not?"

"Lorenzo!" Jill exclaimed. She wasn't used to me being mean to Reaper. "That's unnecessary."

I ignored her and glared at my subordinate. Jill gave me her Death Frown. I had known Reaper since he was a kid. He looked up to me like some sort of father figure. I knew he'd be brave if I required it of him. "I've never let you down," Reaper stated, clenching his hands into fists. "I ain't gonna start now. Screw this guy, he's goin' down."

"That's the spirit. Fuck Jihan. Now here's the plan. Make notes of everything, and I mean *everything*, that you saw in the compound, and we take it to Ibrahim and Exodus."

"So you've decided you trust them?" Jill asked.

"No, not really. Every human being I actually trust is in this room," I said. Reaper looked relieved when I said that. "In fact, before I set up another meet with Ibrahim, I want to poke around town some. We only have their word that it was Jihan's people that took Bob. I feel like Ling was telling the truth and Bob's notes point in that direction. Exodus has similar goals.

Enemy of my enemy is a friend, and all that. If they're going in and if I'm along for the ride, then I can get a look inside that prison building, but trust them? Hell no." I tossed Reaper a notepad. "Start writing while it's still fresh."

"What I wonder is, how did the Pale Man see right through you?" Reaper wondered aloud. "It isn't like you look dangerous or anything. You've done gigs way harder than that. Hell, you convinced the President of Sumatra you were his cousin that one time."

"Beats me," I shrugged. The locals would probably have some supernatural mumbo-jumbo explanation, but we were both men who knew how to sell a roll. Except I hadn't been able to see through his act at all. "He knows me now. So getting a covert look inside that prison isn't likely." I ditched my western style coat, and began rummaging through my bag for some more native clothing. My holster went on, disappearing under a bulky Turkic overcoat. "While I'm gone, don't let anybody in. Don't trust anyone. Not even the Exodus people. Don't answer the door, and if somebody tries to push their way in, shoot them a lot. Keep the fire stoked and toss your notes in there if anything feels off. If I'm not back by midnight, go right to the escape plans. Don't come looking for me, because you'll get eaten alive out there. I'm going down to the fighting pits. That's the last place Bob was seen."

"Sounds safe," Jill said. She was far too smart to even suggest going with me.

"Honey, this is The Crossroads." I chamber checked my 9mm before holstering it. "Nothing is safe here."

VALENTINE
Eastern Kazakhstan
March 13th

Our small caravan of trucks made its way along a mountain highway. Five trucks in all, loaded for bear with Exodus personnel and supplies, had departed the airport in the city of Semey, hundreds of miles to the west. We'd been driving for over fourteen hours. Kazakhstan was a huge country that had nothing equivalent to an American interstate highway. It had been slow going along poorly maintained two-lane highways the entire trip.

We switched out drivers as necessary, stopping only to refuel and for piss breaks. The residents of the little villages along the road to The Crossroads were used to comparatively rich foreigners buying gas from them, so we didn't draw any particular notice. The highway was cleared of snow, just as Ling said it would be.

Along our route there had been very little in the way of local law enforcement. I'm not sure if it was due to such things being bad for business at The Crossroads, or if the Kazakh government simply didn't bother to police the remote areas of the country. Either way, the lack of cops made me feel better. I hadn't had any good experiences with government authorities lately.

We did encounter one army checkpoint, as Ling had warned me we might. It was pretty far from the border. Their sole purpose seemed to be keeping track of, or possibly shaking down, the suspicious types who looked like they were on their way to The Crossroads. You know, people like us.

My heart rate doubled as we approached the checkpoint. There was an entire squad of soldiers, all armed, and we were all trapped in vehicles. I kept my head down and stared at the seat in front of me as a bored-looking Kazakh soldier looked in the window at me. Ling assured me that it was going to be okay. And so it was. A wad of currency was handed over, along with a carton of cigarettes and a couple bottles of booze, and the Kazakh soldiers lost all interest in us. We were left to go on our way without being searched.

We were in the home stretch after that. We slowly rumbled along Highway P-163. All around us were stunning mountain vistas and breathtaking, unspoiled wilderness, and damn, was it cold. The driver of the rattling diesel truck noticed that I was struggling to stay warm and turned up the heat. I didn't feel good.

Ling seemed to notice my discomfort. "It's the altitude. It will take some getting used to."

I shook my head. "Are we almost there?"

"Yes. We are just crossing the border into Russia now."

"No more checkpoints?"

Ling smiled. "Not so close to The Crossroads. It's bad for business."

The Russian side of the border didn't look any different than the Kazakh side. We continued to follow the river down a long, winding valley, until the highway began to veer off to the south. It was then that I saw, in the distance, the river pooled into a huge reservoir. Beyond it sat an imposing, ancient-looking dam.

"That hydroelectric plant was built in the Fifties," Ling informed me. "It powers The Crossroads and most of the small Russian villages in the area. The Kazakh government buys electricity from the Russians as well."

"Why did they build a dam so close to the border?" We were only a few miles from North China.

"1950 was the year the Soviet Union and China signed the Sino-Soviet Treaty of Friendship and Alliance. Stalin wanted to bolster relations with the People's Republic of China. The dam supplied electricity not only to Soviet villages, but to Chinese villages on the other side of the border. The town that became The Crossroads was once called the City of International Friendship. It was intended to be a symbolic beacon of international Communism."

"From what you've told me about the place, it doesn't sound very friendly."

"It was all lies, of course. Hardly anyone ever lived in their city of friendship, even at the best of times. When the Sino-Soviet Split happened in the late 1950s, The Crossroads was all but abandoned. Now the former communist city has turned into probably the most capitalist place on earth. The Crossroads is home to every international crime syndicate and black market imaginable. Anything goes, so long as you have the means to pay for it."

"You will never find a more wretched hive of scum and villainy," I mused.

Ling looked a question at me. She didn't get the reference.

"Seriously? Uh, never mind. What else?"

"The Soviets built a military base here after the Second World War. Joint military drills with the People's Liberation Army were conducted after the Friendship Treaty was signed, but like the town itself, it was all symbolic. During the Sino-Soviet Split the garrison was reinforced. Anti-aircraft batteries and surface-to-air missiles were emplaced. In the sixties, R-5 intermediate-range ballistic missiles were stationed here, and silos were built to house them."

Holy crap. "The Russians put *nukes* this close to the border?"

"Oh yes. They were quite displeased after the Communist Party of China formally denounced the USSR."

"Do the Russians still use the base?"

"Michael, didn't you read the briefing material I gave you?"

"I, uh, skimmed it." I'd slept on the plane from Azerbaijan and spent most of road trip across Kazakhstan sleeping as well. I had only glanced over the information, and mostly read up on what little there was about this Sala Jihan.

Ling shook her head. My physical condition wasn't much of an excuse for pity in her crowd. "There was an incident in '63. Most of it is rumor in any case. Madness high in the mountains, a Soviet drug experiment gone wrong, who really knows? The soldiers at the base mutinied. They turned on their officers and killed them in a ritualistic fashion."

"Ritualistic?"

"There aren't many details. According to the stories, the soldiers went insane. They didn't just kill their officers, they were sacrificed on a crude altar, their organs cut out, eaten, and their blood drunk as some form of sacrament."

"Jesus!"

"I doubt that is true. What is known is that a base, close to the Chinese border, housing nuclear missiles of the Strategic Rocket Forces, mutinied. The government was in a state of near panic."

"They bomb it?" That was the Russian response to most things.

"Yes. The Soviets lost several bombers in the effort, but they managed to destroy the air-defense sites. Elite KGB troops were parachuted in. After two days of fighting they retook the base. None of the mutineers survived. Shortly after that, the missiles were withdrawn from the area and the base was abandoned."

I whistled. "Wow. And I thought I had personal problems in the Air Force."

"They kept it secret, and the secret grew into a legend. The Soviets were afraid of this valley after that, leaving only a small number of troops to guard the dam. That garrison was removed when the Soviet Union collapsed and has never been replaced."

"So who runs the dam now?"

"The Pale Man runs the dam, Michael," Ling said, with a slight change in her tone of voice. "He runs everything through his intermediaries. Crossroads City sits right on the border between Russia and North China. Roads to it run in from Mongolia and Kazakhstan. The rail line from Russia to China is up and running again. The governments of all four of these nations abide the atrocities that go on here so long as they get a share of the profits."

As we passed the dam, I could see Crossroads City in the hazy distance, miles beyond the reservoir. It sprawled out haphazardly in every direction. A brown haze hung low in the air above the town, obscuring the view. I had heard of this place, of course. It was hardly a secret. It had its own Wikipedia page. To the world, it was just another lawless wasteland that occasionally rated a news blurb. It wasn't considered any different than the Horn of Africa, the Balkans, or countless other places where law and order had broken down. But The Crossroads *was* different. It wasn't lawless. It had Sala Jihan's law.

I looked at Ling as she gazed out the windows, and tried very hard to quash the terrible feeling that was eating at me. It wasn't just pre-operation jitters. Something was wrong with this place, and I very badly wanted to go home.

I'd promised these people that I'd help them, though, and I intended to see it done.

Chapter 13: The Arena

LORENZO
Crossroads City
March 14th

The Arena was right where I remembered it. The ramshackle buildings that had sprung up around the ancient ruins were situated high on the banks of the river that bled from the nearby Lake Tansai. If I was to follow the river for about thirty miles, it would eventually lead to Lake Hanas and the village of Kola Su in Xinjiiang. That was one of our possible escape routes if this went horribly wrong.

I had been to Kola Su once before, a very long time ago. It was a beautiful little place, rustic, but with beautiful old buildings and long, graceful, white bridges. Katarina and I had shared a small cottage there for a few weeks while laying low after one of Eddie's jobs. I still remembered one particular moment, waking up on a sleeping mat, and glancing over at Katarina, wearing nothing but my shirt, framed in the glorious sunrise, the crystal clear lake behind her, and her throwing rice balls at some weird looking Chinese ducks. That image had stuck with me for a lot of years. It had actually been a relatively peaceful stretch in an otherwise turbulent time of my life.

I shook my head, forgetting those useless memories, and refocused on the present. The arena was one of the larger structures in town, made of stacked bricks by the long forgotten people that had originally settled this place. It was sloped, with multiple tiers providing seating, so the residents of The Crossroads could watch their favorite sport: *violence.*

It didn't really matter what kind of violence either. The malcontents here were ready for anything that involved blood. The space inside the arena was set up for anything. There were smaller circular pits for cock fighting, dog fights, snakes and mongooses, and wider circles for wild horses to kick and bite each other to death. The losers ended up quartered and hanging from stalls in the marketplace. Eddie had even had the idea of posting these events live on the internet, and taking bets from a worldwide audience. I knew that he had made a particularly large amount of cash on a fight that had involved a Russian bear versus a pack of wild dogs.

The highlight of this casual brutality was the human fights. Nothing brought out the bets like a slugfest between random crazy people, and judging by the size of the crowd gathered around the main fighting pit and cheering from the arena steps, that was exactly what was going on right now. There were about two hundred people, and before I even saw the contestants, I could tell who was involved by the spectators. A group of Russians were the loudest, shouting, and chanting for their guy, while on the other side, a smaller group of Mongolians had some sort of song going on. I merged with the middle group, made up of everybody else who didn't have a dog in this fight, and jostled my way to the front of the pit.

If the fights had any rules, they were usually agreed to by the factions beforehand. If the rules were broken, then the two groups would usually settle the difference by shooting each other. At least that was how it had worked in the past when Eddie was in charge. With the Brothers running the show, I wasn't sure how disagreements would play out. An old Chinese man was walking back and forth around the lip of the pit, big wads of colorful money in each fist, shouting and pointing, taking bets from the mob.

Ah, a knife fight. So much for rules.

Both men were shirtless, even though as the Sun dipped behind the mountains it wasn't even twenty degrees out. The Russian was older, with short, graying hair, and muscles like twisted rope. The Mongol was bigger, younger, looked stronger, with his hair tied back, and was wearing, believe it or not, what looked like pink hot pants. Both of them had a lot of laceration scars, and were armed with very short knives. Of course, long knives make for a shorter fight.

The Chinese bookie was done taking bets. He shouted something unintelligible, both sides began to scream, and the fighters started to circle.

Having no need to watch this, I scanned the crowd. I was looking for information, and watching two psychopaths cut themselves to ribbons for entertainment, pride, and a little bit of money was not my idea of a good time. The market area that Bob had last been seen in was only a little bit further to the north.

One face caught my eye. The easiest way to spot a tail was to wait for some event that naturally draws everyone's attention, like for example, a knife fight. Then all of the normal people tend to look at the action. Somebody up to no good will be looking at you. The man was walking toward me, moving smoothly through the bustling crowd. He was really tall, broad shouldered, blond, with a bristling beard. His eyes were a cold Nordic blue, and he looked away as soon as he saw me turn. Now he was watching the fight like everybody else.

Got you, asshole.

I pushed to the side past a few random peasants, hunching down into my coat, and pulling my fur hat lower on my head. I didn't know who the tall guy was, and I didn't know if he'd brought friends. Best to fade away, then take stock of the situation. I made it all of fifteen feet before somebody bumped into me and tried to pick my pocket, which wasn't really a shock in this bunch. *Amateur.* I blocked the grab, caught the thumb and twisted it in a direction that nature had never intended. The pickpocket cried out, but I was already gone.

I circled toward the other side of the arena, but couldn't spot the tall man. *Damn it.* He had to be moving too, and a split second of being distracted by a random thief had given him enough time to fade. He was good. You would think somebody that tall would be easy to pick out in central Asia, but both the Russians and the Mongols had some big boys.

The crowd went nuts at first blood. One of the fighters had just gotten lit up.

The stone wall at the side of the ruins was in the shade. I scanned both ways, didn't see the tail, and ducked into the dark. There was a tunnel there that ran beneath the seats for about twenty feet before coming out the other side. As soon as I was alone, I tossed my fur hat, took out my black skull cap and pulled it on. Every little bit could help, and if my tail had programmed himself to scan for that hat, it might give me an edge. My sunglasses went on, and if it wouldn't have looked suspicious walking around without one, I would have ditched my Turkic coat.

Who was following me and why? Could it be one of Jihan's men? But that didn't make sense. He ran this place. If he wanted to take me out, he would have just done it back in the silo. Maybe somebody was just looking to kidnap and ransom a wealthy westerner, and I was supposedly Jill's translator. It was doubtful anybody would recognize me from the last time I'd been to The Crossroads.

I stepped over a passed-out drunken Kazakh, thought better of it, went back, and relieved him of his stinking coat. I draped mine over him, and pulled the filthy thing over my shoulders. He really got the better deal out of that trade. Then I was into the light on the other side of the seats, head down, hands in my pocket, walking briskly in the direction of the market.

"Hello, Lorenzo."

I stopped. The noise had come from above me, from the arena seats. Turning slowly, I nodded at the tail. He was good. He must have seen me enter the tunnel, and he had hurried right across the top and waited for me on the other side. He was sitting on the third row of stones, studying me emotionlessly, not breathing hard from what had to have been a good run to catch up. Everyone around us was watching the fight, so nobody noticed the HK .45 dangling from one hand.

His voice was dead calm. I'd seen the gun, so he moved it under the edge of his coat and kept it there, hidden, but still ready. He had spotted me even when I was trying to be grey. He had tailed me without my noticing for an unknown amount of time. Once I'd made him, he'd caught up and revealed himself rather than shoot me in the back. That meant he wanted to talk business. It was rare that I let somebody get the drop on me. This was a professional.

"Do I know you?"

He ignored the question. "You met with Sala Jihan. That makes you an important man around here." He could tell I was doing the math. "I've been told that you're extremely fast, but I *am* faster, so don't do anything stupid. You're coming with me."

An American? "Where are we going?" I saw no opening. My body was relaxed, hands loose and ready, but my brain was flipping cartwheels at a million miles an hour. I would only have a split second to move and get to my gun. We were only a few feet apart. There would not be any room for error.

"Montalban Exchange."

Oh fucking shit.

"No thanks."

"Have a seat." He patted the spot next to him with his left hand. The tall man waited only a moment before adding, "Not a request." He nodded his head toward the far side of the market.

I followed his gaze. Several men were getting out of a 4x4 with tinted windows. "I don't really feel like having a gunfight right now," I said simply as I walked up the steps and sat next to him.

"It wouldn't be much of a fight."

What the hell was he doing? Montalbans? Did they know I'm the one that blasted Eddie? Would they care? The stone was cold and uncomfortable. We were now at bad breath distance. Around us the crowd continued to scream and chant, apparently the knife fight was one hell of a show.

We were both silent for a moment. He was big, and it was obvious even while wearing a heavy coat that he was thick with muscle. He didn't have a neck. Instead, muscles like pot roasts came out of his shoulders and met up under his ears. An anvil-like head sat on top. I sat just to his left, his right hand was crossed over his body, under his coat, pointed at my midsection now.

"No." He shook his head slightly. "I know what you're thinking, because

I'd be thinking the same thing in this situation, but if I was supposed to kill you, you'd already be dead. And even if you got lucky, you wouldn't get back to the Glorious Cloud before we got your people."

Shit.

"I don't get menaced by Vikings that often. So who're you?"

"My name's Anders." I waited, but he didn't elaborate further. He seemed content to sit, half watching the fight, and half waiting for me to try something stupid. Finally after a moment, he spoke again. "So, who do you think will win?"

"Huh?"

"Russian or Mongol?" His voice was emotionless, as if watching a fight to the death was like watching the Weather Channel.

Both of the combatants were bloody now, spinning, and circling, lashing out at each other, then dancing away. Inwardly I was dying, trying to think of something, anything, that I could do. So I decided to answer his question. I wouldn't say I was a master of the blade or any macho horseshit like that, but I had been stabbed, cut, and slashed, and even killed quite a few people with various sharp or pointy things myself over the years.

The fighters were hurting, both were breathing hard, slick with sweat and blood. The Russian had the more serious injury, a cut to the muscles of the abdominal wall that was bleeding profusely.

"The Russian," I said.

"Wanna bet?"

"Twenty bucks says the Russian kills him in the next two minutes."

"You're on," Anders responded. "The Mongolian's bigger, younger, stronger."

"See how the Russian has those faded blue tats? Russian prison tats. They're always blue like that. Means he's done hard time." The Russian twisted and dodged as the Mongol swept in, a flurry of back and forth swipes. "The crucifix means he's the highest possible rank. The crown on top makes him *Pakhan,* a leader."

"So? He's old." Anders looked to be about my age, but it was hard to tell with the beard.

"The skulls mean he's a murderer, and the number means he's done a bunch," I pointed. "The stars on his back are one for each year he was in, and the knives pointing up in the stars . . . "

The old Russian had waited long enough and his boys had placed enough bets at bad odds. The young Mongol thought he was winning, so he pushed in, hard and fast. The Mafioso took a small cut to the chest, but climbed right up the Mongol's arm, driving the short blade in, running it up the limb, opening it like cleaning a fish. The younger fighter screamed.

"Shit," Anders muttered.

"The knives are pointing up, which means his murders were straight up prison fights. If they were down, then it would have been by stealth. So counting from here, it looks like he's won twenty-six knife fights."

The Mongolian stumbled back, blood flowing everywhere. A knife wound is all about running the clock. As soon as you cut somebody, a clock starts. The body can compensate for a lot, but the more you hurt it, the less it can compensate for, the faster the clock runs down. When the clock hits zero, you're done.

The Mongolian was getting wobbly now. The Russian probably could have just hung back and let him bleed out, but that wouldn't have been sporting. He went low, caught the Mongol's wide swing, and ran the blade from the kid's belly button around to his kidney. The Russian jumped back before there was a response, and then a shower of blood doused the side of the Mongol's pink hot pants. The Russian pumped his fist in the air and bellowed as the Mongolian went to his knees in the black dirt of the arena. The Russian side of the arena went nuts, chanting his name. A rope ladder was rolled down for their champion.

"Make that twenty-seven. Now pay me my twenty bucks, asshole."

"I'll pay you when we get back to my place," he said. "Now . . ."

Pain burned through my arm as Anders jabbed a long, spring-loaded needle into my neck.

"Gah!" I stood up and yanked the needle out. "What the fuck?" A thick burning sensation worked its way down my shoulder, into my arm and my chest. It was like hot wax was being pushed through my veins.

Anders was nonplussed. He watched me carefully, ready to pull his .45, but didn't move. "Calm down, Lorenzo. Trust me, you're going want to keep your heart rate down."

I cursed and swore at the pistol-packing viking, but the words didn't come out right. I was mumbling, babbling, not sure of what I was saying. My mind raced but I couldn't focus. Darkness edged into my vision. I tried to back away, but his men had already come up to keep me from falling and making a scene.

As I faded out, I realized Anders was standing next to me. "Shit works fast, don't it?"

Black.

Chapter 14: Hunting Season

VALENTINE
Crossroads City
March 15th

I was roused out of bed early in the morning, long before the Sun came up. Exodus had established a number of safe houses in Crossroads City, spreading themselves out to try to reduce their apparent signature and keep a low profile. Ling and I had been dropped off at one of them with all of our clothing and equipment. Not everyone was in place yet, so Ling was very busy.

The building was one of the structures erected by the Soviets in 1950. Bland and featureless, it was on the far north end of town, crumbling from decades of disuse and tagged with graffiti in four different languages. It had electricity, sort of, but no functioning toilets or showers. Field-expedient means of hygiene were necessary and unpleasant.

We were posing as a group of mercenaries for hire. There were several such groups in town, and while we were sure to draw the ire of our supposed competitors, we were less likely to gain the notice of Sala Jihan. Enterprises of all sorts and varying levels of legitimacy came and went through The Crossroads all the time. With Sala Jihan's own forces keeping the peace, we weren't especially concerned with being attacked outright.

After a brief, frigid scrub in an improvised shower, I dressed myself in some civilian attire I'd been given and found Ling in the main room. Two men, other Exodus personnel I guessed, were with her.

"Good morning, Michael," she said, as I walked in. "Allow me to introduce my comrades." Ling indicated a fit-looking Middle Eastern man with a thin mustache. "This is Ibrahim Barzani, one of our strike team leaders."

Ibrahim offered me a firm handshake. "Mr. Valentine, it is most excellent to meet you. Your reputation precedes you."

"Nice to meet you."

"This is Hideo Katsumoto," she said. An imposing Japanese man with a shaved head bowed politely, a move which I awkwardly attempted to return. He then shook my hand, and though his hands were thinner than mine, he had a grip like a vice.

"Mr. Valentine," he said curtly.

"Michael, we will be working with Katsumoto during the operation."

"I am happy to have Ling at my side during this operation," Katsumoto said. "She will be my second-in-command."

I wondered how Ling really felt about effectively being demoted from team leader, but Ling's face was a mask, as always. "You will be with us, Michael, if you're feeling up to it."

"Doing what, exactly?"

"I must be blunt," Katsumoto said. "I do not like the practice of colluding with outsiders. As I'm sure you can understand, they are often security risks and prove to be less than reliable. Ling has vouched for you, however, and we are short on personnel. If you wish, you may come along on the mission and assist however you can."

"You're not an initiated member of our order, so you will not be in the chain of command," Ling clarified. "But an extra hand with as much combat experience as you have would be a great asset to the operation."

It sounded like Ling was talking me up, trying to convince the others that I was worth the trouble they went through to get me. I figured they were just sticking me with her because they didn't know what to do with me. Fair enough. They could have just left me to rot in North Gap, so I didn't feel I had any grounds to complain. I wasn't sure if I was in any shape to fight, but I tried to conceal my misgivings. These people had done a lot for me, risking their lives in the process. I felt obligated to put on a brave face. "I'll do what I can," I said with fake confidence. "But I don't know what we're doing here. I've only been given the briefest of overviews on this entire operation."

Ibrahim and Katsumoto looked at each other, then at Ling. "For operational security reasons, you won't be given a complete overview, I'm afraid," Ibrahim said. "Please, Mr. Valentine, we mean no disrespect. We have procedures . . ."

I waved my hand. "It's fine." I'd spent too long as a mercenary to expect otherwise. "I don't need to know what I don't need to know."

"No, you do not," Katsumoto replied. "Our swords won't be directly involved in the primary assault on Sala Jihan's compound. That will be Ibrahim's responsibility. Our mission is to capture the hydroelectric plant upriver."

"I see." I was honestly intrigued. "Are we going to disable it, cut off their power?"

"In part," Ibrahim answered. "We have acquired detailed plans of the structure. Our engineers have determined the best possible points of attack. We have more than sufficient explosives to structurally compromise the dam forever."

I thought about the huge reservoir upriver from the dam. "You're going to blow the dam and flood the town?"

Ibrahim nodded. "It is for the best."

I looked at the three Exodus warriors in front of me, and didn't know what to say. Flooding the valley would drown thousands of people. The deluge wouldn't discriminate between the deserving and the innocent. The surprise on my face must have been evident.

"It isn't like that at all, Michael," Ling said.

"The dam will not fail immediately. If our engineers are correct, eventually the dam will collapse and flood The Crossroads. They will have time to evacuate. We expect the people who live here will disperse once the power fails. If any are foolish enough to remain in this wicked place, then they do so at their own risk. Regardless of whether or not the mission to kill Sala Jihan succeeds, we shall cleanse this valley and wipe The Crossroads off the face of the earth."

"You must understand." Katsumoto said. "This place was used for horrible things when a lesser man ruled it. Now someone truly evil is in charge and it has only grown worse. Should Ibrahim's attack fail, this is our only hope of ending the human trafficking in this part of the world. Even if Ibrahim succeeds, there is no promise that the cycle will not continue, with Jihan replaced by another, just as he replaced Eduard Montalban before him. It is necessary."

If the people who lived here didn't clue in and evacuate, they would die. Exodus was utterly committed to their mission, to the fundamental belief that they were doing the right thing. I wondered what it was like to have that kind of certainty in life. On the other hand, everything I'd learned about The Crossroads was unsettling. Of all the places in the world that could stand to be wiped off the map, it was pretty close the top of the list.

These people respected me. Despite my misgivings, I was going to stay professional. "Understood," I said simply.

"We will get into the specifics of the operation later," Katsumoto said. "For now, just know that we have discussed this matter at length. If there were not so many tens of thousands of innocent lives in danger, we would not be taking such drastic action."

Ibrahim addressed Ling. "There is another matter we need to bring to your attention. I have met this Lorenzo you spoke of. He is much as you described, driven, yet shortsighted."

"He is a horrible man," Ling said. "But he grows on you."

"So does a fungus." Ibrahim grinned. "Yesterday, Lorenzo went into the fortress and met with Sala Jihan."

Ling's eyes widened. "Face to face?"

"Yes. One of his people, the skinny young man with the long hair and bad complexion, brought me the intelligence they had gathered."

"Reaper?" I asked.

Ibrahim nodded. "They are staying at the Glorious Cloud Hotel. Lorenzo departed that location after he told young Mr. Reaper to see us. He went to the arena, but was involved in an altercation there and disappeared."

I could see the concern on Ling's face. If the damned fool had gotten himself captured it could compromise everything. I was personally, *bitterly* aware of the consequences of getting yourself caught.

"We believe he was taken," Ibrahim said. "Our operative had to leave the scene, as an altercation would have attracted the attention of the Brotherhood, but he was able to take this picture." Ibrahim retrieved a smartphone from his pocket, tapped the screen a few times to bring up the picture, and handed the phone to Ling.

The picture was slightly blurry; the photographer was probably moving when he took it. Lorenzo was being choked out by a large, muscular man with short-cropped, blonde hair. The beard was new, but I recognized him.

My blood ran cold. "*Anders.*"

I spent the next half hour filling my Exodus compatriots in on everything I knew about Anders. He had been Gordon Willis' right-hand man for Project Heartbreaker. I hadn't seen Anders since the operation in Yemen, where we recovered a stolen nuclear warhead that was en route to General Al Sabah. I had no idea what happened to him after I killed Gordon.

"He was with Majestic," Ling said. "Is he still?"

"I don't know. I sure hope not. He was in on Gordon Willis' dealings with Eduard Montalban, I know that much. I also know that those dealings were off the reservation, done on the side. After everything was found out, he may have had to get out of the country. Gordon's superiors were mad at him, but I don't know what went on with Anders. Hell, they should have been interrogating his ass instead of me at North Gap. Lord knows the son of a bitch has it coming. I guarantee he knows more about Project Blue than I do."

"What is Project Blue?" Katsumoto asked.

"That is the question isn't it?"

The Exodus man humorlessly raised an eyebrow.

"It's a long story and not relevant right now. But you need to know that cold hearted bastard is one of the most dangerous men I've ever met."

Ling looked thoughtful for a long moment. "Why did he take Mr. Lorenzo? It can't be a coincidence."

LORENZO

Gideon Lorenzo sat on the fallen log, leaned his Model 70 Winchester against the bark, and used a handkerchief to wipe the sweat from his forehead. Dad's bad knee was really bothering him today, and it had been a heck of a hike up the mountain. Bob and I stopped to wait for him in the peach-colored light that came just before dawn in the Texas foothills. Bob took the opportunity to take a long draw from his canteen. Both of us were young, and in excellent shape. It was only a few days after my fifteenth birthday.

"Bob, do me a favor."

"Yeah, Dad?" my older brother said as he twisted the cap back on his old Boy Scout canteen. He was a senior in high school now, and was looking more and more like Dad every day, a veritable giant of a man. Unfortunately, Bob had also inherited the bald genes, and his hair was already thinning.

"Run along to the deer camp, and tell your uncle that we'll be along in a minute. Ammon gets all excited if anybody's late, and he'll probably send out a search party. Hector can stay with me."

"Sure thing," Bob slung his .30-06 over his shoulder and gave me a thumbs up, "Take care of the old man for me, bro."

Dad snorted. "Old man . . . And Bob, remember, if you see something," Dad glanced at his watch. "It isn't legal for another . . . fifteen minutes." As a municipal judge, it really shouldn't have been a surprise that the senior Lorenzo was such a stickler for the rules. There wasn't a hypocritical bone in his body, and even if the rule was dumb, he obeyed it, because he had to sit in judgment of others using the same rules.

"Okay, not like I ever see anything anyway. Hector's the killer. See you guys in a minute." He turned and jogged up the hill.

Dad waited for him to leave, then he patted the log next to him. "Take a seat, Hector. Enjoy the sunrise with me."

I could tell he wanted to talk to me about something. I sat, and waited, my old Savage lever action in my lap. The forest was quiet. I was uncomfortable in the woods. It was strange, the farther I got from pavement, the more twitchy it made me. I liked having noise and people. In the woods, it's just you and what you really are. You can't pretend to be something else when it's so quiet and empty. The woods are about truth.

But the Lorenzo family loved the annual deer hunt. The younger kids really enjoyed the camping. I didn't mind hunting. Apparently I was really good at killing animals, and they sure did taste great.

"So, how's the leg, Dad? I can take your pack."

He smiled. "Naw, I'm fine." Which was a lie. His leg hadn't been fine since some communist had tried to blow it off. He lived in constant pain, but you would never know it since he never let it change his attitude. "I just wanted to talk to you for a minute."

"That time of year again? I already know. He's not getting out." The parole board had no interest in talking to me. They knew my opinion. If I had one regret in my life, it was that I had not had better aim when I'd stabbed him with that fork, and gotten my real father in the jugular instead of the eye socket.

"No, not that," Dad coughed. "Honestly, we both know he's not going anywhere. This is Texas, thank God. Men serve their time here. No, it is something else."

I waited.

"I'm worried about your future, Hector."

"My grades are better. I'm trying harder in class," I lied. I hated school. Bob was the one with straight A's, and a football scholarship. Dad was probably worried I was going to end up digging ditches. Either that or he was going to warn me about the dangers of rock and roll music again.

"No, nothing like that. In fact, Mr. Thompson told me the other day that you excel at . . ." he paused, as it was kind of distasteful, "drama. And Coach McClelland says you have a real gift for gymnastics, that you could even take state if you put your mind to it . . . and there's nothing wrong with either of those things," he quickly added. The Lorenzos were manly men, and neither of those things were exactly "manly" endeavors in his view.

"Dad, I promise. I like girls."

He rolled his eyes. "That's not what I meant. It's just that . . . Eh, I don't know how to explain it. I'm concerned about your outlook. You know the kinds of people I've deal with."

"Politicians? Lawyers?"

"No, I was thinking of the people I send to jail, dishonest, thieving, amoral . . . so actually, I suppose most of the politicians and lawyers I deal with would fall into the same category . . . " he chuckled as he thought about it, but then his face darkened, and turned grim. "It's just that sometimes I feel like I get a glimpse of what you're going to be like as you get older. You've got a lot of anger in you still."

I shrugged. Probably true, but all things considered, since I had been taken in by the Lorenzos, I had been a relatively good kid.

"I look at some of those men that I send to jail, and sometimes, I see you, and I worry. Some of them have the same kind of attitude you do. They think that what they are is what they are, and that they can't change. People aren't set in stone."

"I'm not going to do anything stupid, Dad. Don't worry," I assured him. "You guys have been great to me. I won't let you down."

"But I'm not going to be around forever. Just remember, no matter what happens, a man can always repent. They can always change. You know, there're three kinds of people in the world." He ticked them off on his fingers. "Good guys, bad guys, and those that don't care. Now most people, if you ask them, they would say they're one of the good guys, but really, they don't care. They're good as long as it's convenient. Bad guys, well, I'm afraid you know a lot more about them than any young person should ever have to. But you want to be a good guy. Sometimes, life makes it easy to be a bad guy, or for those that don't have the stomach for that, then they fall in that great grey middle ground. But to be one of the good guys, that takes work. It takes honor."

Dad was rambling now. He did that once in awhile. "I'm not going to get in trouble with the law."

He laughed aloud. "Law? Boy, good has nothing to do with the law. You can be the most evil son of a bitch to ever walk the earth . . ." that surprised me, he rarely, if ever used bad language, "and still obey the law. Heck, you can even write the laws. No, good means you do the right thing. Even when it hurts. Bad men can become good. I've seen it happen, and a good man can go bad."

"Okay," I humored him. Sometimes he liked to get philosophical. The Lorenzos were very religious, but Dad had never pushed any of his personal beliefs on his children. He just tried to teach them, and let them choose for themselves. He did make us all go to church every Sunday, however. I didn't really mind, because there were some really good looking girls at church.

There was a crack of a gunshot from over the hillside. Gideon Lorenzo looked at his watch again. It was a very nice watch, inlaid with silver, with an onyx face, and had been given to him as a present from his father when he had graduated from law school. He sighed. "Looks like Bob jumped the gun by four minutes. That's buck fever right there."

"The scoundrel," I said, imitating Dad's voice perfectly. We both laughed.

He put his arm over my shoulder. "Be good, Hector. That's all that I ask. . . . We better get going."

Then the Sun was up.

It was morning.

LORENZO
Crossroads City
March 15th

It was morning.

My head ached. I cracked open my eyes and scanned the room. I was lying on a bed. I'd been dreaming about my foster father, and the last thing I recalled was him looking at his watch. It was the same watch that would cost him his life the year I turned sixteen. Ruthlessly beaten until his internal organs had ruptured by a gang of worthless hoodlums, because they thought his watch could be hocked for drug money. The law hadn't caught them, but I had. I'd dropped off the world to find them, and kill them, and I'd never looked back.

The sheets were bright white and smelled like fresh soap. Outside the window, a rooster crowed. The room was empty of decoration. There was only a small table by the bed with a pitcher of water and a cup, and two chairs near the closed door. Both chairs were occupied by men armed with P90 submachine guns.

"Hey." My head was stuffed with a foggy, hung-over feeling. "Bring me that punk-ass bitch, Anders. We've got some unfinished business."

"Good morning, sir," replied the first guard. They both had that eurotrash look that the Montalban retainers seemed to cultivate. Even with Big Eddie dead, his people still tended to look like something from Sprockets. "Your clothes are under the bed. We took the liberty of washing them. Your presence has been requested at breakfast."

At least they were polite. "Where's my coat?"

"The one you stole off the drunk under the arena?" said the second. "It smelled like piss. We burned it. Now hurry up, the boss doesn't like waiting."

Breakfast with the head of the Montalban Exchange? I just hoped that Jill and Reaper had stuck with the plan and bailed when I hadn't come back to the hotel last night. This very well might be my last meal.

The Montalban Exchange building was large, solidly constructed, and sat on a hill overlooking most of the other faction houses. The architecture was vaguely Chinese, with a red roof with upswept corners. The dining room was on the third floor, with a good view surveying the chaotic town, the mountainside, and the mighty gash in the earth that was Jihan's mines. The walls were made of polished local wood and the floor was covered in thick rugs. A giant rectangular table filled most of the room, and it appeared to have been carved from a single epic tree. There was no one else there.

The guards gestured for me to take a seat. They then left me alone, sliding the bamboo door closed behind them.

I could hop out the window. It was a good drop to the ground, but with my acrobatic skill, I had no doubt that I could roll with it and still walk away. Then all I had to do was somehow make it out of town and then cross a whole bunch of wilderness with the Montalbans after me. And that was assuming that they didn't have Jill and Reaper. Anders had clearly known about them. So I sat and waited. Besides, if they wanted me dead, they could easily have done it already.

Drumming my fingers on the table top, I tried to think of what could be going on. Maybe whoever was in charge now was happy that Eddie was gone. Maybe they were going to throw me a big thank-you party. I scanned the room. No balloons. No cake. *Probably not.*

The roof of the Glorious Cloud Hotel was visible from here. I had let Jill come along against my better judgment. She wasn't cut out for this kind of mission. I'd given in to her, and now she was in danger because of me. I was such a fool.

"It's been a long time, Lorenzo."

The bamboo door had opened so smoothly behind me that I'd not even heard it. The voice was female and hauntingly familiar. The accent was Swiss.

"Seven years," I said automatically, without turning. "Hello, Katarina."

"Really, that long?" I could sense her walk up behind me. One of her hands landed softly on my shoulder. Her fingernails were painted blood red, and she dragged one up my neck, caressing the edge of my ear. An electric shiver passed through my bruised face. "It seems like yesterday," she purred.

"Still working for the Montalbans, I see."

She kept her fingernails on my neck as she circled my chair. She blocked my view of The Crossroads and stopped directly in front of my knees. Always beautiful, she had aged extremely well. Her lips were full and red, her skin was as smooth as the day I had met her, and her ice blue eyes twinkled with a predatory mischievousness. She was wearing a black silk kimono that was entirely inappropriate for polite company.

"Working for the Montalbans?" She laughed as she lifted one long, perfectly muscled leg, and draped it over my own. Katarina settled down onto my lap, with her fingers intertwined behind my head. I could smell her warmth and her perfume. "Lorenzo, my dear, I *run* the Montalban Exchange now."

"You've moved up in the world," I replied in the most noncommittal way possible. She always had been the ambitious one. It wouldn't have been a surprise for her to grab whatever she could after Eddie's death.

"Indeed," she answered, breathing on my neck. Some of her soft blond hair hit me in the mouth, and I could see down the top of her kimono. "I'm very glad to see you."

"Yeah, I got that impression." This was certainly not going the way that I had expected. My ex-girlfriend was the capo of a group of hired killers that should want me dead, but apparently she was all about kissing and making up. I tried to remain stoic, but it is difficult to keep a poker face in a situation like this. "So, if you're so glad to see me, why'd you have your thug knock me out?"

"I told him to bring you in. Anders is an efficient employee. Would you rather he have subdued you by force?" She rubbed one hand down my chest. "Mm, you're still doing all those pushups, I see. Maybe I should've told him to be forceful after all. I should have liked to see that fight, I think. Pity."

"Where's my crew?"

"They're fine," she whispered into my bad ear. I could feel her teeth. "Perfectly safe."

I'm only a man, and it was hard to hide my reaction, but I knew Katarina, the human razor blade, far too well to fall for this kind of thing. Besides that, if I was anything, I was loyal. "Kat, I'm glad to see you too, and I'm real glad you didn't have me killed, *but . . .*" I gently grasped her hands in my own, and pushed them away. "Ain't gonna happen. This trip is all business. Nothing personal."

She guided my hands to someplace *really* unexpected. "All business is personal," she said, punctuating it with that sultry laugh of hers.

This was awkward. I don't usually have mob bosses sit on my lap and try to seduce me, but then again, this was the best looking mob boss I'd ever dealt with. "Kat, get off me."

"Very well. I just wanted to see if the fire was still there. I never felt more alive than when I was with you." She leaned in and kissed me, just like the old days, hard enough to almost draw blood. I didn't respond. She broke away. Disappointed? Who could tell with her. "Too bad . . . " Her warm thigh dragged across me as she stood. Katarina stepped back, adjusted her kimono, put her hands on her perfect hips, and smiled. "Besides, our breakfast guests are here. Please, have a seat."

I glanced back at the door. The guards and Anders were flanking the *guests.* Looking past an obviously nervous Reaper, there was Jill. And the look on her face was a mixture of disgust, anger, betrayal, and shock.

We had just moved to a whole different stage of awkward.

I thought back to Malaysia, and the aftermath of the Independence Day Massacre seven years ago.

"Sorry, Kat, it's over."

"Are you talking about our employer . . . or are you talking about us too?"
She suddenly looked sad, but I knew that was an act. A year ago I would have believed she was capable of sadness but now I doubted it. Any human emotions Katarina had, had long since been expunged.

"Both."

"I thought you loved me . . ." she said, voice cracking, and this time, I almost could believe her. Almost . . . I turned my back on her and walked away.

I had loved her once, to say otherwise would be a lie, but she was broken inside. There was something wrong with Katarina, deep down, just plain abhorrent. She never talked about her past, and all I really knew about her was what she had chosen to reveal to me, and that wasn't much, and over the last few months I'd decided that she had fabricated most of that too. Not that I was somebody who could say much about that.

"Wait!" Her voice was plaintive. I paused, just for a moment, weak. "You can't leave me, Lorenzo. Not like this."

It had been great at first. For the first time in my life I had found someone who was just as conniving and malicious as I was. Ambitious, smart, and for a man like me, who lived his life on the ragged edge of law and probability, she had actually been fun. But that had changed over time.

It was like she was several different people, wrapped into one beautiful, fragile shell. The one that I fell for was a relatively decent human being who had endured a difficult life, a scared girl with a good heart. The next minute she could turn into a cold-blooded murderer, all calculation and ruthlessness, her body a weapon in more ways than one, and when she was off her meds, she turned into a screaming psychopath, flying off in a rage at the slightest provocation. She popped pills like crazy. Not so many at first, but the more jobs we pulled for Big Eddie, the more she had taken. Which Kat you ended up with depended greatly on which personality was running the show that day.

Working for Big Eddie was bad for her. I could see it. No sane person could exist in his world for long without being corrupted, and Kat was now his favorite intermediary. I was never allowed to meet the man. I had tried to get her to leave, but she had refused. Her future was with the Montalbans. That ambition that I had been so infatuated with had required her to turn totally into the cold Kat, with occasional outbursts from the crazy Kat. I was certain that the good Kat was still in there somewhere, but that side of her was weak, so she had locked it away in her cage made of drugs and hate.

Yes, I had loved her, but not anymore.

"Don't walk away from me! Lorenzo!" she shrieked. "Damn you! Don't you leave me! Not like this!" She grabbed onto arm, her nails tearing into my skin. And just like that, she lost it entirely. Kat attacked me, clawing at my eyes, ripping my shirt, her spit hitting me in the face. She was a trained fighter, but when she flew into one of her rages, there was no skill, just savagery. I bore it for a moment, waiting for her to do something stupid like actually start fighting, or to go for a weapon. Finally, I put one hand on her chest and shoved her violently to the ground.

She curled into a ball in the wet Malaysian grass and began to sob. "But . . . But I . . . I need you."

"Goodbye," I said simply and turned back to the house. Carl was watching from the front door. He nodded once and left to get Reaper, Train, and the car. We were out of there. Kat could stay and deal with Eddie all she wanted. A small part of me expected a bullet in the spine, but none came. Apparently she had taken at least some of her medications today.

"You'll pay for this, Lorenzo, I swear to God!" She screamed, cursed, and cried as I walked away. I didn't look back.

"So, what brings you to my neck of the woods?" Katarina asked innocently.

"General thievery. You know how it is. Boring stuff," I answered mechanically.

She and Anders were sitting across from us. Jill was sitting on my right, and Reaper on my left. There was a submachine-toting guard standing at each end of the room. Jill was brooding, her face a mask, barely concealing her emotions. I could understand what she was going through, but thank goodness she was smart enough to let me do the talking. Whatever Katarina was, she was dangerous, and she was also our captor, so Jill was better off holding her rage in for now. I just hoped she would believe me when I had a chance to explain that I was innocent, assuming, of course, that they just didn't drag us all out back and put a bullet in us first.

"How did you know I was here?"

"I was very surprised to hear that a Spanish businesswoman named Maria Consuela Garcia was coming to The Crossroads to do business with Sala Jihan. The coincidence was striking, considering that identity had originally been prepared for my use. I'm such a fan of irony that I felt I needed to meet this person."

"Whoops."

Breakfast had been brought in by servants and sat steaming before us. I had to admit that the bacon smelled really good. A plate was put before Kat first. The boss got a steak so rare it still had feelings. "I had heard you were retired. That was the word on the street."

"This is just a temporary thing I've got to take care of, then back to the old folks home."

"Decent fieldcraft for somebody retired," Anders stated as he helped himself to a heaping pile of pig meat. "By the way . . ." He paused, pulled something out of his pocket, and tossed it across the table. It was a badly crumpled twenty dollar bill. "I always pay my debts."

"So you're out of the business, and you're no concern of ours, but here you are, in our backyard, with a . . ." Katarina sniffed. "*Crew.* Skyler, it's good to see that you're still alive."

"Uh-huh," Reaper muttered as he chewed, keeping his head down. He had always despised Katarina. "And it's *Reaper.*"

"That was such a silly name for a young boy."

"Well, I'm no kid anymore."

"Where are Carl and Train? Oh, wait. That's right. My predecessor here had them both killed. How about that?" Katarina turned to Jill. "And this must be my replacement. Lorenzo always believed in having a pretty young thing on his team. You can get into places that a male thief could only dream of. Oh, but Lorenzo always was *quite* the lady's man back in the day. You have no idea how many times he seduced some poor girl during our scams, whatever it took to finish the job. He could pretend to be anything, for anyone. Quite the heartbreaker, our Lorenzo, but he always came back to his *crew.*"

Katarina was baiting Jill, testing her, and sadly, Jill fell for it. The mask fell away, and her temper shined through. "He's my boyfriend, you bitch. We live together."

"Lorenzo settled down? With *you?*" Katarina laughed as she used a knife to cut her breakfast steak. "What are you, twenty?"

"Twenty-*six,*" Jill answered defiantly. I had a feeling that if it wasn't for the two guards with P90s, she would have gone across the table and twisted Katarina's head off. "What're you, *fifty*?"

Katarina's eyebrows narrowed. "I'm younger than your *boyfriend.*" I had seen that look before, kind of like how she had looked right before shooting Datuk Keng in the head. She turned her icy blue eyes back toward me. "So, when did you start robbing the cradle?"

I was fourteen years older than Jill. "I make up for it by being immature. It averages out."

"Well, he dumped your skank ass, and he comes home with me. Speaking of which, I would appreciate it if you kept your tentacles off my man," Jill said calmly as she scooped herself some breakfast. "Or we'll have us a problem, *puta.*"

Reaper looked over at me, raised an eyebrow, as if asking if it was okay to watch the catfight. I shook my head in the negative, and then nodded toward the guards. "Jill, machine guns." My ex was not the person to provoke.

Katarina pushed her plate away. "It's Jill, right? Well, listen to me carefully, *Jill.* I have been killing people professionally for the world's most dangerous criminal syndicate since you were wearing a training bra. I clawed my way to the top of this organization by pure ruthlessness. And then, when

Big Eddie died, I had to fight every other one of his lieutenants for the scraps. They died. I didn't. So I won." Suddenly she reached across the table, faster than I could react, and stabbed her steak knife into the wood directly in front of Jill. The handle vibrated slightly. I had forgotten how fast Kat was. "So don't think you can come into *my* house and disrespect me in front of my men. Another word, and I *bury* you . . . Now the grownups need to have a conversation."

Jill started to say something, but I reached over and grabbed her hand under the table. She glanced at me, anger flashing in her dark eyes. I shook my head. Jill had no idea what Katarina was capable of, so hopefully the look I gave her conveyed the danger we were in. Anders glanced around, shrugged, and went back to shoveling food in his face.

"Good. Now where was I?" Katarina smiled, and pulled her plate back. Another knife appeared out of her kimono sleeve, one of those fancy, expensive titanium folders. It was razor sharp and zipped through the meat like it was made of air. "Oh, that's right. You were about to tell me why you had the audacity to bring a crew onto my territory to perform a job without my permission."

"Better to ask for forgiveness than permission," I tried to joke. She didn't go for it. There was no laughter when Ruthless Kat was in charge. "If I had known it was you, believe me, I would have asked. I didn't exactly leave the Exchange under the best terms." I was praying that she didn't know that I was the one that had killed Eddie.

"Why are you here?"

"I can't tell you that."

"Very well." Katarina didn't bother to look up from her food. "Diego, kill the girl."

One of the guards lifted his subgun. Jill gasped. "Okay! Okay!" I raised my hands. "Don't shoot. I'll tell you everything." The guard lowered the gun, and waited for further instructions.

Katarina smiled as she popped a piece of ultra rare in her mouth. She chewed with her mouth open, a disgusting habit that had always annoyed me. "Your softness surprises me. You're certainly not the man you used to be. Talk."

"I'm here looking for a man, an American FBI agent. He came to The Crossroads to investigate Sala Jihan. He was kidnapped. If he's alive, then I will rescue him."

"And if he's not?"

"Then I'll kill the people that took him," I stated simply. "Then I'll go home."

"Just like that?" Katarina quipped.

"Just like that."

"Tell me, why on earth would you, of all people, be trying to help an American policeman? Ahh . . . yes. Your brother was FBI, wasn't he? You mentioned that once. Oh, and you were even foolish enough to take on your adopted family's name as your cover." Katarina snapped her fingers, and one of the guards quickly brought her an iPad. He placed it into her waiting hand, then retreated back to his station. She began to read. "Special Agent Robert T. Lorenzo. Disgraced, paranoid, delusional, conspiracy theorist, fired for revealing classified information, disappears from the US, only to arrive in The Crossroads, to immediately stir up trouble by harassing Sala Jihan, which, by the way, is never wise. He's a nosy, self-righteous, goody-two-shoes, law-and-order pig, who meddles in affairs he does not understand, and pays the price."

"So, you've met Bob. Where is he?"

"Sala Jihan has him," Anders spoke up. "By the time I found out, there was nothing I could do."

I turned my attention from Katarina to Anders. "Why would you *do* anything?"

Anders wiped his mouth with the back of his hand. He pushed his chair away from the table and stood. "Because Bob Lorenzo came here to find me."

"I don't understand."

The giant shook his head. "I'm the Fourth Operative."

I opened my mouth, but no words came out. I didn't know what to say. Bob had been right all along. "You're the man that knows about Project Blue?"

Anders dropped his fork on his empty plate. "Take a walk with me, Lorenzo. There are some things you need to know."

Chapter 15: Old Friends

VALENTINE
Crossroads City
March 15th

Our breath smoldered in the frigid air as Ling and I stepped out into daylight. Though the sun only occasionally peeked through the heavy layer of gray clouds, the snow amplified the brightness enough that I put on a pair of tinted goggles. These had the added benefit of helping to conceal my identity. We were dressed in what passed for street clothes in The Crossroads: heavy jackets, knit caps, and thick gloves, most of it either North Chinese or Russian military surplus. All of the high-end cold weather gear I'd been issued might have drawn more attention.

Our armament was limited to what handguns we could conceal. My custom Smith & Wesson .44 Magnum revolver was in its usual place on my left hip, but it was buried beneath several layers of clothing. I could get to it, but it wouldn't be a fast draw by any means. So I'd asked my Exodus compatriots for something smaller, that I could stash in the pocket of my coat. I was graciously offered several compact handguns. I picked a Taurus Protector Poly, a hideous .357 Magnum snubby with a polymer frame. Ugliness notwithstanding, it fit into the hand-warmer pockets of my jacket perfectly. Being a revolver, it could be fired from the pocket without malfunctioning, and I shoot revolvers better than automatics anyway.

Together, Ling and I made our way across the cluttered, crowded mess that was Crossroads City. Shops and stores of every sort lined the winding street, and where there weren't shops there were ramshackle carts or people selling goods out of the backs of trucks. The air stunk of diesel and burning trash.

At the heart of the town was the literal crossroads from which the settlement had gotten its name. The east-west road from Kazakhstan to Mongolia intersected with a north-south road that ran from Russia into North China. Railroad tracks ran parallel to the north-south road. A bustling train station sat just south of the intersection and seemed to be the center of activity. Scores of people crowded the platform as more boarded and disembarked a stopped train. The station itself had once been very ornate, decorated in old Soviet art-deco style. Much of it had been vandalized, stolen, shot up, or crumbled from decades of neglect.

Twin statues of Joseph Stalin and Mao Zedong flanked the main entrance to the station. Each had their arms uplifted in the air, like something off of an old propaganda poster. Only, Stalin's arm had been missing for many years and Mao had been spray painted with graffiti. His arm was being used to hold up a line of Christmas lights strung up over a noodle stand.

Ling and I had volunteered to go looking for Lorenzo. Even though the picture I'd been shown was blurry, there was no mistaking Anders. I had a score to settle with that son of a bitch and was eager to put a .44 slug through him. I didn't tell Ling this, of course. Revenge might seem unprofessional, and I really didn't want to get left at the safe house. I was sick of being cooped up. I'd been locked in a dingy old building for a long time, and I'd had my fill of it.

We didn't bother going to the Arena. It was public and we knew he'd been carried away. That left us with only one place that was worth checking: the Glorious Cloud Hotel. That was where Lorenzo, Jill, and Reaper were staying under their assumed identities. An Exodus informant worked the desk there and Ling wanted to question her. A pair of Exodus operatives, from a different safe house, were supposed to meet us there.

The Glorious Cloud didn't look glorious from the outside, but given the surroundings it was actually pretty nice. It was very quiet inside, decorated sort of like a P.F. Chang's restaurant. Ling told me to wait by the door and stand watch as she approached the desk clerk, an elderly Chinese woman with a hard gleam in her eye.

People, mostly Westerners, came and went as if The Crossroads was just another tourist destination. Just by looking at the folks inside the Glorious Cloud, one might not get the impression that The Crossroads was as nasty a place as it actually was. I could only wonder what criminal business brought most of the guests to this godforsaken corner of the globe.

"Jill and Reaper were taken from here late last night," Ling said, speaking very softly. "Four armed men, Europeans, came into the hotel, went up to the top floor, where Mr. Lorenzo was staying, and returned a few minutes later, leading them out the door."

"No one said anything?"

"This is The Crossroads, Michael. She also told me that if other Exodus members are here, they didn't identify themselves to her."

"We should check Lorenzo's room."

"Yes. She gave me the key. Come on."

✣ ✣ ✣

The top floor of the hotel was quiet. There were only a few rooms on the fifth floor, and they were the most expensive ones available. The entire level was designed to minimize noise and dampen sound. Our footsteps barely made any noise on the carpet. An ornate fountain babbled quietly along one wall. The walls were made of red wood and had beautiful tapestries hung on them.

Ling unzipped her jacket. "That's the room up ahead." I nodded and unzipped my own jacket so I could get to my .44. Upon reaching the door, she tried the handle. The room was unlocked. The Exodus operative looked back at me as she pulled an engraved Browning Hi-Power pistol from a holster on her belt and swiped the safety off. I nodded again and drew my .44, holding it close to my chest, muzzle-down.

Ling quietly opened the door. Somebody was talking inside. We entered the suite as quietly as we could. Ling moved like a cat, graceful and silent. Lorenzo had himself a nice setup there, a multi-room suite. The entrance room was a small foyer that led to a central common room. The voices were coming from there.

We swept into the room, guns raised. There were two men in the room. They were armed too, and startled. I had one, a thin man with a brown complexion and dark hair, in my sights. Ling held up her left hand, "Hold on," so I didn't fire. His eyes were big and white as he stared at my revolver. The Glock 19 in his hands was shaking. *He must be new at this.*

"Diamond," Ling said cryptically.

"Sapphire," the other man responded. Ling lowered her pistol, and so did they. I let my .44 linger on my target for just a moment before pulling the big gun back to my chest.

"Michael, this is the other team that was sent to the hotel," Ling said. "They are from Ibrahim's sword."

"Michael?" the other Exodus operative asked. He was a short man, dressed in dark clothes, his face hidden under a watch cap, Oakley sunglasses, and a scarf. His voice sounded familiar. "Val?" *Very* familiar. He pulled down the scarf.

I blinked hard. "Skunky?"

"Hey bro," he said sheepishly, holstering the two-tone Beretta 9mm he carried. "Long time no see."

"Jesus tapdancing Christ," I blasphemed. "What the fuck are you doing here? I haven't seen you since . . ."

He smiled. "Since Mexico? Yeah. I know. Sorry about that." He stepped forward and wrapped his arms around me in an awkward man-hug, slapping me on the back as he did so.

"Friend of yours?" the other Exodus man asked Skunky.

"We were in Vanguard together."

Skunky's real name was Jeff Long. He'd grown up in California, the son of Chinese immigrants. About a year before Vanguard had landed the Mexico contract, he was assigned to my team, Switchblade 4. He had been there on our last mission, acting as our team's designated marksman, when our chopper was shot down. The last I'd heard, Tailor had tried to recruit Skunky, just like he had for me, for Project Heartbreaker. Now I knew why he'd declined. "You're working for Exodus? How? Why?"

"I could ask you the same thing." He grinned.

"I recruited him the same time I tried to recruit you," Ling said. "You were both instrumental in saving Ariel."

Me, Skunky, and Tailor had been the only survivors of Switchblade 4's disastrous operation in Mexico. "Hell, did you try to recruit Tailor too?"

"He wasn't Exodus material." She didn't explain what *Exodus material* meant, but Tailor was a lunatic.

Skunky laughed. "Tailor was one cigarette being put out on his skin as a kid away from being a serial killer."

"He had my back in Zubara."

"Yeah, I heard that went south . . ."

Ling turned her attention back to Skunky. "You two can catch up later. What have you found here?"

"There is some sign of a struggle," he said, indicating for us to follow him into one of the rooms. "The door wasn't kicked in, but there was definitely a struggle."

A laptop sat on the desk in one of the rooms, a screen saver displayed on its monitor. It was connected to a pair of external hard drives. Another cable ran from a USB port to what looked like a modem of some kind. A cable from that ran out onto the balcony, where a compact satellite dish was set up. A pair of headphones was plugged into the machine, still playing heavy metal. The chair was knocked over. Half a dozen empty cans of Monster energy drink were scattered across the room. Reaper struck me as messy. What gave it away was that a half-full can of Monster had spilled on the desk, around the laptop, and hadn't been wiped up. Messy or not, that boy would never let anything like that happen to his equipment.

"This is Reaper's room alright," I told Ling. "So Anders has got Lorenzo, Jill, and Reaper."

Ling cursed in Chinese. "This is not good. They know too much about our operation."

"Do you know the people we're looking for, Val?" Skunky asked.

I nodded. "You have no idea."

LORENZO
The Montalban Exchange
Crossroads City
March 15th

There was a large balcony that circled the top level of the Montalban exchange. The red tile roof was suspended over our heads by giant wooden beams, and the only thing that separated us from a good plunge to the ground was an intricately wrought iron railing, complete with dragons and swans. The breeze carried the rough civilization smells of The Crossroads up to us. Jill and Reaper had been escorted back to the *guest* quarters. Anders and I walked the perimeter while one of the guards shadowed us, far enough back to not hear anything.

"So, who are you? And what is all this Fourth Operative bullshit?"

"Don't get ahead of yourself." Anders picked a spot with a good view of the mountains, and leaned against the railing. It creaked against his weight. As big as he was, Anders was probably a solid two-seventy of muscle. "Let me tell you a story first."

This man had shadowed me for days without being spotted. I already knew he was dangerous. I wasn't in a story mood, but no need to push him. Anders took his time finding words. I got the impression that he wasn't much of a talker. "I assume you know something about my former organization."

I nodded. "Just what Bob said in his notes."

"I doubt he knew much."

"Enough to throw his life away in some vain attempt to stop Majestic for launching Project Blue."

Anders smiled briefly, still staring out over the distance. "Majestic . . . The name started out as a joke. Our organization had lots of names, none of them official, most of those names were just line items on a budget that went into a big black hole. It was the conspiracy theorists that started calling it Majestic. We laughed at them, but it had a nice ring to it, so it stuck. But that was long before I was recruited."

"From where?"

The big man shrugged, not wanting to say any more about himself. "What I was doesn't matter now. Those days are gone. There is only *now*."

"That's very Zen of you, Leif Erikson."

Anders looked over at me, raising one eyebrow, as if internally debating whether he should just kill me on the spot, but he continued. "There's a secret war being fought. It's a cold war, but both sides have spilt a lot of blood."

"Between who?"

Anders looked at me like I was stupid. "Between my guys and the Illuminati."

"Another joke name, I take it."

"Of course. I don't know what they call themselves. It'll do though. You of all people should know all about them. You've served the Illuminati interests most of your life."

"My brother's the conspiracy theorist. I have no idea what you're talking about."

"Just another pawn then." Anders went back to looking at the view, his unkempt beard fluttered in the breeze. "Majestic was founded to fight commies, but they were bound to butt heads with these other assholes. The Illuminati is made up of thirteen powerful families. They're all old, powerful, and rich. They've been pulling the strings for a long time. Their base is mostly European, but they're involved in everything, same as us. Business, crime, politics, currency manipulation, terrorism, you name it, they've got a piece."

"I've never heard of them before Bob's notes, let alone worked for them."

"One of the thirteen families is Montalban. Ring any bells, jackass?"

"Heard of them . . ." I muttered.

"Rafael Montalban was the head of the family. It was supposed to be hands off, but Gordon had him offed in Zubara. Next in line was his brother Eduard. You killed him. Now their family is in shambles, but the other twelve go about their business, still having their secret war, like nothing ever happened. Whichever side wins steers the destiny of the world."

I could honestly say that I didn't want to root for either side in this one.

"Project Blue was our doomsday contingency plan to destroy the Illuminati once and for all. If the war ever went from cold to hot, my team's job was to cut their heads off in a preemptive strike." Anders cleared his throat and spit over the edge, watching it fall all the way to the bottom. "Majestic is so layered in secrets that nobody ever knows what's going on. The highest levels come up with plans, but they don't want to know how we get the job done. They just want it done. The first operative, his name was Barrington, was given the mission parameters and told to set the contingency plans in place."

"The senator?"

"Former senator. He was the idea man. Gordon Willis was number two, operations, he made it happen. Gordon was my immediate boss in black ops. He picked me and another guy named Hunter to be the boots on the ground."

"Big Boss in Zubara?"

Anders was surprised. "You're better informed than you let on. You met?"

"Nice guy. Had his boys break a couple of my fingers."

"Lucky that's all they did. He was old school, learned his trade fighting Soviets. Me and Hunter did the work for Blue, set everything up, put all the assets in place. It was top secret. So secret that nobody had a fucking clue what they were unleashing. They just gave Barrington a mission and turned him loose."

"So what went wrong?"

"Plan was in place. I never thought we would have to use it. It was too extreme, even for us. When the higher-ups realized just how nuts Barrington was, they freaked. Then Barrington died."

"Killed by the Illuminati?"

"Nah . . ." Anders shook his head. "Somebody above decided he was a liability. Barrington had certain *hobbies* that could lead to blackmail, and that could compromise Majestic. I was ordered to terminate him. He was into some weird, kinky things. Anonymous sick stuff in airport bathrooms, stuff like that. Then one day, when he opened a stall door, it wasn't some messed-up little fag waiting, it was me and I stuck an icepick through his ear hole. We made sure the autopsy said he had a stroke."

"I used that trick once. It doesn't leave much blood."

Anders nodded in appreciation, one professional to another. "Anyway, Blue just sat and waited, kind of forgotten by the higher-ups. Then Hunter died, betrayed to the Zubarans by Gordon. It turned out that my old buddy had cut a deal with Eddie Montalban. Gordon popped Rafael, Eddie got control of his family and deniability, everybody wins."

I'd seen that alliance myself. What Anders was saying jibed with what I'd overheard in Quagmire.

"But then Gordon 'committed suicide.' And then they nab Valentine at the scene? Suicide, my ass. I could read the writing on the wall. Four men knew about Blue, and just like that three were dead, all at the hands of other Majestic operatives. Somebody had decided to make every one of us who knew about Project Blue go away . . . So that's when I went rogue and bailed."

I had to smirk at that. "One problem with your theory. I know Valentine. He wasn't ordered to kill Gordon by anybody. He did that on his own. Gordon's betrayal got his girlfriend killed. It was as simple as that. But yeah, Majestic is upset all right. Valentine doesn't know shit about Project Blue. They tortured the hell out of him and he didn't know a thing. They were torturing him because they're scared of *you*. Now they're panicking."

Anders raised that one eyebrow again.

"Your bosses didn't drop the hammer on you guys. You fell off the face of the earth for nothing." I laughed. "But since you ran, now they think you're a liability. Hell, dude, you could probably be back in America living it up with your fat government salary."

His massive hand flew around faster than I could react. Anders' fingers clamped around my throat, and he slammed me back into one of the beams. He glared at me, not saying a word, breathing hard through his nose.

"Valentine was working on his *own*, you stupid fuck," I grunted as he threatened to crush my trachea. I could see the turmoil on his face as he realized that I was telling the truth. He had thrown away his life for nothing. His nostrils kept flaring, like the bellows on some giant furnace. I spotted something on his forearm, a little tattoo with a trident and the number four, and made a mental note of it for later. He let go. His fingers left indents in my flesh.

Anders slumped back against the rail with a sigh. The guard approached, seeing if he needed to pump some rounds into me. Anders waved him away, seemingly calm again. "Well, wish I had known that . . ." he muttered. "Too late now."

"All those steroids make you dumb." I rubbed my throat. If he tried that again, we were both going to take a dive off this roof.

"When a Dead Six operative got picked up at Gordon's house I figured they'd ordered the hit." He snap punched the railing hard enough to break most normal men's hands. The metal let out a harsh clang. "I was in F—" He stopped himself. "I was on an operation at the time, when I heard about Gordon. I made it look like I'd been killed by Illuminati and took off. I figured they'd be sending their best after me, that son of a bitch Underhill."

"Buddy of yours?"

"Underhill's the most dangerous man I've ever met," Anders stated flatly. "Old-school operative, came up through the ranks with Hunter. He's killed more people than cancer." Any man that put that kind of unease on a mutant like Anders was nobody I ever wanted to tangle with.

"What's done is done. Tell me the rest of your story."

"Gordon had a good thing going on the side with the Montalbans, so I hooked up with Katarina. We knew each other from a prior . . . business arrangement. I've been here ever since."

"My brother knew to look for you here. Why?"

"My part in Blue required me to make a deal with Sala Jihan. I was the one who had the technical expertise necessary. Bob must have found out something about that. I've got to admit, I was surprised to find out he was here."

"You knew Bob?" I asked, suspicious as always.

"From the FBI." Anders paused, knowing he'd said too much. "Hell with it. He was a field agent when I was HRT, Hostage Rescue Team, before being recruited by Majestic, at least. I'd heard about his meddling in Majestic's business, lots of us had. So I figured why he was here right away. That optimistic bastard probably thought he could flip me. Offer witness protection." Anders gave a bitter laugh. "But his poking around spooked Jihan. The Pale Man's soldiers took him before we could meet."

"And you were going to tell him about Blue? Let him expose Majestic?"

"Why not? I figured they wanted me dead," Anders stated flatly. "Fuck 'em."

"So what is Blue?"

He took forever to respond, weighing his response first. "I was going to tell you, but now things have changed."

So the nature of Blue was to remain a mystery. *Fine.* That was Bob's deal, not mine. "I'm assuming there's a reason I'm here . . ."

"We share a common goal."

"And why should I believe that?"

"Because we have a mutual enemy in Sala Jihan." Katarina's voice echoed across the open space. I didn't hear her join us on the balcony. She still moved like a ninja. Kat had wrapped a giant fur coat around her earlier skimpy outfit. She didn't look particularly happy, which told me that Jill was still alive. Kat smiled. If a cobra could smile, that's what it'd look like, and I wasn't falling for it. "The Montalban brothers are dead, the easternmost Illuminati family is in shambles. The remains of their kingdom picked over by scavengers like me, while the other twelve divide up their international spoils. The only thing that stands in the way of me taking back their old glory is control of this place, which means Sala Jihan must die."

"Not my fight, Kat. I'm done with the whole crime war thing. Congrats on the criminal empire, though. You always were better at this stuff than I was."

"*Au contraire.* This *is* your fight. Jihan has your brother, so by your own admission, you plan on killing him. My spies know all about Exodus. They also want to see Jihan dead, but they would never work with me."

"And I can't rightly say that I blame them."

"You are to be our introduction to Exodus. They will not trust me, but you, they respect for some reason. I want you to act as our intermediary. Alone, he is too strong for any of us to take. Between all of us, Jihan *will* fall. Exodus frees their slaves. You get your brother back. And I control The Crossroads."

"Sounds like a win-win situation," Anders stated.

Kat gave me her most innocent look. "An introduction. That is all I ask."

"The only word I have about who really took Bob is from you and Exodus, and frankly, you're both less trustworthy than the crabs on a five-dollar hooker."

Anders glanced at Katarina. She nodded, giving him the go ahead. He turned toward me. "There's a work crew of slaves here in town. They serve Jihan's garrison and the Brothers. If we were to free them, I know for a fact that one of them would be able to confirm that Bob was present in Jihan's prison cells." Anders pulled something out of his pocket and tossed it to me.

I caught it. It was a large coin, one of those military challenge coins that soldiers carried with their unit insignias and slogans on it. This one had been partially smashed, as if by a hammer. The first side was the Army Special Forces logo, 1st battalion, 19th group, with *De Oppresso Liber*, To Free the Oppressed, underneath. The other side was an ODA number that started with 92, but the last number had been crushed. It didn't matter, I knew it. I had seen that same logo on one of the plaques in Bob's basement, from my brother's old National Guard unit.

"That came from one of the slaves at the garrison. Dumb shit tried to *spend* it at a local shop after the Brothers sent him on an errand. You get one guess where he got it from," Anders said.

I was quiet while the deadly duo studied me. I absently bounced the coin in my palm. This was the first indication that I was on the right path.

"Partners again?" Kat asked.

No way in hell. But unless Ibrahim had an army, I didn't see how were going to get into Jihan's compound. We were going to need every bit of firepower we could muster. However, I needed to find out if they were telling me the truth, because I was mighty sick of being lied to. I spun the coin between my fingers before dropping it in my pocket. "Let's go free us a slave."

LORENZO

"You were *kissing* her!" Jill shouted.

"No." I held up my hands, partially to look innocent, partly to block anything she might throw at me. "She kissed *me*. I was an unwilling participant."

Jill's dark eyes narrowed dangerously. "Yeah, *real* unwilling!"

We were in the Montalbans' guest quarters. The room was actually nicer than our accommodations at the Glorious Cloud, but there were no windows, and the only exit led into a long hallway with guards posted on each end. We were only guests in the loosest interpretation of the word.

"I just sat there," I answered, keeping my voice level. "I told you what happened. Okay, damn it, what should I have done then? And give me an honest answer that doesn't involve her skinning us alive."

Jill folded her arms tightly across her chest and scowled at me. She had a fiery temper, but she also knew that I was right. "I don't know!"

"Well, why are you still yelling at me?" I pleaded.

"Because you suck," she answered.

I clenched my teeth to keep from saying something stupid. I gave it a moment before trying again. "Okay, then, as long as you're being rational about it . . ."

Jill sat on the bed, deflated, or just tired of being mad. "I don't trust her."

"No kidding? Jill, listen to me. There is nothing that Katarina won't do. She's a bona-fide sociopath. Trust her? Of course not. But I'm not seeing much choice. Either we work with them, or they kill us." I put my finger over my lips, and pointed toward the ceiling, to indicate that it was possible our room was bugged. Jill nodded. She knew there were other choices, but nothing that I wanted Kat to know I was pondering on. "I'm going with Anders to grab this slave. If I get confirmation that Bob is, or was, in that brig, then I'll arrange a meeting with Exodus."

Jill stood awkwardly, and hugged me close. "Sorry."

"No, I'm sorry. You shouldn't have come."

"Don't be stupid," she answered, before leaning in, and whispering into my good ear. "Did you love her?"

I paused, uncomfortable, with the love of my life in my arms. *Best to tell the truth.* "Yes . . . once."

"But not anymore?"

"No."

"Why?"

I thought about it for a moment. "Because she brought out the worst in me." And I thought of a nightmare with an old Malaysian woman screaming *murderer* over and over while her crone finger stabbed through my heart. I kissed Jill softly. "You bring out my best." I pushed a note into her hand. It was information for her to sneak to Reaper.

There was a heavy knock at the door. It was time.

Anders was waiting for me in the hall. He handed me a canvas backpack. Inside was my pistol, suppressor, spare magazines, holster, and knives. "Don't get stupid," he suggested. "Your woman and the kid are in our *care*."

"Me? *Stupid?* Never. Let's go."

"Here, put this on," Anders passed me a surplus Russian army coat. It was heavy and a little bit too big, which worked out well since I was wearing a Spetsnaz armored vest underneath. "There will be a couple of goons. Take them fast."

"Aren't they slaves too? What are the odds of them putting up a fight?" I rocked and locked an orange bakelite magazine into the AKSU-74 he had given me. The weapon was short, stubby, and at the ranges we were going to be at, incredibly effective.

He shook his head. "They'll fight, I promise. Jihan brainwashes them. His soldiers only stop when you put them down." He pulled back the charging handle on his Saiga 12K, chambering a round. "Everybody knows the garrison buys supplies here, and they always pay in gold. We're a couple of toughs looking to make a buck, got it? How's your Russian?"

"Excellent."

"I do okay. Act Russian."

We were going in hard and fast. Anders had led me through a series of alleys and shadowed paths. We were now in the back room of a Montalban Exchange trade house, watching through the dust coated windows. The building we had under surveillance was a two-story, wooden construct, with no ornamentation and very rudimentary signage proclaiming it as a seller of foodstuffs.

I didn't like going in without a plan, but Anders had been doing his homework. He glanced at his watch, one of those giant black things with every kind of dial and display known to man, waterproof down to the *Titanic*. "The house slave usually goes shopping for the garrison around three. He normally has two soldiers with him. If they're buying a lot, then there will be another slave to help carry it back. He's the garrison cook, and they let him pick his own produce. He tried to pass Bob's coin one day while his guards weren't paying attention to get himself a little something."

"What about the Brothers?"

"I've got a distraction in place. When I call it in, some Uyghur separatists are going to firebomb one of the PLA stations south of town. Those guys all hate each other, so that was easy enough to arrange. That's the kind of thing that will draw those hooded bastards right in. We give them a minute to swarm over there, then we hit."

"So, why's everybody so scared of the Brothers?"

He thought about it for a moment. "Because they're badass mother-fuckers. The most we've ever seen in town at once is three, so hopefully they'll all head toward the bombing."

"What do we do if one shows up here?" I retracted the bolt on the stubby AK, and let it fly forward, chambering a green lacquered 5.45 round.

"Kill him," he answered like I was stupid. "They're tough, but they're not bulletproof. Then run. They pin us down, we're dead. If I die, Kat will assume you did it. If they catch you, and you say a word about Montalban involvement, you know she'll feed your girl to the hogs. If you're really lucky she'll put a bullet in her head first."

"Kat's a big softie like that," I muttered, watching the street. I was wearing a green knit ski mask, rolled up on my head like a hat. "She's all heart."

"She's the devil's concubine," Anders said. "But she's great in the sack."

I turned away from the street, and studied the former G-man. "You're banging Kat, huh? Tapping the crazy?"

"Yeah. Job perk. Jealous?"

It shouldn't have surprised me. Kat always had liked to cement her working relationships with a little bit of lust. "Hell no. Been there, *done that*. Literally. Doing it with a sack of angry porcupines would be safer."

Anders scowled.

I grinned viciously, looking up at the big operative. "But hey, who'd have thought we'd be belly buddies? Small world, hey?"

Anders fumed. I could tell he was contemplating just shooting me on the spot. My hands tightened around the stubby Kalashnikov in my hands. I silently dared him to make a move.

Something caught his attention then. He nodded toward the window. "They're here."

A thin man was walking up the front steps of the shop across the street. He was dressed in rough clothes, and flanked by two soldiers wearing snow camo. The soldiers were in their late teens, if that. Both were armed with AK47s. All three men had brutal burn scars across their faces. They disappeared into the building.

Anders pulled a radio out of his pocket, already set to a predetermined channel, and hit the transmit button three times. Then we waited. I could feel the adrenaline begin to flow. I took long, deep breaths. There were several thumps, and in the distance a black cloud rolled up over the horizon. One of the soldiers ran back onto the porch and watched the rising smoke. We gave it a few minutes to sink in, hoping that most of the garrison strength, and especially the Brothers, would head toward the burning PLA station like moths to a flame.

Anders pulled down his mask, hiding his face. I did the same, rolling my eyes when I saw the skull painted on the outside of his mask. "Remember, no English," he said. "Act Russian." He jerked opened the door.

We were moving. I was only a few feet behind Anders' towering form. The street was crowded with armed men, like everywhere in The Crossroads, but now everyone was looking toward the distant explosion. Jihan's soldier was standing at the bottom of the steps, his AK at port arms, watching the commotion like everyone else. Anders threaded his way through the people, remarkably smooth for such a big man. The slave soldier never saw him coming.

Anders' shotgun had a steel folding stock. It impacted the soldier's cranium with a sound like an aluminum bat driving a home run ball over the fence. The man crumpled in a heap, but Anders was already well past. His giant combat boot impacted the door, and the frame exploded in a cloud of splinters.

We had talked about this beforehand. He buttonhooked hard right, I went left. The main room was open, just tables of local and imported vegetables. The foodie in me marveled at the remarkable selection for this time of year. Everything you could possibly want to feed a hungry criminal underworld. "Nobody move!" Anders ordered in Russian. A young man, dressed in the manner of the Triads, started to get indignant, but Anders kicked him brutally hard in the groin and just kept going.

"On the floor!" I shouted at the shoppers. Even if they didn't understand the language, my tone, combined with the rifle muzzle in their faces, got the point across. There were three people in front of me. None of them were who I was looking for. They complied with my orders and laid down. One Chinese man in an apron began to shout angrily about how he had paid his protection money already.

I didn't glance toward Anders. In an operation like this, each shooter had an area to cover. Leave your area uncontrolled to scan your partner's and you were dead in an instant.

Anders' shotgun belched thunder. A table of weird, pointy fruit exploded in yellow pulp. Something moved behind it, crouched low. *The other soldier.* A third blast of buckshot blasted through the wood and food. Jihan's man was still moving. He came up, swinging his AK, already depressing the trigger, and firing wildly around the shop. My Krink was set to semi-auto. I focused on the front sight, already on the soldier's chest, and stroked the trigger three times fast. He jerked as bullets tumbled through his heart and lungs. The top of his head disappeared in a red blur as Anders found him.

"I said, everybody get on the damned floor!" I bellowed, in Russian, over the ringing in my good ear. "Where's the slave?"

"Over here," Anders called. The slave was on the ground covering his head with his hands. Anders bent down, grabbed him by the neck, and dragged him to his knees. "Talk to him quick."

My partner stepped back, scanning the room for further threats. I squatted before the shaking slave. He was confused, his eyes wide, bits of fruit splattered all over his scarred face. "Hey, look at me. *Hey*!" I slapped him once. That got his attention. I pulled the challenge coin out of my pocket and held it in front of his eyes. "Where did you get this?"

"I not know!"

"*Where?*"

"I not seen it," he sputtered, in bad Russian.

I slapped him again, hard enough to sting my hand through my glove. "Liar!"

Believe me, being a jerk to a man that had spent a good chunk of his life in slavery felt just as bad as you can imagine. I despise slavers. But I needed info, and I needed it now, and there was no way we were going to carry him out of here without getting caught. I had told myself that this was for the greater good, because if it helped end Jihan's reign, then it was freedom for thousands, and not just this one.

Anders stomped to the front door, and scanned down the street, obviously impatient. "More coming." He stepped back toward us, glanced around to make sure everyone else's head was still down, then lifted up his face mask. The slave looked startled, like he recognized him. "Clock's ticking."

"Yes, yes! I seen coin. Took from white man. Big white man. American. No hair. No hair." He rubbed his hands over his skull. "Please, no kill me."

"Is the American still alive?"

Now he appeared really scared, his eyes so wide that they appeared ready to pop out, but he looked hopefully toward Anders, almost as if he was asking permission. "Yes, alive, in master's dungeon. In fort. In Pale Man's fort." Once he had gotten past implicating his master, he seemed to decompress, to almost melt down, like he had gotten past the hard part. "Now you let me free? You take me away?" He pleaded toward Anders, tears of relief in his eyes.

BOOM.

I flinched as blood splattered across my face. Anders lowered his smoking shotgun as the slave thudded lifelessly to the floor.

"What the hell!" I leapt up, shocked.

"He saw my face," Anders stated as he rolled his mask back down. He reached down and took the leather bag filled with coins that would have bought supplies for Jihan's garrison. Now it was just a robbery. "Move. Out the back." He gestured toward the rear of the room, then he was gone.

I stared at the body for a moment as I wiped the blood from my eyes with the back of one gloved hand. Then I followed.

Just like the old days.

We dumped the masks, coats, vests, and long guns in the alley behind the vegetable shop, then walked nonchalantly through the rambling streets back toward the Montalban Exchange. Anders had the audacity to be hungry, and stopped at a noodle cart. "You ever try this stuff? It's probably made from cats and dogs, but it's pretty good."

I sullenly waited for him to get his lunch. I had no appetite. "That wasn't the plan."

He paused in his noisy slurping. "What?"

"Killing that guy."

"Your way wasn't working. We didn't have time. I showed him my face because I've got a rep around here. He had to know he was dealing with someone who would just kill him, otherwise he never would have talked in time. If we let him go, and they caught him, he'd talk, we'd die. And once he told them what we asked about, your brother would die. I'm surprised. Katarina talked you up like you were a mad-dog killer."

"I try to be a little more selective." I shoved my hands in my pockets and watched the passing throng. There was still smoke rising from the PLA compound, but nobody was paying attention now.

"Well, you popped that soldier fast. He was about to shoot me when you got him," Anders said with grudging respect. I had to assume that was his version of "thank you." "Hey man, at least you know your brother's alive." He tossed some coins on the counter as he pulled out his radio.

I had been too preoccupied with Anders' casual murder to think it through, but this meant Bob was here. I still had a mission and a purpose. "I'll set up a meet between Kat and Exodus."

Anders keyed his radio. "It's on," he stated simply, before shoving it back into his pocket. "Your crew will be released and sent back to the Glorious Cloud. We'll be in touch." Anders ordered another batch of noodles to go.

Kat had kept her word, and Jill and Reaper were waiting at the Glorious Cloud by the time I returned. Reaper had even had some time to do some research. He had taken the note that I had slipped Jill at the Montalban Exchange, containing everything I had gleaned earlier, and gone to work.

"Your note said Anders had a SEAL Team 4 tattoo on his arm, and he mentioned being HRT," Reaper said. "So I started there."

"Assuming he's telling the truth." Jill was sitting on the bed next to me, also studying the screen on Reaper's laptop. She hadn't said anything yet about my earlier meeting with Katarina, and I wasn't going to bring it up either.

"Duh." Reaper rolled his eyes. "Do I tell you how to look hot? Do I tell Lorenzo how to steal stuff? No? I used the Majestic files Val took that Bob dropped on the Internet. Then I cross-referenced Bob's conspiracy nut notes. I digitized them while you were screwing around with Exodus, by the way. Then I wrote a—" And as soon as I recognized that he was about to drone on about his anarcho-crypto nerd brilliance I cut him off.

"Get to the point."

"The Project Heartbreaker records had an operative under the name of Anders, attached to Dead Six, and working for Gordon Willis, code-named Drago. But that name was a dead end. He's a ghost. No connection to a real identity."

The way Reaper was talking, I knew he was itching to tell me more. I waited patiently. I had already killed somebody today, so I was feeling kind of mellow. "And with your 'mad skillz,'" I made quote marks with my hands, "I'm sure you got more than that."

"You know it." He started rapidly clicking, bringing up other files. "One of Bob's suspects for the Fourth Operative was a former FBI agent named Simon Andrew Sundgren. Bob said that he had some indication that this guy was a possible because of his prior training, but Bob didn't elaborate what training, but he did mention the guy was HRT. Bob only wrote about the dude for one paragraph, but he was the only one that was former FBI."

He must have noticed that my eyes were starting to glass over.

"Okay, okay." He clicked a wireless mouse and the screen changed. It was a picture of Anders, only younger, clean-shaven, with a sharp buzz cut. He looked like one of those Nazi recruiting posters from World War II, a square-jawed, blue-eyed block of muscle.

"Wow. He looks a lot better without the beard," Jill said. I scowled at her. She raised her hands. "What?"

I turned back to the computer. "So you cracked the FBI database finally?"

"No. I got slapped down hard when I tried that for Bob's file. This is from Google," he explained. "See, just like all the guys working at North Gap had shady pasts, and some of the people that Majestic recruited for Dead Six had legal problems, I figured the rest of their operatives would be similar. Special Agent Sundgren is a bit of an internet celebrity." He brought up the next window. "He apparently shot some people in a standoff in North Dakota. They turned out to be unarmed and were trying to surrender. One of them was a pregnant lady."

"I remember that one. I saw a thing about it on TV once," Jill said. "There was this big standoff with some people that refused to pay taxes. When they teargassed the place, he said that the people came out with guns. The survivors said that they were unarmed and trying to surrender. Gotta love NatGeo."

"So all the intel gathering about our new buddy, Anders, has already been done for us by the internet. Hell, he's even got his own Wikipedia entry. It was really controversial. North Dakota tried to prosecute him. The Feds wouldn't release the official records of what happened, and he claimed immunity. The next thing you know, he just quit the FBI and disappeared.

We know he was recruited by Majestic."

"Congratulations. You won the Internet." I gently pushed past Reaper and stole his laptop. Anders had quite the resume. Annapolis graduate, US Navy, started out as a nuke tech on a carrier, and then transferred into Naval Special Warfare. Olympic athlete. Won a bronze medal in freestyle swimming. So not only could he fight, he was apparently one hell of a swimmer too. Multiple citations for bravery, left the Navy, joined the FBI, and eventually the elite Hostage Rescue Team. Until he jumped the gun and massacred some people. Then nobody had seen him since. And now former Special Agent Sundgren was kind of an iconic figure for governmental abuses of power.

They had no idea.

"So apparently we're now in business with a jackbooted thug that shoots unarmed pregnant women. Majestic certainly wouldn't want to let a set of skills like this go to waste."

"Friggin' awesome," Jill muttered.

"Okay. Keep looking. None of this tells us what Project Blue is. There's got to be something about Anders that keyed Bob in on him, and when we know what it is, maybe we can figure out what Blue really is."

"I thought you didn't care." Reaper sounded surprised.

It really wasn't my business, I need to take care of my family and get the hell out of here. The world's affairs weren't my problem. That altruistic bullshit was best left for good guys like my brother.

"Well, now I guess I'm curious."

Chapter 16: Dead Leprechauns

VALENTINE
Exodus Safe House
Crossroads City
March 16th

Skunky and I sat and talked for a long time. I hadn't seen him in a couple years, and both of our lives had been irrevocably changed after that ill-fated operation in Mexico. We had much to discuss. He had, of course, heard of the unrest in Zubara, hell, the whole world had. After reading the Project Heartbreaker Commission report, Skunky was sure that I had been killed there.

What was once the Confederated Gulf Emirate of Zubara was now the Zubaran Arab Republic, run by General-turned-President-for-Life Al Sabah and his so-called Arab Socialist Party. He ruled with an iron fist that would have made Saddam Hussein proud. I'd heard you could find videos of Zubaran security forces machine-gunning protesters in the streets on YouTube.

Fat lot of good we'd done there. I was personally responsible, at least in part, for the suffering of the people of Zubara. It took me the better part of an hour to tell him the convoluted tale of how Exodus helped me escape from Zubara, and Sarah's death. I described my encounters with the Lorenzo brothers, the Montalbans, my falling out with Tailor, my capture and rescue, all of it.

When I was done talking, my former teammate closed his eyes and took a deep breath. "Holy crap, dude."

"You're telling me. You know, every morning I get up, I try not to think about it. By rights I've got no business even being alive. Almost everyone I care about is dead. Sarah is dead. The guys I worked with at Vanguard are, except for you and Tailor, and I'm not even sure about Tailor. I can't even contact Hawk because it might put him in danger. Almost everyone that took part in Project Heartbreaker is dead, too. I don't even know what the fuck I'm doing half the time. It's like I'm running on autopilot. I just go along with the flow because I don't have anywhere else to go."

"Is that why you're here?" he asked, a worried expression on his face.

I looked around, to make sure Ling wasn't listening. "At first, that was my reason for coming along. I owe Ling—and I owe Exodus—my life. She pulled me out of hell, risking her own life and killing a bunch of people in the process. I can't just walk away from that."

"Even if you really want to," Skunky interjected.

"Even if I really want to," I repeated. "But honestly, as crazy as it sounds, this feels right to me. I feel like I'm where I'm supposed to be."

"That doesn't sound crazy to me. I was lost when I got home from Mexico."

"That was a bad op," I said.

"Yeah," my friend agreed. "Bad op. I got home, I tried to go work for my parents, do a regular job. I tried really hard at that for almost a year."

"So did I, Jeff."

"What did you do?" he asked.

"Security guard."

"I sold camera equipment." He had always been an avid photographer. He had taken about three quarters of the pictures I had from my Vanguard days. "I did that for a while, but I got . . . I don't know, restless. I couldn't sleep at night and had nightmares when I could. When I thought about some of the shit we did, man . . . I don't know. Someday we're all going to stand before God to be judged. What am I going to tell him? How am I going to explain the shit we did? We got paid really well? It seemed like it was necessary at the time? It was what I was told to do?"

"I think I'd ask him where in the hell he was when all of those horrors we saw were going on."

"It started eating me up, Val, bad," Skunky said.

"Me too, sometimes." In our former profession, we put on a legitimate facade, prettied up what we did by saying we were providing security, ensuring stability, or protecting VIPs. All of that was basically true. We got our hands dirty and fought other people's wars. You can tell yourself that it was just a job, that they were bad guys you killed, but when you're alone on a quiet night, you can't fool yourself with that crap. You know what you did. It ate at me too, sometimes.

"We killed people for *money*." Skunky was more religious than most of my teammates had been. He was the only one on Switchblade 4 that made any effort to attend regular church service. He was a good man, a better human being than a lot of the people I worked with. He didn't really seem cut out for the work we did. He looked right through me. "So now what are you killing for?"

I didn't deny it. What Hawk had said about me was right, whether or not

I realized it back then. I'm a *killer*. It's what I do. Everyone is good at something, and God forgive me, that's what I'm good at. I couldn't imagine doing anything else. When I tried to do something else, I was miserable, and that was how I ended up in Zubara. I think that's how I ended up at The Crossroads, too. Maybe it was just my calling.

"I don't know."

"Well I do." Skunky was a more decent human being than I was, but he was a killer too. Deep down, he knew it. "Same reason you're here now, I think. I was falling to pieces back home. The only time I'd find any peace was when I'd go camping up in the mountains alone. Even working for my parents I felt completely alone. They didn't know what I'd been doing overseas. I think my dad sort of knew, but I never talked about it. I couldn't bear to tell them. How do you tell your parents that, yeah, this one time, we mowed down a bunch of protestors in front of a government ministry with automatic weapons?"

I winced as I recalled the incident. That, too, had been a bad op. "Those protestors were shooting at us, Jeff. That's how Roberts and Bigelow bought it, don't you remember?"

"I know, I know. But how many people did we kill that day? Dozens? How many women and kids? God help me, Val, it was eating me alive. Once I got home, and had peace and quiet, and lived in the normal world, it was eating me alive."

The protestors in that incident had deliberately brought as many women and children as they could with them. Many of the women and children were armed and were shooting at us. Not that that makes you feel any better when you're surveying a mound of corpses.

"I couldn't talk to anyone. I couldn't relate to anyone. I was alone and I was miserable."

"You had PTSD," I said bluntly. "It's okay, I've been told I do too."

"I know. I didn't know it at the time, but I know now. We're both pretty fucked up, you know that? So then I get this email from Ling, asking me to join Exodus."

"I got the same one. I damn near did it, too. If Tailor hadn't approached me, I probably would've taken Ling up."

"I did it. It took me all of a minute to decide."

"So what's it like?"

"I've been on a couple of missions. I can't really talk about what I do. You're not a sworn member of the order, blah blah blah."

I grinned. "No worries, don't get yourself in trouble."

"Anyway, most of what Exodus does isn't violence. I know that's what gets all the press, but that's not what it's about. We help people. We free people from slavery. We bring down warlords. We allow food aid to get to starving people. We bring dictators and warlords down. Exodus helped overthrow Muammar Gaddafi, did you know that? We were in Syria too."

I scoffed. "Look how well *that* mess turned out. I've been in the business of overthrowing nations, man. It never works out the way you think it's going to."

"I know. You can hand people liberty but you can't make them keep it. After that, and what you guys pulled in Zubara, the order got much less enthusiastic about operating in the Middle East."

"That's a smart decision, I think. So I take it you're a true believer? No offense. You just seem into it."

"You have to be, dude. It's given me a purpose. Once you learn about Exodus' history, its founding, and the role it's played in shaping history . . . we are trying to make the world a better place. And we're not trying to do it by social engineering, or telling people how to live, or trying to take control or gain power. We believe in freedom, and that freedom is worth fighting for. Dying for."

"Killing for," I added.

"Yes," he agreed grimly. "And that's why we're so damned good at what we do."

I wasn't sure what to say to that.

VALENTINE
Crossroads City
March 18th

I found myself sitting in the left-hand passenger's seat of a right-hand-drive Toyota Hilux Surf SUV. Ling was at the wheel, beeping the horn at a slow-moving ox cart as we tried to make our way across town.

She swore in Chinese as she stepped on the clutch, shifted gears, and passed the cart. Another horn sounded as we only very narrowly avoided hitting a huge Russian 6x6 truck head-on. Ling cursed again and stepped on the gas. I'd just learned that Ling had a case of road rage, but I still didn't know where we were going. I'd been roused out of bed in the predawn darkness and told to get dressed. I had no idea what was happening.

"Mr. Lorenzo told Ibrahim that he has a proposal for Exodus. Ibrahim is the overall commander of this operation, but he wanted to consult with the leadership before making any decisions. We're going to that meeting."

Exodus spies had told us that Lorenzo and his team had safely returned to the Glorious Cloud. They did not approach him to ask where he'd been, though, for fear of tipping their hand.

"So why am I going?" I asked. I wasn't even a member of Exodus, much less part of the leadership.

"You know Lorenzo better than most of us," Ling said.

I supposed that was true. "Only because we've tried to kill each other."

"That is the best way to truly understand someone." She smiled. "Ibrahim doesn't know him at all, so any of us who have worked with him will be there. We want to get a feel for what he has to say, whether or not he is telling the truth."

"The man is a professional liar and that's a giant understatement. I'm not sure having us there is going to help anyone know that Lorenzo's being sincere. I'm sure he's very, very good at feigning sincerity."

"I'm well aware," Ling insisted. "But you and I also know more of his background, and we've seen his home. We have leverage over him that he's undoubtedly unused to. It might give us an advantage."

I rubbed my eyes. "All this skullduggery is giving me a headache."

"It won't be so bad. Think of it this way, at least we get to—" Ling cut the wheel hard to the left as a rusted fuel tanker truck pulled out in front of us from a narrow alley. She laid on the horn and what she was saying melted into a swath of Mandarin obscenities. I grasped the "oh shit!" handle and hung on for dear life. Such was rush hour in a place with no traffic laws.

Somehow, we made it to our destination unscathed. We parked behind a deteriorating Soviet-era warehouse and, after having our identities confirmed, were hurried inside by the guards. The warehouse was dimly lit, and full of vehicles, supplies, shelves, and stacks of crates. The air stunk of dust, must, and years of neglect.

There were many Exodus personnel present, going about their daily tasks. Some were working on a truck engine. Others were cleaning weapons. Some were doing push-ups and pull-ups. We were hurried past them, through the warehouse, into a small office in the back. The echoing sounds of the building were muffled as the door was closed.

Lorenzo was there. I barely recognized him since he was dressed in dirty, drab clothing, topped with a surplus Russian military parka. He looked exactly like a resident of The Crossroads. I probably would have missed him completely if he hadn't nodded at me. His eyes gave him away, though. I recognized his eyes. They darted everywhere, trying to scan every angle of the room. I had no doubt he'd arrived at the safe house unnoticed, like some kind of hobo ninja.

Also in the room was Ibrahim, who was quietly speaking with Lorenzo, as well as Katsumoto and a handful of other Exodus people that I didn't recognize. From their demeanor and their presence in the meeting, I gathered that they were the leadership of this operation. Whatever Lorenzo had to say had certainly gotten their attention.

One of the Exodus men put an electronic device on the table and activated it. "The room is secure," he told Ibrahim. It must've been some kind of electronic jammer.

Ibrahim nodded, then turned to address the room. "Gentlemen," he began, then turned to Ling. "My lady," he said formally, grinning. Ling, to my astonishment, blushed and looked away briefly before regaining her composure. Ibrahim was a flirt. "Our ally, Mr. Lorenzo, comes to us with an interesting proposal. He was told to bring it to us, which has some disturbing implications. It seems our operational security has been compromised."

Everyone in the room was taken aback. Ling's eyes went wide, but Ibrahim held up his hands. "Not to fear, my friends. As far as we can tell, our presence here is not known to Sala Jihan or his subordinates. However, a third party has become aware of us."

"Who?" Ling asked. Though considering this town, none of the options were good.

Lorenzo stepped forward. "The Montalban Exchange."

"You gotta be shitting me," I muttered to myself. The Exodus leadership began to murmur to each other.

"As far as I know, it's just a name. It's a remnant of the criminal organization that Big Eddie, Eduard Montalban, controlled. The Montalban brothers are both dead, as I'm sure you're all aware. Valentine back there killed one of them, and he was there when I shot the other one out of the sky. They're dead and good riddance." Lorenzo's normally calm composure cracked slightly; he hated Eduard Montalban with every fiber of his being. The fact that the man was dead gave him little comfort, it seemed, and he could barely conceal his contempt.

People began to bombard Lorenzo with questions. Before it could get out of hand, Ibrahim raised a hand, silencing the room again. "Mr. Lorenzo, why don't you explain to them what you told me?"

Lorenzo pinched the bridge of his nose, obviously annoyed, but took a deep breath and continued. "A couple days ago I was approached by a representative of the Montalban Exchange."

"Was it Anders?" I asked pointedly, interrupting Lorenzo. Most of the Exodus leadership looked at me with surprised expressions on their faces.

Lorenzo looked grim. "Yes." He must've seen my hackles rising. He very subtly moved his hand, quietly telling me to tone it down. I figured he'd fill me in later. He was right. I didn't need to go airing my grudge with Anders in front of all these people. "So when I say approached, I mean he tailed me, caught me at gunpoint when I made him, and then doped me. I get the impression they're a shadow of what they were under Rafael and Eddie, but they still seem to have a lot of resources, and they have a big problem with Sala Jihan and they want him dead. They want in on your planned operation. They're offering intelligence, personnel, and logistics."

"Intelligence, personnel and logistics?" one of the Exodus leaders asked. "What does that mean?"

"I'm assuming that personnel, means they'll provide personnel," Lorenzo said dryly. "I don't know what they meant by logistics. Maybe supplies, maybe transportation. Intelligence is pretty self-explanatory."

"Who made you this offer?" Ling asked.

Lorenzo paused for a moment, as if lost in a memory. "A woman named Katarina. I used to work with her, a long time ago. She was on my team. I know her well."

"How is it that this woman came to head the Montalban Exchange?" one of the Exodus commanders I hadn't met yet asked.

"She's absolutely ruthless," Lorenzo answered. "That's really all it takes."

"Can we trust her?"

Lorenzo looked surprised by the question. "What? No. No, no. Not even a little bit. She's dangerous and violent."

"Then why should we go along with this?"

"I'm not saying you should," Lorenzo said. "I don't give a damn what you people do. I'm just here to find my brother, and I'm just the messenger. If your raid fails, the chances of me finding my brother go from slim to none. But I can think of some reasons why you might want to consider it."

"What do you mean?" Ling asked.

Lorenzo's mouth split into a mean smile. "I know you guys think you're being all secret squirrel and everything, but you're not. You can't just put this many people into such a small area and not be noticed. I noticed, and I've only been here for a few days. Sala Jihan has been here for a lot longer, and the Montalban Exchange has already compromised you. Also, I haven't seen your battle plan obviously, but how in the hell are you people planning on taking that fortress?"

"We are working on that," said Ibrahim.

"I've been inside that thing. Do you really think you have enough people? How are you going to get them up there? Do you have good intelligence on Jihan's compound? Do you know how many men he has? Do you know where they're all housed, how they're equipped, where their defensive positions are?"

Lorenzo was met with silence.

"Thought so. The Montalbans say they know. They told me to give this to you people." He retrieved a folded piece of paper from his pocket, and laid it on the table. The Exodus leadership crowded around to get a better look.

"This is a map showing the interior defensive positions around the fortress," Ibrahim said. "Including where they house their antiaircraft weapons."

"Katarina says there's plenty more where that came from. She says her spies have infiltrated Jihan's operations. She's ready to make a move, but can't do it without you. You're ready to make a move, and she says you can't do it without her. Look, people, I've been inside Jihan's compound. I've met the man."

The room became uncomfortably silent.

Lorenzo was unfazed. "That's right, I was face to face with Sala Jihan at the bottom of his missile silo. He's not somebody to screw around with. I can give you guys information, but I only saw a little bit, and what I saw told me he's got a lot more armed motherfuckers than you guys have."

"What do you know of our strength?" someone asked indignantly.

Lorenzo scoffed. "Please. You aren't as good at this as you think you are, no offense. I don't know exactly how many people you have here, or what else you might be scheming at, but I know that Sala Jihan has an army in there, a lot more people and weapons than you people could have possibly smuggled into town. So unless you've got an air strike planned or something, you might want to at least hear the Montalbans out."

"And what does she want in return for our assistance?" Katsumoto asked.

"She wants The Crossroads. With Jihan gone, she believes her group can take control of this place and get a share of all of the business that goes on here."

"And trade one monster for another?" one of the Exodus leaders scoffed.

"No," another replied. "We'd be trading an actual monster for a mere criminal."

Katsumoto and Ibrahim looked at each other for a long moment. Lorenzo didn't know about the plan to assault the dam. Neither did the Montalban Exchange, it seemed. The two Exodus commanders nodded at each other.

"I propose," Ibrahim said, "that we at least meet with the Montalban Exchange. They have compromised our OPSEC. If we decline the meeting, they could turn on us, or even expose us to Sala Jihan. We must move carefully, lest we be lured into a trap. You all know the gravity of the situation. Our footing isn't nearly as strong as I would like it to be. We need to be willing to take every advantage offered to us."

The room erupted into loud discussion. Lorenzo stepped away from the limelight and leaned against the wall. He seemed happy to no longer be the center of attention. Ling joined the energetic discussion as the Exodus leadership argued among themselves.

Awkward. I stepped back. The debate reminded me I was an outsider. *What are you doing here?* I asked myself. *This isn't your fight.* I was so lost in my thoughts that Lorenzo was able to sneak up on me. He startled me as he materialized to my side.

"Valentine," he said curtly.

"What the fuck happened to you?" I asked, my voice lowered so the Exodus people couldn't hear. "What is Anders doing here?"

"Come on," Lorenzo said, indicating the door. "I need some air. Let's get away from these crazies." He walked out of the meeting room. We found a dark, quiet corner in the warehouse, away from prying ears, to talk. "You know this Anders guy? He's an asshole."

"You have no idea," I said, not looking at him.

"Then fill me in," Lorenzo said. "The short version. You tend to ramble on when you start telling stories."

I raised an eyebrow at him. "Fine. Anders worked for Gordon Willis. He was, like, his right-hand man or something. Everywhere Gordon went, just about, Anders went with him. He was there in the office the day I was recruited. He was in Zubara. He was there when we raided Rafael Montalban's yacht, too, so I'm guessing he was in on Gordon's schemes."

"How do you know?"

"The yacht raid was not one of our planned operations. It was part of Gordon's plan, part of his deal with Eduard Montalban."

Lorenzo's eyes narrowed. "Makes sense. Go on."

"Anders is an ice-cold motherfucker. I don't know if he feels pain. He kicked the shit out of half my team in Yemen, and he's the only man I've ever met that's a faster draw than me."

"You haven't seen me draw. What were you doing in Yemen?"

I cracked a mean smile. "Oh please, pops, I've got you beat by a tenth of a second, easy. We were there recovering a nuclear warhead that was supposed to go to General Al Sabah."

"We'll settle this on the range someday, kid. So . . . wait, wait a second. Is it my bad ear, or did you just tell me that Anders got his hands on a nuke?"

"You heard me right. An old Russian ICBM warhead. We intercepted the transaction in the middle of nowhere, Yemen. Anders was there for the raid. We lost guys, too. Christ, he let Singer bleed to death. The guy was supposed to be our medic and the cocksucker didn't even open his trauma kit."

Lorenzo thought that over for a second. "Sounds about right. What else?"

"That's all I know. I never saw him after the raid on Rafael Montalban's yacht. I didn't know what happened to him."

"He told me about it. He went underground after Bob leaked all of that information to the press. He fled the country when you killed Gordon Willis. He thought Majestic sent you to clean up loose ends."

I chuckled sardonically. "Yeah, Gordon thought Majestic had sent me to kill him, too. Blew his fucking mind when I told him I was there on my own."

"Were they going to kill him?"

"I think they were going to take him alive, to interrogate him about Project Blue. The guys that were supposed to capture Gordon entered his house while I was confronting him. They captured me right after I shot him."

"Damn. Couldn't have timed that better, could you?"

"I should've just stayed with Hawk. It would've saved me a lot of trouble."

Lorenzo leaned in closer to me, the tone of his voice darkening. "It would've saved us *all* a lot of trouble. You did the worst possible thing: you got *caught*. You *talked*. My brother could be dead because of you."

"You think this is what I wanted? You think I don't regret it every single fucking day I'm alive? You think it doesn't just kill me on the inside knowing that my choices have gotten almost everyone I know killed?"

"I don't give a shit how bad you feel," Lorenzo said. "You got stupid. You let your childish rage compromise you. And you didn't just compromise yourself, you compromised Hawk, my brother, me, Jill, Reaper, everyone!"

"Really? You're going there? Okay, okay, let's talk about your little high-speed chase down a public highway and shooting down a jet. Way to keep it low profile. And using your real last name as your pseudonym? Jesus, Batman, you think they'll ever figure out that you're really Bruce Wayne?"

"First off, that was never *my* last name. Second, that's not even the same fucking thing! I did what needed to be done! And shooting down that jet was awesome and you know it."

I couldn't argue with that, but I felt like arguing anyway. I was sick and tired of Lorenzo jumping my shit. "Whatever. I've had enough of you blaming me for your problems. Enough people have suffered because of me. I'm not going to take responsibility for the people that suffered because of you. I never asked for your help. You didn't have to get involved in any of this. Your brother wouldn't have gotten into this mess if he'd have quit while he was ahead and stopped digging. You're pissed off at him and you're taking it out on me."

Lorenzo stepped back and seemed to deflate a little. I folded my arms across my chest. He thought for a moment, then looked up at me. "I'm trying to help you, goddamn it," he insisted. "I've been where you are. Nothing to lose, nothing to live for, no longer giving a fuck. I lived that way for a long time. Look where it got me. You gave me some advice when were in Las Vegas. Do you remember? You told me to get out of this life, for Jill's sake."

"I remember," I said sullenly.

"I wish like hell you'd have listened to your own advice, kid," Lorenzo said. "It was the first smart thing I ever heard you say."

I sighed heavily, looking around the warehouse. "Yeah, well, it's too late now, isn't it? For both of us. Look at everything that's happened, Lorenzo. Look at all this crazy shit and tell me that it's just a coincidence."

"I don't believe in fate," Lorenzo said stiffly. "Or destiny, or predetermination, or unicorns, or pots of gold at the ends of rainbows."

"If there were pots of gold at the end of rainbows, I can only assume that you'd have a lot of gold and there'd be a lot of murdered leprechauns buried in Ireland."

Lorenzo actually smiled. "Damn straight."

"Yeah, well, I don't believe in any of that stuff either. But look around you. Can you honestly tell me you feel like you're in control? I don't know, man. There's something wrong with this place, with this whole thing."

"It's a third-world, drug-trafficking, slave-trading, arms-dealing hellhole," Lorenzo said, almost like he was trying to defend the place. "It's going to feel wrong."

"Not like that. I've been to places like that too. I worked in Africa for almost a year, you know. This is different. I can't put my finger on it, but there's something seriously messed up here. We don't belong here. I have a terrible feeling about this whole thing."

"Have you told Ling that? She's pretty into you. She might listen."

I raised an eyebrow at his comment, then shook my head. "Not on this. These guys are dedicated. They're going to go through with it one way or another."

Lorenzo sighed and rolled his eyes. "Bunch of fanatics is what they are. No offense. I can't complain, though. This insanity is the only shot I've got at finding Bob."

"What about your friend Katarina? Is she for real?"

"She's for real," Lorenzo said. "And she's not my friend. The bitch is crazy. Genuinely, legitimately, totally screwed-in-the-head bug-nuts. She's a businesswoman, though. She'll uphold her end of the bargain, especially if she thinks she's got something to gain, but if Exodus knows what's good for them, they won't trust her."

"Exodus doesn't strike me as the trusting sort. I have no doubt they'll have a contingency plan."

Lorenzo gave me a hard look after that comment, but I said nothing more. He didn't know about the raid on the dam, and he didn't need to. This whole thing was already complicated enough.

And for the life of me, I just couldn't shake the bad feeling I had.

Chapter 17: Dance Partners

LORENZO
Somewhere in Kazakhstan
March 20th

There was an awkward silence in the small cabin. Terrorists on one side, gangsters on the other, nobody speaking, kind of like the uncomfortable beginning of a middle-school dance when the music starts and the boys are too intimidated to go talk to the girls. The Montalban Exchange was represented by Katarina and Anders, Exodus by Ibrahim and a tough-looking Czech named Fajkus. Outside the single-room dwelling, several other Exodus members and Montalban goons watched each other with nervous alertness while their bosses talked business.

The meeting place had been agreed upon by both groups. The house stood alone in a mountain pasture forty miles into Kazakhstan. It was a cramped, wooden shack, but since it was alone in a sea of stunted yellow grass poking out of the snow, there was no place for either side to set up snipers or an ambush. It was too open for any of us to have been tailed by Jihan's spies. The lone shepherd who lived here had been given a small sum of money and sent off to watch his goats.

I had introduced the various parties, and was now leaning back in my rickety chair, arms folded across my chest, just an impartial observer at this point. I didn't trust either side, but sadly I needed these people to free Bob.

After sizing each other up, Ibrahim broke the silence. "Lorenzo has told me that you wish to assist us. I'm willing to listen to your proposal. However, you must know that Exodus does not need your help. We are more than capable to accomplishing our mission."

Kat smiled. "No. No, you are not. Otherwise you wouldn't be here today."

"I'm afraid you are mistaken," Ibrahim stated flatly.

"Then why haven't you killed Jihan yet?"

Fajkus scowled. The Czech was probably in his mid-thirties, stocky, with bulldog jowls, and short, spiky, black hair. The Exodus XO wore small, round glasses, and it was rather obvious from his expression that he didn't like this meeting. The Pale Man will be dead soon enough."

"Oh, but think of all those poor slaves, dying by the score every day, living in squalor and suffering, while their saviors wait in relative comfort." She gestured at the walls of the cabin. The only decorations were antlers off of some animal that I didn't recognize. "That must be infuriating."

"Don't patronize me, Ms. Katarina," Ibrahim said. "We both know that you do not care about the welfare of the slaves."

"Of course not. I care about profit and competition. But for you, every day you wait, every hour, the odds of Jihan learning about you increase. My spies were able to discover you, so you are vulnerable. Should Jihan learn of you, he'll hunt you down like dogs, but still mighty Exodus hesitates." Kat leaned forward and rested her hands on the plank table. "No, you are not ready yet. You lack something."

Ibrahim and Fajkus exchanged glances, conveying information like only two professionals who had worked together for a long time could. Ibrahim nodded. Fajkus turned back toward Kat. "We are waiting for a few more swords, our strike teams, to arrive. Jihan's compound—"

"Is a fortress. Impenetrable walls, every building a concrete bunker, guarded by a legion of disciplined troops, and even if you carpet-bombed the entire place, your target spends most of his time at the bottom of an armored pit designed to survive a near hit from an atomic weapon. To take it will require a huge force."

Ibrahim raised a single bushy Kurd eyebrow in my direction. "Perhaps by stealth then?"

"They're thorough, no discernible gaps," I answered truthfully. "The gates stay closed. Incoming traffic is searched. Walls are too high to scale. Guards everywhere, and there aren't so many of them that they don't all know each other. It would be difficult, but not impossible. I could find a way."

"Trust me. Your usual methods of disguise won't work. I've sent men in before, impersonating slave soldiers, and they were always spotted. Somehow they just know. You can't impersonate a Brother, because nobody on the outside has ever heard them speak. How will you respond when questioned?" Kat shook her head. "You will fail. Jihan cloaks his people in mystery, but that secrecy becomes a formidable defense. You can't get inside the head of something you can't understand."

"Oh, I'll get in," I responded. Kat of all people should have known that. Every defense has a weakness.

"And then what? Assassinate Jihan?" Kat had a cold laugh, more of a cackle. "Many have tried. Yes, that benefits me if you succeed, but if you fail, he'll suspect the Exchange. And even if you manage to kill Jihan, it would be a suicide mission, which isn't your style, and that does not free your brother. No, you need a full assault to assure his death and destroy his organization. It is the only way to be sure."

"So what's your plan then?" Fajkus spat. "Are we supposed to rely on your hired thugs?" He gestured angrily at Anders. "Murderers and trash? You expect me to believe that Montalban scum is going to take those monster walls and watch our back? I say horseshit to that!"

Anders shrugged, seemingly calm, his massive hands resting in his lap. The big man looked bored. He'd been called worse things than hired thug.

Ibrahim raised a hand to calm his subordinate. Fajkus was done, his distrust for the Montalban Exchange having been noted. I liked the Czech. He was angry. He kind of reminded me of a young Carl. Ibrahim nodded toward Katarina. "Please continue."

"Just because your people are suicidal fanatics, do not underestimate what my *hired trash* is capable of. I offer you more than just men with guns, I offer you resources, and I offer you a way into that compound."

Ibrahim kept up his poker face, but I could tell his interest was piqued. "And how exactly do you propose to do that?"

Katarina glanced absently at her absurdly expensive Swiss watch. She raised her head, and an evil grin split her perfect features. "Like this . . ."

The cabin door flew open. It was one of the Exodus operatives that I had met earlier, the Russian woman, Svetlana. She had a big bolt action sniper rifle cradled in her arms. "Ibrahim, we have incoming." Fajkus rose, his hand moving under his sweater to his holstered pistol.

"Don't worry," Katarina said. "They're with me."

A CZ 97B appeared in Fajkus's hand. "Treacherous—" He was cut off as Anders' .45 materialized right under his nose. The big man had moved so fast that I hadn't even seen the draw stroke.

"Calm down," Anders ordered. Svetlana jerked her rifle to her shoulder and pointed it square at Anders' back, then looked to Ibrahim for guidance. The Exodus commander shook his head slightly as he studied Katarina. Fajkus slowly placed his .45 on the table and removed his hand. Ander's pistol didn't move, and it was obvious that the Exodus man was only a few pounds of pressure on a trigger between life and death.

Then there was a noise. Faint at first, but it quickly grew, as the thunder closed on us. The dirty windows began to vibrate, clay pots rattled, and dust fell from the ceiling like fat brown snowflakes. Then it was deafening, as massive engines drove giant rotors, an endless deep scream, like some sort of leviathan descending on us. The room darkened as something blocked the sunlight.

"That's certainly a large helicopter," Ibrahim said.

"It's a Mil-26. The Halo. Biggest in the world, I'm told," Katarina shouted over the noise. "I have two of them." Kat always had liked to make a big entrance. She was such a drama queen. The noise receded as the huge helicopter tore away, demonstration of speed and mass complete. Anders slowly lowered and reholstered his gun. Svetlana dropped the muzzle of her rifle. Fajkus grudgingly returned to his seat.

"An impressive fly-by, but we've already thought of air insertion," Ibrahim said. "They'll see us coming, and shoot us out of the sky."

"I run the finest smuggling operation in Asia. My pilots are better than yours. We can run the mountain passes on night vision at a hundred and eighty kilometers an hour. Radar won't see a thing until we exit the pass. We'll be on top of the compound before Jihan even knows we're there. I can drop all of your strike teams right into his lap. At the same time my men will destroy his garrison in The Crossroads and the Brothers. Once they and their master are dead, the slave soldiers at the mines will collapse."

Fajkus shook his head. "It'll still take a minute to make it from the mouth of the canyon to the target, and our intel indicates there's a Shilka in the compound. That thing will tear your choppers apart."

He was right. I had seen that antiaircraft monstrosity when we had reconned the compound. Flying right into four quick and responsive 23mm cannons with active radar and an alert crew? *Screw that.*

"How do you propose we deal with that?"

Kat examined her nails like this was boring her. She took her sweet time responding. "You see, this is why Exodus needs me. I've been studying Jihan's weaknesses for quite some time. I have a way to get someone into the compound undetected. I've been laying the groundwork for months. We'll need someone capable of infiltrating when the choppers are in place, then at a predetermined time, that individual will disable the AA. It will be extremely dangerous and require someone skilled."

Every set of eyes in the room turned toward me.

I snorted. "Yeah . . . figures."

LORENZO
Crossroads City
March 24th

The last few days had been spent in preparation. I had gone over my part of the plan repeatedly, and had worked closely with both Exodus and Kat's forces. The choppers were prepped and stashed in Mongolia. Exodus would be riding in style. Kat's choppers could carry a small army, so they wouldn't even be close to full, but if one was disabled, they'd still have a way out. The Montalban foot soldiers were going to assault the garrison in town. The final group consisted of me, Anders, and a handpicked group of Exodus members.

On the other side, Jihan had several hundred fanatical soldiers in his fort. We needed to work fast though, because he and another hundred guarding the dam and around a thousand or so possible reinforcements at the slave mines only a few miles away. We were leaving the dam and mines alone, because it was better to cut off the head and let the body die.

In twenty-four hours the great raid would begin.

Exodus was spread thin. I had not realized at first just how much this operation meant to their organization, but I had pieced together a few facts. Exodus wasn't a huge operation by any means, and the force gathered here was one of the largest they'd ever assembled. Swords had gathered from every corner of the world for this. Ibrahim was their most experienced commander. Exodus literally had all of their eggs in one basket.

The Montalban Exchange was risking just as much. As soon as Kat struck against Jihan, she would either win total control of The Crossroads, or they were done, and they would be lucky to escape with their lives.

I had spent the last four days bouncing back and forth between the Montalban Exchange, the Glorious Cloud, and various Exodus meeting places. Today I was once again on the top floor of the Exchange, near a crackling fireplace, sitting around a table with Ibrahim and Fajkus of Exodus, and Katarina, Anders, and a man named Diego from the Exchange. I'd been told Katsumoto was the other hotshot Exodus boss in town, and I was a little suspicious as to why I'd not seen him at any of the meetings with the Montalbans, but Exodus was probably just hedging their bets in case this was an elaborate plot for Kat to sell out their leader.

Reaper and I were at the end of the table. Jill was at the Glorious Cloud. I was not comfortable having her near Kat, as I was still waiting for my ex to fly into one of her rages and kill somebody. Though she actually seemed a lot more grounded and *sane* than when I had last been around her. This mafia-don thing seemed really good for her.

In the middle of the table was a scale model of the compound. It was actually rather impressive, with carved foam blocks mimicking each building, the wall, and the surrounding terrain, with a red number painted on each structure to help us keep track. The compound was at the border between the windswept valley and the edge of the mountain. Three sides of the compound were exposed to open ground. The fourth hung over the side of the mountain, and had a near-vertical drop to the rock below. A red arrow was painted on the table, pointing to the northeast, the direction of the canyon mouth, where the helicopters would be coming from.

Katarina reached across the table and moved the toy tank that represented the dreaded ZSU antiaircraft cannon slightly. She turned the turret so it was pointing at me, and grinned. "So, you've had a chance to think it through. Can you do it?"

I stood, so I could have a better bird's eye view of the fort. We had been through this a dozen times, but it never hurt to look again, to try and find that one hidden problem that was just waiting to bite you in the ass. There was approximately two hundred meters from the cliff edge to where the ZSU had last been parked, and most of it would be navigable in the dark without being seen.

"Assuming phase one goes according to plan. Yeah. I can do it. Phase one gets hinky, and I'm probably dead."

"Then we'll abort. Turn around and fly back to Mongolia, and be home in time for cocoa," Kat replied. "If not?"

"Phase one complete. I'll initiate phase two, bring up my team, and when we're ten minutes off the ZSU I'll give the signal," I replied mechanically. I would only be on my own for the initial engagement. After that, in theory at least, I would have some help. I had received some good news from Exodus before the meeting. Shen had arrived, and would meet me at the staging point. I had worked with the man before, and had faith in his abilities.

"At Go, phase three will begin," Ibrahim stood, and moved two plastic helicopters across the board, and into the red path of the red arrow. "We'll move off station, and proceed through the canyon at maximum speed. My chopper will be in the lead position. One minute behind will be the second." Ibrahim had insisted that the chopper he was riding on be in front, that way if I failed and the ZSU blasted something out of the sky, it would be his Halo. That way half of his men could still escape. "That is the point of no return." He slowly sat back down. Once the choppers exited the canyon and were seen, we had to win, or Jihan's forces would expunge our existence from the earth.

Reaper looked up from his laptop. "As soon as I see the radar go down, that's when I'll bring in our eyes. By the way, weather still looks good. Chances of snow the next morning, but we should be clear during the raid." I had been adamant that he and Jill would not be placed in harm's way. Later today they would be leaving town, just in case this all went horribly wrong. Reaper still had a job to do, but it could be done remotely just as easy as it could be done in town. Having my people out from under the gun was going to be one less thing on my mind.

"When you leave the canyon, my men will attack The Crossroads barracks and kill any Brothers present." Diego spoke for the first time. He was relatively young, and had cultivated that Big Eddie Euro-trash vibe, down to the puffy hair and a suspicious amount of eye shadow. Ibrahim's spies had confirmed that when Diego wasn't working for Kat, he was cross dressing at one of the local clubs. Typical Montalban employee, but apparently Kat thought he was pretty sharp. He would be leading the Exchange's forces in town as they surrounded and burned Jihan's barracks to the ground. We still didn't know how many Brothers there actually were, but as of this morning, intel indicated that there were at least two in town.

Fajkus spoke directly to Katarina. "How is your men's morale?" His voice implied what he thought of the mercenaries.

Diego cut in. "The Montalban troops are as good as yours."

I snorted, perhaps a little too impolitely.

Diego's plucked eyebrows narrowed into a dangerous V. He lifted his shirt and exposed a well-worn knife handle. Ibrahim's spies had also confirmed that Diego had participated in a few knife fights in the arena, when he wasn't busy portraying a very convincing Celine Dion. He also had a bit of an attitude around me since I still had the reputation of having been Big Eddie's favorite killer. "You have something to say, Lorenzo?"

I leaned back further in my comfortable chair. "I never met a transvestite I couldn't take in a knife fight."

Diego began to rise, but Kat glared at him. He slowly lowered himself back down, fixing me with a glare that let me know we had unfinished business, or maybe he was going to start singing the theme song from *Titanic*. Hell if I knew.

"My men don't know they're doing this. When we initiate, I will tell them that Jihan has already been killed," she stated simply. "That'll fire them up. What they don't know can't hurt them, and if we fail in the compound . . ." She trailed off. We all knew it wouldn't matter for long. And she meant it when she said *we,* since Kat was going to be on the second chopper. That fact alone helped to demonstrate to Exodus that she was just as committed as they were. "How's your troops' morale?" she asked snidely, already knowing the answer.

"Excellent," Ibrahim said with an honest assurance. He wasn't exaggerating either. I had worked closely with his subordinates in planning this. They were fired up. There were still several other Exodus teams scattered around the world that were supposed to be converging here, but Ibrahim was done waiting. The Kurd had picked a course of action and was committed to seeing it through.

The next phase was the separation of the various teams to take over and control different points of the compound. My group got the brig. Ibrahim was going to personally take the missile silo that Jihan called home. I didn't like that part at all. A commander should be someplace he can have a view of everything, and that's not at the bottom of a giant hole, but Exodus leadership seemed to be very *lead from the front* oriented. We went over secondary plans, who would take over what areas of responsibility should some other team be incapacitated, and finally every contingency plan that we could think of.

It had been a long time since I had worked with this large a group. I grudgingly respected Exodus. Their motives were pure, their training top notch, and their fury justified. They were nuts, but they were devoted nuts. The Exchange was the wild card, but Katarina had been nothing but professional so far. Anders was a brute, but he was also cunning, and by all accounts, very good at what he did. Diego was a weirdo, but in typical Montalban fashion could be counted on to be ruthless and efficient.

We went over a few last bits of business. Ibrahim nodded at me toward the conclusion, his bushy eyebrows scrunching together. I had already agreed to meet with him secretly, to discuss a few other contingency plans that we were going to put into place in case the Montalbans fell through. There was not a lot of trust in this business.

Finally, we were done. We had planned about as much as possible in the time allotted. If we didn't go tomorrow, it would be at least another week before we could do this again. That meant a greater chance that my brother would be dead, Exodus would lose more slaves, and Kat lost more money. None of us wanted to postpone. We were a go.

Ibrahim addressed Katarina, very formally, very solemnly. "On behalf of Exodus, I want to thank you. I know that your reasons for helping us are to your own benefit, but know that the lives and freedom of thousands are in your hands. With almighty God's blessing upon us, tomorrow liberty will shine on the ancient Crossroads again."

Katarina smiled politely. She had a glass of wine in front of her. She picked it up as if she were about to give a toast. "Thank you. I—" There was a knock at the door, and she turned briefly. Anders pulled a cloth over the table, covering the model. "Please excuse me, for a moment." Ibrahim nodded for her to proceed.

The door opened, and two Montalban retainers came in, each one holding the arm of a third, his feet dragging limply behind him. They pulled the semi-conscious man into the center of the room. Kat waved her hand. "Leave him." The retainers dropped the man with a thud, turned and quickly left. The man curled up in a fetal position and moaned. He had obviously been severely beaten.

Katarina pushed her chair away from the table, and strolled toward the man, still holding her glass. The rest of us at the table exchanged confused glances, including Anders and Diego. The injured man seemed incoherent. "Everyone, allow me to introduce you to Dieter, one of my employees." Kat paused, and then threw her wine in his face. He jerked awake as the alcohol burned the deep lacerations on his face. He cringed back from Kat's feet, trying to roll away, his hands raised to cover his head.

"Ms. Katarina! I'm sorry! I'm sorry!" he shrieked.

"Shut up!" she screamed back at him, and then flung the glass into his face. It shattered and he yelped and scurried back further. His back collided with the wall, and he had nowhere else to go. Her voice went immediately back to a normal inflection. "Dieter was working closely with Diego on the plans for the raid. It has been brought to my attention that my *employee* has a big mouth."

"I didn't tell anyone anything!" Dieter insisted, still recoiling. Blood was running down his forehead into his eye, and he instinctively wiped it away with his torn shirt sleeve.

"Only because we caught you in the act before you could open your stupid mouth," she said calmly. "How long have we worked together? We were equals under Big Eddie. So, what, eight years? Eight years I've considered you my friend?" She turned back to address the table. "Ibrahim, if you doubted my sincerity in this operation, don't let your heart be troubled. Allow me to demonstrate the depth of my commitment."

"That isn't necessary," Ibrahim said, stone-faced.

Kat smiled. Her teeth were a sharp white line splitting her face. "Oh, yes. It is." A stainless SIG P232 appeared suddenly in her hand. She spun around, and there were two rapid cracks. Dieter screamed as a bullet exploded through each knee. Reaper was the only one to let out an audible gasp.

Dieter just kept on screaming, a hand on each leg, blood welling up between his clenched fingers. "Shut up! Shut up! You haven't earned the right to scream!" Kat shrieked. The injured man choked back his pain. She walked over to the fireplace, removed an iron poker from the rack, and stuck the tip into the coals to let it heat up. She was again calm as she studied the fire. "This meeting is adjourned. We'll rendezvous at the assigned positions tomorrow. Anders will see you out."

So there she was. I was wondering if that personality had finally been put away. She had been so calm since we had reunited, but apparently not. This was Evil Kat, and from the look in her eyes, and the poker in the coals, I knew the Crazy one wasn't far behind.

I was the last one out. Kat was still watching the poker. I shook my head sadly. If Dieter was lucky he would pass out from blood loss before the metal got red hot.

✢ ✢ ✢

"She's irrational," Fajkus insisted. "I say we postpone, and find a way to do it without her."

The Exodus members were clustered under an overhang down the street from the Montalban Exchange. Roland, Svetlana, and another young Exodus operative named Phillips met us there. They'd been tailing Ibrahim to make sure their leader was safe. I scanned back and forth, but couldn't spot any eavesdroppers. We hadn't walked very far, so my good ear was still ringing from the sudden pistol shots.

"No," Roland said forcefully. "Every day we wait, more slaves die."

Svetlana spoke up. "Not only that, we're committed to the Montalbans now. If we back off, they could easily sell us out to Jihan. No. To postpone now means that we will have to fight both of them."

Ibrahim folded his arms. Ultimately the decision rested with him. "Lorenzo. You know her best. You were her lover once." He stated that fact without animosity or judgment, I was simply the best source of intelligence. "Will she fail us?"

I probably knew her as well as anyone could. I weighed my answer carefully. "Is she unstable? Yes. Will she fail you? I don't think so. She's as committed as you are, but in a different way."

Fajkus snorted. "Bullshit."

"Katarina is dangerous, but she's focused like a laser beam. As long as she's targeted on something, she'll see it through to the end. When she's got a goal, nothing else matters and she'll risk anything to achieve it." I hoped I was right, because heaven help us if I was wrong. "She's damaged. By what, I don't know. In a way, she's like some of the slaves you've freed, only she never had someone like Dr. Bundt to help put her back together."

The Exodus members waited for their leader's decision. I had come to like each of these fanatics. Roland was an American, as was Phillips, and they were buddies. How they had ended up here was a mystery, but they were both earnest, smart, and likable young men. Svetlana was a sharp woman and, it turned out, a good friend of Ling. Fajkus was a surly bulldog of a man, but he struck me as honorable and honest.

"This isn't the only way, Ibrahim," Fajkus insisted.

There was a lot Exodus wasn't telling me. They were playing it cool, but I knew they had other plots. First off, the number of men on the choppers was a little smaller than what I estimated they had in The Crossroads, and some of the ones I'd met so far weren't part of the raid. In fact, nobody would tell me where Ling and Valentine were going either. However, you get used to that sort of thing in a business where nobody tells the whole truth.

"Fajkus, old friend. You've seen more combat than the rest of us put together, and I always value your counsel, but today I'm afraid that we must choose to associate ourselves with the lesser of two evils. If we turn back now, then Jihan will find out about our mission, and tens of thousands more will die in servitude. Not on my watch." Ibrahim nodded. "We strike tomorrow."

VALENTINE
Exodus Safe House
Crossroads City
March 24th

"We strike tomorrow," Katsumoto began his briefing. "Our operation will commence simultaneously with the main assault on Sala Jihan's fortress." The Japanese Exodus commander used a laser pointer to indicate the old Soviet fortress on a large Cyrillic topographical map that was years out of date. The map hung on a wooden board propped against the wall. Someone had written all over it in Sharpie, indicating the present-day positions of things.

Next to the map was a large screen, onto which was projected a PowerPoint presentation detailing our assault plan. A laptop sat on a small table at the front of the room, hooked to a projector. I stood off to the side with Ling. Some fifty Exodus operatives, all of whom were taking notes or listening intently, sat in metal folding chairs. Skunky was among them.

Katsumoto continued, using a wireless mouse to advance the PowerPoint presentation as he spoke. "Our first challenge lies here," he said. The laser dot fell on a cluster of buildings on the road that led to the hydroelectric plant. "This is a former Red Army checkpoint that is now being used by Jihan's forces. The road from there to the dam itself is straight, open, and uphill. If we get stalled trying to break through the checkpoint, the enemy will be able to rake us with machine-gun fire and RPGs all the way up to the dam itself. Our strategy will be to smash through this checkpoint as quickly as possible. It's about a kilometer from there to the dam. If we move quickly enough, we will be on top of the dam before its garrison knows what's happening."

Someone raised his hand. "Won't they still be able to hit us with fire on the way up?"

"Yes," Katsumoto said grimly. "Our safety lies in darkness and speed. The raid will commence after dark. To the best of our knowledge, Jihan's forces at the dam are more primitively armed and will likely have limited night-vision capabilities. We will advance up the road without using headlights. This is risky, there is no doubt, but there is no other way. We do not have any personnel to spare to try to infiltrate the checkpoint quietly."

The fifty guys we had were going up against a garrison of over a hundred at the plant itself. They were part of Sala Jihan's slave army, brainwashed conscripts, but what they lacked in training they made up for in fanaticism. If we didn't move quickly enough, the Brotherhood could be called down on us as well, and although we didn't know how many of them there were, apparently they were well trained.

I listened intently as Katsumoto described the rest of the operation. Our initial approach would be made in a small caravan of vehicles, including two old BTR-70 armored personnel carriers that Exodus had acquired in The Crossroads. These vehicles would lead the charge through the checkpoint and up the hill, followed by the unarmored trucks.

The rest of the plan was pretty straightforward. The hydroelectric plant itself wasn't that large, which simplified things. The road that led up from the checkpoint crossed over the top of the dam itself, running from west to east. On the east side, nestled against the mountains on a flat spot, was a cluster of buildings that housed the defensive garrison and part of the dam's operational crew. There was also a group of huge transformers, connected to power lines that led down into The Crossroads. There was only one way in and out of this compound, and that was across the top of the dam.

The reservoir, which was covered in ice that I assumed was thick enough to drive a truck across, was on the north side of the dam. Trying to cross the ice would be too dangerous, as there were no roads that led to the shore, and there was absolutely no cover out there. Also, the water line was about twenty feet below the top of the dam.

The south side was even less accessible. The dam was over a hundred feet tall, with no easy way to scale it. A river flowed from the south side of the dam, but there was no way for personnel to access the interior from down there.

The road across the top of the dam was the only way to access its interior. A large concrete superstructure, centered on top of the dam, contained most of the hydroelectric plant's machinery. You had to go through this building to get inside the dam itself. The actual turbines were buried deep inside, and that is where Katsumoto's team of sappers would be placing their charges. The explosives would have to be expertly placed to permanently disable the dam and compromise its integrity to such an extent that it would collapse, but not right away. That would be quite an accomplishment. Just blowing the thing up right away would have been easier, and I got the distinct impression that that is exactly what Katsumoto had wanted to do.

Our task would not be easy. We were to hold off the garrison, housed in the compound on the east side of the dam, while also holding off reinforcements from the road to the west. We were outnumbered and there was no room to maneuver on top of the narrow concrete structure.

Fortunately for us, Sala Jihan's forces would have their hands full. There would be an attack on his fortress, which would surely draw the brunt of his attention and the bulk of his forces. The Montalban Exchange's mercenaries would attack the garrison in town and create a diversion there. With any luck, the assault on the dam would be low on the enemy's priorities list.

It remained to be seen whether or not we'd have any luck.

Katsumoto surprised me by drawing the group's attention to me. "Mr. Valentine will be joining us on this operation. His reputation, of course, precedes him."

All eyes were on me. I waved sheepishly.

"Mr. Valentine, perhaps you have something to contribute? I have been told that you are a very experienced operator, after all."

Is he putting me on the spot? I looked at Ling briefly. She subtly nodded for me to speak to the group. *Fine.* I didn't know what the hell Katsumoto's problem was, but I wasn't going to be made a fool of. I smiled at the Exodus leader politely and made my way to the front of the group.

"Uh, hello," I began. "My name is Michael Valentine. I'm not one of those guys that likes to blather on about his credentials, so I'll give you the short version just to assure everyone," I looked directly at Katsumoto, "that I know what I'm talking about.

"I began my career in the United States Air Force before moving to Vanguard Strategic Solutions International. I have seen combat in Afghanistan, Africa, the Chinese DMZ, Bosnia, Central America, and Mexico. Though, being honest, that thing in Central America was pretty uninteresting. I was also involved in the recent mess in Zubara." I left out the shootout in Nevada.

"Who are the team leaders here?" I asked. Several of the Exodus operatives in the audience raised their hands. "Okay, good. Now, how many of you have ever worked with each other before? I mean, actually were involved in a combat operation, or even a training operation, where you worked in concert?"

The team leaders slowly lowered their hands, awkwardly looking around the room.

"I don't know much about how you guys operate in the field," I said. "As was pointed out, I'm not a member of your club. But I get the distinct impression that you primarily operate in small, independent teams, and aren't always involved in direct action. Am I correct?"

Several members of my audience, now interested in what I had to say, nodded their heads.

I nodded back. "Right. Well, boys and girls, that can cause problems.

You have multiple teams that will be operating in the same small area. You guys aren't used to working with each other. You may do things different ways. Communication is going to be vital here. This isn't going to be some quick-in, quick-out sneaky secret squirrel shit. We're outnumbered and in hostile territory. It's going to get ugly out there. Things will go wrong. You will take casualties.

"What you need to do, guys, is go over every detail of the plan together. Memorize the terrain as much as you can. Pass that information down to the people under your command. Each person on your team should be able to do the job of another. Everyone should know what the plan is, and what the backup plan is. At no time should anyone out there be wondering what to do. There's always something you can be doing.

"I don't mean for anyone to get discouraged. I've been in combat with Exodus before. You guys are some of the best trained, most disciplined, and most motivated troops I've ever worked with. I wouldn't be coming to this party if I thought it was a suicide mission. Give 'em hell."

With that, I smiled politely at Katsumoto, winked at Ling, and strolled confidently out of the room, even though I didn't really have anywhere to go. I just wanted to make a good exit.

Later on, needing some air to clear my head, I ventured outside into the cold. The sky was overcast, a low blanket of grey clouds blocking out the stars. The world was lit with a dull ambient amber glow from the lights of Crossroads City reflecting off of the snow and the clouds. Snowflakes lazily drifted downward from the sky, and there was no wind. It was almost pleasant. It reminded me of home, of long winters in Northern Michigan as a child.

Behind the crumbling Soviet-era warehouse was a fenced-off lot where a couple of vehicles were parked. Armed guards quietly kept watch. A couple of barrels had fires lit in them. One had a blazing fire going in it, and was surrounded by half a dozen Exodus operatives, talking and laughing.

The other barrel was deserted, and the fire was dying. I made my way over to it and threw on a couple pieces of wood from the pile stacked neatly next to it. I pulled off my gloves and warmed my hands before shoving them in my pockets. That's when I remembered I was carrying my harmonica.

I removed the instrument from my pocket and examined it by the glow of the firelight. It was an old Hohner Super-Chromatic 12-hole that had belonged to my father. I held it in my hands and remembered him. He died when I was young. After all these years, I couldn't remember what his face looked like.

We'd spend summers at his cousin's hunting camp in the Upper Peninsula, deep in a forest at the end of a dirt road. We'd have a campfire every night, and my dad would play his harmonica and tell stories to us. Sometimes my mom would be there too, but usually she'd go inside and make dinner, since she'd heard all of my dad's stories a million times. But my little cousins and I were always riveted, no matter how many times we'd heard them.

My father would tell us stories about being in the Air Force. He'd been a navigator on a B-52. I remembered laughing as he'd talk about playing his harmonica while in flight, driving the rest of his crew crazy. He told us about the time his BUFF got hit by an Iraqi SA-2 during the First Gulf War, and no matter how many times I heard the story, it always had me on the edge of my seat.

"I didn't know you played an instrument," Ling said, startling me. Her breath smoldered in the cold air as she stepped close to the burn barrel to warm herself.

I smiled. "I haven't played this thing in a long time. I keep it because it's the only thing I have that belonged to my father. What are you doing out here? Can't sleep either?"

Ling shook her head. "Not yet."

"Something on your mind? Talk to me, you'll feel better. Something about the plan is bothering you, isn't it?"

"The plan is good enough," Ling said. "We're making the most out of the assets we have. It's risky, but Katsumoto and I discussed it at length and I couldn't come up with any viable alternatives."

"But . . . ?"

"This entire operation is bothering me, Michael," Ling said, shoving her hands in her pockets. "Sala Jihan is a blight upon the face of the earth, there's no doubt about it. It's just . . . " she trailed off momentarily, looking around to make sure no-one else was within earshot. "It's just this whole thing seems rushed. We're trying to get more people in place, but Ibrahim won't wait."

"The longer we wait the more likely it is we'll be found out."

"I understand that. My issue is with the timing of this whole operation. We should have waited, gathered our assets more carefully, and moved from a position of strength. Now we're committed to doing this while understrength, having to rely on outsiders for support."

"Hey, *you* asked *me* to come along."

"I didn't mean you, Michael. I meant the Montalban Exchange. I don't like this deal with them. I don't like it at all. That woman, Katarina, is broken. I've seen such things before. In most cases the people were victims of the most horrific kinds of physical, emotional, and sexual abuse. I don't know what happened to that woman, but she's . . . she's . . ."

"She's fucked *up* is what she is." I hadn't met the woman but I'd heard about everything that had transpired with her.

"As you say," Ling agreed. "And there are disagreements on the execution of our own portion of the operation."

"Disagreements? About what?"

"Katsumoto wanted to destroy the dam outright and flood The Crossroads."

I raised an eyebrow. "Thousands would die if you did that. There are people here that are not involved in this. Women and children."

"That is the argument that Ibrahim made. Katsumoto insisted that it was worth the price to destroy the base of Sala Jihan's power for sure."

"Isn't that why they're going to kill Jihan?"

Ling sighed, a puff of steam forming in the air as she did so. "There are no guarantees that he will be successful."

"You guys keep talking about this asshole like he's Sauron in Siberia. Jihan is only a man, Ling. Everyone has gotten spooked by all this hocus-pocus crap he pulls. He's just a warlord with a bunch of crazy, drugged-up followers. I saw the same thing in Africa."

"Perhaps," Ling said, trailing off. "It's just that if Ibrahim fails and The Crossroads remains, then we will have accomplished nothing here."

"What do you think? Should we just blow the dam?"

"I think if Exodus had had such scorched-earth policies when they found me, I wouldn't have survived to join. Yet Sala Jihan is a far greater evil than the human traffickers I knew in China. The plan is the best compromise we could come up with. I just hope it works."

I smiled at her. "I'm glad you're opening up to me a little bit. You're one of the few people I know here. I feel like the outsider I am."

"I admit I can be . . . standoffish . . . at times," she said slowly. "Please don't take it personally. It's just . . ."

"I know how it is. I haven't been super fun to be around lately either. I damn near shot Lorenzo back on the island."

"So I heard."

"Oh, don't worry, it's fine now. I think." I laughed.

Ling smiled. "To be honest, I feel alone too. Shen and Antoine have been assigned to the main assault. They were the only members of my sword that were still with me."

I felt bad for Ling. There's a certain loneliness that comes with command. A lot is required of you to lead men into combat. "What happened to your team?" I asked hesitantly.

"It's nothing dramatic," Ling replied. "We took casualties in Mexico. I wasn't . . . am not . . . the most experienced team leader. I shouldn't have gotten a mission so important, not with Ariel's life hanging in the balance."

It all came back to that girl and her secrets again. "Don't sell yourself short. That was a bad op from the very beginning, but you accomplished your objective in the face of impossible odds. By rights, none of us should've gotten out of that hellhole alive."

"By rights, I shouldn't have been in charge there in the first place," Ling said. "But there was no choice. My team was in Mexico and there simply wasn't anyone else available. We lacked the means to get to her on our own."

"So you hired us. Decker was an ass. How were you able to convince my old boss to go along with it?" Adrian Decker had been the operations manager and CEO of Vanguard Strategic Solutions International. After the fiasco in Mexico, the UN had wanted to put him on trial at the Hague for war crimes. He got out of it, though. Decker always had a way out.

Ling raised her eyebrows. "You don't know? Michael, Adrian Decker had done work for Exodus before. Several times. We don't like to outsource work but we do build working relationships with outsiders. He was certainly receptive to our propositions."

"He was always receptive to money."

"Indeed, but he was discreet and reliable, and his personnel were the best that could be hired for any price. In any case," Ling said, "You know the rest. You were there. It all went to hell. I lost good men."

"So did we."

Ling nodded. "After that, I was given missions that weren't direct action. Support missions of different sorts. Things where a large strike team was not required. Personnel rotated in and out of my sword as necessary. Only Shen and Antoine stayed with me, by their own choice."

"Did Exodus *punish* you for Mexico? Like that was your fault! You did everything humanly possible, and don't you ever let any asshole that wasn't there tell you any different."

"That's very sweet of you, Michael, but it wasn't like that. My confidence had been shaken. *I* had been shaken, to the core. I thought of leaving the order, but Antoine talked me out of it. So I was assigned to what you might call lower stress operations until they . . . and I . . . felt I was ready. The mission to retrieve you was my first serious combat operation since Cancun."

"Well, you pulled it off like a boss," I said encouragingly. "I'm here, ain't I?"

Ling actually laughed. I was glad to make her smile. "As you say. To be honest, I find I do better at the kinds of missions I've been doing. Espionage and intelligence seem to suit me better than door-kicking, as you might put it."

"There were a lot of times, over the years when I wanted to quit," I said. "Vanguard, I mean. After every big deployment I'd swear to myself that I was done, that I was going to go back to the States and get a real job and become a respectable citizen. See how well that worked out for me. I ended up a security guard in Las Vegas. I almost left, though. A few years back I managed to get my pilot's license, and I had an in to transfer to the aviation support division of Vanguard. Flight pay was about the same as the special duty pay I got on the Switchblade teams and there was a whole lot less death."

"Why didn't you transfer, then, and become a pilot?"

I thought for a moment. "Tailor. Skunky. My teammates. Ramirez, my team leader. He was a good guy. Despite how terrible the work was sometimes, I loved working for him. I didn't want to leave my team. Like you said, they were my family. And also . . ." I trailed off for a moment, looking up into the cloudy sky.

"I don't know how else to live," I said. "This sort of thing is familiar. Comfortable, even, in some crazy way. Standing over this burn barrel in the ass-end of Siberia feels like it makes more sense for me than working in a cubicle somewhere."

Ling put a hand on my arm. "Is that why you came here with me?" She had a worried look on her face. "I'm sorry. I shouldn't have pressured you . . ."

I didn't let her finish apologizing. "No, no, it's not like that. This feels right. I have my misgivings, but . . . I don't know. Ariel said this is where I'm supposed to be. I don't believe in fate, but I really feel like I'm supposed to be here. This sort of thing is what I was born to do. And I might actually get to do some good this time. A lot of the shit we used to do was morally ambiguous, at best. I've done things I'm not proud of. It sounds stupid, but maybe I can make up for it here. Use my skills to help people for once."

"It's why I stay on, you know," Ling said. "What we do is ugly business, but it's necessary. Please don't take this the wrong way, but I'm glad to see that you've stopped running from who you are. I saw this in you in Mexico. And when I saw you risk your life to protect Ariel, I knew that you were also a good man. Don't doubt yourself anymore, Michael."

Ling very subtly moved a little closer to me. I didn't say anything else, not wanting to ruin a perfect, quiet moment of tranquility before the storm.

Chapter 18: Lotus Blossom

LORENZO
2.7 kilometers from Sala Jihan's compound
March 25th

"Spring . . . my ass," I muttered through chattering teeth.

It was damn cold. Mind-numbing, break-your-fingers-off, shatter-your-teeth, fucking-kill-you-dead cold. There was no wind, and the night sky was brilliantly clear, displaying unbelievable billions of stars, but somehow the stillness and clarity made it even colder. All I wanted to do was huddle in my parka and pray to get on with this.

"I got here in January," Phillips replied, with that typical, abnormally-high-morale, Exodus can-do attitude. "This is *nothing*."

"Yeah. Remember when we had that big storm last month? Dude. Now that was cold," Roland radded. "We were way up the mountain trying to survey the compound with telescopes and—"

"And there was like this . . . ice tornado. It was awesome." Phillips made a twirling motion with his hands.

"Well, until Rasheed froze his toe off."

"Yeah, broke it right off."

Both of the young Americans laughed. Even though it was dark inside the ice cave, my eyes were adjusted well enough to see Anders regarding the two like they were dimwits. Shen was squatting at the cave mouth, rubbing his hands together and occasionally blowing on them to keep the circulation up, as enigmatic as ever. He had his gloves off so that he could better operate the thermal camera. Luckily it was plastic, so the odds of him freezing his skin to the machine were relatively low.

Shen had only recently arrived. His usual partner, Antoine, was not exactly built for stealth, and would be on one of the choppers. Shen hadn't fully acclimatized to the altitude yet, but he was in such good shape that it didn't seem to affect him nearly as bad as it had hit me when I had first gotten here.

The five of us were inside a rock indentation, surrounded by fat, shiny icicles. There was a faint touch of wood smoke and yak in the air, drifting up the canyon from the nearby bunch of yurts. The cluster of fur dwellings was far too small to be considered a village, but it was something, and the nomads that made it their home seemed comfortable enough through our thermal and night-vision devices.

All of us were dressed for warmth, in state-of-the-art camouflage parkas and face masks. We looked like a mottled pile of white lumps. Even our weapons had been spray painted or wrapped with white tape. But despite the fancy gear, we were still freezing. The sudden drop in temperature had been unexpected. We probably should've huddled together for warmth, but every one of us was too stubborn or proud to do that.

"Hey, Lorenzo, you know Valentine?" Phillips asked.

"Sadly . . . What about him?"

"Is it true he single-handedly fought off like a hundred soldiers in Mexico?"

Ling had said Valentine had developed a bit of a rep with Exodus. "Hell if I know. Valentine's just another asshole with mental problems and a gun."

"Oh . . ." Phillips sounded disappointed.

"He'll fit in great with Exodus. Anything yet, Shen?" I was ready to get this show on the road. Worst case scenario, the mark would decide that it was too damn cold and just stay in bed. Then we would have to abort the mission and try again next week. Shen shook his head. A mist of ice particles fell from his hood as he did so, and it hung suspended in the small window of light from the thermal cam. "Shit. He's probably not going to come."

"He'll be here," Anders stated.

"It's a little cold for romance," I replied, annoyed, but knowing that overall, Kat's plan was a pretty good one, and she had been laying the groundwork for months.

"You haven't seen this girl . . . "

"Whatever." I still had a hard time picturing one of Jihan's minor business functionaries leaving the comfort of the compound once a week for a clandestine meeting with some nomad's daughter, especially when Jihan had a bunch of slave girls available. Kat had assured me that there was more to it than that, and that the young functionary was actually in love, and had plans of running away with the girl. The functionaries weren't slaves. They were the business people that kept Jihan's finances in order while he was busy being creepy in the bottom of a missile silo.

The young businessman had met the nomad's daughter in town. It was love at first sight, and though Jihan's people were not allowed to leave the compound unescorted, this one had found a way. He had been meeting the girl once a week for the last few months. It was a forbidden love, and if Jihan found out, the young man was toast. However, once a week he risked it anyway. Of course he did. Kat had picked the girl herself, and trained her to be irresistible, a classic Juliet sting.

We were some distance from the compound, but the lights from the walls could be seen reflecting off of the mountain snow above us, giving the place a slight pink glow. The canyon we were watching led directly to the base of the fort. The climb was virtually impossible, but the mark had found a way back and forth, and tonight we intended to exploit it.

Provided he actually showed up.

Roland stirred as something buzzed inside his parka, and he had to struggle through multiple zippers to access his tac vest. There was a flicker of light as he opened the sat phone and studied the message.

"Ibrahim?" Phillips asked.

"No. My girlfriend sent me a text message." He laughed as he read it. "She's back in the States. She thinks I'm doing an internship with Toyota." He pulled off one heavy glove so he could type with his thumb. "Hang on."

Anders reached over and unceremoniously grabbed the phone. The giant pointed a massive finger at Roland's face and wagged it condescendingly, before tossing the phone back to Roland. Anders was a singularly humorless individual. Roland shoved the phone back into his coat and sulked.

Every Exodus team was a little bit different. My experience had been with Ling and her highly formal men. Zack Roland and Nathan Scott Phillips didn't really seem to fit that mold. They were attached to my group tonight because they were both supposed to be very good at this kind of infiltration mission, and they always worked together. Both of the Exodus operatives were in their mid-twenties. Roland was dark haired, and Jill said that he looked like the kid from *High School Musical*, which I hadn't seen, while Phillips was blond, stocky, and perpetually jovial.

"Hey, Shen. I thought you Exodus types were all fanatical and intense. Where'd you find these two?" I wasn't worried about being quiet, since if the mark showed up, he would glow on thermal as soon as he entered the canyon. Plus talking made me not think about the onset of hypothermia. Shen shrugged.

"Brazil," Phillips said.

"We were mission companions," Roland followed.

"Mormon missionaries."

"You know. White shirts. Ties. Name tags."

"Then we ran into some soldiers for a drug cartel. They raided an Amazon village we had been teaching in. And we weren't going to stand for that."

"I thought you guys didn't go for violence," Anders said.

"No, those are Quakers. We're awesome at violence," Phillips said.

"Yeah, we met Ibrahim when Exodus wasted those slavers. After we finished up our two years, we joined up, been on board ever since."

Both of the young men made fists, and knocked their knuckles together, scattering snow. "Heck, yeah!"

I nodded as if this made perfect sense. The Lorenzos were Mormon, and Gideon Lorenzo had been extremely devout. Bob had been a missionary himself, and had gone to Russia, or so I'd been told since that had happened after I'd run off. Exodus seemed to be made up of a bunch of religious types, Christians, Jews, Buddhists, Muslims, and Other. Ling had been wearing an Orthodox cross. I was surrounded by religious nuts. Personally, I didn't know if there was a God, but I was pretty sure there was a Devil. Me and him were old acquaintances. Anders glanced at me and shrugged. Apparently he was also a member of the Church of Moral Ambivalence and Whatever's Convenient.

"Contact." We all perked up at Shen's voice. I was glad to see that the screwing around ceased immediately. Everyone was totally still. "Individual entering the canyon. Heading toward the village."

Unable to make out anyone in the darkness, I slid forward and hunched down behind Shen's view screen. A single blob of white trudged through the hip deep snow. The man positively glowed with heat compared to the frozen black backdrop, a halo of waste heat from exertion escaping his coat and leaving a trail behind him. He was heading toward the nomad's yurts.

Well, I'll be damned. That's true love for you.

"I've got him," I stated as I slid my night vision monocular over one eye and tightened the strap around the top of my head. My head began to freeze as soon as I dropped my hood. The world turned into brilliant green pixels as the lens settled into place. I quickly cinched the hood back up. I studied the other four in the green light. They were intense and ready. "You know the plan. Proceed on my signal. Roland, contact Ibrahim and tell him we're on."

The other four nodded. The great raid had just begun.

It took me longer than expected to traverse the snowfield leading to the yurts. I had hoped to take down the mark outside the village, but the snow was deep, and I kept stepping on hard bits that immediately cracked and plunged me down to my hips. I had to be careful, as noise seemed to travel forever across the stillness. My target was not bothering to conceal his movement, and I could hear him sliding, crashing, and grunting from a hundred meters away.

I could have just shot him from here, but I wanted to talk first. He had an accomplice who lowered a rope so he could secretly reenter the compound. I wanted to find out if there was a code word or something of that nature. *Then* I could shoot him.

There was no pity for this man. He worked for a force of pure evil, and right now that force was my opposition. Even the three good men behind me—and Anders—would have no mercy on him because of who he worked for. In fact, they would have even less pity than Anders. The fact that the functionary was out here because he was being manipulated by Katarina was just too damned bad for him.

It took me too long to catch up. The snow was packed hard closer to the dwellings by constant stamping of the animals and the residents. He was now on more solid footing, and made really good time to the closest yurt. There was a flash of light as the fur door was opened briefly and a shape moved inside. The smell of spices and perfume hit a moment later.

Gliding up outside the entry, I listened, but couldn't hear anything. The fabric walls were surprisingly good at sound dampening. I waited five more minutes for him to get comfortable. There were no sounds from the other yurts, since people who work this hard to survive go to sleep early. I stuffed my night vision set back into my coat. It was handy, but that strap around the back of my head gave me a headache. Luckily there were no dogs barking an alert. Since it had been a long winter, they had probably gotten eaten. Even if the nomads knew I was here, they too were being paid by Kat not to get involved. Montalban money was also the reason they were settled at this particular point, rather than at a lower altitude where life would be a lot less miserable.

The girl didn't know when we would take the mark. Kat told her only what she needed to know, and even then probably half of the information she'd been given was false. So even if she talked too much, nothing would come back to incriminate the Exchange. She just knew that during one of these weekly meetings, somebody was going to pay her boyfriend a visit and she wasn't supposed to do anything about it, other than collect her bonus money.

Finally, tired of freezing, I decided to enter. I figured five minutes was plenty of time for the two of them to start playing Rogue Businessman and the Nomad's Daughter. It assumed that the rules to that would be similar to Heidi and the Storm Trooper. They should be plenty distracted by now. I unslung my Remington ACR, checked the Aimpoint sight, and used the attached sound suppressor to part the airlock-like fur entrance. There was one layer, a small spot of dead air, and then a second layer.

"Going in," I said into my neck microphone.

"Go," said Anders' voice in my ear.

Pausing, listening, no response, I pushed through the thick furs and into the dwelling. Slinking in low, quiet as I could be, it took a moment for my eyes to adjust to the firelight. The interior of the yurt was actually much warmer and comfier than expected. In fact, the heat differential was almost painful. The mark's fur coat was discarded on the floor. The two occupants had their backs to me, and they were speaking quietly, sitting crosslegged on blankets, staring into the fire, which was not exactly the scene I had expected.

He was maybe twenty-five, definitely Han Chinese. Anders had been right about the girl. There was no way he was going to stay away. She was beautiful, probably in her late teens. They were holding hands. Either she was as superb an actor as Katarina, all dopey and moon-eyed, or the two really were in love.

So now I needed to go beat some information out the guy, then kill him. *Some days I hate my job.*

The furs absorbed any noise my boots might have made as I stalked closer. With my head tilted slightly to favor my good ear, I could hear them clearly now.

"Come away with me. Please," he said, the tone of his voice was desperate.

"I can't. My people are here, my family. Your home, so far away, as if on the other side of world." Her Cantonese was rough. He must have been tutoring her.

"We must leave soon. The Pale Man is evil. You know what he'll do to me if he finds out about us," he pleaded. I thought of the grinning skull faces propped up on stakes on the railway into The Crossroads. I'm sure the functionary had seen that kind of thing a few times.

"I know . . . He has hurt my people before, taken many of us away. But this is my home. I am afraid."

"I'll protect you. I promise," he vowed with the intensity that only the young and stupid can muster.

Judging by how badly the functionary flinched, the metal end of my Silencero sound suppressor must have been staggeringly cold against the base of his neck. "You're in no position to promise anything, kid. Don't you fucking move." My Cantonese was pretty rough too, but I think I got the point across. And to think that Jill said *I* was bad at communicating.

The girl squealed, leapt to her feet, but tripped on the blankets that she had wrapped around her legs, and fell back down. She rolled over and scrambled on her hands and knees back to the far wall of the dwelling. The functionary didn't move. He knew damn good and well what the cold metal lump resting on his spine was.

"So Jihan knows . . . " he said with resignation, the breath leaving his lungs in one long, painful sigh. Slowly, he turned so he could see me. I kept the gun on him the whole time, until he was staring at my mask. I reached back with my left hand and pulled it down. His eyes widened in surprise. "But you're not one of Jihan's men . . . who are you? Bandit! Leave her be. She has nothing. I'm the one you want. Do what you will with me, but please don't harm the girl. I can—"

I put my left hand back on my gun's vertical foregrip, then stabbed the whole gun forward, ramming him in the face hard enough to chip a couple of teeth. "Will you shut up already?" He stumbled back and raised his hands to his bloody lips. I turned my attention to the girl. She had gotten over her initial shock, and was apparently glad to see that I wasn't a scar-faced slave-soldier. "It's time."

"What?" he mumbled through his hands, glancing between me and his girlfriend. I reached into my coat, pulled out the rubber-banded stack of currency from the Montalban Exchange and tossed it to her.

She caught it in one hand, and immediately used her thumb to fan through the bills to make sure they were all large denominations. "About time," she responded. "Now my family can leave frozen shithole." She stood to leave. "Do what you have to. Tell Mrs. Katarina thanks for money."

"But . . . but . . . *Lotus Blossom*?" The functionary began to cry. "What . . . . what are you doing?" He got up and stumbled toward her, pleading.

Now she was angry. "My people taken away to be slaves by your boss. You think I could love you? Stupid. I was paid to love you. You die now. Serve you right." She paused long enough to face him, look him squarely in the eye, and then kick him squarely in the balls. It was damn hard too, like she was kicking a field goal. He doubled over. "Goodbye!"

You can't really slam a fur door, but she somehow managed to. "That sucks," I said cheerfully as I shoved him to the ground. "Now let's talk."

"You're an American?" The functionary responded in English. He moaned for what seemed like forever, then started to cry. "Just kill me. I have no reason to live." His English was better than my Cantonese.

"Man, that's harsh," said the voice in my ear piece. *Phillips.*

"Just shoot him, Lorenzo. That would totally be a mercy killing." *Roland.*

"Guys, stay off the radio," I hissed. I pointed my gun at the sobbing functionary. "The rope to the compound, is there a code word?"

"Lotus Blossom!" he shrieked.

I groaned, and took a seat on the rug. This was going to make for a long evening at this rate, and I had two helicopters full of terrorists and mercenaries waiting on me. "Listen, kid, you're not the first guy to ever get taken advantage of. That's just business. I've been shafted myself a few times. What's your name?"

He took his hands off of his groin long enough to wipe the blood from his lips, and muttered "My name is Wing."

"Okay, Wing. I'm going to break this down for you. I heard what you said earlier. Sala Jihan is evil, we both know it, and as soon as he finds out that you've been sneaking out to meet that hot little nomad and compromising his security, he's going to torture you to death. So you help me out, and I'll go kill him, so you won't have to worry about it."

"You can't kill the Pale Man."

"Oh, I'm pretty sure I can. I'm good at killing stuff."

"You cannot kill what does not die," Wing insisted. "The Pale Man will destroy us all. I was a fool to betray him." Wing started to cry again. He really was afraid of Jihan. "Lotus Blossom! How could she betray me?"

"*Wing*. Focus. You're not helping me, buddy. If you don't tell me about how to get into the compound, I'm going to hurt you until you do. Do you understand?"

Wing curled up in a really pathetic fetal position, heartbroken and afraid, and probably nauseous from the nut kick. It was actually kind of sad. I could only imagine that if Jill were here she would probably like . . . *comfort* him, or something, and within thirty seconds he would be giving me the keys to the front gate of the compound.

"Hurry up, Lorenzo. Start cutting off his fingers already," Anders said over the radio.

"This is your last chance, Wing. You're pretty much screwed. You either help me, or I kill you. You help me, and I let you go. If I kill Jihan, you're home free. If I fail, at least you've got a head start."

"I don't deserve to live. I've been helping a monster. My Lotus Blossom can't love me because of the evil I've done."

New strategy. "Then this is your chance to atone for you sins." He looked at me, confused. "Atone, make up for, say you're sorry, fix past mistakes. You help me kill Jihan, so we can free the slaves that are her relatives, and then maybe Lotus Blossom will forgive you, and take you back." It was stupid, but from the look on his face, it seemed to work. "You'll be a hero. Come on, Wing. Do the right thing." *You idiot.*

The wheels were spinning. "Yes. I will help you. You will still fail, because I don't think you know what you're dealing with. At least I can go to her and beg forgiveness." He smiled through bloodstained teeth. "Then she'll love me again!"

"Yeah, sure. That's awesome. Code word?"

"The man who lets down the rope, his name is Tausang. He works for me. I just call to him. I pay him as soon as he pulls me up. Don't yell from the bottom, or the guards will hear you. Wave your arms with the flare in the pocket." Wing gestured at his coat. "He'll see the movement, and toss down the rope. When you're close enough to the top to whisper, call him by name. Otherwise, he'll cut the rope, and you will die on the rocks below."

I could tell he was telling the truth, the poor deluded moron.

"Now, I'm going to go and find my love. I'll beg her forgiveness!" Wing stood, a man on a mission. "I know she loves me!"

"Good luck with that."

Wing ran out the exit, not even bothering with his coat, just blundering out into the cold, to go randomly barge into the other yurts. I took off my fancy Goretex, and put on the functionary's grey fur coat. He was bigger than me, but that meant my gear could still fit beneath. My radio crackled in my ear. "You think he told you the truth?" Anders asked.

"Roger that. I'm heading for the canyon now."

"Why didn't you kill him?"

Outside, I could hear someone calling out "Lotus Blossom!" over and over, as well as a few guttural responses in a language I didn't recognize.

"I have a feeling somebody else is about to do that for us." I pulled the stolen coat tight, picked up my rifle, and ducked back into the night.

I stood at the base of the cliff and slowly waved my arms back and forth, road flare burning red in my hand, casting an unearthly glow on the surroundings. The spot I was standing in was basically a tube cut through the black rock by a long-since-disappeared glacial runoff. Now smooth ice covered the walls and hung in bizarre shapes all around, with a single slash of moonlight visible overhead. Through the gash in the ice was the slick wall that seemed to leap up for nearly a hundred feet before terminating at the back of the compound.

My rifle was stashed further down the canyon. It was too large to conceal, and the last thing I wanted was for Wing's accomplice to think something was up and cut the rope while I was halfway up. Anders and the others were coming up behind me, but had to hang back far enough in the darkness to not be spotted.

"Come on . . . Come on . . ." I whispered, ice crystals forming in my goatee as the vapor from my lungs instantly froze. I had to put away my face mask, and Wing's bulky coat was not nearly as warm as my previous garment. There had been a scarf with the coat, and I pulled it up over my face to disguise the fact that I wasn't a twenty-something Chinese man. It still smelled of perfume.

Wing had really loved the girl. This was unbelievably dangerous. All it would take to end his charade was a single slave soldier happening to patrol this area at the right time, and his whole plan would have been toast. He had done this over and over. With my luck, his accomplice, Tausang, had already bailed, and I was waving this stupid flare at some sniper up there with a Dragunov.

Finally, a thick hemp rope flailed out of the darkness and landed with a *thump* against the ice. I tossed the flare and kicked snow over it until I was back in blessed shadow. So either Tausang had seen me, or some slave soldier had a twisted sense of humor. I fashioned a basic harness around my waist, and then gave the rope a tug to indicate readiness.

The rope was pulled taut, cutting into my midsection. I put my boots against the wall, wrapped my extremely expensive neoprene shooting gloves around the rope, and waited. It would have been faster to just climb, but that would have aroused suspicion. I had no idea what Wing weighed, and hadn't even thought of the possibility until now that I would be drastically different enough for his accomplice to notice while he hauled me up. I'd left my equipment below, he was bigger than me, but I had a lot more muscle packed onto my frame, so hopefully it was close enough not to matter.

Now I was up out of the crevasse and dangling in the open moonlight. Somehow the air seemed even colder, or maybe it was just my nerves. The trembling in my hands was either from hypothermia or adrenaline, I wasn't sure. The rope creaked above, and I bounced slightly as Tausang did something with the line. He probably would hoist me up a bit, and then loop it around something so that if he lost me, I wouldn't plummet back into the rocks.

"Looking good, Lorenzo." Anders could see me. The downside was that if the guys below could, anyone looking over the wall above could too. "The choppers are airborne. They'll wait until we're secure before entering the canyon."

The pull continued. I would ascend a few feet, and then pause for about thirty seconds, and then ascend another few feet. At this rate, assuming Tausang had good cardiovascular fitness, I was only minutes from the top, and with that thought, a sudden bolt of dread traveled down my spine and lodged in the pit of my stomach. I rummaged through my vest until I found my radio, and clicked the dial over to another predetermined frequency. I really didn't have time for this, but I needed to hear her voice.

"Jill, come in."

"Lorenzo, I can hear you."

"I'm almost at the top. I'll make this quick."

"Go."

". . ." I stopped. What was I going to say? That this was dangerous? That my odds of survival were low? That there were a million things that could go wrong up there? That if the raid failed her and Reaper needed to flee the country as fast as possible, and not look back? We had talked about all of that before.

"Lorenzo? Come in."

"I . . ." Honestly, I was selfish, weak, uncharacteristically nervous, and had just wanted to hear her voice. The words didn't come out.

"I know."

The radio was silent. I took a long, deep breath. Cold air filled my lungs and burned.

Jill's voice was authoritarian. "Now get your head back in the game. I need you to come back safe. Got it?"

"Got it. Lorenzo out." I clicked the radio back to my team's channel. For some stupid reason, I felt better. So I relaxed and enjoyed the view.

The sheer ice wall gave way to black rock laced with fat rivulets of ice, rough enough to actually climb. The lip of the cliff was now just ten feet overhead, and I could hear the grunts of exertion as the rope jerked to another stop and was tied off. A large fur ball, no . . . a head in a hood, appeared over the top, and gazed down at me, as if waiting for something.

"Tausang," I hissed, keeping my face driven as deeply into the scarf as possible.

The shape paused, and the hood tilted slightly to one side. "Password?" he queried softly. *Oh, give me a break.*

"Tausang," I said, louder this time.

The head disappeared back over the lip, and I prepared myself for the final pull to the top.

Then I heard something. A metallic click, like a clasp of a folding knife . . .

Damn it, Wing. Then I heard the sawing. It hadn't been just addressing his accomplice by name. When I had been interrogating Wing, *'The rope to the compound, is there a code word?'* I had asked.

"Lotus blossom. Lotus blossom!" I hissed, but it was too late. The rope was severed.

Panic. The rope made a hissing noise as it shot across the rock lip, pulled by my weight. My hands shot out, scrambling for purchase, for anything. My gloves struck the black rock. My shoulders screamed as I swung like a pendulum and smashed into the mountain.

I opened my eyes. By some miracle, I was dangling by my right hand from a tiny lip of stone. A few more feet down and there would have been nothing at all to grab onto. The glove began to slip. I raised my left hand, bit down hard on the glove, tore it off, and barely had time to put my naked skin on the freezing stone and find another groove before I lost my grip. I spat the glove out and watched it tumble. Then I hurried and repeated that with the other glove, and was able to get both hands grasping tiny bits of stone, legs dangling over the abyss.

I tried to pull, every fiber of my being screaming in pain, fire and electricity scorching through my fingers as the frozen rock cut through my skin, and the outer layer of skin died from the cold. I found a deeper pocket with my left hand, and latched on tight.

The fur shape reappeared above. I was ready. Hanging by one hand, I reached into Wing's coat, and pulled my STI 9mm from the holster, the long suppressor seemingly taking forever to clear. The long tube extended, there was a single match flicker of light from the muzzle and ejection port, and a noise that sounded like closing a fat book hard.

The shape reeled back, and for a brief moment I thought that I had missed, but then he reappeared, and sailed silently over the edge. Tausang's body hurtled past me, close enough to brush the snow off my back, and disappeared into the darkness below. I didn't even hear the impact.

I struggled to shove the long pistol back into the coat, got it roughly secured, and turned my attention back to climbing. Each inch was pure pain, and the rock was jagged and sharp. Blood seeped from my palms and instantly froze into a red crystal pudding. Finally I was high enough to get my boots above the ice layer, and onto a toe hold so I could take some weight off my protesting finger tips.

"Lorenzo's down. He fell off the cliff."

"Son of a bitch. Ibrahim. Abort. Abort."

I paused, keyed my mic, and then realized I was breathing too hard to talk. I forced the words. "No . . . I'm alive. Not me . . . down there."

"What happened?" Anders demanded.

". . . cut rope . . . climbing," I grunted.

"Status?"

". . . little busy . . . right now . . ." I almost added the word asshole, but I was a little distracted.

It took me another five minutes to make it up those last few feet. There was almost nothing to hold onto. I was an experienced climber, but had never done anything like that before. I finally pulled myself up over the lip, and sprawled face first into the packed snow, my legs still hanging over the edge, but not really caring. Hell, if a slave soldier had walked up right at that moment, I would have been too spent to notice until they poked me with a bayonet to make sure I was alive.

Finally, I rolled over. The stars glared back down at me. It took me a moment to catch my breath before I got to my knees, and studied my surroundings. The lip was hidden from the rear of the compound by a few piles of stone and some discarded vehicles, their origin impossible to tell since they were covered in snow. The whole area was cloaked in darkness. The nearest light was sixty meters away in the rear of the compound. I untied the rope from around my waist and tossed it.

"I'm up. Hang on, I'll send down the rope." Tausang had been securing the rope between two heavy stakes pounded into the ground. My hands burned and ached as I unwound it, made sure one end was still tightly secured, and then threw the remainder over the side.

"Rope is down. I'll secure the perimeter." I studied my palms as I spoke. They looked like cheese graters, practically shredded. Gloveless, my hands were freezing. This was off to a great start. You know how little kids' moms will clip their mittens onto their sleeves to keep them from losing them? Yeah, that didn't seem like such a stupid idea right about now. "And bring up my rifle."

Chapter 19: Joy Ride

VALENTINE
Exodus Safe House
Crossroads City
March 25th

This is it. With all of my weapons and gear, I stepped out of the safe house, into the cold night air. My G3 rifle was slung at my side, and my vest was full of magazines for it. I carried in my hands an AKMS with an under-folding stock, loaded with a seventy-five-round drum. This was to be my dump weapon, something I could lay down some fire with and discard if it got in the way.

The 6x6 trucks that formed the heart of our convoy were in the vehicle yard. They had been hastily fitted with improvised armor. Sandbags lined the beds, and thick metal plating had been affixed to the sides of the trucks. Large-caliber machine guns were bolted to the backs of two of the vehicles, positioned so they could fire over the top of the cab. Heavy 14.5mm KSVs, as near as I could tell, a machine gun nearly twice as powerful as a standard .50-caliber.

I walked up to one of the trucks and yanked open the passenger's side door. The driver, a young Exodus operative who I guessed was from the Philippines, nodded at me as I climbed in next to him. The crew cab was not armored and was vulnerable, but the heaters worked. I chose to be warm over being slightly better protected.

They offered to let me ride in one of the BTR-70s, with Skunky and Ling. These vehicles were in a different yard, being readied at the same time. I politely declined the offer without telling them why. Basically there was no way in *hell* I was going to ride in one of those claustrophobic commie deathtraps. Prudent mercenaries make it a point to avoid old Russian APCs on general principle. More to the point, being the only two armored vehicles we had, they were going to draw fire like a turd attracts flies. They weren't any faster than our trucks and weren't particularly maneuverable. The only way in and out of the troop compartment was through a small hatch on either side, just between the third and fourth wheels. I'm probably five inches taller than the Soviet conscripts those hatches were designed for. If you had to get out while the vehicle was still rolling, there was a good chance you'd get crushed under the wheels. God only knew what condition the internal fire suppression system was in, if there even was one.

So, I said no thanks. I felt better in the truck, where I could see what was going on and could unass the vehicle in a hurry if I had to. Not that that would do me any good if a hail of bullets came through the windshield, but what can you do?

There was no point in worrying about it now. We were about to start our Thunder Run through Crossroads City to the first checkpoint. We'd quickly link up with the other vehicles in town, forming the convoy, and haul balls toward the dam. We were waiting for the signal, the notification that whatever they were doing to infiltrate the compound was happening as planned. If we left too soon we'd tip our hand. If we left too late they might have time to reinforce the dam.

As I adjusted the seat belt around the bulk of my body armor, Exodus troops climbed into the back of the truck and took up positions around the bed. Equipment was loaded into the beds and strapped down. Nobody wanted to get hit in the back of the leg with a crate of grenades that wasn't secured if the truck had to stop in a hurry.

My radio, and that of the Exodus operative in the truck with me, crackled to life at the same time. I turned down the volume on mine as Ibrahim's voice came through. He was transmitting on all of our channels simultaneously, broadcasting from wherever the Montalban Exchange's helicopters were being staged out of. Our radios were encrypted, frequency-hopping types, so there was no chance anyone else could be listening in.

"*Attention all elements, this is Sword One Actual. The operation will begin soon. We undertake the greatest, most daring mission Exodus has attempted in any of our lifetimes. The risk is great, the enemy is fanatical and merciless. Offer no quarter, for none will be given to you. Know that our cause is worthy! We go forth into the night, ready to wipe the scourge of Sala Jihan from the face of the Earth. And here, in this place, where the rocks and soil have been stained with so much blood, where the very mountains have bore witness to so much suffering, we will be remembered for this. This will be our finest hour! The defining moment of our lifetimes! God be with us all.*" He paused for a moment. "*Commanders, conduct final pre-operation checks. Stand by for orders. Sword One Actual, out.*"

While I hadn't done any long operations in the Middle East during my time with Vanguard, we did spend a couple of months training the Iraqi Army before they sent me to Central America. It was an easy gig that paid well. I learned there that Iraqi commanders loved giving big pep talks before operations, and often put more effort into their speeches than they did their actual mission planning. Ibrahim didn't fit that stereotype, of course, but the dramatic speech didn't surprise me. Exodus was an old-school organization that did things the old-school way.

The other Exodus leaders checked in. First was Fajkus. "*Sword Two acknowledges,*" he said tersely.

Next was Katsumoto, his voice imposing and serene at the same time. "*Sword Three copies.*" And so it went with the others.

My driver seemed to have taken Ibrahim's words to heart. He was young, couldn't have been more than nineteen. I could see the uncertainty in his face, the fear, which he stoically tried to hide. *My God,* I thought. *Was I ever that young?* I remembered then that I wasn't as old as I felt. Only seven years had passed since I was the baby-faced tyro getting his first taste of war.

"Hey, what's your name?" I asked him.

He seemed almost startled by the question. "Paolo," he said. "Are you Valentine?"

"Call me Val. Where you from?"

"Manila."

"Are you new to Exodus?"

"I am, sir. I have only been on a sword for five months."

"Holy shit, kid," I grinned. "You picked a hell of a first op. Go big or go home, hey?"

"As you say, sir," he stammered.

"How is it you came to work with Exodus? If you don't mind my asking."

"I am an orphan, sir. I was a . . . servant . . . of a drug-trafficking gangster in the Philippines. I was not allowed to leave, until one day Exodus came and killed him. I begged them to take me with them. I didn't want to be left alone. So they accepted me. I am honored to be on this mission, and to be working with someone of your reputation."

Reputation? "What reputation? What have you heard?" I didn't mean to put the kid on the spot. We were getting ready to roll into combat and he was nervous as hell. I figured by talking him up I could get him to relax a little bit. I didn't want a wound-up driver. I was scared too, of course. You're always scared. If you're not, you're a fool. You just get used to the fear, learn to control it.

Young Paolo was new at this, though, and it showed. And he kept calling me 'sir' for some reason. "I was told . . . I mean, I heard that two years ago, in Mexico, you saved Ms. Ling's entire sword."

"Uh-huh. And how did they say I did that?"

"S-sir, I mean no disrespect. I only know . . . I mean, I am only telling you what I heard from my friends."

"Yeah, I know," I said, raising my eyebrows bemusedly. "Please, tell me what you heard." I wanted to keep him talking, keep him focused on something besides our impending mission. The worst part of combat isn't the actual fight. It's before the fight, when you're waiting to go. Even a short wait is agonizingly slow when you're amped up. It drives you crazy, makes you impatient, and causes bad decisions.

Paolo shifted nervously in his seat. "Is it true that you carried Ms. Ling out of the wreckage of a crashed helicopter?"

Hoo boy.

LORENZO
Sala Jihan's Fortress
March 25th

I watched the closest guards through my night vision monocular. Kneeling, I slid around the rear of the derelict truck and tracked the two of them as they rounded the corner. Luckily the back of the compound was where the Soviets had dumped their unrepairable vehicles. There were plenty of places to hide. I was now about fifty meters from the crumbled concrete that had been the rear wall of the fort. There were soldiers positioned on top of the wall, but they were mostly huddled together for warmth on the corners in their machine-gun emplacements. I had seen at least four individuals walking back and forth near the hole in the wall. I knew that we had to make it through that gap to reach the ZSU.

There was a small noise as Anders approached. The former SEAL moved like a ghost. He was not even breathing hard from scaling the rope, and he was a big dude. He looked like some Viking cyborg with his bristly beard sticking out from under his PVS-15 night vision goggles. He squatted behind me and waited. Shen joined us a moment later. The quiet Exodus operative passed me my rifle. It was so cold it burned my hands as I got the single-point sling over my head and one arm. Phillips and Roland took up a position on each end of a frost-coated APC five meters behind us.

Turning back to the others, I held up my hand, two fingers down in a wagging motion, then four fingers up, then pointed at the gap. *Four infantry patrolling.* Then I made the universal sign for gun, and indicated both machine-gun emplacements that I had spied on the wall, then two fingers, for two men at each position. Then to Roland, I pointed at my eyes, then at the left emplacement, then the right for Phillips. Both men had suppressed Micro Tavors, and if anybody started for those machine guns, they needed to pop them fast. If it came to that, there would be enough noise that the mission was hosed. I looked at Shen and made a throat-cutting motion, then jerked my thumb at the sentries. Shen nodded.

After all of that abbreviated sign language, Anders extended his middle finger to me. And to think that I had said he was humorless.

I took point, leaving bloody handprints in the snow behind me as I crawled to the next truck, axle long since broken and left out here to rot. Anders and Shen were right behind me.

We were all armed with suppressed weapons. Everyone had one magazine of 5.56 75-grain subsonic loaded, but even then, the action of the weapon could be heard some distance away, especially on a night this quiet, and subsonic 5.56 frankly sucked at putting people down quickly, being basically a glorified .22. My other 30-round magazines were loaded with standard-velocity Hornady TAP, which through the short barrel of my gun and Silencerco suppressor sounded like a regular .22 long rifle, but at 2700 feet per second tended to leave softball sized exit wounds.

My secondary weapon was my STI Tactical 4.15 9mm, also with a can on it. The 147-grain hollowpoint loads were subsonic and relatively quiet, as Tausang had already experienced. Then I had my knives, because though a suppressor was quiet, these were quieter when used correctly. I was traveling relatively light tonight, as my mission depended on stealth rather than slugging it out. That job belonged to the guys in the choppers. All I had was a plate carrier and a battle belt with a few pouches for magazines.

We waited long enough to get a general idea of the guards' patterns, but *pattern* was a misnomer. Tonight it consisted of trying to stay warm. There was a steel drum with fire licking out of it just inside the gap. Two guards would stand next to the drum to warm up, while the other two would patrol outside the compound wall for a few minutes, before trading off. This worked to our advantage, since the fire ruined their night vision.

I positioned my single point sling so that my rifle was slung behind my back, and pulled my fixed-blade Greco. Shen drew a long, thin blade, nodded once, and glided to the side. Anders raised his HK 416 and covered us.

My pulse was beating in my ear, and strangely enough, I was no longer cold. I leaned back into the shadow of the rusted vehicle. I could hear the crunching of snow beneath boots as the guards approached. They stopped only a few feet away, glancing side to side, their scarred faces visible in my night vision. I exhaled slowly through my nose, hoping to not cause a steam cloud. My lacerated hands were leaving a red skin paste in the textured handle of my knife. The two guards, arms folded, weapons slung, hands constantly rubbing together for circulation, took one last look at the graveyard of discarded vehicles. They turned and began to move back to the small circle of firelight and warmth.

Shen and I were on them in a flash. I couldn't watch my teammate as he came around the other side of the truck. I had to concentrate on my own responsibility, and trust in the Exodus operative's skill. I clamped my hand over the guard's mouth and jerked his head to the side. I rammed my knife into the base of his skull, twisted it violently, and yanked it out. Spinal cord severed, he fell, instantly lifeless. I hugged him tightly and dragged him back to the side of the truck. I could feel hot, sticky blood flowing down my arms.

I looked up. Shen and the other guard were gone. There was only a splatter of blood and some disturbed snow. He was good. I wiped my blade on the guard's arm and put it away. I tried not to notice that the slave soldier was probably barely old enough to drive in my home country.

Shen materialized at my side. He patted me on the shoulder, then bent down and gently closed the slave's staring eyes. He whispered something, not to me, but rather to the dead man. I unslung my rifle and raised it to cover our next move.

Anders was now moving forward, through the gap created by us. The last two soldiers were standing around the burning barrel, hands extended, leather gloves hardening just outside the plume of smoke. They were looking right at Anders as he approached, rifle muzzle down in his left hand. The big man's head was lowered, as he slouched forward, appearing shorter than he really was. The guards looked up, their eyes adjusted to the licking flames, just seeing a black mass approaching.

Anders raised the little Ruger MKII and put two rounds into each of the guards' craniums. *Tick-Tick . . . Tick-Tick . . . .* The low mass of the action and tiny, low pressure round made it so that the integrally suppressed .22 was literally about as loud as a staple gun, but both soldiers went right down. The big man paused just outside the circle of light. *Tick . . . Tick.* He put one more into each man, just to make sure. Anders shoved the .22 back into his armor, then stepped forward, grabbed one guard by an outflung arm, the other by his boot, and effortlessly dragged them both back into the dark.

Shen and I sprinted through the gap, snow flashing around our ankles as we leapt through the broken slabs of concrete and bent rebar. We slowed to a walk as we approached the burning drum, the knowledge of what we had to do unspoken, born of years of experience. We stopped next to the fire, hands extended for warmth, as if we were the fallen guards. To anyone further inside the compound, watching this area, the two guards had only disappeared for a moment, and now there were two more black blobs clustered around the light, just like before. I scanned across the compound, but saw no other movement. The fire felt good.

There was more motion and a whisper of noise behind us as Phillips and Roland moved through the gap. I nodded my head toward the steel ladder leading to the top of the wall. There were still two machine guns mounted up there. Anders and the young Exodus operatives knew what to do. I made a motion toward the right, and Shen turned that direction, back to the fire, so he could watch that position. I watched the emplacement on the left.

"Psstt . . . Lorenzo," Shen whispered.

"Yeah." My eyes never left the two hunched shapes on the wall. There was an angular black thing mounted on a pintle up there, probably a 12.7mm DhSK heavy machine gun, and if those guards gave any indication that they had seen Anders, Roland, or Phillips, I was going to light them up with my ACR. Something thumped into my shoulder, and sat there, a slightly damp weight. I reached up and grabbed it. They were thin wool gloves.

"You looked like you needed them more than the soldier I removed them from," Shen said simply.

"Thanks." I pulled the gloves on and flexed my fingers. At least they had finally gone numb.

"Target spotted," Shen said, both to my side and in my ear, as he had keyed the radio. "Two hundred meters to the north."

Sure enough, there it was. The antiaircraft vehicle was a brutish, squat thing, sitting on top of a small hill. The only reason Shen had seen it was from the twirling motion of its radar, constantly spinning, seeking targets for its huge guns.

"*That's no ZSU.*" Anders' voice was a whisper on the radio. I could see his shape halfway up the ladder to the top of the wall. "*That's a Tunguska.*"

I looked at the shape through my night vision. It looked a lot bigger than it had before. "That's a different one. The one I saw had four guns. This one's taller and has two guns."

"*And missiles,*" Anders said. "*Plan's changed. We've got two antiaircraft systems in the compound.*"

The vehicle I had seen when I had toured the compound had been closer to Jihan's silo. This second vehicle was a bad complication. So much for good intel. "We're going to need more time."

Shen fiddled with his radio. "Ibrahim's not responding."

The choppers had already entered the canyon. They would be here in less than twenty minutes. As we spoke, the choppers were tearing along just above the tree tops, navigating a narrow pass. Our radios were not powerful enough to reach them with mountains in the way.

"Take out those machine guns. Fast," I ordered. Then I flipped my radio to Jill and Reaper's channel. "Jill, come in."

"*Go.*"

"Unexpected problem. There are multiple antiair vehicles. We can't reach Ibrahim. Try to reach him. Tell him we need more time. Over."

"*On it.*"

I flipped back to my team. Hopefully Jill could reach Ibrahim, otherwise those choppers were going to fly right into a stream of giant tracers. I returned my attention to the emplacement. A third shadow was stalking up to the men on the gun, then the shadow went low, below the railing. I bit my lip, ready to open fire. There was some motion, a small bit of noise, and one of the shapes flipped over the wall and plummeted to the ground outside the compound. The second guard started to rise, then appeared to get a whole lot shorter as his head flopped to the side, mostly severed from his neck. A noise like someone chopping firewood hit my ear just a moment later.

I glanced around. There were no other guards close enough to have heard the noise.

"*This is Phillips. Southern position secure,*" he panted.

A moment later, Shen stiffened up as he took aim at the northern point. Then he relaxed and lowered his weapon.

"*This is Roland. North secure.*"

"*I was faster,*" Phillips replied.

"*Yeah, but listen to you. I heard you from here.*"

"*Whatever, dude.*"

"Guys, on my signal, use those machine guns. Kill everything that isn't us. Anders, Shen, on me. We have to reach those tanks. Now."

I checked my watch. We were almost out of time. I made a spinning motion with my finger in the air and gestured toward the Tunguska. *Move out.*

The next few minutes were a blur. The three of us kept to the shadows under the wall. We would move quickly, sprint to the next piece of cover, scan for threats, and then move again. I spotted guards, but all of them were moving in directions away from us. We had also seen no sign of dogs, which was lucky, as they would have sensed us long ago, but Katarina's intel had indicated that Jihan hated dogs for some reason.

We reached the rear of one of the concrete bunkers, Number Five when it had been a Styrofoam block on Kat's table. There was a ten-foot alley separating the wall of the compound from the back wall of the bunker. There was a single steel door on that back wall, and Shen and I crouched down as we passed it, since there was light coming through a glass slit at eye-level through the door. Anders stayed back, covering the way that we had come from.

I peeked around the corner. We were now only twenty meters from the Tunguska. It was straight up a small snow-covered hill. I could see a few men milling around outside the beast, and could hear the diesel engines running from here. *Good.* The noise would mask our approach.

What the hell, the noise should be enough to mask suppressed gunfire as well. I scanned the Tunguska through my night vision. A thing like that should have at least four people manning it, but I only saw two on the outside. The other two were probably sitting inside, actually running the radar and the guns. I signaled for Shen to approach the tank, and if either of the guards noticed him, I would shoot them.

Shen nodded once, and pulled that same long knife. Hopefully from the Tunguska's vantage point, we could spot the ZSU.

CREAK.

The metal door to the bunker opened slowly. Shen pushed himself back against the wall, knife blade held flat against his chest, the door shielding him from view. A squat figure stepped into the alley, pulling round goggles down over his masked face, an AK47 slung over one shoulder.

A Brother!

He stepped into the snow, goggled head swinging in my direction, the door closing automatically behind him. Shen was up in an instant, the knife a pixilated blur through my goggles.

The Brother sensed him somehow, and impossibly, at the last possible instant moved fast enough that I thought my night vision had malfunctioned. The Brother ducked and sidestepped, Shen's knife flying through the space where his throat had been a second before. At the same time, the Brother's palm struck Shen's chest. The Exodus operative flew back, colliding brutally with the wall.

I turned, my finger already flying to the trigger of my rifle as the Brother stepped toward me, his body uncoiling like a spring, but then the rifle was knocked out of my numb hands, snow from his boot struck me in the face. The son of a bitch had kicked the gun out of my hands. Then he kicked me. *Hard.*

The concrete impacted my back with a great deal of force. My night-vision device went flying into the distance. I went for my pistol, but with the suppressor mounted, I had to carry it in a shoulder holster. Slow to draw, too slow. As I reached across my body, the Brother's leather glove clamped onto my wrist. I jerked my knee into him, but it swept through nothing but empty furs. I locked my left hand onto arm, and tried to leverage him into an arm bar. He was impossibly strong. Those blank goggles stared into my face and he didn't make a sound.

Shen was back up. I saw him rising behind the Brother's back. Shen latched onto the Brother's slung AK with his hands, pulling back while he kicked his boot into the back of the Brother's knees, a move sure to take the little man down.

The brother grunted at the impact, but didn't drop. He threw a backhand that hit Shen like a sledgehammer. The Exodus operative and the AK went down.

I struck out with my left. He took the blow to the face and barely budged. He swung me back into the wall. I shook loose, the STI coming out of the holster. He smashed me in the elbow, *CHUFF,* and I fired my pistol uselessly into the snow at his side. Now somehow he was holding onto my gun, and bending it back into my stomach.

TickTickTickTickTick.

The Brother turned toward the source of the impacts. Anders was striding forward, the little Hush Puppy extended in one hand. The bolt locked back empty, and Anders dropped the spent magazine. The Brother was still locked onto me, and he spun me, like a discus thrower, and launched me into Anders. We collided, both of us slipping in the snow.

I sprang to my feet. My pistol was in the snow somewhere, so I pulled my knife. The Brother was standing in the center of the alley, in a wide stance like some old-west gunfighter. He put one hand to his side, then slowly raised it, studying his own blood. Anders had hit him several times, but .22s suck. His black mask cocked to the side, incredulously, and then looked back at us. Anders grunted as he got to his feet.

Anders raised his carbine, but the diesel noise died with a cough. They had shut down the Tunguska. There was some yelling from the top of the hill. They probably just ran it long enough to charge up the batteries for the radar. Our opportunity for gunfire had passed.

Shen pulled himself off the ground, the Brother's AK in his hands. He looked at it in frustration, knowing it was too loud. He dropped the mag and racked the charging handle back to eject the chambered round. Shen was prepared to use the rifle as a club. Anders and I were on one side of the alley, the wounded Brother in the middle, Shen between him and the Tunguska crew. I don't know why the Brother didn't shout for help. He had already soaked up several .22 rounds, but he didn't make a sound. Anders stepped past me, a SOG knife held low at his side.

The Brother waited for him, his head swiveling slightly to keep all three of us in view. The goggles were cold and almost insectile. Anders moved first, charging forward, the knife coming up in an eviscerating arc, but the Brother was faster. The knife cut through a layer of wolf pelt and cut the cord of a bear tooth necklace, but no flesh. Then the Brother hit Anders, once, twice, three times, before the big man was sliding through the snow on his face.

Shen clubbed the Brother in the back, and having been clubbed by Shen myself, I knew that the man knew how to put some juice into it. The Brother stumbled, but mule kicked Shen in the ribs. I leapt over Anders, my knife leading the way, and drove my blade into the Brother's side. He jerked away, but I knew that I had scored a hit. Then a black clad fist slammed into my jaw and sent me sprawling.

All four of us were up again, the Brother still in the middle, hands up and open in front of him, his back to the compound wall. He still hadn't made a sound, but now I could hear him breathing, the leather of his mask bulging slightly as he exhaled. My knife was dripping.

Then it was on. All three of us closed on him at the same time. We were all experienced fighters and the Brother had to be losing a lot of blood. It should have been over in an instant.

It wasn't.

It was a flurry of motion and flying frost, yet it was eerily quiet. Shen smashed the AK into the Brother's raised arm. The stock broke off and flipped past my head. Anders and I both waded in, blades singing, but somehow the Brother stayed ahead of them. He danced through the steel, forearms and elbows colliding with ours with bone-jarring force. Shen hit him with the rifle again, hard enough to bend the barrel. The Brother moved like part of the shadows, disregarding the impact, and the next part was confusing because he had kicked me in the side of the head, but somehow Shen was upside down, in the air, then corkscrewed violently into the ground.

Anders finally scored a hit, driving his knife through the Brother's wrist, the blade erupting out the other side, blood spraying everywhere.

Without a tourniquet, that was a fatal hit.

The Brother jerked the knife away, slammed Anders in the throat, sending him sprawling, and pulled the knife out with his other hand. I could hear it grind through the bones of his wrist.

"Shit. Now he's got a knife," I muttered as I got back to my feet. The Brother closed on me. Anders' blade aimed at my heart. I readied myself, but I knew that he was too fast.

THUD.

The Brother stopped, the hilt of another knife sticking out of his back. Shen had apparently found his and hurled it down the alley. The Brother stumbled slightly, then stabbed toward me. I dodged aside, his knife striking sparks off the steel door behind me. I kicked him in the knee, them slashed my knife across his stomach, driving it in deep. He rolled into me, both of us locked together, churning down the wall, the unkillable Brother leaving a trail of fluids.

The clock was ticking.

Not fast enough. The point of the knife was inches from my eye. Somehow I had grabbed his good wrist, and muscles straining, was holding it back. I stabbed my blade into his chest, levering it around his ribs, slicing toward his heart and lungs. But still he fought, the knife descended slowly as he overpowered me. I could see my reflection in his goggles.

CHUFF.

The Brother's head snapped forward violently, colliding with mine in a spray of warmth. His head rolled back limply, and one goggle instantly pooled with blood that then came leaking out the sides. I shoved him back, and he collapsed silently into the powder, his brains leaking out the back of his head into the snow.

Anders was holding my 9mm.

I stumbled back over to the corner and peered around. If the guards had heard that noise, we were screwed. It was dark, but the reflection from the snow was giving the surroundings a faint, almost pink glow. I had no idea where my night vision had landed. There were a few lights around the Tunguska, and I could see shapes moving. Someone was running a hose into the beast. That's why they had shut it down. They were refueling.

There was movement at my side as Shen stumbled forward. He still had his night vision. He scanned back and forth, and gave me a thumbs-up sign. We were okay. I checked my watch again. The choppers would be arriving soon.

"*What's the holdup?*" Roland asked over the radio. "*We've got guards headed our way. I think it's the shift change.*"

I secured my rifle. "We ran into a Brother."

"*Ooohhh,*" he whistled. "*Is everybody alive?*"

"Barely," Shen grunted.

"Guys, pop those guards if you have to. Wait as long as possible though. Anders. Let's go . . ." There was no response. "Anders?" I turned around. The big man was kneeling next to the still twitching Brother and had pulled back his mask and goggles. It was too dark for me to see what he was looking at. The Majestic man stood, dusted the snow off his knees, and joined us. He handed me my pistol.

"What?" I asked as I secured my gun.

"Nothing . . ." He shook his head. "I just had to see if the stories were true."

"What stories?"

"Sala Jihan cuts their tongues out. Okay. Let's do this."

We hit the Tunguska crew hard just as they had finished refueling and turned the engine back on. I took down the man standing at the pump, jerking back his head and plunging my Greco down over his sternum and through his aorta. The other guard looked up in surprise, his mouth forming a perfect O, but he didn't have time to make a sound before Shen's arm encircled his neck. The two of them slunk down on the other side of the Tunguska and disappeared.

Anders bounded past us, clambered on top of the armored vehicle, ducked under the spinning radar dish, and was on top of the turret in a flash. Luckily the hatch wasn't locked. He pulled it back, reached inside, grabbed the man sitting in the commander's seat by the hair and pulled him out. This one did have time to shout, and you would too if a baseball-mitt sized hand suddenly hoisted you out of a tank, but Anders tossed him over to Shen's side, where I heard a hacking noise, and the screaming stopped.

We were past the point of stealth. We had to take these guns out *now*. The choppers were probably already leaving the canyon. I could only pray that Jill had been able to reach Ibrahim. I walked around the front of the Tunguska, to the driver's compartment. He must have seen what happened to his associates, as his head popped down before I could play Whack-a-Mole, and the steel hatch came down, but it landed on the rail system of my rifle. I levered the rear of the gun up, and fired three rounds into the driver's body.

I threw back the hatch, aimed, and fired one more round into the man's face. By this point I was soaked with blood, but didn't have time to care. "Tunguska down," I said into the radio.

"*Guards are almost on us,*" Phillips hissed.

"Shen, Anders, look for that ZSU!" I spat. They both still had night vision, and their odds of seeing it were far better than mine. A light came on in a nearby bunker. Somebody had heard the Tunguska crew's cries. I took cover behind the front of the tank, and braced my rifle.

"Northwest. Four hundred meters," Shen said. I glanced in that direction, but couldn't make it out in the darkness. I would have to take his word for it. "Near the missile silo."

"We'll never make it in time," Anders stated. "We need to get out of here."

The bunker door opened, and a slave soldier stepped into the night air, an SKS in his arms. I shot him three times. The feeble subsonic loads barely made a sound, but they didn't have much hitting power. The soldier looked down at his chest for a long moment, before stumbling back into the bunker. Five seconds later an alarm began to sound.

"Screw that. Anders, can we run this thing?"

"Hell if I know."

"I drove an armored vehicle once," Shen said.

"Let's do it!" I grabbed the dead driver by the shirt and hauled him up and out of the hatch. "Inside!" Shen vaulted into the driver's seat. I crawled on top, and followed Anders into the top hatch.

It was cramped. There were red lights and buttons everywhere. I flopped into a seat. Anders was smashed into a seat behind me. There was a popping noise that I didn't recognize at first, but then I realized that it was small-arms fire bouncing off of the turret.

There were controls in front of me, a darkened screen, flashing LEDs, and a joystick like off of a 1980s-era arcade game. "How do we make it shoot?"

Anders didn't answer. He was scanning across the Cyrillic labels, his mouth moving as he tried to read them. He had pushed his goggles up on his forehead, and it was obvious that reading Russian wasn't one of his primary skills.

I pulled a small flashlight from inside my coat, turned it on, and started going over the controls. "What, they didn't teach you that in Navy SEAL school?"

"It never came up. There!" He did something, and the screens lit up. Behind him was a larger screen, obviously a display for the radar dish. Two bright green blips had just appeared on it. At the same time, Shen must have been playing with the controls, as the giant beast lurched painfully forward, slamming us all into various pointy bits inside before rocking to a stop.

I grabbed the joystick. It was articulated to only move in four directions. Through the screen, I could see the darkened shape of the compounds walls. My best guesstimate was that we were about thirty degrees off of where the ZSU was parked. I pushed on the stick, and the turret rotated, surprisingly smoothly and way too fast. I had to hit the stick the other way to move it back.

"I can't see it!" I shouted, which was totally unnecessary considering we were inside a steel tub together. The small-arms fire had stopped, which meant that the soldiers were now going to do something effective, like set us on fire, or bust out some RPGs. Anders popped out the top of the hatch and started firing his 416.

The screen was mostly dark shapes. This vehicle was pretty advanced, so it probably had some sort of IR floodlight or something, but I had no idea where the controls were. It probably tracked aircraft automatically, as there was no way a human being could track a jet fast enough with this joystick to shoot it down.

There had to be a way. This thing was Russian. Everything they built was made to be run by third world, illiterate goat herders. I cursed under my breath as I read the labels. Too bad Reaper wasn't here. He had probably played a video game where he had driven one of these at some point.

"If you're gonna do something, do it fast!" Anders shouted. Then there was an explosion, and he shouted and fell back down into the hatch. "RPG!" Then he was back out the top, firing wildly.

Then the fates smiled at me. The ZSU must have picked up the incoming choppers, because suddenly there was movement, and headlights, actual headlights, came on, two brilliant white beacons, just on the left side of my monitor. I thumped the stick, so that I was now even with the two lights, then thumped the control down to lower the cannons. There was a illuminated circle on the screen, and I filled it with the black shape that had to be the ZSU. I mashed the trigger.

Nothing happened. *Damn it*. I looked at the stick. There were buttons on the side of it. I pushed one of the buttons, and then mashed the trigger again.

The roar was unbelievable. It sounded kind of like an air wrench removing rusted lug nuts from an old wheel, only magnified a hundred billion times, and reverberating through a steel shell until it vibrated your fillings out of your teeth. The twin 30mm cannons fired explosive shells at a rate that had to be around 4,000 rounds a minute. I had only depressed the trigger for a second, but a line of tracers longer than a football field stretched across the compound. The ZSU exploded in a brilliant cloud of flame and sparks like Thor had gotten pissed off and personally came down from Valhalla and whacked it with his hammer.

"Holy shit!" I shouted. "Drive, Shen! Drive! Back the way we came." There was infantry running around now, and with Phillips and Roland on those machine guns, maybe they could keep them off of our back.

The Tunguska lurched forward with a grinding noise. Anders dropped back down inside, his hands shaking, pulling another magazine from his vest and slamming it into his gun. "When it shoots, it blows fire out the side for like twenty feet!" Then he bounced back up, and kept shooting at random people.

With the sounding of the alarm, every light in the compound was blazing, which helped me see a whole lot better. There were soldiers scurrying everywhere, and I could make out other machine-gun emplacements along the walls. Apparently they hadn't gotten the word yet to rip the Tunguska to shreds. *What the hell?* I had a giant tank, I might as well have some fun.

I jerked the stick, stuck the emplacement in the center of the glowing circle, and mashed the trigger. The jackhammer noise gave me permanent brain damage, but when the thing stopped vibrating, the machine gun, the gunners, and fifteen feet of wall was gone. I glanced back to the radar screen. The two green helicopter blips were right on top of us.

Shen drove the Tunguska like a madman. I was stunned how fast this thing moved under the roar of a twelve-cylinder turbo diesel. I kept sticking various valuable-looking things into the glowing circle and blowing them to bits. Anders popped down and screamed, "Left! Left! LEFT!"

Shen cranked it hard, and the Tunguska spun like only a tracked vehicle can. Something heavy hit us, and sparks flew through the compartment. "Heavy machine gun!" Anders shouted, pulling me by the shoulder, apparently in the direction he wanted me to shoot. There were specks on the view screen, coming from the top of a bunker. *No.* Not sparkles. Muzzle flashes. I mashed the trigger and ripped the concrete roof off the bunker entirely.

"Out!" Anders shouted. He jerked his thumb, and when I twisted to look, I saw fire. We were on fire, lots of fire, and there were missiles sitting on this thing.

"Shen! *Run!*" Anders was already out the hatch and gone by the time I levered myself out after him, and leapt off the top of the still rolling tank. I hit the ground, rolling over as I lost momentum, then sprang to my feet, and sprinted as fast as I could away from the burning hulk. I had no idea where we were and I had no idea if Shen had made it out, but I knew that if I stopped to look, then the damn thing was going to explode.

It did, but thankfully not before I made it around the corner of another bunker. Fire and noise billowed around behind me as the Tunguska's missiles cooked off. Without even thinking about it, I was on my face with my hands covering my head.

Boots stopped in front of my face. I jerked up, raising my rifle. Shen batted it aside. "Let's go."

"You *are* Jet Li," I said in awe. Anders joined us a second later, shoving yet another magazine into his carbine. Heat mirage was rising off of his suppressor. A giant black monster screamed overhead, causing the rising smoke of the burning Tunguska to form pinwheel vortices. The choppers were here, and judging from the volume of tracers flying down from their doors, they were entering a target-rich environment. They tore past, heading for the landing area near the missile silo.

"Roland. Phillips. Report." I shouted.

"*Shooting lots of people!*" one of them shouted over the drum of a heavy machine gun.

"*Bad people!*" said the other.

It took me a moment to get my bearings, but then I tracked in on the noise and the stream of tracers flying from the rear of the compound. A soldier came running around the corner. Shen and Anders dropped him with a volley of quick shots. "Okay, we'll rendezvous at the gap. Don't shoot us."

I could still hear the scream of the choppers' giant engines, and there was a whole lot of gunfire coming from that direction. The compound had devolved into a state of primal chaos. Anders took point, firing as more soldiers appeared ahead of us. Shen had gotten us back nearly to our entrance point, and it only took a few frantic minutes of leapfrogging from wall to wall to near the gap. The alarm was blaring from sirens located on the tops of the bunkers. Random soldiers, slaves, and functionaries were exiting the buildings. We shot anybody that was armed or that looked at us funny.

"*Belt-fed's empty! Moving to Roland's position,*" Phillips warned us. Now only one big gun was blazing at this end of the compound. We had to hurry.

The thrumming beat of the last heavy machine gun was near. We approached the final corner, almost back to the junkyard. A group of half a dozen soldiers were ahead of us, crouched behind a broken concrete pillar. They were trying to sneak up close on Roland's emplacement so they could overwhelm it with rifle fire and grenades. Just beyond the bad guys was a pillar of sparks and flames as Roland worked over anything that moved with absurdly powerful bullets.

"Roland, you've got a bunch of rubble fifteen meters in front of you. You've got soldiers hiding behind it. You might want to do something about that," I suggested.

"*On it.*"

A split second later, the lance of fire shifted to the concrete debris. The giant 12.7 rounds zipped right through the soldiers' cover, blasting shrapnel everywhere, sending up giant gouts of snow, dirt, blood, and meat. There was a secondary explosion as one of the soldiers dropped a live grenade. Anders stepped around the corner and fired a few rounds, just to make sure all of the targets were down.

"Cease fire, cease fire. Get off that wall." The two Exodus men were sitting ducks if they stayed up there any longer. We needed to get the hell out of here and meet up with the rest of Exodus by the choppers. "We're at the corner of building . . . six."

"*Okay. Cover us.*"

The three of us spread out, scanning for threats. I was missing my night vision, but every light in the compound was on now. I took the chance to switch out my pathetic subsonic magazine for something better. There was a veritable storm of gunfire coming from the helicopters' landing spot, and it sounded like a lot more fire than what should have been coming from the expected number of enemy troops. In fact, it sounded like this compound was hell of a lot better manned than we thought.

I flipped my radio to another setting. "Reaper, where are my eyes?"

"*Little Bird will be on station in two minutes,*" he responded hastily. Our little UAV had to stay circling in the canyon until the radar had gone down, only it wasn't nearly as fast as the choppers. "*I'll be feeding to you and Ibrahim.*"

"Okay, switching to the command channel." There were so many separate strike teams operating at one time that Exodus was using a bunch of encrypted frequencies to keep from crowding each other. "Come in Ibrahim. This is Lorenzo."

The radio picked up to a live line, but there was a pause as somebody on the other end hammered something with what sounded like short barreled .308. "*This is Sword One Actual. Status?*"

"My team's okay. We're on the rear wall."

"*You did well to destroy not only one, but two of those AA guns, my friend.*"

"Yeah, how about next time we know that there are two first?"

Ibrahim laughed heartily. Even in the middle of a gun battle, the man was chipper. Friggin' Exodus. "*Yes. Your friend, Mr. Reaper, was able to relay to us your message. As soon as he saw the radar go offline, he gave us the signal.*"

"How's it going over there?"

"*If you would like to come and lend some assistance, it would be much appreciated. There seems to be no end to how many men Jihan has. Once we secure the LZ, we can destroy the Pale Man once and for all.*" There was more gunfire. "*I must be going now.*"

The plan was for Exodus to control that one portion of the compound long enough to take control of the silo. With Jihan dead, it was believed that his troops would collapse. None of us wanted to have to clear every one of these bunkers. Personally I just wanted to get into that prison, find Bob, and get the hell out of here.

Roland and Phillips came sprinting in behind me. Neither one appeared to have any bullet holes in them. "Head for the LZ!" I ordered.

Chapter 20: False Gods

VALENTINE
Crossroads City
March 25th

"You should put your earplugs in," I told Paolo. The Ural truck rattled and crashed down a potholed road at a high rate of speed, bucking and jarring all the while. Everything I saw was illuminated in green through my night vision goggles.

"Why?" he asked. To my eyes he appeared slightly blurry; the focus on my NVGs was set for a longer distance.

I pointed to the roof of the truck's cab. "When that big-assed gun opens up, it's going to be really loud." The Ural 6x6 truck we were riding in had a KPV 14.5mm heavy machine gun mounted in the back, behind an armored gun shield. When the gun was pointed forward, its muzzle was right over the cab. "Seriously," I continued, "It'll be louder than hell and if it gets ugly up there I'm going to be firing right out the window. Either put your ears in now or have tinnitus for the rest of your life."

Paolo shakily nodded his head and, while driving with one hand, put rubber earplugs in one at a time. I had on electronic earphones that protected my hearing and kept my ears warm.

Katsumoto's calm voice broadcast over our radios. "*This is Sword Three Actual. We are about to engage the enemy. Prep for combat.*" On cue, the BTRs in front of us sped up. Where we'd been traveling in a column, the rear vehicle pulled up alongside the lead. Both APCs had an armored turret with a 14.5mm KPVT machine gun and a coaxial 7.62mm PTK machine gun. The two surplus Soviet vehicles formed a wall of armor and firepower for the rest of the convoy.

Young Paolo steeled himself and gripped the steering wheel so hard it was a wonder he could still turn it. My own heart sped up as the truck accelerated. Adrenaline hit my system in a pleasant rush. My concerns and distractions faded away as *the Calm* washed over me. My muscles relaxed and I rolled down the window. A rush of cold air blasted my face as I stuck the muzzle out of my AKM out the window. I clicked the safety lever to the full auto position, and checked to make sure that the 75-round drum magazine was locked in. *This is it.*

We caught them completely off guard. All that Jihan's soldiers, sitting idly at the checkpoint, could have seen was several streams of green tracers lancing out at them from the darkness before they died. The checkpoint was just a couple of shacks, a feeble wooden roadblock, and a pair of parked 4x4s. Heavy machine-gun and small-arms fire tore through the shacks and the trucks alike. The noise was terrible. The BTRs blasted through the barricade without hesitation, breaking it off and crushing it beneath their wheels.

We slowed down to make the ninety-degree right turn up the hill to the dam. *Movement in the shack!* The AK roared as I squeezed the trigger, hosing the wooden building with a long burst. Paolo winced at the noise. He looked like he was going to piss himself when the KPV machine gun above us opened up on a vehicle coming down the road to our left. The concussion from each shot was like having a metal bucket on your head while someone banged on it with a hammer.

Just like that, we were around the corner and speeding up the hill. It had taken us less than a minute to shoot our way through the checkpoint, leaving nothing but dead bodies and burning trucks in our wake. We had surprised them so completely that they had only gotten a couple of ineffectual potshots off at us.

The convoy sped up after rounding the corner, beginning the long charge up the hill. The dam loomed over us at the top, brightly illuminated through my NVGs. I couldn't hear anything over the roar of the truck's diesel engine but I had little doubt that alarms were sounding up there. A mix of red and green tracers zipped down the hill at us. There was no cover. The road was straight, two lanes wide, flanked on either side by six-foot snow banks. There was nowhere to go but up.

The two BTRs maintained their armored wall up front, sending bursts of automatic weapons fire forward as we charged. The huge machine gun behind me roared, each burst sounding like a maniac was pounding on the roof with a sledgehammer. I had no targets. There was nothing I could do but sit and wait. The road to the dam was only a kilometer long, but a klick is a long way when you're being shot at.

PING! "Shit!" Paolo cried. He flinched and ducked down in his seat. An incoming round ricocheted off of one of the BTRs and loudly nicked the corner of the cab. Staying close to the armored vehicles didn't help a lot, as our truck was considerably taller than they were, but it was better than nothing.

I involuntarily gasped as an RPG rocket zipped to my right in a flash, barely missing the truck. We'd be at the top of the hill momentarily, but the enemy fire was getting more accurate as we drew closer. Another RPG hit the ground and detonated in front of one of the APCs, causing it to swerve and sending a cloud of dirt and snow into the air.

"Oh God!" Paolo swerved the truck at the last instant to avoid the pothole left by the RPG.

"Just go straight!" I shouted. "Stay on line!" There was a horrible sound of holes being punched in metal and glass. I hunched down in the seat. Holes appeared in the windshield as a burst of machine gun fire tore up the front of the truck. Paolo grunted. He was hit. The Exodus operative slumped over to the right, turning the wheel as he went. I frantically grabbed for it, but it was too late.

I barely had time to brace as the massive Ural truck cut sharply to the right. My stomach lurched as the left-side wheels left the ground. The snow, bright green through my NVGs, flew up at me in what seemed to be slow motion. Every bone in my body was jarred as the truck dumped over on its side. The last thing I remember seeing was a sideways snowbank speeding toward my face.

Everything went black.

Cold.

That was the first thing I consciously thought. I wondered if I was back on the mountaintop at North Gap left out in the elements again. I didn't know where I was, and couldn't remember how I got there. I opened my eyes to pale gray light. Nothing was in focus. I couldn't feel anything. I couldn't hear anything. For what seemed to be a very long time, I was utterly alone.

A long burst of automatic weapons fire echoed in the distance. It was answered by a slow-firing heavy machine gun, and several small explosions. I was able to lift my head slightly. My face was numb. I was on my side, half buried in snow.

Well I'll be damned, I thought whimsically. *I'm still alive.* I lifted my head some more, shaking the snow from my face. My night vision goggles were gone. The sky was clear and the Moon was rising. The snow glowed gray under the white light of the Moon. As I fumbled with my seat-belt latch, I felt something wet and warm dripping on my face. I looked up, to my left. Paolo was still strapped into his seat. His arms dangled lifelessly, as if he was reaching out for me in death. Blood trickled from several wounds on his body and was dripping on my face.

Freeing myself from the seat belt, I searched for my weapons. The truck had slid sideways on the icy road, right into one of the tall snow banks that lined it. The windshield smashed, the cab had half filled with snow, and I had been all but buried alive. I couldn't find the AKM rifle I'd been carrying, but my G3 was still slung to my chest. I habitually patted my left side for my revolver. My lucky S&W .44 was still there, and seemed to have saved me once again.

The sounds of battle roared from the top of the hill as I slowly dug my way out through the front window. I had to get up there and rejoin Exodus. I didn't know how long I'd been out, or how the battle was going, but I couldn't stay where I was. Somehow I'd gotten left behind, probably in the mad rush up the hill. There was no way they could stop on the road for very long without getting shot to pieces. Exodus probably saw that I'd been buried and assumed I was dead, like Paolo.

I managed to dig my way to the top of the snow bank, breath smoking in the frigid night air. I looked around briefly, then trudged through the snow away from the road. I took cover under a nearby pine tree with low-hanging boughs. I needed a minute to catch my breath and didn't want to do it out in the open.

The Ural truck had been abandoned, front end shot to pieces. It lay on its right side, blocking half the road. The heavy machine gun mounted in the back hung uselessly, barrel pointing toward the ground. I didn't see any other bodies. Everyone in the back must have survived the crash and probably climbed onto the next vehicle in line to continue the assault.

Looking through the pine boughs, I could see the dam, even without my night vision. It was illuminated by a multitude of amber lights, as well as the moonlight that was now streaming through the dispersing cloud layer. The Moon was low in the sky, barely clearing the mountains. Trees cast long, ominous shadows in the snow, and I began to shiver. I had to keep moving.

It looked like it was about half a klick uphill to the dam. *Shit.* Five hundred meters is a long way uphill, in the open, when the enemy holds the top of the hill. I wore a snow camouflage smock over my clothing, but I was hesitant to bet my life on overwhites. The road was the only option. Trying to plow through hip-deep snow on foot would make the trip take a lot longer and leave me just as exposed.

I reached for my radio. "Sword Three, this is, uh . . ." I didn't have a callsign. Or if I did nobody told me. "This is Valentine," I said. Fuck it, the radios were encrypted. "I'm still alive. I'm at the site of the truck crash. I'm alone, but I'm mobile. I'm going to try to make my way to you."

There was no response. I looked at the radio briefly, then repeated my transmission. Still no response. I swore and changed the setting to unencrypted broadcast, and turned the power up. Somebody had to hear me. "Sword Three, Sword Three, Sword Three," I said, "This is Valentine. I got left behind at the truck crash, but I am still alive, how copy?"

My radio crackled to life. "*Holy shit! It's you!*"

The voice sounded damned familiar. "*Who is this?*"

"Dude! It's Reaper!"

You have got to be fucking kidding me. "Listen to me. I got left behind. I'm alone, and I'm in trouble. Are you in touch with anybody?"

"*Why are you broadcasting on an open channel? Everyone can hear you.*"

"My crypto shit the bed, or my radio got fucked up. I was in a truck crash. Listen, you need to tell somebody that I'm alive."

"*Where are you? No wait, don't tell me! The enemy could be listening!*"

I sighed heavily. "Look, just tell Sword Three, or someone in that element, that I'm alive and I'm trying to get to them. I'm going radio silent after that, but I'll be listening. Keep me updated, okay?"

"*I don't know where Sword Three is.*" Of course, we'd kept Lorenzo in the dark about the attack on the dam, but Reaper was just glad to help. "*But okay. Good luck! Be careful!*"

Be careful, he says. "Roger, out." I shuffled out from under the pine tree and slid down the snowbank onto the road. Before I could even get going, the road ahead of me was illuminated by bright white headlights coming from behind. *Shit.* I ran back to the wreck of the Ural. There was nowhere else to hide.

Shit, shit, shit! My heart was racing. My breath was ragged in the thin, cold air. I hadn't yet regained my *Calm.* I was alone, scared, and was about to get caught. I huddled by the shattered windshield of the Ural truck, crouching in a dark spot by the snow bank where I had first crawled out. With my winter camouflage, they probably wouldn't see me unless they walked right up on top of me. I readied my rifle, which was wrapped in white gauze, and tried to hold still.

There were two vehicles. I couldn't tell what they were, but they weren't big trucks. Probably 4x4s of some kind. One stopped about fifty yards down the hill, its headlights illuminating the rear end of the truck. The other slowly crept up the road, to the left of the crash.

They're looking for survivors. I huddled even lower, hoping both trucks would just drive past. Mere seconds ticked by at an agonizingly slow pace. The lights of the approaching truck drew nearer and nearer, then stopped.

Oh hell. I heard two car doors slam shut. Harsh voices in an unfamiliar language. There were two of them. They approached cautiously. I only caught glimpses of their movements as shadows in the truck's headlights, but I knew they were going to find me.

A dark silhouette came into my view, stepping around the bumper of the overturned truck. He had an AK-47. I was out of time.

I snapped off two shots. *Crack! Crack!* Heavy .308 rounds tore through the man's chest. I jumped to my feet, weapon shouldered, and moved forward. The other man came around the truck suddenly and crashed right into me.

Our eyes met for a split second. I was more than a foot taller than him. His face was young. His eyes were black and empty. A strange character was branded into his cheek.

BOOM! Another gunshot rang out, surprising me. The young man's stomach erupted in a horrific wound. My overwhites were splashed with blood. He grabbed his abdomen and crumpled to the ground, writhing in the pink snow.

I realized that my .44 was in my left hand. I'd fired from the hip. My rifle hung across my chest on its sling. I lowered my revolver and fired again, killing the young slave soldier, and holstered the big gun. I had no time. The other truck was still there.

Turning around, I struggled through the deep snow at the front of the wrecked truck. Lit up in the headlights of the second truck, I trudged out of the snow bank next to the truck's bed. The huge KPV machine gun was still on its pintle, muzzle hanging down in the snow.

I squatted down and grabbed the machine gun's heavy barrel. It was still warm. I pushed up, flipping the gun over so it was pointing to the rear. It took all of my strength to hold the heavy beast level. Grasping the gun sideways, I pointed it at the headlights down the road and mashed the trigger.

The gun roared and bucked in my hands. It immediately climbed up to my left, until it wouldn't traverse anymore. I realigned it and fired another burst. Tracers lashed out into the night, each shot producing a blinding muzzle flash. The driver of the truck threw it into reverse and backed down the hill as fast as he could. I had no idea if I hit him or not.

It didn't matter. I had my chance. The gun's heavy barrel swung down and hissed as it contacted the snow. I bounded around the rear of the overturned Ural truck, then back up the hill. The 4x4 the first two soldiers had arrived in was still running. I threw open the driver's door, climbed in, and put the truck in gear. It sputtered and rattled as I sped up the hill toward the dam. I had to rejoin the fight.

It only took me a few minutes to get to the top of the hill. Another guard shack sat on the west side of the dam. It had been shot to pieces, and two dead bodies lay in the snow next to it. Beyond that, I could see the two APCs and the remaining trucks on top of the dam. They'd all stopped near the superstructure. One of the APCs burned brightly in the night, sending thick black smoke curling into the frigid air. The other vehicles continued to fire on the barracks and utility buildings on the east side of the dam.

Exodus was still in the fight. I wasn't going to risk getting my ass shot off approaching in the truck. I put it in park and killed the engine and lights. I left the keys in it, thinking we might need it later.

On foot, I hustled across the road, digging into one of the pouches on my vest as I did so. I found an IR ChemLight, which can only be seen through night-vision goggles, and cracked it. With my left hand on the grip of my rifle, I held the chemlight in my right hand and waved it over my head as I jogged toward the Exodus convoy, wheezing as I went. The cold burned my lungs on every breath. My chest felt tight. I was already out of shape from my exile in North Gap and wasn't close to acclimatized to the altitude. I just hoped to hell Exodus wouldn't shoot me down before I could reach them.

Between the amber lights along the top of the dam and the burning BTR, I could see Exodus personnel scurrying about. A group took cover behind the vehicles and sent fire back across the dam. Others, weapons slung, were hauling supplies from the back of one of the trucks down into the dam itself. In the confusion of battle and the dark of the night, I was able to get pretty close before they noticed me. Multiple weapons were raised at me.

I stopped dead in my tracks and let go of my rifle. "Friendly!" I gasped, struggling to catch my breath. I frantically waved the chemlight over my head, expecting to get shot at any moment. "Friendly!"

"Val?" someone asked. "Val!" It was Skunky. He waved the others off. "It's Valentine, stand down! Stand down!" He jogged to me, his weapon held at the low ready.

"Holy shit, Val!" he said excitedly. "What the hell happened to you?"

"I got left," I panted. "At the truck crash. Left for dead."

"Damn. Sorry about that. I didn't even know we lost one of the trucks until we were at the top of the hill. I was in one of the BTRs."

"You actually rode in that death trap?" I asked. "Man, Exodus really has got you over a barrel."

My friend cracked a smile. "C'mon, this way. I'm glad you made it."

"How's it going up here?" I crouched slightly and moved toward the vehicles with him. Bullets snapped past high over our heads, but the gunfire was getting more sporadic.

"We caught them completely off guard," Skunky said. We stopped behind the intact APC. "Medic!" he shouted.

"I'm fine," I insisted, but he was having none of it.

"I just want to get you checked out real quick while I fill you in."

I looked down at myself. "Oh, yeah. Listen, this isn't my blood. I'm okay." An Exodus medic, dressed in winter camouflage just like mine, appeared at my side despite my protests.

Skunky kept talking as the medic gave me a quick once-over. "We took the dam pretty easily. The garrison was almost all in the barracks over there to the east. We overran the guards on the dam itself and just poured suppressing fire on those buildings." He pointed. One of the indicated buildings was burning. "Yeah," Skunky continued, "we lit 'em the hell up. Rockets, machine guns, grenades, everything we had. I think we caught most of them in bed. They're still over there, and they've tried to move on our position a couple of times, but we have them caught in a funnel. They're disorganized as hell, too. Like, ten minutes ago a dozen guys just tried to bum rush the convoy. We shot 'em all down before they got within a hundred yards."

"They're fanatics," I said. "Where's Ling?"

"She's downstairs. We've more or less secured the dam. We're placing the explosives now." A long burst of automatic weapons fire, followed by several shouts, then more gunshots, resonated from within the dam. Skunky shrugged. "More or less. Casualties have been light." Before I could say anything else, one of the Exodus operatives up by the intact APC shouted a warning to us. "Shit," Skunky said. "Here they come again. C'mon, get on line!"

I followed my friend around the side of the BTR-70. It was parked perpendicular to the dam so as to form the core of Exodus' improvised road block. The trucks were parked next to it. The burning BTR was farther to the east, blocking the top of the dam even more, and when an APC caught fire, they really *burned*. Any attackers coming from the east side had to run a serpentine of debris and vehicles in order to get to the convoy, while being covered the entire time by Exodus' heavy machine-guns. It was no wonder they hadn't had any success.

But damned if they weren't determined to try. I took cover behind a concrete jersey barrier that looked like it had been sitting on top of that dam for sixty years, leveled my rifle, and steeled myself. Skunky huddled next to me. I'd fire around the left side, and he'd fire around the right. Exodus troops hurriedly took up positions on the line, pointing rifles and machine-guns in the direction of the enemy.

Tortured, malevolent screams echoed from the smoke and darkness. It sounded like dozens of men, or boys. *RAAAAH!* they screamed. *RAAAAH!* again. *RAAAAAAAH!* On the third shout they charged. They fired wildly from the hip, their shots flying high and wide. There were a lot of them, bearing down on us full tilt. I'd never seen such a fanatical mass banzai charge before.

Before I could even get one in my scope the machine guns opened up. The 14.5mm on the BTR roared like the Wrath of God, with a chorus of lesser belt-fed angels backing Him up. I put my crosshair on one of Sala

Jihan's soldiers and snapped off a shot. He was ripped apart by machine-gun fire before I could even tell if I'd hit him. I adjusted and kept rocking the trigger. Hot brass belched out of my rifle as I fired, a shot here, two shots there, laying rounds into anything that moved.

The enemy was cut down as they came into view. Their fire was inaccurate and largely ineffective. Few of their rounds even came close to us. There was nothing on top of the dam, except perhaps the burning BTR, that could stop the huge, armor-piercing bullets from the 14.5mm machine-gun. They had no cover. Hell, they didn't *try* to use cover. They just charged, screaming and firing as they ran.

"Reloading!" I shouted to Skunky. I'd gone through a twenty-round magazine just like that. I dropped it out of my rifle and ripped open the velcro on one of my magazine pouches.

"Shit, reloading!" Skunky said. He was out too. *Goddamn.* He had open-topped magazine pouches, so he was a little quicker on the reload than me. We both sent our bolts forward at the same time, leveled our rifles around the concrete barrier, just as a screaming fanatic with a grenade in each hand bore down on us. We shot him down in hail of fire, shouting "Grenaaaade!"

We ducked. The double concussion was skull-rattling. Fragmentation buzzed angrily as it zipped overhead, and pockmarked the far side of our concrete barrier. A few more random shots and it was quiet. Skunky and I made eye contact briefly, then leaned out from behind cover to survey the carnage.

Bodies were strewn across the cracked, snow-dusted pavement. The APC still burned, black smoke blotting out the tepid moonlight, its firelight illuminating the carnage. Most of the enemy had been dressed in a mishmash of Russian and Chinese military gear, leathers, and rags. I estimated that we'd been charged by something like forty soldiers, and we'd killed them all.

"Jesus Christ," I muttered, standing up. My rifle was hot to the touch.

"There can't be many more of them," Skunky hoped, spent brass rolling under his boots as he walked.

"I hope you're right." Something golden glinted briefly in the moonlight. I noticed it as I took a long swig of water. I squinted, straining to make out what it was. A little statue or idol, made of gold (or something that looked like gold from a distance) was lying on the ground. It was on the end of a staff about five feet long. The staff was still clutched, in death, by the slave soldier who had been carrying it. His weapon was slung across his back, unused. The little idol gleamed in the light of the Moon and the burning vehicle as it was slowly enveloped in a pool of blood.

"They're insane," Skunky whispered. "What kind of man inspires that?"

LORENZO
Sala Jihan's Fortress
March 25th

"Damn them! Move Johan's team to the south. Reinforce Nagano," Ibrahim ordered into his mike, one hand pressed against the speaker in his ear so he could still hear over the roar of the nearby machine gun, his other hand dangling with a G3K in it. He saw me coming and nodded. "Do it now! Sword One Actual out. Hello, my friend. How goes it?"

"Not as good as we'd hoped, apparently," I said as I jogged up to him, my team right behind me. It had taken us awhile to make it to the LZ. There were a lot more troops stationed in the compound than we had expected. Anders ran for the second chopper. He needed to check in with his boss.

The two massive Russian helicopters were parked in the snow. One of them was canted at a very awkward angle, its front end broken and smoking, its blades pointing at a drastic downward angle. It had caught an RPG on the way in, and the only reason anyone had walked away from the crash was because of how close it was to the ground when it had been hit. Katarina was probably going to be pissed about the loss of such an expensive thing.

Ibrahim and a handful of Exodus operatives were clustered around the choppers calling the shots, while the remainder had formed a rough semicircle around it. On the far edge of that semicircle was a bunch of really angry fanatics protecting a hole in the ground. On the opposite side was a bunch of other fanatics trying desperately to get to said hole. We were right in the middle. They were unloading explosives and tools from the choppers.

"We have to beat these soldiers back. Many of them protect the silo, and we're having to dig them out like ticks," Ibrahim shouted over the noise. There was an oily explosion in the distance behind us as something else highly flammable detonated. Our plan relied on us to secure that damn silo, because as long as Jihan was alive, we believed his slave soldiers would continue to fight, and fought they had, unexpectedly hard, and with suicidal ferocity.

We were behind schedule. It was only a matter of time before reinforcements arrived from the mines. And if they came before we took the silo, we would have to retreat. Luckily the Halos were so big we could easily fit everybody into one.

"Lorenzo, I need you to help eliminate the guards around that silo," Ibrahim ordered.

I shook my head. "I have to get to the prison."

"Then you will go by yourself," Ibrahim snapped. "Shen, Roland, Phillips, reinforce Solomon at the silo."

"Yes, sir!" shouted the two younger operatives. Shen looked at me, and nodded slightly. He was going to do his duty, no matter what. The three of them ran immediately in the direction of the most gunfire.

"Damn it!" I shouted. "My brother—"

"Your brother is as dead as the rest of us if we cannot kill Jihan!" Ibrahim spat back.

I bit my tongue. He was right, but that didn't make it any easier. I glared at Ibrahim, then took off after the others.

We passed the still-functioning chopper. In the dark, it was difficult for me to ascertain who was standing near its rear door, but as I drew closer, I recognized Anders' massive bulk, and Katarina's slender frame and almost silver hair. She finished telling him something, then slapped the big man on the shoulder. He turned to rejoin us.

"Lorenzo," Kat shouted over the noise. She had a familiar weapon in her hands, and she gestured for me to come toward her. I slowed up, the others quickly leaving me behind.

"What, Kat? I see you've still got Mr. Perkins."

"Yes. He is my favorite." She held up the M79. She had used that same old 40mm grenade launcher on quite a few jobs. It had been a little unnerving when she had given it a name, but she was an artist in its use. "I'm glad to see you made it."

"Thanks, look, I've got to go," I started walking. I didn't have time for her bullshit.

"I just wanted to tell you one thing." She grabbed my arm. I could see her white teeth glowing in the dim light as she smiled. "No matter what happens here tonight—"

Something impacted the sheet metal of the chopper over her head, showering both of us with metal fragments. I flinched down. Kat's smile disappeared, and Mr. Perkins moved to her shoulder as she zeroed in on the muzzle flash from the sniper.

BLOOP

A full three seconds later, there was a small explosion on a bunker's roof and the sniper was permanently silenced. "No matter what happens tonight," she continued talking as she popped open the single-shot weapon to shove another huge shell in, as if nothing had happened. "I just want you to know that I'm really glad you showed up. It was good to see you again."

"Uh, yeah. Me too."

"It has helped me set some things straight, to reexamine my life, if you will." She suddenly leaned in and kissed me gently on the cheek. My face was so frozen that it almost burned. It was strange in that she actually seemed calm and in control. "Goodbye, Lorenzo."

Another bullet impacted near us as somebody opened up from the far wall with an AK. Katarina shrugged and aimed her 40mm. I used the opportunity to run after my team.

The warhead had screamed by so close I could have reached out and touched it.

"Son of a bitch!" I shouted as the RPG exploded fifty feet behind me. Anders rolled around cover and started shooting at the shadows where the rocket had come from. "Reaper!" I hit my mike and shouted. "Come in, Reaper!"

"*You've got ten of them moving in a trench ten meters in front of you, and I saw at least one move into the elevator shaft.*" Reaper sounded relatively calm, but he should, since he was sitting in a truck miles from here. "*You've got to remember that when they're under a roof, I can't see them on thermal—*"

Yeah, whatever. I tuned out the technical explanation and refocused on the crazy people trying to kill me. I saw a man leap out of the trench and sprint for the elevator. I put the Aimpoint dot on him and started shooting. I must have hit him in the legs, as they flew out from under him and he sprawled in the snow. Somebody nearby with a larger caliber rifle finished him with a shot through his face.

"Phillips!" I shouted over the din. The remaining soldiers must have had a lot of ammo stashed, and they weren't trying to save any of it. The young man looked up from the stock of his rifle. "Cover the elevator door. Somebody's in there."

"Got it!"

There were two full teams of Exodus operatives converged on this spot when we had arrived. We had moved up right between them and hit the soldiers from a third angle. A few feet to my right was an Exodus sniper with a Sako bolt action. It took me a moment to recognize that it was Svetlana under that fur hood and tac gear. A soldier started out of the trench, and she rocked under the recoil as she took the top of his skull off.

I had scrounged up several frags on our trip across the compound. There had been plenty of them just lying around, and the previous owners had been in no shape to argue with me about taking them. They were those nasty little Southeast Asian ones that were wrapped in pre-stressed wire. I yanked a pin and tossed one, waited just a second, then followed it with another. Amazingly enough, even as cold-numbed as my hands were, I managed to land both of them in the trench, but I had gotten a lot of experience chucking grenades back in Africa.

The soldiers in the trench were on the ball, though, because both of the grenades were tossed back out to explode harmlessly in the snow. Sure, I could have pulled the pin and waited a second before throwing them, but I had learned not to trust Third World grenade fuses.

The Exodus team leader to the right must have decided that they were out of time. With a ragged battle cry, the entire group of them popped up and ran toward the trench. It was brave, and maybe suicidal, but no more suicidal than still being inside this compound when the reinforcements arrived from the mines.

The elevator door popped open, and a soldier with an RPG launcher stepped out, but Phillips had been doing exactly what I had asked him to do, and the soldier went down in a spray of arterial blood before he could launch the rocket.

Muzzle flashes erupted from the trench and some of the charging Exodus people went down, screaming as bullets tore through their flesh, spilling their blood into the snow. But some of them made it through, and I could see them silhouetted in the moonlight as they stood on the lip of the trench and fired downward into the remaining soldiers.

Finally, the gunfire stopped. The only sounds were the moans and screams from the wounded.

"Reaper?"

"*They're still warm, but they ain't moving.*"

"Ibrahim. We've got the silo," I said quickly.

"*Understood. Assault element moving in,*" he said breathlessly.

I moved forward, my team right behind me. The young guys looked slightly shocked. These were their comrades that were in front of us bleeding and dying. They each moved to help one of the wounded. I saw Svetlana sitting in the snow at the lip of the trench. Her big Sako was in her lap, and she was staring stupidly at her hand.

I knelt at her side. She had pulled off her glove, and held her delicate left hand up to show me. Her smallest two fingers were missing, just jagged bone stumps sticking out of her palm. "I didn't even feel it . . ." she said.

"Don't worry. You will," I responded as I pulled a roll of bandages out of my pocket and started wrapping it tightly around her hand.

"Ooohh . . ." Her eyes rolled back into her head. "Yes, I believe you're right."

"You're going to be fine," I said reassuringly. The only good thing about the cold was the blood flow to the extremities was slower than normal. "Your friend's charge was stupid. You know that, right?"

She spoke through gritted teeth. "We are Exodus."

"Yeah, now get your ass back to the chopper before you pass out," I ordered. She shook her head, being stubborn. I saw Roland standing nearby. The man that he was trying to help had just stopped breathing. "Roland! Get Svetlana back to the chopper." He quickly complied, helped her to her feet, grabbed her sniper rifle, and half-escorted, half-carried her back in the direction we had come from.

Ibrahim sprinted up to the pit. Behind him was the assault team, each of them carrying climbing rope, tools, and explosives. The doors of the silo itself had been designed to withstand a nuclear war and would take hours to break through, so they were going to go down the same shaft I'd used when I had visited before, but they'd probably still have to cut through multiple blast doors to reach Jihan's quarters.

I noticed for the first time that in addition to his stubby .308, Ibrahim also had a sword on his belt, an actual friggin' scimitar, and it looked like an antique, complete with rubies on the hilt. I had to admit, these guys had *style*. The Exodus commander surveyed his men as they circled the top of the silo. He spoke when he saw me. "Lorenzo, take your team and get your brother. I will be out of contact from here on out. Fajkus is now leading the operation." He was very somber. "Godspeed, my friend."

I nodded once, then went after Bob.

Chapter 21: Poor Life Choice

VALENTINE
The Dam
March 25th

The interior of the dam was dark and smoky. Many of the lights had been shot out in the firefight. I pulled a small flashlight from my vest and used it to help me navigate.

The narrow corridors were filled with the low-pitched hum of the dam's turbines. Above that, voices echoed throughout the structure. Scattered Exodus personnel hurried to and fro, carrying supplies and moving the wounded. An aid station had been set up just inside the doorway. A pair of medics tended to the wounded and covered the dead.

I ran into Ling in the upper level of the dam, almost literally, as she and another Exodus operative were hurrying the other way. "Michael!" She threw her arms around me and embraced me tightly, for just a moment. My slung rifle clattered against the SIG 551 that hung from her shoulder. The air was cold but she was warm.

The other Exodus operative maintained a poker face and said nothing. Ling stepped back, blushing slightly, and cleared her throat. "I was worried when you didn't arrive with us."

"I got left at the truck crash."

"As I feared. And your driver?"

"Yeah, the kid didn't make it," I said. "His name was Paolo."

Ling closed her eyes for just a moment, and took a deep breath. "There is no time to mourn now. We must hurry. The raid on Sala Jihan's main compound is well underway. I just heard Ibrahim on the radio, they're about to breach Jihan's personal quarters. Come with me," she said, and I followed her back outside.

"What kind of nutjob lives at the bottom of a missile silo?" I asked, as we stepped back out into the night air. "And how much longer until the explosives are in place?"

"Not long," Ling replied, before shouting orders to some other personnel in Mandarin.

"How will you be initiating it?"

"Two ways. We're going to have time fuse as a backup. Our primary means of initiation will be radio. We'll spool a firing wire out to the surface, hooked to a receiver, as we withdraw across the dam. It's redundant."

That was good. If for whatever reason this huge demo shot misfired, it was very unlikely we'd be able to get in, fix the problem, and get back out alive. We only had one shot and Exodus was leaving as little to chance as possible.

Ling changed the subject. "I'm glad that you're well, I truly am. We need every able body we can find now."

That sounded ominous. "What's happening?"

"Reinforcements are coming from the mines."

I closed my eyes tightly and sighed. It wasn't exactly a surprise, but it was far from good news. "How many?"

"Many. Lorenzo's man has a small drone that is tracking them with thermal cameras. They're on their way here now. I don't know what's happening. The Montalban Exchange's mercenaries do not seem to have begun their attack on the garrison in town."

"That's not good. How are things going at the fortress?"

"I have no news of Mr. Lorenzo, if that's what you're asking. Though no one has called me to tell me that he is dead. So far, all seems to be going according to plan there."

"How long do we have?" I asked.

"Maybe ten minutes, fifteen if we're very fortunate. I need you to help me get everything organized up here. Katsumoto is down below with our engineers and demolitions men, supervising the final placement and priming of the explosives. Right where he should be, as that is the primary mission. I have been charged with holding the line up here until we are ready to leave."

"Is there any chance that we can get out of here before they get to the road at the bottom of the hill and cut us off?"

"That is the hope," she said. "But it is not likely."

"We'll hold them, Ling," I promised.

We spent the next few minutes hurriedly trying to reorganize the defense of the dam. The focus was now on the west, where we'd come from, instead of east, even though the east side hadn't been completely cleared and we couldn't ignore it. If we were pushed back across the dam, there probably wouldn't be any escape for us. The terrain on the east side was too rugged for vehicles, and we wouldn't last long hiking around the mountains on foot.

Everybody who could hold a weapon, wounded or not, was put on the line. We were likely outnumbered. If they broke through, none of us would survive. Certainly no one wanted to be captured and taken to Sala Jihan alive.

Our barricade was moved to the very west end of the dam, near where I had parked my stolen truck. The BTR-70 that was still intact rolled into position, once again sideways, blocking off almost the entire road by itself. The other trucks were lined up in such a way that they could leave in a hurry once the explosives were in place, assuming they had anywhere to go.

Sala Jihan's forces would face the same kilometer-long uphill battle that we did. Unlike us, they lacked the element of surprise, they lacked night vision, most of them lacked body armor, and they faced a much more competent foe.

On the other hand, there were less than forty of us that weren't preoccupied setting the charges. Hundreds of Jihan's slave soldiers were on their way from the mines, and more could come from town at any time since the Montalbans had not begun their diversion for some reason.

It wasn't looking good. Skunky joined me on the line, and he seemed to read my mind. "Having second thoughts?"

"Honestly?" I began, as I took up a position behind the armored personnel carrier. "I kind of am. I'm beginning to think this may have been a poor life choice." I cracked a smile, and my friend laughed.

The levity was forced. Beneath it, I was grappling with the growing realization that I was probably going to die in this godforsaken place. Everything I'd managed to survive, from Mexico, to Zubara, to North Gap, and look what I'd gotten myself into: outnumbered with no hope of rescue on the ass-end of the world, fighting somebody else's damned war. I swear to God, it's the story of my life.

I looked over at Ling. She briefly smiled at me, then returned her attention to what she was doing. My bitterness faded. I'd come here for her. I'd had nothing to live for, so I'd gone along to help somebody who did.

The cloud cover had been thinning all night. The Moon was now high in the sky, and pale grey light poured over the land and reflected brightly off the snow. Even without my lost night vision goggles, it was easy to see a long way through the darkness. What I could see wasn't comforting. At the bottom of the hill, turning onto the road that led to the dam, was a long line of vehicles carrying Sala Jihan's soldiers. Their headlights pierced the darkness in front of them as they rounded the corner and started up the hill in a single column.

I zoomed my rifle's scope in to maximum magnification and clicked the elevation knob up to 800 meters. Our best bet was to pour fire on the advancing forces as they climbed the hill. They were vulnerable, and we could make them pay for every inch of ground they covered. I was glad that I'd brought a lot of ammo.

The BTR-70 opened fire first with its turret-mounted 14.5mm machine gun. The weapon's roar would have been deafening if not for my hearing protection, and even so it was loud as hell. Tracers speared out into the night, peppering the convoy from a range of nearly a thousand meters. The machine guns mounted on the trucks opened up next, followed by a few crew-served machine guns manned by Exodus troops. The symphony of automatic weapons fire pulsed in my chest with each shot as *the Calm* enveloped me in its cool, leveling embrace.

If I was to die here, then so be it. I looked over at Skunky, who was holding fire. His SIG 551 was equipped with an Aimpoint, not ideal for long-range shooting. He shook his head slightly at me, smiling in the darkness. "You're kind of scary when you're in the zone like that, you know that, brother?" he said, raising his voice to be heard over the cacophony of gunfire.

Tracers were zipping up at us from the hill now. Sala Jihan's forces were returning fire. *PING! DING!* Incoming fire ricocheted off the armored hull of the BTR-70. *PING! BING!*

I set my scope's reticle on a set of headlights midway through the convoy and squeezed the trigger. My rifle recoiled over and over again as I cracked off an entire magazine. "Reloading!"

"I've got you covered!" Ling said. She leaned around the front of the BTR and fired off several short bursts from her carbine. Bullets buzzed overhead. They were shooting back at us, but inaccurately so far.

"I wish I had my M14!" Skunky said, firing over the rear of the armored personnel carrier. An RPG rocket streaked down from our position, detonating as it impacted a vehicle in the convoy. The truck rolled to a stop and was quickly enveloped in flames. Burning men jumped out of the back and rolled in the snow, trying to extinguish themselves. My active hearing protection allowed me to hear their agonizing screams between bursts of machine gun fire from the BTR. The convoy didn't stop. Not a single vehicle, other than the ones we immobilized, stopped. No one got out to aid the wounded or recover the dead. They hardly even slowed down.

"Keep firing!" Ling shouted. "Kill as many of them on the road as possible!" Sala Jihan's forces continued their relentless push. Several of their vehicles had been disabled or destroyed, but the rest drove around them. Troops dismounted and began to run up the hill at us, screaming like madmen the whole while. The enemy's incoming fire was taking its toll on our defensive position now. One of the trucks with a 14.5mm machine gun mounted on it was shot to pieces. RPGs streaked up and down the hill.

Struggling to overcome the chaos, I fired shot after shot, magazine after magazine, as rapidly as I could accurately manage. My rifle was hot to the touch. The enemy convoy was almost on top of us. Two vehicles, beat-up old cars, swerved out of the line and sped around the others. They accelerated up the hill toward our position. The gunner in the BTR-70 turned his attention to it, pouring fire into the car. Riddled with huge holes and burning, it veered off into the snow bank and exploded. The concussion from the blast rattled us all.

The other car was already on top of us.

"VBIED!" I screamed, pronouncing it "vee-bed," but it was already too late. I barely had time to get down as the little car crashed into the side of the BTR-70 and detonated.

The next thing I knew, I was face down on cold pavement. My ears were ringing. Muffled sounds of gunfire and screams swirled all around me, but I just couldn't focus. A bright orange light was behind me, and I felt heat on my back. The BTR-70 was ablaze. The big truck next to it, closest to the four-foot wall that marked the northern edge of the dam, was mangled. The stench of diesel and burning interior filled my nostrils.

I pushed myself up to my elbows and tried to focus. Someone ran past me, coming around the burning APC, then stopped in his tracks. He was dressed in camouflage pants, a tattered brown great coat, and carried a Mosin Nagant carbine with the bayonet locked into place. His eyes were wide as saucers. He leveled the rifle at me and screamed as he charged.

I rolled to my right and pulled my revolver. No time to align the sights, I just shoved it out and rocked the trigger. It bucked in my hand as it roared. The fanatical young soldier's stomach splashed red. His scream turned into a shriek, but he kept coming, stumbling, falling, rusty spike bayonet slicing the air toward my face. I pushed myself out of the way just as the point of the bayonet struck the pavement. The screaming fanatic was carried forward by his momentum, pivoting around his rifle and landing on top of me.

Struggling to sit up, I tried to push the dead weight off of me. Two more soldiers appeared around the side of the burning armored personnel carrier. One had some kind of pump shotgun in his hands and was firing from the hip. The other carried nothing but a satchel full of hand grenades. The shotgunner noticed me just as I acquired him in my sights. The .44 Magnum roared two more times as I ended him. The grenadier had a frag in his hands, pin pulled, when I shot him. He fell over backwards. I barely had time to hide my face behind the dead body on my chest before the grenade exploded.

We were being overrun. There was no time to lie under a corpse in a daze. I managed to sit up and pushed the slave soldier's body off of me. Someone grabbed my arm. Every muscle in my body tensed. I swung my revolver around to fire over my right shoulder. The tritium front sight aligned on Skunky's face.

"Whoa whoa whoa!" he cried, eyes wide. "Holy shit, it's me!"

"I almost shot you in the face!" I snarled, hand suddenly shaking. "Fuck!"

"C'mon, dude," he said, helping me to my feet. "We need to get out of here. We've been— *Get down!*" My friend pushed me back, snapped his carbine to his shoulder, and cranked off half a dozen shots. Hot 5.56 brass bounced off my shoulders and burned the back of my neck. "Damn it, they're everywhere!"

I picked up my rifle and came to my feet. "We need to fall back. We can't hold them here." Everyone else seemed to be engaged in a fighting retreat back to the superstructure of the dam. "Wait, where's Ling?"

"I don't know!" Skunky said, quickly changing magazines. "Come on, we have to go!"

"Ling!" I yelled, trying to make myself heard over the chaos. Bullets snapped past us in both directions. The Exodus operatives were running and gunning their way back across the dam. The extremely motivated, but completely disorganized, slave soldiers were still trying to take advantage of the hole they'd punched in our defensive position. Their own vehicles had piled up, and many seemed to be milling about without direction. They had no leadership and weren't sure what to do. It gave us a brief opportunity to regroup. "Ling! Where are you? *Ling!*"

Skunky shook his head. "Come on, man, she's probably on her way back to the dam. We can't stay here! We gotta go!" The smoke from the burning vehicles was so thick that it was impossible to see very far. Despite the moonlight, we were enveloped in darkness. Ling was out there somewhere, and I couldn't just leave her.

Her voice rang through the hellish scene, clear against the low-pitched roar of battle. She called my name.

"Where are you?" I shouted back. Skunky looked around frantically. We couldn't see but a few feet in any direction now.

"I'm here!" Ling said, stumbling through the smoke. "I'm he—" her words were cut off in a fit of coughing.

"Ling! Oh my God!" I ran to her and grabbed her arm. She'd been injured. Blood trickled from under her wool cap down her pretty face. Her cheeks were smeared with soot. "What happened?"

She was in a daze. "I don't know. I . . . we have to get to the . . . the . . ."

"Come on, we're going back!" Ling only nodded. She was too out of it to argue.

I raised my voice as loud as I could. "Exodus! Fall back! If you're still here, fall back to the east! Move, move, move!" Several shouts of acknowledgment rang through the haze. With Skunky's help, I used the smoke as cover and led Ling back toward the superstructure of the dam.

✢ ✢ ✢

The chaos caused by the enemy's vehicle-borne improvised explosive device gave us enough of a break in the onslaught to retreat back across the dam. That was the only good news, though. We were now stuck on top of the dam. The only way we had to retreat was east, which would put us on the wrong side of the river and leave us stranded. We had too many wounded to move without vehicles.

I told the remaining Exodus operatives to set up a defensive perimeter around the superstructure of the dam. We'd lost our trucks and our heavy machine guns, but there were still a couple belt-feds on the line. Sala Jihan's forces now had to come from the west, straight across the top of the dam, with no cover. It would cost them dearly. But they were utterly relentless and oblivious to their own casualties. There weren't enough of us left to win a battle of attrition.

Skunky joined the defensive position outside as I led Ling into the dam. I called for a medic and had her sit down against the wall. The Exodus medic, a young woman whom I guessed was from India, knelt next to Ling and began to administer aid.

"You have a gash on your head," the medic told Ling. "It's not very deep. You are very fortunate. Two centimeters closer and this would have killed you."

"She was close to the vee-bed when it detonated," I told her. "The car bomb, I mean. She may have been close to the blast." The blast overpressure is the most destructive component of an explosion. It has a very short lethal radius, depending on the size of the blast, compared to fragmentation. Being caught in it can do instant, horrific damage to the human body, including traumatic brain injury. Having experienced a TBI myself, I was very worried about Ling.

As the medic talked to her, she seemed to come around. "I think it is just a case of shock," the medic said with a slight accent. "She's responsive. Her wound is dressed and I have not found any other injuries. Please stay with her, I need to attend the others."

I nodded and the medic ran off, aid bag in hand. There were many wounded and we were likely running low on medical supplies. Inside the concrete superstructure, the sounds of gunfire outside echoed throughout the corridors. The lights dimmed and flickered with the occasional grenade or RPG detonation.

Ling sat up against the wall and just slowly shook her head. She then buried her face in her hands. I moved closer to her and put my hand on her shoulder. She didn't look at me, but she put her gloved hand on top of mine.

"Michael, I am so sorry," she said.

We didn't have time for her to be sorry. But she needed a moment, she needed help, and I was all she had. "You don't have anything to be sorry about."

"I do," she insisted. "I'm afraid I've led you to your death. I don't think any of us are getting out of here."

"What's going to happen? Will Katsumoto blow the dam even if we're still on it?"

Ling shook her head. "Not if there's any way for us to retreat to safety. I don't think we'll have that chance, though. I think today is the day we die." She squeezed my hand. "I'm sorry, Michael. You've been through so much. You've seen enough of war. I pulled you out of hell and led you right back into it, and I had no right."

I managed a smile for her. "I'm supposed to be here." She actually laughed in that musty, dimly lit corridor. "And I haven't given up yet. Come on now," I said, standing. "Can you walk?" She nodded. "Okay. Your people need you now. They need a leader. If there's any chance at all of us getting out of this alive, it'll be up to you and Katsumoto to make that happen."

Ling nodded again. "You're right, of course. You're right. Thank you."

"They're holding the line up there for the moment. I don't think the enemy has regrouped for their final push yet. Let's go downstairs and see how things are going. Katsumoto needs to be up here leading this fight." I turned down the corridor, but Ling grabbed my sleeve.

I turned around. "What—" Ling stepped forward, closed her eyes, and kissed me. The warmth of her lips, her breath, her body against mine contrasted starkly against the cold, dingy air of the old hydroelectric plant.

She stepped back after a moment, blushing slightly. "I wish we had more time," she said with a sad smile. "There is . . . much I would like to say."

I didn't know what to say, or what to do. I hadn't touched a woman since Sarah died. Before Ling pulled me out of North Gap, I hadn't even *seen* a woman, except for Dr. Silvers, in months. Ling was beautiful, with dark almond eyes and shiny black hair. There was no denying that I was attracted to her. Tailor had teased me about it when we first met Ling, a lifetime ago in Mexico.

You don't have time for high school drama, goddamn it, I scolded myself. I looked into Ling's eyes. "We're not dead yet," I managed, trying to sound reassuring. "Come on, let's get going."

We found Katsumoto and the Exodus engineers in the heart of the dam. Explosive charges had been placed all around the roaring turbines, and daisy-chained together with many strands of red, yellow, and green det cord.

"Katsumoto-sama," Ling said, using a formal honorific. "We are out of time. Our perimeter has collapsed and most of our vehicles have been destroyed. If we wait much longer will we be overrun completely and the mission will fail."

Katsumoto, though small of stature, was a proud man who commanded great respect. His demeanor hinted at a quiet intensity, but he was completely calm and collected. "I know," he said simply. "And I am sorry. The placing of the charges took too long. This is my responsibility. I fear I may have killed us all. This is why I wanted to just destroy the dam. We would not have taken nearly so long to place the charges."

Before Ling could say anything, one of the demolition engineers stood upright. He maintained composure but looked like he was fighting back tears. "Commander! It is I who is responsible. This is my fault!"

Their willingness to assume responsibility for failure was noble, but we didn't have time for finger pointing, even if they were pointing fingers at themselves. "Guys, guys, guys," I said, interrupting. "The question is what the hell do we do now? Your troops are fighting for their lives up there. The enemy is fanatical but disorganized. It's all Jihan's conscripts. We haven't seen any of the Brotherhood yet."

"They must be all at the fortress," Ling suggested.

"That makes sense," I agreed. "And it's the only good news we have. We still have a chance to get clear of this, even if we have to retreat to the east side of the dam and blow it from there."

"We will be stranded," Katsumoto reminded me, "on the wrong side of the river. It shouldn't collapse from the explosion, but once we move off the dam to the east, getting all the way back across it under fire may be impossible."

"I know. But a few people making it out on foot, or at least having the shot, is better than everyone martyring themselves here. Live to fight another day, right? If the dam is disabled, we've accomplished the mission. It's not hopeless yet."

"What do you suggest?" Katsumoto asked.

"They broke through our defensive line but they still have a big choke point there. We're pouring fire on them as they come through, and we can keep that up until the ammo runs out. Then we'll be overrun. So we can't stay here. We have to push."

"The odds are not good."

"No, they're not. But they can only bring so many across the dam at a time, and there's not much cover. Their numbers don't mean much in a fatal funnel like that. We can suppress them with whatever machine guns and grenades we have left. We use smoke and advance under concealment. We only have to push them back west to where the car bomb went off. We can pick up weapons from their dead if we need to."

"Then what?" Ling asked.

"At the western edge of the dam we're at least on the right side of the river. If we have to cut across country on foot, we can link up with the others or get back to town. We can use the stretchers as sleds and drag the wounded across the snow if we have to. The vee-bed wasn't that big. I don't think it disabled all of the trucks. If we break their assault completely, we might be able to get in a vehicle and make it back down the road. Either way, it's better than being stuck on the east side, and it's a hell of a lot better than everyone getting wiped out. It's not much of a chance but it's the best one we've got."

Katsumoto looked thoughtful for a long moment, then nodded his head slightly. "Yes. Yes. Mr. Valentine, you are indeed an asset. We will do as you suggest."

"Your people need you up there on the line," I said. "Are the charges ready?"

"They are," Katsumoto confirmed. "We have only to spool out the wire and initiate the charge. We will have to do it quickly, though. If we delay, if their forces back-fill behind us as we withdraw, they might be able to get down here and disrupt the explosives before they detonate." Katsumoto then looked at the demolition engineer. His winter camouflage smock was stained with dirt. "Prepare the explosives for initiation. Do not begin the time fuse yet. That will be the last thing we do before we make our push to the end of the dam. We have to make sure we can move the wounded before we do that."

"How long will we have?"

"Fifteen minutes. We can initiate sooner if we get off of the dam in time. Everyone needs to be clear in case the dam actually collapses."

"Understood, Commander!" the engineer said. He then gathered his teammates and ran off to complete his task.

"Come," Katsumoto said. He reached behind his back and brought his weapon, a SIG 552 carbine, around. "Let us finish this."

The battle was raging when we returned to the surface. The remaining Exodus defenders were holding the enemy at bay, if only barely. Most of the amber lights across its topside roadway were intact, illuminating the bodies that littered the roadway. Black smoke poured into the air as both BTR-70s continued to burn, one on either side of the dam, giving the scene a hellish glow.

Skunky was among the defenders waiting for us when we emerged. He and several other Exodus operatives came to Katsumoto while the rest held the line. They needed to know what the plan was. Katsumoto took a knee with them, behind cover, and outlined our strategy. The word was passed along to everyone that was still alive. A couple of the 4x4s we'd convoyed up in were still parked by the superstructure and operational. The immobile wounded would be piled into them. The walking wounded would make the final push with us.

I'd done my best to sound confident to the Exodus leadership, but we really didn't have much of a chance. Oh, I thought we could hold them off until the dam blew. I was actually very sure about that, but I was more concerned with getting home alive, and I didn't really think that was looking likely. We had enough firepower to push the enemy back for a while. We didn't have enough to fight the entire column down the road and make our escape. The best we could hope for would be to scatter into the woods, trudging through the snow, hoping to get to friendly forces without being captured, shot, or succumbing to the cold. The wounded almost certainly wouldn't make it.

I made sure my rifle and revolver were both topped off. The hideous plastic Taurus snubby was in my coat pocket if I needed it. The fifth and final round in that gun's cylinder might be for myself, I decided. I had heard enough horror stories about Sala Jihan that I resolved not to be captured alive. Taking a deep breath, I drew my bayonet from its sheath and snapped it onto the end of my rifle. The blade glinted dully in the firelight from the burning vehicles. There were a lot of bad guys out there, and we were going to have to punch through them all.

Skunky saw me fix my bayonet. "It's ugly out there, bro. No matter what happens, I'm glad you're here with me. It's good to fight with you again."

"You too, brother. You too. Now don't get all squishy on me. We've got to shoot some motherfuckers in the face." *The Calm* was overtaking me, and my fears and doubts were falling to the wayside. It's not that I thought I wasn't going to die. It was just that I no longer cared, at least not on the surface.

We that remained were split into several smaller elements. Some would provide suppressive fire while others advanced. This would maximize our chances as opposed to blindly rushing the enemy. Jihan's forces were using that technique and they were dying by the bushel. Ling and I were in the vanguard. Skunky was to remain in Katsumoto's element. I slapped him on the shoulder and joined the troops I was going to be fighting with. We were discouragingly few in number, but that didn't change anything. We had to do what we had to do.

Katsumoto stood up, raising his voice so well that it sounded imposing over the raging fires and the snap and hiss of incoming rounds. "This is it! Our sacrifice will not be in vain! For the Order! For honor! For freedom!"

"For freedom!" the people in my element echoed, Ling's soprano voice standing out from the rest. The passion in their voices was undeniable. These people knew they were going to their deaths, and they wanted to die well. I can respect that, even if it's somewhat antithetical to the mantra of a career mercenary such as myself.

"Suppressing fire!" Katsumoto shouted. His entire element opened up on anything that moved through the remains of our roadblock. He looked over at Ling. "Advance!"

"Let's go!" Ling shouted. "Move, move, move! Advance on me!" Her people formed a tight wedge. They readied their weapons and jogged up the right side of the dam, giving the support element some separation as they fired past us. I lagged behind with the wounded, being out of shape, out of breath, and having had a pretty rough night.

Sala Jihan's army continued to advance around the destroyed roadblock and burning APC to the west like so many ants. The people in the front of my element opened fire as well. Incoming rounds zipped back at us, snapping past my ears and over my head. I just put my head down and ran harder, plodding along in my heavy vest and pack, hoping I wouldn't trip or slip.

A man in front of me screamed. Enemy fire cut through our little formation, tearing through his leg. He fell. His teammates paused, but they didn't have time to pause. "Keep going!" I screamed, kneeling next to the fallen. "Keep going, goddamn it! I'll take care of him!" I got him to let go of his mangled leg long enough to let me see the wound. The bullet had hit his shin bone and shattered it. He wasn't going to be able to walk. There wasn't much I could do. I pulled a tourniquet from my med pouch and looped it around his leg. A couple of inches above the wound, I cinched it down and twisted the windlass three times. The Exodus operative, who was swearing in German, shrieked at the pain, but it needed to be done.

"Stay here! Hey! Listen to me, damn it! Stay here! Stay down! The truck with the other wounded will pick you up. Do you understand me?"

He jerkily nodded his head, his teeth clenched from the pain.

"I've stopped the bleeding. Hang in there. Good luck!" I slapped him on the shoulder, then was on my feet, running as hard as I could to catch up with the formation. I didn't want to get left behind again.

Ling's element paused about halfway to the wreck of the BTR-70. She had her people firing at the roadblock while Katsumoto advanced his element. As soon as he moved, the time fuse on the explosives was initiated. Ling stopping her element allowed me to catch up and rejoin the formation. I took a knee next to the Exodus operatives, shouldered my carbine, and opened fire at the hoard of slave soldiers descending upon us. Icy wind chilled my neck as hot brass ejected past my face. Bullets snapped past us and over our heads. An RPG rocket screamed by and exploded in the distance somewhere. The pile of bodies at the gap was mounting.

My safety glasses were spattered with blood as the Exodus woman next to me was hit. She didn't even scream; the round went right through her face. I paused only long enough to check her condition. Her pretty face had been obliterated. This horrific sight was burned into my mind, but there was no time to dwell on it. "She's dead!" I said to the man next to her, and resumed firing. *The Calm* kept the emotion at bay. For now.

"On me, move, move, move!" Ling screamed. The other element had caught up with us. It was their turn to provide covering fire while we advanced. We didn't have time to screw around. We were all vulnerable on the top of the dam. Bullets zipped back and forth, finding targets on both ends. Exodus operatives had the benefit of good training and body armor, but they were still dropping. Every second we delayed cost lives.

Another smoke grenade was tossed ahead of us. The white cloud billowed up, concealing us from the enemy and vice versa. Their already poor accuracy only worsened, and we used the opportunity to push ahead.

Another young man in our formation went down in a gurgle of blood. Three of his teammates stopped to help him. "No! Only one of you stop!" I yelled. "Come on you two, keep up! We gotta push! Come on!" Almost losing each other in the smoke, we reached the burning wreck of the BTR-70 at the western edge of the dam. We used the cluster of vehicles as cover and laid into the enemy so the other elements could advance. We had to get clear and survive until the charges. After that? If any of us were alive after that, we'd figure it out then.

There were several ways a person on foot could get through the wreck of the roadblock, and Sala Jihan's slave army streamed through all of them. There were just so many of them! I crouched behind a pockmarked jersey barrier and leveled my carbine at the gaps. *BAM BAM,* two shots here. Swing left, *BAM BAM BAM,* three more shots. *Shit! More of them!* Swing right, *BAM BAM BAM BAM! Change magazines!* It was chaos. We were right on top of them as they crossed through the roadblock. Gunfire rang out in every direction, drowning out the screams of men. The air was filled with heavy smoke that stunk of burning vehicles.

I moved forward. Next to the burning APC was a Ural truck that had been mangled by the explosion. The heavy machine gun mounted in its bed was unusable. There was a small gap between the truck and the north wall of the dam. Jihan's soldiers kept squeezing through one at a time. It was time to close that gap.

I zigzagged around debris and dead bodies in my approach. I rounded an old car that was parked behind the roadblock, its windows shattered, and kept my gun trained on the gap.

BOOM! I flinched as a grenade detonated somewhere to my left. The blast made my ears pop and scared the shit out of me. I snapped my head back to the gap when I heard a blood-curdling scream coming from that direction. I looked back just in time to see one of Jihan's soldiers lunge at me, running at full speed.

His SKS had its folding bayonet locked open. The wind was knocked out of me as the tip of his bayonet slid in between the magazine pouches on my vest and hit me dead center. I was pushed back, back, nearly falling, until I was slammed against the side of the car. The slave soldier's eyes were wide, and glazed over. His mouth frothed as he screamed at me in a language I couldn't understand. He was trying to nail me right to that damned car.

The ceramic plate in the front of my vest stopped his bayonet. My rifle was hanging uselessly on its sling. My left hand fell to my side and found the grip of my .44 Magnum. I brought it up, pushed it forward, and let it roar. The fanatical soldier's head exploded into mush and the pressure on my chest was gone as he collapsed to the ground.

I raised the gun higher, putting the glowing tritium front sight on the gap, and fired off five more shots in rapid succession as more men tried to squeeze through. At least two of them fell, landing on top of other dead bodies.

I took the second I'd just bought myself to duck behind the car. I opened the revolver's cylinder, held it muzzle-up, and punched the ejector rod with the heel of my left hand. Hot brass tinkled on concrete as I grabbed a speedloader from my vest, rotated the gun muzzle-down, and twisted six fresh rounds into the cylinder. I snapped it closed and reholstered it.

Two Exodus troops took cover next to me behind the old car. The other element had caught up with us. "We need to close that gap!" I shouted, pointing over the hood of the car. They nodded in affirmation as I stood up to move.

I raised my carbine again, approaching the gap cautiously. My bayonet led the way as I stepped over bodies and vehicle parts. My nostrils were clogged with soot and smoke. The heat of the fire was making me sweat through my parka. I stumbled on a dead man's leg as I approached and nearly fell.

I looked up just in time to see a skinny enemy soldier in a green coat several sizes too big for him lunge through the gap. He charged through so fast, jumping over the bodies of his fallen comrades, that he crashed right into me. I pushed him back and plunged my bayonet deep into his guts. He screamed like a wild animal, dropping the bag of hand grenades he was carrying. I brought a boot up and kicked him off of my rifle, sending him flailing back. He hit the wall at the north edge of the dam, leaving my bayonet smeared with blood. I tried to stab him again, but he was too fast.

He grabbed my rifle as I lunged and pulled it past him. Freakishly strong, the wounded fanatic pulled me right into him.

He was screaming at me as we met, face to face. His frothy spittle spattered against my eyepro as he tried to wrap his fingers around my throat. His breath stunk of gruel. He hardly had any teeth.

I slammed my elbows down on top of his forearms, breaking his chokehold on me. Grabbing his coat with my right, I viciously jabbed him in the face with my left fist, over and over again. I knocked out one of his few teeth, then punched him right in the goddamn eye.

Seizing the opportunity, I grabbed his coat with both hands. Grunting, I lifted the skinny fanatic up and shoved him over the edge. I ran to the wall and looked down, just in time to see him crash to the ice of the frozen reservoir, twenty feet below. He landed on his back in a puff of snow and didn't move.

God damn. Out of breath, arms and legs shaking from adrenaline, I picked my rifle back up and looped the sling around me. Coughing and hacking in the smoke, I grabbed the skinny guy's bag of grenades and handed it over to my Exodus comrades. The APC continued to burn, but the sounds of battle began to die down.

Clearing the narrow gap and the pile of enemy dead, I found myself on the west side of the roadblock. Surrounded by dead bodies were more than a dozen cars and trucks parked haphazardly, many still with the doors open.

Jesus Christ, I thought to myself. *Did we kill them all?* That would have been nice, but it wasn't the case. There were dozens, maybe scores of bodies on the ground here and more on the dam, but plenty of Jihan's soldiers were still alive. They were just retreating down the hill. That was odd. We hadn't seen them retreat before.

"Michael!" It was Ling. Her voice cut through the night like a clarion call. She appeared through the destroyed road block, approached, and squeezed my hand. "I'm so glad you're still alive."

"You too," I replied, breathing heavily. "Are you okay?"

"I'm fine. What's happening?"

I pointed down the hill. "We didn't get them all, but they're retreating. See?" In the moonlight, reflecting brightly in the snow, it was possible to see dozens of figures running down the road, away from us.

"I don't understand," Ling said. "They don't retreat. They never retreat. Something is wrong. Where is Katsumoto?" I shrugged. Ling stepped around me and jogged along the road block, crossing through it at another one of the openings. "Katsumoto?" she shouted. There was no response.

"Ling!" It was Skunky. I was relieved to see him. He held his weapon at the low ready as he made his way to her.

"Where is Katsumoto?" she asked, concern obvious in her voice. "Did he fall?"

Skunky hesitated for a moment. "No, Ling. He stayed behind. At the dam, I mean."

"What? Why? Never mind." She grabbed her radio and hit the transmit button. "Katsumoto, this is Ling," she began, ignoring callsigns and protocol. "Where are you?"

There was no response at first. Ling repeated her query. Then, surrounded by static, Katsumoto's smooth, calming voice crackled over the radio.

"*My lady,*" he said. "*I am afraid I chose to stay behind. You are in command now. I apologize for not telling you. It would have been a distraction.*"

Tears welled up at the corners of Ling's eyes. "Why are you doing this? Your place is here, leading your men! Are you injured?"

"*I am,*" he said. "*I can barely walk. But I am at peace. Child, my place is here. I have wounded that cannot be moved. There is nothing we can do for them. It is not right that they die alone. It is not right that I ask my brave warriors to lay down their lives if I am not willing to do the same.*"

"This is madness!" Ling insisted. "Come on, there's still time!"

"*I'm staying here,*" Katsumoto replied calmly. "*To ensure the demolition goes as planned. I did not ignite the fuse when you left. I wanted to ensure you had enough time to escape, and that the enemy was not able to disarm our explosives.*"

Tears trickled down Ling's cheeks, almost steaming in the frigid air. "I understand," she said simply, maintaining her steady demeanor despite the tears.

"*I knew you would. Let me know when you are a safe distance from the dam. Go with God, Song Ling. One day, we will meet again.*"

"Until that day," Ling agreed. "Go with God." Ling placed the radio back in its pouch, lowered her head, and took a deep breath.

She wasn't given long to cope. Skunky came running up. "Commander! We have a problem here!" It seemed like it took a second for her to realize he was speaking to her when he began with "Commander." My heart sank into my stomach. I knew it was too good to be true.

Skunky led us back through the roadblock, into the mess of vehicles that Jihan's soldiers had left behind. A kilometer down the hill, through the darkness, a stream of headlights pierced the night as many trucks turned to go up the hill. The enemy hadn't been retreating. They were regrouping and waiting for reinforcements.

I looked back across the carnage. There were few of us left, and we were already cut off. We were out of time.

Chapter 22: The Digging of Graves

LORENZO
Sala Jihan's Fortress
March 26th

"How many of these motherfuckers are there?" Anders shouted as bullets zipped through the air over our heads. The big man waited a moment, then jumped up and fired his stolen AK47 back in the direction of the enemy.

"Apparently lots," I grunted as I leaned around the wall and fired several rounds into the nearest bunker's doorway. The slave soldiers inside hunkered down as my rounds ricocheted harmlessly past them. I wasn't going to hit anyone. I already knew that. I was just trying to keep their heads down for a moment. Roland used that opportunity to cover the distance, get a better angle, and hurl a grenade through the door.

There was a resounding crash as the Russian frag detonated. One of the soldiers inside started screaming. Phillips limped around the corner, hung his Tavor inside, fired two rounds and the noise stopped.

We had been fighting for what seemed like forever against a neverending stream of men. I would have run out of ammo for my ACR a while ago, except that Anders' 416 had been shot out of his hands and I had taken the rest of his magazines. Shen had a flesh wound across his hip, and Phillips had twisted his ankle, but other than that, my team was surprisingly fine. I couldn't even begin to calculate how many people we had shot to get this far.

"*Chief, you're only thirty meters from the prison,*" Reaper told me. "*There's one more squad of soldiers ahead of you. Maybe a dozen of them.*"

"Okay, how's the center holding?" The gunfire from the Exodus perimeter around the choppers was sporadic now. The soldiers had fought with suicidal intensity, but Exodus had held.

"*Just pockets of soldiers keep throwing themselves at the silo. Ibrahim's pulled the perimeter around so that most of Exodus is there covering the assault team. There's just one team guarding the chopper and the wounded. I'm feeding info to Fajkus, and he's moving his guys around to intercept any soldiers as they get close. But I think most of them are dead.*"

News like that made me really glad that I had dropped almost a million dollars into Little Bird. It was like my own personal spy satellite. "How about reinforcements?"

"*I was able to jam the radio signals from the compound when the attack began, but somehow the soldiers at the mine knew anyway. There's a column of trucks coming up the road now. Fajkus sent one team to stall them at the front gates. Those bastards are going to have a real hard time getting through those big ass gates. But . . .*"

"What?"

It wasn't Reaper that responded, rather it was Jill. "*I've been listening to the local radio chatter while Reaper's been playing flight simulator, and I haven't gotten anything from town.*"

"At all?" Kat's mercenaries should have assaulted the Brothers and the garrison in town by now.

"*Nothing. Especially nothing about a battle in The Crossroads.*"

"Shit," I muttered. Diego must have chickened out. Which meant that we had a bunch more bad guys in town coming to help.

"*And there's something going down at the dam. There's a big fight going on there that Exodus didn't tell us about. Lots of vehicles went that way from the mine, too.*"

What? Talk about biting off more than they could chew. What the hell was Exodus thinking? "Okay, be ready for anything."

"*Love ya. Bye.*" It wasn't proper radio etiquette, but I liked Jill's methods better. Jill and Reaper were stationed well out of town, using a vehicle that we had bought on the down low. I didn't trust any of the sides here, and wanted my own ace in the hole. Nobody but me knew where they were parked.

"Anders, we've got maybe a dozen between us and the prison." I flexed my aching hands. The insides of the wool gloves were stained with red, and I figured that quite a bit of it was mine.

"Here's what we do." Anders had, by far, the most actual combat experience. I'd spent my career avoiding straight-up fights. He signaled toward Shen. "I want you to flank right. We'll cover—" He was cut off by a sudden thunderous chain of explosions. The sky back toward the silo was suddenly bright as yellow flashes reflected off all of the compounds' walls and buildings. Ibrahim had breached the elevator shaft.

Anders' plan went out the window then. The remaining slave soldiers all began screaming. They rose up from behind their positions of cover, and began to run wildly toward the silo, which meant they had to go right through the five of us. It was like the Exodus banzai charge earlier, only it made even less sense.

I opened fire, pumping round after round into the charging fanatics. Red dot moving to one, *tap tap*, then on to the next, repeat. One of them tumbled face down into the snow as my rounds pierced his chest. He continued to claw his way forward for a few more seconds. I watched him in disbelief as I reloaded, but he wouldn't give up until his pulped heart could finally pump no more.

Then it was over. The remaining soldiers were all dead, splayed about in the street, blood slowly staining the snow into pink slush, steam rising from their torn open corpses.

"What was that?" Anders asked in disbelief.

"They were trying to get to Jihan . . . it's like they went crazy," I replied.

"But . . . but . . . they're slaves. Why would they do something like that?" Phillips asked. He was sincerely shaken. Shen shook his head. The quiet man had no answers either.

What kind of man was Sala Jihan, that he could inspire such psychotic loyalty in people that he had kidnapped from their own homes?

"Screw it. Let's get my brother."

VALENTINE
The Dam

Ling, Skunky, and I stood at the breach, staring down into the darkness. Another line of vehicles was slowly headed up the road toward us. They would be on top of us in minutes. Our only hope now was to spread out and scatter, try to escape on foot through the snow. There was no hope for the wounded who couldn't walk, like the German whose leg I'd put a tourniquet on.

Ling watched in silence. I could see something I'd never seen in her eyes before: *fear*. It was all over Skunky's face as well. And if I was being honest with myself, deep down, hidden beneath *the Calm*, I felt it too. I took the fact that after surviving so much, I was probably going to die in this place, to be a grave injustice. My mind raced for a way out, for some other option besides death and something worse than death, and I was drawing a blank. Ling didn't say anything. She just watched our approaching doom and shook her head slightly. Behind us, the rest of the surviving Exodus personnel were gathering at the burning remains of the roadblock. They were all watching her, waiting for orders, waiting for *something*.

"Jeff," I said, looking at my old friend. "Go back there and make sure the wounded are still being treated. Get everyone together and start figuring out a way to drag the wounded that can't walk across the snow. We don't have a lot of options right now and we have no time. Make litters or something."

"But what about . . ."

I cut him off. "Just do it. I'll take care of her. Go!" He nodded his head and ran off to do as I asked. Ling and I were alone. I put my hands on her shoulders and looked down into her eyes.

"Listen to me," I said. "Your people need you right now. They need their commander. They're counting on you."

"I have already failed them," she said. "Don't you understand? We're all going to die here."

I agreed. "Seems that way. But that doesn't give you the right to just quit on them when they've fought so hard for you. It's not over until the last one of us is dead. You owe it to them to keep fighting until the last. They've earned that."

Ling looked down at the ground for a moment, her face resuming its usual mask. "Yes. Yes, you're right." She looked up into my eyes. "You are a remarkable individual, Mr. Valentine."

"If you say so. No offense, but I just want to go home."

She actually laughed. "As do I. Come, please help me carry the wounded. We don't—" She fell silent as her radio crackled to life.

It was Ibrahim. "*Stand by to breach. Fire in the hole, fire in the hole, fire in the hole.*"

"What's going on?" I asked.

"He must be breaching the missile silo. Michael, look," Ling said, pointing back down the hill. "They've stopped." Sure enough, the enemy column that had been slowly advancing up the hillside had stopped in place.

"What the hell are they doing?" It didn't take long for me to get my answer. In the most haphazard and erratic fashion imaginable, the enemy column tried to turn around on the narrow road. It was almost comical. Vehicles crashed into each other. The shouts of Jihan's men were carried on the wind to our position. They reversed as fast as they could, seemingly in a panic.

"Holy shit. Is it because of Jihan? Are they going back because they're going after him? Did the fortress call in reinforcements?"

"He's calling to them," Ling said. She spoke into her radio then. "Sword One, this is Sword Three. The enemy from our position is apparently en route to your position. Prepare yourselves for enemy reinforcements."

There was a long delay before Ibrahim answered. "*This is Sword One Actual. Understood. Can you delay them?*"

"Negative, Sword One. We have taken heavy losses. We were about to be overrun when they retreated. Our entire egress plan is going to have to be revised on the fly."

"*Understood,*" Ibrahim repeated. "*Godspeed, my lady. We are about to enter the abyss.*"

"Godspeed to you as well," Ling said solemnly. "Shine a light into the darkness."

I was confused. "What's going on? What's he doing?"

"He's preparing to take his team down into the silo after Sala Jihan," Ling answered, sounding distant.

"It's just a single missile silo, right? It shouldn't take them long to find him."

"There are many places to hide down in that dark hole." Ling paused for a second. "Sala Jihan has proven difficult to kill in the past." Before I could ask her what in the hell *that* meant, she switched channels and spoke into her radio again.

"Sword Three Actual! This is Sword Three X-Ray! Come in!"

Katsumoto took a moment before responding. *"This is Sword Three Actual. Are you clear of the dam?"*

"Negative! Stand by, we're coming to get you! The enemy has retreated. We have time to gather the wounded and commandeer vehicles. No one else has to die here!"

There was a long silence. *"I hope you don't think less of me if I admit to being relieved,"* Katsumoto said wryly.

Ling laughed as her eyes teared up a little. "It can be our secret. Please hold on. We're on our way."

LORENZO
Sala Jihan's Fortress

The steel door to the prison was open. The walls were still painted that sick pea-green that the Russian military painted everything. Starkly naked lightbulbs burned and flickered on the walls. Water dripped from exposed steam pipes. I rushed through first, my muzzle sweeping back and forth, the three Exodus operatives followed me, and Anders brought up the rear.

"Chief, you should turn back to the command channel. Ibrahim and his guys are roping down the elevator shaft," Reaper informed me. *"Oh, man, they're jumping down. The Pale Man is pwned! Go get that creepy motherfucker!"*

I clicked my radio over. The men behind me did as well. It all came down to this. Even though my mission was to find Bob, what happened in the next few minutes would determine all of our fates. The first floor of the prison was empty. We moved from cell to cell, but the doors were unlocked and nobody was inside any of them.

One of the functionaries was hiding behind some crates. I recognized him from the business meeting with Jill. He was barefoot and wearing flannel pajamas, probably chased out of his nice bunker by Exodus. He started pleading for his life as soon he saw us, but Anders shot him in the heart.

At the end of the floor was a flight of industrial steel steps. We headed up.

The second floor was dark. I turned my Surefire light on and shined it down the hallway. There was a single door made of iron bars that was currently hanging open, a chain and open padlock dangling from it. I stepped through. My light illuminated a long corridor of heavy cell doors. It was musty and claustrophobic.

We all heard Ibrahim's voice come over the radio. *"We're heading down. Be wary."*

"Bob!" I bellowed at the top of my lungs. "Bob Lorenzo!" There was no response except for the echo.

Something moved at the end of the corridor. I lifted my gun. A skinny, shirtless man leapt out of the darkness. He had a Nagant revolver in one bony hand. He screamed at us, his lips spread wide over toothless gums. He started to raise the pistol. I fired a single shot, splattering his brains all over the wall.

The rest of my team turned on their flashlights and started checking rooms. Shen spoke softly. "Lorenzo, it doesn't look good."

I glanced over Shen's shoulder. Inside the first cell was a body. It was a younger Mongol man, but he had a single bullet wound to his head, his body still backed into the corner. The next cell was the same, with another recently murdered prisoner. The man that I had just shot had been systematically executing them rather than letting them be freed.

"We're at the bottom. There is extensive damage from the explosives." I could almost imagine the sounds of his team's ropes rebounding against the wall and the clacking of their weapons. *"Fan out. Wait . . . The blast doors are already open. We won't need to cut through."*

Someone in the background of Ibrahim's radio said something that sounded like *what luck.*

"No. He is waiting for us . . ."

I moved quickly from cell to cell, just long enough to shine my flashlight inside each one. More dead bodies. None of them were Bob. With a great deal of hesitation, I approached the final cell. My light flooded the little room through the bars. There was a large body face down in a pile of dirty straw in the back of the cell.

Ibrahim had left his radio on transmit, as every member of Exodus was eager to hear what happened next. *"Rasheed, cover our exit. We are heading into the center. The launch pad is clear. No sign of life. He's here somewhere. Carmen, check over there . . . Wait . . . What was that?"*

My boot impacted the cell door. I smashed it as hard as I could, over and over, the impacts traveling up through the bones of my feet. "Damn it, damn it, damn it, damn it. Bob!" The lock was too heavy. Shen materialized at my side, having lifted a large ring of keys from the dead jailer. He started trying keys. *Oh, God, my brother is dead.* "Bob! *Bob!"*

The ancient lock clicked open with an audible snap. I shoved it open and tore toward the body.

Ibrahim's radio was sending the sound of nervous, heavy breathing, in the distance someone else on his team says something that sounded like *there's something in the water.*

I grabbed the arm of the dead man and pulled him over. He was a huge, bald Caucasian. The Exodus operatives raised their lights to help me see. I stared into the dead man's face.

The radio transmitted the sound of splashing, then gunfire.

I stared into the dead man's face. Involuntary tears started to roll down my cheeks.

"Show yourself, demon!" Ibrahim bellowed.

It wasn't Bob. It was somebody else.

The radio was a cacophony of chaos. The noise from the silo was indescribable. Something had gone horribly wrong.

I sprang to my feet. "Let's go." I ordered. The three Exodus operatives were standing there, speechless as they listened to their command channel.

There was a sliding, metallic crashing noise from the end of the hall. Somebody had just slammed the main gate. I shined my light down the hallway. Anders stood on the other side of the now locked gate. "So long, Lorenzo."

"Anders!" I raised my rifle, but he moved swiftly around the corner. The muzzle of his AK appeared around the wall as he triggered a burst. I narrowly dodged back into the cell as bullets skipped around me.

"It's nothing personal. We just needed your help, and now we don't."

"You son of a bitch!" I shouted, ignoring the screaming and shooting in my earpiece. It sounded like Ibrahim's team was getting torn apart.

"We needed a way to take Jihan down. Then you showed up. We were afraid something like this would happen, but it was worth a shot."

There was enough space between the walls and the cell doors that a thin man could squeeze in there and have cover. I leapt across the hall and slammed myself into the next doorway.

"You see, it's not just about control of The Crossroads. Sure, that's a plus," Anders explained patiently. He must have realized that I was trying to get closer as he fired a few more rounds down the hallway to pin me down. "But it is bigger than that, way bigger. You have no idea what Project Blue is."

"Why don't you tell me before I kill you, then?"

Anders laughed, that traitorous bastard. "Sala Jihan knew about my part in Blue. Hell, I couldn't have done it without him. He had to go. The Pale Man's a loose end. See, when I figured Majestic fucked me, I decided to fuck them right back. Majestic didn't have the balls to complete Project Blue, but I do."

I jumped across to the next door. I could hear one of the Exodus operatives doing the same behind me. Anders fired another shot, but was answered by a pair of suppressed shots in response that sparked off the bars.

"Seeing your brother here was a surprise. I hadn't seen Bob since he helped get me thrown out of the FBI, that self-righteous asshole. He had finally figured it all out, put all his paranoid conspiracy theories to work, and actually ended up with the truth. That's why I had to grab him."

Jihan never had Bob.

"Oh, just figuring it out now? Yeah. Sucks, don't it? Hell, Bob was locked in the basement of the Exchange while you were there. I'll tell you though, you showing up helped us. It enabled me to get Exodus to do our dirty work for us. That slave we killed back in town? I contacted him beforehand, told him that if he told you a story, I'd sneak him out of the country. We were afraid that the stories about Jihan were true. Personally, I thought they were bullshit, but I've seen stranger stuff. I mean, seriously, Majestic agents get to do some freaky shit, but we needed muscle, and that's where Exodus came in."

"Did you kill my brother?"

"Not yet. He's my Lee Harvey Oswald. When he dies, it'll be on the world news. Not that you'll be around to see it, because it looks like Jihan is going to fuckin' kill all of you. Too bad I couldn't tie up that loose end, but I've got another contingency plan in place for him. Kat loses The Crossroads entirely, but Blue is going to get us something a whole lot better."

I moved again. One more.

"And speaking of loose ends, your hot little woman and your dipshit sidekick? Yeah, Diego's going to take care of them. We triangulated the radio signals they need to drive your little toy airplane. They'll be dead soon too, just like you."

I took a deep breath and jumped for the next doorway, but there were no more gunshots. I was close enough now that I could get a grenade through the bars and not just bounce it down the hallway back into us. I chucked it through the iron. The explosion came a moment later. It shook dust from the ceiling.

Sprinting the rest of the way, I slammed into the bars, shoving my muzzle through, but Anders was already gone down the stairs.

"Everybody okay?" I shouted. I got three quick yes answers.

The padlock was huge, and shooting it would've just hit us with lots of ricochets. "Breach it," I ordered. Phillips moved up, pulling a block of explosive out of a pouch on his vest.

Ibrahim was on the radio again, except I was having a hard time understanding him. His breath was coming in ragged gasps. He was talking, in short, clipped sentences, apparently in Kurdish, obviously in a great deal of pain. He was tying up the command channel, whispering a prayer. I heard him commend his soul to Allah. There were a few more gun shots, then a loud crack.

A moment later, I could hear something else on the radio, a crunching noise, like bones being snapped. Finally another voice came on. I recognized it, and could picture the pale white flesh and solid black eyes. He had warned me not to come back here.

"Trespassers . . . " Sala Jihan muttered. Then the radio went dead.

"Jill. Reaper. Come in."

No answer.

"If you can hear me. Get the hell out of there now. Diego's coming to kill you." I flipped back to the command line as I ran through the snow.

"Sword Two, on me. Move up on the pit," Fajkus ordered over the radio. There was a huge volume of gunfire coming from that direction now. My team was sprinting through the compound, heading toward the choppers. "What the hell is going on down there? Somebody answer me!"

"Fajkus! Come in. This is Lorenzo. Anders is a traitor. Watch out." I panted as I ran. I got no response. It was no surprise. The radio net was in complete disarray. Something very bad was happening at the missile silo.

"Oh God who art in heaven," somebody gasped. "Hallowed be thy name . . ."

"Get off the fucking radio!" Fajkus ordered. "Somebody give me a sitrep."

Then there was screaming. The praying stopped with a series of tearing noises, and that signal died.

"Fajkus. This is Nagano. Retreat. They're all dead. We've got to— Aarrgghh—" then that one was gone too.

I flipped back. "Jill! Reaper!" I tripped and sprawled face first into the slush. Rolling over, and bounding back to my feet, I had tripped over the body of an Exodus operative. It was dark, but it was obvious that he had died horribly, his chest torn open, white ribs sticking out.

"Lorenzo!" Jill finally responded.

"You've got to get out of there. The Montalbans are coming to kill you."

"I know. I just shot two of them, I think," she replied, sounding rather flustered. *"They showed up, but I had stuck out those claymores just like you showed me. I'm driving now. We're both okay. I don't know where we're going though, I don't think they're following me, but I don't know how they found us."*

"Tell Reaper that they're triangulating off the radio signal he uses to fly the Little Bird. I'm glad you're okay," I said, still running. "Put Reaper on . . . Reaper? What do you see? What's going on at the silo?"

"A counterattack. Exodus is getting slaughtered." Reaper didn't sound very good. He sounded kind of confused and out of it. *"I . . . I don't know."*

"What do you see?"

"Something . . . I don't . . . I don't know . . ."

"Come on man, focus, I'm going to be there in a second."

"Don't go there. Run, Lorenzo. Run away. Get out of there. Get on the chopper and fly away. Please." His voice was desperate, and . . . afraid? He was miles away staring at a video screen.

"What is it?" It was unlike Reaper to freak out like this. He was young, but he had seen a lot. He had never choked on me before in all the years we had been doing this together. "What's going on?"

"Quit yelling at me!" he cried. *"I don't know what it is, okay? Just get away from it!"*

"Damn it! Reaper, listen to me. Take down Little Bird. The Montalbans found you because of that signal. Take it down now!"

"Okay. Okay. Okay," he stammered. *"Here's Jill."*

"Honey, I'll be in touch. Just keep driving."

"Be careful, Lorenzo." The line clicked off.

Then the choppers were in view. The four of us tore toward them at a full run, our breath leaving clouds of steam hanging behind us. The one working chopper's blades were turning fast, only seconds from lifting off. There were a shockingly small number of people milling around near the choppers, and most of them were spread out in a skirmish line between the Halo and the pit, muzzle flashes indicating that they were firing against the silo.

Suddenly the chopper was airborne, blowing snow everywhere in a giant tornado. As I got closer, I could see a figure standing in the open door of the Halo helicopter. I only recognized that it was Svetlana by the big sniper rifle in her bandaged hands. She turned and shouted angrily back into the chopper's interior, then turned around and gestured for them to go back down to pick up the other survivors.

There was a muzzle flash from inside the chopper, and Svetlana dropped from the back door of the helicopter and plummeted about twenty feet to the ground. She actually landed on her feet, but her legs immediately crumpled, broken beneath her.

"No!" screamed Phillips as we charged onward.

The rear of the chopper swiveled toward us as it continued to rise, tracers strobing from the door gun down into the Exodus wounded as Anders murdered everyone he could. A lone figure stood in the door, braced against a strut, her blond hair billowing in the turbulent wind around her. Katarina waved.

"Kat!" I shouted as I raised my gun and opened fire at the retreating chopper, but it was moving too quick. "Damn it!" That was our way out.

"Where's the chopper going?" Fajkus shouted across the radio. *"Wait, what the hell is tha—"* His radio cut out suddenly.

"Attention, Exodus. This is Katarina. Our business arrangement has, sadly, come to an end."

We're screwed.

My team reached the remaining members of Exodus at the LZ. There were only a handful left, and all of them appeared to be injured. Anders had shredded the skirmish line with the chopper's door gun, and there were screams from the dying. Shen and Phillips tried to help them while Roland attended to Svetlana, who was moaning in the snow, a jagged chunk of bone sticking out the side of her pants.

"Fajkus! This is Lorenzo. Come in." There was only static on the line. I realized that all of the gunfire from the silo had ceased, and with the chopper getting further away, the compound was gradually quieting. After so much commotion, it was rather disconcerting. I glanced around. "Who's in charge?"

The shell-shocked Exodus survivors looked at each other, trying to ascertain who was the senior member still standing.

"I believe that would be me." A deep voice from the direction of the silo. I turned my flashlight on the approaching figures. One large man had a second smaller man over his shoulders in a fireman carry. I recognized them immediately.

"Antoine," I said, glad to see it was somebody I could count on. "What happened?"

"I don't know. Fajkus is unconscious," the tall African grunted as he gently lowered the other man to the ground. Fajkus's parka was covered in blood and torn open in several places. "Everyone else is dead."

"We have to get out of here," I said tersely.

"Agreed," he glanced upward. "Why did the helicopter leave? Why did it fire on us?"

"Long story," I replied, looking over the carnage. Exodus had been exposed. "Fucking Anders. We can grab some vehicles and head for town."

"Negative," Antoine shook his head. "Reinforcements from the mines are blocking the road. They will be here soon." What went unsaid was that whoever had just killed most of Exodus in the last few minutes was still in the compound with us.

I scanned the compound. Flames were billowing upward from a dozen points and the air tasted like burning rubber and diesel. "Okay, we take the back way out, the way my team came in. We rope down to the valley floor, and then hoof it up the canyon."

Antoine glanced around at the many wounded, both of us already knowing that many of them were not going to make it. The Plan C escape route was a worst-case scenario even if you were healthy, let alone carrying a bunch of injured. He raised his voice so that everyone could hear. "Exodus, my brothers. Move quickly. Take ammunition from the dead and the other Halo. Everyone that can walk, help those that cannot. Follow Lorenzo. He will show us the way out."

"Brother," Shen said. I jumped, adrenaline-soaked nerves expecting another one of those silent, hooded freaks to have shown up, but Shen was just talking to Antoine. The two men embraced. "I'm glad to see you made it."

"We must hurry." Ling's former teammates began helping the wounded. There were only a few of us in any shape to fight; me, Shen, Antoine, Phillips, and Roland. There were four others a lot worse off. I couldn't believe it. I didn't know how many men Exodus had brought it, but it had to have been at least sixty or seventy. Svetlana screamed as Phillips shoved the bone back into her leg and wrapped it in gauze.

"Damn you, Katarina," I whispered to myself as I led the way back across the compound, a horde of fanatics only minutes behind us. This was going to be tight.

My radio chirped in my ear. I hit the mike, expecting news from Reaper or Jill. Instead it was Katarina, calling to gloat. I felt an indescribable ball of rage bubble up from inside my stomach. It made me warm.

"*Well, well, well, you're in a predicament now, aren't you, Lorenzo, my dear?*"

"I thought you wanted The Crossroads more than you'd want revenge. I was a fool to believe you."

"*Yes, and I was a fool to trust you all those years ago. Now you know how it feels. You abandoned me when I needed you, and now I'm abandoning you.*"

"So that's what this is about, then?" I spat. I moved quickly through the wreckage of the compound, running forward, and taking up a cover position as the others followed more slowly. "You're willing to let all these good men die just out of spite?"

Kat laughed over the radio, having a good old time. "*No, of course not, silly. That's absurd. I was going to betray them no matter what. That's just sound business. This was a gamble for me to not only utilize Project Blue, but also to become the sole ruler of The Crossroads, like Big Eddie before me. Being able to destroy you along with Exodus was just a happy bonus."*

I didn't respond. Half of my brain was trying to watch my surroundings, the other half was a calculating how I was going to track Katarina down and kill her. I paused, waiting for Exodus. Something moved in the shadows ahead. I hit the spot with my flashlight, but whatever it was had already moved.

"Do you know why I'm calling you?" She didn't bother to wait for my response. *"I just wanted to explain myself, and perhaps, to hurt you a little bit more. I feel I owe you that. After all, I loved you once."*

"You chose Big Eddie over me."

"Oh, how stupid you are. You still don't get it, do you?" she asked as I leapt over more dismembered bodies. An arm dangled from a nearby roof, drizzling blood. *"Of course I was loyal to the Montalbans. I always have been. Back when we worked together, all those jobs that we did, you were Big Eddie's right-hand man, and yet you never met him. I was always the go-between. I was the one that had to prove myself to the Montalbans, not you. I had to earn their respect."*

"Sounds like a personal problem."

"Do you remember, once, so long ago, you always warned me about how people like us should never reveal our real identities to anyone? I heeded your advice. I never told you my real name. You were weak, and you told me yours, Hector Romasanta. So allow me to return the favor. My real name is Elizabeth . . ."

One of the Exodus operatives slipped in the snow behind me. The injured man he was carrying screamed as damaged nerves struck the ground.

"Katarina . . ."

I kept seeing shapes moving ahead of me, just out of the view of my light, but I couldn't catch them. I kept moving.

". . . Montalban."

I stopped. "You've got to be shitting me."

Her laugh sounded distorted through the radio. The chopper was getting further away, and the reception on my portable was starting to break up. *"No. My older brother was Rafael Montalban. He was father's favorite, as he was the legitimate heir. Eduard, or Big Eddie, as he insisted on being called, was next in line, but Eduard was always a little off, a little crazy, but at least his mother was respected English royalty. Rafael was a prodigy, Eduard liked to burn things and hurt animals. I was the youngest, and least legitimate of all my father's children. My mother was a Swiss whore."*

"Crazy and sleazy runs in the family," I snarled.

"Yes indeed. Eduard hurt me many times, but I thank him for it now, for it made me strong. After Father died, Rafael took care of the legitimate family business. Eddie inherited the dark side. There was nothing left for me. I was unwanted, unloved. So if I could not receive my family's love, then I would earn it. That is when I went to work with you, to prove my worthiness to my brothers."

"You used me, even back then." This changed nothing. I was still going to get out of here and kill her, but at least it put her damaged nature in perspective.

"Oh, at first, but I really did love you. You were the one that made me choose, choose between happiness and destiny. You never should have done that, Hector."

A thought flashed through my mind, a memory of Thailand, a few years ago, as the Fat Man, Big Eddie's indomitable bodyguard, had arrived to blackmail my team with information about our real families. I had never understood how Big Eddie could have learned so much about me. "You . . . It was you that gave Big Eddie my family. It was you that forced me into the Zubara job."

"Of course. When Eddie told me he needed the best for Zubara, you were the only man for the job. I was glad to give him your real name. I prayed for your death every day. But somehow, impossibly, both of my brothers died instead. Brave Rafael murdered by Majestic, and beautiful Eduard, dead by your hand. The great Montalban dynasty, one of the great Illuminati families for over five hundred years, shattered, and now scorned by the other legitimate families. But fate has smiled upon me. Anders has given me the key to Project Blue, a brilliant plot to put the Illuminati in their place, and with it, I will reclaim my family's glory. The other families will kneel at my feet."

"You're toast. Jihan will destroy you."

"The Pale Man's power ends at the border of The Crossroads. I hoped to use Exodus to end him and regain this kingdom that Eddie built, but I don't need it anymore. I am on to bigger and better things."

I reached the gap in the back wall. The guards' bodies that we had left in the shadows under the broken rebar were gone. I saw no movement, so I proceeded to secure the rope, my mind still reeling from the information I had just been given. "What about my brother?"

Her voice was breaking up badly now. I could barely hear her through the static. *"Hector, always so loyal to everyone except for me. Your brother is still alive, for now, but only because Anders has a use for him. Blue is coming—"* Static interrupted the transmission. *"When it—the world—"* The signal was fading.

I smashed the button on my mike. "You know what the last thing I told your darling Eddie was before I blew him to pieces?"

"What was that?"

"I'll see you in hell."

The signal was gone.

Chapter 23: Weakness
Leaving the Body

VALENTINE
The Dam

We'd been given a second lease on life. At least, that's how it felt. The situation was still dire. We'd lost a large chunk of our force, we had many wounded, and our exfil plan had gone to shit, but we were accomplishing the mission, and it looked like we would actually live to talk about it.

Despite the good news, we were in a real hurry. There was no telling when Sala Jihan's forces would return to the dam. We had no idea what was going on at the fortress. No one was answering the radio over there, and the distance and terrain made communications difficult to begin with. Nothing seemed to be happening in town as near as we could tell.

Only one of our original vehicles was still in driving shape, but it didn't matter. We had plenty of trucks to choose from. One had only to pull out the dead driver and not think about sitting in someone else's blood. In this fashion we put together a new convoy and tried to contact the people that were waiting for us at the rendezvous point.

Despite our heavy losses, Ling was actually smiling. Katsumoto, limping badly from a bullet in his leg, was still alive, and we'd beaten back the enemy, at least temporarily. There's a certain rush that comes with completing such a dangerous mission that's hard to explain to anyone who hasn't experienced it. The look on her face gave it away.

It never lasts. Sooner or later reality always catches up with you. It caught up with us when the two of the wounded who had been at the dam with Katsumoto succumbed to their injuries. It was driven home when Katsumoto received a static-filled radio transmission from Antoine.

"Sword Three, Sword Three, this is Sword Four."

Katsumoto and Ling exchanged a knowing look. Ibrahim had been Sword One. Fajkus was his support element, Sword Two. Sword Four was Lorenzo's team.

"This is Sword One," Katsumoto replied calmly. "What is the situation?"

There was a long pause, filled with static. *"We have failed."*

Katsumoto closed his eyes for a couple of seconds. Ling lowered her head. "Understood. What happened?"

"I do not know. Sword One took his element down into the pit. They are all lost. Sword Two attempted to come to his aid, and they suffered severe losses as well. Sword Two Actual is catatonic. I am in command now."

"Are you egressing on the helicopters?"

"Negative. One helicopter was lost. The other left without us. The Montalbans have betrayed us. That woman took her remaining men. They fired on us as they left, killing several more men."

"Treacherous whore!" Ling snarled, her hands balling into fists.

"We are cut off by reinforcements from the mines. Our only means of exfiltration is down the cliff, on foot."

"We will come get you, brother. It will take us some time, but we will come get you. You will not be left to die. We will meet you at the emergency rendezvous point with enough vehicles to extract you."

"We will lose radio communications as we go down into the valley. It is a long walk to the rendezvous point, and we are carrying wounded. Our chances of making it are not great. Do not wait for us too long."

Katsumoto's face was a mask of resolve. "The Montalbans have betrayed us, but they will pay dearly for it. Our part of the operation has succeeded. We are preparing to initiate as we speak. This foul place will wither and die."

Antoine actually sounded happy about that. *"That is the best news I've heard all night,"* he said. *"Good luck, my friend."*

"And to you," Katsumoto replied.

"Wait," I said, before the Exodus commander signed off. "Is Lorenzo still alive?" Katsumoto relayed my question to Antoine.

"He is still alive, Mr. Valentine. He is with us. Do you wish to speak to him?"

I took the radio from Katsumoto. "Not really. Did he find his brother though?"

"I'm afraid not. He tells me that that, too was a Montalban ploy. His brother was never here. We've all been deceived." The radio went to static for a moment. *"He also suggests that you go fornicate with yourself."*

"Likewise. Valentine out."

As the last of us cleared the dam, Ling and Katsumoto consulted on a plan. We had too many wounded to all go to Antoine's rescue. Some would not last the night if we had to fight our way to our friends. There was little choice: we'd have to split up.

Katsumoto wanted to lead the element that rescued Antoine, of course. He was the senior Exodus commander on scene now, and saving his people was his duty. His right knee had been shattered by a bullet, though. He could move under his own power only with the aid of an improvised crutch, and he'd lost a lot of blood. He looked tired and pale.

The rescue mission fell to Ling. She'd been through a lot this night, but she only had minor injuries. She accepted her task solemnly and swore to Katsumoto that she'd get Antoine out if there was any possible way. The call then went out for volunteers, those who were still able to fight and wanted to go. As near as I could tell, every single Exodus operative still walking (and some that weren't) raised his or her hand, Skunky included.

Their loyalty to each other was impressive. They were bonded as tightly as any professional army I'd ever worked with. You couldn't help but feel respect for their level of dedication to one another, despite coming from widely different ethnic, national, cultural, and religious backgrounds.

Not everyone could go, and there weren't very many to choose from. Of the original fifty Exodus operatives, only thirty were still alive. Of those, only sixteen were uninjured. Of those, not all could be spared for the rescue.

In the end, six Exodus operatives were to accompany Ling, including Skunky. It was a small element to potentially have to fight across hostile territory. They would have to bring enough vehicles to carry all of Antoine's surviving people. Many were low on ammunition and had to scrounge for what supplies they could get.

For my part, I was leaning on one of our wrecked trucks, drinking a bottle of water from a case that'd been inside. I'd sucked the hydration bladder in my backpack dry and was thirsty as hell. I was leaning because my arms and legs were shaking. Adrenaline dump was hitting me hard. I was exhausted. I just wanted a hot shower and a warm bed to lay in. I think Ling sensed this as she approached, because she seemed to do so cautiously. "How are you doing?"

"I'll be okay," I said. "I just need a moment. What happens now?"

"I will lead my team to the rendezvous point to extract Lorenzo and Antoine's element. I owe Antoine my life several times over. And Lorenzo . . . I asked Lorenzo to come here. Practically coerced him. I owe it to him to not leave him to die without trying to come to his aid. That is not the Exodus way."

"I know," I said. "I just needed a drink before we go."

"Michael, you don't have to go," she said levelly, looking up into my eyes. "I can ask no more of you. I thought I'd brought you to your death, but by the grace of God we came through. All you need to do is go with Katsumoto. It is as close as you can get to being safe."

"And Jill would never forgive me if I just left his stupid ass there. Besides, you need all the bodies you can get. So stop arguing with me, please. I'm going. I'm in this thing to the end."

Ling looked at me the way Sarah had, very briefly, before putting her mask back on. "Thank you," she managed. "But please, take your water with you. We need to get going."

Damn it, I thought. All of this and I wouldn't even get to see the explosion.

LORENZO
The Cliffs

The last of the injured was tied to the rope and sent spiraling over the edge that I had climbed over just a few hours before. There were only three who couldn't walk now. We had not been able to control the bleeding from a man named Solomon, and his body was behind us in the snow. I would be the last man to leave the compound, which was good, because we'd kicked the hornet's nest.

There was a lot of movement inside the compound. I could see a lot of shadows moving in front of the fires. The gates had been flung open to let the reinforcements inside. I took one last look before going over the edge, and froze. A lone figure was standing silhouetted in front of the burning Tunguska. It was dark at the lip of the chasm. There was no way he could see me, but I felt an involuntary shiver anyway. The black sliver of a man was perfectly still, and somehow I knew he was watching me with deadly, soulless eyes.

Sala Jihan had come up out of his hole.

"You win this one, you son of a bitch."

I went over the edge quickly, a makeshift harness strung around me. My boots would impact the glasslike ice, kick outward, and I would plunge another twenty feet at a time. I hit the ground too fast. The others were already prepared to move out. Exodus was silent, each of them burdened by heavy thoughts and internal pain. Shen was mashing a claymore into the snow just ahead of us. The first soldiers down that rope were going to get a surprise. Hopefully an occasional booby-trap would keep our pursuers cautious and moving slow.

We took turns carrying the wounded, one unburdened man on point and the other at the rear. We passed the nomads' tiny settlement and found it was abandoned. No sign of Lotus Blossom, her family, or their yaks. They apparently had the good sense to get the hell out of the area after I had shown up earlier. Wing's body was probably stuffed into one of the many ice crevasses nearby.

We had memorized terrain maps of this area, not only because it was where my team had inserted, but also because it had been our last-ditch possibility of retreat if everything had gone horribly wrong. The canyon was far too rocky for vehicles to follow, so now we had us a foot race.

My team had been dropped off on the main road, and we had walked to the nomad village. Now that road was crawling with Jihan's reinforcements from the mines. So our only other options were to hide or to try to walk out the other end of the canyon, which was about ten miles of brutal terrain that finally terminated on a Russian plain just off the Mongolian border. Judging by the ant's nest we had just kicked, the smart money wasn't on hiding.

The going was hard. The footing was treacherous and slick. Only half of the group had managed to retain their night vision, and we took turns wearing it, so that the person on point and the man bringing up the rear could always see. Luckily, the sky was still clear and the snow was so bright and reflective that none of us were totally blind.

Antoine set a brutal pace for the first thirty minutes. We needed to get as much of a lead as possible before the soldiers zeroed in on us. Finally, he called a brief halt. We needed to tend to the injured and better secure their wounds before anyone else ended up like Solomon.

Fajkus was still out. He was badly concussed, with a deep laceration on his scalp and several more cuts on his arms and torso. Nobody knew what had happened to him after he led the counterattack against the silo, but at least we had gotten the bleeding stopped.

The next was an Exodus operative from Korea, named Kim. He had taken a round through the forearm. It had struck him in the wrist, traveled right up the bone, and exited out his elbow. The flesh was totally pulverized. Shen had tied a tourniquet just above the elbow. Kim wasn't looking good. He could scarcely walk, and kept stumbling. He had lost a lot of blood and was barely coherent.

Svetlana was hanging in there. The Russian sniper was in terrible pain, with bones in both of her legs shattered. She had to be carried, and the burden was increased for whoever had her on their back because she refused to put down her heavy sniper rifle. None of us could really disagree with that because all of us knew what the chances of us getting away were, and none of us were the type that would give up without a fight.

Phillips was limping badly now. His ankle was terribly sprained, and the flesh sticking out the top of his boot was black, purple, and swollen to twice its normal size. He grimaced at every step, but would not quit.

There was a muted thump far behind us. Somebody had set off the claymore. Antoine signaled for us to continue. It was my turn in the middle, so I helped Kim to his feet, locked his good arm over my shoulder, and helped drag him up the mountain.

LORENZO
The Mountain

"How many are there?" I asked.

Antoine shook his head grimly and passed me the binoculars. "Too many."

I scanned down the mountain. The glass wasn't night vision, but I could make out the dark shapes moving on the white surface far below us. He was right. There were hundreds of them down there. It was a full-fledged hunting party. Occasionally there would be a flicker of lights as they came across some part of our trail they wanted to examine in the dark.

"They're not having any problem tracking us," I muttered.

"Not much we could do about that, I'm afraid." Which was true, we were leaving a trail that a blind man could follow. "We must go. They're moving much faster than we are."

"Come dawn, they'll be able to track us even faster." I exhaled, leaving a cloud of steam that instantly crystallized in the stubble on my face. If anything, it had only gotten colder as the night had gone on. Stopping briefly to check on our pursuers drove that point home as all the sweat from our exertion froze instantly to our bodies. My hands ached with a throbbing pain that was warning me that something was seriously wrong.

"And dawn will be here soon. It is spring, you know," Antoine said.

"Antoine? Was that a joke? Exodus issued you a sense of humor?"

"Do not tell Ling. She would not approve."

I tried my radio again, but still no signal from Jill. The mountains had to be between us now. Antoine and I ran after the others, following a rocky trail that had to have been created by goats or something else narrower than a person. We knew that it wouldn't take long to catch up. Antoine was breathing hard. He and Shen had only been at this altitude for like a week, and had not had a chance to fully acclimatize before the raid. Both of them were feeling it now.

We caught up to the others a moment later. They had stopped for some reason, and were clustered together under a rock overhang. "What's going on?" Antoine demanded. "We must continue."

Roland looked up at us as he rubbed his eyes. "Kim . . ."

Antoine nodded once. "Let us say a few words over him. Then booby trap his body. Leave him on the trail." The tall African studied our surroundings for a moment. "There. If we're lucky, it will cause a rockslide and take a few of the hounds with it."

Now there were only seven of us.

Every step was agony. My legs burned and cramped. It would have been a difficult trek even under normal circumstances, but I had Svetlana riding piggyback with her arms encircled around my neck and her legs dragging behind. She was actually taller than me.

"The map said that this canyon was sixteen kilometers long," Svetlana said, "I did not realize that meant an average of thirty up and fourteen down." Her English was good, but her accent was thick.

"It only feels that long because of the painkillers," I responded. "We're on a beautiful mountain walk is all."

We stumbled on for a few more minutes in silence. The snow crunched under my boots. The other surviving members of Exodus were just darker shadows around us.

"So, Lorenzo . . ."

"Yeah?"

"You have a girlfriend, no?"

"Actually," I replied as I struggled over a fallen tree. "I'm in a serious relationship."

"Too bad. You have a nice butt."

"Now I know you're high."

The beautiful Russian laughed weakly. She was not faring well. "If you left me behind, the rest of you could make better time."

"Shut up," I grunted.

At least we were walking generally downhill now, not that that was any easier, as the ground was uneven and I kept tripping and sliding. There was probably another mile of downgrade, but then we faced a difficult uphill battle over the highest point of the pass.

"They're gaining on us," Roland gasped as he sprinted up from behind.

"How far?" Antoine asked.

"They've got an advance party, maybe twenty men. They're about eight hundred yards behind us. The main group was still around the river bend. I don't know how far. I set our last claymore."

That was grim news. An hour ago they had been twice that distance behind us.

"Antoine. Let me slow them down," I suggested. "If we're going to do it, we might as well do it now. We haven't seen any of them equipped with night vision."

"You would be overwhelmed. No. We should stick together."

"You forget something. I don't take orders from you. Sorry, Svetlana," I told her as I stopped and tried to lower her to the ground as gently as possible. She whimpered in pain as her damaged legs touched down. "Antoine, I'm going back there to kill a few of these guys. That'll slow the others down. I'm a way better murderer than pack mule."

Antoine knew better than to try to argue with me. "Very well." Shen raised his hand. Antoine shook his head in resignation. "You too?"

Shen shrugged.

Roland and Phillips started to speak, but I cut them off. "Wrong. Somebody has to be on point, and Antoine isn't going to carry two people by himself."

"Leave me," Svetlana said from the ground. "I'm endangering the rest of you."

"No," Shen said with grave finality. "We will hurt them, then return."

"But—" Svetlana began.

"No. I was there when your brother died on the side of a mountain, and I'll be damned if the same thing happens to you. Phillips, pick her up. Good luck, my brothers. Hurry back." Antoine said as he adjusted the still unconscious form of Fajkus on his back and lumbered on.

I was unbelievably exhausted as I slid in behind the patch of rocks. Shen and I had scrambled up one of the almost-vertical rock faces, tearing our clothing and our skin on the jagged bits, to get above the approaching soldiers. Once we were at the top, I went to one side, Shen to the other. We would try to hit as many of them as possible before retreating. With any luck, the expectation of further ambushes would slow them down from here on.

There we perched, the advance party of slave soldiers now only about a hundred meters and closing. These men were moving quickly. If I had sneezed loud, they probably would have heard it. I tried to take a drink from the Camelbak I'd taken from the crashed helicopter, but the liquid had long since frozen into a block of solid ice. Add dehydration to my list of complaints.

The thief in me told me what I should have been doing. I should have told Exodus to fuck off, and I should have left them. I didn't owe them anything. On my own, I could have already made it to the other side of the canyon or, worst case scenario, I could have hid, and then escaped during the confusion of the soldiers slaughtering the remaining survivors.

Be good, Hector. That's all that I ask . . .

For some reason I kept hearing the voice of Gideon Lorenzo in my head. What I was doing here was suicidal. It was asinine. If I was the man that I had been even a few years ago, I would have ditched Exodus hours ago.

But I wasn't.

I studied the terrain. We were in a good position. We could probably get most of the advance party into the open before we opened fire. The soldiers were moving in the trees, but they had to cross a pretty good-size field of snow with very little cover to get to us. Hopefully we could catch a bunch of them in the open.

Shen signaled me and started passing hand signals. Both of us were wearing night vision. I was wearing Fajkus' pair since he was still unconscious. Shen and I were on the same page: wait until the last possible second and then nail as many of them in the open as possible. I signaled that I would start close and work my way to the rear, he would start at the rear and work his way forward.

The soldiers moved into the kill zone. They were in pairs, and keeping a bit of distance between each pair. Doing the math, the best we could hope for would be to get ten of them in the open at once, and that was pushing it. The others would still be in a copse of trees, and they would probably take cover and start shooting back. Hopefully, without night vision, we would be able to retreat without getting hit.

I had been able to scrounge up one more 5.56 magazine from the crashed chopper, so I had one full thirty-rounder and one other that I estimated was mostly full. By my calculation, I had already fired about two hundred rounds through my ACR since the fighting had started in the compound.

The soldiers were getting closer, spaced pretty far apart, our earlier claymores having taught them a lesson. I signaled to Shen. *It's time.*

It's difficult to be accurate at anything more than short range with a red dot sight through night vision. My ACR had an IR laser invisible to the naked eye, but through my monocular, it was a brilliant beam. I put it on the closest soldier and he was totally oblivious. I flipped the selector to semi and pulled the trigger. The round spat from the muzzle with a muted hiss, a small spark of light the only visible indication I had fired. There was a high pitched sound as the tiny projectile traveled at a rate greater than the speed of sound before the bullet struck the soldier in the top of his chest. He stopped dead in his tracks, then fell flat on his back.

Shen opened up at the furthest visible pair while I quickly shifted my gun to the second soldier and popped him once. Normally I liked to shoot everybody a bunch of times, but I didn't really have a whole lot of ammo left at this point. Besides, if we were lucky, maybe the main body would slow down to tend to their wounded. *Doubtful, but what the hell. Worth a shot.*

I moved from pair to pair as quickly as I could. I was firing on the second group before they realized what was happening. Our suppressed weapons and ability to see in the dark was a huge advantage. Shen and I met in the middle pair as both of us hit the soldier on the right at the same time, and the soldier on the left dove into the snow. It had only taken a few seconds to work across the group.

"Go!" I hissed. We both leapt up and began to scramble back down the rocks. Muzzle flashes erupted from the tree line. Bullets violently struck all around us as the soldiers hosed our general area with automatic fire. I tripped, and tumbled down the last few feet of the slope, sprawling forward, but managing to catch myself with my already-abraded hands. Shen grabbed the back of my coat and pulled me upright. The two of us ran as fast as we could back toward Exodus.

The gunfire behind us didn't let up for almost a minute straight.

And come dawn, they would actually be able to aim.

It was going to be a tough morning.

VALENTINE
The Mountain Road

The dam was crippled, but we weren't out of this yet.

Dawn was fast approaching as our ersatz rescue party wound its way through barely passable mountain roads. I drove a beat-up 4x4 with Ling next to me, and it was slow going. Some effort had been made by someone to keep the roads relatively free of snow, but we continually got bogged down in soft spots. Ling, using a map and her GPS navigated, while trying to stay in contact with Lorenzo's group on the radio. They were constantly fading in and out, as the terrain did a marvelous job of limiting radio range.

We *were* in good contact with Reaper and Jill, who had taken it upon themselves to make a beeline for Lorenzo's location on their own. Reaper was feeding us real-time information from his little drone aircraft, and it was a godsend. Otherwise we'd have had no chance of finding them in time. He said the Montalbans had been tracking his signal somehow, so he would put the plane on standby, where it would just drift in circles on autopilot, they'd move, and then he'd reconnect.

The situation was dire. The survivors of the raid on Sala Jihan's compound were on foot, trudging through deep snow and over rugged terrain. There were only a handful of them left, and half were wounded. They were pursued by a mob of Jihan's fanatical soldiers, numbering well over a hundred by Reaper's best estimate.

Ling was finally able to get someone back on the radio. "What's your status?" she asked.

Antoine answered. *"It is good to hear your voice,"* he said, panting.

"We are on our way. What is your status?"

"Not good, I'm afraid. I hope you have good news."

Ling read off coordinates to Antoine. "This is a place northeast of your position where the canyon reaches the road. If you can get there, we'll be waiting to pick you up. It's as close as we're going to be able to get without walking. There are no other paths."

"I understand," Antoine said breathlessly. *"Stand by . . . "*

Lorenzo's voice squawked over the radio next. *"Okay, I'm looking at those coordinates you gave us. Shit, that's a long way. Are you sure there's nowhere closer?"*

"I'm positive, Chief," Reaper said, stomping Ling's transmission before she could reply. *"I'm looking at maps and footage from Little Bird. That's the closest place anywhere near your path of travel where you'll even come close to the road. There's another spot up a different canyon from there, but it's even farther away from us, and it looks like it'd be a pretty steep climb to get up to road level. The coordinates Ling gave you are your best bet."*

"Acknowledged," Lorenzo said. *"Do you still have eyes on us?"*

"Little Bird's running low on fuel, but I'll be your eyes in the sky for as long as I can. The Exodus guys will probably catch up with us before we get to the rendezvous point. We'll all be there."

"Yes, we will," Jill said suddenly, transmitting before Lorenzo could reply. *"You damned well better get there, Lorenzo. I mean it."*

The radio was silent for a moment. *"It's good to hear your voice, honey,"* he said.

"Hang on," Jill said, sounding like she was trying to keep her fear under control. *"We're on our way!"*

Chapter 24: Pick a Direction and Run

LORENZO
The Mountain

"You're alive. Good," Antoine said as Shen and I caught up.

"We got a few of them, but they're still coming," I bent over, put my hands on my knees, and retched into the snow. Running at this altitude was killer. I stood, wiped my mouth, and noted, "Fajkus is awake?" Ibrahim's second in command was sitting on a rock, his face in his hands.

"Yes, but he is incoherent. He took a severe blow to the head," Antoine nodded toward him. "He awoke screaming, talking about . . . *things* coming out of the silo. Now he is not speaking to anyone."

I watched as Fajkus wrapped his arms around his chest and began to rock back and forth, glancing nervously side to side. I had seen people lose it like that before, especially back in Africa, brains just overloaded with awful shit. "He's shell-shocked." In the light of my magnified vision, I could see that the other survivors were deeply disturbed by Fajkus's behavior, their eyes shining bright, wide, and afraid.

"No," Shen shook his head. "He's one of our most experienced men."

Antoine agreed. "Fajkus has seen more battle than any two of us put together. He has been fearless before certain death many times, and his courage has inspired the rest of us. No . . . this is something else."

I felt an uncomfortable shiver, and it wasn't from the cold. "Don't matter what it is, because if we don't keep moving, we're dead." I strode over to Fajkus, grabbed him by the sides of his head, and jerked his face up. He looked confused. "Hey. Listen up." I slapped him, hard. This seemed to startle the others.

And I learned why, really quickly. Fajkus moved, way faster than I thought a stocky fellow could, one hand clamped around my throat as he jerked me forward, and something cold and metallic slammed into the side of my head, a pistol apparently, as I heard him cock the hammer.

"No, you listen, asshole. I'm just fucking fine," Fajkus snarled as he screwed the gun into my ear hole. "As fine as you could be considering that I just met the fucking devil himself. If you had seen whatever the fuck I just saw, then you would need a *moment* too." He sounded calm, rational, but there was something just beneath that, something that indicated that this man was well and truly *freaked out.* "I saw hell open up and take a shit on *my* men, on *my* friends, and now Jihan is going to catch us, and swallow our souls, because apparently we're walking, because *your* girlfriend betrayed us and left us to die, and if I remember right . . . " he shoved the gun in even harder, and the hand around my throat clenched off even more precious air, "*you* were the one who said we could trust her."

"Sir, please, Lorenzo is on our side," Antoine said calmly. "We do not have time for this."

Fajkus's eyes flashed down as he felt my knife press up between his legs. "I'll make time," I growled back as I put enough force to indicate that I was feeling real serious. The pressure released enough from my throat to let me talk. "Get your hands off me."

He let go, and lowered his gun. "Well, I guess you are walking too, so at least you aren't in league with that Montalban Exchange bitch."

"No, I've been taking turns carrying your unconscious ass up a mountain for hours. If I was walking, I would already be out of here." I rubbed my throat, but I didn't put away my knife. "What did you see back there? What happened to Ibrahim?"

He shook his head, mind distant. It took him a long moment to respond. "I don't . . . don't really know. All I know is that Jihan is more dangerous than the Council knew, more than Ariel expected."

I had no idea who that was, but Fajkus was a man whose faith had been shaken.

"And now this is all that remains of Exodus' warriors." He gestured at the survivors, ragged and tired. "We are ruined."

There was random gunfire behind us as the soldiers mistook a menacing tree for one of us. The noise was way too close.

"Keep moving," Antoine ordered, unconsciously taking command. The mystery would have to wait. Dawn was coming fast.

We plodded forward. Roland and Phillips were behind, setting up another ambush. They had demanded a turn. I had turned my borrowed night vision over to Roland and was stumbling along through the shadows beneath the trees, Svetlana again on my back. But it wouldn't matter for too much longer. Dawn was coming fast.

Already we had moved from real darkness to a fuzzy gray reflecting off the snow. Last night, the sky had been brilliantly clear, but now a fat wall of clouds was coming in from the north, the direction we were traveling. We hoped it brought with it fresh snow and the possibility of evading our pursuers. The weather was actually warming up.

According to the map, we had crossed the highest point of the canyon during the night, and it was mostly downhill from here on out. There was one more bulge on the topographical map, but after that we were heading into Mongolia. Jill would be there waiting. As it stood now, we only had one option: forward. That also meant that the bad guys had a pretty simple path to follow in order to catch up.

Gunfire echoed behind us, bouncing wildly off the mountain walls. Roland and Phillips had sprung their ambush. Hopefully they would live through it. Antoine was on point, and he glanced up, listening, trying to ascertain how far away the shooting was. Shen was helping Fajkus, who was stumbling indomitably along, but the head wound had left him dizzy and uncoordinated.

Now that it was quickly brightening, I could see our surroundings better. I had no doubt that Jill would think that it was beautiful, a pristine, virgin-white, winter wonderland. The canyon was only a mile wide at any given point, and we were trekking along the bank of a river choked with ice flows. Sometime during the night we had lost enough altitude to be back in a real forest and the air smelled clean. For a city boy like me that was kind of scary. At one point, I noticed that there were wolves watching us from the trees. Giant, scary dogs, like Reaper had read about on the internet. They looked at us curiously before moving on to eat something without guns.

"—in. Come in, Lorenzo." The chirping of my radio startled me so badly that I almost dropped the sleeping Svetlana in the snow. She snorted loudly in my ear.

"Jill?" I gasped, my throat parched and aching.

"Oh, thank God. You're alive," she said. "Where are you?"

"We're most of the way through the canyon, heading into Mongolia. We're close to the coordinates Ling gave us."

"We're almost there. Reaper's got the Little Bird in the air . . . He's looking at the guys following you right now. He says he can walk you in to us before they catch up."

I was too tired to think. "Careful, the Montalbans will find you." My words were slurred.

"Reaper says he can handle that. He started to talk about trigonometry and the curvature of the Earth or something, I almost drove the truck off a cliff because it put my brain to sleep. Keep going. You're almost there. Reaper can walk you in."

"Awesome," I spoke up so the others could hear. "Guys, we're almost to our ride."

"Excellent," Antoine said just before the bullet hit him.

FFOOoooooommmm!

The shot had come from quite far away. It took the sound a moment to catch up. Antoine fell into the snow, clutching his side.

"Sniper!" Shen shouted as he and Fajkus dove to the ground. Svetlana gasped in pain as I took us down.

"I'm hit!" Antoine shouted, scrambling through the snow and finally coming to rest behind a log.

"Where is he?" Fajkus said. I raised my head and scanned the mountainside. They had to have been paralleling our path on the mountain above us, there was no other way.

The bark on the tree next to my head exploded in a shower of splinters and pulp. "Damn it!" I flinched back down. "I don't see him!"

"Antoine. Status?"

The big man didn't answer.

Shen leapt up, heedless of danger, and dove toward where Antoine was hiding. The two men were like brothers. He was only up for a split second, then back down. A bullet whizzed through the space that he had been occupying, sounding like an angry bee on steroids. The sound of the muzzle blast came a moment after.

Fajkus popped his head up to look, and the snow next to him erupted. That one had been very close. The Exodus leader began to speak into his radio, trying to raise Phillips and Roland to tell them to take cover.

Svetlana was lying on her back, Sako across her chest, bloody and bandaged left hand hugging the rifle close, as she calmly scanned the mountainside. "Six hundred meters," she stated flatly.

"You see him?" I was scared to lift my head again.

"Not yet," she grimaced as she rolled over and began to low crawl into the trees, dragging her broken legs uselessly behind her. "I could tell by time takes sound to travel."

"What are you doing?"

"What I do best," she said.

"You can't even walk."

"I don't need to," she glared at me.

"Let me do it. You're missing fingers."

She held up her right hand, and then extended her middle finger. "I still have all these. Are you a trained sniper?"

"No."

"Then shut up and spot."

I was kneeling behind a rotted stump, now damp as the temperature, by some miracle, was moving slightly above freezing. Svetlana was on her belly, ten feet ahead of me, covered in pine needles, and scanning the mountainside through her scope. I was amazed how far we had crawled, how fast.

"Reaper, come in."

"*Yeah, Chief?*"

"Do you have us on thermal yet?"

"*I lost you under the trees. It doesn't have X-ray vision.*"

"I've got a sniper on the mountain approximately six hundred meters to the northeast. Find him, Reaper. Fajkus?"

"*Go.*" Everybody was switched on to the same channel now.

"Svetlana is going to try to take this guy. As soon as he's distracted, you three need to move. We'll catch up." The main body of soldiers had to be almost on top of us by now. "Where're the Mormons?"

"*Almost there,*" said one of them over the radio. I couldn't tell which because the speaker was breathing really hard. "*The soldiers are right behind us. Roland took a round.*"

"Shut up . . . Just a flesh . . . wound . . ." Roland was gasping. "*Jerk.*"

This was going to be close.

"Lorenzo," Svetlana hissed. "There are three places I think he could be hiding. I need your help."

"Okay," I answered, scanning the mountainside, waiting for her to tell me which spot to watch.

"When I tell you to . . . stand up."

"Are you nuts?"

"Not for a long time, stupid. Just get up and move to side. When he shoots at you, I kill him."

"That sounds like a good plan," I said sarcastically. But we didn't have much time. "Okay."

Svetlana let out a long breath. "Now."

Despite my brain telling me not to, and every fiber of my being screaming *no*, I stood, ran to the side, and dropped. No shot came.

"Did you see him?" I gasped.

"No. Do it again."

"What? *No.* Screw that."

"Not from same spot. He will blow your brains out from there. Crawl first. Then move when I tell you."

Son of a bitch. I started low-crawling, slush moving up my sleeves and down my shirt.

"Now."

Aw, man. I stood, and it took my brain a split second to process that the burning sensation I felt across my scalp was a hot piece of lead moving at just over 3,000 feet per second. My legs buckled without me even telling them to.

Her big rifle roared.

"Got him," Svetlana said as she worked the bolt. "Lorenzo, are you alive?"

I rubbed my hand across the top of my head. The bastard had creased the top of my skull. My stolen glove came away covered in fresh blood to match the dried blood from earlier. "You sure you got him?"

"Yes. It was one of the Brotherhood. I was a little off center, but with a .338 Lapua, you can be a little off. He won't be shooting back, that's for sure."

I sure hoped she was right. I keyed the radio. "Sniper down. Move. Move." That was two Brothers dead. Through the trees, back the way we came, I could make out Shen and Fajkus, with Antoine hoisted between them. A split second later, two other shapes came running up behind them, Phillips and Roland. "We'll catch up. Jill will walk you in to her position."

"*Moving,*" Shen replied.

"Come on," I said as I stood up, fully expecting to get shot by some yet unknown danger, and ran over to Svetlana. I squatted down next to her, so that she could clamber onto my back. My muscles ached and burned and I hoisted her up. She wasn't light.

"See? And you wanted me to drop my rifle," the Russian insisted.

"You were right, that what you need to hear? Now hold on." Now we had to sprint to the finish. We had to make it through some pretty thick brush, but so did our pursuers. It was a good thing I worked out a lot, because all I wanted to do right about then was curl up in a ball and die. I couldn't ever remember being this tired. Svetlana's bandaged hand was bouncing right in front of my face, and I tried to ignore the missing fingers, and concentrate on my footing, as I half ran, half stumbled forward.

"*Lorenzo!*" Reaper shouted in my ear. "*Your sniper's back.*"

"Impossible!" Svetlana screamed in my good ear. "I shot him in the chest."

"Maybe you missed," I suggested, but from what I knew about the Exodus sniper, I really doubted that.

"No. He must be wearing armor plates," she spat.

From what I had seen earlier in the compound, I could assume that the Brother was probably a dead man walking, and it wouldn't make a lick of difference until his heart finally quit beating, damn fanatical bastards. "Where, Reaper?"

"*He's moving downhill. Wait, there's two of them. One's moving fast, and he's got a short gun with some big drum on it, the other's moving slow, like he's injured, and has an old-fashioned rifle.*"

"Shit!" I hunched forward so I could run faster. We were heading due north, the other survivors were ahead and slightly to the west. The Brothers were to our northeast, and if they could get ahead of the others or get into a position to slow us down, then we would be overtaken by the soldiers.

Svetlana must have realized the same thing that I was thinking. "Get me to higher ground."

LORENZO
The River

"This is good!" Svetlana yelled in my good ear. "Put me down."

I lowered her as gently as possible, which wasn't very gentle considering that I had just sprinted up a rock slope with a hundred-and-fifty-pound woman and her fourteen pound rifle on my back. We had a good view from here, with the river at our back and the forest below us. The Exodus survivors were almost out of the canyon, three quarters of a mile ahead of us. The mass of slave soldiers was even closer, and would be passing below us in the next few minutes. I could already hear snatches of their excited voices on the wind.

Svetlana grimaced as she dragged herself up and braced her Sako across a fallen log. "There. That's where the Brothers will try to intercept." She was aiming at another spot along the riverbank, between us and the others. "They will have to get on top of that hill to get a shot, and then I'll have them."

"Reaper. Status?" I commanded.

"The Brothers are heading toward the river, a hundred and fifty meters north of you. They're blocking your escape. And you've got a shitload of bad guys about to be on top of you. You've got to get out of there now!"

The Sun was coming over the side of the canyon. I could clearly see the path I had to take to reach extraction. My best bet was to head right down the riverbank, right through the Brothers. It was rocky and uneven, and would be treacherous with Svetlana on my back, but it was the only way now.

"Pop these guys, and we've got to go."

"We don't have time to wait for them. Go through the Brothers, and I'll cover you from here," she stated.

I turned back to her. "There's no way I can make it down there and back to get you and still make it."

She gave me a tired smile. "I know."

"Bullshit," I spat. "I didn't carry you this far for nothing."

"Go, Lorenzo. We're out of time."

I started toward her, then hesitated. She was right. We had to take out the

Brothers before they pinned down the others. There was no time to argue. I nodded once, hoisted my rifle, and turned to leave. It was suicide. Suddenly my eyes were burning.

"Wait!" she cried out. I spun, expecting her to have come to her senses. Instead, she had pulled her Makarov and set it on the ground next to her. "Let me have your grenade." I pulled the frag that I had found in the Exodus helicopter and passed it back to her. She took it in her uninjured hand. and shoved it in the top of her coat. "I'm not going to let them take me alive. Now hurry, I'll cover you as long as I can. Kill the Brothers."

There was no time for sentiment. I sprinted down the riverbank in the direction of the next high spot, leaping from rock to rock. I kept the stock of my rifle against my shoulder, muzzle swinging wildly back and forth in front of me. I could hear the almost musical noise of the river flowing about twenty feet below. The rocks were slick, and the dirt between them had transformed into clingy mud. There was no way I could have made it with Svetlana in time. That didn't make it any easier.

"The Brothers are almost on top of the hill. Antoine's guys are still vulnerable for at least another minute," Reaper warned. There was a loud *BANG* behind me as Svetlana engaged some of the approaching soldiers. I tried to go faster, but my boot streaked out from under me as it hit a damp stone and I fell painfully to the ground. I shoved myself back up and kept going. The bank was on my left, the hill to my front, and the forest to my right.

I was counting on the Brothers being focused on the others and not watching this direction. I was almost to the hill. It was more of a dirt pile, with one side eroded away by the sluggish river. Raising my rifle, I scanned, looking for movement. Something black passed between the trees, running upward, his back toward me. I snapped the red dot onto him, led the target for just a split second, and fired. The black shape went down into the weeds. I continued running. I had to get to cover.

The other Brother appeared to my right, materializing out of the shadows, a stubby PPSh in his hands, the muzzle already flashing. I flung myself face first into the mud as the bullets zipped overhead, tearing up rock chips and dirt around me. I was a dead man.

Then the shooting stopped. I waited for a moment, then popped up, looking for a target, but the Brother was gone.

"Got him!" Svetlana shouted over the radio.

"They're both still moving! I've got one heading north, one low crawling east." Reaper said. *"Svetlana, you've got about ten soldiers in the open, due south of you."*

"Damn it," I spat through a mouth full of mud, and I rose and headed for the trees. These sons of bitches were hard to kill. The one with the PPSh was wounded nearby in the trees, but I had to take out the one with the rifle right the hell now.

"Lorenzo, you're on your own. I've got company," Svetlana stated calmly, then she started hammering that big rifle.

I was in the trees now. There was blood on the bark of a nearby tree, and a splatter trail leading back into the brush. The Brother with the subgun was hit bad. Maybe he would just do us a favor and crawl off to die. I picked my way through the woods. It was thick, dark, and tangled with underbrush. I kept heading uphill. I knew I was making too much noise, but I was exhausted, in a hurry, and out of my element.

There was a roar of a high-powered rifle ahead of me, and I instinctively ducked. But the Brother wasn't shooting at me. He was shooting at Shen and Antoine. Somebody screamed over the radio. I flipped my selector to full-auto and charged forward. I saw the Brother as he saw me. He turned, still working the bolt of his old M44. I didn't take any chances. I mashed the trigger and hosed the entire rest of the magazine into him. The Brother went down in a spray of fluids and meat, and tumbled over the side into the river below.

I dropped my spent mag, shoved my last one in, and slammed the bolt closed as I approached the edge. I hung over quickly, just to make sure. The Brother lay broken in a spreading cloud of red, half submerged in a shallow slush of ice. I took my time, aimed, and put a final round through the Brother's skull.

"Lorenzo, last one is coming up—" Reaper started to warn me, but I didn't hear the rest. Something small and black came sailing out of the trees and landed in the mud in front of me. *Grenade!* No time to think. I stepped back off the edge and plummeted into the river.

The grenade detonated above with a violent concussion. I braced myself to hit the water, but instead of a splash, there was a crunch as I smashed into an ice sheet. It shattered beneath me, and my legs plunged into unbelievable cold. It was shallow, and I hit the gravel bottom way too fast. It was like an electrical shock traveled up my legs as the ice water hit me. I fell over on my side, and then half my body was submerged in the freezing cold. I pulled myself back onto the ice, and rolled into the mud on the bank.

The final Brother appeared over the top, emotionless goggles studying me for a moment. I had to move, my numb legs clumsy beneath me. The PPSh came over the edge and the Brother ripped a long burst, the ice and water billowing up at my side. I jerked my rifle up and fired wildly at him. He disappeared back over the edge.

I stumbled to my feet and started downstream, wading through the water before he decided to toss another grenade. He must have been out, as he hung the subgun over the side and fired another burst. This one was even closer, striking a string of water plumes right past me. A mist hung in the air. I extended my gun and returned fire, the two of us strobing bullets back and forth. I stumbled, sprawled backward on the ice, and broke through again.

The cold was so intense, so invasive, that I almost blacked out. I exploded out of the water, every nerve on fire, my muscles not wanting to respond, and my hands automatically clenching into fists. I thrashed through the ice and the mud, and flopped face first onto the bank, my body shivering uncontrollably.

I forced myself to breathe and grabbed my rifle. I was shaking so badly that I couldn't even aim. I just raised it toward the Brother and jerked the trigger a few times. I wasn't even close. The empty ACR slipped from my quivering fingers and fell into the water as I struggled to draw my pistol.

"Lorenzo!" Reaper screamed over the radio. *"Hang on!"*

I fumbled the draw, my pistol shaking badly. The Brother fired and something burned down the inside of my arm. I jerked as the bullets hit me like a sledgehammer. I extended my hand but my STI was gone, torn right out of my grasp. My body was frozen but a flash of heat was spreading on my side.

I was done.

The Brother took his time. His subgun was empty, so he nonchalantly dropped the drum, and pulled another from a pouch on his belt. I knew I was hit, but I was so cold I didn't even know how badly. In the distance there was a huge amount of gunfire coming from where I had left Svetlana. I was so cold and in so much pain that I could barely understand the words over the radio, but somebody had gone back for her. I saw my pistol laying just beneath the crystal surface of the river, but it might as well have been a million miles away.

The Brother shoved the drum in, flipped the lever to lock it in place, and drew the bolt back. He took one final look at his dead comrade floating face down a few feet from me, and shook his head sadly.

"Lorenzo!" Reaper was shouting. *"Hang on, man!"*

There was a strange buzzing sound. At first I thought it was from my bad ear, but the noise was growing. Now it was whistling.

The Brother aimed the Russian subgun at my face.

"Fear the Reaper, motherfucker!"

A black shadow zipped by overhead. The Brother heard the approaching noise, looked up, and then got hit right in the face by Little Bird.

The flying wing smashed into pieces. The UAV didn't weigh much, but it was enough to knock the Brother off balance, and he went over the edge, arms and legs windmilling, until he crashed through the icy crust of the river.

I plunged my hand into the icy water.

The Brother came up thrashing, water droplets flinging in every direction.

My hand closed on my pistol.

Goggled eyes fixed on me, then he scanned around. The Brother had lost his gun. He looked back up at me, then began struggling forward, waist deep in the slush, pushing my way. He reached into his furs and his gloved fist came out clutching a curved blade.

The STI came up, water pouring out of it. My hands were shaking so badly that I couldn't even find the front sight, so I sprayed and prayed, pulling the trigger wildly. Ice cracked. Dirt puckered along the banks. A 9mm round struck the rocks and whined off into the distance. There were splashes all around him. And then I hit him. He staggered a bit. I hit him again, and again, and again. He stumbled, slipping on the slick rocks beneath his boots. He went down in a splash, but then he was right back up, lunging toward me.

I shot him several more times before the slide locked back empty. Blood was spurting from the side of his neck, drizzling down a necklace of sharp teeth.

He was only five feet away as he slowly sank to his knees, the river trailing red around him. It was almost like the Brother drifted off to sleep, as he sank to his side to bleed out onto the rocks of the bank.

"Thanks, Reaper," I gasped, but I didn't know if he heard me.

I wanted nothing more than to follow the Brother's example . . . I'd been shot. I was so cold I couldn't even tell how many times or where. Then I tried to get out of the river, and the pain told me. Blood was running out of my side, just beneath my armor. Crawling, splashing, I made it onto the rocks and lay there for a moment.

This is very bad.

Chapter 25: The Good Guy

VALENTINE

The Mountain Road Rendezvous Point

Distant gunshots echoed off of cliff faces as they drew closer to our position.

We bailed out of the trucks. The Exodus troops with us, few that there were, spread out and took up defensive positions around us. If Jihan's forces were following us down the road, they were sure to catch up with us now. It was a risk we had to take, though. We weren't going to leave anyone else behind.

Ling, Jill, and I waited nervously by the edge of the road. Down to the southwest was a deep, narrow rocky canyon filled with trees. That was the direction they were coming from.

The radio crackled to life. It was Antoine, breathing hard. *"We're here. I have eyes on. We're coming out."*

"I can see them!" one of the Exodus troops said. He and a couple of others ran forward to help their comrades.

Below us, a handful of haggard-looking people trudged out of the trees. They were all dressed in camouflage, so I couldn't tell who was who except for Antoine. The six-foot-four African was hard to mistake for anyone else. He was weaving badly, and his whole right side was covered in blood.

My heart sank when I saw how few of them remained. The look of shock on Ling's face was difficult for even her to hide. Reaper had warned us that there weren't many left, but it didn't really sink in until we saw it with our own eyes. Jill took off down the embankment, sliding into the snow, and ran forward. Ling and I looked at each other, then followed. They were going to need help getting up to the road.

I followed Ling as she ran to Antoine. Next to him, another Exodus operative whom I didn't know was helping Fajkus, the second in command of the compound raid, along. "My God," Ling asked. "What happened? Is this all that's left?"

"I'm afraid so," He bent over to catch his breath. "Forgive me, I've been shot."

"There's no time to talk now," Fajkus growled. "The bastards are right behind us."

"Where's Lorenzo?" It was Jill. She was running around the clearing almost in a panic, checking every person that had come out of the trees. Someone else came out of the trees, carrying a body over their shoulder. "Lorenzo!" Jill cried, but it was Shen, limping badly, but carrying a blonde woman. "Where is he?"

Ling looked up at Antoine. "He was with you. Was he killed?"

Before he could answer, Jill came running up to us, her breath smoking in the frigid morning air. "Where the hell is Lorenzo?" she barked, her dark eyes flashing with anger. "He was supposed to be with you! You tell me what happened right now!"

"Lorenzo went the wrong way to draw them off."

Jill deflated a little, and covered her mouth with her hands. "Oh no. No, no, no."

"He was alive when I saw him last. He intercepted our pursuers. We all would have been overrun had he not done that," Fajkus said.

"But . . . but he's still alive?"

"I don't know."

Jill tried her radio. "Lorenzo! Come in, Lorenzo!"

Shen stumbled up the clearing as the others rushed to help him. He looked exhausted. Two men took the blonde woman between them, and she screamed as they bumped her legs. They were flopping about below the knees, obviously broken.

"Lorenzo was alive a minute ago." She grimaced through the pain. "The enemy was right on top of us though."

"Well, then, what the hell are we waiting for? We're going to go get him!" Jill turned to run away, but I grabbed her arm. "What are you doing, Val? Let me go! We don't have time to waste!"

"I'm going," I said flatly. "You're not."

"Fuck you, I'm going," Jill retorted.

I didn't let go.

Ling stepped in. "Jill, please. Let us go get Lorenzo. It is our responsibility. It is because of us . . . because of me, that he's even in this situation. I owe it to him. Michael and I will go. If he's still there, we'll bring him back."

"He's still there!" Jill shouted, pulling away from me. She turned to walk up the embankment again.

"Jill!" I said. "So help me God, you're staying here if I have to have Exodus tie you the hell up. No one else is going to die here, do you hear me? Enough people have died tonight. What in the hell do you think you're going to do, other than put your own life, and Reaper's life, in jeopardy, huh?"

Jill obviously hadn't thought about that. She wasn't even carrying a rifle. She didn't even have body armor. Letting her go would probably be sending her to her death.

"Jill, please . . . We're leaving right now. We'll find him. We're not going to abandon him."

Tears welled up in Jill's eyes. She was visibly shaking. "Hurry, please," she said quietly.

The door of one of the big Russian vans slid open and Reaper began shouting. "I lost eyes, but Lorenzo's in the river! He's in the river!"

I nodded, then noticed that Shen had a large bolt-action rifle slung across his back. "What's that?"

"It's Svetlana's rifle," he said. "She's a sniper."

It was a *long* way down to the river. "Give it to me," I said, "It might come in handy."

Shen nodded, and unslung the long weapon. It was a Sako TRG-42 wrapped in white webbing for camouflage. I slung my carbine behind my back as he handed me the heavy beast. I worked the bolt to verify that there was a round chambered, and looked through the scope. It was a five-to-twenty power.

"Here," the woman said. She tossed me a single five-round magazine for the rifle. "That's all the ammunition I have left for it."

.338 Lapua. That'll put a hurting on somebody. "Let's move."

Ling turned her attention to Antoine and Fajkus as I began jogging away. "Do not wait for us here. Rendezvous with Katsumoto's group. We will try to stay in contact, but do not linger for our sake. Enough of us have died here already. If we don't make it back, don't come looking for us."

"I understand," Antoine said solemnly. "Go with God, my friend."

VALENTINE
The Mountain Road, above the Canyon

The path was narrow and treacherous as we made our way toward where we thought Lorenzo was. Ling was trying to raise him on the radio, but had no luck so far. Without Reaper to guide us in, there was little we could do but hope. I was on edge, exhausted, and afraid. The woods were swarming with Jihan's men. What I really wanted to do was turn around and head back with the others. I just wanted to get as far away from The Crossroads as I possibly could, and never think about it again.

But as much as I disliked Lorenzo, I was determined not to leave anyone else behind. Not now, not after all this. Twice in my life, I'd been left behind, abandoned by the people I was working for. I know what it feels like and I wasn't about to do that to somebody else.

If Lorenzo was alive, I hoped to God he wasn't bringing a lot of company with him.

"We can get a clear view of the river from there." Ling pointed.

"Keep your head down. We don't know who's down there."

Approaching cautiously, we took stock of the canyon before us. The ground just dropped away in a gap between thin evergreen trees. The grade was steep, all the way to the canyon floor and the river. We had a good view of the river from here. Ling lifted a pair of binoculars and started scanning back and forth.

On the valley floor, in a clearing five hundred yards away was the rusting hulk of a big airplane. I recognized it as an old Soviet Tu-95 bomber. One of its wings could be seen, half covered by a snow, some distance behind it. The other wing was nowhere to be found. A faded red star still adorned its tail. It looked as if it had been there for decades, forgotten. "Looks like they tried to ride it in," I mused. There was no way the bomber was going to do an emergency landing in a place like this, but it was obvious it hadn't just plowed straight down into the ground, either.

We had concealment from the foliage and cover from the boulders, plus a commanding view of the narrow valley ahead of us. It was as good as we were going to get.

I unfolded its bipod and set up the sniper rifle as Ling tried to raise Lorenzo on the radio. "Lorenzo, Lorenzo, this is Sword Three X-Ray. Can you hear me, over?"

Nothing.

"Lorenzo, this is Sword Three X-Ray, please respond. What is your status?"

Ling looked over at me and shook her head.

"Well, we can wait here for a little—"

The radio crackled back to life. *"This is Lorenzo. I'm here, I'm still here."*

"Sword Three X-Ray copies, Lorenzo. Where are you?"

"Fuck if I know. I see lots of fucking trees. I've got a lot of pissed off assholes on my tail. That narrow it down for you?" His breathing was ragged. He sounded horrible. *"I see an . . . airplane?"*

"We're waiting for you at the road past that, Lorenzo. As you come out of the trees, there'll be an open area covered with boulders. Past the wreck, there's a steep, rocky grade up to our position. I don't think it'll be an easy climb. Do you copy?"

"I hear you," Lorenzo replied. *"Fuck. I'm in bad shape here. I've been*

shot . . . a couple times, and I'm hypothermic and running out of ammo. I hope you got a lot of guys up there."

Ling and I looked at each other.

"Just make for the plane wreck. We'll cover you as best we can." Ling said. "Get ready. I think he's almost here."

"Take my rifle," I suggested. "It's got a scope on it and more range. It'll be better than your carbine."

I hunkered down behind Svetlana's heavy sniper rifle, scanning the canyon for movement. The tree line we expected Lorenzo to come out of was at least eight hundred yards away, maybe a bit further. The rifle I was using could hit playing cards at that distance, but it had been a long time since I'd done this kind of long-range shooting, and I only had ten rounds. Lorenzo had a lot of open territory to cover past the trees, with only boulders for cover until he got to the wreck of the bomber. And even then, I had no idea how he was going to get up the grade without getting shot to pieces.

Focus, damn it. Can't worry about it now. I slowly pivoted the rifle on its bipod, looking for movement.

"There! I have eyes on."

A lone figure appeared from the trees, slogging through deep snow as fast as he could. Even at twenty power magnification, he was too far off to ID, so I reached for the radio.

"Lorenzo, this is Valentine. I have eyes on one individual that just exited the tree line. Is that you?"

There was a pause before I got a response. "*Valentine? Fuck me. Yeah, yeah, that's me. Where are you guys?*"

"We're up at the top of the grade. We've got you covered."

"*Get ready. They're right behind me.*"

Lorenzo wasn't kidding. Sporadic gunfire erupted from the trees before I could even see anyone else. First, a couple of figures, dressed in brown and green coats, appeared from the trees, hot on Lorenzo's tail. Then a few more, then dozens of them.

"Holy shit."

LORENZO
The plane wreck

I was in very bad shape. The wound in my side was deep. I had my left hand jammed against it, but blood was pouring between my fingers and leaving a trail in the snow behind me. The ice bath had done something to my mind. Everything was foggy and I was having a hard time thinking straight. My heart was pounding in my chest and my mouth tasted like it was filled with pennies.

The soldiers were all around me, moving between the trees. I could hear them shouting. My legs burned as I had to hoist each foot high enough to clear the snow. There were boulders in the clearing. I could use them for cover, then get to the plane, then—

The bullet pierced my left arm. Blood hit the snow in front of me. I let out an incoherent cry, lifted my pistol and cranked off a couple of shots in the direction that it had come from. The snow puckered around me as they fired back.

I made it to the nearest boulder, stumbled, and crashed into it. I slid along it, leaving a smear of blood, then forced myself onward.

The ringing in my ears had gotten worse. I tripped and fell on my face. *Not like this* . . . And I forced myself back up and headed for the crashed bomber.

Valentine and Ling were shooting. I could hear their bullets buzzing by overhead. What sounded like thousands of bullets were immediately launched back at them.

The cockpit of the bomber was mangled, smashed, and rusty. There was a huge gap past that, and I stumbled inside as fresh holes were punched in the aluminum around me. I turned and saw a soldier moving up to my red-stained boulder. The STI's front sight wobbled past and I put a round into his chest. He slid down the rock and collapsed into the snow.

My gun was empty again. I couldn't even remember firing that many shots. I went to reload, but my left arm didn't want to work and my left hand wouldn't close around a fresh mag. "Damn it . . . " So I tucked the 9mm in my armpit, got a mag out with my good hand, and tried to shove it into the mag well. My hand was shaking so badly it took me several tries.

There was movement everywhere. The clearing was swarming with soldiers. There was no getting out of this one.

How'd I end up here? This was what I deserved for putting somebody else ahead of myself. This was all because I'd gone after Bob. I was going to die, and I still hadn't saved him.

I got the slide dropped on another round and shot a soldier who'd run up to the cockpit.

But that wasn't all. I could have left Exodus. I could have dumped them and run for it on my own . . . Yet I hadn't. I could have abandoned them, but I didn't.

The old bomber smelled of animal piss. Bullets were flying through the metal all around me. A scarred face appeared in a decaying window hole and I blew the young slave's brains out.

I could have abandoned them, but I didn't . . .

I'd made my call.

I'd decided to be the good guy.

And then I knew that old Gideon Lorenzo would have been proud of me.

"I'm still getting out of here, damn it. You hear that, Dad?" I fired wildly out the door, driving some soldiers to cover.

Another bullet exploded through the wall and my leg went out from under me. There was a flash of fire and searing pain, and then blood was spilling from my calf.

I rolled over, tried to stand, and fell over. I ended up face-to-face with a grinning skull, probably the remains of one of the bomber's long-forgotten crewmembers. I couldn't walk. The skull sat there, mocking me.

My leg wouldn't respond. I could no longer run.

And just like that, it was over.

VALENTINE

The powerful rifle bucked into my left shoulder as I squeezed off another shot. Two of Jihan's soldiers were taking cover from Lorenzo behind a rock, but I had a clear shot. The heavy slug tore through both of them, and down they went. That's what they got for bunching up. *Fuck you, assholes.*

I worked the bolt with my right hand, angled the rifle down some more, and found another target. *BOOM.* Another dead enemy soldier, I worked the bolt again. The rifle was now empty. I changed out the magazine. "Last five rounds!"

Ling was still using my rifle, firing slow, aimed shots. "How many more magazines do you have for this?" She'd already gone through one magazine and was working her way through another.

I checked the pouches on my vest, retrieving a single twenty-round mag. "Last one."

"I'll make it work," she said. "Keep shooting."

I scanned the snow-covered wreck of the bomber. I could see Lorenzo, holed up in a gaping tear in the fuselage that faced toward us. He was armed only with a pistol, and was only firing when the enemy got close to his hideout.

Two more soldiers were running toward the gap. One had a bag of hand grenades! A moving target, from a few hundred yards away, with a rifle I had no experience with. *C'mon, c'mon* . . . I tracked my target, leading him slightly, and squeezed the trigger.

He crumpled to the snow in a puff of blood. His friend tripped and fell.

I worked the bolt and put a round into him, too. A hand grenade went off, throwing up a circle of snow and dust. "Two more down!" I told Ling.

"More are coming," she said flatly, before firing off several more shots.

One of Jihan's soldiers appeared from behind a boulder, carrying a belt-fed. "Machine gun!" They were aware of our position now, but most of the fire they directed at us fell short. I didn't want them peppering us with a belt-fed. I put the crosshair on the machine gunner's chest and squeezed the trigger.

I missed. *Damn it!* I worked the bolt, got control of my breathing, and fired again. *Splat.* Down he went. *Fuck you, too.*

Ling changed magazines again. "Lorenzo has to move now, before we all get pinned down here."

I agreed, and grabbed the radio. "Lorenzo, listen up. This is getting worse every second. They just keep coming. You need to make your move, now. Get your ass up the hill. They're trying to surround the bomber now, and— shit!" We ducked down as rounds pockmarked the boulders we were using as cover. Splintered rock chips and snow rained down on us from the barrage of gunfire. I keyed the mike again. "They know where we are. We're taking fire. You need to move, *now!*"

There was a long pause before I got a response. My amplified hearing protection enabled me to make out a few pistol shots from Lorenzo's position, over the slow, steady snapping of gunfire from Jihan's forces. They were being smart, moving from cover to cover, and now applying suppressing fire against us.

"*I'm out,*" Lorenzo said. "*I'm out of ammo. Shit.*"

We had to duck back down as more gunfire peppered our position. "Lorenzo, just give me a second, I'll figure this out."

Another pause.

"*I'm not going to make it.*" His voice was flat.

"What? No, goddamn it, you move your ass and get up this hill!"

"*I can't.*" He sounded so tired. His voice wavered as he spoke. "*I don't know if I can even stand. There's no way in hell I'll make it up that hill.*"

Ling and I exchanged a glance.

"What . . . what do you want me to do?"

"*You guys have to go,*" Lorenzo replied bluntly. "*You have to leave me here. Get out of here before they get you too.*"

"I'm not going to leave you there, goddamn it!"

"*Yes, you are. You don't have a choice. There's too many. They're out for blood. If you don't get out of here, you'll die too.*"

Lorenzo was right. Ling placed a hand on my shoulder and nodded her head slightly.

Damn it, damn it, damn it. My mind raced, looking for a way out.

But there was no way. I had one round left for the .338, and Ling was running low too. There were still dozens of enemy troops down there, and they were all heavily armed. It was quiet. They were regrouping. I crept around the edge of the boulder. It only took me a second to find Lorenzo in the scope.

It was like he was looking right at me.

I took a deep breath and keyed the microphone.

"Lorenzo, if they take you alive . . . it won't be good."

Another long pause. "*I know.*"

"Do you want me to . . . I mean, I've got a clean shot. I have one round left . . . "

Ling's eyes went wide, but I ignored her and awaited Lorenzo's response. Killing him was probably a hell of a lot more merciful than letting Sala Jihan's fanatics get a hold of him.

Lorenzo let out a raspy, wheezing laugh into the radio. "*That would be funny, wouldn't it? After all this, you're the one who kills me. That'd be precious.*" He laughed again, like that was the funniest thing he'd ever heard.

I could see his face behind the crosshairs. I put my finger on the trigger. "Say the word."

He seemed to think about it. The interior of the bomber was splattered with his blood. "*You know what? No. Just get out of here. I'll take my chances.*"

"You sure?"

"*I am. Is Jill safe?*"

"She is. She's with the others. Reaper too."

"*Good. Do me a favor. Get her out of here. Get her far away from this place. Please.*"

"I . . . I will, Lorenzo. I swear."

"*Don't tell her what happened to me. If she thinks there's any chance I'm alive she'll try to come back for me. They'll get her too. Make something up, but don't let her come after me.*"

Ling took the radio from me. "Lorenzo, I'll tell Jill that you died a hero, so that others could live."

"*That's a little dramatic, don't you think?*"

Ling smiled sadly. "It's mostly true."

"*Heh . . . How about that?*" His voice had grown very quiet. "*I'm the hero. Never figured that's how I'd die.*"

Ling looked like she was going to cry.

"*One more thing, Valentine,*" Lorenzo managed. "*Find my brother.*"

"I'll try."

"*Okay,*" he hesitated. "*Now get the hell out of here. I'm turning off my radio.*"

"I'll see you around someday, Lorenzo."

"*So long, Valentine.*"

We left the heavy Sako rifle as we scrambled back up to road level. A few stray shots hit the rocks around us, but none of them were close. As we headed for the road, I could see the wreck through the trees. It was hard to tell, but it looked like Sala Jihan's soldiers were about to drag Lorenzo away.

"Michael, we have to go!" Ling insisted. I turned and left without looking back.

LORENZO

I dropped the radio on the bloody floor. It lay there in a pile of spent shell casings.

The soldiers were approaching cautiously. They could see that I was done.

Poor Jill . . . but she deserved a better man than me anyway.

My eyelids were too heavy. The world was getting very dark.

I could hear angry shouting, but I couldn't understand what they were saying. My chest was rising and falling. Rising and falling.

There was movement inside the plane. They were approaching cautiously. Someone squatted next to me. He was wearing a heavy coat and a fur-lined hood. Beneath the hood was skin as white as a corpse and two pitch black eyes.

"Greetings, son of murder. I warned you not to return." The devil turned back to his minions. "Take him."

A rifle butt smashed me in the face. Boots stomped on my ribs. Rough hands grabbed me and pulled me through the rust. I was lifted up and carried into the cold.

Gideon Lorenzo was standing in front of me, big, strong, and kind. Nothing like the broken, battered, dying shell I'd last seen on his death bed.

I felt him put his arm over my shoulder.

"*You were good, Hector. That's all that anyone could ever ask. We better get going.*"

Then the Sun was up.

It was morning.

VALENTINE
The Rendezvous Point

Ariel had told me that Lorenzo had been trying so hard to live a peaceful life, and Ling and I dragged him into this mess and got him killed. I didn't say it out loud, but we were both thinking it. I could see the pain on Ling's face.

We caught up to the other survivors at a predetermined rally point.

"I can't tell her, Michael." Ling rubbed her face with both hands. "I just can't."

Jill came running up as we got out of the truck. There was a flicker of hope as the doors opened. It was painful to watch it die. "Where . . . where's Lorenzo?" she asked. There was fear in her voice. Reaper stood a few feet behind her, not saying anything. "Val, where is Lorenzo? You said you were going to go get him!"

I steeled myself. "Jill . . . "

"No. No. Please." Tears welled up in her eyes. What little color there was on Reaper's pale face drained out.

I gently placed my hands on Jill's shoulders. "He's gone, honey. There wasn't anything we could do."

"Damn it, Val," Jill sobbed. She buried her face in my shoulder and cried, while hitting me with her fist. "Damn it. You said you'd bring him back. You *said*."

Reaper just sat down in the snow, not saying anything.

Ling spoke up, softly. "Lorenzo's action is what allowed everyone else to get away. These people owe him their lives, and we all owe him a debt of gratitude. His sacrifice was noble. I'm sorry for your loss."

Jill continued sobbing. I held her in my arms and wished like hell there was something I could say that would help.

"We need to get going," someone said. "The longer we stay here, the more likely it is none of us get out of here alive."

He was right. We had to go. But Jill needed a moment, and I was going to give her that moment.

"I'm sorry," I told her. The words sounded hollow and pathetic. "I'm sorry this happened. I wish there was something I could have done. But listen to me. We need to go."

Jill didn't move.

"Jill, Lorenzo made me promise that I'd get you out of here, you and Reaper both. So we need to get going right now. Don't make a liar out of me."

"He told you that? He thought about me?"

"Of course he did, honey. He loved you."

"Did he say that?"

"Yes he did," I lied. "Now come on, please, let's get out of here."

Jill collected herself, and shakily nodded her head. A cold wind blew through the mountains, and she shivered.

Epilogue: Finest Hour

VALENTINE
Exodus Safe House
Olgii, Western Mongolia
March 26th

The town of Olgii was less than a hundred miles, in a straight line, from The Crossroads. Even still, it had taken us hours and hours to get there on narrow passes and around mountains.

There wasn't much to the Exodus safe house. It was one of the bigger buildings in the remote Mongolian village; an old warehouse with snow drifted up against one side of it. Exodus personnel were, as Ling suggested, waiting for us. We pulled the vehicles around back. Medics rushed out with stretchers to carry the wounded. A few guards nervously kept their eyes open, afraid that Jihan's forces would appear out of the blowing snow. I couldn't shake the unnerving feeling that we weren't nearly far enough away from The Crossroads.

The inside was dimly lit, but plenty warm. One side of the main floor was set up as a small medical facility. The other had cots and blankets. They told us they were preparing a hot meal, which sounded good. I was starving. I felt disgusting, too, covered in sweat and blood, and wanted to take a hot shower if one was available. Both of those things could wait, though. I was completely exhausted. I had been running on adrenaline for far too many hours now, and I just could not go on. I found a cot in a dark corner of the warehouse, stripped off my boots and socks, and flopped down on it. I was asleep within minutes.

I awoke some time later. The howling wind outside rattled the old building. No light came in from small, high windows. It was dark out now. I'd slept through the entire day. Someone had been thoughtful enough to leave a big bottle of water next to my cot. A small crowd of Exodus personnel had gathered at the other end of the warehouse, like they were having some kind of meeting. I grabbed it and took a sip as I left my bunk to figure out what was going on.

A rough semicircle had formed around Ling, who had a printout in her hands. The Exodus members looked to her expectantly, even though she wasn't technically their leader. I didn't know where Fajkus was, or what had happened to Katsumoto. No one paid me any mind as I moved through the group, bare feet on the cold concrete floor, to hear what Ling had to say.

". . . have fully briefed the Council on everything that happened. In case anyone here hasn't heard the full story of what happened . . . we failed." The demeanor of the crowd darkened slightly, but Ling continued. "Sala Jihan lives. We few here are all that remain. Of those not with us, we don't know how many are missing and how many have died. It's . . . probably better to assume the worst."

Just like with Lorenzo, I thought bitterly.

"We have, however, arranged transport out of here. It will take them about twenty-four hours to get here, but they're sending an aircraft to Olgii to pick us up. This safe house will be abandoned, and no one else will be left behind here. We've left enough behind as it is."

The small crowd solemnly nodded in agreement.

Ling paused for a moment, trying to decide what to say. "I want . . . I want you all to hold your heads high. You all fought well. Be proud of that. For every one of us that fell, it cost the enemy twenty of his own. But I will be blunt, for you all deserve nothing but the truth, ugly as it may be. This is the worst defeat Exodus has experienced in any of our lifetimes. But such is war. In war, sometimes you win, and sometimes you lose. We have been bloodied, and we have been set back, but we are *not* broken!"

There were a couple voices of agreement in the crowd. Others nodded.

"Even in our darkest hour, do not give up hope. Do not give in to despair! Mourn the dead, but honor their sacrifice by finding the strength to carry on. For six hundred years, Exodus has stood alone against the darkness. For six hundred years, we have known victory and defeat, success and failure. Our order, our brotherhood, our fight continues, because our cause is just. We will recover from this setback. We will recover and carry on, learning from our mistakes and coming away better prepared than ever."

Ling had the crowd transfixed. Even as an outsider, I found her appeal to be moving. She was a much better leader than she gave herself credit for.

"The road ahead will be hard," Ling said, lowering her gaze slightly. Her dark eyes shimmered, as if she was fighting back tears. "We have all lost . . . so very much. But even on such a terrible day, let us not forget where we came from. Let us not forget why we do this, what we fight for. If we give up, if we say it's too hard, if we don't continue on, who will? Who will stand for the weak against the strong? Who will fight for the oppressed and the enslaved?"

There was no answer from the crowd.

Passion filled Ling's voice, giving it clarity and purpose. "Our work is just, and noble. Our work is necessary. We cannot turn our backs on it, even now. For if we give up, if we do not continue on . . . no one will. The cycles of suffering that we struggle to break will continue, and the world will grow that much darker."

Ling paused, taking a deep breath. Her voice was lower when she spoke. "You all fought magnificently. You are the finest men and women I have ever had the honor to serve with." A tear trickled down her cheek. "I am proud of you. I am proud to count myself as one of you. So please, hold your heads high." She fell silent, and quickly made her way out of the room.

A man stepped in where Ling had been standing, taking over from her. "Yes, thank you, Ling. Let us all take a moment to say a prayer for the fallen."

As the group bowed its head in prayer, I headed back to my cot to put my boots back on and find Ling. I wanted to make sure she was okay.

I found Ling outside, alone.

Mercifully, the howling wind had died down. The sky was overcast low, and the lights of the town gave the clouds an amber glow. Ling's breath steamed in the cold air as she stood, arms folded across her chest, staring into the distance. As I approached, I could tell she was crying.

I surprised her when I gently placed my hand on her shoulder. She turned to face me, with tears in her eyes. Ling then surprised me by wrapping her arms around me. She pulled me close to her, buried her face in my shoulder, and quietly wept.

Reciprocating her embrace, I held her tightly, and rubbed my hand up and down on her back. She squeezed me even tighter as she cried, struggling to regain her composure. I didn't ruin the moment by opening my stupid mouth.

After a little while, Ling looked up into my eyes, but didn't let go of me.

"Hey, you," I managed.

She sniffled. "I'm so glad you're okay. I just . . . I just couldn't bear it if I lost someone else I care about. I couldn't bear it. I'm barely holding on, Michael."

Looking down into her eyes, I agreed with her. "I know. It's been—"

My eyes went wide as Ling leaned up and kissed me, deeply, passionately. Her soft skin was hot against mine in the cold air. She pulled me tightly against her.

I didn't know what I was doing. I didn't think I was ready for this. I didn't know what 'this' even was. We were in shock, exhausted, both badly needed a shower, and had barely escaped with our lives. It was the worst time for something like this.

But God help me, it felt right. I held her tightly, reciprocating her embrace and her kiss. After a moment, we pulled apart. Ling's eyes were locked onto mine, studying my face for approval. I smiled at her, and she kissed me again. I held her close to me, closed my eyes, and for a wonderful moment, forgot all the horrors I'd seen.

The next morning found the Exodus safe house bustling with activity. It was only a matter of hours before the plane that was taking us away was to arrive, and Exodus was busy preparing to leave. Everything they couldn't take, they intended to destroy, leaving behind as little evidence as possible.

I barely saw Ling that morning. At first I was worried, wondering if she was avoiding me. Had we jumped the gun? Was she regretting kissing me? Did I take advantage of her? Did it get weird?

I saw her for the first time that morning when she came out of one of the back offices with Fajkus. At first she didn't acknowledge me, and I was concerned. But when her compatriot had his back turned, she looked over at me, dropped her professional demeanor for just a moment, and smiled at me. Then she winked at me, and a stupid grin split my face. As soon as Fajkus turned to face her again, the mask was back on, and she was as solemn as ever. I couldn't help but laugh at the rapid transition.

"How are you holding up, man?" It was Skunky. I was outside the safe house, getting some fresh air for just a moment. The air was cold and still. It wasn't snowing, but was still overcast, and thankfully the wind had quit. It was so cold out it froze your boogers right in your nose, though.

I turned my attention to my friend. "All things considered?" I asked, but just left it at that.

Skunky nodded knowingly. "What about your friends?"

"I don't know. They're both still in shock. Jill is . . . was . . . Lorenzo's girlfriend. Reaper's been with him for years. I guess another member of their team died in Zubara. You know how it is, man."

"Will they be okay? Do they have a place to go?"

"Are you kidding? Lorenzo practically owned an island in the Caribbean. He was loaded. They'll be fine, but money doesn't replace the man."

Skunky looked around the snow-covered valley that Olgii sat in. "What about you? Where are you going after this?"

I hadn't actually thought much about it. Now that it had been brought up, I didn't have a good answer. I just shook my head. "I don't know, man. I guess it depends on where Exodus drops me off. I don't know where I could go. It's not safe for me to go home. They're looking for me. The government, I mean. For all I know they have every federal agency looking for me.

Anyway the only place I could go in the States is Hawk's, and all I'd do is put him in danger. He already stuck his neck out too far getting involved in this."

"Have you . . . I mean, I don't want to sound like I'm pressuring you, or giving you the sales pitch, but have you thought about becoming a member of Exodus? You already know more about the organization than most of us do. You've been on our biggest op in living memory. There are plenty of us that would sponsor you in. You'd just have to, you know, take the oath and commit. We'd take care of you, though." Skunky lowered his eyes just a bit. "And we could really use new people right about now."

My friend had a look in his eyes that I hadn't seen since the debacle in Mexico, our last operation as employees of Vanguard. There was uncertainty in his eyes, even fear. I could see it on the faces of all the Exodus operatives. It was plain in how they carried themselves now, and in how they spoke. There was precious little laughter or joking. Their ridiculously high morale had been shattered. Those missing or dead would likely never be found, and never be giving a proper burial. It was heartbreaking to watch such a proud organization, one that I owed my life to, smashed like that.

As much as I liked them, though, and as much as I didn't want to disappoint Ling, I didn't feel that joining Exodus was the way I should go. They asked for my help, and I gave it. "I don't know. Let's wait until we get out of this godforsaken place before we start talking about my future. I need a vacation. I can't go back to Hawk's, but there's got to be somewhere I can go."

Skunky looked thoughtful for a moment. "Speaking of Hawk, have you contacted him at all? You just dropped off the map last year. He probably thinks you're dead."

I suddenly felt very guilty. "I wanted to call him when I was on Lorenzo's island," I said, "to tell him I was okay. But it would've put him in danger. They might be watching him, monitoring his phone. Hell, they might've picked him up. They fucked with my mind when they had me, man, drilled into my head. I don't know what all I told them. For all I know I betrayed Hawk and he's dead already." A pit formed in my stomach as I thought about it. *Oh God, what did I do?*

Skunky read the look on my face. "Listen, we have encrypted satellite phones. You can call him. The odds of them tracing the call are pretty slim, and even if they do, we'll be out of here in a few hours, and I'm pretty sure we ain't coming back."

"It's still risky. I'm sure your boss won't approve."

"I don't plan on asking my boss, bro." He retrieved from his pocket a Benchmade *Infidel* automatic knife. Each member of a Switchblade unit was issued one. "I was Switchblade 4 first. Knife check!"

Allowing myself to smile, I retrieved my own Benchmade and snapped the blade out. "Check!" We both chuckled.

"No time like the present," Skunky said. "Let me go get the phone." It turned out that Skunky's satellite phone was much nicer than any I'd ever used. I had to have him show me how to use it. "Do you remember Hawk's number?" he asked.

I thought about it for a second. "I think so. Hang on." I dialed the long sequence of numbers necessary to connect with a US phone number, pressed send, and waited. It rang several times, then stopped, beeping at me.

I showed Skunky the screen. "What's it doing?"

He squinted and looked at it. "They're requesting a video chat."

"This thing can do video chat? I bet that's expensive."

"Yeah. There'll be lag, too. Just 'press accept' and hold it a couple feet from your face."

I told Skunky to keep quiet while I was talking, and rotated the phone so that the only thing visible behind me was the wall of the warehouse. I suddenly had a bad feeling, and wanted to give as few visual clues to my location as possible. I took a deep breath, and pressed accept.

After a short pause, Hawk's face appeared on the screen. He looked like hell.

Oh no. "Hawk? Are you—?"

"Val?" he asked, sounding hoarse and raspy. "Goddamn it boy, you're dumb as a stump! Why the hell did you—" Hawk grunted in pain as someone punched him in the head. My heart dropped into my stomach. The phone on the other end was pulled back so I could see him, bound and handcuffed. A man in a suit pushed him onto the floor and kicked him in the stomach.

Somebody has Hawk! I mouthed to Skunky. His eyes went wide.

A new face appeared on the screen. I'll never forget it for as long as I live. He was an old man, with gray hair and hard lines in his face. His eyes were pale and piercing.

"Mr. Valentine," the man said. "We've been waiting for you to call."

"Who . . . ?"

He interrupted me. "Now you listen to me, boy. You have no idea the world of shit you're in. My name is Underhill. You know who I work for. I was retired up until about two weeks ago. They called me out of retirement and gave me every resource at their disposal for the sole purpose of finding you."

My eyes narrowed. "What do you want?"

"If you want Mr. Hawkins to live, you'll do exactly as I say. You will tell me where you are, and you will wait for me there, for however long it takes me to arrive. Then you'll come in with me, and we'll sort this whole thing out. If you refuse, I will kill this man, and I'll still find you. That part is inevitable, nonnegotiable. One way or another, I'm bringing you in. You only get to decide how much you, and Mr. Hawkins here, suffer before it's done."

Before I could answer, Hawk shouted to me. "Val! Don't listen to him, boy! I'm already dead! You run! You—" I couldn't make anything out for the next few seconds. The phone was tossed around so fast, with the lag, I couldn't tell what was going on. There was commotion, yelling, a fight. Somebody shouted at Hawk again.

"Fuck you!" was the old gunslinger's reply. Then a pair of gunshots, then silence.

I felt the color drain out of my face. I looked up at Skunky. His eyes were wide, and he covered his mouth with his hands, but he said nothing. My knees went weak. I wanted to throw up. I struggled to maintain my composure as my heart raced and my head spun.

After a moment, Underhill's face returned to the screen. He looked as ice cold as ever. "Mr. Hawkins is dead," he said flatly. "His choice, not mine. Now you have a choice, son. No one else has to die. Tell me where you are, and this all ends. If you don't tell me where you are, I will kill however many people it takes to get to you. Either way, I'll find you. So what's it going to be?"

My heart rate slowed. My senses were heightened. Everything slowed down just a bit as *the Calm* washed over me. My blood ran as cold as the arctic wind blowing against my face.

"I'll tell you how it's going to be, old man," I said slowly. "You people have taken everything from me. I have nothing left to lose. You won't have to find me, because I'm going to find *you*. I'm going to find you, Mr. Underhill, and I'm going to kill you. I'm going to kill *all* of you. That is a promise."

There was a pause from the lag of the satellite connection, before an unpleasant, predatory smile split Underhill's face. "We'll see about that."

I pressed the end button, hanging up before anything else could be said. Skunky stared at me wide-eyed as I slowly lowered the phone. My hands started to shake. My teeth ground together. An icy rage bubbled up from deep inside me.

This isn't over.

Peter Nealen is a former Recon Marine, a veteran of Iraq and Afghanistan, and has written both fiction and nonfiction, primarily on military subjects. He is the author of the American Praetorians thriller series, the Jed Horn supernatural thriller series, and the recent paramilitary thriller Kill Yuan. *This story marks his first time writing in two other authors' sandbox. This story is set within the time frame of* Alliance of Shadows. *It is part one of a two-part story series.*

Rock, Meet Hard Place
(Part 1)

by Peter Nealen

Jimunaizhen, North China

"Target is moving."

I took my hand off the sand sock that I had crammed up under the bolt gun's buttstock and picked up the phone. "Roger," I said, holding it up to my face, without taking my eye off the scope. Cell phones, even in this shithole, got lost in the traffic a lot more easily than tac radios.

"You know, I think I am going to get that Maserati," J.D. said. He was sitting at the table beside me, his own eye on the spotting scope. "It's just nicer than the Beemer."

I shook my head a little, without taking my cheek off the rifle. "Dude, you're Stateside, what, four weeks out of the year? When the hell are you going to drive the damned thing?"

"Hey, I've got a really small window to convince the high-end chicks that I'm the heat," he said. "The fancy car is a shortcut. Stateside women are all gold-diggers, anyway. This way I get to be picky." He laughed. "Besides, what else am I going to spend the money on?"

He had a point. I honestly didn't know what my bank account looked like at the moment; I hadn't been home in over a year. I was probably relatively rich. Our employers certainly paid well enough.

The equipment we were using kind of highlighted just how much money they were willing to throw around. I was sitting behind an AX50 rifle with an MP-7 PDW lying on the table next to me. J.D. was sitting behind a top-of-the-line Zeiss spotting scope, with his MDR bullpup leaning against the cinder block wall next to him. There were tens of thousands of dollars' worth of weapons, optics, and comm gear crammed into our little hide site.

Ten years ago, we never would have been using this stuff. Even when working clandestinely, where being seen means compromise, we'd still use mostly local weapons and gear. There was always that unlucky time where you get spotted, and if your kit looks like it doesn't belong there, people start digging. It screws with the deniability our employers prized so highly. Back then, you simply didn't see high-end gear in Xinjiang, much less high-end Western gear. But our employers had been funneling so much hardware into North China for the last decade that the only ones who *weren't* using NATO equipment anymore were the North Chinese People's Liberation Army itself, which was increasingly outgunned by the Triads in the east and Al Qaeda and their affiliates in the west.

"I think I've got the target," J.D. said, suddenly all business, his eye pressed to the spotting scope. "Three Yongshis passing the stadium; looks like one's a gun truck."

I shifted my position to bring the big sniper rifle to bear, peering through the scope. Sure enough, there were three of the boxy SUVs driving past the soccer field, which J.D. had generously called a "stadium." I didn't need to pick them out of traffic, either; out here in Bumfuck, Xinjiang, right across the border from Bumfuq, Kazakhstan, most traffic had been reduced to mule carts. The only other cars on the road were going to belong to the PLA, the Russian Mafia, the local Communist Party boss, or the Uighur militias that were getting a lot of support from AQ.

Helpfully, the target had a North Chinese flag fluttering from his antenna. The Commissar was the target; we weren't getting paid any extra for killing his escort, and clearing them out meant staying in place longer than I cared to.

The North Chinese had put enormous amounts of resources into fortifying and manning the DMZ along the Yangtze. It seriously dwarfed the standoff between North and South Korea, and rivaled the Great Wall itself. But they had used so much of their precious resources and manpower that the border with Kazakhstan might as well be wide open. So, naturally, our employers used that border to bring most of the disruptive stuff in, where it was sold to militias, organized crime groups, and whoever else might give the Reds heartburn.

At least, it may as well have been wide open, with the border guards waving convoys of trucks through while they counted the bribes the lead driver had handed over, until this little prick had come out and started getting efficient. He'd had an entire platoon of border guards shot the first week he'd been out on the border, and it had gotten a *lot* harder to get the goods over the line. So we'd been called in.

I already had the range marked, so I didn't have to do any range estimation. The vehicles were moving, though, so I still had to lead the target. I took a deep breath and let it out, settling into the gun, my finger already taking up the slack on the trigger as I searched the darkened windshield for the shape that would be the Commissar in the back seat.

He wasn't in the back seat, I realized suddenly. He was riding shotgun. So much the better, then. I had to shift my position a little, to get solidly behind the weapon as I got my lead, breathed one more time, and squeezed.

I've never shot a .50 that didn't feel like getting punched in the face when it fired, and the AX was no exception, even with the enormous muzzle brake that did a pretty good job of attenuating the recoil. The rifle bucked bruisingly against my shoulder, and I lost the sight picture momentarily.

J.D. hadn't, though. "Good hit," he said. "Took old boy right in the face. Hello, twenty-five grand."

"Time to go, then," I said, kicking back the chair I'd been sitting on and pulling the rifle back from the mesh-draped window. I had nothing against the Commissar's guards, and any further shooting was just going to draw them like flies anyway.

I hastily shoved the AX50 into its drag bag and slung it on my back, scooping up my MP-7 and making sure I hadn't dropped anything else. J.D. had already shoved the spotting scope in his day pack and slung his MDR. "After you," I said, pointing to the stairs. The mesh over the window could stay where it was. Taking it down was too likely to attract attention.

J.D. headed down the stairs, as I pulled the phone out of my pocket and sent a pre-loaded text to Ivan and Carlos. "Done," was all it said. They'd know to break down and head back to the safe house.

J.D. and I moved down the dim, dirty stairwell, J.D. keeping his rifle up as we moved. I took up security on the second floor landing as we passed it, letting him cover downstairs and to the front.

We burst out of a back door into an alley, where a dirty Dongfeng pickup was waiting, with Sergei sitting behind the wheel. I shoved the drag bag into the back seat and climbed in after it, while J.D. got in the front. Sergei already had us rolling by the time the doors slammed.

I'd taken the back for a reason; I had the MP-7, which was going to be a lot easier to maneuver if I needed to shoot Sergei in the head. Sergei was a Kazakh; he was also a *brodyaga* for Nursultan Kunaev, the mob boss who ran a cut of every smuggling route that came over the border near Lake Zaysan. Kunaev was a bastard's bastard, but Sergei, though quiet, had been a pretty good dude, so far. I'd still kill him in a heartbeat if I thought he or his boss were going to sell us out, and I was sure he'd do the same to us, but as long as our money was good, we'd get along fine.

He didn't drive for the border, but headed south, out of Jimunaizhen. We had our own little border crossing a few miles away, near Shali Haji, courtesy of our pal Kunaev.

Once we were out of town, I dug in my kit and came up with a pack of Sobranie Black Russians and a lighter. I rolled down the window a little before lighting up; J.D. didn't care for the smoke, but I needed some nicotine after that. I still didn't relax, exactly, as I puffed on the harsh cigarette, but then, I probably hadn't really *relaxed* in at least six years. You don't tend to relax much when you work for the kind of people we work for.

"You know," J.D. said, turning halfway around in his seat, "there are a lot more pleasant ways to kill yourself than smoking those nasty fucking things."

"I know," I replied. "I contemplate them every time you start hounding me to quit smoking."

He laughed, and we lapsed back into silence, hands on weapons and eyes out the windows, scanning the fields around us. We sure as hell weren't going to talk about anything more than banal superficialities around Sergei.

The border crossing was pretty straightforward. Hell, until our dead friend the Commissar had shown up, we could have just used the main road, the North Chinese border guards having been paid off handsomely to look the other way. We had to be a little bit more careful now, and the river crossing had needed to be concealed, but we still got across without too much trouble, and in a few minutes we were in Kazakhstan and making tracks for the safe house.

The safe house was an old farm out in the weeds; Ul'ken-Karatal was *way* too small a town for a bunch of strangers not to stand out like a sore thumb. Fortunately, there were enough ethnic Russians floating around that we didn't stand out like we might have in the Middle East. Granted, Carlos was brown enough that he might raise eyebrows; Kazakhs don't look much like Mexicans.

Sergei trundled the Dongfeng up to the whitewashed farmhouse and stopped with a squeal of brakes. J.D. and I piled out, dragging our gear with us, and I dropped an envelope fat with rubles in Sergei's lap. He picked it up, rifled through it, gave me a gap-toothed grin, and ground the pickup's gears into reverse before pulling out and leaving.

I was still tempted to move the safe house, since Kunaev knew where it was. So far, with the enormous amounts of cash our employers were willing to throw around to cover our operations and support, he'd left us alone. But a crook is a crook, and they all get greedy after a while. I should know; I'd spent most of the last decade working with crooks, rebels, terrorists, mercenaries, and all sorts of other unsavory types across Eurasia.

Dropping our gear in the entryway, J.D. and I set about checking the perimeter, making sure that none of either Kunaev's guys or the Kazakh NSC thugs had been poking around. By the time we were both satisfied that it was secure—it should have been, as the IED wired to our comms room door hadn't gone off—Ivan and Carlos were pulling up to the front door, Ivan's huge frame somehow squeezed behind the wheel of a creaking, rusty '79 Lada.

Ivan parked the car, levered himself out of the driver's seat, slammed the door hard enough to almost break the glass, snatched his gear out of the back seat before slamming that door almost as hard, and stalked inside. J.D. and I looked after him, then turned to Carlos, who had gotten out of the passenger seat rather more sedately. Carlos just shrugged.

"I don't know," he said. "He's in one of his moods again."

"Ivan is always in a mood," J.D. said. "I think it's part of his Russian genes or something."

"You could always try taking him on one of your hooker safaris," I suggested. "Might mellow him out a little."

J.D. gave me a look that suggested I was a complete idiot. "First of all," he said, "I don't use hookers." He waved to indicate himself. "You really think that *I* have to pay for it? No. Just, no."

"What about that Maserati?" I asked, following Carlos inside.

"That's for the American chicks, I told you," he replied. "It's a shortcut, not a payment. And second," he continued, undeterred, "there is no way I'm taking that misanthropic gorilla out to the clubs with me. I'm pretty sure he'd look at a girl, go into lock, drink three bottles of vodka and start a fight."

Considering that I'd first run into Ivan in the middle of one of the nastiest bar brawls I'd ever seen in Pavlodar, that was not outside the realm of possibility.

Carlos was just shaking his head. Ivan was in his room in the back of the house, doing brooding Russian things. The guy was the ultimate case study in disillusionment meeting clinical depression. He was damned good at his job, though.

I had more pressing matters to worry about than Ivan's mental state at the moment, though, namely getting paid. I knew Ivan would snap out of it eventually, whatever *it* was.

After carefully disarming the IED, I stepped into the windowless interior room that housed our comm setup, flipping on the light as I went. The single, bare light bulb hanging by its wiring from the ceiling illuminated one of the most high-tech comm setups Eastern Kazakhstan had ever not seen. The funny part was, if anybody outside of the team ever did set eyes on it, they'd think we were working for the CIA.

It didn't take long to get the VTC setup linked back to the office. For us, the "office" was a nondescript back room in an industrial park in Philadelphia. Most of the time. When we really needed to talk to the Office, well, that was different.

Ginger was staring at me through the screen, chewing her inevitable bubble gum. She had a real tendency to dress and act like a stereotypical early-'60s secretary, even though she was usually alone in the windowless closet she called her workspace. I knew for a fact that she was a lot smarter than the gum-chewing bubblehead she presented to the world, but the one time I'd said as much she'd just winked and shushed me. Given what we'd been up to the night before, I'd just smiled and nodded.

She wasn't wearing the airhead act this time, though. She stared out of the screen at me with a dead serious, one hundred percent professional look on her face. That didn't bode well.

"Frank," she said, "the Office called. They want to talk to you, five minutes ago."

I frowned. "Why? I didn't think Komrade Kommissar was that important."

"They didn't say," she replied, "but it sounded like a pop-up. It sounded serious, too."

I shook my head. "They should know better than to hit us with 'serious' without some sort of big number attached to it," I said. "But fine," I continued, when a worried look crossed her face. "I'll call 'em."

A look of relief crossed her face before she signed off. That was kind of worrisome. Generally speaking, our employers had been pretty good about keeping their distance. They got us the jobs, we executed them, we got paid. We tried not to ask too many questions. Knowing too much of the big picture tended to result in people, even contractors like us, mysteriously disappearing.

I knew that Ginger was worried that, just through sheer time on the job, we were getting too close to the threshold where they decided to make us vanish. They hadn't been as effective as they had been for seventy years by taking chances with leaks, that huge internet file dump on Operation Heartbreaker in Zubara notwithstanding. If anything, that had made our position that much more precarious.

I typed in the link to the Office. I didn't know where it was physically located, and I had no desire to know. We didn't keep the link anywhere on anything, and on the rare occasions that we had to use it, we were careful to wipe as much trace of it off the computer as possible. If it came to the possibility of the laptop falling into unfriendly hands—which pretty much meant anybody outside of the four of us—we'd destroy it first, making sure we got the hard drive. And we'd make sure we had proof of destruction if our employers asked for it.

The VTC link connected immediately, suggesting that somebody was just sitting there waiting for me to call in. Considering it was pretty early in the morning Stateside, that suggested that Ginger was right, and they were taking whatever it was really seriously.

I didn't recognize the face that appeared on the screen, which was surprising. Our employers liked to keep the stable of people who knew about the contract side of their operations small. This man had a shaved head and small goatee. He was lean, though there was a softness to him that suggested that he had spent the majority of his career at a desk. His next words suggested that my assessment was wildly erroneous, though.

"Mr. Dragic," he said, his voice dry, with a hint of a Midwestern accent, "my name is Forsyth."

That was chilling. I'd never met Forsyth, but the stories floating around among those in the know were not terribly pleasant. He had once been one of the top HVT hunters out there. In more recent years, as he got older, he tended to handle more . . . internal affairs. If Forsyth came after you, you were boned. If Forsyth took *any* interest in you at all, it probably meant you were boned.

"We have a mission for you," the man continued, even as I pulled out another Black Russian and lit it, trying not to let my fingers shake as I did so. I usually tried not to smoke in there; there wasn't really any ventilation aside from the door that was shut behind me. But I was talking to one of our employers' scariest errand boys. I needed the nicotine.

"Whoa there," I said, trying to maintain my tough-guy image and not let him see how much that name had rattled me. I was slightly relieved by the fact that they didn't want me to come in, but anything Forsyth touched was something I wanted to stay away from if possible. "That's not how this works. I work contract, and I pick the jobs you offer. I'm not one of your Dead Unit dupes. You ask, I say yes or no, you pay my price."

The cold-eyed man on the screen didn't change his expression one iota. "Yes, I'm aware of your rather unique arrangement," he said. That was bullshit; there was nothing unique about my little team of hitters. I'd been kicking around doing dirty deeds for these people for the better part of ten years. I'd linked up with other teams half a dozen times. And that wasn't even mentioning the Project Heartbreaker files. The Office had dozens of us running around the world, knocking people off to nudge events here or there. The Dead Units were the big offensives; we were the skirmishers. "And that arrangement depends on you maintaining your usefulness." That wasn't a subtle threat at all.

"There is a time-sensitive target that just popped up. It is considered of serious enough import that *all* available assets are being called in, even those that might be at some distance." A faint smile crossed his lips, that didn't extend to his dead, shark's eyes.

While I really didn't like the sound of that, I also realized that I'd probably blustered all I dared to. I looked at him through an eye-watering cloud of harsh cigarette smoke. "Who's the target?"

"Mr. Anders," he said.

That made me sit up and take notice. As bizarre as it might be to hear that

Anders, one of the Office's chief killers, was now an HVT, quite frankly it was like hearing that Christmas had come early to me.

He'd come out to Xinjiang with a few more of his high-speed, low-drag meatheads five years before. I'd had a five-man team at the time, and had been instructed to liaison with Anders. I'd done what they'd told me, even though a gigantic, blond mountain of muscle who looked like he belonged on a Wehrmacht recruiting poster didn't exactly blend in with the locals.

One of my guys, Imad, had been a Uighur and a Muslim. He was the best terp I'd ever worked with, and one of the best liaisons with the various Islamic groups that we interacted with in Xinjiang there had ever been. He knew every tribe, every clan, and he knew just whose ego to stroke to further work against the PLA. He was also what I called a jack Muslim. He drank, swore, and was one of the biggest porn hounds I'd ever seen. We were the only family he had; he knew that if AQ got their paws on him, he was just as dead as if he wound up in PLA hands.

Anders hadn't liked him. He made no secret of the fact that he didn't trust the "towel-head slope" and told me to kick him to the curb. I told Anders to pound sand; Imad was one of mine, and Anders didn't call the shots where my team was concerned.

Two days later we got ambushed. We never saw who it was; they shot at us and ran. They might have been one of the many AQ offshoots that had gained traction in Xinjiang the harder the PLA cracked down on the Uighurs. In the course of the ambush, Imad went down. He'd been shot in the back of the head.

I couldn't out-and-out prove it was Anders or one of his meatheads. There was no real court or chain of command to prove it to anyway. Anders all but dared me to do something about it. I swore then and there that one day I'd see him dead.

Maybe this was my chance. *If* it was legit.

"When did Anders wind up on the Office's target deck?" I asked, unsure that this wasn't some kind of elaborate loyalty test. It sounded too good to be true, and if it sounds too good to be true, then it probably is.

"Some time ago," he replied coldly. "You do not need to worry about the details. All you need to know is that he is a target, you are being hired to capture or kill him, and you need to get moving quickly." It wasn't an unfamiliar mission statement, except for the ID of the target.

"I take it you have some intel about his whereabouts?" I asked.

"Yes," Forsyth replied. "We have actionable intelligence that he is presently in Stepanakert." When I stared at him blankly, he supplied, "That's in Nagorno-Karabakh. Azerbaijan. At least it's still Azerbaijan officially. There's something of an ongoing ethnic war between the Azeris and the Armenians, and Stepanakert is right in the middle of it. Which is, we presume, why he's there.

War zones are notoriously good places to do business with the underworld, something with which, I am sure, you are quite familiar."

I was, but that didn't make this better. Azerbaijan was not our usual AO. It was most of a damned *continent* away. We had no contacts, no resources there. I said as much.

"Doesn't matter," Forsyth replied. "This is high priority, and we're calling in all hands. *All* hands. So that means that you pack your shit and get on the next thing smoking for Azerbaijan."

"How reliable is this report?" I asked, stalling for time. I *really* didn't like this. Whatever was going on—and I had no illusions that Forsyth was telling me the whole story—going half-cocked into a country I'd never worked in to pull a "Capture or Kill" mission was not my idea of a good time, or a good idea.

"Very," the man replied. "He's apparently now working as muscle for the Montalban Exchange, which means he hasn't just gone rogue, he's actively gone over to the Opposition."

I knew vaguely that the Montalban Exchange was involved in all sorts of underworld operations that our employers were always looking to counter, but the mysterious "Opposition" was something I'd never looked into that thoroughly. It all sounded like some kind of conspiracy theorist bullshit to me, anyway, cooked up to justify half of our dirty deeds in distant places. Sort of like the people who called our employers "Majestic." There were plenty of webs of criminals, terrorists, and rich people hiding the fact that they were criminals without some kind of big-time shadow-clash of massive conspiracies going on.

"How long has he been there?" I asked, stubbing out my cigarette and lighting up another one. The smoke was raw on my throat, but I'd been smoking Russian cigs for so long that American ones just seemed tasteless now.

"We don't know for sure," he replied. "Nor do we know how long they can be expected to stay there. We're not sure what the Montalbans are up to, but you should move quickly. I'm sending you a file with the locations where he may have been sighted, along with any other information we have on Anders and his movements."

I held up a hand. "Hold on," I said. "I'm sure you are already well aware of my past with Anders." He just nodded impassively. I'm sure they had an entire file on the incident. "There's still the matter of our fee."

He held up a piece of paper with a number on it. There were a lot of zeros after it. "Enough?" he asked.

I just nodded, taking another deep drag off the Black Russian. It was a good payday, almost enough to justify going halfway across the Eurasian continent to kill a very dangerous man. It was also enough to make me nervous about our future even if we did succeed. Our employers paid well, yes, but there were limits, and this was pushing it. Especially after what had apparently happened to Dead Six in Zubara, an offer that big had me looking over my shoulder.

"I'll need to discuss it with the team," I said, but he shook his head.

"Let's dispense with the free market bullshit," he said coldly. "This is a high value, time sensitive target. You do the job, you get paid, and the wheels keep turning. You turn the job down, or you hem and haw and make it clear to me that you don't have any actual intent to follow through with it, and your stock with the Organization fucking *vanishes*. And given your experience, Mister Dragic, that means that I will start to take a very personal interest in enforcing our non-compete agreement."

There comes a point where the bluster and the facade of being your own man has to give way to reality. We'd just passed that point. The truth of the matter was, as much as I had a bad feeling about attempting to pull a snatch and grab— or just an assassination, which would be fine with me—on unfamiliar territory, I really did want Anders dead, even more than I didn't want this cold-blooded bastard turning his baleful eye toward me and my team. So, as much as it galled me to be their dutiful yes-man, I just nodded. "Understood," I said, in as close to a tone of absolute professionalism that I could summon up anymore. "Send us any intel you've got, and we'll get it done."

He gave me the same thin, vaguely sinister smile. "The packet is already in your inbox," he said. "As is the contact to reach when the job is done." He started to reach up as if moving to cut the connection, then paused. "Mister Dragic?" he said. "Just so we're clear. Taking Anders alive would be preferable. There is information in his possession that the Organization is very interested in extracting. However, given that it is Anders . . . dead is almost as good."

"Roger that," I replied flatly. If they thought I was going to try to take that mutant alive, they were out of their damn minds. He nodded with a sly, knowing look on his face, and cut the connection.

My cigarette had burned down to my fingers. I crushed it out and immediately lit up another one before going out into the main room, rummaging through a cupboard until I found the fullest bottle of Stolichnaya in the house. Without a word, I popped the top and took a long, burning swig.

J.D. and Carlos watched me as I slugged back the vodka, exchanging a glance. Ivan was off being Ivan somewhere else in the house, but he'd be along as soon as I called him; moody he might be, but he was still a professional.

"That bad?" J.D. asked. "I was sure we whacked the right guy."

"We did," I replied, after coming up for air. "No, this is because of the new mission we just got handed to us. Along with a not-so-subtle hint that if we didn't do it, we'd be the next ones on the chopping block."

Eyebrows climbed. "That's a little unusual," J.D. said. Carlos just looked concerned. Usually the pay was considered enough. "What's the job?"

"Anders," was all I needed to say. Expressions hardened, and a dangerous, brittle edge entered the atmosphere in the little safehouse. The name even brought Ivan out of the back room, where he loomed in the doorway, his expression thunderous.

"He's apparently pissed off our employers," I continued, before any of the muttered cursing could gain any real volume. "Whatever he did, he's now on the target deck, and apparently there's a full-court press offensive to capture or kill him. And when I say 'full-court press,' I mean that we've been brought in to help. Whether we like it or not."

There was a note of enthusiasm and slight confusion in J.D.'s voice. "We get a chance to kill *Anders*? What's not to like?"

"Oh, I don't know," I retorted. "Maybe the fact that he's in fucking Azerbaijan, where none of us have worked in years, if at all. Not only that, but I don't like being railroaded. We've done everything these motherfuckers have asked for years, and demanded nothing but our paychecks. And now they want to threaten to put us on the target deck if we don't take this job."

J.D. looked a little taken aback. Ivan glowered. Carlos got quiet, his face very still.

I studied Carlos a little. The fact was, even though we'd worked together for close to five years, I still knew next to nothing about Carlos' life before I'd met him. He was a devout Catholic, which sometimes seemed a little strange in this business, but he'd told me that he justified it by the fact that most everybody we killed really had it coming, and that his prayer life kept him steady. But there were little hints that didn't quite fit; little reactions—like this one—that suggested that he hadn't always been as . . . centered. The clouded look in his eyes suggested that this was not the first time he'd been faced with a situation like this. Considering that even in my admittedly cynical view of the U.S. military, American soldiers were not really treated as expendable pawns, I had to wonder.

But Carlos' mysterious past was not our primary concern at the moment. "Something is very, very wrong," Ivan said, his existential moment apparently over with the onset of a new mission. "They would not make threats if they were not desperate. Anders was golden boy. If he has defected, is something more going on." Even though he was an American citizen and had spent twelve years in the Army, Ivan still had a pronounced Russian accent. I'm sure that all the time we'd been spending in Eastern Russia had contributed to it; I sometimes caught myself speaking English with a bit of an accent and even dropping articles every once in a while.

"Are we seriously considering *not* taking the job?" J.D. asked, looking around at the rest of us. "I mean, sure, there's a risk operating in a new place on short notice, and I'm sure that Ivan's right and there is something more going on. But I'd say that between our employers' potential displeasure if we don't do it, and the chance to finally give that psychopathic prick what he's got coming, that's two pros to one con."

I took a deep breath, took another fiery swing of vodka, sighed, and shook my head. "No, we're taking the job. Forsyth made it pretty clear that we're in the cold if we don't. Doesn't mean I've got to like it, but we need a flight west, pronto."

"I'll get on it," Carlos said, heading into our little comms room. He had been the only one not to weigh in on the problem. He was like that. He rarely said what was on his mind, and most of the time we had no idea what he thought of any of the stuff we did. He just did it, coolly and professionally, and rarely said a word about it.

Stepanakert, Nagorno-Karabakh Republic

The Stepanakert International Airport wasn't the smallest "International" airport I'd ever seen, but it was up there on the list. The single paved runway was in decent shape, though any painted markings had worn off a long time ago. The terminal wasn't actually that much bigger than the control tower, which was also part of it. The flag of the Nagorno-Karabakh Republic, which was basically the Armenian flag with a white chevron at one end, fluttered from the flagpole on top of the control tower. The green hills of this part of the Caucasus Mountains loomed above the terminal in the distance.

Wrangling a flight into an active war zone, even if it had been technically active for most of thirty years, had been an interesting trick. We'd ended up hitching a ride with a cargo flight that may or may not have been legit, ostensibly running medical supplies into Stepanakert from Astrakhan. I was pretty sure that the pilot was, if not drunk, at least heavily fortified with vodka, and the An-24 he was flying had clearly seen better days. Fortunately, it was a Russian bird, so it could still fly with a bunch of parts missing and fluids leaking everywhere.

I stood up, still having to hunch over in the cramped cabin, and tried to work a few of the kinks out. It hadn't been a straight flight; we'd had to go an extra hundred miles to the west to make sure we stayed away from the front line between the Nagorno-Karabakh Armenians and the Azeris. That front line had apparently been fluctuating more in the last couple of months than it had in the last five years, which was probably part of why Anders was hanging out in Azerbaijan.

The plane rolled and rattled to a stop on the crumbling apron, and we shouldered our relatively small packs and filed off once the crew chief, whom I was pretty sure *was* drunk, opened the door and let down the steps. Since we weren't sure what we were going to run into in the way of Customs officials, not to mention the Nagorno-Karabakh Defense Army, we hadn't brought a lot of gear. We were going to have to obtain most of our weapons and kit on the ground. Fortunately, Forsyth's briefing packet had included the locations of a couple of caches that should have most of the weapons, ammo, and gear we'd need. I supposed it was the least they could do, given how they'd been jerking us around so far. We hadn't even gotten any assistance on transportation.

I'd definitely be billing the office for the fat bribe we'd paid the Antonov pilot.

As we walked down the stairs, I couldn't help but notice that the airport looked, well . . . dead. There was a single short-range jet parked on the apron, and it looked like it had seen better days. I couldn't see anyone working, either; no ground crew, no baggage handlers, nothing. I glanced back at the Russian crew chief, who just grinned. Apparently, we were lucky to have been able to fly in here at all. The briefing packet had said something about lots of trouble about flights into and out of Nagorno-Karabakh, but I'd kind of skimmed over that part, and when we'd found a pilot willing to fly into Stepanakert, we'd jumped at it without asking too many questions.

There were also no cars waiting in the parking lot. Which meant we had a problem.

Chagrined, I turned back to the crew chief. "Is there some way to get ride into town?" I asked in Russian.

He grinned again, even wider. "Our friends will come for cargo soon," he said. "You can ride with us, maybe buy car in town."

From the looks of his grin, it was going to cost us even more rubles or dram. Fortunately, our employers have a tendency to throw money around like confetti, so we usually had a pretty sizable bribery budget. I just nodded, unable to keep some of the disgust off my face, wondering just who this Russki smuggler was going to tell about us before all was said and done. We'd have to sweep any vehicle we bought from these people *very* thoroughly, and take a good half a day to make sure they weren't following us before we found a safe house. It was somewhat contrary to the time-sensitive nature of the mission that Forsyth had gone to such lengths to stress, but fuck him, he wasn't the one out here with his ass in the breeze. Let these fuckers sell us out to Anders, and we were screwed before we'd even gotten started.

But if there was one thing I'd learned over most of a decade working in shitty, chaotic parts of the world with a lot of shady people, it was that you just smiled, nodded, looked for trouble, and stayed patient. So we settled in to wait for the Russians' contacts.

The safe house was a small, red-roofed cinderblock house with the whitewash peeling off the walls, surrounded by ancient oak trees and what looked like half a century of fallen leaves and weeds. The Office hadn't provided any prep for it, so we had to settle for renting the place from the Russians we'd hitched a ride into town with. If it wasn't bugged, I was sure that it would be under surveillance. We'd booby-trap the hell out of it the first chance we got. We had barely gotten inside when the phone rang.

I just looked at it for a moment. We'd been working our asses off to shake any surveillance that the Russians might have planted on us, dig up the weapons cache—which was now scattered across the floor, a combination of AKMs and AK-74s, AKS-74U Suchkas, Makarovs, Tokarevs, and an RPD, along with ammo, magazines, and chest rigs for same—get to the safe house, and unload our shit into it to start prepping. I was pretty sure that it was Forsyth on the phone, and I wasn't eager to spend time talking to him.

But the alternative could be worse. Our employers didn't like to get blown off. I answered the phone. "What?" I asked, by way of greeting.

Forsyth was about as pleasant. "Are you on the ground?"

"Yes," I replied. "We're starting the planning and prep." I left the *and you're wasting my prep time* part out.

"Will you be ready to move on the farm tonight?" he asked.

Are you fucking kidding me? "We just got our base of operations set up, hopefully without the Russians or Armenians knowing about it," I replied. "We haven't done any reconnaissance on the farm to make sure that he's there, or get a good idea of the layout and possible opposition. These things don't happen with a snap of your fingers, you know."

"You have the imagery and the briefing packet," he said. "There isn't time to fuck around."

I bit off the acid retort that his words deserved. What kind of amateurs did he think he was dealing with? That was a bit of a rhetorical question; the Organization had never shown a great deal of regard for its subcontractors, even the ones who had been working for them for years.

"Rushing this sort of thing gets people killed, and gets missions botched," I told him, trying not to sound too much like I was lecturing a twelve-year-old. "How can we even be sure that Anders is there? There aren't any photos in the briefing packet; we have to get eyes on to confirm or we're going to miss him and he'll be gone."

"We have enough indicators to be eight-five to ninety percent certain that he's there," Forsyth said impatiently. "If he moves, we will let you know. We don't have time to do this the traditional way. Get your weapons and gear prepped, and hit that farmhouse tonight." He hung up.

I stared at the phone in a mix of disbelief and fury, then tossed it on top of my pack in disgust. As tempting as it might have been to throw it against the wall, I wasn't pissed off enough to do something that stupid.

The other three were watching me, though Ivan kept loading AK mags, his fingers pushing the rounds in with a mechanical regularity, as if he was a machine. J.D. was frowning. Carlos was as impassive as ever, though there was a hint of concern in his eyes.

"Forsyth is insisting we go tonight," I told them. "He says that they are certain that Anders is there, and that we should have enough from the briefing packet to launch. He tells me that if he moves, they'll let us know."

"What?" J.D. snarled. "They've got surveillance on this asshole, and they're just now telling us?"

"That's presuming that they actually have surveillance on him," I pointed out, "and they're not going off of some electronic chicken entrails and trying to bullshit us. Either way, Forsyth doesn't seem to be too inclined to brook any delay. As much as I don't like it, we're going to have to move fast, because I don't want my head in the Organization's crosshairs." I took a deep breath, then checked my watch. "Offhand, that gives us about four hours to get a general CONOP set up and try to do at least a drive-by recon. We can't do anything in-depth, but hell, it won't be the first time we've had to do things on short notice."

J.D. was fuming. Ivan just turned back to loading mags. Carlos shook his head as he finished going over his RPD. It was going to be a long one.

Ivan, J.D., and I slipped through the trees, moving toward the target house. Carlos had split off earlier to set up a combination of overwatch and base of fire on the house. Being the smallest guy on the team, naturally he had just sort of ended up with the RPD.

The rest of us were going to execute the actual hit. We were all dressed similarly, in camouflage that looked like some sort of Flecktarn knockoff, canvas AK chest rigs, and carrying the two AKMs and one AK-74 that had been hidden in the cache. We'd unanimously left the Suchkas behind; they may look cool, but if you're hoping to hit anything past a hundred yards, good luck. Even the Spetsnaz didn't like those things.

The house was dark, though we'd seen the flicker of a flashlight through the trees some time earlier. We had briefly considered simply driving up to the door, piling out, and kicking it in, but with Anders involved, that idea hadn't lasted more than a minute. Anders would have some kind of security out, and booby traps were definitely a possibility as well. So we'd stay nice and quiet and sneaky, up until it was time to go loud.

We kept a fairly tight formation, mainly because there hadn't been any night vision in the cache. I had no idea how old it was, but I suspected it was mid-Cold War old.

There was enough illum that we could just see the whitewashed walls of the house through the trees ahead. It was a long, low, one-story farmhouse, not dissimilar to our safe house in Ul'ken Karatal. There were a few outbuildings under the trees near it, including what had looked like a garage to the north on the overheads.

I was keeping my eyes peeled for sentries as we approached. It was a cool night, but my hands were sweating on the AKM's Bakelite grip and forearm. My heart rate was a little elevated, and I was trying to look into every shadow at once. That happens when you're on a half-baked, rushed op with three other dudes in unfamiliar territory, trying to hunt down one of the nastiest killers you've ever seen.

I took a knee next to a towering oak only a few paces from the house. So far, I'd seen no movement, no lights, no nothing. The place looked deserted. Given how much I trusted the intel from our employers, it might well *be* deserted. But I also knew that if there was a chance that Forsyth was right, and Anders *was* there, getting overconfident and sloppy would mean we wouldn't see the dawn.

Ivan and J.D. had joined me at the tree, spreading out around it to cover our six as well. I brought the compact little ICOM radio up to my lips and keyed it, my voice barely above a whisper. "Any movement?" I asked.

"No movement that I can see," was Carlos' reply. "There are two vehicles parked out front. There's another one sitting at the Y down south, too. I can't see if there's anyone in it, but it looks wrong. It's out of place."

I clicked the mic twice to acknowledge. I didn't want to talk too much that close to the target house. If anything, a suspicious vehicle nearby served as a positive indicator that this might be the right house, after all. I just hoped that we hadn't been spotted by anyone sitting in the vehicle with a belt-fed.

After another couple of minutes watching and listening, I started to get up. If there was a lot of security in there, they were inside, waiting for somebody to kick the door in. Or they were asleep. Either way, we couldn't wait any longer. It was go time.

The AKM up in the low ready, J.D. and Ivan flanking me a step behind, I flowed toward the back door. I kept the muzzle generally pointed toward the far corner of the building, except when I had to cross a window. There were two before we reached the door, and I quickly pied them off, covering every angle inside with my muzzle as I walked past, before snapping back forwards when J.D. moved up to take over for me. The maneuver was mostly pointless, since the interior was pitch black. But old habits can be a hell of a thing to break, and that's one that's saved my life a few times.

Getting to the door, my focus narrowed. I pointed the AKM just above the door handle, even as I reached forward to test the latch.

It was unlocked. I carefully turned the handle, and tried to ease the door open. I wanted to stay soft for as long as possible.

The door creaked loudly, as if the hinges hadn't been greased in years. There went staying soft. I flung the door open and stepped through the threshold, stepping aside as fast as possible to clear the way for Ivan, even as I triggered the flashlight taped to the rifle's forearm, scanning for threats.

The back hallway was empty. Flashlights played over bare plastered walls and a stone floor. There was no sound except for our own movement and harsh breathing.

Now that we were inside, we didn't dare stop moving. Hallways are deathtraps, and I had no intention of staying in that one for more than a few seconds. I swept forward, gun up and watching the three doorways ahead.

There were curtains over the one to the front and the left. So I went right, pausing just long enough to get a bump from either J.D. or Ivan behind me before charging into the next room.

It was a kitchen, dominated by a large hearth with iron racks for cooking bolted across the deep fireplace. There were hooks set into the wall above the hearth, and there were shelves made of old wood and brick along the far wall.

There were also two Russian 152mm howitzer shells sitting upright in the fireplace in a tangle of wires and det cord, with a cell phone sitting on top.

"Avalanche!" I bellowed. It wasn't original, but it was the standard code word in the U.S. mil that we'd all trained with for, "There's an IED, get the fuck out!" I suited actions to words by promptly diving through the window in a shower of glass and broken window frame.

Well, it was sort of a dive. It wasn't nearly as graceful as the word makes it sound. I kind of went through the glass shoulder-first, cut myself, lost my balance, and fell out of the window. I hit heavily and off balance, knocking some of the wind out of myself, only made worse when Ivan's big ass landed on me, followed by J.D.. J.D. wasn't as heavy as Ivan, but it still hurt.

Both of them rolled off, and I levered myself to my feet, painfully, but probably a lot faster than I would have under different circumstances. I wanted away from that bomb disguised as a farmhouse, *right fucking now*. Wheezing, favoring my side, which twinged painfully when I tried to take a deep breath, I started jogging away from the house, with Ivan and J.D. on my heels. I wasn't moving *that* slowly, but between the pain of my rapid exit and the desperation of having a whole lot of high explosive right behind me, it felt like I was swimming through tar, even as we plunged into the trees.

Just because we were running for our lives, though, didn't mean I'd dropped all semblance of situational awareness. I'd survived too long in too many dangerous places. So I saw the figures moving up through the woods even as we ran toward them, and instinctively slowed, bringing my rifle up. Then the house blew up behind us and knocked me on my face.

Fortunately most of the blast went up, throwing cement, stone, wood, and sheet metal high in the air. We were still close enough to catch a good bit of the shockwave, though, and more fragments were flying through the air and smacking into the tree trunks. It was momentarily raining debris, bark, and shredded leaves, and my ears were ringing as I picked myself up off the ground, feeling like I'd just been hit by a truck. I'd still had my AKM's sling around my neck, so I hadn't lost it, though I still had to grope for the controls as I got up, pointing it vaguely toward the team that had been coming at us. I didn't know who they were, but the odds were good that they weren't on our side. The only person on our side who wasn't within arm's length of me at the moment was Carlos, who wasn't exactly in a position to intervene, being some two hundred yards away on the wrong side of the farm.

I couldn't see much in the dark, especially with the pall of dust and smoke from the explosion that was settling over the woods. But I could just make out the shapes picking themselves up off the ground, a little faster than we were managing. We'd been closer to the blast. I didn't want to just start hosing down the woods without knowing what my targets were, but we were not in a good place. I brought the rifle to my shoulder, trying to focus on the sights, though this was going to be point shooting more than anything else.

I still hesitated. I just couldn't see. Decades of conditioning were cautioning me about shooting at any target I wasn't sure of. So I held my fire, even as the dark shapes of men started to approach out of the shadows and smoke. J.D. and Ivan would follow my lead; neither one was easily stampeded, as much as J.D. might seem a little hyper from time to time.

Four figures loomed out of the dark. Two of them were big dudes, the lead one carrying what looked like a G3, which was presently pointed in my general direction. Which was a problem, except that I had my AKM pointed at his face at the same time.

I couldn't see many details in the dark, but I could tell that this was no Armenian militiaman. I didn't know what kind of people Anders had around him, but the general circumstances suggested that he was either one of Anders' or he was competition. If he was competition, I really didn't want to shoot him. Okay, maybe I wanted to shoot him a little bit.

Before either one of us could decide whether or not to pull the trigger, a long burst of machine gun fire from the north ripped through the trees, driving us all back into the dirt.

It was really turning into that kind of night.

In moments, at least two more guns had opened up, rounds going past overhead with hard, painful *snaps* and smacking into trees with heavy *thuds*. They were hitting close enough that they had to have some pretty good night optics; they weren't just hosing down the woods.

Flat on my belly, I scrambled behind a tree, which promptly started getting chewed up by bullets. Green tracers were skipping by, and, in a rather surreal moment, I saw one only a few feet in front of me spinning on the ground, like some kind of deadly firework.

Looking to my right and left, I saw that Ivan and J.D. had managed to take cover, though J.D. was holding his arm as if he'd gotten hit. We had a momentary breather, but it couldn't last. We were pinned down, with little hope of suppressing machine guns with our little 7.62x39 rifles, and it was only a matter of time before more shooters closed in under cover of that withering storm of metal and finished us off. We had to get out of there.

Looking toward the unknowns that we'd almost started shooting at before the machine guns opened up, I could just make out their shapes huddled behind trees and flat to the ground, not unlike us. Whoever they were, they weren't on Anders' side. Either that, or Anders' mooks were way more incompetent than I had any business hoping.

Getting Ivan's and J.D.'s attention, I pointed to the south, the way we'd come and, helpfully, pretty much straight away from the machine gun fire. Fire superiority was out, so we were going to have to break contact the old-fashioned guerrilla way. We were going to have to get down in the dirt and do a lot of crawling.

Gripping my rifle with one hand, I managed to turn myself around even in the very, very small space that constituted the slowly eroding cover of the tree I was huddled behind, and started skull-dragging my way away from the fire. Rocks and roots dug into my cheek and hands, and leaves and grass seemed to slip and slide under my boots as I pushed and dragged myself over the ground, but as much as high-crawling might have been easier, the continued hiss and snap of rounds going by all too closely overhead was a great reminder of why that would be a bad idea.

The canvas AK chest rig that's been ubiquitous in the Eastern Bloc since the rifle first entered service with the Soviets is a thin, minimalist piece of gear, that doesn't add much bulk beyond that of the magazines themselves. It was still lifting me way too far up off the ground, especially as I actually *felt* a round go by only inches over my head.

Inch by inch, yard by painful yard, we got some distance. After a while, the machine gun fire let up, and I could hear a few voices calling back and forth in Russian from back by the wreckage of the target house. Somehow, I didn't think that they were the unknowns we'd almost collided with; either they were dead or they'd evaded like we had. At that moment, I didn't care.

A painfully long five hundred yards away, I finally got up on a knee behind a tree. There was a fair bit of forest between us and the flashlights that were now shining through the trees near the ruins of the target. We weren't safe yet, but we had some cover and concealment. I lifted my radio and called Carlos.

"Carlos, we're clear, break off and meet us at the rally point."

No reply.

I checked the radio as best I could in the dark. It was on, and I was pretty sure it was still on the right channel. "Carlos, this is Frank. If you can hear me, get to the rally point. We're moving now." There was still no answer, but we couldn't stay where we were, and trying to get to Carlos' position would mean crossing an open field and exposing ourselves while still well within the effective range of those PKMs or whatever the machine gunners had been shooting at us.

A Russian-accented voice came over the radio. "Hello, Frank. I am afraid Carlos cannot answer. Do not worry, though. You will see him very soon."

With a muttered curse, I switched the radio off. There would be time to mourn Carlos, and plot vengeance for his death, later. I couldn't afford to forget that we were still in a very bad tactical position, and we needed to get out of it without doing anything stupid, or we'd be just as dead as Carlos.

We were far enough from the enemy that we could start moving somewhat normally. Of course, with the NKDA everywhere, we'd have to be even more careful getting back into town and to the safe house with our camouflage and hardware. Everyone within twenty miles would have heard that shitstorm.

But that would come later. Our rally point was out in the weeds, for obvious reasons. Getting to my feet, I led out, rifle at the ready. J.D. and Ivan fell in behind me silently.

None of us said a word, but we knew each other well enough not to have to. There was a lot of retribution brewing for the disaster that this night had turned into.

It was morning by the time we got back to the safe house. We'd had to dodge several NKDA patrols, who were predictably stirred up by the explosion and the gunfire. They were far too close to the front line to take a roaring gunfight right outside the Nagorno-Karabakh Republic's capitol city lightly. We'd had to stash the weapons and gear under the seats of the old, broken-down UAZ that we'd paid entirely too many dram to the Russians' contacts for, and even stripped down and stuffed our filthy cammies in over them, donning simple work clothes in their place and frantically trying to scrub the camouflage face paint off.

If we had gotten stopped, we'd probably have been screwed. We were pretty obviously not locals, and not Russians, which would have immediately put us under suspicion. But we had managed to get into town and to the safe house before the mad scramble had managed to lock down the streets. The Armenians weren't quite the most professional or quick-reacting army I'd ever seen, and that worked in our favor.

We dragged the gear inside in a couple of duffel bags, dumped them on the floor in the kitchen, and stood around the table for a moment. Nobody said a word for a long time.

"I don't suppose there's much of a chance we could retrieve his body?" J.D. asked.

I just shook my head. Any chance at it would almost certainly be a trap. That Russian bastard was trying to goad us into doing something stupid on the radio; he could probably be trusted to be waiting for us to try something like that.

It was something we'd all had to come to terms with, over the years. We were mercenaries working for a shadowy, pseudo-governmental paramilitary/spy organization, in various places where Americans in general usually weren't welcome, never mind well-armed paramilitary operatives. If things went sideways, nobody was coming for us. If we went down, we'd be buried where we fell, if we got a burial at all. It sucked, but it was the nature of the game.

"So, what do we do now?" Ivan asked. "Element of surprise is lost. And now there are only three of us."

"I'm not sure we ever really had the element of surprise in the first place," I said. "That was an ambush, no two ways about it."

"You think someone leaked that we were coming?" Ivan asked.

"Possible," I said. "More likely, to my thinking, is that Anders dangled it in front of our employers to draw out anyone hunting him."

"And just our shit luck," J.D. put in, "that the Organization sent a handful of expendable contractors to do the job."

"Maybe," I said. I was getting a bit of a nasty suspicion about the whole thing. J.D. looked at me and frowned.

"You think that Forsyth sent us in there to hit the tripwire for him?" he asked quietly, after a moment.

"I think it's entirely possible," I replied. "It would go a good way toward explaining his insistence on haste and as little preparation as possible. Though I don't know why they felt the need to drag us halfway across the continent for it."

"Question still stands," Ivan said. It must have been the strain; his accent had gotten *really* thick, even while his voice was as stolid and unemotional as ever. "What do we do now?"

"It might be a good time to start looking at one or another of our fallback options," J.D. mused.

"We'd have to be damned good and sure that our employers think we all died," I pointed out. "And that's pretty hard to do. Remember Tarasov?"

Nikolai Tarasov had been one of our targets, a Mafia *Avtoritet* who had done a lot of work through the Crossroads. The Organization had marked him, and he had apparently been assassinated in Vladivostok. Except that he'd faked it, and somehow the Organization had tracked him down and put us on him. We'd found him in the Crossroads, followed him to Belyashi, and put a bullet in his head behind a barn that had looked like it belonged in the tenth century. The Organization had ways of finding people. And if we all vanished at this juncture, Forsyth was likely to get suspicious and start digging. "Live and let live" was not in the Organization's vocabulary.

"We don't have the resources here to pull a vanishing act," I pointed out. "And on top of that, we don't just have Forsyth to worry about. Anders and whoever that Russian bastard was know we're looking for them now, and they'll be looking for us."

"Not to mention whoever the hell that other team was," J.D. pointed out.

I looked over at him. So, I hadn't been the only one to notice that they didn't fit. A small team moving toward the same target we'd been after, that had been taken under fire by the same machine gunners who had been trying to kill us. Again, unless Anders' mooks were way, way more incompetent than I thought they were—and nothing about that ambush suggested that they were—those guys were working for somebody else. The only question was, who?

Then I shook my head. They were the least of our worries. My guess was that they were another team sent after Anders, which made them competition, but not necessarily more of a threat than that. "We'll keep an eye out for them, but we've got bigger fish to fry. Obviously, the intel Forsyth gave us was crap. We lost Carlos, and Anders now knows we're here. Which means he's going to be hunting us, not to mention the fact that the NKDA is going to be on heightened alert after last night. We try to run, we're probably going to get rolled up, especially if we try to fly—presuming that the same Russians who flew us in here aren't in cahoots with the Russians that Anders had waiting in the trees.

"I think our best bet is going to be to lie low and watch for an opportunity to ambush Anders, take him on the move. If we can take him out, Forsyth might just send enough support to get us out of here in one piece."

"You really believe that?" J.D. asked.

I sighed. "Not really," I admitted, "but it's a chance."

The phone rang. I'd actually been expecting this earlier. When I looked at the number, it was simply "Unknown," but I knew who it was.

"Your intel was shit," I said, as soon I answered, without giving Forsyth time to say anything.

"Hardly," he said dryly, apparently unfazed by my attitude. "If it had been, you'd have found nothing but an empty house. It's evident that you're on the right track."

"So, you *were* watching."

"Of course," he replied. "We've had assets overhead ever since we determined that Anders was in Stepanakert. We saw the whole little drama, in real time."

I bit off a bitter curse. They'd been sitting, fat and happy and safe, probably in some trailer in Nevada or somewhere, watching while Carlos died.

"Do you have anything useful for me," I asked tightly, "or is this just a reminder that you're watching?"

"Consider it touching base, and an assurance that you're not on a wild goose chase," he answered coolly. "I'm not calling the op off, if that's what you're hoping. However, check the email I sent the briefing packet to. I've attached some of the overhead footage." I grimaced. We could watch Carlos die, since we hadn't seen it on the ground. "That other group on the ground is a concern."

That got my attention. I'd presumed that if they weren't Anders' people, they must have been sent by the Organization. It would fit the "Need To Know" Nazis not to tell us about a backup team.

"I thought they were another team you'd sent," I said. "You did say that this was an 'all hands' evolution." Ivan and J.D. traded a glance before going back to watching me, Ivan impassive, J.D. with one eyebrow raised.

"Negative," Forsyth said, ignoring my thinly veiled jab at our lack of support out here. For full court press, we were awfully alone, suggesting that more than just the intel Forsyth had given us was bullshit. "We don't know for sure who they are, though there are a couple of possibilities. We need you to keep an eye out for them. If they know about Anders, they might present a security leak that we need to plug as soon as possible. They are not your primary target, but if you can find out any information about them, we need to know."

Well, that's just plumb gracious of you, I thought viciously. My team down by a quarter, not a word of condolence or promise of support, just another target to add to the deck. *Asshole.*

"Can we expect any more in the way of support?" I asked, trying to unclench my teeth before asking. "If you were watching, you know that we're down a man."

"And that's unfortunate," Forsyth said, utterly without feeling, "but at this time, we can't send anyone. Nagorno-Karabakh is getting more non-permissive. The Russians are starting to take a more active role in supporting the Armenians, and that means more eyes that could compromise us. Best to keep the footprint small." A sarcastic edge entered his voice. "You should be fine, Mr. Dragic. I've read your file. You're a professional, after all." He hung up before I could even ask for any additional information.

"Cocksucker," I muttered, as I resisted the urge to throw the phone against the wall. If he was watching from his eye in the sky, he had to know more about Anders' movements than he'd told us. If that file he was supposedly sending didn't have that info, when this was all said and done, scary reputation or no, I was going to find Forsyth and put a bullet in him.

The imagery wasn't nearly as helpful as we might have hoped. The drone operator had tried to keep eyes on both the ambushers and the other mystery shooters, and as a result, lost both of them within a kilometer of the target site. The ambushers looked like they were heading in our direction, while the mystery shooters had headed for the hills to the northeast.

That was interesting. While I wasn't shifting fire—Anders and the Russian on the radio were still my main focus—that told me that they were either camping out in the woods or they had more resources in the area than we did. Or maybe they had a safe house with some distance from Stepanakert, which, given more time to prepare, I might have done as well.

Leaving them aside, we were reasonably certain that Anders' people had gone into the southwest portion of the city. Somewhere. There were actually two semi-intact villages spread over the hills to the south, Kerkicahan and Haykavan. I say semi-intact because we'd all noticed that there were a *lot* of ruins scattered around Stepanakert. How much was because of shelling during the war, and how much was because of the Armenians ethnically cleansing the Azeris from the region, I didn't know. At that point in time, I didn't particularly care. The ruins might make decent observation sites, and probably wouldn't make for very good safe houses. We might be able to use them for recon, and we could probably safely write them off as Anders' local base of operations.

We'd start recon that afternoon, after we got a few hours sleep.

Even with only Ivan and me in the canvas-topped UAZ 469, dressed in the dark clothes that seemed to be the most common in the area, with the Suchkas under our seats, trying to stay low-profile in Kerkicahan was not an easy task.

The UAZ was a large part of the problem. While there were still a lot of ruins around the outskirts, central Stepanakert itself was a pretty modern city, with high-rises, parks, paved streets, sidewalks, and plenty of cars. Kerkicahan, while just outside, was an old-world village, not that far removed from the Middle Ages. The roads were unpaved dirt, most of the houses standing were stone or brick, though most of them had been re-roofed with corrugated sheet metal, and internal combustion engines were about as common as electricity. I saw a few carts and a few donkeys, but this place was Afghanistan poor. It wasn't all that strange to us; we were used to working in some of the poorest, shittiest parts of Eurasia. But it made it difficult to cruise the roads looking for a safe house.

Of course, it should make it hard for Anders to hide a safe house, too. Not only would the blond giant stand out, but the vehicles they'd probably be using would, too.

The village sort of wrapped around the hillside in a crescent, with the roads forming something akin to switchbacks as they wound around the hill. We were rolling through the ruins of the upper half of the village when we saw another car on the road.

It was an ancient, ugly LuAZ 969, colored a mix of faded yellow and rust. I couldn't see the driver and passenger clearly, but a vehicle in this ancient dump of a village was an indicator. I just pointed, and Ivan nodded. We'd see if we could tail them; if they were Anders' people, they might lead us back to their safe house. Then we *might* be able to plan a proper, and less suicidal, hit on the place. Or at least set up more low-profile surveillance so that we could take them on the move.

We were going to lose sight of them if we kept going the way we were; they were on the next road downhill, and were going to pass behind some more ruins and thick stands of trees. But without going full car chase on them, we wouldn't be able to avoid it. Looking at the crude map I'd drawn based on the overheads, the two roads should come together up ahead, anyway.

The road entered the trees, ruined houses looming on either side, and I put out a hand to have Ivan slow down. I didn't want to run into them unprepared or unawares; if this was going to be an ambush, I'd rather be the ambusher than the ambushed.

We crept forward, Ivan's foot just off the brake, as I drew my AKS-74U out from under the seat and slid it under a jacket on my lap. For the most part I was just being careful, but if by some chance that was Anders in that car, I was going to have Ivan sidle up to it and hose it down. Even that huge freak would die with enough 5.45 holes in him.

By now, I was keyed-up, scanning the woods and the gaping, darkened holes of the abandoned windows and doors in the shells of the village houses as we rolled past, looking for an ambush, a triggerman, or even any signs of IEDs in the piles of rubble alongside the road. After having that farmhouse blow up and narrowly avoiding going with it, I was a little more paranoid about explosives than usual.

I wanted a cigarette, but we had the windows rolled up to make it harder to see us, and while Ivan smoked, he didn't chain-smoke the way I did, and even I wasn't all that keen on hot-boxing the UAZ with Black Russian smoke.

"There he is," Ivan said, nodding toward where the LuAZ was coming around the bend just downhill and in front of us, barely visible through the trees. If the house at the bend hadn't been reduced to little more than a rubble-strewn foundation, we probably wouldn't have spotted it at all.

The vehicle turned right, heading further downhill and away from us, and Ivan pressed the accelerator, picking up speed to catch up. It would be easy to lose them in this labyrinth of empty, crumbling buildings and steadily encroaching trees, but it would be just as easy to get burned and wind up in a fight we weren't ready for. We had to find a balance.

We hit the intersection at just the same time that the LuAZ turned left on the next road down. A quick glance at the map told me we had a little bit of leeway, provided they didn't floor it as soon as we lost sight of them.

Ivan glanced at the rear-view mirror just as we turned down the road after the LuAZ. "Who is that?" he asked.

I hunched down and looked in my own rear-view mirror. There was another car behind us. An ancient, rusty Lada sedan, it had just come up on us from the same road the LuAZ had been on.

"Son of a bitch," I muttered. We'd gotten focused on the LuAZ and hadn't noticed that they were being followed. But who was who? There were two big dudes in the Lada, both looking hunched and uncomfortable in the little car, but I couldn't see much more detail than that, at least not in the tiny, cracked and scratched mirror that wasn't at a very good angle. I turned in my seat and looked back.

"Well?" Ivan asked as I turned back forward. We were still following the LuAZ; there was no point in doing anything else until we decided to break away and try to lose the Lada.

"I don't know," I answered, still peering in the rear view while trying to keep an eye on the LuAZ, which had just trundled past a Y intersection and was continuing straight ahead. "The driver is a big black dude. I don't remember anything in the intel about Anders having a big black dude on his team."

"Nothing in intel said anything about booby-trapped house or Russian *brodyagi*, either," Ivan pointed out. "What do you want to do?"

"Keep driving," I said, my hand on the Suchka's grip under the jacket. "Let the situation develop." We really didn't have much of a choice, aside from opening fire, and I was pretty sure that Anders wasn't in that Lada, so starting a gunfight just had the potential to get us both ventilated without getting any closer to our target. Even so, I was looking for an escape route. We were *not* in a good position.

The LuAZ suddenly turned off the road, heading toward a larger house some way off the road and back in the trees. At the same time, an open-top UAZ surged out of the same side avenue and up onto the road in front of us, blocking the way.

As if that wasn't enough, a pair of Lada 4x4s came roaring down the road behind the sedan. I caught a glimpse of what might have been an AK in one of the open windows.

I tensed and flipped the jacket off my shorty AK. We were boxed, and it looked like things were about to get loud.

"*Yub tvoyu maht*," Ivan muttered, reaching down to drag his own Suchka out from under his seat, even as he wrenched the wheel to the left. We were just past the Y, but Ivan was going for it anyway.

There were three shooters in the open-top SUV in front of us, dressed in civilian clothes but wearing Russian plate carriers over them. Three black AK variants were leveled at us, even as I finished rolling down the window, stuck my Suchka out, and opened fire.

It was a fifty-yard shot, so it was entirely doable with the stubby little AK subgun, but we were bouncing over dirt and rocks, and I'd just yanked the selector down to the first slot, auto, and mashed the trigger.

The Suchka only has an eight-inch barrel, so the muzzle blast is an impressive blossom of flame. It strobed in front of my face as I did my best to riddle the other UAZ with bullets, though I'm pretty sure out of the forty-five round mag, only about ten actually hit anything.

It was enough to get their heads down, at least, and I thought I saw one drop into the back, hopefully shot. I pulled the weapon back inside just in time to avoid having it smashed out of my hands by a low-hanging tree branch, as Ivan got us onto the other road, heading back up the hill.

The Lada was right behind us, the passenger leaning out of the window and firing what looked like a Dirty Harry revolver of all things at the 4x4s behind them. One of the 4x4s looked like it had swerved off the road and smacked into the ruin of a house; there was a pile of rubble on the smoking hood. The other one was still coming after us, with the occasional muzzle flash of an automatic weapon coming from the passenger side. Rounds snapped and hissed past, audible even over the roar of the UAZ's engine. One hit my rear-view mirror with a *bang*, sending bits of glass and metal flying.

"*Chyort!*" Ivan yelled, even as another round ripped through the canvas top just over our heads, tearing a long slit through it. We'd come around the long curve in the road, only to see that it dead-ended at a bombed-out house surrounded by low stone fences about four hundred yards away.

I rocked the next mag into my Suchka and turned to hang out the window again. Ivan could find us an escape route; I needed to suppress our pursuit. The UAZ was moving, though I could only see two guys in it now, and it was right behind the other 4x4. I didn't have a shot at either, however, without hitting the asshole who was hanging out of the Lada's window with that big wheelgun.

"Who the fuck is that?" I wondered. At that point in time I really couldn't give less of a damn about Forsyth's Request For Information; they were shooting at the same people we were. Of course, it looked like they sucked at not being followed, had probably blown this whole op, and what kind of amateur brings a revolver to a gunfight anymore? But then the guy put a bullet through the windshield of the 4x4 behind them, and the sporadic AK fire from the passenger side window suddenly ceased, so maybe he wasn't that much of an amateur after all.

Ivan, rather than slowing down as we rapidly approached the end of the road, floored the gas and sent us hurtling alongside the low stone fence around the ruined farmhouse ahead. He spun the wheel as we came abreast of what had once been a gate leading off the road to the left, almost flipped the vehicle, and then we were bouncing and roaring across the overgrown remains of some Azeri farmer's barnyard, heading uphill and toward the trees.

Unfortunately, I now had no shot at all, as our pursuers were now on the wrong side of the vehicle, and eclipsed by another crumbling farmhouse. I did get a glimpse behind us of the Lada continuing the way we'd been driving, heading for a gap in the trees. That dude was still shooting that enormous hand cannon, and it seemed to have dissuaded the pursuit somewhat, even though the sedan was now rocking way too much for him to actually be able to hit anything. Then the Lada disappeared into the trees, even as the UAZ tried to make the turn to follow us.

I braced the Suchka as tightly as I could against the door column, and squeezed off a burst at the driver. At least, I tried to aim at the driver; Ivan wasn't slowing down to give me a good shooting platform, so I sprayed the general area with about ten rounds. Then Ivan gunned it over the low remains of a gap in the stone fence, I damn near bit my tongue off as we hit the ground on the far side, and by the time I'd un-rattled my brains enough to try and shoot again, he'd taken another turn, and there were trees and a ruined wall between us and our pursuers. I couldn't see shit, so I hauled myself back inside and slumped in the seat.

"You good?" I asked, already starting to check him for bleeds even before he could answer. I'd seen a teammate bleed out before he'd even realized he'd been shot. Considering that Ivan was driving, and we were hurtling along a rocky hillside at what I would not consider entirely safe speeds, having him pass out from blood loss would not be a good way to live to get paid, much less to old age.

Once I was confident that Ivan wasn't going to keel over from blood loss, I slumped back in my seat and started checking myself, wondering what the hell we were going to do now.

"Wait, wait, wait. Stop," J.D. said. "Go back. He was carrying *what*?"

"A big-ass, Dirty Harry Magnum revolver," I repeated. "I thought it was weird, too."

J.D. had a frown on his face, though, rather an odd expression for Mr.

Always Obnoxiously Cheerful himself. "No," he said, shaking his head, thinking so hard I could hear the hamster about to have a heart attack. "It's not just that. Something about a revolver . . . "

I looked over at Ivan as I lit up. He just shrugged. He didn't know, either.

J.D. suddenly snapped his fingers. "There was a BOLO, came out about a year ago," he said. "I bet I can find it somewhere, still. Something about an HVT who uses a Magnum revolver."

"A signature weapon, particularly one like that, doesn't seem terribly smart for somebody playing the HVT game," I commented, taking a deep drag on the cig.

J.D. wasn't listening, but was poring over the "sensitive" laptop, that we used for comms and such things as mission files. "Here it is!" he said excitedly. "I knew I remembered it." He turned the screen so that we could see.

The picture was remarkably good quality for an HVT shot. It looked like a mugshot, except there was no prisoner number under the young man's face. His head had been shaved, and he had a couple of nasty scars, one across his forehead, another that looked like it had barely missed taking out his left eye. For all that, he still looked like a kid. Just a kid who'd seen some shit.

He was also pretty high up on the Organizations "Capture" list. Strangely enough, there didn't seem to be a "Kill" portion to it. Whatever Constantine Michael Valentine was wanted for, it had to have been something he was carrying around in his head. The Organization wasn't usually all that eager to go for "Capture Only."

"Fuck me," I muttered, taking another deep drag on the Black Russian and trying to let the nicotine keep the headache at bay. That was all we needed. Another snatch-and-grab on top of the time-sensitive one that had already gone south.

After a moment, staring at the kid's picture, I snorted. "Constantine Michael Valentine, huh?" I said. "Damn, his parents must have hated him. Well, it's lover-boy's lucky day. Because we're sure in no position to do anything about him."

"We could send the sighting up the chain," J.D. said.

"And then what?" I retorted. "You know damned good and well that as soon as Forsyth hears that there's another HVT here, he's going to task us with both. We're already down a man, and we were undermanned for the Anders mission to begin with. Fuck Valentine and fuck telling Forsyth about him. Let somebody else worry about that one. We've got enough on our plate. Now, can we get back to the mission at hand? This is twice we've clashed with what I can only assume are Anders' people, with no sign of the big bastard himself. This isn't that big a city. He's got to be somewhere."

J.D. looked uncertain. Ivan just looked grim. But without any further complaint, we got back to planning. The clock was ticking, Forsyth was probably going to be calling about the dustup in Kerkicahan any minute now, and I was now fairly certain that Anders' people were actively hunting us.

We needed to hurry up and get this job over with before it killed the rest of us.

"Why am I getting impression that this is waste of time?" Ivan muttered.

I just grunted an irritated monosyllable that might or might not have been a word. I was driving, Ivan was riding shotgun, and we were following one of the 4x4s that had shot at us in Kerkicahan a couple days before.

"We have seen all of these *brodyagi* several times," he continued. "Still no sign of Anders. He is not type to stay inside and hide when there is killing to be done."

I had to agree. We had gotten to the point over the last couple of days where we could recognize most of the Russian shooters. And the man in charge was definitely not Anders. Short, stocky, scarred, with a shaved head, no appreciable neck, and a nose that looked like it had been broken at least a half-dozen times, the guy I was mentally thinking of as The Bulldog was pretty obviously the team leader for the shooters, most of whom were hanging out in paramilitary uniforms and kit, openly armed.

The reason they were getting away with being so blatant was pretty evident from what we were seeing. The 4x4 ahead slowed and stopped at an NKDA checkpoint, and the Russians got out leisurely. Two of them hung out by the vehicle, while the other two walked up to the ancient BTR-52 and started handing out cigarettes and shooting the shit with the Nagorno-Karabakh soldiers.

As I watched, I decided that this wasn't just the Russians trying to win over the locals. There was a certain camaraderie in evidence that wasn't explicable by the Russians paying the Armenians off to look the other way. These guys had seen action together.

Ivan was watching the byplay going on next to the old BTR as well. "Russian 'volunteers,'" he said. "Russians have been supporting Armenians here for decades. Naturally is corruption and *mafiya* involved. Probably some 'volunteers' also *brodyagi*. Makes sense that Anders paid *brodyagi* already here for fighting against Azeris."

I had slowed and pulled over to the side of the road as the 4x4 had stopped at the checkpoint. I didn't want to drive into the middle of that, and even as we sat there, a block and a half away, watching, I was looking for an escape route. One of the difficulties of our situation was that we didn't have multiple teams with multiple vehicles to do our surveillance with. That meant that sooner or later, we *were* going to get burned, assuming we hadn't already. Ivan and I had carjacked a creaky, wheezing GAZ-24 to replace the UAZ that had gotten shot up, but the same vehicle with the same two mopes in it was going to start to stand out after a while.

I was about to say something more about Anders' presence or lack thereof, when The Russian turned, looking around, and looked right at me. At least, he seemed to. He paused for a moment, puffing on his cigarette, looking at us.

"I think we might be burned," I said.

"I think so, too," Ivan replied. "Just play it cool."

"Do I look like I'm panicking?" I asked, as I took my hands off the wheel to light another cigarette. Let The Russian think that I had just pulled over to light up. Plus, the initial cloud of smoke would help conceal my features.

Of course, of the few people who drove around here, most wouldn't actually stop to light up, but I was making do with what I had.

The Russian was still looking toward us as he leaned over to his buddy and said something. It was definitely time to go. I still kept it casual as I put the GAZ in gear and started us rolling, taking the first turn before the checkpoint.

The Russian and his cronies watched us the entire way.

"Fuuuuuuck," I said, as I started on a long, meandering route back to the safe house. We'd been burned, all right. And for what? If Anders really wasn't there, we were about to get killed for a fucking red herring. Carlos already had been.

Neither of us spoke much on the way back. We managed to avoid most of the checkpoints, though at least one had been unavoidable. We'd been careful that all the weapons and gear were carefully hidden before driving up and handing the NKDA soldier our fake documents, which had been hastily turned out by the Organization. They were shit copies, and wouldn't stand up against any serious scrutiny, but the kid just looked bored and disinterested as he checked the documents, gave the inside of the car a cursory glance, and waved us by. He probably had some serious drinking and porn watching to do, and having to check vehicles was cutting into his "me" time.

Getting back to the safe house, we were presented with a problem. The car was burned, no doubt about that. Parking it in front of the safe house would only burn the house as well, and we didn't have a backup. But walking too far with the gear, even stuffed in the big backpacks we had in the back, might raise some eyebrows as well. We weren't locals, and this part of Stepanakert, hell, any part of Stepanakert, was a little sensitive to out-of-towners. These people had effectively lived under siege for decades. Strangers were noted. That was why we'd exposed ourselves as little as possible.

But the car was going to be a bigger target indicator, so we parked it five houses down, stuffed our Suchkas and chest rigs in our packs, and walked the rest of the way. J.D. was at the door, his AK-74 held just out of sight.

"Where's the car?" he asked, as we walked in.

"Down the street," I answered. "We got spotted." I dropped the pack on the floor and picked up my AKM. I'd be keeping it close for the moment.

"Um," was all J.D. said. I turned and frowned at him. Usually, he'd have a lot more to say, especially about a compromise. But he wasn't looking at me. He actually looked a little guilty, which was a new expression for our resident hedonist and serial womanizer.

"What the fuck did you do?" I asked, concern about The Russian eyeballing us suddenly eclipsed by J.D.'s demeanor.

He was saved the necessity of answering immediately by the call signal from the laptop in our makeshift comms room, which was just a former bathroom, the toilet having been ripped out to leave nothing but a noxious-smelling hole in the floor. With a glare that promised a continuation to the conversation, I went inside to answer it.

I was expecting Forsyth. But the face that came up on the screen wasn't Forsyth. I'd never seen this guy before.

Forsyth had a dangerous rep, but he looked like an office geek who got to the gym regularly. Whoever this was, he was older, decades older, but even with thinning white hair and wrinkles, he looked like one dangerous, scary old bastard. His neck was almost as thick as The Russian's, and his eyes were probably the coldest I'd ever seen, and I've looked into the eyes of some very nasty people.

"You Dragic?" he asked. His voice was low and gravelly. It fit him.

"I am," I said. There probably wasn't any point in trying to beat around the bush with this guy. He didn't look like the type to play games. "Who are you?"

"My name's Underhill," he replied. "I'm told you've made contact with Michael Valentine."

I felt a sudden cold rage at his words. So that was why J.D. had looked like a kid caught with his hand in the cookie jar. He'd talked about Valentine. Fucker.

But somehow I got the impression that showing this man anything but the utmost professionalism was not a good idea. "That depends on how you define 'contact,'" I answered. "We've tentatively ID'ed him, based on a couple of chance encounters in the course of our own operations. We're pretty sure he's here after Anders, just like we are. If it is him."

Underhill's expression didn't change a whit. Nor did he apparently give a damn for my qualifications. "Your mission profile has changed," he said bluntly. "You are to get eyes on Constantine Michael Valentine, and maintain surveillance until I get there. Do not try to engage him or his companions."

"Dammit," I snarled, momentarily not caring about how scary this oldster appeared. An old guy working for the Organization was usually not one to trifle with. He'd probably been around a long time, and done some things that would give most normal people nightmares. But after ten years of working for these people, we were being used as expendable pawns, and it pissed me off more than this guy scared me. "We're already in over our heads with looking for Anders. I'm ninety-five percent certain that he's hunting us as much as we're hunting him. And as near as I can tell, we're the only assets you've got here looking for him. And you want us to add another target to the list?"

"No," he said, with the grinding patience of a glacier. "You're shifting targets. There are plenty of other teams out doing the same 'confirm or deny' game that you've been playing with the three dozen or so mostly spurious Anders sightings that have been cropping up. This is a higher priority."

I saw red. We were out in the cold, with Carlos dead already, for a target that probably had never been there, and the Organization had known that? "And how many of those teams have been ambushed?" I asked through gritted teeth.

"Several," he replied, with about as much feeling as a man talking about how his stocks were doing. Less, actually. A man talking about his stocks would have some actual stake in their success. Underhill didn't care. At all. "That was always to be expected. Enough of that. Stick to the matter at hand."

It was a tribute to just how menacing this emotionless, gravel-voiced oldster was that I quit bitching and went ahead and played along.

"Why Valentine?" I asked. "What did he do that makes him more valuable a target than Anders?"

"He's not," Underhill said. "You're being re-tasked because we're now fairly certain that Anders isn't in Azerbaijan, while you've got a pretty solid lead on Valentine. As for what he did; that's need-to-know, and you don't need to know. Just don't underestimate him."

"He looks like a kid," I said.

"That kid was a Vanguard merc before he became an Exodus terrorist," Underhill said. "He's seen plenty of combat, and he's a survivor. If he was just any schlub with a gun, they wouldn't have hauled me out of retirement a year ago to find him."

"You've got your instructions," he said, his voice low, hard, and brooking no dissent. "Get eyes on Valentine and don't lose him until I get there and can take him in. He's my target; you're now spotting for me. Don't screw this up." The screen went blank. He'd ended the call.

To my credit, I didn't yell, I didn't scream, I didn't even curse under my breath. I just sat there for a minute, staring at the laptop. Then I got up, went out into the main room, without looking at either J.D. or Ivan, and lit a cigarette. I smoked the entire thing down to the filter, then crushed it out on the filthy floor before turning to stare at J.D.. He didn't look at me, not at first.

"I specifically said we were going to leave well enough alone," I said. "We are undermanned, all but unsupported, and in unfamiliar territory. Let's stick to the job at hand until we can either bag the target or otherwise get back to our own AO, where we know the terrain and the people, I said. So tell me, J.D., since I'm pretty sure it was you, why did you decide to throw that decision completely out the *fucking* window and tell *fucking* Forsyth that we'd seen *fucking* Valentine here?"

He lifted his head and looked me in the face. Suddenly his guilty look was gone, replaced with a flash of anger. "Because somebody had to," he snarled. "We've been through two ambushes and several days of recon, with no sign of Anders. Forsyth was getting impatient. If we wanted to have a chance in hell of getting out of here in one piece, I had to give them something, some reason not to just write us off and make us disappear. They wouldn't even have to take us, you know that. A word here, a file deleted there, and we're international fugitives. Fuck that."

He stepped closer to me, lowering his voice. "This isn't about your pride anymore, Frank. It isn't about your idea of somehow being above it all, a gun for hire, totally uninvested, doing the job well enough to keep below the level of a threat and above being a pawn. Guess what, Frank? We're fucking pawns. We're no better off than the Dead Six guys that you pitied so much, all the while telling yourself that you had it figured out, that we could walk the tightrope and come out fine." He stepped back and shook his head. "We're not fine, Frank. This isn't our game, and we can't play it the way we want to. I had to give them something, and it bought us time. So you can get off your damn high-horse and accept that if I hadn't told them about this Valentine character, we'd be dead in a week."

I just glared at him, but at the same time, I knew that he was right. We'd been playing a game of brinksmanship for years, banking on our usefulness to keep us from being too expendable. But to the Organization, *everybody's* ultimately expendable, particularly contractors. We weren't special. We'd just bucked the odds for longer than most. Now we were out of options. I had no doubt that Underhill would make it his business to hunt us down and finish us off if we screwed this up. Forsyth might have a nasty reputation, but even without knowing *anything* about Underhill, something about that old man just scared me.

But that didn't make the fact that J.D. had gone behind my back to the Organization any easier to swallow. I'd trusted this man with my life for years. And he'd just betrayed that trust as surely as if he'd slid a knife into my back.

Part of that tightrope act we'd pretended was going to end in anything but a fiery crash and burn had been the understanding that we could never entirely trust the Organization. We had to trust each other instead. Yet J.D. had gone to the Organization in spite of Ivan and me. I didn't know if I could ever trust him all the way again.

I'd always known that J.D. had an amoral streak. He was a hired killer and a serial womanizer, and not much else. But this . . . it was all I could do not to just shoot him in the face. He was the same guy, but I'd be watching him like a hawk from here on out. Because I couldn't know when he'd decide to sell us out the rest of the way.

Ivan hadn't said a word, but the expression on his flat Russian face was thunderous as he looked at J.D.. Loyalty was a big thing with Ivan; he'd followed me without hesitation—though occasionally with some rather pointed questions—ever since I'd pulled him out of Pavlodar just ahead of the friends of the *brodyaga* he'd nearly killed in the bar. He wouldn't like this. And when Ivan really didn't like something . . . well, things could get a little *physical*.

"You should not have done this, J.D.," he said, his voice sounding a little deeper, his accent a little thicker, than usual. "Not without consulting us."

"Both of you would have just doubled down on your walk-the-line bullshit," J.D. answered harshly. "You wouldn't have done it. So I did it for you." He turned away, toward his room. "You can thank me later."

Ivan and I watched him leave the room, neither one of us saying anything. Ivan didn't look pissed anymore. His expression was blank, dead. Ivan with the dead face was *way* worse than Ivan pissed off. It meant he was seriously contemplating killing J.D. in the next few minutes.

He turned to look at me, and I shook my head. "We still need him," I said, reading the unasked question. I sighed bitterly. "We'll figure out what to do after this is all over."

"He knows all fallback plans," Ivan pointed out quietly.

"He won't tell anybody," I said, starting to get over the anger. I could see why J.D. had done it, even if it still pissed me off. He hadn't suddenly turned into an Organization drone. He was scared that we were going to fail and pay the ultimate price for it, and had acted out of that fear.

Still, I could tell that the team's days were numbered. *If* we survived this nightmare of an assignment, we wouldn't be working together anymore. More than likely, we'd activate our fallback plans, and disappear into the shadowy corners of the world, to live out the rest of our lives under assumed identities, hoping the Organization overlooked us.

But that was dependent on that big, ugly *if*. If we survived. We needed to get to work on that part, and worry about what came after if there was an "after."

"Come on," I said. "We'll start planning to track down this Valentine character. J.D. can come join us when he's done sulking."

✣ ✣ ✣

In the end, we didn't have a chance to find anybody. They found us.

The fact of the matter was, we had no idea where Valentine and his Exodus pals might have been. We'd only ever seen them in passing, while hunting for Anders—or, rather, hunting The Bulldog, since Anders didn't seem to actually be on the ground in Nagorno-Karabakh. The only lead we had was that the Russians had apparently been following Valentine when we'd had our little dust-up in Kerkicahan. So we decided to go looking for Russians.

J.D. had come out of his room after Ivan and I had only been planning for a few minutes. We kitted up and got ready to move without much conversation. There wasn't much to say. At least, until Ivan looked out the front window to see if the coast was clear.

"We have company," he said. I joined him at the window, trying to peer out without exposing myself too much to the outside. We hadn't drawn too much attention from the neighbors, but it was probably bound to happen. It was just a *really* bad time for it.

It wasn't the neighbors. Valentine had ditched the Lada for a UAZ. They were trying to be casual, but I could see enough through the rolled-up windows to tell that it was the same big black dude in the passenger seat.   The thought that they should probably have left that guy at home went through my head. It's hard to be inconspicuous in the Caucasus when you're damn near seven feet tall and black as the Ace of Spades.

"Oh, hell," I muttered. Ivan had a stream of Russian profanity going under his breath. We didn't have to look for our target, but one of the keys to successful surveillance is that the target *doesn't know you're there.* And apparently, Valentine had come looking for us.

"We don't know that he knows we are here," Ivan said. "He could only be looking. Maybe he is not even looking for us."

"We haven't seen any of The Russian's people in this neighborhood," I pointed out. "Either he's *way* off, or he's not looking for them. And right now, I'm not trusting in coincidence."

"So what do we do?" J.D. asked.

I blew a deep breath out past my nose. "We've got to take him."

Ivan's eyebrows climbed toward his hairline as he turned to look at me. I kept watching Valentine's vehicle through the window.

"Take him?" he asked. "In middle of street, during middle of day? And how will we avoid Russians and NKDA while getting him out of town, while dismantling safe house, and making contact with Underhill to tell him change in plans?"

"I don't fucking know, all right?" I snapped. "This is 'desperate times, desperate measures' time here. I'm spitballing." The truth was, I had a sinking feeling in my gut that said we were fucked, no matter what happened over the next five minutes. "The only other option is to try to run out the back, try to lose 'em, set up somewhere else, and try to find 'em again. What are the odds we can pull that off, given how the rest of this job is unraveling around us?"

"Is not good plan," Ivan said.

"It's no fucking plan at all," I replied, throwing on my chest rig and grabbing my AKM. "It's nothing but a desperate roll of the dice. We're probably dead either way. May as well go down shooting, if that's what it comes to."

Ivan shrugged, though he didn't even look at J.D. as he grabbed his own gear and weapon. J.D. didn't say another word, but he kitted up as if he was fully on board.

"J.D., you stay here, cover us from the window," I said. "Ivan and I will go out the back." He nodded, staying back from the window, but shouldering his AK-74 and bringing it to the low ready. Ivan and I beat feet out the back door.

The back was mostly overgrown, with trees overhanging the yard between the safe house and the house behind it, one of the few on Shahinyan Street. The yard was overgrown, but not overgrown enough to conceal the four men in Russian digital camouflage and black chest rigs moving toward the safe house, their black AK-107s held ready.

I don't know who was more surprised to see the other; we had been a little focused on Valentine out front, and they thought they were sneaking up on us. Everybody reacted about the same way and at about the same time, though.

I barely aimed as I ripped a burst at the first green and black silhouette that rose in front of my muzzle, even as I ran for the corner of the house and some kind of cover. Ivan was going the other way, and the Russians were diving for the ground, all of them shooting at the same time. Bullets snapped past, hitting the side of the house with loud *cracks*, spraying concrete fragments and plaster dust into the air with each impact.

Diving onto my belly behind the corner, I found that it really didn't provide that much cover; it cut off one of the Russian shooters, but I was still pretty exposed to the other three. Worse, I could hear more fire coming from out front, both rifle fire and the *booms* of Valentine's hand cannon.

Caught in the open, the Russians charged the house, firing as they came. I was in the prone, though, and shrank back against the wall, aiming in on the closest, and fired three fast shots. They tracked up his chest, and he staggered, but didn't go down. He had to be wearing a vest. So I raised the rifle a bit and shot him three times in the throat and face. Red splashed and he stopped dead, kind of went up on his tiptoes, and fell flat on his face.

The others slowed, and the covering fire started to get uncomfortably close. I shrank back further against the wall, trying to make myself as small as possible, but I had to finish this fast. The shooting from the street was intensifying, and I felt *really* exposed. There wasn't much between my ass and the street, after all.

Flipping the AKM back up to auto, hoping that there were still enough rounds in the mag, I rolled out from the wall and dumped the rest of the magazine at the charging attackers.

The AKM bucked with the recoil, the muzzle rising as I tracked it across the two men I could see. One doubled over as a round took him right beneath the plate, and stumbled to his knees. The other one tried to duck, and took a round to the top of the head. He wasn't wearing a helmet, either. A bloody chunk of skull went flying, and he fell on his face. Then the rifle *clicked*. Empty. It was a bit of a frantic scramble to get the next mag out of my chest rig, which I was lying on, strip the empty, and rock the new mag in. That guy I'd gut-shot, while he was rolling around on the ground and screaming, wasn't dead yet, and I never trust a bad guy until he's dead.

I racked a round into the chamber, got up on a knee, and started to bring the rifle to bear on the wounded Russian, when a burst smacked more concrete chips into my face, the deformed bullets whining past as they skipped off the corner. I'd forgotten about the fourth guy.

Where the hell is Ivan? I thought, ducking back away from the storm of AK fire. As soon as it slackened, I surged out around the corner, leading the way with my rifle.

I damn near hit the Russian in the face with the muzzle. If I'd been a split second slower, he probably would have grabbed my rifle and I'd have been in a world of hurt, down on the ground fighting him for the weapon. But as soon as his ugly, lumpy, scarred-up face appeared in front of my front sight, I was squeezing the trigger.

I hadn't dropped the selector lever down to semi, either. A five-round burst turned his head into a canoe. Blood and brains splashed back in a muddy red spray, and then splattered on me as his momentum kept him falling into me. We went down in a tangle of limbs, guns, and gear, as the liquid contents of his skull spilled across my chest.

With a grunt of mostly effort—I was too far in the zone to worry about disgust or what kind of STDs a Russian mobster might be carrying around in his blood—I shoved the corpse off of me and scrambled to my feet, desperately bringing my rifle to bear, scanning for any more threats. That was when I saw Ivan.

He was slumped against the wall, only a few feet short of the corner, not moving. A red splash against the plaster behind him told me all I needed to know.

I stared at his body for a moment, a moment I probably couldn't afford. I should have run after that. I really didn't have a team left. I didn't have anything left. I was watching what was left of my life unravel in front of my eyes. But for some reason, I turned and headed back around to the street, trying for one last chance at Valentine; one last chance at not ending up on Underhill's hit list.

Moving in a crouch, rifle up and ready, I approached the front of the safe house and the street beyond.

There was no fire coming from the house. Whether that meant that J.D. had chickened out or was dead, I didn't know. All the fire seemed to be going up and down the street. A two-and-a-half ton truck was parked almost right in front of me, with half a dozen Russian shooters trading fire with Valentine and his buddies, who were just down the street to my right, crouched behind their UAZ, which wasn't providing very good cover, but it wasn't going to be much of a getaway vehicle after that, either. There were several Russian bodies strewn in the street, as if they'd tried charging the UAZ.

I didn't really think about it. The Russians had killed most of my team; target or not, Valentine hadn't. So I opened fire on the Russians.

They weren't expecting it; they were entirely fixated on Valentine's team. No one even appeared to be watching their six o'clock. They must have been pretty confident that the NKDA wasn't going to interfere, and that their buddies in the trees would have taken us out without too much trouble.

If there's one thing I'm not, it's "not too much trouble."

I knew they were wearing body armor, so I didn't just spray. I clicked the selector down to "semi," and started putting controlled pairs into bodies.

Most of my work in recent times may have been sabotage and assassination, striking without warning against targets that usually have no idea that there's a threat anywhere near, but I'm still a good combat shooter. It's one of those skills I've always taken pride in maintaining. I'm fast, and I'm accurate. So it didn't take long to track along the ragged line of men crouched in the vague cover of the truck, putting two rounds into each of them. The AKM's rattling roar wasn't much compared to the storm of noise that was already roaring across the street, and I started at the back, so they only realized they had been flanked when the second guy from the rear fell onto his buddy, blood and brains leaking from his perforated skull. That threw off my aim, and the shots meant for his buddy went into the side of the truck, but I corrected and hammered three shots into that guy's side before continuing on.

The last guy, who was crouched at the front wheel well, almost got me. He realized what was going on and spun, bringing his Suchka around to point it at my face. His finger was tightening on the trigger when I shot him in the eye. His head snapped back and hit the fender, leaving a red smear on the green paint as he slid down to the pavement.

Still not certain I'd gotten all of them, I sprinted toward the bodies to check the back of the truck. Sure enough, there was one last Russian back there, and he let off a blind burst at me as I dove to the street, scraping my knees and hands, my AKM clattering as it hit the asphalt. I rolled quickly to the wheel well to get my feet under me, shoving the rapidly cooling corpse of the last man I'd shot aside.

Glancing down at him, I saw he had a couple of grenades on his kit, and I briefly considered it. But that would probably just blow me up, too, and I was in combat mode at that point. Depression and the inevitable destruction of my life were about as far from my mind as they could be.

I got into a crouch, then surged forward. There was only one thing in my mind at that point: *Attack*. The blind fire from the back of the truck had died away, and I wasn't going to give that sonofabitch a chance to try again.

I came around the corner and collided with The Bulldog, his bald head and lumpy nose unmistakable. He was frantically reloading, but I knocked the AK-107 out of his hands when I hit him. At least, that was what I tried to do. He let it go quick enough, and grabbed my rifle, trying to wrench it away. I held on for dear life as I fell on top of him, trying to get my knee under myself so I could get some leverage, buttstroke him, knee him in the ribs, *anything*.

He suddenly let go with one hand and snatched a knife off his chest rig. That made me let go with both hands and grab for his knife hand. I caught his wrist just as the tip of the blade touched my shirt beneath my chest rig. I held on, my knuckles turning white, practically doing a static pushup above that nasty piece of steel, trying to keep my weight off of it while I tried to twist his wrist.

He let go of the rifle entirely, and suddenly we were in a wrestling match for the knife, guns completely forgotten. Either I sagged a little, or he managed to push upward a little, because I felt the white-hot pain of the point going into the skin over my stomach. I surged backward and to one side, trying to get away from it. In the process, I got off the point, but lost my grip with one hand.

As fast as a striking snake, he was up off the ground, pressing his attack, my one hand no longer enough to hold off his two. He got on top of me, pressing down on the knife, which started to inch closer and closer to my chest.

I still only had one hand on his wrist. I drew the little backup Makarov on my hip with the other and shot him.

He grunted, a confused look in his piggy little eyes turning to shock as I pumped the other seven rounds of 9mm into his guts. The strength had gone out of him, and it was easy enough to roll him off of me, though I was bleeding from a couple of knife wounds now. The Makarov was smoking slightly, the slide locked back. The Russian looked up at me, that puzzled look still on his face for a moment, and then he wasn't seeing anything ever again.

A boot scuffed on the asphalt. I spun, instinctively pointing the empty Makarov, knowing it was too late. I was staring down the barrel of a G3 in Valentine's hands. That big revolver was in a leather holster on his hip.

Valentine was studying me. I don't know why he hadn't just shot me. Maybe it was because so far, we'd both been shooting at the Russians. Maybe he really didn't know what to make of me. I knew what he saw. A gaunt, prematurely gray-haired man, fit but with too many lines in his face from too much stress, too many cigarettes, and too much vodka, soaked in blood and brains and aiming an empty pistol.

"Who are you?" he asked. Strange, his eyes were different colors.

"Me?" I asked, glancing over at the safe house. The front windows were shattered, the wall pocked with bullet holes. "I'm nobody. Not anymore. Just one more expendable pawn who's been expended. Go ahead. Do it. You'd be doing me a favor."

"Listen," he said, lowering the muzzle so it was pointed more at my chest than my face, "you don't have to die today. I just wanted to ask you a few questions. This can work out so we both walk out of here, alive. We don't have a lot of time, though."

"Yeah, no shit," I replied, dropping the useless Mak on the ground. "Every Russian *brodyaga* and Armenian henchman is going to be descending on this place in the next hour. You'd better go."

He wasn't going to make it that easy. He frowned, the rifle muzzle twitching upward a fraction of an inch. "Yeah, no, I think you're missing what I'm getting at here. You're coming with me. Get the fuck up."

I briefly considered just letting him shoot me. It would solve a lot of problems. With the safehouse as shot up as it was, the fact that J.D. wasn't blasting Valentine and his buddy to pieces told me all I needed to know. I stood up and looked him in the face. "You're Valentine, right? The one they're looking for?" For some damned reason, I felt like validating my targeting, and making sure I hadn't blown it completely for the sake of some random merc who wasn't even the target.

But I'd hit paydirt, apparently. He tensed up, his face going blank. "I am," he said, "and right now, your survival depends on you answering one question. Where is Simon Anders?"

I felt an insane, hysterical laugh rising up, but managed to keep it to a chuckle. "Fucking hell, this is too much."

He didn't like that, and went back to pointing the rifle at my face. At that point, I couldn't care less. "Last chance, asshole," he said.

"You don't get it, do you?" I snapped. "Anders isn't here. He was never here. This whole thing? It was a fucking setup. He's put out false trails everywhere. Looks like we both took the bait."

The big black dude came to Valentine's side. "We need to go," he told him. "This was an ambush. They knew we were coming."

"I don't think so," Valentine said, studying me. He jerked his head at me. "I think they knew this guy was coming."

The big dude looked at me. He wasn't an American; his accent was wrong. "Who is he?" he asked.

"He's a fucking dead man if he doesn't start being useful," Valentine said.

Go ahead, tough guy, I thought. *Do it. Do me the favor.*

But I knew at that point that, depressed as I was, lost as I was, my damned survival instinct wasn't going to let me just lie down and die. Valentine wasn't going to just let me walk away, yet, and there was no way I was going to get the drop on him right away. Maybe, just maybe, he could be my way out of this clusterfuck. For damned sure the Organization's secrecy rules no longer meant shit to me. I'd play along with Valentine long enough to get out of this damned kill zone, then I'd fade. I'd run, and find one of our fallback bolt-holes and disappear, just like Ivan and I had planned to do. It might take some doing, but I could be patient.

Ulan Bator, Mongolia
Eight Weeks Later . . .

My safe house, a small apartment in a nondescript brick apartment building in Ulan Bator, was dark as I came in from a supply run. I easily passed as a Russian, blending into the considerable Russian population of Ulan Bator. A bigger city is an easier place to disappear in than a small town or village out in the country, even if there was more risk of hostile eyes there.

This was one of the places that Ivan and I had set up as a fallback, a number of years before. I'd taken my time getting there after ditching Valentine, bouncing through a few other places and a few other identities to make sure I wasn't being tracked. We'd visited it every once in a while, though never for long, just enough to make sure the bills were paid and nobody was squatting there. I was living there as Dmitri Kuznetsov, a semi-retired professor. It wasn't much, as cover stories go, but it would do until I could come up with something better.

If I had so much time. As I closed the door and bolted it, a match flared in the living room. I froze.

As far as I knew, only my team had ever known about this place. How had they found me? I started to reach for the Tokarev concealed in the small of my back.

"I wouldn't do that, Frank," the man in the living room said. The match briefly illuminated his features as he lit the cigar in his teeth, but I saw little except his glasses. "Turn on the light."

I did. He had an old revolver pointed at me, a .357, I thought. I briefly wondered what the hell it was with revolvers lately? I reconsidered reaching for the Tok.

"Sit down," he told me. I complied, studying him as I did.

He was old. His ears stuck out a little from snow-white hair and a face that was a mass of wrinkles. His eyes, though, were as keen as any young man's even as they watched me from behind a pair of round-lensed, wire-rimmed glasses. He was eighty if he was a day. There was an oxygen bottle sitting next to his chair, yet he was puffing on a cigar. The muzzle of that Smith never wavered.

"We need to talk, Frank," he said.

"How did you know about this place?" I asked. "Nobody knows about this place."

"I've been watching you for a long time," he replied, puffing on his cigar. "I keep tabs on a lot of people. When one of them might be useful, I might have to act. I had to move quickly, in your case."

I just felt tired all of a sudden. "Did they drag you out of retirement like Underhill?" I asked.

"Did who drag me out of retirement?" he asked.

I frowned. I was confused now. "The Organization?"

"Like that bunch of schemers and lickspittles could drag me anywhere. Pshaw!" he snorted. "Most of them think I'm dead."

Now I was really confused. "So why are you here, and why have you been watching me?"

He stared at me. "Frank, how much do you really know about the Organization you've been working for for the last decade?"

"Not that much," I admitted. "Some black agency buried so deep that it's existence never gets mentioned outside of shows like *From Sea to Shining Sea.* Conspiracy crap."

He grunted again, taking another puff from the cigar, then reaching down to hold the oxygen mask to his face and take a deep breath. "Fair enough assessment, these days," he replied. "Wasn't always like that, though."

"You were with the Organization in the old days?" I asked.

"With the Organization?" he harrumphed. "Boy, I was one of those *started* the damn Organization. And it served a purpose back then. I'd been killing Communists on four continents before you were even born. That was what the Organization existed for. To stop the dominoes from falling. Ultimately, to win the damn war and bring the Soviets to their knees." He took another puff off the cigar, then another breath off the oxygen bottle.

"Now it's all power games. Influence operations, PsyOps, using secret police tactics in the U.S. The whole shooting match has gotten corrupt. These damn kids don't give a shit about their country, they only care about their power and influence, their damned games. Most of us oldsters who are still alive have just gone deep, waiting out our time until we go, wishing it was different."

"But not you." I was starting to see where this was going. I wasn't sure I liked it, either.

"Damn straight," he said. "I might be retired, but I still hear everything, and I've got contacts everywhere. The pattern's still faint, but it's there, if you've got eyes to see and the experience to put two and two together. Things are coming to a head. Bad times are a'coming. It's getting to be time for us old guys to step in and set things right. The new generation's screwed it all up." He eyed me keenly. He might look like somebody's kindly old grandpa, but when you looked into his eyes, you saw that this was one hard old man. If what he'd said was true, this kindly old grandpa had probably killed more people than cancer. "That's where you come in. I need people. You've already got yourself in one hell of a position. Underhill's no joke. I should know. I trained the sonofabitch."

"This is where you make me an offer I can't refuse," I said, weary down to my bones.

"Smart boy," he said. He stood up, that Smith still pointed at my heart, his cigar clamped in his teeth. The oxygen bottle was on a cart, but he didn't seem to need a cane. "You've got a choice. You can be like that Valentine kid, looking over your shoulder for the rest of your life. Or I can use my resources to help you stay under the radar. Underhill will never find you. The only price is that occasionally you've got to do some work for me. So, what's it going to be?"

I squinted up at him. "No, old man, what it really comes down to is I work for you, or you put a bullet in me and disappear. If you're really the shadow player you say you are, you're not going to chance me getting rolled up and telling them about this conversation."

He smiled. "See, I said you were a smart kid." His eyes went cold. "So what's it going to be?"

I sighed. "Hell, that's no damn choice at all," I said. I wasn't ready to be murdered by Commie-Killing Grandpa in a shitty apartment in Ulan Bator. "If I wanted to get killed by my erstwhile employers, I'd have stayed in Stepanakert and waited for Underhill. I'll be here when you need me."

Rock, Meet Hard Place
(Part II)

by Mike Kupari

VALENTINE
Disputed Zone
Nagorno-Karabakh Republic

Quiet, unsettling quiet, descended on Shahinyan Street as the firefight abruptly ceased. The last of the Russians was dead, but more would be coming. Even in a war-torn hellhole, a firefight between groups of foreigners in broad daylight warranted investigation. The locals would show up sooner or later, and Antoine and I weren't equipped to fight off a platoon of pissed-off Armenians by ourselves.

We didn't have a lot of time. We'd been able to track the Americans back to their hidey-hole, a house in a ruined neighborhood on the outskirts of town, but those damned Russian mercenaries had shown up again. I had guessed that the Russian mercs were working with the Americans, and that they were all working for the Montalban Exchange, but then the Russians started shooting at the Americans and that theory went right out the window.

Driving the point home was the grim-faced American man, splattered with the blood and brains of the dead Russian mercenary lying next to him, defiantly pointing an empty Makarov pistol at me. I wasn't sure who was who, and the dead Russians scattered around the house sure as hell weren't going to tell me. That left this asshole, whoever he was. I stood over him, rifle pointed at his face, but held my fire.

"Who are you?" I asked.

He looked tired. I've worked with a lot of guys who had spent too long in the business of war, and this man's thousand-yard-stare was a dead giveaway. "Me?" he asked, resignedly lowering the Makarov. "I'm nobody, not anymore." He mumbled something about being expendable, and glanced over at the house. "Go ahead, do it. You'd be doing me a favor."

I should've just shot him. My G3 was pointed at his face, the safety was off, and my finger was on the trigger. Killing him would have been the safest thing to do, because there were some very bad people looking for me. Yet I hesitated, slowly taking my finger out of the trigger guard. What I needed more than another dead man on my conscience was answers, and this guy was the only chance at those I was going to get.

"Listen," I said levelly, lowering my rifle slightly, "you don't have to die today. I just wanted to ask you a few questions. This can work out so we both walk out of here, alive. We don't have a lot of time, though."

"Yeah, no shit," the man said, distantly. He dropped the Makarov. "Every Russian *brodyaga* and Armenian henchman is going to be descending on this place in the next hour. You should go."

I frowned, having no idea what a *brodyaga* was. "Yeah, no, I think you're missing what I'm getting at here. You're coming with me. Get the fuck up."

He stood up, slowly, leaving the empty pistol on the ground. He kept looking past me, at the house he'd come out of. His clothes, drab, local garb, were stained with blood. He had a chest rig full of AK magazines, but didn't reach for his rifle as he came to his feet. He looked at me for a long moment, his face a mask. "You're Valentine, right? The one they're looking for?"

My stomach twisted a little. *Damn it.* I'd been made. Coming out here had been a big risk. "I am," I said, "and right now, your survival depends on you answering one question. Where is Simon Anders?"

A humorless smile split the man's face. He chuckled like a condemned man laughing at the gallows. "Fucking hell, this is too much."

I moved my finger back to the trigger and pointed the heavy battle rifle at the man's face. "Last chance, asshole."

"You don't get it, do you? Anders isn't here. He was never here. This whole thing? It was a fucking setup. He's put out false trails everywhere. Looks like we both took the bait."

Again, I hesitated. The simplest answer was that he was lying, trying to bluff his way out of getting his head blown off. Yet, there was something about the look in his eye, the harshness in his voice, and in his bitter resignation that seemed familiar. I remembered that look on my comrades' faces, after one nearly-suicidal mission or another, as they realized that their only reward for surviving the last mission was to be sent on the next. It's one thing to know that you're expendable. It's another thing altogether to realize that you've been *expended*.

Antoine appeared at my side then. Like me, he was dressed in muted tones, with a tactical vest and a G3 rifle. His rifle, however, was fitted with a 40mm grenade launcher. "We need to go," he said flatly. "This was an ambush. They knew we were coming."

"I don't think so." I nodded toward my captive. "I think they knew *this* guy was coming."

"Who is he?"

"He's a fucking dead man if he doesn't start being useful," I answered, my tone changing slightly. I could tell that Antoine was uncomfortable with the idea of shooting an unarmed man. I was too, to be honest, but the stakes were too high. Anders was working with Katarina Montalban now, and was the last living person who knew what Project Blue was. I didn't know, at the time, what Project Blue was, but I knew it was big, and I knew it was bad. I didn't want to do it, but if I had to have Antoine hold this guy down while I cut pieces off of him to get him to talk, then that's what I'd do. I could tell he was mulling it over; I could almost see the gears turning behind his eyes, looking for a way out.

"My name is Dragic," the man said, finally. "Frank Dragic. I was sent here by the Organization to track down Anders, but he's not here. We contacted higher authority and they told us as much. Anders set out bait, and we were sent to spring the trap on the off-chance that he might actually be here. They were just going to leave us to die."

I lowered my rifle, but kept the safety off. "Which organization are we talking about here?"

Dragic looked at me like I was stupid.

"I mean, I'm pretty sure, but there are, you know, a few different organizations looking for me. You work for Majestic, right?"

He actually laughed. "That's what the conspiracy nuts call them, but yeah. Majestic. You were Dead Six, weren't you?"

"I was. Right up until we became inconvenient, and they left us to die."

Antoine spoke up. "Gentlemen," he said, his voice deep and serious. "Perhaps now is not the time for swapping war stories?"

"The big guy is right," Dragic said. "Those Russians we killed? They're working with the NKDA. Once they realize they all got smoked they'll come down on this place in force. Either let me go or let's get the hell out of here."

I looked over at our ride, a rusty old Russian UAX 4x4. It had been riddled with bullets and was leaking fluids from several places. The two-and-a-half-ton truck the Russians had rolled up in was pretty shot up too, and several of its tires had been perforated. "Do you have a ride? We can call for one, but it'll take them a while to get here, and I don't think we have a while."

Dragic seemed to hesitate. "I do, but it's been made. The NKDA is looking for it. It's parked down the street."

"It's better than walking," I said. "None of us blend in, and we just need to get to a place where we can ditch it. I have backup, and they can pick us up."

"I need to check the house first," Dragic said.

"Forget it. Let's get to that car."

"One of my teammates was in there! I'm not going to just leave him."

Antoine gave me a look. I sighed. "Fine, let's go." Dragic bent down to pick up his AK-47. "Whoa, whoa, whoa, killer," I said, shouldering my G3. "You just leave that right where it is."

He stood back up, slowly, raising his hands, but looking at me like I was stupid. "Are you fucking serious right now?"

"What, you think because I decided not to shoot you a little bit ago that we're besties now? Into the house, you first. We need to get off the street."

If looks could kill, Dragic would've stopped my heart cold with the glare he gave me, but he complied with my command. Leaving the Kalashnikov on the ground, he headed toward the front door of the house. I followed, closely enough to keep eyes on him, but not so closely that he could turn around and grab my rifle. Antoine followed, watching our six.

The inside of the house was mostly barren, save the areas where Dragic and his team had obviously been set up. In one room was a bunch of computers and communication equipment, all of it portable, next to a stack of Pelican cases. In the main room, the one facing the street, a dead man was crumpled beneath a window in a pool of blood.

"JD," Dragic said, quietly. He exhaled heavily, and looked back at me, a tired expression on his face. "You know, he always was an asshole." He looked back at the body and shook his head. "That's it, then. I'm the last one left. I guess going with you is my best bet now."

It was his *only* bet, as I was resolved to shoot him if he ran, but I didn't need to say that. "I'm sorry about your team."

"There's something you should know, Valentine," he said, distantly. "Before he died, JD over there notified higher authority that we had a tentative sighting of you. There's been a BOLO out on you for over a year."

My hands tensed on the heavy rifle in my hands. "What did they say when you told them you saw me?"

"A guy who called himself Underhill called us and said he would be en route. He was an old guy, but—"

"I know who he is," I said, coldly. "How much time do we have before he gets here?"

Dragic shrugged. "Hell if I know. You got some history with this guy? What the hell did you do to piss off the Organization that much?"

"It's a long story. A *really* long story. Short version is, I survived being liquidated in Zubara and then escaped their custody later on. They didn't like that."

He raised his eyebrows. He didn't quite look *impressed*, but I could tell that he either thought I was bullshitting or that there was more to me than met the eye. "No, I bet they didn't," he said, chuckling.

I was barely listening. Underhill had been hunting me ever since Exodus helped me escape from Majestic custody at North Gap. No surprise there; after months of torture and twisted mind games, my captors had come to realize that I really didn't know anything about Project Blue. I was as in the dark as they were. They still couldn't just let me go, though. I knew too much, I'd seen too much, and that made me dangerous. I'd been inside their black sites, I'd seen faces, known names, and could potentially corroborate other evidence. For an organization built on layers of secrets and lies, having someone like me on the loose was unacceptable. For that reason alone, they'd never stop chasing me.

I was tired of running, though. I was tired of always looking over my shoulder. I had important work to do, trying to find Anders, find Katarina Montalban, and stop Project Blue from happening. It was too important to waste time playing cat and mouse with shadow government operatives. The stakes were too high, and there was no time to waste.

Maybe, just maybe, I thought, if I killed this Underhill guy, they'd finally give up and leave me alone. If they sent their best after me only to have him disappear, or turn up dead, maybe then they'd get the fucking point. I owed him, anyway; he'd murdered Hawk in cold blood. Beside the fact that a government organization had summarily executed an American citizen with no due process whatsoever, Hawk had been like a father to me. Beyond the outrage over the injustice of it, this was personal, and I swore to God that I was going to find a way to kill Underhill myself.

As if on cue, the satellite phone in one of the pouches of my vest vibrated. It was all I could do to not roll my eyes as I pulled up the Velcro lid and checked the phone. Sure enough, it was a text message from Ariel. She denied it up and down, but I swear the girl was psychic.

Status update?

Watching as Dragic rummaged through his safe house, I thumbed a brief explanation of everything that had happened, including how Underhill was on his way.

You're thinking of staying behind, aren't you? she asked me. *To lay a trap.*

I am, I replied, honestly. Ariel was incredibly perceptive, and I'd long since learned that there was little point in lying to my little Oracle. *I can't do what I need to do while being hunted.*

It won't work, she sent back. There was a long pause, more than a minute, before I got the next message. *If you try, you will either be killed or captured again. Even if you do succeed, it won't change anything. They're afraid of you and they will never quit. If not Underhill, they'll send men like Frank Dragic after you, one after another.*

I can't keep running forever.

You won't have to, she assured me. Even via text message, she always seemed so damned confident in everything she told me. *Your paths will intersect. But not today. Dragic is a rogue variable. He complicates things. Just get out of there. Please. Come home.*

Dragic interrupted my text message conversation. "Are you done? I mean, every armed and angry asshole in the area will be descending on this house in the next hour, but sure, finish your status update or whatever."

I ignored him as I put the phone away. "I'm going to be honest with you," I said quietly to Antoine, "I was thinking of laying a trap for Underhill."

"I assumed as much," Antoine said. "It was all over your face the moment this man mentioned his name."

Am I really that easy to read? "The Oracle strongly advised against it. She said it won't work, and she's right. The Armenians or Russians or whoever will be here long before Underhill gets here."

"You should listen to her," Antoine advised. He didn't add that any personal quest for revenge would jeopardize my entire team, but I could tell he was thinking it from the intense look on his face. Being responsible for others often means not doing what your base impulses tell you to do.

I sighed again. "You're right. You ready, Dragic?"

He shouldered a full-looking backpack, probably his bug-out bag, and nodded. "We should go out the back."

Driving his point home, a big, green military truck rumbled down the street and pulled to a stop in front of the house. Ten men, wearing camouflage uniforms, helmets, and mismatched gear, sporting AK-74s, spilled out of the back, appearing one after another from under the canvas top. *That was fast.*

"Get down!" Dragic hissed, and we all dropped to the floor. The house was dark, save the light coming in through broken windows. "This way," he said, crawling on his hands and knees toward the back of the house. Antoine and I followed, scuttling along, trying to get low and stay out of sight.

"Who are *these* guys?" I asked Dragic.

He looked at me incredulously as he scurried across the floor. "Seriously? They're the Nagorno-Karabakh Defense Army. The *NKDA* I've been talking about? Armenian nationals, probably with some Russian *volunteers*. Did you do any research on this AO before you got here?"

I had left the Exodus compound in the rocky desert of Azerbaijan in a hurry, upon Ariel discovering information that led her to believe that Anders was on the ground in the disputed zone in the western part of the country. There was no way, I thought, that him turning up so close to one of the few remaining Exodus strongholds could be a coincidence. Antoine, Ling, Skunky, and Shen had all volunteered to accompany me, though the latter three were still at our safe house outside of the city. I hadn't really bothered to read up on the convoluted politics of this region before setting out, something Ling had also scolded me about. *She'd probably get along great with this guy.*

Dragic was out the back door as the NKDA squad kicked in the front. I could hear them shouting and the tromp of combat boots on a bare wooden floor as they searched the house. The ramshackle structure wasn't that big, and they'd be on top of us before we got through the backyard and into the concealment of the foliage beyond.

I looked up at Antoine. "Go, stay with him! Stay low!" Before he could say anything, I rolled onto my back, sat up slightly, and flipped the G3's selector lever to full auto. The German battle rifle roared throatily as I emptied the twenty-round magazine through the wall in a matter of seconds. When the rifle clicked empty, I rolled back onto my stomach and furiously low-crawled out the back door, into the yard. The angry shouts and one scream told me I'd tagged at least one of them.

A few yards in front of me, across the yard, Antoine took a knee and shouldered his rifle, also a G3. The Armenians in the house blindly fired through the walls, as I had, but they still didn't know where they were and their little 5.45mm rounds didn't have the same punch as the 7.62mm from my weapon. Still, some of their rounds got through, ripping through the back wall of the house in little puffs of plaster dust.

I was a few yards out into the yard, still low-crawling, when Antoine opened fire. He fired shot after shot, his rounds snapping angrily overhead, as the NKDA troops were caught in the fatal funnel of the back door. He was joined a moment later by Dragic, who had taken a weapon and a black chest rig off one of the dead Russians. His carbine, some AK type I thought, had no discernable muzzle rise as he fired off burst after burst on full auto.

As I reached their position at the back of the yard, Antoine told me to get down and shouted, "Grenade out!" The 40mm launcher bolted under the barrel of his G3 popped, and a split-second later the round detonated inside the back door of the house. I used the moment to roll to my left side and retrieve a mag from my vest. I pulled back the rifle's charging handle and locked the bolt open. Rocking in the fresh magazine, I slapped down on the charging handle, sending a round into the chamber and reloading the rifle. Looking back, I saw several dead bodies in the doorway.

I looked up at Dragic, who was reloading the weird AK-type rifle he'd gotten off the dead Russian. "Where's that car?"

"We can't get to it now," he said, pulling a pack of cigarettes off the dead Russian. "It's five houses down, but it's on the street. We need to get out of this neighborhood before they cordon it off completely. They're looking for us now, and none of us can pass for locals." He nodded toward Antoine. "Especially not the big guy. No offense."

Antoine just frowned, but Dragic wasn't wrong. "Lead the way," I said. "We'll follow." Now that he was armed, I wanted to keep him where I could see him. Besides that, he obviously had done a lot more scouting of the area than I had, and knew his way around better. Ling would never let me hear the end of it.

I spoke up, quietly, as we made our way through the overgrown foliage of the crumbling neighborhood. Few signs of life were evident. What locals still lived in this part of town were probably hunkering down because of all the shooting. It looked post-apocalyptic. "If we can get clear of this and get to a safe spot, I can radio the rest of my team and have them come pick us up. They're holed up in an old barn outside of town." I didn't want to head straight there. It was a long walk, in broad daylight, while we were being hunted, and I didn't want to risk leading the locals to my comrades.

"I think we need to find a good spot to secure until it gets dark," Dragic said. "The Organization has, or at least had, aerial surveillance of the area, too. Probably a UAV. If it's still on station, then they're watching this shit-show from above. Nightfall won't give us a lot of cover, but we'll at least be harder to ID on thermal than we are in daylight." Off in the distance somewhere, the distinct *thwup-thwupping* of a chopper could be heard, but I couldn't see it. We'd really kicked the hornet's nest.

We came to a deserted street. We crouched in the bushes and scanned the area before crossing the danger area that the open road presented. Where houses had apparently once stood, there were only crumbling foundations on overgrown lots. "What happened here?" This looked worse than the usual crumbling infrastructure you see in post-Soviet Central Asia.

"Ethnic Armenians, backed by the Russians, have been fighting with the Azeri for this part of the country for years. They shelled the fuck out of this part of the city, and engaged in some serious ethnic cleansing later. This was back in the Nineties. There was a cease-fire, but both sides have violated it over and over."

The helicopter sounded like it was getting closer, though I still couldn't see it through all the trees. "We need a vehicle. If they've got air support, it's going to be that much harder to get out of here on foot."

"Do you see any vehicles around here?" Dragic asked, obviously frustrated. "This isn't the rich part of town, okay? Most of the people that live here don't have much."

"Actually . . . " I trailed off, peeking my head out of the shrubbery just a little. A smallish van, light blue with a white roof, was headed in our direction. Its rounded contours and utilitarian aesthetic gave it a distinctly eastern European look.

"Un-fucking-believable," Dragic said. "Okay, here's what we do. I'll . . . hey!"

I stood up and stepped out of the bushes before Dragic could finish his plan. We needed a ride right-goddamn-now, and we didn't have time for this guy to come up with an elaborate scheme. I walked out into the middle of the street, rifle in hand, and stood facing the oncoming van. Antoine followed, pointing his rifle at the vehicle from the side. Dragic reluctantly stepped out a few seconds after that.

The driver was a middle-aged local man, wearing blue jeans and a polo shirt. He slowly raised his hands off the steering wheel. I didn't point my rifle at him, but Antoine had him covered. Even though I didn't speak his language, carjacking transcends most language barriers. I jerked my thumb to the side, indicating for the driver to get out. He did so, slowly, flushed white with fear.

I actually felt bad. This guy probably had a hard enough time of things without three foreign assholes stealing his van, too, but this was a life-or-death emergency. As he stepped away from the van, Dragic strode past me. "I'm driving," he growled, and grabbed the old man by the shirt. He said something to him in a language I didn't understand. The old man looked terrified, and with shaking hands produced a small cell phone. Dragic grabbed it and smashed it on the ground before shoving the old man away. "Well? Get in!"

Antoine and I jogged over to the van. The big African opened a side door to the rear cargo compartment, which was presently empty, and climbed in. I jumped into the passenger's seat next to Dragic and closed the door. I handed my rifle back to my teammate while Dragic laid his on the floor between the seats. Getting a good look at it, I realized it was an AK-1-0-whatever, one of those rifles with the counterweight that's supposed to negate recoil.

"You know," I said absentmindedly, as he put the van in gear, "I did this exact same thing once in Zubara. It was a French car, if I remember right, driven by a British guy, not a . . . " I looked around the cabin of the van. "Whatever this is."

"It's a *Yeraz*," he said tersely, lighting up a cigarette. "That's what the locals call them. Armenian produced for about thirty years."

"Yeraz," I repeated. "Cool. Okay, what's the best way out of the city?"

"Reach in my bag, the outside pouch. There's a map of the city. I've got a couple of egress routes highlighted, but that wasn't accounting for the entire NKDA looking for me. Fuck. They'll have checkpoints everywhere."

"That's why I wanted to get us a vehicle." I pulled the map out of Dragic's bag, waving the coarse smoke out of my face. "They might have God-knows-how-many dudes scouring the city for us by the time it gets dark. We need to get out of Dodge before they can get their shit together."

The grizzled mercenary puffed his cigarette and looked at me sideways. "That's surprisingly solid thinking."

"Surprisingly?" *Asshole.*

"To be honest, I'm kind of surprised you've lived as long as you have, after seeing how you operate. You just barge in and start shooting. You showed up and fucked everything up for us."

I chuckled. "Yeah, that's what I do. Besides, if you know anything about Project Heartbreaker, then you should realize I might know a thing or two about sowing chaos and escaping in the confusion. I helped bring down a nation, once." I rolled down my window a bit, to clear out the acrid smoke from his cigarette. "And I got away alive."

"Yeah. Cute. My team's dead and my life's barely worth the cost of a bullet, all because you barged into the middle of my op. I'm glad you think this is funny."

The tone of my voice changed. My left hand habitually dropped to the butt of my revolver. "Fuck you. Don't act like you don't know who you were working for. How did you think it was going to end, Dragic? You thought you were going to retire from this someday and die of old age? I risked my life to tell the world about Project Heartbreaker, tell them how we were betrayed and left to die. Even after that, you still kept working for *them*."

He looked over, giving me an icy glare. "Now you listen to me, kid—"

I didn't let him finish. "No, you listen to me, you son of a bitch. Your employers didn't just leave us to die when we were inconvenient. They sold us out, had us liquidated. I watched the woman I loved die in the mud. After they caught me, they didn't just interrogate me. Hell, they didn't just *torture* me, they turned me into a *science project*. So don't you fucking *dare* get on your high horse with me, dude. If I had known you didn't know where Anders was, I'd have shot you dead or left you for the Russians."

Dragic didn't say anything. He puffed his cigarette angrily. He was gripping the steering wheel so tightly his knuckles were white. Every muscle in his body was tense. He was seething with anger. I think that had Antoine not been just behind us, gun in his hand, Dragic would've tried to murder me right there.

Too fucking bad. Sooner or later, we all have to face what we've done. You can only lie to yourself for so long. When the truth can no longer be denied, it's a terrible shock. The realization of what you've wrought, the consequences of the choices you've made, it all weighs on you.

"Anyway . . . .I'm sorry about your teammates. I've been there, more times than I like to think about. It was a bad op. You got used, and when you weren't useful anymore, they threw you away. It's not right."

He relaxed his grip a bit and exhaled, heavily, filling the cabin with foul-smelling smoke. "Once you get in, there's no getting out."

"That's not true. I got out. You're getting out right now. As long as people like me and Anders are still on the loose, I doubt they'll commit any resources to tracking down a runaway door-kicker."

"Yeah, well, we gotta survive the day, first. Now check that map and find us a good route out of here."

"Hey, kid."

I kept my eyes on the map of the city. "Yeah?"

"What's with the revolver?"

"Huh?"

Dragic pointed at the .44 hanging from my hip. "The Dirty Harry magnum. Why do you carry that thing?"

"I like it," I said. "And I shoot revolvers better."

"Yeah, but it's huge, and has to weigh a ton. You could carry two Glock 19s for that weight, and have more than twice as much ammo."

I thought about it. "Yeah, probably." I looked back down at the map.

"No, seriously. Nobody carries a revolver anymore. They went out of style in the Eighties. A modern gun is smaller, lighter, easier to conceal, has less recoil, can be suppressed, and is quicker to reload."

"You're right about that."

"And for someone in your position, carrying a weird gun like that is fucking stupid. That's how we ID-ed you, you know. We saw that revolver."

Hmm, I thought. *Maybe a little more discretion wouldn't hurt.*

"So why do you insist on carrying it?"

"Like I said, I shoot revolvers better. And this gun? It's always kept me alive."

"That sounds like a bunch of sentimental bullshit to me," Dragic said. "I once knew . . . *shit.*"

Dragic's, snarled expletive and change in tone was enough to get my attention. I looked up from the map and down the road. We'd been driving for almost an hour, having had to change our route and double back more than once. The Nagorno-Karabakh Defense Army had mobilized in a rapid fashion. They were setting up expedient checkpoints along every road out of the city. I'd hoped that this road, at least, would get us out of town without being spotted.

So much for that. We came to a stop. Up ahead, an old UAZ 4x4 was parked in the road, blocking one lane. Four bored-looking, but armed soldiers stood around it. One had one of those flashlights with a red cone on it, and was motioning for us to come forward. Antoine ducked further into the back of the van, his rifle in his hands.

"What do we do?" I asked.

"This piece of shit can't outrun them. If we turn around, they'll get suspicious. If we go forward, they'll either capture or kill us. There's no way I'm going to be able to bluff my way through without getting the van searched. If it was just me, maybe, but with you two?"

"Well, this sucks," I said. The soldier with the flashlight-cone was getting impatient, waving the glowing implement faster. "We can't just sit here, either."

"I can try to gun it," Dragic suggested. "Run a couple of them over. Maybe we'll get around that bend before they shoot us up."

The bend in the road he was talking about was a long ways off. I shook my head. "They'll start shooting before we even get to them."

"I *know,* goddamn it! We have to do *something!*"

"Pull forward," I said. "Be ready. If you have earplugs you might want to put them in," I said, putting in a pair of my own. I drew my .44 Magnum and put it in my lap. "It's about to get loud."

Dragic looked at me incredulously, shaking his head. He lit another cigarette, probably the fifth one he'd had since we'd been driving, and put the van in gear. "Fuck me, we're gonna die." He wasn't losing his cool; he was frustrated, but still level headed. It was more resignation than anything else.

I took a deep breath, feeling my heart slow down as we approached the checkpoint. Everything else seemed to slow with it. My senses were heightened, my thoughts clear. I was scared, and I was amped up, but that all got pushed into the periphery. With the adrenaline came the *Calm.* "Trust me. I've done this before."

Of course the last time I'd done this it had cost Wheeler his life. There was no other way, though. I looked back at Antoine. "Don't shoot until I shoot."

We slowly rolled toward the checkpoint. It was late in the day, and we were headed in an easterly direction; the sun was at our back, which worked in our favor. As we drew near, I got a good look at the four NKDA soldiers. All of them wore camouflage. To our left was a young, skinny man with a unibrow. His helmet was too big for him and the chinstrap dangled from the side of his face. He had an AK-74 slung over his right shoulder, muzzle-up. I saw that the safety was on.

In front of us, standing next to the parked UAZ, was an officer. He wore a soft cap with a shiny badge on it. A green pistol belt was fastened around his ample waist. A pistol in a flap holster hung from his right hip. He was fiddling with a radio and wasn't really paying attention.

On the right side of the road was a more seasoned-looking soldier with a big mustache. He looked squared-away, and held an AKS-74 at the low-ready. He was also wearing a plate carrier—the biggest threat. Next to him, with the flashlight-cone, was another young man, this one with glasses. He had an AK-74 slung across his back.

Everything seemed to slow down as Dragic brought the van to a stop. When *Calm,* I perceive things like you do when you're in a traffic accident, when everything seems to move in slow motion. It's more than that, though. I tend to notice every detail, and I remember everything I see later. It's an overwhelmingly intense focus that I wish I had better control over, but as is it's rarely let me down.

Unibrow-guy stepped to the driver's side window. At the same time, flashlight-cone-guy stepped to the passenger's side. Both of their eyes went wide as I brought my gun up in both hands, pushing it out over the dashboard. The big, stainless-steel Smith & Wesson roared. Glass fractured as .44 Magnum slugs punched right through the windshield. I fired once, twice, three times, aiming at the veteran NKDA soldier with his weapon in hand. The first round went way low, impacting on his front armor plate. Bullets do funny things when they go through glass. The second shot I pulled to the left, and it clipped his shoulder. The third hit him in the face and blew his brains out the back of his head.

At the same time, Dragic reached out the widow and grabbed unibrow-guy's uniform collar. He jerked the skinny soldier to the window with his left hand. His right hand came up with a knife and plunged the blade up into his head, under the jawbone. He twisted and yanked the knife out in a spray of blood.

As unibrow-guy and the veteran were both falling to the ground, I shifted my gun to flashlight-cone-guy. He had dropped his light and was backing away from the passenger's side window, struggling to bring his rifle to bear. He wasn't nearly fast enough, and he wasn't wearing body armor. The .44 bucked in my hand as I put a round through his heart.

The fat officer looked up, an expression of shock on his face. He dropped his radio and went for his pistol, but Dragic stomped on the gas. Antoine's rifle barked from the back of the van. I felt the muzzle blast as the bullet zipped between Dragic and me, punched through the windshield, and struck the NKDA officer in the stomach. He doubled over and started to fall. *THUMP!* The bumper of the van clipped him before he hit the ground, launching him into the grill of the parked UAZ as we sped past.

Just like that, it was over. Time sped up to its normal rate. I noticed that my ears were ringing despite the earplugs. My hands started to shake. "Is . . . is anybody hit? Everybody good?"

"I'm fine," Antoine assured me. "Are you injured?"

"No! No." I was just spun up. My heart was racing now. "Dragic, you okay?"

He looked over at me with an intense expression on his face. He'd been splashed with blood and looked primal. "I'm good," he said haltingly. "I'm good. Holy fucking *shit*."

I exhaled heavily. I couldn't believe that had actually worked, either.

"You weren't kidding about being good with that revolver, were you?"

We drove for probably another hour, putting distance between us and the city. The road was narrow and winding, so it was slow-going. As darkness fell, we learned that the NKDA officer's fat body had busted our left headlight. Antoine was on the radio with Ling, updating her on our location. We weren't actually going toward the safe house. We were going to find a secluded spot, ditch the van, and have her come pick us up.

We pulled off the lonely highway, turning north, and followed a dirt road for a couple miles as it plunged into the forest. Finding a good spot, we came to a stop, and climbed out. "Here," I said, handing Dragic my GPS. "Figure out where we are, exactly, and find a good spot for my team to meet us. They have a four-wheel drive, so they can go off-road if they have to. Antoine and I will push the van into the trees."

"Good," the mercenary said, taking the GPS from me. The glow from the screen made his haggard face look even more unsettling. "We should move under tree cover in case the Organization still has a UAV overhead."

Nodding, I turned my attention to the van. Antoine had already disengaged the parking brake. We both sidled up to the back of the van, put a shoulder into it, and pushed. I was glad to have Antoine with me; he's big and made of muscle. We were able to get it over the hump at the edge of the road, and from there the van started rolling on its own. I stood back and watched as it rolled a short way down a hill, coming to a stop only when it crunched into a tree. The hill was steep enough that anyone driving by wouldn't see the van from the road, and the trees were so dense that it wouldn't likely be spotted from the air.

I wiped my brow on my sleeve and turned to Dragic. "Okay, where do we . . . Dragic?"

He was nowhere to be seen. I immediately knew what happened. *Son of a bitch.*

"It seems this is where we part ways," Antoine said quietly.

The asshole had stolen my GPS. "Probably a waste of time trying to go after him. He could get the drop on us too easily if he decides he doesn't want to be followed." More than that it was dark, it was getting cold, I was tired, and I'd had enough fun for one day. I looked up at Antoine. "I probably should've shot him when I had the chance."

The big African shook his head. "I don't think so, Mr. Valentine. I think you stayed your hand for a reason. I doubt he'll try to return to his former employer."

I doubted it, too. As near as I'd been able to tell, Frank Dragic hadn't been a Majestic insider. He was kind of like I had been on Dead Six, hired help, only told what he needed to know and not privy to anything too sensitive. Deniable and expendable. "Underhill will be on the ground here soon enough."

Antoine actually put one of his huge hands on my shoulder. "Believe me when I say that I know what it's like to desire vengeance for someone you love.

Please, also believe me when I say that going down that road will only get you killed. You may get your shot at this Underhill person yet, but now is not the time. We should regroup with the others and return to Azerbaijan while we still have the chance. We've pushed our luck enough."

"Yeah . . . yeah, you're right." Setting my rifle down, I unzipped my tactical vest and dropped it on the ground at my feet. Ripping open Velcro straps, I pulled my body armor off over my head and tossed it aside. My shirt was soaked with sweat and I was suddenly cold. I picked up the tac vest, put it back on, even though it fit loosely without the armor, and slung my rifle. "I guess we're hoofing it. Let's get out of here, find a good spot to have Ling pick us up, and call for a ride. Hopefully they can figure out where we are. Oh, and tell her to burn the safe house, too. We're not going back."

Antoine nodded and quietly spoke into his radio as we set off into the forest, under the cover of a moonless night.

ALLIANCE OF SHADOWS

by Larry Correia and Mike Kupari

Chapter 1: The Stakeout

VALENTINE
Salzburg, Austria
September 3rd

Bullets pinged off the helicopter's hull as we lifted away from the port. Through the chaos, the scream of the engines and the roar of the machine guns, time seemed to slow to a trickle.

The crew chief ripped off burst after burst from the door gun as the NH-90 maneuvered violently, her pilot trying to avoid the incoming fire. My team leader, Ramirez, was wounded, bleeding out. Tailor was talking into the radio, trying to hide the fear in his voice. Skunky was firing his M14 out one door, while the mysterious Exodus operatives were on the other side of the cabin, huddled protectively around the young girl they'd just rescued. Her hair was silver, almost white. Her face was dirty, and there was fear in her eyes.

We hadn't gone onto the ship with them. That was their op. We were just supposed to provide transportation and security, supposedly the easy part. Exodus performed the extraction—several of them died in the process—but they got the girl. I didn't know who she was. I didn't know why she was so important, why the arms dealer, Federov, kidnapped her in the first place, or why Exodus paid us so much money to help recover her.

The girl's eyes, intensely blue, unnervingly clear, locked onto me, and everything else seemed to fade away. The fear left her face for just a moment, replaced with . . . curiosity? Interest? She cocked her head very slightly to one side as Ling, the Chinese woman who led the Exodus operatives, and their medic looked her over. She was staring right at me.

"Only you can save us."

BANG! I came crashing back to reality when a large round blasted a hole in the hull of the chopper. The screams of men were joined with the scream of a warning klaxon. I was pinned against my seat as the chopper began rotating. Through the open door I could see Cancun spinning all around us. The ground rushed up to meet us.

My eyes snapped open. A bead of sweat trickled down my head as I quickly looked around, breathing heavily, trying to remember where I was.

"Are you okay?" Skunky asked. I was sitting in the driver's seat of a car. It was dark out.

I took a moment to catch my breath. "Yeah . . . yeah, I'm fine."

"Did you have a bad dream?"

I closed my eyes for a long moment, trying to will my heart to slow down. "The chopper crash in Mexico again."

Skunky winced. He had been on that op too. His real name was Jeff, and we'd been through a lot together. Riding a helicopter into a swimming pool wasn't the worst thing we'd been through. Not even close.

"How long was I out?"

"About an hour," he said.

"You kept watching the house, right?"

"Naw, man, I zoned out playing *War of Battle Clans* on my phone. Of course I was watching the house. One of us actually has to work." He had a night vision scope in his hands, and a big camera on the dash. We were parked down the road a bit from the target, away from the street lights, in the shadows beneath some trees.

I stretched. "I'm the brains of this operation. I need my rest."

Exodus had sustained terrible losses in the operation at the Crossroads, and was desperately short on manpower. There were only six of us in Austria, trying to prevent the end of the world. I kept telling myself that was the reason I was here, that they needed me.

They say it is good to be needed. I didn't know about that, since the only thing I'd ever been needed for was war.

I shifted uncomfortably in my seat. We had been sitting in this BMW M3 for hours. "Whoever would've thought this is where we'd end up? From a helicopter crash in Mexico to a Beemer in Austria?"

Skunky shook his head. "I think it was meant to be. I don't believe in coincidences like this."

"You know, Ariel told me I was right where I needed to be."

"You should listen to her. She's a smart girl. She knows stuff."

That was an understatement. Ariel was the girl we'd rescued off that ship, the weird one from my dream, only she was all grown up now, and palling around with Exodus—a secret organization dedicated to protecting the weak in all the places the civilized world didn't give a damn about—but which was unfortunately considered a terrorist organization by every law enforcement agency in the world. So she'd come a long way.

"Knowing stuff . . . I can't argue with that."

"I still think she's got psychic powers, man."

"Dude, shut up. She's not psychic." I opened my door. We'd shut off the car's interior light to not give our position away. "I'll be right back. I need some air."

Salzburg is beautiful. It was a clear night, and the city was lovely. Moonlight reflected off of the snow-capped Alps and the Salzach River, which ran through the city. Behind me, at the top of the hill, was Hohensalzburg Castle. The ancient fortress was the most prominent feature of the picturesque city, and was a very popular tourist stop. Narrow, winding streets cut back and forth up the hill leading to the castle. This part of the city was terraced, with houses lining the streets, packed in together. The street I stood on, Nonnberggasse, was at rooftop level with the terrace below me, and I could see down into people's windows. The street was virtually deserted, as the castle was closed at night.

There was some kind of festival going on in the heart of the city. The city center was lit up, and even from where I was, I could hear music. I wondered what it was like to just be able to go to things like that, to live your life without worrying about staying off the radar. I was sick of the cloak and dagger bullshit.

My phone vibrated in my pocket as I made my way back to the car. I had a text message from Ling.

How are you doing?

The phones were a bit of a risk, but as long as we were careful about what we said we were safe. *Cramped,* I texted back. *I had to get out to stretch.*

How are you boys getting along?

Bored. Talking about the old days. How are you?

Same, she wrote back. *S. and A. are up front. I tried to sleep for a while, but got a cramp in my neck.*

Aww. When this is over, I'll massage it out for you.

I can't help but notice that whenever you try to give me a massage, I end up with my clothes off.

I don't see how this is a problem.

I didn't say it was a problem. I just think that, perhaps, with you being as easily distracted as you are, the therapeutic quality of your massages is dubious, at best.

I couldn't help but smile at Ling's judicious use of proper grammar, punctuation, and capitalization in her texts. It was adorable. *I disagree,* I sent back. *Those massages always make me feel great. Hey, you should send me a picture.*

Is that so? Fine. Let me find one you haven't seen yet.

"Val, look," Skunky's tone had changed. It was all business now. "There's a vehicle arriving at the building."

Damn it. I grabbed the radio. "Alpha Team, this is Bravo. We've got a vehicle approaching the building of interest, I say again, vehicle approaching the BOI. Late model Mercedes sedan, four-door, dark color. We're getting it on camera, how copy?"

"Understood," Antoine replied. His deep voice boomed over the radio. *"We're moving now. Keep eyes on until we get to you."*

"Roger," I said. We had kept our vehicles separate so as to be as discreet as possible, and to watch different paths of entry. Ling's team was in a nondescript Range Rover. This part of Salzburg had too many curvy little streets, so it was impossible to cover all possible routes with just two vehicles, but we had to make do with the assets we had.

"Two people getting out," Skunky said.

"Let me see," I said, taking the camera from him. Resting it on the steering wheel, I zoomed in and studied the two men climbing the steps to the four story house. It was a narrow building, constructed right up against a rocky outcropping on the hill. It didn't have a yard, but it did have an adjacent garage. "Bravo Team, Alpha. I think that's our boy."

"Copy," Antoine said. *"Stefan Varga?"*

Our radios were encrypted and secure, so he could use our target's real name. I studied the zoomed-in image intently, and compared to a picture I had saved on my phone. "Affirmative."

"Are you sure?"

"Sure as I can be. Get up here."

"Copy that," Antoine said. *"We're moving."*

"Roger. As soon as you guys get into position we're going in."

"We need him alive," Antoine reminded me.

"We'll do the best we can. We . . . stand by."

"What's wrong?" Skunky asked.

"Shit," I growled. "Bravo Team, I got a quick look inside when they opened the door. There are more dudes inside. The guy that answered the door had a weapon, submachine gun maybe." We had thought the house to be empty. There was no vehicle parked on the street—though we couldn't see into the garage—and no one had passed by a window in the time we'd been watching the place. They'd kept a low profile. "Security is better than we thought."

"Understood, Alpha," Antoine said. *"Have we been compromised?"*

"I don't think so. I don't know how many guys are in there, though. This could get ugly. How do you want to run this? We got two options. We can kick the door in and do it the hard way, or we can wait until Varga leaves and try to nab him off the street. Either way is risky."

Ling's clear soprano voice came over my radio. *"If Varga gets away, the last two months have been for nothing."*

"Copy that, but if there are six armed dudes in there plus our new arrivals, we're gonna have a bad night. Everything will be for nothing if we all get killed."

"*This is your op, Valentine,*" Ling said, much more formally than she had been via text a minute ago, but she kept our relationship private and separate from our work. "*It is your call. If we try to catch Varga in town, you know what can happen.*"

Shit. My mind raced. I'd done this sort of thing before, though door-kicking was not something I was particularly fond of—it's an easy way to get killed—but if this thing turned into a running gun battle downtown, we'd be lucky to avoid getting arrested by the Polizei, and countless innocent people would be endangered.

Skunky started tapping me on the shoulder as I brooded. "Dude. Dude! We've got another vehicle approaching, a motorcycle."

I keyed the radio. "Bravo Team, stand by. We've got a motorcycle rolling up to the house. Bullet bike of some kind. Only the driver. He's wearing riding gear and a full face helmet. He has a messenger bag. Skinny guy, maybe five foot nine, and I'm sorry I can't convert that to centimeters or hectares or whatever for you. He's got a package in his hands, heading up to the door."

"*What do you want to do?*" Antoine asked.

"Hold up for a moment. Maybe he's just making a delivery or something. It looks like he left the bike running. He'll probably leave in a minute. We'll wait until he's clear before we move in."

"*Understood.*"

I watched on my little screen, recording, as the newcomer walked up the steps to the door of the house. He opened the bag and pulled something out of it.

"Is that a weapon?" Skunky asked.

BOOM! The stranger blasted the door handle with a sawed-off shotgun. He kicked the door open and went inside.

What the hell? There had been no hesitation there. It was roll up and breach. It had taken me by surprise, so it was probably a whole lot worse for our target. I keyed the radio mic. "Bravo, Alpha, shots fired, shots fired!" More gunfire erupted from inside the building as I spoke.

"*Say again?*"

"There's a goddamn gun battle going on in there!"

"*We need Varga alive,*" Ling said.

"I know!" But I didn't want to jump in the middle of somebody else's gunfight.

"You want to take a look?" Skunky asked.

Seconds ticked by. *Who'd want Varga dead?* Well, besides us? The man worked for a slave trading, arms dealing, drug running, organized crime syndicate. It was probably a long list. More gunfire came from the house. We'd spent months waiting for a chance to grab this guy. "Damn it . . . Come on." I pulled a ski mask over my head and drew my Smith & Wesson 629 revolver. The big .44 Magnum glinted dully in the moonlight as I opened the door. I looked at Skunky. "You ready?"

He got his mask on, drew his Beretta, and nodded.

I hit the radio and warned Ling's team, "We're going in."

"We're on the way."

We moved quickly but cautiously across the cobblestone street, guns drawn, toward the house. The muffled pops of gunfire could still be heard from where we were. This was a sleepy neighborhood, and one of the neighbors was sure to have called the cops by now.

"It sounds like a deathmatch round going on in there, and someone's got a kill streak going."

"I just hope the fuck Varga is still alive," I said as we neared the house.

Skunky pointed toward the top floor. "There's movement in that window."

"What the hell is—" *CRASH!* A body smashed through the fourth-story window and tumbled to the cobblestone below. The man landed with a sickening crunch. I don't know if he'd jumped or been pushed, but that landing was all ribs and skull.

I ran up, saw who it was, lowered my revolver, and sighed. "That, right there, is Stefan Varga."

Skunky knelt next the target whom we had hoped to take alive, probably to take his pulse, but when he saw the brains sliding out, that wasn't really necessary. He looked at the dead man, then at me, then back at the dead man. "Well, crap. What now?"

"Come on," I said, moving past the newcomer's still running motorcycle. "Maybe we can still get some intel from this place."

"It is on the scanner. The police are on the way," Antoine warned. From the tire squealing noise over the radio, he was headed our way fast.

I hesitated. I was still wanted by a shadowy arm of the U.S. government, and they had a long reach. Any involvement with the police would end up with me either being renditioned to a black site or shot in the back of the head. They wouldn't risk letting me escape again. I'd had more close calls than I liked already.

Skunky noticed my hesitation. "Maybe we should just split? He hasn't seen us. We can back off and tail the assassin."

"Unless he's bleeding to death inside." After all, it had only been one man, and he'd shot it out with at least four of them. With Varga dead, our only hope of this operation not being a total bust was to get some answers from *somebody.* I spoke into my radio. "We're going in."

"*Understood,*" Antoine said. "*We'll be there momentarily. Faster, Shen.*"

Decision made, I raised my gun, pushed forward, and made it halfway up the house's front stairs when someone flew out the front door and kicked me in the face. Off balance, I lurched backward, crashing into Skunky, and we both tumbled down the stairs. A boot stomped on my chest as the interloper ran right over the top of us. Dazed and still rolling, I saw the shooter running for his motorcycle.

Ling's team came blazing around the corner in their Range Rover, but without slowing the shooter extended a pistol in both hands and cranked off several fast shots. Shen swerved to the side and hit the brakes. The shooter got on his bike, revved the engine, and took off.

I rolled over onto the cobblestone, brought my gun to bear, but it was too late. I didn't have a shot without putting a round into some poor Austrian's house. I pushed myself off the ground, pulled Skunky to his feet, and we sprinted for our car. If we lost sight of him there'd be no way we'd catch up with that bike.

As I buckled myself into the BMW, Shen came back over the radio. "*I tried to ram him. I missed. He's headed down Nonnberggasse. I'll try to go around. Hurry.*"

I started the engine, put it in drive, and stepped on it. My face hurt. Blood was trickling from my nose, making a wet spot in the ski mask. Our car was fast, but that bike was faster. And he could fit through things that we couldn't. This would take a miracle, but I intended to catch this son of a bitch.

The rider killed his headlight so it would be harder for us to spot him, but Skunky had a night vision device he couldn't hide from.

"Left, left, left!" Skunky said excitedly. I saw him, but he was still leaving us behind. The motorcycle took a sharp turn, tires squealing, and for a moment I thought he was going to lay it down on the cobblestone street. He recovered and hit the accelerator, having cut a hairpin turn off of Nonnberggasse and onto a street that joined it in a Y-shaped intersection. I nearly spun the BMW out trying to keep up.

"Shit," I snarled, "he's going downtown!" In the heart of the city there would be more lights, but even at this time of night there would still be a lot more traffic. Which he could go through, which I couldn't.

"*Do you still have eyes on?*" Ling asked.

"Roger, but he's making distance. I'm going to lose him unless he screws up!"

"*Do not lose him!*" Ling ordered. "*Shen found a shortcut through someone's garden. We're going to try to cut him off.*"

I wished I could have seen Shen drive the Range Rover through somebody's garden. An angry motorist in a little hatchback laid on his horn as I swerved around him. I was just trying not to kill anybody.

The short switchback road ended in a T-intersection, which was clogged with traffic. The rider easily picked his way through, probably confident that he was getting away. Suddenly, the Range Rover appeared from the left, speeding out of a narrow alley between buildings. Shen turned hard and flew right in front of the bike. Narrowly avoiding the impact, the rider turned to the side and laid his bike down, hard. One of its mirrors snapped off as it hit the pavement, sliding into the side of a parked Volvo with a crunch. It looked like it hurt. Shen could have had him then, but apparently the Range Rover's brakes weren't that good, and he smashed their front bumper through a plaster planter and killed some shrubbery.

Reaching the intersection, I threw the Beemer into park and jumped out, drawing my gun. Skunky bailed out too. Shen was trying to back up. Motorists honked and cursed at the crazy Range Rover, but the ones who saw two men in ski masks with guns shut their mouths and ducked. The rider had already gotten to his feet. The assassin was small, but he must have been really strong as he dragged the heavy bike upright, mounted up, and took off before any of us was even close to grabbing him. I almost fired, but stopped myself, but there were too many bystanders behind him. I swore aloud and ran back to my car as the motorcycle rider maneuvered through the stopped traffic.

"I didn't have a shot," Skunky grumbled.

"Me either. Get back on the radio, keep telling Shen where he's going."

"Roger! He's turning right onto, uh . . . Erhardg . . . Erhard . . ." Before Skunky could pronounce the name of the street, I jumped the curb, laying on the horn as I sped down the sidewalk, clearing the intersection and keeping eyes on him.

"The police scanner is going crazy. Someone called in the gunshots and the police are en route. Most of them are pulling traffic duty for the festival, but they're being redirected this way."

"Understood." They'd also be calling in our high speed chase now. "We need that diversion!"

"Roger that," Ling said. Our diversion was simple enough: call in emergencies all over the city, spoofing the police. They would have to respond to them all, and it would tie up their resources.

He was still blazing along, getting away from us, but the motorcycle appeared to be wobbling badly. I really hoped he'd damaged it somehow when he'd laid it down. We followed the bike through a roundabout and across a bridge over the Salzach River.

With just that brief straightaway, he nearly lost us, but across the bridge, the motorcycle screeched to a halt. There were two lanes in each direction, but another roundabout on the far side was also jammed with traffic. Just as I was closing in, the bike moved through the tightly packed traffic, and sped off to the northwest. I couldn't afford to lose sight of the faster vehicle for very long, so I cut the wheel to the left, laid on the horn, and Skunky gasped as I drove the BMW onto the sidewalk, sending pedestrians running for their lives, hoping to God I didn't clip somebody. There were police sirens in the distance. A car on the sidewalk would draw attention. I had to get back on the street, blend in, but still keep up with the bike.

The street we were on followed the river northwest. The bike was still a lot faster than my car, and far nimbler, but the rider looked like he was really struggling with it. I was right, it had gotten damaged somehow. I kept him in sight, driving in the margins and on the sidewalk when I had to.

"I think his bike's dying. Get ready for him to bail on foot. Where are you guys?"

"Behind you. We got cut off."

As the river curved to the north, the motorcycle made a hard right, wobbling, nearly wrecking again. The road dipped down and ran under railroad tracks here, but he turned onto a perpendicular street that ran parallel to the tracks. I nearly collided with another car, barely maintaining control, but managed to make the turn and stay with him. The street was separated from the railroad tracks by concrete barriers.

"Where did you go?" Ling called.

"He turned east along Humboldtstrasse! Parallel to the tracks! He's . . . oh, shit!" Riding up an earth berm, the bike jumped the barriers and disappeared on the other side. "He just fucking jumped the fence!"

"What?"

"Val, I lost him!" Skunky said.

"No we didn't!" *There.* There was an access gate in the barriers blocked by a chain link fence a couple hundred yards up the road. "Hang on!" I said, gritting my teeth, and stepped on the accelerator. The car groaned and made a sickening crunching sound as we smashed through the fence. The window cracked. I nearly spun out, but we were through, and I was relieved that the airbag didn't deploy in my face. I stomped on the brakes and launched the chain link gate, which was still on the top of my car, forward onto the tracks.

"Are you okay?"

"There he is!" Skunky pointed. The rider was a short way up the tracks, picking up the bike. He must have lost it on landing. He'd probably been thinking he could get out of sight for a second, and ditch us in here. *Wrong, asshole.* He looked up, saw me, and gunned his accelerator. For a second I thought he was going to crash right into us, but he swerved at the last second, accelerating down the tracks. I cut the wheel to the right, stomped on the gas, and followed.

The car rattled and bounced as we followed the tracks, weaving around parked sets of train cars. It felt like we were going to vibrate our car to death. The bike was producing smoke, and making a lot of noise, but not a lot of speed. His ride was toast.

"I think I can get a shot," Skunky said, Beretta 9mm in hand.

"Hold your fire. Just hang on, I got this."

"Dude, you're going to get us killed trying to catch this asshole and we don't even know if it's worth it!" We flew past a railroad station, under a highway overpass, and the tracks curved to the right. They made a wide loop, turning back to the south. "If we lose sight of him he's gone."

"I know!" I pushed the gas pedal all the way to the floor. The rattling increased so much that I thought the doors were going to fly off. Each bump threatened to send the Beemer out of control as I tried to navigate the tracks by my one remaining headlight. "Okay. Shoot him."

"About time!" Skunky said.

"Try not to make it fatal." Or at least immediately fatal, because we really needed to interrogate this guy.

He leaned out the window a bit, pistol extended in his hand, and popped off shot after shot. "Damn it," he snarled. The car was rattling so badly from driving on the tracks that he couldn't hold his gun steady.

"Holy shit, man, just shoot him!"

"I'm trying! Drive better!" He leaned out the window again, further this time, holding his gun in both hands, and fired again, then again and again. The motorcycle suddenly cut its wheel to the side and fell over, sliding to a stop. "I got him!"

More like Skunky had finally put the bike out of its misery. The rider was on his feet and running away. I cranked the wheel and hit the gas, the BMW bucking over row after row of tracks. The rider sprinted as fast as he could, though obviously hurt. He had nowhere to go. At the edge of the tracks was a metal security fence. *Got him. Wait, what?*

"You have got to be fucking kidding me!" I snarled. The rider scrambled up the eight-foot fence like a monkey and vaulted himself over.

"Dude's got some mad parkour skills," Skunky observed. "Stop the car, you can't crash through that fence. We gotta go on foot!"

I threw the car into park and opened the door. Skunky was already out of the car. He hit the fence, sturdily constructed from steel, and started to climb. "I see him!" he said, at the top. "Come on, hurry!"

"Jesus," I wheezed, hitting the fence as Skunky dropped to the other side. "I'm hurrying!"

Now we were having a foot chase. This really wasn't how I planned my evening to go. The assassin was fast, but Skunky was a damned good runner. I just tried to keep up.

Ling's voice was in my ear as I climbed. *"Where are you?"*

"He wrecked. We're off the tracks now," *pant pant.* "On foot." *pant pant.* I looked at a street sign affixed to a lamp post. "Robinigstrasse, I think." The street was short and ended at what looked like a yard for parking trucks. At least the place was closed down for the night and there weren't any witnesses.

"Come on!" Skunk yelled from down the street. "This way! He went into that building!" Two small warehouses marked the end of the street, which was lit only by a couple amber streetlights.

"He went . . ." *pant pant* ". . . into one of the buildings," I said, relaying it all to Ling. "You got my location?"

"Affirmative." She could track me by GPS, but there was lag when I was moving. *"We'll be there in a few minutes. Don't enter that building alone!"*

I acknowledged Ling and slowed to a fast walk, breathing hard. *Damn, I'm out of shape.* The warehouse was butted up against some trees. If there was a back door, the rider could get away and I'd never see him.

Skunky was waiting for me at the door. "About time," he whispered.

I flipped him off, still breathing hard. The door of the small warehouse was still open. I took a quick peek around the corner, into the darkness. I didn't see anything, but was immediately answered by shots. I flung myself out of the doorway and pushed Skunky to the ground as a hail of gunfire peppered the corrugated metal behind where I'd been standing. I rolled back over and came to my feet. I transferred my revolver to my right hand, stuck it around the corner, and blindly fired off all six shots.

The gun roared and echoed in the metal building and throughout the neighborhood. I hoped to hell our police diversion was working. I could hear sirens in the distance, but none seemed to be closing in as I twisted a speedloader into my gun's cylinder. I keyed my radio. "Ling, I think I got him cornered in the warehouse. He's armed. Shots fired. What's your ETA?"

"Less than a minute."

"Roger. I'll stall him." I pulled off the ski mask so I could speak more clearly, and so my face could breathe. The sweat was stinging my eyes, making it hard to see, and my face still hurt from him feeding me a shoe on the stairs. "Listen, asshole," I said, shouting into the doorway. "You're trapped. I'm not alone out here, and I've got more backup coming. The cops are coming too. We don't work for the owners of that house. We were doing surveillance. We don't have to be enemies. We just want to talk to you."

There was no response.

I tried to hide the frustration in my voice. "Do you speak English? Can you understand me? I'm not a cop. I just want to talk to you, figure out what the hell is going on. You killed Stefan Varga. We were looking for him. Just come out. I'll put my gun away."

After a long pause, the rider finally spoke. "You have got to be fucking kidding me!"

"What?" I moved away from the doorway when I heard footsteps approaching. I looked over at Skunky and signaled that our guy was coming out.

A moment later the rider stepped out of the shadows. I kept my gun on him, but he came out with his hands up and empty. He ditched his helmet. The face looked familiar, but it still took me a second before I recognized him. Then my heart dropped into my stomach. I knew this man, but he was the last person in the world I'd expected to see here, mostly because he was supposed to be dead.

"Lorenzo?"

Chapter 2: Whispers in the Dark

LORENZO
Sala Jihan's Fortress
Date Unknown

The shackles bit into my wrists as the soldiers pulled on my chains. I stumbled through the dim hall, pain tearing through me with each halting step, trying to keep up. If I fell, they'd just drag me. I knew from experience that would probably reopen my wounds, but my legs were too weak. When I fell my captors didn't even bother to slow down, and my arms wrenched in their sockets as the chains snapped tight. My stitches pulled, scabs broke and wept blood, but the slave soldiers didn't care. They dragged me until stone turned to soft dirt, and out into the searing daylight.

It really wasn't much light, just a hole in the roof above. I'd been kept in the dark for so long that my eyes were having a hard time adjusting. I couldn't see where I was, but the slaughterhouse smell gave it away.

We were back in the pit.

Time didn't mean anything here, but it had probably been weeks since my last fight. I told time by how healed my wounds were. What would I have to fight today? Slave soldiers? Other prisoners? More vicious dogs?

The soldiers hauled me roughly to my feet and began unlocking my shackles. I didn't struggle. I'd need the energy for whatever was going to come next. My abraded wrists throbbed. My ankles burned where the irons had rubbed off my skin. The soldiers' cheeks had been branded with Sala Jihan's mark. Their eyes were emotionless and vacant as they took the chains away.

There was one other door into the pit, but it was still closed. My opponent hadn't arrived yet. Blinking against the sun, I looked up and tried to see *him*.

As usual, I could see nothing but shadows inside the observers' alcove above. Was the Pale Man here? That was the worst part. Each time I was tortured or made to fight something for Sala Jihan's amusement, I didn't even know if he bothered to watch.

The other heavy door creaked open. More slave soldiers dragged in another prisoner. His tattered rags had once been a North Chinese uniform, but he was fighting the guards, and appeared healthy, so he hadn't been here long. A deserter? A border guard who'd crossed the Pale Man somehow? It didn't matter. Nobody here retained their identity or their sanity for long.

I had nothing against this man. I didn't know him or anything about him, but if I wanted to survive one more day I'd have to kill him.

A slave soldier dropped a knife at my bare feet. "Pick it up," he ordered in Mandarin.

I looked down at the little knife, stuck point first into the dirt. The handle was antler, wrapped in leather strips, stained with dried blood. Last time I'd been forced to fight it had been with bare hands. The time before, I'd been given nothing but a sharpened stick.

I left the knife there. "Why doesn't the Pale Man just kill me and get it over with?"

The soldier backhanded me hard in the face. It barely registered. Blood dripped from my split lip and down my rags. I knew if we didn't fight, they'd just execute other prisoners in front of me until I provided them a good show, women, children, they didn't give a shit. "Pick up the knife."

Instead, I shouted at the alcove. *"Why won't you kill me?"*

Surprisingly, there was movement in the shadows above. "The better question, Lorenzo . . ." Sala Jihan's voice was cold, distant, ominous. "Is why won't you die?"

I picked up the knife.

"I'm Lorenzo," I said through the crack in the wall. "What's your name?"

The prisoner in the next cell didn't respond, but I could hear his labored breathing. I'd heard him in there for the first time today. There were no lights in the cells except for what the guards brought with them, so I'd never seen the man, had no idea who he was, but was extremely thankful for the company anyway.

"I was part of the Exodus mission to assassinate Sala Jihan. We got our asses kicked. Never even saw it coming. I got shot a few times on the mountainside trying to get away. How about you?"

Still no answer. Keeping my voice down, I tried a few other languages. The guards didn't tolerate noise, and I was in no condition to take another beating.

"Do you know what day it is? What month?"

More breathing, sort of wet and gurgley.

"Yeah, me either."

I'd been delirious from blood loss and hypothermia when Jihan's men had carried me off the mountain. I'd woken up in surgery. Well, surgery is an overstatement. No anesthetic. Just some slaves yanking bullets out of me with pliers, and piecing me back together with needles and thread. Even then, barely coherent and half dead, I knew Sala Jihan was keeping me around only because dying quickly was too good for a trespasser.

Healing, I'd spent days in the dark, alone, with no sense of time. Unidentifiable, tasteless food had been shoved into my cell. Occasionally I'd wake up to someone tending my bandages, but asking them questions always ended with a beating. They would give me shots, probably antibiotics, because dying of infected gunshot wounds would be insufficiently painful.

Once I was healed enough to handle the stress, the torture had really begun.

It was purely for sport. They never even asked me any questions. Thankfully they didn't cut any parts off of me, break any bones, or drill any holes. The really invasive stuff tended to kill the subject, so I figured they'd work up to that eventually. It had been things like electrical shocks from a car battery or drowning me in a bucket over and over. Then they'd drag me back to my cell, burned or soaked, and leave me all by myself in the dark for who knew how long. Once I was recovered, they'd do it again.

But the worst part wasn't the torture, it was the noise. I can't explain the sounds in this place, or what made them, but they never stopped. They were always there, just past where you could make sense of what they were saying. Sometimes there was chanting, even singing, but the only sounds I could tell for sure were human were the screams.

"Do they make you fight in the pit too?"

The other prisoner panted and hissed.

"I don't have a choice."

Fighters who refused got shot in the head, and then they'd just haul in the next one. Those that didn't have the will left to put up a fight simply got murdered by their opponent, and I'd seen some savage bastards in the pit. Fighting was the only time I'd interacted with anyone else, but I'd quickly discovered that many of the other prisoners in this place were mentally gone, full-on psycho killers, little more than animals. They'd been here too long, the constant whispering burrowing into their heads, twisting everything. Hell, when I put some poor bastard out of his misery in the pit, I was doing them a favor.

Wheeze, gurgle.

"Don't judge me."

I wouldn't break like the others. I couldn't die, because I had things to do. I was going to find a way out of this hole. I was going to find my brother, stop Katarina, and get back to the woman I love. Love was an alien concept in a place like this, but when the anger and determination ran out, it was all I had left. I'd spent most of my life alone. To survive as a criminal at my level, you had to be willing to abandon everything as soon as you sensed danger.

I'd always thought that falling in love was a weakness. Only now, when there was nothing else but the darkness and the whispers and the pain, remembering Jill, imagining her alive and happy somewhere beneath the sun . . . It kept me sane.

The other cell was silent. The breathing had stopped. He'd either died or melted through the floor, I couldn't tell anymore. I was alone again.

Sala Jihan had seen right through my disguise, even recognized what I was, and called me *son of murder.* He'd warned me not to come back here. I should have listened.

Without any sort of reference, it was impossible to keep track of time. When you can't even tell if it is night or day, scratch marks on a wall are pointless. Food came at random times. The temperature never changed. It was always hot and muggy. It stank like a zoo, that kind of cloying, rancid, primal stink of spice and fear and waste. There was a pipe in the floor for waste. When it would rain, water would trickle down through the rock and make a puddle in my cell. That was the closest I came to bathing, well, that and the occasional waterboarding.

Blind, I explored every single inch of my small cell with my fingertips. I knew every crack and bump, but there was no discernible weakness. My chains were heavy-duty and sunk into the rock. I had no tool that could pick the lock on the shackles. It would be virtually impossible to break free, but I picked what I thought was the weakest link, and then I spent most of my time rubbing steel against steel. I had nothing but time. The chains were thick enough to pull a truck, but I worked on them constantly anyway. I did it so often that I could reach down on instinct and immediately find the right link. I'd rub them together until the metal was so hot from friction that it burned my fingers, but I still kept going. I didn't know what would erode first, that metal, or my sanity.

The bad thing about working on the chain was that while my hands were busy I couldn't put my hands over my ears. I was blind, but I wished I was deaf. That damned indescribable background noise never stopped. I tried to make plugs out of scraps from my ragged clothing, but I could still hear it. It was like the noise got inside your head. I slept with my hands clamped over my ears, and if I did it tight enough, the sound of my own pulse would keep the haunted noise out of my dreams. Sometimes.

I seriously contemplated scratching out my own eardrums, but truthfully, part of me was afraid that even then the noises wouldn't stop. I was already mostly deaf in one ear, but even in that one I thought I could hear the whispers. And if I did destroy my hearing, but the voices were still there, then that meant this place had succeeded in driving me crazy.

The only time I saw light was in torture sessions or when they'd drag me into the pit to fight. Even then there was no schedule to it. Strangely enough, I started to look forward to the fights. Despite it being bloody, horrific, and awful, at least I knew it was real. And for a few brief minutes, at least I didn't have to listen to that damned chittering in the walls.

The food was cold slop with chunks in it. It was so devoid of flavor I couldn't tell if the chunks were animal or vegetable. I was so malnourished that I was having a hard time concentrating. I hadn't had much fat on my body to begin with, but there was nothing left now. There were barely enough calories and nutrients in the gruel that I could still fight in the pit, but that meant I was strong enough to get out of here.

After enough time passed for the gunshot wounds to harden into scar tissue, I was ready to escape. The instant I was given an opportunity, I'd take it.

Then one day the chain broke.

When the guards came for me again, I made my move. Their light was blinding, but I was used to not being able to see. I struck the first one in the throat hard enough to crush his windpipe. I beat the second one over the head with his big aluminum flashlight, plunging us all back into the dark. I caught the last one in the hall and choked him to death with my broken chain before he could scream for help.

I swear, as I killed those men, the noises in the walls got louder. I dragged the bodies inside my cell and closed the door. They'd only had the one, now broken, light, so I had to blunder around in the dark, hands on the stone walls, looking for a way out. The prison was a maze. There was no rhyme or reason to the layout. I knew where the pit and the torture room were, and that was it. As I moved through the darkness, I couldn't tell if the voices were cheering me on or ratting me out.

Another guard died by my hand before I found the stairs, but at least now I had another flashlight. The crumbling prison was a maze of passageways. This place had to be ancient, and put to use more recently by the Pale Man. I found rooms filled with nothing but dried blood and scraps of clothing. There was an empty wheelchair in the hall. Eventually I found a set of stairs. The noise seemed to be louder downstairs, so I went up.

The cells on the next floor were separated by iron bars, and each one was packed with people, children mostly. The older males would go to the mines to be worked to death, the younger branded and brainwashed into the ranks of Jihan's army. The females would be sold to vile, horrible men around the world. They stared at my light, fearful, but I was in no position to do anything for them. Exodus had tried to save these people, and gotten themselves slaughtered for it. The only reason I was in here was because I'd been soft and stupid enough to make myself into a distraction to buy time for the Exodus survivors, and I didn't even know if any of them had made it out.

I knew Jill had escaped though. Sala Jihan had seen us together. So if he had caught her, he would have taunted me about it. If he'd killed her, he would have showed me her body. No matter what Jihan did to me, she was beyond his reach, and knowing that was plenty to live for.

They caught me before I could find the way out. I never figured out how they tracked me down, but somehow they knew right where I was. Maybe the whispers told on me. Despite me doing my best to gouge their eyes out, the slave soldiers fought like fanatics and accepted their casualties, determined to take me alive.

It seemed the Pale Man wasn't done with me yet.

Ears ringing from the beating, I woke up chained to a different wall, but from the humidity and the animal stink I knew I was still in the same prison. There was light here though, coming from a bright orange fire burning in a nearby metal tub. There were guards there, and one was holding a metal rod in the fire, the end glowing red hot.

Branding irons. This was new.

I was hanging there, arms stretched overhead. There was no give when I tested the chains. The guards noticed I was awake, but paid me no heed. I was no threat. My body was covered in fresh bruises, cuts, and scrapes. My muscles were cramped and trembling. I was so weak I could barely think. If they were going to burn my face like they did to mark his slaves, there wasn't much I could do about it. The ringing in my ears subsided enough that I could hear the crackle of flames, and then I could barely make out that damnable noise, the whispers and mutters. It was like they were laughing at me.

The door creaked open.

There was one man there, wearing a long black coat, leather and fur, with the hood up. The guards saw who it was and silently bowed their heads. In the shadows beneath the hood I could only make out his jaw, skin deathly white around neatly trimmed black facial hair. He studied the scene for a moment, before pushing back the hood with one gloved hand. His skin was somewhere beyond albino but his eyes were black holes. It was the Pale Man himself.

A feeling of terrible dread formed in my stomach and radiated out through my limbs as Sala Jihan entered. His age was impossible to guess. Neither old nor young, he just *was.* He'd claimed for himself the name of a villain from local folklore and lived at the bottom of an abandoned missile silo. He was a man who had built a kingdom in place where there was no law, reigning over people who believed he wasn't a man at all. The mountain tribes thought of him as a vengeful demon from their past, and feared him accordingly.

The first time I'd met the slave-trading warlord, I tried to tell myself it was all an elaborate act, a mind game to fuck with his opposition. That was before he'd slaughtered the Exodus strike team sent to kill him, and before I'd been exposed to this godforsaken place.

The Pale Man didn't speak for a very long time. He said something to the guards in a language I didn't recognize, but probably meant *leave us*.

The guards closed the door behind them, so it was just me alone with the devil.

"Just kill me already," I croaked, my mouth so dry that I could barely talk at all. "Get it over with." *At least then the whispers would stop.*

He tilted his head a bit to the side, as if listening. "What whispers?"

I didn't remember saying that part out loud.

Sala Jihan came closer, smelling like wet earth. He muttered something else, but it was in no language I recognized, and I'd heard them all. He grabbed me by the hair and violently jerked my head back so he could better see my battered face. Holy shit, he didn't look it, but he was incredibly strong. Somehow I knew he could twist my head off if he felt like it. Those terrible black eyes cut right through me

If I'd had enough saliva, I would have spit in his face. Sala Jihan noted my effort however. The warlord wasn't used to such disrespect, but he refrained from snapping my neck. He spoke in clear, precise English. "What am I to do with you, son of murder?"

"Unlock these chains and fight me like a man."

"I am not merely a man, and you are only a serpent. You invaded my home and killed my servants. You have deserved all of this suffering and more." His words were calm, measured, aloof, yet threatening at the same time. "What you have experienced thus far is nothing compared to the punishments I could inflict next. You exist entirely by my whim."

"Fuck you."

Jihan showed very little reaction, he seemed more curious than anything. "I've known many like you, wretched *hashishin*, wolves who hide among the sheep. Death follows wherever you go. Friend or foe, it does not matter. Yet you are special, a unique variable."

"What the hell are you jabbering about?"

"Fate has not determined a path for you. The son of murder is outside of destiny. Even when captured, you remain defiant, tempting me to end you. I did not because you could still prove useful. If your escape had not failed, what would you have done with your freedom?"

As tempting as it was to talk more shit, I told him the truth. "I'd run as far away from here as I could go."

"And then?"

There was no point in lying. The Pale Man would know. "Find Katarina Montalban and kill her."

"Yes. The woman who was deluded enough to think she could steal my kingdom. Her treachery is the reason you are here. Is it only your desire for vengeance so strong that it has kept you from breaking in this place?"

I clenched my teeth together. The Pale Man could never know what I still lived for, because he'd find a way to take Jill too.

"I know there is more, son of murder. Do not mistake my idle curiosity for caring. Love and hate are equally meaningless to me. I do not care about your motivation, merely the outcome. After you finished killing off the Montalbans, would you return and try to take your revenge upon the great Sala Jihan?"

"No." Even if I managed to survive taking on the Montalban Exchange, I was never coming back to this hell hole. "I swear."

"I believe you mean that, for now." Sala Jihan actually seemed pleased with my answer. "Katarina Montalban did not merely betray you and Exodus, she betrayed me as well."

He had been Exodus' target because he was an evil, slave-trading madman. Kat had nothing to do with that. Exodus was gunning for him no matter what.

"Exodus has tried to destroy me before. They have, and always will be my enemy. Thus, they are irrelevant. Now, I speak only of you. Katarina made you believe it was I who stole your brother. She tried to silence me, to usurp my throne. You were merely her weapon. She was naive enough to think she could use *you* to destroy *me*."

The first time we'd met, the Pale Man had told me that though death had always been my servant, in this place, death only answered to him.

"Yes . . . In this place." Jihan slowly lifted one gloved hand and gestured around the room. "For now my kingdom ends at the borders of the Crossroads. Yet, I desire revenge on Katarina Montalban. I do not like wanting things I cannot have. She must pay for her trespass, only she has moved beyond my reach."

The idea that there was a limit to Sala Jihan's dominion would make me sleep a little easier, at least until the whispers invaded my dreams and turned everything to blood again. "Let me go . . . I'll take care of her for you."

"An intriguing offer, only because the time of her triumph draws near. The Montalbans' plan, this *Project Blue* as you have heard it called, is far more ambitious than you can imagine. Eduard Montalban tried to enlist my aid in this plot. He intended to buy my allegiance with this." The Pale Man pulled a small object from the interior of his coat. There was a slight golden glow between his fingers. "This, too, had once been beyond my reach."

In the palm of his hand was an ancient piece of jewelry. I recognized it immediately. It was the Scarab.

I'd stolen it from a Saudi prince's vault. Being coerced into that heist was what had dragged me back into Big Eddie's world. A lot of people, including two of my best friends, had died to get it. We never even knew what it did. The last time I'd seen the Scarab it had been inside an abandoned building in Nevada as it burned to the ground. How had it survived? *How was it here?*

"That is not your concern." Sala Jihan closed his fist and the Scarab disappeared. "All that matters to you now is that it serves as evidence of your ability to reach that which I cannot. This was kept from me for a very long time, until you freed it."

"You're welcome."

"You would not be so flippant if you understood what you have done." He sneered at me, but I had no clue what that thing was for. "I am patient. I waited a lifetime to retrieve this device. I would do the same to have my revenge on the Montalban family. Only Katarina is too impetuous. She will act soon. If she is triumphant, the balance of power will change. Old orders will fall into chaos. That I will not allow. It appears once again the son of murder must go where the Pale Man is barred, and take for me that which I cannot take myself."

Between the beatings and my overall awful condition, I was having a hard time following the creepy weirdo. Were we cutting a deal? "Take her life?"

The Pale Man nodded slowly. My freedom in exchange for assassinating Kat? That was a no-brainer. Or was he was he dangling freedom in front of me, just long enough to give me hope, only to snatch it away and toss me back in the dark? Was this just a creative new form of torture?

"In exchange, I grant your freedom and declare your punishment fulfilled."

"Agreed." And as soon as I said that, it felt like I'd literally made a deal with the devil.

"I suspected it would come to this. The only reason I did not have hot ash poured down your throat was so that you could still speak your lies. The only reason I have not castrated you was so that you would not lose your will to fight. I left your fingers so you can hold a blade and eyes to find your prey."

Jihan went over to the fire and pulled out the branding iron. He held up the orange glowing metal, the firelight dancing in his black eyes, and satisfied that it was hot enough, turned back to me.

I cringed back as far as I could as he held the hot metal next to my face.

So close that it singed my beard and I could smell burning hair. "We have a deal!"

"You still have a face, only because my mark would make it difficult for you to disappear amongst the sheep." Jihan slowly pulled the glowing metal away from my eyes. "You will need all of these things where you are going."

He jammed the branding iron against my chest.

I screamed and thrashed as my flesh sizzled. With shocking force, Jihan held it there, crushing me back against the stone. I screamed until I couldn't scream anymore. When he finally pulled the glowing metal away, a lot of skin went with it.

I must have blacked out, because by the time I came to, Jihan had put the branding iron back into the fire and the whispers had turned to shouts. Hanging there limp, I retched against the stench of my own charred flesh. If there'd been anything inside my stomach, I would have vomited. If I hadn't been so dehydrated, I would have wept.

"Because you would die rather than break, that is not a mark of ownership." The Pale Man returned, crouching next to my sagging body, so we could be eye to soulless black eye. I was flickering in and out of consciousness. "This mark is my final gift. You say you will not return to my kingdom, but I know that in time vengeance would tempt you. Fear would fade. Memories would grow dim. Then you would come back for me, and I would utterly destroy you. Thus I bestow this scar upon you, so wherever you go, for the rest of your days, you will never forget the cost of trespass against Sala Jihan."

Daylight . . . actual daylight.

At first I wasn't sure if I was alive, dead, or back in my cell hallucinating. The pain convinced me it was real. Moving at all caused unbelievable agony as the burnt hole on my chest pulled on the raw red skin around it, but despite the pain, I still had to raise a hand to shield my eyes from the piercing light.

I'll be damned. That really was the sun up there.

I was on an uneven metal floor. There were great jagged tears in the roof above. There were holes—bullet holes—in the walls. Motes of dust swam through the beams of light. When I shifted my weight a bit more, I found that there were shell casings beneath me. Everything was covered in rust, vines, and cobwebs. When I lifted my aching head, there was a human skull watching me. There were mice living inside of it.

I'd been here before. This was the old crashed Russian bomber I'd taken cover in while running from Jihan's soldiers. They'd left me in the exact spot where they had captured me. I listened carefully. There were birds singing and bugs buzzing. The wind rustled and sighed through the trees.

There were no whispers.

I couldn't believe it. For the first time in months, there was quiet. I was out of the prison. It had to be some sort of trick.

Pulling myself up the wall, I saw mountains and trees through the bullet holes. Through the front of the cockpit, I could see the slope I'd climbed up from the river. There was the boulder where I'd been shot in the arm. My eyes weren't used to all this glorious unimpeded vision, so they began to water badly. Okay, maybe part of that was emotion, I'll admit it.

I reached out and touched one of the jagged bullet holes. One of these had pierced my leg. The last time I'd been here, this valley had been covered in snow. Now it was hot. Things had grown, and begun to die. It had to be late summer. That meant I'd been in Jihan's prison for at least four or five months.

It was amazing that I'd survived that long.

Slowly, I dragged myself to the twisted doorway, and flopped through onto the dry grass. Everything hurt, especially the fresh burn on my chest, but I'd been burned before. I'd live. I lay there for a long time, just feeling the sun above and the grass below. Sala Jihan had actually let me go. Either that or this was just a twisted game, and slave soldiers were going to show up any second to take away my last shred of hope.

No . . . If I'd learned anything over the last few months, it was that Sala Jihan was tyrannical and evil, but there was a twisted code of honor in that madness. He'd said he'd set me free in order to stop Kat only because he couldn't. The Pale Man wasn't a liar. He didn't need to be. But he'd also left me miles from civilization, injured, tired, hungry, dehydrated, barefoot, and in rags. So, the Pale Man may have had a peculiar code of honor, but that didn't make him any less of an asshole. I was in no shape to make it out of this forest.

I laughed for a few minutes straight. And then I wanted nothing more than to sleep.

Focus, Lorenzo. Kat and Anders were going to do something horrible, and then they were going to murder my brother and pin it all on him. I couldn't stop them by sitting here on my ass. The Pale Man wouldn't have let me go if there was time to dick around. I didn't just survive a stay in hell to die of exposure on a mountain or get eaten by a fucking wolf, so it was time to man up and get the job done.

Besides, I *really* wanted to murder Kat.

And once that was done, I could find Jill. My time with her had been the best days of my life. Was it possible to actually be happy again? I'd been living off of stubborn determination and hate for so long that I'd forgotten what it felt like to *hope*.

Ignoring the pain, I forced myself to stand up. I knew jack and shit about wilderness survival. I was more of an urban survivalist, but I remembered the maps of the region from when we'd been preparing for the raid. The nearest settlement was Sala Jihan's compound, but I would be avoiding that haunted shithole. If I followed the river, it would take me back to the Crossroads. Once I was back in a town full of criminals I'd be in my element.

I limped toward the Crossroads.

It took two miserable days to reach the Crossroads. When you haven't seen the sun for months, you sunburn like a bitch. After roasting during the day, it still got damned cold at night. There wasn't a security system in the world I couldn't circumvent, but I didn't know how to rub two sticks together to make fire. Bob had been the Eagle Scout, not me. Sure, I'd been a mercenary in Africa, but we'd ridden in trucks to battle, and when we did occasionally have to sleep in the wilderness, I'd had a lighter. So, fireless and miserable, I huddled next to a tree and shivered the night away. Even then it was the best night's sleep I'd had in a long time because of the *real actual quiet.*

In the morning I took what was left of my shirt and wrapped the rags around my feet because I swear the canyon was covered in sharp rocks, just because Mother Nature is a bitch. On the bright side, the horrific burn on my chest was so incredibly painful that it distracted me from torn feet. Yeah, I'm an optimist like that.

There was plenty to drink. The river water was wonderful, colder, clearer, and fresher than the cups of brackish sludge I'd been given in the prison, but I was still weak with hunger. Luckily, I found a fresh animal kill, half eaten. I don't know what killed it, and don't even know what the animal was—what was left had hooves kind of like a little deer—but it wasn't rotten, and that's all I cared about. I used to be a connoisseur of exotic food, the weirder the better, and Carl often said that I could eat things that would make a goat puke, but let me tell you, you've never really vomited until you try to choke down chunks of bloody raw meat after months of eating nothing but gruel. On the second try I kept some inside, and that gave me enough calories to make it the rest of the way. I'd probably get some parasites and microbes or shit, but if I could get back to civilization, they had pills for that.

The Crossroads may have been run by a bunch of criminals acting like competing fiefdoms, but it was a real town. I was going to find some criminal faction to con or suck up to, get myself real food, see a real doctor, then find a way to steal some clothes, shoes, money, and a ticket back to the world. Then I was going to find Kat's people, and torture them until one of them gave me her location, so I could shoot her in the face. Then I was going to find my woman, put this place behind me, and never think about it again. I was really looking forward to my exciting new life plan.

But when I got there, the Crossroads was *gone*.

Well, not gone, but mostly underwater and abandoned. Many of the buildings were still standing, but they were flooded, only the roofs or second stories sticking out of the new lake that had formed where a city had been. There were still people living around it, mostly in yurts and shacks made out of scavenged materials, but the criminal empire, the trading houses, the chaotic businesses, the gun runners and drug dealers, the world's best illicit flea market, it was all gone.

There had been tens of thousands of people in this boomtown just a few months ago, now it was maybe a few hundred, tops. Before, there had been representatives of every regional group. Now they appeared to be mostly nomadic traders. Men with rifles watched me suspiciously as I approached their settlement.

The rail line was on the high ground, and since plants weren't growing over the rails, I assumed trains still passed through here. When I got closer, I saw that the train station had been burned down, and all that remained was an ashen wreck with a collapsed roof. What the hell had happened here? Last I'd heard, the Montalban Exchange was supposed to have made a move against Sala Jihan's garrison in town, but they'd chickened out. Had the Pale Man run everyone out after that? But the Crossroads didn't feel like the victim of a battle, more like a derelict ghost town, and where had this friggin' lake come from?

I hailed the nomads when I got close enough. They didn't shoot me, probably because it was obvious the emaciated scarecrow hobbling in on bloody feet wasn't too much of a threat. I went through a mishmash of languages until they responded with really bad Russian. I had nothing to offer, nothing to trade, but I hoped they'd show some hospitality to a starving man.

When I got close enough that they saw the brand on my chest, they fled in terror.

It wasn't what I expected, but I could work with it. As the nomads retreated toward the other yurts and huddled there for safety, I went to the closest tent and started looting. I was too worn out to run, and if they were going to come back and shoot me, I'd at least die with a full belly. There was a pot of rice, still warm, and I sat down and ate it with my fingers.

While I ate, I looked over the new lake. Though it was leaning to the side now, the Montalban Exchange building was only partially submerged. It had been built to look sort of like a pagoda. My search for my brother had brought me there, and it was only later that I'd learned he'd been prisoner there the whole time, locked in a cell in the basement. I'd thought Bob was in Sala Jihan's compound, and he'd been right there, under my nose the whole time. I'd visited the Montalban Exchange building several times during the preparation and planning for the raid. It wouldn't have surprised me if Anders, being a dick, had taunted Bob about my searching for him the whole time.

Looking at that lopsided pagoda gave me an idea though. Bob was crafty. Everywhere else he'd gone, he'd tried to leave bread crumbs. Why not here?

A few minutes later a single nomad approached. Dressed in lots of wool, leather, and strangely a really faded Chicago Bulls t-shirt, he was probably in his forties, so close to my age, though it was hard to tell because he was so incredibly weathered by the sun, and I couldn't even guess which of the minor regional groups he belonged to. He had an old Mosin Nagant rifle in his hands, but he was polite enough not to point it at me. He stopped near the tent and squatted there. "We are not enemies or friends, but you may eat this meal." His Russian was pretty good, which meant he was probably their leader, or at least their main trader or negotiator.

"Thank you."

He pointed two fingers at my burn. "You are the one *he* freed?" the man asked suspiciously. I hate the pronoun game, but in this case there was no doubt who *he* was.

"I'm guessing that doesn't happen often."

"You are the first. Enjoy our hospitality, and then be gone. You cannot be our guest. We do not want his eyes upon us. Everything he touches is cursed."

"Agreed." I kept chewing. "When does the train pass through?"

"Toward Russia or China?"

"Either."

He pulled back a sleeve and checked his watch. I don't know why it surprised me that a nomad at the ass end of the world had a big fat digital watch. "About three hours." I grunted acknowledgment and kept shoveling rice in my face. I was probably going to get sick, but it was worth it. The nomad seemed happy that I would be leaving. After a minute passed, he got up the courage to ask. "My people tell stories about his prison. Are they true?"

I didn't know what the stories were, but I could guess. "Worse."

He nodded thoughtfully, expression hard to read, but I suspected he might be taking pity on me. He went into the tent and came out with a can of some Russian soda. He tossed it to me. I cracked open the warm can, took a drink of the Motherland's version of Mountain Dew, and it was so magical, it made my teeth hurt. I'd always been a health nut, but I'd missed sugar.

"Oh, man. Thank you. You have no idea. Thank you so much . . ." Right then it felt like the nicest thing anyone had ever done for me. "So what happened to the city here?"

"The night they attacked the Pale Man, they hurt the dam too. A bomb started it leaking. It could not be repaired. The city began to flood. The criminals fought each other. Business slowed. The bazaars moved elsewhere."

Blowing the dam must have been Exodus' backup plan. If they couldn't kill Sala Jihan, at least they could cripple his empire. That explained why Ling and Valentine hadn't been on the raid, too. The sneaky bastards had managed to shut the whole place down and keep the death toll to a minimum. I had to hand it to Exodus, that was clever.

The nomad gestured toward the leaning pagoda. "A year later, it is like this."

A year? It was summer. I'd been captured in spring. That couldn't be right. "What's today's date?"

The nomad looked at me funny, then he checked his giant watch again. Of course it had the date on it. "It is the twenty-second of August."

So I'd been captured five months ago . . . But if the Crossroads had been abandoned too long, that made no sense. "What year?"

He told me. It took a moment for it sink in.

I'd been in prison for almost *a year and a half.* For a long moment, I couldn't even wrap my brain around the number.

"Are you alright?" the nomad asked.

I didn't know. A year and a half . . . *Damn.* What else had I missed? "I will be." I looked toward the leaning Montalban building. I'd noticed something when the nomad opened to tent flap to get the soda can. "Can I borrow that flashlight?"

I swam through the flooded hallway, the borrowed LED flashlight cutting a narrow beat through the dark. Silver fish scattered ahead of me.

This was stupid. Repeatedly diving into the lower floors of a flooded, rotten, collapsing building would have been dangerous with a wetsuit and an air tank. Doing it while freezing and holding your breath, when you were already in bad shape, was suicidal. I swore, not for the first time, that someday I was going to choke the shit out of Valentine. In the most convoluted way possible, he'd once again managed to make my life more difficult. I wasn't going to leave the Crossroads emptyhanded, though, one way or another.

This was my fourth trip down. Most of the lower rooms had been easy to reach, but none of them looked suited for holding someone prisoner. The Montalbans had left all of their furniture behind. It wasn't as if once you betrayed Sala Jihan, there was much time to pack, so it was pretty easy to tell what each room had been used for, and the ones I could reach had been barracks for their employees and hired muscle mostly.

Part of the ceiling had collapsed, so I had to squeeze between the boards. I stuck the flashlight between my teeth, and used my hands to pull myself along. I cut my thumb on a protruding nail, but I got through. I'd have to squeeze back out though, which would take even more time, so I couldn't spare a second in this next room.

It was eerie as hell down here. The water was fairly clear and free of sediment so I wasn't blind, and the flashlight helped a lot. Sadly, nomadic traders in the Golden Mountains didn't stock swim goggles, but I could see well enough to get by. The flood had been so gradual that it hadn't even knocked over chairs. There were still billiard balls on the pool table, though the cues had floated away. Things were starting to decay and the walls were getting fuzzy with moss. There was still a TV mounted on the wall. I'd found the Montalbans' rec room. *Useless.*

My lungs were starting to hurt. I'd been a damned good swimmer, but it had been a long time. By the time I squeezed back through the debris a little bit of panic was starting to build in the back of my mind. I'd pushed too far. I was going to run out of air and die down here. I swam down the hall as fast as I could, passing other rooms I'd already cleared. As the pain grew, I cursed myself. It figured that I'd be the one to survive a prison that no one ever survived, only to drown myself inside a house two days later. Desperate, I reached the stairs, got my hands, then feet on them. The glue had melted so the carpet was a floating bubble, tacked at the edges. I half swam, half walked the last few feet, and gasped in precious air as my face broke the surface.

Dripping and gasping, I stumbled out of the water, sank to my knees, and lay down on the damp floor.

Damn it. That was as far as I could go, yet I'd found nothing.

I began to shiver uncontrollably. We were way up in the mountains, so even in the summer the water was cold as hell, and I had no insulation left. There was a fireplace ten feet away, but no way to light it, and everything here was too soggy to burn.

There was one more room past the rec room, but I couldn't reach it. I knew my brother. If Bob thought there was any way Exodus could find him, he'd leave a clue. He was so dedicated to his investigation, so worried about Project Blue, that he'd been willing to sacrifice his life—and mine—to stop it. Bob had months to piece together more about Blue after those journals of his I'd read, plus he might have learned something from Kat and Anders, or maybe even had an idea of where they would be taking him next. He had to have left something in there. I knew it.

Bob wasn't a quitter. It ran in the family. I'd not given up in the dark for a year and a half—that still boggled my mind—And I wasn't going to give up here either. I was getting into that last room one way or the other, and if there was nothing, then I could get on that train knowing that I'd at least done my best. The Montalban Exchange was big, but it was just a fancy house. I hadn't given up when I was surrounded by solid rock. There was an iron poker next to the fireplace. I got up, went over, and picked it up. It was rusty, but that was fine. I just needed it to last longer than the soggy floorboards.

I made an educated guess about where the last room was, and went to work on the floor. Smashing into the Montalban Exchange gave me a chance to think, and to focus my rage. If there was no clue, no bread crumbs, no answer, then I'd just declare war on the lot of them. I used to work for Big Eddie. I used to know some of his operations and many of his lieutenants. Some of them still had to work for Big Eddie's psychotic little sister. I'd pick them off, one by one, until somebody gave up Kat.

As I pounded the floor into splinters, I had to stop to rest several times. It gave me time to think through the repercussions of going to war with an organized crime family. I'd been elated to get out of the dark, but enthusiasm can only get you so far when you're trying to kill a bunch of professional killers.

There were good odds I'd die. Kat was damned good at her job, and Anders was probably better. Anyone who helped me would be in danger. Kat knew what Jill meant to me. I'd stayed alive for Jill, but once the Montalbans knew it was me, they'd go after her again. I had to keep her out of this. I had to keep Reaper out of it. They were probably still in hiding. They needed to stay that way. Big Eddie had targeted my family to manipulate me once, and if Kat found out I was still alive, she'd do the same thing. Right now, my best defense was them thinking I was dead.

I had to do this the old way, the way I used to operate, back when I truly did not give a shit about anyone or anything. When I was a ghost, faceless and living job to job, doing whatever it took to win, without mercy, without thought, without hesitation. The only way to beat them would be by being worse than them.

Jill had helped me become a better man, and I loved her for it, but being a decent human being was a luxury I couldn't afford. I had to become that perfect killer again, and that meant I had to be alone. If I was going to do this, I could afford no distractions.

In my condition it still took me a while, and by the time I'd pried up enough floor to squeeze through, I was exhausted again. I was going to be cutting it close on catching that train, and if I missed today's, it wouldn't surprise me if one of the nomads just decided to kill me in my sleep to keep life simple. Hospitality is nice and all—until it draws the Pale Man's eye.

Making the hole had at least warmed me up, so it sucked extra when I lowered myself through the moldy insulation and back into the frigid water. I took a deep breath, and dropped into the last room. My vision was blurry, but when I shined the light around, I knew that I'd hit the jackpot.

The four walls were made of solid wooden beams instead of sheetrock like the rest of the place. The door was metal, and looked like it had been looted from an old Russian military bunker when they'd built this place. The only piece of furniture left was a metal bed frame. There were leather straps bolted to the side of the frame. The Montalbans had probably used this room for interrogations. Someone could have screamed their head off in here and the people upstairs would have never known.

If Bob had been here, there hadn't been much to work with in the way of tools, but he would have improvised something. He couldn't have done anything in the open, or they would have seen it when they took him away. I swam down to the bedframe and put the flashlight between my teeth so I could use both hands again. The little flashlight had a yellow plastic body, so at least it was soft enough not to chip my teeth. It still tasted better than Jihan's gruel.

I felt around behind the metal bars. Sure enough. One of the bolts was really loose. That had been his tool. He'd been smart enough to stick it back in the frame so they wouldn't notice. Anders was observant and smart, but Bob was smarter.

My chest was starting to hurt. I felt along the wall. It reminded me of exploring my cell in the dark, looking for any vulnerability I could exploit. *There.* Something was scratched into the wood, placed at an angle that any guard who entered wouldn't see it behind the frame. I had to practically drag myself beneath the bed to get eyes on it. It was too blurry to read, so I had to feel it out with my fingertips. It was rough, and must have taken him forever to do it with the end of a bolt.

Varga.

I knew that name. I swam for the hole. I had a train to catch.

Chapter 3: Rampage

LORENZO
Budapest, Hungary
September 1st

Ten days later I was in a nightclub in Budapest, looking to take down a Montalban stooge.

Big Eddie's employees loved places like this. Lots of coming and going, big crowds, so much obnoxious music noise that bugging it would be impossible, it was a perfect place to exchange information, collect bribes, plot crimes, and then fade away. The combination of black lights, glowing body paint, and half-naked people was distracting enough that a regular boring criminal—like yours truly—drinking at the end of the bar was practically invisible.

It had taken me a while to get to Hungary. Playing hobo across Siberia isn't as fun as it sounds. I couldn't call in any favors, because I couldn't risk word getting out that I was alive. Once back in the civilized world, I'd stolen money and clothing, and got treated by a shady doctor who'd given me a bottle of antibiotics. Then I'd hotwired a car to get to one of my stashes in Volgostadorsk. That storage locker I had rented years ago had netted me some IDs, a fake passport, and more money. I'd found a Roma caravan. That's how my dad had grown up, before he'd been such a scumbag that they'd tossed his ass. I'd picked up a couple of dialects over the years, and knew how to pay my proper respects—and money—which had bought me a ride to Hungary. Being a passenger had given me time to rest and recuperate. They'd dropped me off in Budapest, I'd stolen a car, and come straight here.

I scanned the crowd for Stefan Varga. Back when I worked for Big Eddie, he'd run this club. It seemed like a legit establishment, but if you knew where to look there were signs and signals to the other criminals that this was Montalban turf. There was still plenty of hired muscle wandering around, partying between their criminal endeavors, but nobody I recognized from the old days. Varga had been a major smuggler for Eddie when I knew him, and smarter than he was tough. Kat had probably promoted him after she took over. She'd always had an eye for talent.

There had to be some reason Varga was important enough that they would have mentioned his name in front of Bob. Unless it was a different crook with the same last name and this was a dead end. Or the right guy, but he'd moved on. But if that was the case, one of these mooks would know where their old boss had gone.

I'd gotten cleaned up in Russia and bought nice clothes so I wouldn't look like the Unabomber. I must have done something right because I got flirted with twice in the last forty minutes, by one woman and one dude. Apparently this scene was into that emaciated, spent a year and a half in a lightless hole chic. I told them that I was waiting for my date and went back to my scotch. I wasn't wearing a disguise, but my hair was longer, my beard was trimmed, and I was probably twenty pounds lighter and a decade older than the last time I'd been here, so I wasn't likely to get recognized by a crew that thought I was dead. However, I probably shouldn't have blown the flirts off, because if I was here alone for too long I'd look suspicious. I couldn't afford to get made. I wasn't even armed. I knew the club would have metal detectors, so the only people in here with guns would be working for Kat.

I got up and walked toward the bathrooms, trying to get a better view of the VIP area. Varga had never been a back office type. He'd always liked to conduct his criminal business out in the lights and music, snorting coke off the table while getting a blow job from an expensive hooker under it. Big Eddie's people were classy like that. If Varga was still here, hopefully he hadn't mellowed with age, because if he was in the offices, I was going to have a hard time getting back there without being seen.

The music was shit. It was better than the horrible noise of Jihan's prison, but that was it. Music had peaked with Black Sabbath. This was just repetitive electronic noise over a bunch of bass and what sounded like a power drill. The DJ looked like a crackhead. The air smelled like pot and sweat. The dancers were sleazy, stoned kids. It made me feel old, but Reaper probably would have loved this place. Damn I missed him. Five minutes on his computer and he'd probably be able to tell me exactly where Varga was right now and what he'd had for breakfast. But I'd made my call. I couldn't risk my old team's lives. This was on me alone.

My target wasn't in the VIP area. In the bathroom I splashed some water on my face and stared at my reflection in the mirror. I was getting stronger, but I still looked like death. The sunburn from the mountains was healing and I was getting my color back. I'd been eating, exercising, and actually sleeping. Sure, the sleep was riddled with nightmares, and I kept waking up in a cold sweat freaking out that I'd imagined my whole escape, but I was getting better. When I woke up now all I had to do was focus on sweet revenge until my pulse slowed down, and then I was fine for another hour or two.

You got this. Satisfied that the hollowed-out, used-up killer staring back at me in the mirror could still do the job, I headed back to the bar.

Back out in the electronic noise and fog machine chaos, for just a moment it felt like someone was watching me. I turned to see a shadowed figure on a balcony above, white skin, black hood. I felt a flash of panic. It was the Pale Man. *He followed me!* But then the spotlights shifted along the rafters, and the figure was gone. It was an illusion. Nothing more than a trick of the lights and smoke. My fear was irrational.

Calm down, you big pussy. I'd been through hell, but that was no excuse. *Focus.* Then, through the dancers, I caught a glimpse of another ghost from my past. Only this one turned out to be real.

Hello, Diego.

It was hard to tell with the flashing lights, but I was certain it was him. The last time I'd seen that lunatic had been at the Crossroads. One of Kat's best men, he was also the asshole she'd sent to try and kill Jill and Reaper during the betrayal, and afterwards Kat had *gloated* about it. Diego had shaved his head since then, but there was no mistaking him for anyone else. See, Diego was one of those guys who was too *pretty.* He stood out, even in a place like this.

Carefully, I followed him, keeping a lot of people between us. Diego was an effeminate crossdresser in his free time, but he was a psychopath and underestimating him would get me killed. From what I'd heard he was a ruthless, efficient killer. Hands on, preferred to work with knives, and good enough at it that most of the Crossroad's resident professional killers had given him a wide berth. It takes a *lot* of skill to build that kind of rep in a place like that.

Diego went past some security guys and up the stairs to the club's offices. I went back to the bar and ordered another drink. Diego was one of Kat's insiders. I might not get another opportunity like this. One of the bartenders had been slicing lemons. There was a little knife on the cutting board. When nobody was looking I snatched it. It was only a skinny, five-inch kitchen knife, with a clumsy square wooden handle. Not exactly a properly balanced killing blade, but it was solid, and when I tested the edge with my thumb I knew it would do.

This asshole had tried to kill my woman. That sort of thing demands retribution.

Normally I liked to plan things out, take my time, look for angles and plan for contingencies, but a few minutes later Diego came down the stairs and headed for the back exit, and I followed him. There was an alley behind the club. He'd probably parked there. I might be able to tail him to someplace quieter, but my car was parked half a block away. By the time I reached it, I might lose him. Diego paused to talk to another security goon in a suit, who handed Diego a motorcycle racing jacket and a helmet. Diego took them and went out the door.

Palming it so the blade was concealed along my forearm, I quickly walked toward the back exit, passing between unsuspecting Hungarians. The big guy in the suit was moving toward the stairs. *Good.* If I'd had to slash his throat in here there'd be too many witnesses. There was a sign that warned opening this door would cause an alarm to sound, but Diego had just proven that was bullshit designed to keep patrons from letting their friends in. I pushed the door open and entered the alley.

The night air was cool. The light was bad. There was a security camera mounted on the bricks high above me. I wouldn't have much time. The annoying techno music faded as the door closed. I looked right. *Clear.* To the left was a green dumpster. I stepped around it. Fifteen feet away Diego was walking toward a parked BMW motorcycle. I'd cripple him, then question him. Simple, nice, fast, and clean.

Making no sound, I flipped the knife around in my hand and started toward him.

Diego must have seen my reflection in the bike's chrome, because he reacted instantly, spinning and hurling the helmet at me. I dodged to the side, but it still caught my forearm, slowing me. I lunged, directing a cut at his face. He blocked my arm with his palm as he moved back. I slashed again. Our arms and hands collided. The man was *quick.*

So much for simple.

Trying to make distance, Diego reached for his side. *Gun!* Kitchen knife flashing back and forth, I followed. His hand came up with a black pistol, but I elbowed it aside, kicked him in the shin, and with the flick of my wrist sliced open his knuckles. The pistol went skittering down the alley. He hit me, but I shoulder checked him into the brick wall. I kept on him, slicing, but I'd lost track of his other hand, and barely avoided getting cut by the blade that had appeared out of nowhere. I leapt back as a six-inch tear appeared in the fabric of my shirt.

We stood there for a moment, a few feet apart, knives pointed at each other. His folder was designed for piercing skin, severing tendons and arteries. Mine was for cutting lemons. But Diego was bleeding and I wasn't. I could still hear that damned techno music. His baby smooth face contorted in rage as he realized I'd already cut him several times. "You realize who I am? You know who you're fucking with, you little bitch?"

"Where's Kat?"

"Lorenzo?" Diego's anger turned to shock. I had a rep too. "But you're dead!"

"Where's Anders?"

Diego rushed me.

The knife was aimed at my eyes, but mostly to steal my attention long enough to nail me with a knee or an elbow. If I'd not had the element of surprise, he might have taken me. He was scary fast, but I was too focused, too angry. All the fights in the Pale Man's dungeon had changed me, honed me. Now? I felt alive. It was amazing the difference food and a purpose could make.

I blocked his knife hand and cut him. I ducked under his fist and cut him. I caught his knee with my forearms and stabbed him. He grunted as the blade punched a hole through his abdominal wall. I shoved Diego back into the dumpster. He left a big streak of blood across the sheet metal.

"Where's Kat?" My voice was cold.

His knife came back around, but I caught his wrist with the edge of my blade. Lemons weren't the only thing it could slice in half. His knife landed at my feet. He punched me in the ribs, but he was losing too much blood and weakening. His next punch was easily dodged, and I stabbed him in the shoulder. I twisted the knife and Diego screamed in my ear. *"Where?"*

"Fuck y—" My elbow knocking out some of his teeth cut that right off.

"Talk." I threw my knee into his side. I felt at least one rib break. As he slid down the metal, I put my palm on his forehead and used his face like a cheese grater on the rusty metal. Back and forth as Diego wailed in agony. He wasn't going to be pretty anymore. I let him fall. "Where's my brother?"

Diego was dazed and hurting, but the important thing was he knew he was beaten. His only hope of survival was my mercy—fat chance of that—or stalling until help arrived. "I don't know," he gasped. "That's Anders' deal."

My eyes flicked to the camera. Any second somebody was going to look at the screen and Montalban goons were going to come out shooting. I retrieved Diego's gun, a Glock 19, then went back and knelt next to him, but kept glancing at the door. "Tell me what I want, and I'll call for an ambulance." Blood loss made you stupid. He might believe me.

He laughed in my face. "Go to hell."

From the amount of blood coming out the hole in the top of his chest, I'd severed his brachial artery. Diego was dying, he just didn't know it yet. I didn't have much time to get answers. "Look at me. Look at me, Diego. I survived Sala Jihan's dungeons. I learned things about suffering you can't ever understand. But I'll share them with you, one by one, until you tell me where they are." I stuck the knife into the meat of his thigh.

Diego bellowed as I turned it. The kicking and thrashing only made the wound worse. "I swear I don't know! There's a number in my phone if we need to speak."

If he was lying, he was damned convincing. "Is Varga still here?"

"No." I pulled the knife out, and moved it to his other leg but he hurried, hoping that giving me something would make the pain stop. "Anders sent him to Austria a year ago."

I pushed the point of the blade into his leg, but stopped short of piercing his skin. "*Where* in Austria?"

"S . . . Salzburg!" he stammered, trying to talk while in agonizing pain.

It felt like the truth. Diego was beginning to fade out. "Hey." I slapped him in the face a few times to bring him back to reality. "What's Project Blue?"

"She took it on after Eddie died. It's like her monument to him. That's all I know. Don't kill me. I don't . . . Please . . ." Diego begged. He must have finally realized how badly he was bleeding out. "Nothing. I know nothing. She kept it secret. Please. I don't want to die."

"Too late." Diego's clock was running down fast. I stood up as he grasped at me uselessly with his ruined hand. "You died when you betrayed us at the Crossroads. You just didn't know it yet."

My trendy new suitcoat was ripped and covered in blood, so I took it off and threw it in the dumpster. The bike was closer and would be a faster getaway than my car. With luck, they'd think that Diego had just driven off and be unaware that anything had happened. By the time I'd taken his wallet, keys, and cellphone, Diego had passed out from blood loss. So I hoisted his body over the side of the dumpster and dropped him inside. He landed with a crash. I took a few seconds to cover him with trash bags. By the time I was done he'd stopped breathing. I smashed the nearest light bulb on the way out to leave the alley in shadows. Hopefully nobody would see all the blood until tomorrow.

The motorcycle racing jacket hid the fresh blood on my shirt and the helmet hid my face. I'd have to get out of Hungary, and Salzburg was on the opposite side of Austria, but I could be there by morning.

The Pale Man had kept calling me the *son of murder*. By the time I got done with the Montalbans I'd earn that title.

LORENZO
Salzburg, Austria
September 3rd

Stefan Varga had been easy for me to find. Criminal scumbags were sort of my peer group. Knowing the right kind of assholes to threaten could get you a list of Montalban hangouts, and there weren't that many. Salzburg wasn't that big. Big Eddie had run a much tighter ship than his little sister. While Eddie had preferred being quietly dreaded, Kat seemed to like flexing the muscles and being openly feared. It seemed like the only thing Kat was tight-lipped about was Project Blue. For the rest of her criminal empire, she liked a bit of flash.

One of the drug dealers I'd kicked the shit out of that morning had told me the top Montalban man in town spent a lot of time at a local freight company. Using legit businesses to cover for smuggling had been Varga's bread and butter, so it fit. I'd lucked out and seen Varga getting into a car there, and tailed him. I'd had to hang back a bit when they'd gotten into these narrow, residential streets, but his Mercedes was parked just ahead of me in front of an old, but very nice, four story house.

Varga had a man with him, probably a bodyguard, not that I'd gotten a good look. There were an unknown number of people inside. The smart thing to do would be to play it cool, plan it out. Despite being a creepy, inscrutable motherfucker, the Pale Man had still acted like time was of the essence, but rushing in would only get me killed. Going after Diego in that alley had been stupid, and I'd been lucky I hadn't gotten hurt, especially in my suboptimal condition. Careful planning was the only reason I'd survived as long as I had in this business. Going head to head against an unknown number of Montalban soldiers was stupid. I needed to wait, study it, find an angle.

Screw it. I got off the bike and walked straight to the front door.

Though I didn't see any on the street, Europeans loved cameras, so I left the helmet on. I had two guns, Diego's Glock, and an old double-barrel shotgun I'd taken off the drug dealer's doorman. The barrels had been hacksawed off just ahead of the forearm. The stock had been cut down so that there was barely anything to hold onto. It would be awkward as hell to shoot, but on the bright side it fit inside a messenger bag. As I walked quickly up the front steps, I pulled the 12 gauge.

First, I tried the doorknob. Of course it was locked, but you never know. So I pressed the shotgun's lopsided muzzle against the lock and pulled the trigger. The buckshot blasted a jagged circle of door and frame into pieces. I kicked it open and rushed inside.

A man in a suit had been sitting not too far from the door, but he'd fallen out of his chair when the shot had gone off. He was fumbling for the subgun slung across his chest, so I simply turned the shotgun on him and gave him the other barrel. With the choke cut off, the pattern was garbage and did more damage to the floor than his body, but he still got hit by a *lot* of double aught buck. He was still thrashing, so I pulled the Glock from my waistband and shut him up with a shot to the brain as I went past.

The helmet muffled sound, so I was lucky I heard the next man coming. He was sloppy, leading with his gun, and the muzzle cleared the corner before he did. I knocked his pistol down with a swing of the shotgun, and as his body followed around the corner I shot him, several rounds fast to the body, and as he stumbled, a final 9mm hollow point through the side of his face. That had been meant for his forehead, but I was out of practice.

I dropped the shotgun and helmet—I'd grab it when I left—and moved down the hall. There was noise above. Thumping, crashing, panicked people taking cover. I took the stairs three at a time. On the second floor landing, somebody started shouting a challenge in German. When I didn't respond, he decided to fire a few rounds through the wall. I knelt down behind an antique table while he put useless holes in the wallpaper around me. He did a real number on the furniture, and the instant I heard panicked swearing as he ran his gun empty, I went through the doorway.

The shooter was an older, overweight, blond man—not Varga—so I shot him four times while he tried to reload his little pocket pistol. I was a little rusty, but shooting was like riding a bicycle, so you might suck, but it isn't like you forget how. He fell across a desk, scattering papers and rubber-banded stacks of euros.

I ran up the next flight. I didn't see anybody on the third floor, and I didn't have time to look. There was more noise above, from the sound, at least two men, moving in different directions. I moved to the side. If they were smart, they'd hunker down, call for help, wait, and blow my head off if I appeared on the next floor.

Luckily, they weren't tactical geniuses. Instead of waiting, the bodyguard came for me. *Sloppy.* I heard him running down the stairs. I only had to wait a second for his feet and legs to appear, pounding down the stairs. I put the front sight on a knee and fired. Blood flew, and he fell, screaming, momentum taking him face first down the stairs. When he hit the landing, I waited long enough to confirm it wasn't Varga before I shot him a few more times.

The Glock was at slide lock. I'd not realized I'd fired that many rounds already. I picked up the dead man's gun, an FN 57, checked to make sure there was a round chambered, and started up the final set of stairs.

"Whoever you are, there is money and drugs downstairs. It is yours. Take it all. Come any closer and I'll shoot you!" he shouted in German. It had been a long time but I recognized the voice. It was Varga. He repeated much the same thing in Russian, probably because he wasn't sure who the hell had just massacred all his men, but it was clear he thought this was just a robbery.

While he talked, I crept down the hall. He'd placed himself in the back bedroom, probably behind something that would stop bullets. I didn't know if he'd had time to phone for help or not. But I'd just made a lot of noise, and somebody was bound to have called the cops, so time was on his side.

The lower floors had been carpeted and nicely decorated. This floor was all bare and utilitarian. As I passed the other bedrooms, I saw they were filled with bunk beds, each one with handcuff rails and tiedown straps. Then I knew what this house actually was. This was a clearing house. They'd take in runaways or clueless immigrant girls, get them addicted and trained, then ship them off to be pimped out somewhere else. There was a medical cart in the hall, with needles, syringes, and medicine bottles on it. There was huge money in an operation like this. The fact they could get away with shit like this, in a quaint little picturesque neighborhood, extra pissed me off.

I *hate* these people *so much*.

Varga was still shouting, but he'd have a gun trained on the doorway, and there appeared to be only one way in. I needed to get his eyes off the door. If he thought the Russian mafia was moving in on him, I was going to give him Russian mafia. I spoke in Russian, but not to him, but rather like I was speaking to someone right next to me. *"Granata?"* Then I changed the pitch of my voice, and answered myself. *"Da. Granata."* Because of course, the answer to *grenade?* Is always *yes, grenade*. Varga heard that and quit his yapping as he realized he was about to get fragged. Then I tossed one of the medicine bottles through the doorway. It made a very ominous noise rolling across the hardwood.

Since he thought he was about to get blown to hell, Varga instinctively ducked for cover. I used that chance to rush through the door. I found him cowering behind an overturned table. By the time he realized there was no boom and looked up, my stolen pistol was aimed right between his eyes.

Knowing he was screwed, Varga let go of his pistol and slowly raised his hands over his head.

I'd run up four flights of stairs, killed four men, and captured their leader in well under a minute. Not too shabby considering my sorry state and lack of recent practice. I hate to admit it, but it felt good to be *on*. But I couldn't get cocky. I hadn't cleared the place, so there could still be someone else downstairs waiting to fuck me up, or the cops could roll in. I had to make this fast.

I noticed his phone was lying on the floor next to him, and the screen was lit. He'd already called for help. Hell, if they could hear me, anything that might make the Montalban reinforcements hesitate was worth a shot. Keeping the gun on Varga, I picked up his phone and shouted in Russian, *"Vladimir, send ten men to secure the first floor, and another ten to watch the street."* Then I hit End. I switched to English. "I've got some questions."

Apparently, he didn't recognize me. "You think you can rob me, asshole?"

Varga hadn't changed much. He was still a thin, heavy lidded, hook nosed scumbag, just a little more gray and with a more expensive suit than the last time I'd seen him. Keeping his hands raised, he got off his knees, and stood up, probably thinking he could bluster or threaten his way out. "This house belongs to—"

I casually raised the pistol and shot him through the palm of his hand.

He flinched, and even managed to blink a few times before the pain hit. The zippy little 5.7 round had blown a perfect hole through his palm, like a high-velocity paper punch. He was lucky it hadn't hit a bone or it probably would have blown up in a meat cloud. He made an awful noise as he clutched his injured hand to his chest, but to his credit, he didn't start screaming. He was tougher than I thought.

"I'm here *because* you work for the Montalbans."

"You shot my hand!" Varga shouted, like I didn't know.

"Each time you don't answer, I put another hole in you. Where's your boss?" I'd settle for either Kat or Anders.

"France!" I moved the gun toward his knee. "Paris! Don't shoot! Katarina is working on something in Paris. I don't know where. She moves from safe house to safe house. Nobody can touch her."

"If Diego had been this forthcoming, he would have lived longer." From the look on Varga's face, they must have found his body in that dumpster. "Yeah, that was me. Don't make the same mistake and force me to bust out my talking knife. Where is Anders holding Bob Lorenzo?"

"Who?" Varga seemed genuinely confused, but I aimed at his knee anyway. "Shit! I don't know who that is! You've got to believe me!"

Good thing he talked fast, there wasn't a lot of slack in this thing's trigger. "Big, bald American. He mentioned your name in the Crossroads." I moved to the window and checked the street. Two figures were moving this way. I couldn't get a good look at them. Maybe Varga's men? Maybe the law? Stupid curious neighbors? Either way it was time to go.

"Anders never told us his name. He was sedated and tied up when I got him. My men flew him to Paris. That's all. Just a package. I move things. That's all I do." I thought about the empty beds down the hall, and resisted the urge to shoot him in the dick. "Anders' men picked him up from my place by the airport. I swear on my mother that's all I know."

I moved back to the door and looked down the stairs. That was my only way out. I couldn't get cut off. I had to make this fast. "Tell me about Project Blue."

Varga was in pain and terrified of me, but when I said those words, his expression slowly changed. I knew that expression well, because every time I'd looked in the mirror since I'd gotten out of the Pale Man's prison, I'd seen it in my own reflection. It was a fatalistic knowledge of certain mortality. As if me simply asking about Blue had sentenced him to death. Just like that, I'd just killed all his hope.

"I moved the cargo for her. As of last week everything is in place, but I never thought Katarina would actually go through with it. She wouldn't." Varga looked wistfully at the window. He'd been willing to give up his employers, but he'd rather try to escape that talk about Blue. "Millions would die!"

Millions? That made me sick to my stomach. "I'm going to stop her."

"Kill her and the plan launches. That's her insurance." Varga looked to the window again, he was doing the math. Four stories onto cobblestones *might* not kill him, but anybody who knew about Blue certainly would.

"Wait—"

Varga went for it.

The glass barely slowed him.

VALENTINE
Salzburg, Austria
September 3rd

Salzburg was in chaos, the *Polizei* were setting up checkpoints across the city, and we had to get out of town while we still could. We had executed our emergency egress plan, the one we'd put together in case things went sideways. The BMW and the Range Rover had both been doused with gasoline and torched. We switched to backup vehicles we'd prestaged nearby. Months of research and weeks of reconnaissance were all down the drain, thanks to Lorenzo.

Lorenzo who—I was surprised to learn—was somehow still alive.

Four of us were piled into a Mercedes Sprinter van. Antoine and Skunky were in a different vehicle, a tiny little Hyundai i20, leaving the city by an alternate route. Ling and I shared a bench seat behind Shen, who was driving. Behind us, Lorenzo sat by himself, leaning back against the wall of the cabin. His eyes kept darting back and forth, like he thought we were about to come at him.

No one spoke for a few moments. "Well, this is awkward," I said, breaking the uncomfortable silence. "I didn't recognize you for a second there."

Lorenzo watched me, but didn't say anything. His eyes were different than I remembered, sunken into his skull a little more. He looked older. He looked like he'd been through hell. His hair was longer, and he wore a short beard now.

Ling turned around and met Lorenzo's thousand-yard stare. "I'm glad you're still alive, Mr. Lorenzo," she said. "Please don't take this the wrong way, but may I ask how?"

Lorenzo shifted his gaze, staring off into space in silence for a moment. Ling looked back at me; I just shrugged.

"Jill is safe," I said after a moment. That got his attention. "We got her out of the Crossroads and into Mongolia. I think she and Reaper flew home from there. I'm not Facebook buddies with them, but we e-mail once in a while. All encrypted and everything, Reaper set it up. Last I heard they were both doing okay. As okay as they could be, I guess."

Lorenzo looked down at his lap for a moment, then up at me and Ling. "Thank you."

"No, thank *you*," Ling insisted. "Many owe you their lives. We thought . . . we assumed you were dead."

"I thought I was too."

"What happened to you?" Ling began to grill him. "How did you survive? Did you escape? What are you doing here? Why did you kill Stefan Varga?"

Lorenzo shook his head. "Give me a minute, will you? This is a lot to process. Where are we going?"

"Wels. A city just over an hour northeast of here. We have a house there that we've been operating out of, owned by a real estate shell company the organization uses. It's as safe a place as we're going to find."

"It's getting harder and harder to get around Europe," I said. "Police checkpoints are popping up all over. There are riots and mass protests happening all over the place. Terrorist attacks are on the rise, too."

"I heard," Lorenzo said simply. He fell silent then.

"So, uh, listen," I said, struggling to find the right words. The last time I saw Lorenzo, it was through a rifle scope from several hundred yards away. He was taking cover behind the decaying wreckage of a Soviet bomber as Sala Jihan's forces surrounded him. He'd run some kind of diversion, leading the pursuers off so that the few survivors of the raid on Jihan's compound could get away, and had gotten shot in the process. Ling and had tried to hold them off, but we were running out of ammo and there were just too many of them. I had offered to shoot Lorenzo, then, with the thought that it'd be more merciful than letting Jihan have him. He declined the offer. We had retreated and he'd been captured.

Like a cockroach, you just couldn't kill this guy. Believe me, I had tried.

As if reading my mind, Lorenzo raised a hand. "Don't worry about it. I told you to leave me. You got Jill out. That's all that matters."

"For what it's worth, I'm glad you're alive." It was Shen, looking at us in the rearview mirror.

Lorenzo nodded. Shen never had much to say, but I learned that he and Lorenzo had . . . well, I don't want to call it *bonded*, but they'd understood one another. "I'm glad you guys made it out, too." He looked back at me. "Before I tell you my story, you tell me yours. What the hell are you people doing in Austria? Why were you tailing Stefan Varga?"

"We're trying to track down Katarina Montalban. Our intel suggested Varga knew how to contact her."

Lorenzo simply nodded. "What happened after the Crossroads?"

Ling took a deep breath. "Exodus is . . . not at its strongest right now," she said honestly. "We got our asses handed to us, as you might say. Katarina is a lunatic, and all indications are that Project Blue will have apocalyptic repercussions."

"What the hell *is* Blue?" Lorenzo asked.

"We still don't know," I admitted. "We've tried to find your brother, he probably knows, but haven't had any luck."

"Maybe. Probably. I interrogated Varga. He squealed on Kat's location, no problem, but Blue? He took a swan dive rather than talk." He pointed directly at me. "But what the hell are *you* doing here? These people— Exodus—I get. They're idealistic do-gooders who think they can unfuck the world. No offense, Shen."

"None taken."

"But why you, Valentine?"

"It's a long story."

"Sounds like we've got a long drive ahead of us. Talk. And this time, I want to know everything."

Chapter 4: The Princess in the Tower

VALENTINE
Exodus Compound, Azerbaijan
Several months earlier . . .

"Well? What do you think?"

Dr. Bundt turned off the flashlight he'd been shining in my eyes, and glanced down at his iPad. "Mr. Valentine, you're very healthy. The last time I examined you, you were underweight and injured. You have made a remarkably swift recovery. Aside from some scar tissue and the fact that I performed the procedure myself, I wouldn't have guessed that you had been treated for a traumatic brain injury."

"Okay, that's good, right? So what's wrong?"

"Wrong?"

"Something is obviously bugging you, Doc. What's wrong?"

Dr. Bundt looked at his iPad again. "I'm not sure how to explain this."

"Okay, now you're scaring me. Do I have cancer or something?" That would be a hell of a way to go, after everything I'd been through and survived: fucking *cancer*.

"Cancer? No, no, my boy, you're as healthy as a farm horse. That's just it: you shouldn't be this fit. You should have barely been able to participate in the battle of the Crossroads, given your condition when we recovered you from North Gap."

I couldn't stop myself from wincing at the mention of the black site where I'd been held, interrogated, and had God-knows-what-else done to me.

"Have you read the files on you that we found there?"

I shook my head. "I kept meaning to, but . . . you know."

"I understand." I guess there's no shame in not dredging up unpleasant memories. "Dr. Silvers was conducting certain, ah, procedures on you. The notes we retrieved are vague, but she was working off of a template, a plan of action. The program is called 'XK *Indigo*.' Have you heard of it?"

Now I was scared. "XK what? Was she experimenting on me or something?"

"I wouldn't call it experimenting. She knew exactly what she was doing. I have not been able to find any real specifics on XK Indigo. A search on the internet reveals nothing but rumor and conjecture from conspiracy theorists. As near as I can tell, though, it's a mental and physical conditioning program."

I suddenly felt uncomfortable. I didn't want to talk about this. "Hey, maybe this is my superhero origin story. That's basically how the Canadians made Wolverine."

Dr. Bunt raised an eyebrow. I don't think he got the reference.

"So you're not a comic book guy, Doc? He was a mutant, one of the X-Men. The second greatest Canadian ever, behind Wayne Gretzky."

Dr. Bundt cocked his head slightly to the side, ignoring my attempt to change the subject. "Tell me . . . how much do you remember about the program?"

"Almost nothing," I lied. You can block some of it out, but you don't exactly forget months of drug-cocktail fueled torture sessions. "It doesn't matter now anyway."

The doctor wouldn't let it go. "Mr. Valentine, you have been a patient of mine for some time. I need you to be honest with me, and tell me how much you remember. It does matter. It matters a great deal. You're not the only one who has been through such conditioning."

What? "There are others?"

Dr. Bundt nodded. "I can't give you any specifics, for privacy reasons, but no, you are not the only one. However, you have dealt with the aftereffects of that program better than most, I believe it's due to your ability to enter into a serene mental state during extreme stress—"

"I've always called it *the Calm*." To me it wasn't anything special, it just was what it was. When things get really dangerous, I get detached. Not from reality, if anything I was even more rational when I was Calm, but things seemed to slow down, or maybe I processed everything faster, but it was handy in combat.

"Indeed. I have friends in the mental health industry who would love to be able to bottle that and sell it. Regardless, you're the only one who has been through this Indigo program retaining much at all. So please, tell me what you remember."

I took a breath, and looked down at my lap. "It's hard to remember a lot of it. It's like a dream, how it slowly fades after you wake up. I wrote a lot of it down in a journal, like you told me to, last year. I haven't gone back and read it. I get . . . I don't know, I get itchy thinking about it. It makes me uncomfortable."

"It is good not to dwell on such trauma, but I think there is more to it than that. This aversion to recalling the process, to discussing it, I believe that is part of the conditioning. I believe the same of the memory loss. I was concerned such a thing would happen, which is why I asked you to keep that journal after your recovery. You really should go back and read it."

"No. Like I said, it makes me uncomfortable." I squirmed on the exam table a little. I wanted to get up and walk out of the room. I didn't like it when he dug like this, but Dr. Bundt was the man who put the people Exodus rescued back together, both physically and mentally. He wasn't going to let it go, but I didn't like thinking about what would have happened had Exodus hadn't gotten me out of there. What kind of brainwashed, screwed-in-the-head asset for the Majestic organization would I be today?

So the doctor and I had a bit of a stareoff for a while. He folded his arms and looked like a really disapproving Albert Einstein. Sadly, he was such a nice guy that I couldn't just tell him to buzz off.

"Are you done with him yet?" someone asked, startling both Dr. Bundt and I.

Ariel was standing in the examination room doorway. There wasn't much left of the terrified adolescent I'd first met in Mexico. She was a lovely young woman now, with platinum blonde hair and intensely blue eyes. I suspected that if not for being sequestered in the Exodus estate in the middle of nowhere desert of Azerbaijan, she'd have her pick of young men.

"Yes, my dear," the doctor said. "Not to worry, he's quite physically healthy."

"Note, he specified physical. I'm still a mental basket case."

"Okay great, Michael. Will you walk with me? We need to talk."

Relieved at the distraction, I stood up. "I need to go, Doc. Thank you."

Dr. Bundt seemed reluctant, like there was more he wanted to ask me, but he let me go. The Doc was a really important man in Exodus circles, but everybody around here usually gave in to Ariel's wishes. He wasn't the only one. I'd gotten used to all of Exodus' secretive paramilitary badasses deferring to a kid, but that didn't make it any less weird. I'd spoken with her several times, and had even saved her life, but the girl was still a mystery to me.

She led me to the garden. The Exodus manor was built in the restored ruins of a medieval fortress. The modern part of the structure was U-shaped, with a nice garden in the middle. Being out in the desert, the garden was well watered, climate controlled, and protected from the blowing sands by a glass ceiling. It was, essentially, a large, beautiful greenhouse.

Ariel ditched her shoes. "I like to walk barefoot on the grass," she said idly, even though I hadn't asked.

"You're a weird girl."

"I like you the best because you're at least honest to me. Not wearing shoes reminds me of when I was small, when I was home."

"Where are you from anyway?"

She smiled at me but didn't say anything.

I cocked my head to one side. "What is your deal, kiddo? The sworn Exodus people won't say a word. Why all the hocus pocus and mystery? I mean, look, I don't know anything about you. Why are you even here? Why are you so important to Exodus? Why—"

Ariel shushed me. "So many questions."

"Well nobody else is going to answer them for me. They just tell me you're so observant you see patterns other people don't." Even Ling wouldn't tell me the whole deal. It isn't fun to ask your girlfriend questions and get blown off with BS like about recognizing patterns. "Asking why you'd have a little girl planning combat operations seems like a pretty reasonable question to me."

"You're right to ask them. I know so much about you, and you don't know anything about me. It's not fair." She looked sad for a moment. "Okay, I'm from Fresno, California. I haven't been there since I was a toddler, but that's where they say I'm from. I don't talk much about my past, mostly because I don't remember a lot of it."

Ariel was young, but her eyes looked older. Sad. Seasoned. I knew that she was frighteningly intelligent and almost unbelievably observant. She was probably a certified genius, if there was any sort of certification for that. She was weird, too. Like, sometimes you got the vibe she acted the way she did just because she was trying to mimic the people around her, to blend in. I didn't spend a lot of time around teenagers, but remembering how things were back when I was in high school, I could tell she wasn't typical. She almost reminded me of myself at that age, but only after my mom had been murdered, and after I had taken a human life. That was a crappy thing to be compared to, but there it was.

"When I was a little girl I was kidnapped. Like you, I was taken, tested, experimented on. They changed me, just as they changed you."

My heart sank for the poor girl. "Who took you?"

"You know them as Majestic, but that's not really what they're called."

"Oh, I've got plenty of names for them."

"The one I've heard you use the most is *fucking assholes.*"

"Language, young lady."

That made her smile. She paused to smell some white flowers. Then she plucked one and stuck it in her hair just over her ear. "You'll laugh at why they took me. It was because I was good at chess, puzzles, math problems, that sort of thing. I don't remember most of those days. It's like there isn't room enough in my brain for things like that anymore. They had problems with me, I know that. When they were done, they put me with a family to be monitored. I guess I needed a *normal environment* to see how I'd turn out. It was under a fake name. I don't even remember my real one."

Now that really was sad. "How did you end up on a Russian arms dealer's boat in Mexico?"

"Federov wasn't just some gunrunner, Michael. He was an asset of Russian foreign intelligence. They watched me for years, and then they grabbed me one day while I was walking home from school."

"What about your foster parents?"

"I don't know if Doug and Linda were working for Majestic or not. Either way, it's better to let them think I'm gone forever. I never even asked to go home. I don't have a home to go back to. None of that was real. It was all a puppet show, a fabrication. It was *fake*." Her tone and her pretty face both darkened. "It's not real and it's not my life."

I took a deep breath. I could certainly sympathize with her situation. "That's a tough break, kiddo."

"Exodus was watching Majestic's program the same way the Russians were, so after they grabbed me, Exodus grabbed me back. I've been with them ever since. It's not so bad, you know. I have a good life here. I don't want for anything."

"This isn't a life. This is a gilded prison." I looked around the lush garden make sure no one was listening, and leaned in closer to her. "Are you being held here against your will?"

She laughed at me and shook her head. "No, Michael. You're such a sweet man, though. You were going to try to rescue me, weren't you?"

I didn't admit to anything, but as a matter of fact, the gears had already been turning in the back of my mind.

"I'm not a princess locked in a tower. I'm here of my own free will. This is where I belong, for now. This is where I can do the most good." There was an uncompromising certainty in her voice that made me understand how grown men could take her advice seriously. She didn't sound like a teenager just then. "But I think that's changing, which is kind of why I had you brought here."

"I thought Exodus invited me here to stay off the radar." Majestic's best operative, Underhill, was hunting me. I'd gone out on a couple operations in the last few months and had had some close calls. Exodus probably didn't want me dragging them into a war they couldn't win against Majestic. "I'm confused."

"I know, but just listen. There are things happening out in the world right now. Big things, and they're not good."

"That's . . . not really helping."

Her intensely blue eyes almost burned holes in me. The shift from out-of-her-depth teenager to commander was a little unnerving. "The time has come for you to find Katarina Montalban. You need to stop this Project Blue, whatever it is, from happening. If you don't do anything, if you just sit here in exile, she will succeed."

"There's like half a dozen people in the world who know what that even is, and none of them are talking to us. How do you know all this?"

"Because I *know*, Michael!" she snapped. "Okay? I can see things other people can't see. I know things other people don't know. That isn't just some line Ling feeds you to get you off her back. It's hard to explain. I see lines of causation, strings, patterns, whatever you want to call it, and I can see where it's all leading. You have to find her and stop her. You will probably, like, have to kill her though, but that alone might not stop her plan. She's very smart, but she's crazy and she's dangerous. The important thing is you stop Blue."

I really wasn't sure what to say. "Um, okay then. Take out the leader of a powerful organized crime family, but first dismantle her wacky scheme that nobody understands first. I'll get right on that."

She shook her head. "I know you think I'm crazy. I'm not. You asked me why Exodus thinks I'm valuable, why the Russians thought I was valuable, and why Majestic thought I was valuable. This is why. I know things and see things and feel things that other people can't, and I'm usually right."

"So . . . you're like a psychic?"

"No! I'm not . . ." She was obviously frustrated. She pointed at a nearby bench. "Sit down." I did, and she plopped down next to me. There was a little fountain gurgling in front of us. The garden even smelled nice. It was a rather pleasant place to talk about the apocalypse.

"I hate when people call me psychic. Making what I do sound like magic is insulting to my intelligence. Look, I don't read tarot cards or palms or whatever. It's about facts and probabilities. Some things fit and others don't, but everything goes somewhere, and when you get enough things together, it is pretty easy for me to see what comes next. No offense, I don't know how to explain this to you in a way that you'll really be able to understand. Regular people just don't get it. You just have to trust me."

"I do trust you. I'm just trying to understand. You know, wrap my feeble mortal mind around it all." I shot her a lopsided grin.

She shook her head, looked up at me, and smiled back. "I said no offense. That means you can't get offended, stupid."

"Yeah, that's not really how it works."

"But listen, okay? I'm totally serious. I read everything that Robert Lorenzo found out about it and everything from the Majestic info that was dumped. I can read between the lines based upon Majestic's reactions, and now that they've lost control, they fear it more than anything else, ever."

"I figured that when they were torturing me for information I didn't have."

"This is what we *do* know: Majestic thought Blue up as a doomsday scenario. Four operatives were given the mission to prep it, but their superiors were in the dark on the details. Of those four, one was assassinated, the second died in Zubara, you killed the third but only after he'd cut a deal and given Blue to Big Eddie Montalban, and when the last operative, Anders, saw that everyone else was dead, he assumed Majestic was cleaning house, and threw in with Big Eddie's successor."

"Katarina."

"Exactly. Majestic opened Pandora's box, and then promptly handed it to a psychopath, so now they're freaking out. I don't know what they're planning, but I see where it leads. There will be war, chaos, and worse. The world is on the brink of falling apart already. This might be all it takes to push it over the edge."

"Colonel Hunter . . ." That was Ariel's *second operative*, but he had been my commanding officer in Zubara, so I couldn't just give the man such a casual designation. I'd been there when he'd died. Crushed and bleeding, his dying confession was how I'd learned about Blue, and his barely coherent last words had been to command me to find someone named Evangeline to stop it. Majestic had tortured the hell out of me to try and find out who that was, but all I had was her name. "Hunter's journal mentioned a Project Red in China. Millions of people died in the Chinese Civil War, and I think Majestic caused it, just like they used my Dead unit to destabilize Zubara. He said Blue was even bigger."

"So you know I'm right, then," Ariel said levelly as she squished her toes back and forth in the grass.

I sighed. "I'm afraid you might be. That's pretty close."

"This isn't about me or what I see, Michael. We're way beyond that. This isn't even about Exodus, or Majestic, or any of the other factions fighting for scraps. This time the world is at a crossroads, one path leads to an unknown future, but the other takes us to a hell that even I can't wrap my brain around."

"It's not fair, you know."

"What's not fair?"

"You're too young to have this burden on your shoulders. The world's about to blow up, but you think you're the only one who can see it coming. The only people who buy into your theory are a handful of fanatics who think they can make the world a better place if they just shoot enough bad guys."

Ariel smiled. "It's okay. This is how it has to be for right now."

"Why me?"

"Why you what?"

"Why me?" I repeated. "Why do you think I'm the one who can do anything about this?"

She shrugged. "I just know. You always seem to be in the right place at the right time. Trust me."

I'd made my living kicking doors and pulling triggers. Ariel talked about a world on the brink, but it was men like me who'd put it there. I had spent my whole life fighting somebody else's war. *Here I go again.*

"This isn't someone else's war, Michael," Ariel said softly. "If you're going to win, this has to be *your* war."

We sat in the garden for a long time, quiet except for the fountain. I didn't know if she was crazy, or if I was crazy for believing her. "What should I do first?"

VALENTINE
Salzburg, Austria
September 3rd

Lorenzo raised an eyebrow at me. "Just so we're clear, you're here because a teenage girl told you that you need to save the world."

"It sounds bad when you put it like that, but yeah, basically."

He shook his head slowly, looking between me and Ling as if we were inmates in a mental ward.

"There's something else you should know," I said hesitantly. "Hawk is dead."

Lorenzo was quiet for a long moment. "How?"

I took a deep breath and looked down. I couldn't look Lorenzo in the eye anymore. "It's my fault. It happened right after the Battle of the Crossroads."

"Your fault? You were on the other side of the planet."

"The people that held me . . . Majestic, whatever you want to call them. They're looking for me. They couldn't find me, so they went after the one person they could find. They killed him over the phone while I listened."

"Hawk," Lorenzo said, the word coming out as a harsh accusation.

"Yeah, I don't remember it, but I probably said something about him under interrogation. They had me so jacked full of drugs that I didn't even know what was real."

That sounded pathetic. Shameful. I thought Lorenzo would be angry at my excuses. From him, there would be at least harsh words, or maybe even a gun in my face. Instead he just exhaled and said, "It happens. Don't blame yourself. What's done is done."

"That's . . . mighty charitable of you."

"You do what you need to do to survive when you're in captivity. Every man breaks, sooner or later."

From what I knew about Lorenzo, that was a strangely humble thing to say. Whatever he'd gone through had left him changed. Had Sala Jihan broken him?

"I called Hawk after the battle. I hadn't spoken to him since I was captured. I wanted to let him know I was okay. They already had him. The Majestic operatives were waiting for my call. He said his name was Underhill. Older guy, maybe in his sixties. Hawk tried to fight back and they shot him down in cold blood, right on the fucking phone."

"Anders mentioned something about a guy named Underhill, and being worried that was who his old bosses were sending after him. Anders is probably the deadliest man I've ever known, so anyone who worries him is one scary motherfucker. He's probably still after you."

"Underhill didn't strike me as the easily discouraged type."

"Good. That makes it easier for us to find him and kill him, doesn't it?"

"I don't mind being the bait, for Hawk."

"For Hawk," Lorenzo agreed.

"Boys, please," Ling said, interrupting. "Let's put our penises away and focus on the here and now." She looked at Lorenzo. "Have you spoken to Jill?"

"No," Lorenzo admitted. "I wanted to. I thought about it, but the fewer people who know I'm alive the better."

"Mm-hm," Ling said, looking down at her phone. She had been sending text messages while I'd been telling my story.

"If they're not expecting me, I have the advantage. Kat doesn't know I'm coming for her. She won't until it's too late."

"You keep tossing her guys out of windows," I said, "and she'll figure it out."

"Varga jumped, but no. She'll be suspicious, but she won't think it's me. She has a lot of enemies. I intend to become Kat's worst nightmare, and Jill doesn't need to see that."

"You know," I said cautiously, "it wasn't easy for Jill. They came after her." I raised a hand before Lorenzo got too worked up. "It's fine. She's fine. She ran. I guess Kat pulled some strings. The government of the Bahamas seized most of your assets. Tax adjusters went to your house. Nobody was home because Jill had already bugged out, so the police searched the place. She destroyed all your documents, scrubbed everything, but they found your armory. All those guns are illegal in the Bahamas, so . . ." I trailed off.

"I'm glad I never paid taxes, then. Where is she now?"

"I'm not sure. She went back to the States for a while, I think. She's using one of the other identities you guys had set up, and Reaper was watching over her too. I haven't talked to her in a while but she's okay. I promise you, Lorenzo, she's okay."

"Good. She was always tougher than she gave herself credit for."

Ling's phone buzzed. "Hello?" she answered. "Yes. No, I didn't know. Yes, he's here. Okay." She reached past me and held her phone out to Lorenzo. "It's Jill," she said. "She wants to talk to you."

Lorenzo's eyes went wide. "What? How?"

"I texted her and told her. The only one you're fooling with all of that *she's better off without me* prattle is yourself. Being a stoic loner will not help you. Here. Take it."

Jill spoke loudly enough into her phone that we could all hear her, even though it wasn't on speaker. "You son of a bitch, you pick up the phone right fucking now!"

Lorenzo meekly took the phone. I turned back around and slumped into my seat. It was about to get even more awkward in the van.

LORENZO

Ling held out the phone to me. I hesitated before taking it. I was a con man who could smooth talk his way out of anything, but I didn't know what to say to the woman I loved. I was . . . scared? That wasn't the right word. Maybe *ashamed* was more appropriate, not that I'd ever been good at feeling shame like most people. Jill had never seen me at my worst, and that was where I'd descended in order to survive Jihan's prison, and where I'd planned on staying in order to get this job done.

"Damn it, Ling. I can't drag her into this."

"*Seriously, Lorenzo? I can totally hear you!*" Jill yelled.

"It's for the best, Lorenzo. I can see that prison damaged you. There is an emptiness in you, a wound, here," Ling said, placing one hand over her heart. "The choice is yours how you will fill that hole."

Metaphysical Exodus bullshit. The only thing over my heart was a big-ass burn from a branding iron. Hooking up with Valentine had turned Ling sappy. I snatched the phone from her, put it to my ear, and took a deep breath.

"It's me."

The line was quiet for a really long time, but I could hear Jill breathing. "*You're alive.*" It wasn't a question, more of an accusation. I couldn't tell if Jill was shocked or angry or happy or what.

Suddenly, my chest hurt. My face burned. "Yeah." There wasn't a lot of personal space in the back of the van. I looked at Ling and Valentine. "Give me a minute." I didn't want to cry in front of the terrorists.

Ling nodded. "This line should be secure and encrypted, but it would still be best to avoid names."

Valentine gave me one last odd look before turning around, like he actually got it. But fuck him and his pity. Trying to get as much privacy as I could in the van, I slunk down, and spoke quietly. "I got out. Are you okay?"

"I thought you were dead."

"Me too. Are you okay?"

"Am I okay? I grieved for you. They told me you were dead." She sounded out of breath, like she was walking fast or had just gotten done running. *"I'm too shocked to cry. Where have you been? How did you escape? When?"*

"I was locked up until a couple weeks ago."

That had to be a slap in the face. *"Why didn't—"*

"It wasn't safe to contact you. It still isn't."

"Come back to me. Come home."

This stung. "I can't yet. There's something I've got to do first."

"Then I'm coming to you."

"It's not safe—"

"It never is with you. But a lot has changed since you've been gone. I need to see you."

I missed her so much. She was the one who'd kept me alive and sane in the dark, and she didn't even know it. I wanted to be with her. But then what? I was on a cross-country murder spree. To win, I had to embrace the hate. I couldn't drag someone so good and decent into that. "Please, Jill. Just stay where you are."

"I'm in Paris."

That didn't make any sense. To Kat, Jill was just another loose end to tie up. She was hiding from the Montalbans, why go where they had so many eyes? "What?"

"I'm here to take care of your ex. Our friends know how to reach me. I've got to go."

Jill was trying to assassinate Katarina Montalban.

I could hear sirens in her background. "I love you." But Jill had already hung up.

That hadn't gone the way I'd hoped, and it sure as hell hadn't lived up to my dreams in prison. "Fuck!" I smashed my fist into the side of the van.

Valentine turned back around. "What's the—"

I cut him off. "Damn it, Ling. What the hell were you thinking?"

Ling faced me. "I misled Jill to believe you had died, so she wouldn't throw her life away trying to get you back."

It was blunt, incredibly cruel, and we both knew if Jill had come back for me, the Pale Man would have destroyed her. I was pissed off, but I did manage to mutter, "Thanks for that."

"And now I have stopped you from throwing away the one thing in your life that makes you an actual human being. She loves you very much, and she needs you, almost as much as you need her. Jill balances you, Lorenzo."

"Whatever, Ling."

"Do you truly think you are the first warrior so tempted to do evil, that you'd set aside all the good in your life because it might hold you back? You know what kind of broken people end up in Exodus? Freed slaves, refugees, and former child soldiers who have lost everything. They hunger for revenge more than even you can understand, yet, if we have to destroy everything we stand for to achieve victory, then what's the point?"

"I'm not in the mood for Exodus' cornball philosophy. Here's the deal. I'm going to Paris. Contrary to Valentine's assurances that Jill is okay, you must have missed the part where she's stalking Katarina Montalban."

Valentine was stunned. "She's doing *what?*"

"You didn't know, did you? I gathered that by the stupid look on your face when I said it. You're hunting Kat, it's your business to know. Varga told me Anders shipped Bob to Paris. He's their patsy. If Kat's there now, that's got to be where Project Blue is based out of. After I stop Jill from getting herself killed, I'll see if I can't track down my brother's whereabouts."

"Exodus has contacts in Paris," Ling said. "I will reach out to them for information. If Katarina has moved her operations there, we will find her."

"Good. Because Jihan made it sound like time is running out."

"So did Ariel," Valentine said.

"So your little angel and my devil are on the same page then. Fantastic. Before Varga took a header he talked about Blue killing millions." Valentine and Ling seemed discomfited by that, but not shocked. The description must have matched up the general idea they'd gotten from Exodus' weirdo mystical teenager. And here I'd been hoping Varga had been exaggerating. "Bob talked about it being big, but I don't know if he ever realized it was that big."

They were tight enough now that Ling and Valentine had reached that point where they could share a lot of information just in glances. Valentine gave Ling a questioning look, like *hey, I guess I'm supposed to be the leader, but what do I do now, honey?* And she nodded in the affirmative, as if to say, *go for it.* He swallowed, then turned back to me, looking a little uncomfortable. "We're shorthanded, Lorenzo. We could use all the help we can get. Work with us."

"The last time we partnered up, I collected several exciting new gunshot wounds and ended up rotting in the Pale Man's prison."

"It was your idea to team up with the Montalbans," Ling said pointedly.

She had me there. "Oh, believe me, I'm full of regret for that little partnership. It gave me something to focus on during the beatings."

"Call it an uneasy alliance then, but Blue has got to be stopped," Valentine said. "Are you going to help? Or would you rather keep bouncing around the countryside murdering assholes and ruining months of our work?"

"Yeah, I can't imagine how that feels."

Valentine frowned as he realized he and Dead Six had done the same thing to my carefully laid plans in Zubara. "No wonder you were such a prick when we first met."

"Falah, Adar, Hosani? Because if we're keeping score on ruined plans and general fuckery, you've still got a lead."

"I do, don't I?" he asked smugly.

"Enough. Our goals are the same," Ling said. "Let's not waste any more time getting in each other's way. We will do what we can. If fate is in our favor, perhaps we will learn enough to tip off the authorities, and they will stop Blue for us."

"Fat chance of that. You saw what the FBI did to Bob when he started poking around in Majestic business." Not that I would mind Kat and Anders getting arrested. I could arrange for them to get shivved in a prison way easier than I could pop them on the streets myself. "Fine. Whatever works. But I figure this doesn't end until we put a bullet in them ourselves."

"I don't have a lot of faith in the system either. Does this mean you're in?" Valentine asked suspiciously.

Normally when somebody tried to persuade me to do something, my instinctive reaction was to tell them to go to hell. As much shit as we'd gone through, he'd never like me, and I'd never like him, but I knew he'd shoot straight with me, and that was better than *at* me. Say what you will about him, but Valentine knew how to get a job done when he stopped moping long enough to focus.

"I'm in." My one-man rampage had somehow turned into another messy teamup. I needed some air. "Let me out somewhere I can boost a car. I'll see you in Paris."

VALENTINE
Exodus Compound, Azerbaijan
Several months earlier . . .

I stood off at the edge of the room, not saying anything. The faces of the other twelve appeared on a large screen, in two rows of six, as part of a secure video teleconference. They were electronically distorted so I couldn't make any of them out. Sir Matthew Cartwright, the councilman who owned the Azerbaijan estate, stood off to the side, hands behind his back, while Ariel addressed the bank of screens. Ling was with me, arms folded across her chest, looking unhappy.

Ariel turned out to be an eloquent speaker. Her conviction and confidence was impressive, even if she did still say *like* too much. She had just explained to the council what she had previously explained to me, except in greater detail. Once again, the teenage girl sort of disappeared, and all of a sudden there was this brilliant tactician in her place, making her presence felt.

She was a strange kid.

Despite Ariel's reassurances that this was all for the best, I still felt bad for her. A girl that age should be going to college, hanging out with friends, not making life-or-death decisions and weighing the fate of the world.

"It's unfair, getting robbed of her childhood," I whispered to Ling.

My girlfriend smirked at me. At that age Ling had already been conscripted into the Chinese army to fight in their civil war. She didn't even have to say anything.

"Yeah," I agreed. Compared to Ling I'd had it easy. When I was about Ariel's age, I had been in the Air Force. "Never mind."

Ariel was still making points. Her skills as an orator would have given any politician a run for his money, but it was a tough sell. She was arguing that Exodus should focus all of its present efforts on stopping Katarina Montalban and preventing Project Blue from happening, whatever that entailed. Only Exodus was—by legal definition at least—a terrorist organization. And though they were absolutely committed to stopping evil, righting wrongs, and all that good stuff, they had just gotten their asses kicked at the Crossroads.

She was trying to convince them that Project Blue, if allowed to continue, would set in motion a chain of events that would end with the deaths of millions and possibly trigger a major war. Only she seemed unwilling or unable to get into the specifics of how this was going to come about.

Our host, Sir Matthew, was one of the dissenters. He was one of those distinguished, proper English gentlemen types. I barely knew the guy, but I had a hard time imagining how somebody who looked and sounded like he did had risen through the ranks of a secret vigilante army that spent most of its time blowing up warlords and freeing slaves, unless he'd had some swanky James Bond thing going on in his youth.

"My Lady, we all appreciate your conviction, but you must consider our position. We lost a significant percentage of our strike steams at the

Crossroads. Word about the battle has gotten out. There are rumors of it on the Internet, satellite photos showing the damage to the dam and the resulting flooding. We have attracted the unwanted attention of the world's law enforcement and intelligence agencies. It is my belief, and has been the belief of the Council, that our best course is to take some time to collect ourselves and recover from our losses."

Ariel glared at him. "You mean retreat? Go into hiding? Give up on the work because of a setback?"

"No, child, I don't mean retreat." Ariel's eyes narrowed at being addressed as *child*, but Sir Matthew either didn't notice or didn't care. "It's more of a strategic realignment. We are operationally limited right now. We need time to recover, recruit, and train. When we are ready, we shall reenter the fray from a position of strength."

"There is no time! None of you seem to understand this. We are *out of time*. Project Blue is happening *now*. Katarina Montalban isn't going to wait while we sit in the corner and lick our wounds."

"You are being impetuous. Exodus has survived for centuries because we have operated in the shadows. That has become increasingly difficult. Yes, many powerful people have known about us, but have allowed our work to proceed because we were doing the things that they could not, things which their governments lacked the stomach to do. One slipup now, while we are so weak, could mean the end of us."

An Exodus councilwoman, hailing from India from the accent, spoke up from the screen. "We've all read the projections of the Oracle." From the look on Ariel's face, I could tell she thought her designation was absurd. "We know that Project Red, whatever the specifics were, was an American operation to destabilize China."

"We don't know that," another council member protested. He had a slight Canadian accent. "Mr. Valentine provided that information." That was the first time I'd been recognized in this little shindig. "There's no way of proving that the journals of this Colonel Hunter are genuine, and even if they are, there's no way of knowing if he was correct in his assessment. We're making far too many assumptions for my taste."

At least he didn't cast any aspersions on my character. Considering how much blood I'd spilt and shed on their behalf, that was nice.

The Indian woman protested. "The Oracle has made it clear that—"

"The Oracle was the one who said we should go into the Crossroads in the first place! Have we not had enough of her mystical nonsense? Have enough of our people not died because of her?"

The councilwoman from India looked aghast. "James, please. Things didn't go exactly as planned, but—"

938

"No, it's okay." Ariel raised a hand, and the Indian woman fell silent. "He has a right to speak his mind. Go ahead. Tell us how I screwed up everything."

"As I was saying, on her advice we went into the Crossroads, and how many people did we lose to that butcher? I admit that our so-called Oracle has been right on many occasions, but on this one, she was spectacularly wrong, and we paid for her error in blood."

That was remarkably impolite for a Canadian. I kept waiting for him to say *sorry*.

Another councilman chimed in. His accent was thicker than the others, some kind of Spanish. "I agree with our colleague. Will we continue to place stock in this, this nonsense? She may be brilliant, but she is still human. Her advice to concentrate on the Crossroads led us to disaster."

Ariel looked up at the screens, her face a mask, in silence. She lowered her gaze and looked at me briefly, as if considering what to say next. She nodded to herself, looked up again, and spoke. "The councilman says that I was spectacularly wrong. Was I? Did I say that the operation in the Crossroads would go as planned? Did I say we would not suffer casualties? No. I warned you not to underestimate Sala Jihan, and I had no role in the tactical planning or execution of the operation."

"So you'll lay the blame on Ibrahim?" Sir Matthew snapped.

"Of course not. He did the best he could. I simply told you what most of you already knew, Sala Jihan is a force for evil in this world, thousands die in his mines every year, and that he had to be stopped."

"But we failed," Sir Matthew insisted. "Now we are unable to conduct other missions, missions that could save lives, in other places in the world."

"We did not fail!" Ariel insisted, raising her voice, her hands balled into fists. "Sala Jihan lives, yes, but the Crossroads are gone. His mines are flooded. It will be years before he can regain the power he's lost. It's not the ideal outcome, just as it wasn't the ideal outcome the last time Exodus took him on. We suffered major losses then, too, but Sala Jihan was left impotent and powerless. It took him six decades before he showed his face again."

I had no idea what she was talking about. Sixty years? Lorenzo had met the warlord in person, but he'd not described him as old.

Taking a deep breath, Ariel looked directly at the portion of the screen that displayed the Canadian's image. "Had anyone told me about making an alliance with the Montalban Exchange, I would have advised them to abandon the mission altogether. I could have told you that was going to end badly. And, if you remember, I was the one who said Michael Valentine was important. I was the one who said we needed him. If not for his leadership, the effort at the dam would have also failed, and the whole mission really would have been for nothing."

The council remained silent for a moment. I was awkwardly looking at the floor. I knew Ariel was playing up my role in the battle for the dam to get her point across, but it still made me uncomfortable.

Ariel shifted her intense gaze across all of the faces on the big screen. Her eyes reflected the light of the screen and seemed to burn with a blue fire. "You think I didn't predict the cost? You think I haven't felt every single loss? None of you hurt as badly as I did. None of you."

Ling had told me that Ariel had gone nearly catatonic when the results of the battle came in. They'd even called Dr. Bundt in because they were afraid she would try to kill herself. She had retreated to her room, barely eating, not coming out for over a month.

Today, though, Ariel was resolute. "But that doesn't matter now. The work has to continue, even if we suffer losses, even if we have setbacks, even if we fail. There's too much at stake to stop. You all know this. If we don't do it, no one will. People will suffer without hope. For this operation, we don't need a bunch of soldiers. We can get by with a few volunteers, but from the organization we need logistical and intelligence support. I can't see for certain what will happen if we attempt this, but I do know what will happen if we do nothing. So please, let's not give up now. Too much is at stake. Authorize the mission."

"No." the Canadian said.

"I agree, no!" said the Spanish-speaker. "Young lady, we've had enough of your fortune telling. Am I the only one who sees it? Are we so blinded by her that we don't realize what we're doing? We're letting this American girl have a say in life-or-death decisions while a thousand miles from the action. She's clearly out of her depth, and quite possibly out of her mind."

The Indian woman tried to defend Ariel again. "Marco, the Oracle—"

The Canadian cut her off. "Enough of this talk of oracles! Enough! This has gone on for too long. It's time to put the adults back in charge. She doesn't know anything. She's no gift from God. She's a charlatan who's been fooling us all along!"

Ling looked at me with a worried expression on her face. This was not going well, and it was pissing me off. I started to step forward, but Ling put a hand on my arm. "You won't help here," she said quietly.

I stopped. Ling was right. I was an outsider.

Ling stepped forward, as if to say something, but before she could, Ariel balled her hands into fists and shouted. "I don't know anything, you say?" she asked, looking up at the screens. "James, I know about that torrid little affair you're having with your secretary, and that the only reason your wife hasn't left you is because of your money."

Too bad the image was blurred, because I imagined the look on his face would be priceless.

"Matthew," she said, addressing the Englishman in the room, "I know *you* haven't yet found the courage to come out to your family. Believe me, it's the twenty-first century, nobody cares."

Sir Matthew looked aghast, but didn't say anything.

"The clues are everywhere. It isn't my fault the rest of you are too stupid to put things together. All I have *ever* done," Ariel said, her small voice booming with conviction, "is give you people the best advice that I could. It was you who sought *me* out! It is you who came to *me* with your questions! The half-baked mysticism came from you guys. All this oracle talk is your words, not mine."

Ling looked me in the eye, and stepped forward, until she was in view of the screens. Dressed in fatigue pants, a t-shirt, and combat boots, she looked out of place in the luxurious office. "I think it's a sad day when this exalted council seeks to blame its failures on a mere advisor," she said coldly.

Sir Matthew seemed taken aback. "Ms. Song, I've allowed you to watch these proceedings, but I'm afraid I must ask you to—"

Ariel cut him off. "Let her speak! She's been there for all of this, while you've been reading about it from the safety of your offices afterwards."

Ling gave Ariel a really nasty scowl, and I think the little genius realized that she was being a hypocrite, and shut up. They might have been on the same side of this debate, but Ling was a whole lot more hands-on.

Ling spoke softly. I was pretty sure she did that on purpose, not through any sort of meekness—trust me, not an issue—but rather because it forced everyone to listen carefully. "I was involved in the planning of the Crossroads operation. The decision to meet with the Montalban Exchange was made by the commanders in the field. Ariel had no part in those discussions. We had our reservations, but given the situation, we made the best judgment call that we could."

"Your call cost hundreds of lives!" Marco insisted.

"I was there," Ling said coldly. "We made a gambit and it failed. I accept responsibility for my decisions. Ariel was not wrong about Sala Jihan. Having seen his operation firsthand, I can tell you that it was even worse than you can imagine. His reach was expanding daily, as more innocents died or were enslaved, and—as is our mission—we rushed to stop it. Our greatest failing was, I believe, in moving too soon. I point this out to this council, because the timetable for the operation was your decision, not Ariel's."

The council had no immediate response to that.

Ling continued. "I do not know how this girl knows the things she does. God help me, she's tried to explain it to me, and I'm still unsure. But she is right more often than she is wrong. So here we are, with this esteemed council calling her a false prophet on one hand, yet denouncing her for not foreseeing everything on the other. Is this what defeated Exodus has become? Is this how we honor our fallen, by trying to assign the blame to someone who was not there?"

"The situation is more complicated than you know," Marco said. "Katarina Montalban is a very well-connected woman, above the law, who now has total control of one of the most powerful organized crime groups in the world. She hasn't forgotten about us. Ever since the Crossroads, international authorities have been haunting our steps, breathing down our very necks. We've been subjected to countless cyberattacks and attempts to steal our information. Safe houses have been compromised, and many of our suppliers have gotten nervous and have severed ties. Our connections in national governments advise us to go to ground for a time, stay off the radar, especially in Europe. And in the midst of this, after suffering the biggest defeat in generations, with unprecedented assaults on our operation from every angle, you propose we try to take the Montalban woman head on?"

"That is exactly what I propose," Ling stated. "Was I not clear?"

Ariel butted in. "I'm aware of all of that stuff, Marco. You think I'm naïve, but I understand what's at stake way better than any of you do."

"You are not helping now," Ling muttered under her breath. Then she addressed the council again. "Katarina Montalban is a psychopath, an unstable, amoral, ruthless psychopath, who has been given the keys to Armageddon. Apparently Project Red destroyed my country and caused the death of millions. If we let such evil proceed unchecked again, then everything Exodus stands for will mean nothing."

Ariel spoke up one last time. "If we don't find a way, no one will." Without another word, she turned her back on the council and stormed out of the room.

After some searching I found Ariel in her room.

"Go away!" she demanded when I knocked on the door.

"It's me, kiddo," I said, leaning in close to the heavy wooden door. Music loudly thumped from the other side. She didn't answer, but after a moment the door opened. She didn't say anything after opening the door; she just went back to her bed and sat down. It was obvious she'd been crying.

Cautiously, I sat down next to her, and looked around, trying to think of what to say. Her room was cluttered and messy, but smelled nice. Scented candles were burning on her dresser. A couple strands of Christmas lights were tacked to her ceiling, giving the room soft, moody lighting. Band posters decorated her walls. Of course I didn't recognize any of them. Wrinkled clothes were piled in a heap by the wall. An electric guitar and a small amp sat in one corner, next to a TV and a Playstation.

"The council voted no," I told her.

"There was an eighty-two percent chance that they would, but I got my hopes up anyway. What are you going to do?"

"What I have to." I wasn't going to back down, and Ling was pissed. "Could you turn that down?" I could barely hear myself think over the racket of her music. It sounded like little girls singing heavy metal, but I think it was in Japanese.

"Okay, grandpa," she said, tapping a little remote control. The music volume went down to where I could hear her talk.

"Thank you. I've been around a lot of gunfire. My hearing's not so great."

"What do you want?" she snipped. After a second, her expression softened. "I'm sorry, Michael. I don't mean to be bitchy to you."

"No, it's okay. You have good reason to be upset. A bunch of grown-ass men are blaming a bad op against a bloodthirsty warlord on a teenage girl. It's ridiculous and they should be ashamed of themselves."

She sniffled and wiped her eyes. "They're not wrong, you know. I didn't see everything. I didn't know how badly the Crossroads would go."

"Will you listen to yourself? You told me you're not psychic. How in the hell do they expect you to predict the future, then? Don't listen to them. It's probably been a long time since any of them have gotten their hands dirty, if ever. It's easy for them to second-guess you."

"I know, but . . ."

"No buts. I've made decisions that have gotten people killed. It's the nature of the beast in this business. You can either forgive yourself for not being perfect or you can let it eat at you until you're paralyzed. Either way, it doesn't change the past or bring back the dead. And, honestly? Sometimes, you do everything right, and still lose. Sometimes, even if you win the fight, good people still die. Turn left instead of turn right, die. I don't care how good you are, you're not going to predict that. You guys, you're fighting a war, right? This is war. People die in war, even if you win every battle and execute every operation perfectly. There's no getting around it."

"I know that up here," she said, pointing at her head. She then put her hand on her chest. "It just hurts here."

"Ariel, how old are you?"

"I'm eighteen." She paused for a moment. "I'm pretty sure. My records aren't, you know, complete."

I raised my eyebrows. "Wow, there's a way to get some guy in trouble."

"What?"

"Nothing. Look, what I'm getting at is, you're too young to be doing this stuff. You're making life-or-death decisions for others and you haven't even lived your own self yet."

"I already told you. I'm right where I'm supposed to be. This is where I can do the most good."

"Is it? Seems to me that those guys just scapegoated you, and probably won't be listening to you much from here on out."

"I don't know," she said quietly.

"Yes, you do. Hell, if anybody knows, you do. Just like you knew all that other stuff about them. You know. So you probably know what I'm going to suggest next."

"I can't just leave."

"Why not? You don't owe these people anything."

"They saved my life and gave me a home. They took care of me."

"No, Ling rescued you. I helped, by the way. Besides that, you've more than paid your debt. Has it ever occurred to you that they've just been using you?"

"It's not like that," she said, a little defensively.

I shook my head. "I was a mercenary for years, kid. I know what it means to be an asset. To be honest? Your services are worth a hell of a lot more than room and board. I've heard what you can do. They give you an Internet connection, feed you intel, let you see what's going on and connect the dots and you're a goddamn oracle. How many successful operations have you fed them?"

She sniffed. "Sixty-four."

"They are the ones who owe *you,* Ariel, not the other way around. They saved your life, granted, but that doesn't make you an indentured servant, and it's pretty hypocritical of an organization like Exodus to treat you like one."

"It's not like that!" she insisted, more forcefully. "They asked me, you know, if I wanted to go home. I didn't. I have nowhere to go."

"How's Europe sound?"

"What?"

"You've been cooped up in this mansion for years. Have you been out, even once, since you've been here?"

"Yes," Ariel said softly. "I've actually traveled quite a bit, but it's usually to some safe house or base or whatever place. The last time I got to actually go outside was a few months ago. They took me shopping down in Baku. I even got to go out on a boat on the Caspian. It was so awesome that I wanted to sing. It was like in *Tangled* when Rapunzel got to leave her tower."

I didn't admit to having seen that movie, but in fact we'd watched a bootleg copy of it, with Chinese subtitles, in Mexico. I didn't want to lose points off my man card.

"Why?" she asked. "What are you getting at?"

"Catch up, genius. That's where the heart of the Montalban family business is. I can use you more than Exodus can right now. Come with me."

"They won't like that. That's where Katarina Montalban will be."

"You said I had to make this my war? Then fine. I'm drafting you. Help me figure out Blue. And frankly, I don't trust that these guys are going to let me talk to you once I leave here. I want you to come with us."

Ariel suddenly looked very unsure of herself. Her eyes darted back and forth. "I don't know. It's unexpected. I didn't think of this. It's an unknown, a rogue variable. I don't like rogue variables. I don't know about this. I need to think about this. There are implications that—"

"To hell with the implications. You're overthinking it. Stop trying to see every end, every possibility. You can't. I don't care if you actually are psychic or whatever, you're not omnipotent."

I could almost see her thinking. "You . . . you're right. I do need to go with you. I can't do much from here, not anymore. There isn't a lot of time left, Michael. I think I can see the end of the world from here."

"Then pack your shit." I stood up. "We're going on a road trip."

Sir Matthew Cartwright was, as I expected, not happy.

"Absolutely not!" he insisted, raising his voice. His secretary, Penelope, hurried alongside us, her heels clicking and clacking on a polished wooden floor. "You can't take her!"

I got in front of him and blocked his way. The aristocrat and his secretary were quickly surrounded by Ling, Shen, Antoine, and Skunky. Four badass Exodus operatives, all of whom had been there to rescue Ariel in Mexico, all of whom had been at the Crossroads, and all who were ready to openly revolt, and me, the meddling outsider. It turned out Ling's guys were a lot more loyal to Exodus' mission than to the parties running it. They took this protecting the helpless stuff real serious.

I looked Sir Matthew in the eye, coldly. "Try and stop us, Elton John. Ariel is an adult, and she's going with us of her own free will. We'll be driving her right out the front gate. I suggest you not be in the way."

"Ling," Matthew said angrily, turning toward the woman he'd worked with for years. He should have known better. "When the Council said no, I knew you'd disagree. Yet, I said I'd allow you and your assets to leave without repercussion if you felt you must. Those assets did not include the Oracle."

Ling glared right through him. "Exodus fights against slavers. It is a sad day when we become them."

"You know it isn't like that! We need to keep her here."

"What difference does it make?" Ling asked, pointedly. "You've made that abundantly clear you won't listen to her. What good does she do here, literally locked away in a castle tower, if you're not going to use her talents?"

"Bloody hell, it's not about that!" he insisted, lowering his voice a little. "It's about keeping her safe. She's safe here. She won't be safe out there in the world."

"Kid's gotta grow up sometime, man," Skunky said.

"Not like this! You understand nothing." Desperate, he turned back to Ling. "If you do this, you will be cast out of Exodus. You would throw away everything you've worked for, everything you stood for?"

"I'm standing now," Ling stated.

"I won't allow it! Stop this madness at once or I'll get security down here!"

"Do not do this, Matthew," Ling stated flatly. "Not like this."

I felt for Shen, Antoine, and Skunky. They were true believers. They'd devoted their lives to this outfit. The *security* they were being threatened with were their friends, but they didn't back down. Ling was like a rock. Her principles never wavered. If doing the right thing meant turning her back on Exodus, which had freed her from slavery, which she'd fought and fled for ever since, she would, in a heartbeat. That was one of the reasons I loved her.

"Penelope, get the guards."

"Don't, Penelope," I warned. This poor woman looked like she was going to faint. She looked at me, looked at Matthew, then back at me. She then hurried off down the hall without another word.

A pulse went through my body, a muscle twitch, and my heart rate slowed, ever-so-slightly. I was carrying one of Ariel's bags in my left hand, my *gun hand*. I slowly set it on the floor and stared Sir Matthew down. "If that's how you want to play it, we'll paint the walls red. I promise you this, bullets start flying, you won't make it out alive."

He didn't bend. Sir Matthew may have put on airs of being a foppish rich guy, but right then I could tell from the way he carried himself that he was made of sterner stuff than that. He wasn't going to come out of this confrontation alive, but I doubted I would, either.

"Stop it!" Ariel shouted. I had not heard her approach. "All of you, stop it!" She pushed her way in between Shen and Antoine, and walked up to Sir Matthew. "Please," she said. "Don't do this."

"My Lady," Sir Matthew said, "I can't let them take you. It's too dangerous."

"Matthew, you're such a sweet man," she said, putting a hand on his arm. "But I need to go where the work is, and it's not here, not anymore."

"But, Ariel . . ."

"You've kept me safe for the last few years, but you can't keep me safe from the world forever." She looked at me, then back at Sir Matthew. "Besides,

Michael isn't joking. This time the future is perfectly clear: he will kill you. But the five of them would not make it out of here alive. Among these are beloved heroes to the rest of your soldiers, and their death at Exodus' hands will shake the conviction of your remaining soldiers, leading to desertions and betrayal. Exodus would never recover. In the next few seconds you will decide the fate of the entire organization. It's not worth it, not for me."

He clenched his jaw, torn, but believing. *Do the right thing, man.* I really didn't want to get into a gunfight with people I nominally liked.

"So just let me go. Please. I need this."

Sir Matthew looked up at me, bitterly, daggers in his eyes, then back down at Ariel. His expression softened, and I could tell that he really did care for the girl. He wasn't protecting her because she was an asset; he protected her out of love. "Perhaps you're right."

The Exodus operatives all breathed a sigh of relief. That had almost gone sideways.

"I pray you are right. In any case, as you say, you're an adult now, Ariel. You're free to go. Exodus is not in the business of keeping captives."

"Thank you, Matthew." She hugged Sir Matthew, squeezing him tightly.

"Just mind yourself, child. It's an ugly world out there. Worse than even you know." The British councilman then looked at Ling. "Promise me you'll keep her safe. She's more important than you know."

"We are in the wrong line of work for guarantees, Matthew, but I will do my best." Ling began walking away. She was done here. "Come on."

"One last thing, Mr. Valentine. If anything happens to her, I will hold you personally accountable. Please believe me when I say that I have great resources at my disposal."

I picked Ariel's bag back up. "Yeah, well, get in line."

Chapter 5: Rogue Variables

VALENTINE
Wels, Austria
September 4th

Ariel was waiting for me when we arrived at our safe house.

"Oh my God, what happened?" she said, as we made our way through the door. The three-story house on the outskirts of Wels had been our base of operations for several months at this point. Progress had been slow in our efforts to track down Katarina Montalban and her cronies; there had been many days when we had nothing to do, so we just sat around the safe house trying to stave off boredom. This was the most excitement we'd had in a while.

Ariel was freaking out. "You need to tell me everything!"

"Okay, okay, everybody is fine," I said, setting my gear bag down on the floor.

"Something went wrong," she said pointedly.

"Indeed," Ling agreed. "Stefan Varga is dead."

"Well, okay, yeah, Varga's *not* fine. I meant none of us got hurt."

Ariel looked confused, like she sometimes did when things didn't go how she expected them to. "What? How?"

"Lorenzo's alive," I said.

It wasn't often that I left Ariel speechless, even momentarily. "*What*? I didn't . . ." She trailed off, eyes darting back and forth. "He's a variable. Too variable. The probability is . . . I didn't see this. I should have. It makes sense."

"I'm glad this makes sense to you, honey, because I was surprised as hell."

"Ariel," Ling said, "did you suspect Lorenzo was still alive?"

"No . . . I mean, yes. Kind of. I didn't want to say anything because, well, if he was alive, that meant that Sala Jihan was keeping him alive, and that was just too awful. I need everything you have, the video, the pictures, and you need to tell me everything Lorenzo said. Where is he? I have so many questions for him. He's a rogue variable. Don't you see, this totally changes everything?"

948

"Slow down," Ling said. Ariel tended to talk faster and faster the more excited she got, as her vocal cords struggled to keep up with her mind. "You can debrief us after we get cleaned up, I promise. Here are the SD cards from our cameras."

That seemed to satisfy Ariel. She took the cards from Ling, hugged me, and headed upstairs, to where her personal command center-slash-bedroom was. The house had six bedrooms, enough accommodations for all of us to have a bit of privacy. This was good, since Skunky's hobby was playing the banjo, and Ariel enjoyed listening to Japanese heavy metal.

Like I said, she was a strange kid.

Despite our earlier disagreement with the Exodus Council, occasionally a runner would stop by, bringing either supplies or information that was deemed not safe to transmit. Apparently kidnapping their oracle had forced their hand. Better to help us not get caught than to stay out of it and lose their precious asset. Aside from that little bit of aid, we were more or less on our own.

Ling looked over at me, smiling. "You called her *honey*."

I thought about it for a second. "I did? So?"

"Then she hugged you."

I was confused. "Is that bad?"

Ling sighed, shaking her head. "Michael, you are incredibly dense sometimes. Think about it for a moment. That girl doesn't have any family, just like us. You know what happens. You find yourself a family. She's picked you as a father figure."

"I'm not old enough to be her father." At least, I didn't feel old enough. Still, what Ling was saying made sense. After losing my parents, I'd found myself a family first in the military, then later on with Switchblade 4. Skunky had been like my brother, as had Tailor, whom I hadn't heard from since we left Zubara. I still thought of Hawk almost like he was my father.

Looking smug, Ling watched me as I came to the uncomfortable realization that she was right. "Well, that's intimidating." I had spent a lot of time with Ariel during my stay in Azerbaijan, but I figured she liked hanging out with Ling and me because she didn't have any friends in the sprawling estate, and certainly not any friends her own age. "It's just, you know, she's a grown woman."

"Is she now?" Ling asked, as we made our way upstairs. "Were you all grown up when you were eighteen?"

"I was in BMT at Lackland," I said. "But not really."

"I had already been conscripted into the PLA. This was before Shanghai was destroyed and the ceasefire talks began anew. But I was still very much a child, and I missed my parents dearly." She paused. "I still do."

I put my hand on her shoulder. "I know. Me too."

"If that poor girl needs a stand-in parent, then so be it," Ling said. "She's been through enough hell. I'm glad you brought her with us, Michael. That was a good decision."

"Does that make you Mom then?"

"Oh, of course not. I'm far too young. And . . . hip? Is that what they call it? In any case, I'm more like her big sister."

Ling was actually a couple of years older than I was. "Sure, baby, hip. I'm just glad Sir Matthew didn't have me shot." I stopped at my door. I had my own bedroom, but spent most nights in Ling's. The others in the house were polite enough to pretend they didn't notice. It was the sort of thing that was probably frowned upon in Exodus' bylaws, if they had such a thing, but I didn't really give a damn about such nonsense anymore. I was a fugitive working for a paramilitary organization that had been labeled as terrorists by the UN, the European Union, and Interpol; breaking Exodus' fraternization rules with Ling didn't even register, compared to all that.

"Hey, I'm going to get cleaned up and maybe take a nap. Wanna meet downstairs in a few hours for dinner? We all need to sit down and have a hot wash about what happened, too, make sure everybody's on the same page."

Ling raised an eyebrow. "Hot wash?"

"Air Force jargon. We'll just go over the operation, what went right, what went wrong, stuff like that."

"I see. Right? Lorenzo didn't shoot you. Wrong? The man we needed to question fell to his death. Good call. Yes. I'll see you at dinner." She kissed me on the cheek and continued down the hall.

I usually didn't leave the house if it wasn't necessary. Majestic, and every organ of the United States government that it could influence—which was probably all of them—was still looking for me. If I were spotted, I'd have to run, and the entire effort to stop Katarina Montalban would be compromised. Even though Dr. Silvers had finally believed me when I said I didn't know what Project Blue was, they weren't just going to let me go after escaping from their black site, especially since I was the one who gave Bob Lorenzo the Project Heartbreaker files. Shadow governments weren't big on forgiveness or loose ends.

I thought about exposing them, from time to time, just going public with the whole thing. Calling up some big network news outlet back in the States and saying "My name is Michael Valentine, I was the one who originally acquired the Project Heartbreaker files, and boy, do I have a story for you." I doubted it would accomplish anything, though. One way or another, it'd end badly for me. If Majestic didn't kill me outright, they'd use the legal system against me and I'd end up in prison. I'd broken countless laws back home, killed people, and there were those who thought that whoever released the Project Heartbreaker files was guilty of treason. My only hope of avoiding that would be to try to defect to another country, live in exile, getting worked over by their intelligence organizations. *Fuck that.* I'd spent enough time being interrogated and held captive. Just because my own country had gone to hell it didn't mean I wanted to work for somebody else's.

No, trying to come clean, tell the truth, shine the light on everything, would end up with me discredited, imprisoned, and probably dead. That was the way the world worked. All I really wanted to was to go home and live a quiet life, but I doubted that that would ever be an option for me.

Bob Lorenzo was such an idiot, I thought bitterly. The damned fool thought it was still possible to work within the system, to effectuate positive change. After the incident in Quagmire, Nevada, he'd practically begged me to go with him. He talked about the "legitimate government" and called Majestic a "cancer." What he failed to see is that Majestic wasn't the cancer; Majestic was a symptom of a much, much bigger problem. He acted like his so-called legitimate government wasn't giving materiel support and tacit approval to the operations of Majestic. Even shrouded in layers of secrecy like they were, none of it would be happening if they didn't have approval from on high. One man wouldn't be able to fix that problem. I doubted the problem could be fixed at all.

Hell, I'd given Bob all the info Colonel Hunter had given me on Project Heartbreaker, and he had gone public with it. He exposed Majestic to the cold light of day, and what changed? Nothing. They scattered, laid low for a while, but that was it. It had just been one more scandal out of dozens, whitewashed by the politicians and a compliant media. The whole exercise was for nothing.

Still, I wondered, what would have happened if I had taken him up on his offer. I probably wouldn't have been captured by Majestic and sent to North Gap. Colonel Hunter's last words had been about somebody named Evangeline, who was somehow related to Project Blue, and Silvers had drilled my mind into Swiss cheese trying to figure out who the hell Evangeline was. Maybe if I'd gone with Bob I would've been able to find out. I certainly wouldn't have given him or Hawk up under interrogation. Hawk would still be alive and Bob wouldn't be missing.

There was no sense second-guessing the past, not now, not here, alone in my room. I was exhausted, and needed to take a shower before my housemates used up all the hot water. After that, I badly needed a nap.

It was hours later when I awoke to someone gently knocking on my door. I opened it to find Ling waiting for me. Her black hair was done up in a messy bun with a pair of sticks shoved through it. She wore a purple spaghetti-strap t-shirt and black yoga pants, and was barefoot.

"Did I wake you?" she asked, stepping inside.

"Yeah, but it's okay. I need to get up anyway. All these stakeouts are hell on a sleep schedule."

"You look like you got some rest," she said. "I thought I'd come check on you."

"We still need to sit down and have that hot wash."

"Dinner, or perhaps it is closer to breakfast, is cooking now. And you are right, following criminals makes setting a reasonable schedule difficult. We will all sit down together and discuss what's happened shortly. Since we are short on time, I have some proposals, but no matter what, I want you to know in front of the group that I will defer to your judgment. This is your operation."

"Is it?"

"This mission is your doing. The group looks to you for leadership. It's good to see. It comes naturally to you."

"I'm glad one of us is confident in my abilities," I said glumly. "Half the time I feel like I don't know what I'm doing, like I'm just winging it and hoping for the best."

"To a large extent, that's exactly what we're doing. But it's all we can do right now. This is unfamiliar territory for all of us."

"I wouldn't be able to do any of this without you," I said. I squeezed her hand. "You keep me sane."

Ling leaned forward and gave me a quick kiss. "I've seen you at your finest, Michael. You have every reason to be more confident."

"I've gotten too many people killed."

Ling shook her head. "That is the nature of this business. People die."

"I told Ariel that same thing before we left. But, I've been thinking, I really should have gone with Bob Lorenzo when I had the chance. None of this would have happened. Not like this."

"You don't know that," Ling said. "Perhaps it would have worked out better, perhaps not. Bob would have been found out eventually, even without you being interrogated. There was no way a lone FBI agent could go up against an organization like Majestic without penalties. It was only a matter of time. In any case, perhaps this is selfish of me, but I'm glad things went the way they did."

"Why is that?"

"Because now I have you." Nobody ever accused Ling of being tender, but with me she tried. "And you have me. Things work out. They always do. The Crossroads ended badly as it was, but it would have gone even worse without you."

I leaned forward and kissed her again, longer this time, more deeply.

After a moment, she moved to get up. "I need to get dressed."

I didn't let go of her hand. "I don't think so."

A playful, mischievous smile appeared on her face. "Oh really?"

I nodded. "As a matter of fact," I said, kissing her on the neck, "I think you're overdressed as it is."

"Is this how it's going to be?" Ling asked, eyes closed as I kissed her neck and shoulder. "You use your authority to take advantage of your subordinate? Shameful."

"Shameful," I agreed.

Ling pulled away, her dark eyes twinkling. She gave me a gentle shove, pushing me back onto the bed, and climbed on top of me.

"Well then," she said, straddling me, hands on my chest. "Let's see who's really in charge."

Sometime later, Ling and I lay together, naked beneath a sheet. She had her head on my shoulder and was listening to me breathe, something she often did after sex. If you didn't know Ling, and only judged her from the public face she wore, you'd think she was an ice queen. She tended to be standoffish and, often, needlessly formal. She'd lived a hard life. I knew full well why she put up the walls that she did, but that didn't make it any less striking when they came down.

For someone normally so distant, when we were alone, she was very touchy. She liked to hold hands and cuddle. She was never one to engage in public displays of affection; a quick peck on the corner of the mouth was the most I would get out of her if there was any chance anyone would see. But behind closed doors, she was a different person: sweet, sensitive, passionate, enthusiastic in the sack. One time, we even watched *Steel Magnolias*, and I held her while she bawled her eyes out.

Other times, we talked about the bad stuff. She had seen as much combat as I had, and the horrors of the Chinese Civil War were well known. Cities burned, mass starvation, fields of bodies. I could talk to her about the bad days, about the things I'd done, about how I desperately tried to cling to my humanity, and she actually understood. I could talk to her about the friends I'd left behind, the people I'd watched die, the things I'd swore to lock away, and she didn't just listen, she *got it*.

When I woke up in the middle of the night, soaked in sweat, reaching for a weapon to fight an enemy that wasn't there, she held me until I calmed down. When she found me drinking myself stupid, crying, regretting the past and feeling sorry for myself, she didn't judge, didn't shame me for cracking, didn't look down on me for not always being able to keep it together. She just wrapped her arms around me and told me it was okay.

Fate had brought us together, time and time again, against all odds. Ariel had insisted that Ling and I were meant to be, and even though I told myself I didn't believe in such things, I was beginning to believe it with her. Ling wasn't just my girlfriend, or my lover. She was my partner, my other half, my warrior, my beautiful angel of death. I couldn't imagine life without her.

I wanted to tell her. I wanted to tell her so badly what she meant to me, how I'd be dead without her, how my heart skipped a beat when she smiled. I wanted to tell her, but I couldn't. I didn't have the words, I didn't know how to say it in a way that wouldn't sound stupid.

"I love you," was all I could manage.

"I love you, too," she said.

Somehow, that was enough.

We sat around the dinner table, scheming. The house in Wels had a large dining room with a round dinner table, big enough for all of us. We six were all the manpower we had, and that included Ariel, whom I wasn't about to take out on a mission. In fact, we'd gone over contingency plans over and over again covering what she was supposed to do if we were compromised in any way.

Our crew was small and our resources were limited. We were down two vehicles now, in the aftermath of the fiasco in Salzburg, limiting our transportation options. We had a small pile of cash, guns, whatever information we could get our hands on, and not much else. Against us was a crime family with limitless resources.

Sometimes it seemed hopeless, but I couldn't let the team think I had my doubts. Ling had been right; this operation was my baby. These people had volunteered to follow me on this fool's errand, and I owed it to them to not let uncertainty get the better of me.

If I was trying to seem upbeat, Antoine was dour. The hulking African always struck an imposing figure, even when casually hanging out at the dinner table. He was actually a very kindhearted, gentle man, but ferocious in his convictions, and not the sort you wanted to piss off. Shen was, as usual, quiet and unassuming. It was as if he wanted people to forget he was there. Skunky was a bit of a smartass, but he was damned smart. Shen and Antoine had worked with Ling for years. Skunky was one of my oldest friends, and we'd been in Switchblade together before he joined Exodus. Despite our challenge, I couldn't ask for a better team.

"The information Lorenzo presented is disturbing. It seems that we have less time than we thought," Antoine said.

Nods and grunts of agreement came from around the table. Even Ariel was quiet. She chewed her food absentmindedly, seemingly zoned out, but I had seen her like this before. Her mind was racing, trying to process everything, account for every possibility.

"Varga says the pieces are in place, but if we just pop Kat, it'll launch. So what do we do about it?" I asked. "How do we stop this when we don't even know where to start?"

Ariel blinked hard a couple of times, swallowed her food, then joined the conversation. "I've been thinking this over. The answer is there; I just can't see it yet. Elusive, you know?"

"No," Skunky said. "Not in the slightest, scary computer brain girl."

"We need more information. I need more if I'm going to be able to put it all together."

"Yeah," Skunky agreed. "I'm on board with you guys until the end. You know that. But I'm not gonna lie, bro, I'm pretty lost."

"Perhaps," Antoine suggested, "it would be helpful to start with what we *do* know. Katarina's operation has moved west, and so must we."

"Varga told Lorenzo that Katarina Montalban is in Paris, so that's where we need to go."

"Agreed," Ling said.

"Yay!" Ariel cheered. "I've always wanted to see Paris. It's the city of love."

"I thought it was more the city of ham sandwiches myself," Skunky said. "Seriously, they've got like a little bakery like every twenty feet there, and they're all awesome."

"I guess it could be both," Ariel said, thoughtfully. "If you love sandwiches, I mean."

Ling was not impressed by love or sandwiches. "Let's stay on topic, yes? Operationally speaking, Paris is solidly Montalban territory. We have been able to operate with relative impunity over the last few months because we have been poking around the outskirts of the Montalban empire. Paris is the heart of it. They will have eyes everywhere and informants in the government and among the police. Any contacts we have with the criminal underworld can be assumed to be compromised."

"Assume that anyone we speak with will immediately inform our enemies," Antoine grumbled. "To find intel among Paris' criminals will be difficult. That is something we could use Lorenzo for."

"True that," Skunky said. "We spent how many months tracking down this one Varga dude without getting caught, and your old buddy from Zubara found him in what, a couple of days after getting out of a torture dungeon?"

"Something like that," I mumbled. Yes, Lorenzo knew the underworld better than anybody, but I suspected the reason he'd found Varga so fast was that he just didn't care about getting caught. I'd seen it in his eyes in the van, he simply didn't give a damn if he lived or died as long as he took his target with him. I recognized the look because I'd seen it in the mirror when I was after Gordon Willis. Maybe Ling had saved his life by putting Jill in his path, maybe not. Time would tell, but in the meantime I had people to take care of. I didn't have that luxury of risking him dragging us down with him. "We'll work with Lorenzo, but I'm not sure we can count on him for anything."

"Because he's traumatized," Antoine said.

"More like kamikaze," I corrected.

"We may be flying blind, but I have received word from Sir Matthew," Ling suggested. This was probably the part she'd warned me about earlier. "He has made contact with another player who may help us, and believes he may be of use."

"Could you be more vague?" Skunky asked.

"Oh, trust me, she can be," I answered.

Ling scowled at me before speaking. "His name is Alastair Romefeller."

"So who is this guy?"

"The chair of Romefeller Fund Management and head of the Romefeller Foundation, his philanthropic apparatus. He's a hedge fund manager worth something like twenty billion U.S. dollars. He is also the sole owner of a think tank and private intelligence gathering firm called Romefeller Military Intelligence."

"He's Illuminati," Ariel said flatly. "One of their power-hungry overlords who imagines himself ruling the world. You can't trust him."

"Whoa, whoa, wait a sec," Skunky said. "*The* Illuminati? That's conspiracy theory bullshit. It's just a bunch of rich bastards who like to do favors and pull strings for each other. The Montalbans belong to that social club and you want to talk to *them?*"

"It is not ideal," Ling said, "but there's a mutual interest here."

"The Illuminati are real, and they have always stood in the way of Exodus and the work!" Ariel protested.

I couldn't let this degenerate, and ultimately, I had to make the call. It may have sounded crazy, but I knew there was something to it. Gordon Willis had me assassinate Rafael Montalban as part of the secret war between Majestic and the Illuminati.

"Bob Lorenzo said that Project Blue was Majestic's way of destroying the Illuminati. We know both sides are assholes, but let's back up. Everything I've heard about the Illuminati comes from pop culture, a bunch of wealthy elites who secretly run the world, and all that. If anybody is actually running the world, they're doing a terrible job since it's falling apart, so I know that's nonsense. What's their actual deal, Ling?"

"We don't know everything," Ling said. "Much of the truth is buried in layers of misinformation. This conspiracy theory bullshit, as Jeff calls it, helps obscure their real objectives. As soon as someone starts talking about the Illuminati, he's immediately dismissed as a nut."

"But the actual conspiracy is real," Antoine said.

"Yes, they're very real," Ariel said. "Once you get past the lies and legends and bullshit, they are basically an alliance of descendants and heirs of European aristocracy. Their leadership all comes from several powerful families. The Romefellers are one of them, as are the Montalbans. The different families' influence goes up and down over the years."

"Well, I checked Google," Skunky said as he placed his phone on the table. "Wikipedia says that the Illuminati were founded in Bavaria in 1776."

Ariel rolled her eyes. "That's not true. They go back way further than that."

"Like I'm going to trust you over Wikipedia."

"Older than Exodus?" I asked.

"Exodus and the Illuminati share common origins, according to the lore," Ling said. "Both were products of the Crusades and, later evolved during Enlightenment. Both were founded with the goal of bringing justice to a base and, at times, unbearable world. Exodus chose the path of direct action, fighting evil wherever it showed itself. The Illuminati chose . . . well, another way. Manipulation through the levers of power. They do not seek to combat injustice so much as they wish to implement order and control."

"With themselves in charge, of course," I said.

"Obviously!" Ariel said. "And that's why you can't trust them! They think that people can be managed. They don't get probability. They freaking started World War One!"

"What? How?"

Ling just shook her head, but Ariel went off.

"Well, not started, but made it spiral out of their control. Their attempts at manipulation, gaming the system, were at an all-time high. They thought they could manage a regional conflict to gain more power, and bring about a tide of internationalism. It backfired. They got their League of Nations, but they didn't predict the rise of communism or fascism. This took away the base of their power for a while, so they watched, and waited. They were key players in the founding of the United Nations and, later, the European Union. They are, I think, more powerful today than they've ever been. They are rivals of Majestic."

I scratched my head. "Why would a secret U.S. government organization want to attack the Illuminati? Jesus, this sounds crazy just talking about it. Majestic was formed, originally, to fight communism. That's what Hunter said."

"The Illuminati long supported communist expansion—that's just another kind of lever to them—but that made them natural enemies of Majestic. After the Second World War, Europe had lost its power base. The United States emerged as the superpower, so the power shifted, but Majestic kept the Illuminati from getting their hooks in. It was a turf war. So the Illuminati did their best to help the Soviet Union along as a hedge against the Americans. Ultimately, they wanted a unipolar world with themselves at the top. In the meantime, they settled for a bipolar world on the brink of nuclear war. When the Soviet Union collapsed, and then China fell apart, the Illuminati saw a chance to reshape the world. The Illuminati never wanted the United States to be the military and economic power it became. They've funded efforts to counter American supremacy for decades."

"It's working," I said sadly. "My country is in decline. It's a mess."

"When your country has a civil war that involves the use of atomic weapons," Ling said, "then you can call it a mess."

"Fair enough," I admitted. "So how is this Romefeller guy going to be able to help?"

"They have a thousand times our reach," Ling replied. "Hopefully the threat of catastrophe will make him listen to us."

"Hmmm . . . They do not want the world destabilized," Ariel mused. "That's not to their benefit. Plus, regardless of what Blue is, it was designed with them as the target, so it can't be good for the Illuminati to have it executed." She obviously didn't like where her current train of thought was taking her.

"Say Romefeller does listen, and he's smart enough to see that Katarina's nuts. What's in it for us? Because they're part of the same *social club* he finds her for us?"

"That's the idea," Ling said.

"Then what?" Skunky asked. "I'm sure this is a dumb question, but is there any reason we can't just shoot her in the face and call it a day?"

I shrugged. "Varga told Lorenzo that that isn't good enough. She dies, Blue goes off. It's insurance. Is that true? I've got no idea."

Ariel gave me a long look, one of those unsettling gazes that reminded you of just how intensely, almost unnaturally, blue her eyes were. "Maybe. She's dangerous. I think you will have to kill her before all of this is over with. I'm sorry, but you probably will have to."

"I'm okay with that," Shen stated. Which I believe was the first thing he'd contributed to the conversation in days.

"But that won't do it, by itself. She's not dumb. She's very, very smart, actually, and more sadistic and vindictive than you know. She's angry, so angry. She would burn the world down if it meant she could be queen of the ashes. She'll have everything planned out so that even if she's gone, Blue will still happen."

I sighed, a little frustrated. The kid was probably right. "What are the odds Romefeller sells us out to Katarina, or otherwise screws us?"

Ariel tilted her head to the side as the whole group watched her. Strangely enough, this group of trigger pullers actually put that much faith in her opinion.

"Flip a coin."

It was my decision to make. "Romefeller it is, then. Anybody disagree?"

There were a lot of uneasy glances exchanged, but they didn't have any better ideas.

"Just be careful, Michael," Ariel said. "Making deals with devils out of desperation is the main reason the mission at the Crossroads fell apart. Romefeller *cannot* be trusted. Promise me you'll be careful."

"Okay, kiddo, I . . ."

"*Promise me!*"

Yikes. "Okay, okay, I promise. I won't trust the son of a bitch as far as I can throw him. The feeling will probably be mutual, considering I offed one of his golf buddies a couple years ago."

Chapter 6: The All-Seeing Eye

VALENTINE
Zurich, Switzerland
September 10th

"You know," Ling said, looking up at me as she straightened my tie, "you clean up rather nicely. It's nice to see you in something besides cargo pants and combat boots for once."

I looked her up and down as I smoothed some wrinkles out of my suit jacket. It had been a long train ride. "You're not so bad yourself." Ling's gray suit looked like it had been perfectly tailored for her. Her skirt was short enough to be attractive without looking unprofessional. From the way she walked in them, you would have thought she wore heels all the time. Her hair was done up in a tight bun, and she wore a pair of thick-rimmed glasses. She didn't need them, but even a bit of Clark Kent level disguise helped when you were traveling through unfriendly territory.

"You look like a naughty Asian librarian."

I never would have teased her like that in front of her team, but it was just the two of us. She struggled to keep from smiling as she told me to keep quiet and focus on the task at hand.

"Yeah, you shushing me isn't doing anything to diminish the librarian thing." That actually got her to laugh a little before she put her serious face back on. Truth be told, I was cracking jokes because I was nervous. I was unarmed, in an unfamiliar city, and I was a wanted fugitive. So far, the fake identity that Exodus had given me had held up: I was allegedly a Canadian citizen. Probably backpacking across Europe, seeing the sights, I liked to imagine. Ling told me that I had, perhaps, gone overboard in my fake backstory, but it's not my fault the woman has no imagination.

The people we were seeing today knew who I really was, and I wasn't comfortable with that. I scanned the busy streets of Zurich nervously, expecting Underhill and a Majestic black ops team to pop out at any moment. But it had to be this way. This was my mission, and my real identity lent authenticity to my claims. My fake Canadian alter-ego couldn't get a last minute, one-on-one private meeting with a billionaire. Michael Valentine, the soldier of fortune, who had exposed Project Heartbreaker, and was supposed to be dead, could.

We entered the lobby of the gleaming office building and made our way to the reception desk. "Yes?" asked the bored-looking looking receptionist. She had a thick French accent.

"We're here to see Mr. Romefeller," I said quietly.

"He's expecting us," Ling added.

The receptionist looked at one of her computer screens. "Ah, yes, there you are, Monsieur, Mademoiselle." We hadn't even given our names. "He is expecting you. Please, take a seat, and someone will be along shortly to take you to where you need to go."

Ling and I sat in the lobby, next to a fountain, for an agonizing twenty minutes—there weren't even any magazines to read—until a pair of security men came to get us. They were dressed alike, in dark suits, with ID badges hanging from lanyards around their necks, and radio earpieces. The taller of the two, a German man with closely cropped blonde hair, politely asked us to follow him. He led us out of the lobby into a secure area, swiping his badge to get the door to unlock. Inside, we were checked with a metal detector. The German patted me down very thoroughly, while a Swiss woman in a blue security guard uniform did the same to Ling. Once they were satisfied, we were led to another elevator.

The security man once again swiped his badge and punched some numbers onto a keypad, calling the elevator, and indicated for us to step inside once it arrived. "This will take you directly to the correct floor. Someone will be there to meet you. Good day."

"Word," I said, stepping into the elevator. Ling rolled her eyes at me and thanked the man. The secure express elevator took us all the way up to the top floor.

"Tread carefully, Michael. By all accounts he is a charming and reasonable man, but one does not rise to the top of such a conspiracy unless possessing merciless cunning."

The elevator came to a stop with a soft, electronic ding and the doors slid open.

"This is it," I said to Ling. The room we found ourselves in was huge and well-lit, a luxurious foyer. Floor-to-ceiling windows along one wall gave us a spectacular view of Zurich. Ling's heels clicked on a marble floor as we made our way to yet another reception desk. Leather couches and wooden coffee tables, set upon an expensive-looking rug, made for a nice waiting area.

The woman behind this desk was expecting us, but before we reached her, a door off to the side opened, and a trio of men in suits approached. Two of them carried suppressed MP9 submachine guns, and my body tensed up. Ling put a hand on my arm, warning me to chill out.

The man leading the security detachment wasn't openly carrying a weapon. His suit jacket was unbuttoned, and he was a good bit shorter than his compatriots. He wore sunglasses indoors for some reason, but something about him seemed immediately . . . *familiar.*

It hit me like a ton of bricks a split second later when the bastard opened his stupid mouth.

"Well, well, well," Tailor said, taking off the shades. He'd lost some of his Tennessee twang and more of his hair, but there was no mistaking that lumpy, misshapen head. "I can't believe what I'm seeing. Michael Valentine, showing up here? You got a lot of balls, Val, I'll give you that."

"Tailor?" I hadn't seen him since after Exodus had snuck the survivors of Dead Six out of Zubara. We'd been friends for years, but our last parting hadn't been on the best of terms. I eyed the pair of armed goons flanking him, both of whom stood a head taller than him. This would have been awkward even without the hired muscle, but they weren't helping.

"And if it isn't the mysterious Miss Ling," he said, nodding at her. "I don't believe I ever thanked you for getting us out of Zubara."

"You most certainly did not," Ling said coldly. As with me, every muscle in her body was tense, though she tried to hide it.

"What in the hell are you doing here, Tailor?"

"That's it? Seriously? No 'hey, man, good to see you'? No 'I'm glad you're alive, buddy'? Just 'what are you doing here'? I work here, that's what. The question is, what are you doing here? I oughta have my boys here shoot your ass."

I shook my head slowly. "Then fucking do it. Get it over with. Any world where you can get a supervisory position is a world I don't want to live in." I looked at his men. "Trust me. He used to be my boss. Get out while you still can." I looked back at Tailor. "Get on with it."

His face twisted into a smile, and he started laughing. His men looked at each other awkwardly as he cackled. They looked outright confused when he stepped forward and hugged me, slapping me on the back. "Holy shit, Val! I can't believe you're here! Sorry, man, I was just fuckin' with you. Couldn't resist. How the hell are you?"

What an asshole. I looked down at his name badge. "Wilhelm Schncider? Really?"

"Yeah, well, I don't really pass for Swiss."

The whole thing was bewildering. "What . . . what in the hell are you doing here? How did you end up in Switzerland?" I looked at his two men again. "And what's with the mooks? No offense," I told them. "Mooking is honest work. Is it mooking? Mookery? Whatever. You know what I mean. I used to mook myself."

The security men scowled at me, but didn't say anything.

Tailor just shook his head. "You got a reputation around here, you know. You killed Rafael Montalban."

"Motherfucker, you were there, too!" I protested.

Tailor raised a hand to calm me before I got too riled up. "I know, I know. Just relax. Look, it's a long story. Believe me, it took me a long time to work my way to this position. You're going to see the big man in just a minute. He's been waiting for you. Later on, when we get time, I'll catch you up."

The receptionist at the desk looked over at us. "Mister Romefeller will see you now, Mr. Valentine." Her English was perfect. Way better than Tailor's.

I nodded at her, then looked back at Tailor. "I'm glad you made it okay."

"You too. Good luck in there." We shook hands and parted ways.

As we headed for the office door, Ling whispered in my ear, "Don't trust him."

"Of course not."

Alastair Romefeller's office was palatial, to say the least, and huge. It took up the corner of the building, with floor-to-ceiling windows on two walls and a waterfall decoration on another. The fourth wall was lined with bookshelves and mementos of military service, including a UN officer's beret and a suit of medieval armor. An ornate wooden desk filled one corner.

Romefeller himself was standing by one of the windows, hands behind his back, looking out over the city. As Ling and I approached, he turned to face us, and we were looking at a very unassuming man. He was older, probably mid-sixties, with hair that had skipped gray and gone right to silver. Romefeller had probably been a very handsome man in his youth. He was thin but appeared fit, and wore a dark blue three-piece suit.

He stepped forward and shook my hand firmly. "Good to see you, Mr. Valentine," he said cordially. He gave Ling a much gentler handshake. "Ms. Song. Thank you both for coming." He had a hint of an accent that I couldn't quite place.

"Thank you for agreeing to meet with us," Ling said.

"It was an unusual enough request that it piqued my curiosity." He indicated the chairs in front of his desk. His attitude was confident, but not smug, like he understood he was important, but wasn't going to be a dick about it. "Please, have a seat. We have much to discuss."

The chairs were big and plush. Ling sat down, crossing her legs primly, and adjusted her fake glasses. I sat down next to her, feeling out of my element. Romefeller's desk looked as if it had been carved by hand. The engraving seemed innocuous from a distance, but upon closer inspection some of the imagery was odd, with things like all-seeing eyes above pyramids. It wasn't exactly subtle. Miniature flags of the United Nations and the European Union were mounted in a wooden holder on his desk.

"Drink?" He offered. Ling and I both politely declined. "I hope you are not offended if I have one." Romefeller produced took a bottle from his desk and poured himself a shot of golden liquor before sitting down in his gigantic leather chair. The floor had to be raised on that side, because even though I was taller than he was standing up, he now appeared to be looking down at us. That had to be some CEO psychological trick. It made his chair seem vaguely thronelike.

"This is unorthodox," he said, almost apologetically. "I don't normally agree to meetings with known members of a terrorist organization. It has, as you might say, poor optics. As such I greatly appreciate your discretion in this matter."

"Discretion is something we also value, Mr. Romefeller," Ling answered. "This is unorthodox for us is well."

I exhaled heavily. "Yes, yes, we're all very mysterious and secretive. Forgive me for being blunt, sir, but we have a serious problem on our hands."

"Oh? Do you now?"

"I said *we* have a problem, as in what's about to go down is going to ruin your day too. That's why we're here."

Ling looked at me like she was trying to kill me with her brain. Romefeller leaned back in his chair. The leather was so soft it didn't even creak. "I appreciate your candor, Mr. Valentine. I'm afraid I don't get enough of it these days. What is it I can do for you?"

"Are you familiar with a program called Project Blue?"

Romefeller's demeanor barely changed, but that had gotten his attention at least. "Vague rumors, that's all. It was some manner of plot against . . . let's call them European interests."

"You know who I used to work for, so let me clarify what I do know for you, Mr. Romefeller. Project Blue was originally concocted to be a master stroke against the Illuminati meant to disrupt their operations and remove their influence from the world. The groundwork was laid, but it was never intended to actually go forward, except in the gravest extreme."

He nodded slowly. Apparently that matched what he'd heard. "As I said. Rumors."

"Do you know what Katarina Montalban has been up to?"

Romefeller was quiet for a moment, processing what I had just asked him.

Those two questions in a row were like asking *do you know where the matches went*? Followed with *by the way, how is our local arsonist?*

"Though I've not seen her recently, I know Katarina Montalban. You could call her a family friend."

"I didn't think that psychopaths had friends."

"Ah, so you're acquainted with Kat then." He was playing it cool. "This must be about the recent unpleasantness in Asia. I heard a bit about that, terrible business. I can see why Exodus would want to have a word with Ms. Montalban, but I'm unclear how that relates to me in any way."

"She has Blue."

At first he just shook his head and chuckled, like *silly terrorist, quit pulling my leg.* But then he slowly realized I wasn't lying, and as he thought through the implications of a crazy woman inheriting a shadow government plot to really fuck up his world, the cool demeanor cracked.

"Dear God. It's worse than we feared. Please tell me everything you know."

So I did. Ling and I spent the next twenty minutes or so explaining what little we actually knew. From the genesis of the project, to Hunter spilling the beans, to Gordon selling it to Big Eddie, and culminating with his little sister inheriting it and a whole bunch of baggage.

When I was done, Romefeller sat there in silence, his liquor untouched in front of him.

"Does the name Evangeline have any significance to you?"

"I'm afraid it doesn't mean anything to me," he said. "Why?"

"Evangeline was the last thing Colonel Hunter said to before he died. The name is related to Project Blue somehow. Even the men who authorized Blue didn't know how, and the only living person that helped set it up has defected. So they don't even know, but whoever Evangeline is, she was important enough to torture me for months trying to find out, so I was kind of hoping the name rang a bell."

"It's an extremely common name here. Without knowing details of their foul plot, who knows? Perhaps it was a code name for someone? Katarina Montalban, perhaps? Your former employers were quite fond of their code names and such."

"Evangeline is the key to this whole thing. At least, the people plotting your downfall seemed to think so."

"We know Project Blue could potentially kill millions," Ling said. "Perhaps it's some kind of attack, or a weapon of mass destruction. Everything we've gathered so far indicates it is a mass disruptive event. We need to know more."

"So your sources claim. May I assume, Mr. Valentine, Ms. Song, that this isn't merely some convoluted trick to sow dissent among my . . . business alliances? Or perhaps even an attempt to get me to take care of Exodus' problems for you? My understanding is that you are currently short staffed."

"That's a polite way to say that half of us died recently," Ling stated.

"I'm unfailingly polite. However, if I found out you were lying to me in the hopes that I'd remove Katarina Montalban on your behalf, I would be greatly offended, and the limits of my courtesy would be severely tested."

Romefeller had been a perfect gentleman, but I assumed when he got offended people got murdered. *Hell, why else would somebody hire Tailor?*

"Don't take our word for it. Perhaps a discrete look into Katarina's affairs would be in your best interests," Ling suggested.

"She is . . ." Romefeller tried to find the right word. "Erratic. If you had come to me with this outlandish story about anyone else, I would have dismissed it out of hand. But Katarina, even an allegation like this is plausible. Frighteningly so."

"Don't you have people that can police your own? It seems like you know full well how dangerous Katarina Montalban is. Why would you let her be a member of your secret club when she's a nut job?"

Romefeller scoffed. "Secret club?"

"Is this really the time to be coy?" I leaned forward and tapped one of the all-seeing eyeballs on his desk. "I know about the Illuminati, so does she, so do you. There's nothing to be gained from pretending otherwise."

"I assure you, Mr. Valentine, that you know *nothing*. We are merely a confederation of altruistic individuals dedicated to human progress and enlightenment. If anything, we have stood as a balance against the aggressive, militaristic, meddling of your nation's darker elements."

"You pull strings in secret."

"We organize and guide decision-makers, so that humanity can achieve its potential. Amongst members of my *club* there is an order, and there are rules."

"To hell with your rules. Big Eddie Montalban paid off Gordon Willis to have Dead Six murder his own brother, so he could take over. That sounds pretty dirty to me."

"Each family refrains from interfering in other families' internal affairs, unless it threatens the security of all. Though loosely allied, each of us has our areas of interest, whether geographic, or pertaining to certain industries, and we do not meddle in each other's business."

"Turf."

"A crude way to put it. We merely manage events behind the scenes for the greater good of all. Do you really believe that a system so complex could survive without guidance? No. Society requires management, and that role had traditionally been quietly filled by the families. The Montalbans were once a respected family. Sadly, things went rather astray for them after Rafael's untimely death." He looked pointedly at me as he said that. "Perhaps if such a powerful family had remained under sound leadership, we wouldn't be having this predicament now."

My eyes narrowed. Sure, maybe if I'd not shot Rafael with a .44 and tossed him from a moving helicopter into the Persian Gulf with his hands tied, everything would be sunshine and happiness. "If you're fishing for an apology or something, you won't get one. I made the best decision I could with the information I had."

"There is no use dwelling on the past." Romefeller downed his drink, and poured himself another. He offered drinks to us as well. I declined again, but Ling accepted this time and had a shot of brandy. After taking a sip, the billionaire was quiet for a few moments, and looked contemplative. "Rafael was a friend of mine, and a colleague of many years. We rarely saw eye-to-eye, and he would argue with me to the very end, but we were friends. I never thought I'd be sitting here sharing a drink with his killer."

"I never thought the Illuminati were real, and that I'd be explaining to them how the sister of a guy I killed is trying to burn the world down with a shadow-government plot." I shrugged. "It's been a weird day for all of us."

"Burn it?" Romefeller shook his head sadly. "Perhaps you do not know Katarina nearly as well as you think you do. Yes, she is destructive, but she is not suicidal, nor is she a nihilist. She was the unloved bastard child of a harsh, manipulative man, who spent her life trying to prove herself worthy of their family name, first to her father, and later to her brothers, the rightful heirs. Rafael humored her, and Eduard tormented her in what was rumored to be vile and despicable ways, yet she never quit. Deprived of her family name, she still rose through their organization using intelligence and cruelty, until now she is the last of the Montalbans. Someone who has risen above so much does not simply throw it all away out of spite. No, Katarina does not want to burn the world, she wants to rule it."

"But if Blue was designed to destroy your organization, that means Kat thinks you're what's in her way."

"A reasonable assumption." Romefeller was quiet for a long time. I could tell there was a lot going on in there, but he showed very little of it. He played the affable businessman really well, but beneath that he was something else entirely. "Mr. Valentine, I don't mean to pry, but I must ask . . . how did Rafael die? How did . . . how did it happen?"

"He didn't suffer, if that's what you're wondering. I pulled the trigger. He looked me in the eye. He didn't beg or plead. It was dignified." I kept it vague, because I didn't know what Tailor had told his new boss.

Romefeller seemed satisfied with that, and nodded. "Good, good. I respected Rafael, but his inability to keep his family under control has brought us nothing but trouble. His brother Eduard used you. He was . . . well, I needn't get into that. To say he was an embarrassment doesn't nearly go far enough."

Embarrassment, to describe Big Eddie? Romefeller was a master of understatement.

"Sir," Ling said, "we come to you with all of this in hopes that you understand our sincerity. Your organization and mine have clashed over the years, but right now we have a larger problem and a common enemy. We would not be coming to you with this if we could take care of it ourselves, or if we thought the normal authorities would stop her, and, to be blunt, she is one of your own."

"I do not jump to conclusions," he cautioned. "However, if you are correct, this has the potential to spiral out of control. Whatever else you may think of my associates, we are a force for order and stability. I will look into this."

"That's it?" I scoffed. "You'll look into it?"

Romefeller's expression grew stern. The cordial businessman was replaced with the kind of hardliner you'd expect to run an international conspiracy. "You've made assumptions about my people, yet not all of what you believe about us is incorrect. I assure you, Mr. Valentine, when the all-seeing eye turns its mighty gaze upon you, the results can be most *unpleasant*."

Again with the understatement.

VALENTINE
Zurich, Switzerland
SEPTEMBER 10th

Tailor and I had a lot to discuss. I hadn't seen him since our escape from Zubara. I had been wounded and was recovering on a freighter that belonged to Exodus. Tailor and the other survivors of Dead Six decided to disembark in Mumbai, India, and dispersed from there. Tailor had been my best friend, like a brother to me, but we didn't part on good terms. Basically, he had wanted me to go with him and I—if not in so many words—told him to go fuck himself.

In my defense, the woman I loved had just been killed and I had a traumatic brain injury, so I hadn't been in the best state of mind. Years had passed since then, and I never imagined I'd see Tailor again. The survivors of Zubara were liabilities, and Majestic would kill any they found. So I figured he would be dead or in hiding. I certainly never expected to find him working for a European billionaire in Switzerland.

Both of us had been through a lot, it seemed, and I wanted to catch up. Not just because he was an old friend; Tailor was also security for a big shot whose help I needed. That's how I found myself in one of the nicest McDonald's restaurants I'd ever been in sitting across from Tailor.

Ling had gone back to the hotel, and Tailor had told his mooks he was taking a lunch break, so it was just the two of us. I thought about telling him that Skunky was with me—Jeff Long had been our sharpshooter on Switchblade 4—but I thought it better to keep that to myself. Right then I wasn't sure where Tailor's allegiances lay, and we could always have our Switchblade reunion later.

"Are you sure this is where you want to eat, Val?" he asked as we sat down. "You know I actually make good money now, right?"

I opened my box of McNuggets and peeled the lid off of a little tub of barbecue sauce. "I've missed good old American junk food. I don't get to eat out much, and the people who do the shopping where I'm staying like to eat healthy. I'm sick of it. If I have to suffer one more plate of kale and baked fish I'm going to flip the fuck out."

"Where are you staying?" Tailor asked, sipping a Dr. Pepper.

"Don't worry about it," I said, bluntly.

"Eat a bag of dicks. I wasn't gathering intel. I was going to say you could crash at my place while you're in town, asshole."

"What are you doing working for Alastair Romefeller?"

"What are you doing with Exodus?" He shot back.

Fair question.

"Isn't it obvious? They saved my life."

"What happened after we got off that boat?"

I didn't answer his question. "What happened to the others? Hudson and the other survivors, I mean."

"Everybody went their separate ways. We were stranded in India with no documentation and nothing but cash on hand."

"I don't want to say I told you so, but I told you so. I stayed on the boat for a reason."

"You stayed on the boat because you were being a mopey bitch."

I glared at Tailor. He just grinned at me. "What happened to Hudson, at least?" He was one of the original members of our four-man chalk in Zubara. We'd gone through a lot together.

"Last I heard he made it back home to Detroit, legally dead and living under an assumed name. He has cousins there or something, if I remember right."

Like everyone selected for Project Heartbreaker, Hudson had no immediate family. It made us easier to dispose of without anyone noticing. "Good. I'm glad. Detroit is a good place to disappear." Motor City hadn't been doing so well. I hadn't been there in years, but I'd heard half the city was abandoned and crime was sky high. A place like that wasn't a bad choice to hide when there were people looking for you.

I paused for a moment to chew my nuggets. I had to know the truth. "Tailor, level with me, man. How in the hell did you end up working for Alastair Romefeller? Zurich is a long way from India."

Tailor looked out the window and sighed. We were on the ground floor, and the street outside was lined with parked cars and bicycles. Pedestrians went about their business, walking, talking on phones, or going shopping. Zurich was a clean and beautiful city, a model of modern Europe.

"Remember the last time we had lunch like this?" he asked.

"Yeah. Ruth's Chris, Las Vegas."

"Do you remember what I told you about the real world? Look at those people out there, Val. They don't live in the real world. They live in their own little worlds, worried about phone reception and going on holiday or some stupid soccer match or whatever. I study medieval history, you know, as a hobby."

I interrupted. "You? Study? Really?"

"Shut up. Yeah, I study medieval history. Europe went from centuries and centuries of warfare, topped off by the two most destructive conflicts in human history, to decades of peace and prosperity. That didn't happen by accident. World War Two is what happened when the people I work for lost control and got sidelined. They're not some shadowy cabal secretly controlling the world. They're just people with the means, who got together to ensure peace. They make sure the right people, stable, reliable people, get into positions of political power. No more crazies, no Hitlers or Mussolinis. They do what they do so those people," he nodded at the pedestrians, "only have to worry about whatever stupid bullshit they worry about."

"That sounds exactly like a shadowy cabal secretly controlling the world," I pointed out. "Also, a lovely defense of fascism."

"Oh, fuck off." This time Tailor scowled, and I grinned. "It's not even like that, Val. We've both seen what happens when order breaks down, shit, we made a living off it. You think the world has to end up like Mexico? Or Africa? You see how nice this place is? This is what the world can be like if we let it."

I wasn't about to get into a political and economic debate with Tailor, but his last comment did cause me to raise an eyebrow. "Wow. You sound like a true believer. You've changed."

He smiled and shook his head. "I believe in the big-ass paycheck I get, and the nice flat in the city they provide for me."

"Flat? You're calling apartments flats now? Jesus, you've been Europeanized." It sounded all the more hilarious to me with Tailor's southern accent. "But you didn't answer my question; how did you end up working for the Illuminati?"

"That's a stupid fuckin' name for it," but Tailor looked thoughtful as he took a bite of his burger. Chewing gave him time to think of an answer that wouldn't sound like bullshit. "They found us in India. They'd been keeping an eye on Zubara from the start, but after we killed Rafael Montalban they got real interested. It wasn't too hard for their intelligence guys to locate a bunch of bewildered Americans stranded in India. They offered us jobs, some of us took 'em up on it."

"So that's it? A job? What kind of job?"

"Like you have to ask." Like me, Tailor was good at one thing, and it wasn't the sort of thing you bragged about in a public place.

"So now you're all in, lecturing me about World War Two and world peace? I don't buy it. This isn't like you."

"How do you figure?"

"I told your boss, and I'm assuming he told you, about Katarina Montalban. The woman is a dangerous lunatic, and he's all, 'oh, we need more proof,' and 'hey, let's not jump to conclusions.' The Tailor I knew would tell his boss to let him go put a bullet in the bitch and be done with it."

"There are rules. These people have their own way of doing things. It keeps everything stable."

"See? This is what the hell I'm talking about. Since when does William Jefferson Tailor give a fuck about the rules, or stability?"

"Not so loud," he warned.

"What? Your real name? Oh, like it matters. The sheep around us aren't paying attention and you know it. This isn't like you at all. You know damned well how to solve this problem, and stop this Project Blue from happening. We need to find and kill Katarina Montalban. Problem solved, problem staying solved." I'd been warned that killing her wouldn't stop anything, but I didn't buy it. If we could get close enough to her to put her down, then we could track down the rest of the operation and interrupt it.

"It doesn't work like that!" Tailor snapped. A couple of nearby restaurant patrons looked up at us briefly, before returning to their meals. He exhaled heavily and lowered his voice. "Look, Val. These guys have their rules and their methods. A lot of it doesn't make sense to me, either, but they've been doing this for hundreds of years and they're pretty set in their ways. I'm not in a position to change the way things get done. I'm just the hired help."

"Bullshit. You're a fucking sellout."

"Fuck you. I have a pretty impressive résumé, you know. After Rafael Montalban bought it, people like Romefeller started to get real worried about their personal security."

"You helped kill him!"

Okay, that had been a little too loud, and since most people around here understood English, several people looked our way.

Exasperated, Tailor put his face in his hands, shook his head, then put his hands flat on the table and tried again. "No shit, Sherlock. Who better to help him plug the holes than a guy who had been involved in that mess? He knew it wasn't personal. Besides, what else was I going to do? I'm sure as fuck not going back to East Knoxville, even if it was safe to return to the States, and we both know it's not. Hudson's living in a shack out of *Mad Max* to stay off the grid. I got a pretty good gig here. More than a gig, man. I've got a life."

I looked at him for a long moment. Tailor was totally sincere. "Holy shit . . . There's a woman, isn't there?"

"What does that have to do with anything?"

"It has everything to do with everything. You met someone and now you're all settled down. Domesticated. Housebroken!"

Tailor got even more defensive. "What's wrong with that? I'm over forty, Val. I've been all over the world and done all kinds of crazy shit, but I'm tired. I'm too old to be out there door-kicking, riding around in helicopters, and all that. Now I go home every night and Sophia makes me dinner. I sleep in a real bed, wear nice suits, and make six figures without having to roll around in the mud. Do you know how long it's been since I've stabbed somebody? Like fucking forever! That's a good life."

"Okay . . . how'd you meet her?"

He was still pissed at me, but you could tell he was proud because Tailor immediately took out his phone and showed me a picture. She was a really attractive blonde woman, younger than him by at least ten years, with her hair done up in a tight braid. "This is her. She works as a bartender in the Widder Bar, a few blocks from here."

"So you went out for a drink and one thing led to another, huh?"

"It helped that I grabbed a drunk asshole tourist who was harassing her and showed him the door. Tossed him out on his face, actually."

"Well, look at you, all civilized, big salary, nice apartment, and a pretty girl."

Tailor put his phone away. "You know, I told her about you, Val."

"What you'd say?"

"That I loved you like my brother, and that you'd saved my life a bunch of times, but I didn't know what happened to you, and I figured you were dead."

"Yeah . . . sorry, man."

"So you want to give me shit for getting respectable, kiss my ass. Like you know anything about respectable. Vanguard? Left us to die. Dead Six? Left us to die. I'm tired of being left to die, Val, and you should be too."

"I am. That's why I'm still with Exodus. I'm not really *with*-with them, but anyway. They came back for me, well, Ling did, at least."

"Sure," Tailor said, obviously not believing me about Exodus.

"No. Really. The assholes we worked for in Zubara, they had me in a secret prison, and Ling got me out."

"How'd you end up in prison?"

"Remember Gordon?" Of course he remembered Gordon. "Yeah, well, I kind of murdered him."

That made him grin. "Serves that fucker right." Now that was the Tailor I remembered. "Ha!"

I spent the next little while catching Tailor up, about my time in North Gap, and what had gone on since, though I kept the recent details fuzzy. I gave him shit about having a girlfriend, he would give me far more if he knew I had one too, not to mention, *oh yeah, I'm doing this because a teenage girl who can predict the future asked me to* would go over great.

Surprisingly enough, he tried to be comforting about what I'd gone through in North Gap. Of course, being Tailor, he sucked at it. "Man, Val, that's bullshit what happened to you, but you got through. That's what matters."

I realized then that I hadn't told him everything.

"Val, are you okay?"

"Hawk's dead, Tailor."

"What? How?"

"I think I gave him up under interrogation. They couldn't find me, so they went and got him instead. I called him to let him know I was okay, and they were waiting. He tried to fight back and they shot him, right there on the fucking phone."

Tailor's face started to turn red. Tailor had been nearly as tight with Hawk as I had been. "Who shot him?"

"Majestic. You know who."

"No, *who*. I want the name of the motherfucker that pulled the trigger."

"Underhill. He was an old guy named Underhill, and he's still after me."

"Oh, fuck . . ." Tailor glanced around, suddenly nervous. He leaned in and whispered, "No shit? Underhill? *The* Underhill?"

"You know him?"

"Of him. He's a fucking legend, Val. I'm talking old school, wild west days, Cold War, Phoenix Program, shit like that. The people I work for now are at odds with the people we worked for in the Zoob, so we keep tabs. I've seen a lot of intel about them since I've been here, and I've heard a lot of stories. Underhill is the unrelenting motherfucker they let off the chain when they absolutely, positively, need somebody caught. They call him the bloodhound, because when he finds your trail, you can't shake him. Everybody I work with thought he was retired. If they pulled him back, Majestic really wants you."

"It doesn't matter."

"Listen to me real careful, Val, I'm saying this as your friend, get out, and go someplace far, far away. Take Ling, she's really rocking that sexy librarian thing, whatever, but get the fuck out of Dodge. Because otherwise Underhill will find you, and you're dead meat."

Tailor really was worried about me. Regardless of his cushy job working for the bad guys, he was still my friend. "I can't do that, man. I've got to stop Blue first."

"Well, look," Tailor said. "I know the boss was pretty skeptical of what you had to say, but I was still told to give you whatever support you need. I've got people. I'm a pretty big deal in this outfit now, and the boss trusts me. We'll find the Montalban woman and end this, I can promise you that."

"And Underhill?"

Tailor had an evil glint in his eye. I'd seen that look before, it meant he was getting fired up. "There's a truce between my boss and Underhill's people. If he's operating in Europe without permission, he's breaking the rules. You can talk shit about the rules all you want, Val, but they're there for a reason. They keep wars from happening. If that Majestic son of a bitch comes here, I'll show him this is *my* house. Now finish your fucking nuggets so I can get back to work."

It was good to have Tailor back.

Chapter 7: La Ville Lumière

LORENZO
Paris, France
September 10th

Things had gotten tough in Paris since the last time I'd been here. There had been several nasty terrorist incidents recently and sporadic rioting. I'd never seen so many armed cops on the streets in a European city before. There were four-man military patrols, complete with rifles and armor, wherever large numbers of people congregated. Some of the immigrant neighborhoods were no-go zones, and the *gendarmes* didn't enter them unless it was in large numbers. If they did arrest somebody inside there was a good chance the incident would turn into a full-blown riot.

Personally, I think the French get a bad rap. I've worked with way too many tough, sensible, pragmatic Frenchmen to disrespect the culture. From my outsider's perspective, their problem was similar to my home country, in that people with a clue how the world worked were outnumbered by easily manipulated wishful thinkers with their heads up their asses. But it was still pretty damn sobering, driving through some immigrant neighborhoods and seeing flags I recognized as belonging to terrorist factions being openly flown. I'd never expected to see that in a place like this.

Being in a hole for a year and a half had put me behind on current events. I'd read a few newspapers on my trip, but as usual the news coverage was naïve garbage written by twenty-something journalism grads who never ventured outside of Manhattan, making stupid assumptions about how the world worked. The way I saw it, the fall of Zubara had been the beginning of a chaos avalanche, and many parts of the Middle East were eating themselves. That led to lots of refugees, who the kindhearted first-worlders naturally wanted to take in. Unfortunately, among those masses were the parasitical scumbags the refugees were running from in the first place. To the psychos, refugees were just a delivery vehicle to hide in so they could start trouble in vulnerable new locations.

So the countries taking in the refugees got fucked, the refugees got double fucked, and the fanatics had a field day. Some countries went soft on them, which just made them look weak. Trust me, I made my career off of conning and robbing terrorist organizations. You can't reason with people who think they're righteous conquerors and Western civilization is a minor stumbling block. On the other hand, when a country goes too harsh, out comes the big brush and they start pushing in the wrong direction, it pisses people off and increases recruiting. Rooting out fanatical assholes requires a fine touch . . . and governments' fine touch is more like Captain Hook, Proctologist.

One street I drove past was covered in trash, debris, and a few stores that were ashen wrecks. It was clear what had gone down here; I'd seen a lot of riots in my day. You can't make a career out of profiting off the collapse of society without being around for some. Rich country, poor country, it didn't matter. Everybody had some disaffected, angry bunch ready to blow up. When you are a professional thief, riots make for a fantastic diversion. In the western world they usually handled things with kid gloves and let the assholes burn things until they tired themselves out, but in the third world, they just machine-gunned the troublemakers and got on with life.

Strangely enough, from looking at the bitter cops, annoyed soldiers, and tired locals, the normally civilized, law-and-order types were getting mighty sick of the state of things. You could almost sense it in the air. They had tried to help by opening their doors to people in need, and got smacked in the face for it. You know things were getting bad when a major European capitol city gives the same bad vibe as Zubara did.

Paris felt *tense*.

The address Jill had given Ling was next to an old industrial park on the west side of the city, in the surrounding department of Hauts-de-Seine. She'd picked an area far from the nice, shiny, business and tourist parts of town. The majority of the factories here were closed down, and judging from the nearly empty parking lots, those that *were* still making things were running at less than capacity. Even then it was nicer than some of the other communes I'd passed through to get here. At least there weren't any burned-out cars abandoned on the sides of the road in this neighborhood.

I parked on the back side of the old tenements, in one of the few spaces that wasn't covered in broken glass. The apartments were old and shabby. The asphalt was cracked and weeds were growing through it. Some young men were sitting on some nearby planters. They were the unemployed, disaffected, bored types. When they glanced my way, seeing if I looked like an easy victim, I gave them my best *don't fuck with me* look and they were smart enough to realize I wouldn't be worth their time.

Inside, the apartment building was even sleazier. There were junkies hanging around and winos sleeping in the corners. Somebody on this floor was playing really loud rap music. The elevator was out of order, so I took the stairs to the fifth floor, found the right room number, and after the briefest hesitation, knocked on the door.

This was awkward. It felt like I should have brought flowers or something. I was really excited, happy, but nervous. It was hard to explain. While I waited, I realized that a very discreet camera had been installed at the end of the hall. The peephole was already dark, so I never saw when she looked through it. From the sound of metal being moved on the other side, the door had been reinforced. Apparently Jill had been paying attention all those times I had lectured her about how to survive in this lifestyle.

The door opened. She'd changed her appearance. Her hair was shorter, and dyed lighter. She'd put on a little stress weight, and looked tired. But it was Jill. *My* Jill.

I could still read her expression like I'd never been away. It was a mixture of joy, disbelief, relief, and a little bit of bitterness.

Without a word, she stepped out of the way so I could come inside. While she closed the door and put down a heavy security bar, I looked around. Unlike the rest of the building, her tiny apartment was clean, orderly, and there was a half-assembled bomb on the table. There was a tablet next to the Semtex, with the screen showing feeds from four different camera angles around the block. I'd only spotted the one.

"I missed you," she whispered.

I stretched out one hand for her, but she moved away, just the tiniest bit. But then she realized what she'd done and froze there. I stayed where I was. She'd thought I was dead. Jill had gotten on with her life. I couldn't imagine what she'd been through, and she had no comprehension of what I'd been through, and I wanted to keep it that way. Tentatively, she reached out and touched my cheek, as if testing that I was real.

"Sorry I didn't call." It was a remarkably lame thing for me to say right then, but then we were pulling each other's clothes off, so words didn't really matter.

Later, the two of us lay in bed, listening to distant sirens through the open window, content to enjoy the human contact. Jill's head was resting on my shoulder. It felt good to be alive. I had told her a little about the prison, but I'd glossed over or left out most of it, especially the parts I wasn't sure had been real.

Jill ran her fingertips across the bandage on my chest. "What happened here?"

"Nothing. It'll be just another scar."

She'd seen the newer puckered bullet holes and fading knife lines, but she sensed this one was different. "You already had a ton of those when we met. What makes this one nothing special?"

"Sala Jihan burned me with a branding iron. Like a parting gift."

"So you'd remember him?"

"More like a warning to never come back."

Jill gently traced the edge of the bandage with her fingertip. "Would you go back?"

Normally I liked to finish what I started, but I was never going back to that place, no matter how much that evil son of a bitch deserved to die. "I'm never leaving you again."

There was a lot of bitterness in Jill's laugh. "Liar."

That was fair. "No, I . . . I mean it. I just want to forget that place ever existed. I just want to be done." I turned my head enough so I could look into her eyes. "I swear to you."

"What about this thing you've got to do?"

She had me there. "Well, there is that."

"That's why you didn't try to contact me." She shifted slightly against me as she said it. It was remarkable how you could be this close to someone, yet distant at the same time.

"Listen, Jill, I had to do some horrible things in that prison." How do you explain what it was like, putting a knife in some other poor unlucky bastard, just so you could maybe live one more day? Fighting for a warlord's amusement, again and again, losing track of the lives you take as the days bleed into months in the perpetually whispering darkness. You can't make someone understand what that's like, and that was my problem.

"I don't care what you had to do."

"The only way I could survive was to go back to being the man I was before I met you. When I got out, it was easier to stay that way."

"What was it Carl called it? Monster mode?"

"Heh . . . Yeah. Carl had a funny way of putting things." Only Carl hadn't been joking. I could never admit it to her, but part of me enjoyed being that way. Offing Diego and Varga's men? I'd enjoyed that. Living with a complete disregard for dying was why I'd been the best. It was a cruel addiction. My foster father had seen that in me, and he'd done his best to steer me away from it, but ultimately failed. Jill had gotten me to live in peace for a time, but that had been nothing but a brief illusion. It turned out the evil was always there, eager to be used. "It isn't the kind of thing you can just turn off and on, Jill. I didn't ever want you to see that side of me."

"I saw how you were in Zubara and Quagmire. Give me some credit. I don't care."

Jill was right, but knowing that and admitting it were two different things. She'd blundered into this world as a poor innocent victim, wrong place at the wrong time, but she'd risen to the occasion. She'd kicked ass, taken names, and was probably as stubborn as I was. But most importantly, she'd seen me at my worst, but still stuck around. We were a team, and I was an idiot to throw that away.

"I know."

"Running from me still hurt, Lorenzo."

I squeezed her tight and kissed her forehead. "I had to do something first, and I wanted to keep you safe."

"Killing Katarina."

"The same reason you're in Paris, apparently." We'd got the fun part of the reunion out of the way, so now we were getting into the messy, emotional, accusatory parts. I'd always sucked at that those. "Stalking the head of an organized crime family? She's a billionaire, and probably one of the most powerful women in Europe now. What the hell are you thinking, Jill?"

She had an endearing smirk. "You weren't around to stop her. Nobody else would. I thought she was responsible for your death. What did you expect me to do?"

"Take the vast sums of money I've squirreled away, go somewhere safe, and have a long and happy life."

"That was my plan. Right after I killed that bitch," Jill muttered. "What? You think you're the only person who ever dreamed about getting revenge on the people who've screwed you? I guess you rubbed off on me, Lorenzo."

"Damn right I did."

"Jackass." She laughed. Most couples, lying there naked, probably weren't contemplating murder, but we were weird like that. It worked for us. "You know what I mean. She had to be stopped. Period. Exodus was toast. The government still wants me dead. Who was I supposed to get to help? Either I had to do it, or nobody would."

I'd never seen this side of her before. Jill had always been tough, but I'd fallen for her because of her tender side. Now she sounded like me. "Really? You were going to take down Kat by yourself."

"Reaper's helping, sort of."

"Well, that's something. How is he?"

"Not good. I think he took your death worse than I did. I don't know if it's PTSD, or what, but he won't talk about it much. Me? I got drunk a bunch and wallowed in self-pity for about a month, but then I decided to focus on getting even."

I stroked her hair. "I've always been a fan of the healing power of murderous revenge."

"But Reaper, he saw something at that missile silo. I don't know what, but it shook him. I kind of dragged him into this last year, to keep tabs on Majestic and Kat's people. I needed his help, but more than that, I knew he needed something to work on."

"Good." It was kind of hard to imagine a purposeless Reaper. He was like this hyperactive ball of fixation. A Reaper without direction was scary.

"I was—I'm still—worried about him. You'll see for yourself. He should be here soon."

"Did you tell him about me yet?"

"Unsecure line," she explained, though she was probably lying. Reaper was too paranoid to talk to anybody over a regular phone call. She probably just wanted me to have to explain to my best friend why I'd not bothered to tell him I was still alive as soon as I could.

"Jill and Reaper versus the world . . ." The least experienced members of my old crew, up against some of the best professional killers I've ever known. It was amazing they were still alive at all. "How far were you willing to go?"

She mulled that over for several seconds. "Far enough . . . Look, I don't want to talk about it right now."

I was too naked and comfortable to want to fight. So I dropped it.

She was silent for a moment, like she was trying to think of how to phrase something difficult. "I was with the Exodus people afterwards, while we were escaping through Mongolia. Ling gave me a number to contact her. I think she was trying to recruit me."

"I kind of thought you might have joined up." They were a bunch of self-righteous busybodies, trying to make the world a better place. Typical, except unlike most idealists, they were actually willing to get dirty. I could see that kind of idealism appealing to her. She had a good streak a mile wide.

"I kept in touch with Ling, but I'd never join Exodus. I blamed them for your death too. The Exodus survivors told me you could have left them behind and made it out by yourself, but you stuck around, taking turns carrying the wounded. Roland, Svetlana, they all said the same thing. They all would have died otherwise. You stayed behind to delay the brothers to save their lives, even though you knew you'd get caught."

"Something like that."

"Ling and Valentine let me think you'd died."

She didn't understand right now, but they'd been doing her a favor. "There wasn't anything anyone could have done for me."

"They said you were a hero, and it wasn't just to make me feel better. They believed it. *Lorenzo died a hero.*" She gave me a sad little laugh. "I bet you never thought you'd hear anybody say that. But I didn't see it that way at first. It just made me mad at you."

"At first?"

Jill snorted. "I thought you were gone, Lorenzo. How was I supposed to feel? I know it sounds selfish, and they were just trying to comfort me, but . . ." she trailed off. "I don't know."

"I understand."

"You always talked a big game about looking out for number one, being the merciless hard-ass thief, get the job done and get out, all that. From the day I met you, that was how you acted, how you saw yourself, so I thought I'd been rescued and given shelter by a selfish, greedy, self-centered asshole."

"Man's got to keep up his rep." I'd gone down some dark paths and done some things I wasn't proud of. Hell, I'd done some unforgivable, horrible things that I could never atone for, but saving someone as good as Jill from someone as evil as Adar al Saud must have made some sort of dent in my karmic debt.

"Past all that swagger, I saw how much you loved Carl and Reaper, and you were there to try and save family you barely even knew. Then in Quagmire, you risked everything for me. That's the man I fell in love with."

"Sucker."

"Don't be an asshole. I'm trying to have an honest sharing relationship moment here. So yeah, I was mad at you for dying in the Crossroads, but then I thought about it. You gave up your life to save people. How could I hate you for doing what I fell in love with you for to begin with?"

As I'd lain in that crashed bomber, incoherent and bleeding out, with soldiers closing in on me, I'd heard the ghost of my foster father, congratulating me for being the good guy for once. All in all, it hadn't been a bad way to die. Any goodness I had, it was only because I was trying for her sake.

An hour later, showered, dressed, and happier to be alive than I had been in a very long time, Jill walked me through what she'd been up to.

I hated to admit it, but other than being stressed out and trying not to show it, Jill had been doing a pretty damned good job without me. She'd shown a real knack for shady business back in Zubara where I'd taught her some rudimentary fieldcraft. Then in the Crossroads, she'd done extremely well, and if we'd been trying to pull a con on anyone other than the Devil himself, it would have worked. Jill had taken to heart everything I'd ever taught her, and then kept on learning while she'd devoted herself to ridding the world of Montalbans.

I was impressed. On her own Jill had gotten ahold of some illegal guns, surveillance equipment, and quality fake IDs. She had clothing and props to pull off several different roles, from bland work clothes, to outfits that screamed tourist, to a slinky party dress that I was afraid to ask about. She'd been gathering intel on Kat's people for months, and was still alive.

"I've planted cameras around the block, and I've got some of the local drug lookouts double dipping. They're watching the block anyway. I slip them some Euros every week, and they call this burner phone if they see anything out of the ordinary. If I see anything that smells like Kat, I've got three escape routes."

"I saw two on the way in."

"I figured so would Kat's men," she answered with just a bit of pride. "But I rolled a rope ladder down the out of service elevator shaft, and I made a copy of the keys to the electrical service tunnels in the basement."

"Nice. Other hideouts?"

"Two. I bounce between them using a couple different vehicles."

"How's your French?"

"Pas tres bien," she said. *Not very good.* "The fake IDs Reaper prepped say I'm from Barcelona." That was a good call. Jill was American, with a Mexican father and a Filipina mother, but she was good at tweaking her accent to sound like a Spaniard. "Or I wear a hijab and pretend not to understand French at all. Lots of service workers in Paris are Muslims. Either way I mostly avoid talking to people. Usually I eavesdrop, record them on my phone, and piece it all together later. The rest of us can't do your language tricks."

"If crime didn't pay so well, I could have been one hell of a voice actor. Got anything to eat?" I checked the tiny fridge. There was food, but sadly, it was all bland, packaged garbage. I'd always been the cook in our relationship. There was a little .32 automatic hidden in the egg carton. "Cute. Want something?"

"Sure." Jill sat down at the table. "You need to eat more. You look terrible."

She should have seen me when I had first gotten out. I had been practically stuffing my face over the last few weeks and had started exercising hard again. I hadn't exercised much in prison. You don't have enough calories to spare for training when you were living off of watery gruel. "Well, you look amazing."

"It must be because you've been blind for a year, because I look like crap right now."

Women got hung up on the stupidest things. Sure, hard living wears you down, but she was still gorgeous. I found some white bread, crappy lunch meat, boring American style mustard—French's, ironically—and processed cheese slices wrapped in plastic. "This is barbaric. Who comes to the culinary capitol of the world and buys plastic cheese?" I sat down across from her and started making sandwiches.

"I've been busy." Jill pushed the tablet across from me. It was a map of the city and its surroundings. "Six weeks ago I followed Katarina here from

London. The red dots are places she or Anders have shown their faces. I've got dates and times for each one, but no discernible pattern yet. She doesn't even sleep in the same place more than a few nights in a row, and judging by the times she's been seen and the distances between them, either she can get through traffic like a champ, or I've got a suspicion she's hired body doubles."

Kat had the resources, skills, and mindset to be a hard target. She knew how to be a ghost. Sadly, she'd learned from the best. Despite that, there were still quite a few dots on Jill's map. "Did you get these yourself?"

"In person? No way. Don't worry. I'm angry, not suicidal. Mostly, she stays out of sight and runs her business by phone or proxy. When she does go somewhere, it's never without a convoy of armored cars filled with armed mercenaries. Since you talked Anders up like he's got eyes in the back of his head, I've been too worried he'd make me to ever try following him. These are mostly from snitches and Reaper stealing security video. The problem is, by the time we pin her down that way, she's already moved. I started putting together dossiers of her security people and coffee-fetchers. I've got a lot of names, but since she pays really well, they're not super talkative."

I finished making a sad little sandwich and passed her the plate. "What was your next move?"

"Use one of her employees to figure out where Kat is going to be, get there first, and leave this for her." Jill nodded at the bomb she'd been putting together.

She said it so matter of factly that it took me a second to have that sink in. Jill really had changed. "Just like that?"

"As opposed to what else? It seemed easier than getting into a gunfight with a bunch of hired muscle, a former Navy SEAL, and their boss, the professional assassin, by myself." She gave me a look, like she was daring me to continue.

"I think Exodus will back us up now. There aren't many of them, but Valentine brought a few friends."

"I don't know. I'm still pissed at him for lying to me."

That wasn't fair. Valentine had only been trying to protect her from Sala Jihan . . . But I wasn't going to argue with my woman to defend the asshole who'd shot me and wrecked my hearing. I wandered over to study what she'd been working on.

The bomb was pretty straightforward. Two blocks of Semtex with a commercial blasting cap. The cap was wired to a cheap cell phone, and there was a spot for a nine-volt battery. The phone wouldn't have enough juice to set off the cap, that was what the battery was for. The ringing would close the switch, causing electricity to flow from the battery to the cap. Removing the battery would render it safe, and also keep a stray cell call from blowing her up. The Semtex was wrapped in duct tape. A second layer of tape was stuck with hundreds of nails to serve as frag. It wasn't a complicated device, but it was meant to blow up Kat, not befuddle a bomb squad. Reaper must have been tutoring her.

There wasn't much of an explosive payload there, but still, it was dangerous as hell. "And what if the next place she's going to be is next to a daycare or a school?"

"Or a teddy bear hospital? Really, Lorenzo? You're going to try and play the morality card with me? If there were innocents who might get hurt, I'd wait and try again later."

"Don't get defensive. I'm just asking."

"Why? You afraid I'm turning into Kat? You think I'd just wipe out anybody who got in the way?" Jill seemed really agitated on this point.

"Bombs can be sloppy. That's all I'm saying. They're really easy to hurt the wrong people with."

"If there was any chance of that, I'd back off. You know I would."

"I know." Despite having to do some terrible things to survive, and proving way harder than she appeared, Jill had always retained a gentleness in her soul. Relatively speaking, obviously, since we were arguing about her homemade bomb. I couldn't see it just now, but I figured that gentleness was still there. Well, I hoped it was, because Jill wouldn't be Jill anymore without it. "If there's even a chance of collateral damage—"

"Of course," she snapped. "That's how Kat got away in London. I had her. I found out about a meeting, I snuck in early and hid a bomb in a planter. When Kat showed up I was down the street with a cell phone. She sat at a table like ten feet away. All I had to do was make a call, and poof, she was gone . . ." Jill trailed off, staring into space. "I was *so* damned close."

"What happened?"

"Nothing. Other people showed up. I bailed. That's it . . ." She was remarkably stone-faced as she talked about it, acting like the idea of premeditated murder was no big deal. I'd seen that act a lot in this business, *fake it until you make it.* "See? No reason to worry about me."

I'd never seen Jill this haunted before. "How long have you been at this?"

"Almost the whole time you've been gone. I started almost as soon as Exodus got us out of Mongolia. I've tracked her from city to city ever since. It's sucked. She's got a lot of rivals, so she's nervous as hell. She's also got a lot of powerful friends. When they get skittish, and find out somebody has been looking into them, they send people. So I run, and work other leads while I hide, and then come back and try again."

No wonder she was fried. "I can't believe you've been dodging Montalbans for over a year."

Her expression softened. "Why? Were you worried that when I got over crying for you I'd gotten back on the dating scene?"

That made me smile. "There hasn't been a man who has ever been incarcerated in history who hasn't wondered what his woman was doing without him around."

Now Jill grinned. "Don't forget, I was hanging out with Exodus for part of that. Have you seen Zach Roland with his shirt off? That dude is chiseled." I must have scowled, because Jill laughed at me. "Okay, I'll be honest. You got me. In my time of grief I was so vulnerable that I messed around with *Valentine.*"

"Now you're just being cruel."

"Relax, Lorenzo, I'm kidding. No. I've been a little too focused. The closest I've come to getting any action is dressing up like a call girl to spy on a Montalban party."

"How was that?"

"Lots of techno music and the overpowering stench of cologne." Jill tapped the tablet screen and brought up folders of pictures and documents. "I've not accomplished much recently, but that's because they've been extra jumpy for the last week. Apparently somebody has been offing Montalban employees across Europe." She gave me a very pointed look at that. "Between me on the ground and Reaper being Reaper, we've got a ton of information on their operation. I've been limited on what I could do with it though. Now that you're here, and if Exodus is helping, then we've got a lot more options."

I knew it was doubtful. "Any sign of Bob?"

"Nada. I'm sorry, but I gave up on the idea of him still being alive about the same time I gave up on you."

"Never count a Lorenzo out. Anders wants him alive for some reason. Bob's supposed to be the fall guy for Project Blue, whatever that is."

It was obvious that Jill thought Bob surviving was wishful thinking on my part, but she let me keep my comforting delusions. "Blue, huh?" Jill tapped on another folder. It was titled *Crazy Town.* She opened up a Word document. "Reaper's been doing a lot of digging on that, nothing concrete of course, considering it was top secret and most of the planners are dead, but he's come up with some theories. Get ready for some fun reading. I mean like Sea to Shining Sea AM talk radio stuff."

After the things I'd seen over the last few years, it was getting harder and harder to make fun of Reaper's crazy conspiracy theories. "Please tell me he isn't wearing a tinfoil hat and living in a single-wide trailer out in the desert yet?"

"Not quite, but the sad thing is I've started to believe him."

A couple of days ago I'd had a conversation with a man I'd sprung from a secret government black site about the secret war between Majestic and the Illuminati. My life was a conspiracy theory.

"Screw it. Let me catch up on your intel, and we'll go from there."

"About that . . ." Jill trailed off as she studied me.

"Yeah." I pushed the tablet away. As interesting as Reaper's strolls through crazy town could be, there was some stuff we needed to get out in the open first. "Normally now would be the part where you'd urge me to let it go."

"And the part where you'd worry about me too much, and try to shuffle me off to somewhere safe," Jill stated flatly.

"I'm still just a man. I'd be lying if I said I wanted you anywhere near this mess." I thought about what the Pale Man had told me before we'd cut our deal, friend or foe, death followed wherever I went, and I wanted her to be safe.

But I also really didn't want to be alone anymore.

"This isn't the life you chose, Jill."

"But it's the one I wound up with when I decided to stick with you."

The truth hurts. "Which is why I'm saying this now. They know about Saint Carl, so we can't ever go back there, but I've got plenty of money stashed around the world, enough to live long, boring lives away from all these nut jobs and their plots. We let it go. Kat can be Exodus' problem. Valentine can figure out whatever the hell Blue is without us. We can walk away. There's nothing stopping us."

She was quiet for a long time, deep in thought. She flicked the edge of her plastic cheese with one finger. There wasn't much point to a revenge mission, when the man you were trying to avenge turned out to be alive and sitting there with you.

"What about your brother?"

I had no answer for her.

Jill pushed away her uneaten sandwich. She'd already come to the same conclusion I had and lost her appetite. "You said Varga told you that Blue would kill millions. Could you just let that happen, Lorenzo? Sipping margaritas on another private island, knowing we could have stopped it, but didn't?"

I shook my head. "Not really."

That was actually a pretty profound realization for me. Jill really had been a bad influence.

"Then that's settled. We're committed. I don't think either of us is the kind of person who can do anything half way." Jill gave me that sad little smile again. "I know why you avoided me. You were prepared to do some horrible things to see this though. It's hard to let someone you love see you like that. Believe me, I understand that better than you think."

"I can't let Kat win. That means doing *whatever* it takes."

"I know." Jill reached across the table and held my hand. "Then we'll do it together."

She didn't understand that the hard part wasn't going down that road. It was coming back.

Reaper stood there in Jill's apartment, mouth hanging open.

"Hey, Reaper," I said again.

"Dude . . ." He'd already said that a few times, like it was the only word his brain could process. "Dude!"

Jill closed the door behind him. "Surprise."

"I'm back. I got out."

"Dude." Reaper was blinking rapidly. He was looking a little weak in the knees. He'd gone whiter than usual, and that was saying something. It was like he'd seen a ghost. "Lorenzo?" Articulating my name was good progress.

"Yeah, Reaper. It's me."

He cocked his head to the side, studying me carefully. This wasn't just surprise. It was like he didn't believe me, like this was a con. "But are you still you?" What the hell that was supposed to mean?

"I'm alive. I'm here. I'm me."

That must have finally registered, because Reaper came over and gave me a hug. "Lorenzo! Holy shit, man!" Reaper was holding me so tight that I flinched when he hit the burn on my chest. The kid actually started to sob, but then I realized that wasn't fair. He wasn't a kid anymore. He was a man who'd been through some awful shit. "I thought the Pale Man got you."

"He caught me, but he couldn't kill me." I patted his back awkwardly. Reaper was nothing but skin and bones. *Damn.* He was even skinnier than I remembered. He was in worse condition than I was. We broke apart and I led him toward the kitchen table. "Hey, come on, sit down."

Reaper wasn't in good shape. He never had been, but now he was looking downright ragged, and it wasn't from the sudden emotion of seeing me in one piece. He'd never been one to get out much, living off of Red Bull and junk food in front of his wall of computer screens, but his complexion was worse. I was used to Reaper often having dark circles under his eyes, but those had been his weird goth makeup style when he'd gone out. These dark circles now were from insomnia. It was obvious he'd not been eating or sleeping well. When he sat down, he rested his hands on the table in front of him, and there was an unconscious nervous tremor in his fingers.

"Dude, Lorenzo, shit . . . Man. What the fuck?" The poor guy was bewildered. "I tried. I tried to find out what happened to you, but my world, my world is like, you know, *electrons*, and the Pale Man . . . It's like the stone age there. I can't. I couldn't get in. It's like a different time. Different world, man." Reaper leaned toward me, eyes wide. "He's *outside*."

I looked to Jill. She grimaced and nodded. This was what she'd been warning me about. She went over to the little fridge, got out two cans of beer and put them on the table for us. "You boys catch up. I've got to go check with one of my snitches downstairs to make sure nobody new has been poking around the block. I'll be back in a bit."

After Jill left, I got right down to business. I'd known Reaper way too long to mess around. "Damn, man. What happened to you? You look like I do, but I was in a dungeon, so I've got an excuse. Are you on meth?"

"Of course not! You know I don't mess with that shit. No drugs. No pills, man. I knew I was messed up from . . ." He trailed off, not sure what to say. "I tried to get help after the Crossroads. The shrinks all gave me prescriptions, Zoloft, Paxil, Lexapro, but I chucked them in the trash." He tapped the side of his head. "Pills slowed me down. No time for that."

Reaper had a super genius level IQ, and apparently when the wires got crossed in a brain like that it wasn't pretty. I shoved one of the beers toward him and opened the other. "It's just, you look like—"

"I know. I know. I'm frazzled, man. I don't sleep so good anymore."

"How come?"

"Bad dreams." Reaper grinned at me. It was a kind of crazy grin. "But you're back, so it'll be cool. Everything is cool now. You know what I'm saying? You being alive puts it right! But . . . But I just gotta know, when you were in there with those cavemen, did you see anything . . . *weird*?" He looked strangely hopeful.

"What do you mean by weird?"

"I don't know. I can't explain it." Reaper looked really uncomfortable, and his lip began to tremble as badly as his fingers. "I saw some things on the drone camera, from the silo, but there's no record. We lost Little Bird's recordings when we ran. Ever since then, I don't know if I imagined it, or I'm just going crazy, but I still see them in my nightmares. What happened to those Exodus guys around the Pale Man's silo."

I remembered our mad escape across the canyon, pursued by Jihan's soldiers. During that, whatever Reaper had seen on those cameras had truly freaked him out. The Exodus commander Fajkus had been the only other surviving witness from the missile silo. Even though the Czech was an extremely experienced combat veteran, whatever he'd seen there had screwed with his head too.

I thought about how to proceed. It wasn't just that I needed Reaper in one piece, but whatever he thought he saw, it was slowly killing him. "I didn't see anything while I was there."

He appeared absolutely dejected when I said that. "You know, Lorenzo, when I do sleep, which isn't much, it's with the lights on. I can't even go to a strip club because I'm too scared of the dark. That sucks."

Back in Varga's old club, for just a moment, I thought I'd seen the Pale Man watching, and it had been enough to paralyze me with fear. I understood what he was going through, I just dealt with it differently. As much as I'd tried to compartmentalize and forget it, I had to tell him the truth. "I said I didn't see anything. They kept me in the dark. But, I *heard* things."

"Like what?"

"Things that weren't there, couldn't be there."

Reaper was suddenly curious and strangely hopeful. "And?"

"I'm only going to talk about this once, and then I'm never going to say it again. Jill doesn't need to know what I went through. No one else does, because that shit can stay in the Crossroads where it belongs. Yeah, Reaper, I heard things in the walls, in the floor, in my head, things that couldn't be. There were voices, whispers, even when there weren't people there, and maybe things that weren't people. It never stopped. I could feel it, just burning little holes in my sanity. Like fire ants in my head." Surprisingly, it felt good to tell someone about this.

"But you didn't lose!" Reaper exclaimed. "You never lose, Lorenzo."

"Hell no. I knew that place wanted me to go crazy, to give up, to fall apart. I saw what it did to the other prisoners, it strips away who you are and leaves nothing but an animal behind. You remember Precious?"

"Eddie's dog you shot?"

"Yeah. I used to wake up because something in my cell was growling at me. I just knew it was that fucking poodle. I could feel it there, but I wouldn't reach out to touch it, because I was afraid of what I'd actually feel. I knew it wasn't going to be soft and fluffy, you get what I mean?"

Reaper nodded vigorously.

"It was too dark to see most of the time. I guess I was lucky for that. Was it haunted? Something else? Hell if I know, but it wasn't *right*. Whatever you saw come out of that silo, wasn't *right*."

"So I'm not crazy?" Reaper asked with complete sincerity.

I shook my head. "No. You're not. It was a bad op in a bad place, and we messed with something that we shouldn't have. Some of us caught a piece of it. The rest were lucky. Let them stay that way."

"I knew it." He slammed one skinny fist down on the table hard enough to knock over his beer. Reaper's whole body had begun to shake. Relief, exhaustion, beats me. I bet the psychology types would call it *catharsis*. I let him have his moment. This emotional stuff was more Jill's area, but I could tell he needed it.

"You okay?"

"I couldn't tell anybody else, Lorenzo, you know, because they'd think I was nuts. I tried to talk to Fajkus in Mongolia. Only he wouldn't talk about it. He lied and said he couldn't remember what happened at the silo."

"He didn't want to remember. Big difference."

Reaper wiped his eyes with the back of his hand. "Last I heard, Fajkus left Exodus to become some kind of priest."

"You could have tried that. Father Reaper has a ring to it." We both laughed at the absurdity of the idea.

"Dude, I'm a stallion that needs to roam free." Reaper gestured at his skinny, geeky self. "You can't cage this."

"No kidding. Who is going to put all those strippers' kids through college? Look man, whoever, *whatever*, Sala Jihan is, it doesn't matter now, because we're done there. You understand me, Reaper? That's in the past. That world? We never have to go back. I know it and you know, and it dies with us, because nobody else needs that burden. This world?" I gestured around the ratty little French apartment. "This world is real, and we can still make a difference in it."

"Since when do *you* give a shit about the world?"

"Maybe I'm just tired of sharing it with a couple specific assholes. The people we're after are just flesh and blood, like you and me. They're flesh and blood scumbags who *only* want to kill a million people. I need your help to take them out. Can you handle that?"

"That, I can handle." Reaper picked up his knocked over beer, popped the top, and held it out toward me. "The crew is back together. To kicking ass like old times!"

We hit the beer cans together. "To old times." It was a good toast.

"And murdering your ex-girlfriend. You know I never could stand her." Reaper drank a bit, coughed, then read the label. "What's this cheap shit? Who buys American beer imported to *Europe*? Okay, if we're working together again, Jill is not allowed to buy supplies. Period."

There was a little nagging part of me that was angry, like these moral human beings were going to somehow hold me back from my path of righteous vengeance, but right then it mostly felt really good to be back with my people. It felt *normal*. Ling had been right to call Jill. I'd been prepared to lose my soul to get this done, but maybe I didn't have to. "We've both been living in fear for too long. Now it's time to make Kat afraid."

"You're one scary bastard when you're on a mission, Lorenzo, but we both know there's stuff in the dark way worse than you."

I could drink to that.

VALENTINE
Paris
September 15th

The drive from Wels, Austria to Paris was long, more than twelve hours, and it was also lovely. We drove across southern Germany in a two-vehicle convoy, before cutting to the north. Ling, Ariel, and I rode in front in the little Hyundai; Shen, Antoine, and Skunky followed in the van. We drove carefully, adhering to posted speed limits and staying off the main highways, which were full of traffic cameras. We had enough to worry about already without getting pulled over, especially since the van was full of guns, ammunition, and gear, most of it very illegal.

As it was, we'd had to go out of our way to avoid checkpoints, especially as we got closer to the big cities. The security situation in Europe was deteriorating and national governments were responding in kind. We had to sneak across the border into northern France on a narrow two-lane road close to the border of Luxemburg, where there weren't any checkpoints. The major routes, including all the bridges across the Rhine, had police stops on them.

I had crammed myself into the back of the diminutive car so that Ling could drive and Ariel could sit in the passenger's seat. She snapped hundreds of pictures with her phone, and despite the severity of the situation seemed to be having the time of her life. It made me smile to see her so happy, just enjoying something as simple as a road trip without the weight of the world on her shoulders. She even got Ling to sing along with her when some catchy American pop song came on the radio. I'd never seen her like this, just acting like a normal girl without a care in the world.

God only knew how this would end, but I resolved to find a way to make sure Ariel didn't go back to Exodus. Sequestered away in a castle, cut off from the whole world is no way for a girl to grow up.

Exodus had had, at one point, a safe house or two in the seedier parts of Paris, but with the near collapse of that organization, they had been liquidated. Lorenzo thought it was a bad idea for all of us to pile into the same accommodations, and I think he was correct. A safe house is safe by virtue of it not drawing attention. Having a bunch of suspicious foreigners coming and going at all hours is how you draw attention to your safe house.

Tailor had taken care of us, though, and made available to us a place to stay, courtesy of his employers. Following the GPS, we eventually arrived at a nice stucco house with a red slate roof in the Parisian suburbs. The house and its small yard were surrounded by a high fence and a carport big enough for the van. With the car parked in the drive and the gate closed, no one on the street would be the wiser.

It had been nice to see Tailor alive and well, but I hadn't been lying when I told Ling I didn't trust him. With various electronic bug detectors and RF locators in hand, we scoured the house from top to bottom for listening devices. I was honestly surprised when we didn't find any. Still, we remained cautious, just in case there was anything we missed.

As excited as she was, Ariel got right to business once we arrived. She opened up her laptop, pulled out some notebooks, and set up a little command center in the study. Tailor had come through with a bunch of information on Katarina Montalban's operation, and we had been given a lot of leads to chase down. He explained over the phone that his boss kind of liked having us doing the poking around for him. It gave him plausible deniability. The Illuminati bigwigs were insistent on playing their stupid cloak and dagger games. I could tell it frustrated Tailor, too, even if he wouldn't admit to it over the phone. He swore up and down that Romefeller didn't actually know where Katarina was hiding. I didn't trust the old billionaire, but I didn't think he was lying about that. Kat was a hard mark to track, and she was paranoid as hell. Even with the leads, finding her would take a lot of leg work, a lot of luck, and maybe a goddamn miracle.

We had help, though. Romefeller's private intelligence company, RMI, was doing a lot of the digging for us. Tailor was coordinating, and would feed the intel to Ariel. One of the barren walls of the study soon became plastered with pictures, snippets of printed-out documents, and sticky notes. She'd even put lines of colored string up between them, like something out of a cop show. It was fascinating to watch her work, her brilliant mind moving at Mach 2, connecting the dots, finding the patterns in the deluge of information she was being fed. I could see why Exodus considered her such an asset, even if calling her an *oracle* was a little dramatic. It took a few days, but we finally got our first break.

"Who's she?" Tailor asked. We were video chatting over what he insisted was a secure connection while Ariel laid it all out for us. The rest of my team stood around the study, listening without saying much. Since they weren't big on the idea of allying with the Illuminati, most of them stayed away from the camera. Since Ariel was giving the briefing, she didn't have that luxury.

"Don't worry about who she is," I said. Tailor had been there in Mexico when we rescued her, but he didn't seem to recognize her all grown up. He didn't need to know about Ariel. More importantly, his employers didn't need to know about her. "The girl works for me."

Tailor frowned. "I know that, dumbass, I'm talking about the lady your little friend is showing us right now." Ariel had printed out a picture, taken from afar with a zoom lens, of a woman in a slinky black dress and red high-heeled shoes. She had night-black hair, long legs, olive skin, and a figure most women would kill for. "Who is *she*?"

"I was getting to that," Ariel said impatiently.

"She's how we are going to get close to one of Kat's men without tipping her off," I said.

"She goes by the name Eloise. She's a prostitute. Word is she's very exclusive and costs about a thousand Euros an hour," Ariel explained. "Is that a lot for a prostitute, Michael?"

Ling folded her arms and shot me a half-smile. "Yes, Michael, is that a lot for a prostitute?"

"What makes you think . . . how the hell should I know how much a high-end French hooker costs?"

"He's got a point," Tailor said, over the video chat. "The whores didn't cost that much in the places we used to work."

Ariel frowned. "Gross."

"Indeed," Ling agreed.

"Look, can we stay on topic here? Keep going. Tell everyone why she's important."

Ariel took a deep breath. "She works for a local, uh, courtesan service that usually serves the rich and famous, businessmen, politicians, people like that. She came to our attention . . ." Jill DelToro had taken that picture. Ariel was having to tread carefully here, because Tailor didn't know about Jill and Lorenzo. They were another thing the Illuminati didn't need to know about. "One of the men our source has been following is a *frequent* customer."

"One of Katarina Montalban's men?" Antoine asked.

"She has a lot of hired muscle for a billionaire philanthropist. It makes her harder to get to, but a little easier to track, since she has this big entourage everywhere she goes." She pointed to a different picture, connected to the photo of Eloise by a length of red yarn. "RMI has identified him for us. His name is Georges Mertens, a Belgian national who was on the international bodyguard market right up until last year, when he dropped off the radar. His career has been spent working for organized crime, he's been implicated in several murders, but he's never been convicted."

"The types Mertens works for hire good lawyers," I said.

"Our source has seen him as part of Katarina's security detail," Ariel finished.

Tailor's brown wrinkled up in thought. "So, you want to use the hooker, to find the bodyguard, to find the target?"

"It is possible he confides in this prostitute," Antoine suggested. "We could bug her."

"Now hang on," Tailor said. "It may not matter what she does or doesn't know. Someone like Katarina Montalban isn't going to hire guys that can't keep their mouths shut. But we can use her to get to him, roll him up and bring him in."

"That's pretty ambitious. Might tip Kat off, too if her men start disappearing." *Not that Lorenzo's reappearance had been particularly helpful in that respect.*

"It might," Tailor agreed, "but our only other option is to follow this asshole around hoping he leads us to our target."

"We may not have that much time," I said. "Who knows what their schedule is like? This guy might just be working in the city, and might not get anywhere near Kat again. I don't think following him around and hoping for a break is a good way to go. I think we need to talk to him."

"You're talking about kidnapping someone off the street and sequestering him away for interrogation. Paris is not Zubara," Ling said. "Coming to the attention of law enforcement here is extremely risky."

"I think I can help with that," Tailor said. He held up an ID badge to the camera on his phone, but it was hard to make out.

"What is that?"

"Interpol credentials." He grinned. "No shit. I am the law! Special Organized Crime Task Force. Gives me a lot of leeway, and the local cops are usually pretty deferential."

"Are you really a police officer, Mr. Tailor?" Ling asked, incredulously.

"Technically, sorta. Enough for this situation, anyway. My boss pulled some strings. Interpol doesn't actually have arrest powers, but most people don't know that. Besides, I'm only gonna flash my creds if I have to. I'd rather just snatch the guy and never have him find out who we are."

"We can use your creds to get the hooker to cooperate, too," I suggested. "She'll probably be less worried about client confidentiality if she thinks she's keeping her own butt out of jail. Maybe if you roll him up on some human trafficking or vice charge, it'll be less suspicious to Kat than him just disappearing?"

Tailor smiled. "I like how you're thinking, Val. I can make up some crimes. I'm flying over first thing tomorrow morning so we can plan this out in detail." He looked at Ariel. "Good job, kid. Call me if anything comes up tonight." The call was ended and Tailor disappeared from my phone.

"Are you sure about this?" Ling asked me.

Antoine was really not liking our current arrangements. "The Illuminati *and* Interpol? This carries a lot of risk."

"Until we have something better to go on, this is worth at least looking into. Get in touch with Lorenzo and let him know what's going on. If we are going to grab Mertens I want to run it so we risk the minimum number of our people. It'll probably just be me and Tailor."

"Stop trying to protect everybody!" Ariel blurted. "You can't do this all by yourself." Ling looked like she agreed, but she was an experienced leader, and knew the last thing you wanted to do was undermine the decision maker's authority in front of everyone.

"You said this is my war, then this is my call. When Tailor gets here we'll hammer everything out, including a backup and a bugout plan. We'll have you guys on standby, in case we need to call the cavalry."

"In other words, Val here doesn't know if he can trust our old buddy Tailor or not," Skunky spoke up for the first time. He'd been standing off camera, but since he'd been on the same Switchblade team, Tailor would have recognized his voice.

"What do you think?"

That was a tough question. I thought of Jeff as a man of principle, which was why he'd wound up with Exodus, sucked into trying to do the right thing. Tailor was a pure mercenary to the core. We'd all been like brothers, but it was hard to guess how strong Tailor's loyalty would be when we were working for different sides.

"You know I love the guy, but Tailor is Tailor. He's a hell of a soldier, a good leader, but we both know he can be a company man. He's the sort of guy who'll take orders for a paycheck, and not think too hard about what those orders are. It's been a long time." Skunky shrugged. "But I do know one thing for sure, I don't need any more evidence that the Illuminati are pure evil."

"Why do you say that?"

"They trusted Tailor with a *badge*."

Chapter 8: Spy Games

VALENTINE
Paris
September 16th

"Jesus, dude, traffic here sucks."

Tailor nodded without looking at me. The two of us were in his rental car, trying to make it across town. "I fucking hate Paris, man. Between the regular congestion and the police everywhere, it's impossible to get around."

"What's the deal with all the checkpoints? It's like the city is under martial law."

"Almost, but not yet," Tailor said. "They've left most of it to the Gendarmerie, but there are French army units on the ground in the city, too. They got 'em mostly over in the poor parts of town, where the Africans and Middle Easterners live."

I should have been doing a better job keeping up on the news. "They been having some kind of ethnic tensions or something?"

"It's getting pretty bad—oh, come on!" he snarled as a little hatchback pulled front of us, causing Tailor to stomp on the brakes. "People in the States bitch about traffic. They have no idea. Anyway, yeah, there's been a rash of attacks recently. Tribal shit, some of it, but also targeting Jews. Things are tense with that G20 summit coming up in London, too."

"Why does anyone care about a summit in another country?"

Tailor shrugged. "French economy is struggling same as everyone else's. The word is, the government will announce some more austerity measures after the summit. There are a lot of people that depend on welfare. They're gonna be pissed. Paris cops are worried there'll be a riot. Another riot, I mean. Maybe a big one this time."

I smiled and shook my head. "Do you know how weird it is to listen to you, of all people, get me up to speed on current events? There was a time when we didn't know or care what was going on back in the regular world. It was just one third-world shithole after another, and that was all we worried about."

"Yeah, well, things change." Tailor looked almost uncomfortable. I couldn't remember ever seeing him like this.

"You've changed," I said.

"So have you, Val. You're different than you were when I left you on that boat."

The car fell into an awkward silence as we crawled through stop and go traffic. The only people getting anywhere were the motorcycle riders creating their own lanes on the dotted lines.

"You were right, you know," Tailor said after a long moment. "Right about me."

"What are you talking about?"

"Last time I saw you, you said I was a war junkie. That really pissed me off, but you were right. I didn't give a damn about anything but our next job. I lived for the thrill, the adrenaline, the . . ." he trailed off. "The killing."

It was weird to have Tailor open up. "Yeah, it's a rush. There's nothing like it." Combat is terrifying, but also a sort of primal thrill. Like Mark Twain said, there's no hunting like the hunting of armed men.

"But after Mexico, then Zubara, you know. Getting left for dead twice in a row is kind of a bad deal," he muttered.

"It is."

"I guess you came to the same conclusion I did. You just beat me to it."

"Yeah, well. Circumstances."

"I don't think I ever said it, Val," Tailor said, glancing over at me, "but I'm sorry about Sarah."

She had been communications and interrogations for Dead Six, and we'd fallen in love. It felt like a lifetime ago, but I could still see her death as clearly as the second it happened. Not a day went by when I didn't think about her. I didn't talk about it with anyone, not even Ling. Especially not Ling.

"It eats at me sometimes," I managed finally.

"It wasn't your fault, Val. You were the one who saw what was coming. You were the one trying to get everyone out."

"I know. But it doesn't change anything."

He was right, though. A few months into Project Heartbreaker, I could see the writing on the wall. Suffering unsustainable casualties, being sent on virtual suicide missions, all as the tiny Emirate of Zubara spiraled into chaos, my goal had become getting me and Sarah out alive. In the end, it hadn't mattered. Majestic pulled the plug. Gordon sold us out. And nearly everyone, including Sarah, died.

I will likely never forgive myself for that.

"For what it's worth," Tailor said, "I wasn't thrilled with how it turned out either. It don't matter now anyway. I know you're being all secretive about your people, and I get it. It's insulting, and kind of hurts my feelings that after everything we've been through you don't trust me, but hey, whatever. I just want you to know I'm done getting sold out."

Of the few people still alive whom I called friend, I'd known Tailor the longest. He'd been like my brother. He was assigned to train me on my first job with Vanguard, in Africa, right after I got out of the Air Force. He'd been there with me through some of the best and many of the worst times in my life. I wanted to tell him everything. I wanted to trust him. I wanted there to not be any kind of ulterior motive. Only, what I wanted didn't really matter. The people Tailor was working for were nothing but ulterior motives, layers and layers of lies, deceit, and manipulation.

"Well, I don't have faith in your bosses like you do."

"Faith? I ain't got faith in *shit*, Val," Tailor said, an edge in his voice. "I got . . . well, don't worry about what all I got. Let's just say I got contingency plans."

That actually made me feel better. It told me Tailor was still being pragmatic, and really hadn't just bought the Illuminati bullshit hook, line, and sinker.

Night had fallen as Tailor and I waited in an upscale hotel room. He had booked both the room and an appointment with the lovely Eloise. As far as her *escort service* knew, Tailor was an American businessman, with very specific tastes which—if they thought about it too hard—sounded just like he'd been describing her from Jill's photographs. If Eloise was unwilling to help us, we had ways of applying leverage. I was more worried that she'd be un*able* to help us. If Georges Mertens didn't have an appointment with her anytime soon, our lead could go cold before we were able to exploit it.

"She should be here soon." Tailor was sitting on the bed, watching a German cop show that had been dubbed into French, munching on a bag of potato chips from the minibar. *Were they crisps here? Or was that a British thing?*

I was standing, looking through the glass door to the balcony, taking in the sights. I'd never been to Paris before, and it really was beautiful. The Eiffel Tower was all lit up. Boats slowly moved up and down the River Seine, tourist cruises from the look of them, and the entire city seemed to glow gold in the dark.

"Someday," I said wistfully, not looking at Tailor, "I'd like to visit a place and not be on a mission. Just go somewhere as a tourist without anyone trying to kill me."

"Hell, and you called me housebroken," he said, through a mouthful of half-chewed potato snacks.

"No, I get why. I'm just surprised that you settled down. It didn't seem like something you'd want to do."

"People change, Val. Even me."

I didn't respond.

Tailor persisted. "What happened to you, man? You said you got captured by Majestic. What did they do to you? I ain't the only one who's changed. You're different. More mopey than usual."

"I learned a lot of things the hard way, bro," I said, still looking out the glass door. I turned to face him. "When this is over, your employers might ask you to kill me."

"What the hell are you talking about?"

"You know goddamn well what I'm talking about, Tailor. They'll want me dead for the same reason Majestic wants me dead: I know too much. It makes me a threat. Having you do it makes the most sense. You can get close to me without it being suspicious."

"Val, you might have changed, but you're still a big drama queen. I can't believe we're having this fucking conversation right now. If it makes you feel better, I promise I won't betray and kill you. Feel better?"

I laughed. "You're such an asshole."

"Nice to be working with you again too, brother."

"Just don't make promises you can't keep. If you do decide to come after me," I warned, "you better bring your A-game."

"Fucker, your A-game is whiffle ball."

There was a gentle knock at the door. Eloise had arrived. Tailor used the remote to shut off the TV, then he walked over to the door. "Now shut the hell up and let me do the talking." I stepped off to the side as Tailor loosened his tie and opened the door.

"'Ello," Eloise purred in a French accent. She was stunning, like movie-star pretty, which probably explained how she made more per day as a hooker than I had as a mercenary. She sauntered into the room in a short blue dress and high heels, clutching a small handbag. She noticed me, awkwardly standing by the bathroom door, as Tailor closed and locked the door behind her.

She didn't miss a beat. "I see. That's fifteen hundred an hour for the both of you. Eleven hundred if one of you only wants to watch."

"Mademoiselle," Tailor said, pronouncing it *mad-am-mow-zell*, "you got it all wrong." He pulled out his INTERPOL identification. "I'm Special Agent Wilhelm Schneider, and this is my partner."

"Not the kind of partner you were thinking of," I added.

"Shut up," Tailor said to me. "I need to ask you a few questions."

Eloise stepped back, dropped the sex kitten act, and got very defensive.

"I have done nothing wrong," she said angrily. "I work freelance. You are the ones guilty of solicitation."

"Actually we're not," Tailor said. "I didn't say I wanted to have sex with you, lady, I just said I wanted to see you."

Eloise folded her arms across her chest and glared at Tailor. "What is it you want, then?"

Tailor raised his phone and showed her a picture of Georges Mertens. "This man is one of your clients, correct?"

Obviously she recognized him. "I do not discuss my clientele. I'm leaving."

We were ready for that reaction. "Eloise, wait." She paused and looked over at me. "We're not trying to bust your customer for hiring you. We're trying to protect you."

"Protect me?" she scoffed. "As if."

"We don't care about prostitution. Our division profiles serial killers. Georges is a very dangerous man. We've been tracking him for weeks. He's covered his tracks very well, but we've tied him to a string of murders of sex workers in five different countries. If he's hiring you, especially if he's a regular, that's his pattern. You are in a lot of danger."

"He . . . he is a murderer? I don't believe it. I just saw him last week."

Tailor, following my lead, thumbed his phone screen a few times. He approached the woman and showed her a gruesome picture of a beautiful young woman who'd been stabbed to death. He'd just picked some from Google earlier. "This was his last victim. Her name was Greta, and she was from Frankfurt."

Eloise cringed at the photo. "A hazard in my profession."

"We need your help, Eloise."

"I want nothing to do with this! I'm leaving!"

"Please, you're the only connection we have to him. If he gets away, he will kill again. He's a predator. More women will die by his hand."

"We won't let anything happen to you," Tailor added. Originally I was going to be good cop, and he was going to be bad cop, but it was obvious from the expression on her face that she was softening. So there was no need for him to get all threatening. "We're not going to put you in harm's way."

"What . . . what is it you need me to do?" she asked with trepidation.

"We just need you to help us catch him. Could you contact him and set up a meeting?"

She nodded. "I can. It is not how I usually do business, but I can. I have a phone number. I think he is still in Paris."

"Can you come up with an excuse to call him, see if he wants to see you?"

"I do not do business that way," she insisted. "My clients come to me."

"Yeah, but he's a regular, right?" Tailor asked. "Tell him you had a cancellation or something, and you wanted to see if your number one client wants to take that time slot instead."

"Time slot? I am not some . . . some *street walker*, Monsieur Schneider. I do not see multiple clients in a day."

"Fine then." Tailor tried to hide the exasperation in his voice. "Tell him you have a date that opened up, whatever. We just need to get this guy off the streets. He's got an EU passport, and he's been staying one step ahead of the police by moving from country to country. If we lose him here, there's no telling where he'll go next. You're our best shot."

"Will you help us?" I asked, gently.

Eloise looked thoughtful for a moment. She shifted uncomfortably on her high heels, her hands tucked tightly under her arms. "I will," she said, looking up at me. "If it will save another girl from this monster, I will."

I felt bad about lying to her, and not just because I'm a sucker for a pretty face. What she was offering was actually very brave, and I found it to be a very noble gesture on her part.

"You must still pay my hourly fee, though," she added. "My time is valuable."

Okay, so it was only a *little* noble.

LORENZO
Paris
September 18th

After getting settled in at one of Jill's hideouts, picking up some more clothes and another motorcycle, I made a trip to the bank.

I hadn't worked in Paris very often. My specialties—blending in to rob tyrants and scumbags—had ensured I'd spent most of my career in poorer countries. Plenty of swaggering targets and second-rate law enforcement kept things simple. But this city was such an important center of international business, the odds were good that I'd find myself here often enough to warrant setting up a stash.

Having once had to escape across war-torn Africa with what I could scrounge on the fly had been an educational experience, so I'd gotten into the habit of hiding rainy-day stashes wherever I went. Without the money and papers I'd left at a storage unit in Russia, I wouldn't have made it here so quickly. This safety deposit box had been one of my first, toward the beginning of my professional thieving career. My Paris stash was almost twenty years out of date, but it still had some useful stuff in it.

Most of the guns Jill had gotten were the type of cheap, unreliable trash you could procure off of low-budget street punks. Reaper knew better quality illegal arms dealers around these parts, but they would know the Montalbans. Exodus had good equipment, but I didn't like relying on others too much, and I knew the stuff I'd left here would run.

After the bank employee left me alone in the privacy room, I opened the safety deposit box with one of the keys from the ring I'd picked up in Russia. Smart crooks made copies of their keys and IDs to leave at other stashes in the same region. The whole point of a stash was using it when you didn't have anything else, and getting a replacement key required prolonged conversations with bank managers who might remember you later.

A strong smell hit my nostrils. *Cosmoline.* I'd packed the guns in the oily sludge to prevent corrosion. I'd probably used way too much for a climate-controlled room, and it would be a pain in the ass to clean, but then again, I'd been pretty new at this business back then and a little overzealous at preventing rust. I'd come prepared now though, and took the latex surgical gloves out of my pocket before I lay the empty suitcase on the table. I didn't want to get grease spots on my new clothes.

The biggest thing in the box was a Steyr TMP submachine gun. They'd quit making these back in the 90s and sold the design to a Swiss company later. Come to think of it, Carl had gotten popped with one of those. But this one had been a reliable piece. If the French cops ran ballistics tests on this one, they'd match up to a bunch of bullets pulled out of a gun runner and his goon squad in Toulon. Carl and I had done a little job for them, and afterwards they'd tried to *aggressively renegotiate.* It hadn't gone well for them.

There were several thirty-round magazines stuck into a canvas chest rig I'd never worn because it was too big and obvious. The TMP had come with a suppressor when I'd bought it, but that can had been a piece of crap anyway and this was a terrible gun to silence. Anytime you shot it on full auto all the extra gas back pressure venting carbon in your face was enough to gag you, so I'd ditched the can. If I needed to shoot somebody without making a lot of noise, that was what the other gun I'd left in the safety deposit box was for.

I'd taken the .45 one off of a hitman sent to kill me once. I'd learned to shoot with Gideon Lorenzo's old GI 1911. I'd always been fond of that style of pistol, so I'd kept this one. It had been a basic Springfield before some mystery gunsmith had done a lot of work to it. The giant C-More red dot sight mounted on it was obsolete—or *retro*, depending on how you looked at it—now, but back then it had been the hotness. Really, it just made it an impractical pain in the ass to conceal because the only holster I had in the box for it was a goofy nylon rig. Of course, when I checked the sight, the battery was long dead. I'd have to pick another up before I needed to shoot anybody. The suppressor for it was an old, original Gemtech. The tube was bulky and heavy by modern standards, but still pretty damned quiet. At least, nobody I'd ever popped with it had complained about the noise afterwards. Can and pistol went in the case too.

There was an envelope stuffed full of money, only it was francs and marks. Those were completely useless now. I didn't even think I could trade them for euros anymore. It was a waste, but Reaper had brought lots of cash. Another envelope held IDs and passports. They were all expired and way out of date. I'd burn those, just to keep the number of pictures of me in circulation to a minimum. There was a little disguise kit, but the makeup was long since dried out, and besides all of those facial prosthetics were amateurish by my current standards.

I'd forgotten about the other manila envelope.

When I looked inside I saw a sealed plastic baggie with a single old Polaroid photograph inside. I shook it out far enough to study it. The picture was a group shot of my foster parents and all their kids, including me. I stuck out as the skinny dark one. Everybody else was bulky and super white. The Lorenzos were good people, the kind of family that kids who grew up like I did thought were a myth. The picture was cracked, yellowed with age, and water stained. This had been the one memento from my too brief, temporary home that I'd taken with me when I'd fled Texas. I'd carried that Polaroid in my kit the entire time I'd been with Switchblade. It wasn't like I'd ever looked at it, but I'd carried it anyway. I couldn't tell you why.

I'd put together this stash when I'd made the final jump from semi-illegitimate mercenary to full-on criminal. I wonder what it said about me that this was the place I'd finally left my old life behind. I studied the picture. Gideon Lorenzo had been a good man. He'd been a judge, but one of the rare ones who actually balanced justice with compassion and didn't go too stupid one way or the other. Despite knowing my juvenile record, he'd taken me in after sentencing my real father to prison. Any understanding I had of mercy, decency, or honor had come from him. He'd hate that it was my avenging his murder that had put me on this path.

One nice thing about a privacy room was that nobody could hear the fool talking to himself. "Be good, Hector, you said. Well, dad, I tried to follow your advice," I told Gideon's image. "Okay. *Eventually.*" It had gotten me shot and imprisoned, but hell, who was I kidding? That didn't mean he would have changed his advice one bit. There had been nothing flexible about Gideon's principles.

I swear, he did look kind of proud of me in that picture though.

Then there was Bob standing next to me. Even though we were both teenagers there, I looked like a midget next to that man-mountain. Of course, I was the only one not smiling for the camera. I'd gone on to be a crook, and he'd become a cop. It was Bob's quest to expose Majestic that had gotten him captured in the Crossroads.

"This is your fault, Bob." Only that was bullshit. It was my involvement with Big Eddie that had introduced Bob to Valentine and the wealth of Majestic secrets he'd gotten from Hunter. Without me dragging him into that, Bob would have gone on as just another oblivious crusader, far beneath Majestic's malicious notice. Bob had pulled the trigger, but I'd given him the ammo. I started to put the photo with the envelope back in the safety deposit box, but then I changed my mind and put it in the suitcase too.

The last thing in the box was a stainless steel knife . . . Man, this was turning into a regular trip down memory lane. It was the old, custom Italian switchblade I'd carried in Africa, not that I'd ever used it much. My working blade had been a surplus US Air Force combat knife. I'd never used this flimsy little decoration for anything more strenuous than opening a package. But because his merc company was named Switchblade, Decker had given his troops these as gifts. He talked a big game about brotherhood and loyalty, but the second he needed to spend our lives to accomplish a mission, he did it, and slept like a baby afterwards.

If Gideon Lorenzo had shown me how to be an actual human being, Adrian Decker had taught me how to be a merciless bastard who got things done.

I picked the knife up, slid the button forward, and the skinny blade popped out. *Click.* It made me smile. This was a toy compared to the folders I usually carried, with a locking mechanism that would probably break if I ever had to really go to town on somebody and hit a bone. I tested it with my thumb. It still held a good edge. What the hell, I was feeling sentimental and would never be coming back here again, so I closed the blade and stuck it in my pocket.

Suitcase full of useful implements of destruction, I left the bank. Valentine had cooked up a scheme, and I was going to tag along and make sure he didn't screw it up.

VALENTINE
Paris
September 20th

It took a couple of days for Eloise to set everything up. I had been afraid that she'd want to back out, or would just bolt, but with reassurances from me and daily cash payments from Tailor, we kept her on board with the plan. She contacted Mertens and gave him some story about how a client had cancelled on her, freeing up her entire weekend. He—quite understandably in my opinion—took her up on her offer. We dealt with the rest.

I was standing in the rain on a busy street beneath an umbrella, waiting for Tailor to pick me up, talking on the phone Reaper had given me to stay in contact with Lorenzo. That was one of the three phones I had to carry now. This spy stuff was complicated. The umbrella wasn't really that necessary, but it kept my face off any security cameras that might be around here.

Unbeknownst to Tailor, I was keeping Lorenzo in the loop. He was desperate to get his hands on any of Katarina Montalban's people, and he was probably better at this sort of information extraction than anyone on my ragtag team, so he could have Mertens. Part of my decision there was that I was still worried that Lorenzo was going to go off half-cocked and expose us all if he got impatient. Sala Jihan had messed him up, and my gut was telling me that Lorenzo was one setback away from going on a rampage. Regardless, there was no way we could get any information out of him and then let him go. He'd tip off Kat, and we'd lose her. It was cold, but having Lorenzo dispose of Mertens was easier. Also, despite what you see in the movies, it is hard to get rid of a body in a major city without getting found out.

Tailor knew I had my people, but he was under the assumption they were all Exodus personnel. The last time he'd encountered Lorenzo was in Zubara, where Lorenzo's partner had whanged Tailor on the head with a shovel. Tailor didn't know about Quagmire, St. Carl, or the Crossroads, and I wasn't ready to explain it all to him. It was just simpler this way.

"*You have everything you need?*" Lorenzo asked.

"I think so. We're waiting for a message from our girl. She thinks he's in Vaugirard, but didn't have his exact address yet."

"*I know it. Nicer residential area, some good bakeries. You need to keep control of the situation. Things go wrong, it's not like it is in the slums. The cops will be there in a hurry, especially if there's gunfire. Don't shoot anybody.*"

"Fine, Mom, I'll try not to shoot anybody."

"*This isn't a game. Don't fuck this up. I've watched you work for a long time. Catching people really isn't something you're good at.*"

I chuckled. "We caught you that one time."

Lorenzo didn't have an immediate answer to that. He just breathed through his nose a couple of times, angrily. "*You had a small army and I still had to break into you oblivious bastards' fort. Just stick to the plan, Valentine.*"

"Are you sure Kat won't get spooked once this asshole disappears?" It didn't help that Lorenzo had already left a bloody trail of dead Montalban toadies across half of Europe. She had to know someone was gunning for her.

"She won't run. I know her. She's too territorial. Push her here and her instinct will be to push back. She's going to be well protected, and she'll be confident that nobody can get to her. She'll already be on alert, but if we get good info from Mertens, something actionable, it might not matter. Either way it's the best shot we've got."

"You're not wrong," I agreed. Tailor pulled up, this time in a different black rental sedan that probably had no connection to his employer's expense accounts. "I gotta go. I'll call you when it's done."

"Do not fuck this up," Lorenzo repeated.

"I love you too," I said as I got into the passenger seat.

"Was that Ling?" Tailor asked. "You guys are pretty serious then, huh?"

"Huh? Yeah, we're pretty serious."

"I just got a confirmation from Eloise. The appointment is on. She's supposed to be at his flat at nine-thirty. I got the address."

"You tell her to split?"

"No, we need her to get us to the door without spooking him. She agreed. She doesn't seem as scared now. This might actually work."

"I sure as hell hope so. Text me the address. I'll relay it to Ling, tell them to start getting ready. We've only got a couple hours."

Darkness fell over the City of Lights as Tailor and I drove down a quiet street in Vaugirard. It was a nice, middle-class area, free from most of the commotion that had rocked the city recently. The streets were tight, with little cars crammed into every space they could possibly be parked in. Apartment buildings lined both sides of the street, built into one another so as to make me feel like we were driving down a narrow canyon.

A few cars ahead of us was a nondescript blue Renault Clio, Eloise's car. I was sure she made enough money to afford something nicer, but that particular model was one of the most popular cars in France. For a professional who valued discretion, using a common car, even if it wasn't fancy, made a lot of sense. In Tailor's Audi we followed from a safe distance, keeping a few cars in between us when we could. I received a text that Shen and Antoine were in our Sprinter van, approaching our destination from a different direction. They would cover the back of the apartment in case our target bolted. Ling and Skunky were in another vehicle ready to fill any gaps or to provide extraction.

"Not too many people out," Tailor said, scanning the sidewalks. The rain had turned to a thunderstorm and it was keeping people indoors. The wipers were keeping a steady beat. He even had to turn on the defroster because we were fogging up the glass. "This is good."

"Once we bag him, I'll have my people bring the van up and we'll toss him in. If any lookie-loos show up just flash your badge and tell them to move along."

"Then we'll take him to meet my people and hand him off." Tailor was still under the impression we were going to drive Georges across town, to meet with some of his own people.

"Right," I lied, not missing a beat. I was hoping he wouldn't be too mad when he found out I had no intention of doing that. He was my friend and my former partner, but I didn't trust his employers, and I wasn't giving Romefeller our sole lead. Giving him to Lorenzo kept Tailor's hands clean, and by extension his employers', which seemed really important to them. Tailor would be pissed at me, but he would just have to deal with it.

I watched the GPS' screen. "We're almost there."

"This brings back memories, huh?" Tailor asked, after a moment.

"What do you mean?"

"Zubara, man. Think about it. We're rolling down a street in a major city, trying not to get noticed, planning on snagging some asshole to drag him back for interrogation."

"Hopefully without getting our asses shot off or bringing the cops down on us. Yeah, this all feels familiar."

"Right? You nervous?"

"A little," I admitted, but that was mostly because I was lying to Tailor about what we were going to do with our target once we grabbed him. "There's a lot that can go wrong."

"Stop being so negative, Val. We'll be fine."

I chuckled. "You sure about that?"

"Always remember, I am never wrong."

We were prepared just in case. We didn't have long guns, but my team in the van did. My big .44 was riding under my right arm in a vertical shoulder holster. I was wearing a concealable soft armor vest under my jacket, which wouldn't stop rifle bullets but would protect me from anything less than that. I was also packing a CZ-75BD 9mm pistol on my left hip, with a couple of spare magazines. The barrel was threaded and I had a sound suppressor for it hidden in my jacket pocket. I didn't ask, but I was sure Tailor was packing too.

"Alright, she's parking," Tailor said. I watched as Eloise found an open space and pulled into it, parallel parking like a pro. Unfortunately, there was nowhere for us to leave our car. "Shit, I can't see another open space."

"Let me out," I said. "We've got comms. I'll keep eyes on her. My team is in position." I opened the door as Tailor came to a stop. "You find a place to park and get your ass back over here."

"Got it," Tailor said, before he drove off and left me there alone. I immediately realized I'd left my umbrella in the car, and the rain was cold.

I scanned the street as I made my way up the sidewalk, walking with my hands in my jacket pockets and my head down, hoping my baseball cap would hide my face from any high-mounted security cameras. There were very few other pedestrians out that I could see, and only the occasional car drove past.

Eloise was waiting for me near the door of the apartment building. She wore a long coat that came down to her knees, undoubtedly over some classy but too-tight dress. "Where is your partner?"

"Parking." I touched the mic on my neck. "Where the hell are you?" Far down the sidewalk, a pair of policemen rounded a corner and turned up the street, headed my way. *Shit.*

He sounded exasperated. *"I'm stuck at a light!"*

"I don't like this waiting out here," Eloise said. "He is expecting me. He will become suspicious."

"Tailor, I can't wait, man," I turned away so Eloise wouldn't hear what I said next. "I'm too exposed out here. There are cops coming."

"What? Why?"

"Routine patrol, I don't know." They might not even give me a second glance, but a foreigner standing around in the rain in a residential area was suspicious, but worse, if the cops stopped to talk to me, it would be obvious to Eloise that I wasn't the law. And I still needed her to get inside. "Look, I can't stay here. I'm going in with the girl."

"Val, just wait, damn it!" Tailor argued. *"Give me a minute."*

I made my decision. "Eloise, how do you get into the building?"

"He is in flat number 3B. But the door is locked. He has to, how do you say, buzz us in."

"Right. Tailor, apartment 3B. The lobby door is glass. Just smash it if it's an emergency. I'm taking her up." I let go of my throat mic and looked at Eloise. "Let him know you're here."

"As you wish," Eloise said, more calmly than before. She pulled out her phone and sent a text message. A few seconds later, the door unlocked with a loud click. I held the door open for her then followed her in.

The lobby of the apartment building was a small room with mailboxes built into the wall. Eloise made her way up the stairs, her heels clunking loudly on bare wood. I followed, cautiously, heart racing, feeling exposed. There were no cameras that I could see, only the clunk of Eloise's shoes, the scent of her perfume, and the incessant buzzing of fluorescent lights.

On the third floor, we turned down a carpeted hall, so our approach was a lot quieter. The hall was, thankfully, deserted, and apartment 3B was the first one on the right. This was it. I drew the CZ 9mm from my belt and screwed the suppressor onto the muzzle.

"That is not a policeman's gun."

"Interpol standard issue."

My heart rate slowed as I did so, my senses seemingly heightened. I noticed every detail of the hallway; the carpet was a dark blue, a light at the end flickered irregularly. The doors were heavy wood, and there were eight apartments on the third floor. Eloise was suspicious of me now, but kind of stuck. She shifted nervously, but seemed more collected than I expected she'd be. It was odd.

I was ready. I was *calm*.

"Let's do this," I said quietly. I positioned myself to the side, so that I couldn't be seen from the peephole. Tailor spoke into my earpiece, telling me he was on foot from a block away, having finally found a parking space. I clicked the mic to acknowledge, but didn't say anything. I held the pistol in both hands, tucked tightly to my chest, as Eloise softly knocked on the door. Footsteps approached. *Click, clack*, locks were undone. The door swung inward.

"Ello," Eloise said.

Calmly and smoothly, I pushed her aside and went past, raising my weapon as I moved. The man that had opened the door was young, probably in his twenties, with dark skin and short curly hair—*that isn't Georges Mertens*—and he was aiming a gun right at me.

I'd walked right into a goddamn trap.

I just reacted. He'd been ready to shoot me, but I was faster. Somehow, Eloise knew to duck. As the prostitute hit the floor, I pushed the gun out in both hands and shot him three times.

The gunman went stumbling away. Behind him, there was a short entryway that opened into a larger room. Another man was standing there, and he didn't even wait for his friend to fall out of the way before he started shooting. His shotgun blast tore a chunk out of his associate and the frame next to my head. There were more people moving behind him. I thought one of them might be Mertens, but he'd already disappeared around a corner. Bullets zipped past me. I fired a barrage into the apartment, as they took cover amid the cloud of plaster dust and gun smoke.

Reaching down, I grabbed Eloise by the arm and pulled her to her feet. "Come on!" I yanked her away as a hail of gunfire echoed throughout the building, bullets peppering the wall on the other side of the hall. I squeezed my throat mic. "Compromised! Ambush! Get up here now!"

"I'm at the lobby!" Tailor said. Glass shattered as he smashed through the

door two floors below me. I kept my gun trained on the doorway to the apartment as long as I could, firing off a shot whenever his men tried to poke their heads around the corner, until we were out of view down the stairs. Even then I tried to keep my body between their bullets and Eloise. Footsteps thumped on the wooden stairs as Tailor ran up to meet me.

"Eloise, you need to get the hell out of here. Run!" She went down as Tailor came up past me, suppressed VP9 in his hands. He popped off several muffled shots as one of Mertens' men came blundering into the hall with a short-barreled shotgun. That one was dead before he hit the floor.

The terrified occupant of apartment 3A cracked her door open. I was certain some of the stray rounds had gone through her wall. "*Interpol*," Tailor shouted with authority, and then a rapid bunch of half-mangled French that was probably *lock your door and stay down*. Whatever he said worked, because the lady fled. "Come on, Val, we gotta get out of here. This has gone to shit."

"I think he's still in there. We can—" A cylindrical object flew out of the doorway, bounced off the opposite wall, and hit the stairs.

The flashbang detonated before I could even warn Tailor.

LORENZO

The first thing that went through my mind when the bullets started flying was that I'd told Valentine not to fuck this up.

I had been tailing him all evening. I'd even been watching Valentine while we had been speaking on the phone, sitting under an awning at a brasserie a hundred yards away enjoying a cappuccino and his lame attempt at blending in. Valentine was one hell of a soldier, but he would have made an awful thief. When the other guy had picked him up in an Audi, I'd followed on a used Ducati I'd bought for cash.

They had never even come close to making the tail. Paris was a motorcycle-friendly city. There were thousands of them here, so I didn't stand out. Bikes made sense, since you could cut through their awful traffic, parking sucked, and for me in particular a helmet kept my face off of the security cameras. Sure, riding was miserable and dangerous in the rain, but many of the locals just used these zipup leg covers to keep the water out of their laps, and called it good.

When the mystery driver had dropped Valentine off, I parked. And unlike them, I could park damn near anywhere. I picked another building down the street with an awning to keep out of the rain, and hung out there. When the cops Valentine had avoided walked by, I simply wished them a pleasant evening in perfect French. I don't normally smoke, but carried a pack and a lighter anyway, so to Paris' Finest I just looked like a regular dude having a smoke break while avoiding the worst of a shower. Once they were past I went back to watching.

Valentine would probably be torqued if he found out I was following him, but unless something went wrong, he'd never even know I was here.

So of course, something went wrong. Valentine is a shit magnet.

A couple minutes after Valentine and the hooker went inside somebody started shooting. My first thought was *I told him not to fuck this up.* Then his friend—I still didn't know who he was—ran up and kicked in the front glass. I checked the other way, the cops had turned the corner and hopefully mistook the noise for thunder. That wouldn't last long. "Damn it, Valentine," I muttered as I tossed the cigarette and reached for the little plastic Steyr subgun stashed in my bag.

But then I realized something was up. The door had opened on one of the apartment buildings across the street and four men had come running out, heading directly after Valentine and his buddy. They had their hands down at their sides or inside their jackets, trying to hide their weapons. They'd been camped this whole time. This had all been a setup. *But how—?*

Before I'd even finished thinking the question, I got my answer. The hooker ran outside, but rather than getting gunned down, the man in the lead shooed her out of the way, and neither of them seemed surprised to see the other. She had tipped off the Montalbans.

The Kat I knew, if warned beforehand, would have just left a claymore in the apartment and blown them all to hell. The fact that she hadn't—and this was a relatively restrained amount of gunfire for her people—suggested that she wanted to take somebody alive, probably because she was curious who had killed Diego and Varga. Was it someone moving in on her business? Was it personal? Or were they poking into Blue? She'd want to know.

So technically, since Valentine hadn't been smoked immediately, by raising those questions in Kat's head, it was like I'd done him a favor. And since I was now walking toward the four armed men who were about to storm the lobby, I was about to do him another.

I ran, crouched, along the parked cars, keeping my gun low so hopefully they wouldn't see it until it was too late. A flashbang went off inside and the window over the second floor stairwell blew out. The four dudes must have been waiting for that as a signal, because three of them rushed through the broken glass. The gunfire had really picked up to an unmistakable level, so those gendarmes that had been here a minute ago were probably calling for backup and hauling ass back. This was about to get really complicated.

They had left one man as lookout. He saw me coming, assumed I was a law-abiding citizen, pointed his subgun my way, and started shouting about how this wasn't any of my business. But I simply lifted my TMP to waist level, and put a burst through the windows of the Peugeot parked between us. Hip firing is stupidly inaccurate, but I still winged him. As he flinched back, I raised the gun, put the front sight on his torso, and the next burst stitched him from nipple to neck.

I ran toward the entrance, but out of the corner of my eye I thought I someone in the shadows off to the side. White skin and black eyes. I spun, ready to fire, but there was nothing there but rivulets of water pouring from a broken gutter. For just a split second I thought the Pale Man had been there.

CRACK.

The bullet passed through the air where I would have been if I'd not stopped. It smacked into the concrete and fragments flew. I dove behind a parked car, cursing myself as I realized that the men hadn't come out of the lobby across the street. They'd been waiting in one of the apartments above it, and they'd left a shooter in the window to cover them. Using something big and semi-auto, he went to town on the car I was using for cover, pounding rifle rounds through the sheet metal as I hugged the gutter. The burn on my chest ached when it landed in the cold water.

I glanced back the way I'd come from. The two cops were running this way. They had drawn their pistols and were heading directly toward the sound of gunfire, balls to the wall. It was brave as hell, but Kat's men would have no compunction at shooting the police. I shouted a warning and tried to wave them back, but the Montalban shooter had already seen them. He turned on the police, and bullets started smacking the walls around them. One cop got hit in the leg and crashed. His partner skidded to a stop, and by some miracle didn't get hit as he dragged the wounded man behind a planter.

It sucked for them, but I used the distraction to scramble up and bolt for the entrance. By the time the rifleman had swung back toward me, I was already through and heading for the stairs.

VALENTINE

That had been one hell of a bang. The stairwell was filled with so much smoke it was hard to breathe. All I could see was flashing purple lights. I could barely hear Tailor shouting over the ringing in my ears. There were men above and below us, and they fired a bunch of rounds through stairs to let us know they were there. We were surrounded and there was no way out. One of the men below was shouting something in French.

"What's he saying?" I asked. "And when the hell did you learn French?"

"Asshole wants us to surrender. I told him I was Interpol. Didn't faze him. Guy's a pro."

There were tears in my eyes as I kept blinking, hoping my vision would clear up in time to shoot somebody. One of the men yelled something else. "What's that?"

For once, Tailor sounded worried. "He said there's two of us, but his boss only needs one alive. They're going to count to ten, and then start shooting."

"I'm not getting taken alive. Not again. Call their bluff, let's see how brave they really are."

Tailor shouted back something in French, then for my benefit said. "I told him his mom gives lousy head. We only got a second here. Up or down?"

The man downstairs started counting.

It was a bad situation to be in, but I was *calm*. Down was the most obvious direction to go in. Down would bring us to the street and give us room to maneuver. Trouble was, we didn't know how many of them were below us. I thought I had seen Mertens above, there couldn't have been too many stuffed into that little apartment, and we'd already killed at least two of those. There would be a fire exit or at least a window at the back. Antoine was covering that side, and if we could get to him, we had our egress route. By the time the count had reached *trois* I had made my call.

"We're going up."

LORENZO

"*Quatre!*"

I didn't know why the jackass at the base of the stairs was counting, but he was armed and jumpy. The other two were ahead of him, further up the stairs, so all I could see were their legs. They were all focused in the other direction. They must have thought my shots had come from the man they'd left guarding the door, and that he and their rifle guy still had their asses covered. They assumed wrong.

Before he could say *cinq*, all hell broke loose. Val and his friend must have gone for it, because there was a chain of suppressed *pops*, the sound of feet pounding stairs, and somebody above started screaming bloody murder.

"*Merde*," the man muttered, right before I bashed him upside the skull. Plastic guns make shitty clubs, but I still hit him hard enough that he spun around and crashed into the mail boxes. Before he could shout a warning, I throat-punched him with the hot muzzle of the Steyr. This thing had a vertical foregrip too, so with both hands I really put some oomph into it. He went down hard enough to bounce his face off the tile floor.

By the time I looked up, the other two were gone, chasing Valentine. I went after them. Taking the stairs two at a time, I caught them just as they were drawing a bead to shoot Valentine in the back as he ran down the hall. Valentine's little friend had been faster, and had already dived over a dead guy and through an open door. I opened up, stitching the rest of my magazine into Kat's men. Valentine heard the shots, spun around, and fired a suppressed pistol at them. One of Kat's men went down spraying blood all over the carpet, and the other flipped over the railing to plummet back into the lobby.

The instant Val's pistol had locked back empty, he'd switched guns, and I had that big stupid shiny revolver aimed at me *again*. The dude was quick, I'll give him that.

"Point that somewhere else or I'll stick it up your ass," I warned as I reloaded.

"Lorenzo?" He lowered the hand cannon. "What're you doing here?"

"Cleaning up your mess."

"Val! Mertens is getting away!" his friend shouted from inside the apartment. "There's stairs down the back!"

Valentine went in. I followed. I would have loved to get back to my bike and get out before half the cops in Paris descended on this place, but I didn't know how dedicated the rifleman across the street was. He might have run at the first sound of sirens, but I didn't want to risk getting my head blown off if he was feeling stubborn.

There were bodies in the hall, and another in the entry. It smelled like blood and smoke. The apartment was small, but there was a back balcony. The glass door was open, the curtains were billowing, and rain was coming inside. There was a circular metal staircase leading down into the alley. Valentine started talking into this radio, it sounded like to Antoine. I pushed past him and hit the stairs. They were shaky, wobbly, and slicker than snot in the rain, but I managed to bound down the steps, two and three at a time, without killing myself. I spotted a shape that had to be our guy, twenty yards ahead, leaping over garden fences like they were nothing. Georges must have been a track star. Valentine's friend was already at the bottom and had taken off after him.

The rain was really coming down now. Beyond that rumble was the sound of sirens, *lots* of sirens. The neighbors had heard the gunfire and there were a lot of faces pressed against windows, trying to figure out what was going on. Unfortunately for us, this back area was lit, so witnesses were sure to see the four of us having a foot chase, and they'd vector the cops right in on us.

I sprinted after Georges. That son of a bitch was *fast*. He'd already reached the end of the block. Lucky for me, rather than turning right or left and heading down the sidewalk, he crossed the little side street and entered another foot path between apartment buildings. Montalban connections or not, he didn't want to get busted by the cops. Valentine was coming down the stairs behind me, shouting directions into his radio. Valentine's friend reached the street and nearly got creamed by a passing car. They hit the brakes, he wound up in their headlights, briefly, before sliding across their hood like T. J. Hooker. Somehow he stayed on his feet and kept up the chase as the car honked at him.

I scrambled over a metal fence—glad that I was wearing a motorcycle jacket as the spikes stabbed at me—and hit the other side running. I even looked both ways before crossing the street and managed not to get hit by a car. *Way* ahead, Georges was still booking it. My lungs were burning and my legs were on fire. There's not a lot of space to practice your wind sprints in a dungeon. These apartments had their own little yards, and hurdling the little fences was killing me. Dogs were barking. A little schnauzer tried to bite me. I dodged it and hoped it bit Valentine when he caught up. It would serve him right.

We cleared another street. There were flashing red and blue lights zipping through the intersection at the end. *Don't look this way. Don't look this way.* One of their own had just got sniped. They were going to be pissed. I'd almost caught up with Valentine's friend, who was soaked, gasping, and starting to lose steam. Ahead, at the end of the *next* block, Georges was damned near out of sight. He'd already crossed another street, and this block was mostly shops and hotels with living quarters above. It would be really easy for Georges to dart into one of the buildings and disappear. He turned into a skinny alley behind a café. I pushed myself harder to keep him in view.

A van appeared, tires sliding on the wet street, as it took the corner way too fast, and followed him in. I sure hoped it was the Exodus guys and not Montalban reinforcements. It was too close to drive far inside, and I saw brake lights. Luckily, I learned it was Exodus when Shen leapt out of the passenger side while the van was still screeching to a halt.

This was it. This street was clear. I didn't see anybody looking at us. The cops were going in the opposite direction. There would be some confusion before they were pointed our way. We had a few seconds where we could still pull this off.

By the time I reached the back of the van, our quarry was stopped in the headlights. There was a chain link gate behind him, he didn't have time to make it over, and Shen had him at gunpoint. Antoine had the driver's door open and was using it for cover. Georges' chest was heaving from the exertion. The bodyguard slowly turned around.

"Gun," Shen warned.

There was a pistol in his hand.

Antoine barked at him to put it down. The other man who'd been pursuing Georges with me moved up on them, his handgun aimed at Georges too. He was terribly out of breath but he started shouting for Georges to surrender in really bad French.

A strange look came across Mertens' face. It was the expression of a man who knew there was no way out.

I never knew why he went for it. We had him dead to rights. He couldn't know who we were, but maybe he assumed anybody trying to capture one of Kat's men weren't the type to let him live when we were done. Or maybe Kat had told her people that if they let themselves get caught she'd assume they'd flipped on her and she'd kill their families. I wouldn't put it past her. Hell if I know. Whatever his reasoning, he had made a fateful decision. I could see it in his eyes. *Resignation.*

"Don't do it!" I shouted.

He swung his gun toward Shen.

Several bullets punched Mertens' chest.

I couldn't blame them. There was none of that *shoot him in the legs* or *shoot the gun out of his hand* bullshit. When somebody is about to send a bullet your way, you put them down. Period. Anything less just resulted in a wounded man killing you.

Georges Mertens fell backwards, rattling the fence as he slid down, until he came to rest sitting in a puddle.

"Son of a *bitch*!" the man who'd chased him all this way shouted, in English, with a southern American accent . . . that sounded strangely *familiar*. "You fucking asshole!" I don't know if he was yelling at Mertens for basically committing suicide, or at everyone who'd shot him. Which included himself, since his pistol was now at slide lock.

Keeping their guns up, Shen and Antoine approached cautiously. Shen pushed Mertens' pistol away with his shoe. Antoine felt for a pulse. He looked back at me and shook his head.

Everyone who'd just fired was using a suppressed weapon, so hopefully nobody inside the café had heard the noise. We could still get out of here. I looked back. Valentine had almost caught up. He was a lot bigger and heavier than me or the other guy, so not nearly as fast on foot, but his giving directions over the radio had worked. I glanced back at the corpse. *Kind of worked.*

Another setback, and worse, from the ambush, it was clear Kat was hunting us while we were hunting her. Things were about to get a lot more difficult. I walked in front of the headlights, swore, and kicked the bumper.

Antoine was already patting down the body for intel. He found Mertens' cell phone and stuffed it into one pocket. "I am sorry, Lorenzo. He left us no choice."

"Shit happens."

"Lorenzo?" The little angry dude looked over at me. "Who the hell is . . ." He was still breathing hard. He fell silent when he got a look at my face.

I couldn't quite place him. The voice was familiar, an angry Tennessee twang that I'd heard before. It came to me in an instant. A mosque in Zubara. Valentine with his arm around Jill's neck, using her as a shield. And *this* asshole . . . they called him *Xbox* then.

"You!" He didn't even blink, just threw a punch. Lucky his gun was empty or he probably would've shot me. I narrowly blocked his arm, and pointed my subgun—which was very much loaded—at his dick.

"Back off, stumpy."

"Whoa, whoa, whoa!" Valentine came running up. "For fuck's sake, guns down!"

The Southerner was seething, but he wasn't stupid enough to try anything else. I took a step away and lowered my weapon. What the hell was Tailor doing here? Or at least I thought his name was Tailor, as we'd never been formally introduced. We had met during a gunfight . . . on opposite sides.

"Val, this is the guy from Zubara, the asshole that hit me with a shovel! What the hell is he doing here? Are you *working* with him?"

"Technically my partner hit you with a shovel."

"Yeah, sorry I'm a little fuzzy on the memory details there, bub, because *I'd just got a concussion from a fucking shovel!*"

Valentine got between us. "Everybody calm down, we're all on the same side here."

The Southerner had been Dead Six. "He's Majestic."

"Mr. Tailor is Illuminati now," Shen corrected helpfully.

"Don't tell him my name!" the Southerner, Tailor, protested.

"You've got to be kidding!" They were the last people I wanted to know I was still alive. "Those are Montalban allies!"

"Gentlemen," Antoine boomed, "the police are coming. We don't have time for this nonsense! Sort it out in the van!"

Chapter 9: Breaking Point

LORENZO

I made it back to one of Jill's—hideouts—one step above a crack house, late that night, exhausted and bitter. I gave her a quick debrief, and then tried to go to sleep, angry at Valentine for being stupid, angry at Kat for being smart, and basically angry at the world for not cooperating.

Yet despite all that anger, with Jill resting next to me, I actually calmed down enough to rest. No matter what, as long as I had her, everything would be okay. She'd been my anchor in prison, and out.

Only I had another terrible dream that night. Nothing elaborate, nothing special, just Sala Jihan standing in shadows of the bedroom, whispering that I was not focused enough, that I had lost my way, and that the *son of murder* had no time for distractions.

I had bolted awake, chest burning, snatched up my .45, and pointed it at the darkened corner . . . to see nothing. Still, I waited, until I was absolutely sure there was no one there, and the whispering had stopped.

"Go away, Pale Man," I muttered. "You can't have her."

"Huh?" Jill asked, mostly asleep. "What's wrong?"

"Nothing." I put my gun away and went back to sleep.

Nothing at all.

Jill was suspicious, but she'd done as I asked. I told her to dress nice, because our stakeout would be in the classy part of town, the rich, touristy part. So when she met me at the riverside, just before sundown, she was wearing a fashionable dress, a nice jacket, and a scarf that was probably really expensive. Jill wasn't big on the hair and makeup, but she'd gone all in tonight. She was gorgeous. I had just gotten this new suit tailored this afternoon. We actually made a really cute couple.

I offered her my arm. "Right this way, my dear."

"What's the deal, Mr. Secretive?" Jill glanced around. There wasn't really anything of much note here. Behind us were some businesses, ahead of us were boats. "You made it sound like a party."

I led her down the stone steps. "Kind of."

"At least warn me if there are going to be metal detectors. I'm wearing a thigh holster under this thing."

"That's actually kinda hot, but don't worry. There's no security. It should be pretty quiet."

We followed the walkway closer to the Seine. Now it was obvious we were heading for the docks. One nice thing about all the rain yesterday was it knocked the city stink down and left the air nice.

"Okay, seriously, Lorenzo, who we spying on? I didn't bring my snorkel. Look at all those cute little boats. You know, I really miss having our yacht." Then Jill saw the boat we were heading for. It was a long rectangle. It had one floor that was enclosed in glass, while the top was flat, open, and had tables with umbrellas. "Ooh, floating restaurant. Fancy."

"This is supposed to be one of the best ones in town. The guy who runs it even won on 'Iron Chef.'"

"American?"

"No way. Old school Japanese."

"*Nice* . . . Let me guess, some Montalban dickweed has reservations for tonight, so we're going to spy on him? Score. I guess that's way nicer than impersonating a maid and cleaning hotel rooms." But then Jill realized that there were no other customers inside. "Are we early . . . No . . . Please don't tell me we're pretending to be wait staff. I'm a terrible waitress. The only reason I got tips at that greasy spoon in Quagmire was because of my legs."

"No, now be cool. And if anybody asks, I'm a rich, eccentric Bollywood film executive producer."

"Okay then." It said a lot about our relationship that Jill took that in stride. "What does an executive producer even do?"

"Produce things? Executively. I don't know."

"As long as I don't have to dance and do a musical number, I'm happy. I can't dance in heels."

There was a hostess waiting for us. She greeted me as Mr. Kumar (the single most common name in India, which made fake IDs a piece of cake) and told us our table was ready. I'd specified that if the weather was nice, I wanted the best spot on the roof.

We were seated at a very nice table, with a great view off the front of the boat. There were even fresh flowers and candles lit. I swear they'd perfumed the air. Nobody did this sort of thing better than the French. I even got her chair for her, very gentlemanly like.

Jill waited until our hostess had left. "Where is everybody else?"

I made a big deal of looking around, like the fifty other empty chairs up here came as a surprise. "How about that? Must be a slow night."

"Lorenzo . . ."

"Go big, or go home. Hang on." They were bringing out the wine. I knew a bit about the subject, enough to fake it in polite society, but I played it safe and had ordered a bottle that cost about the same as a good used car. When the server was gone again I explained, "I took the liberty of ordering drinks, but if you want a Diet Coke or something—"

"Lorenzo!"

"I wanted to give you a nice night on the town, but all the classy places are in public with lots of witnesses and cameras. But not this, so I rented the whole place."

She was cute when she was incredulous. "What did that cost?"

"One of Reaper's suitcases full of Euros, but he knows I'm good for it." There was some noise below as our boatstaurant began moving away from the dock. "We're taking a little cruise and seeing the lights while enjoying a fine gourmet meal. We'll head past Notre Dame, that big wheel thing, and by the time we get to the main course, we should be down by the Eiffel Tower."

"Are you crazy? With everything that's going on, this?"

I reached across the table and took her by the hands. "Tonight, it's just us. No mission. No business. Just us. We've both been through a lot. Tomorrow, we'll go back to work. But tonight . . . Tonight I just want to remember what it is that we're fighting for."

As I said that she had gotten a little choked up. "I don't deserve this."

"You deserve the world." I didn't know where her attitude had come from. She was awesome. I was the crook who would have a rap sheet as long as my arm—if I wasn't so good at not getting caught. The last year had beaten her down, and it was my job to bring her back up. "Let me do this for you, because I love you, and because you saved my life in more ways than you can ever know."

For once, Jill was speechless. She was so surprised, that for a moment I thought I might have broken her brain. "You? You're trying to be romantic?"

"Trying?" I spread my arms wide, with the lights of Paris stretched out behind me. "More like *nailing* it."

"What are you *really* doing, Lorenzo?"

I thought about the whispers in the dark, and the still aching burn on my chest, about revenge and justice, and about how *none* of that mattered without her.

"I'm taking my life back."

She smiled, and for the first time since I'd been free, that was the smile of the Jill I used to know.

LORENZO
Paris
September 23rd

It had been Reaper who had demanded a face-to-face meeting with Valentine. His latest snooping had turned up some really bad news. Valentine also promised that he'd share all their new intel, which was mighty considerate, considering he'd teamed up with the Illuminati without bothering to tell me. It might be just Reaper's paranoia, but he said Majestic had access to some *next level* tech, and didn't trust phones when they were the topic. Since Reaper's fieldcraft and ability to move through a foreign city unnoticed was nonexistent, I got to be the bearer of bad tidings.

We picked a café in Goutte d'Or to meet, specifically because it was in a poorer neighborhood that was mostly North African immigrants. All the police cameras around the place had been smashed by the residents. I didn't think my face was in Majestic's database, but Valentine's certainly was, so better safe than sorry.

The place wasn't crowded, but I asked for a table in the back where it was quiet. Two minutes after I was seated by the waiter, Valentine joined me, wearing a hoodie, ball cap, and big black Ray-Bans. "You look shady as fuck," I told him. "You'd blend in better if you dressed like a tourist."

"Yeah, well, this secret agent bullshit is still new to me. Are we actually going to eat? I'm starving."

"If you want. I've got plans for tonight, but I'm free until then. Oh wait, that's right. You already know about me scouting the smugglers by the airport because I filled you guys in beforehand."

"I *said* I was sorry. What do you want, flowers? Did you drag me out here to try to guilt-trip me, or do you need help with your thing tonight?"

I shook my head. "It's just a sneak and peak. The less presence nearby the less chance they'll ever know I was there."

"Do me a favor. I want you to keep one of my people in the loop tonight."

"Oh, are we keeping each other in the loop now? Is that what we're doing?"

"Jesus Christ, do we need to go to marriage counseling over this?"

It was so entertaining getting him agitated like that. For someone who was so eerily calm during combat, it sure was easy to push his buttons the rest of the time. "Who's this person of yours? Backup?"

"Not like that. She's not going out there. She's . . . it's hard to explain. She's good at analyzing stuff. Pieces of information that seem random to you might reveal a pattern to her."

"Fine. I thought about inviting an Illuminati hit man too, but I didn't because I'm a team player like that."

"You're not going to let that go, are you?" The waiter came back with our menus. Outside of the trendy, touristy parts of the city, the service was actually a lot better than the stereotypes. Even there, if you weren't a stereotypical douchebag tourist, people still tended to be pretty cool, and you wouldn't end up with a stereotypically snooty waiter.

"*Merci.*" Valentine's French was truly awful. The waiter left. "So what's the bad news you have for me?"

"Next time you're caught on camera, try to smile. Somebody got some cell phone video of an *Interpol agent* the other night after a shootout."

"How bad?"

"It's a little blurry, but it got uploaded to YouTube."

Valentine sighed. "Super."

"Look, Reaper thinks this is really bad. He walked me through how the latest facial recognition software works. Glasses aren't enough to throw off the programs anymore. The good stuff measures your available face, maps your bone structure, builds a 3D model, and extrapolates out anything you cover. If you do have to move in the open somewhere with cameras, best thing to do is keep your head down and watch your feet. Most of them are mounted up high so they don't get vandalized. Reaper says the software still struggles with angles and profiles."

"It's hard to keep your head down when you're chasing a guy and trying not to get lost. If Majestic knows I'm here, that complicates things."

"Being a left-handed shooter with the right height and build probably sealed the deal if they had any doubt."

"This stuff is your wheelhouse or whatever, right? What can I do?"

"Have Antoine's complexion. No, seriously. Darker skin makes it harder for the cameras to measure facial features. Something about contrast and shadow depth. If you were any whiter you'd be translucent."

"Sure, I'll take some time off to hit the beach, get my tan on."

"For future reference, I've got my super genius hacker trying to get into the local police system so that if you show up there, it doesn't get flagged. He can't know about every camera phone upload in the world, though, so you need to be more discreet from now on. We can't afford another fuckup like that."

"Fine. How is Reaper, anyway?"

"Better . . ." *Maybe.* He seemed happy to be working, but I was a little worried I might have validated his fears by telling him about my experiences in prison. "He's working on that police thing, but apparently Paris is a lot harder to crack without getting caught than Zubara. Go figure. But if we need to meet again, this neighborhood is a good one. Rough enough there's not a lot of cops, but not so rough that French intelligence is camped on it looking for terror cells. Just don't go a mile that way. It's Jihadi asshole central."

"How can you tell?"

"Graffiti mostly, and lopsided signposts." Valentine nodded when I said that. He'd been around disintegrating cities enough to know that trick. The local hooligans would shake any pole stuck in the concrete so that it was loose. That way when—not if—a riot broke out, all they had to do was yank the already loose pole out of the ground. They were handy for smashing windows, and the holes broke the surrounding concrete to give them a supply of useful throwing rocks.

"I'll skip that leg of the bus tour then."

"Trust me, you'd need a lot better disguise. You're too tall, too white, and too corn-fed-looking. You look like you just stepped out of a John Deere ad."

"Number one, you're just mad because you're short. Number two, that's racist. Number three, what are you anyway? Like, what ethnicity?"

I could pass for lots of things when I put my mind to it. "Mutt mostly, but my real dad was a gypsy."

Valentine thought I was messing with him. "Right. And for your information I'm not white. I identify as an albino Samoan."

"I'm serious. My birth parents were Roma."

"Whatever. Listen, don't stress too much over Tailor. I didn't tell you because I didn't want the distraction. I haven't told him anything about you, and believe me, he wanted to know how it is I'm working with you. I don't think he'd believe me if I told him the whole story anyway. He works for one of the Illuminati families, but we've got kind of a deal worked out with them right now. They're helping us track down Kat. That's where we got the lead on Georges Mertens from. They also helped steer the investigation of the aftermath so that we don't have to worry about the cops looking for us. Tailor's employers can pull a lot of strings when they want to. Right now we need every advantage we can get, especially if Majestic shows up again."

"You ever wonder about the screwed up life choices we've made to end up where we're talking about Majestic versus the Illuminati and it's not a joke?"

Valentine raised his eyebrows over his sunglasses. "I wonder about my life choices every day. I had to work really hard to get this screwed up. Anyway, Tailor's boss is Alistair Romefeller. Know him?"

"Not really." That name sounded familiar, but when I'd worked for Big Eddie, I'd been in the dark about all this global conspiracy stuff. "Was Tailor your contact with him?"

"Actually, no, if you can believe it. I had no idea he was working for him. It just so happened."

"I'm a professional con man. *Nothing* 'just-so-happens'. Assume any coincidence is probably somebody like me trying to manipulate you. You trust this guy?"

"Tailor? I knew him from Vanguard. We were on Switchblade 4 together, and Dead Six after. He was like a brother to me."

"My brother got me into this mess."

"He got me into some shit, too. Like, Zubara. He recruited me. I want to trust him, but his boss? As long as what we're doing benefits him, we're okay, but once we stop being useful we start being a liability. Tailor doesn't think it's that bad, but he always was the optimist." Valentine chuckled. "You know what's really screwed up? I actually kind of trust you."

"That's not funny. It's sad."

"No, really. I mean, you're probably a sociopath, but you're a consistent sociopath. I understand your motivations. Tailor, the Illuminati, Majestic? That whole mess is so convoluted I doubt they even know what they're fighting for. The truth is buried under layers and layers of secrets and lies. You, you're straightforward. A guy who tries to murder you is, at least, being honest about his feelings toward you."

That was actually a nice compliment. Our waiter came back and I asked for the spiciest thing on the menu. I'd missed flavor almost as much as I'd missed sight. Valentine surprised me by ordering some chicken tagine. I'd kind of figured the big corn-fed Midwesterner would have asked for a hamburger or something.

"What are you going to do if Underhill comes to Paris looking for you?"

An evil smile split Valentine's face. "He'd better hope he doesn't find me. You should know, it's pretty likely he'll turn up if they manage to ID me. He's been haunting my footsteps since we left the Crossroads. It was enough that I had to lay low for a few months, let the trail go cold. He's a persistent bastard."

"Look, I get it. He killed Hawk and you want to kill him back. Awesome. Me too. But know going in that Underhill is a beast. Anders is one of the toughest, sharpest, meanest bastards I've ever had the displeasure to meet, and Underhill *frightened* him. Anders faked his death because he was worried they'd pull Underhill out of retirement to go after him. That old man is the best hunter-killer Majestic has ever had, and let me accentuate, *old man*. You realize how hard it is to live long enough to get old in this business?"

"Like Hawk?" Valentine's demeanor changed subtly. I'd seen him get like this before. It was like flipping a switch. One second he was a normal, almost likable, guy. The next he was a killing machine. There was no emotion when he was like that, no fear, no remorse. Just action and reaction. That switch was what made Valentine so damned dangerous, and I had just managed to move it a little. It was weirdly fascinating to watch. And to think, this nutjob thought *I* was a sociopath!

I leaned back in my chair. "If he comes for you, he'll probably have some sort of official credentials to hide behind and diplomatic immunity. You're a fugitive, a wanted criminal. The French government will be backing him. You've got jack and shit. Local cops are going to be on the lookout. They'll be working their CIs and it wouldn't surprise me to see your face plastered all over the news soon. That's the surface. I'm betting Majestic sends an army with him. They won't risk you being picked up and talking to regular cops. They'll kill you or disappear you into another black site like before."

"I'm sure they'll try."

I had no doubt he'd stack the bodies when they did. "You think that's what Hawk would want? This isn't about just you anymore, Valentine. Exodus doesn't need another bloodbath. They need a leader."

Just like that, I was talking to normal Valentine again. It really was that quick. They'd done some weird shit to his brain in North Gap. Or had they? He was like this before that, too, if not as intense. "I told them everything Hunter told me, but Silvers wouldn't let up. *Who is Evangeline? What is the Alpha Point of Project Blue?* I don't know who Evangeline is or what Project Blue does. I told them, I fucking told them everything. What the hell more do they want from me?"

"Underhill wants you dead, or in a cage."

"He doesn't even care what I know, as long as he's got the thrill of the chase," Valentine muttered.

We didn't know much about Underhill beyond his rep. He'd been some CIA type back in the old days, before Majestic had taken him down the rabbit hole. All the rumors since were that he was a tenacious son of a bitch, and that no matter what rock you were hiding under, he would find you.

"You need to watch your back, Valentine. A man like that searching for you is going to make it tougher to catch Kat."

"I'm not going to run away, if that's what you're suggesting."

"I wasn't suggesting anything. I'm just telling you like it is."

"I'm going to kill that son of a bitch, Lorenzo, or I will die trying. He's going to know it was me, too. My .44? Hawk gave me that gun. Tuned it himself. The muzzle of that revolver will be the last thing Underhill ever sees. But . . ." he trailed off, looking around uncomfortably. "There'll be plenty of time for that. They'll never stop hunting me. In the meantime, what we're doing here has to come first. It's more important than my grudge."

He said it in a way that almost sounded like he wanted my affirmation. Either way, it was a lot more level-headed than I expected from him. "You're not wrong. I think Ling is making you soft."

Valentine was distracted, lost in thought. "If killing Katarina isn't enough, and Blue would launch anyway, we've got to derail the whole damned thing somehow. Maybe we can use Underhill?"

"What're you getting at?"

"All we know about Project Blue for sure is that it was a Majestic scheme to wreck the Illuminati. They never thought they'd actually launch it. Now Majestic is pissing itself over their doomsday plot actually happening. If they have a team looking for me in the same city as Katarina . . ."

He might be onto something. "You want to aim Underhill at Kat."

"If we can get them killing each other, everybody wins." Valentine thought about it for a moment. "I don't know how to make that happen, though. Everything we've learned so far makes it sound like the two sides have a truce. That's why Gordon having me kill Rafael Montalban was such a big deal, because it broke their precious rules. Hmmm. I'll need to think on this."

He had gotten smarter since I'd first met him. Then he'd just been a kid, really good at killing people, sucked into a bad war. The man I'd freed from North Gap had been a suicidal mess. Now he seemed more squared away, like he had a purpose and a clue, or maybe I was wrong. It wasn't that Ling had made him soft. It was that she'd actually given him something to live for.

LORENZO
Paris
Later that night . . .

It took me nearly twenty minutes to break into the truck rental company in Villepinte. Sure, I was out of shape, and I had to dodge security guards and attack dogs, but still . . . *Twenty minutes.* That was embarrassing.

Reaper's digging found that one of Varga's shell companies owned this facility a few miles south of Charles de Gaulle airport. Their call history showed that both Diego and Mertens had both called this business. I'd checked the layout on Google Earth, and then done a drive by. It was the sort of close to everything but secluded spot that was perfect for a smuggling operation.

Dressed in an innocuous dark gray hoodie, I'd come back in the middle of the night to work. This was just a little sneak and peak. I wasn't expecting trouble. I'd packed light. If I was spotted, my plan was to run and hide. That way hopefully they'd think I was some junkie looking for an easy petty theft.

There had been a couple of security guards on duty, but they appeared to be the typical, just-over-minimum-wage, rent-a-cop types, and they were mostly interested in guarding the fenced enclosure that held the trucks, trailers, and heavy equipment. There was a regular boring office building and a modern garage in front. I skipped all that stuff. Customers and normal employees would be through there all the time, and Varga wouldn't conduct his real business in front of potential witnesses. So I avoided the guards and went right to the interesting part.

There was a large workshop at the rear of the property. The satellite images had shown that it was secluded, fenced off from the rest of the facility, and had its own gate leading to a side road. It was only a short ride to the airport, so this was perfect for sorting and storing illicit cargo.

I made my way through the maze of broken-down heavy equipment and rusted out trucks. Weeds were growing through the tracks and over the tires. There wasn't much light back here, but I reached the back fence without banging my head or shins too much. There were places to park around the workshop, but no new cars. The chain link fence was topped in razor wire, and the scent of dog shit warned me what was inside. A couple of big, nasty Rottweilers had smelled me and come over to bark and raise hell. I could have just shot the dogs with a suppressed pistol (which was why they'd nicknamed them *hush puppies* after all) but my goal was to recon the place without Varga's men ever knowing I was here. You can't exactly do that if you go around leaving dead dogs all over the place.

Besides, I'd come prepared for dogs: a Ziploc baggie with some tranquilizer-loaded steaks. I dumped it over the fence, and ten minutes later the slobbery Rottweilers had wandered off, stoned and drowsy. Once I was sure nothing else was going to come out and bite my nuts off, I climbed the fence and went to work. The good thing about there being dogs was that meant there weren't any motion detectors around the garage, because otherwise they'd be setting them off nonstop.

The shop was made out of cinderblocks and rusty sheet metal, but the door was heavy duty and had multiple locks. The windows had bars on them and were probably wired, so I picked the locks with my bump keys. My out-of-practice fingers were clumsy, and it took me far too long, like almost a minute for the first lock. Once I'd gotten all the locks off, I suction-cupped a little octopus-looking device to the door. I didn't understand the science behind it, but Reaper said it screwed with the magnetic fields for door alarms. Once the light on the octopus turned green, I opened the door.

There were a couple of lights on inside the garage, but most of the place was in shadow. For supposedly being for truck maintenance, I didn't see much in the way of tools or machines inside, just lots of shelving for storage. There were a couple of vehicles parked inside by the roll up door, but most of the place was stacked full of boxes and crates. I didn't go right in. There could be motion detectors inside, but probably no cameras. They wouldn't want any recordings of what they moved through this place. I spotted one motion detector mounted high on the wall to the right of the door. The little white box was a familiar brand and about five or six years old, so I pulled out my little IR flashlight and shined it on the motion detector to blind it. Then I closed the door behind me and moved in, looking for other detectors. I didn't spot any. Once I was out of its field of view, I turned the IR light off and checked my watch.

Twenty minutes . . . Shit. Sure, most of that was waiting for the dogs to get sleepy, but prison had still kicked my ass.

I keyed my radio. "Reaper, I'm in."

"Sweet. I was monitoring the tower. No signal sent. You're good to go." If I had screwed up, Reaper had set up a rogue tower—a decoy cell phone relay—to hopefully intercept the alarm call. And trust me, in this business? The alarm company wouldn't be calling the cops.

"What took you so long?"

"The dogs were massive. It took forever for them to doze off. You should have used more drugs."

"Too much Ketamine makes the meat tastes funny."

"You know this from experience?"

"Still better than your girlfriend's cooking."

Jill cut in. *"I'm on the same the channel, dumbass. My cooking is fine."*

The banter made me smile. After so much time alone it felt good to have the company.

Jill was parked a mile down the side access road, at a truck fueling station. Reaper had dropped me off in front and was waiting on the main street. It never hurt to have multiple escape options. While the other two bickered, I went to work. Behind the parked cars—newer and nicer, so probably stolen—there was a desk with a computer on it. It was on and flicking through a screen saver loaded with porn. I stuck the evil-looking thumb drive with the bigass antenna that Reaper had gotten me into the USB port. While his malware or worms or whatever he called them molested the smugglers' privacy rights, I started looking for a good place to hide our bug.

Contrary to what you see in the movies, you can't just stick these anywhere. A listening device needs a power source, and unless you want to sneak back in repeatedly to change the batteries, you want it connected to a steady power supply. This one used both. I found an old phone jack on the closest wall, used my multitool to unscrew the faceplate, clipped the bug in, and then screwed the plate back on. That would provide it with its power normally. It had a battery backup just in case.

"Testing, testing."

"Got it," Reaper confirmed. *"Loud and clear. Hopefully Varga's guys will say something stupid into it soon."*

I doubted the smugglers knew anything, and it was unlikely they were stupid enough to leave any incriminating records on their computer either. As much material and money as the Montalbans moved, they had to keep some records, probably vague and in code, but all large successful criminal enterprises needed good accounting. Would they actually write down anything related to Kat's pet project? Probably not. This whole snooping visit was a crapshoot.

I retrieved the drive and took pictures of every paper on the desk. It was probably useless, but Reaper had surprised me before with the connections he could make from seemingly random bits of data. "Reaper, I'm sending you some pictures."

"Their shitty computer is already giving me everything. I'm sending it all along to our little friend as requested. They call her The Oracle." He snorted. *"What a pretentious call sign."*

"Yeah, that would be like calling you *The Reaper.*"

"That's totally different."

The bottom file drawer was locked, so I picked it. Inside were more file folders. I picked the ones that looked interesting, cargo manifests mostly, and started taking more pictures.

Reaper's scary computer brain read them in less time than it took me to move the papers around. That wasn't a joke. I'd seen him read whole books over breakfast. *"Wow . . . Huh . . . This could be something."*

"What?"

"It's interesting." He sounded distracted. *"These are shopping lists. This is stuff the bosses want their thieves to be on the lookout to steal. But it's weird stuff, not valuable movable merchandise they'd normally be taking. Hang on. I've got to make a call."*

I kept on taking pictures. They'd either burned the really incriminating stuff, or they were lazy and overconfident, because there was a lot of paperwork.

It took a while to get through all of it. It was the middle of the night, the roads were empty, and the dogs were still asleep. I figured I had time. I started searching the rest of the place. The shop was huge and packed, so going through every box would take all night, but I figured anything interesting would stick out. It appeared to be a fairly typical smuggler's stop. There were some stolen prescription drugs, but most of the crates were filled with things like auto parts, electronics, bundles of clothing still wrapped in plastic, cigarettes, basically anything that might *fall off the back of a truck.* Petty criminal stuff, nothing special. If there was anything good staging through here right now, there would have been real live human guards posted.

There were several side rooms. They were mostly full of more stolen junk that they hadn't found a buyer for yet. I kept taking pictures in case any of it turned out to be useful. All of them went right to Reaper and Valentine's brainiac.

Reaper sounded kind of excited. *"Why are the Montalbans collecting tons of mundane stuff they can just buy? I need to check these manifests against insurance company claims from the shippers."*

He was working off of a couple of laptops from inside a rental car. "How do you even do that?"

"By being a badass. I'm cracking and retrieving. Oracle is analyzing. She's actually pretty cool, boss . . ." He was quiet for a second. Reaper was probably working with an earpiece in each ear. *"She says hello. You worry about the breaking and entering and shooting people, chief. We've got this."*

His brain really wasn't right.

I found a curtained doorway hidden behind a rolling shelf. They always kept the human smuggling out of sight, probably so whoever was guarding the door, answering the phone, or doing paperwork wouldn't have to listen to all the sobbing. That sort of thing really grated on all but the most psychotic criminals, and your violent nut jobs—though useful—weren't your best day-to-day operations types.

The next room was divided into a few cells made of chain link, like a dog kennel, only each one held a cot. Each cell had a drain hole in the middle of the floor and a coiled garden hose for "sanitation". I figured this part would currently be unoccupied, because if any sex slaves were being held in here, there would have been real guards. It was a relief to see I was right and nobody was home, because freeing any captives would have tipped off the Montalbans that I'd been here. If this was where they moved Bob through, there was a possibility he had left me another bread crumb. I started searching the cells.

"There's something to this . . ." Reaper muttered. I hated when he felt the need to narrate his extremely convoluted thought process to me over the radio. He was hard enough to keep up with him when I was wasn't in the middle of a burglary. *"Most of the stuff they got ordered to steal makes sense, stuff you can move quick for a profit, but . . . no, some of these shipments they took don't make any sense at all. Industrial goods, chemicals, some medical stuff. What? Yeah. No. Yeah, this shit is too specific to unload . . . Whoa. You're right. It's too specific. Right."*

It turned out it was even worse when Reaper was having two simultaneous conversations.

I got on my hands and knees and started checking under the cots for scratches. It was a lot faster going this time, since I wasn't under water.

"But why steal this stuff when they could just buy it anywhere? Yeah, Katarina's got billions . . . There has to be something in each of these they needed, something special, and the rest is just junk. What pattern?" I could hear the furious typing. *"Okay, you look at that."*

There was nothing in any of the cells except for old blood stains. If Bob had been held here, it hadn't been for long enough for him to do anything. I wondered how much misery this place held. It filled me with disgust.

"You're right, buying those parts would raise terror alert flags. But stealing bits and pieces mixed in with a bunch of other stolen goods spread out over months, and nobody catches on. But what could you build out of this junk?"

Reaper was quiet for a long time. Now I was curious.

"Don't leave us hanging here, Reaper," Jill said.

"Yeah, suspense is killing me," I muttered as I left the last cell. Next time the junior think tank could do their brainstorming while I wasn't trying to be sneaky.

"Dear God . . . No." Now that wasn't a very Reaperly exclamation. *"No way. No way. Shit. I think you're right."*

"Right about what? Spill it, man."

"Sorry. Oracle thinks Katarina has a nuke."

Suddenly very cold, I stood there amid the empty slave cells as a terrible pain developed in my guts. "Hold on. You're telling me Kat built a nuclear fucking bomb out of this junk?"

"No. She probably already had the bomb, or maybe she's planning to get one soon. I don't know. But mixed in all these tons of stolen cargo, is everything you'd need to deal with an alpha particle emitter."

"Particle emitter? Like what?"

"Like uranium or plutonium, chief. As in, detection and concealment. Oracle says it's probably not in good shape or even a complete weapon. She thinks a . . . what? Physics package. She says the physics package could have been clandestinely transported or maybe damaged."

"What the hell is a physics package?"

"It's the part of the bomb that actually makes the nuclear reaction. That's what they call it."

"Who is *they*?" Reaper and this Oracle had come up with that insane theory after a few minutes of doing a jigsaw puzzle with cargo manifests. "Bullshit." I almost never doubted Reaper, but I didn't know the girl who was working for Valentine. I hoped that they were wrong. I wanted them to be wrong. I didn't want to think about Kat with a nuclear bomb.

"Lorenzo, there's some traffic down here," Jill warned in my ear, snapping me back to the present. *"You read?"*

"What've you got?"

"Headlights heading your way fast. Hang on. They're turning onto the access road. Definitely headed your way."

I didn't think I'd set off any alarms, but it was possible that this was just regular seedy middle of the night Montalban business. Either way, it was time to go. "Understood. Heading for the front. Reaper, get ready to pick me up."

"Hang on, chief. Two big, black cars just blew past me. They're . . . shit, they're stopping at the front gate!"

I must have tipped them off somehow, but there were a lot of them, and they'd gotten here fast. There was no way three cars were going to simultaneously roll up on a random alarm, so they must have been expecting an intrusion and staged nearby.

"Both of you stay put. I'll evade, and once I'm past I'll call for a pickup." I ran for the front of the garage. It would still take a minute for those cars to get here, and by then I'd be in the wind. There were plenty of places to hide around—

The front door was open. I was sure that I'd closed it.

A cardboard box next to my head exploded.

I hit the floor rolling, and then scrambled forward on my hands and knees between the shelves. A crate went flying, a pattern of holes torn through the wood. A box just above my head violently flew into pieces. *Buckshot.* Motivated by that thought, I ducked even lower, and made it around the corner as a dozen holes appeared in the shelf behind me.

The gunfire had barely made a sound.

The shooter didn't have a bead on me, so I crept along behind the shelves, looking for better cover. Whoever was firing at me was using some sort of suppressed shotgun. He wanted to keep this quiet. I pulled a Hungarian FEG pistol, one Jill had bought from the local hoodlums, out from beneath my hoody. I was about to make this loud.

I heard footsteps on concrete. The first shooter had moved behind one of the parked cars. "Come out," he ordered in rough French. It was a deep, commanding voice. "The place is surrounded." He sounded really familiar.

Son of a bitch. It was Anders.

I gave my radio three rapid taps. The signal for *oh shit everything has gone to hell.* I was pinned down by one of the best killers alive. We fought together in the Crossroads, and I watched him drop dozens of Jihan's men. He was ruthless, calculating, and supremely skilled. I had come a long damned way to find him, but this was *not* how I wanted it to go down.

Mind racing, I looked at the pistol in my hand. It was a clunky knockoff of a Browning Hi-Power, not my first choice for getting into a gunfight against one of the baddest motherfuckers I'd ever met. For Anders? That would have been an RPG or a Carl Gustav. I kicked myself for not bringing something bigger. I'd wanted to be discreet, though, and you aren't very discrete with an antitank weapon strapped to your back.

Anders switched to English. "When Diego bought it, I got nervous. The way he'd been cut, it told me somebody interrogated him. I wondered what that little freak might have said before he died. Then Varga shattered his skull on the sidewalk? No way that was a coincidence. It got me thinking, what could he have given up before taking the plunge? You probably knew about all his places at least."

I risked a peek past the edge of the desk, but I couldn't see Anders. I didn't want to stick my head any further out, because I had no doubt he was ready to blow it off. My best defense was that he probably didn't know exactly where I was. If he did, I'd already have extra holes in my body.

He spoke again, a little to the side from where he'd been a moment before. Anders was searching for an angle, trying to spot me. "Then after that shit-show the other night, I knew whatever you fuckers wanted, you weren't going to let up. You're operating in our hometown. You know who you're coming after. It's ballsy. Stupid, but ballsy. Figured I'd get ahead of you, have a talk face-to-face."

Anders was talking because he knew time was on his side. He had reinforcements on the way, no doubt. He'd said the place was surrounded, but I figured that was a bluff. I needed to get the hell out of here now. Preferably, right after I put a bullet in his brain.

Leaning out, I cranked off a quick shot into the side of the car he was behind, hoping to make him jump, but Anders wasn't the flinching type. The little 9mm was a whole lot louder than his suppressed big gun. He retaliated by quietly blowing a massive hole through the side of the desk next to me. Firing wildly to make him keep his head down, I leapt up and ran behind another set of shelves.

Taking cover in one of the doorways, I waited in the shadows, listening. My good ear was ringing now. My bad ear was *always* ringing, thanks to Valentine, but I couldn't tell where Anders was now. Had I got lucky and hit him? Fat chance.

"You've been a real pain in my ass," Anders called out. He wasn't wounded. Hell, he didn't even sound flustered, just mildly annoyed. There was the roar of an engine outside and tires on gravel. "Those are my associates. You got nowhere to go. I don't want to kill you. I only want to talk." He managed to say that while sounding perfectly calm and rational. Of course, he wanted to know what I knew first, and *then* kill me. "You don't need to stay quiet. I know who you are, Jill DelToro."

Huh?

"I didn't know you'd gotten out of the Crossroads until that bomb in London. You've got to be a pretty careful bomb maker nowadays because it's amazing the forensic evidence they can lift off of an IED, especially one that fails to detonate. Your signal got through, but your detonator was faulty. It was just blind luck you didn't get Kat that day."

That was bullshit. Jill had told me she'd not set that bomb off on purpose. Anders was trying to goad the wrong person. There wasn't time for this. I peeked around the side of a crate. There were shadows moving in the doorway. More shadows went bounding past the closest window. I was cut off.

"If it makes you feel better, it wouldn't have mattered. Even if had killed her, her plans would've kept going. She's more stubborn than you are. How many of my guys have you killed over the last year? Ten? Twelve?"

Jill must have been busier than she'd let on.

"That's dedication. Seriously, young lady, I'm impressed. If I'd known how much potential you had, I wouldn't have tried to kill you in Zubara. I would've told Gordon to hire you. But right now? You're out of your element. I don't know how the fuck you managed to do the things you've done, but no clever tricks are going to save your ass now. Stop being stupid and come out."

One of the men at the door asked Anders something.

"Form the perimeter. I've got this." He raised his voice again. "We're just having a little conversation, right, Jill?"

It was time to put Anders off his game. "Guess again, fucker."

Buckshot slammed into the crate in front of me, but I saw the tiny flicker of suppressed muzzle blast, and opened fire. I put out the passenger side window of a new Mercedes, but Anders had already ducked back down. He was big, but he was fast, too.

Someone darkened the doorway. It was too dark to see the front sight, but I pointed it, yanked the trigger, and was rewarded with a surprised yelp. The shadow disappeared.

"I said stay the fuck out!" Anders roared at his men. They did as they were told. "Well, holy shit. I've never talked to a ghost before. How you been, Lorenzo?"

"Rotting in Sala Jihan's hellhole prison because of you."

"You escaped the Pale Man?" Anders had been a Navy SEAL, HRT sniper, and Majestic hitman, but even then I think mentioning Sala Jihan freaked him out a little. "Bullshit. Nobody escapes from there."

"You're right about that: I didn't escape. He sent me to kill you."

The silence dragged on too long. Anders laughed, but it was forced. "Heh. How's that working out for you, killer?"

Quietly as possible, I reloaded. It was too dark to get a bead on Anders. Sooner or later he was going to get tired of talking, and then a whole bunch of assholes were just going to start shooting in this direction until there was nothing left for me to hide behind. Someone shined a flashlight through the closest window, searching for me. I needed to think of something fast.

"Lorenzo, stay away from the west wall," Jill warned through my ear piece.

I couldn't risk responding to her out loud. I was ten feet away from the westernmost wall of the shop, couldn't risk moving again, and had no idea what she was planning on doing. So I clicked the radio once for *negative.*

"Shit . . . Okay, in sixty seconds I'm going to make a new door in the middle of the west wall. If you're close to that, you're going to want to move."

She didn't specify the definition of *close,* but my options were pretty limited just then. I clicked the radio twice. *Affirmative.* Now I just needed to stay alive for a minute. "Hey, Anders, I know about Project Blue."

"The fuck you do."

I still hoped Reaper was wrong. "I know about the nuke."

The silence was damning.

"You don't want to do this." I had no idea what *this* actually was. "Innocents are going to die. Eddie was nuts. Kat is worse. You spent your life preventing this sort of thing—"

"You don't know shit about my life, Lorenzo." There was a bitterness in Anders' voice. "I've lost count of how many people I've killed for them, and it didn't make a bit of difference. Majestic had me, Gordon, and Hunter prepping to level cities on a *whim.* On a fucking *contingency.* It's one big game to these people."

"We've both worked for some truly evil bastards," I agreed.

This time Anders' laugh was sincere. "Yeah, well, when this is all over, Majestic will be ruined, and the Illuminati will be unopposed on the world stage, under new management. I never could stand those stick up their ass, snooty Eurotrash cocksuckers. I'm done working for anybody but myself."

"You're working for a psychopath right now!"

"Katarina is more of a strategic partnership. She needs me and I need her. She's got clout and vision, but you get one guess who really calls the shots in our organization. She's not exactly the management type. Trust me, Lorenzo. The world will be a lot nicer place with me running it behind the scenes."

"So the mighty Project Blue, the doomsday plan for one shadowy conspiracy to destroy another shadowy conspiracy, has become nothing but a power play?" I shouted back at him. "A coup, and you assholes are willing to kill millions of innocent people to pull it off?"

"You think this is unique? Like some special event in the grand scheme of things? Jesus, Lorenzo, the whole history of the world, the real history, has been like this forever, games within games. Powerful screwing the powerful, while the guys like us bleed. I'm done being a pawn, and I'm done with you."

Anders opened fire. Buckshot slammed into the boxes around me.

A truck crashed through the wall.

The corrugated steel wall barely even slowed the big Renault. Shelves and crates were tossed aside as I was pelted with debris. I got a brief glimpse of Jill in the cab, practically standing on the brakes, but the truck still flew past me, smashing into the Mercedes and sending it spinning across the shop before the truck screeched to a stop.

Anders' man with the flashlight moved in front of the window, probably surprised he'd almost been hit by a truck, but I shot him in the head. Then I leapt up and ran through the swirling dust and the bright yellow headlights. This was my chance to take Anders out. Gears ground as Jill tried to get the stolen truck into reverse. I moved around the back of the crumpled luxury car.

Anders was gone. He must have gotten out of the way. "Shit!"

Men were piling through the doorway, shooting wildly at the truck. I opened fire, trying to drive them back. Windows shattered as other gunmen opened up from outside.

"Lorenzo, come on!" Jill shouted. The big truck made a *beep beep* warning noise as she backed it through the wreckage of the shop. I ran to the passenger side of the truck, hopped onto the lowest step, and held on with one hand, pistol extended in the other. A thug in a suit rushed through the doorway, firing a subgun from the hip, but I clipped him and he went to his knees, rolling beneath the Mercedes.

I got the door open and climbed up into the cab. "Drive!" But the encouragement was unnecessary, because Jill had already put the hammer down. These things were built for torque and had surprisingly quick acceleration. Bullets were striking the truck. Holes appeared in our windshield.

"Hang on," Jill warned as she backed the truck through the improvised door. There was a sudden *clang*. Jill screamed, a combination of pain and surprise.

I looked over. A circle of holes had appeared in the driver's side door. Stuffing had been blown out of the seat and was floating between us. There was blood on her arm. Blood on her chest. "Jill!"

Anders had flanked us and shot her right through the door. But then we were outside. "I'm hit. I'm hit!" She had one hand on the wheel and one pressed against her side. Eyes wide, teeth clenched, she was too focused on trying to drive us backwards through the junkers to think about the pain just then. If she struck something solid enough to stop us, we were dead. "I'm fine."

They shot Jill. "Motherfuckers!" It must have been the adrenalin because I didn't even remember kicking out the window. Then I started shooting at anything that moved. Anders' men were running into the lot after us, firing. I picked out each muzzle flash, aimed, and popped off a couple of rounds at each one. We were lurching and bouncing, so I probably missed a lot. These things were pretty damned fast when they weren't attached to a trailer.

Despite getting hit, Jill kept her head turned, watching her mirror, trying to drive the giant vehicle too fast in reverse without crashing us into some of the abandoned heavy equipment. The light stuff, though, she didn't care about, and our rear end slapped the side of one of the recently parked cars. I barely felt it, but from the horrible metallic rending noise, that car wouldn't be following us.

We were putting distance between us and the shooters. "Are you okay?"

"I'm okay," Jill insisted, but she didn't sound okay. The words came out dripping with pain and focus.

I was shoving in my final magazine as the truck crashed through the outer fence, beeping the whole time, and out onto the access road. She kept us straight for another twenty seconds, giving us a good lead. "Flip around here." Only we kept going, across the road, and into a field. "Stop!" I shouted as we ripped through the bushes, but Jill didn't respond. Her chin had dropped to her chest. I reached for the wheel, *too late,* because then we were tipping backwards, and our rear end slammed hard into the bottom of a ditch.

The impact caused me to bounce my head off the ceiling. The padding there didn't do much. I blinked myself back to reality a second later, staring up at the night, our one unbroken headlight launching a beam at the stars.

"Jill?" All I got in response was a moan. I reached out and found her in the dark. My hand landed in hot, sticky blood. There was blood *everywhere.* She was hit worse than I thought. "Come on, we've got to go." I found my radio. "Reaper! We're on the access road. We need extraction, now!"

"Already on my way."

Jill's door was stuck against a tree. Mine still opened. She was groggy, with the clumsy, drunken movements of somebody with dropping blood pressure. I pulled her tight against me, and fumbled my way out of the steeply angled truck. I don't know how I kept hold of her, but I did. I fell backwards into the weeds, Jill on top of me. She gasped when we hit. "It's going to be okay." I kept repeating it, like a mantra. "It's going to be okay."

I dragged Jill up out of the ditch. "Can you walk?" But she didn't respond at all. She'd passed out, dead weight. Anders and his men would surely be here any second. Desperate, I looked around for Reaper's headlights, but I couldn't see them yet. I couldn't afford to wait. I didn't know where she was hit, or if this was going to make it worse, but I didn't have a choice. I hoisted her over my shoulder and started jogging through the bushes with her body over my shoulder. I could feel her blood pooling in my clothing and running hot down my shoulder. "It's going to be okay."

I could hear Jill's ragged breathing on top of mine. I needed to stop the bleeding, but I had to keep running. To stop, even for a second, was to die.

They'd gotten closer to the truck. Someone spotted us. "There!" A bullet whizzed past my legs. I turned, found that asshole, thirty yards away, and popped off a shot at him. I don't know if I hit, but he put his head down, so I kept running.

Headlights appeared ahead of me. *Please be Reaper.*

Someone else shot at me. It was so close I could feel the vibration of the bullet. It whined off into the darkness. *It's going to be okay.* Another bullet smacked into a tree right behind us.

Reaper's little rental Peugeot was speeding this way. I waved my gun overhead as his headlights engulfed us. He was going so damned fast that he had to slam on the brakes to keep from hitting us. I don't think he intended to skid sideways, putting us right next to the rear door in a cloud of rubber dust, but it worked.

Opening the door, I shoved Jill's limp form inside. "What happened to Jill?" Reaper shrieked when he saw her. I ended up knocking several laptops and tablets onto the floor.

"Drive," I shouted as I got in behind her. To punctuate the severity of the situation, the Peugeot's back window shattered.

Wheels spinning, Reaper got us moving. Terrified, he looked back over the seat at her. "Is she alive?"

"Get us out of here *now!*" The lights from the screens were enough for me to see by. I already had her shirt open. There were a bunch of scratches from the glass fragments, and right there, weeping blood, was a bullet wound on her abdomen. Then I saw another, and another, right next to each other. "Fuck."

"There's a first aid kit under the passenger seat," Reaper said, as he took us around a corner way too fast. "Hang on."

The only thing I was hanging onto was Jill, and she was barely hanging onto life. *Stay cool.* I'd seen lots of gunshot wounds. I got the bandages open and got pressure on the wounds. There were three entrance wounds, low on her left side. I rolled her over a bit. Two exit wounds. The exit wounds were small, and appeared to have gone through the muscle and fat at a pretty shallow angle, thank God. But the innermost round was still in there. If she was hit in the liver or kidney . . . *Shit.* Her breathing didn't seem strong enough. *Shit. Shit. Shit.*

I didn't see headlights behind us yet. She needed a doctor now, but when Anders saw the blood in the truck, every real hospital would be watched by Montalban. But in every major city the criminals always had people they could call on for emergency medical attention. "Get us to Doc Florian's place."

"I can't. He committed suicide last year. I heard about another guy. His place isn't too far."

I kept pressure on the wounds. I could feel her weakening pulse beneath my palms. I'd gotten the bleeding slowed, but I had no idea how much internal damage there was. Projectiles could do crazy things once inside a body, I'd seen it all, on myself and others, but never felt it like this. I've got a reputation for being a focused, no bullshit, get the job done type, but when it is the woman you love bleeding to death right there, under your hands, you start to come apart at the seams. "Faster, Reaper."

"I'm already doing a hundred!"

"Go *faster.*" I used one bloody hand to stroke Jill's cheek. "It's going to be okay, Jill. Stay with me. Please."

She was fading in and out. "It hurts," she mumbled. "This is my fault. All my fault."

That didn't make any sense. "You saved my life. We'll get it taken care of, just hang in there."

"I deserve this."

"No. It'll be okay." But she'd already lost consciousness again.

Then I heard Anders' voice. For a second I thought it was in my mind, taunting me, but then I realized it was coming from the floor of the car. Careful to keep pressure on Jill's wound, I picked up a tablet. It *was* Anders' voice. I turned up the volume, leaving bloody streaks on the glass.

"*We got a problem.*"

"That's from my bug!" Reaper exclaimed.

"*What now?*" It was Katarina. Anders must have had her on his phone's speaker. I could barely hear her, but that smoky voice just filled me with revulsion and hate.

"*Lorenzo is still alive.*"

The line was quiet as Kat digested that revelation. "*That's impossible.*"

"*I was camped at Varga's place. Lorenzo's alive and he's here. He said Sala Jihan sent him. He got away, him and that Del Toro bitch, but there's blood all over so I plugged at least one of them. Don't worry. We'll catch him.*"

"*You don't know Lorenzo like I do. He's harder to kill than a cockroach. He'll find a way to ruin everything.*"

"He knows about the package," Anders stated flatly. *"I was fishing and got the impression he doesn't know the target or the timetable though."*

"Unacceptable! We can't afford an interruption now! Find him and kill him!" She hung up.

"Bet your ass I will," Anders muttered to himself. Then it was quieter, as he walked away from the bug. *"Let's go."*

"Lorenzo!" Reaper exclaimed. "My rogue tower is still up for intercepting their alarms. Anders' phone was using *my* tower."

"So?"

"Jill and I could never crack the Montalban's encrypted communications, but with this, I can tell you approximately where Kat is, or at least which cell tower she's closest to." Even though we were going extremely fast, Reaper reached down and began reading the screen of a tablet he had resting on the center console. I probably should have told him to keep his eyes on the road, but I wanted Kat *dead*. "She's way over on the other side of town. But I know that area! There's a fancy hotel there that the Illuminati have used for meetings. That's got to be where she's at."

We had to get Jill medical attention ASAP. There was no way I could get over there before Kat was gone.

But Valentine could.

Chapter 10: Poor Life Choices

VALENTINE
Paris
September 24th

The quiet moments in my life always turned out to be like a lull between storms. It made it that much harder to enjoy them, knowing that it was only a matter of time before everything went to hell again, but I tried my best.

Unable to sleep, I lay there in bed, staring up at the darkened ceiling, and wondering what would happen next. Ling was asleep next to me. She denied it, but she snored. I thought it was adorable.

Sleeping was the one time she looked at peace. Like me—like so many other people I knew—Ling had just seen too much. I rarely slept for more than five or six hours at a time. Ghosts haunted my dreams, and I saw dead faces almost every night. People I'd watched die, people I'd killed, people I couldn't save, all blurred together, until they were hard to tell apart. I'd lost track of how many people I'd killed. There'd been so many, from the Skinner Brothers back in high school to the Battle of the Crossroads, everywhere I went I left a pile of corpses in my wake.

Some deserved it, others were just fighting for the other side, and some were just in the wrong place at the wrong time. I'd never been religious, but as I stared at that darkened ceiling I wondered if hell was a real place, and if I was truly damned.

Ling stirred and brushed the hair out of her eyes. "Can't sleep?"

"Sorry, I didn't mean to wake you."

She snuggled up close to me, resting her head on my shoulder. "You didn't. You're not the only one who has a hard time sleeping. Just try to relax."

Without any new leads, we had entered one of those dreaded lulls. There was nothing for us to do until we got something new, leaving the team with little to do but wait. Lorenzo was off grasping at straws, but Ariel was monitoring it. She insisted that there might be something worthwhile there, so we just let her do her thing and hoped for a break. Tailor was on standby in case I needed him, but until we had something solid to go on there wasn't anything he could do, either.

"I've just got a bad feeling."

"Are you actually worried about Lorenzo's operation?" Ling asked.

"Maybe a little. I'm more worried about what happens if we fail."

"We won't."

I yawned. Having Ling with me was terribly comforting, and not just because I was curled up with a beautiful, naked woman. She understood what was going through my mind. It was rare enough that I met someone who understood me at all, much less someone I could really relate to. I was damned lucky to have her and I knew it.

"Are you going to fall asleep on me?" Ling asked.

"I might actually get back to sleep, yeah." I yawned again.

"I don't think so," she said. Before I could say anything else she climbed on top of me and kissed me. A moment later she pulled away from our embrace. She looked down into my eyes, her hair hanging in my face, and smiled. "I love you."

It always sounded strange to hear her say that. "I love you, too." I meant it. I loved this woman with all of my heart, and I would do anything for her.

Ling leaned in closer to me, eyes twinkling in the darkness. "You know what I think we should do?"

"Well, that's pretty obvious."

BRRRRRRT.

She sighed. "I think you should answer your phone. It's probably important."

BRRRRRT.

"Goddamn it," I growled. Ling laughed and moved off of me so I could reach whichever of my three phones was vibrating on the nightstand. *BRRRRRRT.* This time it was the one Reaper had given me.

"It's Lorenzo. He must have found something." I tapped the screen and put the phone to my ear. "Go ahead."

"*Valentine!*" Lorenzo was out of breath. Something was wrong. "*We've got a problem!*"

"What's going on?"

"*Jill's been shot.*"

"What?" Ling looked a question at me as I sat up. "Jill has been shot." I spoke into the phone. "What happened? Is she okay?"

"*No, she's not fucking okay!*" Lorenzo snapped. "*She's losing a lot of blood.*"

I put him on speaker phone so Ling could hear. "Where are you? What happened?"

"Reaper is driving us to a doctor. We can't go to a hospital." He said something I couldn't make out, talking to somebody else. *"I fucked up, Valentine, I fucked up. This is all my fault."*

I'd never heard him like this. It was bizarre, hearing Lorenzo on the edge of panic. "Calm down."

"Don't tell me to fucking calm down. Anders shot her."

"Listen—"

"No. You listen. Reaper knows where Kat is right now. She's at the Hotel Gueguen, or at least really close to there."

"Okay, what do you want me to do?"

"Valentine, she has a nuke."

I felt my heart drop into my stomach, and hoped I'd misunderstood him. "I'm sorry, what?"

"She. Has. A. Nuclear. Weapon!"

"At the hotel?"

"No! Fuck, I don't know. I don't know where it is, but she has one. That's what Blue is. They're going to nuke a city!"

"What city?"

"I don't know!" Lorenzo roared. *"Get over there and kill her!"*

Ling had gone to work and had already pulled up the hotel on her phone. She showed me the display. It was a five-star establishment not too far to the northeast of Place de la Concorde. It was a short walk to the Louvre or the Grand Palace from there. The area would be covered in cops.

"Just like that? Just waltz into a hotel and have a shootout in the middle of fucking Paris?"

"Like you haven't done it before!"

"What does he expect you to do?" Ling asked, concern in her voice.

"Alright, alright. Lorenzo, take care of Jill. I'll handle the rest."

"Handle it how? You have to take Kat out."

"Just trust me. Take care of Jill. As soon as he can, have Reaper send me whatever he has on that place. I'll talk to you later." I cut the call before he could say anything else.

"What is it you plan on doing? We can't just rush in there. There are only five of us." Ling didn't count Ariel on a combat op for obvious reasons. "Katarina will have twice that." Ling was right. We didn't know anything about the situation. Going in blind, guns blazing, was a sure to get some of us killed, or all of us caught. "Her security detail was extensive *before* she knew someone was hunting her. Now she expects trouble."

I set down the phone Reaper had given me and picked up the one Tailor had given me. "Yeah, but they won't be expecting *this*."

LORENZO

Reaper had called ahead and woken up his contact, who had agreed to meet us. Before hanging up, Reaper had offered him a whole lot of money to keep his mouth shut. It wasn't like off-the-books doctors were super honest types to begin with. The address he'd been given wasn't a hospital, but a clinic in an immigrant neighborhood, and it had been closed down for the night. Most of the lights were off, but there was a fat, sweaty man, smoking a cigarette by the open back door. When he saw Reaper tear into the parking lot, he wheeled out a gurney.

"What you got?" he asked, with a thick Serbian accent as I got out of the back seat.

"Three gunshot wounds to the abdomen. She's unconscious and lost a lot of blood."

He *tsked* disapprovingly. "Why you bring girl to gunfight? Get her on cart." Reaper ran around to help me, and the two of us, as quickly—but gently—as possible, lifted Jill out. With the cigarette still dangling from his lip, the Serbian wheeled her inside. "Shoot with what? Big bullets? Little bullets?"

I remembered the sudden pattern of holes. "Buckshot." *Fucking Anders.* "From maybe ten yards away, but they punched through a truck door first."

"Is good. Pellets not fragment, but maybe bounce around a little. No problem." He pushed the gurney down the darkened hall and into a small operating room. A man and a woman were already waiting inside, wearing scrubs and masks. The woman's eyes were bleary and red from drinking. The male was probably still a teenager. They took the gurney, lifted the bandages to inspect the damage, and then waited, not doing a damn thing.

Why weren't they working? "Save her."

"Cash first," the fat doctor said. "Then we start."

Before I could say anything, Reaper stepped in. "This is what I've got on me." He held up a thick wad of euros. Reaper slammed the wad down on a stainless steel table. "You know who I am, so you know I'm good for the rest."

The fat face broke into a scowl. "Yah, I know you, Mr. The Reaper, which is why I know who shot this girl probably. The Montalbans already put out call for extra doctors for the men you shot tonight. They have more money than sense, but they will wonder why I did not answer. Which is why you pay extra up front."

I got in his face. So close I could taste the cheap cigarette smoke, and glared into his greedy pig eyes. "If you know who he is, then you can guess who *I am*." I put as much menace as I could in the words, and right then, pissed off and covered in Jill's blood, I had menace to spare.

"You are him?" He looked me over suspiciously, but he wasn't the easily intimidated sort. "I heard infamous Lorenzo was dead."

"You heard wrong. That's my girl. So get your ass to work. Save her and I'll make you rich." It wasn't unusual for off-the-books doctors to double dip, as in get paid to take the bullet out, and then rat out their patient to the people who put the bullet into them in the first place. "Cross me, and they'll be picking pieces of you out of that drain."

Apparently, he believed me. The Serbian nodded toward the other two, and said something in his native language. Despite their shifty appearance, they immediately flew into action, and even appeared to know what they were doing. The fat surgeon went to the sink, spit his cigarette out, and began washing his hands. "For you, Mr. Lorenzo, special price of only double my usual fee for bullet holes. This is good?"

"This is good."

"Then go to waiting room. Drink coffee. Have a smoke. Read magazines. Clean off the blood first. You look like shit. Do not get blood on the couches or I must explain it in morning. I'll save your woman."

"You better." I turned without another word. In a daze, I walked out of the operating room. Reaper asked me where I was going, but I was having a hard time hearing him. I said something about ditching the car. We couldn't have a car with broken windows and bullet holes sitting out in the open parking lot. He tossed me the keys. Then I went and sat in the car, stared at the blood, and punched the steering wheel until my hands hurt, worrying that Jill was going to die, and cursing myself for being powerless to stop it.

I prayed for a chance to murder everyone who'd wronged me. I shouted, and cursed, and slammed my fists against the dash, so incredibly furious and filled with hate that I couldn't even contain it. I'd never wanted to kill anyone that badly before. Until the ringing in my ears got so bad that for just a moment, the briefest of moments, I thought I heard the familiar whispers of Sala Jihan's dungeons.

I stopped. Put my face in my aching hands, and wept.

VALENTINE

The Hotel Gueguen had once been a Directorial-style manor house. According to the info Reaper had just sent me, this small luxury hotel only had five suites, but all of them were currently being rented on the same credit card, which more than likely belonged to a Montalban shell corporation.

The streets were nearly deserted as the dawn began to overtake Paris. It was a cool but lovely morning. Next to the street-level entrance was a small coffee shop, where a few early risers sat drinking the local brew and eating croissants, conversing, or staring at their phones. There were a few tough guys, trying to look inconspicuous. Security men, undoubtedly Kat's. With a ball cap on, I looked like just another tourist. In any case I'd never met Kat. They would be looking for Lorenzo, not for me. I was six inches taller than him, so there was no mistaking us for one another.

This is insane. You are out of your goddamn mind, I told myself. I'd made Ling drop me off a couple blocks away before falling back a safe distance. She was adamantly opposed to my plan, but for once I got her to listen and do as I asked. She had been really angry with me, though. If I somehow lived through this I was going to catch hell from her later.

Actually, all of my Exodus comrades had been angry at me. Once we roused the team, they all thought my plan was stupid. Skunky called it "suicidal," which I thought was melodramatic. In any case, Katarina Montalban apparently had a nuclear weapon. There was no more time to screw around, and it was better to risk just my life. They had decided that I was in charge of this show, so it was my call to make.

The only person who *hadn't* disagreed, surprisingly, was Ariel. But that was mostly because when we'd found her, she'd been staring at a computer screen going through shipping manifests, mumbling about Kat having a nuclear weapon. So it wasn't so much that she was opposed to my plan, but that she was too distracted by potential Armageddon to notice.

When I asked her if she was sure Katarina had a nuke, Ariel swore that she was certain. That was enough for me. This was worth the risk. If I went down, it would be by myself, and Exodus would still have another shot.

My phone buzzed in my pocket, a text message from Tailor. He called my plan stupid, but he still backed my play. He had called in his reinforcements. Now his team was in position and standing by. *Good.* Now there was only one thing left to do.

I bought myself a hot chocolate from the little coffee shop, sat down at one of the tables on the sidewalk, and pulled out a different phone, a prepaid flip phone I'd paid cash for. I paused for a moment, heart racing, and dialed Hawk's old number. It rang, and rang, and rang, and I just let it go. After about twenty rings with no answer, I hung up, and waited. *I hope this works,* I thought to myself. Part of me hoped it didn't.

After about five minutes, the phone buzzed in my hand, a call from a hidden number. My heart was pounding in my chest now. I didn't want to answer it. Taking a deep breath, I flipped it open, and brought it to my ear.

Underhill didn't waste time on pleasantries. *"You evaded me for a year and a half, and now you want to talk?"* He sounded like he was in a moving vehicle, but I couldn't be sure.

"I'm assuming you've triangulated my location and are en route as we speak."

"What's your game, Valentine?" His voice was gravelly and cold. He sounded weary, and he should be, since they'd pulled him out of retirement for me. *"Just go quiet. You try anything stupid and more innocent people will get hurt."*

"I'll save you time trying to zero in on my exact location, old man," I growled. "I'm at a little coffee shop next to the Hotel Gueguen." I didn't bother trying to pronounce the French name correctly. "Staying in that hotel is Katarina Montalban."

"I don't care about some Illuminati harpy. What is it you think you're doing?"

"I know what Project Blue is. You remember, the thing you guys tortured me for months for? I didn't know then, but I know now."

"We can talk about it when I get there."

I gave him a sardonic laugh. "Hard to talk with a bag on my head. Listen to me. There's something bigger going on here than you assholes wanting me dead. Katarina Montalban has a nuclear weapon. I don't know how, I don't know where, and I don't know when she plans to use it, but that woman has a nuke. If you want to stop Project Blue, if you're really so goddamn worried about it, come get me. How far out do you think you are?"

"Just stay where you are and nobody else has to die."

"Right, threatening bluster. Where are you? Will I be waiting long? Should I have another hot chocolate?"

I could tell that Underhill wasn't used to being talked to like that. I knew I was pissing him off, but he kept his cool. *"You just sit tight."*

"Whatever. Look, I'll be waiting for you, with the Montalban woman. Valentine out." I ended the call and snapped the phone in half, dropping it in a trash can as I made my way toward the hotel lobby. I sent Tailor a text: *He's coming.*

Tailor's only response was, *Rgr.*

An Illuminati strike team couldn't do anything to Underhill, and vice versa. For the same reason, Romefeller wouldn't let Tailor and his team simply grab Katarina Montalban. I had kind of assumed that shadowy organizations operating above the law wouldn't have so much bureaucratic red tape to deal with, but that's what you get for making assumptions. These people took their gentlemen's agreements seriously. In any case, Underhill might not care about Katarina Montalban, but her guys would probably start shooting the moment Underhill showed up, especially since they were paranoid that Lorenzo was gunning for them. If this worked, I'd take out both of them in one move, and I might even get out alive.

If it didn't? Well, I told Ling I loved her and said goodbye. It was about all I could do. I even left my custom .44 Magnum with her. My lucky charm had seen me through countless bad days, but not today. If the worst happened, I didn't want Underhill taking it as a damned trophy.

I was unarmed. There was no way they'd let me get close to Kat with a gun on me, and having a gun wouldn't matter when I was this badly outnumbered. The chances of this working were slim. Ling was right: it was stupid, but somebody had to do something. Better me alone than everyone. I thought about how anguished Lorenzo had sounded with Jill bleeding in his arms. I'd done that once with Sarah. I'd be damned if I was going to do it with Ling.

The small reception area of the hotel was ornately furnished, including a sitting area with plush furniture. Two guys, also trying to look nondescript, watched me over their newspapers as I walked in the front door. The newspapers weren't for reading, they were for hiding the guns on their laps. I smiled at them but didn't say anything as I made my way to the reception desk.

"Good morning, Monsieur," the woman behind the desk said. She was a pretty thing, wearing a tight dress, her hair done up in a bun. I must look American, because she spoke English to me. "I am so sorry, but we are completely booked at the moment. I can direct you to other hotels in the area if you are looking for a place to stay."

"Thank you, darlin', but I'm not looking for a room. I probably couldn't afford it anyway. I'm here to speak to one of your guests."

That certainly got the security guys' attention. The receptionist didn't seem to notice the change in the wind, and was oblivious to the fact that a gunfight could break out any second. "I see, but, I cannot disclose who is staying here. We value our guests' privacy."

"Could you send Katarina Montalban a message for me? Tell her that I know where Lorenzo is."

"Monsieur?" The receptionist seemed confused. The two security men both stood up, and the woman behind the desk got very nervous.

"It'll be okay, I promise," I said reassuringly. I stopped her before she could pick up the phone. "I think you should deliver the message in person." If they were going to just blast me, she really didn't need to see that. I could see them in the mirror. Both were staring me down, and one was on his phone, but neither approached.

She nodded at me slowly, then stepped back from her desk. "*Oui.* I will go knock on her door. Please, ah, wait a moment." Her shoes clicked on the floor as she hurried out of the room.

One of the goons, a muscular man with blonde hair cropped into a flat top, walked over to the main entrance and locked the door. The other, a short, skinny fellow with long hair, remained staring. Neither one was bothering to hide the pistols in their hands.

My heart rate slowed, and the anxiety receded. I felt the muscles in my face relax as *the Calm* washed over me. I didn't want to die, but I was prepared to.

"Nice morning, huh?"

They looked at each other and blinked. The long-haired man stepped toward me.

"Relax." I raised my hands to show they were empty. "I'm here to talk to your boss about the guy trying to kill her. She'll be mighty pissed if you do something stupid and she doesn't get that information."

"Indeed I would be."

I heard multiple people coming down the marble stairs behind me, including the distinctive sound of a woman in high heeled shoes. I turned around. A woman in a white dress stood on the stairs. With her were four armed men, guns all drawn.

"I do not like people interrupting my breakfast; however, I am *very* interested in where Lorenzo is." Katarina Montalban was blond and could've been a supermodel ten years ago. She had a little bit of a Swiss accent, and a smoky voice that put sex line operators to shame. "If you are wasting my time, I will be most upset."

"Right. I'm just here to talk. I'm unarmed. I'm not trying to start anything."

She nodded and the two lobby guards grabbed me and roughly patted me down, not being shy about getting all up in my nooks and crannies. Katarina Montalban slinked down the stairs. Once they were done with the search, they still held onto my arms.

"Now, that's better," she purred, stepping close to me. "Who are you?"

"Michael Valentine."

She tilted her head, a little taken back. "It must be the real you. Only a fool would come here claiming the name of the man who murdered my older brother. How did you find me, Michael Valentine?"

"It's a long story."

"Do not worry, you will tell it. Because I need to know which of my men needs to have his tongue cut off for talking too much." Her guards shared nervous glances. Apparently that wasn't a bluff. She sensually ran a fingernail down the side of my face. I could smell her perfume, and her sleeveless dress was both tight and low cut. Who the hell dressed like that before six in the morning?

Lorenzo had warned me about his ex-girlfriend. She was frighteningly intelligent, but loved when men just assumed she was some dumb sex bomb. Everything about her was a weapon, including her looks and her charm. She could go from flirting to murder in seconds. He swore that she'd had good qualities once, but I didn't particularly believe him.

"But first, tell me, how do you know Lorenzo, and where is he hiding? I miss him. I want to see him again."

I glanced at a clock on the wall behind her, then looked Kat in her cold blue eyes. Her features were lovely, her lips were full and pouty, her makeup was perfect, but her eyes were dead. She had the eyes of a killer. "It's . . . complicated. But I can tell you what you want to know."

She ran a hand down my chest, to my pants, and rested it on my crotch. Even though *the Calm,* I winced a little as she grabbed my junk and squeezed. "I should hope so, or I will cut your cock off and fuck you with it." She let go, smiling again. "Now, you may talk as I finish my breakfast."

My survival depended on my ability to bullshit a manipulative psychopath for a while, until another psychopath showed up to arrest me. Not for the first time, I found myself questioning my life choices.

"And that's how it happened," I explained. "Lorenzo took off on his own and left us to die. He's a fucking coward, and I hope you skin him alive." I was sitting in a very plush chair in Katarina Montalban's hotel room, which was probably the nicest hotel room I had ever seen. She sat on her giant bed, her long legs crossed, daintily picking at a bowl of fruit. There were four armed men in the room with us, and none of them looked happy I was there.

"Mm," she said. "That does sound like my Lorenzo. He was never one for commitment."

Yeah, I simply couldn't *imagine* why Lorenzo hadn't put a ring on that finger.

"But, Michael, I find myself curious . . . why would an Exodus operative come to me, all things considered?"

"I'm not an Exodus operative." That much was true. I had never officially joined. "I'm an independent contractor. I go where the money is, and they offered a lot of money for my expertise. I had worked with them before, in Mexico."

"Anders told me of your involvement in Zubara as well. He also told me should I ever have the opportunity, to just kill you. He said you are most troublesome."

"You can tell Anders to go fuck himself. I still owe him a bullet to the face." That was also true. Lying is easier when you're sincere about it. "I'm not here because I want to be your friend, lady. I'm here because Lorenzo took off and left my team to die in the snow. I'm the only one who made it back. I've wanted payback ever since."

"I don't recall seeing you at Sala Jihan's fortress," she said coolly, leaning in a little.

Truth be told I had never been inside Sala Jihan's fortress. I was on the other side of the valley, at the dam, during the battle, but I had been briefed on what happened well enough to lie about it, convincingly. "I remember you," I said, ice in my voice. "I remember you taking off in that big fucking helicopter and leaving us to die."

She smiled a hateful little smile, like abandoning a bunch of brave men and women to die at the hands of a bunch of fanatics was amusing. "Indeed. So tell me why you're so concerned with Lorenzo, and not concerned with me? After all, you would not have been stranded on that mountain except for me. I would hate for you to harbor such vengeful feelings toward me." She popped a grape into her mouth. "Perhaps I should just have my men shoot you now?"

"You want to know the truth? I can't do anything to you. I never trusted you. I advised them to leave you out of the operation. You did exactly what I thought you were going to do. I *trusted* Lorenzo. I trusted him and six men died because of it. So no, he doesn't get to escape Sala Jihan's mines and live his life while my friends are still buried there. He doesn't get that." I took a deep breath. "Besides, I figure that when you try to kill him, there's about a fifty-fifty chance he'll kill you in the process. Either way, I win."

Had I not still been under the influence of *the Calm*, Katarina's glare may have been intimidating. Even still it was unsettling. After a moment, the mask went back on, and she looked much more pleasant. "I see. I must say, Michael, I appreciate your candor. I'm . . . unused to people being so casually blunt with me. I daresay it's refreshing."

"I don't deny that I'm the one who shot Rafael, either."

She barely reacted to that, like I'd just said I was the one who ate the last donut. "So Anders said. I never thought much of that stuffy fool."

It was the death of Rafael at my hand, and Eduard at Lorenzo's, which had put Katarina into her current position of power. Ultimately, whatever she did, it was on our heads.

"So you screwed me over at the Crossroads, sure, but I screwed you over first. The way I see it, we're even. And I'll give you Lorenzo in exchange for a small fee. He's in Paris, and I know where he's been staying. I don't know what happened to him in Jihan's mines, but he's sloppy now. He's not as good as he thinks he is. I was able to track him down."

Katarina cocked her head slightly to one side. "Why not just go after him yourself, if you're so certain?"

"Because I'm one guy with a couple of friends who do intelligence stuff. He's still dangerous, and I'm pretty sure he has a crew with him. Besides, I can risk getting killed doing it myself, or I can bring it to you and have it done for me, and maybe make a little bit of money in the process."

One of her guards stepped out and took a phone call, but the Montalban woman ignored him and continued to focus on me. "How much is *a little bit of money*?"

"Two million Euros sound good to you?"

Katarina sat back a little bit, looking perplexed. "Is that all?"

"Lady, I'm pushing my luck enough just coming here, and I'm under no illusions that this Cruella de Vil bit is just an act. You have a reputation. It'd be stupid to get greedy. I figure you're a billionaire, so this won't be a big deal for you. It's plenty for me to go retire someplace. I can't go back to the States. Your buddy Anders' old crew is still looking for me."

"You know I could just *make you* tell me."

"I know. But torturing people takes time. We both know Lorenzo won't stay in one place for long. You hand me the cash, I give you his location, and nobody has to get their hands dirty or waste any time." *Underhill, where the hell are you?* "In any case, if I don't walk out of this hotel, alive, and with all my bits and pieces right where they're supposed to be, my friends will tip off Lorenzo and you'll never catch him. I may be crazy, but I'm not stupid."

That actually made her smile. On some level, I think my brashness impressed her. "You have placed me in such a predicament, Michael! Honestly, at first I was just going to kill you. I could not stand Rafael, as he was always daddy's favorite, and standing in my way, but it would be awful for me to let such an insult to my family name pass unchallenged. But giving me Lorenzo inclines me to like you."

"Thanks?"

"The money means nothing to me. That's done. Now . . ." The security man who'd taken the phone call approached. He whispered something in her ear about a problem outside. Underhill's forces must have arrived. "I see." She looked back at me with a glare that could freeze boiling water.

"What's going on?"

"Just what do you think you're doing?"

The Calm pushed that all to the background. I had to fake looking scared. "I don't know what you're talking about."

"I'm talking about the Majestic strike team that is currently surrounding this hotel." She got off the bed, kicked off her heels, opened the closet door, and went inside. "Inform the Americans that I'm inside, and that if they do not want an incident, they should pull back. The council will not stand for overt action."

"Ma'am," the guard said as he went to the window and peeked through the blinds, "we should get you to the garage—"

"In a moment." She came out of the closet holding a really big knife with a wickedly curved blade, and she looked really comfortable with it. "Now where were we, Michael? Oh yes, you were about to tell me where Lorenzo is, and I was deciding how painful your death is going to be."

"I thought we had a deal."

"That was before you brought Majestic to my doors."

Underhill was here, and Katarina was done screwing around, but so was I. "I know about Blue. What do you think you're going to accomplish?"

"World domination." She answered without exaggeration. "But that answers my question. Painful then."

"Ma'am," the man with the phone said. "They say they only want Valentine."

"Did they specify if he needs to be in one piece? Because that is looking exceedingly unlikely right now. You know what, never mind. The Americans can go to hell. They can have him when I'm done. Where is Lor—"

Before she could finish, a window shattered, and a metal can spewing smoke landed on the floor. My eyes immediately began burning. *Tear gas.* I had guessed right about the Bloodhound. He wasn't big on diplomacy.

The Calm helped me focus through the water in my eyes and fire in my lungs. It was a frustrating state, where I could think and process everything so much faster than my body could react, but everyone else seemed so much slower. They were coughing and partially blinded. Kat was too far, so I lunged at the closest security man. He wasn't ready for it. I was on top of him in a flash, and I was bigger than he was. We both went down, rolling across the floor. He had a death grip on his pistol. So I bit down hard on his hand. The hot, coppery taste of blood filled my mouth as he thrashed. He shouted a warning as I got control of his pistol, stuck it under his chin, and pulled the trigger.

BLAM!

Blood and brains stained the carpet. I rolled off the dead man, and stuck the gun—a Steyr M9—out in both hands and shot the nearest of Kat's guards four times before he could get a shot off. The other two bodyguards were dragging Katarina Montalban from the room. I turned and opened fire just as they shoved her through the door. I cut one of them down and wounded the other, but Katarina was gone.

She won't get far. Gunfire erupted from the lobby. The Montalban guards were in a firefight with Underhill's men. It was only a matter of time before somebody won, and whoever won would kill me. I didn't have a lot of time. I ran after Katarina.

The wounded bodyguard was waiting for me. I came out of the smoke shooting, and dropped him. But where had Kat—

She crashed into me, trying to stab me in the chest. Rather than fleeing, she had moved to the side to ambush me. I narrowly avoided the blade as I twisted my gun toward her body. Her blade struck the pistol and traveled toward my hand. I lost my weapon but managed to keep my fingers. Though partially blinded, Kat swung hard for my throat. I dodged it by an inch and she embedded the knife deep into the door frame.

I tripped over the dead man in the doorway and fell to the floor. She was on me in an instant, enraged, seemingly oblivious to the gun battle going on downstairs and the room full of tear gas. She kicked me on the side of the head. The impact of her bare heel almost made me black out. She went to kick me again, but I grabbed her ankle. She fell on top of me, fighting like a wild animal. Her nails tore down my cheeks, then she jammed her thumbs into my throat, trying to crush my windpipe.

"You can't stop me! It's mine! It's all supposed to be mine!"

Katarina was vicious, but I was a whole lot bigger than she was. She was losing her mind with rage, and I was *Calm*. She was frothing, snot leaking from her nose, spittle shooting from between clenched teeth as she tried to choke the life out of me. I slugged her.

She let go, dazed. I hurled her off me so hard she bounced off the wall. I didn't give her any time to recover. This time, my hands clamped around *her* pretty throat, and I squeezed. She thrashed, and kicked, and tried to scratch my eyes out, but I squeezed and squeezed. She turned red. Her eyes looked like they were about to pop out of her head. Everything started to go dark around me as I focused on choking the life out of this horrible woman. I saw Dr. Silvers' face for a moment, but this time I didn't let up. I shook off the image and squeezed. Katarina Montalban was going to die.

Then someone kicked me off of her, pulled a bag over my head, and dragged me away.

When they pulled the bag off of my head, I wondered if it was because my captors wanted to gloat, but Underhill didn't even look smug. This was just another day at work for him. We sat facing each other in the back of a big panel van, speeding along, just the two of us. His face was unreadable. He was an unassuming man in his sixties. His hair had thinned out, and his face had the hard lines of someone who drank too much. He had a thick neck and muscular features, staying in shape despite his age. His wide chin and cold eyes made him look like a TV show's idea of a mafia hit man, except he was dressed in a blue windbreaker and slacks. He could have been somebody's grandpa.

There were empty bench seats along each side of the back. I was handcuffed, my wrists were chained to my ankles, and my ankles were chained to the floor. I certainly wasn't going anywhere.

"Took you long enough."

Underhill was silent.

I was undeterred. "Did you kill Katarina Montalban?"

He just stared at me.

"Damn it." My plan had failed. I was a fool. "I was hoping you'd kill her. Either that or that she'd kill you. If you'd have waited one more goddamn minute, I'd have choked the life out of that psychotic bitch and saved us all a lot of trouble."

He finally spoke, in that same rough voice I remembered from our phone conversations. "I couldn't let you do that once I was involved. It's against the rules."

The Calm was gone, and my temper flared. "Man, *fuck your rules!* Do you know what that woman is going to do? She's going to use a *nuclear weapon!* She's the one who is going to execute Project Blue, the thing you assholes have been so worried about for the past two years, and you *let her get away!* Do you have any idea how royally, how totally, you screwed this up? Jesus Christ, Anders is working for her! I know damned well you're looking for him, too!"

Underhill raised an eyebrow at the mention of Anders' name. "I'll be sure to pass that on. The rest of it is not my problem. My orders are to bring you in, not start a war. The rhyme and reason aren't for me to decide."

"You stupid asshole! Project Blue *is* the reason! It's the reason you people tortured me for months! It's the reason you're looking for me!"

"Not the only reason. You made some bad choices. Now you got to answer for them."

"Will you spare me your folksy homespun wisdom bullshit? I know who you are, and I know what you do. You shot an unarmed man down in cold blood."

"Your pal, Hawk. Sure, I did. I'd do it again, if I had to. You'd have done the same thing in my place. You have. I read your file. You're a killer, just like me. If you hadn't been stupid, you'd be me in thirty years. None of us are clean, kid. It's just a matter of who we work for."

I jerked at the chains binding my wrists to my ankles. "Yeah, well, we all have to answer for our choices, don't we? And believe me, you're going to answer for yours, too."

"No shit." He shook his head slightly. "You think you got it all figured out, don't you? Boy, you don't know a goddamn thing about me. Your old friend Hunter? I was fighting communists with him before you were born, you jumped-up little shit. We protected our country so regular folks could live their pointless, mundane lives without worrying when the Soviet missiles were coming. The enemy changed, but we stuck around. We did the dirty work that kept most of the world clean."

I stared back at him as the van rolled through the streets of Paris. "I'm sure that's what they told you, old timer. You ever think that maybe they were lying to you? All they do is lie. They'll tell you whatever they want you to hear to get you to do what they want. You were protecting America from communists; well, guess what? The Berlin Wall came down and you assholes had nothing to do with it. The only thing you fought for was to keep your bosses in power."

To my shock, Underhill actually laughed. A brief, sardonic chuckle, but before that I didn't think the man could smile lest he crack his face. "Everything you know about the fall of communism is the story we wanted you all to hear. People would accept that rah-rah-America bullshit, that optimism or patriotism, or economics, or whatever brought the Soviets down. You know what really brought them down? Us. Guys like me and Hunter. Years, decades of planning, of covert action, of infiltration, assassination, and sabotage. You know how many men we lost over the years? How many people we killed?"

"You're taking credit for the CIA's work now?"

"The CIA is a joke." Underhill scowled. "After the sixties they lost their nerve, so we stopped working with them. Our leadership had no balls, but some of us kept on doing what we needed to do. Not every politician is a pussy. Those backed us in secret. We put together our own outfit behind the scenes, black budgets, all the best intel, no babysitters, and it grew from there. Since you didn't grow up speaking Russian you should thank God every day we did what we had to do. Presidents come and go, administrations change, people are stupid, and voters are fickle, but we're there behind the scenes no matter what, making sure the shit that needs to get done, gets done."

"Thanks for the Majestic history lesson."

"Majestic?" He snorted. "Whatever you want to call us, the world is fucked up, but we're there to keep it on track. When we do our job right, nobody even knows we exist, and people go on living."

Underhill sounded just like Romefeller. They were opposite sides of the same megalomaniacal coin. "Funny, I heard damn near the same exact thing from the guys Blue was designed to destroy. What's your point?"

"The point is, kid, that nuclear war that all the expert analysts, all the supercomputers, all the data said was almost inevitable? Never happened. Red China, rising to be the next superpower after the fall of the Soviet Union? Never happened. Communism is dead. It's preached in college campuses, but only four countries in the entire world claim to be communist. You think you know about us, about how we do business, about what we fight for? You don't know a goddamn thing. You had your chance to be on this team and you threw it away. Now you're going in a hole so deep you'll never see the sun again."

I laughed at him. "You tried that already."

He shrugged, then leaned back in his seat. "Silvers was sloppy. Nobody's going to make you a science project this time. Nobody will know what happened to you. Your survival now depends entirely on your cooperation."

My chains jerked taut as anger pulsed through my body. "*Cooperation?* Motherfucker, I *handed you* the woman executing Project Blue, with the help of Anders, and you *let her go!* What the fuck else do you want from me?"

"Not for me to decide. Your statements regarding Project Blue, the Montalban woman, Anders, all of it, will be vetted and if they're determined to be genuine, followed up on. You might be lying, or you might just be wrong. Ever consider that, that maybe you don't have it all figured out, smart guy? Of course you didn't. You're a damned fool."

"When a nuke goes off in some city somewhere, it'll be on you. Your bosses will be looking for a scapegoat to hang, so I expect I'll see you in the cell next door in whatever hole you're sending me to."

Underhill shrugged again. "We'll see."

I was at a loss for words. I slumped back in my seat, jingling my chains. "I have to piss."

"Go ahead. I'm not the one who has to clean this thing."

The driver of the van looked at me in the rearview mirror, but didn't say anything. He turned his attention back to the road. I glared at Underhill, trying to read his face, but he was unflappable. He stared at me blankly. I hated him for killing Hawk. I wanted to wrap my chains around his neck and throttle him until his eyes popped out, but I could tell it really hadn't been anything personal. It was like being mad at an attack dog for biting when commanded. He was a professional, and he was just doing what he was trained to do. He clearly felt no remorse, but I doubt he took any pleasure in it either. To a man like him, killing was just work to be done.

To men like us.

Was I really so different? Did I really have the right to hate someone for taking a life, at this point, or was I just a self-righteous hypocrite?

CRASH!

There was a spine-jarring impact. Metal crumpled and glass shattered. Underhill wasn't wearing a seatbelt. He seemed to float in space for a moment, looking slightly surprised, but that was it, and then the van was rolling over. We landed on our side, grinding to a halt.

I must have gone out for a moment. When I opened my eyes, the van was still and filled with dust. Hanging there from my chains, I was listening to the sound of metal twisting and squealing in protest. The back doors were being pried open.

Underhill was lying there, blinking, just out of my reach. He grimaced in pain as he sat up, and drew a government model .45 from under his windbreaker. He aimed it at my head and waited. Daylight flooded the sideways interior of the van as they broke the doors open. Men in tactical gear and masks stormed in, hunched over, weapons ready. Three laser dots appeared on Underhill's chest, but he stayed where he was, his face as unreadable as before.

One of the masked men spoke. It was Tailor. "By order of the Council of the Thirteen Families, Michael Valentine is under our protection. He's coming with us. Any interference on your part will be considered a hostile act and a violation of our organizations' agreement."

"You're not taking him," Underhill said calmly.

"Tailor, shoot him!" I screamed, still dangling, chained to the bench seat, Underhill's .45 pointed at my face. "Shoot this asshole! He killed Hawk! Shoot him!"

"Shut up, Val," Tailor said angrily. "Let me handle this."

"This man is my prisoner," Underhill stated plainly. "You can't take him."

"You're in our territory now, buddy. You being here at all is a violation of the rules and you damned well know it. Now pack up your shit and get the hell out of Europe. You have no business here."

Underhill's finger was on the trigger and I was staring down the barrel of a .45. "Valentine is my business, and you Illuminati fucks aren't taking him. Shoot me and there will be hell to pay."

"Tailor, just fucking shoot him!" I screamed again.

"Val, shut your damned mouth!" he snapped back. Sirens wailed in the background. "Time's running out, Underhill. My team? We've got proper Interpol Special Enforcement Operations IDs and the best lawyers in the country. My boss says one word and the French government says thank you very much. You guys are a bunch of trigger-happy Americans on temporary visas, with CIA creds, who just shot up a hotel in the capital of France. You wanna try me? Walk away right now, or rot in a French prison for the next thirty years. I guarantee your superiors will just disavow your ass, and have you shivved if you cut a deal. You know how they work better than I do."

Underhill mulled that over for a moment. He was stuck. It was surrender or shoot me. Underhill wasn't suicidal. He was a professional. The old killer took a deep breath, safetied his pistol, and put it down. "Fine. We'll do it your way for now." One of the Frenchmen grabbed Underhill by the sleeve and dragged him out. He gave me that same blank stare as he went past. It told me that he wasn't done with me.

"That man killed Hawk!"

"I know, Val, I know. I'm sorry, buddy. I don't have a choice." Another operative, fully kitted up with a slung shotgun, handed Tailor a pair of bolt cutters. The sirens were right on top of us. Tailor spoke to one of his teammates. "Claude! Talk to the police, keep them off our backs. Don't worry, Val. I'll get you someplace safe and explain everything."

I hung there, head throbbing, as Tailor cut me free.

Chapter 11: A Force for Good

VALENTINE

Ancient secret societies sure know how to keep a guy waiting. It had been hours since Tailor and his team had rescued me from Underhill. I was dragged out of one van and stuffed into another, rushed off as Tailor's men worked it out with local authorities. It turned out that Tailor's credentials had a lot more official backing than he'd originally let on, or Romefeller had a lot of officials under his thumb.

From the back of a windowless van, I had no way of knowing where they'd taken me. When we stopped, I got out in a high-security, underground parking garage. I was whisked inside and brought to what looked like the building's security office. I wasn't a prisoner, exactly, but the security guards kept telling me to sit down and wait in broken English. I was looked at by a medic or a doctor—I'm not sure, he didn't speak English—had bandages applied to my surprisingly minor injuries, took a bunch of Tylenol, and was left to wait.

So wait I did, for what seemed like forever. I sat in an uncomfortable plastic chair, sipping water from a paper cup, wondering what in the hell was taking Tailor so long. I was getting frustrated. Katarina Montalban had a nuclear weapon, and God only knew what she planned to do with it. I hadn't been able to contact Ling and let her know I was okay, and she was probably going crazy by now. This was no time to be screwing around. I got up and started to pace around, much to the annoyance of the security guards watching over me, but to hell with them.

I looked up when an elevator chimed. Tailor and two of his men stepped into the security office. One of Tailor's men spoke with one of the guards briefly, in French, before I was waved over.

"Sorry that took so long, Val." Tailor had removed his armor; his black combat shirt was still damp with sweat. "There is so much bureaucratic bullshit in this organization that I don't know how they get anything done. Come on, you're going to talk to the boss man again."

I followed Tailor into the elevator, noting quietly that his two men were still wearing armor and still carrying submachine guns. "Are they here to make sure I don't make a run for it?"

"Dude, shut up. I've had enough of your self-righteous bullshit," Tailor spat. He hit the button, and the door closed, leaving his men behind. We started going up.

"None of this would be happening if we'd just shot the psycho and been done with it!"

"Goddamn it, Val, it doesn't work like that!"

I wasn't in any mood for his excuses. "That guy that had me? That was Underhill. He killed Hawk in cold blood, and you just let him go."

Frustrated, Tailor reached over and hit the hold button. We were going to have this out in private. "You think I don't know that? I can't just go around killing whoever I want, Val!"

"When Katarina Montalban blows up a city, I hope it's Paris, so you, and Romefeller, and all of you Illuminati assholes can die thinking 'man, I'm so glad I stuck to those rules!' *She's* not following your rules."

"No, but Underhill is. And that's the only reason you're still alive. You're welcome, by the way. This whole thing was stupid. I told you it was stupid, and you just wouldn't listen."

"What would you have me do, Tailor? Pass up a chance to put a stop to this? If that woman goes through with Project Blue, a lot of people are going to die!"

"Would you listen to yourself, Val? Christ, you sound like one of your Exodus buddies. You can't save the world if you're fucking dead, alright? That wasn't just stupid, it was suicidal."

"Some things are worth dying for, Tailor."

He laughed at me. "Holy shit, Ling has done a number on you. She's got you wrapped right around her little finger, doesn't she?"

"No." That was crap, and it made me want to punch him in his mouth.

"All this hero bullshit is going to do is get you killed. It's not going to change anything, and it's not going to save anybody."

"Hero thing? And what, your way is better? You traded in the dirt and the blood for some civilization, you cleaned up and got a suit, but you're still doing the same damned thing, pulling triggers for money. I'm not a hero, but I'm not just going to sit by and let a psychopath blow up a city."

"Neither am I!" Tailor shouted. "For fuck's sake, Val, I'm on your side here! I'm trying to help you!"

"You had the chance to help and you walked away, because you're more worried about your cushy job and your stupid rules than you are about doing the right thing. I thought you changed, but you haven't. As long as you've got yours, you'll watch the world burn down."

To my surprise, Tailor wheeled around, grabbed me by my shirt, and slammed me against the wall, hard enough to shake the whole elevator. "You don't know a fucking thing!" I don't think I'd ever seen him that angry. "I've been risking my ass for you, for this pet project of yours. I risked my life, and the lives of my men, saving you back there. Not only could you have gotten yourself killed, but you could have gotten me killed too, but I went along with it anyway because I *am trying to help you*. What the hell did you *think* was going to happen?"

"Let go and back off," I ordered.

Reluctantly, he did, but he stuck an angry finger in my face. "I told you this wouldn't work, but you were so ready to be the hero that you just wouldn't listen. Tell me straight, man, no bullshit. Did Ling put you up to this? This is the kind of shit Exodus would do."

Anger pulsed through me, but I kept it in check. "No. She thought it was stupid and would get me killed too."

"Well, you're just a brain genius then, ain't you?"

"I never claimed to be smart, man. I'm just trying to do the right thing. I'm sick and tired of everybody sitting around, wringing their hands, saying there's nothing they can do. Well, I'm doing something."

People say violence never solves anything, but that's a lie they tell school kids to try to stop them from fighting. Violence solves everything, if applied correctly. Whatever the problem, if you shoot enough people, it will go away. It's just a question of logistics, time, and maintaining the resolve to keep bringing the violence to bear for as long as necessary.

"Look," Tailor said, more quietly this time, "I told you, it frustrates me too. I need you to trust me here, okay? Believe me, I was hoping this scheme of yours would work. If it had, if Underhill had gone in and actually killed Katarina, then I could've put him in the dirt for violating détente. We could have killed two birds with one stone. Those are the limitations we have to abide by, whether we like them or not."

"*You* have to abide by," I corrected.

"Listen, don't cop this attitude with Romefeller, okay? Can you be cool?"

"Yeah. I'm cool."

Tailor collected himself, nodded, then pushed the button. The elevator started moving again.

"Did you tell your boss about Katarina's plans?"

"I told him what you told me. I didn't tell him that I knew you were going in there as bait. I have to cover my ass. So don't volunteer that shit, please." The elevator chimed again as we reached our destination level. "Take a deep breath and explain what happened, calmly. He doesn't respond well to people getting all huffy. You stomping around like a teenage drama queen isn't going to get this done any sooner. Okay?"

"Fine," I said, as the elevator doors opened. "But we are running out of time."

I found Romefeller waiting for me in an office that was just as ornate, if rather smaller, than his one in Zurich. We were on the twelfth floor, and his office afforded a good view of the city. He was leaning on the glass, gazing out across Paris. The Eiffel Tower cut its iconic image in Paris' skyline. It was a beautiful day, the sun was shining, and a secret society was mad at me.

"That was a bold, brazen, but foolhardy act, young man," Alistair Romefeller said as he turned around. Today he was wearing a charcoal gray suit with a red vest, and he did not look happy. He saw Tailor, and dismissed him with a nod, like he was a butler or something. Tailor left without a word. "If I had known that your plan was to go in there and murder her, I would never have sanctioned it."

"The plan was to let Majestic do it for me. It didn't work out."

"You've made the situation worse. Now you've tipped your hand, and she'll be that much more careful in future. Do you realize what you've done?"

I wasn't sure if he was actually mad that I'd made the situation worse, or if it was just sour grapes because I had the gall to violate their precious rules. "I improvised."

Romefeller groaned, and ran his fingers through his silver hair. "And now Underhill is here, confined to his embassy. He is a relic from another era, when both Majestic and my associates were more willing to engage in, how would you say, direct action. If they dug up that Cold War dinosaur for your sake, you must have really, really gotten on someone's bad side."

"It was a string of unfortunate coincidences." I shrugged. "Most of the time I was simply along for the ride. That doesn't matter now though. I know what Blue is."

"I heard from Mr. Tailor. How confident are you in your assessment that the Montalbans have such a weapon?"

He was being mighty goddamned nonchalant about it. "The assessment that psychopath has an atomic bomb? Pretty good. What part of that doesn't scare the crap out of you?"

"How did you come by this information, exactly?" he asked, skeptically. "That's a serious charge."

Is he for real right now? "What difference does it make? Hell, even if I'm wrong, don't you think it's at least worth looking into? Why in the hell do you think I would go in there, risking my life, trying to kill that woman? If there's even a chance—"

Romefeller raised a hand, silencing me. "Mr. Valentine, listen to me. I don't doubt that you believe that what you say is true, but I can't very well level such a charge at one of my peers going on just your word. You keep talking about how she is crazy and dangerous, but think of how this looks from the outside. You're the one who tried to murder her."

My eyes narrowed, but I didn't say anything.

"I suspect I know where you got that information. I would urge you not to trust Mr. Lorenzo so much. He may be playing the role of your ally now, but his reputation is well known. I assure you it is only an act. The only thing motivating him is a personal vendetta against the Montalban family, and it looks to me like he tried to use you to carry out his revenge fantasy for him."

"How did you know?"

"About Lorenzo? I have my sources. After an event last night at a truck depot, Mr. Anders is not only convinced that Lorenzo is alive, but has put out a bounty on him. Minutes later, you were sent on a this fool's errand."

"Doesn't it bother you that a guy who was once the sworn enemy of your organization is now advising one of your members? Anders doesn't raise any red flags up in your little clubhouse or whatever?"

Romefeller actually chuckled at me, as if I were a child who had just said something adorably naïve. "We operate in a complex world of shifting shadows and temporary alliances. Allegiances change. People aren't chess pieces. They can change sides, move around as it benefits them. Men such as Mr. Tailor. You can't see the big picture, from where you sit, but you should be grateful for our liberal attitude concerning the matter. Otherwise, we would have placed a price on your head for having killed one of our members, much like the substantial one that is being offered for Lorenzo."

I raised an eyebrow. "How substantial?" *Just out of curiosity.*

"Ten million U.S. dollars, and another ten million for you."

"What?"

"You can't be surprised. Considering what just transpired between you and Katarina it should not come as a shock that she just put out the same offer for your head. You went in there, announced who you are, and then tried to strangle her. That's rather insulting. The optics are bad, as they say."

"I got the same price as Lorenzo, huh?" *That'll piss him off.* I smiled.

"You needn't worry about it, though. You're still under my protection, as I believe you're still useful to me." In other words, Romefeller was suggesting that our *friendship* was the only thing keeping me alive. "It would be ironic if you are in this situation because Lorenzo lied to you."

Lorenzo may be wrong, but I trusted Ariel. "I got an independent confirmation of the data."

"Interesting. My sources suggest that Exodus has an exceedingly brilliant intelligence analyst. The mind boggles at what someone with my resources could accomplish with such a mind in my employ. She wouldn't happen to be involved in this confirmation, would she?"

I didn't like that somebody like Romefeller knew that Ariel existed, let alone that his sources were good enough that he knew she was female. I could tell he was fishing for information, but I wasn't going to give him anything. I used a different tactic instead. "You know how I know she's got a nuke, how I really know?"

Romefeller didn't answer.

"Because I helped her *get it.*"

That got his attention. "I'm sorry?" he said. "Did I hear you correctly?"

"I didn't have any reason to think about it until last night. One of our missions during Project Heartbreaker, we left Zubara and landed in Yemen, where we intercepted a stolen Russian ICBM warhead that was being delivered to General Al Saba's forces. Anders led the mission, and after letting one of my teammates bleed to death, took charge of the warhead and took it Christ-only-knows where. Do the math. You think Anders' involvement in all of this is just a coincidence?"

I could see the realization in Romefeller's eyes, but he kept his composure. "I . . . see," he managed.

"No kidding. Now you guys need to quit dancing around and commit."

"It doesn't work like that, I'm afraid."

"Are you serious right now? You people keep telling me it doesn't work like this, or it doesn't work like that. You dither and let innocent people die, because you're too polite to violate Robert's Rules of Order? You put on this big show about how you're trying to guide the world, but you act like a pompous model UN club. Tailor gave me a big spiel about how you all are working so hard to maintain peace and order, but when it gets down to it, you're too chickenshit to do anything without voting on it first!"

"Enough!" Romefeller roared. It was strange, hearing a man like him raise his voice. I could tell he was normally too dignified for that sort of thing. "Overt action would lead to family on family violence. If you're so concerned with innocent lives, tell me, how many people will die in the crossfire when my men have a gun battle with hers in the streets of every city in Europe?"

"A lot less than if that bomb goes off."

"Perhaps, but then what? Do you know for sure that taking her into custody will stop this from happening? Do you know where this hypothetical bomb is?"

I didn't.

"I thought as much," Romefeller said, smugly. He moved in closer. "I understand your position, and I'm not dismissing you. I can only imagine what it must be like for you, having helped recover that weapon, only to find out that it may be used for some terrible purpose. I can see how weary you are. I understand the impulse to make things right."

I rather doubted he understood any of my impulses. "Alert the authorities and tell them there's a rogue warhead on French soil. That will get their attention. They'll listen to someone like you."

"Perhaps, perhaps not. She has as many politicians on her payroll as I do on mine. It all comes back to your word and Mr. Lorenzo's, with no evidence to speak of. Do you know how many false threats of a weapon of mass destruction attack the authorities get every year? I can tell them that the Montalbans have such a weapon. They may even go arrest her. Then what? What evidence do we have? All it would do is strengthen her position in the council and weaken my own. It would amount to nothing, and may serve only to buy her more time."

"Then convince them."

"I will. I have called for a face-to-face meeting of all the families to discuss matters. We share lofty goals, but we can be a fractious and argumentative lot. You must understand that a grand council is a rare and momentous occasion, reserved only for times of dire crisis. Katarina will have the opportunity to defend her actions there. In the meantime I need you to continue your mission, only tread softly. Investigation, but no overt action. Do not make it easy for Katarina to play the victim. If we can provide them with evidence the other families will have no choice but take her into custody."

"And then what?"

Romefeller nodded toward one of the weapons hung on the wall. "That is an executioner's ax. It is not just a decoration. My organization takes our traditions very seriously. You will continue to have Mr. Tailor and any of my assets you need at your disposal, but please, before you do anything rash, keep me in the loop. Mr. Lorenzo is welcome to show himself, too, if he cares to. I assure you I won't turn him over to the Montalbans. I own paintings worth more than the price on his head."

Well, la-de-freakin'-da, Richie Rich. "I'm sure. I'll pass that on."

Romefeller came over and put a comforting hand on my shoulder. "I am on your side, Valentine. I took a solemn oath to use my resources to better the world. I've spent my life and my fortune trying to give humanity a better future. I will not allow Katarina to undo all of the good the families have accomplished. You have my word that I will get to the bottom of this."

I nodded. "Understood. I should get going. My friends don't know where I am."

"I would not dream of standing in your way. Mr. Tailor will take you wherever it is you wish to go."

"Thank you for your help. I'll be in touch."

"Godspeed, Mr. Valentine."

LORENZO
Paris
September 28th

As soon as it was safe to move Jill—and even that was questionable—we'd taken her back to one of her hideouts. We picked the flat in the boring working-class neighborhood because it was the least likely to get noticed. The doctor had said it wasn't safe to transport her, she was better off staying, and that nobody at his clinic would talk, but I didn't trust him or his people to not get greedy. So I'd stolen a work van, rolled the gurney right into the back, and left as soon as we could. I also had Reaper take any medical equipment and supplies he thought might be useful, but to make up for it I paid the doctor a *lot* more than the doctor's agreed-upon fee. He'd saved Jill's life. He could consider it a tip.

She had lost a massive amount of blood and was lucky to be alive. Deprived of actual medical care, she could still die here. The next twenty-four hours passed in a haze, with me sitting next to Jill's bed, sleeping occasionally, and waking up from nightmares to check on her. It gave me a lot of time to fret and to think.

There was a two-sided conflict going on inside my head. Part of me wanted to lash out, pure violence, vengeance. If couldn't get to Anders, I'd find someone, I didn't care who, but I'd dismantle Kat's organization brick by brick, man by man. I didn't need a plan. I'd leave a pile of mutilated corpses across this city, and eventually I'd get the right one. On the other side of my internal debate was the mature, rational, sane part, which knew that was stupid. Sure, I could start popping more Montalbans, but I'd eventually get killed or caught before I stopped them all. We needed to continue with the plan, looking for opportunities to ruin Blue. That side of me was right, but useless.

So I spent a day being useless. Antoine came by to drop off some supplies, check on Jill, and gave me a quick rundown of what had happened with Valentine and Katarina, and the resulting clusterfuck with Underhill.

I sat next to Jill's bed, she was still unconscious and I was in a daze, while Antoine stood in the doorway to the tiny bedroom. "So Kat is still out there, plotting, only now she knows exactly who's gunning for her."

"She will be hunting us," Antoine said. "Worse, Majestic will do nothing to stop her. They will not risk starting a war. The Illuminati are fickle allies at best. It is up to us."

"It always was. Damn it. I wish Valentine would have gotten her. Regardless, tell him thanks for trying. I mean that."

Antoine seemed a little surprised.

"What?"

"You do not strike me as the gratitude type, Lorenzo." I'd grown to like Antoine during our rescue mission at North Gap, and I'd saved his life in the Crossroads. He and Shen were good dudes, honorable men, and I didn't have many friends like that. I actually kind of gave a damn what he thought about me. "I know Valentine has caused you quite a bit of trouble over the years."

I could understand his confusion. Normally when I was in this bad of a mood, I'd be tempted to rip apart any convenient target, but I was just too damned worn out. Today, I was the only convenient target. "Valentine has been a huge pain in my ass. But that was a crazy stunt, and he's lucky to be alive. Walking right in there like that took guts. I can respect that."

"Valentine has changed much since we first met. I saw great potential in him, to be not just a fighter, but a leader. The importance of this mission has brought together the noble. Together, we are a force for good."

"Not counting me, obviously."

"Ha! Of course not! Such a terrible man, sacrificing himself to save the wounded after taking turns carrying them on his back across a mountain all night."

"Don't let that get out. You'll ruin my image." Like the Pale Man said, death followed me, and there had been a lot of death on that mountain. I didn't even know who else had made it out. This was the first time Antoine and I had gotten to really talk since I'd gotten out. "Since you mentioned it . . ."

"The rest of us made it because of you. Svetlana had to retire due to her injuries. She'll be glad to hear you're alive. You did good there."

"Yeah? Well, I blew it here."

Antoine looked at poor Jill, drained and sleeping. "Jill is a strong woman. She will pull through."

"I know she will."

"Call if you need anything else." Antoine turned to leave. "We will continue the search."

"Hey," I called after him. The big Exodus operative paused. "I know what I look like right now. I know I look all fucked up, but don't worry. I'm still in. No matter what, I'm still going to finish this."

"I know. I can see it burning in you. You want to strike out. But for now, we have this. Even if she can't speak, savor this time with her, Lorenzo."

"That's easy for you to say. I need to do *something*, man."

"I have been there." When Antoine folded his thick arms, he was truly an imposing man. "When I was young, rebel militia raided my village. While my wife lay dying, I had to abandon her. I could not be there with her at the end."

"Why?"

"Because they'd stolen my daughters. I had to leave my dying wife to chase after them."

Other than knowing he was from West Africa, I'd never heard him talk about his life before Exodus. "Did you get them back?"

He shook his head.

"I'm sorry." It was a trite thing to say, but that's all I had. That certainly explained why he'd become a warrior for Exodus.

"Keep your loved ones close while you can. The killing time will come soon enough. I can feel it . . . And whether you like it or not, you are on the side of the angels now, Lorenzo. Goodbye."

After he left, I'd cleaned some guns, changed some bandages, and continued being angry.

Reaper had gone back to shaking the trees to see what would fall out, but even he had limited success. Kat wasn't stupid. If she knew I was involved, that meant Reaper was involved too. She would hunker down and send her legions of minions to search for us. She had always hated my *little sidekick*, as she'd derisively called him, but she knew what he was capable of. She also had enough money to hire the best nerds possible to counter him. The idea of, hell, I don't know what to call them . . . *anti-Reapers* scouring the digital world for traces of us was frankly terrifying. I don't know what Reaper took as the bigger insult, them shooting Jill, or Kat thinking some other hackers could beat him on his own turf. I didn't know what Reaper had been up to in the other room for the last day, and he didn't have time to slow down and explain it to me. He was acting like he was waging his own private war. Whatever, at least when he was working, he wasn't being all weird and traumatized about the Crossroads.

Meanwhile, I played nurse or watched Jill sleep, knowing that she'd almost died because of me. Damn Ling for contacting her. It was better for everyone when she'd thought I was dead. I was a fool for not doing this on my own. But that damned rational part of me knew that was bogus. I hadn't dragged her into this. She'd been hunting Montalbans the whole time I'd been imprisoned. It was a miracle she'd survived as long as she had.

The irrational part of me suspected that this was all the Pale Man's doing, and that he'd tried to take her from me, because love was a distraction. It made no logical sense, Anders had pulled that trigger, and Sala Jihan was a continent away, but I still knew it was true. My brand ached as I thought about it, but if Jill died, then I was going to go back to the Crossroads and make the devil pay.

She woke up the next morning.

"Lorenzo?"

Jill's voice was barely a whisper, but I woke right up. I'd been sleeping right next to the bed, dreaming about Kat finding us somehow and Anders kicking the door in to finish what he'd started.

"You're awake."

"Hey," she croaked. Her normally olive skin was far too gray, and her eyes seemed sunken into her face. Her black hair was spread across the pillow, and the contrast only made her look too pale and small. "I'm thirsty."

"I've got you." Of course, an IV would keep you hydrated but it just wasn't the same. I should have thought of that ahead of time. I ran to the kitchen and came back with a cup of water. I held it to her lips. "Easy." I sucked at this sort of thing and ended up spilling most of it down her chin. I was going to have to find a straw.

It took Jill a few seconds to collect herself. That was normal when you'd nearly bled to death and been unconscious for days. There were huge dark circles under her eyes. I'd never seen her looking this frail before. I was scared to touch her. I thought she might break.

"What happened?" At least with the water her voice sounded a little better.

"You got shot." I didn't know how much she would remember. She was still on a lot of painkillers, and would be for quite a while. They'd had to cut her wide open to stop all the internal bleeding. I didn't know how many stitches and staples were holding her side together, but I'd seen them when I'd changed the bandages, and it was a mess.

Jill blinked a few times. "I remember driving backwards. Then this pain, like a lightning bolt. It hurt a lot, and that's it. Is everyone else okay?" Now she was looking at me, panicked. She was more coherent than I expected. "Did you get hurt? Where's Reaper?"

"Try not to move too much." I put a gentle hand on her shoulder to keep her from trying to sit up. Of course, Jill would be worried about the others before she even thought about herself. That was just the kind of person she was, and one of the reasons I fell in love with her to begin with. "They're fine. Everyone else is safe."

"Did Anders get away?" Suddenly, it was the new, focused, scarier Jill talking, and I was still getting used to her. "Please tell me you got that son of a bitch."

I shook my head *no*.

"Damn it . . ." Jill winced and started to move one hand to her side.

"Seriously, don't move. If you start bleeding again, we're screwed."

"How bad is it?" From the look on her face, even with the drugs she was still in a lot of pain. "I feel terrible."

"Anders shot you with a shotgun."

Jill blinked slowly. "I should be dead."

No kidding. At close range a 12 gauge hit like a meat hammer. If you got nailed in the torso up close with one, it was game over. A dozen pellets—each one with as much energy as a .380—hitting you in one instantaneous clump made a real mess. Like you could put your hand in the hole and have room to wiggle your fingers kind of mess, but get a little distance and the pellets spread out and bled energy fast. "You're lucky. He was far enough away that the door slowed them down, and the seat caught most of them. There was still a lot of internal bleeding. It was really close."

"How close?"

She'd damned near bled to death while that fat bastard doctor had taken his sweet time, but right now she needed to remain upbeat. "You just need to rest. You'll recover just fine, but it is going to take a while. That was pretty badass though. I didn't even know you knew how to drive a big truck."

Jill gave me a very tired smile. "I drove a dump truck one summer. My dad got me a job at his friend's construction company so I could pay tuition. That truck I stole handled like a sports car in comparison."

"You're one tough chick."

She started to laugh, then grimaced. "Ouch. Don't be funny."

"I rarely am. You just think I'm funny now because you're high."

"I feel like shit."

"The doctor said that's expected."

"Doctor?"

"Some Serbian war criminal Reaper knew."

Jill sighed. "You called, needing a way out. I couldn't figure out what to do. But this poor trucker had just pulled in to get diesel. I just reacted. I stuck my pistol in his face and stole it. I think I scared the hell out of him. I feel awful about that."

"You saved my life." I lowered my head and gently kissed the back of her hand. "Thank you."

Jill didn't say anything in return, she'd gone back to staring at the ceiling. Beyond the pain and the weakness, there was something else there. Jill was really troubled.

I tried to cheer her up. "Carjacking? That's some straight-up hoodlum level stuff. I'm impressed. When we met you were a law-abiding citizen. I've been a terrible influence on you."

Her eyes looked shiny, like she wanted to cry, but was trying hard not to. Her lip began to quiver. "I've done some bad things, Lorenzo. I'm not a good person anymore. You were dead. I lost myself. I didn't know what else to do. But I still had to stop them, you know?"

"I know." I'd been thinking about what Anders had said, both about the Montalban body count and the attempted bombing in London. I'd been hoping he'd just been trying to mess with me, but that damned rational part had been worried he had been telling the truth. Barely conscious, life passing in front of her yes, Jill had declared that she deserved this. "Believe me, I know."

"I lied to you. I lied to you about what I've done."

"I don't care."

"I thought I had Kat in London. I'd put so much work into it. I damn near died finding out where she was going to be. There was this crew she was trying to arrange a meeting with. They caught me snooping, but since they just thought I was one of the working girls trying to steal some credit cards, they only beat the shit out of me and left me in a pile of garbage."

"Who?" I immediately felt the need to find and kill them.

"Some British mercs. They took turns kicking me, but I didn't fight back, because I'd heard what I needed, so I took that beating. It was awful, but there wasn't anything I wouldn't do to stop her."

"Whatever you did, whatever you had to do, it's in the past."

But this was her confession. I'd spent my life around criminals. I'd seen it before, when the weight someone was carrying simply became too much, and they needed to dump it on someone else. Jill pushed on. "They'd arranged to meet in a little outdoor restaurant on the Thames. It was like a nice little garden inside a wrought iron fence. Great view of the Tower Bridge. I limped straight there, climbed the fence before they opened, and hid my bomb in a planter. That evil killer bitch thought she could kill you and then do her business right out in the open because it was a pretty day.

"I was watching from the bridge, lots of foot traffic so I could stay hidden. Anders and his guys got there twenty minutes early and swept the place, but they missed my bomb. The British merc she was meeting with showed up right on time. Last time I'd seen him was when he was kicking me and calling me a whore, and he sat down not ten feet from that planter. I was really tempted to just blow him up as payback right then, but I waited for her. It was risky, out there in public, but I wasn't just avenging you, I was stopping Kat from doing something horrible, right?"

"Yeah . . ." I held her hand. *Saving the world,* according to Valentine's mystical teenager. "You don't need to tell me this. I'll always love you, no matter what." I didn't know if I'd tried to stop her for her own good, or because I really didn't want to know.

"There were people around, but they were far enough away I was positive they wouldn't get hurt. Sure, I felt bad about blowing her to pieces in front of all those witnesses, but she *deserved* it." Tears began to roll out of her eyes and down her cheeks. "She was supposed to have the whole place to herself. That's how she operates. But then this young couple showed up with sack lunches. They walked past the restaurant, but then they stopped on the railing on the other side of the fence and watched the river, eating sandwiches. I kept praying that Anders would chase them away, but he didn't."

"Oh, Jill . . ."

"Kat showed up ten minutes late—longest ten minutes of my life—sat down, and started talking to the British merc. And I was screaming inside, telling that couple to move, to get up, go to the bathroom, get a drink, go for a walk, something. But they sat there, stupid and laughing. Maybe they were on their honeymoon. I don't know. They looked so happy, like we were on Saint Carl, but I just needed them to fucking *move* and they wouldn't! Kat finished her meeting, all that and she didn't even bother to eat. It was too short. She got up and started to walk away, and I knew I was going to lose her. I had the phone in my hand. All I had to do was push a button."

It sucked. It hurt. I knew exactly what had gone through her head in those fateful few seconds. "You did the math."

"Months, Lorenzo. That's all I'd thought about, all I'd lived for, was stopping Kat. I was standing there, with a concussion. My face covered with a scarf, not to hide from Anders, but so the pedestrians and tourists wouldn't see I was still bleeding, one eye was swollen shut, and I was wheezing from the broken rib I'd gotten a few hours before. Were those innocent people far enough away to not get killed? It wasn't a very big bomb. Probably. But I didn't know for sure. But right then I convinced myself they were out of the blast radius. They'd *probably* be okay." She turned her head to look directly at me, stricken with guilt. "And I pushed the button."

"But it didn't detonate."

"How'd you know?"

"Anders told me."

She began to sob. "It doesn't matter. I'm a monster. I risked innocent lives to get what I want. I had no right. There's no way to justify what I've done."

This was killing me. "That's not true. Jill, listen to me. You know I worked for Big Eddie. Kat and I did his dirty work. You know I've hurt people, good people, on accident, and sometimes on purpose. But you still had faith in me. You pulled me out of that hole. You gave me something to live for beyond looking for the next challenge, the next thrill. I only survived the Pale Man because someone *good* loved me."

She went back to staring at the ceiling. "I lost that at the Crossroads."

"No. You became what I used to be, because you had to."

"I chose it."

"Yeah? So what? Bad things happen in war, and don't kid yourself, this is a war. I got drafted when Bob tried to make a difference, but you had guts, saw something that needed to be done, and volunteered. All that stuff you've said over the years about believing in me, it applies to you now too."

"I made a mistake."

"You think you're the first?" I was heartbroken and angry at the same time. I remembered waking up injured in a hotel room in Las Vegas to the sound of Jill singing in the shower. Even after surviving Quagmire she'd been a ray of sunshine. Valentine had warned me then to get out of this life and stay away, not for my own sake, but for hers, so that she wouldn't end up screwed up like us. Valentine had been prophetic. "I don't know. Maybe you did, maybe you didn't. Hell, maybe God dropped that call. Shit happens. When you're tangling with the evil assholes, sometimes law abiding citizens get in the way . . . I can't complain about that too much, since it's how we met."

Jill looked back and gave me a sad smile. The kind, loving woman I'd fallen for was still in there, only she'd been stained and hurt by the cruel world I'd introduced her to.

"No matter what, I'm with you, Jill. We're in this together."

Then she squeezed my hand.

I hoped she'd be okay.

VALENTINE
Paris
September 28th

Focus. I took a deep breath, and squared myself off with the mirror. *Go.*

I drew my gun and dry fired at my reflection. *Too slow.* I reholstered and tried again.

Go. My left hand found the grip of my .44. I rocked the gun back, out of its holster, and then pushed it forward. My hands came together as my arms extended, and everything was blurry except the glowing tritium front sight. My arms reached full extension, the sights aligned on my own reflection in the mirror, and I smoothly worked the trigger: *CLICK.*

It took less than a second. *Too slow.* I sighed in frustration. *Too damned slow.* If I'd been just a bit faster, just a bit more accurate, when I'd had my shot at Katarina, I could have shot her and solved half my problems right then and there. I habitually opened my revolver's cylinder, verifying that it was still loaded with dummy cartridges, and reholstered it. I'd ditched the shoulder rig I'd been using for my .44 and went back to a leather hip holster. It wasn't as comfortable when sitting down, but it was a speedier draw.

Go! I drew again. The hammer spur snagged on my shirt, screwing up my draw stroke. "Damn it," I said aloud, returning the gun to its holster. *Again.* Better this time, a little smoother. Smooth is fast. Trying to rush ends up costing you time, every time. *Again.*

Repetitive practice was a good way to lose yourself in thought. As I repeatedly sighted on him, I barely recognized the man looking back at me from the full-length mirror. I had picked up so many scars that it often surprised me when I saw my own reflection.

I was far from being a chiseled pretty boy, but I was more muscular than I'd been in a long time. I was no longer the gaunt shell of a man I was when they'd pulled me out of North Gap. Regardless of what Dr. Bundt thought, I'd gotten back to a healthy weight, and a modest exercise regimen had paid off for me. Actually, considering just how modest it was, I was far better shape than I should have been. I suspected that had something to do with Dr. Silver's science experiment.

Dr. Bundt had called the project XK Indigo. I had no idea what they'd been doing to me in there, but I vaguely remembered Dr. Silvers telling me something about my fulfilling my potential. They had put me in a thing called "the Tank" countless times, and I still didn't know what that machine did other than make nightmares. There was conspiracy theory stuff on the internet about XK Indigo, but it was all stupid rumor and wild conjecture. Popular—if you can call a few dozen kooks commenting on a web forum that— belief held that it had its origins in Nazi Germany, some kind of desperate, late-war program. It would have been nice to have answers rather than comic book bullshit, but I wasn't going to get that online.

It occurred to me then that Reaper might be of help. Lorenzo's buddy was a huge conspiracy theory nut, but he was actually smart. I resolved to ask him about it next time I saw him. I'd have to do it delicately, though. I didn't know what the hell had happened to him at the Battle of the Crossroads, but the kid just wasn't the same after that. He hadn't even participated in the fight, as far as I knew. He'd just been flying Lorenzo's little UAV, but he probably saw a lot of people getting killed. I knew a thing or two about PTSD, and Reaper displayed a lot of the obvious symptoms. Maybe it would help if I sat down and talked to him about it.

Enough thinking about things that didn't matter. It was time to get back to practicing.

Sooner or later, I was going to have to face Underhill again. He was old, but he got to be old in his business by being fast and lethal. I swore to God, or to whoever might be listening, that when I met him again I'd be ready. *Give me the strength, Lord,* I thought to myself, *and the swiftness, to shoot that bastard in the face and send him straight to hell.*

I paused when someone quietly knocked on, then opened, my door. "Is everything alright?" Ling asked. She stepped into my room and closed the door behind her. "What are you doing?"

I was standing in front of a mirror with a gun in my hand. A few hundred repetitions and I had sweat rings on my shirt. "It's, uh, not what it looks like."

She folded her arms across her chest. "You were practicing quick drawing your gun, I take it?"

"I guess it's exactly what it looks like, then."

"You know, you might be faster if you carried a more practical pistol."

I smiled at her, unloading the dummy cartridges from my gun as I did so. "The lady with the engraved Browning 9mm is going to lecture me about practicality, now?"

"It was a gift from my team."

"And this," I said, loading real rounds into my .44's cylinder, "is my good luck charm. If I'd have brought this when I went after the Montalban woman I might have succeeded."

"You never struck me as the superstitious sort."

"I've had this gun with me everywhere and I've always come home alive. Can't argue with success. But it isn't superstition. I just shoot this better."

"We need to talk." *Uh oh.* Ling was giving me that look that told me that this was serious. "What you did at the hotel was stupid, Michael."

"I had to improvise."

"You were improvising *stupidly.*"

"The plan could have worked, and Tailor was ready in case I got captured."

"And that would not have mattered if the Montalbans had shot you immediately, or if Underhill had executed you on the spot."

"Damn it, let it go, Ling! I saw an opportunity and I took a chance! You know what could happen if we fail. It's worth the risk."

"You would risk one, but not six." Ling put her hand on my arm. "Listen to me. Risks are necessary, especially when so much is at stake. I understand that, but we can't afford to lose you. We need you."

There was something else going on. Sure, she was mad at me, but it felt like she wasn't telling me everything that was on her mind. "What's wrong, Ling?"

"*I* need you. That's all. Don't tempt fate unnecessarily. We may die, but let's make sure our deaths mean something, yes? Don't throw your life away on a long-shot gambit." She gently touched the side of my face. "Promise me."

I looked into Ling's dark eyes. She was right, of course. I wasn't much for arguing, especially when I knew she was right. I had known, going into it, that my idea was desperate and risky, and all it had really managed to do was drive Katarina underground.

"I promise," I said after a moment. "I'll only die if it's for a good reason."

"Good," she said, giving me a quick kiss. "Now stop sulking and come downstairs. It's almost dinnertime. Antoine made a lovely fish and vegetable soup. You need to eat."

Ugh. I needed to introduce these people to junk food or something. I forced a smile onto my face. "Sounds great!"

"You are such a terrible liar. I am amazed Katarina did not cut your throat as soon as you opened your mouth." Shaking her head, Ling turned for the door. "Oh, and fetch Ariel."

"Is something wrong?"

"She's been acting strangely, holed up in her room, buried in her work. She's barely eaten and barely slept."

"Okay, I'll go talk to her. I knew this was too much pressure for her. I'll see you downstairs."

The Oracle was in her room, listening to music through headphones. I had to bang on the door several times before she heard me.

"What?" Ariel sounded annoyed when she opened the door. She really looked frazzled. "I'm busy!"

"Dinner."

"I'm *busy.*" She tried to close the door in my face, but I blocked it with my foot. "Michael!"

"First off," I reached out and picked one of the ear buds off her shoulder. I could hear the music clearly from an arm's distance. "This is too loud. You're going to damage your hearing, and worse, if we have an emergency and have to bail, we're not going to have time to keep uselessly shouting your name, so turn it *down.*"

"Fine, *Dad.*"

"Second, come eat something. You look like hell, kiddo."

She looked down at herself self-consciously. Her hair was a mess, and it was obvious that whatever sleep she did get, she got in the clothes she was wearing. "I'm *working.* Reaper's been sending me packets of information. He's a gold mine. He can reach anything, I mean nothing is safe from that guy, but he can't put the pieces together like I can. The Montalbans are up to something. I'm the only one who can figure it out."

"You can figure it out after you get some food in you."

"No time. I've got to make the pieces fit, Michael. This keeps getting bigger. They've hired a bunch of hackers, really good ones. They're moving money, paying bribes. There's pieces within pieces, but they're all secrets covered in lies. Until I make it work in my head, you guys are going to be in danger. I have to make the pieces *fit*. Garbage in, garbage out. If you guys don't know what's going on, you can't make good decisions. That's my fault."

Suddenly it made sense. She was working herself to exhaustion because I'd nearly gotten myself killed. "Hey, come here." I took her by the shoulders and pulled her out of her room. "Look at me. None of this is your fault."

Ariel's expression softened to the point where I thought she was going to start crying. "You almost died."

"But I didn't. Ling just made me promise not to unless I had a good reason." I gave her a hug. She squeezed me tight, and I could tell she was scared. "It's all right," I said, trying to sound comforting.

"I know." She broke away, and rubbed the moisture from her eerie blue eyes. "We can make it better."

"Now come on. You can fix the world after you have some of Antoine's nutrient-rich fish gruel."

Ariel wipe her eyes, then grimaced. "I'll eat, but can we order a pizza?"

Chapter 12: Beauty and the Beast

LORENZO
Paris
September 29th

"Lorenzo, get in here!" Reaper shouted.

I entered the flat's other room with a gun in my hand. My first worry was that he'd seen something threatening out the window. "What?"

Reaper was sitting in front of a little table that had several computers running on it. He'd probably be using even more if the Internet here was faster. "You've got to see this." He was pointing at something on one of several screens. I was afraid that it was the feed for one of the security cameras Jill had hidden around the block, probably showing Anders and a team of murderous scumbags bearing down on us, but those were all clear.

"What am I looking at?"

"Kat!" Reaper pointed at the screen like it was obvious. There was a black box flashing the word *pending*. "She wants to talk to you."

"Hold on. Katarina is calling us?" She was crazy, but not that kind of crazy. If she was reaching out there had to be a reason, like keeping us in one place while we were being surrounded. "Does she know where we are?"

"No way. Her guys are good, but they're not that good." He started talking about drop something cache packet cryptofuckery, but Reaper trailed off as he remembered everything he did was voodoo to me. "Basically I've made it look like we're somewhere else." Reaper was jittery and excited, but replacing sleep with Red Bull had that effect on him. "They know I'm all up in their shit, and they're having a hard time keeping me out. But look, she pinged me, asking for you, wanting to video chat."

It had to be a trap. "Can she trace the call?"

"Trace the call . . . Man, you are old. No! It doesn't work like that, but sort of, not really, but I won't let her."

"Could you trace it back to where she is?"

"Unless her dude screws up, I probably won't be able to. It's worth a shot though."

I liked how Reaper thought it was possible Kat's equivalent to him could slip, but Reaper making a mistake was impossible. "You sure about that?"

Reaper snorted. "Obviously."

"Hang on. Where's the camera?" He pointed, and I made sure there was nothing on the wall behind me that could give her a clue to our location. The curtains were closed. The room was dark. But to be safe I picked up one of Reaper's empty snack wrappers and put it on top of the camera anyway. This flat was in a quiet neighborhood. I couldn't think of any sounds that would give us away. We weren't even close enough to hear any public transportation that she could match up against a bus or train schedule.

Once I was certain she'd get no clues as to our whereabouts, I pulled up the other chair. "Go." It wasn't even a question of whether to answer or not. When she was rational, Kat was damned smart, but when she was furious, she made mistakes. And I'd always had a gift for making her furious.

"You sure you want to talk to your psycho ex right now?" Reaper asked hesitantly.

"I might be able to get her to slip up and give something away. Record this. Maybe she'll say something we can pass on to Underhill or Romefeller to push them over the edge. Kat's manipulative and sharp when she's being rational, but get her riled up and she's got serious rage issues."

"And you don't?"

"Not like that," I snapped. Though to be fair to Reaper, with Jill getting shot, I hadn't been in the brightest of moods over the last few days. "Answer the call."

Reaper hit the button. Katarina Montalban appeared on one of the screens.

She hadn't covered her camera. Kat had always been gorgeous, and she'd aged well. Maybe she was prideful enough to think she could still charm me like the old days. There were some recent bruises on her face, mostly covered with makeup, and she was wearing a scarf, probably to hide the marks Valentine must have left on her throat. Behind her was a plain white wall, so I'd be getting no hints about her location that way. She tilted her head to the side when she saw nothing but black.

"Lorenzo? Is that you?"

"Hello, Kat."

She had this kind of white, blonde, too smooth Nordic look, and her attitude was either fire or ice, no in between. Since she was a superb actor—anyone who didn't know her found her remarkably charismatic. Those of us who got to know her—without getting killed in the process—knew she swung between charming and terrifying. Even when we'd been lovers, I'd always suspected I was one mood swing away from getting shot. She flashed me her big, fake smile, with her perfect, capped, bleached white teeth. Her eyes twinkled. This was fun for her. Say what you will, psychotic or not, Kat really loved her work.

"You can't imagine my surprise when I found out you were still alive."

"Despite your best efforts."

"Indeed. Why don't you show me your face? I've missed seeing you."

"I don't feel like giving your boyfriend a current snapshot of me to pass around."

"Ah, yes. It is unfortunate how easily you change your face." Kat's accent—when she didn't bother to hide it—was Swiss, and she often turn the S into a Z. "I thought perhaps Sala Jihan had put his brand on it and you were too ashamed to show me."

Just saying that name made my chest hurt. "I'm still plain and boring as ever."

"Better to sneak up on me then."

"I promise. You'll never see me coming."

Kat laughed. It seemed genuine, but most things with her did. "Oh, Lorenzo. Never change. Lucky for you, I didn't fall for you because of your looks."

Or my charm. "How's your neck?"

"You know I don't mind getting a little rough. Mr. Valentine has strong hands." She ran her fingers down the red silk scarf suggestively. Despite the act, I could tell she was still sore. She flipped the subject to something personal to try and throw me. "How is Jill?"

"She's fine."

"Really? I'd love to speak to her again."

"Jill can't come to the phone right now."

"Because Anders shot her?" Kat had a malicious, evil grin. "Did she live? Die? Did you have to bury her in a shallow grave? Or are you too pragmatic, and she didn't even rate that? I bet you put rocks in her pockets and shoved her corpse in the river. I wonder, Lorenzo, can you even truly love someone?"

I didn't say anything. I wasn't going to let her get off on my pain.

"But I think you can. You certainly loved me once. We had some good times, you and I." Kat leaned toward the camera and winked. "Remember our vacation in Northern China?"

"No." I lied. "But I remember dumping your crazy ass in Malaysia."

"I truly wish you hadn't done that. Just think what might have been."

"What do you want, Kat?"

"To make you an offer."

"Let me guess. I step out of your way until you're done with Project Blue?"

She wasn't going to waste time playing innocent, but she wasn't going to admit to owning Blue when I might be recording the conversation. "I simply need you to leave Europe and stay out of my affairs for a time. An extended vacation would be splendid."

"And what would I get for that?"

"Twenty million dollars." That was a little higher than expected, but Kat controlled the Montalbans' fortunes now, so she was easily good for it.

"That's double what you're offering to have me killed for."

"I could have you killed for far less, but then I'd have to go through all the trouble of waiting. I like to expedite things. Take this offer, Lorenzo. In addition, I will let you and all your people live. All of our prior business will be water under the bridge. Your crimes against my family will be forgiven and forgotten."

Fat chance of that. "What about my brother?"

"What of him?" Kat asked innocently.

"I know Bob Lorenzo is still alive." It was more of an educated guess than knowledge. Because Bob had the skillsets, had been missing for two years, and had that whole dishonored federal employee background that Gordon Willis likely would have recruited, Bob made a viable, believable fourth operative. Anders could easily pin Project Blue on Bob. He was the perfect patsy.

Kat just smiled. She wasn't going to say anything that would be passed on to Majestic or the other Illuminati families later. "I've not seen him since the Crossroads. I wish you the best of luck in your continuing search, as long as you do it somewhere far away from here."

Reaper passed over a Post-It he'd scribbled a quick note on. *They tried to pin us. I sent them on a goose chase.* Reaper seemed really smug about it too.

Kat looked down, probably at her phone. Her lip curled back in a snarl before she turned back to the camera. "I am fairly certain you are not hiding at Euro Disney. You are not tall enough to ride all the rides. Well done. My compliments to Skyler."

"His name is *Reaper*." My sidekick was so pleased at that, he stuck out one fist. I obliged his fist bump. Reaper wiggled his fingers and mouthed the word *boom*. "Now, I've got a counteroffer. Do you still have Mr. Perkins?"

"I don't leave home without him." Mr. Perkins was a cut down M79 40mm grenade launcher. It was Kat's personal favorite weapon. It fit under an overcoat, but I'd seen her drop grenades through the open window of a moving car at 300 yards. She was an artist with it.

It was time to start provoking her. "Then stick Mr. Perkins up your ass, and give yourself a beehive round enema."

"So that is a no?"

"I'm not leaving Europe until I take your scalp."

Kat began to unconsciously drum her fingers on the table in front of her. Despite the cool act, she was still a bundle of nerves. "You're not in a position to make threats."

"You know me, Kat. I don't make threats. I'm just describing a series of events that are going to occur as a result of your pissing me off. You can't pay me off. It's never been about the money."

"No. All the things you stole, the impossible places you broke into, it was about doing what others said couldn't be done. You were always such a narcissist."

"I know what I am. And I know exactly what you are too. Which is why I can't let you go through with this. Blue could kill millions of people."

"Since when do you care about *people*? Spare me the sanctimony, Lorenzo. If our circumstances were reversed, you would do the same exact thing I am."

"Bullshit."

"I suppose we will never know." She was starting to flare up, but we weren't quite there yet. "Because I'm the one fate put into this position. I was the illegitimate daughter, unwanted, unwelcomed, and forgotten. They saw me as nothing more than a curiosity, a plaything for when Eduard got into one of his moods. Yet where Rafael lacked the courage, and Eduard was taken too soon, I will succeed where the inferior Montalban heirs failed."

"You're nuts."

Kat still didn't take the bait. "I am a visionary."

"Your brothers died stupidly. Valentine capped one and I shot the other out of the sky. You've already proven them wrong. You took over. You saved Big Eddie's crumbling empire, and from what I've seen, it's stronger than ever before. What more do you want?"

"My birthright!" Kat hissed. "My destiny! I was meant to rule my family, and my family was meant to rule the world. For centuries the Montalbans have been denied their place at the head of the table. Thirteen families have secretly steered the course of the entire world, yet my family was always the weakest, the runt of the litter, making do with the illicit scraps. No more!"

"The other families aren't going to step aside for the likes of you." If I could get her to cop to conspiring against the Illuminati, I could at least give this conversation to Romefeller. Maybe that would get the Illuminati off their ass at their big meeting. "You need professional help."

"Don't be so bitter, Lorenzo!" She wasn't stupid enough to give me what I wanted. "I couldn't have done this without you. I took up with you, my brothers' best unwitting hireling, in order to earn their respect. My ambition, my strength, the total commitment, the willingness to die in order to achieve your goals, I learned all those things from you."

I refused to believe that. "Incest and child abuse made you who you are, Kat, not me."

"That was merely the beginning of my journey." Even talking about her messed-up childhood was failing to provoke her. She remained remarkably grounded. Plotting world domination had done wonders for her. "Who I am, what I am today, I owe that all to the example you set for me."

We had been through some terrible things together, pulling off job after job on behalf of Big Eddie, I'd sunk lower than whale shit, but there were still some lines I'd never crossed. "You're willing to kill all those innocents to reach your goals. I'd never do something like that."

"Only because you lack the spine! I have progressed beyond you. Despite your fearsome reputation, the unstoppable assassin, I saw the real you beneath. There is a frailty to you, Lorenzo. Deprived of morals, you made up your own code, and it binds you far tighter than any law."

If I couldn't anger her, maybe I could appeal to whatever was left of the young woman I'd once known. "You were frail once too, Kat, but I kept you alive."

"That was your mistake. I stamped out that remaining weakness a long time ago."

"This is insanity. You've got to stop," I pleaded. "You want to gain power, take over your old money conspiracy, fine, but give up that nuke. If you set off that bomb, the whole world will hunt you down."

Suddenly, Kat smiled. It was far too devious an expression. That smile was genuine, which meant I'd screwed up somehow. "Why, Lorenzo, you are not as well informed as you think you are."

Shit. What did that mean? This wasn't going very well at all. I needed to switch tactics. *Maybe paranoia?* "Anders is planning on taking over your crime family. He's using you."

"Is that supposed to surprise me? Plant seeds of doubt? Are you hoping I have him killed? Anders is a man of appetites, certainly. He's taken enough orders and now he wants to give them. I respect and understand that. Soon, the Montalban Exchange criminal enterprises simply won't matter to me anymore. He can have Big Eddie's empire, because I will have the whole world to play with." Kat turned the other direction. "Isn't that right, my love?"

"Sounds good to me," Anders said as he leaned in and his stupid Viking face blocked half the screen. "What's up, Lorenzo? It was good running into you again the other night."

Right then I about lost it. Jill had nearly died because of this son of a bitch. I must have looked really pissed off, because Reaper reached over and grabbed my arm. He shoved another Post-It over. *They're getting closer.* Oh, *now* Reaper was wide-eyed and frightened. So much for his earlier confidence.

"That was pretty funny with your buddy, Valentine, trying to sic Underhill on us. I worked with Valentine in Zubrara. He's a fucking mope. Neither of you assholes get the big picture. What did Valentine think was going to happen, going after Kat half-cocked? A Majestic operative like Underhill can't just pop an Illuminati family head. You've got to know the game if you want to play with the big boys."

"I'll pass that on," I muttered.

"They aren't going to listen to you Exodus pussies. Both sides have been wrapped up in this turf war since before we were born. There's traditions and protocols and shit. I can understand you guys being mad though, since I'd just shot your girlfriend. That sure was a lot of blood all over that truck. I bet she's all fucked up. Is she dead? Or just crippled? Where did I hit her? It would suck if she's in a wheelchair. Or did I mess up her pretty face?"

I was quiet. Reaper was shaking his head *no*. I'd gone into this, hoping to goad Kat into giving me something to work with, and instead it was Anders who had me close to bubbling over with rage. Kat had planned this perfectly. She'd saved Anders to taunt me, probably even coached him on what to say to get under my skin.

Reaper added more to his last note. *Can't hold them.*

Anders kept pushing me, while Kat sat there, enjoying my misfortune. "Come on, Lorenzo. I'm looking forward to finishing this. For someone who is supposed to be such a badass, you've been a real letdown in person. If you're going to get us like you promised, you'd better hurry up. I've got some of the best mercenaries in the business descending on this city like a plague. It's going to be biblical. There won't be a rock left for you to hide under . . . You still there, Lorenzo?"

Reaper hit *end*.

That was good. I hadn't known what to say anyway.

VALENTINE
Paris
September 30th

A depressed Lorenzo was a dangerous Lorenzo, so I volunteered to check in on his crew. We'd barely heard from them for the past couple of days, and I knew that he had taken Jill getting hurt very hard. Ling didn't want to go with me. Since she had been the one to tell Jill that Lorenzo was still alive, I suspected Ling was feeling guilty about how things had panned out. She wasn't ready to face her, so I didn't push the issue.

Shen and Antoine were doing surveillance somewhere in the city. Ariel had wanted to come. She'd been cooped up in the safe house since we arrived in Paris, and I actually thought that her getting away from her computer for a while would do her some good. I couldn't risk it, though, especially not going out by myself. Romefeller's words had chilled me to the bone. He knew about her. She was valuable to people like him. For the time being, Ariel was safest at the house with Skunky and Ling. I ended up making the drive across town alone.

Lorenzo met me at the door. He had bags under his bloodshot eyes, and a look of worry on his face that I'd never seen on him before. Antoine had warned me that he was beating himself up over Jill getting hurt, and he sure looked it. "Come in."

"How's Jill?"

"Not great, but okay. She's on a lot of painkillers but she's awake more often. See for yourself." He led me toward the back of the apartment. We passed another room where Reaper was working on his computer, oblivious to the rest of the world. The other bedroom had enough equipment in it that it looked more like a hospital room.

"Valentine is here to see you," Lorenzo told her.

I hadn't seen her since the Crossroads. Jill looked like hell. She was lying in bed, bandaged up, and pretty obviously high on painkillers. She was pretty lucid, all things considered, and perked up a bit when I approached.

"Val? Come here," Jill whispered.

I went to the side of the bed. "How are you feeling?"

"How do you think? I got shot." Her words were slurred. "Lean in closer."

I did so, and Jill slapped me across the face as hard as she could. I recoiled back, rubbing my stinging cheek.

"Whoa! Easy," Lorenzo cautioned. "Don't strain yourself."

"That was for lying and telling me Lorenzo died at the Crossroads, you son of a bitch."

"He probably saved your life," Lorenzo said, quietly.

My face still stung. "No, it's okay. I had that coming."

"You deserve more than that. You're lucky I can't get out of bed or I'd break a chair over your head. Now beat it," she mumbled. "I just took my meds and I'm going back to sleep."

I walked back to Lorenzo, rubbing my cheek. The douchebag had found that funny, and smirked at me. "Don't take it personally. Jill's Filipina. She says all the women in her family have a temper. If she was actually mad she would have stabbed you."

"Val?" Jill called after me. "I still love you, Val." The drugs were kicking in. "You're my spirit guide and I love you!"

"I, uh, love you too, Jill." I shook my head. "Get some rest." Once we were out of her drug addled throwing range, I asked Lorenzo if she was going to recover.

"Yeah," he said, still looking tired. "The doc got her cleaned up and patched up pretty well, all things considered. Hey, give me a minute, will you? I've got to change her bandages and it's easier when she's asleep."

That was okay. There was something else nagging at me anyway. I went back to Reaper's room and knocked on the door frame. "Hey, can I talk to you?"

Reaper didn't hear me. He was wearing a set of headphones as he sat at his computer. The workspace he had set up in Lorenzo's hideout seemed, at first glance, to be a cluttered mess, but if you looked at it more closely you saw a method to the madness. He had a full tower PC, hooked up to no less than three monitors, and a couple of laptops open. Each screen had something different going on. Reaper bobbed his head in tune with whatever he was listening too, quietly clicking away on his mouse. His dark hair was shorter than I remembered, and he looked older. Empty Red Bull cans filled a small garbage pail.

I entered the room and tapped him on the shoulder. "Reaper?"

"Augh!" he blurted, startled. He turned around wide-eyed, suddenly breathing hard, not so much looking at me as through me. His right hand had moved under his desk, to the butt of a Glock pistol. It was in a plastic holster mounted to the underside.

I raised my hands and showed him my open palms, slowly taking a step back. "Whoa, hey, relax. It's just me. Sorry to scare you."

He took off his headphones. "You didn't scare me. I was just surprised."

"So surprised you were ready to shoot me?"

"Like that's so weird around here lately? What do you want, Valentine?"

"You got a minute? I need to ask you about some stuff."

"I'm pretty busy here."

I leaned forward to look at his screens. "What are you doing?"

"I'm trying to track down Isla, She-bitch of the SS . . ." I must have looked at him funny. "I mean Kat. She's got people trying to track us down, people like me, but they're not as good as I am. It's a challenging game of cat-and-also-cat. She's hiding since you almost popped her, but she can't go completely dark, not with an evil empire to run, so sooner or later I'll find her. Why?"

"That's not what I came to ask you about." I took a deep breath. Even after all that time had passed, it was still hard for me to talk about my experience in captivity. There was a folding chair leaning against the wall. I opened it up and sat down next to him. "Lorenzo told me you took most of the files recovered from North Gap."

A look of understanding appeared on Reaper's pale face. "Oh. Ohhh. Believe it or not, I never really got too far into them. After we, you know, rescued you, I was busy with mission prep and everything. Then the Crossroads happened. Then . . ." He trailed off. "You know."

"That was a bad op."

"You can't possibly imagine how right you are about that."

"A screaming teenage fanatic with the Pale Man's brand on his face tried to bayonet me with a Mosin Nagant. I've fought in a lot of wars, and the battle at the dam was the most vicious close combat I've ever seen. It was . . . it was medieval." I tapped the side of my head. "One more helping of nightmare fuel to lock away in the vault."

Reaper gave me a really sad, burned-out look, and it really sank in how much he'd changed. "Is that how you cope? You just lock it away?"

"I used to. Not so much anymore." I could tell Reaper was messed up. I'd seen it before, but maybe I could help him out. I was no stranger to trauma. "It works for a time, but sooner or later it catches up with you. You have to confront your demons eventually, or they eat you up from the inside."

"Demons?" Reaper asked, slowly. He stared awkwardly at me for a bit, then he shook his head. "Oh, not literal. You mean like *figurative* demons."

"Um, yes. I have not, as far as I know, confronted an actual demon." Sometimes, late I night, I wondered about that, too. "It's like this: I had a long talk with God when I was in that hole in North Gap." I remembered my weird nightmares from the Tank, of me murdering people. *God can't find you here. It's just you and me.*

"You don't seem like the religious type, Valentine. No offense."

"Never been to church in my life. I mean owning up to the things that I've done and the mistakes that I've made, forgiving myself for things that weren't my fault, like Sarah's death. And last of all it means finding something worth fighting for, something to get me out of bed in the morning, when it would've been easier to lie down and die."

"Lorenzo said you think you're trying to save the world."

"The world is going to hell one way or another. I can't do anything about that. It's not about saving the world, it's about picking my battles. It's not very often that you find yourself in a position to stop something horrible, when shit like this happens, you know? My whole life, I've been governed by forces beyond my control. Not anymore. This time, I'm fighting on my own terms. I took ownership of this. That's how I cope. That, and having people I can talk to on bad days."

He brushed a few strands of his long hair out of his eyes. "I didn't have anybody. Lorenzo was gone, Jill wasn't the same, and I don't have many friends. I avoided people. I thought I was going crazy. I couldn't prove I saw anything."

"What is it you saw there?"

Reaper didn't say anything for a long moment, looking at me askance. "You know . . . the battle." He wasn't telling me everything, and then he tried to change the subject. "After everything that happened, you'd think it would leak out somehow, but nada. Some bullshit on Russian TV about separatists and militias and that's it. It didn't even make *Sea to Shining Sea AM*."

"That's the world we live in, man, secret battles in places the world doesn't care about. I swear, someday I'm going to publish my memoirs."

"Heh . . . Cool, man. I'll buy a copy if you autograph it." Reaper seemed a bit happier. "Thanks for talking, Val. What did you want?"

Now it was my turn to be weird and traumatized. "Have you ever heard of a program called XK Indigo?"

Reaper tilted his head to the side, giving me a puzzled look. "Whoa . . . Dude. Holy shit. Why didn't I see it?"

"See what?"

Reaper ignored my question and turned back to his computer. A few mouse clicks pulled up a folder labeled *Valentine Stuff*.

"You have a file on me?"

"Of course I do. I have a file on everybody. Lorenzo asked me to put it together before we sprung you from North Gap."

Of course. "So what do you know?"

"Lots. You're not very good about information management."

"Yeah, well, I've been busy."

"That book you want to write? I could probably save you a bunch of time." he said, scrolling through his files. "You're like the most interesting man in the world. But XK Indigo? No wonder Majestic wants you dead. That's some weirdass voodoo tech right there."

"So, you've heard of it?"

"Of course I have. Everybody tuned in has. I just didn't think it was real. It's supposed to be about making perfect assassins for the government. I can't tell you what's real because most of the hard drives Lorenzo recovered from North Gap were encrypted enough that I couldn't do anything with them."

"You can't, I don't know, *hack* into the encrypted drives?"

Reaper sighed. "No, I can't hack into it." He made finger quotes when he said the word "hack". "It doesn't even work like that. I wish guys like you and Lorenzo would take a computer class or something. Cracking is math, not sorcery. Without a key there isn't a whole lot I can do. But not everything was encrypted. That Silvers lady was sloppy at times. All I've got is stuff like this. Here, you might find this interesting." He opened a video and set it to playing.

The camera was focused on me, strapped into a chair. My head was shaved and I was extremely pale and thin. Numerous wires connected my body to different monitoring devices. An overlay in the margins of the screen displayed my vital info, like heart rate and other physiological conditions. They were sticking me with needles and probes.

"I don't remember this."

"There are dozens of videos like this. Most of them are uninteresting. This one is flagged, though. Watch."

My vital signs started spiking and falling, fluctuating rapidly. From the convulsions, I think they were shocking me.

"Turn it up."

"There's no sound."

"What the hell were they doing to me?"

"It's labeled *negative stimuli*. I think they were running a current through different parts of your brain. Mostly it looks like they were trying to piss you off."

"It worked," I said, noting how I began to thrash around in the chair.

"Is this uncomfortable for you?"

"Yes? A little. It's weird."

"Okay, good. Keep watching. This is where it gets interesting." With my thrashing and convulsing, I managed to get my hand free of the restraints. A black-clad security man moved in to resecure my arm.

"That's Smoot. I remember that son of a bitch. Hey, what . . ." I trailed off as most of the visible readouts flatlined. I had stopped thrashing. My vitals all leveled off, abruptly. I recognized *the Calm*. As Smoot approached, I reached out, trying to grab him. He hit me with his baton, but I managed to get my one free hand on a pen in his shirt pocket. As Smoot leaned forward to push me back into the chair, I plunged it into his leg just above the kneecap. Smoot howled soundlessly, grasping his knee and falling backward. Another guard, Reilly I think, shot me with his Taser and zapped me while Smoot crawled away. Remarkably, the Taser seemed to do nothing, and I quickly freed my other hand.

With shocking speed, I went after the guards. It was obvious I was going to kill them.

But then Dr. Silvers said something. Without the sound there was no way to tell what it was. And just like that, I stopped, went back to the table, and sat down, meek as could be.

The video ended.

"I don't . . . I don't remember this. I remember, vaguely, stabbing Smoot with the pen, but this?" A sense of dread crept into me. Seeing a video of you doing something you don't remember is unsettling.

"Dr. Silvers had the file flagged as a *success*, that the *conditioning* was working. Now this is conjecture, okay, most of it is probably bullshit, so take this for what it's worth. The XK Indigo conditioning is like brainwashing. It's supposedly meant to heighten someone's abilities while making them easier to control. The idea is that your loyalty is ensured through a series of psychological controls and triggers."

"My God. This is . . . it's almost sick."

"Yeah. Your former employers are some real, evil bastards."

"What did they put in my head, Reaper?"

"Beats me, man. I don't know if you were conditioned to take orders from just that one doctor, or if there was more. There's no clue in here. I can send you everything I've got so you can check it out when you've got time."

"I think that would be best," someone said. Reaper and I both turned around to see Lorenzo standing in the doorway. I didn't know how long he'd been watching, or if he'd seen the video of me rendered into a murderous zombie. "And you're welcome for my rescuing your ass from that place."

I stood up. "What did you do with Smoot, anyway?"

"I doubt they ever found his body."

I smiled, just a little.

LORENZO
October 2nd

Jill was sitting up in bed. Even that much exertion freaked me out a little bit. The two of us had the place to ourselves. Valentine had gone back to work and Reaper had finally crashed. I'd seen him work in streaks before, not sleeping for days at a time when he got all spun up, but never like this. Since Jill had gotten shot he'd been bordering on mania, attacking the Montalbans' networks and finances.

"Try not to move around so much."

"Quit being a big baby," Jill muttered as she flipped through the photo album on Reaper's tablet.

"I just don't want you to hurt anything."

"Says mister I got third-degree burns all over my back, but I'm going to walk it off while I shoot down an airplane," she responded, not looking up from the pictures.

"When you pop some of those staples out and start leaking blood all over, don't come crying to me. I don't know if Reaper's war criminal doctor network makes house calls."

"I'll be fine. Except I'm probably never going to wear a two-piece bathing suit again."

I almost said *they're only scars* but I didn't think that was what a woman was going to want to hear. I sat next to her on the bed. My complaints to the contrary, she was looking a lot stronger, and she was motivated to get back to work, which was good. I changed the subject. "Reaper said Ling stopped by this morning."

"Yeah." Jill pointed at the fresh flowers on the desk. "She actually bought me a get well card."

"Ling is the sweetest paramilitary vigilante I know."

"She felt guilty for getting me involved and came by to give this big, formal, honor-bound apology. It was adorable. I forgave her. We talked."

"What about?"

"You know, girl stuff. She's the only chick over there, and I guess I'm the closes thing she has to a girlfriend. She's pretty freaked out about . . ." Jill went back to scrolling through the surveillance photos. "Never mind."

"Whoa. Hang on. You can't just say something like that and leave me hanging."

"It's a secret, Lorenzo. OpSec, you know?"

"Jill . . ."

She sighed. "Okay, don't tell her I told you. She'd never forgive me. Ling just found out she's pregnant."

"From Valentine?"

Jill looked at me like I was stupid. "Yes, from Valentine. But he doesn't know yet. He's focused on the mission right now and she doesn't want to mess him up with it. I told her that was stupid, but you know how intense the Exodus people are. Swear you won't say a word."

"I promise." The idea of Valentine and Ling having babies was amusing, and kind of frightening. I hurried and changed the subject in case Jill was thinking about talking about our future. I pointed out some of the faces in the picture she was looking at. "Shen took those. He was tailing these guys based on the intel you gave Exodus. That's in front of a bar downtown."

"I know that one for sure," Jill picked the middle one, an ugly, stout young man with a squished nose. "The rest, no idea. As far as I know though, he's just one of the rank and file Montalban goons. Nothing special, usually he's a driver. I called him Pig Face. He's got a brother, or at least a guy who looks a lot like him. I call him Pork Chop."

"Fitting." All of the Montalban crew she had followed that Jill didn't have names for, she'd just assigned nicknames. None of them were flattering, Dickhead, Big Ears, Stinky, and so on.

For the last few days Jill had been bored out of her mind, and demanding to help. That was good, because nothing helped you heal like the motivation to get on with life, but I'd told her she still needed her rest. She called me a *pendejo*, and told me to get her something to do or she was going to walk out of here.

Like I said, Jill was one tough chick.

"Shen tailed Pig Face to a chop shop. He thinks the Montalbans own it."

"Stolen cars? Really? Is there any criminal enterprise Eddie wasn't involved with? Drugs, piracy, counterfeiting, you name it," Jill complained. "It's like he was trying to be a comic book supervillain."

"Eddie was a big proponent of diversifying his assets. A lot of this was, I don't know, like a hobby for him. A game. He was living out a crime boss fantasy by being an actual crime boss, even though he was so rich he didn't actually benefit, financially, from all the crime." Most of his power base had been in Asia, with its heart in the Crossroads, but he'd had a little piece of everything in Europe too. While his family's legit businesses had been out in the open, Eddie had worked in secret. Unlike Kat, he had kept his identity on the down low, and for most of the time I'd worked for him, I hadn't even been sure *Big Eddie* was one person.

"It wasn't just a game. There was a reason for it. I've learned a lot about how the Montalbans work. Now Rafael, he was mostly a legit businessman. He owned stock in everything and ran a bunch of companies. But on the side, he used his little brother for everything shady. Rafael's construction company built most of the high-speed train lines and stations over the last decade. He even bankrolled that new three-hundred-mile-an-hour super train. But on the side, the freight companies still had to pay protection money to Eddie to make sure the trains run on time, and their shipments don't get stolen. They were in everything, Rafael in the open, Eddie in the dark. That's why Rafael indulged Eddie's crime boss fantasy, because it was useful for him. Now, Kat? If anything she's even more ambitious than her brothers. She wears both hats, CEO and mobster. She's expanded a lot in just the last year."

"Regardless, this is a score. This could be the place Kat parks her big armored convoy when she's not using it. I'll ask Reaper to see if he can steal some traffic camera footage or something to confirm it."

"That's useful. If that's home base, do you think you could ninja in there and put a tracking device on one of her cars?"

"Maybe." I liked the way she thought, though I'd been tending more toward a car bomb myself. I didn't say that though, because she still might be a little sensitive about the topic, and I didn't want to sound like a hypocrite. "Exodus couldn't have found this place if you'd not done all that leg work."

"You're just trying to make me feel better," Jill said as she went back to flipping through the pictures. "It's not working. I'm useless stuck here. And since you refuse to leave me alone, I'm making you useless."

"There's nothing for me to do," I lied. There was no shortage of people I could be murdering. "Underhill's superiors have to know about the nuke by now, so they'll have no choice but get off their asses and take her out. Gentleman's agreement be damned, they can't be that stupid. If that doesn't work, Romefeller told Valentine they've arranged a big secret meeting with all the families, scheduled soon. Once he tells them about Kat having a nuke, they'll lose their minds, and put out a hit on her."

"You actually expect the Illuminati or Majestic to come through for us?"

"Sure," I said, while simultaneously thinking *not really*. But Jill was recuperating and I wanted to keep her spirits up. "They'll be motivated."

"Don't blow smoke up my ass, Lorenzo. You read what Bob thought of those people. If they accomplish something good it's by accident. All they care about is themselves."

"Well, having a nuclear bomb go off in Europe has to be bad for business. Majestic has been exposed. Getting blamed for it could destroy them permanently."

"I like you better when you're honestly seeing the worst in everyone," she stated, completely aware that I was full of it. Jill went back to flipping through the pics the Exodus operatives had taken, but she was distracted. "You know, when I was young and naïve I used to dream about taking a romantic trip to Paris someday."

"Why?"

"Because that's the kind of thing teenage girls think about. It's the city of love. The Eiffel Tower, and the museums, and the cafes, and . . . I don't know . . . Mimes. But not me. Oh no. When I get here for real, I spend my time skulking around seedy bars and drug dens spying on terrorists, and then get shot stealing a truck. I'm just lucky I guess."

"Fire your travel agent."

Jill sighed. "On the bright side, Paris will always be where I found out you were still alive. That's what matters."

"Our fancy boat dinner date was nice."

"Yes, you did good with the boat ride." She grinned. "As for the rest? Sometimes a woman just needs to vent."

That was the regular old Jill I knew and loved, even with bullet holes in her side she was in a better mood than I was. I couldn't even make a crack about this being a honeymoon. It was kind of hard to describe a relationship when you didn't legally exist. Our fake identities in the Bahamas had been legally married, so I guess you could say our status was *complicated*. "Once this is over, I'll take you on a real romantic getaway."

"Knowing you, that's what, robbing a bank?"

"Don't laugh. I've looted a diamond exchange. You should see the size rock I could get you for a ring."

"Why, Lorenzo, is that an official proposal?"

I shrugged.

"Man, that's some emotionally stunted bullshit. You suck at this. Next time you . . . hang on." Jill looked like she'd seen a ghost. She showed me the picture. "Where'd Shen take this one?"

It was a man walking along a sidewalk, wearing a gray suit and black shirt. He was tall, athletic, mid-forties, prematurely white hair, and a scar that split his chin. He was in the process of taking a fat envelope from Pig Face or Pork Chop.

"Outside Le Bon Marche." I remembered that because it was across the street from the best gourmet grocery store in Paris. "Shen said the white-haired guy was smooth. Good field craft. No words. The exchange was a drop pass, and they both kept walking. Since Shen didn't know who he was, he peeled off and tailed him for a while, but lost him when he got to his car. Exodus couldn't ID him."

"I can. I'll never forget that face." Jill had gotten a lot more serious. There was no flippant nickname here. I could tell Jill was shaken.

"What's special about him?"

Jill was staring at the photo so hard it was like she was trying to burn a hole through the screen with her eyes. "This is the man Katarina was meeting in London."

"The one that had you beaten?"

She nodded slowly.

My anger was building. Even if he wasn't working with the Montalbans, I'd kill this particular fucker on principle. "What do you know about him?"

Chapter 13: The Limey

LORENZO
Paris
October 3rd

"The target's name is Aaron Stokes, mercenary, British national, and all around scumbag," I told the Exodus operatives as they passed around the photo Shen had taken. There were seven of us in the smoky little back room of the underground gambling establishment. It was the kind of place where shifty people could gather and count on not being noticed. We'd reserved the room for a *private game*. Private game, planning a hostage rescue, it was all good. "I want to hit his place ASAP."

"It is not your way to rush into things, Lorenzo," Ling said. "You were uncomfortable moving on North Gap on short notice. Why strike so quickly this time?"

That was fair. Ling thought my stay with Sala Jihan had put me off my game. My blitz attack in Salzburg hadn't been particularly well thought out. I could say something about her being unreliable for emotional reasons too, but then Jill would kill me for blabbing their secret.

"I think Stokes has Bob."

That got their attention. Ling, Shen, and Antoine exchanged glances. Her old team knew my brother from his search for Anders in the Crossroads, and there had been some mutual respect there. It had been Bob who'd coerced Ling into roping me into this mess to begin with. Valentine met my gaze and nodded. He knew Bob better than anyone here but me. He got it. I didn't know the American nicknamed Skunky at all, but I figured if I could convince Valentine, the rest would follow his lead. The weird little blonde girl . . . with her, I had no idea.

"What makes you think he's holding your brother?" the girl asked.

"From what Reaper has been able to dig up last night, Stokes was British Army before he got a dishonorable discharge for doing some things of questionable legality in Afghanistan. His background got him a job doing freelance work for some shady parties."

"Valentine knows about that kind of thing," Skunky said.

"I got an honorable discharge. I just wasn't allowed to reenlist. Huge difference," Valentine said. "I'm guessing Stokes' particular set of skills are what set you off?"

Exodus didn't need to know that it was his breaking Jill's ribs back in London that had caused me to sic Reaper on him. The clues Reaper had found were legit, so I didn't want Exodus thinking I was flying off half-cocked because of a personal vendetta.

"His official training was in interrogation and prisoner handling, but now that he's in the private sector Mr. Stokes specializes in kidnapping people for corporate espionage purposes and then holding them for ransom. Basically, freelance rendition on behalf of people who are probably on your buddy Romefeller's Christmas card list."

"Snatch a target and send him somewhere the authorities don't know about while you torture the hell out of them." Valentine sounded a little bitter, but he'd been on both sides of that equation. "Majestic has places like North Gap. I suppose it makes sense the other side has similar resources."

"So this Stokes is the perfect sort to keep a dangerous prisoner in one piece," Antoine mused, "until it is time to use him as their scapegoat."

I held up one hand and began to tick off my reasons for thinking he was our connection. "The Montalbans are paying him for something. Paris isn't Stokes' normal AO. Jill saw him meeting with Kat in London a few weeks before Varga moved Bob to Paris. One day after that meeting, a shell corporation controlled by Stokes purchased a big, isolated property north of the city. He's got to be our guy, and *this*," I held up a printout of the old real estate listing, "has got to be our location."

Valentine took the picture. "Is that a castle?"

"Technically, it's a chateau. Think of it as a mini-castle, without all those bothersome tourists taking pictures, and no neighbors to hear your prisoner get uppity."

"It sounds plausible," Ling stated. "Assuming your brother is still alive."

"Did Bob strike you as a quitter, Ling?"

"No. He did not."

Shen spoke up. "I saw Stokes had a bodyguard. Do we know how many other men he has?"

"This ain't Mexico," Skunky responded. "Down there you could flash your guard force patrolling the grounds, sporting machine guns and wearing armor. This here is a civilized country, so they won't show us their hand easily. Their protection will be hidden, and hard to scout out."

"If this is basically an Illuminati black site, there will be many guards and an excellent security system," Antoine said.

"That's pessimistic," Skunky said.

"Realistic. You have not met Lorenzo's brother. He was an American Green Beret, and he is my size. Would you go into a cell with someone like that without help?"

"As big as you are, Antoine, I'd bring my whole family and extra batteries for the Tasers." Skunky laughed as he pulled over the map Reaper had printed of area around the chateau. I'd marked the boundaries with a highlighter. "Plus, I bet the Montalbans beefed up security after Val choked their boss. This is a nice area, but it's not too far from other known Montalban turf. They'll call for help as soon as we hit it. How fast can we get out? Assuming we can get in there before they kill the hostage, what shape do you think he'll be in?"

"Bad," Valentine and I answered at the same time. He gave me a knowing look. We both understood how rotten being locked up could be. I'd gone old school, basically medieval, and Valentine had been subjected to one continuous drug-addled sci-fi mind-fuck. I'm guessing either of us would laugh at a stint in a normal prison system, not that there was much danger of that, because if we got caught we'd get disappeared long before any trial.

"Perhaps not," Ling said. "If they've kept him around in order to kill him at the scene and frame him as the rogue Majestic operative, it will raise too many questions if he has been tortured or if there are traces of suspicious drugs in his system. His captivity may have been far easier than yours was."

I gave her a grim smile. I could tell Ling was just saying that for my benefit.

"Assuming they don't simply set him on fire or something like that, so the police can only identify him by his dental records." Antoine stopped speaking when he saw me frowning at him. "Or what Ling said. That's more likely."

"It's fine." By my standards these Exodus types were all optimists. Thinking you could actually make the world a better place had that effect on people. "Bob might be messed up, but he'll still be alive. Anders is smart. He was the last surviving Majestic operative that put Project Blue together. They were all so compartmentalized that his superiors don't know that, though. He needs someone with Bob's résumé, and he needs it to be unquestionable that Bob was the one recruited by Willis to do this mission. They're going to use a nuke, so you know it isn't going to be a half-assed investigation afterward. Bob's death and frame-up will have to be really convincing."

"Look, I'm not trying to be an ass here," Skunky said, "but they could have killed him a while ago and got rid of the body, still pin it on him, and then say he escaped just as easily. He's still on the news, only now he's the subject of a worldwide manhunt instead of suspect dead at the scene."

"They don't need to convince the press or the public, that's easy. But the

Majestic leadership is tough. Kat wants to take over the Illuminati. She's not going to want a war with Majestic. She's going to want them thinking one of their own went rogue for the last couple of years and got killed in the act. Bob's still alive. I know it."

Skunky sighed and looked to Valentine and Ling. I was right. Ling was the official decision maker, but everybody here trusted Valentine's opinion. "That's a lot of risk without much preparation or intel based on a hunch."

"The longer we hold off, the more likely we are to get compromised. Twenty million dollars in reward money between me and Valentine, and Paris is crawling with thugs now."

"We need enough time to scope this place out, observe it, see who comes and goes, try to get a handle on what's in there first." Skunky was growing exasperated.

"Normally, I'd agree. I love planning. Planning's great. But it's out by itself away from the city. Look at that map. Where are we going to watch it from?" It was surrounded by grassy fields and hills, but there wasn't a whole lot of cover. The nearest neighbors were farms. "What if we get made between now and then? What if they launch Blue while we're still dicking around? I'm sneaking in there soon, by myself if I have to."

"So jeopardize the whole mission, because you're grasping at straws?"

"Who the fuck are you, again?" I was getting a little tired of Skunky's devil's advocate act. "I made my living getting into places nobody was supposed to be able to get into. What's your background?"

"High-end camera sales and *not throwing my life away* on futile noble gestures on dumb suicide missions! You got a problem with that?"

"Oh my God, both of you, chill the fuck out," Valentine said. "Skunky was on Switchblade Six with me and Tailor. Ramirez and Hawk trained him. Skunky, Lorenzo is old school Switchblade, from back in the Africa days. Decker trained him. We're all family here, and this dick measuring contest isn't helping."

Switchblade? Okay. I had to give him some props for that. He was young enough that he must have been in during their Vanguard era, when Decker had gone all corporate and legitimate businessman, but even then, the Switchblade teams had maintained their reputation of being tough as nails mercenaries who took the shittiest jobs and came back for more. And ironically, for the first time in years, I even had the stupid little knife Decker had given me. I pulled it out of my pocket and pushed the button. The pointy little blade popped out. I held it up in front of my face and wagged it back and forth. "Knife check." That had been Decker's stupid running joke.

Skunky gave me a respectful nod. Young Switchblade must have heard a lot of stories about old Switchblade. I returned the nod. I could still think he was wrong, but it wasn't because he was a wimp. I closed the knife and put it back in my pocket.

"We'll all hug later. Right now, can we figure this out?" Valentine sounded weary.

"Fine." Maybe they were right. I was pushing it. I was angry, frustrated, out of practice, and all that combined was making me sloppy. "Tonight's pushing it. I'll admit that. Look how willing I am to compromise. But it's either soon or never, and you all know it."

All seven of us were quiet for a bit as the maps were passed around. The house itself was twelve thousand square feet with a couple of outbuildings and a big garage. They could have an army inside and we wouldn't know until it was too late. There was four acres of lawn inside the fence. It was hard to tell from Google Earth, but there were some trees and bushes I could use for cover if I got inside the perimeter, even some statuary around the pool area, but there were also balconies on the second floor that would probably have guards posted.

"There is only one lane in," Shen warned us.

"It is entirely fenced in. I wonder if the gate is light enough we can ram through or if we'll have to use explosives?" Antoine asked. "It is possible Stokes installed hydraulic bomb blocks too."

"There is no way to see from the road." Shen ran his finger down the map. The lane was a windy quarter mile that would make it hard to build speed. "It would be suspicious to get close enough to look."

"Two of us they wouldn't recognize could take a rental car, pose as tourists, drive up this lane looking lost, then turn back," Antoine mused. "One visitor is not so suspicious. A minute of looking around is better than nothing at all."

"Good call," I told him. "The real estate listing says the fence is iron bars, but no height given. I wish I could tell if we're talking topped in razor wire or what . . ."

"I bet decorative fleur-de-lis. Only a fat fool would get stuck climbing over," Shen said. I could tell he was thinking what I was thinking. When we'd worked together before, I'd learned that he was *really* good at not being seen. Maybe even as good as I was.

"Shen and I could get in there, pave the way and take out the exterior guards and any dogs."

"I'm betting the Dobermans have poodle haircuts," Valentine said. "Look at this rich bitch neighborhood. My hometown didn't cost this much."

"Spare me, American. I grew up in a hut." Antoine ran one hand across his shaved head to wipe away beads of perspiration. That was one problem with crappy meeting places. You couldn't exactly complain about the inadequate air conditioning to the management, who in this case was an old blind Vietnamese lady. "Despite the price, I can see why Stokes chose this property. There is no way to insert quickly short of a helicopter. Could your Mr. Reaper get us some more current photographs?"

"I've got him working on it now." Sadly, since Reaper had been semi-retired and gone all weirdo hermit since I'd been gone, he hadn't replaced Little Bird after he'd crashed it in the Crossroads. I was missing our drone already. "He's also checking for any possible angle of getting in there. Lawn care, pool cleaner, food delivery, I don't care. Anything Stokes' assholes have brought in from the outside gives us a potential in. Reaper is all up in his business. If Stokes spent money on anything recently, he'll find it."

"There's nowhere we can get close enough to use a parabolic microphone on the windows." Skunky was checking the elevation on one nearby hill. "If the grass is tall enough here still and they've not run a bush hog over it, I can put on my ghillie suit and crawl in from the main road. I can provide overwatch and cover to three quarters of the property from there."

I checked the scale. "That's five hundred yards away. Are you good for that distance?"

Skunky just grinned. "Heck yeah, man."

"Jeff is very talented with two things, Lorenzo," Ling assured me. "A precision rifle that he babies as if it were his child—"

"It's got a lot of carbon fiber on it," Valentine interjected. "He thinks it makes it go faster, like a sports car."

"What's the other thing?"

"A banjo." Ling waited for that to sink in. "I am not joking. He plays the banjo."

Shen just shook his head sadly.

"Hey, country is cool, Ling. Don't judge," Skunky protested. "I know Shen's all Mr. Tradition but my folks ditched Taiwan when you guys' civil war started getting ugly. I'm all-American."

I'd heard Ling was from Northern China, before she'd been conscripted by the commies. I glanced at Shen. "Hong Kong," he said nonchalantly, which was by far the most information he'd ever shared about his past. So half the Exodus team was of Chinese descent, representing both North, South, and American . . . So of course the American played the banjo. Skunky probably owned an orange Dodge Charger with a Confederate flag on the roof, too.

"We need to figure out their numbers and their security system. You and Shen can't sneak through that field if they've got FLIR cameras up. That means we'd have to kill their power supply, but do they have a backup generator? How long will it take for their reinforcements to arrive?" Valentine was really thinking through all the ramifications, and all of these experienced operators were actually looking to him for guidance. I'll be damned. At some point he'd really turned into an actual leader.

Then I got a big surprise, when all of those supposedly experienced badasses looked to the teenage girl. "What do you think, Ariel?"

She was deep in thought, twirling her hair. "It fits. Bob is an important piece of the puzzle. Everything I can see points to Katarina using Blue for its original purpose to weaken the Illuminati, so she can take it over. Placing the blame for a Majestic operation on a rogue Majestic operative prevents their retaliation against her, and furthers her overall goal. So I think Lorenzo's hypothesis is correct—"

"Thank you."

"But we still need more information," she finished. They all nodded like she was brilliant.

"Why the hell does her opinion count? Are you even old enough to drive?"

Shen tried to placate me. "Ariel is very smart."

"Fantastic. I've got a smart person too, and Reaper agrees with me."

"She is like a girl Reaper—"

"Greaper?" Skunky asked.

"But smarter," Shen finished.

"I'm just saying we're going to need more time to figure things out." Ariel rolled her eyes. "Lorenzo changes things. I never thought he'd come back from the dead or be involved now. He's special. He's a unique variable."

I froze. Sala Jihan had said the same thing. I snapped, "What the fuck did you just call me?"

Ariel was taken aback. "Huh?"

My manner had changed so abruptly that I think I startled Exodus. The room got really quiet. "Easy, Lorenzo," Valentine said. His left hand had dropped under the table. I had no doubt it was resting on the butt of that big, stupid sixgun he liked to carry. "She's just trying to help. She didn't mean to, like, offend you or whatever. What the hell is your problem, anyway?"

I was staring at her, really looking at her for the first time. Ariel looked frightened, but was she really? There was something off about this little girl, and it wasn't just because she was too clever, or had a gift for seeing patterns, or whatever that bullshit was. I was really good at observing people, you had to be in order to copy their mannerisms or mimic their voices. I was a master at pretending to be someone I was not. This wasn't a young woman. This was something else pretending to be a young woman. And just for an instant I heard the whispers, pushing against the edge of my sanity.

"So I guess what your Oracle is saying is that *fate hasn't determined a path for me yet?*"

The others didn't notice, but Ariel was suddenly very nervous when I used Sala Jihan's words back on her. Now she was as suspicious of me as I was of her. None of the Exodus people saw what was going on, but somehow . . . I knew this little girl did.

"It's fine." She gave me a nervous smile. "My methods are probably a little weird for him. Mr. Lorenzo and we can talk about it later."

"Yeah . . . sure we will."

Valentine had no clue what had just gone down, and looked bewildered. "Alrighty then . . . so it's settled. Stokes is our next target, but we're going to take our time and do this right. We can't afford any more screw-ups."

"I'm sorry, Lorenzo." Ling put one hand on my shoulder. It was a remarkable display of gentleness and familiarity by her publicly reserved standards. "I understand your frustration, but if Bob has survived this long, he will survive a few more days."

That meant I'd have to wait a bit before I could start killing assholes and get my brother back, but I put on my happy face, because at least I didn't have to try and tackle it on my own. "I'm the spirit of compromise."

After we'd brainstormed and gotten our assignments, the meeting had broken up. Ariel was supposed to ride back to their hideout with Antoine. The street in front of the building was kept dark on purpose. Antoine went to get their car. I waited until she was alone before I approached her. For a while, I thought Valentine would never stop hovering over her like a mother hen.

She saw me coming and looked apologetic. "I didn't mean to upset you, Mr. Lorenzo. I know I sound weird sometimes—"

I cut her off. "Drop the act. What are you?"

Ariel was quiet for a moment. I could still see her blue eyes in the dark. "What do you mean?"

"The whole super-genius thing is a con. Yeah, you can see things, but not the way they think you do. They can't see it, but I do. You actually can see the future."

She didn't say anything. She just looked at me like I was a ranting madman.

"I've seen the other side. You're like *him*."

"I'm not like him!" she snapped. "I don't know of anyone like him."

"You know what? I believe that. He's unique."

"He's evil."

"Trust me, girl, that's really hard to miss." My chest was burning. "He's a force of nature. But you're just this innocent little thing, with a mind that the most powerful secret organizations in the world would kill to possess."

"Something like that," she said. "You wouldn't understand."

"Sala Jihan is evil, you're good. Flip sides of the coin, yin and yang, that's the deal?"

"You sound delusional, you know that?"

"Maybe I am. Or maybe whatever Kat intends to do would mess things up so bad that both the angels and the devils agree it needs to be stopped. If you can see the future, then tell me what's going to happen."

"Don't you get it yet?" She was exasperated. "Nobody can predict your future. That's why you're here! That's why the Pale Man let you go. It's the same reason I talked Michael into taking on this fight. Nothing is predictable once *either* of you get involved! On its current path, things fall apart. *Everything* falls apart! The world is crumbling, it's just a question of how fast. But with you two, we have a chance to change the course." She looked frustrated. "I just wish you could see."

Antoine pulled up with their car.

"Good night, Ariel."

"You know, Mr. Lorenzo, if I were you I would keep your crazy ramblings to yourself. You've been through a lot. The others will lose confidence in you if they think you've cracked." Ariel opened the passenger side door and got inside. "You don't need to be an oracle to see that."

They drove away, leaving me alone in the dark.

LORENZO
Outskirts of Paris
October 5th

I'd learned that it really didn't matter what country or culture you were in, you could always spot the ex-cons, and Samuel had hard time written all over him. If the shoddy prison tats on his forearms and neck hadn't given him away, the bad attitude would have.

Samuel looked me over long enough to know that I wasn't a cop, or whatever they had equivalent to parole officers in this country, then went back to working on the car engine. Shen and I had just wandered into his place of employment and interrupted him at work. The garage was busy, and he had stuff to do. At least he didn't waste my time by pretending he couldn't speak English. "Go to hell, man. I don't know no Samuel."

"You sure?" I looked to Shen, who as usual, just shrugged. "Because you look a lot like the picture of the guy we're looking for. Doesn't he?"

"Yes. The spitting image." Shen wandered over to a workbench and picked up a big wrench. I shook my head in the negative, and looking a little disappointed, Shen put the wrench down.

I knew this was our guy, though the nametag on his coveralls said his name was *Francoise*, that was all fake. Nobody else who worked here would know who this jackass really was. Reaper's digging said this garage was legit, and not even affiliated with any Montalban businesses. A few other mechanics looked our way, but nobody seemed inclined to question what we were doing here. When a place hired low rent scumbags like Samuel, this sort of visit was just another Human Resources issue.

I knew Shen was perfectly happy to beat the information we needed out of this douchebag, but I was trying to keep it diplomatic. "Then there must be another Algerian guy who works here who looks exactly like you, then. Help me find him." I laid a stack of Euros on top of the car battery next to him.

Samuel glanced over at the cash, then went back to work. "Man, I don't know nothing. You're wasting your time."

"This Samuel guy—not that I'm saying you're him, just making conversation—I hear he's really mechanically inclined. The right kind of people can hire him for all sorts of odd jobs involving things like cameras, security systems, and safes."

"Installing them, or getting through them?" Shen asked rhetorically.

"From what I've heard, both. Which is why our guy Samuel needs to have a fake identity at a boring day job so all the many angry Frenchmen he's robbed don't come and cap his ass."

Samuel kept turning a bolt with a ratchet, but he was sweating. "I don't do that anymore."

"I? Look at that, Shen. I think we've had a communications breakthrough." I put more money down on the stack. "You did a freelance install job a few months ago. It was the sort of thing you used to do for Big Eddie all the time."

Now Samuel was really scared. The ratchet was turning faster. Big Eddie wasn't a name you tossed around casually. "The whole time I was in prison, I never said nothing about who I was working for when I got arrested."

"It's cool, Samuel. Big Eddie's dead."

"I don't know nothing about that."

"I do." I was tired of messing around. I got right next to him, leaning over the engine as if I was trying to see what he was up to. "Because I'm the one who killed him."

The ratchet stopped cold. "Oh shit, man . . . You're that guy?"

"Yeah, I'm that guy. Hi, Samuel. I'm Lorenzo." The other mechanics were far enough away and there was enough tool and engine noise they couldn't hear me. This might not be a Montalban affiliated joint, but that didn't mean they weren't clued in enough to know about Anders' bounty on me. Every criminal and dirtbag in France had probably heard about that by now. "Nice to meet you. Now quit wasting my time. Big Eddie's in hell. I'm here. Which one do you think you should be more worried about?"

"But his sister is still around and she's just as nuts." And then he realized that he'd said way too much. Knowing about Kat's takeover meant he was still up on current events.

"I thought you said you were out. Are you working for her?" That was a loaded question, since I knew the rumors flying around Europe right now were about how I was murdering the hell out of Montalban employees, so if he was, and answered truthfully, I'd probably kill him, and if he wasn't, and answered truthfully, and I didn't believe him, I'd still probably kill him. Sucks, but that's what he deserved for being an asshole.

"No way!" he exclaimed. "I don't do anything with them anymore. The Montalbans left me to rot. When I got out, they'd forgotten about me. But my name's still out there, man. I just freelance once in a while, but never for the people you've got a beef with. I avoid Big Eddie's old people like the plague."

"Then let me clarify the nature of my visit, Samuel. A few months ago you were paid a bunch of money by a British mercenary named Aaron Stokes to beef up the security on a chateau in the countryside."

"How'd you know that?" That was supposed to be a secret. Now he'd moved into terrified. *Good.*

"I know everything." That was a complete lie.

Skunky had played lost tourist and taken a detour down Stokes' private road. He had to turn around before the Brits got suspicious, but when Exodus checked the hidden cameras they'd placed on Skunky's car, Ariel noticed that new cameras had been installed along the fence. She identified the brand and model by comparing images on the Internet. Somebody must have put those in recently, so Reaper had checked everyplace that sold expensive security cameras in the region. A large cash purchase in the right time frame had led us back to this clown. A little more poking and a few bribes and we knew Samuel's criminal record, his rep, and the fact that he'd paid off all of his considerable debts and stuck a bunch of money in the bank, all in the right time frame, told me this was probably our guy.

I tell you, criminals make the best detectives.

"Considering what Stokes paid you, either you overcharged him, or you did a whole lot of work to that old place."

"Part of that was him paying me to not talk about it. I haven't talked to them or said a word about them since the job was done. You can't mess with those Brits! His boys are killers, man."

Shen snorted.

"I need to get into that chateau, and you're going to help me."

"You want to die, man?"

"The only thing I'm in danger of dying from right now is boredom. You're boring me, Samuel." Before he could react, I cupped the back of his head and shoved his face against the engine block. From his wailing it turned out that it was still hot. Then I caught the car hood and pulled it down on his body. He squealed when it hit, but let's be honest, it really wasn't a good angle to really hurt him. So I wacked him with it a few times, squishing him. The money was sent flying by the wind gusts. I smashed him as far into the engine compartment as I could, and then leaned my weight on the hood. His legs were kicking and he was letting out some muffled screams, but he wasn't going anywhere. "Check it out, Shen. I'm not bored anymore."

"You need a hobby."

Two other mechanics had seen my *negotiation strategy* and were coming our way. They probably didn't know who Samuel really was, but there was a certain international blue collar code of honor that declared you needed to step in when some outsider started kicking the shit out of one of your coworkers. Both were big, burly, tough guys with nearly as many prison tats as Samuel had. One of them had a jack handle. The other carried a ball-peen hammer.

Shen stepped right in front of them, hands on his hips. All he said was "No," and smiled. The two big guys stopped, looked at Shen, who was half the size of either of them—or one quarter of their combined mass—yet seemed completely confident anyway, and realized this probably wasn't the dude to mess with. They walked away, muttering. Apparently Samuel wasn't popular enough to risk an ass-beating over.

I opened the hood, pulled Samuel out by the ear, and then dragged him out the back door so we could have some privacy while Shen stuck around to make sure none of the others suddenly felt like using the phone. Once we were in the back parking lot, and satisfied there weren't any other witnesses, I let go of his ear.

"Okay, okay!" There was blood trickling from his nose and bruises spreading on his cheek. It turned out I'd gotten more leverage on that hood than I'd thought. "I swear I don't work for the Montalbans anymore! Back when nobody knew who Big Eddie really was, there were rules, you know? You obey the rules, you don't get clipped. But the new boss is all up in everyone's shit. She'll have you killed if she imagines you did something wrong. The money's good, but I'm avoiding that outfit. I swear. If Stokes is in with them, I didn't know it. He told me he's a free agent."

"I believe you, Samuel, which is why I'm offering you two options. Weigh them carefully. I pay you more than what Stokes paid you to begin with to walk me through every aspect of their system, and then you can forget this conversation ever happened. Or I beat it out of you for free. The only part of this which is completely non-negotiable is the part where you tell me everything you know."

"Stokes will kill me," he protested.

"He might later, but I'll for sure kill you sooner. So, bribe and run, or severe beating and probable death? I've not got all day."

I must have been really persuasive, because his decision didn't take too long. "I'll talk, it's good! I didn't like those pricks anyway."

"Fantastic." That was easy. I whistled for Shen that it was time to go. Then I pulled out my key fob, and pushed the trunk button. "Climb in."

Samuel got a really sick look on his face when he saw the Audi's trunk pop open. "Don't make me get in the boot. Come on, man, I said I'll tell you everything."

"Oh, you will. And then you'll hang out with us until the job is over. If we get caught, you get caught too. That should guarantee you don't forget any pertinent details. Plus, I'd hate to be all merciful and let you go, only for you to have second thoughts and warn them we're coming."

"I wouldn't do that!" he protested as Shen joined us.

"Yeah, because you've been a rock so far." I probably didn't need to make him ride in the trunk, but I'd just stolen this car, it was clean, and he had grease all over his coveralls.

Shen wasn't as patient as I was. He just snap kicked Samuel in the stomach, and while he was bent over, gasping, Shen hurled him head first into the trunk.

"At least it's roomy in there," I said as Shen slammed the lid.

As we were driving away, I called Reaper and told him we were on our way back.

"Did you get the package?" Reaper asked, having watched too many spy movies.

"It's in the trunk."

"Oh . . . Did you make sure there wasn't one of those emergency exit pull tab thingies? They mandated those for like when kids play hide and seek in the trunk and get trapped."

"Yes, Dad." I hung up on him. "Sheesh, you'd think I'd never kidnapped anybody before."

As usual, Shen sat quietly, watching out the window as the outskirts of Paris scrolled by.

In the few times we'd worked together, I'd found that Shen wasn't exactly a man of many words. Which meant he was probably the safest person I could say the following to: "Between what we've heard about Stokes' crew, and Samuel's rep for doing quality work, I hate to admit it, but Valentine made the right call. If we'd gone when I wanted we probably would have gotten spotted and chewed up . . . Probably would have gotten Bob executed in the process."

"Yes."

I drove in silence for a moment. This was eating at me, and I kind of wanted to talk about it with somebody. I hadn't wanted to bring it up with Jill since she was injured and had enough on her mind, and Reaper was still dealing with his weird personal demons. But what the hell, Shen seemed like a good listener.

"Ever since I got out, I've been off. I've been making too many mistakes. I've gotten sloppy. That place screwed me up, Shen. If I'd taken my time at the smuggler's shop maybe I would have seen Anders staking it out. Jill wouldn't have gotten shot. This is all on me. I know better, but it's like ever since I got out of that dungeon, I've been seeing red. Like I can't think straight until I end these people. The Pale Man got in my head. I can't explain it."

"Desire for vengeance clouds your vision."

"Is that like the Zen Buddhist way of saying I'm too bloodthirsty?"

"Because I'm Chinese, you assume I'm profoundly philosophical?" Shen looked over at me and grinned. "That is racist."

"Motherfucker, I've seen you fight. You're like a kung-fu master, snatch the pebble from my hand grasshopper, badass. If anybody on Exodus is going to get all philosophical *Art of War* on me, it should be you."

"I checked that out from a library once. It is actually a very good book."

"And here I was thinking you'd spent years meditating under a freezing waterfall and punching rocks before you joined Exodus."

Shen shook his head. "I was a killer for the Triads."

I glanced over at the unassuming little man. In my business that was one hell of a resume item. "No shit?"

"No shit." Shen sighed when he realized I was still staring at him, waiting for him to continue. "Pay attention to the road, please."

I did. Traffic wasn't bad here, but I didn't want to do anything that would attract police attention while I had a kidnap victim in the trunk. I'd stolen money from Chinese organized crime a few times over the years. They were an unforgiving, merciless bunch. "I know the Triads. They're not known for their retirement packages."

"My past is not something I am proud of. When I was a boy, I was a typical Hong Kong thug, but I was clever and had ambition. I worked my way through the ranks and developed my skills. By the time I was twenty, I was a trusted associate."

"That's a big career jump from Triad assassin to Exodus do-gooder. What happened?"

"One day my employers asked me to kill someone. I decided not to."

"I'm guessing that's the abridged version."

Shen was quiet as a police car went speeding by. We both watched it in the mirrors for a moment to see if it flipped around. Samuel's ex-con coworkers didn't seem like the types to call the cops, but you never knew. Once he was certain we were clear, Shen continued. "Being ordered to kill a man who has broken our agreed-upon rules is one thing. Killing his wife and children to set an example is another. The assignment forced me to examine my life choices."

I laughed at that. Shen was like the master of understatement. "And?"

"I hesitated. The Triad does not tolerate disobedience. They decreed I would die along with my assigned targets. I returned to Hong Kong and killed my employers instead." He said that like it was no big deal.

"You're telling me you went to war with a Hong Kong Triad."

He shrugged. "Only with enough of them to settle the matter."

"See? I knew you were a badass. Damn, Shen. Did you wear a white suit? Did doves fly by in slow motion while you used a Beretta in each hand?"

Shen didn't seem to think that was funny. "Nothing so dramatic. When it was over, I agreed to never return to Hong Kong. I had no purpose and nothing to live for. There had been conflict between the Triads and Exodus. I knew they fought for what they believed to be good. To atone for the evil acts I had committed, I offered Exodus my services. It took years before they trusted me. Some still do not. The ones with us here are my family now . . . Very well, Lorenzo, you wish to know what I think?"

"Go for it."

"Like me, you are experienced in these matters. You understand that only death can satisfy some debts. Regardless of what you have suffered, you must . . ." Shen paused, trying to think of the correct way to phrase it, "Keep your shit together."

"You don't need to worry about that. On my worst day I'm still more than a match for these dickheads." But that was just talk. I was worried. I knew it, and Shen knew it.

"You want to lash out. I have been there. But too much is riding on this mission. We can feel the pressure. The time is close. As you Americans say, it breathes down our neck. You have made mistakes, recognized them, and made fewer. You were still recovering from Jihan's prison. My friends have no such excuse. I respect Ling. I love her as if she was my own sister. She was one of the first to accept me in Exodus. Only her heart follows a flawed man. Valentine is dedicated, but too passionate. He rushed, trying to pit Underhill against Katarina, and nearly paid with his life. It was foolish."

"Harsh."

"Yet true." Shen trailed off as we stopped at an intersection.

When it was a little quieter we both realized Samuel was yelling for help from the trunk. The carbon monoxide was probably making him stupid. "Keep it down in there," I shouted toward the back seat.

"I accepted death long ago, but when it comes I pray it serves a purpose. We can't afford to die without results, Lorenzo. I truly believe the world depends on what we do here."

"The world, huh?" I tapped my fingers on the steering wheel as I waited for a light to change. "You talking about Ariel's predictions?"

"I am."

"While we're on the topic of mystical bullshit philosophies . . ." Under the cold light of day I wasn't going to tell him my crackpot theories. "Never mind."

"I think she sees patterns others do not. I leave it at that. All that matters is that she is usually right."

The light changed. "Damn, Shen, that was remarkably unhelpful."

"Now you understand why I do not make small talk."

Chapter 14: The Rescue

VALENTINE
North of Paris
October 8th

The plan was simple enough: Lorenzo and Shen would sneak up in the dark and try to get the gate open, while Skunky would provide overwatch with his rifle. Reaper—and his unwilling passenger, Samuel the security installer—was parked a ways off with our secondary getaway vehicle. Ling, Antoine, and I were in our van, hidden off the main road, ready to roll in when the infiltrators got the gate open. We had nothing to do until then, and it was maddening.

I sat in the back, with Antoine, dressed out in full combat gear. I had on body armor, with plates, and a load-bearing vest on top of that. Beneath all of that we were wearing normal clothing, so we could ditch the heavy stuff and not look like weirdos if we needed to. Antoine and I both carried German G3 rifles. I had the same one I'd used since the Battle of the Crossroads. Like mine, Antoine's had the sights cut off and was fitted with a Spuhr stock. Unline mine, his also had a 40mm grenade launcher mounted under the barrel. We were really hoping not to use grenades, however, since this was supposed to be a hostage rescue. Regardless, we were ready to provide heavy fire support when the time came.

Ling was in the driver's seat, she was fully kitted out too. Of course, we had left Ariel behind. Despite her enthusiasm, she had zero training, and quite simply wasn't cut out for this kind of work. I had suggested that she stay with Jill to keep an eye on her. Jill was still recovering, and wasn't in good enough shape to get around, only Ariel had begged off, saying she was too busy. For whatever reason, I had the feeling Ariel wanted to avoid Lorenzo's people. She was still at our safehouse.

We were really shorthanded, especially since we had no idea how many men Stokes had. It was too risky to keep the place under surveillance directly, but a little cautious poking around with the farmers in the local villages told us there had been several people staying at the chateau, but the number of cars coming and going had jumped dramatically right after I'd tried to strangle Katarina. That probably meant she had called in reinforcements.

I wished Tailor could help. We'd have a lot better luck getting Bob Lorenzo out alive with a properly equipped tactical team on our side, and from what I had seen Tailor's guys seemed to really know their shit. However, there was the slight problem that I hadn't told Romefeller we were doing this. He thought we were still investigating and searching for the bomb. The big Illuminati meeting was in the morning, so I was afraid he'd declare any direct raid against Katarina Montalban's employees to be *unsanctioned*, and then we would be out of luck. I wasn't just worried that he'd tell us not to, but after the mess at the hotel, Romefeller might actively send Tailor to stop us from going in. But if we could retrieve Bob, Kat would lose her patsy and Blue would be delayed. Romefeller might not like doing it my way, but tough shit.

Antoine must've read my face, even in the darkened van. "You look pensive, Mr. Valentine."

"Pensive," I repeated, keeping one ear on the radio. Skunky was slowly crawling into position. Lorenzo and Shen were doing the same. Since they were going low and slow, the wait was downright nerve-wracking. "That's one way of describing it, I guess."

"It is understandable." It must've been difficult to find body armor that would fit somebody as large as Antoine. He had to be six-foot-five, with at least a fifty-inch chest. The G3 rifle he carried, especially with a grenade launcher attached, is not a compact or especially handy weapon. It looked almost like a toy in his hands. His voice was deep and accented, but despite his imposing figure, he always spoke like a schoolteacher. "There is much that could go wrong. Do you still think this is the right thing to do?"

I exhaled, wiping sweat from my brow. We didn't have the engine running and it was getting warm in the back of the van, wearing all this gear. "I think this is crazy," I said, bluntly. "But it needs to be done. We can't let them frame Bob for mass murder."

Antoine simply nodded.

"Besides," I continued, leaning back in my seat, "Exodus roped Lorenzo into this mess on the promise that you'd help him get his brother back. He went through God-knows-what because of that. It would be incredibly screwed up to not uphold your end of the deal."

"Exodus keeps its promises," Antoine agreed, "no matter how long it takes. But I was not speaking of us, I was asking about you."

"You guys and Lorenzo came and rescued me when I was being held. You risked your lives for me. Bob's in the predicament he's in because of me. Getting him out is the least I can do. It's the right thing to do."

We got the signal over the radio. They were almost there.
Good luck, asshole.

LORENZO
The Chateau

"Do you have the shot?"

"*I have the shot.*"

"Take it," I whispered.

The sound suppressor hid the gunshot, but the impact of the bullet came as a wet *thwack* as Skunky blew the guard's brains out. There was a *clack* as his rifle dropped from nerveless fingers. A shadow passed in front of the light as the man fell flat on the balcony. A red mist hung in front of the lamp for an instant before dissipating in the wind.

"*The guard is down.*" Skunky's voice came through my earpiece. He was excitable in person, but on the job it turned out he was all business.

We had been crawling for hours. Now that Skunky had shot a guard, it was a race against the clock before they realized we were here. No alarm sounded. The compound remained quiet. That wouldn't last forever.

That had been a damned good shot. There was a strong breeze tonight, and it was even harder to judge wind through a night vision scope. My own night vision device was stowed in a pouch on my belt, because it sucked to wear while crawling through the dirt, caught on branches, and after a while the weight killed my neck and gave me a headache.

"*Keep holding position. The camera is turning left.*"

All the cameras tracked slowly back and forth. We were so close that I imagined I could hear the little servo motors, but that was wishful thinking from my hearing damaged, half deaf self.

I waited, hoping that nobody inside had heard the guard fall, but the yard around the big house remained clear. Shen and I had spent three miserable, filthy hours low crawling through the weeds and brush, moving when the camera was pointed away, and taking cover when Skunky warned us it was close. It had to be nearly as exhausting for him, watching it through the scope and repeating the countdown a few hundred times now.

"*Four, three, two, one. And clear. Go.*"

Shen and I leapt out of the weeds and sprinted for the fence.

Samuel had given us the stats, and since he was a mile away, tied up in Reaper's car with the promise that if I got caught, Reaper was just going to leave him there, I was certain he'd been completely forthcoming. There were no motion or contact sensors on the fence. He'd talked Stokes out of it because there were too many deer in the area, and they would always be setting it off. The fence was fifty years old, ten feet tall, and made of thick iron bars, spaced four inches apart, with—Shen had guessed right—decorative pokeys on top, that was it. So it would be a piece of cake for guys like us to get over. My biggest concern was that it would rattle and make a bunch of noise as we climbed it.

We had thirty seconds before the camera on the roof came back around. We reached the fence with fifteen seconds to spare. Shen bent next to it, so I could step ladder my way onto his knee, his shoulder, and as he stood up with my weight on him, I grabbed the top bar. The fence shook a bit, but the metallic noise was less than the sound of the wind. I rolled on top, balancing, letting the fleur-de-lis poke into my soft Kevlar body armor vest as I swung one hand down to Shen. Gloves hit my exposed forearm as Shen pulled. He was pretty damned acrobatic, and made it over the top in a flash, dropping smoothly and silently onto the grass on the other side.

I rolled off and dropped next to him, hitting with a grunt. I'd been pushing my body hard since I'd gotten out of Jihan's dungeon, training as hard as I could while limited to an apartment with no exercise equipment, so I wasn't even close to being in prime shape. Shen was crouched and listening, one hand on his slung weapon. There hadn't been any dogs when Samuel had done his install work, but that might have changed since. There wasn't any barking and no big angry German Shepherds descended on us, so that was good.

I pointed toward the nearest patch of bushes. Shen and I moved out in a fast crouch. The grass was thick, hadn't been mowed for a while, and had gone to seed. Secret prisons were lax on their lawn care. The wind was blowing the leaves and shaking the branches. That was a huge benefit for us, as the noise and movement would help hide us from the patrols.

"Camera coming back in five, four, three—"

By the time Skunky got done, we were already on our bellies in the dirt and roots. This would be the last countdown. After this, we'd be beneath the exterior camera's field of view, and we could push for the front gate. Skunky's earlier lost tourist scout drive-by had confirmed the gate was too solid to ram. Blowing it up would be messy and time-consuming. Short of a tank we didn't have, the terrain was too rough to crash the fence at any other angle. So if we wanted help to roll in, we needed to open that gate.

However, there was now a dead man leaking the contents of his skull all over the rear second-floor balcony. Any second somebody was going to miss him or trip over him, and then we were screwed. So time was of the essence.

On my knees and elbows I crawled through the bushes. I could tell they'd been well trimmed once, probably styled into animal topiary, but now they were lumps of wonderful concealment. The wind helped hide any inadvertent shaking I caused. I reached the edge of the leaves and surveyed the back of the house. There were a lot of lights around the chateau, so I'd made the right call leaving off my NVGs. In fact, there were too many interior rooms lit up for comfort. Hopefully that just meant they liked to sleep with the lights on, and not that there were a bunch of them still awake, but probably not.

Seen up close, this was a really nice estate, but a little too snooty, Euro artsy for my tastes. Everything between the buildings was landscaped into gentle curves and cobbled paths. There were terraces, columns, and even imitation Greek statues. The pool was full, but judging from all the leaves and bugs floating on the water, it hadn't been used for a while. Lights hitting the rippling water cast odd reflections on the walls and statues.

I checked my watch. It was after 4 AM. We were behind schedule. I'd wanted to hit while people tended to be at their natural deepest sleep rhythm, but that weed crawl in had been agonizingly slow and put us behind schedule.

"*This is Skunky. Ghost and Slick are in the compound,*" he reported to the assault element.

Exodus had made up the call signs. I looked toward Shen, like *fuck you, I should be Ghost.* In the dark, with his artificially blackened face, all I could see was his teeth smiling back, like *up yours, I'm Mr. Exodus Cool Guy. You have to be Slick.*

"*This is Nightcrawler. We are ready to move at your signal.*" That had been Valentine's Dead Six call sign, and what I'd first known him as. So in that case, I was lucky my call sign hadn't ended up as *Asshole.*

I had the 9mm TMP subgun hanging from a single point sling at my side. While crawling through ditches all night, the compact weapon had been handy. Now that I was in a compound with an unknown number of heavily armed mercenaries, I wished I had carried something chambered in an actual grown up sized rifle cartridge. Shen had one of those Czech EVO subguns, with some short, fat European suppressor I didn't recognize. I pulled out my 1911 with the old suppressor screwed onto the end of its threaded muzzle. We would keep this quiet as long as possible.

This was my element. There was something addictive about sneaking around in the dark. If we needed to bail, I was ready to disappear in plain sight too. Though I was dirty and sweaty and had my face painted, beneath my soft vest, I was wearing regular clothes. I could ditch the guns and vest, and a quick scrub later I could disappear back into society, not that there was any society within a couple of miles, but you never know. But until we had to run, I owned these scumbags. I felt alive.

Shortly, we'd be clear to move. Then we'd either succeed and get Bob back alive, or we'd fail, and probably all get shot in the process. At this point there was no use dwelling on it. We'd made the best plan we could. This crew was motivated, experienced, and extremely skilled. If something went wrong, we'd adapt, and we'd win.

While we lay there in the shadows, Shen unslung the EVO and quietly opened the folding stock. Skunky began our final countdown. *"Camera is past in three, two, one. Go."*

I was out and moving quickly toward the edge of the pool shack. Shen and I had talked it over beforehand, and he veered toward the right, staying with the bushes. We had the same target. Two different paths let us watch more angles for threats, plus—let's be honest—this whole alpha predator in the dark thing is mostly instinct, so having somebody up close on you is awkward. I kept to the darkest spots, moving from shadow to shadow. I caught one brief glimpse of Shen as he rolled beneath another bush, but then he was gone. The dude was really good.

We knew there were patrols around the interior. For the last few hours Skunky had told us about each one he'd spotted and the path they had taken, but they'd been sporadic enough that there didn't seem to follow a scheduled route. It was just two dudes with guns walking around periodically.

I began to slide around the edge of the pool house, then realized there was gravel here, and gravel is too loud to walk on, so I backtracked and took the other side.

"Slick, this is Skunky. When you go around that corner, I won't be able to cover you."

I tapped my transmit button twice in the affirmative, then I went that way anyway. Like I said, you had to go with your instinct. I made it twenty feet closer to the gatehouse before Skunky transmitted again.

"I've got more movement on the rear balcony. Another guard. He's a few seconds from seeing that body I left."

The angle was such that I couldn't see the balcony anymore. I kept pushing on. I was just going to have to count on our sniper.

Skunky must not have realized he was still transmitting. *"Come on. Turn around. Don't open that door . . . Don't . . ."* There was a long pause. I was far enough away that I didn't hear the sound of the supersonic bullet travelling through the air or the impact against flesh. *"There's another guard down on the rear balcony."*

That was probably the first guard's relief. When he didn't go back inside, the rest would realize something was wrong. They'd sound the alarm, wake everybody else up, and then all hell would break loose. The clock was ticking down fast now. It was tempting to rush, but that would get me spotted, so I just kept on slinking along from shadow to shadow.

Slowly, very slowly, I peeked around the corner. Quick jerky movements were what got you spotted in the dark. The gatehouse was in view, but unfortunately, so was one of the random patrols. Two men were strolling my way, with maybe ten feet separating them. They weren't smoking or joking. They were relaxed, but alert. Heads up, glancing around, these weren't just goons. Their attitude and appearance said they were pros. The ones Skunky had seen during the daylight drive by had been wearing contractor chic, khakis and photographer's vests to hide their pistols, so they looked like security, but not so militant as to make witnesses nervous. Apparently that went out the window after dark, because now they were wearing tac vests and carrying shorty AR carbines.

Skunky couldn't see us. They were going to be on top of me in a few seconds, and I didn't have time to back up out of their way. I'd need to pop both of these guys before they saw me, and I had to do it clean and fast enough that they couldn't shout or yank a trigger. I had been working out, but there hadn't exactly been ample opportunities to hit the shooting range. This was going to be tough.

Then Shen surprised me by appearing behind the man in the rear, wrapping one hand over his mouth and simultaneously running a black knife across his throat. That guard made enough of a noise to catch the other's attention. He saw Shen, opened his mouth to shout something, but then my bullet caught him in the back of his skull. He dropped in a heap.

We'd put them down in the light. If anybody had been looking out a window, we were fucked. I rushed over next to Shen, who was already dragging his body into the shadows behind a stone bench behind the pool house. I grabbed mine by the drag straps of his armor and pulled. Between the armor and mags, the dude weighed a ton. His carbine dragged along through the grass behind him by the sling. It left a red trail. Looking down, I realized the .45 hollow point had gone through his brain and exited through his mouth. Then the fucker blinked at me and I nearly dropped him. It was like he was really confused and trying to ask me something. He was probably my age, had a big mustache, and I'd seen that same look on the faces of many of the other prisoners I'd had to kill for Sala Jihan's amusement. Thankfully, he was dead by the time I caught up to Shen.

"How'd you know I was going to be there?" I whispered.

Shen was wiping his knife off on his guard's pant leg. "I just did."

Nothing else needed to be said. I noted our position. If we had to fall back, we now had a convenient stash of extra guns and ammo. We moved out.

"This is Skunky. I've got visual on Ghost and Slick again, approaching the gatehouse. There is one guard in the gatehouse. I have a shot, but he's behind glass at an angle. Do you want me to take it?"

"Slick. Negative, Skunky. We got this." Rifle bullets could deflect in weird ways hitting heavy glass. A hole would be one thing, but if the whole window shattered, it would make a lot of noise. Besides, I could see the guard now. He was sitting down inside the little building. The interior light was on. Outside was dark. He wouldn't be able to see very far. This guard was younger, buzzed head, military look, pistol on his belt, but street clothes and no armor. Probably in the unlikely event some local farmer rolled up asking questions about the place and they didn't want the neighbors talking about paramilitary looking dudes living here.

Samuel said there was a keypad at both sides of the gate for a driver to put in the code, and a button in the shack. He didn't know what the code was, so that meant button.

I scooted right up on the door and rested one hand on the knob. Shen went down, crawled past me, and got under the window. I'd try the knob. If it was open, I'd sweep in and drop him. If it was locked, the guard would probably hear the knob move, and then Shen would come up and pop him flat through the glass with the EVO.

I put one gloved hand on the knob, pistol in the other. Shen nodded when he was ready.

And then a phone rang. We both froze.

It rang twice more before the man inside answered it. He must have been zoning out. I could barely hear the guard through the door. "Yeah, mate . . . Stokes is coming back?" There was a long pause. "What? We're done! The fuck you say." Another pause. "About bloody time that fucker Anders told the guv what to do with the prisoner."

There was an electric hum, and then a metallic rumble as the heavy gate began to move. The guard had pushed the button for us. We had incoming.

"*This is Skunky. The gate is opening. I repeat, gate is opening.*"

"*Nightcrawler. Rolling.*"

They must have thought we'd done that. Shen hurried and tapped one for negative. They were opening it for somebody else. That meant Exodus would cross paths with them on the road. Sure enough, Valentine came right back. "*We have a single vehicle moving toward the gate at a high rate of speed.*"

The guard started laughing. "We're done! So let's deliver that big bald fucker so we can get paid and go home."

They're moving Bob.

I heard another noise inside, like a chair being shoved back. "I'm on my way."

The door opened. The guard was beaming as he dropped his phone back into his pocket, probably thinking about how he was going to spend all that money he was getting paid for holding my brother prisoner all these months.

He was so excited he damned near walked into me, crouched in the doorway. I jammed the Gemtech under his chin and painted the ceiling with blood. He crashed back, hit the wall, and began to slide down. I shot him again before he hit the floor, just to be sure. A .45 shell casing bounced across the sidewalk.

I glanced back toward the house. More lights were coming on. They hadn't sounded the alarm yet, but they were going to move Bob. They were now five men short, and things were going sideways as soon as they realized that. But even worse, the guard had been acting like their job was done. That could only mean one very bad thing.

I came to a very terrifying realization. There was only one reason to move Bob.

Blue!

I keyed my radio. "Nightcrawler, can you intercept that car?"

"We can try."

"Our secondary target is in the car." That was Stokes. "Take him alive. Anders just called him. The target knows the Alpha Point."

"Damn it." I could hear the squeal of tires over the radio. *"We're on it."*

"Project Blue has launched. I repeat, Project Blue has launched."

VALENTINE
The Highway

Blue was in motion? *What the hell?* Lorenzo said Stokes knew the Alpha Point, the very thing Majestic had spent months torturing me for. But there was no time to think through the repercussions now.

"Got them," Ling stated with the utmost calm. Our lights were off and she was driving with NVGs. There was a pair of taillights moving along the dark and windy road ahead of us. Our man Stokes was in there, and if they arrived while Lorenzo and Shen were still on the ground, our infiltrators would be caught in the open. Ling mashed the accelerator and we began closing on the sedan.

"Get us closer," I said. Hopefully running dark we could close the gap before they realized we were on them.

I pulled open the sliding door on the passenger's side. Wind rushed in as trees whizzed by at a hundred and thirty kilometers per hour. As *the Calm* settled over me and my heart rate slowed, I took a deep breath. "Antoine, slide over and grab onto my vest so I don't fall out. Ling, come up on them and match speed."

"Affirmative."

I leaned outward, bracing myself on the door frame, hoping to hell Ling didn't swerve and send me flying. Antoine had hands like a vise, and he had remained buckled in, but I really didn't want to test his grip strength if I didn't have to. The sedan was just ahead of us and we were closing fast. They hadn't yet realized what was happening yet. I aimed at the rear of the car as best I could while hanging clumsily out the door of a speeding vehicle, flipped the selector to auto, and squeezed the trigger.

The G3 bucked against my shoulder as I fired the short bursts, trying not to lose the target. I didn't know where Stokes was sitting, so I concentrated on the rear tires. The car began skewing wildly side to side. Brake lights flared as a tire burst.

I had went through twenty rounds in just a few seconds. "Reloading!" I shouted as I dropped my mag, but Antoine was already handing me another.

Ling used that lull and put the hammer down. She put the edge of our front bumper on the wounded car ahead of us. A couple of muzzle flashes blinked at us from the back seat, as the surprised occupants desperately tried to return fire, but we had the initiative. Ling cranked the wheel into their back end, forcing them into a hard turn. The sedan flew off the road, spun through the grass, and crashed through a fence, disappearing in a cloud of dust.

Ling stomped on the brakes and we slid to a stop on the gravel. Through the swirling dust I could see the car's headlights. They had smashed into some trees. A car door was already open.

"They bailed out!" I leapt out of the van. Antoine was right behind me. Ling jumped out too. "We need Stokes alive!"

That was going to be difficult, because shots rang out from the darkened woodline. The moon was out, but it was hard to see through the trees. From the muzzle flashes, it looked like someone was firing wildly while moving away from us. The three of us crouched, as we moved up, keeping the crashed Mercedes between us and the shooter.

When we got to the car, the driver was still buckled in. His air bag had deployed, and from the way he was clumsily trying to get out, he had been dazed by the impact. From the his size and hair color, I could tell it wasn't our target. When he saw us moving up he went for a pistol on his hip. Ling and I simultaneously shot him through the glass.

"Nice." The back seat was clear. Stokes was our runner.

"Contact," Antoine shouted as he spotted our target moving through the trees. Tall guy, white hair, that had to be him. He must have gotten hurt in the crash, because he wasn't able to run too fast through the brush. Antoine fired a couple of rounds into the trees ahead of him, blasting through branches and bark. He didn't want to kill him, but Stokes didn't know that, and he dove for cover.

"Ling, go around to the left. Antoine, stay with me." Guns up, Antoine and I pushed forward, jogging toward the trees while trying to stay low. Ling moved to our flank, but remained in sight. We were close and he was cornered, but a stupid mistake could still get us killed.

"Come out, Stokes," I shouted.

"Piss off!" Stokes responded, as he hung a handgun over the top of a log and fired off several wild shots. "Do you have any idea who you're fucking with?"

"Screw this," I muttered. I took aim and smashed several rounds into the log next to him.

Odds were that he got pelted with fragments and splinters. That must have put the fear of God into him because he cried out, "Alright! Enough!" His breathing was labored and he sounded like he was in pain. He tossed his gun into the dirt, then slowly stepped into the open. "I'm coming out! Don't fucking shoot!"

Ling turned on her weapon mounted light, blinding him. There was a bunch of blood on his face, but sure enough, he was our target. "Aaron Stokes," I said, more as a statement than a question. "You're lucky we didn't kill you."

"Who the fuck are you people?" he sneered. "Do you have any idea who I am? Who I work for? You're in a world of shit, mate, a world of shit."

I walked up and hit him in the chest with the buttstock of the G3. Not hard enough to break anything—I needed him to talk—but hard enough to let him know I wasn't playing. He landed on his butt, coughing. I realized that he had something in his hand.

"Give me the phone, asshole." I snatched it from him, stepped back, and looked at the screen. He was in a call with somebody, trying to give them information about us. I ended the call. "Nice try, bro, but I saw that movie too."

"Get on your knees," Ling ordered. She had pulled out some zip ties.

"Fuck you, cunt," Stokes snarled. "I'd like to see you make me."

"Oh?" Antoine really didn't like anyone talking to Ling that way.

"We need him alive," I warned Antoine, as I scrolled through Stokes' phone.

"Indeed," Antoine said, right before he slugged Stokes in the face. He crumpled to the ground, knocked silly.

"Jesus," I said, looking up. "I said we need him *alive.*"

"He'll live," Antoine said, sounding a little defensive, as Ling hurried and zip-tied Stokes' hands behind his back.

"You could have put him in a coma."

"Being in a coma is still alive."

"Haul him back to the van. We need to go. Lorenzo and Shen need our help." I let my rifle hang on its sling and keyed my microphone as Antoine hoisted Stokes up and dragged him back toward the road. "Slick, this is Nightcrawler, we got him."

"Say again?" Lorenzo replied, with lots of static. Down here in the trees our reception was garbage.

"Reaper, Nightcrawler, come back."

Reaper responded much more clearly. He was in a vehicle with a more powerful radio. *"Send it."*

"Relay to the others, we have our boy, I say again, we have our boy. How copy?"

"Understood, Nightcrawler. Is he alive?"

"Affirmative." I glared at Antoine. "Probably. I'm going through his phone now."

"Awesome!" Reaper said. *"Probably useful intel on there."*

"And lots of porn. I mean, wow, lots of porn." Lorenzo had said that Anders had just called and given Stokes the Alpha Point. I scrolled through his recent calls. The contacts were listed with really innocuous nicknames, but there was a call from Draco less than fifteen minutes ago. That had to be Anders. Then Stokes had placed a few calls immediately after. One number appeared twice, probably to tell his men to get ready, and then another to call for help when we attacked. But there was one other number he'd dialed immediately after speaking to Anders. I tried that one.

It didn't even ring. It went straight a recorded message being spoken in French. Something, something, *Gare d'Evangeline.*

Evangeline?

I must have twitched or something, because Ling asked me what was wrong.

I couldn't answer. I was lost in a memory. Colonel Curtis Hunter, buried in the rubble of a collapsed roof, trying to tell me something about Evangeline. He died before he could explain what he meant. *It couldn't be a coincidence.*

Then there was something I understood. *"For English, press two."* I quickly lowered the phone, brought up the keypad, and tapped 2. Raising the phone back to my ear, I listened. *"Welcome to the automated directory for the Evangeline Station. For train schedules, press one. For ticketing, press two. For customer service, press . . ."* I hung up.

"Evangeline . . ." Images of Dr. Silvers asking me who she was over and over again filled my head. "My God. It's not a person, it's a place."

"What are you talking about?" Ling asked.

I got on my radio. "Reaper, listen to me very carefully. Evangeline isn't a person, it's a train station. That's has to be where the Alpha Point is! Evangeline is where Hunter hid his fucking bomb! Tell Lorenzo they're moving it by train!" I let go of my radio. "Quick, get back to the van."

"What about Stokes?"

"Leave him." Before I'd even finished saying that, Antoine tossed the stunned man into the dirt. "Reaper, we're on the way to Evangeline to stop that bomb."

"What about the mission?"

Shen and Lorenzo were in a compound filled with mercenaries, and since their boss had called them, they knew they were under attack. I looked toward the lights of the chateau. It was *so* close . . . But if Anders was moving that bomb . . .

"I'm sorry, man, this *is* the mission. Tell Slick he's on his own. We don't have time."

"But Lorenzo . . . shit, I mean, Slick and Ghost, they're counting on you!"

"I know!" I didn't mean to yell at the kid, but the hour had just turned out to be a whole hell of a lot later than we thought. "We have to go. Do you copy?"

There was a long pause before Reaper said anything. *"Understood."*

I looked to Ling and Antoine. Skunky and Shen were like family. Lorenzo had saved Antoine's life on the mountain. But from their grim faces, they understood what was at stake. "Slick, Ghost, if you guys are receiving this, I'm sorry. Nightcrawler out." I let go of my mic. "Let's go."

LORENZO
The Chateau

Stokes' men had come pouring out of the chateau when Exodus ambushed their boss. Judging by the sound, there were a lot more of them than we'd hoped. Shen and I were still hiding behind the gatehouse. They'd not spotted us yet, or realized we'd killed some of them, but they would soon.

With Valentine ditching us to go after that bomb, there went most of our firepower and our ride out of here. We could abort, and then Shen and I would have to make a break for it on foot, link up with Skunky, and have Reaper pick us up. Or badly outnumbered and on enemy turf, we could try to grab Bob, and fight our way out. Either way, we were fucked.

The sad thing was Valentine was still making the right call. I would have done the same thing in his shoes.

I gave Shen a look. He was thinking what I was thinking. Run or fight? Shen gave me a determined nod. *Let's do this.*

There was a lot of movement around the front of the house. The garage door was open. Engines were turning over. This outfit was loyal enough to go after their boss. There hadn't been enough time for them to get Bob ready, so he still had to be inside. I whispered to Shen, "We let those assholes drive out of here, then we hit the house."

"Divide and conquer," Shen stated.

"There you go, all Sun Tzu again."

"That's far older than Sun Tzu," he whispered back.

I keyed my radio. There were only four of us left, so this was about to get really informal. "Skunky, hold your fire until their rescue car is down the lane. When I give you the signal, shoot everybody who isn't us."

"Got it."

"Reaper." Deprived of his usual bag of technical tricks, he was our secondary ride out, Samuel's babysitter, but sadly, not super useful in a gunfight.

"I'm ready, chief."

"Boot your hostage and tell him to start walking." Samuel had been honest, and leaving him in the countryside hadn't been part of the deal, but it beat being hogtied inside a car that was probably about to get shot at. "Then be ready to drive in here and save our asses."

"You want me to come in guns blazing?"

Hell no. Reaper was a terrible shot and had the tactical awareness of a potted plant. "Skunky has eyes on the place. He'll tell you when it's safe to move up." What went unsaid was that if me and Shen got shot to death in the next few minutes, then Skunky would also have a good view of when it was time for him and Reaper to run like hell.

A Land Rover gunned its engine and flew out of the garage. Shen and I stayed low as headlights lit up the guardhouse. It drove past us, through the gate, and down the lane. The glass was tinted, but there had to be at least a driver, somebody riding shotgun, and probably another in back to drag their wounded inside. So that was a few bad guys out of our hair for a minute. Sadly, I didn't know what we'd started with, but X minus three was better than X.

Shen tapped me on the shoulder, then pointed back the way we'd come in. We'd hit the house from poolside. *Good call.* It had been glass double doors there, and most eyes would be on the front toward where Stokes had been hit. Shen moved first while I covered him.

There was a bunch of angry shouting from the back of the property.

"This is Skunky. They just found the bodies on the balcony."

The SUV was far enough out that they'd be committed to their rescue now. They'd push on to the ambush site rather than try to turn around in the field and rush back to help their buddies. This was as good as it was going to get. "Open fire."

While I ran, I shoved the pistol back into the old nylon holster on my vest, and brought up the TMP. The little subgun didn't have a butt stock, but between the vertical foregrip and keeping tension pushed out against the sling it made for a decently solid shooting platform.

I didn't hear the shot. *"Winged him. Bad guy is still up,"* Skunky exclaimed. *"He's retreated back inside."* Oh well, nobody was perfect.

Shen had barely reached the poolside before he was spotted. *Too soon!* There was a flash of movement through a window above, the sudden opening of a curtain, and then a pane of glass was shattered as a muzzle punched it out. The man in the window just opened up, hosing down the area on full auto. Shen dove over a railing and crashed behind a stone bench as bullets zipped past him.

I crouched behind the base of a statue. They'd not seen me yet, so I extended the TMP and ripped a burst through the window. The little 9mm roared. More glass panes broke. I couldn't tell if I hit him, but the shooter pulled back inside.

"Are you okay?" I shouted toward Shen as I covered the window, but that indestructible little bastard had already popped up and was running to the next available piece of cover. The curtain moved, maybe the gunman, maybe just the wind, I didn't know, but I put another burst through the window anyway.

"Hostiles moving up on you from the front and rear of the house," Skunky warned. *"Some are holding back. They probably think you two are just a distraction."*

Sadly, we were the whole damned assault element now.

Shadows appeared around the front corner of the house. I turned and fired. At nine hundred rounds per minute, it didn't take long to burn through the rest of the magazine. I ducked back behind the statue as I dropped the mag and pulled another stick from my vest. There was a *thwack* and a yelp from the rear of the house as Skunky popped somebody coming around that side. We had to count on Skunky to hold that flank, and he was five hundred yards away shooting through wind.

Someone moved on the other side of the glass doors. Shen fired at them, the suppressed EVO sounding like a series of rapid *pops*. I couldn't tell if he hit them through the glass or not, but whoever was in there was smart enough to kill the interior lights so Shen couldn't see them.

There was a muzzle flash ahead of me and bullets hit the statue. Bits of hot stone hit me in the forehead, but I was too busy aiming to flinch. He stumbled back and fell on his ass as I put a short controlled burst into him, but he stayed upright, and shot at me again. That round hit the statue so close to my face I had no choice but to drop.

I must have hit him in the armor, and 9mm wouldn't do shit to it. More guys were coming up behind the man I'd hit while he kept shooting. I kept the pedestal between us and sprinted back toward the poolhouse. Of course, that's when the asshole in the upstairs window decided to pop up again. I pushed the TMP upwards and stitched bullets across the top of the house as I ran. We were catching fire from all over. There were too many of them.

Then a flashbang went off right at my feet.

Sound punched my ears and light kicked me in the eyeballs. I crashed into the wall, tripped, and landed face first on the gravel. The movement in the upstairs window hadn't been him popping up to shoot. He'd been tossing a bang out the window.

At least it hadn't been a frag.

Half my vision was swimming purple blobs. When I pointed the TMP at the approaching gunmen and pulled the trigger, I couldn't hear the gunfire. At first I thought my gun had jammed, but then I realized it was still bouncing around and a stream of hot brass was flying out the ejection port. I was just deaf again. The man I'd shot had rolled over and was trying to crawl back around the front corner. *Fuck that guy.* I didn't have a shot at his head, couldn't see my front sight, but I stuck the muzzle in the general direction of his legs and fired the rest of the magazine at him. He jerked and kicked as bullets ripped into his legs and pelvis. I pulled back to reload again. His buddies were shooting my way, putting a lot of lead in the air, and, I realized too late, a whole lot of holes in the walls around me. So half blind, all deaf, I crawled across the gravel until I hit sidewalk, popped up, found the door—*locked*—and kicked it in.

I couldn't tell you what the inside of the poolhouse looked like, purple blobs and flashing stars mostly. It sounded like ringing. I took cover behind what I think was a couch, blinking and rubbing my eyes.

My hearing was starting to clear up enough to realize that Skunky was yelling in my ears. *Something. Reloading. Incoming. Something.*

I crawled across carpet, bumped into a wall, found the window, and looked up in time to see somebody trying to peek inside, looking for me. We saw each other at the same time. Through the tears and stinging he appeared to be a tall black man wearing body armor, so I was pretty sure it wasn't Shen, and I shot him. The window between us shattered and he flinched back. I guessed at his direction and speed, and kept firing through the wall, chasing him down with bullets as he stumbled toward the pool.

"*—Land Rover returning. I'm engaging.*" I could hear Skunky better now. Stokes' rescuers were coming back.

I could see a little better now too. At this rate, I might even be able to aim again. Adrenalin is one hell of a chemical. There was another door on the other side of the pool house. It would put me closer to the main building and where I'd last seen Shen. I ran toward it.

That doorway was clear. The lights in the narrow path between the pool house and the mansion had been knocked out. I saw Shen—or at least I hoped it was Shen—fifteen feet away, apparently pinned down next to the fountain. There was a chain of splashes as the dude on the second floor hung his gun out the window and rattled off wild shots downward. The TMP's front sight was really blurry right now, but I stuck it up there anyway, and was rewarded with a bloody red flash as I put a 9mm hollow point through the man's elbow. He jerked back inside, but lost his gun in the process. The M-4 slid down the shingles before falling on the concrete.

I rushed over toward Shen. He was busy shooting at the men who'd come from the front. He didn't see the one coming from inside, but I did. He was moving through the darkened living room. This one hadn't had time to get dressed in anything but a pair of sweatpants, but in one hand he had a pistol and in the other he had a *motherfucking hand grenade*.

His arm was moving forward, almost in slow motion, as he went to underhand toss the grenade at my friend. I opened fire. Red holes puckered across his bare chest. He lurched to the side, hit the wall, and slid down in a red smear. But the grenade had still popped out of his hand and was rolling, lopsided, across the hardwood. "Shen!"

I grabbed Shen by the drag handle on the back of his armor, yanked him away from the doors, and shoved him toward the pool. Shen trusted me enough to throw himself face first into the shallow end. I dove in after him.

I hit the water, then the concrete bottom of the pool just as the grenade went off above us. Even submerged I could feel the blast as it vibrated the pool. *That was close.*

Underwater, holding my breath, I thumped into a body. A hand touched my face, and just from how it touched me, limp and floating, I knew it belonged to a dead man. I rolled over, thinking it was Shen, and that he'd caught a round while we'd been diving for cover, but it was the man I'd shot through the poolhouse window. His eyes were wide and staring at nothing. There was a gaping hole in his neck that was turning the water around us red. He must have fallen in after I'd shot him and the weight of his armor and ammo had taken him right to the bottom.

I popped my head out of the water and gasped for breath as bits and pieces of debris rained from the sky. The grenade had blown a smoking black hole in the side of the chateau. Shen had already waded to the side, hung his EVO over the edge, and was shooting at the men toward the front, turning the shallow end of the pool into an improvised foxhole. I lifted the TMP, angling it forward for a moment so the water would pour out the barrel, then joined Shen, trying to drive them back.

The bad guys must have realized the two of us weren't just a distraction, because there were more of them heading our way. I fired, clipping a runner, who went down behind a railing. Shen was chewing up a statue that someone else had taken cover behind. He saw I was back in it, and shouted, "Moving!"

Which was smart. If we were in the same spot too long, we'd get flanked and murdered. "Covering." I shot the railing and the statue as Shen rolled out of the pool and ran to the side, but my 9mm didn't penetrate for shit. Between their armor and use of the terrain, I was having a hell of a time stopping these guys. I kept firing until my bolt locked back on an empty mag. I needed something bigger, and I needed it before somebody wised up and tossed a grenade into the pool.

While bullets snapped by, I kept my head down and waded back to the corpse. Somebody got brave enough to stand up enough to get an angle, and bullets smacked into the water around me, sending up geysers of water just as I reached the body. The dead man had landed on his rifle. I kicked him over, and saw that he had a bullpup of some kind. Splashing around, I wrestled him over until I got the sling over his head and pulled it free, only to realize that this fucker had brought a grenade launcher. It was an Israeli Tavor, but even better, there was an M203 mounted. I cracked the launcher open and confirmed it was loaded. There were more giant 40mm shells on his vest.

Party time.

The Tavor had a Meprolight reflext sight on top. The glowing dot reticle was super convenient when the light sucked and your eyeballs were fucked up from a flashbang. I popped up, aimed at the top of the statue Shen had a man pinned behind, and pulled the forward trigger. The grenade launcher thumped my shoulder. The 40mm shell flew across the yard to strike the statue. It exploded in a rapidly expanding cloud of white dust and shrapnel, but I didn't stick around to study my handiwork. I'd already sunk back into the water to fish out more grenades.

I shoved another big round in, pulled it closed, then rose from the water already pointing toward the rail. That grenade smacked it solid, throwing hot bits of metal and stone in every direction. The men ducking behind it never had a chance. By the time I loaded the third grenade, gray smoke was obscuring most of the front, but I put a grenade into the corner of the chateau just because it looked like a good place for somebody to hide behind.

It was a good thing they hadn't just lobbed one of these through the poolhouse window when I'd been hiding inside, but these guys were living here. The thought of blowing up their own place probably hadn't even crossed their mind. Me? I loved blowing shit up.

I came up with the last grenade ready, but I didn't have any more targets. Over the ringing in my ears, I could hear screaming and coughing. I'd managed to wound a bunch of them. Nobody had come around the rear to kill us yet, so apparently Skunky had locked that side down.

Now was our chance. I began wading up the steps. "Shen! I'm going for Bob. Cover me."

Shen stayed in position, searching for targets as I got out of the pool, soaked and dripping. Glass crunched beneath my sodden, now heavy shoes as I moved to the blackened hole in the side of the chateau. My nostrils were filled with the stink of carbon and chlorine. This had been a living room of some kind, but now it was just a blasted mess. The half-naked guy I'd shot had blown himself into hamburger with his own grenade. Once I had a good position, I signaled for Shen to run around the pool and come over.

"Skunky. Can you hear me?" I thumped my radio a few times, hoping that the Exodus gear was decently waterproof. We'd only gone hot a couple of minutes ago, but the SUV sent to retrieve Stokes was probably on its way back, and I wanted to know if they'd be waiting for us. "Skunky?" But I got nothing. Shen slid in next to me. He jerked his head toward the hallway and where we thought the kitchen was. I nodded. The chateau was so old there were no blueprints or floor plans on file anywhere. Samuel hadn't spent too much time inside, so his descriptions were crap. But he'd alarm wired the door of the one windowless storage room that was this place's entire basement, so that was the most likely place they'd be holding Bob. The stairs down were just off the kitchen.

We started down the hall, moving fast, with me on point and Shen watching our tail.

The interior of the chateau was as fancy as the outside. Stokes had bought the place fully furnished, so it felt more like a rich grandma's house than a staging area for mercenaries. I glanced down and saw Shen was leaving bloody footprints on the thick white carpet. I realized there was blood all over his leg. "No time. It's just a scratch. Go."

We'd killed over half a dozen of them for sure and wounded I don't know how many more, but we didn't know what they'd started with, so there were an unknown number of threats remaining. We didn't know their plans for a rescue attempt either. They might have already executed Bob. Or, they might think they were losing, and were saving him to use as a hostage or bargaining chip. Lacking time and manpower, we didn't slow to clear each room. They could be lurking around any corner, or they could be forming up somewhere out of sight getting ready to converge on us.

"Come on! Up the stairs. We've got to move." Someone with a British accent was shouting ahead of us. "If you try anything I'll blow your fucking head off."

I took a knee behind a bookshelf. I didn't have a target, but he hadn't been yelling at me. The voice was coming from the direction Samuel had told us the kitchen was.

"Easy . . . I'm cooperating." The man who responded to the agitated Brit had a deep voice and was playing it cool. I recognized that voice.

Bob.

"To the garage, we're getting out of here! Now, you fuckin—"

There was a crash, followed by a gunshot, then another and another. A man began to scream, but it turned into a horrible, gurgling, choking noise, which was suddenly cut off by another violent impact and the sound of plates breaking. There was a burst from a submachine gun and the sound of bullets tearing through wood.

I rushed through the dining room and swept into the kitchen, stolen Tavor at my shoulder. Suddenly, the door to the kitchen flew open as a man with long blond hair was hurled through it. He crashed hard against the table, a pistol in one hand. Snarling, not losing a beat, he struggled to get up, pointing his piece back toward the kitchen. "Fucking Yank cocksucker!"

Shen and I both shot him repeatedly, practically riddling him with bullets, before he went down.

The kitchen was wrecked. Everything was broken. There were bullet holes in the walls. One of Stokes' men was on the floor, twitching, his neck snapped, probably from the impact that had left an obvious dent in the side of his head.

And standing in the middle of the kitchen, panting and breathing hard, barefoot, wearing sweats and a t-shirt, and holding a frying pan with some blood and hair stuck to it, was the man I'd come all this way to find, my brother . . . Bob Lorenzo.

Bob looked up as we swept in, snarling, obviously ready to fight us to the death with a frying pan. Bob was a huge, scary dude when he was just being his friendly, optimistic self. I'd never seen him in berserker mode before. Considering what he'd just done when provided with a distraction demonstrated why Kat had hired a squad of professionals to keep him contained until she needed him.

"Bob, it's me!" I shouted before he tried to remove my head. I raised the Tavor so the muzzle was pointing straight up. "We're here to rescue you."

He made it a couple of steps then stopped. I'd blackened my face, and that was probably a running mess from the pool water, so I would've been hard to recognize even without the red haze of rage. He tilted his head and asked incredulously, "Hector?"

There weren't many people who used my real name. "It's me. Come on, bro. We've got to get you out of here."

It was like he couldn't believe it. He'd been a prisoner for too long to grasp the idea of being able to just walk away. I understood the feeling. "It's really you. You found me."

"We're not clear yet. There's more of them."

"Fourteen total, as far as I could tell." Bob said quickly. *Good.* That accounted for most of them. "Stokes called and told his men to get me out of the cellar and ready for transport. Then the shooting started." Emotional moment or not, once a professional, always a professional. "We've got to get out of here. You got a ride? Otherwise the one I tossed through the door had car keys."

He was in better shape than I'd hoped. Ling had been right. They'd needed to keep him fed and healthy so there would be no suspicion that he wasn't the fourth operative. We'd be able to make a run for it . . . Only Bob got a puzzled look on his face, stumbled, and had to put one big hand on the counter to steady himself.

"You've been hit," Shen stated.

"Yeah." Bob turned until I could see his left side. There was a black hole right through his bicep and his white shirt was covered in blood. "But did you stop Blue?" Despite the shock of beating a man to death, getting shot, and being rescued, Bob didn't mess around. It was that crazy focus that had made him into Majestic's mortal enemy to begin with.

"Valentine's on his way to the train station now." I picked up a kitchen towel from the counter and stuck it against the wound to slow the bleeding. The bullet had gone clean through, but the exit wound was nasty.

Bob winced at the pain. "Valentine's here, and you know about Evangeline. Thank Goodness." But then Bob got a stricken look on his face. Whatever he'd just thought of was much worse than the gunshot wound. "Hang on. If Anders is pulling me out now, that must mean some of the nukes are already in transit."

"What do you mean *some* of the nukes?"

Chapter 15: Project Blue

VALENTINE
North of Paris

Ling was driving again, flying down French highways as fast as she could without getting us arrested. Even going way too fast, Evangeline was still at least twenty minutes north of the chateau. Thankfully, at this time of night, the highways were fairly deserted, but we did blow through more than one traffic camera. Had our van's plates been legitimate, we would be getting some huge fines later on.

I was in the passenger seat, talking to Tailor on the phone. I had interrupted his beauty sleep. I stopped to read a text message from Reaper. Lorenzo was too busy to communicate but there had been a lot of gunfire and explosions. *The Calm* was wavering and I was tired. *Focus.*

"*Val?*" Tailor asked. "*Did I lose you?*"

"No, I'm still here." I put him on speaker phone.

"*You did what?*"

"Raided one of Kat's holdings in the country."

"*You weren't supposed to make any moves without us! Son of a—*"

"Shut up and listen, I know where the bomb is."

"*No shit? Where?*"

"A train station near Amiens called Evangeline. We should have known."

"*There's like fifty thousand things in this country with that name. Hang on. I'm pulling it up . . . It's just a little place, but it's a hub. A bunch of lines converge there.*"

"That's where Hunter stored the nuke, and I bet they're going to deliver it to its target by train."

"And immediately after detonation, Bob would have been conveniently shot to death at the launch point by helpful local police," Antoine said from the back.

"*Evangeline isn't close to anything vital. What's the target?*"

"That I don't know."

"*Wait, there's a G20 summit in London right now!*" Tailor said, the

1133

realization creeping into his voice. *"They just put in a new line that is a direct shot to the Chunnel, for that new super train, Paris to London. Holy shit, Val."*

Holy shit was right. Leaders from all over the world were going to be there. London was clogged with functionaries, visitors, security, and protestors. The President of the United States, the British prime minister, and French president, and God-only-knew who else was going to be there.

"That is the most reasonable target," Ling stated flatly.

"Look, Tailor, I don't care what you need to do. I don't care if you have to go around your boss on this, okay? He's been really hesitant to break your stupid rules, but I have no idea if we'll get there in time. You need to alert the French government and tell them you have a credible threat of a weapon of mass destruction on one of those trains."

New Tailor would probably want evidence before causing an incident, but old Tailor had always been ready to shoot someone in the face. *"I'll alert the authorities on the way. My boss will cut through the red tape, trust me, he'll call up GIGN."* That was France's premier counterterrorism force. *"Hell, he'll get the Foreign fucking Legion if we have to, but don't wait up for me! Go kill those assholes!"* Luckily, I got old Tailor.

"Will do. I'll keep you posted." My phone beeped. It was Lorenzo. I switched over to him.

"Valentine, I've got Bob. Shen and Skunky are okay. We're on our way out."

Ling smiled at the news. "Ha! Excellent!" Antoine shouted.

"Don't celebrate. We've got a huge problem."

"I know, the bomb could be moving already, Reaper told me."

"No, damn it, listen to me. There are four bombs!"

Ling's eyes went wide. "What did he say?"

"There. Are. Four. Bombs!" Lorenzo repeated, each word a forceful statement.

My heart dropped into my stomach. I felt like I was going to throw up.

"Valentine! Are you still there?"

"Yeah, yeah, I'm here," I stammered. "I copy, four bombs."

"Bob says Blue doesn't have one target, there's four. The Alpha Point was just the staging ground. He doesn't know what the targets are, but Blue was designed to decapitate the Illuminati in one move. Four simultaneous detonations to wipe out their power base forever, blame it on terrorists, and Majestic has one less competitor."

"Where else do trains from Evangeline go?" Ling asked.

"Christ, all over Europe!"

Antoine had pulled up the information on his phone. "The north-south line goes through the Chunnel to London, and down all the way to Rome.

The east-west line goes through Frankfurt, all the way to Prague. The line's not done yet, eventually it's supposed to go all the way to Moscow."

"So basically anywhere could be a target." If we knew where they were going, Tailor could get the authorities to intercept them. But there was no way we could figure it out in time. "Antoine, call Ariel. Fill her in. It's up to her to guess where the targets are."

"Give your angel her puzzle pieces but don't count on her," Lorenzo muttered. *"Stop those bombs, Valentine. We'll catch up."*

LORENZO

After telling Reaper and Skunky to extract, and updating Valentine, I'd gotten us out of the chateau. If any more of Stokes' men were still in the fight, they were keeping their heads down. Not that that was a comforting thought. They could be waiting to ambush us, but we had no choice except going out the front. Bob had lost a lot of blood, and Shen's *just a scratch* had turned into a bad limp. We weren't going to be running across any fields.

Luckily, nobody took any potshots at us when Reaper drove through the open gate. He'd picked up Skunky on the way. As soon as the rest of us piled into the back of the sedan I smacked Reaper's seat and shouted "Drive! Drive!"

With all of us pointing guns out the windows, Reaper flipped the car around in a spray of gravel, and got us the hell away from the smoking ruins of the chateau. I kept waiting for a bullet to shatter the back window for a tense few seconds, but we were clear. It was a tight fit, especially since Bob was huge and squished between me and Shen. Skunky was in the passenger seat, still wearing a ghillie suit made out of layers of tattered burlap and covered in local weeds so it looked like Reaper was sitting next to a bush. Inside the Audi it was hot, and smelled like blood, sweat, and gunpowder.

"This remind you of anything?" Bob asked.

"I'm having a flashback to Quagmire."

"Only that time it was your little buddy who got shot in the arm, not me. By the way, good to see you again, kid."

"You too." Reaper was way too focused on the country road to look back at my brother. He was doing the best he could, but as soon as I was sure we were clear, I was going to make him pull over so I could drive. No offense to Reaper, but his video-game driving skills didn't translate over to real life worth a damn, we needed to get our asses to Evangeline fast, and he would be way more useful on a computer figuring out how to stop those trains.

There were headlights just off the side of the road ahead of us. It was the

Land Rover that had peeled off to pick up Stokes. It had crashed into a ditch on the way back. "I went by that on the way in," Reaper said. "I didn't see anybody alive."

"We haven't cleared it." Skunky warned. "I put a magazine through the windows as they were coming back." Skunky's rifle was too long to maneuver in the confines of the car, so he'd drawn his Beretta. As we got closer, I could see the mess of bullet holes in the SUV's windshield. That was some damned good shooting. "Movement." Skunky said as he angled his pistol out the window.

The back door of the SUV had opened, and a man had spilled out onto the grass. Before Skunky could open fire, Bob shouted. "Stop the car!" Bob wasn't the one giving the orders around here, but with a command voice like that, Reaper automatically hit the brakes. We slid across the gravel, raising a great cloud of dust. "Let me out."

I had no idea what he was doing, though I could tell now that the injured man who'd gotten out of the SUV matched our pictures of Aaron Stokes. Bob was a pro. Maybe this asshole knew something else important about Blue. "Make it quick," I told Bob as I opened the door and got out of his way.

Bob grimaced as he got out, one arm dangling, slick with blood. Skunky took the opportunity to shrug out of his burlap-covered jacket, and went to check on Shen's leg. I followed Bob over to the wreck. The engine was still running. The inside of the glass was painted red. The mercs who'd rescued their boss were either dead, or really convincing at pretending. Stokes was covered in blood, but I couldn't tell how much of that was his, and how much was from the men Skunky had ventilated. As he slowly tried to crawl away, Bob followed after him.

Stokes was messed up, moving with that dizzy, disoriented, seasick-looking motion of somebody who'd just gotten a severe head injury. I didn't know how much information my brother was going to be able to get out of him in this shape. "Hurry up."

"This won't take long." Bob put his foot on him and kicked Stokes over onto his back. Even in his bewildered state, Stokes seemed really surprised to see Bob looming over him.

From the utterly terrified look on Stokes' face, and the merciless, righteously angry way Bob was glaring at him, I realized this wasn't an interrogation. This was an execution.

"Hey, come on, Lorenzo. I was just doing my job. I'm begging you, mate. You'd have done the same, if our situations were reversed."

"No. I wouldn't." Then Bob lifted a stolen pistol and shot Stokes in the chest. Not just once or twice, but Bob just kept on pulling the trigger, over and over as Stokes jerked and twitched. He kept shooting until the gun was empty, and then I watched the pistol's muzzle wiggle as Bob pulled the trigger uselessly a few more times.

"You done?"

He looked down at the smoking pistol. If he'd not been at slide lock, he would have kept going. For the first time since we'd found him, Bob actually seemed a little out of it. He was a professional, but even professionals can get personal. He took one last look at the perforated corpse then started toward the car. "I'll be done when those bombs are stopped."

We went back to the car. "Move over Reaper, I'm driving."

VALENTINE
Gare d'Evangeline

Gare d'Evangeline consisted of a concrete and glass enclosure over a whole bunch of tracks. On the other side of that was a depot with several large buildings for maintenance and storage. The train station was quiet this time of night, but the doors were still open. Beneath the street lights, a couple of police officers were patrolling, as could be expected for any mass transportation hub these days. The problem was, there should have been a lot more. With a credible threat of a weapon of mass destruction this place should have been covered in cops.

"I thought your friend Tailor said he was going to involve the authorities," Ling said. We were in our van, parked in the nearly empty lot on the north side of the station.

"They should be here." I checked my phone, but I had no signal. That was odd. We weren't exactly in the wilderness. It had been fine when we had spoken to Ariel a few minutes ago, and Reaper had been sending me information about the station up until about that same time. "Anybody else having a problem with their phone?"

Antoine tried. "I am getting a prerecorded message that the system is out of service."

"Even our GPS says it cannot find a satellite." Ling was scowling hard at the train station. "It must be a signal jammer."

Even if the Montalbans were using a device like that, it wouldn't stop communications outside of the jammer's zone, where our help should have been coming from. "Tailor said help would get here, it'll get here." But even as I said that, I was worried that something had gone horribly wrong. "If Ariel can figure out the other targets, she knows how to reach him."

"That is a lot of ground to search with only three of us," Ling said.

"Ariel said that this is a working station, but there's another section that's not open to the public yet. It's for this new maglev that's supposed to do Paris to London in record times, like the world's fastest train. It's still in testing, but she thinks that part is where the bombs would have been stored."

"How come?" Antoine asked.

"The construction company that built it was owned by Rafael Montalban, and it went up around the time Hunter got killed. Kat owns the whole thing now. We've got to walk through the regular station, and head for the back." Going in like a SWAT team would only end with us in a firefight with French police. "Ditch the tactical gear and long guns, go low profile. The longer we can look around without being spotted the more likely we are to find those bombs."

I stripped off my load bearing gear and pulled a hoodie on over my armor. It was a little bulky, but from a distance nobody would notice. I had my .44 in a pancake holster concealed under my sweater, and had filled my pockets with spare speed loaders. The Taurus .357 snubby I'd had since the Crossroads was stuffed in my front pocket.

"This is it. Once inside, play it by ear."

Antoine slid open the side door and got out. Before I could, Ling reached over and grabbed my sleeve. Normally at a time like this, Ling would be stone-faced, but right now her concern was obvious.

"What is it, Ling?"

"It's . . . nothing. Let's go."

LORENZO

I was tempted to try and call Valentine again to get an update, but since I was driving as fast as I could, passing the other cars like they were standing still, it was probably better for me to concentrate on the road. Thankfully it was still early enough in the morning that the traffic hadn't gotten thick. If we picked up a cop, they could just chase us to the train station.

"What else do you know, Bob?" I glanced in the rear view mirror. "Anything you can think of that might help?"

"Maybe." Bob was gritting his teeth as Skunky tended the nasty hole in his arm. "Gordon's plan was aimed at the Illuminati leadership."

"Killing thousands to get to a handful of old men," Skunky muttered as he kept wrapping gauze. He'd been busy back there. "Assholes."

"The problem was the Illuminati leadership stays spread out on purpose. It's hard to get more than a handful of the family heads in the same place at the same time. Every now and then, when they've got something really important to discuss, one of them can demand a big mandatory meeting and the whole council has to gather. It's tradition, but it can only be called by a family head. That's why Gordon originally approached Eduard Montalban. Majestic intel said he was the loose cannon and the most likely to sell out the others."

"That's why Dead Six killed Rafael Montalban, to put Big Eddie in charge," I muttered.

"Only Eduard and Gordon Willis cut themselves a side deal instead. Gordon was paid to switch sides. Eduard would get a meeting called, Blue would blow it up, and the Montalbans would be the last family standing to inherit the whole damned thing."

Eddie was a psychopath, and his little sister had taken his dream and made it her own.

"Oh, shit. Exodus cut a deal with an Illuminati boss named Romefeller. He called one of those big meetings."

"Because of us hunting Katarina," Shen said as he came to the same conclusion I just had. He was gray and sweating badly. Skunky had gotten the bleeding stopped from the gash on his leg, but Shen wasn't looking good. "The actions of Exodus caused Blue."

"If it wasn't you, it would've been called for something else eventually," Bob said. "That council is what they've been waiting for this whole time."

"Wherever that secret meeting is being held is one of the targets."

"I don't know. They never said anything in front of me about that. All of this is working off of what I've overheard, my investigation from before, and a whole lot of time with nothing better to do than think about it."

"Reaper, relay that to Valentine's buddy. Tailor will know where that meeting is. He can at least get an evacuation started." Not that I gave a shit about the Illuminati, but I felt bad for whatever city their little party was in.

Reaper was in the passenger seat, staring at a tablet screen and typing fast. I didn't know what the hell he was trying to do, but it was important enough I was hesitant to interrupt him. He didn't look up. "Something's wrong, Lorenzo. Everything is falling apart."

"What's happening?"

"The systems are going down. All the systems." He was either frightened, or in awe. It was hard to tell. "Every system in western Europe is under attack. I'm trying to warn the authorities, but they're all swamped. They're making it impossible for me to even call in fake bomb threats to force evacuations. They're hitting police, military, phone networks, utilities, banking, the works, but I think that's just a smokescreen to hide what they're really doing. All the transit hub systems are down, no GPS tracking, nothing. I can't tell where anything is or where it's going. Nobody can."

"Who is doing what now?"

"It's a coordinated cyber-attack," Bob explained. "Nobody in charge has a clue what's real and what's not. It's the ultimate diversion."

"No shit! That's what I just said!" Reaper was freaking out. "Remember when I said Kat had hired some people like me? More like a hundred of me. They must have been working on this for months. Each one targeting different systems. They probably never even knew they were part of a team effort, just hey, here's a million dollars if you break this when I tell you to. I think she just turned them all loose at once. Nobody has ever done this wide of an attack before. It's kind of amazing, actually."

"Can you fix it?"

Reaper laughed at me.

"I'm not fucking around, Reaper."

"Sorry, chief. It's like she just drove a truck loaded with dynamite into a dam and you asked me to plug the hole with my finger."

I punched the steering wheel. There wasn't a damned thing I could do about cyber-attacks, and we were still several minutes away from being able to shoot anyone. "Okay, so the Illuminati meeting is one target, but what about the other three?"

"Some of the second-tier Illuminati leadership will be held back from the main meeting. These people have been in the treachery business for a thousand years. The bombs will be wherever her biggest potential rivals are congregated. This way Katarina pops a bunch of other surviving potential competitors too, and it looks more like acts of terrorism to the rest of the world rather than just a directed assassination against one group."

"There's a summit in London this week, lots of world leaders there." Skunky said.

"Even if the Illuminati aren't present, she might blow them up just so everyone thinks they were the real target." Bob was just making educated guesses now, but my gut told me he was right.

"Where the hell did she get four nuclear bombs from?"

"One was seized by Dead Six. The others were stolen from a Russian demil site and sold by Sala Jihan."

"Son of a bitch." *Should have seen that coming.* No wonder the Pale Man had let me free. He didn't want this to come back to bite him. I knew Kat better than anybody else here, so I tried to think like her. *What would I do if I was Kat?* "She'll probably time the bombs to explode at the same time. That maximizes her chances of getting as many important targets as possible."

"Anders is running the details. This whole thing was his and Hunter's op," Bob said. "I know Anders well. He's one efficient son of a bitch. He likes to run his ops like clockwork. He had Stokes lock me up near for a reason. He wants me to get killed at the launch site as close to the time of detonation as possible."

"He must really not like you."

"I got him fired from the FBI. Majestic never would have recruited him if I'd not ruined his career. But that's just a side benefit. I've got the right résumé. Anders needs to frame me as Gordon's recruit so he can get away with it. No, the bad part is that timeline means that the bombs headed for the furthest targets must already be on their way."

I looked to Reaper. "Any ideas?"

He sure didn't seem happy. "I'm on a tablet with a shitty connection in a speeding car but I'm trying to go around all these cut-rate Chinese hackers Kat hired, break into NATO's command net to warn them they're about to get nuked. So quit bugging me!"

I was too busy trying not to crash into early commuters at two hundred and twenty kilometers an hour to think through all the implications of that. If Bob was right, some of the bombs were already on their way. But the ones intended for closer targets might not have left yet. "Can you stop the trains or not?"

"I've never seen anything like this. I don't know," Reaper said, and that honesty was a little scary.

The rest of Exodus had to be at Evangeline by now. "Then it's up to Valentine."

VALENTINE

The interior of the station was clean and orderly. There were several food stands but they were closed for the night. There weren't very many passengers present in the station, and most of those were dozing on benches, but the cleaning crew was out in force, scrubbing floors and emptying garbage cans. There were elevated screens showing arrival and departure times. I went to the closest and checked. It was sparse until commute time. The next arrival was in twenty minutes, departing in thirty to Paris.

"We must check that one." Antoine said.

"Yeah, but nothing toward London for hours though."

Ling shook her head. "But the experimental line is not open yet. It would not appear on this schedule. Magnetic levitation trains do not run on normal tracks." There was an interactive map on a nearby touch screen kiosk. Ling found the portion of the train station blacked out as still under construction. "They are building a new section for those. The experimental train should be there."

"Assuming it hasn't left yet."

"We can pray," Ling said. "This way."

There were no trains parked under the enclosure yet. Pigeons were nesting in the rafters above. Ling led us to a section blocked off with caution tape and signs warning us to keep out. None of the custodial staff had paid us any mind. I didn't see the cops. None of the weary travelers looked like hired mercenaries keeping watch, but that could be deceptive. So we went down an empty corridor marked with a bunch of signs that I assumed said *keep out* in French. The next area was lined with scaffolding and lit only with work lights. At the end of the corridor, we ducked under some hanging plastic sheets and entered the new, half-built section of the train station. It wasn't very well lit, and it was very quiet. We didn't see anyone.

I looked back at my Exodus compatriots. "Fan out a little, keep your eyes open. There may be night crews. ID your targets before you shoot. I've had a shitty enough day without accidentally murdering a janitor or something."

"No flashlights," Antoine suggested. "Let us keep the element of surprise."

It took us a few minutes to navigate the labyrinthine construction site. The large, open central area was divided up with scaffolding, construction barriers, and more plastic curtains. We moved as quickly as we could without making noise, in case the Montalbans had patrols, but we didn't encounter anyone. I noticed a vantage point that would allow us to observe most of the station, a platform where a large window would eventually be installed. Now it was just a skeleton of metal beams. While Ling and I found a ladder up, Antoine stayed at floor level to keep watch.

A cool night breeze drifted across my face as we observed the yard from our elevated position. Numerous sets of tracks split off the main line, allowing trains to park or get out of each other's way. At least, that's what I thought they were for; I'm not really familiar with the ins and outs of railroading. The maglev track was taller, much wider, and being shiny and new definitely stood out from the others.

Ling pointed. "Those are the service hangars." All four of them were lit up, though there was no movement. The experimental super train was on the other side of those buildings. It was silver, had a bunch of sleek cars behind it, but the important thing was that it wasn't currently moving.

"There's not a lot of cover out there." If there was anyone inside, it was going to be really hard to get close enough to check without being spotted.

"Perhaps they won't shoot first and ask questions later," Ling said. "They are trying to be low key about this, yes? They're also in what is supposed to be a secured area. If we're lucky, they're not being as vigilant as they might be."

"I hope so, but we can't count on it." I checked my watch. That train to Paris would be here soon.

"Listen," Ling warned. At first I thought the sound might be a distant train, but then I realized the noise was from a helicopter. It was running dark, no lights, and the only reason I spotted it was that it moved in front of some of the city lights. It was coming in low and fast from the south. "We have company."

"Hopefully Tailor got ahold of someone."

"If that is French special forces, they are just as likely to shoot us as the Montalbans. Wait. I don't think . . . that isn't a military helicopter."

She was right. It was a little civilian helicopter, and it descended to land near where we had parked our van. The authorities didn't need to *sneak* in. It could have been Tailor, but somehow I knew it wasn't. I just had a gut feeling who it was. Tailor must have gotten the word out about the nukes, but Majestic had been listening. Majestic was *always* listening.

"It's Underhill. He knows I'm here."

"You can't know that," Ling insisted.

I shook my head. "No, it's him."

"Either way, we must hurry." Ling went to the ladder and effortlessly slid to the ground. I followed, not nearly as gracefully. We set out for the nearest hangar.

The cement ended with the construction zone and the ground turned to gravel. We were out in the open now, so stealth was out. "Spread out." If there was a guard posted, it would be harder to shoot us if we weren't clumped together. Then we simply ran for it.

Breathing hard, I reached the edge of the hangar. Nobody had shouted an alarm or started shooting. When I peeked through the nearest window I discovered why.

"They've already left."

Antoine tried the closest door. It was unlocked. Pistol raised, he swept inside. I drew my .44 and followed. Ling was right behind me.

There was a concrete enclosure inside the hangar. It was covered in signs that I assumed meant *danger, high voltage*. It had an extremely heavy-duty metal door, but it was hanging open. Inside the room there were some shelves and four big metal cradles. They were stenciled *War, Pestilence, Famine*, and *Death*. All of the cradles were empty.

"Shit." I glanced around. On the shelves were some plastic jugs, and I recognized the labels as being from the shipments Ariel had keyed off on. There was a Geiger counter and a bunch of tools I did not recognize. The work area looked suspiciously clean, like the Montalbans had probably scrubbed the place so that the only forensic evidence the authorities would find later would belong to Bob Lorenzo. "Where'd they go?"

"Not far," Antoine said. He had gone back into the empty hangar. "Look over here."

I came out to see that he was pointing at a small puddle on the concrete.

One of the pipes in the wall had been leaking. There were lines of water, like someone had driven a big cart through the puddle, and it had been recently enough that it hadn't had time to evaporate. There were also a few footprints, big ones, boots, from the treads. They went a few feet before drying into oblivion. They were headed down a walkway, back toward the station.

"The last bomb is going to Paris!" Heedless of danger, I sprinted down the walkway. Ling and Antoine ran after me. That cart couldn't be too far ahead.

Sure enough, a few seconds later, I turned the corner and spotted several men driving a motorized cart up a ramp. There was a big metal box on that cart, about the size of a coffin. There were six of them in total, two ahead, one on each side of their precious cargo, and two bringing up the rear. And those two saw me as soon as I saw them.

I was *Calm*.

I took in everything in that second. They were dressed casually, but had that contractor vibe, not Montalban regulars. Of course, Katarina wouldn't use anybody who could be tracked back to her for this assignment. Short haircuts, a few operator beards, none of them old, all of them fit. If they hadn't been wearing drab jackets to hide their weapons, I bet I would have seen tats from their old units. Deniable, expendable, they were probably doing it for the money, and a few years ago I had been exactly like them.

But that didn't matter now, because they were reaching for their guns, and I needed to stop a nuclear holocaust.

Still running forward, my .44 was already in both hands, punching outward. The rear guards were twenty yards away. I shot one, then the other, before either could clear leather. The sudden roar of gunfire caused the others to reflexively jump and turn. The two by the bomb were even further and I was still moving. I hit the one on the right. My gun jumped, and came smoothly back down as I stroked the trigger. The one the left fell off the ramp.

Then Antoine and Ling were behind me, blazing away.

Of the men at the top of the ramp, only one had managed to move to cover before they nailed him. Antoine began hammering the pillar he dove behind. Everyone else was dead or wounded, and Ling methodically put 9mm rounds into all of the fallen to be sure. I reached the motorized cart as it slowly plodded up the ramp with a methodical hum. It seemed simple enough. There was a green button for go and a red button for stop. The last man risked a quick peek around his cover and I reflexively shot him through the forehead. I punched the red button.

The cart stopped.

It was quiet. There were dead bodies everywhere. We had just saved Paris from destruction.

One down, three to go.

LORENZO

It had been one hell of a quick ride. The car was pretty sporty, and I kept it as fast as I could without flying off the road. There wasn't much traffic, trucks mostly, and I blasted past those. The street lights along the highway were out, and all of the houses along the highway were dark. There were blackouts everywhere. The town was still lit, but the traffic lights on the way to the station had been blinking. The police bands were a mess, with hundreds of fake emergency calls flooding in, right before it all crashed. Our chateau shooting was probably in there too, lost among the sea of bullshit.

The phones were still out, but as we got closer Skunky tried to get hold of his comrades on the radio. So far he hadn't had any luck. It could have just been a matter of range and material between us, or they could already be dead. There was no way to tell.

None of us had never been here, and the GPS was down, but Reaper had downloaded a map of the region before he lost the Internet, and since this was newly-built Europe, instead of old cobblestone streets designed for horses Europe, the streets were actually laid out in a way that made sense. We were getting close.

"How are you guys doing?" That was aimed at Bob and Shen, since they'd both been wounded.

But Reaper answered. "Frustrated. I can't accomplish dick from here."

"Reaper, when we get inside there's got to be some sort of control center for the station. See if you can do something from there."

"Yeah. They've got to have an emergency radio to call the conductors. I'll force them to park those trains someplace that isn't too populated in case the bombs are on timers. I'll take the whole place hostage if I have to!"

"That's the spirit. Shen? Bob? You up to fight?"

Shen snorted, like that question was offensive.

"I can shoot one-handed," Bob sounded weary, but pissed off. Probably because we were taking him to the very place he was supposed to get framed and murdered. This was really going to suck if we failed, and still managed to deliver Kat her patsy.

"I was talking about the blood loss, Bob."

"It's not squirting."

"You sound like Dad when you say that."

"Thanks."

"We get in there, split up and spread out. If those bombs are here, do not let them leave."

Gare d'Evangeline looked like a pretty normal train station. There weren't crowds of panicked citizens fleeing the place so the shooting probably hadn't started. I didn't see any cops yet, so I pulled up right in front of the main doors. All of us bailed out and left the car in the passenger unloading only zone. They could just tack that parking violation onto the other hundred felonies I had committed already tonight.

VALENTINE

I stood next to the nuclear weapon and reloaded my revolver. As I reholstered, there was panicked shouting from inside the terminal. The passengers had heard our gunfire, but it had happened quickly and was over. They were probably still trying to figure out what was going on, but they'd start running sooner or later. If there were any more of Kat's hired goons around, they'd have heard the noise, too. We'd stopped one of the nukes, but we had no way to secure it with just the three of us.

"I've reached someone on the radio," Antoine said. "It is Mr. Long. They have arrived." He keyed his microphone. "We have recovered one device. The others are status unknown."

I looked over my shoulder. The maglev train was still parked, but now its lights were on. That was strange, I thought, as I stared at the high-tech locomotive.

"What is it?" Ling asked.

I didn't answer.

"Michael?"

"There's a bomb on that train."

"What? How do you know?"

"I just know! Holy shit, there's a bomb on that train! There has to be! Antoine, tell the others that we're heading back toward the hangar." I started down the ramp. Antoine and Ling were closer. "Get to that train!"

A voice came over the PA system. It was Underhill.

"I assume you can hear me, Valentine. We intercepted some coms earlier. Seems you've been busy."

"Oh, come *on!*" I snarled. I didn't have time for these assholes now.

"Don't worry. Help is on the way. This will all be over soon. I can't let you get away again. You were one hell of a fighter, son, but you can rest now."

Then he said something I didn't understand. It was in foreign language, Latin maybe? Pain, blinding pain, exploded behind my eyes, like I was suddenly beset with the worst migraine of my life. My legs went limp and I tumbled down the ramp. Ling shouted at me. I thought it was my name from the shape of her mouth, but I couldn't hear her over the buzzing in my ears. She skidded to a halt, turned, and started back toward me.

"Keep going!" I shouted, the struggling to force the words out of my mouth. "Don't stop!" *Please don't stop.* An image of Sarah flashed through my mind, cut down by gunfire as she came back for me.

Ling did as I asked. She hesitated for only a moment, then turned and continued on, leaving me alone. *Thank you.*

Struggling, head still pounding with pain, I grabbed the handrail and pulled myself up. Holding on for dear life, I struggled to get down the ramp without falling again. I was dizzy, I was nauseated, I could barely hear anything. I didn't know what was happening, and it terrified me.

Underhill kept talking over the PA. *"That's right. Just relax. Your time is done."* He said the gibberish word again, and the pain hit me with full force. It was like getting boxed in the ears. My knees buckled, and I fell down again. The pain in my head was unbearable. I thought I was having a stroke. I lay there, face down on the concrete, muscles twitching, in so much pain that I just wanted to die so it would stop.

"That is the idea." I could still hear a voice, only now it was the ghost of Dr. Silvers in my head. *"The control phrase activates the emergency kill switch I have placed in your mind. If there is any hope that the project can be contained or salvaged, the phrase should not be used, for once it is utilized, there is no turning back. The subject is programmed to experience an immediate disintegration of his nervous system, so painful that he will willingly die to make it stop."*

"No," I hissed through gritted teeth. Silvers was gone, but she'd left something inside me. I couldn't tell if her words were a memory or a hallucination.

"Why aren't you dead, Michael? I did this to you as a favor. You were always my most obstinate subject. I could have used this when you tried to escape, but I felt you were still salvageable. You are special, this unique bundle of psychological trauma, brain injury, and life experiences that left you perfectly suited for my program. The sad thing here is that when you give up, my life's work will have been wasted."

I was blinking in and out of consciousness. My heart was beating so fast it was going to tear itself apart. I saw Sarah, and Hawk, and Hunter. Wheeler, Ramirez, then my mom, and everything Silvers had twisted up in my head was telling me to give up and join them. The pain got worse and worse, and more images flashed through my mind. Violence, suffering, death. So many dead faces, staring at me, judging me, damning me, screaming at me. I put my hands over my ears to make it stop, but I could still hear them.

Then there was another voice, a clarion call amongst the chaos in my mind. This time I think it was an angel. She sounded just like Ariel. *"You are stronger than they are, Michael. Calm yourself and fight."*

I gasped for breath. My heart rate began to slow. The voices and the screaming faded. *The Calm* began to push back the pain. Reaching out with one shaking hand, I grasped the railing, held tight, and pulled myself upright. I was in control again.

"The brief said that was supposed to have killed you dead, given you a stroke or something." It was Underhill, and he was no ghost. My vision was still blurry, but I could make him out at the top of the ramp. "Hocus-pocus science project bullshit I told them. You can't make better soldiers in a lab, but they wouldn't listen. Guys like me and you, we're forged in a crucible."

My eyes cleared up enough to see that he had a pistol pointed at me. It was a 1911 with a threaded barrel.

"I beat her," I told him. "I won."

"Good for you, kid. You gave me a hell of a chase too. I'm almost sorry this is over."

Now I could see with perfect clarity. I was so *Calm* that I saw his grip tighten as he lined up the sights and swiped off the safety.

"This is your last chance," he said. "Get down on your knees and put your hands behind your head. I'm supposed to bring you back alive, but I'm not going to risk your getting away again."

My body moved slowly, so infuriatingly slowly, as my hand moved to my .44. I didn't have time to aim. The instant the muzzle of my revolver cleared leather, I rocked it upwards, tucked my elbow against my body, and fired. The gun bucked in my hand.

Underhill's eyes widened as my bullet hit him in the stomach. The .45 barked and flashed as he lurched.

His bullet smacked hard against my vest as I pushed the big Smith & Wesson outward. I brought my hands together. Underhill fired again. A hot burning pain slashed across the side of my neck, but I acquired a flash sight picture, focusing on the glowing green front sight as I aligned it higher on Underhill's body.

My .44 roared again, earsplittingly loud on the loading dock.

I watched Underhill fall to the ground, slowly, gracefully, losing his grip on his gun. He landed unceremoniously on his back, and the pistol clattered off the ramp to the concrete below.

I stood there for what seemed like a long moment, revolver extended in both hands, pointed up at Underhill. One deep breath and time seemed to return to its normal speed.

The pain was gone. I could feel hot blood trickling down my neck, but I didn't take my hands off of my gun. Muffled gunfire erupted from inside the building, punctuated by people shouting. I ignored it, kept my gun trained on Underhill, and approached slowly.

The old man was still breathing. His breaths were short and ragged, punctuated by a gurgling sound. A dark red blot stained his button-down shirt. I'd shot him right through the upper sternum, just over the top of his vest. Some distant part of my brain thought, *Hawk would be proud.*

I stood over Underhill for a few moments. He didn't say anything. His eyes were focused on me, but his face looked eerily serene. He died doing what he'd been born to do. "I told you this would happen."

Underhill didn't answer. He didn't even try to move. He probably couldn't. That bullet had probably shattered his spine.

"Are you the best they've got? Is this it? How many of you sons of bitches do I have to kill before they leave me alone?"

Underhill still didn't answer. His ragged breathing slowed. The pool of blood under him expanded. I got closer until I was standing in the puddle, big, stainless steel revolver pointed at his face. He didn't look scared. He looked perfectly calm.

"That was for Hawk," I said defiantly.

Underhill didn't respond. His breathing slowed a little more, then stopped. Just like that, he was gone. Then there was nothing. No satisfaction, no remorse, no adrenaline rush, no adrenaline dump. Just an old man dead on a loading dock of a train station in France.

I lowered my gun. I realized then that I had blood trickling from my nose.

LORENZO

It was the quickest draw I'd ever seen.

The old man had him dead to rights. Only Valentine had been faster. *Way* faster.

Back on Saint Carl I'd talked some trash about being as fast with a pistol as Valentine was . . . *Damn.* Not even close. Valentine said something to the man I assumed was Underhill, and then left him there to die alone. Hawk would have been proud.

"Valentine!" And since he looked really jumpy, I immediately added. "Hold your fire, it's me." He was standing near a big metal box on a cart. "Is that what I think it is?"

He looked a little out of it, and had blood trickling from his right nostril. "Yeah."

Well, that was intimidating.

"Where's everybody else?" he asked.

"Converging on those hangars like you said."

Before I had finished speaking, Valentine was running in that direction.

I took one last look at the bomb. It seemed wrong to just leave it sitting there, like I should hang a warning sign on it, *do not touch,* or something. Since all the law-abiding citizens in the station were fleeing for their lives now, I pulled my .45 before I went after him. Across the yard was the sleekest train I'd ever seen. In fact, it looked more like a spaceship than a piece of mass transit. Valentine hopped off the concrete platform and ran across tracks and gravel directly toward it. I went to the other side of the elevated tracks and jumped down too. At least there were a lot of shadows here.

Antoine came over the radio. *"They are loading the train. I am in position."*

"Almost there," Valentine said. "Wait for us."

Far ahead, I spotted a group of men standing on the platform by one of the futuristic cars.

"Down," I hissed at Valentine as I took cover behind a concrete barrier.

They were dressed in contractor garb, cargo pants, vests, and ball caps. From the way they had their guns out and were nervously scanning, they had heard Valentine's gunfire. One of them spoke into a radio, and a few seconds later a man came off the train, driving an empty cart. Behind him was a tall, blonde woman. She had her back turned, but the way she was supervising, that had to be Kat. Of course she needed to see her crowning achievement launched in person. One more person got off the train. Towering over Kat was the gigantic, unmistakable form of Anders. As Anders scanned for threats, I pulled back further behind the barrier.

"I can no longer wait," Antoine whispered over the radio.

There were several security men visible, an unknown number out of view, and probably more still on the train, because Kat was the kind of awful person who would hire somebody to guard a cargo and not tell them it was going to explode. Not to forget Anders, who I'd seen in action in the Crossroads, where he'd been like the fucking Terminator, and Kat was still deadly as hell. I was no hero, but in a few seconds that train was going to leave, and if I let Kat blow up a city Jill would never let me hear the end of it. I'd already been lucky to survive one lopsided gunfight tonight, and unlike the men we'd surprised earlier, these were alert and ready for trouble. They were out of effective pistol range, so we'd have to get closer. I took a deep breath and crept around the barricade.

Apparently Valentine had to do less soul searching, because he was already way ahead of me. I was close enough now to hear Kat shouting orders. The job was done. They were leaving.

Antoine must have made a move. Only with a reaction time that rivaled Valentine, Anders spotted them, lifted a stubby black weapon from beneath this jacket, and fired. From the lack of noise, it was that same suppressed shotgun he'd used to shoot Jill.

"Take them!" Valentine shouted as he took off running. I lost sight of him around the front of the engine.

I was still a hundred yards away, which was too damned far to be shooting a .45, but I opened up on them anyway. I put the red dot on top of the closest man's head, hoping that was sufficient holdover, and popped off a shot. There was either enough drop or wobble in my aim that I only hit him in the chest. The 230-grain hollow point made an audible *slap* against his concealed body armor. Most of the security guys weren't well trained enough that they'd turned to see who Anders was shooting at, but of course the asshole covering my sector was a professional. He saw me, shouldered a subgun, and stated shooting.

Bullets smacked into the concrete in front of me as I took a knee, leaned out, and cranked off a few more quiet shots. The shooters were breaking off and moving to cover. Anders was still shooting down the hall. In the middle of it all, Kat was standing there, actually *grinning*, like this was incredibly exciting, and she was having the time of her life. But then they started taking fire from the far side of the train, and Kat had to duck as bullets went whizzing past. I caught a glimpse of Skunky and Shen coming up the platform at the opposite end of the train. The man standing closest to Kat spun around as they nailed him.

The security men opened up on them as Skunky took cover behind some construction equipment. Only they weren't fast enough. I couldn't tell where Skunky had gotten hit, but he just collapsed in a heap. Shen grabbed him by one arm and dragged him behind cover as bullets struck all around them.

By the time I leaned out to shoot again, we'd broken them. Several of Kat's men were out of the fight, and they were taking fire from three sides. They had nowhere to go except inside the train. The security men dragged their wounded into the train after her. Anders calmly walked backwards toward the door, still firing down the hall. I shot at him, but some stupid bastard stepped right in front of him and I clipped the guard instead. His head snapped back, flinging blood and brains all over my real target.

Anders saw me. We locked eyes, and he knew I'd almost gotten him. But then that bastard was inside the train and out of my line of sight.

The sudden lack of gunfire made it feel far too quiet. Then the radio chatter started.

"*Skunky is down,*" Shen reported.

"*I'm hit,*" Antoine gasped.

The train started to move.

It was shocking how fast it took off, and even worse, how remarkably fast it was building up speed. It was coming my way, but all I had was a pistol, which wasn't anywhere near enough to stop a friggin' train. Not wanting to get run over, I hurried and clambered up onto the platform. I took cover behind a pillar and watched helplessly as the engine floated by, then the first car, but then the second was filled with scumbags who blew out the windows trying to murder me, and I was too busy trying to become one with the floor as they hammered the concrete pillar between us into dust to pay attention to much else.

The gunfire let off, and I leapt to my feet, cranking off a few futile rounds after that second car as it rapidly accelerated away. There was no time to think. I shoved the 1911 into the holster. I was going to need both hands for this next bit of reckless stupidity. It was already moving way faster than I could sprint, but I started running alongside it anyway. I'd hopped plenty of trains before, and I searched for something to grab onto, but this thing was sleek, round, and aerodynamic. There was nothing to grab hold of. It was a hobo's nightmare.

There had to be *something*. I kept running as it kept passing me by, faster and faster. My chest hurt. My legs burned. Tonight had already kicked my ass. Then I was next to the final car. Thankfully, there was a rear door with a safety rail, and a bumper sufficient to stand on. I reached out, and the train was already going so damned fast that the rubberized metal bar hit my palm like a bat. I latched on, and it damned near took my arm out of the socket as it yanked me off the platform.

My boots hit the bumper. I was hanging on for dear life, but I'd made it.

Apparently on the other side of the train, Valentine had come up with the same bright idea, only he wasn't nearly as acrobatic as I was. He caught the rail on that side, and was jerked around and swung hard into the metal door. His shoulder hit way too hard, and he probably would have bounced off and eaten track if I'd not grabbed onto his arm. I pulled him back onto the bumper.

"This is insane!" Valentine shouted.

"No shit." There were handholds leading to the roof, but this thing was supposed to go three hundred miles an hour, which meant going that way would be suicidal. "See if you can get the door open."

Valentine tried the handle. "Locked."

We needed to get inside before Kat's men came back here and just machine-gunned us through the wall. The train station was flying past us. I leaned back to the left to see if maybe I could reach around to smash out the side window and climb through, but I had to pull my head back to keep from ripping it off as another pillar flashed by.

I stuck my head out again. Ling was on the platform ahead, frustrated, and glaring at the escaping train, when she saw me hanging there. Without hesitation, she keyed her radio. *"Grab my hand, Lorenzo."*

We were going much faster than when Valentine and I had made it across. This was going to be tight. As the distance closed, I could see that Ling was focused on me like a laser beam. She'd either make it across or die trying. If anybody could do it, it would be Ling. She stuck her arm out.

But then I thought of what Jill had told me about her.

It wasn't even a conscious decision. I hesitated for just an instant, it was too late, and then we were past, leaving Ling alone on the platform. She watched me, furious at the missed opportunity.

"What are you doing?" Ling demanded.

"Why didn't you help her?" Valentine asked a split second later when he saw his girlfriend hadn't caught our ride.

"You'll thank me later," I snapped at him. "Get that fucking door open." I keyed my radio. "Ling, you've got to find those other two bombs. Use Reaper. He's going for the command center. We've got this one."

"Roger," Ling said, tersely, obviously pissed that I hadn't snagged her.

"Try to get Tailor. That one we caught might be armed," Valentine said into his radio.

I hadn't even thought of that. Maybe I hadn't done Ling any favors after all.

He went back to kicking the door. "We could have used her help."

"We're probably going to die if you don't hurry up."

There was a little Plexiglas window. Valentine tried to break it a couple of times with his elbow, but when that failed he pulled his .44 Magnum. *Man, I hated that stupid gun.* "What do you mean I'll thank you later?" He asked as he used the butt of the revolver to bash the little window in.

"You're going to be a dad."

Valentine froze, arm shoved through the door, searched for the handle. He looked like I'd nut-punched him. *"What?"*

"Congratulations, Pops."

Chapter 16: As Above, So Below

VALENTINE

"What do you mean?" The train was speeding up rapidly as I, hand through a broken window, fumbled for the emergency door release.

Lorenzo, his long hair whipping in the wind, looked at me like I was stupid. Judging by how fast we'd left the station, we had to be going over a hundred miles an hour already. "Biology 101! You knocked her up! Now open the fucking door!"

I found the handle and cranked it. An alarm sounded inside the train car. They probably knew we were here now.

Lorenzo readied his pistol as the door slid open. Nobody had shot my arm off, so maybe they weren't watching the back door yet. As soon as it was open, Lorenzo was in, and I was right behind him.

We found ourselves in a tiny room about as big as a walk-in closet. The walls were made of rubber. The connectors between cars must have been like flexible airlocks. There was another door just ahead of us and stairs that went up to the second level.

"Wait, how did *you* find out Ling was pregnant?"

He exhaled sharply. "We don't have time for this, okay? She told Jill, Jill told me, she was going to tell you, but didn't because, I don't know, she loves soap opera bullshit like this. Will you focus? Can't you do that creepy calm-face thing you do? We need to go kill a bunch of assholes."

He was right, but I wasn't going to give him the satisfaction of admitting it. "We're on a train with who-knows-how-many dudes with guns, Kat, Anders, and the bomb. They can't be planning to detonate it if they're stuck on the train with it, right?"

"You sure about that?" Lorenzo asked.

"Uh . . . hell." I wasn't. Not really. The mercenaries probably didn't know they even had a bomb. Anders? No way. But Kat? If she couldn't get off in time, she might set it off, just out of spite.

Lorenzo glanced through the door, then pointed skyward. "Okay, this looks like other bullet trains I've been on. Two levels, stairs at the beginning of every car. We go up. Top level is how you get from car to car. Bottom will dead end."

"What if someone hides below us, let us go over, then comes up behind us?"

"Then we get shot."

We went up the stairs. I risked a quick peek through the window on the door. Armed men were moving this way, guns shouldered. I pulled back and held up two fingers. "The second we go through this door we're toast."

"Not necessarily." Lorenzo removed something from his jacket pocket.

"Is that a grenade?" I asked, hopefully.

"No," Lorenzo whispered, shattering my hopes. "I wish, but I wasn't planning on using grenades when I was going to rescue my brother. Ended up using a bunch anyways, long story. It's a stun grenade, a Canadian nine-banger. After that, it's gonna get ugly. We've got to push straight through. Don't let up. You ready?"

Even though Lorenzo was a real bastard, I couldn't think of anybody I'd rather be doing this with. I checked the cylinder of my revolver. "As ready as I'm going to get. Do it."

Lorenzo nodded and slid the interior door open just a little, his suppressed 1911 at the ready. He tossed the flashbang grenade in and slammed the door shut.

BANG BANG BANG BANG BANG BANG BANG BANG BANG! True to its name, the nine-banger rapidly blasted off nine head-splitting concussions. As soon as the last pop had sounded, Lorenzo shoved the sliding door open and moved in. He didn't give the two stunned men in the room any time to react. *CHUFF CHUFF CHUFF!* Three shots on the closest guy, then *CHUFF CHUFF CHUFF CHUFF,* four shots on the next. Both went down with bullet holes in their heads and necks. Lorenzo ejected the magazine from his .45 and was slamming a replacement in as the empty hit the floor.

The train car, surprisingly quiet now, was filled with smoke.

"Cover the door," I said, crouching down by the nearest dead man. He was dressed in black and had been carrying a compact assault rifle. It was a 5.56mm SCAR with a ten-inch barrel and a holographic sight. He had a couple of spare magazines in his pockets, which I took, before standing up.

I leveled my carbine at the door. "Hurry up, check the—" I didn't get to finish that thought. Bullets tore through the thin door between cars. Lorenzo ducked back down the stairs while I tried to use the economy-class seats for cover. Leaning out, I flipped the selector to full auto and dumped the whole magazine in return fire. The noise of the short-barreled weapon in the confines of the train car was head-splitting, but I ignored it as best I could. "Reloading!"

Lorenzo pointed his gun toward the door and ran up, stepping over the other dead man without stopping to grab his weapon. "They're running." He fired after them. "Move up!"

Nodding, I quickly ran up the aisle, weapon at the ready. I had shredded most of the couchlike seats in this car, and fabric was floating in the air. Lorenzo and I found ourselves on opposite sides of the door that led to the next car. "Got any more tricks?"

"You're not going to like it," he said. "Go prone on the floor in the aisle. Get ready. When I pull the door open, you shoot low, and I'll shoot high."

"Why am I the one that has to lie in the line of fire?" I asked, dropping to the floor of the train car.

"Quit being a bitch. You're *below* the line of fire. You ready?"

"No," I said, looking through the holographic sight. "Do it anyway."

Lorenzo was right. I was below the line of fire. You should've seen the look on the man's face when the door opened and he fired, his rounds passing above me. I stitched him up, firing a long burst into his guts, going under his hard plate. He fell.

Another guy rolled out and tried to blast me with a short shotgun. But I was *Calm*, and he was painfully slow. I rolled to my left, out of the way, with a faction of a second to spare before his buckshot obliterated the carpet I'd been lying on. Before he could pump another round into the chamber, Lorenzo came around the corner and started shooting. He was out and moving before I could even get up. His pistol, that custom 1911 with the can and the old electronic sight, was firing so fast it sounded like an MP40. The shotgunner was hit repeatedly and crumpled.

Lorenzo looked over the top of each seat until he reached the flexible connection. "Clear!"

"If this is the best she's got," I said, pulling magazines out of the pouches on a dead man's armor vest, "we'll be home by dinner."

"Don't get cocky," Lorenzo warned.

Kat's men didn't wait for us to enter the next car. The door slid open and all of them rushed through, weapons shouldered, firing. A burning pain shot through my side as the second man in the stack lit me up with a P90 submachine gun. As I fell, Lorenzo dropped to a knee and opened fire with the shotgun, blowing the lead man's head off in a spray of blood and buckshot. Stumbling backwards, I landed hard on the armrest of one of the economy-class seats, lost my carbine, and flopped to the floor. I rolled onto my side, pulled the .44 from its holster on my hip and jabbed it outward, rocking the trigger, firing up the aisle toward the man who was now trying to retreat. He didn't make it.

"You good?" Lorenzo asked as he dragged me up.

I nodded jerkily. It burned, and I could feet something hot and wet under my armor vest. A round must've gotten through.

It didn't matter. We couldn't stop now. "I'm good. Let's go."

LORENZO

Entering each new car was a nightmare, but we had to keep pushing.

The doors were a fatal funnel, but there was no other way to go around. I couldn't tell how fast we were going, but judging by how quickly the countryside was flying past the window, it was *really* fast. If this had been a normal train I could have taken to the side or the roof to bypass the choke points and ambush the ambushers, but on this thing that would've been like trying to walk across the wing of a jet plane. Despite that the ride was remarkably smooth. If we hadn't been fighting to the death this would be a pleasant way to travel.

Valentine was leaning against the huge, flexible rubber gasket that served as the bridge between cars, waiting for me while I hurried and looted a corpse. He still had that eerie *Calm* thing going on, but he was breathing too hard.

"You hit?" I asked as I took the dead man's FN P90. The magazine was translucent and looked almost full. Good. I was out of .45 and had dropped the old 1911. I flipped it over and checked the chamber. *Hot.*

"Vest stopped it." But I think he was lying. He went back to trying to get a peek through the glass door into the next car to see how many of them were waiting to kill us. "I don't see anyone."

I risked a glimpse through the glass door. The next car was the food car, with rounded couches instead of packed seats like our current economy car, and a bar down the opposite side, but I didn't see anybody waiting for us. "They're there."

"I know." He'd picked up a SCAR off one of the men we'd killed, and kept that at his left shoulder while he put his right hand on the door to pull it open for me. I got into position, and when I nodded back, Valentine yanked the handle.

I dove through, hit the floor, and rolled behind the end of the bar. Somebody must have shown themselves because Valentine started shooting over my head. I crawled forward as bottles and glasses shattered above me. I flinched when I stuck my palm on something sharp, but I was too occupied to care. By the time I popped up, there was a bunch of stuffing floating in the air, as Valentine tried to peg one of Kat's men hiding behind a couch. There was another man hiding at the opposite end of the bar, so I opened up on him. He ducked further down as he was pelted with splinters and flying glass.

"Moving," Valentine shouted as he came through the door. I kept hammering the boxy little subgun at the two men, alternating between them, fast semi-auto shots, trying to keep them pinned. Apparently there was some sort of solid metal frame beneath the rounded couch, because I couldn't seem to hit the bastard through it, but from the swearing and shouting, I was pretty sure I'd gotten the one behind the bar.

Valentine went right down the middle, gun shouldered, aggressive as could be, and by the time the men realized he had an angle on them, it was too late. He pumped half a dozen 5.56 rounds into the one behind the couch. The barman leapt up to engage Valentine, but I put a bullet through the side of his skull on the way up. He jerked the trigger as he fell, shooting through the side wall and spraying rounds across the French countryside. Valentine reached him and put one more into his head to be sure.

"Clear!"

I ran up to him. It wasn't until I looked down to see how much ammo I had left that I realized I was bleeding all over the P90. I'd cut my hands on broken glass. But that wasn't as important as the fact that the gun was almost empty. Fifty rounds went fast when you were really motivated.

The glass door had been struck and broken during our firefight. Valentine had an unobstructed view into the next car. He took a knee by the wall and signaled for me to stay low. There were more waiting for us. And as if to punctuate that, somebody started randomly launching bullets through the wall. Valentine hunkered down as I crawled toward the nearest body.

While I was searching for another weapon, a voice came over the intercom.

"*This is your captain speaking,*" Katarina said. "*Apparently we have some uninvited stowaways on our five-thirty nonstop to London. Whichever one of you kills these annoyances will receive a ten-million-dollar bonus. That is all.*"

The man we'd nearly decapitated had been armed with a P90 as well, so I started rifling through his stupid contractor vest looking for more magazines. Valentine fired back through the door. "Just one shooter. He's retreating," he reported.

Fresh magazine in the gun and another one stuffed in my back pocket, I got up. "Keep pushing." The two of us rushed into the next car. We both had to pause and take cover as the man we were chasing decided to start firing indiscriminately through the walls again.

"*Are they dead yet? I'm getting impatient up here. Is that you, Lorenzo? Valentine? I knew it. You just couldn't let it go.*" Kat was getting agitated. "*Bonuses be damned, if you idiots don't hurry up and take care of them, they're going to kill you all.*"

We reached the next wall. There were brass casings rolling beneath our boots. The glass between the two cars was already shattered. Valentine did a quick peek through the hole, then pulled back and held up one finger. The shooter was waiting for us. Another fucking fatal funnel.

I didn't know who her security was. They looked more like PMCs than typical Montalban criminal stooges. They probably didn't even know they were protecting a maniac with a nuclear bomb. Not that they'd be inclined to believe us over their current employer, since we had just killed a bunch of them, but what the hell? It was worth a shot.

Signaling for Valentine to hold, I shouted, "Hey, asshole. Do you know what's in that box you're protecting?"

There was a brief pause, and then somebody shouted back. "Why don't you tell us then?"

Valentine's eyes narrowed. He slowly moved his weapon along the wall, estimating where the voice came from.

"It's a nuclear bomb. Kat intends to blow up London with it and I don't think she's going to stop and let you morons off first!"

He must not have believed me, because he opened fire, punching holes through the rubberized walls. I nearly got my head blown off. Valentine emptied his magazine through the wall in response.

Except for the ringing in my ears, it was quiet. "Fuck diplomacy!" I shouted.

"You're really bad at it," Valentine stated flatly. We both looked in. The gunman was flat on his back, dead. He'd been hiding behind a table, but Valentine had shredded it and his body. "Go." We moved in, leaping over the dead man, and headed for the next car.

There couldn't be many left. I didn't see anyone inside the next one. This car must have been intended for business meetings and taking calls. There were little glass privacy enclosures inside, each one crowded with comfy chairs and tables. It was all very fancy. It was a good thing the maglev line didn't actually have passengers yet, because we'd indiscriminately fired so many rounds through this place we would have accidentally killed a bunch of them.

There was movement at the far end of the car. *Anders!* Unfortunately, he saw us coming and jumped down the stairs before I could get a shot off. I'd forgotten just how freaking fast he was for a big dude. Val had seen him at the same time, and both of us instinctively rushed inside, hoping to take him out fast. Since the glass partitions ran down the middle with aisles on the sides, Valentine automatically veered left and I went right. Anders was a high-value target. He had to die.

It wasn't until the gunshot went off that I realized we'd walked right into a trap. Valentine shouted a warning as he caught a bullet in the back. I spun around to see the shooter, but I was too late. He'd been lurking in a corner, hiding behind a shelf, and since we'd focused on Anders we'd gone right past him.

We fired at the same time. The glass partition between us exploded. I know I hit him, but then it was like a fiery fist punched me right in the sternum. He punched a few holes in the glass behind me before there was a flash of heat down my forearm and the P90 was torn from my grasp. I crashed against the heavy window hard enough to crack it, and then launched myself at the floor before he could shoot me again.

I know I'd plugged him repeatedly, but the stubborn gunman was still up and coming my way. He lined up the sights of his subgun on my face and I knew I was going to die.

But then Valentine rolled over, pulled his .44 and blew the back of his head off.

My chest was on fire. Because I'd needed to be mobile and stealthy low crawling through the weeds all night, I'd only worn an old Level II soft vest beneath my shirt. I put my bloody hand on my sternum and found the slug flattened there, still hot to the touch. Then I realized his other bullet had cut a shallow bloody line down my arm before it had smacked the FN, but like Gideon had always said, the wound wasn't squirting . . . So I crawled forward, trying to find a gun so I could finish off Anders before he could—

Anders came out of nowhere and kicked me so hard in the ribs that it launched me through another glass partition.

It was like being mule kicked. I'd broken the glass with my head. I lay there on the floor, stunned, cut, in a pile of broken glass, trying desperately to breathe, as Anders crunched after me. He had that little suppressed shotgun pointed toward where Valentine had been. Apparently Anders didn't have a shot at him through the furniture separating us, but that didn't stop him. He simply switched the shotgun to his other hand, aimed it at me, and ordered "don't move" as he pulled a pistol from beneath his jacket to keep pointed toward where Valentine was hiding.

"Yo, Valentine, show yourself or I'm killing your partner here."

"You think he cares?" I gasped.

"Shut up." The 12 gauge hole on the end of the boxy shotgun remained pointed at my mouth. His finger was on the trigger.

"What are you doing, Anders?" Valentine shouted back. He sounded like he was in a lot of pain, but he was smart enough not to show himself. Anders didn't miss much. "You're not suicidal."

"You think I wanted to end up on this train? That's your fault. From here on Kat can see her glorious dreams come to fruition without me. I'm getting off here."

We were riding the world's fastest train, how in the hell did he think that was going to happen without turning into paste? But then I remembered that he'd been doing something in the floor between the train cars.

"He's decoupled the cars!" I shouted. "You've got to reach that bomb, Valentine!"

Anders just scowled and dropped one big boot down on my chest, stomping the remaining air right out of my lungs. *Damn. That hurt.* But shutting me up had been a mistake. Anders was now in reach.

"Hell, it wouldn't be the first time. Valentine helped us retrieve this bomb. Isn't that right, kid? We couldn't have done Project Blue without you."

Fuck it. He was going to kill me anyway, and we couldn't afford to let that bomb go off. I had to go for it. Only before I could make a grab for Anders' shotgun, I saw something silver sliding across the floor, beneath the couches, directly toward me.

It was Valentine's .44 Magnum.

Valentine leapt up, not heading for Anders, but rather sprinting for the next car. I went for the shotgun.

Anders reacted and pulled both triggers, firing his pistol at Valentine and his shotgun at me. I *barely* knocked the muzzle aside as it blasted a dozen holes in the floor next to my head.

Glass shattered between Anders and Valentine. Blood spatter decorated the walls, but Valentine just put his head down and kept running.

With one hand pushing the shotgun's muzzle away from my face, I desperately reached for Valentine's revolver with my other. Only to discover that the .44 had stopped just out of range. *Damn it, Valentine. Good idea, shitty execution.*

Anders was still trying to shoot both of us, only the instant he wasn't busy aiming at Valentine's moving target, I was dead meat. I gave up on trying to grab the .44 and went after the suppressed shotgun with both hands, this time trying to pull Anders down toward me to twist it from his grip. That was even harder than it sounded considering he was stepping on my chest and was twice my size. I managed to pull him off balance, and his next few shots at Valentine went wide. Snarling, Anders turned his pistol on me.

Only Anders didn't realize I hadn't been trying to take his shotgun away. I'd been trying to *aim* it. I shoved my thumb inside the trigger guard on top of his finger and fired the shotgun directly into the closest interior window. The buckshot hit the already damaged safety glass—

FOOOOOOOOOOOOOM!

And a three hundred mile an hour wind came ripping through the cabin. It was like stepping into a tornado.

Everything that wasn't bolted down was hurled around the car. Anders instinctively raised his arms to cover his face as he was pelted with debris. He stumbled aside, trying to protect his eyes. I rolled over and went for Valentine's gun, only to discover that it had been blown away. I scrambled and rolled behind a couch before Anders could get his bearings.

I had to hand it to Anders, he was one committed son of a bitch. He fired wildly toward where he thought I was, then still managed to try and kill Valentine again one last time. Anders dropped his pistol and pulled out a radio detonator. I could only hope that Valentine had made it through the gasket before Anders mashed the button. There was a bright flash at the front of the car, but I couldn't hear the little explosive over the rushing wind.

The cars separated. Within seconds the engine was leaving us behind. Kat was getting away.

I'd failed. Valentine was now London's only hope.

As for me? I was still on a train car with the bastard who had shot Jill. I was determined to find that .44 and kill this fucker once and for all. Only my search was interrupted by an incredibly loud noise, and I suddenly found myself flying through the air.

One thing I hadn't known about high speed maglev trains: when a car gets decoupled, it has some *serious* emergency brakes.

VALENTINE

I had barely made it through the gasket before the explosion, but Anders had clipped me on the way. There was a shallow tear through the skin and muscle along my hip. It burned. I could feel sticky wet blood under my shirt from where I'd been hit earlier. I was dizzy and weakening. *Gotta keep moving.* I was only down for a few seconds, but by the time I looked back, the rest of the train cars were a shrinking dot in the distance. Lorenzo hadn't made it across. I was on my own.

Anders had used an explosive device to separate the coupling. It had cracked the safety glass of the next door, but hadn't blown it out. The next car only had one big floor with a tall ceiling, but it appeared clear. I went through. When I slid the door closed behind me, it was all at once eerily quiet. Out the window, we were passing through what appeared to be a seaside town. Then suddenly everything out there was black. At first I thought we were going through a tunnel, but then I realized this was the Chunnel. We were travelling beneath the ocean. Outside, safety lights flew past at a frightening speed. I didn't know how long we had until we emerged on the English side of the channel, but certainly not long aboard this thing.

Sweating, breathing hard, and bleeding, I limped down the stairs. This was a luxury car, and it was decked out in sleek, ultramodern décor. There were even potted plants and a crystal chandelier. The car was divided into several alcoves, providing privacy to passengers as they sat on plush couches. There was an information screen mounted on the wall but now it was just flashing an error message. There was no bomb on this car.

You can't just stand here and bleed. As if to drive the point home, the doors at the front of the train car slid open. I took cover in an alcove, then risked a peek down the aisle. Two men entered, pistols drawn, and they moved down the stairs cautiously. I pulled back. I'd lost the carbine in the last car. I'd given my .44 to Lorenzo. All I had left was the hideous, plastic Taurus .357 snubby that I'd been carrying since the Crossroads. It only held five shots.

Unlike the guys in tac gear we'd faced when we first boarded the train, these guys looked like Kat's regular bodyguards. *What the hell are you people still fighting for?* Maybe she told them they'd have time to escape before the bomb detonated. Maybe they were just that fanatically loyal to the woman. Maybe they didn't know what Kat was doing and thought they were just protecting her.

I shouted at them. "Do you know what this train is carrying? Do you have any idea what you're doing? You're protecting a nuclear fucking bomb, and when this train gets to London you, me, your lunatic boss, and a million innocent people are gonna die! Whatever she offered you, whatever she pays you, it isn't going to matter when we're all dead!"

One of the men said something to the other in a language I didn't understand. The other answered him harshly, and my plea was answered with a hail of gunfire. Bullets tore up the seat, the floor, and punched holes in my cover. One of them fired shot after shot, not letting up, but the other held his fire, waiting for me to make a move. I scrunched down lower, trying to merge with the floor. The gunfire ceased as suddenly as it had started. All that shooting and he hadn't hit a damned thing. But they knew where I was, so all they had to do was wait for me to pop out. I wasn't playing that game.

Only they were moving up on me, leapfrogging forward. One covering my position while the other moved to the next alcove. Next time they opened up, my bullet riddled cover would be insufficient. Except they stopped when the door to the last car slid open again. Kat was staying behind cover, but I could hear her clearly as she asked her men something. One of them answered. Then she raised her voice. "So there's only one of you left? Which one is it?"

"Give it up, Katarina. This is insane."

"Valentine? Disappointing. After everything we've been through together I thought Lorenzo would come through for me at the end."

"He's busy murdering your boyfriend."

"Anders is a strong man, but he does not share my level of commitment. Very few do."

"So you're going to ride this nuke to London and go out in a blaze of glory." I still hoped that her men were in the dark, and they would balk when they realized what was happening.

"I would rather not. The train is programmed to slow when it enters the metro area. I'll be getting off there with plenty of time to get out of the blast radius and seek shelter."

"I hope you like radioactive fallout."

"I'm not entirely happy about how this is working out, but that is your fault. I should be on my way home right now to enjoy some wine and a relaxing bath while I watch news reports of how my rivals perished in cleansing fire."

One of the guards said something then. He must have caught enough of our exchange to realize what was going on. *That's right, morons. Your boss is insane.*

"So tell me, Valentine. Have you met Mr. Perkins yet?"

I was bleeding out, so the name didn't immediately ring any bells. I risked a peek, only to see Kat aiming a cut-down M79 grenade launcher at us.

One of Kat's men began shouting something in French. I didn't need to speak the language to understand that he was begging her not to use that thing in here. A panicked *you're going to kill us all* sounds the same everywhere.

"But, if you die, I don't have to pay you," Katarina told him. Then she blew up the train.

LORENZO

The sudden stop had been hell on the furniture. Whatever hadn't been bolted down ended up in a pile at one end of the car, including me. Unlike a regular train coming to a surprise stop, there weren't any sparks or screeching noises followed by a violent derailment. This was more of a *whoosh*, like when an airplane lands, but a whole lot more abrupt. I ended up pressed against a broken table, up to my eyeballs in broken glass, and as the G forces subsided, the table toppled over and fell on top of me.

I was having one hell of a night.

As we came to a shuddering halt, I heard Anders coughing. He'd landed ten feet away, only he wasn't crushed beneath a bunch of debris. I struggled to get out from under the table, and of course, it weighed a ton. I tried to do a push up, but the stupid table was somehow wedged on top of me. It was stuck. I started clawing my way through the glass, grabbing handfuls of carpet, trying to wiggle out from beneath it.

"Damn, Lorenzo, you're one obnoxiously hard-to-kill son of a bitch. No wonder you screwed up so many of our operations in Zubara." Anders must have lost hold of his guns, because if he still had one, he'd be shooting rather than talking. Not that a monster like Anders needed a gun to kill me, and he proved that when he stomped the table and knocked the ever living shit out of me beneath it.

I was screwed. He kicked the table several times, but it was enough of a shield that he grew frustrated.

"I told Kat I should have just murdered you when I had the chance at the Crossroads, but oh no, she said you had to suffer first! She loved the idea of Sala Jihan catching you." Anders was like two hundred and seventy pounds of solid muscle, so when he reached down and grabbed the wreckage, he flipped it off of me like it was a card table.

I sprung up. The instant my Benchmade knife snapped open in my hand, I slashed for his guts. But he'd been waiting for that, and his open palm hit my forearm so hard that it felt like I'd bashed my bones on a pipe. Anders caught the back of my knife hand and twisted, trying to snap my wrist. Once he had me off balance he swung me against a window. I tried to twist out of it, but his grip was as hard as the Pale Man's shackles. I lost my knife as I dropped all my weight on his thumb, but I broke free. Luckily I accomplished that the microsecond before his fist put a dent in the wall where my head had been.

I launched myself at his legs. I got an arm around one ankle and threw my shoulder against his knee, trying to lever him down. It would have worked against most people, but Anders just kicked his back leg out to steady himself. I couldn't topple him. He dropped a hammer blow on my back, then encircled my torso in his massive arms, hoisted me off the floor, and flung me against the wall.

Damn, he was strong, but I'd fought a lot of men a lot bigger than I was, and no matter how tough they were, anybody could be crippled. I came off the wall, swinging. Anders blocked my arm, but he'd known that was just a feint and easily dodged the snap kick I'd aimed at his knee. I ducked beneath his jab and then danced back.

"Slippery little bastard," Anders growled as he went after me.

I met him in the middle of the train car, doing everything I could to hurt him. We collided, knees and elbows flying. I'm a damned good fighter, but physics were unforgiving, and he was one big, powerful motherfucker. The only advantage I had was speed.

And it turned out I didn't have nearly enough of that when he swatted my arms out of the way, slugged me in the side of the head, kneed me in the stomach hard enough to lift me off the ground, and spun me around into a couch. I went over the top, rolled across the floor, and only stopped my momentum by carpet burning my face.

"You know all that fucked-up shit Silvers did to Valentine? I wasn't interested in her mental games, but I *volunteered* for the physical part."

I got up, far slower that time, remembering Valentine telling me about how Anders had singlehandedly beaten the hell out of an entire Dead Six chalk. That story didn't seem very far-fetched right now. My chest was on fire. It was like I couldn't breathe fast enough. My head was swimming, but he was already charging me again.

There was no finesse this time. Anders just tackled me, swept me off the floor, and drove us back into the wall. Another window broke out of its frame. Then we were sliding down as he got on top of me, slamming his fists into my face. His knuckles dented bone and split skin. Each impact put a lightning bolt through my skull. I tried to get my hands up to stop him, but he had me, and just kept punching down through my defenses. I tried to lift my body to close the gap, but he just kept on striking.

With perfect rational clarity, I knew that he was going to render me unconscious, and then cave my skull in, and I had no idea how to stop him.

The better question is, Lorenzo, why won't you die?

It was like the Pale Man's voice awakened all the savagery I'd learned in the dark. The son of murder doesn't die. He kills.

I caught one of Anders' hands before he could retract it, pulled it close, and bit down on his wrist as hard as I could. Blood filled my mouth. Anders screamed in my ear and tried to pull away, but I wouldn't let go. I jerked my knee into his crotch. Anders shouted as he clubbed me with his other hand, but he didn't have as good an angle now, and I'd gnaw his damned hand off before I'd give up.

Anders flung himself backwards to escape. I think I might have left one of my teeth embedded in his wrist, but I was too dazed to tell. Anders was waving his bloody hand, spasmodically clenching and unclenching his fingers as I pulled myself up the wall. I must have bit through a tendon. *Good.*

I spit out a mouthful of blood. This time I charged him. He hadn't been expecting that. He was so much taller than I was that I practically had to jump to strike him in the face, but I still sunk my knuckles deep into one eye socket. Anders reeled back. I kept on hitting him, trying to tear him down. I don't think I've ever hit anybody that hard, that many times, and it still didn't seem to do shit.

Anders clocked me again. The only reason his fist didn't break any ribs was that my bulletproof vest spread out the impact. He struck me with a shockingly quick jab that split my lips open, then he got a handful of my shirt, rolled me over his hip, and tossed me hard on the floor.

I landed in a pile of broken glass and debris. The back of my head struck something round and metallic. I rolled off it, only to discover that it was Valentine's Smith & Wesson.

Anders was on his way over to finish me off, blood and snot leaking down his chin. His face was contorted with rage, but he froze when he saw what I was reaching for. Realizing he was unable to close the distance between us in time, he lurched desperately toward the broken window as my hand fell on the grip.

My eyes were nearly swollen shut. My hands were shaking so badly I couldn't even find the front sight. Anders was a blurry mass climbing through the window. I jerked the double action trigger. My first round punched a useless hole in the wall next to him. My second shot, I think I missed again, as Anders fell out the window and disappeared.

It took me a few seconds to get up, and a few more to wobble to the window. I was so dizzy that I tripped over my own feet, fell down, and then had to catch my breath before trying again. I probably had a concussion.

When I pulled myself up I saw the orange vapor lights of an industrial park. It was nearly dawn. The train cars had come to a stop on a small rise. Squinting, I looked down, hoping to see Anders lying next to the tracks in a pool of blood, but there was nothing but gravel and litter. There was a gentle slope of dried grass down to a chain link fence fifty yards away . . . Which was shaking back and forth because Anders was climbing over it. I'd only grazed him.

The front sight was wobbling badly as I pulled the heavy trigger.

I missed. "Fuck this thing!" I snarled, and fired again. Another miss.

Anders landed on the ground on the other side, glaring at me, and then he took off running across a parking lot.

I hate revolvers. I always have. Even back when Gideon Lorenzo had tried to teach me how to use one of the old-fashioned things, I had sucked with them. It didn't help that this particular gun had offed my business associates, wrecked my hearing in one ear, and shot me in the chest, *twice*. Valentine's gun really had it in for me.

But this time I slowed down, braced my arms against the window to steady myself, and thumb cocked the hammer. That took the trigger pull weight down to nothing. Blood was running into my eyes, but I just squinted through it and kept tracking Anders through the red haze. He was running between parked cars. I led him a tiny bit, and exhaled as I squeezed the trigger.

BOOM!

Anders spun around and crashed against a parked car. He slid down the hood and fell from view.

That was more like it.

Then I realized there had been multiple witnesses to my shooting an unarmed, fleeing man in the back. A few men and women, most of them in coveralls and work clothes, had come out of the nearby buildings to see why a train had stopped here. Some of them had gotten close enough to hear our fight, which certainly explained why they'd been hesitant to cross the fence. When they saw me, ragged and bloodsoaked, with a big stainless cannon dangling from one hand, hopping down from the train, the smart ones fled back inside, while the dumb ones pulled out their phones to call the police.

Well, shit.

My survival instinct told me to get the hell out of there, but I was too damned angry and started limping down the hill anyway. I'd just survived a knock-down, drag-out, literal tooth and nail fight, and I wasn't leaving until I was one hundred percent sure Anders was dead. It took my rattled brain a moment to remember that this fucker still had two more bombs out there unaccounted for, and suddenly I found myself in the weird position of hoping that I *hadn't* actually killed Anders. If I could find out what the other targets were, the authorities might still be able to stop them.

My radio was missing, probably somewhere back in the train. I still had my phone, but when I checked I had no service, probably because of Kat's cyber-attack. On the bright side, it looked like the witnesses trying to call the *gendarmes* weren't having much luck getting through either. By the time I reached the fence, the remaining witnesses had retreated. As pissed off and messed up as I was right then, I probably looked like death incarnate.

I clambered over the fence and practically fell over the side. My balance was all screwed up, but I got right back up and wobbled after Anders. Gun leveled, I approached the car, and sliced the pie around the trunk. There was blood there, but Anders was already gone.

He was out of sight, but had left a red trail for me to follow. I could tell by the smears he'd crawled across the asphalt, keeping the car between us. Then it turned to droplets as he'd stood up again. The dots got farther apart as he'd started running—I glanced around—into a construction site. He was bleeding bad, but Anders was slippery. If I gave him too much of a lead he'd hijack a vehicle or find some other way to escape, which meant I needed to hurry. Only he was also a malicious, clever bastard, he'd know I was thinking that, and he could be lying in wait to ambush me, which meant I was better off taking my time while his blood pressure kept dropping.

Except I wasn't exactly in good shape either. I just wanted to lie down and pass out. Plus, for all I knew somebody had gotten through and the cops were on their way, and oh yeah . . . don't forget the nuclear bombs speeding toward their targets. So I set out at a run toward the construction site. It wasn't much of a run, but it was the best I could do since my chest felt like it was on fire and my legs were made of lead.

The construction site was still laying a foundation. It was nothing but dirt holes, footings, and rebar. If there were any workers here this early, they had better have seen Anders coming and gotten out of his way. Which was good, because if he'd taken a hostage, I was in a bad enough mood I probably would have just shot through them, and I had enough baggage already.

There was some shouting ahead of me, followed by a meaty impact. I moved around a stack of concrete forms and spotted Anders at the edge of a drainage ditch filled with muddy yellow water. He'd just brained a construction worker over the head with a stout length of rebar and was in the process of stealing his car keys. Anders looked like shit. He'd been cut by glass, fists, and teeth. The bullet had hit him low, through the side of his abdomen. It looked too shallow to have punched any vital organs, mostly just muscle and subcutaneous fat, but that wound was bleeding profusely and running down his leg. I'd been aiming at his center of mass, but in my defense, I could barely see my distant moving target, and Valentine's gun hated me, so it had been good enough.

I stopped twenty feet away and aimed the revolver right between his shoulder blades. I cocked the hammer. It was just for dramatic effect. Even I couldn't miss with this damned thing at conversational distance.

Anders slowly turned. His chest was heaving from the exertion. I wouldn't say he looked defeated—I don't know if a warrior like him could even understand the concept of defeat—but he knew I had him dead to rights.

"Do it then."

"Tell me where the other bombs are, and I'll let you walk."

He laughed. Even I'm not that good of a liar. But the fact I'd not simply just blown him away told Anders he had something to bargain with. He pressed one hand against his bloody torso. "How about this, Lorenzo? I give you two targets, you let me drive away, then I'll call and give you the other two."

"I already know two."

"Fuck it then." Anders grimaced, as the blood continued to roll between his fingers. "I'm not that committed. I only wanted to take over Kat's empire . . . I would've made a great crime lord." Anders was acting cooperative, but he hadn't let go of that piece of rebar or those car keys. "Then I'll give you one more. You'd better decide fast. Paris, London, and Brussels, they're rigged for a simultaneous detonation, and you're running out of time."

Exodus had stopped one at Evangeline. That had to be the Paris bomb. I could only hope Reaper and Bob had figured out the Belgian one. "And the fourth?"

Anders gave me a malicious grin. "Kat's primary target, the council. That one left hours ago. Hell, I think some of the Illuminati leaders were actually riding on board with it. Those clueless fucks were heading to their fancy secret meeting. The whole cabal, all her competition, all in one spot, and the best part is they're all there just to talk about what to do about her. Kat has a sick sense of humor that way. Toss your piece and I'll tell you how to disarm all of those bombs."

It had to be a trick. "You think I'm stupid?"

"You think I ever would have tried to escape on that train with one if I didn't have a way to stop the countdown? I can transmit a code that will shut them all down." Anders was hard to read at the best of times. Bleeding, in pain, and with nothing to lose, it was even harder to tell. "Let me go, and the code is yours."

My gut told me he was jerking me around. He'd ended up on that train because they'd been surrounded, taking fire, and it was the one way out. "You're lying."

"You willing to take that chance, cowboy?"

I had to follow my gut. "You might not be that committed, but Kat is. With her there's no backing down. No second thoughts, no cold feet. When she launched, that was it. There's no magic code to take it back, because Kat knew if there was, then someone close to her might be tempted to use it. She's willing to burn the world to get what she wants, but someone else involved might turn out to have a soul." I shook my head. "No. There's no code. She wouldn't allow it."

Anders eyes narrowed. Damn it, I had been right. "How'd you know all that, Lorenzo?"

"I made her that way."

Cool as could be, Anders lifted the big chunk of rebar like it was a club. He was done playing games. He was going to go for it.

I pulled the trigger.

Click.

It was the loudest sound in the world.

Click. Click.

Valentine's revolver was empty.

I hate this fucking gun.

Anders smiled. His teeth were stained red. It was the most murderous, bloodthirsty, confident expression I'd ever seen. And then he came over to beat me to death.

VALENTINE

There was an angel standing over me when I opened my eyes. She was speaking but I could barely hear her. Every sound was muffled, as if I were underwater, except for the rapid pounding of my heart. *Am I dreaming? Am I dead?*

I knew I had been here before, only that angel had turned out to be Ling, and she had saved my life. Not just there, but ever since. That had been Mexico, where we had saved Ariel. Now I was beneath the English Channel and had to save London.

This time the angel was speaking with Ariel's voice, urging me to wake up, to get back in the fight.

Please, get up.

Then the angel was gone, swept away in the wind.

Groaning, I sat up. The main lights were out in the train car, but there were small orange emergency lights on the floor. From the screaming noise whipping past, all the windows had been blown out. The air tasted like smoke and copper. My clothing was hanging in tatters, and then I realized that some of that was my skin. I realized that there was a big chunk of metal embedded in my vest, and it was still hot. When I tried to pull it out, my right hand wouldn't work. My fingers couldn't close around the slick piece of frag hard enough to get it out. I had to put my gun down to pull it out with my left. Blood came welling out of the hole. That was bad. Probably should've left it in.

Then I noticed my right leg was worse. From the knee down, the flesh was shredded. My calf was a pulverized mess. I could actually see the bone. I was sitting in an expanding pool of red.

It doesn't matter. Get up. You're almost there. I was beyond *Calm;* I was serene.

Everything hurt. I'd been flayed. There was so much pain that I should have passed out, but instead it just faded into a sort of background noise as I calmly opened the first aid kit in my cargo pocket and pulled out a tourniquet. I tied it just below my knee, cinched it up, twisted the windlass—spitting blood and spittle through gritted teeth at the agonizing bolt of pain—and locked it in place. That would keep me from bleeding out in the next few minutes. *Long enough.*

I picked up my gun and began to crawl onward. The interior of the car was a twisted mess. Kat's last two men were dead, their bodies mangled and bloody. Above, the Chunnel flashed by at frightening speeds, as I followed the orange lights to my destiny.

Hurry, Michael. You are going to be a father. Don't you want to meet her?

I shook my head. I kept hearing voices. I had lost a lot of blood. I was in shock. Soon I would lose consciousness, and then I would die. I was okay with that. It didn't matter, so long as I stopped the bomb. As I dragged myself along, beneath the English Channel, alone and bleeding, I was at peace.

The bomb had to be in the next car, where Kat was waiting for me with that damned grenade launcher. I pulled myself up the stairs, trying to keep the snubby pointed ahead of me, hoping that I'd get a shot off at her fast enough. If nothing else, I was inside the arming distance of a typical 40mm grenade round. It wouldn't detonate at such close range, a safety feature designed to prevent grenadiers from accidentally blowing themselves up.

She wasn't waiting for me at the door, so I pulled myself up and looked through the glass. The lights were on in this car. It was similar to the other luxury car, except in the middle of the room was a big, green metal box. Katarina was pacing back and forth next to her bomb. I could tell she was scared, that she didn't want to die and was trying to think of a way out. She hadn't come to terms like I had. I thought that her line about getting off in London had been a lie. She had a ring of keys in her hand, and the safety lock on the side door was green instead of red.

Startled, she looked up when I slid the door open. Before she could do anything, I shot her.

Katarina Montalban took a couple halting steps. There was a red hole in her shirt, about where her belly button would be.

"It's over." It was a strain to say every word. "Now open the box and disarm that bomb or I swear to God I'll kill you."

"Nothing's over!" she shrieked. Katarina put her hands on her stomach. They were quickly covered in blood. Grimacing, she walked to the side and sat on one of the couches. "You shot me. It's not supposed to be like this."

"Shut it off."

"I can't stop the timer." She was obviously in terrible pain. *Good.* "The train's failsafe mechanisms have been overridden, and the controls are locked out. Even if we stopped, once in motion, if the bomb remains stationary for too long, it'll detonate. I win no matter what."

"There has to be a way!"

"No." Blood was spurting from her body, and had rapidly formed a puddle on the couch cushions. Katarina was dying, just like I was. "This *is* the way. These men have controlled the world for too long. It is time for someone else to have a turn."

Using the seats to brace myself, I hobbled to the case. The locks and latches on the box were heavy duty. Bullets would have bounced right off.

Even if I had known how to disarm it, I couldn't get to it in time. The box weighed a ton. It had probably taken two or three men to lift it off the cart.

Kat kept rambling. "But it was supposed to be my turn. All I ever wanted was what was mine. I worked so hard, sacrificed so much. Why couldn't they just let me have what was mine? My father, Rafael, Eduard. None of them. Why couldn't Lorenzo? Why couldn't *you*?" Katarina stared at me. Her eyes were filled with anger, hate, but then her expression softened. She turned her head to look out the window. Her reflection stared back. "I'm tired."

Anders had decoupled the cars, maybe I could find a way to separate us from the engine? Better for the bomb to detonate under the ocean than on land. Except Anders had used explosives. Just the metal-on-metal friction, at the speed we were travelling, would mean the cars wouldn't separate without being forced. Even if there was a way to stop the train, or decouple the cars, I didn't know what it was and I didn't have time to figure it out.

Wincing at the almost unbearable pain, I undid the Velcro fasteners and lifted my armor vest off my head tossing it into the aisle. I was too weak to keep it on; it was slowing me down. My shirt was soaked with blood. Blood was running down my legs. I was so cold as I lurched to the door control and the now-green button.

Katarina's voice was a whisper. "Look, a light . . . a light at the end of the tunnel. Watch the end of the world with me, Valentine?"

It was too late to make a difference, but no matter what happened, she wouldn't get the satisfaction of seeing her plans fulfilled. I raised the .357 and shot her in the side of the head.

There was only one way left to stop this bomb. I hit the button. The doors began to hiss open, but they had never been intended to open at this speed, and with a screech of metal, were violently torn open. Cold tunnel wind blasted into the car. I fell on my back.

I crawled to the bomb. The physics package from the Topol warhead we had recovered in Yemen was heavy, the metal case added even more weight. I put my shoulder against it and shoved hard. It barely scraped an inch across the carpet, but it *moved*.

My body was shutting down, but I kept pushing. My blood was all over the metal, making it slick. I drew myself back, and then flung my body against it, again and again. It slid further and further. There was more blood, but the wind was closer. The end of the case was through the gap. I was freezing, shivering, but sweat was pouring out of me, cutting tracks through the blood. I could see the light now, too. I didn't know if it was the end of the tunnel, a hallucination, or the afterlife waiting for me, but I kept pushing. The case began to tilt. Everything was fading into oblivion. My vision went dark, and I drifted away.

LORENZO
France

The first blow hit me in the upper arm. I tried to get out of the way, but Anders still hit me with the chunk of rebar across the shoulder. It sent me spinning over the edge. I landed in the mud and rolled, splashing into the drainage ditch.

Desperate, I tried to stand in the knee-deep slippery muck, but Anders was already sliding down the bank after me. He was bleeding badly from the gunshot wound, so with his heart pumping this hard, he'd weaken eventually. I just needed to stay alive however long that took.

Anders brought the rebar down hard. I barely got out of the way as it sent up a plume of yellow water. He had a reach advantage on me anyway, giving him a three-foot length of metal wasn't helping. In the muck, I couldn't move fast enough to get out of the way, and he caught me flat on the chest on the back swing.

I hit the water again. That had to have broken a rib, but I thrashed my way back up beneath a pouring drainage pipe. He was splashing after me. Trying to negate that length advantage, I threw myself at him, and wrapped my arms around his waist. He kneed me in the chest, and now I was sure that rib wasn't just broken, but might actually have just punctured a lung. He broke away and shoved me back. I ducked as the rebar whistled past my head.

As I tried to get up, Anders brought the rebar down across my back. I can't even begin to explain how badly that hurt. Then he kicked me in the stomach, flipping me over, deeper into the ditch.

"You should have let me go, Lorenzo!" Anders swung his club, barely catching the edge of my scalp. It split my head open, but my skull escaped in one piece. I was down. He put his boot on my chest and shoved me beneath the surface. The water was hip deep here, but pinned beneath him, it might as well have been at the bottom of the ocean.

He was still shouting, but I couldn't hear him. There were only bubbles and the sound of my own heart pounding. I thrashed and fought, clawing at his leg, trying to get free. He was going to drown me in a few feet of water.

Desperate for air, the sound of my pounding heart was replaced by something else. *Incomprehensible whispers.* The whispers wanted me to give up. They had always wanted me to fail. My damaged vision was turning black as the Pale Man's prison. I'd been to hell once before, and I was about go back, only there wouldn't be any escape this time.

Why won't you die, Lorenzo?

Because *fuck you* is why.

I'd forgotten something, probably because I thought of it as a souvenir, merely a letter opener, or toy, more than a weapon, but at that brief moment in time, my life hanging in the balance, it might as well have been Excalibur. I let go of Anders' leg, reached for my pocket, and by some miracle, the little switchblade Decker had gifted me in Africa all those years ago was still there. I got it free, pushed the button to release the blade—I could only hope that it would still pop open under water—and then I slammed it upward into Anders' leg.

I ran the blade up his thigh.

The boot came off my neck. The pressure was gone. I sat up, bursting out of the water, and gasping for air.

Anders was standing there, staring in disgust at the blood *pumping* out of his leg. I'd been right about the cheap little Italian knife. The blade had broken clean off the first time it had gotten some serious use . . . but not before it had sliced through several inches of muscle and his femoral artery. There was no stopping that here. Sever the femoral and unless it was clamped off, it meant death in a matter of minutes.

He knew it. I knew it. Anders was a dead man walking.

"You killed me," he stated, so matter-of-factly, it was like we were talking about the weather. "Fuck."

I could only cough my response. "You deserve it."

Bleed a man, a clock begins to run. When it reaches zero, it's over. Anders lifted the rebar. He could still take me with him.

And he tried damned hard. I was too messed up to even dodge. All I could do was make sure it hit my shoulder instead of my head. But Anders was weakening, slowing, and his next shot only broke the surface of the water. He fell to his knees. We were face to face, breathing hard, as he shifted the rebar so he could try to stab me in the throat with it. I shoved it away. He fell on his face with a splash.

Anders was still struggling. He got his hands beneath his body and pushed himself out of the water. Give him an inch and he'd find a way to kill me with it. He'd remain deadly until his heart quit beating. So I climbed onto his back and wrapped my arms around his face.

But I wasn't going to try to choke him. *Oh no.*

I clamped down with all the strength I had left. The tough son of a bitch still tried to bite a chunk out of my bicep. But I twisted hard, straining against his thick neck, craning his head around until his chin was pointed at his shoulder. Then I put all my weight into it and flung myself back.

SNAP.

I lay there against the muddy bank. Gasping for air as my chest filled with fire instead of air. Anders floated to the top of the yellow water, face down, but with his head at a horribly unnatural angle. I got to my feet as Anders' body slowly began to float away. I was pretty sure there was a bone sticking into my lung, but the horrible choking noise I made right then was actually supposed to be a laugh. I was in so much pain that I wasn't sure if I was going to die or not, but for just a moment, I was triumphant. The darkness had come to take me away again, but I'd won.

There was light on the horizon.

I looked toward the sunrise.

It was in the wrong direction.

Chapter 17: The New World Order

VALENTINE
Location Unknown
Date Unknown

The first thing I remember was a muted rattling sound. After a while, I realized it was rain on a window. It took some doing, but I forced my eyes open. After a few moments, things came into focus, and I found myself surrounded by medical equipment.

"I'm not dead," I said, my voice little more than a raspy croak. "How about that?"

I tried to sit up, but it only brought me pain, so relaxed and stayed down. I wasn't in a hospital. It seemed like a bedroom in a nice house somewhere. I had IV tubes running into my arms, and my body had been bandaged. I remembered the train, I remembered shooting Kat, and I remembered pushing the bomb off. Somehow, I had survived, but I had no idea where I was.

My leg ached with a dull, but relentless throb. I remembered how badly it had been mangled. I was scared to look, but forced myself to sit up enough to see. There was an empty flat spot beneath the sheets where my right leg should have been. My leg was gone from just below the knee.

My leg is gone. I laid back down, surprisingly calm about the whole thing. I guess it hadn't really sunk in yet.

There was a TV on the wall. It was on BBC news, but it had been muted. A tired-looking anchor had a grim look on his face. The crawl along the bottom of the screen said something about thousands still missing. The screen changed, and it was a picture of a mushroom cloud.

My heart dropped into my stomach. I was dizzy. I felt like I was going to throw up. We'd failed. God forgive me, we'd failed.

"Hey," someone said then, startling me. It was Tailor. I hadn't noticed him sitting in a chair in the corner. He looked exhausted, his clothes wrinkly, with dark circles under his eyes. He hadn't shaved in a couple of days, and was smoking a cigarette. He dragged his chair over and parked himself at the edge of my bed. "How you feeling, man?"

How the fuck do you think I'm feeling? I pointed at the TV screen. "Is that London?"

"No. London is safe. You stopped the bomb."

"Where is that, then? What happened?" I tried to sit up.

"Just relax, man. I'll catch you up."

"What about Ling? Is Ling okay?"

"I don't know. We haven't been able to contact anyone from Exodus, or your buddy Lorenzo." He nodded at the TV; now the video was of buildings in flames. "We got three out of four. The London one detonated at the English end of the Chunnel. It's gone. The Chunnel, I mean. It collapsed and flooded. But the explosion was underground and the radiation was mostly contained. Casualties were, well, minimal, all things considered. A lot of traffic had been stopped because of the cyber-attack. The normal trains weren't running. It could've been a lot worse. Anyway, you were found passed out on the train at a station in London. The thing blew right through the stops it would have made under normal circumstances and went straight to the city. It was a miracle you survived that long. You lost a lot of blood."

"How? How did you find me?"

"London was in chaos. A nuclear bomb just went off in the Chunnel, man. They were trying to evacuate the city and they hadn't realized where that train had come from yet. Our people knew where it was going, though, and snatched you up before the British authorities found you. Probably did you a favor, since they'd think you were the terrorist who blew up the Chunnel."

"What about the other bombs?"

"You guys caught the one headed to Paris. The other was intercepted on the way to Brussels, and a NATO special ops team took care of it. We can thank your little girl for reasoning out that target and putting us on it. She saved a lot of lives."

I was staring at the TV, lost. Now they were showing video of the wounded, people badly burned, and children crying for their parents. "Where is that?"

"It detonated on the rail line between Saint-Omer and Calais." Tailor sounded incredibly weary just then. "It's bad, but it could have been way worse. The government is saying that the terrorists had probably intended it to go off in a different city, but it detonated prematurely."

That wasn't true. The bomb had gone off right when it was supposed to. The cities weren't the main targets. They were secondary targets, intended to sow chaos, clean up loose ends, and further damage Kat's rivals. The primary objective had always been to cut the head off the snake. "That was where the Illuminati meeting was, wasn't it?"

Tailor nodded slowly.

"What happened? We warned you! I thought you warned your boss?"

"I did. I don't know what happened. The estate they were meeting at was wiped off the map. They're all dead. The leadership of the other families is gone."

"What about Romefeller?"

Tailor took a long drag off his cigarette. His hands were shaking badly. "Romefeller got held up. He hadn't arrived yet. He's the only one left."

That son of a bitch. "You told him, but he didn't warn his associates to get out in time. He didn't find some way to stop the train like they did in Brussels. You don't find that suspicious?"

Tailor took a deep breath. "Listen, you need to stow that line of thinking for now. Romefeller wanted to talk to you when you woke up. Don't go pointing fingers. It'll just make this harder on you."

"Am I a prisoner?"

"No, Val. You're a hero."

I sure as hell didn't feel like a hero. "I need to rest now."

"Hey, listen . . ."

I didn't let him finish. "Just get out."

"Okay, man. Get some rest. I'll talk to you later." He left the room and closed the door behind him. The TV continued to show images of horror and destruction. I closed my eyes and tried not to cry.

The next time I woke up, Alistair Romefeller was sitting next to the bed. Tailor was wearing a fresh suit and standing in the corner like a dutiful toady. He looked like worn out shit. Romefeller seemed as cool and collected as ever. Why not? Everything had worked out for him, and he hadn't gotten his hands dirty.

"Welcome back, Mr. Valentine. I apologize for the loss of your leg. I promise you'll get the best prosthetic available. I owe you a great deal, and millions of people owe you their lives."

"We didn't stop all the bombs." Tailor was standing behind Romefeller, so his boss couldn't see him. He quietly shook his head in the negative, like I should shut up.

Romefeller sighed. "What happened was a dreadful tragedy, simply dreadful. We did the best we could, but Katarina was too well prepared. Her disruptions of communications and emergency response protocols were just too thorough. I, personally, lost many friends and colleagues to her madness. But we are still here, and we will rebuild, and together we can manage real global problems. Resource inequality, climate change, overpopulation, conflict, poverty . . . these are real problems that are causing real suffering. My peers talked about building a better world, but they were little more than a . . . how did you put it? Model United Nations? A debate club. No more. Things will start to change, now, and I owe all of this to you and your friends. In the end, the whole *world* will owe you a debt of gratitude."

I looked him in the eye. "Right. Tell me, when did you figure out that Blue was intended to target an Illuminati council meeting? Because it seems mighty convenient that that's the one bomb that got through, and even more so that you're the only one left. Things really broke your way, huh?"

Romefeller was quiet for a long time. The billionaire bit his lip as he mulled that over. Tailor was distressed, but didn't say anything. "That is a serious allegation, young man, especially after my surgeons saved your life. You are here, enjoying my hospitality as a guest, rather than being turned over to the British government for questioning. You have to know that had that happened, your own government would take you back into custody, and your former employers would undoubtedly acquire you again. You should feel grateful."

Grateful. "You're a cold son of a bitch, I'll give you that. You told me you people liked to pull strings, and you sure as hell played me. Your rivals are gone, you're in charge, European governments will be panicked and vulnerable. Either a rogue American organization or one of your dead rivals planned and set up the whole thing, depending on who you care to blame. A few thousand people had to die, but you won, didn't you? You got your new world order, and you come out looking squeaky clean."

Romefeller leaned forward, put his elbows on his knees, and rubbed his face with both hands. "Ah, I see. Very well." Tailor looked crestfallen, like I had just signed my own death warrant. "I was worried it would come to this." Romefeller finally lowered his hands and looked me in the eye. "You're reckless, but you're no fool. So let's dispense with the pleasantries and get down to it, shall we? Your survival depends on your cooperation, so I suggest you consider your words very carefully before you speak."

"What do you want from me?"

"Two things, Mr. Valentine. First, what did those Exodus fanatics do with the nuclear weapon intended for Paris?"

"It was still at the train station, last time I saw it." That much was true. "What, you couldn't even take care of that without me? I left the bomb sitting there and it disappeared?" I shook my head. "Unbelievable."

Romefeller scowled, but ignored my defiant sarcasm. "Enough. Tell me about the Oracle."

I laughed at him. "I don't know enough to tell you anything. Besides that, fuck you."

Tailor looked aghast, silently pleading with me to keep my mouth shut, but his boss also ignored my insult. "She is special, isn't she? After the bombings, I sent someone to collect her. She was alone in the residence we'd provided for you, after all, and in danger. She's much too valuable to be left alone like that. I sent one of my best, someone who I knew would see her to me safely." Romefeller reached into his breast pocket and removed a folded, yellow piece of paper. "Later, a second team found her, my operative, I mean. She was alive, but in a coma. She'd had an aneurism. The girl was nowhere to be found."

"What's that?" I asked, nodding at the piece of paper.

"We also found this. It's a note from the Oracle herself, addressed to you. Would you like to read it?"

I lurched up. "Give it to me, you son of a bitch!"

Romefeller actually smirked and tossed the folded piece of paper onto the bed. I snatched it up and opened it. It was written in neat cursive, with a purple ink pen. The I's were dotted with little circles.

> *Michael,*
>
> *For better or for worse, it's done. By the time you get this, I'll be long gone. Please, don't worry about me, and don't try to find me. It's not safe for either one of us. Too many bad people are looking for you and me both for us to stay together. I know you'd die to protect me, but I don't want you to ever been in that position. You've done enough for me. You deserve to be free of all these burdens, and to live a happy life.*
>
> *I have to follow my own path now. I don't belong anywhere now. I need time. I need to find myself. I need to find out who I really am, what I really am, and where I really belong. There are so many things I wanted to tell you, but I just couldn't, and I'm sorry about that. I was afraid you wouldn't understand, and I guess I was afraid you wouldn't believe me. I know better, now. I know you'd stay with me no matter what, and that's why I have to go. They're coming for me, and I'm done being a pawn in someone else's game.*
>
> *I don't know what the future holds now. The old constants are gone, leaving only variables like you. I can make guesses, but there is no certainty anymore, just probabilities. I guess this means humanity is on its own now. No more puppet masters, but that's for the best. That's the way it's supposed to be. Those who want to force a certain order on the world have brought more death and suffering than anything else. Now the world has a fresh start, and a chance to do better.*
>
> *Please don't be sad. I will miss you so much, but I promise I'll see*

you again. I just have a lot of things I need to do, and I need to do them on my own. Thank you for being my family. Thank you for showing me what it means to be human. Say hi to your little girl for me, when she's born.

I love you.

—Ariel

My hands were shaking as I lowered the note. My eyes teared up as I carefully folded it back up.

"Imagine the good that I could accomplish, with a mind like that in my employ," Romefeller said. "I've learned much about your young oracle, and I understand now why so many have fought for her. Tell me, where do you think she would go? You can't tell me that she really just disappeared, a teenage girl, in an unfamiliar country."

"Wherever she is, she's out of your grasp."

The smug bastard chuckled at me. "I assure you, *nothing* is out of my grasp. Either you're lying, or you really don't know. In either case, I'm afraid that makes you a liability."

I said nothing. I clutched Ariel's note and stared the old Illuminatus down.

Romefeller looked over his shoulder. "Mr. Tailor?"

Tailor's face was a mask as he stepped forward. Without a word, he reached under his suit jacket and drew his pistol.

I looked him in the eye. "I told you it would come to this."

"Val . . ." he trailed off.

I shook my head, but didn't avert my gaze. "Do what you have to do, man. You should know something, though: she told me that humanity is on its own, now. No more puppet masters."

Tailor looked at me, but said nothing else. He looked over at Romefeller, then back down at me.

"Mr. *Tailor*," Romefeller repeated, his very tone a threat.

After another couple seconds, Tailor nodded to himself. In a flash, he turned and cracked Romefeller in the mouth with the butt of his gun. I saw a tooth go flying as the billionaire stumbled backward, stunned and in pain. Tailor then grabbed him by the lapels of his expensive suit, spun him around, and pushed him down onto my bed. The old man kicked and thrashed, but my friend didn't hesitate. Grabbing a pillow with his free hand, he stuck it over Romefeller's face, stuck the muzzle of his pistol into it, and pulled the trigger.

With a muffled pop and a puff of feathers, Romefeller stopped kicking. Tailor stood up, straightening his suit jacket as the dead billionaire slid off the bed, leaving a bloody mess on the sheets, and crumpled to the floor in an undignified heap.

It was suddenly intensely quiet in the room. Tailor and I stared at each other for a moment, not saying anything.

"Jesus Christ!" I finally blurted, breaking the silence. My heart was racing. "God *damn*, dude."

Tailor crossed the room and returned with a wheelchair that had been parked against a wall. "Yeah, well, he can consider that my two weeks' notice. Come on, Val, we're getting the fuck out of here. We don't have a lot of time."

He helped me out of bed and into the wheelchair. My right leg ended at a stump, just below the knee, so it wasn't like I was getting out on my own. "Where are we going to go?"

"Bob Lorenzo went to the U.S. embassy in Paris and gave them everything your people have collected on both Majestic and the Illuminati over the last couple years, all the evidence you've recorded, all the puzzle pieces that your girl put together. Here." He dropped a Glock 26 into my lap before unlocking the brakes on the chair. "Hide that, don't pull it out unless I tell you to. I can still talk my way out of here. The shit's hitting the fan all over. Two nukes went off in Europe. NATO is on full alert. The U.S. is at DEFCON 2. I really don't want to be here when the French government puts everything together."

He started to wheel me out of the room. As he asked, I concealed the little pistol in my lap, along with Ariel's note. "Where are we going to go?" I repeated.

"I've got a contact with the CIA. Don't freak out, it's the CIA, not Majestic. Believe me, I did some digging. Majestic has a lot of reach, but they're not everywhere, and they're on the run now. Things are going to change, fast. Now shut up and let me get us out of here."

"Tailor?" I said, as he rolled me down a quiet hallway. "Thank you."

"Yeah, well, it's only fair, I guess. If it weren't for me you'd still be a security guard in Vegas, and you'd still have both your legs."

I actually chuckled.

LORENZO
Ostrava, Czech Republic
Three weeks later . . .

Europe was in chaos. It was like Kat's bomb had set off every simmering bit of built-up anger and resentment on the whole continent. There were riots in every major city. And then there were counterprotests that turned violent because people were sick of the rioters' bullshit. Militant assholes used the chaos to strike. Governments cracked down on threats, both real and imagined. In my old life it was exactly the kind of volatile situation that I would have found a way to take advantage of.

But I was retired. And this time, I meant it.

I hadn't seen Exodus since the night everything fell apart. Antoine had gotten hurt, but Skunky had taken a bullet to the chest at Evangeline, and had been touch and go for several days. Reaper's war-criminal doctor network had gotten a little richer, but Skunky had pulled through. Exodus had gotten out of France their own way after that. As for my brother, I had not even gotten to tell him goodbye before he'd gone to the U.S. Embassy and started raising hell. Before he had turned himself in, he had made a bunch of calls, so there were enough law enforcement and intelligence VIPs there watching like hawks to make sure Majestic didn't just murder him.

After I had gotten patched up, Jill and I had fled the country too. I told myself if I hadn't just been used as Anders' punching bag I might have felt up to trying to relieve the decapitated Illuminati of some of their wealth, but to be honest, my heart just wasn't in it. So we had headed east until the rioting stopped and we found a quiet place to hide out. Jill and I were both still a mess, and we spent most of our time lying in bed and healing. Reaper caught up a few days later, and tried to take care of us. He was a terrible nurse.

Jill kept healing, and one day while she was watching the news, and they were showing something about London—and it wasn't a smoking radioactive crater—it finally sank in what we had accomplished, what she had spent a year fighting for. She looked over, tears in her eyes, and didn't have to say a word. I went over and held her, and that was the day she began to forgive herself for being human and having to make a call.

She was going to be okay. We were going to be okay.

It kind of blew my mind thinking about it. Valentine, Skunky, his buddy Tailor, and me; four former Switchblade mercenaries, all trained by Hawk, brought together by crazy coincidence, and we'd changed the course of history. I knew Hawk would be proud. Hell, I think even Decker would have been proud, if he knew. If nothing else, it demonstrated how capable his guys really were.

Reaper was being even more jittery than usual, and that was saying something. But it wasn't the pensive, mopey, afraid of the dark Reaper I had been dealing with recently. He was excited about something, and after a couple weeks of relative quiet, he finally let me in on his secret.

Wincing at every step because of my ribs, Reaper had led me down the narrow stairs to the private lane behind the house we were renting. There was an unremarkable van parked there.

"Okay, Lorenzo, before you freak out, I just want you to know that this is a little scary, but I think it is the best idea I've ever had."

"I have no idea what you're talking about."

"Sala Jihan is still out there. It's about that burn on your chest. Yeah, you've been talking in your sleep ever since you got out. I know about the nightmares. I know you can still hear stuff occasionally, just like I can still see stuff once in a while when I close my eyes, and it scares the hell out of me, you know?"

"Sadly, I do." I had fulfilled my part of the bargain, but I still wore the devil's mark. One day he might decide to reclaim what he owned. "Wait, have you been watching me in my sleep?"

"Don't worry about it. I got a message from the Oracle. She said because some of the bombs came from him, he'll be hiding for a bit, but after that he'll start rebuilding his empire. She said that with time she could figure out how to get him, that *you* could get to him."

I still didn't know what that girl was, but she was on the opposite side of the Pale Man, and that was good enough. "Reaper, I just want to find a home, and go there. Just me and Jill. No more of this . . . whatever it is."

"And what if the Pale Man decides he's not done with you?"

"I can only hope we're done with him."

Then, grinning like a maniac, Reaper opened the van doors and showed me his souvenir from France. "What if this time we could make *sure*?"

Epilogue: The Blood of Patriots, and Tyrants

VALENTINE
Hays, Kansas
Three Months Later . . .

Kansas was cold and windy in January, but today was a pretty nice day. The sky was blue, the sun was shining, and I was sitting on the back porch of an old farmhouse, bundled up, sipping hot chocolate as I talked with my visitor. Tailor and I had been moved from safehouse to safehouse ever since we'd been brought back to the United States. We'd been smuggled into our own country on an Air Force C-17, and hadn't stayed in one place for too long since. The old farmhouse was heavily guarded.

Bob Lorenzo was leaning on the railing, looking out over the snow-covered field behind the house, awkwardly trying to make small talk. "So how's Ling?"

"She's fine," I said tersely. She was out of the country, far away and safe, and Bob didn't need to know where she was.

"How's your kid-to-be?"

Ling had told me in an encrypted email that she'd been examined by Dr. Bundt. The pregnancy was going fine so far. It was too early to tell if it was a boy or a girl. "Fine."

"Parenthood is great. It changes everything. I sure missed my kids while I was locked up. Still do, but at least I know they're safe. And they know I'm alive. Having children really puts things in perspective. It makes you realize the importance of leaving them a future."

"I already agreed to testify about Majestic in exchange for a pardon, Bob. What else do you want? I'm giving my full cooperation."

"First things first. I have something to give you. Here." He handed me an ornate wooden case that he retrieved from an attaché case.

"What is this?" I asked. I undid the brass clasp and opened it. The case was lined with silk padding and contained some kind of medal. It hung from a long red neck ribbon, connected to an ornate badge by an enamel laurel

1186

and oak wreath. At the very center of the badge was an engraved image of a woman's head. The inscription on the badge read, *République Française.* The inside of the lid had a plaque affixed to it, which read, *On Behalf of The French Republic,* in both English and French.

"You've been inducted into the National Order of the Legion of Honour, at the rank of *Commandeur.* It's the same award they gave General Patton. There are similar awards, though ones of lesser rank, available to your former teammates if you ever to decide to give the French their names."

"I don't think that would be a good idea."

"I understand your caution, but you saved Paris from a nuclear bomb. The whole thing is being kept secret for the time being, but they love you more than Jerry Lewis now. There's rumblings that the British want to grant you a knighthood, too, for saving London."

"You'd think they'd be mad I collapsed the Chunnel."

Bob shrugged. "We've briefed the Ministry of Defense on everything that went down, and gave them your sworn statements. Nobody who matters thinks there was anything more you could have done. You need to quit beating yourself up."

"Fine," I said again. "Is this why you came all the way out here?"

"No, Valentine, it's not. Listen, we both know that a cancer like Majestic isn't something that can be rooted out with just hearings. They're still out there, sinking their claws into everything, trying to rebuild their shadow government. But they're on the ropes. This is our chance to root them out, once and for all."

"Did the FBI give you your old job back or something?"

"No. This is bigger than the FBI. The president gets it now. He knows how dangerous Majestic is, and he wants them gone. He's created a special task force. Since he wanted somebody motivated, and somebody he thought trustworthy, he put me in charge. Now I'm recruiting people that *I* can trust." He turned around and gave me a very solemn look. "Your country needs you again, Valentine."

I scoffed and sipped my hot chocolate. "You know, Gordon Willis told me the same damn thing. You know how that worked out for me."

"I need people who hate Majestic just as much as I do, who know what they're capable of, who can't be corrupted by them."

Is he for real right now? "So you get a secret government task force, to fight the last secret government task force that went out of control?"

"I've got men who can follow orders and pull a trigger, Val. I want people like you running it specifically so we don't turn into the very thing we're fighting against. It isn't about just building an operation; it's about having the courage to tear it down when we're done."

I looked up at him incredulously. "Do you have any idea what you're asking me? I've lost friends. I was tortured. They screwed with my mind in ways I still don't understand, I should be with the woman I love while she's carrying my child, and let's not forget," I knocked on my prosthetic right leg, "I'm crippled. You want me to do *more*?"

"Yes," he said, so earnestly I wanted to punch him in his big, stupid face. "I know the gravity of what I'm asking, but I also know what's at stake. I think you do, too. Are you willing to do what it takes, or will you sit back and hope things work out for the best?"

"The question isn't whether or not I'm willing to do what it takes. The question is, how far are *you* willing to go? What needs to be done won't be pretty. It won't be within the confines of the law. It can't be, because *they* don't operate within the law. We can't use due process when they can corrupt the process itself so easily. In order to do what you're suggesting, we will have to do things that are illegal, unconstitutional, and unacceptable to the American people. We're going to have to hunt down and probably kill American citizens, and there's no guarantee that we'll succeed. Sure, this president says he's on board, but as soon as things get ugly he's liable to change his mind. Politicians won't have the stomach for what needs to be done, and God only knows how many of them Majestic has its hooks in. Even if we do pull it off, even if we uproot Majestic from the ground up and wipe it out, then what? Now that the dirty work is done, we're a liability. We're a liability and sooner or later they'll be tempted to come after us."

Bob nodded. "I know."

"Then why are you doing this? Why should *I*? What is the point if we do all of this, only to end up in prison or in an unmarked grave someplace?"

He was quiet for a long time. "Project Red tore China in half. Project Blue was supposed to do the same thing to Europe. Those aren't the only such projects out there. There are rumors of another one, aimed at the United States itself."

My titanium and polymer leg creaked as I leaned forward on it. "What are you talking about?"

"Project Black is the Majestic contingency plan to overthrow of the government of the United States. It was originally cooked up, way back in the 1950s, as a hypothetical failsafe in case the government was compromised by communist agents. Well, more than half a century later, we've backed a rabid dog into a corner. We have no way of knowing how much of this contingency was set up, how many assets are in place, or what all it would involve. But you know what they were willing to do to China, and you saw what they were willing to do to Europe. These are the same people that left you all to die in Zubara as soon as you became a liability. These are the same people that use American citizens for science projects. You *know* what they're capable of. You know what kind of state the country is in already. Something like this? It could be the end, Valentine. Your country is at stake."

"I'll think about it."

"The Tree of Liberty must be refreshed, from time to time . . ."

I didn't let him finish the quote. "Yeah, yeah, I took American History too. I said I'll think about it."

"I'm confident you'll make the right choice. Mr. Tailor is already on board, and we've got other leads we're chasing down. He's trying to contact your teammate, Hudson, I think, from Dead Six. I want you to know, too, that if you do this, I'll guarantee the safety of your family. They'll be given the same protection as mine. So please, think it over." He turned to leave. "Oh, there was another package for you. I left it on the table. I'll be in touch." He zipped up his jacket. "Stay warm. It's a cold one, this year."

I waited until I heard his car leave, then I limped to the kitchen. I was still going through a lot of physical therapy, learning to walk all over again. It made me glad Ling couldn't see me like this. Standing over the package, I hesitated for just a moment. It was a plain cardboard box. *No.* No more fear. I snapped open my automatic knife, and cut the tape holding it closed. Bob wasn't the type to leave a bomb or anything for turning down his offer, and the house had his people in it, guarding me. It was stupid paranoia, and some days it was a struggle to overcome it.

The box contained my Smith & Wesson 629 revolver, my custom sidearm, my lucky sixgun, completely caked in dried mud. Knocking hardened clay off of the frame, I got the cylinder open. It still had six fired brass cases in it. I was going to have to detail-strip the gun to get all the crud out.

There was also a note.

Thanks for the loaner. I used it on our mutual friend. I heard you dealt with my ex. Thanks.

I saw my brother. He made me the same offer he's going to make you. I told him no. Any organization that would hire me is too disreputable to work for. Besides, I've got my own business to handle. But I know you won't say no. You'll take his job. I don't know how you'll justify it, but you will, and then you'll go ruin some assholes' day, because that's what you do best. A warrior needs a war.

This time, I'll try and stay out of your way. You need me for something, you can figure out how to reach me. I don't say that lightly. I don't have many friends. I consider you one of them.

I set the letter down, looked at my gunked-up gun, and sighed. I had a revolver to clean. Then I needed to call Ling, tell her I love her, and hope she wouldn't be mad at me for taking a new job.

LORENZO
Altay Mountains, Russia
Three Years Later . . .

My message had been delivered. The face that haunted my nightmares appeared on the screen. Sala Jihan stared through me with his unnatural black eyes. Even though I was sitting in the back of a truck, upwind, twenty miles away, his gaze was still unnerving. It was like he could reach through the glass and rip out my soul. Maybe he could, I didn't actually know.

"I warned you never to return."

The scars on my chest burned as he said that. "The two of us had some unfinished business."

"You have made a grave error." He must have been holding the device too close to his face, because now all I could see was his teeth. That was somehow even worse. *"You will pay for this trespass."*

"Probably."

"Why has the son of murder called upon the Pale Man?" As he said that, he turned the camera enough that I could see the concrete walls of the missile silo he called home.

Location confirmed. "I'm returning something you lost."

When Reaper had shown me what he had taken from France, I hadn't believed it, at first. It was hard to comprehend the fact that my friend had stolen one of the four horsemen of the apocalypse. Guided by the Oracle, it had still taken a long time and a lot of meticulous planning to get the nuclear warhead buried into the mountainside next to Sala Jihan's fortress. Ariel had insisted on that to minimize fallout to the regional villages. I had been all in favor of an underground detonation, because it didn't matter if he lived at the bottom of an impenetrable missile silo, if I dropped a whole mountain on top of him.

I opened the control box, and turned the key, and placed my finger on the red button.

"What do you think you are doing?" the Pale Man demanded.

"You once told me you like digging in the earth. Dig your way out of *this*." I pushed the button. There was a roar like thunder. The earthquake hit a moment later. The screen went black.

Reaper's voice was in my headset. "Detonation confirmed, Chief."

VALENTINE
Flagstaff, Arizona

I leaned in the doorway of my daughter's bedroom, watching her sleep. Sarah

Mei Song-Valentine was an energetic toddler, to say the least, and she wore me out. Even after running around the house all morning, she stubbornly refused to take a nap until she was so tired she fell asleep on the floor in the middle of her toys.

My wife appeared next to me, leaned her head on my shoulder, and looked in on our daughter. "You finally got her to go to bed," she said, quietly.

"It was a struggle today," I said, smiling.

"It will be a struggle tomorrow," Ling agreed. "She's so full of energy."

"I hope you got in a nap yourself." She had taken Sarah to the park that morning, and apparently there were a bunch of screaming toddlers there. I was gone a lot, so I tried to do as much parenting as I could while I was home. Raising a kid was a full-time job, and I felt guilty about Ling doing it by herself so much.

Task Force 151 had kept me busy for the past three years. When Bob first approached me, on the porch of that old farmhouse in Kansas, I'd never have imagined that his proposal would grow into what the task force had become. What started as a handful of patriots grew into over a hundred, backed up clandestinely by the FBI, the CIA, the NSA, and the military. The tentacles of Majestic and its subsidiaries went farther and deeper than we ever would have guessed, too. We'd made a lot of progress in the first three years, and Majestic was on the run. Many of its key personnel were in witness protection, prison, or buried out in the desert. The president had kept his word to let us do what needed to be done, and we kept our part of the bargain by keeping him in the dark about it.

Someday, the country would know the truth. Someday, these stories would be told. Until then, we worked in secret, trying to undo decades' worth of damage without turning into the very thing we were fighting. It was a fine line to walk, and we'd had some pretty major successes. We'd gone deep into the base popularly known as Area 51, tracking down a Majestic supercomputer/AI called Prometheus. This machine had given our information warfare guys all sorts of hell, but in the end, Reaper helped us pin down the physical location of the AI, hidden in the DOD black budget, in a bunker that few had access to. After we pulled its drives to comb for intelligence, I dropped a Thermite grenade in its CPU and burned it to slag.

No, I'm not at liberty to discuss anything regarding extraterrestrials that may or may not have been there.

After a year-long operation, we were able to find and secure a pair of nuclear weapons that had officially been missing since 1961. The two hydrogen bombs had supposedly never been found after a B-52 carrying them crashed in a North Carolina swamp. Information from Prometheus' drives led to the realization that an arm of what became Majestic had clandestinely secured the weapons, and later held them in reserve. Tailor and I oversaw the capture of these weapons and their long-overdue return to the Air Force. They were eventually sent to Oak Ridge and decommissioned. Each one had a yield of 24 megatons, far bigger than the warheads used in Project Blue. Getting those out of Majestic's hands was one of our greatest accomplishments to date.

There were setbacks, too, of course, and the matter was anything but settled. But three years in, I felt that the tide had turned. Majestic was on the run, and for the first time in my adult life, I was cautiously optimistic about the future of my country. Oh, don't get me wrong, politicians are still crooks, Washington, DC is a sewer of cronyism and corruption, and the nation is still polarized, but I didn't go into this expecting to fix any of that.

Lorenzo had been right about me, though. A warrior needs a war, and this was *my* war. It felt good to be fighting for something I believed in, for my daughter's future, when I had spent so much of my career fighting for a paycheck.

"I slept for a while," Ling said with a yawn, "until your phone went off. Your work phone."

"Oh, God," I said, taking the plastic rectangle from her. "What is it now?"

She smiled. "Go see what they want. Don't forget, it's your turn to make dinner tonight."

"Okay. Do we have any hamburger left?"

"We're not having hamburgers again."

"Okay. Do we have hamburger so I can make tacos?"

Ling shook her head.

"Well . . . how about I order a pizza?"

"Just go," she said. "I'll get dinner started."

"Love you!" I said, walking into my office with my phone. Once inside, I unlocked it and checked my messages. There were a bunch, as usual, but an urgent one from Tailor.

Val, check this out. That seismic disturbance the other day was definitely a subterranean nuclear blast. It was located in the Altay Mountains, right on the border of Russia and China. Bob is sending Dragic's team in to assess the situation on the ground, but it looks like the old Russian missile base there was destroyed. A mountain fell on it. Will keep you posted. Sorry to bug you when you're on leave.

I opened the files Tailor had sent with the message. Satellite imagery, wind analysis, seismic activity recordings, things like that. What was left at the Crossroads was now gone. I had no way of knowing for sure what happened, but I had a pretty good idea. *Lorenzo, you amazing son of a bitch.* I was just glad he didn't accidentally start World War Three.

There was a second message, this one from an unknown sender. That immediately set off alarm bells in my head. This was my work phone, and it was supposed to be secure. I wasn't supposed to get spam. *I swear to God, if this is random junk mail I'm going to tear someone a new asshole over at tech division.*

It was a picture of a lovely young woman, a selfie. It took me a moment to recognize Ariel, but when I did, I almost dropped the phone. She had purple streaks in her platinum blonde hair now, and had on a pair of those big sunglasses that girls like to wear, but there was no mistaking her. With the image there was a brief message.

Michael:

I'm sorry you haven't heard from me. I had something I needed to do. Tell Ling that the Pale Man is gone, for good this time. Also tell her I miss you guys, and I love you both, and I can't wait to meet Sarah. I just knew you were going to name her Sarah! Oh, and happy birthday, Merry Christmas, etc., times three. I hope I can see you soon. Until then, please don't worry. I'm okay.

Love, Ariel

"Michael?" Ling startled me when she said my name. I'd been engrossed in my phone and hadn't heard her come in. "What's the matter?"

I looked up at her, smiling, and handed her the phone.